LONELY CONFLICT

a novel of the Vietnam war

the unexpurgated edition
GARY GENTILE

Bellerophon Bookworks

Bellerophon Bookworks
P.O. Box 57137
Philadelphia, PA 19111

Additional copies of this book may be purchased from the same address by sending a check or money order in the amount of $30 U.S. for each copy (plus $4 for domestic shipping per order, not per book). For a list of available titles that can be ordered by credit card, visit the author's website:

http://www.ggentile.com

Picture Credits
The front and back cover photographs are courtesy of the National Archives.

International Standard Book Numbers (ISBN)
1-883056-25-X
978-1-883056-25-4

Original copyright - 1986

Printed in the U.S.A.

Author's Preface

Although *Lonely Conflict* is a work of fiction, the scenes depicted in the book represent actual events. Many of the incidents I experienced firsthand, others I witnessed, some I heard from the participants. Except for one incident, the depicted situations actually occurred - no matter how absurd or preposterous they may seem.

In this respect, *Lonely Conflict* personifies historical fiction. I did not create or originate any of the plots or subplots. Rather, I compiled the storyline from my own experiences in the Army and in Vietnam, along with other events which I know to have occurred, and arranged the narrative in a sequence that presented those events in such a way as to maximize the dramatic appeal.

Each scene is therefore a combination of various situations that I parsed, rearranged, merged, or blended in order to create a cohesive whole, and to achieve a semblance of allegory. The only scene that is truly fictional is the escape from Fort Dix and the subsequent car chase (although, some individual components are factual, each occurring at a different time).

The characters are composites or extrapolations of real people. I recreated the dialogue, but based the words, thoughts, ideas, opinions, and dialect on those of people I actually met. My purpose in this regard was to convey the polemics that ran rampant during those tempestuous times, when the United States was embroiled in, and torn apart by, the Vietnam conflict. The characters symbolize controversial attitudes.

The story is intentionally idealistic, as is the teenaged protagonist.

The purpose of this novel is to exemplify for future generations the turmoil of the Vietnam era. In one way or another, every American citizen, no matter how tangentially, was affected by the political appeal to arms. Particularly affected were those men who fought in the war, those draft-age males who avoided the war, those dissidents who actively protested the war, and those fortunate youths who - due to physical disqualification, sexual discrimination, or pure luck of the draw - managed to escape the war. Never in American history have such a large percentage of citizens demonstrated *against* a war.

When my agent submitted the manuscript to the major publishing houses, the final draft elicited an incredible amount of editorial abuse - much of it due to caprices of the editors, some

of it purely arbitrary. Here are some examples taken from discussions and marginalia.

One editor wanted to delete the first ten chapters, starting the book with Chapter 11 in order to grab the reader with an action sequence. I have begun all my other novels in this fashion - but those were fast-paced, action-oriented novels, not thought pieces that relied heavily on theme. In writing *Lonely Conflict*, I wanted to emphasize the growth and progression of a high school graduate, from a bucolic and unsophisticated beginning, through a series of traumatic and stressful situations that accelerated his emotional development, to a mature but violent conclusion.

Another editor wanted furthermore to delete or drastically curtail Books Two and Three. These Books deal primarily with army training procedures: Book One with basic, Book Two with jungle warfare. Because he was a Canadian citizen (working in New York) who had no military experience, he lacked understanding of what peaceable and uncorrupted American draftees were forced to endure along the savage path to the battlefield. He failed to recognize army training as a mechanism for annihilating innocence, while indoctrinating impressionable young men with irrational adherence to obedience, no matter how immoral or absurd. This training was accomplished by means of threat, intimidation, and fear of consequences, not by willful compliance or voluntary willingness to learn. The point he missed was that this kind of training does not make loyal soldiers.

For those who read Books Two and Three, my message is directed at two audiences. Veterans will applaud my forthright and honest depiction of humiliating training tactics, because that was the way it was. Non-veterans will be chagrined and astonished to learn about the brutal and dehumanizing nature of enforced military training.

In addition to glossing over the training experiences, the Canadian editor with objections also wanted character sketches kept to a bare minimum in order to jump to the blood and guts of combat. He leaned toward publishing Book Five (combat in Vietnam) as a stand-alone novel.

Other editors wanted large sections of Books Two and Three deleted, primarily sections dealing with the nuts and bolts of combat training to which they could not relate. These editors also failed to recognize the purpose of those sections; they could not place those sections in context with the manner in which combat training affected impressionable adolescents who would otherwise, in all likelihood, have retained most of their innocence.

One editor wanted to delete the letters from home. Apparently, she did not realize that the letters served as a convention for keeping the reader apprised of concurrent events that were beyond the view of the protagonist.

Another editor noted that the politically correct word for Negro is Black. That may have been true at the time she made her editorial comment, but the book takes place in the 1960s, when Negro was in common usage and was descriptive rather than pejorative. The usage was acceptable at the time, before Black came into vogue. To employ modern usage in a period piece would produce anachronism.

Likewise, characters make references to their contemporary people and events which the modern day reader might not recognize: the G.T.O. was a high-performance sports car that was made by Pontiac, the Temps was short for a singing group known as the Temptations, and so on. Some editors wanted those references deleted because the references held no meaning for them due to their age or lack of experience. This is equivalent to excluding the arbalester in a novel about medieval warfare.

Another editor wanted to delete references to homosexuality in the army. It existed, therefore I included it - not out of prurient interest but because it affected ingenuous teenagers who were introduced to alternative sexual practices.

With respect to smoking marijuana - which one character called "sniffing" - one editor wrote in the margin, "I've smoked dope since 1965 and I've never heard it called this." I do not doubt her word, but she lived on the East Coast, and the recruit who told me that smoking marijuana was called "sniffing" lived in California.

One editor who resided in New York City objected to a character's negative comments about New Yorkers.

Several editors expunged dialogue in which characters made comments to which they objected (such as political assumptions or ideological arguments). Since each editor had pet peeves, a great deal of dialogue was censored simply to satisfy a particular editor's ego. They wanted to use my book to make social commentary that either conformed to their own beliefs and opinions, or at the very least did not contradict their beliefs and opinions.

In some cases, an editor deleted an entire character's existence because he or she did not care for that character's attitude or his statements about the war and about life in general. They did not care that I purposely formed such characters for the very specific purpose of expressing attitudes, opinions, and beliefs of real people - including attitudes, opinions, and beliefs to which I myself took exception, but which were important threads in the tapestry woven by historical context. A true historian does not imbue his narrative with personal convictions, but relates historical events and attitudes in perspective to the reality of the times, so that they can be compared to current events and attitudes.

One female editor objected zealously to any female character who exhibited traits or flaws that made her less than perfect. She wanted every female character to be mature, wise, and self-assured - without any room for growth - despite the fact that most of these female characters are teenagers.

Most editors wanted to obliterate any text which they construed as controversial (homosexuality, student demonstrations, overbearing parents, manipulative people, killing techniques, army brainwashing, political propaganda, combat realities, drug use, and so on). How much of this expurgation was the result of subliminal defense mechanisms or deep-seated guilt complexes, I never ascertained.

None of these editors exhibited any sense of comprehension of the totality of the work. They did not appear to see it as a rite of passage: for the country as well as for the protagonist. The fact that none commented on the theme indicates that they did not understand the theme; or perhaps they failed to recognize the book's thematic importance, or even the theme's very existence.

In addition to these extensive bowdlerizations to suit the editors' personal preferences, they then deleted large chunks of text arbitrarily, simply in order to condense the book to a length which could be printed economically. The fallacies of such a maneuver are manifold. In some instances, they deleted scenes that foreshadowed coming events; this made follow-up scenes appear contrived. In other instances, they deleted scenes that had been foreshadowed by previous scenes, leaving unexplained or unused the purpose of the prior scenes. Some plot devices were left unresolved; others were resolved without any basis for resolution. Disconnected snippets of dialogue were left hanging, like a classical symphony in the middle of the finale, or were commenced without introduction.

Worse yet, the editors then tried to extract and utilize only that text which forced the final product to fit a very distinct template. Instead of a tough, gritty, and original novel of America at war - with itself as well as with alleged communist aggression - they wanted a commonplace, stereotyped potboiler that conformed to the war fiction genre as it was generally perceived. The result was a bland and meaningless shoot-'em-up just like all the other formulaic war books on the market, the only differences being the cover, the title, and the author.

These editors apparently forgot the meaning of the word "novel." A novel is an art form which, according to the dictionary, is "new, unusual, or different." "Sameness" and "repetitive" are not used to describe such a literary work. I have often wondered how these editors would have butchered *All Quiet on the Western Front*, *Atlas Shrugged*, or *The Grapes of Wrath*, with their predilection for standardization and their refusal to transcend the ordinary.

By the time the succession of editors finished with my manuscript, the redacted text was so mutilated, so eviscerated, so emasculated, that it was no longer the literary effort that I intended it to be. I did not struggle for four years of my life to write a magnum opus that equals five standard books in length, only to have it published as a fragmented hackwork whose superficial treatment was indistinguishable from commonplace shelf fillers. I withdrew the manuscript from consideration.

A novel consists of four elements: plot, character, theme, and setting (not necessarily in that order). *Lonely Conflict* is a work of literature, which by definition places emphasis on character. The book has its greatest impact if it is read sequentially from beginning to end. That is why I have published this unexpurgated edition.

Given below are synopses for readers whose interests are specific rather than global, in order to enable those readers to decide which chapters they can skip. To my knowledge, such a tactic has never been done before in the publication of a novel. The reader is warned, however, that the whole is greater than the sum of its parts. Much of the impact of the ending will be lost upon those who have not perused the book from its simplistic beginnings.

Lonely Conflict is separated into five sections, which span from one spring to the next. This framework allows me to show the changes that occur from one bucolic spring in rural America, to the next spring in combat in Vietnam. The year that transpires is one of growth and coming of age - for the country as well as for Tony.

Book One (Spring) is divided geographically and temperamentally into two parts. The first ten chapters take place in Salisbury, Maryland, where the protagonist's grandparents live on their farm, and where homespun ideals are introduced. Chapters 11 through 36 take place in South Philadelphia, Pennsylvania, where the protagonist lives with his parents in the neighborhood of his friends. Book One introduces the civilian characters who materially affect the life of the protagonist. The Book relates the mores and attitudes that were prevalent in America's pre-drug culture, recounts silly escapades and harmless high jinks in which the protagonist participated, and adds background material to events and relationships that occur after the protagonist is drafted. Book One is the primary literary portion of *Lonely Conflict*: the part that separates the novel from one whose focus is purely military. This Book is intended for present day literati and for future generations.

Book Two (Summer) incarnates the manner in which basic training was conducted; and introduces the ruthless instructors who conducted it (and who were chosen by the army to conduct it the way they did). All veterans will find this section fascinating for its true-to-life depiction. Non-veterans will be appalled by the cruelty, the barbaric realism, and the sadistic lack of sensitivity that ran rampant in the army.

Book Three (Autumn) describes the conduct of jungle warfare training at Fort Polk, Louisiana (known at the time as Tiger Land). Cadre attitudes were different from those that were found in basic training. The instructors cared about their trainees because they knew that the men were only one step away from the bitter reality of combat. Trainees were almost universally draftees; no one I met requested jungle warfare training. Many were misfits and nonconformists with respect to military desirability. By this I do not mean to imply that these trainees were substandard in any way; rather, they were largely military nonconformists. The only army holes into which these pegs fit were foxholes. They were equivalent to the cannon fodder of World War One.

Much of the training was too brief to be effective in the field of battle, especially when pitted against a well-trained, highly motivated, and experienced adversary. Most draftees were disadvantaged because they possessed noncombatant personalities. Many fought to stay alive rather than to win any so-called objectives.

Book Four (Winter) is a literary interlude which reunites the characters who were introduced in Book One, and which brings their various conflicts to the fore. It also demonstrates all too realistically the merciless and inhumane treatment that soldiers received at the hands of the army. These soldiers were being sent to another country to fight for freedoms which they themselves were not granted in the country that sent them. This Book constitutes the final transition between peace and war.

Book Five (Spring) graphically limns small unit action in Vietnam. This Book portrays the culmination of the Vietnam conflict in all its blood, and without any glory. The combat veteran and armchair soldier, who are interested only in the fighting in Vietnam, might consider reading only Book Five.

One of the basic tenets of authorship is to write about what you know. I know about the Vietnam conflict. I was one of the lucky ones to live through it.

Cast of Characters

Book One (Salisbury, Maryland and
Philadelphia, Pennsylvania)
Anthony Giovanni: the protagonist.
Walter and Pauline Ruark: Tony's maternal grandparents.
Spot and Driver: Walter's hunting dogs.
Frank and Elizabeth Giovanni: Tony's parents.
Robby Giovanni: Tony's baby brother.
Kitty: the Giovanni's family cat.
The fraternity gang: Ben Clark, Pete Robinson, George Hart, Ray Murphy, Teddy Murphy (Ray's younger brother).
The girlfriends: Patty MacDonald (Tony's), Katie (Ben's), Marion (Pete's), Kathy (Ray's).
Mrs. O'Brien: Patty's maternal grandmother.
Helen MacDonald: Patty's mother.
Bob Windsor: Helen's boyfriend.
Jack and Frances Clark: Ben's parents.
Professor Dean: Tony's college English teacher.
Gail Levy and Dennis Kravetz: Tony's college classmates.
Mike Farnsworth: truck driver.
Sergeant Gonzales: induction sergeant.

Book Two (Fort Gordon, Georgia)
Close fellow trainees: Wally Gibson, Hank Gibbs, Thomas Gelbert.
Distant fellow trainees: Diment, Alfredo Gonzalez, Farley, Holloway, Jackson, Jorgensen.
Captain Maxwell: company commander.
Sergeant Hawkins: second platoon sergeant.
Lieutenant Wakefield: executive officer.
Sergeant Abrams: first sergeant.
Other platoon sergeants: Peterson (first), Murphy (third), Wheaton, (fourth).
Sergeant Ralph Breneke: mess sergeant.
Corporal Mead: company clerk.
Military police school
Captain Johnson: company commander.
Sergeant Swansea: platoon sergeant.
Captain Jonathan E. Marshall: chaplain.

Sergeant Jordan: guard detail leader.
Captain Daniels: hospital doctor.
Corporal Miller: hospital medic.

Book Three (Fort Polk, Louisiana)
Close fellow trainees: Alexander Hays, Terry Kurtz, Richard (Pops) Haiburn.
Distant fellow trainees: Pete Gormley, Mack Johnson, Ron Kitson, Bill Larson, Jordon, Kozel.
Captain Whale: company commander.
Lieutenant Satterlee: executive officer.
Sergeant Holtz: platoon sergeant.
Sergeant Waltham: another platoon sergeant.
Sergeant Moberly: first sergeant.
Sergeant Williams: mess sergeant.
Corporal Velden: company clerk.

Book Four (Fort Dix, New Jersey)
Captain Pierson: Overseas Processing CO.
Sergeant Mendez: desk sergeant.
Corporal Ringgold: company clerk.
Captain Hunley: chaplain.
Major Pinchot: stockade CO.
Captain Ralph Masters: prosecuting attorney.
Lt. Granger Roberts: defending attorney.
Sergeant Mattwell: temporary guard.
South Philly
Mrs. Murphy: Ray's and Teddy's mother.
Joey Clark: Ben's older brother.
David: Tony's and Patty's son.

Book Five (Vietnam)
Pleiku in the Central Highlands
Duc Pho in the coastal paddies
25th Infantry Division.
Colonel Charles Bradey Adams: 4th Brigade commander.
Captain Collins: Company B commander.
Lieutenant Blake: 3rd Platoon leader.
Sergeant Miller: 3rd Platoon sergeant and 1st Squad leader.
Corporal Yates: 3rd Squad leader.
3rd Squad PFCs: Burns (machine gunner), Wallace (ammo bearer), White (grenadier), Tait (rifleman), Rodriguiz (rifleman).
1st Squad PFCs: Andrews (medic), Raymonds (radiotelephone operator), Kelsey (machine gunner), Norton (ammo bearer), Belden (rifleman), Renslow (rifleman), Lieterman (rifleman), Riley (rifleman).
Lieutenant Thang: Vietnamese interpreter.
Henderson and Pepper: PFCs from another platoon.
Hanes: rifleman who was wounded before Tony's arrival.

Book One
SPRING

He who knows others is wise;
He who knows himself is enlightened.

Lao-tzu, c. 604 — 531 BC

An oppressive government is more to be feared than a tiger.

Confucius, 551 — 479 BC

Chapter 1

Spring was always a happy time of year for Tony. Not that he had anything against the other nine months, for he fully enjoyed the seasons in their turn. But spring had a freshness to it that was unconquerable. It was a time to climb out of the cocoon and to take on new form; a time to test newfound truths and to move toward newly designed goals; a time to discharge stored up energies kept in harness during the short days and the long lonely nights of winter; a time to feel the fever of life and the stirring in one's groin as pent-up passion ached for release; a time to which to look forward and from which to leap. Each season held its worth, but only spring inspired revelations.

The cool April morn was charged with life, from the dewy green grass and golden daisies on the ground, to the litany of singing orioles and chirping, scampering squirrels in the cone laden trees. The tip of the fishing rod bounced sinuously in time with the motion and sway of his body as he raced down the slippery slope with the exuberance of untamed freedom.

He slid to a stop at the bottom of the embankment and turned back to look up at the road. All six cylinders of the dull red pickup truck strained as it accelerated slowly along the narrow, gravel-covered country lane. A faded flannel shirtsleeve rippled across the rear window of the cab; Tony waved back wildly. Then the arm dropped and the transmission ground into third gear. The engine noise persisted long after the thin mist swallowed the '49 Ford. After the dust settled on the unpaved roadway, there was nothing to show that the serenity of nature had been disturbed. Tony turned and walked into the forest of tall Virginia pines and juniper shrubs.

In these lowlands, the shroud of mist that clung to the road formed a tall umbrella, which glinted like a thousand silent demons as the still-orange sun exploded into colorful fragments, each a tiny, self-contained rainbow. Against the chill of dampness he zipped his unlined jacket to his throat, where goose bumps crowded in flocks. Strenuous walking would soon dispel any discomfort. And before long, the sun would burn off the rising vapor.

For several minutes he jogged along lightly, crunching pine needles, jumping over moss-covered logs, and going out of his way to kick an oversized pine cone for an imaginary field goal.

He did not pay close enough attention to the shrubbery, for suddenly the tip of his fishing rod caught on a low-hanging branch; the pole was nearly torn from his grip. His momentum carried him on as the rod was whipped behind him. The reel brushed against his leg, popping the bail and releasing a dozen coils of monofilament before he could stop it and flip the metal wire back into place.

The escaped line was draped awkwardly over the leafy foliage; it pulled taut when the branch on which the hook was snagged straightened out. "Darn." It took five minutes to retrieve the hook, disentangle the line from the bush, and reel it in carefully so that the line did not coil into knots. It was an auspicious beginning for the first fishing excursion of the season.

The conifers soon yielded to their deciduous brothers, which flaunted their new coats of leaves. The gray trunks of beeches and elms supported green canopies that rose more than a hundred feet into the cloud-filled sky. Infrequent sycamores, shorter but stouter, looked out of place. The sumac grew in thick patches which were easily avoided. Tony had learned to distinguish staghorn sumac by the longer and thinner leaves, but despite his grandfather's patient counseling, he was still unable to differentiate between shining sumac and the poison variety, so he avoided all of it.

When the ground turned soggy, and the first river birch appeared, he knew that the creek could not be far away. He walked along the edge of an almost impenetrable bush line until he found a birch whose shallow, wide-spreading root system had been deeply undercut by the slow-moving water: it had had the misfortune to take its stand at a sharp bend in the water course. The birch had fallen sometime during the past year, for clumps of dried earth still clung to the exposed root ball. It lay at an upstream angle so that its uppermost branches, now short and leafless, lay about halfway between the high banks.

Several miles downstream, in tidewater flowing through the center of town, a weather-beaten wooden sign proclaimed this stream as the Wicomico River. But here in the forest, devoid of civilization, it was really not much more than a quiet creek.

Tony clambered over the outreaching root system with some difficulty, taking care not to snag either his clothes or fishing rod on roots or nearby shrubbery. The rounded trunk measured only two feet in diameter, but the bark was smooth and dry, and it gripped the treaded rubber soles of his new Converse sneakers like flypaper. He walked out on the log as if on a tightrope. He passed over the mainstream of the current where the water was deepest. When he reached the confusion of branches resting in shallow water, he turned around and sat down astride the trunk. His feet barely grazed the glassy, reflective surface of the water. By wrapping his legs around the bole, he could lean outward and see himself looking back up, his olive features partly obscured by tiny ripples caused by chunks of bark that were shredded off by his slight movement. If he looked hard into the dark water, he could see the clear sandy bottom over his reflected shoulder.

At that moment, the clouds in the sky dissolved and the sun shone forth in all its brilliance and warmth. His image faded as beams of yellow light strode down the river and bounced off the top of the water, darkening the bottom so that he could see minute particles of dust floating gently in the current. In the low-angled light, the river became a dark cloak of mystery.

As if the sun were a signal, the sounds of nature suddenly came alive. Somewhere upstream, a chorus frog burped intermittently in a soft, tenor voice. In the depths of the underbrush, a locust rubbed legs furiously, the slow cadence rising and falling stridently like a wailing police siren. A swooping Baltimore oriole chirped loudly as it flew low above the water, dodging tree limbs in its own, uncanny fashion. And in the woods across the creek, a woodpecker maintained its incessant search for beetles and ants, thrumming in short staccato bursts.

Tony balanced the fishing rod across his lap. He pulled about six feet of line off the reel. From his jacket pocket he took a cellophane bread bag; the raucous crinkling sounded harsh amid the peaceful wilderness noises. He removed a fresh slice of bread, folded the wrapper, and stuck it back into his pocket. With a deftness that came from years of practice, he pinched a piece of soft dough with thumb and fingers, and molded it into a diamond shape. The moistness held it together while he forced it onto the hook. From his other pocket he removed a red and white bob, which he snapped to the line some eight inches above the curved metal shank. Then he dropped the hook and bob into the clear water, released the bail, and let the gentle current carry the float downstream.

Almost immediately a school of shiny minnows swarmed around the breaded hook and dexterously nibbled off the bait. Tony scowled, pulled in the line, and pinched another piece of bread onto the hook. With a light, underhand swing, he tossed the float about fifteen feet downstream. It took the minnows longer to find it, but the end result was the same. He reeled in the empty hook, rebaited it, and with a strong, overhand cast, managed to drop the hook beyond reach of the marauding minnows. But the school must have been broken into classes, for another band of robbers charged out from the grass-lined shore, and hastily gobbled the bait. In exasperation, he reeled in the line until the bob caught in the end ferrule. He stuffed the remainder of the bread back into the jacket pocket.

After making certain that he was properly balanced, he drew one foot up on the log, unlaced the sneaker, pulled off it and the sock, stuffed the sock inside the sneaker, and tucked the sneaker in his lap. He rolled up the trouser leg as high as it would go — to just above the knee. Then he reversed the position of his legs and repeated the process on the other foot. He tied the sneakers together, slung them around his neck, and jumped into the frigid spring water. Breaking a dead limb off the tree as a cane, he waded to the opposite bank.

The sand was soft; it sifted between his toes caressingly. By the time he reached the ankle deep water near the muddy shore, his muscles were nearly numb; he felt as if he were walking on frozen stilts that had no physical connection with his legs. A red dot terrapin, only recently roused from winter hibernation, was startled at his approach; it plunged off the log where it had been sunning itself, and took refuge in the muddy leaves at the bottom of the creek.

Tony jumped onto a grassy clump on the bank. He danced from foot to foot, waiting for increased circulation to ease the pain of the cold, and groaned aloud. He calculated that he had been in the water for only fifteen seconds — the temperature must have been barely above freezing.

Walking away from the creek, Tony found a sunny glade and sat down to dry his feet. He lay on his back and kicked furiously in the air until they were nearly frozen, then used his socks as towels to brush off dirt and leaves.

With socks and sneakers back on his feet, he forged through the brush, beating his way through the tangle of weed and springy limbs. Entangling vines played havoc with his fishing rod, even though he trailed it along behind. After about a hundred feet he broke out of the thicket into a wide swamp. His face and hands were covered with tiny tears and scratches, but his jacket and dungarees had protected the rest of him.

A droning bumblebee all but knocked him down as it buzzed past his ear like a high-speed bomber; it made two circuits around his head, then nonchalantly took off at a tangent and disappeared into the forest behind him. He ran his fingers through his curly, dark hair, and ruffled it slightly. Then he set off at a rambling gait, leaping from one grassy clump to another, keeping his sneakers as dry as possible.

Tony reached higher ground a little out of breath, but none the worse for wear. He continued walking, now through pine forest again, regaining his breath as he went. With a general idea of the direction of the stream, he described an arc and in just a few minutes found himself back at the water's edge.

The bread that he had partially used and stuffed into his pocket unwrapped, had dried up and would not stay in a ball, no matter how hard he pressed it together. So he spit into the dough and kneaded it together on the hook. After five minutes of no action, he moved downstream, eating the stale innards and using the crust for chum. He dropped a piece at a time at various spots in the creek as he walked along the edge. Still, the only fish he attracted were minnows: slender gleaming arrows that darted through the water, reflecting the sun off shiny scales, and boiling through the surface whenever too many of them tried to attack the same

piece of bread.

Eventually, he found a spot that was clear and fairly shallow. He saw a sunfish idling in a craterlike depression in the sand of the creek bed. It was a female, and she was defending her nesting area against protesting intruders. Whenever a minnow approached her territory, she darted after it faster than the eye could follow. Yet the minnow was faster, and once beyond an invisible boundary, the sunfish lost interest and glided back to her home.

Tony did not consider it sporting to fish for homebound females (although he had done it as a kid), since they would snap at just about any kind of food placed within reach. Their condition prevented them from foraging, so they were in a constant of hunger. He opted, instead, to fish nearby where he might catch one of her suitors.

About thirty feet downstream, he found a sunny spot where the river bent and formed a deep pool. He took out a fresh slice of bread, crimped a dough ball on the hook, and, after casting upstream into the current, the bob floated past him. Finally, on the third such journey, the hook managed to drift through the eelgrass without hanging up and having the bait stripped off.

On the fourth cast, when the hook was directly in front — and the line was laid out in a loose semicircle — the bob was pulled down violently for one long second. It popped up only to be pulled down in a series of smaller and shorter tugs. By the time he reeled in all the slack line, the fish had escaped with the bait.

Undaunted, Tony molded another piece of bread on the hook and cast upstream again, this time keeping the line taut. As soon as the hook passed over the pool, the fish struck again. He gave a brisk tug, felt resistance, and saw the lightweight pole bend. An instant later, he pulled the golden sunfish onto the grass where it flopped like a toad on a hotplate.

It promptly spat out the hook — not unusual since he had filed off the barb. He usually lost a few fish by doing this, but then, he did not have to tear any fish apart in order to get them off the hook. Meanwhile, the sunfish sprang down the slight incline toward the water. Tony interceded before it escaped altogether. He took a twelve inch cloth tape from his trousers pocket (it was a fragment of his grandmother's old sewing tape), held the squirming fish down with the flat of his hand, and laid the tape across the body from nose to tail. When he had his measurement, he picked up the fish and gently returned it to its own environment, watching it swim away. He did not know if a fish could feel happiness, but it certainly showed relief at being released. He dried his hand on his dungarees and wrote down the length in his notebook. He moved on to a new spot.

An open field appeared close to the edge of the stream. In the middle of the fifty-acre expanse, a rambling, two-story white farmhouse posed next to an equally large barn. A tractor dragged a plow slowly across the gray, bare furrows which rippled in the sun like frozen waves of sand. Soon the land would sprout new life in the form of corn, soybean, or watermelon: the three principle crops of the Delmarva Peninsula.

Tony skirted along the edge of the field, soaking up the heat that reflected off the sandy soil. In a couple of months, during harvesting time, that heat would become unbearable. After a while he charged back into the woods and met the stream where it began to widen.

The dam at Shoemaker Pond had been built mainly for flood control of the lower river, since the zoo and the park bordered its shore. It also formed a respectable pool several hundred feet across, even in low water. Somewhere in the middle, a homemade raft lay on the bottom, sinking into the sediment. Several summers ago he had lashed some boards across two old fifty-five gallon drums, with the idea of poling to the middle of the pond where schools of huge bass and pickerel undoubtedly lived. The rusted drums had leaked, the raft had sunk under his weight, and he had had to swim for shore with his fishing pole and tackle box. After he recounted his experience to his grandfather, the experienced woodsman had explained, with a hardly suppressed chuckle, that predatory fish did not live in schools.

Now the pond was brimming with spring runoff, engulfing the reed-choked banks. Eventually, he reached the road built atop the dam, and crossed the black macadam. He reentered the woods through a well-worn but narrow path that emerged where rapids formed below the overflow. It was a favorite fishing spot, for the water was deep and mysterious, and one never knew what one was going to pull out of it. It was not grassy enough for bass and pickerel which liked to hide and stalk their prey, but giant catfish and even bigger carp inhabited the dark depths.

Tony breaded his line and plopped it into the stream. He wished he had brought an apple core or a chicken leg knuckle, since only sunfish and silversides — and, of course, minnows — would bite on bread. But the fishing was good, and during the next half hour his notebook grew heavier with the addition of three good-sized sunnies.

"Howdy, son," said a deep voice from behind. "Having any luck?"

Tony sat on the ground, back against a tree, knees drawn up to his chest. The bob floated off the edge of the deep pool and rested near the grassy shallows. Looking around, he saw an elderly man wearing blue serge pants and a beige shirt with two flapped pockets, one with a pen protruding. His head was bare, exposing to the breeze a thick shock of white hair that puffed up like a tuft of cotton. He smiled as he sat down on the rock next to Tony.

"Good morning." Perfunctorily, he started reeling in the line. "I've caught four sunnies so far, one of them almost eight inches long."

"Where are they?" His voice conveyed interest rather than disbelief.

Tony laid the rod on the ground and took out his notebook. He opened it to the last written page. "They're all right here. I don't keep the fish. I just mark them down and put them back."

"Why bother catching them?"

"Oh, just for the fun of it."

"How can you prove you really caught them?"

"Why should I have to prove it?"

The man smiled. "Just because most boys want something to show for their efforts. It seems odd, is all."

Tony shrugged. "I don't put back everything I catch. When I go surf fishing with my grandfather, we bring home the fish for dinner."

"Don't like fresh water fish? Or do you think the water's bad?"

"No, they're just too small and bony. There's no sense killing a fish when you're not going to eat it."

A slight southern accent complimented the man's easy-going manner. "Well, I guess maybe you're right."

Tony pinched off another piece of bread to replace the one that had become too soggy to stay on the hook. Then he cast into the stream. The bob caught in an eddy and slowly circulated. He did not bother to recast. "Do you do any fishing around here?"

A broad smile broke out on the man's ruddy face. "Not too much any more, although I did quite a lot when I was your age. But I do keep an eye on them, you might say."

Tony scrunched up his face. "How do you do that?"

"Well, you see, the county needs someone to monitor the fish population — to make sure they're healthy and that the water's not being polluted, and to see that they're not being overfished. Of course, we can't prevent them from dying, or from being taken by natural predators, but we can make sure that there are enough of them to go around, so to speak. What I mean is, there are laws passed to protect the fish from all being caught by one person, so others can enjoy fishing, too. So I sort of check up on fishermen to see that they're doing the right thing."

"I thought the game warden did all that."

"Well, we don't actually call them wardens any more. You see, the word warden implies there's a kind of prison involved, or some fancy legal process. We call ourselves ecologists, because we want to maintain a good environment for all concerned. Of course, all that takes money, and the way we get the money to support these programs, such as raising fish and stocking streams, is to have the people who use those services and reap their benefits help subsidize the work. We do that by asking participating fisherman to pay licensing fees that go to pay the salaries of those who do the work. Now, this doesn't apply to youngsters under the age of sixteen, because they're dependents. But when you become an adult we expect people to put something back into the system they're taking from. And to see that everyone pays an equal share, the state has a set fee which is paid at the time of procuring the license. So, part of my job is to see that people are aware that licenses are necessary, and to remind them to get one."

The man stared out over the brimming water, rubbing one coarse fist over and around his chin. His smile never left his face.

Tony stared blankly for a moment. "Oh, I've got a license." He propped his fishing rod between his legs and fumbled in the back pocket of his trousers. He yanked out a thin leather wallet that was worn with age, the first one he had ever owned, and extracted a still-new and uncreased blue card. He handed it to the man.

The man squinted as he moved the card in and out. "Oh, you're a visitor."

"Yes, I'm from Philadelphia. My grandparent's are from here — my mother's parents, that is. My mother was born right here in Salisbury. We come down every so often for weekends, and during the summer I stay with Grandmom and Grandpop, and pick watermelons for my Uncle Joe. He's really my great uncle, but I've worked for him ever since I was fourteen. When I'm not helping Grandpop, that is."

The man handed back the fishing license. "I see. Well, Tony, my name is Jake Gouty. Pleased to meet you."

"Pleased to meet you, too."

Jake Gouty stretched his legs out in front of him, right to the water's edge. "Don't see many boys — er, uh, young men — here during the week. They're either working or in school."

"I'm on semester break. I'm a freshman at Temple. I came down by bus last weekend, and my parents will be coming down on Friday, for Easter. Then we'll be going home Sunday night."

"Where's your grandpa live?"

"Over on East William Street."

"Oh? What's his name?"

"Walter Ruark."

"The painter?"

"Yes, how'd you know?"

"I guess he's painted my house now and again over the years. Isn't he a deacon in the Immanuel Baptist Church over on Ocean City Road?"

"That's right. But, I don't remember seeing you there."

"I'm Presbyterian. But the only difference between us that counts is that we're allowed to have a nip or two every once in a while. The Baptists are sure sticklers about liquor."

"I know what you mean. My father's a Catholic, and it's a good thing, too."

"Which are you?"

"A little of both, I guess."

"How can that be?"

"Well, when I'm in Salisbury I go to church with my mother and Grandpop — Grandmom usually stays home and does the cooking for Sunday dinner, except on holidays. Then, when I'm in Philadelphia, since most of my friends are Catholic, I go to mass with them. But I'm not baptized in either one." Tony shrugged, then pulled in his line. "Guess I can't make up my mind."

Jake Gouty laughed heartily. "I guess that's being about as borderline as you can get. Don't really make any difference as long as you follow humanitarian ways. That way, too, when you're grown up, you'll be able to make your own choice."

"I keep wondering when that will be. I have an adult driver's license, and I've had to buy a fishing license ever since I was sixteen."

Jake's gray eyes met Tony's sharply. "How old are you?"

"Eighteen."

"Ah, eighteen is a dangerous and confusing age today. You're old enough to pay adult prices at the movies, but not old enough to see adult films. You're old enough to stand trial by jury, but not old enough to be a juror. You're old enough to drink if you're in the service, but not at home as a civilian. You're old enough to kill someone in the name of patriotism, but not old enough to carry a weapon for self-defense. And you're old enough die for your country, but not old enough to vote for it. Yes, it sure don't make much sense. And I don't profess to understand it myself — I just accept it. It's no wonder the young folk are a might addled today. No wonder at all."

Chapter 2

The park was green and verdant and pastoral.

Wild ducks quacked and swam and preened their feathers in a river that was still only fifty feet wide. Harems of drab, brown-speckled females turned and twisted in their efforts to be closest to the seemingly indifferent, colorful males. Snow-white geese, with clipped wings, honked loudly at their feathered friends who chose to live in the domain of the park because of the excess food. Large swans ignored all these avian shenanigans, and paddled the still water in pairs.

The banks of the clear waterway were groomed and grassed, and the tall white pines were carefully thinned to give an impression of vastness. The open ground was lightly covered with pine cones and slender needles from conifers whose lowest branches towered more than fifty feet in height. Picnic tables, benches, and brick fire pits were scattered far enough apart to dispel the oppressive feeling of a crowded municipal park, and were tucked into the seclusion of laurel thickets.

The programmed feeding procedure, which enticed the brightly plumaged teals to live in comparable harmony with the domesticated geese and swans, also kept the trees crowded with warblers of all varieties. Bird feeders swarmed with finches and sparrows, which chirped raucously at encroaching squirrels. On the ground, rabbits nibbled at the lush grass.

Tony tossed chunks of bread crust into the midst of roving geese and ducks, and laughed at the resulting pandemonium as they all raced for the same spot and pecked first for the food, then at each other. A few kernels of corn produced even more delight as the ducks turned tail up to dive for the sinking morsels.

Two gray squirrels, seemingly oblivious to the watery confusion and noise, scampered down the rough trunk of a nearby white pine and alighted timorously on the soft ground. Crouching at the base of the tree, their tails whipped spasmodically in silent communication, punctuated by short loud chirps that sounded birdlike in quality. As if on cue, the conversation ended and they dashed across the open lawn, hopping smoothly like ocean waves, but stopping sporadically to sniff the freshness of the soil and the food that it might conceal.

Tony ran toward them as fast as he could. Their itinerant meandering became a mad dash for the nearest tree. From five feet away they leaped to the trunk of another white pine, and climbed like a barber pole stripe, stopping out of sight on the opposite side. Tony walked around the tree, looking upward, but the elusive pair continued to go around in circles. He left without ever seeing more than a glimpse of a furry tail or the tip of an inquisitive nose.

Although the zoo was free for all visitors, and was sponsored largely by Salisbury's wealthier patrons and businesses, a collection box posted at each entranceway carried a painted sign that hawked: "Help support your zoo. Suggested donation twenty-five cents." Tony dropped a quarter through the slot as he entered the east gate.

The larger mammals interested him the most: the pacing civet, the blundering bison, and the snoozing black bear in his concrete cave. He avoided like the plague the dark-eyed llamas that scrutinized him from a distance, ruminating pointedly. He had encountered their viciousness before, and knew that chewing their cud meant that they were ready to take aim against an unsuspecting visitor with a wad of saliva the size of a baseball.

The highlight of the trip was the peacock displaying his charms to an uncaring female. He strutted proudly before her, but the few weekday onlookers showed more interest than the object of his desires. Finally, discouraged, he folded his feathers in frustrated detumescence.

Some time later, Tony passed under the arch that was the west gate. He followed the paved trail through an area that was scattered with park benches, and veered off toward the river before the road at Beaver Dam. He was out of bread, but not out of ideas.

He turned over a few rocks at the water's edge, and plucked out a couple of slimy earthworms. He left one high and dry on a flat rock where he could keep an eye on it, and threaded the other through his hook. The absence of the barb now made itself apparent, for with enough wriggling the worm could eventually work its way to freedom.

The bridge measured only two lanes wide, and passed a bare three feet over the water. On the other side stood the dam that kept the water level constant at the zoo. It poured a four-foot stream of water into what, in the summer, would become a popular swimming hole.

Tony removed the bob, and cast the weightless hook as far as it would go. He reeled it in at just the speed that would keep the worm submerged but would not let it drag on the muddy bottom. He should have had a crimp weight to increase the casting range, but he had brought none with him.

As it turned out, the lack of a weight did not matter. On the third cast, a dark silhouette streaked out from the shadow of the bridge. A sharp tug caused him to jerk back on the rod. He felt the reassuring wiggle of a captured game fish. He reeled in the coiling monofilament, pinching it through his fingers so it would not tangle. Then the line went suddenly slack, and a moment later he saw that it had been neatly severed by sharp, serious teeth. Leaders were not necessary for the toothless jaws of sunfish, but this was either a bass or a pickerel — and judging from the momentary glimpse, a big one.

He ran back to where the other worm was stored, tied on another hook, triple speared the bait, and left only a short tail dangling free. He knew that it would be difficult to catch the culprit without a reinforced leader, but if he gave it enough line before pulling back, he could hook it through the rear side of the mouth where the formidable teeth did not extend.

When Tony returned to the river, he saw a red pickup truck parked off the side of the road next to the dam. Leaning against the bulbous front fender, an elderly man pulled a paint-spackled peaked cap down over his forehead. "You ran by me so fast I thought a bear must be chasing you."

"Grandpop! I thought you weren't going to meet me until lunchtime."

"It's half past now. I was paintin' the west wall of a two-story bungalow, and couldn't stop in the middle. Doesn't look like you minded waiting, though." He looked cool and comfortable in his work clothes: loose fitting, blue striped trousers, pale blue shirt tucked in around his portly middle, cracked leather belt, once black shoes, and gray socks. Speckles of every color covered his clothing — the result of years of working with the brush. Today, tiny white specks marred his benign face, thickly veined hands, and wire rimmed glasses.

"Heck. Who could think about food when I just lost the biggest pike in the county? Do we have enough time for me to catch him?"

"I guess my breadbox will hold out, but you know how your grandmother is about having us there on time."

"Please, Grandpop? All I need is five minutes."

He shook his head, but his wistful smile never faded. "Seeings as how you already have the hook baited, you may as well use it."

"Gee, thanks, Grandpop."

"But let's not be too long or your grandmother will start to worry."

Tony was careful to cast in exactly the same spot, about midway between the second and third piers. He let the worm sink a little before reeling it in. It came all the way to the shore without attracting any attention.

"I pulled it in too fast."

Grandpop stood by silently as Tony cast again, but this time the hook fell short of its intended location. He terminated the cast and reeled in as quickly as he could. Another cast fell short, but only by a few feet. He reeled in slowly so that the lurking fish would have ample opportunity to see the worm, or to smell it. The hook sank and got caught in the long bottom grass. He jerked it loose, and reeled in quickly again. He shot a furtive glance at Grandpop, then cast again. It fell exactly right, and this time he reeled it in a little too quickly so that the worm floated on the surface. He let it fall back down and then took in the line at a slow pace.

Just when he gave up hope, and was about to pull the line out of the water, something darted out from under the bridge, snapped up the worm, and sped away. It was so close that all Tony had to do was lift the fishing rod up and swing it over, and the pickerel was landed. He leaped to hold it down, and dragged it further away from the water lest it get away unrecorded.

"Look at that! Just look at that!" The fish performed an athletic leap. "It must be a foot and a half long. It's the biggest pike I ever saw."

Grandpop smiled broadly, watching Tony's enthusiasm. When the fish stopped flopping around enough so he could get a hand on it, Tony saw that it had not one but two hooks protruding from its mouth. He retrieved both hooks and tossed the fish onto the grass.

"Wow! I got my other hook back."

He pulled the twelve-inch tape measure out of his pocket while several youngsters gathered around, oohing and aahing. One of them said, "Whatcha gonna do with 'im mister?"

The fish was longer than the tape, but only by two inches. Tony was disappointed, but tried not to let it show.

"What kind of fish is it, mister?"

"It's a pike, isn't it, Grandpop?"

"Well, now, let me see." Grandpop got down on one knee and tilted his head back so he could see through the lower part of his bifocals. " 'Pears to be a pickerel. Don't remember there being any pike in these waters."

"I thought they were the same thing."

The three boys stopped gasping and listened attentively as Grandpop explained. "The pike is usually larger, and lives farther north. The markings are pretty much the same, but the best way of tellin' them apart is by looking at the gill covers. See here?" He stepped on the tail and held the head down with one firm hand. The trapped fish tried to flop, but succeeded only in rippling on the ground. "On a pike only the top half would be scaled, but this gill cover is completely scaled."

"How do you tell them apart in the water?" asked one inquisitive youth.

"That's pretty hard to do," Grandpop allowed. He stood up and wiped his hand on his trousers.

"Whatcha gonna do with 'im?"

Tony picked up the dirt- and leaf-covered fish. "Guess I'll put him back."

"Why you gonna do that?"

"Because he'll die if I don't." Tony slid the pickerel into the water. It was stunned, and for several seconds it did not move even though freedom was only a swish of the tail away. Tony nudged it. Suddenly, it seemed to come alive, and with a flash it was gone.

"I woulda tooken him," said the third youth, until now quiet and wide-eyed, "for my cat."

"I woulda tooken him for my dad."

Tony smiled. "But that wouldn't be fair. This way you'll have a chance to catch him for yourself."

"We never catch anything but sunnies."

"You're not using the right bait. Turn over some rocks and get a couple of juicy earthworms. That'll catch 'em."

The three disenchanted boys stared blankly into the water, as if they expected that their longing gaze could bring the pickerel back onto the shore. They continued to grumble among themselves as Grandpop climbed aboard the pickup truck.

Tony threw his rod in the back, then eased into the front seat. "Do you think they'll learn anything by that?"

"Only if they want to."

Chapter 3

"Land sakes. Dinner's been on the table for 'most an hour. I just don't know what I'm goin' to do with you two."

Grandmom dashed around the kitchen in black, low-heeled shoes, a paisley dress, and a faded, flowered apron. As she talked, she slashed the air with a thick wooden spoon. In the middle of a swipe, she plunged the spoon into a large kettle that was huffing away on the stove; she vigorously stirred a delicious smelling brew. She peered into the kettle, then stepped back as the steam fogged her glasses.

"Now you two wash up and set down while I put the soup on the table."

Neither Tony nor his grandfather said a word, nor made any excuses. Grandpop placed his glasses on the counter next to the cap with the embroidered M-A-B nearly covered with paint, then turned on the faucet and grabbed the soap. He exchanged a silent wink with Tony.

"And the arms."

Tony wrinkled his nose, but reluctantly washed clear up to his elbows before toweling off. Grandpop diligently lathered his face and the back of his neck, and ran a dampened cloth over his nearly bald head. When he was done, his face was fresh with the wrinkles smoothed; his hands were clean, pink, and calloused — but still speckled. He used turpentine only at the end of the day. Paint, he always said, was not dirt.

By that time, Grandmom was ladling hot butter beans and corn into three bowls. She turned down the gas flame to let the pot simmer, and placed the steaming bowls on a table already piled high with fried chicken (room temperature leftovers from the previous night), sweet potatoes, spinach, dumplings, and fresh crust.

Tony piled dumplings into his butter beans and corn and sliced them with his spoon. Since it was still too hot to eat, he buttered a wedge of crust and devoured it while picking up a chicken leg with the other hand.

Grandmom opened the refrigerator door. "Do you want some milk, Honey?"

Tony never missed a chew. "Mn-hmn." He stabbed a huge forkful of spinach and transferred it to his plate.

Grandpop wore his ever-present smile. "Tony, slow down, or you'll make yourself sick."

Tony took the milk and washed down the dry crust. "I'm so hungry I could eat a horse."

"Maybe next time you go fishing you'll have ham and eggs for breakfast 'stead of just a bowl of cereal." Grandmom continued to putter around the kitchen, doing her chores. "You're still a growing boy."

"Aw, Grandmom, I'm not growing any more. Grandpop measured me a couple days ago and I've only grown a half an inch since last year."

"That's because of your mother's cooking."

"No, it's because I was wearing shoes instead of sneaks."

"Well, you may not be growing up, but you're still growing out. Someday you'll be broad shouldered and husky like your father."

"You mean fat, not husky. The only place he's broad is around the middle."

"Your father may have put on a little weight over the years, but times was when he was in the peak of health." Grandmom sat down for a moment and took a bird-sized bite of food. "When he was stationed down at Princess Anne during the war he was the apple of every local girl's eye. You ask your mother."

Tony finished his first bowl of soup and worked his way through his vegetables and another piece of chicken. Grandmom, ever attentive, scooted her chair back and took his empty bowl to the stove. She filled it from the kettle, then set it back in front of him.

"But that was when he was active. He's slowed down a lot in the last twenty years. His elbow is the only thing he exercises now."

Grandpop scooped some sweet potato out of the hard-baked shell. "His work is his activity, and being an electrician must prey on his mind as well as his body. Working with all them volts can't be easy on him."

"Ever since he became a contractor all he does is sit around and talk on the phone and work on blueprints. Sometimes he doesn't go out for days at a time, and then he only checks up on the jobs. He says he can't stand the cold any more."

"A man of his age shouldn't have to work all day in the cold. That's why he went into business."

"He did not. He went into business to get rich. And besides, you still work outside, even in the winter."

"Not when it gets really cold. I always save some inside jobs for when the weather's bad. Besides, I'm a country boy, and being out in the cold is a way of life on the farm."

"The only reason you don't work outside in the winter is because the paint doesn't stick right. But you're still tough enough to do it."

Grandmom set her beanpole body on the edge of the chair, but remained poised in case she had to get up again. She nitpicked at her food. "Things are different nowadays. With all these newfangled gadgets, people don't have to work their fingers to the bones, so why should they?"

She was as tough as they came. She still used a 1920 vintage washing machine: one that sat on three legs and had a wringer mounted on one side. She laundered Grandpop's dirty work clothes on a glass scrub board. She heated her solid irons on the wood-burning stove, supplied by wood that she chopped herself. She even baked her homemade breads and pies in the cast iron stove because, after all these years, she still preferred a wood fire to gas. And her sewing machine was an original Ideal operated by a foot treadle.

"There's nothing wrong with using them, but my mother wants to buy every gadget that comes on the market, whether she needs it or not. And my father just spends money for the sake of spending."

There was no communication between them, but somehow Grandmom knew exactly when Grandpop was ready for his coffee. She poured it, and he added sugar and milk. He stirred it casually. "That's the way people are today. Always wanting more, always spending more. They're no different from anyone else."

"That's because they don't want to be different."

"It isn't always easy to make a choice." Grandpop tested the too-hot coffee, put it back on the china saucer. "People have to live up to an image, do what's expected of them, be a part of society."

"They don't have to."

"But it's what comes easiest. It's a hard thing to do something other than what's expected of you. You strike out on your own too much and people brand you a radical. You must see them all the time in school."

Tony shrugged, but kept chugging down the food. "Yes, you get your share of off-the-wall people in college, but most of them are doing it just to get attention. I don't think they care whether they're right or wrong, they just want to be loud."

Grandmom pushed the vegetables closer to him. "All this talk don't mean no never mind to me, 'bout radicals and things. But I do know if you keep runnin' through the woods like you do, you got to eat up. Now finish your dinner and talk politics later. We get enough of that when your Dad comes down."

Grandpop winked, and smiled whimsically. Tony reached for another piece of chicken.

Chapter 4

Tony situated the chaise lounge between the two scraggly oak trees in the back yard, where the afternoon sun had a clear path over the furrowed cornfield and Grandmom's flower garden. Despite the blue, cloudless sky and the warm air, frost warnings were forecast for the night. Snuggled in one of Grandpop's thick, woolen sweaters, and a hand-woven shawl that was tucked around his legs, he was deeply engrossed in a geology book. He liked to stay a couple chapters ahead of the class so he knew what was coming.

The back door creaked open, the spring twanging with age, and Grandmom stuck out her head. "Tony, you want to catch me a chicken for dinner? Your mother and dad will be wanting to eat as soon as they get here."

"Okay, Grandmom." Tony leaped up out of the chaise lounge, stuck an ornate leather bookmark between the pages of his book, and laid it down in order to fold the shawl.

"The water's just about boiling, so I'll meet you over by the chopping block." Her snow-white head disappeared, and the screen door shut with a bang.

The long, narrow country house lay between two driveways. The east driveway led to the double car garage, one side of which was used to store farm implements. Behind it stood the chicken coop, and beyond that stood the truck garage, reached by the west driveway, which curved between the yard and the field. And beyond *that* stood the dog pen. With this kind of arrangement, the chicken coop required only two wire fences, since it was nestled nicely between the two garages.

Tony ran along the dirt path between the car garage and the garden to the screen door of the chicken coop. He rattled the door to make sure the chickens would scatter away while he slipped in and fastened the latch from the inside. Chickens were not very smart, but that did not stop them from running through an open door to make good their escape when they knew what was on the menu.

The coop measured about twenty feet square, in the center of which stood a two compartment henhouse: the larger part was for the chickens, and the smaller one for feed, tools, and miscellaneous items such as kerosene for the ever-present wasp nests. The slanted, corrugated tin roof kept the insides at a perpetual incubator temperature. A trellis occupied the space between the henhouse and the side of the truck garage; an ancient grape vine hung from the trellis and draped down along the eight-foot-high wire fence. Many times in the summer, if he was fast enough to beat the hungry sparrows, Tony enjoyed the purple grapes amid the chatter of frightened chickens. And in his younger days, the henhouse had served admirably as a fort in endless fantasy games of cowboys and Indians.

He pivoted the wooden latch on the feed shed door, and reached in for the chicken hook: a five foot long, heavy gauge iron wire which curled into different sized hooks at each end. He carefully locked the door to keep the chickens from stealing food, or else they would eat themselves to death.

Tony peered into the henhouse opening when, out of the gloom, a squawking demon with flapping wings crashed into his chest and flailed him with beak and feathers. He should have been prepared for it. Instead, he fell back so fast that he tripped and sat hard on the ground. The henhouse emptied in a flurry of clucking and loose feathers, leaving him sitting ignominiously in the dirt.

He laughed at himself as he stood up and dusted himself off. He knew there were no chickens left inside, but he checked anyway. Then he rummaged through the straw nests until he found a lone brown-shelled egg tucked away in a corner. Delightedly, he picked it up, carried it to the door of the coop, and cached it by the wooden sill.

Now he surveyed the situation. As long as he was at the back of the henhouse, he could hear the chickens clucking clandestinely at the front. As he walked slowly around the yard, the small flock of seven or eight — they moved too quickly to ever be certain — strutted noisily away. He felt like a sheep dog herding his flock.

Suddenly he charged into their midst, and half a dozen chickens exploded around the henhouse in frenzied flight. Two of them, squawking wildly, flapped their clipped wings hard enough to rise a foot or two into the air. One turned unexpectedly and dashed past him, while another crawled under the stilted building.

Tony pursued the greatest number, then turned suddenly and raced the other way. He met the cluckers head on. Before they rose in mad flight, the iron hook jabbed out and connected with a scaly, yellow leg. The hook slid down and caught on the widely spread, four-toed foot. The chicken protested loudly, but he pulled in the hook hand over hand, and took a firm grip on both legs before she could slip off and get away. He held her upside down in one hand, triumphantly, and replaced the hook in the shed. When he slipped out the door, completely uncontested, he had the brown egg safely tucked in his pocket.

Grandmom's lively step resounded on the five wooden steps, and the door banged shut on the two-story, whitewashed house. She carried a pot full of scalding water in one hand, and a sharpened axe in the other. Her thin arms were like rails and twice as strong. Tender veins popped out along her forearms as she leaned away from the weight of the pot. She navigated the narrow garden path and set the heavy pot down alongside the chopping block.

Tony handed over the wriggling chicken. "Grandmom, I found another egg."

"Land o' mercy. You get right good mileage out'n them hens." Holding the legs firmly, she placed the chicken across the stump that was the chopping block. The helpless hen quieted down to a monotonous clucking, but when her beak picked up the scent of past sacrifices she flew into a rage of fear, with wings flapping futilely.

Tony winced as Grandmom nonchalantly picked up the axe and with one deft stroke lopped off the head. "Can I have it for breakfast tomorrow?"

The body was still squirming when she plunged it into the water. On the ground, the head gasped soundlessly and the beak twitched. The grisly scene lasted only for a few seconds. When the eyes glazed over, Tony picked up the head by the bloodless, yellow beak, ran to the edge of the cornfield, and tossed it as far as he could. Along with food scraps, apple peels, and stale bread, it would nurture the coming corn.

With gloved hands Grandmom plucked the feathers from the softened skin. "I don't see why not. I've even got some country ham to go along with it. Now, pour this water in the field for me, Honey. Spread it out so it doesn't dig a hole, and scatter them feathers good."

"Okay, Grandmom. Will you take my egg in with you?"

"Sure, Honey." She put the egg in the pocket of her apron, then waddled along the garden path, surveying the flowers as she went. When she reached the cement path that ran through the middle of the back yard, she stopped. "Your grandfather will be home soon, but we'll be holding supper off till your mother and dad get here. If you get hungry in the meantime you can have some butter beans and carn — and I made a fresh batch of dumplings."

"Okay."

She went inside to gut, clean, flour, and fry the chicken. But any thoughts of hunger were driven from Tony's mind as soon as he heard the faraway grind of a familiar motor. He dumped the water and tossed the dampened feathers to the wind, then ran down the gravel driveway. He heard two hoots of the horn, then saw the red pickup truck rounding the bend. Tony ran to the garage and laid the big pot to the side. He pulled the chain that released the latch, and swung open one whitewashed door. He kicked up the floor catch on the other door and swung it wide. Then he hightailed it down the driveway to meet Grandpop as soon as he turned off the road. When he slowed down, Tony jumped onto the running board on the passenger side and stuck his head through the open window.

"Hi, Grandpop!"

Grandpop smiled as he drove carefully over the loose stones, between the azalea bushes not yet in bloom, and slowly eased the truck through the narrow opening. "Some day you're going to get the seat of your pants full of splinters."

Dogs barked loudly as the engine died out. "Aw, you're too good a driver. You slide this truck in here just like you were putting your foot into your shoe."

The truck was still rolling quietly. Grandpop pumped the brake until it came to a halt a few scant inches away from the shelving. "Someday I might be a hair off."

Tony squeezed between the red body and the tiers of paint cans. "Never happen."

Now the dogs were jumping and whimpering for their dinner. "I guess I'd better feed those hounds before they scratch a hole through the wall."

He slipped out of the truck and pushed the door closed. Tony climbed over the rear wheel well and into the truck bed, ducking low because of the roof beams and being careful not to step into paint trays or onto cans or brushes. Then he leaped over the tailgate and out the door to the side of the garage where the dog pen was attached. Instead of opening the gate — always a dangerous thing to do when the dogs were riled up this close to supper — he grabbed the lower limb of the black walnut tree, and swung himself over the fence.

He was immediately set upon by two excited hound dogs. They dashed around in circles, jumped all over his dungarees, and barked woefully. It was as if they had not eaten for a week. With great difficulty, Tony fought his way to the food bowl. Spot buried his head in it and sniffed. Driver lapped his face with a wet tongue. Tony had to fight free of the leaping canines.

Grandpop finished washing paint off his hands, put the lid back on the turpentine can, then dried his hands on a tattered cloth hanging from a nail over the workbench. Tony opened the five-gallon can full of brown, dry dog food, and scooped it into the bowl until it was level with the brim. Then Grandpop added some water from a galvanized pail, careful to hold back the leaves that had accumulated on the surface, and stirred the mixture with a long-handled metal spoon. Tony took out a piece of dry meal before he clamped down the lid, and munched on it.

Grandpop carried the full bowl with two hands while Tony tagged along with the water pail. When they rounded the corner of the garage, the dogs went wild with glee, leaping to the top of the four-foot-high fence. Grandpop opened the gate and flung it wide — the dogs would never leave the pen on an empty stomach. And on the rare occasions when they managed to tunnel under the wire through the soft sand, they either wandered around lost until someone brought them back, or they returned of their own accord, begging to be let in.

Spot started eating out of the bowl before it reached the ground. Then Grandpop fitted it into its place on the wooden platform and stepped aside. Driver retired to the doghouse to wait his turn. Closing the gate, Tony and Grandpop leaned over and watched the dogs devour their food. Spot ate exactly half, then stepped aside as Driver charged in and wolfed down the remainder.

"How does Spot know when it's Driver's turn?"

Grandpop smiled affably. He took the bucket and poured water into the adjacent bowl with such force that it washed out all the leaves and bark. "I don't rightly know, but I suppose if he started to eat more'n his share, Driver would let him know about it."

When Driver finished eating, Spot licked the bowl clean of any scraps. They both drank copiously, so before leaving Grandpop had to refill the water bowl. "Have you fed the chickens yet?"

"Yep. Including the one we're having for dinner tonight." He closed the garage doors on well-oiled hinges. "And I found an egg in the hen house, too."

"You sure get your mileage out of them hens."

"Grandpop, that's exactly what Grandmom said. How come you two always say the same thing?"

"Well, I guess when two people live together for so long, they begin thinkin' alike."

"How long have you been married, now?"

"I first met your grandmother in nineteen-fifteen and married her after three years of courtin'. Your mother wasn't born for another five years."

"Wow, that's forty-eight years ago."

"Seems like a right long time."

"I guess it is. It's two and a half times as long as I am old."

Grandpop laughed at that. He worked his way down the path at his ordinary slow pace. Tony danced around him, skipping backwards and swinging the kettle. "You'll be having your golden wedding anniversary soon."

"Pretty near." Grandpop stopped at the yard, took off his cap, and wiped his nearly bald head with his sleeve. He worked the cap back into place by pulling it back and forth a couple of times. "Now who do you suppose that is coming to visit us at supper time?"

Tony followed the blue, staring eyes and saw a shiny new car turn into the truck driveway. It was long and sleek and so quiet that it seemed to float over the stones. The faint crunching of rounded pebbles under the fat, rubber tires was the only sound it made.

Off to the left, the sun was low on the horizon: a dull orange blob partially obscured by low-lying clouds which it illuminated with brilliant colors. The sun reflected off the spotless windshield in such a way that the glass appeared to be on fire, obscuring all within.

For a long moment the engine purred silently, barely audible in the evening stillness. The whispering engine sighed out, and the driver's door swung open. A short, somewhat overweight but well-dressed man stepped out into the fading light and, raising his hands high over his head, stretched like one who has been in the driver's seat for a long time.

Grandpop put the bucket down by the faucet. Tony ran ahead as if on springs. "Dad!"

The stern face retained its mask. "Hi."

Tony quickly changed his attention to the woman getting out of the car on the other side. "Hi, Mom."

"Tony, come over here and help me with the baby. Frank, couldn't you at least help me with the car seat?"

"What the hell do you want from me? I've been driving for three hours. Can't you undo a simple seat belt?"

"Well, it's stuck. I don't know how to work the damn thing."

Tony rounded the long hood and stood by the door as his mother smoothed out her skirt. A ball of fur erupted from the floor behind the front seat, and a black and white blur streaked to freedom in the field.

Frank threw his hands up in the air. "Now you let the cat get out!"

"I did not! How did *I* know she was going to run away?"

Tony got down on his hands and knees and peered under the chassis. "I think she ran back under the car." The black undercoating had not yet been sullied by mud and dust, and the springs and shocks and exhaust pipe shone without a hint of rust. "Here, Kitty, Kitty, Kitty."

Kitty poked her head out from behind the rear tire, meowed once, then marched out and rubbed her silky body against Tony's leg. He ran his hand along her smooth, coal fur; it was clean and shiny like she always kept it. After the third passage across his legs, he picked her up and held her close to his ear so he could hear the music of her purring.

"Tony, put that cat down and get your brother out of the car seat."

"But, Dad, what do I do with Kitty?"

"Forget the damn cat. She won't go far."

Tony's mother said, "Maybe we'll be lucky and lose her."

"Hello, Frank. Hello, Elizabeth. How was the drive?" Grandpop's voice was smooth and calm, and he wore his perpetual smile.

"Hi, Daddy." Elizabeth walked around the car and kissed her father lightly on the cheek.

Frank groaned. "It was a nightmare. We hit all the rush hour traffic coming over the Tacony Bridge, and then we got held up by an accident coming through Dover. Some idiot ran into a tractor-trailer just before we got there."

"I don't know where everyone was going. It was like the Fourth of July."

Tony placed Kitty on the ground, gave her a few reassuring strokes, then leaned into the car. It smelled of freshness and expensive leather. "Hi, Robby." He kissed the tot on the forehead. Robby was asleep and barely opened his eyes in acknowledgement. His head was slumped forward over the retaining bar. Tony loosened his seat belt and slipped him out from under the bar instead of raising it. "Uh, oh." He backed out of the car with his baby brother cradled in his arms. "Mom, Robby's had an accident."

"Wouldn't you know it? He was dry ten minutes ago. You'd think after four years he'd learn to speak up when he has to go. Well, take him inside and I'll change him."

Tony carried the sleeping innocent around the back of the car, where his father was removing luggage from the trunk.

"Tony, give me a hand with these suitcases."

"Dad, can't you see I'm carrying Robby?"

"Give him to your mother. I can't do everything myself."

"Frank, I've got the diaper bag and the thermos."

Tony looked helplessly from father to mother, waiting for further instructions. But Grandpop solved the dilemma. "Here, I'll take the little feller."

Tony handed the sleeping bundle to his grandfather. "Careful, he's damp underneath."

Frank piled all the luggage on the ground. There were two large suitcases, two small ones, and a compact for Elizabeth's toilet articles. He slammed the trunk lid, picked up one large and one small suitcase, and nodded with his chin. "Don't forget the compact."

Tony tucked the compact case under one arm, hefted the others, then went back for the kettle. He stumbled after his father and caught up with him at the back door, where he was at the top of the steps trying to pull the screen door open without putting down the luggage. "Damn it." He let go of the large suitcase, pulled open the door, and caught it with his shoulder when the spring brought it back. He lunged inside and let the door slam behind him before Tony could grab it.

Tony carried first one, then the other suitcase inside. Then, peering out into the oncoming darkness, he called, "Kitty." Green eyes reflected the last glimmer of light from where the cat was fertilizing the flowers. She looked down at the sand, pawed a few more scoops into a hole, and dashed across the yard, up the steps, and into the house. Tony eased the door shut, picked up the two suitcases, and followed her inside.

The kitchen was suffused with warmth, delicious odors, and confusion.

The ancient cast iron stove occupied one entire corner of the room; it weighed about a ton. Split logs were stored underneath it where it stood on four massive legs. It oozed with the smell of rising, homemade bread.

The gas range had three burners going: two covered by kettles of vegetables, and one large frying pan which crinkled and spat grease as the chicken was brought slowly to a golden brown crisp.

Two sconces lighted the sides of the porcelain sink, while overhead the two circular fluo-

rescent tubes of the ceiling fixture poured out a stark white light. The ends of the tubes were blackened, and coruscating rings charged effortlessly back and forth.

Frank went through the kitchen into the dining room, dropped his load on the floor, and returned saying to no one in particular, "I could sure go for a cup of coffee."

Grandmom wiped her hands on her apron. "Let me see that pretty boy." Robby opened his eyes as he was transferred to his grandmother's arms. He was not yet awake. "My, he's getting big, bless his little heart."

"Be careful, Mother. He wet his pants again. I've got to change him before he ruins another new suit."

"I told you not to put on his good clothes. Did you expect him to last three hours without getting wet?"

"He's supposed to be toilet trained, remember?"

"You've been saying that for two years. Hey, don't leave them there. Put them up in the bedroom where they belong."

Tony picked up the suitcases from where he had placed them next to the others, and carried them up the stairs. When he got back down, he saw Kitty going out the other door of the dining room to escape the turmoil and noise for the sanctity of the living room.

"Get those other suitcases upstairs. Do I have to tell you everything?" Frank turned his attention from Tony to Elizabeth. "What do I have to do to get a cup of coffee around here?"

"You know how to put water on the stove, don't you?"

By the time Tony put away the last of the suitcases, Grandmom had laid a blanket on the dining room table and started to change Robby's training pants. There was too much for the plastic liners to hold, and the urine had leaked through and left a large stain down both pant legs.

While Grandmom changed the baby, Elizabeth took a pair of dry pants from the bag. "I swear, I don't think he'll ever get toilet trained. Sometimes I get so mad I feel like sending him back."

"Now, Honey, you know you don't mean that. You'll never have another one quite so precious."

"You don't have to live with him."

Tony placed his hand on Robby's head. It was warm, and the feel of his hair was like down. "Hi, there."

Robby was fully awake now, and he lisped in his baby patois. "Tonwy, you catch any fishes?"

"A whole bunch."

"Can I see?"

"No, they're not here."

"Where?"

"Back in their home — in the river."

"Didn't you save 'um?"

"No. I had no place to keep them."

"Couldn't you keep 'um inna bafftub?"

"Fish can't live in a bathtub. They need lots of room to swim around."

Grandmom stood him up and pulled up the dry pants, then got the shoulder straps in place. Robby giggled when she tickled his belly.

"Did you get any thinkin'?"

Tony laughed at his precociousness, and exchanged embarrassed glances with his mother. She was not paying any attention to him, but had her eyes riveted on Grandpop, who was talking to Frank in the kitchen.

"I did a whole lot of thinking, but I still have to do some more."

Grandmom held Robby in one arm and nuzzled him with her nose. "There you go, pumpkin. Now you're all fresh and clean, you pretty little boy."

"I pretty?"

"Just like your big brother."

"Like Tonwy?"

"Yes, like Tony. And someday you'll be big and strong like your brother."

"Like Tonwy?"

"Yes, Honey. But in order to get big and strong you have to eat lots and lots of food."

"Fwied chicken?"

"Yes, fried chicken. Now you get down here on the floor while I go and finish fixin' supper. Why don't you go see your grandfather?"

Robby threw himself into Grandpop's arms. "Hi, Gwanpop. We gonna have fwied chicken."

Frank's face was a dark mask. "Did you put that coffee water on yet?"

Elizabeth pouted. "Hold your horses, Frank, I've only got two hands. I had to change the baby first."

Tony pulled out the cutlery drawer. "Grandmom, can I start setting the table now?"

"I guess you may as well. And you'll have to bring in an extra chair from the pantry, and one from the dining room."

"Fwied chicken. Fwied chicken."

Grandpop played with Robby, and hustled him to the sink so he could wash the turpentine off his hands. Tony set out the utensils, then brought the chairs into the already crowded room. Frank plopped himself down and waited for his coffee.

Grandmom dashed back and forth across the room like a short order cook: taking bread out of the oven, stirring vegetables, turning over the chicken, washing utensils at the sink, taking out bowls and plates.

Elizabeth tried ineffectually to light the gas burners with a wooden match. "Why don't you get a range with an automatic pilot?"

Robby cried, "Fwied chicken. Fwied chicken," and pulled change and odds and ends out of Grandpop's trouser pockets.

Frank found the *Salisbury Times* and spread it out on the table while Tony was trying to set out the plates. "I have to put in the leaf, Dad."

"Why did you have to wait until I had the paper out before you decided to do that?" Grudgingly, he moved aside while Tony pulled the table apart, popped in the leaf, and smoothed out the plastic tablecloth. Frank immediately spread out the paper again, grumbling each time Tony tried to slip a plate or bowl under it.

Elizabeth stood in front of the medicine cabinet and combed her hair in the mirror. Robby pulled on her skirt to show her what he had found in Grandpop's pockets. She tapped him hard on the knuckles with the hairbrush until he let go, then went back to combing her hair. Robby wailed until Grandpop finished drying his hands, and picked him up. Then Robby returned all the items he had appropriated, one by one, and helped Grandpop put them back in his pocket.

"Is that little boy going to give me them tears?" Grandmom took time from her cooking to wipe off his face and pinch his cheek. He sniffled at her. Then Grandpop took him to the bathroom so he could get his shaving mug and brush.

The water in the pan boiled while Grandmom was taking out the last of the bread from the wood-burning stove. Elizabeth turned off the burner and poured some water into a cup in which she had already spooned the instant coffee.

Frank looked up disgruntled. "Is that coffee ready yet?"

"Can't you see I'm pouring it?"

Frank scowled, then went back to reading his paper.

Grandpop came back with Robby in tow. "Bethy, is there enough water in there for my shaving cream?"

"I think so, Daddy. If not, I can put some more on."

She poured the rest of the water into his mug. He stirred it up until he had a cupful of hot lather, then plastered it on his face with his fine, camelhair brush. Robby started taking things out of his pocket again, so Grandpop playfully dabbed his nose with white cream. Robby squealed with delight.

"Westmoreland's calling for more troops." Frank's eyes were glued to the paper. "A quarter million men he's got and he still wants more."

"No, no, no, Honey. Don't bother your grandfather when he's shaving. He might cut hisself."

Grandpop patted Robby on the head. "I'll be done in a minute." He started scraping lather off his face with a straight razor.

"Fwied chicken?"

"Almost, Honey. I'm puttin' it on the table now."

"Grandmom, can I have an old dish for Kitty?"

"Sure, Honey. Just let me get these turnip greens out'n the water." Grandmom picked up a large pot of steaming water and poured it into the sink. Then she set it down and took two shallow dishes out of the cabinet. "You'll need one for milk."

"Thanks, Grandmom."

Tony took a quart bottle of milk out of the refrigerator and half-filled one bowl. He put it on the floor next to the range.

"Don't put it there, Honey. She might get splattered with hot grease from the frying pan. Put it over next to the ironing board. And put a newspaper under it, too."

"Okay." The ironing board was built into the wall between the pantry opening and the back door. When the milk was in place, Tony called out, "Here, Kitty, Kitty, Kitty."

In a flash she was there, and wasted no time in lapping up the cold milk. Tony opened a can of cat food and filled the other dish. As soon as it hit the floor, Kitty transferred her attention from the milk to the solid food. She might not have eaten for a week.

"Frank, did you bring in my compact case?"

"Yes."

"Well, what did you do with it?"

"I don't know. Ask Tony."

"Dad told me to put it in your room."

"Now why did you do that? You know I need it in the downstairs bathroom."

Frank never looked up from his paper. "How am I supposed to know where you want your stuff?"

"Well, I need my cold cream."

"So whaddaya want from me? Tony, go get her compact and shut her up."

Tony slipped quietly upstairs. When he returned, Elizabeth was in the living room, watching television. Robby was with her, so he patted him on the head. He grabbed Tony's finger playfully.

"I only wanted the cold cream." She opened the case, removed the small milk glass bottle, and handed it back to him. "Go put it in the bathroom."

Tony left the room with Robby still attached to his finger. After depositing the compact case, Tony led him to the dining room where he picked up some of his toys from the diaper bag and kept him amused.

Robby loved to play catch. Tony threw the oversized rubber hall at him, but his reflexes were too slow and he could never catch it. Most of the time it bounced lightly off his chest; then Tony caught it himself and tossed it back at him. If he threw it slow enough to hit the ground, Robby could trap it, then pick it up and throw it somewhere in his direction. The only time he could count on one hundred percent accuracy was when he carried the ball to Tony and crashed with it into his chest. Then Tony would howl and fall backward with the ball, only he would grab Robby at the same time and take him down with him.

"Will you two keep quiet? I'm trying to read the paper." Frank glared angrily from the kitchen. "Go play in the living room if you want to make noise."

"But Mom's watching television."

"Don't give me no argument. Just shut up."

"Supper's almost ready," Grandmom called out. "Why don't you set yourself down while I finish putting it on the table?"

Grandpop rinsed out his shaving mug in the sink - he always shaved in the kitchen because there was more light there - and carried his things to the bathroom. Tony picked up Robby, and sat him down on the chair that was to be his. He did not have a booster seat, so Tony stacked him on top of two telephone books.

"Fwied chicken. Fwied chicken. I want fwied chicken."

Most of the food was already on the table: heaps of mashed potatoes, two bowls of gravy, turnip greens swimming in butter, a simple salad of lettuce and tomato, steaming hot bread, butter, milk, and a huge plate of fried chicken. Frank still read the newspaper, although he held it up so only one corner managed to slip into the mashed potatoes. Grandmom made room for her homemade applesauce and a pitcher of iced tea.

Grandpop took his seat at the head of the table and started filling his plate and passing things to Frank. Elizabeth came in and sat next to Frank, who grumblingly folded up the paper. Grandmom, as usual, ate on the fly — she was constantly taking used dishes and empty plates off the table, then washing and replacing them. She was cook, waitress, and dishwasher all in one.

Tony sat next to Robby. He took the platters as Grandpop handed them to him. He filled his own plate as well as his brother's. "Do you want mashed potatoes?"

"No."

Tony dumped a small spoonful on Robby's plate.

"How about some nice turnip greens?"

"No."

Tony gave him a dollop, at the far edge.

"Some delicious, home-made bread that Grandmom made herself?"

"No."

He cut off a slice, buttered it, then took a bite out of it. Robby immediately swiped it from him and started munching on it. Without asking, Tony placed a chicken leg on his plate, at which point Robby started chanting, "Fwied chicken, fwied chicken, fwied chicken."

"Careful, it's hot."

Robby tasted the chicken testily, waited a few moments, then tried again. He nibbled at it diligently, the forgotten slice of bread still held in his other hand.

"Bethy, what's this your Daddy's been telling me about a new car?"

"Oh, we finally got rid of that old clunker. Two years old and it was already falling apart. I swear, they don't make things like they used to."

"It's a Coup de Ville," Frank said with pride. "The top of the line. It's got reclining seats, tilt steering wheel, AM-FM radio, electric windows, air conditioning, power steering and power brakes — the works."

Grandpop smiled. "It's so quiet we didn't hear you coming."

"And we couldn't figure out who it was. I would never have guessed it was you."

Frank took time out from eating to pile more food on his plate. "Gimme the butter." Elizabeth handed him the butter dish; he smeared butter sloppily on a slide of bread. "I had to get a Cadillac. I was the only contractor on the job driving a Chevy. Even my men got bigger cars than me — they can afford it with what I pay them. Besides, that Chevy was a dog from the day I got it."

"I always thought it was right nice." Grandmom took a small bite of chicken that she had carved off with a knife. "Them Cadillacs are such big cars, I don't see how you can drive 'em around, not that I ever learned to drive, nor ever will. I see 'em on the road all the time, taking up ever so much space you wonder there's enough for anyone else. Don't seem like it can get you around any better than a Chevy, though."

"A Caddy has class, and that means a lot today. How would it look for me to have a meeting with a builder and drive up in an old, beat up car?"

Elizabeth said, "That car wasn't beat up till you got a hold of it."

Grandmom shrugged. "Well, I guess you young people have different idees 'bout things today."

Robby finished his chicken leg — at least, what he called finished — and Tony replaced it with another. He took the discarded bone and had another meal out of it. When Grandmom passed the gravy, he made a hole in the middle of his mashed potatoes and filled it with the thick, brown liquid.

"I want gwavy." Robby smashed his potatoes so hard with the back of his spoon that they squirted over the edge of the plate.

Elizabeth slapped his hand. "Stop making a mess and eat your food. The next time you want something just ask for it, or you'll go to bed hungry. And just for that you're not getting any gravy."

Robby started crying, his mouth full of chicken.

"Bethy, why don't you let the child have some gravy?" Grandmom asked.

"He's got to learn some manners, and this is the only way to teach him." Tony patted him on the head, but his mother yelled, "Leave him alone." Robby eventually stopped crying, but sat there glumly and chewed on the mouthful of chicken that he still had in his mouth.

Kitty jumped onto Tony's lap and made comfortable circles as she started to settle down. "Put that cat on the floor while we're eating!" Tony did as his mother said, but slipped her a piece of chicken skin when he set her down.

Grandmom refilled some glasses from the milk bottle. When it was empty, she carried it to the sink and washed it out. "Frank, there's a program on the television tonight about the spring trainin' them ball players go through. They been advertising it all week."

"I can't watch it. I already promised Marcy and Al we'd go dancing with them at the Elk's Club tonight."

"Oh, Mother, would you mind putting the baby to bed?"

"Well, of course not. I'm sure he'll be good as gold. Won't you, Honey?" Robby nodded his head deeply, each time touching his chin to his chest. Grandpop reached out for his grandson's plate. "He's been so quiet for the last few minutes, I don't see why he can't have his gravy now."

Elizabeth scowled briefly and locked eyes with Robby. He stared back unblinkingly. Finally, she inclined her head. "Try not to make a mess."

Chapter 5

Tony rose early the next morning, but not so early that he did not find Grandmom already bustling around the kitchen, attending to the thousand and one items that kept her in a continual spanking pace. Having the family home, served only to increase her vigor.

"My, but you're up early this marnin', Honey. Did you get your nap out?"

"Pretty much, Grandmom." Tony leaned over the sink and rubbed the sleep out of his eyes with cold water.

"Did you like the movie? I was in bed by the time you got home. I took Robby over to Miss Gertrude's to shell butter beans. Bless his heart, he was as good as gold, and shelled some beans besides. He was plumb tuckered out, an' I had to carry him home an' put him to bed."

While Tony dried his face on a towel, Grandmom drew water from the spigot into a galvanized pitcher with a sprinkler head on the snout. She wore cotton gloves and a straw hat. She never let a day go by without watering the garden and pulling up weeds.

"I thought it was pretty good. It was a Western starring John Wayne." As long as he could remember, Grandpop had taken him to the movies on Saturday night, and then to Johnny's and Sammy's for dessert. It was a ritual that neither of them had outgrown, although now sometimes Tony "treated."

"Is he that tall skinny fella that's got the funny voice?"

"No. John Wayne's big and husky with a deep, creaky voice. You're thinking of Jimmy Stewart."

"Oh, my, I guess you're right. I'm always gettin' the two confused." Grandmom turned around at a bustling sound. "Well, bless his little heart. What's that pretty boy doin' up so early in the marnin'?"

Robby crouched on the dining room floor, half hidden behind the door frame. One eye spied past the white enameled finish, but so did half his face and body. Grandmom put down her sprinkler, pulled off her knit gloves and laid them on the counter, and scooped him up in her arms.

"My, my, why the little fella not even wet."

"I apposed to go inna toilet, Grandma."

"Well, how about if we go to the bathroom right away? That way your mother can't complain about wet pajamas."

"Okay," he sang, as she trundled him off through the dining room.

The screen door squeaked open and Tony ran to the entry in time to see Grandpop coming in. "Did you already feed the dogs, Grandpop?"

"Just did now."

Tony was disappointed. "Aw, I wanted to go with you. Why didn't you wait?

"They was making such a fuss I was afraid they'd tear the fence down if I held off another minute. You know how those hounds are when they're hungry."

"Oh, gee, you should have gotten me up."

"I didn't want to wake you up till you had your nap out. Maybe if you hurry you can still catch them eatin'."

Tony was halfway out the door before he finished saying it. "How about the chickens?" he shouted back as he leaped down the steps in one bound. "Already fed."

By that time he was at the end of the yard. "Did you check for eggs?"

Faintly, he heard, "Thought you looked last night."

A bolt of lightning could not have reached the dog pen faster than Tony, but something faster than either would have been needed to get to those two hungry dogs before they devoured their breakfast. By the time Tony arrived breathless at the gate, Spot was already licking out the bowl, probably for the second time. Driver jumped to the top of the doghouse and whimpered, looking forlorn. Tony climbed over the gate and petted them as they nuzzled him. After a few minutes he climbed up the walnut tree to the flat roof of the truck garage, clattered across the bending tin, and dropped unannounced into the chicken coop.

With squawks and beating wings, the birds scattered madly to the other side of the henhouse. This time there were none inside when he entered, but he could hear their raucous clucking through the clapboards as he felt around in the straw-covered bins. He found another brown egg partially buried under the thick matting. These were not laying hens, but frying chickens, so an egg was a bonus.

The screen door slammed shut behind him as he entered the kitchen. Grandmom entered from the dining room with Robby trailing after her.

"Robby, look what I found." He held out the fragile egg. Robby automatically grabbed for it, but Tony snatched it out of his reach. "Careful, or you'll break it. Then Grandmom won't be able to cook it for you — unless you want it scrambled."

"Where it come from?"

"The henhouse."

"What it doing there?"

"That's where the chickens live. One of them laid it last night."

"Fwied chicken?"

"Well, not yet. Look, would you like Grandmom to cook it for you?"

"Fwied chicken?"

"No, the egg."

"Gwanmom cook egg?"

"Of course I will, Honey. How do you want it?"

"I wanna bloom egg."

Grandmom frowned. "What's that?"

Tony handed the egg to his grandmother.

"He's trying to say balloon egg. He wants it sunny side up."

"Oh, well, I guess I can fix it that way. Let me get some bacon frying so's to grease the pan, then I'll cook it up. You go ahead an' play for a bit an' I'll call you when it's ready."

Robby wandered into the living room and found the television set. He also found his father sleeping in front of it. Grandpop came up from the basement and started washing his hands while Grandmom set aside her gardening and commenced cooking.

"Are you coming to the Easter egg hunt, Grandpop?"

"I 'spect so. What time is it supposed to be?"

"Eleven o'clock. Right after church."

Grandpop sat at the table, poured corn flakes into a bowl, added sugar and milk, and started eating. "Down to the park?"

Tony ate cereal, too, relying on bacon and eggs for a second course. "Yes, across from the zoo."

"Do you want milk or juice, Honey?"

"Juice," Tony said, through a mouthful of flakes. "Mom."

"I don't know how anyone can sleep in this house, with doors banging and all."

"You're up right early, Bethy. I couldn't see the clock without my glasses, but it must have been after midnight when you came in. Set right down an' I'll scramble up some eggs for you."

"Toast and coffee is enough for me. Hi, Daddy. But I've got to get washed up first. My mascara must have run all over my face."

"Mom," Tony whispered.

"What?" she snapped.

Tony glanced in the other room, saw that Robby was engrossed in a cartoon show. "Did you remember Robby's Easter basket?"

"I meant to put it out last night, but I was too busy. Frank was rushing me to get to the dance."

Grandpop pushed aside his half-finished cereal and backed away from the table. "I'll go sit with Robby for a minute and keep his attention. You sneak it onto the dining room table. We'll let him find it later."

Elizabeth pouted. "Why don't I just give it to him?"

There was infinite patience in his voice. "I think he'd like it better if he thought the Easter Bunny brought it. Now you go ahead and get it. He'll never know it wasn't already there."

"Well, all right."

Chapter 6

Grandpop pulled the black '35 Chevy into the east driveway but did not park it in the garage. Instead, he stopped at the front of the house in anticipation of having to go to the store for Grandmom. Not that she had said she needed anything when they left for church, but years of experience told him that she would probably think of some miscellaneous item of which she suddenly found herself short. Grandpop simply resigned himself to this fact, and saved himself the trouble of worrying about it.

Tony opened the door and slid out onto the grass before Robby had the opportunity to climb over him. At that he practically landed on his heels. Elizabeth swung her legs out of the front passenger seat, her knees held tightly together by the narrow dress. Her pointed high heels sunk into the soft loam, and she forgot about the bulbous hat. The decorative veil caught on the overhead sill and nearly pulled the hat off her head. The retreating hat flattened her immaculate coiffeur, forcing her to sit back down on the seat. Robby covered his mouth with his hand and giggled at his mother's discomfiture.

"It's not funny!" Rage crawled over her white skin and blanketed her face with wrinkles. "If you don't watch out you'll be laughing out of the other side of your face."

Robby's smile faded like the image on an unplugged television screen.

Grandpop came to the rescue. "I'm sure he didn't mean anything by it, Bethy." He scooped up the crestfallen youngster and planted a wet kiss on his cheek. "Did you?"

Robby shook his head slowly, never taking his eyes off his mother. With a humph and a slam, she stood up and closed the door, then walked across the lawn and up the red brick steps to the wooden porch.

"Can we sit on the swing, Gwanpop?"

The green slatted chair hung like a pendant on two stout chains. "I don't see why not."

"Not until he gets changed," Elizabeth insisted. "I don't want him playing in his good clothes. He'll ruin them like everything else he wears. And he's already got grass stains on his knees from crawling around on that stupid Easter egg hunt. Now you get inside and get out of those clothes and not another word out of you, you understand?"

Robby was still nodding silently long after Elizabeth entered the house. Grandpop deposited him on the gray painted porch, and swung wide the screen door. "Come on, young man. Let's get those clothes changed so we can go for a swing."

In the living room, newspapers were spread all over the floor and coffee table. Frank lay sprawled on the sofa in dark wrinkled pants and a white t-shirt. His head rested on one brocaded arm, and his bare feet were propped on two of Grandmom's quilted pillows. Robby ran to him and, with pink fingers, pushed the sports page away from his face.

"Hewwo, Daddy."

"Watch. Watch." Frank pulled the paper out of his clutches.

"Guess what I found."

Frank was never in the mood for guessing games. "An Easter egg." Robby held up bent fingers. "Two."

"Yeah, where are they?"

"Can I have them, now, Gwanpop?"

"I suppose so." He reached into his gray suit pocket and extracted two colored eggs, one green and blue, and the other barber-pole striped.

Frank spared a moment from the sports page to glance at them. In a monotone, he said, "Where'd you find them?"

'Inna grass. Nunna the other kids saw 'em — 'cept me."

"That's nice. How was church?"

Elizabeth sat in a rocker and fanned herself with her hat. "Hot and sticky. I swear, I don't remember a more humid Easter. And I thought the preacher was never going to end the sermon. I can't wait to get out of this dress and into something more comfortable. Is that the *Sunday Inquirer*?"

"I had to go to three stores before I could find a Philly paper. They don't believe in news in this town, and the *Salisbury Times* don't publish on Sunday."

"Hello, Bethy." Grandmom entered the living room wearing an apron over her plaid dress. "My, but that's a pretty outfit you got on. You dashed out of here so fast this mornin' I didn't hardly have a chance to look at you. An' it looks right smart with those shoes an' hat. Walter, I plumb forgot to buy milk for the baby, so while you're at the store, pick up some eggs an' flour. Oh, an' get another loaf of white bread, too, just in case we run short o' biscuits."

"It cost sixty dollars at Wanamaker's, so I know none of the girls down here have ever seen anything like it. I bought it for our last cruise." Elizabeth smoothed out the front and looked down at the toeless blue pumps, whose shade perfectly matched the floral design.

Robby pulled at her faded housedress. "Look at my eggs, Gwanmom."

"Land o' mercy, where'd they come from?"

Robby looked puzzled for a moment. Then, his face brightened into a smile. "Fwom a chicken."

Everyone laughed, even Frank and Elizabeth. Grandmom snickered for so long that tears came to her eyes, and she had to wipe them dry on her checkered apron. Robby smiled, not quite knowing what all the fuss was about.

"Can you make bloom eggs, Gwanmom?"

"Well, I 'spect they're hard boiled, Honey. But I can dice them up for you an' put them on toast. Will that be okay?"

"Okay, Gwanmom," Robby chortled. He tagged onto her dress as she turned toward the dining room.

"I don't want to spoil his appetite," Elizabeth said, becoming serious again.

"Dinner won't be ready for a couple hours yet, an' it's been a right long time since breakfast. I'll just make him one an' save the other for later. An' there's butter beans an' carn for everyone else."

Elizabeth gave in grudgingly. "Well, okay. But not till he gets out of those good clothes. I don't want him spilling anything on them." She left her hat on the chair and took Robby by the hand, pointing to the bathroom. "Now you march yourself in there and get out of those things. And don't leave them on the floor."

Once out of hearing, Tony explained to his father. "He couldn't find any eggs because the big kids got them all. So I stole a couple from his own Easter basket and, after the older kids swept through the park, I dropped them on the grass where he couldn't miss them."

Frank grunted, but was absorbed by his newspaper.

Grandpop winked. "Want to come to the store with me, Tony? We can stop at Leo's and get a chocolate Coke."

"Sure, Grandpop."

Chapter 7

As soon as dinner was over, Frank retreated to the living room with his coffee and parked himself in front of the television set. "Don't anybody bother me till after the game."

Elizabeth followed him, but only to pick up the newspapers that he had left strewn over the floor. Tony munched away at his second slice of Grandmom's homemade apple pie. When he finished it, Robby let him have the rest of his.

"Tony, I do believe you have a hollow leg. Where do you put all that food?" Grandmom shook her head disbelievingly. "I never seen a boy eat so much, no bigger than you are."

"He's all muscle," Grandpop said, squeezing Tony's leg beneath the table. "I do declare, you must purty near eat your folks out'n house an' home."

Elizabeth entered the dining room with the jumbled mass of papers in her arms. "I could put up with his eating. It's that damn college that costs an arm and a leg. He must think money grows on trees, the way he's always buying books and lab equipment and such nonsense."

Grandpop smiled. "It seems to me an education nowadays is a mighty important thing. You just can't get nowhere without one."

"So why can't he be an electrician? Tony, Frank wants to have a talk with you about the union. They're interviewing for apprentices next week, and he thinks it would be a good time to join. He's on the Apprentice Training Committee so there's no doubt about your getting accepted."

Tony's stomach contracted into knots. "But, Mom, I don't want to be an electrician."

She purposely looked away from him, put down the disjointed papers and picked up a pile of plates, bowls, and silverware, and headed for the kitchen. "What's wrong with being an electrician? It's good enough for your father."

"I didn't say there was anything wrong with it. It's just not what I want to do. I'm interested in science, like geology and anthropology."

"Well, you'll just have to learn you can't always have your own way, and get what you want. Sometimes you have to do what you can afford. And right now we can't afford to send you to college. It's draining us dry, because we have all our money tied up in the business. Besides, being an electrician is more practical — they make twice as much money as a geologist or a — a — whatever else you said."

"I'm not going into the field to get rich. I'm going into it because that's the kind of work I would enjoy. I want to learn."

"But why spend all that money for an education just so you can be poor all your life? If you think for one moment I'm going to support you till you die, you can think again. Money is tight enough as it is. And I've got to put up with him — " Elizabeth nodded toward Robby — "for another thirteen years. You can bet your life he's not going to college, for geology or any other reason."

Tony gulped down the last of his milk and carried some things to the kitchen. Grandpop sat at the table, hunched over his coffee, and stared out the window. "Bethy, we never told you what to do with your life."

"But I never wanted to go to college, either. You just don't know how expensive it is. Besides the tuition, I have to give him money for carfare, and lunch, and all that. There's no end to it."

"Children aren't cheap, but they are your own. And you should want to see that they get the best of everything."

"They've got a nice house to live in and the best medical insurance. What more do they need? Sometimes I wish I never had any children. Then I wouldn't have these problems all the time."

"Now, Bethy, I never said a cross word to you in my life, but this takes all. How can you say something like that in front of your own children?"

"I didn't mean to. It's just sometimes it makes me so mad. We never have enough money and I just don't know what to do about it."

She stormed out of the kitchen and locked herself in the bathroom. Robby idled over his pie plate, even though it was empty, his face clouded over. He was always unhappy when his parents argued.

Kitty chose that moment to appear from one of her secluded haunts. Dust covered her usually shiny fur, and cobwebs were draped casually over one black ear and her pointed whiskers. She must have been exploring in the basement and had probably wheedled her way into the crawlspace looking for mice.

Tony took some chicken scraps from the big plate in the middle of the table and handed them to Robby. "Why don't you give this to Kitty and see if she'll take it?"

Robby took a piece of skin, got down from his chair, and approached the wary cat. Holding his arm straight out he advanced on her, and dropped the morsel on the floor in front of her. The cat sniffed it suspiciously at first, but once she determined that it was edible, she squatted right down and began to chew.

Grandmom stooped down and, while she petted her back, slipped the comic section under the cat's chin. Then she returned to the sink and began to fill the basin with hot, soapy water.

Since Robby was just as content to watch her eat, Tony took the chicken platter into the kitchen and, after making sure there were no bones, plopped the rest of the scraps on Snuffy Smith's grinning face.

"Do you want some help with the dishes, Grandmom?"

Grandpop came in and placed his coffee cup on the sink next to the dirty dishes.

"Well, I guess you can help your grandfather dry, if you want."

Tony grabbed a dishtowel and stood ready to work.

Chapter 8

Tony bumped the back screen door with his hip, and lunged out with four suitcases — one in each hand and one under each arm. He walked quickly under the weight, and set them all down gently on the grass next to the shining Cadillac. Frank opened the trunk, then went back into the house to catch the sports on the kitchen radio. The screen door clattered, and a moment later Grandpop rounded the corner of the house with two more suitcases. He piled them in the trunk on top of the others.

"Is it all right to put them here, do you think, or should the baby's things go up front?"

"I don't think we'll need anything out of them before we get home."

"How about your books."

"I've already got them on the back seat so I can do some studying on the way."

Tony picked up an old broom handle that had been shortened and left leaning against the house. One end was worn smooth from greased hands, the other end was chewed and gouged. He picked up pebbles one at a time from the driveway, and proceeded to bat them across the corn field, aiming for the big apple tree on the other side of the furrowed but not-yet-planted ground.

Grandpop watched him pelt stones with unerring accuracy. "You know, I was thinkin'. Going to college means a lot to you, and I can understand that 'cause I never had the chance to go when I was your age. Never even thought about it, really. Being brought up on a farm back in the old days, most kids had to stay home and work."

Tony selected his pebbles carefully. The rounded ones that were slightly larger than a marble were the best shape and size.

"Youngsters in those days weren't as lucky as they are today, with all them modern conveniences. But we worked hard, just like you when you're helpin' me shuck corn, or pickin' watermelons with your Uncle Joe. You're a hard worker, ever since you were a boy. Do you remember when I used to pay you twenty cents an hour to pick crabgrass out'n the lawn?"

Tony grinned with fond memories. "Sure."

"And wouldn't take no more because you didn't think the job was worth more than that?"

"Yes, I remember."

"Well, it seems to me you're workin' pretty hard at college, too. You're always studyin', and you got that part-time job at the food store. You must be busy pretty near all the time."

"I guess."

"Well, I been thinking. Now me and your grandmother, not having any more children to raise since your mother got married, we've been putting our extra money in the bank. Our needs are simple, so we built up a little nest egg over the years. Now, I'm planning to retire in another year or so, and your grandmother's going to quit Woolworth's, so we're goin' to need some of that money to add to our Social Security. But it seems to me we got right much more than we need. That plus I'm plannin' to sell this parcel of land 'cause I'm gettin' too old to work in the fields. Plus, that ole horse of mine ain't goin' to last forever. Or maybe I'll rent it to Mr. Gravener. Anyhow, it's goin' to bring in some money, an' I guess I'll have to in-

vest it somehow. Now your grandmother and me, why, we'd be tickled if you'd take some of it — kinda like a loan — to help with your schoolin'."

Tony dropped the pebble that he was about to bat. "What are you trying to say, that you want to give me money that my parents won't give me?"

"Consider it an investment in your education. You can pay us back when you graduate — or start to working."

Tony stared at his grandfather. His face was frozen in a whimsical smile which poured out probity, goodness, and love. He was not a rich man — at least, not in material wealth. But his heart was far richer than anyone Tony had ever known.

"Grandpop, I — I can't take it. I — " Tony groped for adequate words, reaching into his very soul for an explanation that his grandfather could understand. "It's not that I'm not grateful for all you've done for me, but I feel — I feel like I have to do this on my own. I have to handle the situation my own way. I want to stand up on my own two feet and face whatever comes. I can always go to college later, when I'm self supporting — even night school."

"But, Tony, have you thought about what might happen if you drop out of school?"

"I — don't think I understand."

"Well, there's a terrible war goin' on over there in Vietnam. Don't seem like much now, but it's gettin' worse. Lots of young men from around here have already been called in."

"Well, I — I guess you're right. But that's not the end of the world. I mean, I heard from some fellows at Temple who have taken ROTC that the GI bill pays veterans for going to college after they finish their service time. The best thing might be for me to join the Army now and get my commitment over with, then go back to school afterward. It'll only set me back two years, and the government'll pay for it."

"What's the difference between the government payin' for it and us payin' for it?"

"Because if the government pays for it, it's because I will have earned it."

"Tony, children aren't expected to have to earn anything till their growed up an' their schoolin' is over with."

"But I'm not a child any more."

"I didn't mean you were. You're a growed man by many standards, that's for sure, but you're still a minor in the eyes of the law. You're a hard workin' boy, but you don't have to start payin' your way through life yet. Now, some only needs twelve years schoolin', others need more. Don't think because you have to go longer than most, you're gettin' something for nothin'. The time will come when you'll have kids of your own, an' you'll want to do the same for them."

Tony let out a deep sigh. He dropped the improvised bat. He reached out and put his arms around his grandfather, and hugged him tight. He stepped back and took a good look at the weatherworn face that had seen so much of the hard side of life.

"Grandpop, I have to make my own way in the world. Please understand. I'm not saying this just because I'm refusing your help. I would never do that. But I need to do things on my own. If it means dropping out of college for one semester, then that's what I'll have to do. I love you, Grandpop, but that's the way it has to be."

Slowly, he removed his glasses. He pulled a handkerchief from his back pocket and wiped the lenses. "I love you, too, Tony. We both do. You're a good boy, an' you'll do the right thing no matter what happens. God works in mysterious ways. You follow the footsteps you feel are right, an' we'll be prayin' for you."

Chapter 9

"Bye Gwanmom. Bye Gwanpop."

Robby leaned out the window and waved wildly as the huge Cadillac backed smoothly out of the driveway. He sat in the back with Tony, the car seat held in place by the rear seat belts.

Grandmom and Grandpop stood side by side, smiling broadly, as they waved back. When the car reached the tarred roadway, Frank stopped it, shifted to forward, and eased on the gas. The engine purred and the automatic transmission worked effortlessly. Grandmom and Grandpop never stopped waving until the car rounded the bend and the car was out of sight.

"Watch yourself." Robby pulled his arms in as Frank demonstrated the power windows. One button closed them all at once.

Tony fingered the buttons on the rear door console and found that he could operate all the door locks and windows. There was even a cigarette lighter in the recessed ashtray. "Wow, this car is really neat."

"I like Gwanpop's car."

"Why?"

"It has class."

Tony laughed and threw a mock punch at his brother's shoulder. "Robby, you don't even know what class means."

"Do too. It means old."

"Robby, you're a card."

"What's a card."

"That's just an expression that means you're funny."

Kitty struggled out from under the front seat, where she had hidden as soon as Tony had put her in the car. She climbed over Robby's lap and stood with her front paws on the narrow window sill. She meowed mournfully a couple of times, then got down, jumped over Robby without touching him, and settled into the space between the two brothers, leaning against Tony's left leg. Kitty did not care for cars, whether they had class or electric windows. Every now and then she looked up and squeaked.

Tony smoothed out her fur and tried to wipe some of the dust from it. She had led him a merry chase through the house, in a vain attempt to avoid having to go into the car. He finally cornered her in the attic where she had taken refuge behind some boxes. Now she sat in a perpetual crouch, would not relax for the entire trip, would not lick off her dirty fur, and would arrive home exhausted.

"Are these heating ducts back here, Dad?"

"Uh-huhn. Air-conditioning, too. Watch this." A blast of cold air poured out of the vent in the rear panel. The vent was covered with slats that could be rotated as well as directed, so that one could accurately place the flow of air.

"Frank, turn that thing off. It's cold enough as it is without you making it any worse."

"Cold? This afternoon you were complaining you were too hot. Why don't you make up your mind?"

"Because this isn't this afternoon, that's why. Now turn it off."

Frank left the air-conditioning on, but lowered the fan so that a mild, cool breeze still flowed. Tony fooled with the slats until he found that they could be pushed back far enough to effectively close the vent.

"Listen to this radio." Frank switched it on and spun the dial. Instantly there was a blast of static, which settled down to soft music, then switched to popular songs, then switched to a baseball announcer enthusiastically relating the third strike. There were three speakers in the back: one in each door and one on the rear deck. "The FM has stereo and it's the best quality sound you've ever heard."

Elizabeth humphed. "Why do you need quality just to listen to a ball game?"

Frank ignored her. "Notice how quiet the road is, too." There was barely a whisper from outside. "This thing's built like a sound chamber. And it'll go a hundred miles an hour and you'll never know the difference."

"I don't want you showing off by speeding."

"Who's speeding? I just said it'll go a hundred miles an hour and you couldn't tell from the sound."

"I just don't want you to get any ideas, that's

all."

"What ideas?"

"Frank, would you keep your eyes on the road and stop arguing."

"You're the one who's arguing. All I said was the car could go a hundred, and right away you're accusing me of speeding. Now what kind of sense does that make?"

"I didn't say you were speeding. I just said watch where you're going. And turn off that damn ball game. If we have to listen to the radio, turn on some decent music."

Frank switched off the radio completely. "Sometimes you don't make any sense at all, you know that?"

Tony opened his book and settled back for a long, three-hour ride.

Later, as Robby lay hunched over with his face plastered against the window, sound asleep, and Tony read his chemistry book by the fading rays of the sun, Frank switched the radio back on. He listened to the ball game for a few minutes, then spun the dial until he found a news broadcast.

"Frank, let's stop at Kirby and Holloway's in Dover. I want a cup of coffee."

"What do you need coffee for? You're not driving."

"I didn't say I *needed* coffee. I said I *wanted* it. There's a difference, you know. Besides, I have to go to the lady's room, too."

'If that's what you want, why don't you just say so. We can stop at a gas station for that."

"I don't like gas stations. Their bathrooms are always so dirty. Besides, I want a cup of coffee, too."

"All right, all right. But get it to go. I don't want to have to wait an hour for you to drink it."

They all got out at the restaurant. Robby protested sleepily, but Elizabeth insisted that he go with her to prevent an 'accident.' Kitty tried to get out, but Tony managed to hold her in until all the doors were closed. Then he slipped out while she was looking out the window on the other side.

Frank ordered two coffees, cream and sugar, to go. Tony had a drink from the water fountain and swiped a handful of mints from the cashier's counter while his father was paying the bill.

"I wanna Coke."

"Hush up before I pound you. You've had enough to drink, and I don't want you wetting your pants before we get home."

In the car, Tony slipped Robby some mints. Instead of sucking on them, he chewed them right up. Tony put his chemistry book away as they rolled through Smyrna. He had read the last several paragraphs by flickering street-lights and truck headlights, but it was becoming too much of a strain on his eyes. Besides, he found it impossible to concentrate because of the constant bickering in the front seat. He stared at the deepening purple sky, and counted the stars as they appeared.

The radio blared the world events. "On the international scene, President Johnson reiterated his determination to defend the people of the Republic of South Vietnam from foreign aggression. He says he will continue to send foreign aid in the form of troops and military advisers as long as North Vietnam tries to impose communist rule on the free nation. It is reported that North Vietnam is being supplied with food and labor from Red China, as well as weapons and munitions and other war goods from Russia, although both countries disclaim any such involvement. The President also authorized an undisclosed increase in the number of support personnel being sent to South Vietnam, because of demands from General William Westmoreland. The U.S. already has over two hundred and ten thousand troops serving in the beleaguered nation. Secretary of Defense Robert — "

"Frank, would you turn that thing off. I'm tired of hearing about — "

"SHUT UP."

" — McNamara has said in a recent press conference that the bombing of North Vietnam will continue despite rumors to the contrary. McNamara believes that continued bombing is the only way to bring North Vietnam to the bargaining table for peace talks. He also said that it will help to slow down communist military traffic for guerrilla insurgents along the Ho Chi Minh trail. Further in the world market, the dollar rose today against the German mark in heavy trading — "

Frank snapped off the radio. "Goddamn it, Beth, why do you always have to talk when I'm listening to something?"

"If I didn't, I'd never be able to get a word in edgewise. And what difference does it make what's happening on the other side of the world? Why don't they do something about lowering taxes, or stopping inflation, instead of talking about some godforsaken country that isn't even on the map?"

"If you read the papers once in a while you'd see it on the map."

"Geography was one of my favorite subjects in school, and I don't remember ever hearing about Vietnam."

"Mom, before World War Two, Vietnam was part of French Indo-China."

"Well, I'll never understand why those countries keep changing their names. It's just like Siam becoming — whatever it is now."

"Thailand."

"That's it. Thailand. Why do they have to change their names? What's wrong with the ones we gave them?"

"Usually when a country gains its independence, it prefers to be called by its native name. Vietnam and Thailand are ethnic names, but when they were under French domination they were lumped together by the French as Indo-China."

"It still doesn't make sense."

"That's because you don't want to," said Frank. "If you would spend less time bowling and more time learning what's going on in the world, you'd understand."

"What the hell does bowling have to do with it? All I know is it's costing us money to fight a war that has nothing to do with us. What's it all for?"

"Every generation has its war. Your father was in the First World War. I was in the Second. My brother Charlie was in Korea. Now it's Vietnam. War is a fact of life."

"Well, I don't see why we should have to pay higher taxes just so we can support a war in some stupid jungle that can't mean a hill of beans to us."

"It's important because we can't let those communists push us around."

"Now that's the silliest reason I ever heard."

"Silly. Is that all you can say about it? People over there are dying and you think it's silly."

"They're not people. They're Chinese."

"They are *not* Chinese."

"Tony said they used to be Indo-China."

"That doesn't make them Chinese."

"Well, they're all the same to me. They all have slanted eyes."

"Well, how about the American soldiers over there? Don't you ever think about them?"

"Sure, and they have no right being over there spending our tax money."

"Sometimes you can be so thickheaded. Why don't you wise up to the fact that soldiers dying is more important that having enough money to go bowling?"

"Would you stop picking on me about bowling. You spend more money at the bar on Saturday night than I spend in a month of bowling."

"What I'm trying to say is: once you're involved in a war you can't just pick up and walk out of it."

"Why not?"

"Because that's not the way it's done. If we pulled out now, the rest of the world would laugh at us. We're in it, and we're in it to stay."

"Who says?"

"I say. The country says. The President says.

Didn't you just hear him? This country has never lost a war. Don't you think we could cream North Vietnam, a stinkin' little country, if we wanted to?"

"Then why don't we do it and get it over with?"

"Because our hands are tied. We're a big country, with enough men and machines to walk right through North Vietnam. We could drop an atom bomb on them if we wanted to. But the other countries would sneer at us, because we're so big and they're so small. We have to fight them on their own terms. There are rules, you know."

"Now that's the stupidest thing I ever heard: rules for war."

"You forget, this is the most powerful country in the world. We have to keep up an image. Russia ain't gonna be able to pull them out of it — we're twenty years ahead of them in technology. We're gonna win this war if it's the last thing we do. Nobody can talk to us that way. Nobody."

Chapter 10

"All ashore that's going ashore."

Frank expertly backed the Cadillac into a tight parking spot between two banged-up cars. It had begun to drizzle, and the streetlights that alternated along the narrow crowded street cast a yellowish gossamer aura that was like a surrealistic painting: the three story row-homes leered through the mist, their tops invisible; each house breathed dim light of its own, glowing like jack-o-lanterns through windows that were eyes and doors that were teeth; neither end of the block could be seen; and there was not a soul afoot. The world was made of brick, cement, and macadam: there was not a tree or a blade of grass anywhere.

"Thank God. I hate driving in the dark."

Frank played with the electric door locks. "What're you talking about? You didn't do any driving."

"But there's nothing to see. And now my hair's going to get wet in this damn rain."

Tony singsonged in the back seat. "Robby, we're home. It's time to get up." Robby did not stir. Tony unbuckled his seat belt and tickled his ribs. His cheeks twitched dreamily.

"Frank, go in and get my umbrella. It's in the hall closet. I'm not going to the hair dresser until Wednesday and I don't want my hair to get wet."

Frank let himself out of the car, jangling his keys. The door opened on squeaky hinges, and the outside light flickered on. The bare bulb, screwed into a pigtail spliced to two wires hanging out of an exposed metal junction box, cast a weak glow on the faded marble steps.

"Mom, do you want me to take Robby?"

"Well I can't do it — and hold an umbrella at the same time." Her door opened and the black umbrella was shoved inside, still folded. "Well, you could at least open it for me. And hold my arm. I'm afraid I'll slip on this wet street in these heels."

"So who told you to wear high heels? You don't have to get dressed up just to sit in the car."

"I have to get dressed up some time — you never take me out anywhere." Tony carried his limp brother into the house, right behind his mother. "Just put him on the bassinet for now."

The house was a straight-through — living room, dining room, and kitchen — with the stairs in the living room. He carried Robby up to his room, the middle of the three bedrooms.

"Put some water on for coffee. And how about giving me a hand with the suitcases." Frank sat heavily into his easy chair. "My back is killing me."

"Where's my cosmetic case?"

"In the car. Where do you think? Tony will get it for you. I've got to make some phone calls and get the men lined up for tomorrow." But he did not move from his chair.

"And bring in the groceries, too."

Tony ended up unloading everything himself, including the cat.

Elizabeth checked her makeup, then started to get Robby ready for bed. "Praise the lord, he's still dry."

In the kitchen, Tony pulled out a can of cat food and clamped it into the electric opener. He found Kitty's bowls, filled one with tap water and the other with moist food, and put them in the accustomed corner of the pantry at the back of the kitchen. She curled her tail around her forelegs as she sat down to eat.

He opened the refrigerator to see what was available for supper. After a quick appraisal, he started loading things on the table: lunchmeat, cheese, a loaf of white bread, mustard, pickles, and a bottle of Coke. He got a plate and silverware, then sat down and made a sandwich.

Upstairs, Robby was wailing. He knew that pajamas meant bedtime, so naturally he wanted to stay up and watch television. The teapot whistled, and Tony got up to turn off the gas.

Elizabeth shouted from upstairs. "Tony, turn off the stove. I have my hands full. Frank, the water's hot."

A moment later, Tony heard his father bang the bedroom door. "Where's my coffee?"

"Still on the stove."

"I thought you said it was ready."

"What do you want me to do, drink it for you, too? I had to put the baby to bed."

Frank pounded down the stairs and huffed into the kitchen. He took a cup and saucer from the cabinet, ladled in a spoonful of instant coffee and two lumps of sugar, poured in the hot water, and yanked open the refrigerator door.

"Isn't there any milk in this house?"

"Dad, we just got some at the store. It's right here."

Frank spied the bottle on the table, sat down gruffly, and forced open the lid. "Did we get a paper today?"

Elizabeth strode into the room. "Unless one of you brought it in, it's still on the steps."

"That means it's soaked. Tony, go and see if that paperboy left the paper today. You can't trust these damn kids anymore. One time they leave it, the next time they forget, or it gets blown all over the street. When I used to deliver papers everybody on my route was handed his paper."

"Hard to do when you're not home."

Tony scraped back his chair, took a bite out of his newly packed sandwich, and retrieved the sodden mess that was the Sunday paper. "Didn't you already read it this morning?"

"This is the *Bulletin*. What're we having for supper? I'm starved." He took the paper with a sneer and found a dry section.

"I don't feel like cooking so you'll have to have leftovers."

"It won't be the first time. What do we have?"

"Take your pick." Elizabeth loaded the table with cellophane covered dishes, lidded jars, and foil-covered bowls. She never threw anything out until it went bad. "I can put on a can of soup, too. We have chicken noodle, vegetable, and beef barley."

"Beef barley."

"Tony?"

"That sounds fine, Mom."

She started heating the soup. "So what does the *Bulletin* have that the *Inquirer* doesn't?" But Frank was already submerged in the intricacies of the sports page. Tony slipped out the comics, and absentmindedly read Peanuts. "Tony, don't drink out of the bottle."

"But, Mom, I'm going to drink the whole thing"

"I don't care. At the table you'll drink out of a glass or not at all." Resignedly, Tony got up and took a glass from the cabinet over the sink. "Get one for me while you're there. I think I'll have some apple juice."

"Do you want a glass, too, Dad?" After a moment, he said softly, "Dad?" And again, louder, "Dad!"

"*Whaddaya want?*" Frank's face was dark with anger.

"I just wanted to know if you wanted a glass of apple juice."

"Can't you see I'm drinking coffee?" As if that settled the question, he returned to his newspaper.

Tony put the two glasses on the table, filled his with Coke, and engrossed himself in the comics and the sandwich. A couple minutes later, still nibbling, he swung around the front page, ran his finger down the table of contents, and found the section that had the crossword puzzle. He piled the remaining sections of the paper at the end of the table that was his father's permanent pile of clutter: notes written on scraps of paper, phone messages scrawled on the backs of envelopes, opened and discarded letters that somehow never found their way into the waste paper basket, and a backlog of work items that might get done if he ever took the trouble to see what they were. Attention to detail was not Frank's strong point.

As he penciled in the words with a stub, his mother put the soup on the table, and sat down. "Shouldn't you be doing homework rather than crossword puzzles?"

"I don't have any homework. Don't you remember that I had midterms last week? That's why I wanted to get away for Easter break, because I didn't have any tests coming up."

"Weren't you reading a textbook in the car?"

"Yes. I was getting a head start on the next semester. I figure by boning up now on chemistry and geology, I'll have more time to spend on calculus. I'm having a tough time with it."

"Frank, maybe you better have that talk with him now."

Without looking up, he said, "I'm busy."

"You're always busy. I swear, talking to you is like talking to a wall." When Frank made no acknowledgment, she stirred her soup and took a sip. "I still don't understand what this calculus is."

Tony tested his own soup, found it cool enough to sip. "It's a kind of complicated mathematics."

"Higher than algebra?"

"A lot higher."

"What's the use of it?"

"Well, there are problems that can't be solved by algebra."

"Then why not use trigonometry? That's higher than algebra."

Tony pushed the crossword puzzle aside. "Because trigonometry uses different kinds of functions."

"I don't know. I've lived this long without trigonometry. And before you went to school, I never even heard of calculus."

Frank did not look up, but said, "That's because the teachers in that hick school of yours never heard of it. They might have learned it if they'd gone to twelfth grade."

"Frank, we didn't *have* a twelfth grade in our school. It was set up so you only needed eleven years to graduate."

"That's because the farmers needed their kids on the farm."

"Well, at least I got my diploma. I didn't get kicked out in my senior year like you did. And we had good teachers, too. With books. Not nuns swinging rulers trying to beat it into you."

Franks lips moved as he scanned each line diligently, pronouncing every word. He heard only when he wanted to hear.

Elizabeth took a drink of apple juice. "So what's the use of all this arithmetic?"

"Well, with calculus you can do some really complex calculations, such as figuring out the volume of a potato chip."

"Why would you want to do that? Who cares?"

"I'm just using that as an example. It's a difficult problem because it curves in different directions."

Frank said, "You can always stick it in a glass of water and see how much spills out."

"But you end up with a soggy potato chip." Tony alone smiled. "But it has its uses in science, where logic and extrapolation can involve mathematical formulas that would take weeks to find answers to. Calculus is a short cut that makes things easier to figure out."

Elizabeth said, "What? Besides potato chips."

"Well, in geology, radioactive decay rates can be used to determine the age of fossils."

"What good does that do?"

"Because knowing the age of a fossil will tell you how old the rocks are where it was found. For instance, we know that oil-bearing deposits are always found in certain strata. If you dig a well and find fossils associated with that era, you'll know whether it's worth while to drill for oil."

"You mean, you can tell if there's oil in the ground by what kind of rocks you find?"

"Exactly."

"Seems like you can make a lot of money that way."

"Well, the oil company makes the money. The geologist doing the prospecting gets paid a salary."

Elizabeth pinched her eyes. "It doesn't sound fair to me. You do all the work and somebody else gets the money."

"The interest is in the work, the reward is in the knowledge. And that's only one branch of geology. I could work for the Geologic Survey, or a college, doing fieldwork in glaciers, or volcanoes, or earthquakes, or go on digs for dinosaurs. Geology is only a masthead for a wide-ranging field. It has potential in a lot of different directions."

Frank dropped his newspaper. "But no money."

"Money isn't everything."

"Not to you, because you have everything handed to you. You don't have to pay the mortgage, or the utility bills, or the food, or your mother's credit cards. You think money grows on trees. The kids today have it too easy. You think I didn't want to go to college? When I was a kid out on the street, I had to work: shining shoes, selling apples, answering the phone in the corner drug store. I didn't have all day to sit around reading books. It's about time you earn your own living in this world."

"Dad, you stopped giving me an allowance when I was fifteen. Since then I've made enough money in the summers, and doing part-time work, to get me through the whole year."

"Yeah, and you didn't have to pay rent, either. What do you think, you can live by picking watermelons for the rest of your life?"

"No, but I don't want to be pulling wires or installing receptacles for the rest of my life, either."

"What's wrong with that? I done all right by it so far. You don't see me standing in no food line. You wouldn't be living in this house if it weren't for me pulling wires for twenty years. Now I got a piece of property in Bucks County and I'm gonna start building my own house."

It was the same old argument. Tony sighed. "Dad, I'm not saying there's anything wrong with it. I just have different interests."

His father grabbed across the table in a rage. His hand ripped across Tony's shirtfront, but Tony backed out of reach instinctively. Instead, he took the crossword puzzle and tore it to shreds. Now he was shouting so loud that the neighbors must have heard every word.

"Let me tell you something, mister smarty pants. You have a lot to learn in this world. It don't revolve around you. You're a nothing, you understand? A nothing. Now you listen to me, and you listen good. I ain't paying any more money for no stupid college. I've arranged with the president of the union to have you accepted into the apprenticeship program. And you won't have to be just a wireman. They're gonna take you into the commercial school."

"But, Dad . . . "

"Shut up and listen for one goddamn minute. You know what this means? You can go to school — for free — for four years, and get paid besides. No more night school. You work four days a week, and the other day you go to school and the union pays you. And when you become a journeyman, you'll be making twice as much as any damn college professor."

"But, Dad, it's not what I want . . . "

"How do you know what you want? You're just a kid. What are you afraid of, you might have to work for a living?"

"I'm not afraid of anything. It's just not what I want to do."

Frank continued to scream. "Stop contradicting me. You just listen to what I tell you. You be down at the union hall tomorrow night at five o'clock sharp. You don't have to commit yourself to anything, just listen to the orientation. You fill out the application and don't worry about anything else. I'll take care of it from there."

"But, Dad . . . "

"Don't 'but Dad' me. You be there, you hear?"

Tony stared into eyes that were burning with rage, set in a face that was contorted with hatred.

Tony did not answer. He *could* not answer. He just stared.

Then he heard the clicking of claws on the bright linoleum. He turned his head and saw Kitty licking her chops. He made a kissing sound, and she immediately ran forward and with a long bound leaped into his lap. He squinted as she nuzzled his chin, for her breath smelled of cat food. "Put that cat down while you're eating."

"Aw, Mom. She's not hurting anything."

"I said put her down."

"Why?"

"Because I said so."

He petted the cat, and took a big bite out of the sandwich. "You only say that to be ornery. You're afraid you might let me do something I like."

He hardly had time to flinch before his mother leaned across the table and gave him a resounding slap across the face. The sandwich flew out of his hand, and Kitty was jostled onto the floor. Sensing that something was wrong, she clicked away until the lush carpeting of the dining room absorbed the sound of her retreat. Tony's face stung, and he could feel it turning red. His eyes smarted, but he refused to let tears flow in his parents' presence. He stared back at his mother with intense concentration.

"Don't you ever talk to me that way."

Tony tried to swallow the food in his mouth, but it would not go down past the lump. His father stared at him triumphantly. Tony sat quietly, recovered the pieces of his sandwich where it had been splattered across the table, and regained his composure. His mother made believe the incident never happened, and shoved a bowl of soup in front of him.

Tony got up from the table as calmly as he could feign, left the kitchen, walked upstairs to his room, went inside, closed the door, and threw himself down on the bed.

Then he did something that he had not done for a long time.

He cried.

Chapter 11

"*Go!*"

The voice was drowned out by the two rumbling engines hitting the top end of their tachometer's safety mark. The real signal was the dropping of the arms and the flags to the smooth blacktop.

The two stock cars nosed the starting line for a split second longer before leaping into the air. Engines revved and clutches dropped. The deafening roar of raw horsepower was superseded by the wild screech of spinning tires grabbing macadam.

The flagman shrank into his denim jacket, twisted around, and ran back from the painted line: more than one had been sideswiped by cars slewing out of control.

The dull black '55 Chevy pealed rubber in a straight line, and lurched ahead with unerring expertise. The Thunderbird, streetlights reflecting off its fire-engine-red paint, sashayed like a drunken snake as its tires poured out a cloud of black smoke. By the time it gained traction, it was half a car-length behind the Chevy.

Both cars whined out until it sounded as if their engines would explode. A gap measured in nanoseconds occurred when both competitors slammed into second gear simultaneously. As they passed by Tony, still laying rubber, the Chevy had the lead.

"Go, Chevy, go!" Benny Clark's gangly arms gesticulated wildly, but his dirty sneakers only caressed the blanket covering the roof of his own Chevy, a '57.

Ray Murphy ducked the flailing arms. "Yo! Will ya?" He tugged the sleeves of his clean print shirt, and checked the tuck to make certain that it was even. His white basketball sneaks contrasted sharply against his black, pressed corduroys.

Ben swept dirty blonde hair out of his eyes, and kept on cheering. "Take 'im, Chevy. Take 'im."

Sitting on the hood, with his legs dangling over the fender, Tony was at a disadvantage. Fifty cars lined each side of the rural street, all bulging with screaming teenagers. Because he was so close to the starting line, most of the others observers held positions between him and the finish line. The racing cars were swallowed by distance and semidarkness.

At the other end of the makeshift, illegal track, the dueling cars neared the last streetlight. The Chevy hit third gear, followed by a

chirp as the tires burned rubber. The Thunderbird did the same. Both cars flashed through the softly illuminated area, and the race ended a split second later.

"The Chevy took him!" The roof pinged as it dented under Benny's weight. "He did it again."

Ray stepped out of reach. "You're full of crap. The T-bird had him by a mile."

"No way. He wasn't even close."

"Come on, are you blind? He had him right from the line."

"You're crazy, Ray. The Chevy was halfway down the track before the T-bird finished fishtailing."

"Oh, yeah. Which race were you watching?"

"Hey!" Pete Robinson lounged casually against the left fender, his mousey lips pursed. "If you guys will shut up for a minute and wait for the spotter's signal, you'll find out who really won."

Ben said, "The Chevy was in front when they passed us."

"I think it was a tie." George Hart stood on the street next to Pete. He was so big that Benny would not let him on the roof or the hood of his car.

"What do you know?" Ray asked.

"Yeah. You're dreaming," added Pete.

"That was a great race. That was a great race." Ray's younger brother, Teddy, peered up from the hood through black, horn-rimmed glasses. "I'll say it was the Chevy."

"You shut up, you little pipsqueak." Ray punched Teddy on the shoulder. "You can't even see through those Coke bottle bottoms."

"Ray, leave him alone. Hey, here comes the spotter." Benny cupped his hands over his eyes.

Like a well-versed actor, the spotter entered the cone of light at the far end of the marked track. He held a flag in both hands, pointed down. Dramatically, he raised both arms in front of him until they were stretched overhead. The noise died down as the crowd waited for the decision. He poised overlong, waiting for effect. Slowly, deliberately, the right hand took the flag and dropped until it was perpendicular with his body, pointing toward the winning car.

The crowd roared. Pandemonium ensued as hundreds of teenagers screamed and whistled and danced.

Ben pounded Ray on the shoulders and back. "I told you so. I told you so."

"Ah, they both suck." George walked to the front of the car and leaned back heavily on the hood.

Several hundred yards to the east, an airplane raced along a runway parallel to Decatur Road. Duel headlights lifted off the ground, and disappeared as the plane banked. The industrial park that lined the edge of the Northeast Philadelphia Airport was the reason for the newly paved road that served so admirably as a drag strip.

Ben stuck up for General Motors. "There ain't nothing that can beat a Chevy. Nothing."

Ray slid down to the hood and jumped lightly to the ground. "Aw, he prob'ly only won by a hair. I'll bet he coulda had him if he hadn't slipped coming off the line."

Ben's sneakers slapped onto the macadam. "I keep telling you, Ray, those Birds are just too light. If this were a mile track he could probably top end him, but he can't get the traction for the short hauls."

"Wow, that was great, man. That was great. Hey, Tony, wasn't that great?" Teddy adjusted his glasses with an errant finger. He was as thin as his brother, two years younger, and still in high school. His biggest problem with respect to the "gang" was that he was not known as Teddy, but as Ray's brother. "Man, I never seen anything like it. How about you, Ray? Did you ever see a race like that?"

"Shut up, Meathead." Ray punched his brother on the shoulder hard enough to knock him back.

"Hey, what was that for?" Instead of an answer, Ray punched him again — harder. Teddy stumbled into silence.

Pete walked around George and tripped over his sprawled feet. "Hey, you big oaf. Pull your feet in. And watch those hood ornaments." He grabbed George by the arm and gently pushed him away from the car. Pete was small, but strong.

George stumbled clumsily over his own shoes, and fell against the trunk of a pale blue G.T.O. The car rocked slightly at the soft thud as flesh hit metal.

"Hey, jerk," came an angry yell. "Watch what the hell you're doin', or you'll be carryin' those pearly whites home in a shoppin' bag."

George did not bother to look up. "Don't get your dander up. I didn't hurt anything."

The owner of the Goat tramped forward with fearless abandon. If looks could kill, George would have been dead on the spot. He was huge, the size of George, but without the paunch. His chest was as big around as George's waist. His face could have been chiseled from granite, a perfect sculpture of anger and youthful rebellion. The muscles that filled out his white T-shirt were not unaccustomed to exercise.

"What're you, yo-yo, a wise guy?"

George's flaccid features sagged even more. He took a step backward and used the front of the Chevy for support. "No, I was just saying that I didn't hurt your car any. I only touched it."

Tony slid off the hood and stood adjacent to George's right. Pete moved closer on the left, while Ben and Ray climbed down from the roof. Ray hung back, but Ben sauntered up behind Pete.

The big-mouthed bully also had friends. Neither was as imposing as he was, but the three together made up a wall of flesh that was of considerable bulk. Tony stretched out a hand between the two antagonists, making sure not to touch the other. "Look, he didn't mean anything by it."

George's shaky finger pointed at Pete. "It wasn't even my fault. He pushed me."

"That little squirt pushed a big fella like you?"

Pete drew his full five-foot body to its fullest height. "Yeah, it was my fault. I pushed him."

Mr. Muscle ignored all entreaties. He never took his steely eyes off of George's drooping lids. "My argument's with you, big mouth. Now put up your dukes." Balanced lightly on the balls of his feet, he moved closer until he was practically breathing down George's throat. Their eyeballs might have been on opposite sides of a short level.

Tony moved his upraised hand an inch, until it touched the bully on the front of the sweaty T-shirt. "He said he was sorry, all right? What more do you want? Let's forget the whole thing and watch the next race."

Like a hydraulic piston his arm struck out to the side, and his open palm slapped against Tony's sternum, launching him backward. He crashed into the Chevy's headlight cowling.

"I'm talkin' to Mister Big Mouth here." He flexed his muscles as if he wanted to exercise on George for a while.

Tony's heart pounded in his chest. Adrenaline pumped so fast that legs shook uncontrollably. One hand went to the small of his back where the rounded metal implanted a bruise. He made no attempt to retaliate.

Pete fidgeted nervously from foot to foot. "I said it was my fault, so why don't you pick on me?"

"You mind your own business, midget, or you'll get more than a punch in the chest. I wanna hear from fatso, here."

George had long since wilted like month-old lettuce. The only thing holding him up was Ben's Chevy. He clutched the grill with both hands, his front unprotected. "I said I was sorry. What else do you want?"

"I want you to learn not to touch my car, see?"

"Look, it wasn't my fault. It was an accident."

"Yeah, well, people get hurt in accidents."

"All right, I'm sorry. I'll see that it doesn't happen again, okay?"

"You *better* see it don't happen again, or I'll be usin' your tongue to polish my chrome. Get it, bright boy?" His arm jerked back, then came around in an exaggerated swing. George almost fell over himself trying to get out of the way, but Pete never flinched. The fake punch stopped in mid air, and the three toughs roared with laughter. "Youse guys watch it, next time. Huhn?"

The three toughs turned away and joined the two girls at the front of the Goat.

Ben grabbed Pete and George by the shirt collar, and pulled them to the back of the car. Tony followed, still rubbing his back.

Teddy climbed all over him. "Hey, Tone, you okay?"

"It's just a bump."

Ben said, "That guy's I.Q. is inversely proportional to the size of his arms."

Ray peered past his companions, toward the G.T.O. In a lowered voice, he said, "If he had as much matter between his ears as he has in his biceps he'd be a genius."

"His total I.Q. is less than his shoe size. Hey, Tony, you all right?" asked Pete.

Tony stopped rubbing his back, and shrugged. "Yeah. He didn't punch me, it was only a little shove."

"They ain't so tough," Teddy said, in a voice that was too loud.

"Hey, what's the matter with you?" Ray's high-pitched screech was hardly a whisper. He grabbed his brother and punched him on the arm. "You want to get us all killed?"

"Yo, Ray. Lemme go."

Ray punched him again. "Then keep your mouth shut, Pintsize."

Tears welled up behind Teddy's black plastic frames, but he refrained from further comment.

"If this kid had any brains he'd be dangerous."

"Leave him alone, Ray," Tony pulled Teddy behind him.

"Yeah," Pete added. "He didn't mean nothing."

"You tell that to our muscle-bound friend over there. He's not the most reasonable person in the world."

"Just stop picking on him," Pete said.

Ben pulled the blanket off the roof, and bundled it through the rear window. "Yeah, lay off him. If you want to pick on someone, pick on George." George looked up with filmy eyes, and opened his mouth.

Pete burst out, "Hey, we got race on the line."

Tony looked up just as the tires laid four rubber tracks. The '56 Chevy sported a scoop on the hood to make room for the supercharger. It took the '66 Barracuda off the line and stayed in front. By the time the contenders passed Tony, the Chevy was more than a length ahead. With a loud bang the 'Cuda missed a gear. The Chevy rocketed on toward the finish line while the 'Cuda dropped down to cruising speed. Cheers went up for the Chevy.

"Must be some kid in his old man's car," Pete scowled.

"He wasn't going to beat that Chevy, anyway," Ben said.

Ray shook his head. "You think Chevies are the greatest things on wheels, but let me tell you — "

"Get a load of this," Ben interrupted. A '58 Chevy nosed up to the yellow mark. The car was jet black, and polished like a new shoe. Chrome glimmered in the streetlight as if it were gilded jewelry. The door panels were painted with white script: "if you beat me, you can eat me." Ben let out a yell. "This is her! This is her! This is that red hot mama."

The girl who stepped out of the car was short and shapely, dressed from head to foot in blue denim. The jacket was unzipped to reveal a yellow blouse with two bulges in it that might have been cantaloupes, perfectly poised. Her waist was waspish, her hips full and contoured, and her stomach athletically flat. Her pants were tucked into pointed cowboy boots, and a ten-gallon hat perched atop her head. Long, dark hair flowed over her shoulders and down to the tenth rib. A white silk handkerchief was tied loosely about her soft neck.

"Wow," breathed Teddy, through fogging glasses.

"Get a load of that chick," George drooled.

"Get a load of that *car*," said Ben.

"So that's the girl we been hearing about." Pete looked at Tony and nodded with his chin. "Whaddaya think?"

Tony shook his head slowly. "I don't know."

Ben said, "She's the hottest thing on four wheels."

"And two legs." added George.

"She's unbeatable and inedible."

"That's what you think, buddy." The owner of the G.T.O. sauntered by with his two buddies. As he approached the crowd of admirers that was gathering around the girl, he shoved his way through, none too gently.

Another car rumbled up to the starting line. What it was, or had been, Tony could not determine. The homemade hotrod had probably once been a Ford coupe that had been drastically overhauled and customized. It was slanted down in front, jacked up in the rear, and cut out in the middle. Each rear tire was wide enough to span an open manhole. The differential was geared so low that the car moved in spurts, and the transmission was torqued so high that one turn of the flywheel might have been five on the axle. Two chromed, duel exhaust pipes jutted out behind fenderless front wheels.

"He must measure his gas mileage in gallons per mile," George commented.

Boos and catcalls rang out from the bystanders: it was unfair to pit a stock car against a dragster. The driver of the hotrod revved his engine to attract attention. The cowgirl looked at him once, then ignored him.

"Tell me the Chevy's going to win this one," Ray said.

Ben shook his head slowly. "The most she can have under the hood is a 348. He's probably got a 409, with dual quads. She hasn't got a chance.

"Maybe she likes to lose sometimes," George said.

Pete hopped from foot to foot. "Why don't you introduce yourself, Georgy Porgy? Ask her out for a date."

"George has never even *had* a date, much less ate one," Ray said.

"Yeah. Take her out for a whirl in the Green Lantern." Ben punched George playfully in the stomach. "Dazzle her with your driving skills."

George said, "Knock it off."

"The lightest foot in the west."

"Poetry in slow motion."

"Have you filled your gas tank this year?"

"Did you tell your mom how you rolled the car into the garage door?"

"Maybe this chick'll show you which pedal is the clutch."

"I said knock it off." George stared hard at the street. "Just remember who owns the frat house."

"Your mother owns it, Georgy, not you."

"Yeah, well, I can always have you guys thrown out. All I have to do is say I need the room for storage."

"What's the matter? You got so many nudie magazines you're running out of places to hide them?"

"And your mom needs the rent money 'cause your old man don't pay enough support."

"Besides, we'll just rent another garage and forget to tell you about it."

George champed. "I said, knock it off."

"Yeah, knock it off," Teddy put in.

"You shut up, four eyes," Ray yelled.

Teddy stepped back out of Ray's swinging range and raised his hands defensively. The shrill blast of a whistle cut the air, followed by a warning scream.

"*Cops!*"

From the far end of the track, bearing down with incredible speed, three red cars barred escape in that direction by approaching side by side. Flashing bubble gum machines were mounted on their roofs. Instantly, Decatur Road was galvanized into action. Gangs of teenagers bolted for their cars; a hundred engines thundered to life.

Ben leaped into the front seat of the Black Stallion and keyed the ignition. He slammed the transmission into gear and spun the wheel as if the car had power steering. The passenger doors were still open as he pulled away from the curb.

Pete pulled the right front door shut against the terrible centrifugal force caused by the turning vehicle, but Ray was still hanging half out of the left rear door as the Chevy roared past the driverless G.T.O. Tony grabbed George, who grabbed Ray and pulled him in. The thud that slammed the door shut also knocked down the owner of the Goat. He crashed into his two buddies and all three went down in a heap.

Ben forced the car into a screeching U-turn. "Hang on to your drawers."

Tony lost his grip and was slammed against George, who crushed Ray against the door of the rotating car. Tony saw two girls scream and throw up their hands as they dashed out of the path of the rampaging Chevy. Ben pressed his hand to the horn and his foot to the floor. The car fishtailed halfway around before he let go of the steering wheel and let it swing back on its own. Ray was still being crushed; then the weight shifted back to Tony. George banged from side to side, his head grazing the tattered material of the roof.

All along the road, cars tried to pull out of their cramped parking slots, but Ben yielded to no one. With tires still spinning, he raced toward the starting line where the roadster and the '58 Chevy still spread across the road. Beyond them two more police cars ground to a halt.

"It's a trap!"

Ben shifted into second gear, caught rubber, and massaged the floorboards with his shoe sole. The roadster door was open, and one leg hung out.

"Oh, Jesus Christ!"

Pete jammed his hands against the dashboard and locked his arms. George ducked his head into Tony's lap. Tony held his breath as he watched the developing scene through the windows.

"Ben, you're crazy!"

The leg withdrew, the door closed. Tony caught a glimpse of a startled face under a baseball cap, the foot of the roadster's driver as he fell over backward in his seat, people running out of the way. If either car had possessed an extra coat of paint, the Black Stallion would have scraped it off. The Chevy sped through the gap like a ball from a cannon, spewing dust and black smoke.

Tony had an instantaneous glimpse of a blue-jacketed figure only inches from his face. Through the open window he heard, "Hey you, stop." The pointing index finger was almost lopped off by the aerial. Then everything was gone but the trees and the shrubbery of the airport property.

Pete yelled from the shotgun seat. "Watch out for the curve,"

The industrial park was a wedge out of the airport. Like two legs of an L, Red Lion Road began where Decatur Road ended: ninety degrees to the left. Ben continued to accelerate as the car approached the right-angled turn. He spun the wheel sharply long before the car reached the angle of the L. The Chevy slewed sideways, crushing Tony under the weight of George and Ray, and reared up on two wheels. Tony feared it was going all the way over.

With the engine racing and the tires screaming in agony, Ben kept a death grip on the leather wrappings. The forward momentum slowly translated into the new direction in which the car was pointing. It slid around the curb as smooth as could be. The left two tires crashed down onto the macadam, and the Black Stallion charged along Red Lion Road at maximum acceleration. It was the only car to escape the police barricade.

"Jesus H. Christ," Ray muttered.

Half a mile down the road, Ben stood on the brakes as a stop sign approached all too fast. At ninety miles per hour, the car went into a controlled skid. Tony extracted one arm from the melee in the back seat, and punched down the door lock. Screaming tires whined in unison as Ben downshifted and pumped the brakes madly. An array of smells burned from under the hood: brake fluid, transmission oil, and peeling rubber.

The Chevy entered Academy Road sideways, still going fifty miles per hour, described an arc that took it to the other side, then fishtailed back into the right lane. Tony saw headlights in both directions, but there were no collisions. The engine whined and clawed for speed.

"All right, Ben. We're clear." A crowbar could not have loosened the hold Ray had on the back of the front seat.

The road essed around the western extremity of the airport, toward a traffic light that Tony could see was red. A constant flow of cars and trucks filled the intersection. A car sat in the right lane with its signal blinking, waiting for the light to change,

"Hey, Ben. Will ya?"

"Will I what?"

"Slow the hell down before you kill us all."

The speedometer needle touched seventy-five. "Trust me."

Pete was still straight-arming the dashboard. "Or have faith in God."

Ben stayed in the left lane, barreling onward like a loaded freight train. Tony reached out and touched his shoulder. "Ben?"

Again George closed his eyes and ducked into Tony's lap. Ray pounded the back of the sea "Yo, will ya? Hit the brakes, goddamn it."

The Chevy exploded past the waiting car like a speeding missile. The white stop line was gobbled up under the hood. At the precise moment when the front bumper crossed the second white line and entered the intersection, the light changed to green. The cars that were stopped on Grant Avenue were a blur. A split second later, the Chevy careened through a residential district in the comfort of darkness.

"You crazy animal." Ray was breathing like a runner at the end of a heat. "You are trying to kill us, aren't you?"

"Nice timing," Pete allowed.

"Timing hell. It was too goddamn close. Suppose someone had run the red light?"

"But that would have been against the law," Ben said in an innocent voice. He jammed on the brakes and screamed into a tiny side street, a one-laner with cars parked on both sides. Two blocks later, he turned again down another narrow lane, and after one block more he bounced into a driveway separating rows of houses. "Standard evasive tactics." Finally, he slowed down to a normal twenty-five miles per hour, like a law-abiding citizen, and headed for home.

"Oh, my god!"

"Ray, what is it now?" Pete turned around and stared at Tony. "What is it with this guy. Ninety's too fast and twenty-five's too slow."

Tony rubbed his ears in mock discomfort. "I don't know, but I wish he'd watch the decibels."

"What're you talking about?" George asked. "I'm sitting right next to him."

"Shut up, will ya?"

"Stay cool, man. Stay cool."

"We gotta go back."

"Are you crazy?"

"My mom'll kill me. We gotta go back and get my brother."

Ben said, "We sure as hell ain't going back in this car."

"But we gotta. I can't go home without the little twerp."

Pete reached in his pocket for change. "Here's a quarter. Go take a bus."

"But suppose the police got him? What'm I

gonna do then? Goddamn that Teddy."

The blanket floated up off the floor like a rising ghost, and from underneath a muffled voice asked, "Somebody call me?"

Chapter 12

The neon sign read "Gino's." Gino Marchetti was a baseball player who let his name be used on the restaurant marquee for a percentage of the profit. It was rumored that he was also an investor in the enterprise.

Tony climbed into the back seat of the Black Stallion with his fifteen-cent hamburger, fifteen-cent French fries, fifteen-cent milkshake, and marveled at the genius who had come up with the idea of a complete meal for forty-five cents — and who was still able to make a fortune out of it.

With no dining room, no rest rooms, and no overhead, the appeal was limited to the generation whose time was more valuable than flourish. The fineries of life were traded off for the bare essentials: a cheap meal and a place to gather for take-out food that was delivered fast.

"Hey, there goes Sue Rogers." Ben paused between bites to swallow, clean his mouth, and whistle. "Look at her swivel. Wheeeeew."

Pete tossed a French fry into his mouth. "Why don't you go and talk to her?"

"No way. If Kate drove by and saw me within fifty yards of her, she'd skin me alive."

"Kate's ten miles away from here, and don't even know where we are."

"She's psychic. She'd hear somehow."

"That's the trouble with going steady — hey, give me that Coke before I punch you." Ray grabbed the plastic cup and a straw from his brother. "You shake in your shoes whenever you think of another girl."

"Yeah, but I don't have to scramble around for a date, either. I can always count on Kate to go to the movies with me."

"Plus the fringes," Pete put in.

"It would be cheaper if you went by yourself." George ate his fries slowly, because that was all he had bought. He bumped Tony every time he lifted his hand to his mouth.

Ray said, "It may be cheaper, but it's not as much fun. Is it, Ben?"

Ben stared out the window, and munched his burger thoughtfully.

"I'd rather be with one real girl than with all those nude pictures you got in that closet of yours."

"Don't need no elbow grease, either," Pete said.

Everyone laughed, Teddy the loudest — and the longest. Ray elbowed him in the ribs and stole a French fry from his bag. "What are you laughing at, pea brain? You're not even old

enough to know what we're talking about."

Teddy stuck out his lower jaw. "Do so."

Ray punched his brother, shoving him into Ben so hard that his Seven-Up spilled onto his lap. "Yo, Ray, cut it out."

"I didn't do it. It was the pipsqueak."

"But you punched him. Now, leave him alone." Ben reached into Teddy's shirt pocket and extracted a handful of paper napkins. He kept one, and threw the rest in Ray's face.

The meal that Ray carefully balanced on his lap, overturned when he jerked back. The French fries spilled between his legs, the hamburger overturned and the roll opened so the meat fell against his meticulously clean pants. A colorful combination of mustard and ketchup stained the legs like a work of modern art.

"Jesus Christ! Now look what you made me do." He grabbed for the napkins and wiped the inner thigh of his pants.

"Having fun?" George said.

"Serves you right." Pete smirked. Ray punched Teddy again, swinging from the front so as not to jolt Ben.

"Ray, leave the kid alone."

"It's not my fault, Ben. The kid's a damn troublemaker. I told you not to bring him."

Pete put in, "Stop whining. You sound like George."

Ben parked his soda on the dashboard. "Then let me put it to you bluntly: the kid stays. Now either you leave him alone, or you can walk home."

"Ben, I didn't . . . "

"Those are the conditions. You're the one who started it. And look how you messed up my car."

"*Your car?* What about my pants?"

"The pants don't belong to me; the car does. And you never offer to help me wash it."

Ray tossed a wad of dirty napkins out the window. "Look, Ben, I'm sorry about the car. But these pants just came back from the cleaners." He grabbed another batch of napkins from Teddy's pocket.

"Hey, what do you think you're doing?"

Ray stopped in mid wipe. "What do you mean, what am I doing? I'm cleaning my pants."

"You threw that trash out the window."

"So what? It's only a parking lot."

"Did your mother teach you to act that way?"

Ray's face turned bright red in the yellow floodlights. "What the hell is it with you tonight?"

"I don't like littering."

"You don't have to clean it up."

"That's not the point. The cops are watching for things like that. They're just waiting for an excuse to pick on us. Now, get out there and pick it up."

"You gotta be joking."

"I'm not joking."

"Come on, Ben. Will ya?"

"Pick — it — up."

Ray bit hard on his lip; his cheek muscles bulged. "If this is some goddamn joke — "

"Just pick it up."

"All right, already. Don't get your dander up."

Pete mumbled with a mouthful of food, "You better watch it, Ray. You know what happened to George when he said that."

Teddy was the only one who laughed.

Ray got out of the car and picked up the wad of napkins by one unsoiled corner. He carried it to the trashcan as if it were a soaked diaper.

"Drop mine in while you're there." Pete tossed his crumpled bag out the window. Ray caught it in the air and dropped it in the can like a basketball. Then the tumult started as wrappers and bags were passed to Pete to toss to Ray, who danced around as if he were on the court making fancy plays and avoiding seven-footers. When Ben's soda sailed out the window, with half a cup of ice, Ray let it go. It hit the ground, spilled out the ice, and rolled under a white '65 Belair. He picked it up and disposed of it without disturbing the owner.

Ray reclaimed his seat and fished a pack of cigarettes from his shirt pocket. "Plug in the lighter, Numskull." Teddy did it automatically. Ray lit up and puffed smoke idly out the window. "Get a load of that, will you?"

A tall blonde in skintight pants wiggled by. She stared straight ahead and ignored the cat-calls from half a dozen cars. Ben said, "Are those pants for real, or are they painted on?"

"I don't know," Ray drooled. "But I'd sure like to attack her with a can of paint remover."

"Hey, guys, let's go home."

"Uh-oh. Better watch out. George's got a hot date with a closet." Pete thrust his elbow out the rear window. "Those nudie books are in for a rough night."

"What time does your mother want you home?" Ben asked.

George brushed a wisp of corn-silk hair out of his eyes. "My mother doesn't tell me what time to get in."

"She tells you to go out and get a job," Pete said.

"I *am* looking for a job."

"Better not look too hard or you might find one."

"It takes time."

"How long you been looking? I went to work the day after graduation, and Ray started at the jeweler's a week later. You're supposed to an-ticipate these things, apply in advance. So what are you waiting for, for one to come and knock on your door and take you to it?"

"I've been selling papers for six years."

"Oh, that's just great. One night a week, for a couple hours, you hawk the *Sunday Bulletin*."

"Can I help it if I can't find anything I like?"

"I'm not exactly tickled to death about pumping gas, you know. But at least I can pay my folks for food, and have a little cash left over."

"Yeah, and you'll be stuck there for the rest of your life. You have a great future as a grease monkey."

"Hey, at least I'm learning a trade. There're gonna be cars that need fixing for a long time. So what are you waiting for, your old man to kick the bucket so you can get his insurance?"

Tony leaned around George's large form. "Yo, Pete. Don't you think that's hitting below the belt?"

"Yeah, that's not very nice," Ben said.

"True, but not nice," added Ray.

"How about just laying off me for a while, okay? I want to go home."

"Why didn't you say so in the first place?" Ben reached for the key and started the engine. "I've got no beef with you."

The engine sounded abrasively loud in the relative quiet of the parking lot. The exhaust rumbled as Ben backed out slowly. He followed the one-way arrows around the building, gunning the accelerator a couple times for effect.

Just as they reached the street exit, a bright red car streaked by the left side and slammed to a halt diagonally in front of them. The bubble gum machine on the roof rotated and flashed, but the siren was not blaring.

Pete quoted, "What's red, has four wheels, and fuzz on the inside?"

The policeman turned off the flashing lights and stepped stiffly out of the car, as if he had a pole up his back. He left the door open and swaggered toward the Chevy with one hand resting belligerently on the handle of his forty-five, and one hand gripping the billy stick to prevent it from swinging and hitting him on the legs. His shoulders were thrown back so hard that his legs moved like a gunman's waiting for his opponent to draw, and his hat was pulled down so far in front that he had to tilt his head back in order to see out from under the polished brim.

"Oh, shit," Ben muttered under his breath.

The prim blue uniform showed not a wrinkle; the badge, belt buckle, and shoes shone blindingly. He looked like a clothing store manikin, his face waxy and expressionless. He bent over at the waist and peered in the open window, ignoring every face except Ben's.

"Can I see your driver's license and vehicle registration, please?"

Ben switched off the ignition. "Yes, sir. Is anything the matter?" He pulled out a worn wallet and extracted the appropriate cards.

In the time it takes to read the Book of Psalms, the policeman scanned the cards in the beam of his flashlight. George cleared his throat above the preternatural silence that seemed to pervade the car.

"Where are you coming from, Ben?"

He did not hesitate for a moment. "Langhorne, sir. We went to Reedman's to look at old cars — to see if they got any new ones in."

"New what?"

"Old cars."

"*Old* cars?"

"Yes, sir."

"You just said you were looking for new cars."

"No, sir. I said new *ones*."

"What's a new *one*?"

"It's an old car that's new. You see, I can't afford a new car, but they have some nice old ones. Now, I looked at the new ones, too, but just to compare prices. The new ones cost too much. So, then I looked at the new old ones. But they didn't have any, really. Only the same old old ones they had before. The only ones they got in since last week were some new new ones, and I *really* can't afford them."

The policeman's face stiffened from wax to wood. "I see." Only his lips moved when he spoke. Tony studied his clean-shaven face: the razor nick on his chin, the dab of mustard clinging to his dark, bushy mustache, the pimples glossed over with his wife's makeup, the crow's feet next to his eyes, the deep creases on his forehead. How many other cops had he seen from just this close?

He arched his neck back like a goose's, and fixed his stare on Teddy. "How old are you, son?"

"I'm eighteen, and my brother's seventeen," Ray said.

"I'm not talking to you."

"Sorry."

"Well?"

Teddy stared mindlessly out the windshield. "Huhn? Who, me? I'm, uh, seventeen." He flashed a smile, then went back to studying with intent interest something in the street.

"What's your name?"

"Uh, Theodore K. Murphy."

"You have any identification on you?"

"Well, uh, well, uh, not really. I left my wallet, uh, at home. Yeah, I forgot it tonight."

"Freeloading, huhn?"

Teddy nodded.

The policeman paused for a moment as he scrutinized each one. Finally, he consulted his watch. "Weekday curfew is ten o'clock for sixteen-year-olds, so if any of you are under age you've got fifteen minutes to get home."

The head backed out of the window, but he still had Ben's cards. He strolled around the rear of the car, looked at the license plate, at the cards, and the license plate again. He took his time while scribbling on a tablet.

"What the hell's he doing?" Smoke poured from Ray's mouth as he took the final drag. He made a motion to toss the butt out the window, then stopped, and crushed it in the ashtray.

Pete hissed, "Probably holding us up till ten o'clock so he can haul Teddy in. One look at him and you know he's still in junior high."

"I am not. I'm a junior in senior high."

Ben banged the steering wheel with the flat of his hand. "Will you guys keep it down?"

George said, "Do you think he recognized us from Decatur Road?"

"He couldn't have," Tony said, keeping a sharp eye on the cop through the rear window. "That's in the fifteenth district. This is the seventh."

"Suppose they got the license number?" Ray asked, his voice cracked.

"Damn." Ben banged the wheel again. "I forgot to screw in the bulb."

"Maybe they got a description of the car."

Pete said, "There must be a million black Chevies in the city."

"Not with four doors," Ray countered.

Everyone hushed as the cop sauntered back to the driver's door. "Your engine sounded like it was having digestive problems. When was the last time you had your exhaust system checked?"

"Well, sir, the muffler's pretty new, but I might have some leakage where the pipe attaches. I'll put some putty on it right away."

"I know you will. I'm going to forget about it this time, but if I catch you again I'm going to issue a summons for exceeding the noise standards. You can get away with that in South Philly, but out here in the Northeast we like peace and quiet." He tore a sheet of paper out of his tablet and shoved it in through the window. "For now, I'm issuing you a violation for the light that's out over your license plate. You have forty-eight hours to get it replaced. Unless you wish to protest it, you don't need to appear in court. Follow the instructions on the back of the ticket and, along with your ten dollars, submit proof that the repair has been made."

He looked at his watch again. "You now have eleven minutes to get any minors off the streets. I won't ask for identification — I'm just giving you a warning."

"Thanks." Ben stuffed the cards back into his wallet, tossed the ticket onto the dashboard.

"And don't speed on the way home." The policeman walked back to his car, slithered into the front seat, closed the door, and took his time starting his engine and leaving the parking lot. Ben waited until he was half a block away before turning in the opposite direction.

"The lousy bastard."

"Picking on kids instead of preventing crime."

"Got nothing better to do than act tough."

"How we gonna get to South Philly in ten minutes?"

Ben raced through a yellow light. "I don't care about that, but I gotta meet Kate at ten-thirty."

"She's gonna be mad at you."

"She'll get over it. Besides, her girlfriends are hanging with her." He raced south along Richmond street, passed a trolley car with inches to spare, then weaved between the cars along Fifth Street, making more than one enemy. He made record time, and soon raced by a row of brownstones. "There she is."

Tony got the barest glimpse of Kate and three other girls standing on the street corner. At the end of the block, Ben turned right, then left, then right, then squealed to a halt.

"I hate to do this, Ted. But we'd both be in a bunch of trouble if we got stopped again."

"That's all right, Ben. Thanks for everything."

Ray opened the door, pulled in his legs, and made his brother climb over top of him. "Listen, big mouth. Don't say anything to Mom about Decatur Road."

"What do you take me fo — ? Never mind. I won't."

"I know you won't, because if you so much as breathe a word of it, I'll beat you to a pulp." As proof of his intentions, he gave Teddy a resounding punch on the shoulder. "Now keep quiet, you hear?" After the car was underway, he said, "Sometimes that kid talks without thinking."

Pete said, "I wish you would think without talking."

The car sounded unnaturally loud in the narrow street of row homes. Ben stopped the car a couple of blocks away. "Out, George."

George looked stunned. "Huhn? Why?"

Ben turned around and threw his arm over the seat. "Because you said you wanted to go home. So, here you are."

"Oh, yeah. I forgot. Well, I changed my mind."

Ben pushed his long, straight hair from his eyes. "Let me put it to you bluntly. After I pick up Kate and her friends, we may go for a little drive. That means gas. And gas means money.

And that means you have to chip in."

"Come on, Georgy. Sell a couple extra papers. That'll pay for it."

Tony said, "I'll lend you the money if you don't have it with you."

George cleared his throat. "All right. I'll stick with you guys."

"Atta boy, George." Ray lit up another cigarette and puffed furiously.

"But can you blow that smoke out the window?"

Ray cracked open the vent. "Sorry 'bout that." Then he was thrown back in his seat as Ben gunned the accelerator. At each block they raced up to fifty miles per hour between the stop signs, screeched to a halt, checked for traffic and cops, and took off again. In less than a minute, they pulled up in front of Kate, and parked.

"Ben, what's the idea of going by like that without stopping?" Before he had a chance to open the door, her blonde head tipped into the window and she planted a playful kiss on his cheek. Her face was fleshed out fully with smooth, naturally pink skin, and her hair was set in a permanent wave that made her look older than she was: she could walk unquestioned into any nightclub in the city without being asked for a Liquor Control Board card — unless she were accompanied by Ben and his peach fuzz face.

"Look at the time, Kate," he said, through gritted teeth. Kate distracted him with more kisses. He fought her off and held up his wristwatch. "Look, Kate. See that? See what it says? Can you see what it says? Ten seconds to go. Okay? Now what's your complaint?"

"All right, so you're on time . . . "

"What do you mean, on time? I'm early."

"All right, Ben, but you could have stopped and told me you were coming right back. How was I to know?"

"You know because I'm always where I'm supposed to be at the right time. And I had to keep going because Teddy was late for curfew."

"Oh, Ben, I don't know why you bother with that little snigger. Oh — sorry, Ray. But, isn't he a little young to be running around with you guys?"

"That's what I keep saying, but Ben keeps taking him along."

"Thanks for saying hello," Pete said. "Besides, he's a nice kid. Why don't you give him a chance?"

"Yeah," Tony added. "Instead of picking on him like a flea, why don't you treat him like a human being?"

"Who rattled your chain?" Ray turned quickly, and stabbed a finger at Tony. "You sit in that corner all night long and don't say a word, now you're jumping all over my case."

"He's right, Ray. You never give him a chance to be someone."

Kate opened the door and pulled Ben out. "If you don't mind, I'm tired of talking about Teddy. I want to talk to my boyfriend — alone."

She dragged him into the shadow of a corner gas station. Her girlfriends huddled around a phone booth, clearly visible in the incandescent light. Every once in a while, an eye was cocked toward the Chevy.

"This is ridiculous," Ray finally said. "We're sitting here like a bunch of clucks, while those girls are over there laughing at us. If Kate didn't think about herself so much, she'd at least have the decency to introduce us."

"What are you afraid of?" Pete said. "Go over and introduce yourself."

"Why don't *you*?"

"I'm waiting for you to break the ice. One look at those duds and I don't hafta worry about grease on my pants."

"Let's do it." Ray took a last look into the mirror, smoothed down his dark hair, and climbed out of the car. Pete got out on his side.

"Hey, wait for me." George slid over, taking his weight off Tony, caught his foot on the sill and almost fell, then with the help of the door pulled himself out.

Tony stretched his legs out on the rear seat and watched the proceedings. In one direction he could see Ben and Kate kissing quietly in the shadows, in the other he could see three bashful guys talking to three giggling girls. He was lost in thought.

The front door opened and Kate called out, "Ben and I are going for a ride, if anyone wants to come."

In less than a minute the car was overflowing with bodies. Kate sat practically on top of Ben, nibbling his ear. Pete had a redhead sitting on his lap, and introduced her as Marion. Tony crouched in the corner next to George, whose lap was filled with a girl with long, curly tresses. Her name was Patty. Kathy cuddled in Ray's lap as if they had known each other for years.

Ben started the car and eased away from the curb. He drove slowly toward the river. Marion talked quietly with Pete, her freckled face partially concealed from Tony by her long, frizzled hair. Ray and Kathy were completely hidden by George's bulk, but Tony could hear them necking. Patty was having quite a time with George's roving hands: she pushed and slapped at them continuously.

"Tony, you're awfully quiet tonight," Kate said, between nibbles. "Cat got your tongue?"

"No, there's just not much to say."

"Well, don't worry. We won't be here long. Will we, Ben?"

"You're the one who has to be in by midnight."

Tony stared out the window, watching the houses and the closely parked cars go by. On Monday night there was not much pedestrian traffic, and, except for the bars and the delicatessens, all the stores were closed. A church bell gonged eleven times, echoing off the stone and brick two-story houses. Potholes and broken macadam made the ride less than smooth.

By the waterfront, Ben doused the lights, shut off the engine, and rolled up the windows for silence. Moonlight glinted off the Delaware River. The buildings of Camden on the far shore were silhouetted against the stars.

Kate ran her hands through Ben's hair until it was a ragged mop. Marion and Pete made cute pecking sounds. Kathy had a lip-lock on Ray that might have been a strangle hold under different circumstances. Patty continued to fight off George's advances. No one spoke.

Tony closed his eyes.

Much later, Kate said, "George, why can't you act like a gentleman? Maybe Patty just wants to talk."

"Yeah, show some respect."

"Cool it."

"Give the girl a break."

George pouted. "I'm not doing anything."

"Oh, yes, you are." Patty smoothed out her dress and wriggled close to the front seat. "Kate, I can't stay out much longer or my grandmother will kill me."

Ben pulled back and struggled with the crank. "We can't go anywhere with the windows fogged like this. Open 'em up."

The cool river air was a welcome relief to Tony. He stuck his head out and sucked in great gulps as the Black Stallion rumbled over Delaware Avenue cobblestones and back to the corner. The girls disembarked, waving and saying goodbye. Kate lingered with her head in the window, smothering Ben's face with kisses.

When she finally pulled away, she said, "I almost forgot. I'm having a party Saturday night and you're all invited."

"Will Kathy be there . . . ?" Kate was already gone. "Damn, I didn't even get her phone number."

Ben straightened out his shirt and pulled up his collar. "Don't worry about it, Ray. I'm sure she will be."

"What's the matter, Ben? Got something on your neck you don't want us to see?" Pete laughed.

"None of your business." He started the car, pulled out of the parking spot, and drove respectfully along the darkened street. Kate's parents were staring out the picture window as they passed.

"Uh, oh. Ole Blue Eyes did it again."

"Can't you teach that girl to be more careful, so the guys don't make fun of you all the time?"

"Knock it off," Ben said, with mock anger.

"Is the widdle boy embawassed. Aaaaah, that's too bad."

"You weren't doing so bad yourself, Pete. And Ray, I thought you were never going to come up for air."

He parked the car in front of George's house. It was the only place in this sea of row homes with a garage. The double doors were nailed shut, so the gang used the basement door and ducked under the green-tinged copper pipes in the laundry room.

"I'm for a Coke." Ray padded over three layers of variously colored carpet and yanked open the refrigerator. "Who else is drinking?"

Ben sat in an ancient chair with no cushion and sagging springs. He sank down so low that his knees stuck up like a grasshopper's. The tattered edge of a Temptations poster hung by its side. "I'll have one."

The sofa was a hand-me-down with the upholstery worn through in so many places that only long strips of tape held it together. Pete sank into his favorite corner. "Me, too."

"Sounds good to me."

Ray swung around with three bottles in his hands. "George, you don't have any soda in here, remember?"

"Yeah, you didn't chip in with the rest of us," Pete said.

Ben took the bottle Ray handed him and flipped off the cap with an opener. "Speaking of chipping in, you still owe me for gas."

"I don't see you collecting from anyone else."

"That's because they pay up without being asked. It's you I'm worried about."

Ray offered a bottle to Tony. "No thanks. I think I'll have apple juice." He went to the refrigerator and found his jug, blew the dust out of a glass, and filled it.

"All I have is change," George said.

"As long as it's American, I'll take it," Ben replied.

George reached into his tight pants pocket and withdrew a handful of coins. Very carefully he counted out three quarters, one dime, one nickel, and five pennies. "That's all I have."

"I'll take if off your bill."

"For another fifteen cents you can have a Coke." Ray took a swig from his own bottle and popped it with his tongue.

"They only cost a dime."

"That's when you chip in."

Pete placed his own Coke on the chipped chest next to him. "And you always run off with the bottle and turn it in for the two cents."

George tramped out the door. "Never mind. Forget I even asked. I'll get one from upstairs."

"Yeah, and let your mom pay for it."

"You better wash the mold off that money."

"He already ate the mold off. There's nothing left but pocket lint."

"He's so tight his shoes squeak."

Ray brought an empty hand out of his pocket. "Hey, I'm kinda short of funds, myself."

"Don't worry about it." Ben picked up a handful of darts and one by one tossed them across the room to a trash-picked dartboard with hardly any cork left. "You can owe me. Just don't tell George or he'll have a fit."

Pete made a rocket ship out of a dollar bill and sailed it into Ben's lap. "That should cover me for tonight."

Ben held up his hand as Tony reached for his wallet. "You're paid up from a month ago. Besides, we used your car the last time we went to Decatur and you never collected."

"Yeah, Tone. How come you always have money?" Ray sat at the other end of the sofa. "You're not even working now."

Tony tasted his apple juice. It was several weeks old and already past the cider stage. Next stop was vinegar. "I saved it from last summer."

"Wow, watermelons must have been a boom crop."

"Well, I worked at the store for a while, too."

"Speaking of work, I've got to get going." Ben stood up, finished his Coke, and deposited the bottle in the cardboard case. "I've got early classes tomorrow, and I'm working at the hardware store in the afternoon. How 'bout you, Tony?"

He leaned against a wobbly chest-of-drawers, playing with a three-colored sheet of Mendelev's periodic table. "I'm in no rush."

"Late class?"

"No class is more like it."

"Only George ain't got no class," Pete said.

Tony kept fidgeting.

"Temple's not closed tomorrow, is it? LaSalle isn't."

"No, it's open. It's just that I don't really have to be there. I'm dropping out."

The sudden silence in the frat house was broken only by the gurgle of water slurping through the soil drain — someone upstairs had flushed the toilet. Ben froze in mid-stride. "What do you mean, dropping out?"

Tony grabbed a gray-painted wooden chair, sat in it reversed, and buried his head in his hands. "Just that. I'm quitting. I'm joining the electrical union and taking the four-year apprenticeship program."

"But why? I thought you didn't like construction."

"I don't, really." Tony glanced up at the stupefied faces. "But my father says he's having trouble with the business and doesn't have the money to keep me in school."

Pete got up and paced the garage nervously. "Ain'tchu paid up till the end of the year?"

"No, I only paid quarterly, as my father would give me the money. Now, he says he can't pay for the final semester."

"Use your own money. You've got more than the rest of us put together." Ray knelt down in front of him, pulling up his pants so they retained their crease. "Nobody saves like you do."

"Sell your car if you have to," Ben suggested. "Then save up during the summer."

"I'll never save enough, what with the rent and all."

"*Rent!*" Three voices yelled simultaneously.

"Yeah, my parents want me to start paying room and board. They figure I'm old enough to earn my keep."

George charged into the garage like a herd of elephants. "Who's got the church key? I couldn't find one upstairs."

"Shut up."

"Zip your lip, Chowderhead."

"What the hell's the matter with you guys?"

"Tony's folks're makin' him quit school."

Tony took a deep breath. "Anyway, they want me to start supporting myself and sort of — get out on my own. They think it's about time I — how did he put it — see what the world is all about."

Ben spat like an enraged cobra. "That stinks."

"It sounds like a raw deal to me." Pete never stopped pacing. He plucked the darts out of the board and hurled them back with no constraint. "They never wanted you to go in the first place."

"But can't you get a student loan, or something?" Ray suggested.

"I can do a lot of things, but I can't fight my parents. I need some kind of support. Pete's right, they never wanted me to go to college. I don't know how they ever let me start. I guess they were afraid of what people would say if they said no. Now, it doesn't matter to them. Ever since they went on that cruise and got a taste of the good life . . . "

George cleared his throat. "Uh, how does that affect your draft status?"

"Just what a conscientious objector would ask," Ben said.

"He ain't conscious enough to be an objector," Pete added angrily.

Tony waved them to silence. "Once I'm accepted into the union I get the same deferment I have in college. After four years the conflict will be over and the draft dissolved."

"Believe that and you're a fool," Pete said.

"But what about your education," Ben persisted. "What about science? You're an egghead, not a construction worker."

"I guess I can always go to night school later — or even now, if I want to. I can still work toward a degree. But I have to have a job. There's no way around that."

Ben took Tony by the shoulder, and squeezed hard. "Tone, believe me, now is not the time to drop out of college. The draft board is just waiting to pounce on guys like you."

"But if everything happens the way my father says it will, I'll be in the union and on deferment before the draft board gets wind of my change of status."

Ben grimaced and shook his head. "I still think it stinks."

Chapter 13

"*Beowulf* is more than a poem, it is more than a national chronicle, it is more than a novel of war: it is a human epic. Not only does it expound upon the virtues of strength, courage, and heroism, it also expresses the ideals, the character, and the traditions of a people. It occupies an important and respected place in the literature of the English language not just because it is the earliest known work to have survived from olden times, but because the events therein depicted have distinct parallels still today. It matters not whether Beowulf was a real person, any more than it matters whether Homer's Ulysses was modeled after a real man. What matters is that he is the personification of a race and the sum total of its code of ethics."

Professor Dean talked himself quite literally into a corner. Never at a loss for thoughts, or words with which to express them, he had twice circled the classroom during his monologue, and ended with his meandering, oversized nose plunged into a front corner, seemingly talking to an audience of cinder blocks. The sun that streamed in through the plate glass windows highlighted the wrinkles in his dull gray suit. In the second week of the term he had made the statement: "I get more of a reaction from the walls than I do from this class." As a pragmatist, he directed his attention to that element which paid him the most mind.

By a strange acoustical coincidence, his voice carried louder and with more conviction when reverberated by cold cement. If his delivery sometimes failed in eloquence, it never lacked in punch.

"The idealism of *Beowulf* in merry old England is one that has been carried down through the ages, passed from generation to generation, indelibly inculcated in the minds of man and inherent in modern societies. Through words and action, Beowulf was dedicated to eradicating evil from the face of the Earth. Would anyone care to carry that comment further?"

The white-painted cinder blocks remained as obdurate as the class. Two hands crawled tentatively to half-mast.

Professor Dean's back still graced the classroom. "Can you hear me? Is anyone alive out there?"

No one smiled; no one snickered. Finally, "May I say something?" Gail Levy put down her slender arm, brushed back her short hair.

"Ah-*ha*! Not only alive, but awake. I was afraid you had all stopped listening, or had passed away from boredom." Professor Dean turned suddenly, dashed across the room, and stopped like a leering totem in front of the startled girl. He transfixed her with dark, penetrating eyes, not bothering to brush back the long strands of hair that fell down past his nose, nor to tuck in the pulled shirt beneath his outsized jacket. "Pray, don't be so timorous. If you have something to say, *speak up*."

"Well, I was going to say — that is, I mean, could we make an analogy between Grendel the ogre and, um, modern warfaring nations?"

"You mean comparison, not analogy. And warfare is not a verb."

"Yes. I mean, could we make a comparison between Grendel and foreign aggression?"

"You may say anything you like, Miss Levy, but please get to the point. I'm looking for answers, not questions."

"Well, I think an up-to-date analo — comparison, could be made between Grendel and the Germans in World War Two."

"You mean the Nazis in World War Two."

"Isn't it the same thing?"

"First of all, since this *is* an English class, I must correct your grammar. When you refer to a people you do not use the pronoun 'it' — that word is used for inanimate objects. Secondly, the Germans and the Nazis are not synonymous. One is a people, the other an ideology. It may be true that the doctrine of Naziism was embraced principally by the Teutonic countries, but it was touted only by the militarists then in power. Through a clever advertising gimmick, that minority was able to make the German proletariat believe that their country was in danger, that certain races wished to control them, that the world hated and was against them. The common masses were unfortunate enough to be so paranoid as to believe such gibberish. They were made to think that in order to survive as an autonomous people, they must attack before they were attacked, invade before they were invaded. It was the manipulations of a few with the desire for power and territory that fomented aggression against the free nations of the world, and instituted the contemptible pogrom against the Jews. The average, ignorant German citizen simply went along with the crowd because he did not know what else to do. And that sorry situation was allowed to continue until the entire world was embroiled by their pathologic egoism. In any case, the argument is academic since the comparison is a generation out of date."

Gail Levy did not seem the least bit frustrated by Professor Dean's refutation of her argument.

The peripatetic professor glared wolfishly about the classroom; the students stared back sheepishly. "Is there not one of you who can think his way out of a paper bag and come up with a comparison that is perhaps taking place in the world today?"

Never a man to stay in one place for very long, Professor Dean stalked around the classroom, down one aisle and up another, staring up at the ceiling the whole time as if he were in the woods watching for birds. He never missed a step or bumped into an out-of-line chair. He finally came to rest at the back of the room, where a blackboard identical to the one in front stretched across the wall. With a piece of chalk scrounged from the sill, he drew a shapely and over-endowed figure of a nude woman.

"I'm certain that all you enlightened students are aware of what's been going on in Southeast Asia for the past year."

No books moved; no pages turned. A gentle breeze whispered past the windowpanes and rustled through the young sycamores. The professor's artwork evolved with erotic overtones.

The serenity was broken by the faint clinking of Gail Levy's charm bracelet as her hand fanned the air for attention. The expression on her face was the classic idea smile from the Sunday comics; only the light bulb was missing.

"In fact," continued Professor Dean, as he put the finishing touches on the delicate lines of his chalky dream girl, "I am equally as certain that most of you are here only *because* of what is going on in Southeast Asia. Do you realize that the conflict in Vietnam has almost doubled the application rate for college entrance? Many of us are teaching today because of the appalling preponderance of young people who, with no thoughts at all for their country or fellow man, have plopped their rears in college seats in order to avoid civic responsibility. You," he shouted at the blackboard, the smooth surface echoing his crass voice thunderously. "That's right. You, all of you, are malingerers, lounging comfortably in this air-conditioned room, at the expense of your parents or government subsidy, taking up space that could be better utilized for storing horse manure. You are misusing your lives, abusing your political system, and shirking your moral obligations. You have simply discovered a new method of buying your way out of the draft."

Professor Dean spun around at the end of his soliloquy and swept up the aisle before the echo of his last condemning words quite faded away. His sudden movement caught Gail Levy in mid wave. Her hand toppled like a felled oak, but not before he noticed its waving presence.

"What is it, Miss Levy?"

She hesitated, speechless. He stopped, hunched over in front of her, and glared. The third time she opened her mouth, she said, "I don't think it's fair to say that. Half the people in this room are girls, and the draft doesn't matter to us at all. The conflict in Vietnam doesn't even concern us. We're here to get an education."

"Bullshit. You are here to find a husband. Do you realize that fifty percent of the women now attending college will marry and drop out before graduation, and that a further twenty-five percent will marry immediately after the exercises without ever working in the occupation for which they were trained? Are you aware that a further twenty percent will amble about in various jobs in which they were not educated simply because the ratio of men to women is higher, and offers them a better opportunity of finding a husband with the appropriate financial potential? Of all the women now on campus only one out of twenty will actually seek out a career in her chosen field and become a self-supporting citizen."

Professor Dean vaulted clean over the top of his desk and swung around to face the class. He leaned forward on his knuckles and raised one hand after the other, like a revivalist preacher. This was the man who wanted to become dean of the college only to gratify his witty penchant to be known, because of established protocol, as Dean Dean.

"Who the hell do you think you are kidding? Only yourself, young lady. You are the biggest dodger of all, skimming through life on a magic carpet: accepting the privileges of your sex with none of the responsibilities. You want to earn as much as a man, but have him chauffeur you to a fancy restaurant and pay for your meal. You want to have equal rights in running this country, but you want the men to go out and fight for them. And then you have the audacity to say that the draft does not matter to you because you are exempt!

"When are you going to get your head out of the sand? Just because you put something out of mind does not mean that it no longer exists. The ignorance of a fact does not make its existence less real. You must face facts whether you like them or not — and they must be dealt with in their due course. A bullet will kill you even if you do not see it coming. And your freedom can be taken away even if you do not think it is fair."

Gail Levy slapped her hand down on her desk. "I don't know who these women are you're talking about, but I don't want to be grouped with them. I speak only for myself when I say I'm here to learn. I'm proud of my role in society, and I want to grow and prosper in it, not be tied down with a husband and a family."

"That's just great." The professor threw his hands into the air and stared up at the drop ceiling. "How are we to survive as a race if all the women want to give up motherhood and become President? Where is the next generation to come from? Who is going to raise the children of tomorrow?"

"Who's to say I can't have a career and a family, too? What's wrong with that?"

"Nothing, as long as you play the game by the rules. You have every right to be an individual, and a useful member of society as well. But you must use your brain to do it, not your wiggling ass. If you are going to stand up on your own two feet you must do it all the way. Open your own doors and pay for your own entertainment. Get ahead through hard work and ability, not through your boss's penis. Remember that you are taking on a moral obligation. You, and other women like you, have the potential of effectively doubling the productivity of this nation, as well as humanizing the subjugated half of society."

Gail Levy wilted like a week old flower. "I don't think I follow you."

Professor Dean paused to fling his long hair out of his sweating face, and to tuck in some of the loose folds of his soiled white shirt. He closed one button of his jacket, and sat on the edge of his desk with one long leg thrust forward.

"Then let me elucidate: civic obedience is part of the package of individuality and freedom. It is not enough to ride the crest of the wave; you must help generate the tides. You cannot lock yourself away in your own private nook, where everything is beautiful, and ignore the ugliness around you. You cannot expect to be treated fairly unless you see that others are treated fairly as well. You cannot isolate yourself from the rest of the world, because whether you like it or not, that world will have a profound effect on you and your life, your country and its freedom, humanity and its future. Your individual freedom is guaranteed only by the country in which you live, so in order to protect yourself you must also protect the country which gives you that freedom. Nothing is free in this world. You must earn everything — and then fight to see that it is not taken away. Are you ready to accept that challenge?"

"I'll only fight if I have to."

"Well, guess what? You have to. Freedom does not come on a silver platter. It never has. Throughout the ages, men and women have fought against oppression. Every war this great country of ours has ever fought has been for freedom in one form or another. Vietnam is no different."

"But Vietnam is so far away. They're not even our people. I don't see why anyone should be forced to go fight for someone else. We have everything to lose and nothing to gain. We don't need Vietnam, so why should we care about what goes on there?"

"A storm over the horizon may be coming in your direction. Does it not make sense to board up the windows and bolt the doors before it reaches your house? And even if you do not have the vision to see what is coming, do you not think you should care about the people who are in its path? They, too, are human beings, with every right to life, liberty, and the pursuit of happiness that you have. Just because they live on the other side of a political barrier does not mean that they have less claim to those privileges. The only reason you can sit in that chair and preach about your supposed freedom is because for the past two hundred years your ancestors have gone out and fought for it. Freedom is like a car: it needs constant maintenance. Every generation must change the oil and lubricate the bearings.

"Vietnam is just around the corner. As long as there is one subjugated nation in the world, freedom cannot exist as an ideal. Just as we helped England and France and Sweden and Holland and Belgium twenty-five years ago, today we must help Vietnam. We can never relax our vigil because, whether you choose to believe it or not, there is someone out there who will forcibly take what you neglect to protect."

Gail Levy opened her mouth, but Professor Dean shifted his posture, position, and gaze. "Mr. Kravetz, you had your hand up before. Would you like to make a comment?"

Dennis Kravetz sat on the edge of his seat like a sparrow ready for flight. He was bearded and bespectacled, and swept long tresses be-

hind his ears and over his shoulders before talking.

"Well, sir, I was going to draw a parallel between *Beowulf* and the Vietnam conflict."

"Ah, yes, *Beowulf*. Please proceed."

"Well, sir, it seems like you've already done it."

"I may have been leading up to it, but I do not believe I actually made a statement on it. Why not give me your views on the matter?"

"Well, I was thinking in terms of interpreting America as Beowulf and Russia as Grendel, rendering a modern hero-dragon confrontation. That is to say, that the two countries represent the personifications of two ideologies: capitalism and communism, or good and evil."

"I assume that when you say America, you actually mean the United States, and do not include the other countries of North America, or the continent of South America. And by Russia you obviously mean the Union of Soviet Socialist Republics, the contemporary political faction and not the ancient czarist regime. Now, please tell me why you made such specific assignations. What makes one good and the other evil?"

"The fact that Rus — the USSR is an invader whose sole aim is to convert free people to communism."

"The same as the U.S. which is trying to convert free people to capitalism."

"But we aren't trying to take anything from anyone, or to force people to think or live in any particular way. All we want is to see that they have the opportunity to vote for what *they* want."

"And if they vote for communism, we contribute by overthrowing their communist sympathetic government, and installing one that is more receptive to our way of thinking. How is one more right than the other?"

"Because under a capitalist system the people have a say in the way their government is run — "

"Do they now?"

" — they can vote for or against any proposal, and can politic in either direction without fear of reprisal — "

"Politic is *not* an accepted verb."

" — they can continue to exert pressure to change, by vote, the laws regulating the country. If they find the laws unsuitable there is due process by which they can be repealed. If they really don't like the system, they are free to leave the country and live elsewhere — "

"Canada, to avoid the draft."

" — but the biggest difference is that in our society it is the individual who is most important, not the government that runs him."

"Ah-ha. You have finally made a positive

statement, Mr. Kravetz. By the same token, however, does that not make capitalism seem selfish and self-centered in comparison to communism, in which the greatest good is performed for the greatest number?"

Professor Dean pranced across the front of the room like a clock pendulum: he paused at one side to stare out the window, at the other to stare at the cinder block wall.

"How can you equate communism with a system that allows the poor majority to live in slums while the rich minority live in splendor? With one man living on steak while another lives on scraps? With one man driving a Cadillac while another relies on broken-down public transportation?"

Dennis Kravetz kept his eyes glued to his roving mentor. "Communism in theory is not the same as communism in practice. The greatest bane of communism is that it stifles individuality."

"If by individuality you mean the right to let your hair grow long, I fail to see what good it does."

"By individuality I mean that a person can do what he wants in life, not what is prescribed to him by the government."

"Let each give what he can, and take what he needs."

"Let those with initiative be stifled by the lack of adequate reward, while those without initiative live off the fat of the land, and on the excess of those who have worked."

"No one suffers under communism — everyone lives the same. All are equal."

"But I don't want to be just equal. I want the satisfaction of earning my keep, and doing whatever I please with those earnings. I don't want to support some drone, some shiftless malingerer who wants to live off everyone else's productivity."

"Bitter, Mr. Kravetz. Very bitter. You take too shallow a view of your fellow man."

"It's not a view. It's a fact."

"It is not a fact. It is an opinion."

"It's not an opinion. It's a conclusion."

"You have just contradicted yourself. First you say it is a fact, then you say it is a conclusion."

"It's a conclusion based on the facts."

"But only as you perceive them to be."

"I perceive them to be the way they really are."

"I have no doubt that you think you do. And that is all right, as long as you are willing to change your concepts as other facts come to light. That is an admirable state of mind. But remember that the free will you exercise in this classroom is a result of the political system in which you live, and which you undoubtedly

would defend, since it means so much to you. Am I correct, Mr. Kravetz?"

"In what?"

"In assuming that you are willing to defend the very nation that guarantees you the freedom you desire?"

Dennis Kravetz lapsed into momentary silence. Long, bony fingers ruffled the pages of a book.

"How about you, Miss Levy? Are you willing to defend your liberty?"

"That depends."

"On what? Either you are willing to defend it or you are not. Liberty is not conditional."

"I expect my government to protect my rights."

"How?"

"By doing whatever is necessary to protect them for me. By passing laws, and bills, and making treaties."

"And how is the government supposed to protect you from nations which do not ascribe to our particular brand of beliefs?"

"By negotiation."

"And how do you negotiate with a rapist, Miss Levy? How do you negotiate with thieves and murderers? When will you realize that negotiation works only with sane and rational people, and not with animals, whether they be in human guise or not?"

Gail Levy fell silent, but Dennis Kravetz's hand poked into the air. "I think we should ignore them."

"And what's that supposed to mean?"

"I would mind my own business."

"Oh, great. Someone takes a swing at you and you stand there and take it."

"I mean we should run our country the way we want, and let other countries run their governments the way they want."

"Isolationism is a thing of the past. I am not asking you for idealistic views. I am asking about the world of reality, in which people will not let you alone simply because you want to be let alone. Get your head out of the clouds."

"Then we compromise."

"How do you compromise when a charging lion leaps at your throat? Do you negotiate? Do you stop and have a little chat?"

"We're supposed to be dealing with civilized people."

"Were the Germans acting in a civilized manner when they invaded Poland? The Japanese when they bombed Pearl Harbor? Oswald when he shot Kennedy? Come now, Mr. Kravetz. Civilization obviously has different meanings to different people, or at different times, under different circumstances."

Professor Dean was practically screaming, his face flushed. "The answer is war, do you hear me? War. There is no way of getting around it. War means fighting. War means killing. War means death, sometimes to the innocent."

"I don't happen to believe that."

"You do not believe in war? Then read your history books, Mr. Kravetz. Read the newspapers. Watch television. Listen to the radio. War exists, just like the Earth, the sun, and the color blue. And it has always existed in the history of mankind."

"But I don't believe there has to be war."

"And I do not believe there have to be taxes and death, but I pay them just the same and I will die when my time comes. My failure to comprehend their usefulness does not prevent them from happening."

"I don't believe that killing is a way of solving anything."

"Wrong. Wrong. Wrong. War is the ultimate solution to everything. And so is killing — for dead men do not rape, dead men do not steal, dead men do not murder, and dead men do not command."

"But it's not a humane solution."

"Who is talking about humaneness? I'm talking about efficiency. War works. It is the most expedient, the most economical, the most rational and logical way of defense."

The bell signaling the change of classes exploded into the room like a peal of thunder, jolting people in their seats. But not a book closed. Not a leg moved. Not an eye wavered.

"I believe there must be more creative ways of settling disputes than by fighting."

"Not even if enemy ships were approaching our shores?"

"No."

"Not even if bombs were dropping in your backyard?"

"No."

"Not even if your parents and children were being massacred?"

"No."

"Then resign yourself to being a slave, for that is all you really are. You are a robot that goes where it's told, jumps when told to jump, bows and licks the boots of everyone who threatens him with the back of a hand. If that is your idea of individuality and freedom, it is a pretty stupid idea. You create something so someone else can take it away from you. You are nothing more than a spineless jellyfish and, fortunately for the security of this country, there are enough realists out there who are willing to go out and fight to preserve the way of life that you so much desire and so little deserve. Your kind can exist only as long as you are in the minority, as a parasite on the society in which you live. You are the real drone, Mr.

Kravetz. You and your blasted peace movement. Because what you do not realize is that the only reason you can sit here now and spout such nonsense is because the rest of the country is backing you up and doing the real work that you refuse to do. You are the despicable epitome of irresponsibility. And one thing is certain: Beowulf would never have allowed such people to exist in his kingdom. Class dismissed."

Chapter 14

"Excuse me, uh, Professor Dean."

If the professor heard Tony, he made no outward display of acknowledgement. He pushed papers around on his desk, putting them into piles of seeming insignificance. Test papers, essays, and homework assignments were shuffled together without rhyme or reason.

Tony cleared his throat but before he could speak the professor replied without looking up, "What is it, Mr. Giovanni?"

He cleared his throat again. "Well, uh, that was an interesting session we had today."

"Not interesting enough for your participation."

"Well, I wasn't too sure what it was you were trying to say."

The professor looked up sharply, and cocked his eyes like Bela Lugosi playing Dracula. "Say? Say? What makes you think I was trying to *say* anything? I was just blathering when I should have been keeping to the subject matter of *Beowulf*. I certainly did not intend to put anything into statement form. I leave that for the iconoclasts. My purpose here is to stimulate young minds, not to carve them."

"Well, you said an awful lot about nothing, then."

The professor laughed. "Well put, Mr. Giovanni. Now, I know you did not come up here to compliment me on my astuteness, so what's on your mind?"

Tony shifted from foot to foot. With textbooks clutched tightly under one arm, he flicked his other hand nervously. "Well, I sort of — wanted to thank you for, uh, for your instruction."

"Thank me when the semester is over and you have passed the course."

"Well, it looks like I'm not going to make it that far, sir. I've got — I've got to leave school."

"Leave? You mean, drop out?"

"Yes, sir."

The professor was quiet and unmoving, his eyes alive with the intensity of volcanic fire. "Do you realize the stupidity of what you are saying? By quitting now you lose any chance of getting credit for this course — or any course, for that matter. Your half-term credit will be useless, and you will have forfeited an entire year of education. You will have wasted not only your time, but my own as well."

Tony averted the dark stare. "Yes, I know that. I've already checked with my counselor and he told me the same thing. But, it can't be helped. It's not what I want, but there are economic factors beyond my control . . ."

"Oh, God, what is this country coming to? That we should lose our young minds for lack of that most absurd common denominator of the capitalistic society. And then to indoctrinate our children that money is the cornerstone of progress. Do you actually believe that you cannot be helped?"

"Well, sir, I don't see how. I mean, I just don't have the money. And my parents won't, uh, that is, they can't afford to keep paying my tuition and expenses. And there's this job opportunity . . ."

"So borrow money. Get a student loan. Ask for donations. Rob a bank if you have to. But don't quit now. I hate having students walk out on me. It makes me feel so useless."

Tony caught his gaze for a moment, then looked away.

"And what do you mean, 'it can't be helped?' Everything can be helped, if you are willing to make the sacrifice. But you must help yourself, for in the final solution no one cares as much about you as you do. Empty wastebaskets for extra money; skip lunch; anything. Do not be afraid to suffer for what you want. Sometimes it is the only way to get it."

Professor Dean leaned back in his chair and carelessly threw one arm over the back while he propped his feet up on the desk. "Am I making any sense at all?"

"Yes, of course."

"Your mind is already made up, though."

"It's not my mind that's been made up. It's been made up for me."

"By this time next year you will be cannon fodder, and that will be such a waste, such a shame."

"No, I'll be able to get an apprentice defer—"

"Listen to me, will you? You are a good student, a good athlete, somewhat unimaginative but a solid citizen. Not like the wishy-washy nincompoops who are the so-called free thinkers of our society. Admittedly, the namby-pambies have their place in a progressive culture, but they must be checked and balanced by some stabilizing influence, some form of accredited — and I hate to use this word because of its unsavory connotations — establishment. But you will not do a damned bit of good going off to some insignificant corner of the world to fight for some mistaken ideal that has no real meaning."

Tony shuffled, became more alert. "But, didn't you just say in class that someone has to do the fighting, to protect our system of ideals?"

"Do not listen to me. I am a doddering old fool. I said that to shake them up, to make them think. And I meant it, too. But I did not mean for *you* to jump up on your gallant white steed and charge into the midst of battle."

"Why not me? I'm willing to accept military service if that's what's required."

"Because that is exactly what the government would have you believe. This particular conflict is nothing more than a show of force, and a political ploy to boost the economy — trading blood for money."

"And maybe the Vietnamese deserve a fair share of the freedom we enjoy."

"And perhaps they are not ready for it."

"Who are you to say?"

"I am a poor, misguided English professor who is just as confused as the rest of the world, but who shouts loudly enough and gibberishly enough to conceal it." He climbed out of his chair and pulled himself up to his full, stoop-shouldered height. His eyes were even with Tony's and for the moment lost some of their hot intensity. Now they radiated like the mere flame of a Bunsen burner. "Pardon me for seeming to patronize you."

He took the long way around his desk and sauntered in relative calm to the wall-length windows that overlooked the central courtyard. Tony shifted the weight of his books and followed him, standing to one side.

Old, impressive architectural buildings surrounded the square, their stone and brick walls faded and covered with ivy. The spreading maples and chestnut trees, and the smaller shrubs, lent a parklike atmosphere. Some students lounged in spring clothes on the wooden benches that graced the curved paths and the green lawns, while next to them a sea of bustling, varicolored teenagers flowed like an oil slick in motion, dressed like Hollywood extras in everything from monogrammed T-shirts to Russian furs. From a height of five stories, the scene reminded Tony of a smear on a glass slide under a microscope lens.

Professor Dean clasped his hands behind his back and surveyed the world from his aerie. Besides his wayward hair, the only visible clue to his untidiness was one errant cuff that was caught on the back of a dull brown, cracked leather shoe.

"Look at them down there, scurrying about like ants in a honey pot. What appears to be rout and disorder is, upon close inspection, a multitude of unconformities each with a singularity of purpose. Each has his or her private cares and worries, dreams and goals, frustrations and roadblocks — all invisible to us. Each, taken separately, amounts to nothing more than an individualized packet of memories, abstractions, and ideals, bursting like some cosmic explosion in random directions. And separately, their power is wasted.

"But guide them with an overriding force, align them with an ideal, lead them with a common thought, and the whole becomes much more than the sum of its parts. They are capable of generating a power beyond imagination. They have the potential of becoming a great nation — or an awesome mob. And in so doing, they can easily lose their sense of proportion."

The professor twitched, as if a fly had landed on his nose. The wind whispered lightly against the clear panes. "They will do collectively what each would be afraid to do individually. But, their numbers and their ideals will blind them to the result of their actions. Yet, they are to be forgiven, for they are in great pain, like a person on fire, and cannot see clearly. They will oppose for the sake of being different, and like a storm that wreaks great havoc, they will lead a revolt of thoughtlessness — against thoughtlessness. Let us hope that sanity will ensue."

Chapter 15

Tony walked briskly into the kitchen, fumbling with the buttons of his blue flannel shirt and trying not to trip over his untied shoelaces. A bundle of black and white fur erupted with blinding speed from behind the refrigerator and attacked ferociously the darting strings clicking across the floor. Kitty's lunge was poorly aimed, for the claws of one paw sank into flesh above the top of the nine-inch work shoe. Tony's yell articulated his anger to the cat. On extended claws, she scampered across the linoleum, slipping like a dragster peeling rubber until she caught hold of the throw rug and propelled herself into the dining room, ripping around the corner like Charlie Chaplin around a barber pole. Her paw pats faded into the protection of the living room.

"Who let Kitty into the catnip?" Tony said to no one.

He filled the coffee pot with water, the percolator with five scoops of grounds, snapped down the lid, and set it on the range. After tying his shoelaces, he retrieved the morning paper from the doorstep — this morning it was all in one piece.

By the time he finished making two ham and cheese sandwiches for lunch, the coffee was boiling. He turned down the burner and let it simmer. After pouring cereal, milk, and sugar into a bowl, he tore out the crossword puzzle and scribbled absently.

"How long's the coffee been on?" Frank thumped into the kitchen like a herd of elephants, shaking glasses in the cabinets and dishes on the counter. "About two and a half minutes."

Frank took down a cup and saucer and poured out the brew. He sat at the table and buried himself in the paper.

"Sure, Dad, I'll have some, too." Tony got up and poured his own. His father ignored him. As soon as he sat down, Kitty pranced into the room, leaped onto his lap, and after several turns settled herself comfortably.

The telephone rang. Frank slurped his hot coffee, pushed himself back from the table, and grabbed the receiver from its cradle on the wallpapered divider. His voice was throaty after a night out with the boys. "Yeah. Yeah. Okay. What the hell for? Okay. No, give it to me. I'll have my kid bring it over."

He rummaged through a heap of papers, scratch pads, and letters, and with the broken stub of a pencil started writing rapidly on the back of an old envelope. "When do you need it? Okay, I'll send him first thing. You got a place to lock it up? Good. No, I won't be over till late this afternoon. Yeah."

He slammed down the phone and threw the envelope at Tony. "Randy needs this material over at Woodcrest Arms. Pick up the truck at the shop and pick up whatever he needs. And get it to him right away — you're holding up three men."

"Okay." Tony pocketed the envelope, put the cat on the floor, stood up, and rinsed out his bowl.

"Leave that stuff for your mother. She ain't got a goddamn thing to do today. You get out on the job."

"Sure, Dad. What do you want me to do after that?"

"Go back to the shop and wait for me. We got to do something with that place. It's so fouled up I can't find anything any more. Nobody wants to put anything where it belongs, they just throw everything in a pile and leave it."

"Okay." He dropped his sandwiches into a brown paper bag. Kitty rubbed his legs, so he bent and gave her a pat, and picked up her bowl. He found a can of cat food and slipped it into the electric opener.

"Leave that cat alone and get out of here! Those men are on the payroll and they can't work without material."

The opener stopped whirring. "Are you going to feed her?"

Frank flipped a page. "Don't worry about the damn cat, will you? I got a business to run."

"Where are the truck keys?"

"How the hell do I know? Look on the counter."

While he made noise by pushing miscellany out of the way, Tony located a spoon and quickly dumped the food into Kitty's bowl. He set it on the floor with one hand as he rustled through papers with the other, making noise to cover his actions. "Should I take the whole ring?"

Frank did not look up. "Yeah. The shop keys are there, too. Stop stalling, will you? You're holding up the men."

Tony dumped the dirty spoon into the cereal bowl. He picked up his lunch bag and walked out of the kitchen twirling the key ring on one finger. "When are you going to get there?"

"I don't know. I got a meeting with the inspector at Shady Lane and I don't know how long I'll be tied up. I'll get there when I get there."

"Okay."

A chill spiked the air, and a thin mist condensed on glass and metal. Tony buttoned his jacket as he slid into a milk white, 1960 Ford Galaxie. The plush blue interior was clean, the floor recently vacuumed. The engine kicked over at a flip of the key, and purred quietly for a couple minutes until it was warmed up. Newly replaced windshield wipers swept away the moisture. Fifteen minutes later he parked next to a battered, windowless van that was more rust-red primer than original white paint.

Tony picked through the twenty or thirty keys on the ring, most of which belonged to locks lost for years, and separated the shop key. For five minutes the lock defied him until he slammed it down hard. Then the garage door scraped across the cement pad: the wooden panels were split and sadly in need of trussing. Rusted hinges stopped the door halfway.

The thick odor of musk and mildew made Tony gag. Dirty fluorescent fixtures hung from exposed I-beams. Half the tubes were burned out; those that worked cast an obscure, dingy light throughout the decrepit warehouse. The fifty-foot-long room was a junkyard of wire spools, cases of switches and receptacles, handy boxes, electrical panels, meter sockets, and boxes of fixtures. All were piled on top of each other in random fashion, as if the building had been picked up by some giant hand and shaken thoroughly. Most of what Tony needed, he could not find. He untied the loop of wire holding the two truck doors together, and threw in whatever he could scavenge. The truck was in worse shape than the shop: the floor was stained with oil; cartons that were soaked with water, which had leaked in through the roof, melted down one wall and wreaked with mold; the floor was littered with nails, staples, scraps of wire, connectors, tools, breakers, and a thousand other items that should all have been swept out in the trash. The stench was horrifying.

The delivery truck was a mechanical marvel held together by chewing gum and baling wire. The pavement showed through rust holes in the floor, the dirty windshield obscured vision, and the broken mirrors gave a cracked view of traffic. On the road the van clunked, rattled, and coughed like the Okies' junker right out of *The Grapes of Wrath*.

The job site was a large apartment complex outside city limits. What had once been a thickly wooded, out-of-the-way swamp, was slowly being converted to brick, concrete, and macadam living quarters for non-property owners. Each three-story building housed eleven families and one combination storage/laundry room. With sod laid and trees planted, the resulting community blended simplicity with a fake pastoral setting.

"Yo-ho-ho. To-nee."

Tony brought the truck to a bumping halt in the dirt roadway, still wet and muddy from a morning sprinkle, and rolled down the window. "Hello, Randy."

"Heard you were coming to work for us." Randy stood in a framed-out doorway, tool pouch hanging from one hip like a gunslinger's holster, a homemade deerskin vest covering his white T-shirt.

Tony stepped down from the van. He leaped over puddles and mud clumps formed by the huge tires of cement trucks and the squishings of bulldozer treads. "It turns out that my first chore is to see that you've got enough material to get through the day."

A bearlike hand reached down for Tony's. "I told your dad I've got enough for the next two days."

Tony pounded his shoes on the zigzagged wooden forms where the steps would soon be poured. He took the proffered hand and leaped up to the entry. The helping hand turned into a shake. "He said you needed it right away."

A broad grin split Randy's face. "That's just like your dad, always getting everything mixed up. I'm good until the end of the week."

Tony flexed life back into his hand. "Yeah, well, it's a good thing. I couldn't find half of what you ordered. I'll have to pick it up at the supply house."

"Are there any deliveries coming in?"

"Not right away. The service material for Lancelot Place is being delivered directly. And the fixtures for Honey Hollow are all back-ordered — they may not get here for a week or two."

Randy stood with hands on hips, legs spread,

and both feet planted solidly on the plywood flooring. "You seem to know an awful lot about the business."

"Not hard to do when the kitchen doubles as an office. I'm always talking with builders, suppliers, contractors, and the workmen, on the phone."

Randy laughed easily. "Yes, I guess you're right. Well, what do you have for me for now?"

Tony took out the envelope and indicated what he had checked off the list. "Three thousand feet of fourteen-two, five hundred feet of twelve-two, a case of metal ceiling boxes without brackets — I only found six *with* the brackets — and a hundred and seventy-five wall boxes. I couldn't find any sixteen penny nails."

"Your dad won't buy nails. He makes me scrounge them off the carpenter. He thinks he's getting them for nothing, but he knows I have to give him switches and receptacles when he needs them."

"Yeah, well, that's the way he is."

Randy folded the list and shoved it into his vest pocket. "That's enough to keep us going for three more days, so don't worry about the rest. And take this drill with you. Next time you stop at the supply house, get new brushes for it. Oh, and I could use another twenty-four-inch extension and a couple more three-quarter-inch bits. And while you're there — "

A horn sounded in the distance, beeping on and off incessantly. Randy's face brightened as if someone had turned on a switch. "We'll unload this stuff later. Come on, I'll buy you a coffee."

"Sounds good to me."

On the way, Tony deposited the drill in the truck, then followed Randy up the muddy path to where the vending truck attracted men like a light attracts moths. The vicinity of the vending truck became a melting pot of workers of every trade: carpenters, plumbers, roofers, cement men, bricklayers, sheet rockers, and laborers. A frenzied camaraderie accompanied the selection of doughnuts, muffins, and pies, the pouring of drinks, the picking of sandwiches. The driver stood by and made change from a metal coin holder belted to his waist.

The sun peeped through dark, roving clouds, and began to dry up the muddy driveway. Tony unzipped his jacket as they climbed into the apartment. He sat on an upturned mortarboard and rested his coffee cup on a stack of cinder blocks.

Randy took a huge bite out of an icing-covered bear claw. "You've been working for your dad for a pretty long time, haven't you?"

The apartment building was a skeleton of joists and studs, plumbing pipes and electrical wires. Tony leaned back against a stud, and rolled his spine across it until he found a comfortable niche. "My stock answer is that he's been taking me on the job ever since I was old enough to pick up a hammer."

Randy emitted a bull roar laugh. "Yes, you were just a little feller when I came to work for your dad. Collecting soda bottles and scrap wire. Why, you've been in construction longer than I have."

With Randy's screwdriver, Tony stirred in a packet of sugar. He smiled at the recollection. "I made lots of money at it, too. For a kid. My mother was always complaining about taking the bottles to the grocery store."

"Heh, heh, heh. Your mom's quite a gal." Randy sipped tentatively at his coffee."

"My father always tried to split the scrap wire profits with me. Said it was his wire to begin with."

"Never miss an angle, that man."

Tony touched the Styrofoam cup, decided it was too hot, and blew across the top. "I always argued him out of it, though. I had to do all the work of stripping off the insulation — with a dull knife. He never had any sharp ones. Said he couldn't afford the blades."

Randy shoved the rest of the bear claw into his cavernous mouth. Still chewing, he said, "That was because he was trying to build up his business. You know, I always thought your dad was happier when he was working with the tools — back when it was just me and him. He had no bookwork, no deadlines, no headaches." He shook his head, swilled down a mouthful of coffee. "It seems like after he started getting big, taking on a lot of jobs and hiring a lot of men, well, it seems like work got to be on his mind too much. You remember the lean times: not enough work, bills to pay, builders holding out on him, hiring unknowns who laid down on the job or stole material for side jobs of their own. He was always under pressure, always worrying about where the money was coming from. He should have stayed small, done custom houses, instead of this operation work. It ain't good for him."

Tony stared at the floor, made patterns out of the scattered sawdust.

"You know, when times were tough, he never laid me off — even in winter when work was scarce. He was always picking up odd jobs, doing them at cost, just to keep the men busy and keep the checks coming in. But he had to make it big. Driven. That's what he is — driven. He wants to be somebody. And that's what he wants for you."

Tony put down his half-finished Danish. "What do you mean?"

"He wants you to follow in his footsteps. Oh, not the way he did it, working for peanuts and taking correspondence courses. No, he wants you to go to apprentice school, work with other contractors, learn the trade, and take over the business. That's what he really wants, to give you the whole shooting match."

"I don't know if I can do that. I don't know if I *want* to."

Randy bundled the cellophane wrapping and stuffed it into the empty coffee cup. "If anybody can do it, you can. You grew up in the business. You were wiring whole houses when you were fourteen. Didn't know an electron from a proton, or hysteresis from an eddy current. But you had every circuit in the house memorized."

"Well, actually, I did know an electron from a proton," Tony laughed. His coffee had cooled enough to drink. "But I knew it from reading chemistry books."

"Always were a bookworm, weren't you. Well, you take my advice, Tony. Study hard, learn the ropes, be a good apprentice like I know you will. Then come back and run this shop. Someday I'll be working for you."

"Well, I don't know about that . . . "

"Mark my words — you're a natural born leader. All you need is the opportunity to lead."

Chapter 16

There was only one way to attack the shop, and that was from scratch.

The first thing Tony did was to repair the garage doors so they would open all the way. The cinder block construction offered no windows and no rear door, so cross ventilation was impossible. But the fresh air at least made the building habitable.

Half of everything in the shop was trash: empty boxes, torn cartons, crates, cigarette butts, candy wrappers, years old newspapers, and discarded lunches ripe with moldy peach pits and sandwich crusts. With a dilapidated push broom, he swept out everything he could from where he was afraid to poke with his hands, despite the heavy work gloves, and started filling every available cardboard box. After many pilgrimages throughout the course of the morning, Tony quickly overfilled the beat-up dumpster at the end of the block of warehouses.

He soon struggled in grimy pants and a sweat stained T-shirt. His bare arms sported a coat of dust and white plaster. His nose was crusted with black, clinging dirt. But the exercise was exhilarating, and his muscles felt firm and hard.

In the second phase of the project, he carried — box by box, and article by article — every bit of material outside and piled it in the driveway. Pedestrians gave the shop a wide berth.

After the building was completely empty, he swept out every corner, nook, and crevice. It was not until one-thirty that he washed up in the unscoured sink, and sat down outside in the sun to eat a sandwich.

"What the hell are you doing?"

Tony swallowed, but did not otherwise move. "Eating lunch."

"I sent you out here to work, not to take afternoon lunches. And what the hell's all this stuff doing out here?"

"Getting a suntan. You really should let it out more often." Tony, still chewing, slowly got to his feet.

"Don't get smart with me." Frank's dark brown eyes grew darker, and Tony wondered how his mother ever could have fallen in love with them. "This is expensive material. Somebody could walk off with it out here on the sidewalk. This ain't the best neighborhood, you know."

"But I'm standing right here with it."

"Don't mean nothing. They'll steal it right out from under you. An' I got a delivery comin' any min — Oh, Jesus Christ, here he is now."

A truck the size of a small moving van ground to a halt on squealing brakes. A huge, oval head popped out of the window. "Hello, there, Frank. Didn't expect to see *you* here."

"I'm so busy I'm running around like a chicken with his head cut off. The phone's been ringin' off the wall all morning."

The driver handed a delivery voucher to Frank, then turned and offered a ham-sized paw. "You're Tony, aren't you?"

Tony switched the sandwich to his left hand. "Yes, but I don't think we've met."

"I'm Mike. I — "

"Jesus Christ, you back ordered the pipe."

"Let me see." Mike took back the voucher, and studied it for a moment. "But, Frank, you only ordered it two days ago."

"How was I supposed to know they wanted to pour the floor today? These gas stations go up so fast they leave your head spinning."

Mike put his hands on the girth of his walruslike belly. "You know for special orders like that you gotta call in a week ahead o' time."

Frank threw his hands into the air. "All right. All right. Tony, give him a hand unloading this stuff and get it inside. I got to go make a phone call."

"Okay, Dad." Tony parked his sandwich on a ledge. He pulled on his work gloves. Smiling at Mike, he said, "Well, shall we?"

As fast as Mike was able to tailgate the material, Tony carried it inside, selected an appropriate spot, and stacked it neatly. The delivery consisted mostly of fixtures in cardboard boxes that were large, but not heavy.

In the back of the truck, Mike was sweating and grunting like a pig. He weighed half again as much as Tony, but for all his great mass he was surprisingly weak. "I got a headache today and this glare don't help any."

Tony bustled back and forth. "That's all right, Mike. This is my first day on the job, so I'm full of energy. I won't be running around like this next week."

Coils of wire came next, tied in five hundred foot bundles. "Yeah, your old man was sayin' how you were gonna work for him. What happened to college, dinja like it?"

Tony arched his back and rolled his shoulders. "No, I liked it all right. It just wasn't — the right time, I guess. Maybe I'll go back — later."

"Whatcha gonna do for your old man, run the jobs?"

"I won't be working for him that long. This is just temporary until I'm accepted into the union. Then I'm going into the apprenticeship program, and I'll be working for other contractors. You see, my father only has a couple commercial jobs, like gas stations and stores. He does mostly residential work, and that's a different facet of the trade. Instead of apartments and houses, I'll be working on high-rise office buildings and refineries."

Mike stopped to wipe sweat off his forehead with a faded handkerchief. He was breathing hard. "Yeah? Whaddaya hafta do to get in?"

"Just go to the Hall and apply. Then you take a State aptitude test and if you get a good enough score, they call you in for an interview."

Mike sat heavily on the tailgate and let himself drop to the ground. It seemed as if it were an effort for him to move. "Aw, I'm not too good at takin' tests. That's why I never graduated high school."

Tony grimaced, and said haltingly, "Mike, one of the requirements in joining the union is a high school diploma."

He looked crestfallen. "Well, drivin' a truck ain't too bad. I get to do a lot o' travelin', and I never would get to do that on my own."

"That's the way to look at it. Here, let me help you with that."

Mike took two heavy coils of wire off the tailgate, slinging one over each arm. "No, let me. I need the exercise. I'm on a diet, tryin' to lose weight."

"Is that everything?" Tony saw that the truck was empty.

"Yeah, jus' pull down that rope."

While Mike deposited the last of the delivery inside, Tony rolled the truck door shut with a slam, and threw the locking mechanism.

"You got that truck unloaded yet?"

"All done, Dad."

"All right, you gotta pick up the pipe at Passyunk's an' get it to the gas station on Street Road. You know the one I mean?"

"Near Frankford Avenue, isn't it?"

"Right. The foreman there is Eliot."

Mike ambled out of the shop on blubbery legs. "Here's your receipt."

"But, Dad, you didn't tell me I'd have to make more deliveries. I have to put all this material away."

"So whaddaya want from me?" Frank took a wad of money out of his pocket, peeled off a one-dollar bill, and said to Mike, "Here, buy yourself a soda. An' don't forget my pipe next week. I'll need it for the other station."

"Thanks, Frank." Mike stuffed the money into his shirt pocket. "I won't forget it." As he climbed into the cab, he added, "So long, Tony. See you next week." He drove off.

"You shouldn't a started this damn job anyway. Now I got stuff all over the street."

Tony retrieved his sandwich. "So what was I supposed to do for four hours, sit here and wait for you to come tell me what to do?"

"You didn't have to drag everything outside."

"There was no other way of getting through that chaos."

Frank handed Tony a scrap of paper. "I'll stay here an' watch the stuff. You go get the pipe and the fittings. They'll have it waiting for you."

"Okay. And while I'm there, how about if I pick up the rest of the stuff for Randy? We didn't have everything he needed and . . . "

"Forget Randy. Just get the pipe. I don't want you to hold up the men."

"Okay." Tony gulped down the rest of the sandwich as he climbed into the van.

His father slammed the door behind him. "An' watch those commercial men — they're real touchy."

Tony saw the drill on the front seat. He picked it up and shoved it through the open window. "Hey, I just remembered. Randy said this drill didn't work. Thought it might need brushes."

Frank shoved it back in. "So whaddaya want from me? Fix the goddamn thing an' give it back to him. Do I gotta do everything around here?"

On the way to Passyunk Electric Supply, there was time to start on his second sandwich.

"Your father only called twenty minutes ago," complained the counter man. "We haven't had time to get the pipe up out of the basement. You'll just have to wait."

"It's not really a matter of life and death, like he makes it sound. But while I'm here, do you have brushes for this drill?"

The clerk looked at it, turned and disappeared down an aisle, and returned with a plastic coated package.

"Hey, that's great. Listen, since I have to wait, how long will it take to get this stuff together?" Tony handed over the list of material that he had not been able to deliver to Randy.

"This's all in stock. I can get it for you right away."

"Great. Can you put it on a separate slip — for Woodcrest Arms?"

The man nodded, and began writing. When he was done, he started piling items on the counter. Tony found a loose screwdriver and in a couple minutes replaced the worn brushes. He tested the drill in a socket, then carried it to the truck. He signed for the material, loaded it, and by that time the pipe was being hauled up the basement steps. In minutes the truck was loaded and he was on his way.

Center city traffic was heavy. Tony did his best to avoid the main arteries and get out to the new highway that was under construction. Still, he was the better part of an hour getting to the job because he did not know its exact location.

There was not much activity going on at the gas station. Half a dozen men were setting block for the garage, a carpenter was building forms for the pad, and a backhoe operator was digging the trench for the gas lines between the tanks and the service bay.

Tony parked next to a scaffold. He did not see anyone wearing an electrician's tool pouch, but he opened the back of the van anyway and started pulling out pipe.

"About time you got here." The man was middle aged, heavily bearded, and wore an oil-stained jacket over his off-white T-shirt. He leered, rather than smiled, with a seriousness that was all too apparent to Tony.

"Are you Eliot?"

"That's right." In his back pocket he had a pair of pliers and a screwdriver.

"Well, I'm sorry I'm late, but I only got the message an hour and a half ago, and traffic downtown was bad." He looked past the man's shoulder, into the cinderblock building. "I thought they were supposed to pour the floor today?"

"Not till tomorrow. But we gotta get the pipe laid before they do."

"Oh, sure. Well, I've got everything you asked for. Where are you keeping the stuff?"

"Inside. There's a back room with a lock on it. Duke and I'll take care of it."

Duke was short to begin with, but his shoulders were stooped with age, making him look gnomelike in appearance. His hair was thin and gray, but what there was of it was neatly combed. His face was a mass of wrinkles. The tool pouch hanging from his hip looked as if it would pull him over any minute.

Tony hefted a bundle of three ten-foot lengths.

" Whaddaya think you're doin', kiddo?"

"You said you wanted it inside, right?"

"That's right, but me and Duke'll take it in."

"Oh, that's okay. I don't mind helping. Duke can carry the fittings; they're not so heavy."

Eliot reached out and wrapped his fingers around Tony's arm. They clamped down hard and shoved him back a step. "Didn't you hear me?"

Tony looked quizzically. "Yes, you said you wanted it inside."

"What I said," Eliot enunciated slowly, "was that me and Duke will carry it in. We don't need no help from no scabs."

Tony turned beet red. He let the bundle roll off his shoulder and crash on the bumper. The metal retaining straps broke and the three pipes palled apart. "All right, Mister. What's your beef?"

Eliot was relaxed, his hands held calmly at his side. But he spoke with a brusqueness that deepened his voice to make it sound like a command. "My beef is that the union can't say nothing about scabs bringing material to the job site, but once it's here it becomes union work. And it gets done by union men."

"Hey, I'm only trying to give you guys a hand."

"We don't need no help."

"Maybe you don't, but you can't expect Duke to carry this heavy stuff."

"Listen, kiddo. Maybe I can't stop you from driving this truck for your old man, and spying on the jobs, but I sure as hell can stop you from doing any electrical work."

"What electrical work? All I'm doing is carrying a bundle of pipe. And that doesn't require an engineering degree. Now come off your high horse and give me a hand, and let Duke carry the fittings."

"He'll carry the fittings, but *I'll* carry the pipe. The only thing you're allowed to do is tailgate it. You got that?"

Tony was trying hard to keep his temper. "You're not making any sense. We're all working for the same man."

"But we're union men, and you ain't. So you do your job, and we'll do ours."

Tony stepped aside, shaking with anger, while Eliot and Duke unloaded the truck. Not another word was spoken, and when the last of the pipe was removed, Tony quietly slipped behind the wheel and drove away. By the time he reached the shop, he was no longer seething, but he was still upset.

Frank leaned over the shiny, waxed hood of the Cadillac, reading the newspaper. Tony parked in front of the mound of material, then leaned across the opposite side of the hood.

"These goddamn college kids are making another big stink about the draft." He threw the paper down and jabbed a thick finger at the headlines. "They're making a mockery out of this country. Burning draft cards ain't gonna prove nothing. They oughta be locked up, every damn one of 'em."

"In Philadelphia?"

"Naw, some stinking Midwest college that nobody ever heard about. All they want to do is stir up trouble, an' get on television."

"Well, maybe they have something to say and that's the only way they can get noticed." Tony tried to pull the paper from under Frank's clenched fist, but Frank was not ready to relinquish either the paper or the argument.

"How could they have anything to say? They're just kids, still wet behind the ears. What the hell do they know?"

"Maybe they know a lot. They didn't get into college by being stupid."

"These kids today don't know nothing. When I was a kid in school we did what we were told. You don't know. Your mother sent you to public school, but in Catholic school you stepped outa line you got smacked. Today you hit a kid and they got you in court."

"Well, maybe that's because there are better ways to treat people than to smack them around. You think the old way is the only way. Maybe that's why they have to protest, because no one will listen to them. And after all, they're the ones who are going to get drafted, not you."

Frank pounded his fist down on the hood. "What the hell's wrong with the draft? We gotta have an army, this country's at war — "

"It's only a conflict."

" — an' somebody's got to protect us from the Communists. If not, they'll take over the whole world. Then where will we be? Shit, when I was their age I was proud to be in the army. We were poor, we didn't have nothing. These kids today have everything. They don't know what it's like to go without food. They got it easy. My mother had ten mouths to feed. We had spaghetti three times a week and soup the rest. I never had a piece of meat till I was in the army."

Tony kept his voice even. "So what do you want to do, have it tough for everyone so they'll be forced into joining the army in order to get three square meals a day? Don't you want the kids to be better off today than they were in your day?"

"But these kids today don't know what's good for them. They complain about not having

jobs, and when the army says they need men, the bastards won't enlist. I was proud to wear a uniform. It was the only suit I ever owned till I got married."

"Sure, but for you the army was a step up. It gave you all the things you didn't have at home."

"This country wouldn't be here today if it wasn't for my generation going out and fighting. Hell, I had one brother at Anzio, another was a B-29 gunner in the Pacific and got shot down twice. I would have gone overseas if that cannon hadn't rolled over my back. But these kids today don't want to fight for nothing."

Tony sucked in a deep breath. "Maybe they just want to know exactly what it is they're fighting for."

"What the hell are you talking about? The Russians have already taken over Laos, now they want Vietnam. Do you think they're gonna want to stop there? Once they have Indo-China tied up, they'll be looking for some place else. They would have gotten Cuba if it hadn't been for Kennedy."

"Dad, you've got to look at the issues from both sides. Maybe you want to contain Communism, but how is blowing up a lot of villages going to help democracy? Who knows, maybe those people *want* to be communist. And if they do, you don't have the right to take that away from them. Maybe the establishment is fighting this war the wrong way."

"Don't give me that 'establishment' bullshit. Leave that for the hippies. If they were running this country we'd all go down the drain. They oughta try waving those signs in Russia an' see what it gets 'em. They'd throw 'em right in jail. Goddamn hippies'd give the whole country away if Russia walked in an' asked for it."

"And maybe if someone just bothered to listen to what they had to say, they wouldn't have to take such violent measures as a way of expression. I'm sure they don't have as much information as the President has, but — "

"You're goddamn right, they don't. They don't know the half of what's going on in this world. Oh, Jesus Christ. I didn't know it was that late." Frank yanked the paper off the car and slammed it shut. "I gotta go." He piled into the car, activated the window motor, and shook his fist at Tony. "An' get all that stuff put away before somebody steals it."

He roared down the street, the tail pipe echoing past every car as he zipped by. He slowed for the stop sign, then cruised through.

Tony's task was more involved than simply shoving the boxes and cartons inside. He had to put everything in order so that it was highly visible and easily reachable — and so he could tell at a glance when stock was running low.

Wire was heavy, but had a slow turnover rate. Fixtures were light, but came and went almost daily. Seldom used items he stacked by the back wall. He used small boxes to separate miscellaneous items such as screws, nuts, bolts, wirenuts, staples, nails, fittings, clamps, and connectors — each one further separated by type or size.

By sunset everything was at least in the warehouse. He locked the doors and meandered out to a pizza shop for a cheese steak and a soda: he had not had a drink all day. Then he went back and worked until he was done. The eleven o'clock news was on when he got home.

Frank looked up from the set, sipping hot coffee. "Where've you been?"

"Working." Tony sank into the kitchen chair and dropped the keys on the Formica. "I got the whole shop cleaned out, put all the material in order, categorized . . . "

"Did you get the pipe to Eliot? That's all I want to know."

"Sure, I did that before you left." He pulled a scratch pad from his jacket pocket and shoved it across the table. "Then, after I got everything in order, I made a complete inventory of what we have in stock, what we should have in stock, and what we should order right away. It's all there on the list. By the way, I had a little trouble at the gas sta — "

"All right, don't bother me now. Just put everything over there an' I'll look at it later." He turned up the volume on the television.

Wearily, Tony said, "Sure, Dad."

He went upstairs to his room, too tired to take a shower, and lay down on his bed. He stared up at the shadows on the ceiling, listened to the noise in the alley. He was glad to be alone, and in the quiet solitude of familiar surroundings.

Some time later the door creaked, and a splinter of light thrust itself into the room. The bed thumped with the sudden addition of extra weight. As he rolled over, Kitty padded across the blankets and purred in his face. Her nose was a tiny dot of cold, her tongue a belt of wet sandpaper.

Tony ran his hand along her silky fur, watching the sparks of static electricity shoot out like miniature lightning bolts. She stopped licking, and playfully attacked the hand that was causing the static. Her paws batted him like toy jackhammers. She disengaged, and lunged back from different angles. Finally, she calmed down, and cuddled next to his stomach, and began licking her fur.

Tony eased away from her, put his dirty clothes in the hamper, pushed the door shut but did not latch it, and crawled under the blankets. He stretched out tired muscles. Kitty finished washing and snuggled close.

In the moonlight he could see his bookcase and all his books, his desk with its papers and correspondence, his model ships, his radio and record player, his black and white television: all the material things he could possibly want.

Yet within him existed an emptiness. Despite all the things he had, he wanted more.

Chapter 17

"Go get 'im, Tone!"

Pete held onto the dashboard with both hands while he jumped back and forth in the seat. Outside his window, parked cars streamed by at fifty miles per hour, exhaust sounds reflecting with an alternating, sibilant timbre.

A hundred feet from the end of the block, Tony started pumping the brakes just hard enough so the tires did not squeal. The right brake pulled slightly so he had to correct the drag by steering perfectly: South Philly streets offered no room for error. He gripped the wheel hard as he approached the intersection too fast.

"All clear!" Pete yelled.

Without turning his head, Tony released the brake and rushed past the cross street, then floored the accelerator three quarters of the way down the block. He repeated the stopping maneuver, got the all clear from Pete, and sped through another danger zone.

"Darn. I forgot it was one way."

This time he stood on the brakes until the car slid to a halt in the middle of the intersection. He threw the transmission into reverse, peeled rubber, spun the wheel, and careened to the right. Back in drive, he raced to the next street and skidded around the corner.

This street was so narrow that parking was permitted on only one side. Tony raced along with only inches separating his car from the innocent parked vehicles, while the passenger side tires rubbed the broken curb.

"Go for it!"

At the intersection he spun to the left, turned left again up the one-way street, and sailed past a parking space with brakes straining. With one deft turn of the wheel he backed right into the spot, and snugged up to the curb. He switched off the engine and doused the lights.

"Nice going, Tone," Pete said. "You beat him."

Nothing moved in the dimly lit street. "Are you sure?"

"Yeah, here he comes now."

Tony leaned back and looked in the rearview mirror. A pair of headlights turned into the street at the far end of the block, followed by the squeal of tires and the roar of an engine. The headlights grew larger in the mirror until they filled the glass, then the car sped by with a whoosh. An instant later it braked to a halt, reversed on spinning tires, and backed frantically. The '57 Chevy stopped so that the two cars were window to window.

"What kept you?" Tony grinned.

Ray was riding shotgun, his face only inches from Tony's. "What the hell did you do, fly?"

"No, I just took my good ole time. I thought maybe you got lost — we've been here for five minutes."

"Bullshit," called Ben, from behind the wheel. "We were tearing down those streets so fast the vacuum was sucking the leaves off the trees."

Pete leaned forward so he could talk past Tony. "Speed ain't everything. It takes skill, too." He was grinning from ear to ear. "And a little White Lightning."

"Aw, cut it out." Ray pointed at Pete. "Coming off the line, the Black Stallion can beat the White Lightning any day of the week. We just got stuck behind a trolley car."

"Wait — a — minute," Pete screamed. "Did you just admit that a Chevy can beat a Ford? Is that what I just heard you say?"

"That isn't what I meant. But Ben's got more guts than Tony has."

"What's the length of his intestines hafta do with it?"

"Ah-*ha*!" Ben pounded Ray on the shoulder. "So now you admit it: there *is* more to racing than the engine under the pedal."

"I never said there wasn't." Ray spoke out of the corner of his mouth. "All I ever said was that if you put the same man behind the wheel of a Ford, he'll beat himself if you put him behind the wheel of a Chevy."

"George'll beat himself behind the wheel of any car," Pete said, with a loud guffaw.

Ben looked surprised. "Hey, where *is* George?"

"I thought he was with you," Tony said.

"But, Ray told me he was with you."

A long moment of silence ensued. "Oh, no," Ray said, in mock astonishment. "We must of gone off and left him at the garage."

Three voices chorused "Ray." Tony reached out and shook him by the shoulder. Ben started throwing short, pulled punches at his arm. Pete screamed imprecations. Ray finally yelled for mercy.

"Now he'll have to drive his own car," Ben said. "And if he speeds, maybe he'll get here before the party's over."

"Maybe he'll walk."

"And maybe molasses will run uphill."

"Let me go park the car. Wait for us and we'll all go in together." Ben rumbled in reverse to the end of the street before he found a spot. Tony said, "Forget them. Let's go."

They locked the car and ran along the sidewalk to the stone steps in front of Kate's house. Music blared through drawn curtains. Tony knocked on the door and banged the clapper while Pete rang the doorbell.

"Hi, Pete. Hi, Tony. Come on in." Kate flung the door wide and let them into the living room with its Mediterranean furnishings. "Where's Ben?"

"Isn't he here?" Tony said, showing surprise. "He left before we did."

"Oh, he probably went to pick up Ray and Teddy," Pete added.

Kate's face went cold. "I didn't invite Teddy. This isn't a nursery school, you know."

"It's not a kennel, either, but you invited George."

"I couldn't help it, he's part of the fraternity. Well, get out of the way so I can close the door." Blonde tresses swirled as she stuck her head outside and looked up and down the block. She shut the door. "Come on, the party's downstairs."

Faces were hardly visible in the subdued light of the recreation room.

People were packed in so closely that Tony could not tell who was dancing and who was simply standing along the decorated walls and talking. One thing that was apparent was that there were three times as many girls as boys.

Papier-mâché streamers spanned across wooden beams to hide the exposed plumbing and wiring. Lamps were covered with red shades, casting a hellish mien. Candles huddled on shelves around the paneled walls. Old movie posters added a touch of nostalgia that Kate's parents' enjoyed.

"Soda and refreshments are in that corner, the girls are in the back."

"What do you mean, the girls — ?" Tony started. But Kate was already retreating noiselessly up the rubber treads.

Pete shrugged. "I'm goin' for the food."

Tony followed him as he expertly threaded a path through the swinging, singing teenagers, yelling excuse-me's to the wallflowers and watch-it's to the dancers. With life and limb barely intact, they wedged into a nook behind a table covered with potato chips, pretzels, crackers, cheese, Coke, and plastic cups.

"How long?" The song ended, but another began immediately.

"How long what?" Tony asked.

"How long you think we gotta listen to the Temps?"

Tony glanced at his watch. "Kate knows that Ben is always on time within five minutes either way. Since he was supposed to be here at eight, and assuming that this is a twenty-minute album put on to span the time of his arrival, we should only have to listen to them for another eight minutes."

"Good." He stuffed his mouth full of potato chips. "What do you think's holding them up? I thought they were right behind us?"

Tony poured some Coke into a cup. "Maybe they ran into George."

"I hope they were in the car when they did."

A slow song played next, and a lot of the girls who were dancing with each other faded off the floor. The couples that were left hugged closely, moved in slow circles, barely lifting their feet in time with the music.

"Ben!" Except for the deeply engaged dancers, every head turned at Kate's scream.

About three-quarters of the way down the steps, Ray stopped and slowly scanned the occupants of the room. He pulled at his white-dotted blue tie, and stuck the other hand into a pocket of his blue blazer. When the tie was adjusted to his satisfaction, he casually removed the cigarette from his mouth and held it to the side as a wreath of smoke curling up around his face. He peered through the smoke with half-closed eyes.

Kate approached him, her mouth moving soundlessly. Ray jerked a thumb up the stairs, and she raced past him. He looked up for a moment, then reached the floor and wound through the dancing couples.

"Thanks for waiting." He looked up and down Pete's coveralls and dirty sneakers, shaking his head.

Pete had his mouth full of food. He drained his third cup of Coke and poured another. "We were hungry. Where's Ben?"

"Smothering under Kate's mouth. You couldn't pry those two apart with a crowbar."

"It figures." Tony cut a slice of cheese and put it on a cracker. "By the way, what really happened to George?"

Ray poured a Coke and munched delicately on a pretzel, careful not to get any crumbs on his jacket. "You better slow down, Pete, or you'll be peeing your brains out by the end of the night."

Tony laughed. "He won't have much to pee."

"The crackers are making me thirsty. Can I help it?"

"Then don't eat so much, lunkhead."

"I'm not your brother so don't call me names."

"Sorry 'bout that."

"So what happened to George?" Tony repeated.

"Come on, Ray. Out with the story. He was right behind you when we ran out of the garage."

"How would you know? You had your engine started before you even got in the seat.

Man, when someone yells race, you don't waste no time. And we woulda beat you if we hadn't gotten a light on Broad Street. Which way did you go?"

"Some day we'll tell you." Pete stopped eating, and just sipped at his Coke.

"All right, be a hardnose."

"So what about George?"

"Oh, yeah. George." Ray chewed on a pretzel before going on. "I threw the latch down on the storm door and pushed it shut. Then, while he was trying to figure out why it wouldn't open, I propped the stickball bat under the handle. He had to run up through the house to get out. Then I told Ben he was going with you."

"That's a rotten trick," Tony said.

"Hey, this cheese is good. What kind is it?"

"Gouda. The same kind Kate had at the last party. And it's still a rotten trick."

Pete poured himself another Coke. "Who can remember the last party?"

"Not you, you silly sot — oops, sorry — you were intoxicated."

"He was not," Tony said. "He was inebriated."

"I was not. I was drunk."

"Three sheets to the wind."

"Deep into a Bacchanalian stupor."

"Who cleaned up the mess?" Ray asked.

"What mess?"

"The mess you made when you puked your guts out all over the goddamn sidewalk."

"Hey, Tone, did I leave a mess?"

"A big one."

Pete lapsed into silence for a moment. He looked lost, or dazed. "All I remember is waking up on Ben's sofa in the morning."

"What did Mrs. Clark say when she saw you?"

"Nothin'. Hell, why should she? Ben wasn't drunk. He's like you, Tone. Wouldn't touch a drop a likker if his life depended on it."

Ray snorted. "Mr. Goodie Two Shoes."

Tony shrugged. "What did your brother say when he found out you took all his beer?"

"I didn't take it all — only a case. An' all he made me do was pay for it. He's all right. He done enough drinkin' in the marines to know what it's all about. So'd my dad, for that matter."

"Well, just remember, Kate's parents are just going to the movies tonight, not out of town. So they'll be back early."

Pete uncapped the bottle for the fifth time. "Don' you worry 'bout a thing, Tone. There's no beer in sight. Tonight I'm stickin' with Coke."

"I'll drink to that." Ray lifted his cup in the air, and all three rubbed plastic.

"If you've had enough to eat, let's go over

and see our friends." Ray jerked his head for them to follow. Pete took a fresh bottle of Coke, and Tony grabbed a handful of potato chips. Ray walked straight-backed, holding a cigarette and his cup in his left hand, his right held casually at his side.

"So that's what she meant," Pete said.

Tony nodded. "Um hum."

"What do you say, girls?" Ray said clearly, over the beat of the music. "Hello, Kathy."

Pete said, "Hello, everyone," then centered his attention on the girl he had had in his lap. "Hi, Marion."

Tony nodded and pursed his lips. "Hi."

Pete poked him in the ribs. "This is Patty, Tone. She's the one you and George were falling all over."

Patty smiled, and looked away. Tony said, "Hi, Patty."

After an awkward silence, Ray said, "Kate didn't say you girls were going to be here."

Marion brushed red hair, made redder by the lampshades, out of her eyes. "She didn't tell us you were going to be here, either."

Pete put one hand in his jacket pocket. His T-shirt underneath had smudges of grease on it. "She prob'ly didn' wanna scare you off."

After another uncomfortable silence, Ray said, "Nice music. Kate was playing the Temptations for Ben. They're his favorite."

Kathy said, "Yes, she told us he likes them."

"Likes 'em," Pete shouted. "He's in love with 'em."

Everyone laughed until the music ended and the room was flooded with quiet. After a moment, Ray said, "Don't everybody talk at once."

There were more smiles, a chuckle.

"Hey, you girls want some Coke?" Pete held up the bottle. "I brought enough for everybody."

"All right."

"Sure."

"I'm just about empty."

"I could use some more."

Tony began to feel warm in his sweater, and his armpits were damp. He looked around for somewhere to discard it.

"Anybody got a church key?" When no one answered, Pete put the bottle against the rim of the white, porcelain washtub. "Never mind, it's easier this way." He rammed the heel of his palm down on the bottle top; there was a pop and a fizz, and the cap fell to the floor. He kicked it under the washing machine. "Ain't got no ice, but the bottle's cold."

Ray picked up some plastic cups from the dryer, and handed them to the girls. "You all go to school with Kate?"

Pete poured Coke into Kathy's cup. Kathy nodded. "Marion and Patty do, and I used to. Now I go to public school."

"What did you get kicked out for?"

"Oh, lots of things." Kathy did not smile. In fact, she never smiled. "Care to give us an example?"

"Yo, Ray, stop leanin' on her," Pete said sternly. "Maybe she doesn't wanna talk about it."

"If she doesn't want to talk about it, she'll say so. Now, do you want to talk about it?"

"No."

"See, Pete, I told you so." Turning back to Kathy, Ray said, "Why don't you start the conversation, seeing as how I'm screwing it up?"

Marion smiled. "Kate said that some of you are college students — Temple, or something?"

Pete said, "I'm a grease monkey, Ray's a jewel thief — "

"For Bailey, Banks, and Biddle."

" — and Tony here's an ex-con. He just escaped this week."

"Yes, well, it depends on when she told you." Tony bit his lip. He wanted to get rid of the potato chips, and finally laid them on the washing machine. He kept his greasy hand behind him. "You see, I just dropped out a few days ago. I — that is, my parents couldn't afford to keep up the tuition so I had to go to work — full time, that is."

Pete slurped his Coke. "Yeah, they got payments to make on a brand new Cadillac."

"Yo, Pete, will ya?" Ray jabbed his with his elbow. "You don't have to tell the world."

"Sorry, Tone. Guess I got carried away."

"Forget it."

Marion had a voice that was smooth and cultured. "So what are you doing now?"

"Well, for the moment I'm working for my father. He's an electrical contractor. But in a few months I'll start apprentice training with the union. Then, for the next four years, I'll go to school one day a week and work on the job the other four."

"That's if he clears it with the draft board."

"Pete, I told you that would be all right. I can keep my II-S once I'm in the program."

"That's what you say. But Temple's gotta notify the draft board as soon as you quit. They'll make you a I-A so fast your head'll spin."

Patty knitted her brow, and dimples popped up under rouged cheeks. "What do you mean by two ess and one a?"

"They're selective service classifications," Tony explained.

"Draft priorities," Pete added.

"But, what do they mean?"

Tony laughed. "Pete's the local draft dodging expert. Why don't you explain it to her?"

Pete's hand fumbled inside his jacket pocket.

He brought it out and reached for the bottle of coke, refilled his cup. "It's not that hard to understand, though there ain't much sense to the number system. The worst one you can have is I-A. That means you can stand up on your own two feet without fallin' down, you can see at least to the end o' your nose, and you ain't committed any major crimes worsen burglary or assault an' battery in the past week. They can call you on the phone any time, night or day, an' tell you to get your ass down to the induction center to pick up your train ticket for parts unknown. From there on everything else's a deferment."

Pete drank copiously from his cup, taking an extended sip between every sentence, or in the middle of long ones. Inside his sweater, Tony was rolling in a sea of sweat.

"Deferments come in all shapes and sizes, depending on whether you're a student or a minister, or bonkers — or just a plain parasite. Students are classed as II-S, but it only applies to full-time college or on-the-job training. The problem with that is it don't last: they bounce you back to I-A as soon as your time is up. That way they get to use your smarts before you do."

The noise and the music made hearing difficult. Ray and Kathy slipped off to one side, whispering into each other's ears. Tony and Pete and Patty and Marion put their heads together.

"Now you got other kinds o' deferments that are more permanent. If you're a minister or a priest or anything holy other than an old pair o' socks, you get a IV-D. Spelled out that's eye-vee-dee, an' it don' mean syphilis of the optic nerve. Once you get eye-vee-dee you don' ever hafta worry again, 'cept you gotta give up sex an' live with God."

Pete reached for the Coke bottle and drained it into his cup. Kathy had her arms around Ray, and was rubbing her thighs against his. He was not resisting.

"Then you got your IV-F's. That's spelled eye-vee-ef, an' it's an intravenous for flatfoots. It's for politicians' sons who have hangnails an' a cowlick, or for local yokels with a leg missing or who need Coke bottom bottles — Coke bottom bottoms — Coke bottle bottles — who can't tell the difference between a pussy cat an' a pussy willow — or jus' plain pussy. An' it counts for guys who shave their heads and sing on street corners or who think they're Hannibal riding pink elephants over the Alps or howl at the moon an' think they become wolves when it's full — Ray excepted." Pete nodded in his direction. "An' it includes mental incompetents who ain't got the smarts to count to eleven without taking off their shoes an' socks. Guys like George."

"Yo, Pete."

"Yo, Pete, what? I don' like the silly son of a bitch an' I'll be the first one to admit it. He's a IV-F brain, body, an' soul. An' he makes me sick."

"He's not a IV-F and you know it."

"It ain't because he didn't try. His ole man got some quack doctor to fake a heart murmur for him, but the draft board didn' buy it. They had their own doctors examine him from head to toe, every cuticle and pubic hair. They stuck so many needles in him he looked like a pincushion. His lab bill was half the national debt. He talked so much shit they put a rectal thermometer in his mouth. When they couldn't find anything wrong with him he tried to fake imbecility, but he was too stupid to know how to do it."

Tony could not help but laugh. And he knew that once Pete got going, stopping him was like trying to prevent the tide from coming in. He found a napkin on the dryer and wiped his hand with it.

"Then he tried to go III-A, but he couldn't get road service. He was pleading extreme hardship on account o' his ole lady is divorced an' he was the sole support. But he ain't got a soul, an' couldn't support a pair o' socks, an' he never worked a day in his life. Now he's tryin' to claim he's a conscientious objector, only he ain't never done anything conscientious. Hell, he's been through so many classification numbers it'd take a mathematician a year to add 'em all up."

Tony could no longer hold his soda without spilling it, so he placed it on the washer. "Come on, Pete, cut the guy a break. He may not be the greatest friend in the world but he's at least, I mean, he deserves more than that. I mean, it must have been tough on him coming from a broken home and all that. His father didn't want him, his mother got stuck with him . . . "

"Stuck is the word. Jus' 'cause his folks don' live together is no reason to be a nerd. The world ain' made up o' 'Father Knows Best' families. We all got problems. That don' give 'im no 'scuse. My ol' man spends half his life at the bar, but you don' see me complainin'. When my time comes I'll go, 'cause Uncle Sam done all right by me so far. I got things you can' get in other countries, things that were here when I was born an' I didn' hafta work for 'em. But that bastard never does anythin' but complain about what he don' have, and he ain' never done a decent day's work to get what he wants. So why should he skate off scot free?"

"Pete, he just needs a chance to grow up. Don't hold that against him."

"Grow up? Hell, he'll be a bent ol' man with white whiskers to his knees before he learns to tie his shoelaces right. How ol' you think he is? Huhn? How ol'?"

Tony shrugged. "He's our age. Nineteen if he already had his birthday."

"Guess again."

"He couldn't be much older . . . "

"I guarantee he's older 'an anyone else in this room. You haven't known him as long as I have. I lived across the street from him since before I was big enough to run away from him. He was always a bully, an' besides being as big as a bear he was always two years older."

"Oh, come on, Pete."

"Come on yourself. He got left back in first grade because he was such a troublemaker. Then he flunked his freshman year in high school. That's when I caught up with 'im. The only reason they didn' kick 'im out was because his ol' man had some pull with the parish priest."

"I never knew that."

"Lotsa thin's you don' know. You 'spect 'im to brag about it?" Pete swayed against the washing machine, leaned against it for support. "I'll bet you didn' know he registered while he was still in school. That was when he got his first deferment, as a I-S. Then, when he graduated, he never tol' the draft board, an' they didn' fin' out till the school notified 'em. Then, to slow up the paper work, he changed his legal address so they thought he was livin' with his ol' man. After they transferred all his records he changed his address back to his mom's, so he could claim he was the man of the fam'ly. If shit were electricity he'd be a powerhouse. His ol' man got fake workin' papers for him, sayin' he had a job with his tire company. Only you know what? Even his ol' man didn' wanna hire 'im 'cause he knew he's no good. So now he sits in the closet all day with those girly magazines, an' jerks — "

Tony lunged at Pete, knocking him back across the washer, and wrapped his arms around his middle. The empty plastic cup fell out of his hand and clattered to the floor. Tony wrestled him into a corner between the washtub and the wall.

"What've you got in your pocket?" He felt the cool, glassy hardness of a bottle, and pulled out the flat, half-pint flask. Only half an inch of dark liquid stained the lower corner. "So this is what you've been tipping into your Coke."

"Hey, gimme that." Pete got his hand on the bottle and snatched it toward his mouth. Tony pulled it away just as the dregs welled up into the narrow neck. The contents poured out on Pete's jacket and shirtfront. His head crashed into Tony's chest — he was out cold.

Tony pushed him sideways so his middle folded over the washtub. His head lolled forward, his eyes closed. Tony pulled the bottle away and dropped it in the washtub, and held Pete up by the back of his belt. Then Pete began to wretch.

Except for Patty and Marion, no one else seemed to be aware of what was happening. The music still played, the dancers still gyrated. Pete's legs pulled up off the floor, he pivoted on his stomach, and his forehead touched the water at the bottom of the washtub. The noise he made was drowned out by party pandemonium.

Patty backed away, and turned her head. But Marion came forward with a stack of napkins. While Pete painted the porcelain a speckled pink, she wet the napkins under the faucet and held them against his forehead. Then she placed her other hand behind his head. He remained doubled over, but could not hurt himself in his spasms.

After a couple of minutes of dry heaves, Pete started to slip off the edge of the washtub. Tony kicked a chair under him and sat him on it. Marion kept the pressure on his forehead and held him upright. Tony slipped the flask into his own hip pocket. He ran water into the washtub, and splashed it back and forth until every vestige of vomit was gone.

"I'll need a towel," Marion said calmly.

The small tablecloth, folded on the dryer, kept the enameled surface from getting scratched. Tony pushed off cups, napkins, potato chips, and the Coke bottle, and handed the cloth to her. She wet one end and washed Pete's face, then used the other end to dry him off.

"Whaddja do wi' ma bot'l?"

"It's all taken care of, Pete. Don't you worry." Tony glanced around, and saw that they were still unobserved.

"I feel awful."

"You look it, too. Your eyes are like interstate road maps. You had nearly half a pint of straight hundred and twenty proof rum."

"Did not. I mixed it with Coke."

"It doesn't matter what you dilute it with. Eight ounces of alcohol is still eight ounces as far as your stomach's concerned."

Pete burped loudly.

"I think we'd better take him home," Marion said.

"He can't go home like this. His father would put him in worse shape than he's already in."

"We can't take him to my house. My parents wouldn't allow it. Maybe I can drive him around till he sobers up." Turning to Patty, Marion said, "Can you get home on your own?"

Patty shrugged. "Well, I don't know. I guess I could take a bus . . . "

"I can take her home, but how can you — "

"They don't care what time I bring the car back. They're pretty good that way. Just help me get him up the stairs."

"Hey, wha' am I, a bag o' potatoes. I gotta be carried aroun' like some god — ooooohh." Pete fell back into the chair and banged his head against the wall. "Somebody better peel me an' throw away the skin."

"All right, I'll help you get him out to your car." He pulled Pete off the chair, and hunched down so that he could get one shoulder under his armpit.

"Wait a minute. I can make it under my own steam." Pete wobbled sideways and fell against the sink. "Uh, oh. Stoke the holds, I'm havin' trouble with the boiler. An' ma rudder's awry, too."

Marion cradled his other arm and together they sidled along the wall toward the stairs. "Patty, get my pocket book, please."

Pete burped again. "How incongruous."

"The word is ignominious, and you deserve it, you drunken sailor."

"Not me. I'm gonna be a marine. Runs inna family."

"Let's hope you live that long." At the stairs, Tony took the lead while Marion pushed from behind. Just as they got into the dining room, Kate appeared with Ben in tow.

"Omigod. What happened to *him*?"

"Too much Coke," Tony said. "Must be the additives."

"Has he been drin — Ben, he's been drinking. My God, he's drunk."

"Plastered to the gills," Pete said, with a grin.

From the front of the house a key rasped in the lock, and Kate threw her hand to her mouth. "Omigod, it's my parents."

Ben jerked a thumb toward the kitchen. "*Get him outa here.*"

Tony threw his arm around Pete's waist, picked him up off the floor, and carried him behind the partition. Marion worked loose the back door latch and helped maneuver Pete through the doorway. Patty closed the door behind them. The yard was only fifteen feet square, and in a moment they were through the gate and in the narrow alley.

"Ah wanna girl, jush like the girl, that married dear o' dad."

"Quit singing, Pete. We're not out of the woods yet."

"You're worse off'n I am if you think these're trees."

A hand gripped Tony's sweater and pulled it back tight against his throat. He looked back and saw Patty, wide-eyed and open-mouthed.

"I — I'm scared — in the dark."

Tony pulled his neck free and swallowed.

"Just hang on, we'll be out of here in a minute."

Pete tripped over a garbage can. The lid crashed to the cement and clattered away. "Oh, no. I got trash on my sneaks."

"Forget about your sneaks. Think about these girls you dragged out here in their party dresses and nylons."

"Marion, are you mad at me?"

She shuffled Pete along in the dark. "No, I'm not angry. But try to keep your voice down till we get to my car."

"Ain't a offer like that inna lon' time."

"*Pete.*" Tony slapped him lightly in the back of the head. "You're drunk. Now don't go making a fool out of yourself."

They paused at the cross alley at the end of the block. Marion took some of the weight from Tony. "This way." A moment later they stood on the sidewalk of the houses in the next street. Marion pointed to a blue '63 Plymouth. "My car's right over there." She took her handbag from Patty and dug out the keys.

As soon as they dumped Pete in the back seat, he passed out. "Are you sure you'll be okay?"

"Sure, Tony. Thanks for the help. I can manage it from here. Patty, I'm sorry for running out on you like this."

"Oh, that's all right. Tony said he would take me home."

Marion smiled. "Well, I'll see you two later, then."

After she pulled away, Tony looked up at the sky: city lights blocked out most of the stars. The cool air felt good, so he raised his sweater over his head and pulled it off. His shirt underneath was soaked.

"I'm sorry I didn't know what to do. I know I wasn't much help . . . "

"Forget it." In the glow from the streetlights, Tony saw that Patty had sparkling green eyes set deep in a smooth, white face with plump cheeks. Her nose was wide, but short, her lips full. Brown hair barely reached her rounded shoulders. Her hips were broad, the contours hidden by the colored, knee-length dress. A shiny copper coin glinted from the top of each penny loafer. "Uh, listen, I'm, uh, pretty hot. We can't go back in through the back door, so, do you mind if we walk around the long way?"

"Sure, that would be great. I could use the air."

Tony threw the sweater over his shoulder and shoved his hands into his pockets. He ambled slowly, staring upward.

"What are you doing?"

"What? Oh, I was just looking for shooting stars."

"Oh, meteorites."

"Well, actually, they're not meteorites until

they hit the ground. As long as they burn up in the atmosphere, they're just meteors. Unless they explode, then they're bolides."

"Oh, I saw one explode once. It was down the shore, in Cape May. It split in two right over the ocean."

"Wow! Really? I've only read about them. They're pretty rare, you know. I mean, you don't see that many. I guess there are a lot that people don't see, like in the Arctic, or in the daytime."

"Are there meteors in the daytime?"

"Sure, you just don't see them. The sun's so bright it washes them out, but they're there."

A few other people were walking along the street. One or two front doors opened to emit cones of light and sounds of laughter. Cars were parked bumper to bumper, with hardly any room to get through — or get out.

Tony made small talk. "Uh, I guess you'll be graduating in a few weeks?"

"Yes, thank God. I'm tired of school."

"Don't you like it?"

"Oh, school is all right, I guess. It's just so much work. You have to think all the time."

"Well, what are you going to do after school?"

"I don't know. Work, I guess. My mother wants me to work as a waitress in her restaurant."

"Your mother owns a restaurant?"

"No, she just works in one. The Golden Lilly. She's the hostess there. But I don't know. I've been taking business courses and I kind of thought I'd like to become a secretary. Not just a group secretary, but a private secretary. You know, kind of like working for an executive or something. I think that would be fun."

Tony veered left at the end of the block. "I don't think anyone becomes a private secretary right out of school. I think you have to work at it for a while before you can do it. You know, get some experience in general secretarial work first so you know the job."

"My mother always says 'it's not *what* you know, it's *who* you know.'"

Tony laughed. "Yeah, I guess that's true. After all, that's how your mother's planning to get you hired as a waitress. You happen to know the right person. What's her boss going to say about it, though?"

"He's her boyfriend."

"What?"

"She dates him. She dates a lot of men, but mostly him. He's always over the house."

A car with a broken muffler roared by, and somewhere off in the distance a siren blared its warning. "Uh, are your parent's divorced?"

"Yes, for a long time. That's why she goes out with so many men. Rich men, mostly."

Tony veered left again. "Oh. What about your father?"

"I see him every now and then. He doesn't care too much about me because he's remarried and got a family of his own."

"So you live with your mother?"

"And my grandmother. She's a real pain in the neck, always telling me what to do. My mother goes away a lot, especially on weekends if she isn't working. One of her boyfriends has a real nice place in the Poconos. Sometimes she takes me with her. But if she just goes away for the night and I have to stay home with my grandmother, I usually stay in my room and watch TV so I can keep out of her way."

"A house full of women, and three generations besides. What do you do when you need something done? I mean, like repairs, or something."

"My mother doesn't have too much trouble getting help. She just invites somebody over for the weekend and gets him to do whatever she needs done. The house belongs to my grandmother, and she gets a pension from the government for my grandfather."

"Is he — dead?"

"Yes, he died when I was little, so I never knew him. He was a postal worker, so she gets widow benefits plus her social security. Then my father pays my mother for my upkeep, so we make out pretty good. Course, as soon as I turn eighteen he's going to stop paying for me."

"Uh, oh." Tony stopped so fast that Patty kept on going a couple steps before she noticed. George passed under a streetlight, his face wrought with anger. The sounds of the Bristol Stomp poured through a basement window.

Patty looked, and stopped. A door opened and George disappeared inside.

"I don't think he saw us."

"Don't you like George, either?"

"What? Oh, no. I mean, sure, he's all right. He just takes a little getting used to. He's an all right guy, I guess. But the guys are always picking on him, and that just makes him worse."

Patty swung her pocketbook in front of her. "Well, I don't like him."

"How do you know? You only met him once."

"Once is enough. That's how I know I don't like him. He's too handsy."

"Oh, he doesn't mean anything by it. He just wants attention."

"I know what he wants and it isn't attention. Listen, if you don't mind, I'd rather not go back to the party. Can you take me home now?"

"Well, sure, whatever you say. This is my car." He opened the door for her, waited until she was seated, and pushed it shut behind her.

He had cooled off too much and was beginning to shiver, so he put his sweater back on before getting behind the wheel.

"It got chilly out, didn't it?"

"That's what I was thinking." Tony threw some levers on the dashboard. "But this car has a great little heater. It'll warm you up in no time." Patty slid across the front seat, closer to Tony.

"Hey, don't forget your seat belt." He buckled his own before turning on the engine.

"I never use them."

"You should."

"They're too uncomfortable."

"You get used to them. Besides, it's better than wearing a windshield across your face."

"Oh, I heard you were a pretty good driver."

Tony pulled the car out into the street and drove slowly along the tiny streets. "Where did you hear that?"

"Oh, just around."

"Yeah, well, that doesn't help when there are other maniacs on the road. Hey, where am I going? Where do you live?"

"Right behind St. Agnes Hospital."

"Hey, no kidding. That's where I was born. Pete was born there, too. And Ben."

"I guess you've known them pretty long, haven't you?"

"Yeah, although we never went to school together. My mother didn't want me to go to Catholic school — she's Baptist. And my father doesn't let them in the house — they're Irish."

"So am I."

"Doesn't matter to me."

"I'm glad."

"Yeah, uh, hey, where do you think Marion would have taken Pete?"

"I don't know. She's never done anything like this before. Taken a boy home, that is. And drunk."

"Yeah, well, Pete sure had me fooled, hiding that bottle in the lining of his jacket. I wonder where he picked that up."

"I don't know."

"Pete sure knows an awful lot about the draft, doesn't he?"

"Yeah, he likes to know what he's getting into."

"What do you mean?"

"Well, chances are he'll get his notice as soon as he turns nineteen. He's I-A, and pretty healthy, so I know he'll pass his physical. Up till now I've been pretty busy trying to keep up my grades, so I don't know all that much about it. But he watches television a lot and follows the news about the conflict."

"What conflict?"

"The Vietnam conflict. He figures the way the war's escalating, we'll all be over there sooner or later."

"What's escalating mean?"

"Getting bigger, drafting more men and sending them over. Did you see the six o'clock news last night?"

"No, I always turn the TV off when the news comes on. It's so depressing, they never have anything but robberies and murders and scandals."

"Well, anyway, they corroborated last week's announcement that Westmoreland's going to get all the troops he asked for. He says he can beat the North through attrition in three years."

"It's going to last that long?"

"At least. Maybe longer."

Broad Street was brightly lit, and cars raced by with typical city frenzy. Storefronts boasted colored neon signs, flashing gaily, and taprooms called to their clientele.

"What a waste. My mother's always complaining about how much more taxes have been since this thing began. I wish it would end so she would shut up about it."

A horn blasted right next to Tony's ear. He saw a car full of kids, screaming and waving. The driver of the sleek, bronze '64 Oldsmobile kept beeping, and the girl in the front seat leaned out the window and let out an ear piercing, two fingered whistle. A boy and girl in the back crammed their heads out the window and waved maniacally. The car drew ahead, and their whistles and friendly catcalls diminished in the distance.

"Friends of yours?"

Patty shook her head. "No, I never saw them before."

"Humph. Must be celebrating something, I guess. Where was I? Oh, yes, well, when I turned eighteen last summer I had to register. But I hadn't decided on college yet so I couldn't put in for a deferment. Somehow, they got my birth date wrong and called me back for a physical. The next day I got accepted, so I went back and got reclassified."

"You're trying to stay out of the army?"

"Well, no. Not at first. I considered enlisting, or letting myself get drafted, so I could get it over with and go to school afterwards. I would have lost two or three years, but then I would have had the GI bill to help pay my tuition. Pete says the military is a good way to get an education."

Another car came alongside, honking its horn as it raced past. It was an old Falcon station wagon occupied by six girls. Tony heard "Treat Her Right" in chorus before they swept down a side street.

"Did you recognize any of *them*?"

"No," Patty said.

"I wonder what's going on? Is everyone crazy tonight? Well, anyway, Pete's just hanging back to see which way the wind blows. I guess if his mom weren't sick, well, who knows?"

"Can't he get a deferment, like that objector he was talking about?"

"Who, Pete? He hates conscientious objectors. He says they're just drones who can afford to be CO's because there are enough real men willing to go and do the fighting for them. No, he doesn't believe in deferments at all. He thinks everyone should serve his country some way or other, even if it's only in the Peace Corps."

"What about you? What do you think?"

"Well, there's a lot of truth to what he says, although I don't think he's looking at the other side of the coin. My father says that's being wishy-washy, but I always like to see for myself what's going on, and examine both points of view before I draw any conclusions. Right now I just don't have enough information to go on."

"Turn left at the next street."

Tony slowed down and got into the left lane. He stopped at the signal and waited for the green light. A two-tone '63 Impala stopped next to them, and a mob of teenage boys shouted licentious implications. Tony looked straight ahead. "Ignore them."

The light changed, and he squealed into his turn before oncoming traffic could cut him off. "Maybe everybody's drunk tonight."

"Don't worry about it. We're almost home." She directed him to her street. "It's the fifth house on the right."

The street was packed, so Tony parked on the curb. He released his seat belt and was out of the car before the engine whined down. "I'll walk you to the step," he said, as he opened her door.

Patty stepped out of the car. "Thanks."

The facade was like every other house on the block: dull red brick with flush picture windows. Patty searched for her key while Tony stared up at the sky. "Do you know that there are only six thousand stars visible to the naked eye?"

"Is that right?" She found the key and climbed the three steps to the door.

Tony backed away. "Well, it was good seeing you again."

"Uh, well, good night. And thanks for the ride."

"Oh, that's all right. No trouble."

She pushed the key into the lock. "Why don't you call me?"

"You mean, like, on the phone?"

"Sure. Maybe we could go for a walk, or something."

"Oh, sure, we could do that. I guess."

The door swung open and pulled the key ring out of Patty's hand. A figure stood in the dark opening. A robe billowed outward ominously. Light reflected off round eyeglasses, giving an owlish appearance to a tasseled, gray head. The beak and grim-looking mouth completed the gargoyle effect.

"Oh. Hi, Nan. You startled me."

The specter in the doorway spoke with a raspy voice. "I thought you were supposed to be home early. Aren't you going to the shore tomorrow with your mother?"

"She didn't set any specific time, just not too late. This isn't too late. The party was still going on when I left."

"Well, let's not dawdle with the door open. I don't want the neighbors looking in."

"Yes, Nan." Patty turned and flashed a toothless smile. "Good night. And thanks again for the ride."

Still backing away, Tony waved. The apparition in the doorway disappeared, and the black hole seemed to swallow up the girl. The door slammed shut. Tony backed into a trash can and went headlong over it. He rolled along the sidewalk, but the noise woke up the dead in the cemetery three miles away. He stood up and ran before the neighbors flipped their Venetian blinds to watch the commotion.

He jabbed his key into the door lock — and froze. He had just passed the back of the car and something he had seen there was just impinging itself on his mind. Slowly, he removed the key and studied his subconscious mind for impressions. The only sound in the neighborhood was the hoarseness of his own breathing.

Like a cartoon in reverse he took a step backward, then another, and another. He leaned back and peered at the rear of the car. Then he knew how Ben and Ray had spent their time between parking the car and arriving at the party.

Tied to the bumper, with ragged lengths of white string, was a full-width banner proclaiming, "Just Married."

Chapter 18

"What have you gotten yourself into this time?"

Elizabeth nursed a cup of coffee, her face a picture of accusation. The clock on the oven read one-thirty.

"The main charge is robbery with the intent to steal, plus salt and a six-volt battery."

"This is not a laughing matter!" She threw down her spoon. It clattered and slid across the top of the table and over the edge. "You were picked up by the police."

Tony casually leaned against the doorjamb. "It doesn't mean anything. At midnight they stop every car driven by a teenager, hoping to catch one with a junior license. You think I haven't been stopped before?"

"You've never been locked up before."

"Mom, I wasn't locked up. I just sat in the waiting room."

"It's the same thing."

"No, it's not. I got stopped for a routine car check, and when they found an empty bottle in my pocket they decided to make a big stink about it."

"Big stink is right. You had me worried half to death. What am I supposed to think when the police wake me up in the middle of the night and tell me they've got my son in jail?"

Tears welled up in her eyes. She plucked a tissue from its expensive ornamental holder, and blew her nose. Then she dabbed her eyes while she sobbed. Frank slammed the front door shut and swept through the house like a storm. His eyes widened when he saw Elizabeth crying. He rushed at Tony with all the energy of a football team, and bowled him aside with a wild, one-armed shove.

"What did you have to go an' make her cry for?" he shouted.

Tony crashed into the counter so hard that bottles and glassware in the lazy Susan rattled as they jumped off the circular shelf. He felt stabs of pain in his ankle, shin, and hip.

"You got a lot of nerve coming in here and making a scene with your mother, after what happened."

Tony kept his eyes fixed on his father. He refused to rub his injuries. "I didn't start anything. I didn't even get a chance to explain what happened."

"I don't want to hear any goddamn excuses. I should have left you there over night an' let the cops work you over. You deserve it."

"For what? Carrying an empty pint flask in my pocket? Since when is that a crime?"

"It's a crime when the police arrest you an' call your father in the middle of the night to come an' get you out of jail."

"They didn't call you. You were out at the taproom."

"So your mother had to call me. What's the difference? Don't you know that kids ain't allowed to drink?"

"Nobody said I was drinking, not even the police. And there's no law against carrying empty bottles."

"You wouldn't be carrying empty liquor bottles unless you were drinking. An' besides, it makes me look bad."

"Oh, so now I've gone from one bottle to a whole case. As long as you're exaggerating,

why don't you just go ahead and say I stole a whole tractor-trailer full of moonshine?"

Elizabeth dabbed at her eyes with her wet tissue. Frank went to the range, turned on the burner, then put a kettle of water on the flame.

"Don't try to joke your way out of it." Frank swung his arms around like a mad conductor leading a hundred-piece band. The napkin holder happened to be at the extremity of his reach, and it was lifted off the counter. It crashed into the wall, rebounded, and spilled its flowered napkins on the floor. The wooden towel rack fell apart and a new roll of paper towels rolled into the sink, soaking up water. He grabbed it, and threw the roll at Tony. It ricocheted off the opposite door jamb and hit the table, scattering the salt and pepper shakers and overturning the sugar bowl. Then he kicked at the napkins on the floor, lost his purchase, and fell backward, smashing his hand on the toaster. He picked it up and hurled it across the kitchen into the pantry, ripping out the electrical cord and knocking down cans of food.

"Frank, stop it! You're breaking all my things."

"Goddamn it, it's all his fault, coming in here with lame excuses as if he's little mister innocent who didn't do a goddamn thing. What'm I gonna tell the guys when I go back to the taproom? That I had to bail my son out of jail?"

"All right, but you don't have to go and wreck the house."

"And you didn't have to bail me out. You didn't even have to sign a piece of paper. Why don't you just look at the facts instead of making insane interpretations?"

"*I'm* crazy? You get picked up for drunk driving an' *I'm* crazy? I'll show you who's crazy — "

Elizabeth jumped up and threw herself at his arm, stopping him in mid swing. "Leave him alone. I don't want to have to go to the hospital, too."

Frank glared at Tony like an enraged bull, breathing hard through flaring nostrils. "You better watch yourself, mister, or I'll kill you. An' you better believe it."

The kettle whistled, Elizabeth relaxed her hold, Frank kicked a chair away from the table and sat down. She fixed a cup of instant coffee and put it in front of him. He never took his eyes off his son.

A long moment later, Tony said calmly, "All they found was an empty bottle. But that's not proof that I was drinking."

"Then why did they make me go down an' pick you up?"

"Look, if I'd been drinking they wouldn't have let me out."

"Don't play innocent with me. They picked

you up for a reason. You think the cops got nothing better to do than pick on kids?"

"As a matter of fact, they don't."

"Yeah, well, let me tell you something, mister smarty pants. As long as you're living in my house, an' driving my car, any trouble you get into makes me responsible."

"It's not your car."

"It's in my name."

"For insurance purposes only."

"It don't matter. When you do something wrong, I gotta pay for it."

"But what's wrong with carrying an empty bottle, just because it's shaped like a flask? Is that worse than carrying one that's shaped like a peanut butter jar?"

Frank sipped his hot coffee. "What's wrong with it is it's against the law, that's what."

"Oh, but it's not against the law when you sneak back all that liquor from Maryland without paying revenue tax."

"All I'm doin' is picking up a few bottles of Seagrams to save a couple bucks. I ain't doin' nothing wrong. What I do is my business."

Tony stepped away from the jamb, and leaned on the other one. "Then why isn't what I do *my* business?"

"Because you're just a smart aleck kid, that's why. The law says you can't drink, an' that's that."

"But in some states the drinking age is only eighteen. So what you're saying is that I can be a criminal in one state but a law-abiding citizen in another."

"You don't live in another state. You live in this one. An' you gotta 'bide by the law whether you like it or not."

"Even if it doesn't make any sense? Just because some law is on the books doesn't make it sacrosanct. Laws are only ways of describing the moral code of a society, and by themselves have no meaning."

"Don't go spoutin' that college shit, I don't want to hear it. They're nothing but a bunch of radicals teaching you kids how to stir up trouble."

"There has to be a check and balance system in order to keep things in perspective. If it weren't for people challenging the status quo, we'd still be paying tea taxes to England and condoning slavery."

Elizabeth pulled another tissue out but just held onto it, as if for comfort. "What's all this have to do with you getting picked up for drunk driving?"

"He's just trying to change the subject, that's all." Frank threw his hands in the air, and grunted.

Tony straightened his shoulders, and stood upright. "Wait a minute. Who said I was drunk driving?"

"That's what the police said when they called up."

"And you believed them?"

"Of course. They're the police."

Tony sighed, and rolled his eyes. "That's right, they're the police, not the Pope calling from the Vatican. And if they had smelled the least bit of alcohol on my breath they could have done something about it. Instead, the only thing they could do was cause trouble by calling you. And you fell for it like a ton of bricks."

Frank half rose from the table, but Elizabeth held onto one arm. "You better watch your mouth, or I'll smash it for you. You musta broke some law."

"Hey, whose side are you on, anyway? I didn't break any laws. And even if I did fracture some insignificant ordnance, it doesn't mean anything. Laws are in a constant state of change, because what looks good on paper doesn't always fulfill the standards of its intentions."

"Will you stop bringing in that hippy crap?" Frank screamed. He pounded the table so hard that Elizabeth's empty cup fell over in the saucer. "You broke the law, goddamn it, an' that's all there is to it. An' if it happens again I'll wring your throat. You think I want everybody thinkin' my son's a goddamn radical hippy? I don't want that hangin' over *my* head."

From the second floor came Robby's pitiful wail.

Frank pounded the table again. "Now look what you done. You went an' woke up the baby."

Chapter 19

"Good morning, Tony. I see you brought the sun with you. Come on in."

Frances Clark stepped back from the glass-paneled door, sweeping her faded housecoat behind her. Her auburn hair was set in rollers above an angular face whose wrinkles practically told their own story: orphaned at the age of eighteen and left to raise a younger brother and sister, married at twenty-one to a woman-beating man, issued a stillborn child at twenty-three, widowed at twenty-seven with a three-year-old son. Her second marriage at thirty turned out to be the turning point in a life of misfortunes, giving her a loving husband and another dutiful son.

"Thanks, Mrs. Clark. I was wondering if Pete — " As he entered the sun porch, he saw Pete snoring blissfully on the living room couch. The shades and curtains were drawn tight, making the baroque furniture appear even more ominous than usual. "Well, I'm glad to see he made it home all right."

Mrs. Clark shook her head and tiptoed in worn leather slippers over scratched hardwood flooring and threadbare throw rugs. "That boy's going to kill himself someday if he doesn't stop his drinking. I wish somebody could talk some sense into his head."

Tony followed her into the kitchen.

"Have a seat and I'll get you some coffee." The electric percolator was already full of hot, black coffee, and a large plate of doughnuts sat on the table. "Help yourself to the pastry."

"Thanks." Coffee appeared in front of him, as did sugar and cream. Mrs. Clark handed him a spoon. "Ummm. These are still hot."

"Picked them up on my way home from church."

Tony talked through a mouthful of dough. "Six o'clock mass, as usual?"

"Haven't missed a Sunday in twenty years. God knows Jack isn't too particular about attendance, so somebody in this family has to do the praying."

"These are delicious."

"That's what Ben said. And he ate three of them so he ought to know."

Tony did not miss a chew. "Is he still here?"

Mrs. Clark poured another coffee for herself, and sat opposite Tony. "You missed him by ten minutes. He's having breakfast with the Doughertys, then taking Kate to ten o'clock mass. You can catch him at church."

"No, I don't think I'll go today."

"That's up to you. Don't have to go to church to be close to God. He's with you all the time." She stirred in some sugar, sipped the coffee black. "He'll be back for lunch, though. Ben, that is. Not God. Jack and I are celebrating our anniversary today, so we're having people over for cold cuts. I expect you to be here."

"Thanks, Mrs. Clark. That's awfully nice of you."

"Pshaw, you know I can't stand to be alone. I'm selfish, really. That's why I surround myself with company. Now, I want to know why you dropped out of school without so much as consulting me about it."

Tony gulped down the last bite, and swilled some coffee. He stared down at his saucer. "Well, I didn't think — I mean, it came on rather suddenly, and I didn't have time — that is, the decision was already made. It was my problem, and you couldn't have done anything — "

"Your problems are my problems, and you know it. Now you tell me all about it. If you were raised a staunch Catholic, you'd know that confession is good for the soul."

"I don't know exactly where to start. And it's kind of complicated."

Mrs. Clark leaned back in her chair, cup in hand. "You just start at the beginning. I've got all morning to listen."

Tony swallowed. "Yes, well, business has been bad for my father . . . "

For three-quarters of an hour, Tony was grilled under the blinding, kitchen light. Mrs. Clark hammered him with short, poignant questions that led to intricate debate. Her eyebrows arched at every attempt on Tony's part to evade the issues.

"You know that doesn't make a bit of sense. Jack makes bullets working at the arsenal, and you don't see us complaining about Ben's education."

"I know, but my father's money is all tied up in the business. It's not that he doesn't have capital, he just doesn't have cash flow. All his money is out on the street. The builders are slow in paying, so he has to take out business loans to settle with the supply houses and keep up the payroll."

"Then why does he keep taking jobs with builders that don't pay?"

"He says he needs the work."

"He doesn't need work that doesn't pay. And if he can take out a ten thousand dollar loan for the business, and buy a new car besides, what's another five hundred dollars for tuition?"

"It's not just the tuition, it's living expenses: books, carfare, food, clothes, the works. And I don't want to be beholden on them."

"That's a lot of crap. Since when are children beholden on their parents for their upkeep? That's why you have children, because you want someone to take care of. Doesn't he care about your future?"

"Sure. He's going to get me into the apprentice program."

"What you mean is, he wants to run your life for you. No, don't say a word. You know it's true. So why don't you just pay your own tuition? You're no grasshopper when it comes to money, so I know you've got some stashed away in the bank."

Tony fingered his empty cup. "Oh, sure, I could pay the tuition right now. But I'll never earn enough for the next three years. And where am I going to get the money for room and board?"

"Simple. You just move in with us."

Tony's finger froze; his eyes squinted. It was several seconds before he could speak. "Mrs. Clark, how could I — I mean, I couldn't. I mean — "

She reached for a doughnut and dunked it in her coffee. "What's one more mouth to feed when you've got three big eaters like I've already got? I'm used to having four bottomless pits at the table. Now, with Joey in the Air Force, I'm one mouth short and one bed empty.

All we'd have to do is move his clothes into the basement and fix up another desk for you to work on."

"Well, I, uh, well, I just couldn't do it. I can't just walk out on my parents. It wouldn't be right."

"You start making your own decisions and decide what's right for you, not for the rest of the world. Your only obligation is to yourself."

"Well, all right. But I still want to stand up on my own two feet. I don't want to involve other people in my problems."

"Tony, you know what your biggest problem is? You're afraid to let other people help you. Believe me, there's nothing wrong with accepting help when you need it. How many times have you helped the boys in the fraternity? How many times have you chauffeured them around when they needed a ride? How often have you gone out of your way to help someone in trouble?" She jerked her head toward the living room. "The tables work both ways you know. Life is like a bank in reverse. When you're growing up you withdraw money whenever you need it; you operate on a negative balance. Then, when you become an adult, you start putting money back into it — not necessarily into the same account, but into the system. You don't have to help the same people who helped you, because the country, the whole world, is one great big community. You take help when you need it, and you give it back when you have extra. Some give more than others, some take more. It all balances in the end."

Tony toyed with his cup, refusing to look her directly in the eyes. "I know what you're saying, but I just can't live that way. I can't take something for nothing."

"Stop being an idealist. You don't have to prove to me who you are, you just have to keep proving it to yourself. So you just go back to Temple tomorrow, make amends for missing the week, pay them their money, and move in with us."

"Mrs. Clark, I wish it were that simple, but it isn't. I've already given official notification — I can't go back. From now on I can only go forward. And when I do, I want to do it on my own. I don't want to have any debts."

"That's a silly attitude you got from your parents because they never gave you anything without beating it into your head that you owed them for it. Forget that crap. I know you'll give when the time comes."

Tony slowly shook his head. He lifted his cup, saw it was empty, and put it back down. "It won't work, Mrs. Clark. Thanks for the offer, but I couldn't accept it. I have to see this through myself. I have to play it my way."

Mrs. Clark sat up and poured them both more coffee. "Okay, if that's the way you want it. I won't say another word about. You know, in a way, I admire you for being headstrong. It shows your individuality. It's probably one of your best qualities, so don't ever lose it. You just do whatever your heart tells you, and don't take advice unless it suits your feelings. But my offer remains open. You'll always have friends to rely on, and I'll always be here if you need to talk, or anything. Okay?"

Tony nodded weakly. "Sure. I'll remember that."

"Good. Now, what happened to your leg?"

Tony stopped with the creamer lifted over his cup. "My leg?"

"You weren't limping the last time I saw you."

"Uh, well, you know how my father is, getting excited all the time. Well, last night, when I got home from the police station . . . "

The whole story erupted like a volcano, from car stop to police station to the kitchen — all the facts, all the details, all the excuses. Mrs. Clark knitted her brow and listened to it all.

"Gee, Tone, I'm sorry I got you into all that trouble."

Pete stood in the doorway, hands in pockets, propped up against the jamb at such an angle that he would have fallen over if it were suddenly removed. His socks had slipped down so far that they barely covered his heels, and they protruded about six inches past his toes, with the ends curled up like pixie shoes. One pant leg was caught around his knee, his zipper flew at half-mast. His shirt was held together with one button; one tail hung out and the other was barely tucked in, so it bloused widely at his narrow waist. His eyes were horizontal slits that squinted painfully. His hair looked as if it had been combed with an eggbeater.

"How long have you been — I mean, how much did you . . . "

Pete's mouth barely moved. "Enough." With great effort he pushed himself semi erect, wobbled to the table, and collapsed into a chair. Tony pushed his coffee cup in front of him. But Pete just hung his head in his hands. "What the hell's the matter with me? It's bad enough I make a fool out of myself by getting drunk, but then I have to go and get my friends in trouble. What am I gonna do?"

Mrs. Clark pointed an accusing finger at him. "The first thing you can do is stop hurting yourself. You're your own worst enemy."

Pete continued to stare down. "But I can't help it. Sometimes I just don't think right. I start doing things and I don't know when to stop."

"If you'd listen to me you *would* know. I've

been telling you for years that all you need is more confidence in yourself, more self-esteem. You're a great guy, if only you'd believe it."

"No, I'm not. I'm no good — no good at all. I don't do nothing but cause trouble."

Tony patted him on the shoulder. "Yo, Pete. That's not true. You're the guy who makes us laugh, remember? If it weren't for you and your jokes, the garage would be a morgue. We need you."

"Yeah, like you need a hole in the head. Hey, maybe I should go and see a headshrinker."

Mrs. Clark harrumphed. "He'd only tell you the same thing I'm telling you, and charge you fifty dollars an hour besides. My advice is free, all you have to do is take it."

"But I'd prob'ly believe it more if I had to shell out the bread to hear it."

"What you need is a stabilizing factor, and some responsibility to keep you on your toes."

Tony laughed. "Like a nice girl to tie you down and tell you how great you are."

Pete jerked up as if he had been stabbed. "I don't want no girls. I cause enough trouble already without gettin' no girl in trouble, too. Besides, no girls will have me."

Mrs. Clark pushed the doughnuts closer to him. "What about the one who brought you home last night?"

Pete still had not touched his coffee. "Marion? Naw, I wouldn't touch her with a ten-foot pole. She's too nice to get mixed up with me."

"But she's the kind of girl who looks up to a man for his strong points."

"I ain't got no strong points." With a shaky hand, Pete brought the cup to his lips, tasted the coffee. "I'd give her nothing but grief."

Mrs. Clark took another doughnut, broke it in two, and put half back on the plate. "Some girls thrive on grief."

"She's right, Pete. You shouldn't be so hard on yourself."

Pete took the broken doughnut and dunked it in his coffee for so long that it fell apart. He took a bite out of the dry end still in his hand.

Mrs. Clark said, "And if you don't care about yourself, at least think about your mom and dad."

"Yeah, I know. They're pretty good folks. I like 'em a lot. I just wish I wasn't such a burden on 'em."

"Then make up your mind not to be." She nibbled at her doughnut. "Make a resolution today to turn over a new leaf."

"I do that all the time, but the next day my leaves fall off and get blown away. I need to turn over a whole new tree. But if I did, I'd prob'ly get eaten up by termites."

"How about some insect repellent?" Tony suggested.

"What I really need is a good, swift kick in the pants."

"Jack will be glad to give you that. It always works with my boys."

"My brother would do it, too, only it don't mean nothing. I just keep forgetting and fall back on my evil ways."

"You're too young to have formed evil ways. Now, finish your coffee and forget about it. Clean yourself up and let Tony take you out in the sun. The fresh air will do you good."

Pete finished his coffee at a single gulp, and chewed on the soggy dregs at the bottom. "Okay, Mrs. Clark. But I got one question for you. How come your hair is in curlers if you already been to church?"

She pulled her housecoat tighter, and laughed. "God already knows what I look like."

Chapter 20

"Tony! You got another goddamn phone call."

Tony put down his book and went into the kitchen. "Thanks, Dad."

On his way back to the television, Frank said, "And don't be all night. I'm expecting an important business call."

Tony put the instrument to his ear. "Hello?"

"Hi, Tony. How are you?"

"I'm fine. Who's this?"

"Don't you recognize my voice?"

"Uh, well, no. Not really."

"Well, we met at a party last week."

"Patty?"

"I've been waiting for you to call me."

"Well, uh, it's been a pretty hectic week. I've been working a lot of overtime. Besides, I don't even know your number."

"Well, I like that. I bet you didn't even try to find out."

"Well, I couldn't look it up in the phone book — I don't know your last name."

"You could have called Kate Dougherty. That's what I did."

"But, she doesn't know my number."

"No, but Ben does."

"Oh, yes. I guess I could have asked Ben to ask Kate. I just didn't know how to do it."

'It's simple. You just say, 'Ben, I want you to ask Kate for Patty's phone number.' "

Tony twisted the cord around his finger. "Yes, well, I guess I just didn't think of it. I've been so busy with work."

"All right, I'll forgive you this time."

"Gee, I'm sorry. I hope I didn't hurt your feelings."

"No, that's all right."

"Well, I'm sorry."

After a long silence, Patty said, "Listen, why don't we get together tomorrow and go for a walk, or something?"

"Well, gee, I'd like to but, well, I've got to work."

"But tomorrow's Saturday."

"I know, but there are people moving in on Monday and the fixtures still aren't hung. I think it's going to be a long day."

"Oh."

"But, uh, how about Sunday?"

"Well, I'm supposed to go to the Poconos with my mom and her boyfriend."

"Oh."

"But I can get out of it. I like the mountains, and the woods, but mostly I was going so I wouldn't have to spend the day around here with my grandmother."

"That's great."

"When do you want to pick me up?"

"Well, I don't know. What mass do you go to?"

"Nine or ten."

"Where?"

"St. Aloysius."

"Oh. I go to Epiphany. And I'll have to come home and change. How about if I pick you up around eleven thirty? We'll go out to Wissahickon Park."

"Want me to bring a couple of sandwiches?"

"Sure, that would be great. And I'll bring a thermos of ice tea."

"Okay. I'll see you on Sunday, then."

"Okay. Bye."

As soon as Tony hung the phone back on its cradle, it rang again. This time a gruff voice asked for his father. Holding his hand over the receiver, he yelled, "Dad, it's for you."

"Who is it?"

"Smitty."

Frank thumped into the kitchen. "Good, that's the call I've been waiting for." He took the phone and shouted into the mouthpiece, "Smitty, I want to put a hundred dollars on Red Nose in the fi'th . . . "

****

"You know, I've known Ben ever since we were kids. And he's been going steady with Kate ever since junior high. So how come we never met before?"

Clouds dodged around the sun so that the woods brightened and darkened at random intervals. Twigs and pieces of bark from towering oak trees littered the trail, crunching at every step. There was a slight chill in the air.

"I only started hanging out with her a little while ago. Kathy was always my best friend, and she knew Marion, who knew Kate slightly. Then, Kate and Marion joined the cheerleaders and became friends. And Kathy met Kate in history class. So, we started hanging out together. Although, Kathy goes out with a lot of boys so I don't see that much of her any more. I've been seeing more of Marion lately, because her parents let her have the car."

"You go out with them a lot, then?"

"Only on weekends. My grandmother won't let me go out during the week. She makes me stay home and study. Of course, I never do anyway. I just watch television."

Tony kicked a long limb off the rutted trail. "What about your mom?"

"She's not home that much. She works until the restaurant closes at two — they've got a bar, too — and sleeps late in the morning. Then, she's usually out on her days off. And she works a lot of weekends 'cause that's when the business is, and she gets the biggest tips."

"Do you ever see your father?"

"About once a year. He's got his own family now, so he doesn't have much time for me. I get a card for Christmas."

"So how did you end up with your grandmother?"

"I lived with my mom in a one-bedroom apartment, and since she had a lot of company, I got in the way a lot. She used to hate having me, so she'd always send me to my grandmother's — she's got two extra bedrooms. I spent so much time there that eventually she asked my mom to give her the support money from my father, for taking care of me."

"How old were you when you finally moved in with her?"

Patty lifted her feet over damp leaves, careful not to muss her brown, patent leather shoes. "Twelve, almost thirteen."

"I take it you don't like her?"

"She's a bitch. She never lets me do anything, and if I go out she makes me come home early. She always wants to know here I'm going and who I'm going out with and what I'm going to do. Then, when I come home, she sits me down and questions me about what I did. I hate her guts."

Tony raised his eyebrows. "That sounds definite."

Patty shrugged. "Anyway, my mother is going out with this guy who owns a brokerage firm, and has a place in the Poconos. Bob's pretty upset about it, because he thinks he owns her — "

"Who's Bob?"

"Oh, he's the guy who owns the restaurant she works for. Anyway, he doesn't like her going out with other men. But he doesn't want to get married, either. But then, neither does my mother." Patty smoothed down the sides of her dress, and buttoned up her sweater. "You know, I'm getting a little cold."

"Hey, I have an idea. Let's take this trail up to the top of that big boulder. You get a terrific view of the creek from there. And the climb will warm you up."

Patty looked up at the gray rock face. "I don't know. I'm not very good at climbing. And I'm afraid of heights."

"Aw, come on. It's not that steep." Tony started up the trail. "No, you go ahead. I'll watch." She folded her hands in front of her.

"Okay. I'll leave the pack here." Instead of going up the easy way, he climbed directly up the granite wall until he reached the flattened outcrop sixty feet above. "See, it's easy," he shouted down. "Come on up."

Patty shook her head. "I could never do that."

"Come up the trail. It zigzags back and forth."

"My grandmother will kill me if I scratch my shoes."

Tony stood right on the edge, his toes hanging over. "There's nothing to be afraid of."

"I don't like it."

No amount of coaxing would get Patty up the hill, so eventually he climbed back down. "Next time you'll have to wear your sneaks."

"I don't have any sneaks."

"Oh." Tony sauntered closer to the creek, overturned a rock. "Hey, a red eft." He picked up the creature and held it out for Patty to see.

"Yeech. Get it away."

Tony cradled it in his hand. "Sorry. But I thought you liked the outdoors, and nature. I mean, you were telling me how much you liked going to the Poconos with your mother and her boyfriend."

"I like seeing woods, and trees, and flowers — but bugs and worms make me sick."

"This isn't a worm. It's a salamander."

"I don't care. I still don't like them."

Tony put the creature on the moist ground, next to a rock. "Well, I know where there are some really pretty flowers. It's only another mile or so down the trail. We can go down by the creek and come back on the upper — "

"I don't think I can walk much more."

"Are you tired?"

"Yeah. I guess I'm not used to all this exercise."

"Okay, we don't have to go. We can see it some other time."

The patchy sky was growing continuously less patchy, and by now it was mostly cloudy. There was little chance of rain, but the temperature had dropped and the wind was picking up. Patty started shaking.

"You want to head back to the car?"

Patty looked up and smiled.

Tony took off his jacket and placed it around her shoulders.

"I don't like being uncomfortable." She hugged her middle as they walked.

"How about if we stop for a milkshake on the way home?"

"No, I'm too cold for that."

"Well, how about hot chocolate?"

"No, I couldn't. My mother says I've got to watch my weight or the boys won't want to go out with me."

Tony shrugged his shoulders. "I'll still go out with you."

Patty smiled. "You know. I think I like you."

"Well, I guess I like you, too."

"I had fun today. Could we do it again?"

"Well, sure. Why not?"

Chapter 21

"George, what's wrong?"

Tony stepped into the garage and quietly closed the door behind him. George sat alone, in a worn chair in the corner, staring at the ceiling. Tony pulled up an antiqued, wooden chair and sat on it backwards, with his arms resting on the chipped backrest.

George's flaccid face, concealed in successive folds of flesh, wore the expression of a mask, a caricature of disregard for emotional expression. His eyes were tinged with a glassy redness.

"What's the matter, George?"

He blinked rapidly and cleared his throat, but said nothing.

"Come on, George. Open up. What's wrong?"

His eyes did not waver. His mouth moved independently, like an isolated orifice not connected to the facial muscles. "I don't know." His voice was scratchy and indistinct.

"Want to talk about it?"

He shrugged his shoulders languidly.

Tony took a stab in the dark. "Is it about your mom?"

His head hardly moved to one side. But a pearly bead escaped from one eye and rolled halfway down his cheek before a pudgy fist wiped it away. His flaxen skin was whiter than ever.

"Well, what is it?"

George cleared his throat again, and squeaked, "Nobody likes me."

Tony sighed deeply. "Aw, George, come on. You know that's not true."

"They all hate me because . . . because . . . " He choked up again, and a tear glistened delicately in each round eye. " . . . because ... " His huge mass rocked back and forth as he buried his face in his hands.

Tony touched him softly on the shoulder. "George, nobody hates you . . . "

He might have touched the lever of a jack-in-the-box. George's body straightened suddenly, his legs shot out and kicked Tony's chair, his arm swung out and knocked his hand away. "Leave me alone, you. You hate me as much as the rest of them."

Tony massaged the pain in his wrist. "George, I don't hate you — even though you do some stupid things sometimes. Like hitting me when I'm only trying to help."

George bent forward so that his nose almost touched his knees, and cried into his bent arms. "Oh, yeah ... were you . . . trying to help . . . when you left . . . me here . . . and went to . . . the party? . . . Were you . . . trying to help . . . when you sneaked . . . out the back door . . . with Patty?"

"Oh, boy," Tony groaned, rolling his eyes.

"You're no better . . . than the rest . . . of them," George sobbed. Tony touched him again, but George shrank away, shouting, "Get away from me."

"George, I'm not trying to hurt you. All I want to do is help." He stared at his friend for several minutes while his heaving chest slowed down. "All right, now, let's try to talk this out. Now, let's start with your first statement: who is it who doesn't like you?"

"Nobody does. All you guys ever do is pick on me. And I ain't never done anything to you."

"Well, first of all, if I didn't like you I wouldn't be trying to talk with you. And what makes you think no one else likes you? Why would we all belong to the same fraternity if we didn't like you?"

George looked up, red-eyed. "Because my mom owns the garage, that's why."

"Oh, come on. There are other garages we could rent." George said nothing, so finally Tony bridged the silence. "George, I'll have to level with you. You don't go out of your way to be liked."

George's eyes flared angrily. "See, you don't like me either."

"George, I didn't say I didn't like you. I said you don't go out of your way to be liked. You say wrong things at the wrong time and at the wrong place. You're used to being bigger than all the other kids and bullying everyone around — but you're not a kid anymore. You can't keep pushing people around because there are too many people out there who can push back. You've got to learn to get along."

"What for? Nobody tries to get along with me."

"Stop talking in circles. That kind of attitude will get you nowhere. You can't expect people to treat you right if you don't treat *them* right. You've got to start somewhere."

"So why don't they try first?"

"Jesus Christ, George, cut it out and stop playing games. If you don't act like an adult, people aren't going to treat you like one — including the guys in the frat. They're growing up right past you."

"That's easy for you to say." George twisted his sleeve around to find a dry spot, and dabbed his eyes. "You're one of them."

"I'm not one of anyone. I'm just telling you what I know. Since you graduated high school, you've stagnated. You haven't made one new friend, or had any new experiences. You spend your days huddled up in the house. The only contact you have with the real world is when you hand a newspaper to some joker on Saturday night. Maybe that sounds like Petey putting you down, but it's not. It's just the plain truth. I'm laying out the truth, and you'd better learn to accept it."

There were no more tears in George's eyes. "Humph."

"You know why Pete picks on you? Do you? Well, I'll tell you. He picks on you because he doesn't respect you. That's right." Tony waved his arm indefinitely toward the door. "He's out there working every day, busting his ass in that gas station and getting his hands covered with grease, and you're in here reading magazines and dreaming about being a photographer — but not doing a damn thing about it."

"I do, too. I work in the darkroom, making prints."

Tony's voice grew louder. "That's a load of crap. You're copying nudes out of magazines. You're just playing, you're not learning a trade. But what do you do to earn your keep? Do you help your mother with the dishes? Do you take care of the house? You won't even use your own car if you can get someone else to drive you somewhere. You don't have a job, you brag about evading the draft, you talk about girls, but you won't spend a nickel on any of them."

"You should talk. You took my girl away."

"What do you mean by 'your girl'? You can't own a girl: slavery went out with the Civil War."

"You know what I mean." George huffed, and sat up a little straighter. "You knew I was trying to make it with Patty, so you ran off to the party without me and sneaked off with her."

"Now hold it right there, George. How was I supposed to know you were trying to make it with her when you're so tight-lipped about everything? You never said anything to me. And you never asked her out."

"She won't go out with me because of you."

"That doesn't make a bit of sense, and you know it. If she won't go out with you, it's because of *you*. And I didn't run off to the party just so I could steal Patty — I didn't even know she was going to be there. Besides, kidnapping's a federal offense."

"I suppose you didn't lock the door on me and take off without me. I suppose you didn't pull the ignition wire off my car. I suppose you didn't sneak her out the back door before I got there."

"I didn't know anything about the door or your ignition until later. And I didn't sneak her out the back door — she went of her own accord because Petey was drunk and needed help. And I had to take her home because she was riding with Marion. If you had come to the Clark's house the next day, you would have found all this out. And what were you doing at the party anyway when you should have been on the street corner selling papers?"

"Kate knew I had to work, that's why she had the party on Saturday night."

"George, parties are *always* on Saturday night. You're just making the whole thing up so it looks like everyone's against you."

"Yeah, well, that ignition wire didn't fall off by itself."

"All right, I can't dispute that. Someone must have done it. But it was only a joke, and the only reason they play jokes on you is because you get mad and they like to see you mad. Don't you think they play jokes on me, too? But you don't see me getting mad. I just laugh it off because it's so funny. No one's trying to make a fool out of me, just like they're not trying to make a fool out of you. You make a fool of yourself by not going along with the gag."

"But you made a fool out of me by taking off with Patty when you knew I wanted to go out with her."

"George, I said it once and I'll say it again: I did not know you wanted to go out with Patty because you didn't *tell* me you wanted to go out with her. How can you expect people to know things if you don't tell them? I'm not a mind reader, you know. Besides, she wouldn't go out with you anyway."

George looked up sharply, his face took on a pained expression. "Yeah, and why not?"

"Because you made a bad first impression on her, that's why."

"And what makes you so great?"

"Nothing." Tony leaned back in the chair, away from the wooden uprights he was leaning against. "I'm not great, I'm just me."

"And what's that supposed to mean?"

"It just means that, well, we all have our idiosyncrasies and I guess — "

"Our what?"

"Personal habits. Characteristics." When there was no look of comprehension on George's face, Tony explained, "Ben drives a fast car, Ray dresses nattily, Pete can work with his hands, and so on. They all have their own abilities, their own goals, their own ambitions. Ben's probably as good a mechanic as Pete, but to him it doesn't mean anything. He doesn't get any satisfaction out of knowing how to tune up a car or adjust a carburetor. But to Pete it's important. That's because they want different things out of life. By the same token, it takes different — mates — to make each one happy. Ben has Kate, and Pete has Marion. But Marion wouldn't any more go out with Ben than Kate would go out with Pete. You follow me so far?"

"I — guess so."

"All right. Now, it just happens that Patty happens to like me. Why, I don't know. Maybe it's because I have a Ford instead of a Pontiac, or because I have black hair instead of dirty blonde, or because its curly instead of straight. Who knows? Maybe she just doesn't like photographers. I don't know. But now ask yourself the same question. What are you looking for in a girl?"

"What do you mean?"

"Well, like, I want to have a family. So, I'd like a girl who wants to have children rather than one who wants a career. Maybe one who likes the mountains rather than the beach. You see? You're not just looking for a girl, but for a match. Patty and you just aren't matched. But that doesn't mean there's anything wrong with you — nothing, at least, that can't be overcome. You just need more confidence in yourself."

"That's easy for you to say. You always got good grades in school. You were on the track team. You were always the best pitcher in half ball. But I was never any good at those things. And they always laughed at me."

Tony leaned forward on the chair back, and peered deeply into George's eyes. "So what? Look how inexperienced I am now. I've never gone out with girls before — I mean, I've been with them at parties, or on the corner — but I never really went out with one before. And you were always dating. How many have you had here in the garage?" George simply glared. "See. Now, for the first time, I found a girl I like, and she likes me — I guess. I mean, there's a lot about her I'm not sure about, but we seem to be getting along. So, the next time you meet a girl, instead of trying to rip her clothes off, see if she's interested in photography."

"Oh, sure. Girls don't like photography."

"Well, what do they like? What do you think they like? You think they just want to go to bed with you because you're stronger than they are?" George took in a deep breath, swelled out his chest. "Stop sitting around and moping. Set up a goal and work toward it. Go out and meet the world on its own terms. Make something out of your life."

"See, you're just making fun of me."

"I'm not making fun of you. All I'm saying is that you have to act for yourself. You have to go out and embrace the world. It's not going to come to you. No one's going to come knocking on your door and say, 'George, you're the man for the job,' when no one knows what you can do. Find out what you want out of life, then go out and work toward it."

"I want to be a photographer."

"All right. But photographers aren't born. They have to be trained, just like geologists and car mechanics and accountants and jewelers. You need to know more than you can pick up by tinkering around a darkroom. You've got the opportunity, now use it."

George sniffled. He rolled forward and lumbered to his feet. "Forget it. Just leave me alone."

"George, think about it for a minute."

He reached the door to the laundry room. "I don't want to."

"Well, if you want to talk about it some more, let me — "

But George was already gone.

Chapter 22

"I'm Patty's mother," said the gorgeous woman who showed Tony into the house. At first glance she reminded him of an actress, or a model. Her auburn hair was beautifully coifed, her face daintily made up, her shapely body adequately pronounced through a sheer silk blouse and mid-length plaid skirt. She was tall enough not to need the high heels she was wearing, glamorous enough to outshine her diamond necklace and earrings.

"How do you do?"

She ignored the question, smiled broadly, and swept her hand back gesturing Tony in. "I'll call you Tony if you'll call me Helen. Mrs. MacDonald sounds so old and formal."

Tony stepped into a living room that was a picture out of *Better Homes and Gardens*. Gaily flowered wallpaper accented the deep-piled, gold-colored wall-to-wall carpet. The coffee and end tables were polished, modern, and seductive; the sofa and chairs sported soft pastels. The lamps were brass with ornate, braided shades, and the lights were set low.

"Thank you, uh, Helen. It's nice to meet you." On closer inspection, he saw streaks of gray in her hair that made her look neither old nor matronly, but huskily mature.

"I'm glad to meet you, too. It isn't often Patty has such well-mannered boyfriends. But didn't she tell you dinner would be informal? You didn't have to wear a suit."

Tony smiled, and tugged the jacket by the lapels. "Oh, it's not really a suit. It's just a sports coat."

"Anyway, it looks very nice." Helen held out her hand. "Why don't you let me hang it up for you?"

"Oh, thanks." He unhitched the center button and shook it off, then checked his shirt to make sure it was tucked in properly.

Helen hung the jacket in the dining room closet. "Just make yourself comfortable. Patty will be right down, and I've got work to do in the kitchen."

He said thanks, but she was already gone. He picked out a large blue, overstuffed chair, and sank into it so far that his knees were higher than his hips. A moment later, the kitchen door swung open and Helen came out with Patty's grandmother in tow. The yellow incandescent lights did little to soften the harsh lines in her face. Her hair was solid white and piled up on top of her head to add height to her short fleshy frame. Her eyes were stark, her nose square, her jaw angular. There was not a hint of a smile.

"So this is the young man Patty's been talking about," she croaked.

"Mother, this is Tony — Giovanni. Tony, this is Mrs. O'Brien."

Tony jumped to his feet. "Nice to meet you, Mrs. O'Brien."

Mrs. O'Brien tilted her head back and peered through her bifocals. "We've already met, young man. Or have you forgotten?"

Tony hesitated for a moment before stuttering, "Oh, sure. But we hadn't been introduced, so I figured that didn't really count. I didn't think you would remember me."

"How could I forget all the clatter you made when you kicked over the garbage can?" she replied haughtily.

"Gee, I'm sorry, Mrs. O'Brien. It was an accident. It was dark, and I guess I wasn't looking where I was going, and — "

"It's all spilt milk now, so let's not try to lap it up. But next time, you try to be more careful." Without waiting for a reply she turned and fled back into the kitchen.

Helen smiled and tilted her head. "I'd better go help her with the vegetables. You make yourself at home. Patty will be right down."

But Patty was not right down. Besides a single copy of *TV Guide* atop the mahogany set, there was nothing else to read. He studied the pastoral oil paintings several times, sat down, leafed through the book, then looked at the paintings again.

Ten minutes later Helen reappeared, wearing an apron. "Isn't Patty down here yet?" She sighed, shaking her head. She put her hand on the newel at the base of the stairs, and yelled up, "Patty, Tony's been here for fifteen minutes. The least you can do is keep him company." She turned to Tony and flashed perfect white teeth. "She just needs a little prompting. Sometimes we have to throw her out of bed in the morning to get her to school on time."

Tony just smiled.

Helen went back into the kitchen. A few minutes later, after Tony again inspected the paintings, Patty slowly descended the stairs, like a queen entering a ballroom.

She wore a plain, brown above-the-knee skirt with matching pumps. A pink sweater lay open across a sheer blouse that would have been more revealing than her mother's if it had not been for the wide ruffles. A gold chain hung about her slender neck, and a heart-shaped pendant lay against pink skin just above her breasts.

She shook her head so that her hair bounced slightly. "Hi. You're early."

Tony stood, and glanced at his watch. "Actually, I was just about on time."

"Oh, well, it doesn't matter," she shrugged. "We're not ready to eat yet anyway. We may as well sit down."

While Tony took a place on the sofa, Patty turned on the television, adjusted the volume, and sat next to him. She seemed captivated by the commercials.

"Are you getting much homework now that graduation is so close?"

Patty looked away from the screen. "About the same. But I don't bother doing most of it because I know it won't matter. The nuns are just trying to be mean."

"But, don't you have to take finals?"

"Oh, sure, but they're going to graduate us all anyway, so what difference does it make?"

"Well, the grades might make a difference when you apply to business school."

She stared at the program as she talked. "Oh, I don't think I want to go to school any more. I'd rather wait on tables and collect tips."

Tony folded one leg over the other. "Are you going to get that job in the restaurant your mother works for?"

"Sure. I can have it any time I want it. Bob's trying to get me to work weekends now, but I'm too busy."

"Well, couldn't you do both? I mean, couldn't you go to business school and wait on tables on the side? That way, you could do whichever one you liked the best."

"Oh, that's sounds exhausting. Besides, I'd have to take math courses, and I'm no good at math. At the restaurant I don't have to add up the figures. The cashier does that."

"Well, I don't know. I think when it comes to figures, you're pretty good."

Patty glanced away from the screen, and smiled vacuously. "I just don't know why I have to take trigonometry to work in an office. I don't even know what it's used for. And I hate typing anyway."

"Well, trig is useful in science, for making calculations. But when you get into things like radioactive decay, or . . . "

"Oh, wait a minute. I want to see this."

There were cheers from the television set, and someone was about to win a great deal of money. After the question was asked, Helen came in untying her apron.

"Oh, you're finally dressed. Dinner's all ready. I just hope Bob gets here soon or we'll have to start without him. It would serve him right for being late."

Tony looked up, and smiled. But Patty never took her eyes off the screen. The doorbell rang. Helen rolled the apron into a ball and tossed it into a chair. "There he is now."

The man she let in was big all around, but especially where he wore his belt. Even his grin was big. He had a shock of curly, graying hair above a round face, making him look distinguished rather than old. He took more than the earnings from his restaurant.

He kissed Helen lightly on the mouth, then swung a red bouquet from behind his back. "Roses for my little rose. Umm, the food smells delicious. And I'll bet it tastes even better."

Helen took the flowers, sniffed them. "We're having your favorite."

"You're my favorite, Cutie." He gave her the roving eye.

"What did I tell you about flattery?"

"That it would get me everywhere — as long as it was followed with diamonds."

"Stop showing off — we have company. Now give me your coat." After he removed his jacket, he looked even larger. "Bob, this is Tony. Tony, Bob."

Tony stood.

"Well, glad to meet you, Tony." The hand that grasped Tony's ground his knuckles together. "I've heard a lot about you. Heh, heh, heh."

Tony had to look up half a foot to meet Bob's eyes. "I hope it's not all bad."

"Oh, the ladies in this house wouldn't say a bad word about anyone, even if it were true. You're the electrician, right?"

"Well, I'm working as an electrician, but I'm not a mechanic yet. I have to go to school first."

"Always go to school when you have the chance. Education is a rare opportunity. I regret that I didn't go to college when I was a young man. Now I'm too old to learn."

"You're not too old to learn," Helen interrupted. She turned off the television as she walked by. "You're just too old to change. Look, why don't you two carry on your conversation at the table? We're just about ready to serve the food."

"Mom, I was watching that."

"You come into the kitchen and help us serve, and don't talk back to me." Helen hung up Bob's jacket on a hook in the closet, and took the porcelain vase off the dining room table. Patty grudgingly followed her into the kitchen. "You two sit at that end of the table, Bob on this side and Tony on that side."

"I guess we've got our orders. Heh, heh, heh. We'd better not cross the ladies up." He pulled out his chair and filled it with his buttocks.

The table was set with delicate china, real silverware, and two candelabras. "I understand you own a restaurant," Tony said.

"The Golden Lily. And she's been golden to me. First thing you have to know about a restaurant is to have a good chef. You don't have a chef, you don't have a restaurant."

Helen came through the swinging door with a tray of water-filled glasses, and the dozen long-stemmed roses in the vase. Patty was right behind her with condiments and napkins. "Put them down over there. Bob, do you want some coffee now?"

"No, I'll wait till after dinner. Oh, my gosh, I almost forgot. There's a bottle of wine in my coat pocket."

"Mother's uncorking it now."

"But that shouldn't be done until you're ready to drink. The freshness must be preserved."

"This isn't a restaurant, Bob, so we'll do things our way. Patty, don't leave the napkins there, place them under the forks."

"Heh, heh, heh. That's my girl." Bob turned to Tony. "Let them get their way once in a while — it makes 'em think they're important. You treat them right, they'll treat you right." He winked, then said to Helen. "Isn't that so?"

Patty retreated into the kitchen.

"Bob, don't go telling him things like that. You'll give us a bad reputation."

"Heh, heh, heh. No more than you deserve." To Tony, he added, "But all kidding aside, these girls are the best cooks around. I tried to hire Mrs. O'Brien, but she said she was married once and swore she'd never work for another man. I tried to coax her recipes out of her, but they're old family secrets that only get passed down to the womenfolk." He jabbed a fat finger toward the kitchen. "You hang onto that young one there because some day she'll end up with all the secret recipes."

Patty came in at the tail end of Bob's soliloquy. She held a wicker basket with a giant loaf of steaming French bread. "Where do you want this?"

Helen put down the last of the napkins. "Right there." She went into the kitchen, and came out a moment later with another tray, this one laden with bowls of hot soup. "Take these, Patty."

One by one she put the five bowls on the table.

"Thank you, dear." Bob sniffed in the fragrance of the steam. "She'll be a heck of a woman someday. Won't you, Patty?"

She made a pained expression, but her mother wagged a finger at him. "Bob, stop embarrassing her. You know how shy she is. Now you just sit there and eat your soup." While Patty sat down next to Tony, Helen lit the candles.

Bob tore off a huge chunk of bread. "With two lovely hostesses hovering around, it's hard to decide what to eat first."

Helen grimaced. "Bob, stop it. Now you're embarrassing *me*."

"And where's the coordinator of this banquet?" he said in a raised voice.

From the other side of the door came, "I'll be there as soon as I get the range cleaned off." A moment later Mrs. O'Brien appeared and took her seat at the head of the table. She nodded curtly. "Hello, Bob."

"Why, hello, Mom. This soup is wonderful. Just what I need at the restaurant to draw in the customers."

"Well, that's the only bowl you're getting, and the only way it's leaving this house is in your stomach."

Bob grinned at Tony. "You see what I mean. Well, what special delights have you cooked up for us tonight?"

Mrs. O'Brien lifted her spoon. "You just eat your soup and when I put it on the table you'll find out."

"Holding out on us to the end. Heh, heh, heh."

The soup was thick chowder, light on the potatoes and vegetables, thick with chunks of lobster, crab meat, and more than one kind of fish. "Delicious, delicious, delicious," said Bob, slurping.

"And cozy, too," Tony added.

Bob leaned forward. "You'd better watch out. They roped me in with the same technique."

"Bob's always making out as if we're a house full of vampires, out to get him," Helen said. "Isn't that right, Patty?"

Patty wrinkled her nose. She had hardly touched her soup. "I guess so."

"If there's one thing I found out long ago, it's that men are not only harmless, they're malleable."

Bob said, "Mold me, baby. Mold me."

"You just have to know how to manage them."

"If I said you had a nice body would you hold it against me?"

"You just concentrate on your food and stop talking nonsense."

When the soup course was done, Helen and Mrs. O'Brien brought out the rest of the meal: a roast beef that was browned to perfection, mashed potatoes, string beans and yellow corn, and the bottle of wine, on ice, with five crystal glasses. "This is as lovely as those who serve it."

"Cut it out, Bob."

"Let the man ramble on," Mrs. O'Brien said. "I don't mind being reminded I have a beautiful daughter. The reflection makes me look good."

"You look good without a reflection."

"Bob, any time Helen refuses your compliments, you just pass them on to me. At my age I don't get them any more."

Bob's overworked utensils did not slow down. "A woman of such rare talents should receive compliments all the time. Why, if Patty wasn't sitting right there next to you, I would find it hard to believe you were old enough to be a grandmother." He lifted his wine glass. "A toast to the youngest looking grandmother in Philadelphia — no, in Pennsylvania."

Glasses clattered around the table. Tony sipped slightly at the dry wine, but noticed that Helen drained her glass at a gulp. Bob refilled it immediately.

"Thank you, Bob. I like to hear it even if it isn't true. And if Patty were more aggressive, I could easily be a great-grandmother."

"Mother, please, you'll embarrass her. Or Tony."

"Well, it's true. I was married and had Patrick long before I was as old as Patty. And you were only a little older when you started your family."

"What a mistake that was. I was young and foolish. It would never happen that way if I had it to do over again."

"You just happened to get tied up with the wrong man," Bob said, through a mouthful of roast beef. "If I had met you then instead of getting hitched up with Marjorie, you'd have been a mother five times over by now."

"That's what *you* think. I've raised one daughter, and that's all I want to raise. Now I want to have the fun I should have had when I was younger. And if you think I'm going to have more children at my age, you can forget it. The next diaper I change will by my grandchild's — when Patty feels like getting around to it. And don't rush it on my account."

Patty smiled weakly, and picked at her food.

Bob leaned toward Mrs. O'Brien. "I'm trying to talk her into having another family."

Helen slapped him playfully on the leg. "First you have to talk me into marrying you. And even if you did, I know about birth control, now."

Mrs. O'Brien slapped her spoon on the table. "Helen, I think this conversation is getting a little out of hand. There are ears too young for this kind of talk."

"I was just saying that Bob is a conniver."

"He's also good looking and affectionate. Why, if I were twenty years younger I'd go after him myself."

"And if I were twenty years older I'd be courting you instead of your daughter. In fact, if Helen doesn't watch out, I may run off with you anyway."

Helen wagged a finger at him. "And if I catch you running around with another woman I'll fix it so you'll never have any children — and you'll be singing soprano, too."

"Heh, heh, heh." Bob laughed without ever missing a chew. He refilled Helen's wine glass with a free hand. "Great family they got here. Tony, how long have you known this little girl?"

"Well, less than a month."

"Hmmmmn, that's long enough. I only knew my first wife for ten days before I proposed to her."

"And that was a mistake," Mrs. O'Brien snapped. "If you'd taken your time, you'd have seen she wasn't fit to marry."

"Mother!"

"I'm only repeating what he's admitted himself. And those two boys of his would have been better off with a decent mother to take care of them."

"Well, you don't have to say it to his face."

"I wouldn't say it behind his back."

Bob scraped his plate clean, looked around for something else to put onto it. "She's right, you know. Those two boys are the wildest pair I've ever seen. Racing cars and motorcycles. Always picking them up at the police station. I can't control them — never could. They never do anything really wrong, mind you, it's just, well, they could use a steadying influence — "

"Forget it." Helen tipped the wine bottle and filled her glass. "I'm not going to take care of your brats. They need some real discipline, the kind you can't give them. Why don't you get them to join the army?"

Another slice of roast beef and a large spoonful of mashed potatoes found their way to Bob's plate. "I've been hoping they'd get drafted, but Uncle Sam just hasn't gotten around to them. You know, Mrs. O'Brien, this roast is the most tender piece of meat I've had in a long time — even in my own restaurant. Is this the way they cook it in the old country?"

"That's the way my mother taught me to make it." She stood and picked up her empty plate and utensils, and the vegetable bowls. "If you want any more of this you better take it now."

Bob dumped the leftover corn and string beans onto his plate. "No sense letting it go to waste."

"You can help, too, Patty," Mrs. O'Brien said.

The table was soon swept clean and coffee and desert dishes brought out. When they were alone, Bob said to Tony, "You know, I've got this place down the shore that needs a little fixing up, and I was wondering if you'd be interested in doing a little electrical work on the side . . ."

Chapter 23

Like most vacation places, Bob Windsor's Long Beach Island house needed maintenance badly. Even in the fading twilight, Tony could see peeling paint and loose boards, mute evidence of the ravages suffered by the salt air and the rasping, wind-blown sand.

Bob climbed out of the Volkswagen bus and walked around the front to help Helen down the high step. "I seldom come here in the winter, so the place gets a little run down."

Helen clutched her purse and stepped on the gravel lightly, careful not to break her high heels. "The island is so dismal. The beaches are cold and lonely, the streets are empty of tourists, and the local people stay cooped up in their houses. That's when I appreciate the gaiety of Philadelphia, with the neon lights and bustling mobs and evening entertainment."

"Heh, heh, heh. Yes, we spend all winter hustling so we can come down here and relax in the summer. Then it takes the whole season to get the place in shape. By that time, it's winter again."

Patty, carrying a bagful of groceries, followed her mother up the creaking wooden steps to the porch. Tony dragged out the suitcases. "I sure hope I have the right material for the job. I've never done a hundred amp service by myself before."

"Heh, heh, heh. You'll do just fine. Just have a little more confidence in yourself."

"Well, I'll try."

Bob unlocked the front door, then had to kick it open because the wood had swelled against the jamb. He groped across the room until he found a lamp, and turned it on. "I'm gonna have to get you to put a switch in here, too."

Helen and Patty filed into the musky room.

Tony hauled in the suitcases and kicked the door closed with the back of his foot.

Bob swept some faded newspapers off the kitchen table. "Put the groceries here while I go turn on the hot water heater."

"My is this place dusty." Helen ran a red-nailed finger across the tabletop. "This is worse than the apartment. Honestly, Bob, I don't know how you survive as a bachelor."

"What do you mean? This place has personality. Now put things away wherever you can find a spot, while I go turn on the water heater. I'll be right back."

Tony deposited the suitcases in the living room and went about turning on lights. The mismatched furniture was old and scratched, the upholstery worn, the carpet threadbare. Bob was back in a moment.

"I turned on the furnace, too. This place could use a little heating up."

"Mmmm. I didn't know you bought Hershey bars, too."

"Put that down!" Helen took the candy away from her daughter. She swung open the refrigerator door and stowed the eggs, milk, and cold cuts on the rusty shelves. "How can you even think of food after that meal we had?"

Bob reached behind the counter, grabbed an extension cord, dragged it across the room, and plugged it into a wall outlet. The refrigerator light came on, and the compressor started humming. He tucked the cord under the loose baseboard. "That's why I always eat at the Sand Blast."

Helen wagged a finger at him. "You eat there because you don't have to pay for it, don't tell me."

"Heh, heh, heh. Sometimes I think you know me too well. Place don't make me much money," (to Tony, in aside, "I'm a silent partner.") ". . . operating only six months out of the year, but they serve good food. Patty, turn on that faucet and see if anything comes out. I turned the water on a couple weeks ago."

Patty turned up her nose as the fluid gurgled out of the spigot. "It's a little brown."

"Heh, heh, heh. Just let it run a minute or two. It'll clear up. Then put some on the stove. I can use another cup of coffee to warm these old bones."

"I need a drink, that's what I need." Helen pulled a bottle out of the shopping bag, then rustled around inside it. "Bob, you didn't buy any tonic. You know I can't drink gin without tonic."

"Here it is, Mother." Patty filled the saucepan and put it on the stove, then handed the bottle to her mother. "I put it on the counter."

She swiped it out of Patty's hand. "Thank

God. And you wouldn't be so cold if you had come to the house first and turned on the heat, instead of going right to dinner."

"But, Honey, I've got to take care of this stomach of mine." He took hold of his paunch and shook it playfully. "I don't perform too well when it's growling."

Helen rinsed out some glasses and mixed a drink. "You don't perform well, anyway."

Bob gave her a loud peck on the head. "That's my girl, always making jokes."

"Who's joking?"

"Heh, heh, heh." Bob took some cups down from the cabinet, and found the coffee.

"Hey, does this television work?" Patty pulled the knob, but nothing happened.

"It takes a minute for the tubes to warm up," Bob said. "Do you kids want some coffee?"

"I could go for a cup of hot chocolate," said Tony, rubbing his hands. He felt a slight chill. He found the loose packets and broke one over a cup.

Patty made a face. "This is only a black and white set."

Helen drained her glass and mixed another gin and tonic. "You're lucky you got one at all."

Bob filled Tony's cup, then his own. "Patty, do you want hot chocolate?" She adjusted the vertical control knob.

"Okay," she whined.

"And don't park yourself in front of the television. I taught you better manners than that when you've got a guest."

"Mother, I only want to see what's on."

"That's all right. I don't mind." Tony sipped his too hot chocolate.

"I swear, I don't know what makes that girl so lazy."

Bob hugged Helen from behind. "She's young yet. She just needs a little time to grow up." He winked at Tony. "Isn't that right?"

Tony shrugged, and glanced away.

Helen pulled free from Bob's grip. "When I was in high school, I was already engaged and working two jobs besides. And I worked right up till the time Patty was born. Then I went back as soon as she didn't need me for a milk carton. She watches too much television."

Bob took his coffee into the living room, and picked out a worn easy chair facing the set. "Let the kids have their fun. After all, you're only a kid once. Too soon you have to grow up and face the world on its own terms. Then you have the rest of your life for work."

Helen settled down on the couch, glass in hand. "Well, that much is true. I've spent my whole life working and it didn't get me anywhere."

Tony brought two cups of hot chocolate into the living room, and handed one to Patty. She glanced from Tony to her mother. "I would have made it as soon as a commercial came on."

"That's all right." Tony sat on the floor next to her. He picked up a deck of cards from the shelf on the television stand, and shuffled them absently. He started a game of solitaire.

When their drinks were all gone, Bob said, "Hey, kids, Helen and I are going to take a little walk down to the beach. Want to come?"

Tony looked at Patty. She wrinkled her lip and looked away. Tony said, "We haven't finished our hot chocolate yet."

"And I didn't bring a winter coat. It's cold out."

Helen sloshed more gin into her glass. "You can borrow mine. I've got my love to keep me warm." She huddled close to Bob.

He put his arm around her shoulders. "Heh, heh, heh."

"I don't want to go," Patty insisted.

"Okay, you kids keep the home fires burning. We won't be long."

"Can I take my glass?" asked Helen, as Bob guided her out the door.

Tony could hear her cooing and giggling for a while. "Is she always like that when she drinks?"

"I don't know. She's always drinking." After several minutes of watching television, Patty went on, "How about some gin?"

Tony was taken aback. "What?"

"Rummy. Do you know how to play gin rummy?"

A smile swept across his face. "Oh, sure." He shuffled the cards and started dealing. "For a minute I thought you meant — "

"I know."

Tony squinted. "You know, sometimes I don't think I understand you."

Patty's curls shook as she laughed. "That's just part of the feminine mystique. Men aren't supposed to understand women. That would take all the fun out of it."

"Out of what?"

"Being a woman. My mother says that women are supposed to never let a man know what's coming — to sort of keep him off balance."

"And how do you do that?"

For an answer Patty leaned over the dealt cards and kissed him full on the mouth. She pulled back slightly until their lips separated, then kissed him again, lingeringly. They kissed that way until Tony got so uncomfortable that he had to move. Then they lay on the floor and, guided by an instinct older than mankind, ground their bodies together. The cards, and the world, were forgotten. Tony's hands felt the softness of Patty's body beneath her clothes, and roved with a will of their own until —

A loose board creaked on the wooden steps, a deep voice mumbled in the darkness, a high pitched laugh struck a note of disdain, there was a thump at the front door which stubbornly refused to budge.

Tony and Patty rolled apart. Tony picked up the cards and started shuffling. Patty smoothed her clothes and hair and took a seat in front of the television.

Helen sang out, "Hi, we're back," as she tripped over the threshold.

"Careful." Bob kept his arms tight around her. His face reposed in its perpetual smile. "The beach was too windy, so we went to the Pickle Barrel for a warm-me-up. Heh, heh, heh."

Helen burped. "They make the best hot buttered rum than anyplace in the world."

"But, Honey, you haven't drunk everyplace in the world."

She fell into a chair like a limp dishrag. "I've drunk in enough of 'em to know. God, am I tired."

"Heh, heh, heh. Well, I'd better get you undressed and into bed before you fall asleep right here in the living room. I'll have a devil of a time if I have to carry you to bed."

"Thash all right. I like being carried off to bed — eshpecially by big strong men."

"Heh, heh, heh. Well, upsadaisy." Bob picked her up by the armpits and lifted her to her feet. Helen's legs seemed like rubber, and kept bending under her weight. Together, the two of them swayed to the bedroom.

"Patty," Helen called from the open doorway. "You come in here and get your things out of the suitcase and take them into your own room."

"Okay, mother." Patty pursed her lips at Tony, and said in a low voice, "I'd better go."

"Sure."

Tony wandered into the front bedroom, and got ready for bed. The house grew quiet, and soon all he could hear was the wind whistling through the cracks in the windowpanes, an occasional late night driver, and Helen's soft moans. He drifted off to sleep.

Chapter 24

Tony took the glass-encased electric meter from under his raincoat, and hunched over it momentarily while he removed the cardboard protector from the meter socket. It was difficult to handle because of the thick, black rubber gloves. The driving rain pelted his back.

He shook raindrops off his hood and peered into the socket. He lined up the prongs with the cadmium coated forks, and quickly jammed the meter in place; a small arc leaped from the contact point. Then he wiggled the meter all the way onto the prongs until the rim was flush with the metal box.

"Try it now," he shouted.

He could hear the breakers clicking as Bob switched them on in the utility room. Shrugging off the rain, Tony snapped the retaining ring in place; now the electric company could install the tamper seal. He ran inside, to be greeted by darkness.

Bob appeared in the dungeonlike atmosphere, flashlight in hand. "Nothing's working."

"Let me see." Tony took the flashlight and picked his way into the utility room. He kicked aside the old fuse box and peered into the newly secured panel. The wires were neatly formed. He threw each breaker off, then back on again. "Try that switch."

Bob flipped it several times, but the darkness remained. "I sure hope you don't have to go out in that rain to check those connections on the roof."

"So do I," he said for Bob's benefit. He had no intentions of doing so; he knew that the copper bugs were bolted tight under numerous wraps of friction tape. The problem lay elsewhere. "Oh, no."

"What's the matter?" Bob's concern was unconcealed.

Tony gripped a large plastic handle at the top of the panel and shoved it up. It banged into place like a rifle bolt, and instantly the lights flared on brilliantly. "You forgot to turn on the main."

Bob wiped imaginary sweat off his forehead. "Heh, heh, heh. You really had me worried there for a minute."

"You really had *me* worried." Tony flicked off the flashlight and stuck it in his pocket. He spent a couple minutes tightening the panel trim with a screwdriver.

"The lights are on," came Helen's voice. "Everything came on all at once."

"Okay, Honey, we'll be done soon." Bob kicked the old electrical box and ancient, rotting cables further out of the way. To Tony, he added, "That old fuse box never had a main."

Tony tightened the last bolt. "That's all right. It's done now." He slammed the panel lid shut and dropped the screwdriver into the toolbox.

"Heh, heh, heh. I knew you could do it."

"Well, that makes one of us," Tony laughed.

Bob helped him carry the tools and leftover material to the Volkswagen bus. They threw everything inside, then ran up the stairs to the warmth and dryness of the living room.

"You did it," Patty smiled.

"Yes, it went easier than I thought."

"I told you he could do it," Bob said. "This

boy can do anything he sets his mind to."

Helen handed them bath towels. "Will the heat come back on now?"

Tony doffed his raincoat and wiped his hands and face. "The thermostat should have kicked in right away."

"I could sure use a cup of coffee to warm up." Bob rubbed his hands briskly. "And maybe a little kiss would help."

"There's heat coming out of the register," Patty called out.

Helen grimaced and flew toward the kitchen. "I'll put some water on."

Bob followed her with his eyes. "This place will warm up in no time. The heat's only been off a couple hours."

"You know, I could use some coffee, too."

Patty smiled. "Cream and sugar?"

"One teaspoon of sugar and plenty of cream."

"Okay." Patty padded into the kitchen.

Bob stuck out his hand and pumped Tony's. "I don't know how to thank you. You did a helluva job. Better than any of the local men could have done, and with a lot less fuss, too. Maybe next time you can take care of some other things that need to be done around here. I pay cash on the barrelhead."

Tony ruffled his curly hair, then sat in a chair facing the front window. "What do you need?"

"Well, the first thing is a switch by the front door, so you don't have to grope across the room in the dark. I can't tell you how many times I've tripped over that hassock, or banged my shin on the coffee table."

Tony studied the job with a professional air. "Well, I could probably fish some wires up the wall and into the attic, and tie it in with one of the receptacles. Then, whatever lamp is plugged into it will work off the switch."

"Hey, that would be just fine. And, you know, I could use a few more outlets, especially one behind the refrigerator, so I wouldn't have to drag that extension cord all over the place, and be tripping over it, too. Somebody's going to get hurt on it someday."

"Well, I don't have the material with me — "

"Hell, no. I didn't mean to do it today. You've done enough work for one weekend. I always say you have to have some fun in life or else it's not worth living. We'll take the rest of the weekend off and talk about it some other time. Let's go climb to the top of Old Barney, or pick up some knickknacks at the *Lucy Evelyn*."

"In the rain?" Helen whined, bringing in the coffee.

"And afterwards we can go to dinner. My treat. Tomorrow we'll walk along the beach and collect shells."

"Don't you ever relax?"

Patty appeared with a tray of sandwiches and condiments. "Will you buy me something?"

"Heh, heh, heh. I'll buy something for everyone. Isn't it just great to be alive?"

****

Bob parked the Volkswagen bus in front of his Main Line home. Helen twisted around in the front. "Tony, I'm going to stay at Bob's tonight so I won't have to take a bus to work. Would you mind taking Patty home?"

"No, not at all. It's not even out of the way."

"You want to come in for some coffee?" Bob offered.

"Well, I've got to go to work tomorrow. How about you, Patty?"

She shrugged in the semidarkness. "I've got school."

Bob pushed open the door and the overhead lights went on. "Okay, I'll help you with your tools and things. And don't forget the bag with the cedar jewelry." Winking at Tony, he added, "Keep 'em happy with the small things." He packed a sheaf of bills into Tony's hand, payment for the work and material. "There's a little extra in there, too." Tony started to protest, but Bob held up his hand. "It was well worth it."

Tony accepted the money without counting it. He and Patty said their goodbyes, then drove slowly out of the residential district. It was quite different from South Philly, where the houses walled the sidewalks like brick cliffs, and marble steps reached out like tongues. He and Patty sat quietly, side by side, with the small brown bag between then. Tony found a parking spot right in front of her house. The curtains were tightly drawn, and no light leaked out around the edges. In comparison to the brightly lit windows in the houses on both sides, it looked foreboding.

"Well, thanks for — everything. I really like the jewelry." She leaned over and gave Tony a peck on the cheek. "I really had a good time."

Tony was covered with goose bumps. He swung around and threw his arm over the seat. "Well, look, do you think we could, uh, get together sometime this week? Or will your grandmother let you out?"

"Oh, pooh on her. I can go out if I want to. My mother likes you, so she'll tell my grandmother it's all right if I go out with you, school or no school."

The paper bag crinkled between them as they drew closer, and kissed. Thirty minutes later, Tony broke the silence with, "How about if I call you — tomorrow night?"

"Okay."

Tony rubbed his hand along her back, then across her neck. Fifteen minutes later, he said,

"You know, it's getting late."

Their lips met. After ten minutes, Patty said, "I guess you're right." And later, "I really should be going."

After a few minutes, when they stopped for a breath and just sat hugging, Tony whispered, "Maybe we'd better not get started again."

"You're crazy. But that's why I like you."

When they got to the front door, her grandmother was waiting for them.

****

"So how did the job go?" Frank looked up from the eleven o'clock news. "Did I line it out for you right? Did you have all the material?"

Tony deposited his suitcase at the base of the stairs. "Well, it went all right, except that I had to make the hot splice on the roof in the rain."

"Don't mean nothing, as long as you're not grounded. You didn't have no load on the circuits, did you? I told you to turn everything off, then you don't have to work nothing hot."

"I did. I turned everything off, then disconnected the main. It's just that I didn't have a ladder, so I had to lie on the roof to make the splice. I was just afraid the screwdriver would slip and I would short it out. Even with the gloves I could feel a tingling when I touched the hot wires."

"You kids today make me laugh. I used to hook up services in the snow, in freezing cold weather with my bare hands. I don't worry about getting a little shock."

"Well, it was my first time . . . "

"When I was an apprentice I used to make splices from aluminum ladders. But I was fast. I used to do the whole job in four hours, and I had to lay up the cable myself, and put all the lag bolts in by hand with a star drill. I didn't have no electric drill."

"Well, I may not have done it that fast, but as least I did it right." Tony bent and picked up his suitcase. "Do you want me to put the drill in the shop with the extra material?"

Frank was already engrossed in the news. "No. Take it back to Randy — no, take it to Eliot. He's always complaining he don't have enough tools on his job. That should shut him up."

"Okay." Tony climbed the stairs and tiptoed quietly into his room. Robby was asleep and, judging by the closed door in the front room, so was his mother. He threw his suitcase on the bed. A moment later, Kitty leaped down from the window sill. "Hello, cat."

Tony picked her up and rubbed his nose in her soft fur. She licked his face with a sandpapery tongue. He was sitting at his desk with Kitty in his lap when he noticed a letter waiting for him. It was from the Selective Service Board. Was this a call for another physical, or just his change of classification? He slipped a letter opener under the flap and removed the single sheet of paper. It was a preprinted document with his name and address typed in the upper left corner, and it purported to be from the President of the United States. It started:

"Greeting:

You are hereby ordered for induction into the Armed Forces of the United States, and to report at Armed Forces Exam. & Induction Station, 401 No. Broad St., Phila., 8, Penna. on June 8, 1966, at 7:30 AM for forwarding to an Armed Forces Induction Center."

He was in the Army now.

Chapter 25

"Hi, Grandmom. This is Tony."

"Well, land sakes, Honey, what are you doin' callin' on the telephone? I didn't hardly recognize your voice but I knew it had to be you 'cause nobody else would be callin' me Grandmom. Robby isn't old enough to use the phone, is he? And this is way past his bedtime. My, this *is* a surprise. Are you callin' all the way from Philadelphia? Well, I suppose you must be. Mercy me, Tony, you really put a shock in me, hearin' your voice when I was 'spectin' to hear Cousin Gertrude callin' to tell me 'bout her new drapes and ready to talk my ear to a frazzle. Well, what's the matter, that you should call this hour of the night? We're use'ly in bed by ten o'clock, you know, but tonight we went to see your Uncle Joe and Aunt May and got so busy talkin' we plum forgot the time. Aunt May had to go in the hospital, you know, and have a little operation. But now she's home and feelin' fine and the doctor has given her a clean bill o' health so it looks like she'll make it to her golden weddin' anniversary after all. I just know Cousin Gertrude was tryin' to call all night and I'm glad we were out 'cause she can just go on and on 'bout nothin' and I didn't feel like listenin' to her nonsense tonight 'cause I've been weedin' in the garden all day and I'm plum tuckered out. Is ever'body all right at home, or has there been an accident or something?"

"No, everyone's fine."

"Well, I'm glad to hear it. You know, I was sayin' to your grandfather just t'other day that with the way things are goin' on in the world you just never know when something terrible is goin' to happen to you, or to somebody in your family. Why, just t'other day Cousin Bertie was out drivin' around in her car — just shoppin', mind you, not for anything in particular, 'cause she's old and don't get out'n the house much, so she likes to go shoppin', even though she don't never buy anything — well sir, she just looks and finds things she likes and thinks about how nice it would be to have enough money to buy them, but she's not one to splurge. Anyway, just t'other day she went over to that new mall and this man was backin' out'n a parkin' space — you know how they have them lines painted so you know where you're s'posed to put your car so's it don't take up too much space — well, he wasn't lookin' where he was goin' and he backed right into the car in front of Cousin Bertie and without so much as a by your leave he took off before the man who was hit could get out'n his car and nobody got his license number or anything and the poor man was left there with his bumper all smashed in and nothing to show for it. So I'm just glad ever'body's okay 'cause you know sometimes I worry 'bout you, and little Robby, livin' in that big city with all them city folks who don't bother to give you the time o' day when you ask a decent question. Ever'body just rushes around like they was goin' to a fire, or runnin' away from the police. I never saw anything like it in all my born days. Well, here's your grandfather just comin' up from the basement. You know we been havin' a cold spell here and he had to start up the furnace again 'cause he's feelin' a little under the weather lately and his bones get cold easy an' bother him, and we're already almost out'n coal and we wasn't figurin' on buyin' any more this year 'cause it would just sit there for the whole summer doin' nothin'. Well, Honey, I'm sure glad ever'body's doin' fine and I'll just get off now and let you talk to your grandfather. You be good now, and make sure you say hello to your mom and dad for me. Okay, here his is. 'Bye now, Honey."

"Goodbye, Grandmom."

"Tony?"

"Hi, Grandpop. How's everything?"

"Pretty much the same, I guess, 'cept for this cold spell. Is it cold in Philadelphia, too?"

"It's been kind of chilly, and it's been raining off and on for the past few days. That makes it feel colder than it really is."

"Well, we haven't had any rain, but it's sure been threatenin'. I s'pect we'll have some by mornin'."

"Gee, I guess you won't be able to do any outside painting, will you?"

"No, but I'd just as soon take a day or two off, even though there's some inside work I could do. I'm gettin' kinda old and don't want to work ever' day any more."

"Yes, Grandmom was saying you weren't feeling well."

"Oh, it's nothing much. I'm just slowin' down a mite, is all. I'm not as spry as I used to be and every once in a while movin' that ladder

gets me winded. That's all it is."

"Well, that's good to hear. I got the impression from Grandmom that it was something more serious, like maybe your arthritis was acting up."

"No, it's nothing like that."

"Good. I'm glad to hear it. Uh, how are Spot and Driver?"

"They're doin' fine, runnin' around like they had more energy than a barrel o' monkeys, and diggin' holes under the fence as fast as they can. I have to go out there every day and fill them in or I'm afraid they'll get away from me and get hit by a car."

"Ha, ha. I guess they keep you pretty busy, don't they?"

"Yeah, they sure do that."

"Yes, I'll bet they do."

"How are you and your dad gettin' along, now that you're workin' together?"

"Pretty well, I guess. Fortunately, we don't work together too often, so we don't have too many run-ins."

"I guess that's good, then. Are you workin' hard?"

"I sure am. I put in a full day's work with the men, and make all the deliveries besides, at night — picking up a little overtime. And yesterday I even did a side job, on my own. I put in a hundred amp service down the shore."

"You always were a hustler. Are you savin' all your money?"

"You bet."

"Good. You never know when times'll get tough and you'll need it. How much longer will you be workin' for your dad?"

"Well, not too long. Maybe a couple weeks."

"Then you'll be startin' with the union?"

"Well, not exactly. You see, that's the reason I called. I don't think I'm going to work for the union. At least, not right away. I — I've been drafted."

"Drafted? Into the army?"

"Yes, I'm afraid so."

"But I thought you were supposed to get a deferment from the union."

"I was supposed to, but I guess the draft board reclassified me too fast — after I dropped out of Temple. And I couldn't get my apprentice deferment until I got accepted by the union. So I guess I got caught in the middle — between the two deferments."

"Can't you call the union and tell them to accept you right away?"

"No, that's not the way it works. I took the state aptitude test already, but before they'll accept me I have to go up in front of the Examining Board for a personal interview. Then, after they've interviewed all the applicants, they pick out the ones they want — the ones with the highest grades. And that might not be for another couple months, yet. And besides, once you get your draft notice there's no way of getting out of it. I called them today. Technically, I'm already in the Army — I just haven't been sworn in yet."

"Well, I'm sorry to hear that. I know it's not what you want."

"I know. I don't like it either. But I can't do anything about it. And maybe it'll work out for the best. At least it'll get me away from home — a chance to live on my own. And they say that once your service time is over you're eligible to go back to school under the G.I. Bill, and they'll help pay for it. I guess it has some advantages. I mean, I would have had to go anyway."

"Yes, I guess you're right. Right many boys from around here have been called up, and it's puttin' quite a strain on the farmers, 'specially the ones family owned. With their sons away they have to hire hands."

"Well, at least I won't have that problem. My father can always get another man from the union. But, Grandpop, I — I don't know how to say this but, well, I'm scared."

"What are you scared of?"

"Well, I guess the army. I don't think I'm going to like it. I mean, from what I hear they're pretty tough, and I don't know if I can take it."

"You're pretty tough, too, Tony. I think you can take it."

"Maybe, but that's not all. What scares me is the way they treat people. They beat you up, and everything, if you don't do exactly what they want you to do, or think exactly what they want you to think."

"They may be able to make you do what they say, but nobody on this earth can make you think in a way you don't want to think."

"I hear they try to take away your individuality — to turn you into a machine, and to do everything according to their rules. I guess what I'm afraid of is being changed. I don't want my ideas changed. I want to stay as I am."

"Well, changing is a part of growing up, and there's nothin' wrong with it. And it *is* a little scary. But you don't ever let anybody tell you what's right or wrong. You're old enough to know the difference. You've always been a good boy, and you can make your own decisions. Now, you do what they tell you to do, because you have to. But you think the way you want to think. That's part of who you are. Just always remember to do what's right, no matter what anybody says."

"Thanks, Grandpop. I guess that's really what I wanted to hear. I can do that, too. I *will* do it. I won't ever let anyone tell me what to do

unless I know *you* would do it."

"You make that your motto and you'll get along all right. Just remember that you're the one who has to live with yourself, so you don't want anything bad hangin' over your head."

"Thanks, Grandpop. I won't forget. And Grandpop — I love you."

"I love you, too, son. You just be good."

"I will. And thanks. Goodbye."

"Goodbye, Tony. And may God be with you."

Chapter 26

"What's that?" George asked, in a strained hush.

"Where?"

"Over there." George pointed with a shaky finger that was barely visible in the drizzly dark of night. Something took form in the blackness, like a ghost rising up out of the soggy ground.

"It's a bush, you idiot," Pete shouted with derision.

"But it moved."

"It did not."

"I thought I saw it move, too," Ray chimed in.

"Don't you go flaky on us, too," Ben said. "Bushes can't move."

A deep throated whooshing sound echoed through the trees. Ray practically bowled Tony over, then clutched his arm like a vise. "Yo, Ray. Will you?"

"What the hell was that?"

"It sounded like an owl."

"Whoooooooo-oo-oo," came again, then changed into a recognizable voice. "Pretty good imitation, don't you think?"

"Goddamn you, Teddy," Ray screamed, as he leaped for his brother. There was a scuffle in the dark, and several short punching sounds.

"Lay off." Teddy scampered free and pushed through the middle of the tight group.

"Where'd he go? Where'd the little bastard get to?"

"Yo, Ray, will ya?" Ben said. "Leave him alone."

"Well, he shouldn't be scaring us like that."

"Nobody's scared but you, Ray," Pete muttered. "And maybe George."

"I still think we're crazy for coming out here," George replied. Ben said, "We are, but that's beside the point."

Teddy's muffled voice quivered as he spoke. "Hey, there's something up ahead. Yes, there it is. And it's coming this way. It's — it's — oh, my god — it's a — tree stump!"

"Now I got you, you little four-eyed Mongoloid idiot." Ray started thrashing his brother again. The two silhouettes danced back and forth, punctuated by sharp, thwacking sounds.

A thud accompanied one of them hitting the ground. "Hey, who knocked me down?"

"It was me. And if you punch me again I'll land you in a ditch."

Ray climbed slowly to his feet. "Gee, Pete, I'm sorry. I thought you were Teddy."

"If you'd leave him alone you wouldn't get knocked down."

"All right, that's enough horseplay," Tony said. "Will you guys knock off the nonsense?"

"But that little twerp deserves it," Ray protested.

"I said knock it off." Tony stopped suddenly and Ray walked right into him. "Now just leave him alone."

The woods were thick. The tall trees formed a canopy overhead that shielded the road like a tunnel. Tony could see little but the eyeballs of his companions. The shadows played tricks on his eyes, and the rain caused a light mist to effervesce from the ground.

"Well, you tell that dimwit to stop trying to scare us."

"No one's going to scare you but yourself, and your imagination. There's nothing out there but trees, and they're not going to hurt you unless you walk into one. So just stay on the road, and stick together. Okay?"

George blurted out, "I still think we ought to turn back."

"If you wanna go back to the car, nobody's stopping you," Pete said.

"Listen, guys, we've got to stick together." Tony continued to lead the way at his own pace. "If someone gets separated he might get lost."

George sniffled. "That's because you're the only one who knows where we're going."

"Look, you knew what we were planning to do. No one twisted your arm to come along, you know."

"Yeah," Ben added.

"Hey, there's another one?"

"Another what?" said Ray.

"Another tree." Teddy laughed out loud. "The whole place is full of them."

Tony heard a shuffling behind him, as the two antagonists circled the group. Then came a bump and a punch.

"Yo, Ray, will ya?" Ben yelled angrily.

"I'm gonna kill that little creep."

"Hey, how's about keeping the noise down," Pete said. "You wanna let the world know you're coming?"

"Teddy, wherever you are, you cut it out. You hear?"

There was no answer.

After a long pause, George said, "I still think we should turn back."

"Go ahead," Pete chided. "We'll meet you back at the car."

"I'm not giving him the keys," Ben said firmly.

"Ray, you want to go back with me?"

"Are you kidding?"

"Well, you don't want to go on, do you?"

"No, but I sure as hell don't want to go with you, either. I'll stick with Tony."

"Way to go," said his brother.

Tony kept his voice to a whisper. "How about a little less complaining?"

"I wasn't complaining," Ray said.

Pete snorted. "Now you're complaining about not complaining."

"I was not."

"You were too."

"Was not."

"Were too."

Ray's response was muffled as Ben clamped his hand over his mouth. "Cut it out, Ray."

Ray struggled free, and the two of them tripped over each other's legs and almost fell down on the wet macadam. "All right, maybe I was."

The road veered to the left and started a steep incline. Breathing became labored, and in a few minutes Tony could hear the others gasping.

"Aaaagh."

George's blood curdling scream sent shivers down Tony's spine. He stopped dead in his tracks — but this time no one ran into him. "What is it?"

"Something grabbed my shoulder."

"Oh, that was just a branch," Pete sighed. "It rubbed by me, too."

Tony ran a hand through his wet hair. "You know, you'd think you guys have never been in the woods before."

"Yeah," Ben said.

"Now let's go. And cut out the nonsense."

"Yeah."

Tony peered through the drizzling rain into the darkness ahead. He could see absolutely nothing but the shadowy shapes of trees and bushes that adorned Bowman's Hill. As the slope of the roadway increased, he had to lean forward almost to a climbing posture.

"Are you sure you know where you're going?" George gasped.

"Ain't only but one road," Pete said. "So it's kinda hard to get lost on it. And you better save your breath or you won't make it up this hill."

Teddy danced around as if the climb were nothing. "Hey, Tony, did you really drive your car down this road?"

"Sure. Plenty of times. But only downhill. The park entrance is on the south side. That's where you go in to drive up to Bowman's Tower. That road's a lot more windy and not as steep. There's a parking lot at the top where you can either turn around and go back down the way you came, or you can take this road down to the picnic area. You've got to use low gear and ride the brake the whole way."

"Wow, it sure would be fun to sled down here in the snow."

"You sure couldn't sled down here without snow," Pete observed.

"It would be a hell of a ride on roller skates," added Ben. "But I wouldn't want to do it unless my insurance was paid up."

George's wheezing was noticeably louder. Tony tried to placate him. "It's not much farther."

As the trees thinned, the foreboding, cloud covered sky became more prominent. The rain fell a little harder on Tony's face. Then the road leveled out. Tony discovered that he had built up a sweat during the long climb.

After a final bend, the road broadened into a parking lot. A hundred yards away, soaring way above the lean white ashes and their glistening leaves, stood a tall structure that looked like a huge cannon standing on end, with its deadly barrel pointing toward the sky. It would have made a beautiful sight on a moonlit night, silhouetted against a star-studded background. But shrouded in mist, it appeared mystical, fantastic, even horrific. It could have been the castle spire that housed the heart in *Jack the Giant Killer*. Tony could almost feel the slow throb of oversized muscles pumping blood to that distant titan.

"Jesus H. Christ," Ray breathed.

They clustered like a covey of quail in front of a rusting sign mounted on the massive iron door. The park, administered by the state, was closed after sunset, and all trespassers were liable to fine and/or imprisonment.

Ray rattled the loose chain that hung from the twin portals. "Hey, the door's locked."

"Naturally. Do you think it's left open for illegal night visitors?"

"Then how are we supposed to get in? You said we could climb to the top?"

Tony ran his hand over the wet stones, and fingered the mortar joints. He pointed up at a series of rectangular openings that spiraled toward the castellated apex as if they were dots on a barber pole stripe. "We go in through the window."

Ray's head tilted back. "You gotta be kidding."

"Would I kid you?"

"'I forgot my stilts," Ben said.

"Besides, it's got bars on it," Ray went on.

"Don't worry about it. I already cased it when I was up here with Patty. The lowest window has enough room to squeeze through between the bars."

"You ain't gettin' *me* in that window," George protested.

"You can't *fit* in that window," Pete laughed.

"Hey, Tony, this is neat. This is really neat."

"Shut up, mumble mouth." Ray grabbed for his brother, but Teddy was on the ball and ran around the base of the tower. Ray tripped over something unseen in the darkness and went down with a whoof. "Goddamn you, Teddy. You made me slip in the mud."

Pete shouted, "Don't blame him because of your clumsiness."

"Yeah, it's your own fault," Ben added. "If you hadn't been chasing him you wouldn't have slipped."

Ray walked stiff-legged around the side of the tower. "Somebody shine a light. I gotta get the mud off my pants."

"They're only dungarees."

"But they're new."

"We didn't bring any flashlights, remember?" Tony said.

"Well, somebody light a goddamn match, then. I've got to get the mud off before it soaks through."

"Ray, you're the only one here who smokes," Ben said.

Ray growled, reached into his pants pocket, and brought out a pack of matches. "Here, somebody light one for me."

"Why can't you light it yourself?" Pete wanted to know.

Ray screamed through gritted teeth, "Because I gotta wipe the mud off with a handkerchief, that's why."

"Give them to me." Tony took the book of matches and tore one out. The red head smeared off the first and second matches, the third sputtered but refused to light. The next four did nothing. When he finally got one to light, he held it in his cupped hand to keep it out of the steady drizzle.

"Oh, no," Ray groaned. His pants were caked with dark, brown mud, from knees to ankles. He wiped furiously with his thin handkerchief, with little result other than muddying the white cloth. "Teddy, you'll pay for this."

"Stop blaming him," Eddie said.

"Can you hold that steady?"

The match burned down to a stub that Tony pinched as long as he could.

He struck three more before getting one to stay lit. "I'm doing the best I can."

"Somebody give me another handkerchief." When no one made any efforts in his behalf, he snapped angrily, "Come on, will you?"

Very softly, Tony said, "Ray, I don't think anyone else carries a handkerchief."

When the big chunks of mud were wiped off, he tossed the sodden cloth to the ground. "I don't know why I went along with this crazy scheme of yours in the first place."

"Why don't you use grass?" Tony suggested.

"Hey, that's a good idea. Give me those matches." He grabbed the pack too fast, and dropped it in a puddle. "Goddamn it." He broke off whole branches from a nearby bush and wiped them along his pants legs.

Still using his mellow voice, Tony said, "Ray, you shouldn't be tearing up the plant life like that. This is a state park."

"I don't give a shit about no state park. They're not going to pay my cleaning bill." He threw down the handful of leafy foliage. "Well, that does it. I'm going back."

"Going back isn't going to get the mud off your pants. You may as well stick it out."

"We never should have come up here in the first place." Ray turned his face toward the black sky. "Why me, o lord? Why me? Of all the nights, he had to pick one in the rain."

"Come on, Ray, will ya?" Pete said. "You've come this far, you may as well go on with it."

"I already told you I'm not going, and that's final. I'm going back to the car."

"I'll go with you," George said.

"I figured you would fink out on us," Pete said.

Ben shuffled his feet. "Listen, Tone, I don't like running out on you, but I'm pretty wet and cold. I don't have anything on but this thin shirt. So, if Ray and George want to go back to the car, I'll go along with them."

"I'm staying with Tony," Teddy stated firmly, from out of Ray's range.

"Good. And maybe you'll do me a favor and get lost."

"You shouldn't talk that way about your brother," Pete said. "At least he isn't running out on us."

"Oh, Benny isn't running out because he's cold, but I am because my pants are soaked. Is that it?"

"All right, all right. Let's calm down." Tony knew when an argument was about to begin. "Here's what we'll do. Pete, Teddy, you two stay here while I take these guys down to the trail head and show them the way."

"What's wrong with the way we came up?" Ray wanted to know.

"Nothing, but the road is the long way around. It's easier coming up that way, but if you go straight down the front of the mountain you'll be sitting in the car in ten minutes."

"Well, I guess it's all right, then. All I want is to get these wet pants off and sit under the heater. And the sooner, the better."

"Sounds good to me," Ben agreed.

George said huskily, "Let's quit talking and get going."

"That's the first smart thing you said all night," Ray commented.

Tony led the trio over the rocks to an opening in the brush where the trail began. "Now get this right. The trail goes straight down for a couple hundred yards, and it may be slippery, so be careful. Then it splits in two, one way going down and the other way bearing off to the right and around the side of the mountain. Remember to take the left fork."

Ben threw his arms around his chest, shivering. "I'll have the car warmed up when you get there."

They filed into the woods, George trailing. As soon as they were swallowed up by the darkness, Tony headed back for the tower. The rain had died down enough that it was difficult to tell if it was still drizzling or just misty.

Pete wiped water off his face. "I don't understand Ray's beef. He shouldn't a tried to split us up like that."

Tony glanced up at the stone spire. "Oh, it's nothing. He just can't stand being a little dirty, that's all. And I'm that way, myself, so I know how Ben feels."

"I'm glad he went with them, anyway. Those two dodos would never find their way out of here alone — or together. Sorry, Ted."

"That's okay. I didn't choose him for a brother, we just happened to be born that way. Tony, how're we gonna reach that window?"

"Simple: we climb the wall."

Pete looked up at the dark opening some twenty feet high. "You know, Tone, maybe I should have gone with those guys."

"Cut it out. Just follow me." The stone blocks out of which the tower was constructed were large and unevenly spaced, and the mortar was grooved deep enough to afford easy finger and toe holds. "Stand back in case I fall."

Except for the slipperiness due to the rain, Tony found it almost as easy as climbing a ladder. In a moment he reached the window. He took hold of the two vertical bars and swung himself onto the wide ledge.

"See. No problem at all."

Holding one rusted bar in each hand, he levered out and squirmed his legs through the opening. He slid in easily up to his waist, then had to get on his side and wiggle his hips through. His rib cage got hung up, but by exhaling as much as he could, he shrank his chest until he was able to squeeze through the rungs.

"I'm inside, but don't come up till I check it out."

If it was dark outside, it was pitch black inside. Tony had never experienced such absolute absence of light. His eyes played tricks on him, for he kept seeing fireflies at some indefinite distance.

He looked down to where the stone steps should have been. He knew the interior staircase ran around the perimeter of the tower. Holding onto the bars with a death grip, he lowered himself into the void. With his arms outstretched and his toes pointed down, his feet touched nothing. There may well have been an eternal abyss below him. His imagination ran riot. Should he rely on his senses and hang on, or trust his judgment and let go? As the strength drained out of his arms, he was forced to rely on reason. He let go and dropped into the infinite — and fell about three inches. The shock of landing before he expected it threw him off balance. He fell to a sitting position and stayed there as if he were perched on an eagle's aerie atop a tall cliff.

He wiped sweat off his brow and explored his environment. Slowly he pushed out a foot, seeking the edge of the spiral stairs. Instead, it came up against something hard which, after he touched it with his hand, he remembered was the wrought iron railing. With a sigh of relief he climbed up to the window.

"It's okay. Come on up."

Teddy scrambled up the stone with the ease of Dracula clambering his castle walls, crouching on all fours like a great, gaunt squirrel. Little wonder that Jonathan Harker went mad. A moment later his face reached the level of the window. "Hey, Tony, you were right. It *is* easy."

"I told you so."

"Hey, how'd you get in there?"

"Hold onto the bars with both hands, bring your feet up to the ledge, and slide through feet first."

Tony dropped back into the blackness, and a moment later Teddy was standing beside him. "Wow, I almost got my glasses scraped off."

"They won't do you much good in here anyway." He climbed up to the window again. "Okay, Pete, come on up."

Pete climbed the wall with no trouble, and peered into the darkness. "Holy shit, man, now I know we're crazy. How the hell'd you get through these bars?" Tony guided him through and soon all three were crouched on the cool stone treads. "This is really spooky." His voice reverberated ominously in the curved structure.

"All right, follow me."

"*Follow* you," Pete said coarsely. "I can't even see you."

"You'd better keep talking so we'll know where you are," Teddy said.

"All right, you just have to remember one thing. There's a railing on the inside of the staircase, so you can't fall. But just to be on the safe side, we'll hug the wall."

"Hug the wall? I'm gonna marry it."

"Now keep close behind me."

"I sure ain't gonna try and pass you."

"Wow, this is neat. This is really neat. Those guys don't know what they're missing."

"How about keeping it down, huhn?" Pete suggested.

"Sorry."

Slowly they worked their way up the cold, black inner depths of Bowman's Tower. Tony dragged his hand across the icy stone. He had the feeling that the next step would end in midair and he would plummet over the edge of a precipice. They passed another window.

"Hey, Tony, how many steps are there?"

"About a hundred and fifty."

"Wow. Are we going all the way to the top?"

"We have to if we want to see anything."

Every footfall was magnified by the echo chamber effect. Above, below, and all around was Stygian blackness, and the haunting anticipation of death around the corner. Finally, Tony saw a faint glow ahead: the merest pinpoint of freedom, as if seen from the depths of a mine. He entered a small, squared-off chamber surrounded by glassless openings.

"Whooooo-oo-oo. Hey, this is all right."

"Cut it out, Ted." Pete made a fake slap to the arm.

Teddy leaned far out and peered down the vertical wall. Tony put a firm hand on his shoulder. "Be careful, Teddy. I'd have a hard time explaining to your mother how you fell out of a fifteen story window."

"And if you survived the fall, your brother would prob'ly kill you."

Teddy climbed back inside. "It's wet out there anyway. The rain has soaked through the stone."

"Let's go up on the roof."

"Can we, Tony? Can we really?"

"Follow me."

In one corner stood a doorway to another spiral staircase, barely wide enough for one person. In single file they squeezed into it.

"Wow, this is neat. This is really neat."

"Goddamn."

The staircase curled around like a corkscrew. Tony's imagination ran wild, as he could not see what was around the corner. "Don't get so close."

A long shaft of brightness gleamed downward, and a moment later took the shape of a doorway. Then Tony was on the roof, and Teddy and Pete were pushing past to the waist high stone parapet and looking out over the land.

"Wow, this is really super neat."

"Teddy, sometimes I think I understand why your brother picks on you the way he does," Pete said.

Teddy dashed back and forth across the narrow balcony, looking first down into the blackness of the hills, where the trees were lost in shadow, then peering out over the Delaware River, now visible as a silvery streak through the mist: an optical illusion floating in the air as its surface shimmered in moonbeams. Clouds drifted in and out of sight, brightening as they caught momentary gleams of light reflected from the water below, or from the moon above. The storm had passed.

"What are those lights down there?" Teddy pointed from the east side of the tower.

Tony leaned over the balustrade, squinting. "Must be a car in the road." Because of the mist everything was out of focus. Just beyond the light flowed the silky incandescence of the river. "Or near it."

One light winked out.

"Hey, Tone. Isn't that about where the car is parked?"

'I think you're right, Pete."

"But why are there two lights?"

"I don't know."

"Hey, Tony, Pete. Come over here." Teddy was silhouetted against the gray backdrop, his outstretched arm and finger pointing downward. "Take a look at this."

At the base of the hill, a beam of light stabbed through the trees with the brilliance of a searchlight. Nearby, two smaller lights sprayed the darkness with odd, jerky motions. They meandered for several minutes, then converged on the searchlight. In the cold, damp air, two car doors could be heard slamming. The searchlight began to move in a circular path.

"It's a police car," Tony breathed. "And those were two cops searching the picnic area."

"What do you think they're doing?"

"Looking for us."

"Uh, oh," Pete said.

"Double uh, oh," Teddy added.

"What do you think happened?"

Tony shook his head. "I don't know. It could be a coincidence."

"But what were the cops looking in the woods for?" There was astonishment in Pete's voice.

"I don't know, unless the guys got caught and they're looking for us."

"But they wouldn't rat on us."

"Ray would," Teddy said flatly.

"No, he wouldn't," Tony said.

"Maybe he would, maybe he wouldn't," Pete said. "But George sure as hell would."

Tony sighed. "Look, let's not make any wild suppositions till we find out a little more. If those guys are smart, they won't say anything about us being up here."

"Those cops weren't looking for night crawlers."

Teddy said, "So what'll we do now?"

"The first thing we do is get out of this tower. Then we'll go down to the road and sneak up on the car to see if they're alone. I don't know what kind of story Ben made up, but I'm sure he didn't tell them the truth. If the coast is clear, we'll just get in the car and take off. Otherwise, we'll have to play it by ear."

They filed into the narrow spiral stairway and felt their way down to the room below, then continued right on down to the main stairway. It was like descending into the black pit of Hell. They stuck close together, holding hands. The walls were damp and cold to the touch, but its presence was the only grasp on reality in the total blackness. No one spoke; the only sound was controlled breathing, and the scuffling of sneakers on the stone steps.

Tony's foot caught on a projection and he fell headlong. He gasped as he flung his hands out in front of him, expecting to plunge down into a nameless hole. But his knees came up against hard stone.

"Tony, are you all right?" said Teddy.

Tony did not move — did not even dare to budge. "I guess so. But don't anyone move."

"A bulldozer couldn't pry my fingers off this wall," Pete said.

Tony stood up shakily. With both hands flat against the vertical stone he moved forward cautiously. He was on a level floor. When he felt metal he ran his hands along its edges — it was a door.

"Everything's all right." Tony walked back to where Teddy and Pete were waiting. He laughed. "We just missed the window. Must have walked right under it. We'll have to go back up." A moment later he breathed the fresh outside air, and felt the gentle pressure of the wind. "You go first, Teddy."

"Okay." Deftly, Teddy climbed up on the window ledge, reversed his approach, and climbed through the bars feet first.

"Make sure you have a good foothold on the mortar ledges before you let go of the bars," Tony cautioned.

"Don't worry about me. This is easy." Teddy's statement of confident was followed by scraping sounds and a crash. A faraway voice said, "It's a little slippery, though."

"Go ahead, Pete."

Pete climbed through the grating and let himself down easily, making certain that each toehold would support his weight before proceeding to seek another ledge. He grunted when he reached the bottom, and by that time Tony was already through the window and scampering like a spider down the wall.

"All right, let's get going."

He trotted toward the trail entrance with

Teddy and Pete close behind. The rain had stopped, and the moon glowed dimly through low-hanging clouds. The light enabled him to keep up a good pace. Pushed along by the steep trail, they dashed through the tree limbs and bushes and over fallen trunks with uncanny speed. In less than five minutes they reached the bottom of Bowman's Hill, scrambling the final few feet through loose dirt and mud, right to the edge of the streambed. They halted at the water's edge.

"This way. We can't be too far from the road."

A few seconds later, the bridge that crossed River Road loomed out of the mist, the Roman arch limned against the gray background. They climbed up and over some rocks, through a gully that carried runoff from the road, and emerged onto the macadam exactly opposite the Black Stallion. All was quiet.

"Wow, you really know these woods, Tony."

"Ssshhh. You want to give us away?" Teddy shrugged, and started to climb out onto the roadway. Tony grabbed his soggy jacket and yanked him back down. "Not so fast."

"What're you waiting for?" Pete whispered, crouched behind a tree.

Tony put a finger to his lips. They sat on their haunches for several moments. From behind the '57 Chevy, a car door squeaked open and a dome light went on. A uniformed figure emerged from the other vehicle, the weak light momentarily reflecting the rounded peak of a hat and the glint of a badge.

As one, they slid down into the gutter and crawled backward until they reached the stream.

"What do we do now?" Pete said.

"Gee, Tony, I'm sorry I almost walked out there."

"Forget it. Let me think a minute." He shortened the time to five seconds. "I don't think we should be seen coming out of the park. Those guys haven't been caught doing anything other than sitting in the car. So, if we're just walking down the road, there's nothing they can do to us. It may seem strange, but it's not illegal. Let's cut back up the hill and stay on the slope till it comes out on the other road, then walk down to the car as if there's nothing wrong."

"Sounds good to me," Pete said.

"Okay."

Fifteen minutes later, they walked out onto the road and followed it boldly past the intersection, then down to where the car was parked. Teddy and Pete walked right past and climbed nonchalantly into the back seat of the Black Stallion. Tony bent down to the open window of the police car, and leaned in casually, innocently.

"Is there some kind of trouble, officer?"

The policeman looked up with a critical eye. "Are you Anthony Giovanni?"

"Uh — yes — that's right."

He switched on the dome light and glanced down at a notepad. "And those other two were Peter Robinson and Theodore Murphy?"

Tony faltered for a second until he heard a throat being cleared in the back seat. He looked past the officer and saw Ben nodding silently. "That's right."

"Tony, do you want to get in here so I can ask you a few questions?" His tone was light, almost pleading, but it was also a voice of authority.

"Sure thing," Tony said cheerfully. He walked around to the passenger side and climbed in. He exchanged glances with Ben, saw the other shrug.

"Now, Tony, Ben here didn't know your street address, so would you mind giving it to me?"

Tony gave it to him.

"And your phone number?"

Ben knew his phone number. Tony stated it flatly. The officer wrote it down, then flipped a page, and said, "That's right."

"Do you want Pete's and Teddy's addresses, too?"

"No, that information has already been supplied. Now, tell me," the policeman looked up with weary eyes. "What the hell were you doing out there?"

"Well, we were just — out for a walk?"

"In the rain?"

"Well, yes. I mean, we didn't plan on it raining, but when we got here we didn't want to have to drive all the way back to Philly without at least doing something."

"And what was that something you were planning to do?"

"Well, nothing really. You see, I've been here before, and I thought it would be a neat idea to — just kind of walk around out there. You know, in the woods — in the dark. Just for fun."

"Maybe to you it's just for fun, but I still think you're nuts — all of you."

An uncertain smile broke out on Tony's lips. "Well, we weren't doing anything wrong, were we? I mean, we didn't break any laws, did we?"

The policeman sighed. "Don't try to tell me you didn't know the park was closed after dark because I won't buy it. It's posted at both entrances."

"Oh, no, I knew the park was closed. I mean, the upper park. But there aren't any restrictions on the picnic grounds until you get up the road to the nature trails — where the road comes down from the tower."

"Then why did you go on up to the tower?"

Tony shot a quick glance at Ben. He shrugged back silently and glanced away. "Well, we just kind of started up the road, just to see what it was like. Then we saw the bridge, and we thought we'd go a little further, and before we knew it we were at the top of the hill. But we didn't mean to."

"Did you go inside the tower?"

"The door's locked."

"So you tried?"

"Well, naturally. It was just a reflex action. Besides, it must be pitch black inside that tower at night. You'd have to be crazy to climb up those stairs in the dark."

The policeman thought about that for a moment. "Yes, I guess you're right." The radio crackled, and a static-filled voice asked for Captain Hollander. He picked up the microphone and spoke into it. "Hollander here. Go ahead."

"Sir, there's still no sign of that kid, but Mrs. Lambert called again to tell us he had been back a second time."

"What did he want?"

"He was looking for Bowman's Tower. Apparently he's still lost."

"Okay, keep looking for him. The other three have just shown up. Keep me posted."

"Yes, sir."

Captain Hollander turned his attention back to Tony. "Do you have any idea where George Hart might be?"

"Uh, no, not really. I thought he was with Ben and Ray."

Ben cleared his throat and spoke for the first time. "He was, but we lost him on the trail. We got separated in the dark, and when we got down to the road he wasn't with us any more."

Captain Hollander put down his notepad. "We got a phone call from Mrs. Lambert that a suspicious prowler knocked on her back door asking for directions to the tower. The squad car sent to investigate found Ray Murphy and Ben Clark in an unauthorized parking zone — hiding under a blanket. One with his pants off."

"We got soaked walking through those bushes."

Tony stared blindly through the windshield. He stared up at the clearing sky and shook his head. He heard the crunching of stones just as the huge bulk of George stumbled past the car. Without slowing down or turning his head, he went straight to the Black Stallion and opened the back door and climbed in.

"That was George," Tony said, with resignation.

"Okay, all present and accounted for." Captain Hollander picked up the microphone and called in the search parties. "First one back to the station put on a pot of coffee. Now," he looked over at Tony. "Would you fellows like to stop in for a cup?"

"If it's all the same with you, I'd rather pass."

Captain Hollander smiled whimsically. "I'm sure you would. I should run you in anyway."

"Why? We weren't doing anything."

"That's what *you* say. But until I have someone check out the park in the daytime, I won't know that, will I?"

Tony cleared his throat. "Well, I guess not. But how could we possibly hurt a stone tower?"

"I don't know. Maybe you broke up some picnic benches, maybe you tore up some flowers along the nature walks, or maybe you moved the parking slabs in the upper lot. Kids have taken it into their minds to do stranger things. Now, you boys seem all right to me, so I'm going to let you go. But remember, I have all your names and addresses, as well as identification from Ben's driver's license and vehicle registration. Tomorrow I'll have the rangers check through the park, and the tower, and if they find anything broken or damaged or out of place, Ben is going to be the one held responsible. Do you understand that, Ben?"

"Yes, sir."

Tony sighed with relief. "Well, then, I guess we're in the clear. We didn't even walk on the grass."

"Good. I'm glad to hear it. Now get going, and don't let me catch you around here again — at least, not at night. The park's open from sunup to sundown, and you're welcome then. But just between you and me, I think you're all a bunch of nuts to be out here pulling this crazy stunt in the rain. Now get going before I change my mind."

They slipped out of the car and jumped into the Black Stallion before the officer changed his mind. When Tony slid into the shotgun position, Ray moved over without protest.

"What's happening? What're they gonna do to us? Are they gonna lock us up? Do you think they'll call my mom? Will they — "

Pete reached forward from the back seat and clamped a hand over Ray's mouth. "Will you stop your silly jabbering? I'm tired of hearing it."

Tony said, "Ben, let's get out of here before the good captain changes his mind."

"You don't have to tell me twice." The engine was already running, so all he had to do was throw it into gear. He executed a U-turn, slowly, under the full gaze of Captain Hollander, and headed for the city.

"*Are you crazy?*" Ray exploded. "Pulling a U-turn — "

"Ray, do you mind if I turn down the heat?" Without waiting for an answer, Tony lowered the blower switch. In the comparative quiet, he screamed, "Now, what was the idea of telling him our life histories? Did he torture you or something? Did he shove bamboo splinters under your fingernails? Did he put lighted matches under your chin? Did he — "

Pete placed a hand on his shoulder. "Yo, Tone, calm down."

Out of the corner of his mouth, Ben said, "Ray started blabbing as soon as he turned the flashlight on us."

Ray threw his hands up in the air. "There we are, laying on the floor under a blanket like a couple of queers. What am I supposed to do? I had to tell him something."

Tony was still yelling. "So did you have to tell him everything?"

"They would have found out anyway."

"Not if you kept your goddamn mouth shut." Pete banged Ray on the back of the head. Ray turned around so fast his neck cracked. His face turned beet red, visible even in the darkness. "How much did you tell him?"

Tony lowered his voice a decibel. "He had a dossier on me with everything but my mother's maiden name and what I got for Christmas."

"It was all George's fault anyway." Ray jabbed a thumb over his shoulder.

George gazed out the window like a zombie.

"He's the one who went and knocked on that lady's door and made her call the police."

"Yeah, George." Pete reached past Teddy and pushed him hard on the shoulder. "Why'd you go and do a stupid thing like that? On the *back* door, no less."

"I was lost. These guys wouldn't wait up for me and I didn't know where the car was."

"You couldn't at least find the front door?"

"You dumb shit, you coulda had us all locked up. If you had a brain you'd be dangerous."

Tony calmed down a little. "All right, Pete, you don't have to blame him for it. He didn't know what he was doing."

"You can say that again. Neither did his mother when she had him."

"At least we got out of it all right," Tony added.

"That's easy for you to say." Ben followed the curve of the road, then stabbed Tony with cold eyes. "But *I'm* the one they're going to crucify if they have second thoughts. They've got my car on record."

"Stop worrying, Ben. We're in the clear. We didn't do any damage."

" 'Cept for one torn-up bush."

Ray's voice was high pitched and squeaky. "Suppose my mom gets a phone call tomorrow from the police department?"

Teddy laughed. "I'll just tell her my brother made me do it."

Ray swung around, but Tony stopped his fist with his palm. "Forget about it. I'll take all the blame for everything. They can't do anything to *me*."

"And why not?"

"Because Uncle Sam wouldn't let them. You forget — I'm United States government property."

Chapter 27

"I'm glad your grandmother let you come out tonight."

The Delaware River was dark. Clouds kept the stars from reflecting off the ripples, and because of slack tide, shipping traffic was at a standstill. The lights of the Walt Whitman Bridge brought the only illumination through the windshield.

"What brought about the sudden change of heart?"

Patty shrugged. "Well, I guess it's because of a lot of things. I'll be graduating in a couple of weeks. I'll be eighteen this summer. All the other girls are allowed out during the week as long as they get in early. And besides, my mother told her it was all right. She says I'm old enough to take care of myself. And if I start working at the restaurant, I'll be working late at night, so I might as well start now." She flashed a weak smile. "Besides, she knew I was going out with you."

"And that makes a difference." Tony said it flatly, as a statement.

"Oh, yes. Mother likes you a lot. She thinks you're really nice."

"Does it run in the family?"

Patty looked out the window. She was silent for a while, then turned back. "I like you, too. You're — different."

Tony placed his head against the car window so he could see her from farther away. "Is that good or bad?"

"Oh, it's good." She stared out the window again. From this angle Tony could see the up-turn of her nose, the roundness of her chin, the tip of an ear peering out from behind dark curls. "Tony, my mother wants you to come down to the shore again this weekend."

"Your mother does?"

"Well, Bob, really. He wants you to do some more work on the house before — you know."

Tony thought for a moment, resignedly.

"Yes, I know."

"Then will you?"

"I've already told you I can't. I have to go to Maryland this weekend — to see my grandparents."

"But why?"

"Because I only have three weekends left before — I have to leave. And it's important that I see them before I go."

"But I don't want you to," she said, in a pout. "I want you around here. I want you to take me out some more before you go."

Breathing deeply, he said, "I wish I could, but I can't. It's important to me."

"But don't you care about what's important to me?"

"Of course I do. But this is different. I have to have a talk with my grandfather. He's my — he's my — my grandfather. He's very close to me. And I have to see him right away — so we can talk."

"But why do you have to go for the whole weekend? Why can't you just go on Saturday and come back Saturday night? Then you can take me and my mother to Shipbottom."

"For one thing, it's a three hour drive. For another thing, they're expecting me to stay over. And I want to, anyway. That's my — second home. So, when I'm there, I'm not really away."

There was a whine in her voice. "So, call them up and tell them you can't make it."

"Patty, you don't understand. I *want* to go and see them."

"But I want you to stay here."

"I thought you wanted to go to the shore."

"You know what I mean."

Tony shifted his weight, and rested one arm on the steering wheel. "I'm sorry, Patty. I just can't do it. Maybe next weekend."

"Next weekend may be too late." She pulled away, and snugged up to the door. Tony slid over and put a hand on her arm. She withdrew it sharply.

"Something else may come up. You just don't care about me, that's all."

"If I didn't care about you I wouldn't be here trying to explain all this to you."

"But your grandparent's mean more to you than I do."

"They've been my grandparents for a long time — and they're depending on me to see them before I go."

Patty faced him sharply.

"I couldn't let them down — not now. I — I don't know when I'll be able to see them again. I mean, I'll be gone a long time — a couple years — and — I'll be home on leave, I guess, but not for a while. And they mean a lot to me. Can't you understand that?"

Her face remained sour. But she leaned forward and threw her arms around Tony, and cried, "Oh, why did this have to happen to me?"

Tony patted her back as she sobbed against his chest. "Patty, nothing's happened to you. You're all right."

"But you're going away."

"It won't be forever."

"But two years."

"Hey, it's not like I'm not going to exist for two years. We'll be able to write to each other. You can send me letters."

Patty clutched him tighter. "But I want more than that. I want you — around. Where I can see you, and talk to you. I want you to take me places. I want to get away from that horrid old witch. I can't live with her any more. And I don't know what's going to happen to me after school. I don't know what I'm going to do."

Patty was gushing now, the tears flowing down her cheeks like a spring flood. She sobbed convulsively until Tony felt the dampness dripping through his shirt.

He continued to pat her on the back, and crooned, "It's all right, Patty. Everything will be all right."

But she kept crying. And he kept crooning.

Chapter 28

Tony parked the delivery van on the newly paved gas station pad. Nearing the end of the construction phase, the site looked quite different now from when he had first seen it. Two gasoline islands had been installed, a galvanized crosshatched fence had been erected, and floodlights had been mounted atop tall metal poles. What had once been an ugly cinderblock building was now a picture of modern design and decor, complete with stone facade, picture windows, and brightly painted garage bay doors. It looked more like a contemporary ranch house than a fully functional office and workshop.

Two cars were parked on the lot in addition to the painter's van and the plumber's pickup truck, with lengths of copper tubing lashed to the crossbeams of its overhead wooden racks. Tony parked so that the side doors of the van faced the glass office door, which was propped open with a wedge. He climbed over the engine box, opened the doors from the inside, and backed out with a small but heavy cardboard box full of receptacles, switches, cover plates, wirenuts, and extra screws. He carried the box inside and put it on the sawdust-covered counter top.

He inhaled the dampness of fresh plaster. From somewhere in the back of the building he heard the chatter of voices. The double bay garage was empty, so he went through it and into the back room that was a combination storeroom, washroom, and electrical closet. Four men sat on upturned paint cans and cinderblocks as they drank their coffee.

Eliot looked up, but said nothing. He glanced casually at Duke.

"I've got some material for you," Tony said cheerfully. "Mostly fixtures, and a few odds and ends."

Eliot looked up again, this time with a scowl. He glanced at his watch. "Come back after coffee — in about half an hour."

"Gee, I really can't wait that long. I've got other stops to make."

In a deadpan voice, Eliot said, "Then go make them and come back afterwards."

Tony stared at the unfeeling faces. He nodded slowly. He dropped the box of metal parts on the floor from waist high; it hit with a bang. Then he went back to the truck and grabbed two boxes of fixtures. They were large and bulky, but not heavy. He returned to the office with one under each arm and slapped them on the flowered linoleum floor.

On his second trip, he dropped his load on a pile of loose molding, making sure they crinkled and snapped loudly. When he unbent, he saw Eliot standing in the doorway. His mouth was agape, and steam from a Styrofoam cup drifted past his face.

"What the hell do you think you're doin'?"

"Your glasses must be fogged. Can't you see I'm unloading fixtures?"

"How many times do I have to tell you? Nonunion scabs don't do no work on my job."

Tony's voice was the epitome of indifference. "You can tell me as many times as you want, if it makes you feel any better." He flashed a smile, then brought in another armful of boxes.

"Look here, boy. I'm telling you to stop unloading that truck before you get into trouble."

"I can't get into trouble. There's nothing illegal about what I'm doing."

"You'll be in trouble with me."

"That's no trouble at all."

The hand with the coffee in it dropped an inch. "I said get out of here, and I mean it."

"Stop working your jaw and put your money where your mouth is."

Eliot could not have been more stunned if an ant had strolled in and clobbered him on the shin with a two-by-four. He worked his jaw only once — it fell slack. And it stayed that way.

Tony made another trip to the truck. When he got back, he said, "Your coffee's getting cold."

"Buddy, you pick up one more box and you're gonna be in deep trouble."

"You keep threatening me long enough and I'll be done."

"I ain't gonna take this."

"Okay, then take this." Tony threw one of the two-foot square boxes directly at Eliot's midriff. It crashed into the outstretched hand and splashed coffee all over him. The box tumbled to the floor, the fixtures safe in their cardboard packing.

Eliot's face turned cherry red. His eyes bulged and his jaw gritted — or trembled. He gasped.

Tony unbuttoned the sleeves of his flannel shirt, pushed them halfway up his arms. "All right, big mouth. Make some trouble."

Eliot lunged forward, but not at Tony. He stumbled through the front door and, without looking back, jumped into his car and roared off down the street with a squeal of rubber.

Duke peered into the office from the garage. The plumber and the painter stood behind him, peering over his stooped shoulders. "What's going on?"

"Nothing. The rabbit just went off looking for a hole to crawl into." Tony sauntered out the door, returned twice with boxes of fixtures, and stacked them neatly in front of the others.

None of the bystanders uttered a word.

"If your boss has the guts to come back, tell him he's short two P-113s. They're back ordered, and they'll probably be in next week." Tony brushed off his hands and strutted out the door, smiling smugly to himself.

Chapter 29

The world seemed almost normal as Tony lay tucked under the thin blanket and watched the sky turn from a star-studded deep black to light purple, then gradually to pale blue. It was not the place that lent the appearance of normality, for Salisbury was only an association of ideas. It was the memories it held that created meaning. He reminisced fondly of those happy childhood times spent with his grandparents: church suppers, trips to Ocean City and Public Landing, pony penning day at Chincoteague, historic Princess Anne, and the smell of home-cooked Sunday dinners with apple pie for dessert.

Tony rolled away from the latticed windows and surveyed the room that had been his as long as he could remember. There was the lone bureau with the sticky drawers and fogged mirror, the mahogany table that doubled as a desk, the antique cane-bottomed chair, the wobbly nightstand, and the weary mattress with the squeaky springs on the single bed. This was more a home to him than his room in Philadelphia. Here he *belonged*.

He blinked his eyes, and the sun leaped into the sky. He sensed a presence in the room.

"Are you going to sleep all day?"

"Morning, Grandpop." His grandfather used to come up and get him when he was a child and was afraid to walk down the long corridor and dark stairs. "I woke up at sunrise, but I must have dozed off again."

"Well, your grandmother has breakfast almost ready and she was afraid you were going to miss it."

Tony leaped out of bed. "Okay, I'm up."

He pulled on his pants, flung on his shirt, and carried shoes and socks along the hardwood floor. The scent of cooking bacon wafted up the stairs, awakening his hunger.

"Well, land o' mercy, Honey, did you get your nap out? I was beginning to think you was goin' to sleep the whole day away even though your grandfather promised you a horse and buggy ride. Now you just set yourself down an' plow into them carn flakes whilst I get the eggs out'n their shells."

The linoleum floor was cold on his bare feet, so he put on his socks and shoes. Then he did a first-rate plowing job into the cereal. By the time Grandmom put two soft-boiled eggs in a bowl in front of him, he was ready for them.

The hundred-year-old clock gonged once, signaling the half hour. "Gee, it's only seven thirty. I thought you said it was late."

Toast crunched in Grandpop's mouth. "It *is* late."

"But I didn't get to sleep until after one. I was reading."

"I don't know what it is you find in all them books — you and your grandfather both." Grandmom continued her dance steps between the stove, the sink, and the table. "I never could do much reading my own self — it always makes my eyes so tired I feel like takin' a nap."

Tony drained his orange juice. "Well, I'm always interested in what I'm reading."

"Land sakes, Honey, you must be interested in an awful lot o' things. I never did see so many books than when you're around. Right now you get yourself interested in them eggs. And Walter, when you finish your breakfast, you take those scraps out to the chicken yard for me."

Grandpop continued eating. When the pair was done, and the scraps were dumped, they headed across the cornfield for the barn and stable. Tony ran ahead, leaping gaily over the recently plowed rows that were like frozen waves of dirt in an antediluvian plain. Grandpop walked slowly, and with poise. He used that same, unhurried mode throughout life.

The horse stood idly in his corral, munching corncobs from last year's crop. Except for these occasional buggy rides, the only work the horse performed was the plowing of the cornfield, the fruits of which were to be his main staple throughout the next season. It was the nearest thing to perpetual motion that Tony had ever encountered.

The corral did not have a gate, but opened instead into a little room in the barn. This in turn led to the aisle. From outside the fence, Tony coaxed the horse inside with a cube of sugar — he did not want to walk through the straw-covered manure to drag him out.

Grandpop fetched him from inside and led him to the dressing room, outfitted him with a bridle, and gouged the mud out of his shoes. Then he backed him up to the buggy and hitched him in. The old buggy did not get much use any more, but traditions die hard. Grandpop never threw away anything that might have a possible use or value.

The smell of camphor hung faintly around the aged buggy. Tony collected the cans of pellets and placed them on a shelf. With a well-used broom, he swept the dust and cobwebs off the floor, then wiped down the cracked, leather seats with a damp cloth. The buggy creaked and groaned as he clambered over it.

When the horse was firmly in place, Grandpop took an oilcan and squirted the metal joints while checking for loose screws and broken boards. Grandpop lived in an America that was fast disappearing — an America that was pre-industrial, pre-consumerism, pre-disposable, and pre-opulent. It was a slower, saner world — and a happier one.

Even in Salisbury the hinterlands suffered the encroachment of civilization. But Grandpop knew which roads had resisted the progress of paving, and soon the metallic clicking of horseshoes on macadam gave way to the dull thud of iron on loam: the kind of soil that grew corn, tomatoes, watermelons, turnips, potatoes, and soy beans. The metal-hooped wheels crunched through the soil and pushed aside branches that grew close to the narrow, seldom used back roads.

Deep in the woods they stopped at a shallow ford where the rutted road dipped into a clear, fast-running brook. The horse put his front feet into the cold water and bent down for a drink. He was working hard, and sweating. He swished flies with lazy side-to-side motions of his tail.

"Grandpop, how come you never gave the horse a name?"

"Well, I don't rightly know." He put down the reins and wiped his mouth with the back of one wrinkled hand. His paint-flecked baseball cap kept the sun out of his eyes. "I've always had farm animals and never thought about naming them. I've had cows and pigs and chickens that I raised for food. And I've had a slew of horses. They come and go."

"What happens to them?"

"Sometimes they get old and die, and sometimes I trade them in for new."

"Do they really send them to a glue factory?"

Grandpop laughed. "Used to. Nowadays they drag them away for dog food."

"Drag them away?"

"Seems cruel, don't it? I remember one time when your mother was a girl — it was before I took to painting and I was farming full time. Well sir, one of our horses died, and I called up the factory to come and get it. They paid me for it, but I would have been just as happy to pay them for carting it away. Anyway, there's only two ways to get rid of a dead horse — you either cut it up on the spot, or you hitch it to the back of a wagon and haul it out. Well, that's what they did, and your mother couldn't stop crying when she saw them dragging that animal off to the factory."

"Whew, sounds pretty gruesome. But I guess you're right — they're too heavy to pick up and carry."

"Not if you start young."

"What do you mean, start young?"

Grandpop clucked his tongue a couple times, and shook the reins. But the horse went on drinking. "Well, if you took that horse when he was a colt, and every day picked him up on your back and carried him across the field, as the colt grew up and got heavier, you'd get stronger, so by the time he was a full grown horse you'd be able to carry him."

Tony knew when he had his leg pulled. "Grandpop!"

He grinned as he wiped sweat off his brow. "Anyway, when you grow up on a farm and you have animals all the time, you come to look at them different. They're not people. They're not pets. They have a use, either food or draft. And they don't have feelings — only what you put into them. Now you take this horse, he's kind of an unmechanized tractor, or an automobile. Uses corn for fuel 'stead of gasoline. You wouldn't give a name to your car, would you?"

Tony laughed. "Well, actually, we do. Mine's called White Lightning."

"Yes, well, anyway, horses on a farm are just implements. I guess if I had to name him, I'd name him Horse. That way I could never forget."

Tony climbed down from the buggy and stooped by the water's edge. He overturned a few rocks, looking for salamanders. "You know, I don't remember you ever having cows and pigs."

"Oh, that was a few years ago."

"Really? How come I don't remember it. It seems like you've always been a painter."

"Well, it must have been before your time. Fifteen or twenty years, I suspect.

"Fifteen or twenty *years*? But Grandpop, that's as long as my whole life. How can that be just a few years?"

"Well, I guess when you get to be my age, twenty years *is* just a few."

Tony stepped onto a smooth boulder in the middle of the brook. The top was dry, and offered good purchase. As he crouched down to examine the colored pebbles in the water, something splashed in front of him, wetting his face. "Grandpop, did you throw some . . . ?"

He was looking right at him when another splash came. He glanced out at the woods, suspecting country boys. After the third splash he looked down fast enough to see where the ripples originated. Two of the "pebbles" broke the surface of the water, and one had two dimples on it. Then he recognized the head and body of the amphibian and reached out — just as it leaped into his hand.

"Hey, look at this." Tony ran back to the buggy with the squiggly frog in his clenched fist.

"You better bring it around this side, Tony. I'm afraid I'm feeling a might slow this morning."

He ran around the back of the buggy and brought the frog to him. As soon as he opened his hand, the little frog made a leap for freedom, but Tony clamped his fingers around it before it made good its escape. He could feel it kicking. "What kind is it?"

"I'll need a better look than that before I can tell you."

"But if I open my hand to show you, it'll get away."

"You're going to let him go anyway. I'll tell you what. You put him down on the ground so he won't hurt himself, and I'll get a good look as he hops away."

Tony bent close to the ground. "Okay, but you better be fast. Ready?"

Grandpop nodded, and Tony opened his hand. There was not even a moment's hesitation before the frog launched itself on powerful hind legs. A series of short hops brought it to a patch of long grass along the muddy bank, and the next hop kerplunked it into the shallow water. Tony caught a glimpse of it plopping furiously downstream, before the sun's reflection on the smooth surface obscured its flight.

"It looked like a fowler toad."

"Wow. I hardly had time to see it myself, and I was looking right at it. How could you tell?"

"I've been seeing the same toads since I was a boy. Got a white stripe down his back. And a frog would've taken one leap right across the crick."

"But I thought toads lived on land, and frogs lived in the water."

"Mostly that's true. Frogs can't live away

from water because their skin will dry up. But toads can live in and around the water — they can hold their breath just like frogs. And since they all come from tadpoles they both have to lay their eggs in the water."

"Gee, I never thought about that." Tony climbed back up into the buggy. Grandpop clucked his tongue again. The horse shook his head on his massive neck. Flies buzzed around the blinders. He shook his head again, then lurched off, jerking the buggy through the rocky brook. "How come you know so much?"

"I guess I just picked it up over the years — in books or magazines. I just remembered it."

"Grandpop, do you still remember things that happened a long time ago? I mean, like when you were my age?"

"Some."

"Well, I was wondering. Things that happened to you — bad things, unhappy things. Do you remember them? I mean, I never hear you talk about the bad times: the depression, and the war."

"Which war?"

Tony snickered. "I forgot. Your time goes back to the first one."

"Not the *first* one."

"Well, you know what I mean — the First World War. My father's always talking about the depression, and the war — the Second World War, that is. About when his father died, and stuff. But you never do."

Grandpop put both reins in his left hand and reached up with his right to remove his cap, scratch his head, and work the cap back into place. "Bad memories have a habit of getting lost over the years. I guess that's because it hurts and you don't want to remember the pain. You put it in the back of your mind, or cover it up with good thoughts. You never forget, really, you just lose awareness, like in a dream. I can remember once when your mother was a girl. She was in high school then, and right smart for her age. Well, she came home one day with her head so low her chin was draggin' on the ground. And she wouldn't talk none, or tell me what was wrong. Finally, she started to cry, and showed me her report card. Seems she got a bad grade in arithmetic. Well, to her that was just about the end of the world. I didn't pay it no nevermind, 'cause I only went to the sixth grade, so she had a whole lot more education than me. Bet she don't even remember it now."

The trees crowded in, and the woods got darker with the thickness of pine. He separated the reins and pulled on the left one, directing the horse onto a side path.

"You see, when you're young everything seems more important that it should — I guess because you have nothing to compare it to. But when you grow up, your problems grow up too. After a while, it don't seem so big any more. Now, you take me and your grandmother. When we were young, and engaged, we naturally wanted to be together. But then the war came along — the *first* one, that is — and I had to go away in the army, kinda like what you're going through now. Well, we couldn't afford to be married, and we didn't want to be apart, but that's the way it had to be. Then I went away for a little while, and when I got back — "

"What do you mean by a little while?"

"I don't rightly remember — must have been a year or two, though. Anyway, when I got back we got married and bought a farm with the money I saved in the army, and settled down and forgot all about that time we were apart — because we were too busy taking care of the farm and getting enough food to eat to think back on it.

"Next thing you know, along comes the depression and we had more trouble than you could shake a stick at. Living on a farm we had plenty to eat, but most folks couldn't afford to buy our produce. Your mom was walking around in rags. I had to take to painting to make a few extra dollars. There was a time there when we fell behind in our bills and almost lost the farm. And I worried and worried — and so did your grandmother. And Bethy worried, too, but mostly about her marks in school because she couldn't understand our problems. And you know what I found out? All that worrying didn't do a blessed thing to pay those bills."

The buggy broke out into an open glade — a clearing that had once been a field long since fallow. Tall sunflowers were the only crop, honey bees the only reapers. The sun was warm and bright and full of life.

"But Grandpop, when you're young, how can you not worry about things that are about to happen to you?"

"I never said you could. All I'm saying is you got to think about the good 'stead of the bad, what you have 'stead of what you don't. Remember your Sunday school teachings."

"Well, I don't go to church as often as you."

"It don't matter. Understanding God is only a way of understanding people. You got to take what comes, and make the best of it. Don't worry about what other people think, just do what's right. God will always be on your side."

Chapter 30

"What the hell kind of trouble are you getting me into now!"

Tony stopped short at the kitchen door. He was a little tired after the three-hour drive. "Sorry, I must be in the wrong house."

"Don't give me none of your smart mouth

answers." The Sunday paper was spread over the table like used wrapping paper. With a sweep of his arms Frank pushed it aside, along with his coffee cup, empty plate and silverware, and a scrawled-on pad, as if to make fighting room. "Your mouth already got me in trouble with the union."

"And *I'm* the one who had to answer the phone and talk to the business manager." Elizabeth wagged her nail file in Tony's direction.

Frank pushed the papers further away, until some of them went over the edge of the table and onto the floor. "Right? Right? You even got her involved."

Tony looked from one to the other. "Would someone please tell me what this is all about?"

Frank swung his hands about wildly. "Go ahead. Tell him."

Elizabeth drew up her bathrobe and retied the belt. "All I know is they said there was trouble on one of the jobs and they were threatening to put up a picket line."

"Right? Right?" He pushed the papers further away, clearing a territory. "And they're accusing *me* of putting nonunion men on the job. Now tell me it's not your fault."

Tony merely gaped. "I still don't see the connection."

"Don't you work for me? And ain't you nonunion? And didn't I send you to deliver material to the job on Friday?"

"Yes. So what?"

"Don't get smart with me," Frank said, half rising to his feet, "or I'll throw you right through that door. And don't you think I won't. Now answer me, weren't you there on Friday?"

"I already said yes. Do you want a different answer?"

Frank got completely to his feet, scooped up what was left of the paper, and hurled it. Tony jerked back slightly, but the loose sheets fell apart in midair and fluttered past him harmlessly.

"Don't talk back to me, goddamn it!"

"Dad, what are you getting so excited about? Why don't you tell me what's going on before you fly off the handle. I still don't know what job you're talking about."

"Don't try to lie your way out of it. I had to go down there and smooth the whole thing out. Eliot told me the whole story. But there were already two business agents on the job and they threatened to shut the whole job down."

Tony huffed. "That's a little ridiculous, isn't it? I mean, there were only two other men working there."

"It don't matter how many men are there, they can still shut the job down. Now I want to know what you said to him?"

"To whom?"

"To Eliot, who do you think — the man in the moon?"

"But you said he already told you. You aren't going to believe *me*." After a pause, "You never have before."

"I wanta know what you said."

"I said I had some fixtures for him."

"And what did he say?"

"He was drinking coffee, so he said to get lost and come back in a half hour. Seems like an awful long time for a coffee break."

"And what did you do?"

"I did my job — I delivered the material that *he* asked for."

"You musta did something wrong!"

"Yeah, well, did it ever occur to you that maybe *he* was wrong, or do you just automatically assume that everything *I* do is wrong?"

"You can't fight the union. Whatever they say goes."

"So who's fighting the union? I don't have to take any flak off him just because he belongs to the union. He's no different from me."

"But he's got a union ticket and you don't. That gives him the right to tell you to wait till he's ready."

"Don't you care that he's taking half-hour coffee breaks on your time? And what was I supposed to do — sit around and wait till he got ready to do some work? Am I supposed to hold up all the other jobs that needed material just because of him?"

"I don't care. I can't afford to have the union mad at me. How many times do I gotta tell you — you're not supposed to unload material on a commercial job. Period."

"Dad, you're not making any sense."

"Who's not making any sense?"

Tony squinted at his father. "Are you paying any attention to me? I said you, and when I say you, I mean you. Do you want me to spell out your name?"

Frank pushed the table forward, knocking down the opposite chair. The coffee cup overturned in its saucer, spilling its contents across the table top into a pool on the floor. "Goddamn you!"

Elizabeth stepped between father and son and absorbed the shock of Frank's lunge. Her curlers were torn loose from their moorings. "Stop it, you two! Stop it!"

Frank made a feint past her, but she held onto his arm. He stood balanced on both feet, his chest heaving, his paunch shaking like a bowl of jelly. His hair had broken free of its Vitalis grip and fell forward across his face, half covering his eyes. His whole mien was contorted in abject anger.

Elizabeth pushed him back against the wall. He breathed heavily for half a minute with his beady eyes narrowed onto Tony's. Then he bent down and picked up his chair and slammed it back onto its feet. He continued standing. Elizabeth relaxed her grip, stepped aside, and fell against the counter as if it were a brace. She began wailing.

"Now see what you did?"

"What do you mean, me? I'm standing here trying to reason with you, and you're getting yourself into a rage over nothing."

"Who's in a rage?"

"You are. Why do you think you're screaming?"

"I'm screaming because you got me in trouble with the union. I got a business to run and they can put me right out of business. It's hard enough getting a day's work out of a man without you stirring up trouble. If they sit down on the job I can lose my shirt."

"They can't sit down on the job."

Elizabeth's whimpering went unheeded.

"The hell they can't. I got two days work left, and if they want they can stretch it out to a week. And I wouldn't put it past 'em. A hold-up like that and all my profits go out the window."

"If they slow up the job, you fire them."

"I can't fire 'em, don't you understand?"

"If you hired them, you can fire them."

"The union won't let me fire 'em."

"You just got finished saying you have a business to run, and now you're saying the union won't let you fire men who are laying down on the job. Who runs your business, anyway — you or the union?"

"I run it, and nobody tells me what to do. But the union won't let me fire anybody without a good excuse."

"Isn't intentionally slowing down the job and making the contractor lose money a good enough excuse?"

"No, because the union'll back 'em on it."

"What kind of union will give themselves a bad name by letting their men ruin a contractor?"

"Any union. None of 'em are any good. They all stick together."

"Even if the men are in the wrong?"

"That's right. You think they care what happens to me?"

"They should. You're their bread and butter."

"That don't mean nothing. As far as the union is concerned, the men are always right and the contractor is always wrong. And I got to stay on their good side because I have more gas stations coming up and I need those men to do the work."

"You mean you'd hire the same troublemakers again, knowing what they're like?"

"I got no choice. The union sends the men out, and I have to take what they send me."

"You don't have to do anything you don't want to. And you especially don't have to hire men who take half-hour coffee breaks and refuse to unload material when it's delivered. I'm getting paid, too, you know. And not for sitting around waiting for no good reason."

"You get paid to do what I tell you."

"Not if what you told me isn't right."

"Since when are you so high and mighty you get to make decisions about what's right? *I* make the decisions around here, and *I* say what's right. You ain't nothing but a smart-ass kid, and till you're twenty-one you ain't got no rights. You just do what you're told."

"Not when you start telling me to do something wrong. That's where I draw the line. I'll make my own decisions about what's right and wrong. And when it comes to doing my job, I'll do what's expected of me only as long as it's the right thing to do. You may be afraid of those jerks on the job, but I'm not."

"Who's afraid?"

"You are. You. F—r—a—n—k."

"Yeah, well, let me tell you something, mister. I ain't afraid o' nobody."

"Then why are you sticking up for the union and the men on the job if you're not afraid?"

"Because the union has the final say so. I got to do what they tell me, or they'll put me out of business."

"You're talking in circles. You contradict yourself with every other sentence. If you weren't afraid, you'd stand for one set of principles, rather than changing sides whenever it's convenient."

Frank pounded his fist on the table, cracking the surface. "*I'm not afraid, I told you!*"

He charged forward like a mad bull, with both fists in front of him. Elizabeth tried to intervene, but his strong forearm caught her on the shoulder and brushed her aside like a swatted fly. Even as she was falling she caught his arm and hung on.

"Let go of me!"

Frank tried to disentangle himself. While she was wrestling with his left arm, he swung his other in a roundhouse, catching Tony across the face. The force of the blow knocked him past the edge of the counter and onto the floor.

"Stop it, Frank. Stop it. Leave him alone."

She wrestled him back to the wall while Tony crawled away on his back. He tasted salt in his mouth, and felt a hole in his lower lip. Frank rolled past Elizabeth, this time kicking with his right foot. Tony threw up his arms. Frank's socks slipped on the smooth linoleum and, with Elizabeth still pulling him back, he fell down hard. Elizabeth cracked her head resoundingly against the doorjamb, and went slack. Frank scrambled to his feet and, finding his way blocked by the table, picked it up by the corner and heaved it over. It crashed into the refrigerator. Porcelain shattered, silverware clattered, and everything went flying.

He stood with his shirt torn and his hair disheveled, drooling like a madman. Tony jumped to his feet and raced up the stairs to his room, closing and locking the door. A few seconds later he heard elephantine steps tramping along the hall. The door burst open, ripping the latch out of the woodwork and sending the knob through the plaster wall.

"Frank, stop it. Leave him alone. Stop it. You're tearing my house apart."

Frank stood there glaring, with Elizabeth clinging to his arm like a rag doll. Tony backed up to the bed and hopped onto the mattress. He put his hands out in front of him to ward off another attack.

"Listen to me, you son-of-a-bitch. If you ever raise a hand to me again, I'll kill you." Frank's voice was low and guttural. Spittle ran down the side of his mouth. "You've cost me nothing but trouble your whole life. Money for this and money for that. Well, you know what? I'm glad they drafted you, 'cause at least I won't hafta put up with you any more. I'll be glad when you're gone."

Chapter 31

The rat-tat-tat on the window came like a rifle crack in the dark, and brought Tony out of a nervous, uncomfortable sleep. He drew up to a sitting position just as the beam of a flashlight shone through the glass and burned into his eyes. He covered his face with one hand, and rolled down the window with the other.

"What are you doing?"

Tony squinted at the light. "What does it look like I'm doing? I'm sleeping."

"Are you all right?"

"I was until you woke me up."

The light beam dropped, and reflected off highly polished black shoes. Tony made out a blue uniform, a black leather jacket, a badge.

"You know it's dangerous to sleep with your engine on."

Tony turned off the ignition switch, and the smooth purr died out. "Yes, but I got cold. I only meant to leave it on long enough to get warm. I guess I fell asleep."

The voice barked with urgency. "Are you sure there's nothing wrong?"

"No. I mean, yes. I'm sure. There's nothing wrong. I just want to go to sleep."

"You're not supposed to sleep in your car, you know?"

"Whose car am I supposed to sleep in?" Tony followed the pregnant silence with, "Why not? Is there a law against it?"

The light came back up, centered on Tony's chest. "Vagrancy laws."

"Well, right at the moment I haven't got any better place to sleep, so it'll have to do."

"How about showing me your driver's license and owner's card?"

Tony produced the documents, and the policeman wrote down the pertinent information on his pad. "Okay. But I'll stop back later to check up on you."

"Thanks." Tony rolled up the window and promptly went back to sleep. He woke up shivering, turned on the engine, and lay curled up on the front seat under the blast of air from the heater. When he warmed up, he turned off the engine. Later, he woke up and turned it back on again. It as an awful, broken rest.

Rat-tat-tat. "Are you sure you're all right?"

Tony peered from under heavy lids. "Yes, I'm all right."

"Okay. Just checking."

Tony went back to his endless routine of resting, freezing, starting the engine, dozing, turning off the engine, and resting. Sometime around first light he heard another knock at the window.

Without opening the window, Tony shouted, "I said I'm all right."

He heard a muffled, "Sorry, buddy," as the white clad milkman jumped back into his truck and drove away.

He turned off the engine and buried his face in the crook of his arm, but every time he moved, an arc of light bolted into his eyes and woke him up. He turned so his face was against the corner of the seat, but found that he could not breath. He pulled his shirt up over his face, but his back got so cold that it kept him awake.

With the noise of cars starting and people going to work, Tony gave up further ideas of sleep. He winced at the pain in his right eye, and with his tongue he kept trying to dislodge an unidentified mass in his left cheek. There was a foul taste in his mouth.

At a gas station, as the attendant put five dollars worth of gas into his tank, Tony went to the john and tossed cold water on his face. He did not like what he saw through the cracked, foggy mirror, but got cleaned up as best he could, wiping away dried blood and combing his hair.

At a diner he found a secluded booth and ordered toast and coffee. He nursed his agony through a second and third cup. He was in no rush, had nowhere to go, no one to see. His friends were either in school or work. After his fourth cup of coffee, he left a sizable tip and spent the rest of the day at the Free Library.

He found a recent issue of *Time*, with a crude

bust of General Westmoreland on the cover, and a banner with the proclamation, "Man of the Year." He opened it up to a photograph titled "U.S. Marines in Action in Vietnam." In an open rice paddy, a group of baggy-clothed marines crouched behind a low dike, peering over bayoneted rifles at an unseen enemy.

"Nothing is worse than war? Dishonor is worse than war. Slavery is worse than war." After quoting Westmoreland, the article read on like a scenario out of a Hollywood movie. A full-page map of Vietnam, filled with unreadable place names, showed where the fighting was the worst. At the end of the article was an impassioned speech by Secretary of State Dean Rusk:

"All that's left is the question of what we do about the North Vietnamese attempt to take over South Vietnam by force. We're down to the bare bone. Do we stand aside and let them take it? We do not! There are no tricks or gimmicks here. There is no lack of diplomatic energy or effort on our part to bring the war to a peaceful conclusion. We could have peace in 24 hours if the other side stops what it is doing. The only other thing — the only other egg we could add to this basket — would be South Vietnam itself. Just give it to them. And that is what we will *not* do."

Tony replaced the magazine and leafed through several days-old newspapers. The headlines shouted war, fighting, and death:

4,000 GIs Land In S. Viet Nam
Saigon, April 29-(AP)-The United States landed more than 4,000 fresh combat troops in Viet Nam today, boosting the American buildup to nearly 250,000 men.

. . . The new U.S. troops were jungle-trained infantrymen of the 25th "Tropic Lightning" Division based at Schofield Barracks, Hawaii.

. . . General William C. Westmoreland, U.S. commander in Viet Nam, welcomed the GIs.

. . . The division's third Brigade arrived last December and set up camp at Pleiku, in the central highlands 240 miles northeast of Saigon.

. . . The 25th Infantry won its nickname for its combat record in the jungles of the South Pacific in World War II. Some elements of the division, however, descend from units that fought in the Civil War.

. . . No long range limit on the size of the U.S. forces in Viet Nam has been announced by the Pentagon, but the allied command hopes to field a

million Vietnamese, American, and other troops against the Communists by the end of 1968.

At last, he picked up a science fiction novel and lost himself in the adventures of outer space. By the middle of the afternoon, he took the only reasonable course of action left to him. He went to see Mrs. Clark.

Chapter 32

"Ouch!"

"Well, hold your head still."

"I'm trying, but it stings. What is it — iodine?"

'It's only Mercurochrome and it doesn't hurt."

"If you were on my side of my face you wouldn't say that."

"Well, if you had come here first thing it would have been a lot easier. You had no business sleeping in your car when there's a perfectly good bed in Joey's room."

"Ouch!" Tony tried to move his head, but Mrs. Clark held him with a grip of iron. "And who said I slept, anyway? It was like an emergency room on Saturday night out there — everyone was stopping to inquire about my health. And what was I supposed to do, knock on your door at two o'clock in the morning?"

"And why not?"

"Well, I didn't want to impose. Ouch!"

"What are you ouching for? I haven't touched you yet."

"Yes, but you were going to."

"Ouch!" he said again, when she did.

"There. You're finished." After she let him go, he could still feel where the pressure of her fingers had been. She screwed the applicator cap back on the bottle. "Now, what makes you think you'd be imposing?"

Tony felt his lip, tenderly. "Well, I didn't want to wake anyone up."

"Don't touch it or you'll wipe off the Mercurochrome. Then I'll have to put more on." Tony drew his hand away. "Wait till it dries. Now if you had come here last night I could have put a hunk of raw meat on that eye of yours and the bruise would practically be gone by now."

"Aw, Mrs. Clark. That's just an old wives tale."

"Young man, are you calling me an old wife?"

"I didn't say you were an old wife. I said it was an old wives *tale.*"

"Tony, you may be mature for your age, but I won't have you talking about my tail. After all, I'm old enough to be your mother."

Tony sighed deeply. "Sometimes I wish you

were."

She winked at him. "In that case I'm going to treat you like my own son. Now you go bring your things in and put them up in Joey's room. Then you can get washed up while I get supper started." She cuffed him playfully on the back of the head and pushed him out of the kitchen.

"Thanks, Mrs. Clark."

"Don't thank me, just do as I say."

"Okay." He carried in his suitcase, still unpacked from his trip to Salisbury, and his overnight bag. Joey had always been in love with the Air Force, and his room showed it. His bureau had three model airplanes on it, each meticulously painted and decaled; the walls were decorated with photographs of Air Force planes, jets, and enlistment posters; one wall contained a whole shelf of books on fighter planes of World War Two. He had enlisted over three years ago, but his mother kept his room just the way he left it, as if he had only gone away for the weekend and was expected back any minute. The furniture was dusted, the threadbare carpet vacuumed. Tony immediately felt at home in the ordered neatness.

The first thing he took out of his bag was his toothbrush, which he used to great advantage. He washed in the bathroom sink, careful not to disturb any of Mrs. Clark's carefully dabbed ointment. He donned a clean set of clothes and stuffed his dirty ones into a T-shirt. Then he unpacked all his clothes and put them in piles on the bed. His books and personal items he placed on the chest-of-drawers after pushing Joey's things toward the back.

****

"Well, you look like you're pretty well settled in."

Tony motioned to the bookshelves. "This room is almost like my own, except that my books are about science."

"You're both pretty much alike. Joey was always a reader, too. Spent a lot of time in the library 'cause we couldn't afford to buy him all the books he wanted. The little snooker would take five books out at a time — the limit — but never wanted to take them back. He used to hide them so we couldn't find them. Then, one day I'd get a postcard from the library saying a certain book was overdue, and I'd have to tear his room apart looking for it. I can't tell you how much money I paid in late fines. Oh, he's a card, that one."

Tony picked up a pile of shirts and looked in the closet. "I wish I knew him better."

"Wait a minute, I'll get you some more hangers." She was back in a minute with a handful of wire hangers. Tony pushed aside Joey's high school clothes. "Yes, you two would get along well, despite the difference in your ages."

"When's he coming home next?"

"I don't expect we'll see him till Christmas. He was home last summer, after flight school. But airfare from Germany is expensive. Besides, he'd rather spend his time traveling through Europe."

"I guess I missed him last year because I spent the summer with my grandparents. And before that he was always — older. Ben doesn't talk about him much."

"Oh, those two are worlds apart. Not that they don't get along. They love each other as if they were real brothers. It's just that they have different ways of looking at things. Joey's not so — radical." She paused for a moment, staring. "Well, you just go on with your unpacking. I've got to go to the grocery store for a couple things. Would you check on the stew every once in a while and give it a stir? I don't want the bottom to burn."

"Well, okay. But, how about if I go to the store for you?"

"That would be even better — if you don't mind."

"I'll try to fit it into my schedule."

Mrs. Clark laughed. "Good. Give me a minute to make a list." When he met her at the front door a few minutes later, she handed him a slip of paper and a twenty-dollar bill.

"I'll just take the list."

"Don't be silly." She forced the bill into his hand. "You take this money or you don't get the list, and I'll have to do the shopping myself."

"But, Mrs. Clark, all this food is for me."

"Like hell it is. Since when do you need five pounds of sugar and two cans of tomato puree?"

"Well . . . "

"Well, nothing. You're doing me a big favor just by going. Now get."

Chapter 33

"Actually, it's been a pretty good week." Tony crossed his legs and leaned back on his elbows on the soft, gold carpet. "I spent my mornings talking with Mrs. Clark, my afternoons visiting the guys at work, and Ben at college — I even sat in on one of his lectures. I went hiking in Pennypack Park with Teddy. And the evenings I spent hanging out with the guys. Now I'm seeing you. So why should I go back?"

"But what about your mother and father? Didn't you go home at all?" Patty squirmed a little closer. For once, the television was turned off.

"What for?"

"Well, they must be worried about you."

Tony absently fingered the injury. "Oh, yes, the swelling is gone, and I can only feel it if you push against it hard."

Patty caressed it lightly, sending a tingling sensation through Tony's body — one that was not in the least painful. "It looks a lot better without the Mercurochrome, too."

Tony laughed. "I know. I was glad when Mrs. Clark finally stopped putting it on. I dreaded going through the ordeal twice a day."

"Was it really that sore?"

"No, not really. "I'm exaggerating. It only hurt the first couple times."

Patty smiled pertly. "You know, I didn't want to say this Monday night, but you sure looked terrible."

"I *felt* terrible."

"It was nice of Mrs. Clark to take you in, too." Patty looked down at her lap and fingered the print skirt. She rocked slowly back and forth on crossed legs, one knee exposed. "But why did she do it?"

"Because that's the kind of person she is. She's — well, she's just a good person. She's been through some hard times in her life. She likes people, and she loves her family, and — I don't know. Maybe she just took pity on me because I'm the same age as her own son, and she would want someone to do the same for him."

"I still think it's strange. My whole life I've been shuffled around from house to house because nobody wanted me. I just didn't think there were people like that."

"Your grandmother took you in."

"That's different. She only lets me live here because she needs a slave. She needs someone to go to the store for her, and run errands, and someone to pick on when she's feeling mean, and make do the housework. She just likes having someone around to yell at. She couldn't even keep her own husband around. He was smart; he left years ago."

"I didn't know your grandfather was still alive."

"Oh, I don't know if he is. She never talks about him. I only know that he ran out on her a long time ago — before I was born. Nobody's heard from him since. But I'm sure she drove him away."

"Well, she does come on a little strong at times, but I don't see her as being the ogre you make her out to be."

Patty moved closer, her arm touching Tony's. "That's because she always puts on airs for company. But when nobody's around she treats me like dirt."

"Still, she let me see you during the week."

"That's only because I called my mom on the phone and had her talk to her. She knows you're going away tomorrow, and told my grandmother it would be all right if I saw you. Next week, when you're gone, everything will

go back to normal."

"Well, look at the bright side of things: at least you have a place to live."

Patty leaned her head on Tony's shoulder. "You know, I always wanted to live in an orphanage, just so I could get away from my grandmother. I even used to think about committing a crime, like shoplifting, or something, so I could get sent to a correctional home."

"Patty, you wouldn't want to live with those kinds of girls."

"Why not? Kathy used to live in one, for a whole year. She hit one of her teachers with a wastepaper basket and she had to be sent to the hospital for stitches. She had a pretty good time there. Some of the stories she told me sounded like fun."

"Somehow I just don't think of girls being bad."

Patty jerked away as if stung. "What! Are you kidding? Girls are worse than boys. Did you ever see two girls fight?"

"I didn't think girls knew *how* to fight."

"They may not know how to box, but they'll tear your hair out and scratch out your eyes. They don't let up like boys do."

"Sounds pretty gruesome. But why would you want to go someplace where all they do is fight all the time?"

"I didn't say they fight all the time — just some of the time. Mostly they drink and smoke and have wild sex parties."

"Where do they get the booze and cigarettes? And how do they sneak in the boys?"

"Anything can be smuggled in. And who said anything about boys. Girls don't need boys, you know. Boys just like to think they do. Girls can have a pretty good time by themselves."

Tony pushed himself up to a squat. "You know, I could use a glass of water."

Patty shrugged, and stood up. "Well, come on into the kitchen."

Tony marveled at the lavish trim. The cabinets were made of fine-grained cherry, with brass latches. The drawers were lined with green felt. The soffit was set back and the cabinet tops decorated with filigreed brass wire, behind which poised a collection of antique bottles and glassware. Ornate, red-splash tiles replaced the usual wallpaper. All the appliances were Coppertone, and built in.

"How about a Coke? Water sounds pretty drab."

"Okay." She filled two glasses, and handed one to Tony. He drank half right down. "You know, I'm glad you stayed home this weekend. I mean, I know how much you wanted to go to the shore with your mother and Bob."

"Oh, that's all right. I can always go next

weekend, after you're gone."

"I couldn't have done any work for him anyway. I don't have my tools, or anything."

"I didn't want to spend time working, either. I just wanted to walk along the beach, and stuff. But I had fun here, going up to Washington's Crossing again, and walking through the woods. And going out to dinner with Ben and Kate was fun. I still can't believe you climbed all the way to the top of the tower at night. I was afraid just going up those rickety stairs in the daytime. And it's so much work."

Tony sipped lightly. "You should have gone all the way up."

"And get my hair blown all over the place?"

"A little wind never hurt anyone. Maybe the next time you'll make it all the way."

Patty left her glass untouched. "If you think you're going to get me up there again, you're crazy. I only went because everyone else was there. I'd rather do my sightseeing from a car."

Tony shrugged. "Oh, well. Maybe someday you'll change your mind." He swirled the remainder of his Coke in the bottom of the glass. "So where's your grandmother today?"

Patty tilted her head noncommittally. "Oh, she went on a bus trip with the Senior Citizen's Group. I think they went to Washington, or something. Anyway, she won't be back till late. Hey, I almost forgot. Do you want your going away present now?"

Tony hesitated for a moment. "Uh, well, I didn't know you were getting me anything."

"It's not much. Just something for you to remember me by."

"Oh, well. That's nice."

Patty put down her glass and took him by the arm. "Come on. It's upstairs." She dragged him out of the kitchen. "Besides, I want you to see my room. I spent all morning cleaning it."

Tony barely got his empty glass down before she whisked him out the door and up the stairs. Patty's furniture was in direct contrast to the rest of the house. The furniture was cheap white pine, shellacked blonde, and the bureau was covered from end to end with bottles of perfume, nail polish, hair spray, deodorants, and a wide assortment of makeup accessories. Other than the total confusion, it looked more like a chemists workbench.

The closet door was open. Dresses, skirts, slacks, and blouses hung on wire hangers so jammed together that they bulged out the open door. The floor was a jumbled mass of shoes that had the look of being tossed in. The drawers of the chest were half open, with underwear and nylons sticking out.

"It's not always this neat." Patty rummaged through one of the bureau drawers. Tony caught a glimpse of papers, pencils, rubber bands, and assorted trivia. "Well, here it is." She opened an envelope and took out a stack of miniature, black and white photographs. "Kathy and I were just kidding around in the first set. I tried to get her to smile, but she wouldn't stop making faces. I think she uses too much makeup, but she says it doesn't matter anyway because boys only look at your face long enough to say hello. Then they look at your body. She uses her face to get boys to take her out the first time, and her body to get them to take her out again."

Tony made no reply, but took the stack of pictures and leafed through them. The second set featured Patty, from the shoulders up, posing with different smiles.

"I like this one best." One wisp of dark hair was broken free, and curled gracefully across her left eye and cheek. There was just a hint of white between darkened lips, and a touch of a dimple. "You can have them all, if you want, but I figured you could put that one in your wallet."

"Thank you. I like it." He gave her a peck on the cheek. He took out his wallet and slid it into one of the empty plastic holders. "And there it will stay."

"I don't want you to forget me when you're running around the world to all those exotic places."

"You've been reading too many enlistment posters," Tony laughed. "Look, I'd like to keep the others, too. Not the ones of Kathy, just you."

"Okay." She took the pictures he handed to her and shoved them back into the drawer. "Does that mean you're going to think about me while you're away?"

Tony put his arm around her and drew her close. "Of course. And I'm going to write every day — if you'll write back."

Patty leaned heavily into him. "I'm not real good at writing letters, but I'll try. Mostly, I just want to get letters back from you."

"Well, you'll write whenever you can, won't you?"

She nodded, her chin digging slightly into his collarbone. "Do you mind if we sit down?"

"No, of course not." Tony looked around, but there was only one chair in the room, and that was piled high with dirty clothes.

"Over here." She dragged him to the edge of the bed.

Tony sagged into the mattress, and pushed it down with his hands. "How can you sleep in anything this soft? Doesn't it bother you?"

"No, I like it just fine." She fell backwards and rolled onto her side. "See, it's really comfortable."

Tony pushed again, harder. "I don't know.

I'm used to a hard mattress and spring."

"It's not bad when you lie down on it."

He leaned back tentatively on his elbows. "Well, it's not too bad. He lay back, then faced her. He avoided touching her with his hardness.

"Tony?"

"Yes."

"Do you like me?"

"Of course I like you."

"I'm glad, because I like you, too." She snuggled up close to him, sliding one arm around his waist. She touched her mouth to his neck.

Tony backed away, but kissed her on the cheek. Then he found her mouth with his and plunged into a long, grinding kiss. Patty pulled tighter with her hand, kneading his back with her fingers. Tony fought to back away, but her grip was firm. His hips were pressed up against hers. He kept kissing while she ran her hands down to the base of his spine and up over his waist. When the pressure eased he backed away, and her hand ran right down over his erect penis. She squeezed hard, then released him and slid her hand around his buttock and pulled him close again, rubbing him with the warmth and firmness of her hips.

Now he ground against her as hard as he could, his whole world revolving around that thrusting movement. Patty caught the material of her skirt and pulled it up with one finger, first over her knees, then up to her hips. Together they fumbled with Tony's belt. The hook gave them trouble, but once it was loose, Patty deftly snapped open the top button. The zipper slid down easily.

Tony sneaked one hand between their pumping bodies and caressed one breast, felt the crinkling of blouse and brassiere. Patty worked his penis out of the opening in his boxer shorts and squeezed with that same pressure that had almost set him off before. In a second she was on her back, pulling Tony on top of her. He fitted neatly between her spread legs. There were no panties to prevent him from entering.

She held onto his buttocks with both hands and pressed him inside her. He felt the dampness, the warmth, the soft, velvety down of her pubis. He felt her hand on the back of his head as she pulled his mouth down onto hers and kissed him with deep, penetrating jabs of her tongue.

Tony ground into her harder, as if his life were at stake, afraid that he would slip out of her. The end of each thrust was a deep horrible, wrenching pain that forced him to lunge forward again. The world disappeared from his consciousness. Tiny pinpoints of light sparkled in front of his tightly clenched eyes. His awareness tunneled into his own labored breathing,

the incredible energy in his groin, and the sudden expulsion and unimaginable pleasure that covered his body from head to toe — an unending wave that swept over him like a great sea. When it finally stopped — all too quickly — he felt a queer satisfaction, a strange understanding, and a quiet realization that he had accomplished something wonderful.

Tony found himself gasping for breath, and in a cold sweat. Still he clung to Patty, as if she were a phantom that would dissolve in the night. Her hands held onto him like tiger claws, and she continued to move rhythmically. Tony countered each thrust with one of his own, scared by her wild, animal noises whenever he came close to slipping out. He collapsed with exhausted relief when she uttered a final, loud moan, followed by a series of quiet sobs that emerged with each exhalation, until she fell limp and apparently unconscious.

Moments later, Tony rolled softly away, lay down beside her with one arm draped over her side, and drifted off to sleep.

Chapter 34

Tony turned his key in the lock and slipped inside quietly. A lone nightlight cast dim shadows across the living room, lending a garish view of the antique furniture. He tiptoed across the worn carpet to the base of the stairs.

"Tony, where have you been? It's after midnight."

"Oh, hi, Mrs. Clark." A lamp went on, and Tony squinted in the explosion of light. He clinked the key down on the coffee table in front of her. "I guess I won't be needing this any more."

She put down her magazine. "You know you have to get up early tomorrow."

Tony shrugged and sat down beside her. "Well, I was just walking around." He unzipped his jacket. 'It's a little chilly out, too."

"Do you want some coffee?"

"No, not really. I think I'll just go to bed. I've got a big day ahead of me."

Mrs. Clark calmly sipped from her own cup. "You know, your mother's worried about you."

"Wha — what do you mean?"

"I mean that you'd better call her and tell her you're all right. She's worried about you."

"What makes you think so?"

"She called here about an hour ago. And she did nothing but cry the whole time. You know, she loves you very much."

"Well, she has a funny way of showing it."

"People don't always know how to say things properly, or show how they feel. Some people are very good at hiding their emotions — so good that you might think they don't have any. To make them see the light, it sometimes takes a very great shock, sometimes even death. In your mother's case, it only took your absence."

Tony picked up the key and fidgeted with it. It was suddenly slippery and oily. "How did she find out I was here?"

"I called her and told her."

Tony stared at her hard, his eyes narrow and piercing. He tried hard to keep his voice level. "Why did you do that?"

"Because she's your mother, and whether you know it or not she cares about you. She's not a very strong woman. She never learned to do things on her own. But you're stronger than she is, so you have to make up for her lack."

Tony sat quietly for a moment, then slowly climbed to his feet. "I guess you're right, Mrs. Clark." He sighed, and walked quietly to the kitchen. He closed the door before lifting the phone from its cradle. Then he hesitated a long time before rotating the dial. Finally, his fingers spun out the seven digits. He heard five rings before the line was opened.

"Hello." The lone word was pronounced delicately, feebly.

"Hi, Mom."

"Tony." She quickly broke down to a sob. "Oh, Tony, I thought you were going to go away without calling me."

There was a long lapse of silence, during which Tony continued to play with the key.

"How — how are you?"

"I'm okay."

"Where have you been? What are you doing?"

"I've just been hanging around, saying good-bye to my friends. You know." There was another lapse of silence during which he could hear stifled sobs. His eyes became glassy.

"When — when are you leaving?"

"First thing in the morning."

"So soon? I — I thought . . . Are you going to come home first? To pick up your things?"

"No, I don't think so. There's no reason for me to come home. The army will provide everything I need."

"Well, don't you want to — say goodbye?"

"I *am* saying goodbye."

"But don't you want to — see us — before you go?"

"Mom, I think it's better this way. If I come home I'll just get into another fight with Dad."

"Tony, don't leave me out in the cold because of your father. It isn't fair."

There was another, too-long silence. "I'm sorry, Mom, but I can't come home."

She had almost stopped sobbing by now, and Tony could imagine her dabbing her carefully made-up eyes with a tissue. "Tony, I just don't know what to say." Then she started sobbing all

over again.

Tony waited for a lull. "Look, Mom, I'll be home in a couple months. Maybe we can talk then."

After more sobs, he heard, "Wait — a minute. Here's — someone — who wants — to talk — to you."

"Hi, Tonwy."

"Hi, Robby. How are you?"

"I'm f-i-ine."

"Aren't you up late tonight?"

"Huh-huhn. But Mommy said it was alwight if you called. Are you coming home?"

Tony ran his jacket sleeve across his eyes. "No. At least, not for a little while."

"But why?" Robby whined.

"Well, I have to go away."

"But why?"

The room became a blur. "Because the army says I have to."

"But I don't want to." Robby talked in halting snorts.

"Robby, I have a favor to ask. Will you do something for me while I'm — gone?"

"Do something?"

"Yes, I have a special favor to ask." Tony wiped tears on an already wet sleeve. "I'm going to be gone for a long time, maybe a couple years, and I have no one to look after Kitty. Do you think you can do that for me?"

"Kitty?"

"Yes, do you think you can take care of her? She has to be fed twice a day, and her litter box has to be emptied every week."

"Litter box?"

"Yes, and you have to let her out when she wants to go — and let her in again. Do you think you can do that? I know it's a big job, but I'm depending on you. You know Kitty likes you an awful lot."

"I like Kitty."

"But you have to remember not to chase her and pull her tail. Can you do that for me? Can you take care of her till I come home?"

"Okay, Tonwy. I take care of her."

The phone clattered at the other end of the line. "Tony, will you let us know how you're making out?"

"Well, I don't know, Mom. I'm going to be pretty busy at first. They don't give you much free time in basic training."

"Well, whenever you get a free moment, you call and let me know how you are. You can call collect. I'll pay for it."

"Thanks, Mom. But I don't even know if they have any phones in the barracks."

"Well, you check when you get there. Okay?"

"Okay."

"Well, I don't know what else to say. But you

take care of yourself, and — and — "

"Sure, Mom."

"All right, then. Well, goodbye."

"Bye, Mom."

Tony hung the phone in its cradle and leaned his head against the woodwork. After about five minutes of silent chest heaving, he washed his face in cold water from the tap. He got rid of the tears, but not the dull, hollow pain in the middle of his chest. He went back into the living room.

"How did it go?"

"Pretty good, I guess." Was there a frog in his throat?

"I'm sure you did the right thing."

Tony leaned against the newel. "Yes, I'm sure you're right. I — it sure exhausted me. And thanks. Thanks for helping me."

"You would have done it on your own if you thought long enough about it."

Chapter 35

"All right, men, let's get some kind of order here. Line up arm's length apart. When you run out of room, make another line arm's length behind."

The sergeant's ramrod straight back was jammed into starched khakis. The blonde hair was so close-cropped that he might have been bald. He held a clipboard with a thick stack of papers in one gristly hand, and gestured with the other, index finger extended.

"Come on, a little faster there. Can't you guys do anything right? Just start another line. Come on, let's go. We haven't got all day."

Tony joined the confusion. After an hour of milling, the sudden hurry did not make sense. The motley crew of forty to fifty youths was an odd cross-section of American manhood, dressed in an assortment of styles: some casual, some conservative, some outlandish, and some uncategorizable. Some looked like workers, some looked like businessmen, some looked like college students, some looked like riffraff. None looked like soldiers.

"Who the hell's he trying to kid?" a laconic voice next to Tony whispered. "Not only do I have all day, I have seven hundred and thirty of them to waste."

Tony looked at the sallow, hollow-cheeked face from which poked quick, intense brown eyes. The venerability of the neatly trimmed mustache and pointed goatee was more than offset by the straight, light brown, shoulder-length hair. The bright blue shirt was partially covered by an unsnapped, fringed leather vest, from the pockets of which protruded a toothbrush and a comb — he carried no other baggage. The faded blue jeans presented a colorful patch on each thigh with an odd dichotomy:

one was a peace symbol, the other was the lithium atom with three whirling electrons. The day was a bit chilly for sandals.

"Two years, man. And they all belong to Uncle Sam. Life doesn't begin till it's over."

"Seven hundred thirty-*one*," Tony grinned. "'68's a leap year."

He threw his head back in mock chagrin. "Just my luck."

The ranks and files settled out, five rows with nine or ten in each. "All right, men, let me give you a little orientation before we go on. If you're looking forward to an easy day, forget it. By this afternoon you'll all have writer's cramp, and I'll have a sore throat from yelling at all you bozos that don't know how to follow simple instructions."

The room swelled with groans and a mild chatter, and two more teenagers who peeked through the doorway. "Quiet!" The two halted as if struck. "You latecomers get to the back of the room." While they were getting, the sergeant continued, "Now listen up good, 'cause I'm not gonna repeat myself, and that goes for any more dawdlers. My name is Sergeant Gonzales, men, and I'm giving you the benefit of the doubt by calling you men. The army says I got to, even though some of you are trying to prove different by wearing them queer clothes, beads, earrings, and long hair. You ain't gonna be treated like children, so crying ain't gonna help. From now on you're all on equal footing, no matter what you were in civilian life. There ain't no classifications in the army. No difference between black and white, Catholic and Jew, Republican and Democrat — assuming that any of you snot noses are old enough to vote."

"That covers race, religion, and creed," Tony's companion whispered.

Sergeant Gonzales went on. "You're starting a new life where a forty-five ain't a pop record any more — it's a gun. Orders ain't something you give a waiter, it's something you take from officers and non-coms. And a drill ain't something to make holes with, it's something you practice day in, day out, and in your sleep."

Out of the corner of his mouth, the bearded youth murmured, "This guy should be a comedy writer for Boris Karloff."

Now the sergeant read off his clipboard, "All of you are about to enter the service of your country, the highest responsibility for duty minded citizens. Some of you have volunteered for service, some have been called up by Presidential authority. The army makes no distinction for purposes of opportunity, but appreciates from all of you the time you have sacrificed. We are embroiled in a great conflict against communism and communistic aggression. Your country needs you, the free world needs you."

"Cut the hard sell, already. You got us by the balls."

"*Hey! You!* Wipe that smirk off your face or I'll wipe it off for you."

Tony cringed, and switched his overnight case to the hand away from his mimicking sidekick. But the sergeant was stabbing a finger at the other side of the room. Tony took the opportunity to place his heavy suitcase on the floor; he flexed his fingers.

"All right, Smiley. Step forward." Sergeant Gonzales's face became a little more hardboiled, almost overdone, and his voice a little gruffer. The man walked hesitantly to the front of the room. His smile faded under the sergeant's inflexible gaze. "What's your name, mister?"

"McNally, John C."

"All right, McNally John C. I don't know what you think is so funny, but I want to give you a piece of personal advice. You better learn to button your flap, because wherever you go from now on you're likely to find some smart ass sergeant who'd like nothing better than to button it for you. Now, I'm only an induction sergeant, and I gotta make sure you leave this station in one piece. But I'm warning you, get out of line again and I'm going to make an example of military discipline out of you. Now, fall in."

Without another word McNally executed an about face and fell in. His future was no longer in his own hands.

"Now, like I was saying, you're all gonna have writer's cramp by the end of the day, so let's get this show on the road. And if there are any more McNally's in the crowd who think this is a game, start thinking otherwise. Now, I'm gonna call out your names. You come up and take one of these sets of forms and go into the other room — through that door — and find yourself a chair. For those of you who forgot to bring writing instruments there are pencils on the desk — you sign for it, and when you return it your name will be crossed out." He flipped over the sheet and started reading, "Adams! Arnold! Betts! Callahan! Calvert! Crenshaw! Culver! Davidson! Digby! Dorsett! Egbert! Farnsworth! — "

A burly fellow from the third row lumbered forward, pushing his massive weight through the ranks and tripping twice over suitcases.

"Mike!" escaped from Tony's lips an instant before his hand went to his mouth.

A slow smile grew on the pudgy, tanned face. He looked different in an ill-fitting gray suit and baggy pants, but he still moved with the same slow, lethargic gait.

"*Did you say something!*" the sergeant bellowed.

"Uh, I'm sorry, sergeant. I just, uh, recognized — an old friend."

Gonzales glared at Tony. Tony swallowed a smile and tried to look innocent. Mike Farnsworth snatched the forms out of the sergeant's hands and sauntered through the door. Gonzales looked at his empty hand stupidly for a moment before returning his stare to Tony.

"The next man to say a word will be wearing a wastepaper basket over his head for the rest of the day. Fink! Furley! Gallagher! Giovanni! Gibson! Gilbert! . . . "

Tony picked up his suitcase and took his papers. The sergeant stared at him suspiciously, but made no comment. In the next room he took a seat next to Mike Farnsworth.

"What are you doing here, Mike?"

"Same as you, I guess. Joining the army."

"Wow, I sure didn't expect to meet anyone here I knew. I didn't even know you had quit work."

Mike took a pencil out of a plastic holder in his shirt pocket. "I didn't quit till Friday. Couldn't afford to lose the pay."

Someone sat down in the chair on Tony's other side. A right hand jabbed out and clasped Tony's. "Wally Gibson." White, even teeth showed between mustache and goatee. "The alphabet has decreed that we'll be together for the next phase of life."

"Tony Giovanni. Nice to meet you. And this is Mike Farnsworth."

Wally reached past Tony to clasp hands. "Glad to meet you."

"How do you do?"

"Cool. Where'd you get those crazy threads?"

"Huhn?"

"Never mind. It doesn't matter. We're not going to the opera, I guess."

Tony took a pen out of his overnight case. "Hey, your clothes aren't exactly the last touch in sartorial perfection, you know."

"No offense meant. You got another instrument? I don't want to sign for anything I don't have to."

"Just a pencil."

"It'll do. At least I had the sense take my earring out before coming down here. Only one, the left. It's pierced, see?" Wally grabbed his earlobe and stretched it out. There was a tiny puncture mark in it, like half the bite of a vampire. "I'm no queer, though. Just crazy."

Tony zipped up his bag. "I'm glad to hear it."

"*Hey!* When you guys are finished blabbing about old times, you can make some chicken tracks on them forms." Sergeant Gonzales stood with arms folded over a broad chest as the rest of the men found seats. He handed out pencils to those who needed them.

Wally resorted to whispering again. "Uh-oh, I'm feeling premoncholy."

Tony did a double take. "What's that?"

"A premonition of melancholy. I think I'm going to hate this hitch with the army. I don't know why I ever let them talk me into it."

Tony kept scribbling out personal information. "You mean, you enlisted?"

"Douche your mouth with Draino, man. I said I was crazy, not insane."

"Then what do you mean by 'let'?"

Wally penciled in his forms. "Free will, man. Free will. Everybody makes his own choice whether he knows it or not."

"Not me. I was minding my own business when the army came along and drafted me. How is that exercising free will?"

"Indecision or inaction is the same as choosing, except that you choose by refusing to choose. It amounts to the same thing. Now, take me for example. I had choices after I got my masters, ranging from the logical to the irrational. But I had choices. I could have worked toward my Ph.D., and kept my deferment. Or, I could have tried lying low and teaching at some small town university where they'd be willing to overlook my draft status as critical employment — which might not have worked anyway: Or, I could have moved around the country so fast that they couldn't catch up with me, Or, I could have been really stupid and burned my draft card, or gone to jail, or left the country. They're all choices, man. Some are just not very smart ones."

"Well, that's kind of like saying you don't have to do anything but die and pay taxes."

"Wrong. You don't *have* to pay taxes, you just have to be willing to suffer the consequences for not paying them. Death, I'll admit, is a hard baby to avoid. The only choice you have is how soon it's going to be."

Tony thought about arguing the last point, but decided against it. "So what choice did you make that got you drafted?"

"I made the mistake of playing the game according to the rules. Being an intelligent and rational being, I assumed our leaders were the same way. I solicited and collected petitions from other intelligent individuals who were protesting the Southeast Asia atrocities, joined forces with a group which was handling such petitions, and delivered them in person to the White Shack, as is the right of every American citizen. That's when I found out that politics plays dirty pool. You see, the square in the Oval Office ain't working for us any more. He's not doing what the people want him to do — he's doing what *he* wants to do. He got somewhere where he's the kingpin. He's up there pushing people around like checker pieces, and he's lost sight of the reason he was voted into office. He's got his own private war, and he's having fun — Johnson's Joke, that's what we call it. And look out for anybody who gets in his way."

"So what happened?"

"So, I'm down there with this group — small group, say, fifty of us, half chicks. We walked into the White Shack — during tourist hours, mind you, nothing funny — and asked — *asked* — for an audience with the Top Cop so we could present our petitions. Now get this: nobody's making a scene, nobody's yelling or shoving or demanding anything — you can't do that if you're pressing for peace. You gotta be peaceable or you're a hypocrite. Anyway, they start giving us the run around, telling us we're not allowed to present petitions, we're not allowed to protest, we're not allowed to be against anything the Top Cop isn't against. So naturally, some of us start to argue the point. After all, this *is* America: land of the free, home of the brave, and the place where the buffalo used to roam. We got a right to talk — *talk* — not shout. But they saw otherwise. Freedom became extinct with the bison. Before you know it, they're calling in the troops: CIA, FBI, FUCK. Then they're pushing us around, first with hands, then with fists. Then they're beating us on the head with clubs. I woke up in jail with blood on my face and lumps on my scalp — and the bastards wouldn't even give me an aspirin. They let us go the next day, with no food. The petitions we never saw again — they probably burned them. They tell us if we're ever caught in Disneyland again we'll go to the pen for subversion, and so they don't make any mistakes, they take fingerprints and mug shots, just like big time criminals. Hell, all we wanted to do was find out why the hell we're fighting some flea-bitten war and getting our pants kicked off. You ask a question, you expect an answer — not a browbeating. Anyway, we all go home, but things are just beginning. Everybody's folks get letters from the FBI. Don't matter to me because I'm on my own. But a lot of the younger ones get into family squabbles, which is what they wanted. Things didn't really start happening for a couple months, though. They know where we live, where we go to school, and they start putting on the pressure. The chicks have questionnaires sent to their neighbors and start getting kicked out of school; the guys start losing deferments, and get drafted. That's how they get rid of the opposition: get them in Dutch, or send them to the Big 'Nam and hope they get killed."

Tony put down his pen. "Wow, I never heard

of anything like that."

"There's a lot you haven't heard — enough to make you sick. But I got news for the Big Joker. He thinks they can get rid of me by sticking me in the army. But I still have my rights. I'm still a citizen of this country. And I'm still going to fight him, and all the other corrupt bastards in the White Shack. But I'm going to do it from the inside. Got me?"

"I don't know. It sounds like you might get yourself into more trouble than it's worth."

"Yeah, well, you don't get honey without stirring up the bees. I can tell you one thing right now. I'm not taking any shit off anybody, whether he's got stripes down to his elbows or enough brass on his hat to sink a battleship. How about you, Mike?"

Mike slowly pushed his pencil over the paper, straining over answers.

"Hey, how about you?"

"Huhn?"

"What's the matter with you, man? Aren't you paying attention?"

"Huhn?"

"Hey, man, can you hear all right?"

Tony observed Mike's uncombed hair. His eyelids were at half-mast, and his whole face sagged. "Mike, are you all right?"

"I'm feelin' a little sick. I didn't get no sleep last night — partied till dawn. Most of the guys went home before that, but me and my old man, we were tipping the bottles right till the sun come up — celebratin' me goin' in the army. So I don't feel so good."

"What the hell were you partying for, man? That's like celebrating your mother's funeral."

Mike fidgeted with his pencil. "Well, I been trying for a long time to get in the army. They turned me down three times, and the Navy and Air Force wouldn't even let me take the test."

"*You mean you volunteered?*" Tony looked toward the front of the room, but Sergeant Gonzales apparently had not heard Wally's outburst. "Man, you are really sick."

Tony said, "I didn't know you were trying to join the army. I thought you wanted to get into the union."

"The union wouldn't take me 'cause I couldn't get good enough grades in the aptitude test. Then the army turned me down for medical reasons. I was a IV-F till my doctor got them to change it. Now I'm gonna be a soldier."

"You ain't just sick, man, you're pathologic."

"Mike, maybe you should have — " A dark shadow loomed over Tony, and the stern features of Sergeant Gonzales blazed down like angry Zeus. Tony wilted like an autumn leaf in a full gale.

"If you three mother hens have stopped

cackling, I would appreciate it if you would fill out the rest of those forms. Because when you're done with them I've got a couple dozen more for you to fill out."

He left without waiting for a reply.

Under his breath, Wally said in aside, "Don't let him scare you, man. What the hell's he going to do, draft you?"

When Tony finished the triplicate forms, he helped Mike fill in the blanks. Then, while Sergeant Gonzales sipped quietly at his coffee, a Marine sergeant entered the room. He was more straight-backed than Gonzales and, unbelievably, had shorter hair. But bushy eyebrows, fleshy cheeks, and a considerable dewlap put him a notch lower for the Mr. America contest. He pivoted at the waist and whispered into the army sergeant's ear.

Sergeant Gonzales stood up. "All right, men, listen up. I need five volunteers, on the double."

Tony looked around, saw no one moving, and started to push himself out of his seat. A bony hand gripped him like a clamp.

"Keep a low profile, man. Don't ever volunteer for anything. You're not in college any more."

Tony relaxed, then noticed that Mike's chair was empty. He stood with three others at the front of the room.

"Come on, men, where's your spirit? This is for your own good. I need one more brave soul. Now, who's man enough to come up here? I promise this ain't KP or no trash picking detail."

After a long, dead silence, a fellow in front of Wally climbed hesitantly to his feet, and ambled to the front of the room. A smile broke out on Gonzales's face as the last volunteer took his place in line. But it was wiped off when the Marine sergeant jerked a thumb at Mike and shook his head.

"All right, you. Go back to your seat." As Mike walked back sullenly, Sergeant Gonzales went on, "All right, we need one more volunteer. Someone with guts." This time no one moved, or scarcely breathed. The sergeant intimidated each and every man with piercing eyes, like flaming daggers. They rested on Tony for a seemingly long time; he slunk down under the optic onslaught. With his gaze thus fixed, the sergeant said, "If I don't get a volunteer, I'll have to pick one."

A hushed voice to Tony's side said, "How can you pick a volunteer?" Gonzales glanced around the room, returning to stare fathomlessly at Tony. "Last chance."

The silence was so abysmal that Tony could hear the humming of the ballasts in the fluorescent lights. He shrank down in his seat as he saw the sergeant's mouth open to voice his name.

"McNally, John C. Front and center."

Tony sighed with relief as a startled groan emitted from the back of the room. He heard the movement of a chair and the scrape of a suitcase. McNally, John C. picked his way to the front. The Marine sergeant nodded his assent and motioned the men out of door.

"Congratulations, McNally. You just joined the Marines. They'll knock some sense into your head."

As the sergeant laughed at McNally's retreating form, Tony breathed, "I didn't know they could do that — draft you into the Marines."

"They can do anything, man. They own you."

"Well, if I ever try to volunteer for anything again, remind me of my insanity."

The rest of the morning dragged on with more forms, orientation lectures, more forms, tests, and still more forms. Tony was so weary of the whole process that he quit trying to read every form, and simply signed in the appropriate spot. Then the group was escorted to the cafeteria by a specialist — in what, he did not know.

"Shit, man, I thought the army was supposed to give us everything." Wally had only a couple dollars and change in his hand when he was asked to pay for his meal.

"I left all my money in my savings account." Tony put back the sandwich and paid for a package of crackers with some loose coins.

Wally found a table with three chairs. "I don't have a savings account, man. I baked all my bread for an education. Now Uncle Sam's going to get the first loaf."

"I brought lots of money if you fellows need any." Mike had a pile of food on his tray that would choke a horse: soup, bread, three sandwiches, two Cokes, and two slices of cherry pie. He shoved a ham and cheese in front of Tony.

"Thanks, but I'll just wait until we get our first big pay check."

"No. Go ahead. Take it." Mike refused to take it back. "I don't really need it."

Wally nibbled on a bag of potato chips. "You don't need two pieces of pie, either, man. Now tell me, what the hell caused you to sign up and go for the three-year hitch? Don't you know if you held your cards you could have gotten enslaved for only two?"

Mike took a bite out of a sandwich that left only half of it in his hand. He chewed carefully, and swallowed before answering. "I wasn't gettin' anywhere driving a truck, couldn't get into college or the union, and I wanted some kind of education. By signing up for the four

year program, they promised me the MOS of my choice."

"Holy shit, man. Do you mean you signed up for *four* years?"

Mike nodded silently as he took another bite that demolished the rest of the sandwich.

Tony swilled his mouth with free water. "What's an MOS?"

"Military Occupational Specialty," Wally supplied.

"I read all the brochures, and there are lots of opportunities offered by the army, with civilian applications. And besides, it's a steady job and you can't get fired."

"Man, now is not the time to join the army to broaden your horizons. This country is at war — "

"Conflict," Tony corrected.

"Stop sniffing roses," Wally said, loosely paraphrasing Shakespeare. "This country is at war, and war means death, and you can't see much of the horizon from six feet under. If you wanted to join something, it should have been the peace movement instead of the killing crusade."

Tony kept munching. "Then he would have gotten drafted for sure."

Wally snorted, and took another bird bite out of his sandwich. With a sweep of his hand he pushed his long hair away from his mouth and tucked it behind one ear. "But it would have been for only two stinking years. A chance for peace is better than a sure shot for war."

Mike engulfed a roll the way a kid takes a penny candy. "I been following the papers, and the Vietnam conflict seems like a noble cause."

Wally rolled his eyes. "He is blind, so forgive him his blundering."

"My father fought against the Nazis in the last war, so there's nothing wrong in fighting against communism in this one."

"Where have you been, man? The last war was Korea, not Germany."

"That was a conflict," Tony said.

"Man, if you don't get your nose out of the rose bush you're going to get stuck by the thorns. A conflict is a disagreement of ideas, but when two countries fight over it, it's war. Joining the army now is like signing your death warrant — or signing someone else's. You're not only *becoming* a murderer, you're *asking* to be one."

"Murder's a hard word in this case, isn't it?"

"He speaks with the tongue of innocence, he reeks of childish simplicity. Voltaire once said, 'Killing a man is murder, unless you do it to the sound of trumpets.' But that's a bunch of idealistic hogwash, unless he meant it sarcastically. Killing is murder no matter under what authority you do it. Joining the group that's pulling the trigger is the same as pulling the trigger yourself. And if you let someone put a rifle in your hand so you can traipse through the jungle looking for someone to kill, that amounts to murder."

"Unless it's self-defense."

"Only in this case self-defense applies to *them*. We're the invaders. We are the ones going into someone else's territory. It's no different than the invasion of America."

Tony put down his paper cup. "Now wait a minute. The States have never been invaded — by anyone."

"The Eskimos invaded America — and became Indians. Then they were invaded by the Spanish and British and French."

"But that was colonization."

"For the Eskimos is was colonization because the land was unoccupied. But when advanced nations settle upon land already inhabited by another people, no matter how backward, it's invasion."

Tony stared at his water. "Hmmmn."

"It all depends on how you look at it, man. It's just like in the movies. When the cavalry beats the Indians, it's a great victory, but when the Indians beat the cavalry, it's a massacre. It's point of view, just like Einstein's theory of relativity."

Mike polished off the last of his pie. "But the President says the people of South Vietnam are being invaded by the people of North Vietnam."

"The people of South Vietnam *are* the people of North Vietnam."

"But they don't want to be. What they want is to be free."

"Man, most of the people of Vietnam don't know the difference. They're ignorant peasants, and all they want to do is grow rice and have another generation. *We're* the ones who want them to be different. And there are a few high-ranking politicians in South Vietnam who are willing to go along with it so they can keep their high-paying jobs. You think they care about the common people?"

"But the President says we should protect the South Vietnamese from communism."

"Why? Communism is the best thing for poor people, because it results in the least amount of suffering from the aristocracy of a class society. In a country that's ninety-five and forty-four one hundredths percent poor, everybody washes with the same bar of soap."

"But what about the domino theory?" Tony intruded. "What about stopping the encroachment of communism before it spreads to our own shores?"

"That's propagandist bullshit to give you a reason for going out and dying. It's easy to spout patriotism when you're hiding behind whitewashed walls, but you and me are the ones who are going to suffer for it. When you fight a war from Washington, the most you can lose is face, not your arm or leg or — "

"All right, men," said the specialist in imitation sergeant's voice. "You new recruits have about two minutes to finish up. Sergeant Gonzales wants you back at twelve-thirty sharp, and if I don't get you back on time, my ass is grass."

Wally scowled. "He could use a good mowing. Hey, man, you want the rest of this sandwich?"

"Sure. Thanks." Mike wolfed it down in a single gulp.

The afternoon began with medical forms that blended into an extensive physical. There was a mild titter as they stripped down to skivvies and it was discovered that one fellow was wearing flowered silk panties.

Sergeant Gonzales pulled him out of formation. "Miss, you're sure gonna like the next part of this exam, 'cause we got a guy here who's gonna treat you like a bottle of Mountain Dew. When he tells you to bend over, he'll really tickle your innards."

While the sergeant laughed at his own joke, Wally whispered, "Be ready to get goosed. I can smell a proctologist a mile away — by the dirt under his fingernails."

When that ordeal was over, another doctor jammed his hand into Tony's groin and told him to turn his head and cough. He did, as soon as he stopped choking. Dressed again, he had his eyes, ears, and throat examined. Then he endured stability tests in which he was asked to stand on one leg like a stork, close his eyes, and reach around and touch his nose with one finger. Afterwards, an intern checked his pulse and heartbeat to ensure that he had survived the ordeal. It was rumored that anyone who did not survive the physical was sent to the Navy.

It was not until late afternoon, when all the men were together again, that Sergeant Gonzales shouted, "Ten-shut!"

An unlikely suspect for an officer, with buckteeth and wearing horn-rimmed glasses over a cadaverous face, said, "My name is Major Monahan, and I want every one of you to raise his right hand and repeat after me. I swear allegiance . . . "

A moment later, Tony discovered that he had officially been sworn into the Army of the United States.

Chapter 36

Patty was waiting for him at the train station.

Ben grabbed a handful of shirtsleeve. "Where's your uniform?"

"I thought the first thing they did was give you a haircut," Ray said.

"Did you tell those officers where to get off?" Teddy wanted to know.

Pete made a pistol out of his hand and cocked his thumb. "Kill any gooks yet?"

"Wha — what are you guys doing here?" Tony glanced around at the crowd, his jaw slowly recovering. Marion, Kate, and Kathy huddled in a knot, smiling.

Ben jerked a thumb at Teddy. "Mr. Brains here called the induction center and found out what train you'd be leaving on."

"We came down in both cars." Pete swept his arm along the street, where a souped-up '57 Chevy and a sleek, shining, newly waxed '60 Ford Galaxie were parked. "I worked on your car all day. She's purrin' like a kitten, runnin' like a tiger, and lookin' like whi-i-i-te lightning."

"*All aboar-r-r-d.*"

"And we almost didn't make it because Ben ran out of gas," Ray scowled.

"We had to siphon some out of yours with a garden hose," Pete added.

"I didn't have any money, and I thought we could make it." Ben stabbed a thumb at Ray's chest. "I notice you didn't offer to buy any."

"I don't get paid till Friday."

"So this is only Monday. Did Kathy eat up last week's paycheck?"

"Every *other* Friday."

"Uh, listen, fellas. I don't have much time. Do you mind if I talk with Patty alone for a minute?" Tony dragged her away from the confusion, took her around a dirty concrete pillar where they were out of sight of the gang.

"Trooper, just what do you think you're doing?"

Tony glanced aside at the gruff voice and striped armband. "I'm talking to my girlfriend. Do you mind?"

At the induction center, William Stahl had been assigned the duty of temporary platoon leader. He had been given the responsibility of escorting his fellow inductees to the subway, thence to the train station, thence to the army reception center at Fort Jackson, South Carolina. "I want everybody together, and that means you."

"Buzz off, buster."

Stahl's granite face turned a dark shade of red. "I'll report you for insubordination."

Tony was in no mood for intimidation. "Do it. But get out of my sight."

"You're in trouble now, trooper." Stahl executed a perfect about face, and marched toward the cluster of inductees.

Tony turned to Patty. "Thanks for coming."

"I'm sorry about last night."

"What's to be sorry about?"

"Well, you know, my grandmother and all."

"Oh, that's all right. She could have been worse."

"She was, after you left. She really bawled me out. She said I can't go out for a week."

"Then how did you get out now?"

Patty smiled. "Easy. I never went home from school. Ben called Kate and told her what was going on. And, here we are."

"Well, I can't tell you how shocked I was to see you all here."

"I know. You should have seen the expression on your face. But I'm going to catch hell tonight."

"Gee, I'm sorry I got you into trouble."

"Oh, that's all right. It was worth it, I guess."

"*All aboar-r-r-d!*"

"I — I think he means it this time."

The traffic was thinning out as people rushed onto the train. The oily, dust laden lights shone down weakly from the bare ceiling twenty feet overhead, casting a yellow glow and weak shadows.

Tony put his arms around Patty and held her tight. She did not resist — or respond. He gave her a peck on the cheek as he pushed her away. "Well, I guess this is goodbye."

"Yes."

He started backing down the platform. He looked past her and waved at the gang. "See you in a couple months."

"Okay," Patty said weakly.

The train clanked, and jolted forward. "*All aboar-r-r-d!*"

Tony put his hand on the railing of the last car, the overnight case weighing heavily in his other hand. Everyone was looking at him, but he saw only Patty. He whispered, "I love you."

Patty raised her hand and waved. Brown curls lay loose, fell around a smooth face frozen in a perpetual, quizzical expression.

He hopped onto the lower step, waved, then ran inside and back to the rear door. He wanted to shout, but merely mouthed the words he wanted to say through the grimy glass.

Patty's lips closed, then opened again to form a single syllable that seemed to say, "Bye." She continued to wave as she receded in the distance until her face, her body, the train station blurred into an incandescent patch in the tunnel opening of the underground terminal, which itself shrank as the tall buildings and office lights filled Tony's field of view. Eventually, they too diminished, distorting fantastically as if the city were shrinking instead of getting farther away.

Finally, everything Tony knew, and loved, and was familiar with, faded from view.

Book Two
SUMMER

War is a bad thing: but to submit to the dictation of other states is worse.

Thucydides, 471? — 401? BC

The foundation of every state is the education of its youth.

Diogenes, c. 400 — 325 BC

Chapter 37

"Get your asses outa those seats, we ain't got all day. Come on, let's move it. Move It. MOVE IT."

The black giant jumped into the bus so fast that the brakes were still squealing when he started shouting. His round face shone like a bowling ball, with ebony eyes piercing out from under the stiff brim of a brown felt Smokey-the-Bear hat. With every word, his flattened nostrils flared like an angry bull's, and his taut lips grimaced. There was nothing pleasing, pleasant, or platonic about his manner: malevolence exuded from every pore.

"I said move it, and I mean NOW."

Wally pushed Tony out of his seat. "I think he means it."

The men surged forward in uncomfortably starched, newly issued fatigues — but not fast enough for the sergeant. As each shorn head passed his place by the driver's seat, a huge, helping slap was landed just behind the ears, with enough force that Tony had to jump the last two steps to the ground. Others, not fast enough, fell to their knees and were trampled upon by the next recruit in line. Some, like Wally, ducked in time to miss the blow.

"Keep those covers on." The sergeant knocked more than one hat off its perch. Tony secured his by the brim and squeezed it down tighter.

When Mike Farnsworth reached the front of the bus, Tony saw that he towered over the sergeant by a full head. None of the sergeant's attributes of intimidation had any effect on Mike's natural lethargy. He moved with only two speeds: slow, and slower. He walked the gauntlet and took his hit. Men behind him flew

out like machine gun bullets.

"What do you think you're doing? This ain't no beauty contest. Stop fussing with your cap and get over there with the rest of the men."

A moment passed before Tony realized that the clean-shaven, youthful officer was yelling at him. He got. The world was suddenly noise and pandemonium. Everywhere he turned someone was screaming in his face.

"Let's go let's go let's go."

"Hey, you. Move it."

"Line up here and stand at attention.

"Hey, where're you going?"

" — or I'll kick your ass, soldier."

"Eyes straight ahead."

"Put that hat on straight. You ain't no Stepin Fetchit."

"I said *attention*."

"Stand up straight, you're a soldier now."

"I said MOVE IT."

Tony found himself in formation with the rest of the men from his bus. Wally jabbed an elbow into his side to get his interval. "This is worse than rush hour on the subway."

"Yeah, and that sergeant's no Prince Charming, either."

Suddenly there was an officer standing in front of him. He wore dress khakis with the pants tucked into black, mirrorlike combat boots. He was as thin and hollow-cheeked as Wally, but several inches taller. His ruddy complexion was due to either chronic exposure to the hot Georgia sun, or from the constant expansion of his veins, which stood out prodigiously whenever he screamed — which was all the time. He did not seem to have a normal speaking voice.

The lieutenant was in a fury. "What are you

looking at, son?" Tony glanced away.

"I'm talking to you, son." He stepped so close that he almost trod on Tony's boots. He could feel hot breath on his cheeks. "What are you looking at?"

Tony swallowed hard. "Nothing."

"Nothing what?"

"Nothing — at all."

Dark blue eyes bulged from their sockets. "You are talking to an officer, and I *will* be addressed as 'Sir'."

"Yes, sir."

"Now, what were you looking at?"

"Nothing, sir."

The second lieutenant screamed at the top of his lungs. "Are you trying to tell me I'm nothing, son?"

"No sir."

"Then what did you mean?"

"Nothing, sir."

"You must have meant something."

"Yes, sir."

"Then what were you looking at?"

"You, sir."

"And why were you looking at me, son?"

"Because you were there, sir."

"Oh, a smart ass, huhn? Okay, hit the ground and give me ten." Tony raised his eyebrows, and a split second later the lieutenant said, "I said hit it, and make it twenty."

"Twenty what?"

"Twenty what, *sir*."

"Twenty what, sir?"

"Make it thirty for playing dumb. Now git down and push that ground away."

Tony got down on hands and knees, straightened to palms and toes, and started doing pushups. As in school, with each downward motion he touched the red earth with only the tip of his nose. He did not want to dirty or bend the crease in his fatigues.

After about five pushups the lieutenant shouted, "I can't hear you." Tony stopped and looked up. "I didn't say anything — sir."

"Then you better start counting off, or they don't count."

Tony resumed position. "Six. Seven. Eight. Nine."

"You start from one, son, not from six."

Tony scowled. "One. Two. Three. Four."

"I can't hear you."

Louder: "Five. Six. Seven."

"They don't count unless I hear them."

Exasperated, but louder: "One. Two. Three. Four."

"I still can't hear you."

Screaming with all his might: "One. Two. Three. Four. Five. . . . Sixteen. Seventeen. . . . " He was tiring rapidly. "Twenty-three. Twenty-four." He did not think his arms would hold

out. "Twenty-five. Twenty-six. Twenty-seven." He was gasping for air, and pushing up ever so slowly. "Twenty-eight. Twenty-nine. Thirty."

He collapsed on the ground. After a moment, he rolled over and climbed to his feet, dusting himself off.

"Who gave you permission to stand up?"

Tony was tiring of the game. He would rather be informed of the rules before play began. "No one, sir."

"Then git down and give me ten more for doing it on your own."

He moved as slowly as he thought he could get away with, to give his muscles every second of the rest they so desperately required. He counted out each pushup loud and clear, refusing to give in to the second lieutenant's juvenile attitude. Then he poised on the ground with arms outstretched to show that he had strength remaining.

Did he have permission to ask permission? "Permission to stand up, sir."

"I can't hear you."

"Permission to stand up, sir."

"I still can't hear you."

"PERMISSION TO STAND UP, SIR."

In a low voice, the lieutenant said, "Permission granted."

Tony's arms were so tense that he could not push himself up, so he walked his legs under his body and bent up from the waist. The lieutenant seemed to have forgotten all about him. He was prowling back and forth across the ranks seeking other prey. He reminded Tony of a caged tiger pacing in front of a group of gaping tourists.

"That peach fuzzed brown-bar is no older than you," Wally breathed.

"Yes, but he's got the biggest set of tonsils I've ever seen."

The sergeant from the bus strolled by, handing out nasty looks. "Stand at attention there. . . . Keep those feet together, toes pointed forward. . . . Hey, I'm talking to you. . . . Get those hands out of your pockets. This is no time to play with yourself. . . . Stand straight. Keep that gut in."

Wally stifled a laugh. "He should talk. That beer gut he's got came from many a year of elbow bending."

Tony stared straight ahead as the sergeant passed by. The overcast sky lent no relief to the unimaginative beige paint that covered every building in sight. The reddish, sandy turf was only sparsely covered with struggling tendrils of dust-laden crab grass. The occasional greenery of tall, deciduous trees was the only relief to the pale monotones of military expedience.

As the last busloads poured their recruits onto the parade grounds, the Philadelphia forty swelled with two hundred additional men, picked up at the Fort Jackson Reception Station, South Carolina. New Yorkers, Carolinians, and a large contingent of native Puerto Ricans jangled dog tags that made them official members of the United States Army.

Tony's arm still ached from the first of many immunization shots received at Fort Jackson. He had also listened to endless orientation covering a diversity of subjects such as postal service, legal assistance, medical facilities, recreational activities, religious services, leave and pass policies, post exchange practices, medical and financial care for dependents, privately owned vehicles parked on base, visitors, family correspondence, shipment of civilian clothing (some men had brought entire wardrobes), pay and allowances, service obligations, allotments, survivor's benefits, life insurance, and savings bonds. He had also received a twenty-dollar advance, called casual pay.

At the end of one week, they dressed like soldiers, ate like soldiers, marched like soldiers, stood like soldiers, made their beds like soldiers. Some even talked like soldiers — as you were — thought like soldiers. For some it was an easy transformation, for others it had not yet occurred. For a few it never would.

"Attensh-*hut!*" The skinny lieutenant must have forgotten that they were already standing at attention. "Listen up, men. Your company commander will be here shortly for a brief inspection and you'd *better* be looking sharp. I want you looking good, because I know you feel good. And I want you to be proud of the fact that you are in the best goddamn training company in the whole United States Army. Isn't that right?"

The silence was deafening.

"I said isn't that right?"

There was a halfhearted rumble throughout the ranks that sounded vaguely like "yes."

"Yes *what?*"

"Yes, sir."

"I can't hear you."

"Yes, *sir.*"

"I can't hear you."

"Yes, sir."

"I can't hear you."

"YES, SIR."

"And don't you forget it."

The lieutenant continued his restless pacing, and the sergeants tried to find fault with the recruits.

"This lieuy is a real asshole," Wally said, a bit too loud. A second later the lieutenant was standing in front of him with eyes ablaze. Wally returned his stare with half-lidded nonchalance.

"Did you say something, son?" He used his normal shouting voice. Wally merely stared.

"I'm talking to you!" The brown brim of his Smokey-the-Bear hat brushed the olive drab brim of Wally's baseball cap.

Wally rendered a slow blink.

The lieutenant's carotids bulged out so far that they seemed ready to explode. "CAN YOU HEAR ME?"

"Of course I can hear you," Wally screamed, spraying a mouthful of spit. *"You're shouting in my fucking ear."*

The lieutenant jumped back instinctively, and turned three shades darker. He was struck dumb.

About a half second later the black sergeant appeared out of nowhere and pounded a huge, gnarled fist into Wally's chest so hard that it knocked him back a good two feet. But at the same time the pudgy fingers grabbed onto the fatigue jacket, and in the next instant he was jerked forward, off the ground, and across the sergeant's body. On the downward arc the sergeant's left hand came down with a clap to the back of Wally's head, adding thrust to momentum. Wally hit the ground so hard that the wind exploded from his lungs with an audible whoosh. His cap flew off and landed five feet away.

Wally rolled over on his back, clutching his shoulder. His face was contorted with pain. The sergeant put his foot in the middle of Wally's chest and leaned down with his weight. "Don't you never talk back to an officer, you hear me?"

Wally had not yet started breathing.

"You hear me?"

With a froglike croak, he said, "I — hear — you."

"I hear you what?"

"I — hear — you — sir."

The sergeant swung his shoulder around and pointed to the five stripes. "I'm a sergeant, mister, not an officer. You better learn to tell the difference. Now, do you hear me?"

"I hear you — sergeant."

"Loud enough so the lieutenant can hear you."

Wally's breathing came in gasps. "*I hear you, sergeant.*"

"I want the whole company to hear you."

"I HEAR YOU, SERGEANT."

The sergeant reached down, picked Wally up by the shirtfront, and literally threw him back into formation. He crashed into a man in the second rank, and stumbled forward.

"Now apologize to Lieutenant Wakefield."

If blood could boil there would have been steam coming from Wally's ears. He did his best to stand at attention, but his shoulder sagged. The seconds ticked by like dates on the calendar.

Wally gnashed his teeth and stared at the lieutenant. "I'm sorry." After an appreciable time, he added, "sir."

Lieutenant Wakefield looked him up and down, his face set like granite. Then he turned and sauntered away. The sergeant, his nostrils flaring like those of a maddened bull, smiled smugly. "I didn't miss this time like I did on the bus, did I?"

The question was rhetorical. Wally did not answer.

Lieutenant Wakefield called, "Attensh-*hut!*" as another officer strode out onto the parade grounds. He was finely caparisoned with brass buttons, insignia, badges, and ribbons, and moved with a blend of military bearing and slow assurance.

He surveyed the troops for a good ten seconds before raising a voice-powered bullhorn to his lips. "Welcome to Fort Gordon. My name is Captain Maxwell, and for the next eight weeks I'm going to be your company commander. During that time you will receive an introduction into basic military skills before going on to individual training assignments."

He paused dramatically and half lowered the bullhorn. His eyes made another slow sweep. "Most of you men will be going to Vietnam. About one out of every twenty will come back in a pine box. What we aim to do here is see that you have the best training possible, both physical and psychological, so the majority of you can come back under your own power. That's because those pine boxes are heavy, expensive, and take up a lot of valuable space — to say nothing of the paperwork involved. Keep in mind that everything you learn here will help you no matter what military career you choose — "

"What career?" Wally quipped. "I thought we signed up to get merit badges and become Eagle Scouts."

" — You will receive indoor and outdoor classes covering such subjects as military courtesies and customs, close order drill, inspections, code of conduct, military justice — "

"There isn't any such thing."

" — personal health and hygiene, first aid, field hygiene, defensive training, confidence course, rifle marksmanship, hand grenades, and familiarization with combat conditions — and, of course, physical training, popularly known as PT — "

"It's not going to be very popular with me."

" — You won't be seeing too much of me since I will be handling the administration work. But my executive officer, Lieutenant Wakefield — " who took two steps forward " — and his capable staff of sergeants will han-

dle the training. If you do see much of me it means you are in trouble. Anyone with a problem can make an appointment to see me by going through the proper chain of command. I'm sure, though, that your platoon sergeant will be able to answer most of your questions. Now, I'm going to turn you over to Lieutenant Wakefield, who will assign you to your individual platoons. And remember, now you are only men. But in eight weeks you'll be soldiers. That is something to be proud of. Thank you."

Captain Maxwell executed a sharp right turn and left the field, taking his bullhorn with him. Lieutenant Wakefield went on to prove that he did not need one.

"All right, men. At ease. Now listen up, and listen up good. Your walking days are over. From now on, no matter where you're going, whether it's the mess hall, the barracks, or the john — *you run*. And I don't mean jog. I mean run. Any man caught walking will be put on extra duty, and I have a lot of jobs up my sleeve that need doing, so please walk."

Tony stretched his cramped muscles as best he could without attracting attention. The baggy clothes hid any movement. A pale-skinned sergeant handed the lieutenant a clipboard.

"Now, I'm going to break you up into platoons. When I call out your name you will fall out, retrieve your duffel, and report to your respective platoon sergeants. Platoon number one, Sergeant Baker." The pale sergeant nodded slightly. "Aarons. Abercrombie. Adams. Adkins. Anson. Appleton. Arnold...."

After DiMedio, he said, "Platoon number two, Sergeant Hawkins."

"Oh, no," Wally groaned. The black sergeant hefted his bulging belly around and stood with hands on hips.

"Diment. . . . Farnsworth. . . . Giovanni. . . . Gibbs. . . . Gibson. . . . "

Wally and Tony fell out together and raced to where the bus had parked. In its place stood a scattered pile of olive drab duffel bags and half a dozen men trying to read the black stenciled names.

"Hey, Mike," Wally shouted. "Here's yours over here." He dragged the bag out of the pile and kept searching.

"Thanks a lot. I'll help you look for yours."

"Never mind. I just found it. How are you making out, Tony?"

"You two go ahead. I'll catch up in a minute."

The last bag he turned over had his name on it. He dragged the weight to a standing position, slipped his shoulder under it, and stood up. The speed he made back to where Sergeant

Hawkins was forming his men was anything but a run. But the sergeant had already picked out a victim.

"Didn't you understand the lieutenant when he said there would be no more walking?"

Wally breathed insolence into every word. "Sorry, sarge, but I'm new around here. It must have slipped my mind."

"Well, well, well," the sergeant drawled with a grin. "It slipped your mind, did it? *Then I'll give you a little reminder*. Start running around this formation — on the double. And your side-kick — " he glanced at the name tag sewn over his jacket pocket. " — Farnsworth, too. Now, get moving."

Wally sighed, and rolled his eyes. He dropped his duffel bag in a heap and started jogging.

"Wait a minute, Gibson." Wally stopped and looked over his shoulder. "I didn't say put down your duffel. Take it with you."

Mike had not yet moved. Now he easily threw the bag over his shoulder and started out with glacial speed. Wally retuned and picked up his duffel with a grimace. For someone as slight as he was, he maintained a fair pace. He passed Mike after half a lap.

"Come on, men, let's hustle, unless you want to be keeping company with these two jokers." Sergeant Hawkins ordered the last of the platoon into formation.

Wally completed his second lap and was visibly slowing down. Still, he passed Mike for the *second* time. Mike's breast was heaving, and so short were his steps that the heel of one foot barely passed the toe of the other. Finally he could go no further. He stopped in front of Sergeant Hawkins and eased his duffel bag down to the dry earth. His shirt was soaking wet, and great drops of sweat hung from his chin and nose and covered his face.

"Pick that duffel up and get moving, mister!"

Mike breathed hard for several seconds. Then he nodded, tossed the bag up onto his broad, rounded shoulder, and started off again. His gait was little more than a shuffle. Wally passed him again, huffing and puffing. Now the formation was complete, and everyone was watching the two runners doing their laps.

"All right, that's enough. Resume your positions."

Wally walked through the formation and carefully put his bag on the ground. Mike stumbled to a halt, gasping. His duffel slipped off his back and hit with a crash, although he still held onto the strap. He wobbled slightly, staring around sightlessly. He looked as if he was about to collapse from the heat. Tony leaped to his aid.

"Leave him alone!" Sergeant Hawkins pushed Tony aside as if he were shoving a small kitten. "He'll do it himself."

Reluctantly, Tony retreated. Mike dragged the green bag into formation, his eyes rolling and his head smothered with sweat. He found his spot next to Wally only after staggering like a drunken sailor.

"Let that be a reminder that there will be no walking in my platoon. And no talking back. My name is Sergeant Hawkins, and for the next eight weeks I'm going to be your mother."

He stood with his legs spread wide, both feet planted solidly, and hands behind his back. As he talked, his head rotated slowly from left to right, and his dark, ebony eyes seared into the brains of every recruit.

"You will address me as sergeant at all times. I am not referred to as sir, that privilege being reserved for commissioned officers. And don't you forget it. Now, the first thing I'm gonna do is assign you bunk numbers and get you bedded down. You've got an hour till chow time to pick up bedding and unpack your clothes. Civilian clothes are not allowed in your footlocker. They must be put in your duffel bag and hung up on the back of your bunk. Now, when I call out your name, pick up your belongings and run — *run* — to barrack number two, that one over there, and find your bunk."

He started calling names, and the men started running. It did not take Tony long to catch up with Mike, who was still laboring from heat and exhaustion.

"Keep it up, Mike. You can do it."

"Prove to the old bastard you can take it," Wally said.

Mike nodded, and wheezed, and kept moving, however slowly.

Later, Wally commented, "Old Sarge Gonzales was right about one thing: they're not going to treat us like children — they're going to treat us like animals." Then, after a pause, "And Sergeant Hawkins sure is a mother."

Chapter 38

The two-story barrack was spotless, from the waxed linoleum floor to the sparkling bathroom fixtures. "You can eat off the floor and drink out of the bowls," Sergeant Hawkins had said. What bothered Tony was not the display of sterility, but the suspicion that it was expected to stay that way.

The floor plan was simple and utilitarian, comprised mostly of open bunk space. Several doors downstairs led to the latrine, with a shower room (eight nozzles and no spray control), a urinal room (standing room only and no graffiti to read), and the toilet room (six stools with no partitions, and no privacy.) Each floor had a day room, and upstairs there were several private quarters.

Confusion reigned in the aisles between rows of olive drab double bunks and footlockers, and brown floor and walls. In addition to the oversized windows, the room was lighted by bare hundred-watt bulbs, one of which, by accident, was a soft white. On both floors, men worried over their newly issued bedding.

Wally upended his duffel on the floor and started throwing it piece by piece into a footlocker. "Just my luck. Of all the sergeants in the world, I have to get a paragon of humanity and a pedagogue of military science who never heard of the Emancipation Proclamation."

"Y'all in the South now, where things are run different." Hank Gibbs spoke in a drawl that originated far below the Mason-Dixon line. Standing in socks and boxer shorts, his large-boned and fully fleshed frame quivered as he wrinkled his shoulders. He reminded Tony of a pale, stuffed teddy bear. "But if you Yankees hadda let us win the war, things'd be a whole lot diff'rent."

Wally did not look up. "Yes, and we'd all be speaking that rebel miscegenation that you call language."

Tony pulled his blanket tight and tucked it under the mattress. "Just remember that fifty-nine other guys have the same sergeant." He fished a dime out of his pocket, tossed it in the air, and watched it bounce off the dark brown wool. Turning to Hank, he said, "And don't take him personally. He treats everyone with equal disdain and hostility."

Wally slammed his footlocker shut and stood up with his duffel bag. "But fifty-nine other guys don't have the close acquaintance that I have."

"Even a fish would stay out of trouble if he kept his mouth shut." Tony stuffed the dime back into his pocket.

Hank smoothed the pillow on the upper berth, above Tony's. "Hey, y'all supposed to use a two-bit piece, not no thin dime."

"What difference does it make?"

"Weight. A dime'll bounce off'n a sheet that won't bounce a quarter. And you can bet your rosy red rectum that ole Sergeant Hawkins ain't gonna be sweet on us. Why, Ah'll bet he'll stir up more trouble 'n a horny hoag in a sty full o' bitches."

"You've been watching too much Tennessee Ernie." Wally hung up his duffel bag, which held his civilian clothes, on the back of the bunk. "But you're right. He'll probably pull out a silver dollar when he gets to my bunk."

"Now there you go being negative again." Tony surveyed his bunk with a critical eye, shrugged, then emptied his duffel bag and went to work on his footlocker.

"Sure, y'all oughta look at the bright side o' things." Hank tossed a quarter high into the air. It sailed completely over the rafter, soared down onto his bunk, and sagged into the blanket like a stone into a mud bank. Without any change of expression or word of discontent, he pulled the blankets out from under the mattress and started over again.

Several feet away, Wally started on his own bunk. "Hank, I think you could find a ray of light at the bottom of a cave."

"If that's what Ah's lookin' for, Ah'd prob'ly find it."

Wally scowled, and unfurled his blanket over the sheet.

"Excuse me, but I think you're doing that wrong."

The new recruit had a square head, a square jaw, and square shoulders. Faint blue eyes peered down a long, narrow nose. His fatigues were pressed with a knifelike crease, his boots were brightly spit-shined, and his brass belt buckle glinted like gold. His shirt flap, belt buckle, and zipper were aligned to perfection: a gig line that was geometrically faultless.

Wally stared cynically. "And who are you?"

"According to Geneva Convention rules, I am Thomas O. Gelbert, Private E-1, RA48107798. At your service. My place of repose is directly above you."

"Jesus Christ, man, where did you get that accent? Don't tell me! You were brought up on speeches by John Kennedy."

"Massachusetts born and bred. And I made my bunk and stored my gear while you were making introductions."

"Ah cain't say Ah'm glad to meetchu." Hank leavened his words with a toothy smile. "Ah don't know if Ah can associate with a RA."

"Are you fellows all US's?"

"I am, tried and true."

"Ah may have been drafted from low down south, but Ah'm an uppa US."

"Hey, man, I'm not a letter and I'm not a number. I'm a human being with a name and identity."

A deep voice broke in, "And your name's gonna be mud if that bunk ain't made with military corners." Sergeant Hawkins stood rigidly, hands on broad hips. Slowly he eased his arms down to his sides and strode forward, looking with disrespectful eyes at Wally's poorly sagging bedding. If Thomas O. Gelbert *thought* he was doing it wrong, the sergeant *knew* it.

Wally tossed off his best Lou Costello salute. "Hello there, sarge. We were just talking about you."

"I know." He jerked a thumb in the direction of his private room. "These walls ain't as thick as they look."

At the other end of the barrack, those who were blissfully unaware of the sergeant's presence continued their idle chatter.

"Let me show you how it's done." No one stood in his way as he ripped the blankets and sheets off Wally's bunk. "The first thing you have to do is make sure the sheet is tight." Methodically, he went through each step of tucking and tightening. When he was done, the quarter he dropped on the sheet did at least a one and a half gainer, and it looked to Tony as if a bowling ball would have bounced nearly as high. "Any bed that can't do that ends up on the floor." The sergeant returned to his room.

Voices were lowered a full octave.

"Man, what's the sense of making our beds now, anyway? We're going to be climbing into them in a few hours."

"That's what Ah always tole my mammy. But she scolded me right good if Ah didn't do it ever' mornin' — and Ah dasn't git her riled. Ah'd sooner have this nigger sergeant mad at me." Hank flipped his quarter up in the air, over the rafter, and onto his bunk. It settled into the wool. He shook his head and tore the bedroll apart.

Tony touched his blanket with an extended forefinger. He decided to let it go.

"Excuse me, fellows, but I believe our introduction was interrupted. You can call me Tom."

Wally started to sit down on his bunk, then jumped up millimeters before touching the sacred surface. "Hey, man, did you lose out on a pact with the devil, or something? What the hell made you volunteer for this crap?"

A cigarette appeared from behind Tom's back. He inhaled a mouthful of smoke and let it seep out his nostrils while answering. "I got tired of being a BMOC."

"What's a BMOC?" Tony asked.

"Big Man On Campus. I came from a rich family, was an all around athlete, hung out with the pseudo-intellectuals, had to fight off the girls all the time — "

"Are you sure your name's not Kennedy?"

" — It was all cut and dried. I was supposed to go to law school, enter politics, marry into the right station. But it's all a sham. There's got to be more to life than being rich and getting laid — "

"Sounds awl right to me," Hank said.

" — I want to see some action. Wearing fancy clothes and pushing people around with money and power gets old after a while. I want to see what the world is all about first. So I dropped out in my junior year, joined the army, and signed up for airborne. I've got orders cut for the 173rd. Then I'm going to Vietnam for some action."

"Man, you are a first class, number one, grade A Planter's peanut. How did you get out of the can?"

Tom took a drag on his cigarette, turned his head, and blew the smoke away. "That's the wrong attitude to take. You aren't put on this Earth just to go through life, but to experience it. And if you live a clean life and can do some good along the way, so much the better."

"Man, the only thing I want to live to see is old age."

Tom stubbed his butt out in an ashtray nailed to one of the wooden support columns. He reached into his shirt pocket for another, but his pack was empty.

Hank held out some crumpled plastic. "Here, try one o' mine. These are the best leaves in the world — come from my home town."

Tom eyed it askance, but took one. "Thanks. Where are you from?"

"Winston-Salem."

Tony scratched what little hair was left on his head. "Which is it — Winston or Salem?"

"Both. The name of the town's Winston-Salem."

"Where's that?"

"No'th Carolina, the tobacco belt of the world. Right off the Great Pee Dee River."

Tom laughed. "You have to be kidding."

"Ah swear on a stack of fam'ly bahbles. What part o' Massychussetts you from?"

"Cambridge. It's a part of Bahston."

There was a distinct difference between Hank's "bahbles" and Tom's "Bahston."

"Where they grow presidents."

"Wally and I are from Philadelphia."

"Ah, yes, the city of brothelly love."

"That's broth*er*ly love," Tony stressed.

"You mean they have more queers than whores."

"I don't know. I never met any."

"That's a point in your favor." Tom puffed away and seemed to enjoy Hank's cigarette immensely. "I hate queers."

"Hey, man, they just called first platoon to chow. We won't be far behind."

Tony rubbed his stomach. "Boy, I'm starved."

"One whiff of army chow and you won't be any more."

Tony started off down the aisle. Hey, Mike, are you ready for chow?"

Mike's bunk was by the back door, which overlooked the parade ground. He assiduously polished his spare combat boots. At mention of food his face lit up. "I could sure use a good meal."

"Well, I can't make any promises, but at least there'll be plenty of it. Come on, I want you to meet a couple guys." Mike waddled along behind him like a limping elephant. His body was just not designed for grace. "Mike, this is Tom, and this is Hank. Tom, Mike. Hank, Mike."

"Well, it's sure nice to — "

"Second Platoon. Chow."

During the mad scramble for the stairs, Sergeant Hawkins leaned over the railing and called after his descending troops. "And don't forget to run."

Wally, forever with a comment, said, "This time you don't have to worry."

Unfortunately, the food was not free: the men had to work for it. Sergeant Peterson, First Platoon sergeant and sergeant of the day, stood at the chow hall and funneled the men past the door to wait in line in front of a set of overhead parallel bars that were separated by cross braces, like a ladder lying down between four clothes poles. Each man had to go hand over hand from one end to the other before being allowed in the chow line.

Tony flew through the bars as if he had done them all his life. Wally and Tom were slow, grunting all the way. Hank, despite his size, managed to struggle to the end without falling. But Mike never made it past the third bar. He dropped to the ground like a sack of meal.

"All right, mister, get back at the end of the line and try it again."

He did no better on his second try; or his third. Finally, Sergeant Peterson had him do pushups until he groaned and gasped, and collapsed covered with sweat.

The fifteen minutes they were allotted for meals was not enough for Tony. He was forced to scrape nearly half his food off the tray and into the garbage can when the irate mess sergeant picked him up out of his seat and pushed him out the door. Once outside, he ran all the way to the barrack, catching up with Wally at the top of the stairs.

"Jesus Christ, I didn't know they had cyclones in Georgia."

"What are you talking ab — " Tony's chin dropped to his chest when he saw the destruction.

The barrack was an unbelievable mess. Of the fifteen double bunks, only four remained standing, and of the thirty mattresses, only three were in those bunks. All the other mattresses, sheets, blankets, and pillows lay in the middle of the floor. On top of that were the contents of almost every footlocker: underwear, uniforms, and personal belongings. Then the footlockers topped the pile, with the overturned bunks on top of them.

Hank let out a blood-curdling scream that was an imitation of Jimmy Rogers and the Mule Skinner Blues. "Ah think the cyclone is named Sergeant Hawkins, an' he's tryin' to tell us something."

"Yes, he's trying to tell us that he never grew up," Wally said.

Tom walked around the brink of the debris. His bunk was still intact, and his footlocker was still in place. "What he's trying to say is that he pulled a surprise inspection — and we failed."

"Well, shit, man, why doesn't he learn to communicate instead of throwing a tantrum like a spoiled brat?"

"Ah do declare, if y'all don't keep your voice down, he may come chargin' out here an' answer that question."

Tom leaned forward, placed one shiny boot on his footlocker, and pulled out a cigarette. "And toss you onto the pile."

Wally sputtered like a cranky Model T. His face was beet red as he waded into the pile to retrieve his footlocker.

Tony dragged his bunk to an upright position. "That sergeant sure knows how to get his point across."

As the rest of the platoon got over the shock, the men started rebuilding the barrack. It was an hour before form took place in the general melee. But some of the men walked up and down the aisle long afterwards, searching for lost items, or trying to trade things that did not belong to them. Tom sat on his footlocker and watched smugly.

By the time Mike got back from the mess hall, the clean-up was well underway. His bunk had survived the catastrophe, but not his footlocker. However, his clothes were easily identifiable by their size. It was not long before he joined the others. They all sat in a circle shining boots for morning inspection.

"The food was good, but there wasn't enough of it."

"What do you mean, man? I had to scrape most of mine into the garbage. But then, that's what it was before it was cooked."

"Why didn't you just go up for seconds, if you were the last one in line?"

"They wouldn't let me."

"Why not, man? They had enough food there to feed an army."

"I don't know, but the orderly wouldn't let me have any more. Not even a slice of bread. He made me leave."

"Those ignorant jerks. You'd think you were asking them to give you something out of their own goddamn pockets."

"Will you keep it down?"

"I don't care. This kind of chicken shit pisses me off."

"Won't do you no good to get riled 'bout it." Hank rummaged around in his duffel bag and came out with two Hershey bars. "Here, Mike, maybe these'll get you through till breakfast."

"Gee, thanks." He peeled the wrapper off of

one and downed it in two bites. The second one took three.

Tom put his dress shoes down by the bunk. "Look, fellows, why don't you take a look at my footlocker and see how it's supposed to be set up?" Wally scowled. "How come you know so much about it."

"I had three years of ROTC."

Wally put down his boot in the middle of a buff. "That's good enough for me. Show me your stuff, man."

They all gathered around as he opened the lid and took out the tray. "Now, the fatigues have to go on this side, and the dress uniforms on this side. Underwear must go in the middle, with the T-shirts folded so the collar is visible. And socks have to be rolled, not folded."

"What difference does that make?" Tony asked.

"The difference between staying in the footlocker and ending up on the floor." He replaced the tray and pointed to both sides of the divider. "Now, on this side you have your wash cloth, one bar of soap, and a towel, folded in thirds. On this side your toilet articles must be clean and on full display. The razor has to face this way, and there can be no whiskers or rust on the blade. The spare blades go here, with the label up. The shaving can can't have any foam showing. The toothbrush goes across here, bristles toward the top, and the toothpaste up here, again, label up. Also, you're not allowed to have any dents on the tube."

Wally nearly choked. "How the hell are you supposed to get the toothpaste out without bending the tube?"

"Get another tube."

"Huhn?"

"You see, you need two sets of toilet articles: one for show, and one for use. The one you use, you stash in the bottom of the footlocker, under your spare fatigues. The one on top is for inspection purposes only — you never touch it."

"That's more than silly, man. That's plain stupid."

"It sure don't make much sense," Hank allowed.

Tony slowly shook his head. "You forget, you're in the army now. Things don't have to make sense."

Hank snorted. "Now Ah know what they mean when they say they's the right way, the wrong way, and the army way."

Chapter 39

They stopped running just out of sight of the barracks. The afternoon was unbearably hot, and lunch sat in Tony's stomach like five pounds of rising dough. The company had spent most of the morning doing loosening-up exercises — and Tony discovered that he was not in as good a shape as he thought. He had aches and pains where he did not even know he had places.

Wally was hardly out of breath. "That low crawl was the funniest thing ever, man."

"Yeah, what's so funny about crawling around on the ground like a worm?"

"Knowing that Tom's spit-shined boots weren't spit-shined any more."

"Aw, come on, Wally. Don't start picking on him."

"I'm not picking on him, man. I didn't say a word to him. It's just that his perfection gets to me. I'll even bet he was an Eagle Scout."

"He was. He told me this morning."

"Ha! Well, maybe he won't have time to brag so much about himself if he has to repolish his boots every night. Did you see him huffing and puffing this morning doing those jumping jacks? If he's such an all round athlete, why was he dying out there?"

"He said it's the cigarettes."

"Tony, athletes don't smoke. They know better."

"Well, maybe he smokes so he can look tough for the girls."

"After listening to him brag, you'd think he'd quit smoking and start carrying a baseball bat so he could fight them off."

"All right, all right. Just let him go his own way."

"Man, I won't say another word. Scout's honor."

The Post Exchange was something like a department store except on a smaller scale. It carried everything from rubbers to rain coats — to protect a soldier from the elements no matter how harsh the conditions.

"Jesus Christ, man, the place is air-conditioned."

Tony caught the thick glass door and stepped inside. "Feels good." He took off his cap and wiped sweat off his brow with the back of his sleeve. Short hair did have its advantages.

The PX was jammed with recruits from other companies, easily spotted by fatigues bereft of insignia. It was not until after Sergeant Hawkins had dumped bedding, footlockers, and mattresses as the platoon was merrily chomping through breakfast, that he gave a practical demonstration on how things should be done. Tom had been immensely proud to be pointed out as an example. Then two men at a time were allowed twenty minutes to make the PX run for soap, razors, blades, shaving cream, toothbrushes, and paste.

"You'd better put that one back. The end is slightly curled."

"Shit, man, all the others have dents in them."

"This one doesn't — whoops, yes it does." Tony had picked it up too eagerly. With a sigh, he put the dented tube back on the rack. Together they went through the entire stock, but could find none that were not damaged in some way.

"We'd better see the chief honcho." Wally made off toward the back of the store and a door marked "Authorized Personnel Only." He opened the door and went right on in. Tony stayed outside. "Hey, man, do you have any more small tubes of toothpaste?"

The bespectacled manager, a civilian, looked startled. "There should be plenty out on the shelf."

"Yes, but they all have dents in them. Do you have any that aren't dented?"

The manager tilted his head back and peered through the bottom of his bifocals. "I beg your pardon."

"It's for inspection, man. We need tubes without dents or creases."

"I see." He tilted his head down and looked over the top of his glasses. After several seconds he took a cardboard box off a nearby shelf, ripped open the tape, and handed Wally a fresh tube."

Wally scrutinized it all around. "This'll do. Give me another for my friend." He inspected that one, too. "Thanks, pops. And if I were you, I'd keep that box handy. I think there's going to be a run on toothpaste today."

They left the manager agog, and picked up the other necessary toiletries. On the way along the aisle toward the check out counter, they passed a crowd of recruits diligently inspecting the toothpaste display. Tony directed them to the back room, and had the satisfaction of seeing them descend en masse on the manager, who stood at the door and handed out tubes of toothpaste as if they were the best of Havana cigars.

As Tony put his items on the counter, the elderly female cashier counted up his purchases. Wally dropped his can of shaving cream, and chased after it on hands and knees as it rolled away under the adjacent counter. Tony counted bills and the exact change.

"Would you like a sack?"

Tony hesitated, judging the weight of the items. "No, just put them in a bag."

She raised her eyebrows and smiled quixotically, pulled out a paper bag, and placed his purchases into it. Wally stood up with his can of shaving cream and put it with the rest of his items. At the same time, a middle-aged man in civilian clothes showed a carton of cigarettes to the cashier and tried to push past Wally while waving a five dollar bill.

"Hey, man, wait your turn. I was here first."

"Sorry, but I'm in a hurry. My wife's waiting for me in the car."

With one hand Wally pushed back the carton of cigarettes, and with the other he swept his articles to where the cashier's hands rested on the counter. "I'm sorry, too, but I have someone worse than your wife waiting for me."

"Look, soldier, I don't want to argue with you. Just let me pay for this and I'll be out of your way."

"You'll get out of my way by getting in at the end of the line." This time Wally pushed him back and said to the cashier, "Count them up."

She rang up the items that were at her fingertips as the civilian slammed the carton down on the counter. "Just who the hell do you think you are, soldier?"

"Napoleon Bonaparte. Who do you think you are?"

Tony squeezed between them. "He's right, you know. You really shouldn't butt in like that. Lines are made for a reason."

The man gave him a look that was so dirty it would take a week to wash it off. "Look here, you." He reached over and grabbed Wally by the arm and spun him around. Wally reacted like a coiled spring, and flung the hand off him. "Lay off me, mister," he said, through clenched teeth.

"Soldier, I'll have you know I'm an army major."

"And I'll have you know that I'm a history major, with a masters in political science. That and a quarter will get you a cup of coffee. Now bug off." Wally threw a twenty-dollar bill onto the counter — the whole of his casual pay.

"Mister, you're in trouble now. Both of you. What outfit are you with?"

"How the hell should I know. I've only been here one day."

"Mister, I asked you a direct question. I want to know what outfit you're with."

Wally scooped up his change from a cashier who was trying to ignore the whole argument. He picked up his bag and headed for the door. "Ask my friendly army recruiter."

As Tony stepped out into the scalding heat, he could still hear the major hollering until the thick door closed off the sound. On the other side of the glass he gesticulated wildly. "I think we'd better run."

"I'm right behind you."

Back at the barracks, with his footlocker an identical match for Tom's, Wally asked Sergeant Hawkins. "Sarge, if we pass this inspection with flying colors, do we get a weekend pass?"

"There ain't no weekends in the army — just long weeks and short weeks. The difference is the short weeks don't last as long."

****

"I don't know what the hell got into you two, but the shit has sure hit the fan."

Captain Maxwell sat behind a scratched oaken desk, and leaned back in his swivel chair almost with an air of nonchalance, belying the tenor in his voice. He was older than Lieutenant Wakefield, but not by much. He might not have been as old as Wally. His black hair was long by military standards: almost an inch. It was pushed away from the center in order to hide the prematurely balding spears above the veined temples. His face was tinted a dark bronze, but not rough enough to be considered swarthy. And his light blue eyes could not convey the malignity and terror of his subordinate Executive Officer.

"You've been in my command less than twenty-four hours, and already I've got a conduct report on you. You were allowed out of my jurisdiction for twenty minutes, and you managed to stir up more trouble against this outfit than I've had in the past six months."

Tony and Wally stood rigidly at attention, caps in hands, penitent looks on faces, name tags standing out as boldly as they must have in the PX.

"And of all the people to start a fight with, you had to pick on a major — and the adjutant at that. What the hell got into your heads?"

"Well, sir — " Tony started.

"Who gave you permission to speak? Of all the stupid, lamebrain stunts to pull. Well, you men better get something through those thick skulls of yours. You are nothing but privates in this man's army, the lowest thing on the totem pole: the gophers, the broom pushers, and the paper pickers. Everybody — *everybody* — is higher in rank than you. If a PFC gives you an order, you damn well better carry it out. You do what you're told, is that understood?"

"I understand, sir, but this major — "

"This major, *Private* Giovanni, is the adjutant of this base, and in a position to cause me a great deal of trouble. He can have me lifted from this post, or he can have me demoted to Second Lieutenant — at the bat of an eye. I am responsible for every man in my command, and I now find myself in the very awkward position of having to explain why I let two smart-aleck trainees out of my jurisdiction — unescorted — so they could raise havoc with officers in the performance of their duty. What am I supposed to do?"

"Sir, I don't think he was performing — "

"Quiet! And furthermore, I've got to find a punishment suitable to this atrocity. Major Cunningham wants to have you summarily court-martialed, and I may not be able to talk him out of it. The least you can expect is an Article Fifteen. And you can rest assured that I'll find some kind of extra duty so you won't have any spare time in the future to get into any more trouble. I'm going to make sure that Sergeant Hawkins keeps a sharp eye on you at all times. I can't afford to have raw recruits messing up my good service record. Understood?"

Tony bit his lip.

"Is that understood?"

"Yes, sir," Wally and Tony answered simultaneously. Then, swallowing hard, Tony continued, "Sir, I really think this whole thing has been blown out of proportion. I mean, all we did — "

"That's enough! I'm not interested in your excuses. I am well aware of what you did. And it had better not happen again. Dismissed."

Tony stifled a sigh. He saluted, executed a right turn, and waited for Wally to do the same. Wally stood there resolute and immobile, staring antagonistically at Captain Maxwell.

"I think you're forgetting something," Wally started, in a calm voice that might have been an "oh, by the way."

Oh, no. Fort Leavenworth, here we come. Tony said, "Wally — "

"You've already got us judged and sentenced and you never even asked to hear our side of the story."

"Private Gibson, you don't have a side — not against an officer."

"As long as I'm right, I have a side — against anyone. This country is a democracy, not a military dictatorship."

This isn't the time for a history lesson. "Wally — "

"I have as much right to speak my mind as that jerk of a major. I didn't ask to be put in this goddamn army, even though I went along with it. But I will not go along with this miscarriage of justice perpetrated by you or that major — or anybody else. And if you uphold his allegations without so much as listening to my justifications, then you're obviating the freedom for which we are supposed to be fighting."

"That's enough out of you, Gibson. Sergeant," he called out to the adjoining room, "get this man out of here."

The burly First Sergeant came in and grabbed Wally by the shirt collar and dragged him, still screaming, from the room. "Is the truth too much for you, Captain? What happened to all the military justice bullshit you were feeding us yesterday? Or is justice only for officers?"

His voice was suddenly muffled, and Tony heard loud scuffling sounds and furniture banging around. Then the screen door slammed shut and the sounds died away.

"Sir — " Tony shut up, realizing that he had been forewarned not to say anything.

Captain Maxwell stared out the door, seemingly lost in thought. Just before Tony made good his escape, he said, "What is it, Giovanni?"

"Uh, sir, uh — is it all right to speak?"

"Go ahead." The captain's voice was calm, too calm.

"Well, sir, I have to stand behind what Wally — what Private Gibson said. That major over at the PX was way out of line."

Captain Maxwell leaned forward on his elbows. "Giovanni, you look like you've got more sense than Gibson, so I'll tell this to you and you can tell it to your buddy. We've got hundreds — thousands — of new recruits coming through this base every week. We've got street junkies, jailbirds, know-it-all college graduates, and sniveling high school dropouts still in diapers — and they've all got problems. But I've got a problem, too. In two lousy months I've got to turn these kids into something resembling soldiers, so when they find themselves in the middle of a war ten thousand miles away, they have some kind of chance of not getting their asses blown away. I haven't got time to take each one by the hand and lead him around because he's got a chip on his shoulder. As far as my responsibility as a training commander, I don't care what happens to you when you leave here, as long as you make it through my command without making waves. But personally, I like to see every man receive the best training we can give him. The first keeps my record clean, the second keeps my conscience clear. But when you come down to reality, my record is more important than my conscience, because that's what earns my living. Whether you're right or wrong, I've got to look out for myself. And if it comes to a contest of wills, mark my word, I'm going to win. Because whether your friend thinks it's right or not, I've got more power than he has, and if I have to exercise it, I will. Do I make myself clear?"

"Yes, sir."

"Good. Dismissed."

Tony saluted again. The eyes of the company clerk were on him as he gently let himself out of the orderly room.

"Hey! You! *Git* over here!"

Tony ran obediently to where First Sergeant Abrams indicated. Wally stood at attention in front of him. His clothes were ruffled, and smeared with reddish soil. A thin trickle of blood escaped from the corner of his mouth, and there was a bruise on his cheek.

"Face this way! Stand at attention! And don't give me no trouble like your friend here. Now, the first one that moves gets his ass kicked — by me. And I'll be watching from that window over there."

The sun was hot, bright, and dead ahead. Wally whispered out of the corner of his mouth, "I guess that knocks our chances for a weekend pass."

"And no talking, either!"

"Fucking bastards," Wally breathed.

After ten minutes at rigid attention Tony's legs began to ache. After twenty they started to go numb. Discomfort turned into pain. He remembered from his Boy Scout days the trick of relaxing the muscles so as to not restrict the circulation. Inside the loose folds of his fatigues, he slackened the tension by lowering his shoulders, loosening his arms, rocking his hips, and alternating the pressure on his legs, standing first on one, then on the other, all the while appearing to be standing at attention.

The sun beat down relentlessly, like a searing heat lamp. The sand mirrored the heat back up with the awful intensity of a reflector oven. As Tony slowly baked, salty sweat dripped into his eyes and stung like acid. He tried ineffectually to blink it away, while remembering hot August days in the watermelon fields in Salisbury, where the sweat of his brow brought the enjoyment and satisfaction of hard work and accomplishment.

He stiffened whenever the screen door slammed and Sergeant Abrams came out to inspect them. And as soon as he was gone, he went through his exercises: rolling the shoulders and hips, and standing from leg to leg. Shooting pains stabbed down from his neck, and up from his calves. Flies landed on his face, and he had to blow them away or twitch them off. The sun, after a couple of hours, peeped under the brim of his cap and burned into his eyes.

He started playing games to pass the time. He counted all the windows on the barracks: fifteen on each side, top and bottom, thirty all told, one hundred twenty for all four barracks. And each window had sixteen panes, which meant two hundred forty per side, four hundred eighty altogether, one thousand nine hundred twenty total.

The buildings, which stood on three-foot-high concrete pillars, were constructed of wooden frames with overlapping clapboard. There were forty-five rows up to the eaves, and eight more to the shallow peak. The trees in his field of vision numbered only seven, most of them along the main road to the side of the barracks. Four were pines, two were oaks, and one was an ash, standing all alone. There were more in the far distance, but they tended to merge their leafy foliage so that counting them with any accuracy was impossible.

He counted passing vehicles in two categories: those which passed through the training compound by taking the side street in from of him, and those which drove along the main road, which he could not actually see, although he could hear the vehicles: he counted them by their motors. This kept him going for quite a while, and allowed some free time for day-dreaming. Later, he added to the difficulty by reading the serial numbers painted in white on the door panels of those jeeps and trucks and military cars passing by. After an hour of this, Tony came to the startling discovery that the same green army Plymouth had passed by three times.

The afternoon slipped away, and still they stood. Tony tried to find reason where none existed.

And still they stood.

Chapter 40

"This is really the pits, man." Wally took a jar of cherries off the shelf, and tossed it through the open pantry door. In rapid-fire succession, he tossed out jar after can after box.

"It sure isn't fair." As quickly as he could, Tony piled the supplies in the hallway. Cans of peaches, boxes of cereal, sacks of flour, bags of sugar, all came flying out of the pantry like angry bees from a molested hive.

"Life doesn't have to be fair, man; only people can be fair. But there aren't any people, any real human beings, in this whole goddamn army."

How much more food was there? "So much for reason and justice."

"Might is right. Power obfuscates morality."

By the time the pantry was empty, Tony stood knee-deep in canned goods. He picked up the bucket full of hot soapy water, and climbed over the mound of debris. He handed a wet rag to Wally, threw another one on a shelf, and started scrubbing it.

"Hey, Wally. What's an Article Fifteen?"

"How the hell should I know — ask Tom Perfection. It's probably some euphemism for military injustice."

"What's an adjutant? Some kind of big wheel?"

"Yeah, man, one that goes around in circles. Hey, what did you do with those cherries?"

"They're out in the hall. Why?"

"I feel like having some." Wally climbed over the stacks of groceries and rummaged through the heap of jarred foodstuffs. By the time Tony finished cleaning the lower shelves, and was reaching for the footstool, Wally appeared with an opened jar and a red-stained mouth. "Try some, man. They're good."

Tony grinned mischievously as he took the jar. The cherries were so wet and delicious that he turned the jar upside down and let the fruit and juice roll past his lips. "I wish you had thought of this sooner. But what would Sergeant Breneke say?"

"There is no evil in some, but some good in all." Wally took the jar, screwed on the lid and stuck it in the corner. Tony threw his rag into the bucket and sat down on the stool. "Hey, man, let's get these shelves restocked before we take it easy."

"But my feet are killing me. These boots weren't designed with leisure wear in mind."

"And the sooner we get done, the sooner we can get back to the barracks."

"And polish brass and boots. Great." But Tony climbed up on the stool and cleaned the upper shelves while Wally mopped the floor.

Then they reversed their procedure. Now Tony was the pitcher and Wally the catcher. The mass of cans, bags, boxes, and bottles moved through the air from hall to pantry with very little droppage and, fortunately, no breakage.

They were just pushing some of the larger cases across the linoleum when a high-pitched voice sounded behind them. "What are you men doing back here?" The mess sergeant's elocution was loud and brash, but muffled, as if his mouth was full of dough.

Tony swiveled around and smiled at the man in a white cook's uniform, complete with bilious chef's hat. "Almost finished, sarge."

"You can't be. Let me in there." Sergeant Breneke looked closely at each shelf, sniffing through an overlarge and thickly veined nose. He ran an index finger along each painted board. There were visible watermarks, but no dirt. He pushed several cans aside. "Hey, these walls haven't been washed."

"But, sarge, you told us to clean the *shelves*."

"And now I'm telling you to clean the walls *behind* the shelves." He handed Tony a can of spinach. His acned face and incomplete dentition did not soften his demeanor. "And don't think I won't inspect them when you're done."

He was already stalking away when Wally burst out, "Hey, man, why didn't you tell us that in the first place — "

Tony placed a restraining hand on his chest. "Take it easy, Wally. Take it easy."

Sergeant Breneke turned, and said smugly, "Did you say you wanted some extra detail, soldier?"

Tony shoved Wally back into the pantry, then smiled at the mess sergeant. "No, sarge. We've got enough work already. But thanks anyway."

The sergeant stared at him hard. After several seconds, he continued his rounds. Tony could hear him yelling at the other KPs in the kitchen.

"But that bastard could have saved us a lot of work if he had the brains to tell us that before."

Tony loosened his hold. "I know, but it won't do any good to fly off the handle. It'll just get us into more trouble."

"Yeah, man, go ahead and blame me for everything."

"I'm not blaming you. I'm just saying it won't do any good to stir up a hornet's nest. You'll only get stung."

Wally shoved a cardboard box out into the hall. "I'm quickly losing what little respect I ever had for civilized man."

"But we're not dealing with civilized men; this is a militarized man, barking from behind his stripes."

"Yeah, man, I guess you're right. I'm sorry."

Tony started the laborious task of unloading the shelves again in order to get at the wall space behind them. "Hey, why don't we just empty one shelf, clean behind it, then rotate the stuff from the next shelf and work them one at a time? Then, when we're done, we just repack the last shelf with the stuff from the first. Everything will be one shelf advanced from where it is now."

"Good idea."

"And you don't have to be sorry, just learn something by it. The cards are stacked against you, and *they* hold the winning hand. There's no sense fighting when you can't win."

"That, my man, is defeatism. That's resigning yourself to a fate which someone else has decided for you. Well, I don't give up that easily. If you give in to them, you're only encouraging them. If you don't fight back, you're a slave. You have to stick up for your principles, man, or you don't have any."

"But can't you see that picking on some flea-bitten sergeant is not how to get back at the system that employs him? He's not to blame for the way he acts — he's been trained that way."

"He's allowed himself to be trained that way."

Tony scrubbed hard, first with one hand then with the other. "All right, I'm not arguing free will. What I'm saying is that the army's to blame, not the individual soldier who allows himself to be misdirected."

"Wrong, man. The world is made up of individuals, and each one has to stand up on his own two feet, not be led around like a donkey with a ring in his nose. If you allow yourself to be controlled, there's always someone out there who is willing to control you. You have to be the one who decides when to stop being controlled."

"All right, I agree with you. I don't know what the answer is. But I do know you're not going to solve anything by picking on one stupid sergeant. If you do, you're just stooping down to his level, and that's exactly what they want you to do. Part of the training is to break you down to your component parts so they can build you up the way they want you. If you're going to resist anything, you should resist being broken down. Take their crap, like we're doing now, and when they turn their backs — laugh at them."

Wally punched the doorjamb with his open hand. "Yes, you're right, man. It's so easy to lose sight of things." He leaned back against the shelving, stared up at the bare bulb. "But I still don't have to like the son of a bitch."

Tony grinned. "He doesn't want to be liked. None of them do." With the walls finally done, he squeezed his blackened rag in the bucket. The once warm, sudsy water was now cold and dirty. "Listen, what do you say we do the door and the woodwork, too? That way he won't have anything to complain about."

Wearily, Wally said, "Are you looking for brownie points, man?"

"No, I'm just trying to do a good job."

They were just finishing when Sergeant Breneke returned. He performed no inspection, and took no notice of the shining woodwork. "Come with me."

Tony grabbed the bucket, and Wally the mop. They followed the sergeant's awkward gait into the kitchen where the dishwasher was still going, pots and pans were still being cleaned, and the tables were being set for breakfast.

"I want that wall painted." The surface he indicated was behind a long array of stoves and ovens, and splattered with grease. "Get some fresh hot water and scrub it down first. Here's the paint." Sergeant Breneke then proceeded to ignore them.

Wally set up shop in the corner, behind the gas appliances, and started scrubbing. "If he keeps practicing, he may become a training sergeant."

"He's got to get a different hat."

Wally worked fast and hard. His sinewy arms moved ceaselessly, tirelessly, over the tiles. Tony meticulously spread on the paint as his grandfather had shown him, but could not keep up with Wally. When Wally finished, he sat on his haunches, hidden by the bulk of stoves.

"Hey, what's the hold up?" Sergeant Breneke whistled his esses through a missing front tooth.

Tony still had half a wall to go. Wally perked up and brandished his rag. "The floor's pretty dirty, sarge, so I'm doing that, too."

"Well, all right. But hurry up. I wanna be outa here in fifteen minutes."

Wally was just finishing the floor, and Tony was cleaning the brush in turpentine, when the sergeant dismissed the KPs. He eyed the fresh white enamel. "Next time you guys get inna trouble, have 'em send you ta me — I got plenty of work for ya."

Outside the darkness was cool and refreshing. The sky was purple, and limitless. Thousands of stars winked from the broad band of the Milky Way, as if each one held a secret which it was trying to impart. On the ground, the incandescence and clamor of the mess hall was behind, the gloom of the barrack in front. Tony stopped at the street.

"Hey, man, what's the matter?"

Tony stared at his friend, perplexed. His mind had drifted off for a moment. "Sorry, I was just taking it all in: the beauty, and the serenity. I've been so hounded and harassed this past week that I almost forgot there's another, more real, world out there." He looked around the compound, where no people were in sight. The barracks lights were out, and their companions in bed. He sat down on the curb. "No one knows that Sergeant Breneke's done with us, so what's the rush to get back?"

"Yeah, man, I know what you mean." Wally folded his limbs onto the ground. "Christ, it's good to get away from it all for a minute." He followed Tony's gaze up to the star-studded sky. "So where do you think we're headed in all this?"

Tony shook his head. "I don't know. It's all so confusing. Things are happening so fast that I can't keep up. I mean, one minute I'm minding my own business, going to work every day, saving money, planning a future — and the next minute my future's gone, wiped out. I no longer have a life — I'm living someone else's. Suddenly I'm some kind of — robot. A cog in a wheel so vast that I can't comprehend its size. And there are people pushing buttons that make me do this and do that without ever letting me know why I'm doing it. And if I question the logic behind something, I'm told not to think about it, just do it. Well, I can't do things without thinking. When I do something, there has to be a reason to do it. I don't mind doing my job, as long as I know it has a purpose. And if I don't question, if I don't seek knowledge, if I don't strive for awareness, then I'm not human any more — I'm a machine. And I resent that. I reject it — even the implication of it. I can't let the army, or anyone for that matter, turn me into a zombie, because without the latitude to make my own decisions, no matter how wrong they may be, I'm no longer me — I'm just a mindless puppet. And I don't want that to happen."

Wally patted him on the knee. "You know, the two of us have a lot in common. You're a resister, like me. If someone pushes you, instead of moving along, you push back. And the harder they push, the harder you resist. But you have a calmness about you, a level-headedness that I lack. Oh, yes, I'm aware of my shortcomings. I know I'm impetuous, strong-willed, maybe even a little hardheaded. But that's the way I am, and the way I've always been, and more important, the way I want to be. I act impulsively because I want to cause a reaction. But you — you think things through. That's where we're different. It doesn't mean that either one of us is better, just different. And that difference is important. We need a variety of opinions, goals, and ideologies, constantly fluctuating between individuals and nations. We need that adaptability. As a race, the influx of new ideas is our greatest survival value."

"Hey, I'm supposed to be the scientist. You're the historian."

"I had Anthropology I, too, you know. It's a prerequisite for a history major. History, in case you don't know it, is a science. It's the science of human struggle, of human survival, of human striving. It's a predictive, as well as a deductive, laboratory experiment. By studying the past we try to divine the future, the same way a geologist does, except that we're dealing with human values instead of rocks. But the process is the same. And you know what? We're not even sure yet that intelligence, or at least what we like to call intelligence, is a long-term survival factor. It may turn out to be a dead end, nothing more than a cancerous growth gone astray, which dies when it kills its host. Dinosaurs were around for fifty — a hundred million years, and they didn't pan out. We've only been around for a million or so. So we don't know where our future lies, or even if there is one. The struggle between communism and capitalism may be nothing more than a form of natural selection that kills us all off. You see, to man as a race, it doesn't matter who wins. And to Nature, it doesn't matter if *anyone* wins. It's only necessary for the race to survive as far as we personally are concerned. That's why we each have to resist in our own way -- because resisting offsets the balance of power." Wally nudged Tony unexpectedly. He fell sideways and had to put out his hand for support. "Being off balance is what makes you put your foot forward so you don't fall down, and that constantly forward motion carries you in a new direction."

"You'll never make a politician. You're too honest with yourself."

"And I don't want to be. The study of political science doesn't lead one into politics, it leads one away from it. As a scientist you discover that politics is a game — and games are for children. Science is for adults. So we let the children play their games, make their speeches, and wear their stripes, and make believe they're in control. But we hang around on the periphery of human endeavor, giving gentle nudges in the right direction, so the politicians don't stray too far from the playground. Like children, they tend to make their own rules."

"Then how do you explain this conflict? If you listen to the news media, the majority of the people are against Vietnam involvement."

Wally laughed. "That has yet to be proven. All we know is that very few people have very loud voices."

"But what about the demonstrations?"

"That's a biased and invalid sampling because they represent the very ones who are in the position to be sent over to do the fighting — and the dying. They are looking out for themselves, for right now, instead of looking out for the country, or the world, in the future."

"You're not making any sense at all. You're jumping from side to side."

"No, I'm just facing the facts. I'm looking at the big picture, instead of at the little dots it's made of. You have to understand, man, that I'm not a pacifist — I'm a realist. A pacifist is nothing more than a slave to the first person he meets who is not a pacifist. The only way a pacifist can survive is if he's surrounded by realists who are willing to protect them. Your being alive keeps all the parasites that are living in your body alive, too. Tapeworms can't live unless they're fed. The reason I'm against this war is that I can see the inevitable: there is no way we can win in Vietnam — at least, not within the parameters of lives and materiel that will be acceptable to lose. We shouldn't be in Vietnam not because the people don't need us, or because communism doesn't need to be stopped. We shouldn't be there because we have no chance of winning. All we are doing is prolonging the agony."

"Wally, you're not paying attention to what you're saying. You're contradicting yourself. Just because you think you may lose is no reason to quit fighting. You've got to resist, or else you're submitting to slavery. Didn't you just say something like that?"

"Goddamn it, man, you're talking about idealism. I'm talking about reality. What I'm saying is not that we should give up the fight against communism, or any kind of aggression, but that we should choose our own battle grounds, where we at least have a chance of winning."

"So what do we do? Throw the Vietnamese to the dogs while we go chasing rainbows?"

"In the present state of world affairs, yes. It doesn't do any good to win if you die in the process. Pyrrhus learned that in 279 B.C. He defeated the Roman army, but suffered such staggering losses that he was forced to admit, 'Another such victory and we are undone.' The so-called Pyrrhic victory. We'll never win in Vietnam because the people aren't behind us. And I don't mean just the American people, I mean the Vietnamese people. Most of them are ignorant peasants who don't care who rules them, as long as they can grow their rice and raise their water buffalo and have their children."

"But they're not strong enough to fight against those who would steal their rice and water buffalo."

"If they contain such racial genetic traits that prove to be nonsurvival factors, then perhaps they should die out and make room for those who are more adaptable. Nature is nonselective."

Tony banged his fists into his knees. "But that's not the point. We should stick up for the underdog and see that they have the advantage of choosing their own destiny."

"First of all, there's no such thing as destiny. That is something created by man because of his insecurity and uncertainty. And who exactly are we giving power to? The poor peasants plowing the fields or the political machine holding the reins? The aristocracy who wants to maintain power because they are the sole owners of the country, and naturally the promoters of a capitalistic society which gives them all the power and riches? Don't you see that in a backward nation, the people don't benefit from capitalism? They fit naturally into communism by the very nature of their familial and tribal way of life. Those people don't have anything, so offering them capitalism offers them nothing."

"But we're not fighting communism. We're fighting the enforcement of a way of life. And you're fighting your own arguments."

"Okay, so maybe I'm as confused as you are. But at least I'm willing to admit it. I don't have all the answers. All I'm saying is that we all have to make our own stands, we all have to fight for what we believe in. Disagreement does not have to mean discord. It just means free will. And that's what we must fight to preserve — in ourselves first. The world can come later. Because if you don't have it yourself, how can you give it to someone else?"

Chapter 41

"All right, men, up and at 'em! Let's go let's go let's go! You ain't gonna sleep all day."

The barrack exploded into action as Sergeant Hawkins screamed and thumped along the aisle, banging on every bunk with a wooden nightstick. Tony's head happened to be touching the steel crosspiece, and the vibration nearly knocked him out.

He rolled out from under the blankets and buried his face in his hands, rubbing his eyes vigorously to convince them that they should be open. But the lights were too bright, and his sleep had been too short — they could not be convinced. He left them closed while he fumbled around in his footlocker for his fatigues.

"I said move it! You got fifteen minutes till formation." The sergeant descended the stairs to impart the news to the other two squads.

Wally pulled the covers over his face. "Hey, man, why's he waking us up in the middle of the night?"

Hank yodeled from the top of his bunk, Mule Skinner Blues style, leaped off, and landed on bare pudgy feet. "It ain't the middle o' the night. Them roosters been crowing a hour already."

"Yeah, well, tell one of them to stand in formation for me."

Tony groggily buttoned his shirt, wincing at the pain in his eyes. "Hank's right at home, except he doesn't have any cows to milk."

Hank pulled a clean T-shirt over his head. "How many hours sleep did y'all git?"

"I think we're counting it in minutes." Tony sat down on the edge of his bunk and blindly stuck one foot into a boot. "Since we got back too late to get our personal gear in order, Sergeant Hawkins helped us out by giving us guard duty. I spent half the night in the day room polishing my boots."

Tom hit the floor fully dressed, except for his boots, with his toothbrush and toothpaste in hand. "Hey, Wally, you'd better get cracking."

Wally slid the covers down to his nose. "What the hell did you do, sleep with your clothes on?"

"Of course. It's the most efficient way." In his stocking feet he padded down the stairs to the latrine.

Sergeant Hawkins strode back into the room, picked up Wally's mattress in his hamlike hands, and vaulted him onto the floor."

Wally disentangled himself from the blankets, and came up swinging. "Hey, man, who's the goddamn joker? Oh, thanks, sarge. I was just getting up anyway."

"Next time I'll throw you down the stairs." He moved on down the line and debunked each man who was too slow. He got five before he went back downstairs. "When I say get up, I mean get up!"

Wally was a flurry of motion. He threw his mattress back on his bunk and started doing everything at once: donning clothes, putting on boots, making his bed. In the mean time, Tom sauntered up the stairs, zipped on his boots, and stared out the window with time to spare.

Tony tucked in his sheet. "Hey, I didn't see you make your bunk."

"I never unmade it," Tom said.

"You slept in it, didn't you?"

'I slept *on* it, and used my spare blanket for a cover. Then I just tightened it up and stashed the blanket in my laundry bag."

Tony was hardly listening, for something else dawned on him. "Hey, how did you get those boots on so fast?"

Tom's face split into a broad grin as he propped his foot on the edge of Wally's bunk. "I had these made up in ROTC ." The front was permanently laced, with a thin wire wrapped around the knot so it could not come undone. On the inward facing side of each boot was a cleverly disguised zipper, flapped so that only a faint line was visible upon close inspection. "They got me through a lot of inspections."

After he walked down the stairs and out the front door, Wally said, "Man, I just don't believe him."

"Y'all shoulda been here yesterday." Hank buttoned his shirt and tucked it into his ample waist. "He was happier 'n a tick in a stable full o' mares, goin' up an' down an' tellin' ever'one just how to set their footlockers."

"I wish I'd been here," Tony lamented.

Wally harrumphed. "Yeah, even *that* would have been better than roasting in the sun and doing KP. I'll bet they loved him."

"Well, they didn't exactly love him, 'cept for that queer kid down at the end. He'as about to kiss his boots, or anything else he could get his lips on."

"You mean a real queer?" Wally wanted to know.

"Sure thing. That little red-haired boy from South Carolina."

"Oh, great, man. That's just what we need. We haven't got enough troubles without having a goddamn homo in the crowd."

Hank tossed a quarter into the air. It sailed toward the ceiling, over the rafter, landed on top of the two by ten, and stayed there. "Damn."

"Fall in."

If the men were rushing before, they were frantic now. Everyone piled down the stairs, in various states of undress, and collided with the men surging through the hall from the first floor. There was a bottleneck at the door since only one was allowed to be open.

"Why the hell don't they open the other door? What are double doors for?"

"For the same reason they won't let us use the back door."

"What reason's that?"

At five o'clock in the morning it was still dark out, although there was a glimmer of light on the horizon. A few of the brighter stars still shone, and the waning moon was high in the sky.

The two hundred-odd names were called, and all were present or accounted for. Then everyone ran back to the barracks for the rigid schedule of morning chores.

Tom used his fingers to tick off the jobs. "Waste paper baskets and butt cans need to be emptied and disinfected; the floors have to be swept, waxed, and buffed; the latrine has to be sterilized; and the perimeter of the building must be policed and raked."

"Raked? Man, did you say raked?" Wally threw his hands into the air. "Are you out of your fucking mind? What the hell's the sense of raking the ground? There aren't any leaves, just sand."

"Because that's the way they want it done," Tom sighed patiently. "Everything has to be neat and uniform for inspection."

"But raking dirt just to make parallel rows? That's goddamn ridiculous. How long do you think it's going to stay that way? Shit, man, I'm sure as hell not going to do it."

"Okay, you can clean up the latrine today. I'll get someone else to do the raking, but you'll have to take your turn at it. Besides, it's easier than scrubbing out toilets."

"Hey, man, what do you mean *you'll* get someone else to do it? What are you, all of a sudden promoted to platoon sergeant?"

Tom's grin showed pride. "No, I'm acting squad leader."

"I should have guessed."

"There's no need to get up-tight about it. I'm just going to assign chores — and they'll be rotated every day so you won't get stuck with the same one all the time."

Wally sighed, and shook his head. "Okay, man, you got me by the short hairs. What do you want me to do?"

"How about taking the mop and swabbing down the latrine floor? And that includes the shower room, too. Tony, you give him a hand."

"Christ, man, there are still a hundred men in there trying to shit, shower, and shave. What am I supposed to do, mop under their feet?"

"Showers are off limits in the morning, so start in there. By the time you get to the washroom it'll be off limits, too. Do the shitter last. And if anyone tries to get in after you've started scrubbing it down, you tell them they're not allowed in till after inspection."

"Now that's a joke. Half this outfit speaks goddamn Puerto Rican."

"Wally, please, just do your best."

"All right, but when's inspection?"

"During chow."

"That's a long time to hold your cheeks together."

Tony said, "And that means the sarge will be tearing the barracks apart while we're enjoying breakfast."

Wally rolled his head in resignation. "Okay, man, lead me into the shadow of the valley of death, for I fear no sergeant."

Sabbath chow was like that of any other day: line up, climb the overhead bars, stand at parade rest in line, enter the mess hall five at a time, have food slapped into the sectioned tray, gulp down as much as possible as fast as possible, rush to the garbage can and either scrape off or throw up, rush out the door, run back to the barrack.

Sergeant Hawkins stood by the latrine door, threatening to turn the nozzles on the more than fifty mattresses and assorted bedding he had managed to stuff into the shower room. "It behooves you to learn to make your bunk according to military standards."

Tony dragged out a mattress, any mattress, plus an issue of bedding, and carried it up the stairs. "I'm tired of this game already."

"Hey, man, I sure wish the old sarge would make my bed every day."

Wally tossed a mattress onto bare springs and threw a damp sheet over it. Tom was right behind him, struggling the get the mattress on the upper bunk. "But at least I don't claim to be perfect."

Hank let out a shrill yodel. "Well, Ah do declare, mebbe y'all oughta take some lessons from a country boy."

Tom refused to let himself be baited.

The barrack was barely reconstructed before another call to formation was shouted. This time it was for PT. As a warm up, the entire company, in platoon formation, jogged around the block, singing military chanteys. Only the block proved to be a mile and a half around. This was followed by a strenuous half hour of exercises: deep knee bends, arms swings, toe touching, sit-ups, and push-ups. No one was allowed to leave his assigned position: many groveled on the sand when their muscles gave out, others vomited in place.

Mike Farnsworth was having a difficult time. Along with a few others, he had fallen out of formation on the first leg of the jog. Sergeant Wheaton, of the Fourth Platoon, stayed back to plague the dropouts. He and Mike were the last to arrive at the parade ground, with the sergeant screaming obscenities right in Mike's ear. But Mike never gave up. Moving as slowly as he was, he marched right into place and picked up the exercise that was then in progress.

"All right, men, listen up." Sergeant Abrams took charge of the outfit in the absence of commissioned officers, who had the day off. Tony had trouble hearing him because he was breathing so hard. "Uncle Sam says you men who gotta pray every Sunday can have the opportunity to do so. We only have one God in the army, so we only need one church. All men of faith step forward."

Roughly two-thirds of the company formed ranks in front of Sergeant Abrams. Sergeant Hawkins took the rest of the men, including Wally, formed them up, and marched them out in front. When they reached the church, however, they veered off to an athletic field. They formed one long line, double-arms distance. As they passed, Tony heard Hawkins shouting orders.

"Awright, men, we're gonna walk across this here field an' pick up everything that don't grow. I don't wanta see nothing but assholes an' elbows. *Move out!*"

The church was hot, crowded, and cramped. The service was simple, nonsectarian, and uninspired, rendered by a chaplain in dress uniform. But it was the only rest that Tony had had for a week. Afterwards, the company rejoined for more PT.

"Now I know what they mean when they say that godliness is next to cleanliness," Wally quipped.

After a hasty lunch there was an hour of close order drill until the heat of the afternoon, at which time they were taken on a long run-march-run to a medical building where they were given shots. Anyone not carrying his shot record was assigned extra duty. Then they ran-marched-ran back to the company area for close order drill, PT, and close order aril: facing movements, dress right dress, to the rear march, column left, and eyes right.

"Y'all'd think we's bein' trained for inspection 'stead o' fightin'."

At supper, Sergeant Hawkins took Mike's tray away before he was halfway finished. "You could use a little cuttin' down on the intake, mister, an' a little more sweatin' on the outtake."

Mike left the mess hall meekly, sadly, and hungrily. Tony was the last to leave, and saw further evidence of military spending. While hard-worked men cried for seconds, dozens of cooked pork chops, a bucket full of mashed potatoes, trays of corn and peas, and two untouched pans of brown cake were unceremoniously dumped into the garbage.

During silent hour, between nine and ten, Tony fought to keep his eyes open while brushing his combat boots for the tenth time. They simply would not shine. As soon as the lights flashed, signifying fifteen minutes to lights out, he took out his toothpaste, squirted some into his mouth, and rolled back on his bunk, too tired to go downstairs to brush.

Wally crawled into his bunk. "Well, I learned one thing today."

"What's that?" Tony grumbled.

"I found out why there are no atheists in the army. They all end up doing trash detail."

Chapter 42

"Aggression is the key to being a soldier — not just a good soldier, but a live soldier. Understanding the techniques of combat don't mean a thing unless you use this knowledge aggressively. You can be the greatest shot in the world, but if you don't attack with vigor you can't win a battle. And this is all the more true in hand-to-hand combat. The reason for this training is summed up in four letters: SYOA. That means 'Save Your Own Ass.'" The mild titter went unnoticed. "If you're ever caught without your weapon, or run out of ammunition, you'll have to know how to fight hand-to-hand. This probably isn't any revelation to you young hooligans and street fighters, but I'll say it for the benefit of you eggheads and candy-asses: you don't win a fight by being defensive. You win by hittin' first, hittin' fast, an' hittin' hard."

Sergeant Hawkins held up a wooden staff about three and a half feet in length. It sported a rounded ball of tightly woven padding at each end, and was covered with white adhesive strips that gave it the appearance of an oversized cotton swab.

"This is a pugil stick. We're gonna make believe it's a rifle. And I'm gonna show you the elements of armed hand-to-hand combat. The ends are soft so you don't hurt yourself. An' just to make sure you don't scratch up your pretty faces, I'm gonna let you wear a cage mask."

With his other hand he held up a curved iron grille that was edged in rubber and backed by an array of straps. It looked like a baseball catcher's mask. He tossed the cage mask to an acned corporal, a training assistant.

"You hold the pugil stick just like you hold your rifle — with both hands, in the on-guard position, at about a forty-five degree angle. The lower end is the butt, the upper end the barrel. If this were an M-14, even without ammunition or a bayonet, it would be a for*mid*able weapon."

Wally muttered, "Big word for a sergeant, except that it's pronounced *for*midable."

"Shush." As a squad leader, sometimes Tom

got on people's nerves.

The sergeant rushed up to one of the men in the front rank so fast that, for a moment, Tony thought he had overheard the whispered remark.

"With one quick thrust you can knock a man out of action. Like so."

With incredible swiftness he brought the butt end up into the side of the unsuspecting recruit. It hit his rib cage with a resounding thwack and knocked him out of rank. The man grunted and bent over, holding his side. On either side of him trainees jumped out of the way in order to escape further onslaught. The wounded man staggered back into the second rank, where he was held up by a short Negro.

"Let him alone," yelled the sergeant. "Like I said, you can't get hurt with these pads — but you can sure as shit make him think twice about getting hit again."

Sergeant Hawkins left the aching recruit and walked along the front row, staring into each man's eyes. The formation gradually fell together, and the man who had been hit stepped back into place, still holding his side.

"What did we learn so far? That you must be alert, that you must be aggressive, and that this dinky little stick can't hurt no one. Ain't that right, men?"

Everyone in the front row stiffened as the sergeant passed in front of him, anticipating a pugilistic thrust.

"I said, ain't that right?"

From the rank and file there was a belated and half hearted, "Yes, sergeant."

"I said, ain't that right?"

"Yes, sergeant!" Louder, this time.

"I can't hear you."

"YES, SERGEANT!"

"That's better." Without forewarning, and with unerring cruelty, he thwacked a man in the stomach. Caught off guard by the sergeant's nonchalant manner, he doubled over in pain and with an audible expulsion of air from his lungs. The victim refused to fall out of formation; he stooped, hands on midriff.

"Ain't that right, soldier?"

The injured man tried his best to stand straight. Weakly, with only a hint of breath, he said, "Yes, sergeant."

Sergeant Hawkins pivoted sharply on his heel and raced along the line to the first man he had hit. "Ain't that right?"

"Yes, sergeant," he said loudly, and without hesitation.

"Good. Now that you all know you can't get hurt, I'm going to show you how to use these things. Then when you're all experts, you'll try it out on your buddy — just to get the feel of it. Now, listen up. . . . "

For fifteen minutes he lectured on the use and misuse of the pugil stick: the undercut, the thrust and parry, the down stroke, and techniques that were defensive as well as offensive.

"I need a volunteer." There was no mad rush to meet his demand. "Come on, you pansies. Ain't there a man among you?"

Apparently there were not, for no one stepped forward to claim his manhood.

"Farnsworth, up front."

There was a moment's hesitation as Farnsworth glanced around. Slowly, almost confusedly, he worked his way through the formation from the back row. Tony, for one, breathed easier.

"Put the cage on." Sergeant Hawkins tossed it at him — hard. Farnsworth caught it in the pit of the stomach. He studied the array of straps for a moment, then pulled the cage over his head.

"Stand up straight, legs spread apart, and at-arms." Farnsworth assumed the proper stance. "Remember, the defensive position is also the ready position for attack. But you'll never win a fight by standing like some storefront mannequin. You must press forward the attack. Like this."

With blinding speed and amazing brutality, Sergeant Hawkins tore into Farnsworth like a bulldozer into a flowerbed. With the butt of his pugil stick, he smashed Farnsworth in the rib cage, then brought the barrel end down across the side of his head. Farnsworth was forcibly knocked back by the onslaught, but somehow remained on his feet. He was at least as big as the sergeant, if not as agile.

"Now if this had been a rifle, that man would be hurtin' by now."

In delayed reaction, Farnsworth dropped his pugil stick, clutched his side and head, and crumpled to his knees. The cage mask had been knocked askew, and a trickle of blood hit the ground and was soaked up by the dry, sandy soil as if it had never existed.

"And once you've disabled your man, it's an easy matter to finish him off. Like this."

He leveled a savage blow that landed across the top of Farnsworth's head, and pummeled him flat. Tony winced, easily imagining what a wooden rifle stock or steel barrel would have done to an unprotected skull.

"All right, Farnsworth, now I want you to attack me." Sergeant Hawkins did not even look at the fallen man; he stared at the formation of men in front of him.

Farnsworth coughed, then tried to pick himself up. He rose to one knee, and clawed the air as if it would provide a handhold. When he got both feet under him, he stood as tall as a hunchback.

"Cinch up those straps. Pick up that weapon."

Farnsworth wiped blood off his chin, adjusted the straps of the cage mask, and retrieved his pugil stick from the thick Georgia dust.

"Take up a defensive posture."

Farnsworth raised the stick, wavering slightly.

"Now attack."

He hesitated for a moment — obviously a moment too long in the sergeant's mind. Hawkins lunged forward and knocked Farnsworth down with the same one-two motion.

"Attack, goddamn it. I said attack. We're not playing charades. I'm trying to teach you how to save your ass. And you better remember it. Now, let's start from the beginning, men. What's the key word?"

Silence.

"What's the key word?"

A few of the men squeaked, "Aggression."

The sergeant ran up to one man who had dared to speak. "I can't hear you."

"Aggression," said the beleaguered man, in a voice that was swallowed up in the empty outdoors.

"I can't hear you."

"Aggression," he said louder, and more confidently.

"Did everybody hear that?"

When in doubt, say, "Yes, sergeant."

"I can't hear you."

"Yes, sergeant." This time everyone joined in.

"And what's the key word?"

"Aggression," chimed the troops.

"I can't hear you!"

"Aggression!"

"I still can't hear you!"

"AGGRESSION!!!"

"Repeat!"

"AGGRESSION!!!"

"And why do you want to be aggressive?"

Silence.

"You, soldier. Why do *you* want to be aggressive?"

"To save my ass."

"I can't hear you."

He screamed at the top of his lungs, "TO SAVE MY ASS, SERGEANT."

"Did you hear that, men? Now, why do you want to be aggressive?"

Collectively, "To save my ass."

"I can't hear you."

"To save my ass!"

"And what's the best way to save your ass?"

Silence.

"To kill. Repeat."

"To kill."

"I can't hear you."

"To kill!"

"I can't hear you!"

"TO KILL!"

Sergeant Hawkins wielded his pugil stick like a symphony conductor waving his wand. "Repeat."

"KILL!" the men shouted, in time with the plunging pugil stick. "KILL! KILL! KILL!"

"That's better. And don't you forget it. Some day it may save your ass. Farnsworth, get back where you belong."

Farnsworth half trotted around the formation, still clutching the pugil stick and wearing the cage mask.

"Farnsworth! Bring that stick back here unless you intend to use it." He ran back to the sergeant and stood in front of him. He was unsteady on his feet. In a very calm, almost faint voice, Sergeant Hawkins said, "Okay, you can let it go now."

Farnsworth dropped it.

"The cage, too."

He fumbled with the straps for a moment, removed the cage mask, and placed it on the ground next to the pugil stick.

"Now get back in formation." Louder, "Holloway, get up here and take his place."

Holloway glanced all around him, and pointed a quavering finger at his own chest.

"Is your name Holloway?"

"Yes, sergeant."

"Then git your ass up here. Move it."

A look of sheer panic passed over Holloway's face as he moved it — slowly.

Sergeant Hawkins picked up the cage mask and tossed it at him like an underhand fastball. "And make sure it's on tight."

Holloway fumbled overlong with the straps, making certain that they were snug and that the rubber gasket fitted perfectly. Blood was still visible on the mask. "Now pick up that stick and make an attack."

Holloway bent over to pick up the pugil stick. He only just got his hand on it when Sergeant Hawkins stepped forward and brought down the barrel of his stick on the back of Holloway's head. Holloway went down to his knees and pitched forward onto his face. Only the cage mask saved him from a broken nose.

"We just learned another lesson, men: the art of surprise. Stay alert. Never take your eyes off the enemy, and never let him know what you're gonna do. Now git up an' try it again."

Holloway was already up to his knees, rubbing the back of his head. At the sergeant's command, he pushed himself upright and stepped back out of range of the black pugilist. He held his own pugil stick in the ready position.

"Now attack."

The price of nonaggression had already been demonstrated. Holloway stepped forward and executed a thrust with the butt of his weapon. Sergeant Hawkins parried it as one would push aside a child's hand reaching for candy. He countered with a vicious thrust of his own, catching Holloway in the abdomen, then followed through with the barrel to the side of the head. Holloway went down — and stayed down.

"We're not playing games here, soldier. When I said attack, I didn't mean pass the salt. Attack with force, like you meant it. The object of an attack is to kill. Remember, if you don't git me, I'm gonna git you. Now let's try it again." Sergeant Hawkins faced the platoon. "What's the purpose of combat, men?"

"To kill!"

'I can't hear you.'

"KILL!"

"I still can't hear you."

"KILL!"

"Repeat."

"KILL!"

"I do believe something's finally beginning to creep into those scalps of yours." He turned to Holloway. "Now attack, an' this time do it like you mean it. An' don't be afraid of hurting me, 'cause you won't. But if you give me half a chance, I'll beat your ass to a pulp. Now attack, you sniveling — "

Holloway came off the ground like a charging lion. His thrust was met by the sergeant's immovable parry. But he countered right away with the barrel, aiming toward the sergeant's unprotected head. Again Sergeant Hawkins parried, this time countering with his own thrust. Holloway only partially parried, and was overpowered. Sergeant Hawkins followed through with a downthrust, an upthrust, and another downthrust. Holloway backed away frantically, chewing the air with his pugil stick as he tried to ward off the hammer blows. Hawkins stopped, took a half step backward, then suddenly took a new offense by wielding his pugil stick like a battering ram. The barrel tip knifed through Holloway's unsuspecting defenses, and went home with a thud into the solar plexus. Holloway doubled over as a whoosh of air blew out of his mouth. Sergeant Hawkins bestowed the coup de grace with a downstroke that connected on the muscle between Holloway's neck and his unprotected shoulder. This time he went down for the count.

"Very good, Holloway. But you got a lot to learn yet."

Holloway was on his knees and the knuckles of one hand. The other hand he held to his stomach. He stared at the ground for a long, long moment, not uttering a word. His face turned a bright, cherry red. After an unbelievably long time, Tony heard a sharp intake of air — and another long pause before the next one. Finally, Holloway began gasping and choking. After a minute, he vomited on the ground, sucking in air between each convulsion.

"When you're done, you can take off the cage an' clean it. All right, men, listen up. Choose a buddy, file over to the trailer, an' every man get a stick an' a mask. We're gonna practice, an' I'm gonna see if you guys learned anything."

Practice they did — for two grueling hours in the hot sun. They were allowed to take off their fatigue jackets. It was not long before the clean, white T-shirts were grimy and sweaty, and caked with soft, clinging dust.

At first, Tony was unwilling to swing too hard for fear of hurting someone. But Sergeant Hawkins was watching for this, and as soon as he saw someone slacking off, he charged in with his own stick and cudgeled the nonbelligerent. So there would be no chance of cribbing with a friend, partners were rotated every ten minutes. The sergeant buzzed around the field, correcting stance with a sharp kick, ramming pugil sticks into groins and bellies, and screaming "Kill" in everyone's ear.

When Tony was about to drop from the heat and exhaustion, Sergeant Hawkins set up the ultimate contest: a standoff. He selected five men to come forward and be the brunt of the attack. Then he selected five opponents, who had their masks taken away. This put the defenders in the delicate position of not wanting to hurt their unmasked buddies, while making the offenders timid in their approach. The winner of each standoff got to retire to the shade by the water tank. The loser got to take up the cage mask and fight on until he made a win.

Sergeant Hawkins egged on the contestants, chanting, "Thrust, parry. Thrust, parry. Thrust, parry. You're supposed to kill, not play cat and mouse. Thrust, parry. Thrust, parry. Goddamn it, soldier, thrust. You ain't gonna hurt 'im."

If two opponents reached a point at which neither one fought hard enough, the sergeant showed them how it was done by having both of them attack him at once. Invariably, he emerged victorious.

And so the fighting continued: thrust, parry, thrust, parry, until every man could repeat every motion by heart. And the only way to avoid a beating was to pummel the opponent first.

Aggressively.

To kill.

Chapter 43

"This is a gas-operated, magazine-fed, air-cooled, semi-automatic shoulder weapon. It fires a seven-point-six-two millimeter projectile at a sustained rate of fire of thirty rounds per minute, and has an effective range of four hundred sixty meters. With a muzzle velocity of two thousand feet per second, aimed at a target at a distance of one hundred meters, it can penetrate one-eighth inch sheet steel, a one inch board, or go completely through the human body."

Lieutenant Wakefield spoke as if he were reading the specifications right out of the manual.

Wally looked down at the rifle on the table in front of him. "What are all those numbers in English?"

"It *is* English," Tony replied.

"You know what I mean. American English."

Tony located Sergeant Hawkins hovering in the back of the room, out of hearing range. "The metric system has officially been in use in this country since last year. The bullet's a thirty caliber, a hundred meters is about three hundred thirty feet, and four hundred sixty meters is about, let's see . . . " He took a moment for mental calculations. "Fifteen hundred twenty-five feet — a little over a quarter mile."

"Amazing."

"The range, or my computations?"

"Both."

Lieutenant Wakefield cleared his throat and continued in his normal shout. His Adam's apple, bobbing with each syllable, was fascinating to watch. "With a full twenty-round magazine this weapon weighs approximately twelve pounds."

He held the rifle with both arms stretched forward, as if to demonstrate that twelve pounds was next to nothing. Tony was not sure he agreed, especially after toting one around for half a day and performing PT with it. It was not that he minded doing present arms, port arms, hold arms, right shoulder arms, and left shoulder arms. But why did getting from right shoulder arms to left shoulder arms have to be such a complicated procedure?

"Since the speed of sound is only one thousand one hundred twenty feet per second, this means that by the time you hear a rifle shot, the bullet has already hit you or safely passed you by. Now, you've all seen John Wayne standing there saying, 'Too late to duck now.' But in real life you *do* duck, because there may be another, better aimed bullet right behind it. All the heroes who don't duck are either in Hollywood or cemeteries."

The lieutenant received nothing but cold stares.

"All right. Now, remember this axiom: you take care of your weapon, and your weapon will take care of you. What this means is that you never put your weapon away dirty. It must be cleaned of every vestige of carbon, rust, dust, and fingerprints. So the first thing you're going to learn is how to clean it. And you had better pay attention, because no weapon gets returned to the racks unless it passes thorough inspection, either by me or your platoon sergeant. And if you think I'm tough, sergeants are tougher — because they have to answer to me. Sergeant Hawkins here has been inspecting weapons since Christ was a corporal."

"And the lieutenant was in diapers," Wally whispered.

Lieutenant Wakefield was still holding the rifle at inspection arms, and gave no expression that it was in any way tiring. Finally, he jerked it close to his chest, made a few deft, right angle motions, and it seemed to fall apart in his hands. He laid down the bolt, breech, and firing mechanism. Then he continued to strip it down until it was just a junk pile of miscellaneous screws, bolts, and machined parts that had little resemblance to the finished product.

The platoon got its first lesson in field stripping the M-14. At the end of an hour, Tony was doing pretty well: he had only two parts leftover.

****

Alfredo Gonzalez was one of about sixty Puerto Ricans whom Tony had gotten to know. He was tall and lanky, with light curly hair and a jutting nose and chin. He spoke a beautiful brand of accented English in a deep base voice that carried a ring of education and maturity. He did not fit in with his fellow countrymen, for in Puerto Rico he had been a policeman.

"I have wife, two children, boy and girl, and live in big house with, how you say — wife's mother?"

"Mother-in-law," Tony supplied.

"Yes, mother-in-law. And also two younger sisters and baby brother. One sister go to school after high school — "

"College."

"Yes, college. Wife take care of home and babies. Mother-in-law work in store. Other sister — " Gonzalez shrugged his shoulders. "Ehhnn, maybe get marry — she not like work. But she like boys." He stopped and laughed. "Little brother — " Here he gesticulated by holding his hand down by his leg. "He still go to school. Long time yet."

Gonzalez paused to light a cigarette. "I have respect because I am policeman. Know everybody in neighborhood. Friends laugh when I take them to jail because they drink too much and beat up wife. They like me. Then, one day

I get notice from draft board. Appear on morning at nine o'clock for physical. I go in and pass test — easier than test I take for police school. My English is very good. So I enlist right away."

"You enlisted?"

Puerto Rico was a free associated state, or Commonwealth, of the United States, Gonzales had explained. They had a representative in Congress who had a voice, but no vote. The people of Puerto Rico were U.S. citizens with no vote, but who were eligible for the draft. Public school instruction was given in Spanish, with English offered as a high school elective.

"Why did you enlist?"

Gonzales took another puff on his cigarette, and smiled patronizingly. "As policeman I see much wrong. I see fight, I see poverty, I see ignorance, I see people hurt other people. I grow up thinking this is how world is. But I never leave Puerto Rico. I never able afford leave Puerto Rico." Gonzalez rolled his r's inimitably. "I think, is whole world like this? So I read. And I find out that other people have worse off. I can't believe. I want to see. This my chance to see other parts of world. To fly in big plane. To have education not get at home. This my chance to help people worse off than I. To help people of Vietnam have freedom that people of Puerto Rico have. We all same people. I want to help. So I join. If no join, I get draft and have no choice. Now I have choice. I go Vietnam."

"But what about your home — your family?" Tony refused the cigarette that Gonzalez offered him. "How can you support them? You can't be making as much as your policeman's salary."

"College sister get part time job. Other sister get choice — marry or work. She not find husband, so she work. Wife help out with other children, make money. We do all right."

"Son! What're you doing with that trigger mechanism?" Sergeant Hawkins approached the workbench with hands on hips, snarling like an angry black bear. "You were told not to fool with it."

Gonzalez put down his screwdriver and looked up innocently. "I clean."

"Didn't you hear the lieutenant say that nobody was to touch the trigger mechanism?"

Under the sergeant's watchful eye, and with seeming nonchalance, Gonzalez put the trigger mechanism back into the rifle and demonstrated that it worked properly. "I work on many guns at home. I am expert. This gun very simple. Work better if all parts clean."

"Son," Sergeant Hawkins drawled. "Come up to the front of the room for a minute. And bring your *gun* with you."

Alfredo Gonzalez stubbed out his cigarette in a coffee can, and strode confidently to the front of the room.

Addressing the class, the sergeant jerked a thumb at Gonzalez. "This man was asleep when the lieutenant was describing the M-14, so I'll have to repeat this for the rest of you jokers. This weapon is a rifle, not a gun. An' you better call it by the proper military terminology. An' so none of you sleepyheads forget it, I'm going to show you a simple way of rememberin'."

Using Gonzalez's hand as a pointer, he moved it toward the rifle in his left hand. "This is my rifle." He moved the tanned hand down to his crotch. "This is my gun." Back up to the rifle, and then back down to his crotch, he continued with the rhyme. "This is for shooting, this is for fun."

Every man in the platoon grinned as Sergeant Hawkins ordered Gonzalez to repeat the catechism in his broken English. "This is my rifle, this is my gun. This is for shooting, this is for fun."

"Now you remember that, all of you, the next time you wanna ask a question about your weapons. Every weapon has a name, and every weapon has a purpose. You don't want no guns with faulty triggers, and we don't want no rifles with VD. And the next man to call his rifle a gun will low crawl around this building, with his gun in his hand. Do I make myself clear?"

****

"Did you . . . hear about . . . Farley?" Tom gasped.

"I heard he got . . . two stitches . . . in his chin from . . . when Sergeant Hawkins knocked . . . that mask off his face." Tony slipped out of step with the rest of the formation, did a skip, and went on keeping time.

"I saw him . . . tryin' ta shave . . . around it . . . this mornin'." The roly-poly rebel seemed to have no trouble running and talking at the same time. Beads of perspiration dripped down his forehead and stained his clothes, but he never missed a beat.

Wally spoke with hardly a strain, and did not seem to be in the same conversation. "How the hell does he do it, man?" He pointed with his chin at the galloping Sergeant Hawkins, who thumped along effortlessly beside the platoon, while maintaining his monotonous cadence.

"One two one two keep it going one two, one two one two we like runnin' one two, one two one two put your feet down one two, one two one two double-time it one two, one two one two take a rest now one two, double ti-i-i-me, halt."

The platoon kept moving at the normal pace of one hundred steps per minute, long enough to catch some breath before the next double time cadence of one hundred eighty yard-long steps.

Sergeant Hawkins appeared cool, and breathed easily. Without missing a beat, he sang out, "Give me your left, give me your left, give me your left, right, left."

"Fourth platoon had it . . . worse than we did," Tom continued.

Hank was breathing almost normally again. "What y'all mean?"

"They had lieu . . . tenant Wakefield . . . helping them out . . . One guy ended up . . . with a broken rib . . . that may have punctured . . . his kidney . . . and another got . . . out of bed with . . . blurry vision and . . . a blasting headache . . . Might be concussion . . . They're both . . . in the hospital now."

"Lousy bastard," Wally said.

Hank spat on the ground. "Ah hope he rots in hell."

"He'll have lots of company." Tony's rifle felt like a ton of bricks, his muscles like spaghetti.

"Hep, *haw*, hep, *haw*, hep, *haw*, . . . "

Wally was still on his own wavelength. "He's got to have an iron lung and piston legs."

"Ah'd fall down an' die if a dog pissed on his leg. Haw haw haw haw haw."

****

Tom puffed thoughtfully, blew smoke through his nose. "I'll have to give up these cigarettes or I'll never make it to Ranger school."

"Ah thought y'all was gain' airborne?" Hank breathed his own, homegrown brand.

"I am. Then I'm going to Ranger school."

"What's the difference?" Tony adjusted his cap so that the brim deflected the sun. There was no shade anywhere in these open fields, so when they were given a break there was very little relief to go along with it.

"Airborne training is just a three-week school where you learn how to jump out of a plane — "

"And to land on your feet," Wally inserted.

" — but Ranger school is where you learn survival skills. You train in all kinds of conditions, from snow to desert to mountains. You run recon patrols and live off the land. You learn to kill without weapons."

"Sounds screwy, man. Like the Eagle Scouts of the army."

"And uncivilized, too," Tony added.

"What y'all wanta do that fer?"

"For the challenge." Tom's chest seemed to swell several inches. "Not everybody can make it through Ranger school."

Wally sneered, "Yeah, well, you better put those butts down or you won't make it through

basic."

"I told you, I'm an all around athlete."

"You'd better come in off the football field, man, or you aren't going to make it till half time."

"I'll make it, all right." Tom went into a coughing spasm, then took another drag on his cigarette.

****

"Whadja do this time?"

Sergeant Breneke retied the apron behind his back. Despite his throaty voice, his posture made him appear effeminate. And the goofy looking chef's hat did not help his image.

"Nothing serious." Tony twisted his cap in his hand. "Just talking in formation."

"Yeah, well, you better learn that everything is serious in this man's army. Talkin' when you shouldn't means you weren't payin' attention to something. And that means you didn't hear something you shoulda."

"So how much do you think I'm missing while I'm working in the kitchen instead of attending class?"

Tony's logic was too lofty for the mess sergeant. A leonine smile grew across Breneke's face. "Well, come on. I guess it's up to me to teach you a lesson in paying attention. Maybe you won't forget the next time."

Tony followed him down the hall to the pantry door. "Let me see." The three-striper pushed his hat back and scratched his head. He pointed to a cubbyhole in the back of the pantry. "Grab that pail an' a sponge, get a can of paint, an' a clean brush."

"Yes, sergeant." Tony gathered the materials, then leaned into the hall and called out to the retreating figure. "Hey, sarge. What color?"

Sergeant Breneke stopped and turned. "White."

Tony grabbed a can of white paint and started to go. But in stooping he spotted a jar of cherries on the shelf. He checked the hall one more time, then cracked open the lid and stuffed his mouth full of juicy red deliciousness. Since a half filled jar would be noticed, he finished them all and tossed the empty glassware into a trash can.

In the kitchen, the sergeant did not seem to notice Tony's overlong absence. He tossed him a box of soap and indicated the hot water. "Wash it down first before you paint it."

"Okay, sarge. Which wall?"

"The one that gets all the grease. Behind the stoves."

"But sarge, I just painted that — " Tony stopped when he caught a glimpse of the stained surface. By the time he finished doing a double take, the mess sergeant was already yelling at someone else for imagined misdoings. *How did it get so —*

The wall was stained, all right. But some time since he had last been in here, it had been painted black.

Tony shook his head, and filled the bucket with hot, soapy water. After a thorough scrubbing, he painted the wall white.

Again.

****

"How's it going, Mike?" Tony rubbed his arm one last time, and rolled down his sleeve. The shade of the clinic offered a temporary respite before the march back to the compound.

"Oh, all right, I guess." Mike unbuttoned his shirt flap and pulled out a Hershey bar. Ever since Hank had offered him one for his aching appetite, he was never without some form of melted, chocolate nourishment. The pile of candy he had bought in the PX was stored in his laundry bag. Even Sergeant Hawkins was not willing to rummage through soiled underwear and smelly socks to find contraband.

"No, thanks. You need it more than I do. Hey, Wally, what happened?" Wally came up rubbing his arm. With a cotton ball, he dabbed at a thin trickle of blood running down his bicep. "This is nothing, man. Did you see that Puerto Rican jerk around when the doc put the gun to him? It ripped half his arm off, and part of his chest, too."

Hypodermic needles were too slow and inefficient for the amount of inoculations they were getting. "I don't doubt it. I saw the doctor test the high-pressure gun right in front of me. When he pulled the trigger, it sent of stream of liquid right across the room."

"They already had three men faint — one just from watching."

Tony shook his head. "I don't think that guy was hurt, though. The front of his T-shirt was just splattered with blood and skin from his arm."

"Oh, is that all? Well, it's still not a pretty sight." Wally tucked his shirt into his pants. "How you doing, man?"

"Not too bad," Mike replied.

"Hey, is there something on your mind? You look a little green around the gills."

"Yeah, has the sergeant been clamping down on you again?"

Mike looked from one to the other. "Well, we had a little talk this morning."

Wally grimaced. "That man doesn't know how to talk — he only shouts."

"Well, he was kind of different this time. He talked real smooth."

"He's still no candidate for *Father Knows Best*. What did he have to say?"

"He said I might be flunking out."

"Shit, man, you can't flunk out of the army.

If you could, I'd have done it a long time ago. And so would half a million other guys."

As more men came out of the medical building, they started fighting like barn cows for the coolness of the shade. Tony squeezed over so he could share the shadow with Wally. "Mike, what did he mean?"

"He said if I can't keep up with the rest of the guys, I'm gonna get kicked out."

"Man, what do they do with the discards, throw them in the incinerator?"

"No, he said they have a special training outfit for guys who, well, you know, who don't do so well on the tests, or can't do the PT, like guys who are overweight. He said it's almost like basic, only they work on your difficulties, like they give you more time to study, and easier PT. And if you're overweight they give you less food."

Mike trailed off and licked the soggy mess from the wrapper. The only reason he had made it this far was because he always went into the mess hall with Wally and, when Wally had finished all he could eat, they traded trays.

"Aw, Mike, there's no sense worrying about it," Tony said. "Besides, you're trying harder than anyone else in this whole outfit."

He crumpled the cellophane and stuffed in into his pocket. "Well, he was pretty nice about it. He didn't shout, or nothing. He just said he didn't think I fit in with the rest of the men." He wiped his hands on his pants, took off his cap and wiped away the sweat that had accumulated, screwed the cap back down, and quietly sauntered away.

Tony clucked his tongue. "That's really rotten."

"It's more than rotten, man, it's unfuckingbelievable." Wally moved deeper into the shade. "You know, that Mike's a good kid, but he's a loony tune. He must be if he thinks the sarge is a nice guy."

****

"Mail call!"

Instantly, pandemonium reigned. Men shoved, pushed, and shouted, then encircled the poor corporal who was the company clerk. He cringed defensively, threw a bundle of letters into his mail sack, and hugged it closely, lest it be torn away by mail-starved troops.

"Git back there. Git back I said." Sergeant Hawkins plunged into the broiling mob and tried to restore a semblance of discipline, hurling bodies left and right. "*Company, fall in!*"

If discipline had been easily lost, it was slow to return. He had to repeat his command twice more before a half-hearted attempt was made to form into platoons. With help from Sergeants Peterson, Murphy, and Wheaton, the company was finally whipped into order.

As senior NCO, Sergeant Hawkins took over. "You men are in the army, not kindergarten. So you're gonna hafta learn ta act like soldiers. Everybody ready for PT."

The groans almost drowned out Sergeant Hawkins' commands. Tony had already resolved himself to his fate when Wally said, "It's all a game, man — a carefully calculated trick. Military cruelty at its finest. Show them the candy, then take it away."

After thirty minutes of strenuous exercise, Sergeant Hawkins shouted, "Okay, now listen up. Mail call *will* be carried out in an orderly manner. Corporal Mead will call out your names and you will run — *run* — up front and pick up your mail. You will then put it in your pocket and forget about it. You can read it at silent hour. Anyone caught with a letter in his hand before then will receive extra duty — and have his mail confiscated."

"Ain't there Federal regulations about mail?" Hank asked.

"Not in the army," Tony responded.

Corporal Mead had not taken the trouble to alphabetize the mail, so it was given out in a hodgepodge manner. Tony listened carefully for his often-mispronounced name. He anxiously prayed that there would be a letter for him, for some assurance that home was still there, that people still cared, that the life he had been dragged away from still existed.

"Must be from somebody sweet." Tom ran a letter under his nose. "It smells like perfume."

"Son, you better put that in your pocket or I'll burn it."

"*Giovanni!*"

Tony almost bowled over the corporal. He was handed three letters, all forwarded from Fort Jackson. He glanced at the return addresses before stuffing them into his shirt pocket and buttoning down the flap.

Everyone received letters from home except the contingent of Puerto Ricans. Ships plowed slowly through the emerald sea. For those far away from home, the mail would take its time.

"Don't worry, Alfredo. I'm sure there will be something tomorrow."

****

Dear Tony,

I told you I wasn't very good at writing letters. I don't like writing at all. But my Mom said I should write right away since you wrote to me. So, here I am, writing. I don't know what I'm going to say. Although, I guess you really don't say anything in a letter, you write it. My Mom bought me a new dress for graduation. It's really pretty. All white, with fringe and lace, and a matching hat with a veil, although I can't imagine me wearing a veil. I'll probly cut it off, or throw it back over my head.

And she gave me money for my first permanent My grandmother usually cuts my hair, and I put it in curlers, but I've never had it set before, so I'm really excited about it. I'm really excited about graduation too. I can't wait till school is over. I can't stand the nuns any more. They're almost as bad as my grandmother. She made me stay home for a week after you left, mostly because (so she says) I didn't come home right from school. She wouldn't even listen when I told her why I had to go, and why I didn't have time to come home and ask permission first. She still made me stay in. Kathy was allowed to visit, though, so it wasn't too bad. We had a good time together. We're going down to the shore together in her parent's car and stay with Bob and my Mom. It's really getting warm out so I can't wait to walk along the beach, though I won't go swimming til June or so. How's the weather in North Carolina? I saw Kate yesterday and she said to tell you hello and that she'll write later when she gets a chance. I gave your address to Marion and Kathy, so maybe they'll write too. Well, it looks like I'm going to pass everything in school, although my history nun is giving me a lot of trouble. She wants us to turn in term reports, and they have to be typewritten. I've got it about halfway done, and Marion said she would type it for me when it's ready. She and Pete played miniture golf and had a wild time. Pete tripped on one of the greens and fell into the water trap and got his shoes all wet. He laughed, cause he thought it was pretty funny. Kate's going to have a graduation party at her house, and everybodys invited. Too bad you can't be there. I already made Ben promise to keep George away from me, and he said OK.

Well, I'm back. I had to go watch TV for a while because my hand got so cramped. Danny Thomas was on, one of my favorite shows. My Mom says she's going to buy me a TV for graduation so I can have one in my own room. I will like that cause I won't have to sit with my grandmother and watch what she wants to watch. I'm going to ask Bob and maybe he'll buy it for me. Nothing much is happening around here. Kathy got a ticket for going through a stop sign, and boy was she mad. She argued with the cop, but he gave it to her anyway. Isn't that rotten. Well, I guess if she hadn't been drinking she might not have argued so much. Well, I better go. My hand is getting sore from holding this pencil, and its getting dull and I don't have a sharpener. Hope you had a good train ride.

Yours truly,
Patty
****

Dear Tony,

Your grandmother and I were real glad to hear your alright. From the sound of your letter I guess your getting along pretty well with the Army so far, even though they are tough on you. But I know you'll stand up to it. Your a fine boy, and you do your best. Dont let them get you down with their shouting — that cant hurt you, you know.

I saw your Uncle Joe the other day, and he was right sorry to hear you wont be able to help him with the watermelons this summer. He says you and Michael are his best workers, and if he has to rely on local help it will cost him twice as much, and he will get less work out of them. Your cousin, Michael, will be able to help some, but then he's going to VPI (Virginia Polytechnic Institute) and doesn't know if this might not be his last year on the farm till he graduates. He transferred there from the Maryland State College because they have more courses in agriculture and he can get better teaching. Says he might eventually want to become a veternarian. Your Aunt May was saying that she hopes you can stop in during the summer if you get a chance, just for a visit. She misses you.

I talked on the phone to your mother last week and she told me about the fight you had with your Dad. I wish there were some advice I could give, but I dont rightly know what to say. He is a hot tempered man, but he will cool down in a while, I am sure. Deep down inside he has a good heart, even though he has a funny way of showing it. Dont judge him too harshly, but try to be forgiving. He will come around after a while, you will see. Your mother is most upset by your leaving. She loves you very much, and doesn't want to see you get hurt. She is pretty hard to get along with sometimes, but she means well, she just dont know how to express herself well. Honey, I think it would be a good idea if you wrote to her, as she is dying to hear from you. Your her pride and joy. I know you don't have a whole lot of time, what with your studying and all, but please take a minute to drop her a line and tell her your alright. She needs to hear from you. You might also want to say something to your brother. Robby idolizes you, and looks up to you. Write something simple so your mother can read it to him. He will get a kick out of it. And dont forget to include your dad.

Well, I am sorry all these bad things had to happen all at once, but remember that things wont always be bad. You just do your best. And when the time comes for judgement the Almighty Lord will look at you in a good light. Take care of yourself, son. Your grandmother and I love you very much.

All our love,
Grandmom and Grandpop
****
Dear Tony,

I was really surprised to get a letter from you so soon. My mom gave it to me when I got home from school and I opened it right away. Ray was really mad when he found out I had read it first because when I showed him the envelope to show him it was addressed to both of us he said he should have had the right to read it first because it said "Ray and Teddy" instead of "Teddy and Ray." You know Ray. Anyway, it was really good to hear from you.

I can't imagine you in an army uniform with a brush haircut. You must really look different. How's it going so far? I don't guess you're having much trouble with the exercises or the running. You'll probably show those sergeants a thing or two about being in shape. Maybe I should join the army when I get out of school so I can learn how to fight Ray off. Since he doesn't do anything more physical than smoke cigarettes and drink beer (don't let my mom find out, though) he can't run a city block without getting out of breath. Did I tell you I tried out for the track team? I know it sounds a little late in the year, but the try outs for next term are taking place now, and I wanted to get in. I'm pretty sure I'll make it. I've been practicing hurdles and the mile every day, so I think I won't have much trouble. Because I'm so light I have an advantage.

Well, I guess you're all worried about Patty. I haven't seen her since Monday because her grandmother won't let her out. But Kathy has been to see her when she's out with Ray, and she says she's not doing too bad. Of course, she sees her in school, too. She was pretty quiet on the way home from the station.

I went over to the garage Saturday and Petey had your car over there, working on it. He said it needed an oil change and a lube job. I helped him change the oil. Actually, he took the oil out and I put it in. He also adjusted the points and the distributor, and he says it's sounding real smooth. Then he parked it in front of his house where he can keep an eye on it for you. The big news is that George got a job. That's right, his father finally got him hooked up in his tire business. George says that his father wants him to learn the business from the ground up, so he's starting out in one of the garages changing tires. George's also hoping to quality as sole supporting son, since Mrs. Hart doesn't work. (Well, she does sewing and baby sitting, but that doesn't count) The first thing he did was get all new tires for the Green Lantern. Now he's talking about putting on mag wheels! Can you imagine that, a '53 Plymouth with mag wheels? Oh, well, that's George for you.

We're already making plans for a big party down the shore when you come home. It'll be a picnic at the beach, maybe in Wildwood, since Kate's parents have a house down there. So that will be something for you to look forward to. The whole gang will be there. Patty too.

Well, things are pretty dull without you around. No one wants to do anything. I mean, there aren't any more expeditions to Bowman's Tower, or haunted houses, or anything. Nobody thinks much about those kinds of things. All they want to do is go to parties, and drink, and go parking. How boring can you get? And since Kate doesn't like me too much, she won't let me go along with them when she and Ben go places. She's keeping a pretty sharp eye on him because she caught him going to the library with a girl from LaSalle. He told her they were working on a project together, but she didn't believe him. Kate is very jealous.

Well, Tone, I gotta go. Ray told me not to mail this till he writes you a letter, but I kind of thought you wouldn't want to wait that long. He'll have to use his own stamp now. He's been spending so much time with Kathy that I don't think he'll get around to it right away. He's been staying out pretty late, and boy is my mom mad. Not that she minds him going out, even with Kathy, but she hates trying to get him out of bed in the morning before she goes to work. Twice already he overslept and was an hour late for work. And since she got him the job it makes her look bad. Oh, well.

Well, don't take any stuff off those sergeants, especially that one with the big nose. You sure told him off. And don't worry if you don't get a chance to write. I'll let you know how things are going here. See you in July.

Your friend,
Teddy
****

"Well, my girl still loves me," Tom boasted freely from his upper bunk. He made an exaggerated motion of smelling the perfumed envelope.

Wally squinted in the bright barrack lights. "Which girl is that? I thought you had a million of them."

"Most of them are just good lays. This is the one that counts. I even gave her a ring a couple of weeks before enlisting so I'd know she'd be waiting for me when I get back. Not that I had any doubts, of course."

"Do y'all ever have any doubts about enythin'?"

"Can't afford to. It's self-destructive, like being in love."

"Don't y'all love that gurl who loves you so much?"

"Of course I do," Tom laughed. "I love them all. But I'm not *in* love with any of them."

Tony put down his pen. "Would you run that by me again?"

"Loving girls for the pleasures they have to offer is highly enjoyable and deeply satisfying. But being in love implies dependence. It means you can't give them up. I'm not dependent on anybody or anything."

"Except cigarettes," Wally muttered. He lay serenely on his back, hands under his head.

"I'm talking about personal fulfillment and inner security. I'm talking about the freedom of mind to discover your full potential. I'm talking about defining your goals in life, and going out and achieving them. And to do this you can't be tied down with useless sentiment and idolatry and familiarity."

"Hey, mister philosopher, don't people mean anything to you? Don't forget that you're a part of society, of a great gestalt of human consciousness. No man is an island, my friend. We all need companionship."

Having trouble concentrating because of repartee, Tony pushed aside the letter he was working on. "'Because we're essentially and biologically a social animal. Man has thrived because of his attachments to families, clans, tribes, and nations. We're not a solitary animal, but a collection of interdependent units relying on each other, protecting each other."

Tom hung an arm down over the edge of the bunk and eyed both Wally and Tony. "And I say that if what you want relies for its fulfillment upon others, you are bound to be disappointed. You have to find fulfillment within yourself. Everything else is peripheral."

"What's that gotta do with the price a' eggs? What kinda fulfillment you gonna get outa goin' to Vietnam to kill people? Y'all supposed to be fightin' for a ideal, for your country, to preserve freedom in the world. If y'all goin' to Vietnam for selfish motives, y'all got no right goin' there a-tall. You ain't preservin' nothin' but your own vanity."

"At least I'm not afraid to go. At least I'm not one of the goddamned hippies hiding behind banners and long hair."

"Hey, man, define your terms. What's a hippy?"

"A hippy is a radical with no sense of responsibility other than to himself. He's against everything because he needs something to be against, because he has no convictions to be *for*. He's afraid to stand on his own two feet, so he travels in gangs. He's insecure, so he makes a lot of noise to cover up for it. He doesn't want to work for a living, so he dresses in rags and calls it style, lets his hair get shaggy. — "

"Like Thomas Jefferson and Albert Einstein."

" — He's got no sense of civic pride, so he burns his draft card. He spends his life trying to stir up trouble on college campuses, in cities, in the political seats of power. He goes against every grain of rational thought."

Tony could see that Wally was straining to remain calm, but the crescendo in his voice belied it. "Sounds to me like you're describing a Revolutionary War hero from the British side. In case you don't know it, this country is founded on rebellion, and it's the continued rebellion against established principles that adds perspective to those principles. Change is not brought about by conservatism. Somebody's got to have the guts to stand against the tide and say, 'Wait a minute, I think something's wrong here.' Somebody has to open the eyes of those who are too blind to see, or who are too lazy to act, or who are too comfortable to worry about somebody else's discomfort. An individual, by himself, will never grow. He needs interaction with his fellow man to see what's wrong, not only with his fellow man, but within himself. If he's not willing to improve himself, then he has no right to try to improve anyone else. You can't be a loner, and you can't be an ostrich. You've got to accept the fact that you share this world with billions of other people. You have to be willing to try to cope with *their* problems as well as with your own. And you've got to get your head out of the sand long enough to see what the world is all about before you make any decisions about what's right and wrong."

Tom jabbed his finger down at Wally. "If you have so much feeling for people, why are you against this war?"

"Man, that's a whole mouthful of contradiction. I'm against this war *because* I care for people. In case you don't know it, people get killed in wars."

"So you would rather leave the Vietnamese to starvation, and pestilence, and slavery than to try and fight for their survival?"

Wally's head came up off the pillow, his voice became thunderous. "I would rather get my own shit together before I go sticking my nose into other people's business. This country has enough problems to solve without worrying about solving the problems of the world."

"This country *has* no problems, other than ones we imagine. We have the highest technology, the highest standard of living, the best health care than any other country in the world. What should we do, wait until we reach perfection before we start sharing some of that wealth with our fellow man? Perfection can never be met, because as soon as we attain a goal of perfection we change our idea of what perfection

should be. While we raise our standards of living, we raise behind us our conception of poverty. Do you know that the poorest person in this country today is richer than the richest person of a century ago? The worst city slums have electricity, and sewage, and medical facilities that simply were not available a hundred years ago. A wagon train in the eighteen-sixties faced death at every turn, and torture for three months, to cross the continent. Today's biggest hardship during the three-day drive to California is losing your sunglasses. If the people of yesteryear could view their country today, they would think we were all living in heaven."

A long silence overtook the lower bunk. Tony waited for Wally's reply, but Wally just stared at Tom with pinched eyes and a deep frown, and a jaw that worked soundlessly.

"Shit, man, I don't even know why we're arguing." Wally rolled over and flung the blanket over him.

Tom eased back and stared at the ceiling.

Hank sat up on the edge of his bunk and peered between knobby knees. "Hey, Tony, how did we ever get tied up with two?"

"By an alphabetical coincidence."

The room suddenly went dark. There were shouts and grumbles from men still reading or writing letters, but Sergeant Hawkins put a damper on their complaints.

"I need my beauty sleep. An' if I don't git it, I'm gonna be real ugly in the mornin'."

Chapter 44

"Ready on the right!"

Tony tried to relax, to loosen his grip on the rifle's trigger guard and let the sandbag support the barrel. The stock was tightly jammed against his shoulder, his left eye squeezed shut. Other than his cousin's BB gun, he had never fired a weapon before.

"Ready on the left!"

He kept his face several inches back of the breech and squinted down the sights, not on the central bull's eye, but on the bottom edge of the outermost circle. Hours of classroom theory were about to be tested. The M-14 was zeroed in at one hundred meters, meaning that if you aimed at a bull's eye one hundred meters away, and your aim was accurate, you should hit it dead center. But at twenty-five meters the bullet would hit above the target.

"Ready on the firing line!"

According to the textbook, by simple physics and the universal law of gravitation, a projectile starts falling as soon as it leaves the muzzle, no matter how fast its initial velocity. Bullets are actually lobbed, and its drop is called trajectory. At a target closer than the zeroing point of the particular weapon, the projectile will hit too high; farther, and it will hit too low. At a target very far away, you have to aim way above it and let the bullet drop into it.

"Fire when ready!"

Tony tried to remember all the rules: retain a firm grip on the stock, keep your eye on the target, take a deep breath and exhale halfway, slowly — so slowly — squeeze the trigger. Most of the men let loose their first volley immediately, and the deafening roar of discharging shells broke his concentration. After a couple of seconds only a spatter of shots rang out discordantly, randomly, across the rifle range. He took another breath and repeated the procedure, and suddenly the rifle exploded in his hands.

It happened just like it was supposed to, without his knowing exactly when — it was the sudden jerk of the trigger that made shots go wild. Neither had the recoil bruised his shoulder or broken his jaw.

Rifles cracked all around him now, but they no longer bothered him. He wiped his sweaty palm on his pants, inserted another bullet, aligned his target, squeezed, and fired. After the third round, he let the rifle roll out of his hands and tried to remember the post firing procedure.

Oh, yes: pull back the bolt and eject the last shell, click on the safety, lay down the rifle with the barrel pointed down range with the bolt open and the chamber clear, and yell for inspection. Then pick up the brass cartridge cases and back away from the firing position.

"Congratulations, man. You're on your way to becoming an honest-to-goodness soldier."

Grandpop was a hunter. Many times, as a lad, Tony had accompanied him on hunting trips to the Eastern Shore wetlands for marsh rabbit, or to the inland pine forests for quail and duck. He had thrilled to run wild and free after the hound dogs, trudging through swamp and marsh grass, dashing through brush and briars, leaping over fallen logs and dodging low branches, and skirting pits and holes in a vain but valiant attempt to keep up with Spot and Driver, so fleet of foot. But it had always been a game to him: the stalk, the chase, the flushing of wild game. He had always been saddened by the kill.

He shied at the sight of torn and twisted bodies, the torture of animals scared and still-living as they were brought back in drooling canine mouths, the irreverence as they were tossed still writhing in the agony of near death into a cloth bag, to die later when their strength and life blood gave out. Many a rabbit he chased, many a flock of ducks or geese he spoofed, before they came into range of that awful shotgun. He just wanted to see the rabbits dart, the muskrats skulk, and the birds take wing. If Grandpop knew what he was doing, he never let on.

There was a good reason for killing, when the reason was for food. Grandpop ate everything he shot, so it was no different from decapitating chickens in the coop.

"Hey, man, you okay?"

Tony focused his eyes, and grinned. "Well, that was kind of fun. How'd I do?"

Wally peered down range. "Well, I don't know about your grouping, but I'd say you're a little low and to the left."

Bam! At the adjacent firing position, Tom got slapped in the buttocks with a large yellow sign that said 'Ready' in yellow on one side, and 'Not Ready' in red on the other. "Son, you don't pick that weapon up off the sandbags till I check it an' give the okay." Sergeant Hawkins inspected the chamber, nodded, turned, and held up the 'Ready' side of the sign.

From the fire control tower, Lieutenant Wakefield waited until he saw all yellow, then gave the order to check out the targets. In one group, the men left the firing pits and strode across the no-man's-land of craggy clay.

"You must have telescopic vision. The holes are right where you said they were." Tony inspected the paper target. Like the bunks, the three shots had to pass the quarter test — one silver coin covering all three holes. Two of Tony's could have been covered by a half dollar, but the third was in a triangular position which would be beyond the rim.

"Only you're about twenty-five cents out of line."

"Haw-haw-haw-haw-haw," Hank yodeled exuberantly. "That there hole's got two bullets through it."

Tom crouched on his knees, shook his head. "Like hell it is. You missed the target completely with that last shot."

Wally and Tony checked it out. Tony saw only two holes on the paper, separated by a quarter inch tatter. The group could be covered with a dime.

"Looka here." Hank pointed to one of the holes. "See that slight bulge on the one side, that's where the other bullet went through."

From inches away, Tony could see that one hole was slightly oval shaped. "Well, I don't know."

"Shit, man, anybody who can put two slugs that close together has got to know what the hell he's doing."

"Been 'coon huntin' ma 'hol' life."

"Nobody's that good, not even the experts. That's what they told us in class."

Sergeant Hawkins put an end to the argument. "Who's target is this?"

Tony hastened back. "Uh, it's mine, sarge."

"Try to relax a little more. Don't be in a hurry to fire. Take your time and squeeze that trigger gently, like it was your mother's tit." He drew a red circle around each one so it would not be confused with the next volley. He counted the grids with his pencil. "Drop your elevation three points, Kentucky windage four points west."

The barrel is raised when the sights are lowered. It is assumed that the same man looks through the same sight the same way every time. Each weapon he fires has to be sighted for him and him alone. If someone else fired it, he would shoot off center.

The sergeant drew circles around Hank's grouping. "You musta had a blank in there. Down four and west one." He stalked off to the next target.

"Dayam."

"I told you so," Tom chided, leading the way back to the fire pits.

"How would you know? You're just a city slicker. Ah been shootin' rats through the eyeball an' shavin' the whiskers off o' deer since Ah was knee high to a tadpole. Hell, Ah've got guns that'd make this un look like a peashooter."

The foursome split up, and Tony and Wally climbed over the sandbags into their assigned fire pit. Tony made the appropriate adjustments to the sights.

Sergeant Hawkins came by and handed him three more bullets. "Hang onto your brass." When he got to the end of his platoon he waved the yellow signal. Sergeant Peterson held up red for a moment until an assistant corporal cleared the range and crossed over the safety line.

"Clear the firing line!" Lieutenant Wakefield bellowed. He looked both ways from the control tower, saw four yellow signs. "Lock and load!"

Tony pulled back the bolt, inserted a round, and locked it in place. He heard Sergeant Hawkins yell to someone to his right, "Use your index finger, not your social finger." He aligned the pointed tip at the end of the barrel with the U-shaped cup on the breech. His hands trembled slightly: he was still too tense.

"Ready on the right! Ready on the left! Ready on the firing line! Fire when ready!"

Again came the deafening blasts, only this time Tony fired along with the first group.

"Man, you're way off. About six inches too high."

"Darn. I forgot. I aimed right at the bull's eye." He took his time on the second and third shots, aiming at the bottom edge of the great circle. When they went to check out their grouping he found that the last two rounds were barely within the quarter coverage. The first shot was wild.

Hank's target had only a single additional hole, with three round bulges like the famous three-ring sign, just on the edge of the black central dot. "Ah'll get it next time." Sergeant Hawkins just shook his head. Hank was true to his word.

After the fourth set Tony was pretty well zeroed in, hitting the lower left corner of the bull's eye, and his groups were acceptable. Sergeant Hawkins gave him the final adjustment, and Tony changed the sight one increment in both directions.

Wally rested his rifle on the sandbags. "How far is twenty-five meters?"

Without hesitation, Tony replied, "Seventy-seven and a half feet."

"Amazing."

"Actually, it might be closer to seventy-eight feet."

"Show off."

Wally's groups were much better than Tony's. After only one set of sight corrections, he was hitting the target dead on. After that, he just kept plugging away at the bull's eye until it was torn to shreds.

Tom shook his head and grimaced at his own scattered grouping. "I thought you told me you had never fired a gun before."

"That's right, man," Wally said smugly. "But I used to be a damn good shot with a pea shooter. I could hit a window pane from across the street, and the bread man from half a block."

"Well, there must be something wrong with this rifle."

"The only thing wrong with it is the finger that's pulling the trigger."

Tom's features clouded. "Okay, hotshot, we'll just see who ends up with the marksmanship award. I was number one in ROTC."

"You may have been a big man on campus, but that's the equivalent of a big frog in a small pond." Wally laughed at his own joke. "But in the ocean of reality you're just a hermit crab swept along with the tide."

****

"Get your ponchos out!" Sergeant Hawkins tipped his Smokey-the-Bear hat so the faint drizzle missed his face. Tony did not want to don the awkward sheet of plastic, but in the army, personal preference was akin to nonconformity. If one man donned a poncho, everyone donned a poncho. "Get 'em on, I said!"

Tony removed his newly issued pistol belt and released the poncho that was rolled and strapped under the fanny pouch. He donned it over top of everything, including his rifle. A poncho was a poor excuse for a raincoat: its odd cut insured that the trousers got soaked from the knees down, and water trickled along the arms every time they were lifted. And in this heat, it was not long before he was soaked from the condensation of his own perspiration.

Tom poked a cigarette into his mouth before the impending rainstorm prevented smoking. "You know that guy named Stahl? The one who shipped in with you?"

Wally did not smile. "The jerk with the big nose?"

Tony grimaced. "How could I forget him?"

Cupping a match, Tom breathed life into the tobacco. "Well, he's a squad leader in Fourth Platoon, and he's had a little trouble so he's being demoted."

"My heart bleeds for him."

Tony smirked. "Why's he being kicked down?"

Squad leaders had to attend meetings with the platoon sergeants in order to be prepared for upcoming events. They heard all the gossip, and made excellent informants. "Because the men were complaining about him. At least, that's the official word. I heard he's been pretty tough on them."

"He'd better keep away from the firing line, man, or somebody's liable to mistake him for a target."

"And if he lives through basic he'll probably become a lieutenant," Tony laughed.

"I take it you don't like him either."

"He gave me a lot of grief after we left the recruiting office and went to the train station. My friends showed up to see me off. It was the last chance I had to see my girlfriend, and he didn't want to let me talk to her."

Ponchos were not designer made, but Hank looked more shapeless than anyone. "Ah never even met the man an' already Ah don't like him."

Tony shrugged. "He threatened to report me for disobeying orders — *his* orders — but I didn't figure he had any real authority, so I ignored him."

"Well, it didn't take him long to earn a bad rep." The rain started falling harder now, pelting off the plastic. "He's a real nitpicker, and a snitch besides. Every time someone doesn't do exactly what he wants, he puts him down on report. He hands out demerits like confetti at a ticker tape parade. The guys in his squad have done more detail and KP than any other two squads put together. Finally, Sergeant Wheaton decided to find out why his men were fucking up so bad. They all told him the same thing, that Stahl was the big problem. But he still stuck up for him."

"Figures," Wally spat.

"So the men ganged up on him and forced him to quit."

"What did they do, kill him?"

"They came pretty close."

Tony forced sympathy into his voice. "Did they hurt him?"

"Not physically, but they played some pretty rotten tricks on him."

"Such as?"

Tom adjusted his brim; the cigarette was getting wet. "Well, I don't know the whole story. I only got bits and pieces from the new squad leader. I only heard about the little things, like mussing up his bunk so it kept failing inspection, rubbing dirt on his boots so he had to keep shining them, filling his footlocker full of toilet paper because he was such an ass kisser. And some of the paper was used."

"Yuck."

"That's nothing. The grand finale was last night, but I haven't heard — "

"Hey, Williams, got a minute?" Hank called.

Williams was a friend of Hank's, born and raised in Winston-Salem. They had gone to school together, worked for the same company, and drank at the same bar. Their friendship shattered Tony's preconceived notion about southern blacks and whites not getting along.

Williams was tall and lithe, and in excellent physical condition, with strong arms and a broad chest. His buttocks stuck out as if he were wearing a padded dress, like women in the Gay Nineties. Like Hank, he talked with a slow drawl, and always had a smile on his face.

"Hey, Hank, ole buddy. What's happenin'?"

Hank let loose one of his Mule Skinner yodels. "Haw haw haw haw haw. Tom here was jus' tellin' us you got yourself a new squad leader."

"Yeah, an' it's me."

"No shit?"

"No shit. An' I din' even want the fuckin' job."

Tom threw his soggy cigarette on the ground. It refused to stay lit. "What's the dope on Stahl?"

Williams snickered, then spat. "If you wanna hear it, I'm the man to tell it. I was in on the whole thing, right from the beginning — an' he knows it."

Hank lit up a cigarette and passed it to Williams, then lit up another for himself. The rain was coming down a little harder now. The five men gathered into a circle like a football huddle.

"Thanks for the smoke. Well, Stahl sure thought he was a bad mothafucka, but we showed him who's boss. Put a few stripes on a man an' right away he starts givin' orders like he was King Tut or somethin'. I done so much detail inna mess hall I got to callin' the sarge by his first name — Ralph. I found out when I was on orderly duty one night; read it off the duty roster. He ain't a bad guy onct ya get to know 'im. Anyhow, it got so's I just report in, pick up a mop without him tellin' me what to do, an' start in on the floors. I usually got company with me so we knock it off right away an' stand around an' bullshit for a while. But I got better things to do with ma time, an' I got fed up with all the extra duty. That floor gets scrubbed ten times a day an' it don't need another application when I get there. It gonna be worn right down to nuthin'. Jus' a make-work project anyhow. Well, we decide we gotta fix 'is ass but good."

Williams leaned back and blew smoke overhead. Then he hunched his shoulders and shivered a little. There was no comfort in Georgia: it was either blazing hot or rainy cold.

"We started out kinda slow, to try an' learn him a lesson, to see if he would ease off. Somebody — an' I ain't sayin' who — scraped 'is belt buckle up with sand, so he hadda go out an' buy a new one. Then somebody stuck gum all inside 'is pants pockets — got 'em when they first come back from the laundry, folded up nice an' neat in 'is footlocker. He din notice when he send his others out, so he hadda wear 'em. Then somebody filled up 'is boots with toothpaste — 'is inspection tube. You think by now he'd be gettin' the message. Instead, he jus' gets worse an' worse, yellin' orders, callin' us out for no nuthin' thin's. So we know we gotta get tough, fix 'im up good.

"Well, one night, while he's inna shower, we go inta action. We take his can o' shoe polish an' smear it all over the inside o' his blanket — an' I do mean all over. Not thick so you'd notice it, just a thin layer. Then we smear it on the bottom o' his pillow, which he punches aroun' in 'is sleep. So 'e comes back an' goes to bed an' never notices a thin'. 'E rolls aroun' all night an' when 'e gets up in the mornin' he's as black as I am, only he don' know it. 'E walks down the aisle in 'is underwear with ever'body laughin', only 'e don' know why. Well, 'e goes inna latrine, takes one look inna mirror, an' lets out with a almighty scream. 'E come chargin' back with tears in 'is eyes, an' we was all busted up laughin'."

By this time Tony was in stitches, and oblivious to the rain. Hank did a "haw haw haw haw haw" and rolled his shoulders. Tom was noncommittal, but Wally was grinning enough to make up for him. Williams was strutting under his poncho.

"Well, the motha still din' learn his lesson. Like a little baby 'e runs to the sarge, wipin' shoe polish off his face, an' carries on like inna tantrum. You'd a thunk we'd tarred an' feath-

ered 'im the way 'e cried. Well, ole Wheaton, 'e takes one look at Stahl an' busts up like the rest o' us, an' goes back in 'is room so's we cain't see 'im laughin'. 'Ventually, Stahl gets cleaned up, an' Wheaton don' do nuthin'. I guess 'e figgered 'e had it comin' to 'im, an' mebbe this'd learn 'im a lesson. But Stahl, 'e don' learn. 'E takes it out on us all day. One guy — an' I ain't sayin' who — goes right up an' threatens to kill 'im if 'e don' lay off — then 'e spits right in 'is face. Stahl puts 'im on report. Now we start confabulatin', an' we plan to really kill 'im. All we want is an excuse, so we go about makin' one.

"First thin' we do is fill 'is bunk up with sand. Then, just to make sure it don' get away too easy, we empty a whole can o' shavin' cream between the sheets an' smear it all aroun'. We figger this way 'e can't jus' dump it on the floor. Then we start gettin' ideas, and add thin's to the conglomeration: grass, twigs, butts, anythin' we can lay our hands on. Coupla guys even come in with night crawlers. Well, then a bunch o' guys sneak out an' start trappin' ants inna empty beer can — we shake out about fifty ov'im in 'is bunk. One guy comes in with a black, furry spider so ugly I wouldn' even touch it. Anyway, it gets throwed inna bunk with the ants.

"Well sir, we hear 'im comin' up the stairs so we all run to our bunks an' start shinin' boots an' belt buckles an' actin' natural. 'E thinks 'e's got us cowed, but nobody's scared ov'im. When the lights go out we all git in our bunks, an' we can see 'im by the light inna day-room. It's hard not to laugh, but we're all ready to jump up an' beat the shit outa 'im soon's 'e makes the first noise. Well, the mothafucka slips in 'is bunk really easy like, so's it won't get mussed an' 'e won't hafta make it inna mornin'. First 'e puts in one foot, then the other, then 'e slips down 'bout half way an' stops cold. 'E don' move, 'e don' say a word, 'e jus' stays there, kinda crouched. An' we're all snickerin' under our blankets waitin' for the signal to jump 'im. But 'e fools us. 'E don' even look aroun', 'e jus' sticks one foot alla way down, real slow, then eases 'imself under the blanket. 'E lays on his side facin' the wall, an' 'e don' move. 'E never so much as squeaks. 'E jus' lays there all night, an' ever' time somebody goes to the latrine 'e sees 'im layin' there, wide awake, eyes starin' at the wall, an' the blankets shakin'. 'E's scared — scared half to death. Inna mornin' 'e goes and explains to the ole sarge 'e don' wanna be squad leader no more."

It was deliriously funny to Tony, and he was holding his side and leaning against Hank so he would not fall down.

"What the hell are you men rejoicin' about? There ain't no laughin' allowed in my army!"

The laughter died as quickly as a bulb with a blown fuse. Tony eyed Sergeant Hawkins sheepishly. His coal-black stare would have stopped a two-hundred-car freight train going down hill at full speed.

"Pick up those butts! This ain't no trash dump!" The sergeant stabbed a thick finger at the ground. "That's *my* land you're litterin'." The smokers bent to retrieve them. "Now get down on your bellies an' crawl over to them trash cans an' put 'em where they belong. All of you!"

The three smokers dropped, but Wally and Tony hung back.

"Do you know what 'all' means?"

Tony started to protest. After a moment's hesitation, he unslung his rifle, dragged it out from under his poncho, and got down on his knees. He held the rifle across his arms as he had been taught, and fell forward onto his elbows. The damp sand clung to his sleeves, and water soaked through his pants. The poncho hood was designed to be worn over a helmet instead of a baseball cap, so it fell completely over his eyes.

"Don't just lay there. Move it!"

Sergeant Hawkins stood with hands on hips and legs spread wide. In his poncho, he reminded Tony of a huge, olive drab starfish.

"Git those asses down!" He kicked Wally in the rump.

The poncho hampered Tony's movements: chest and hips touching the ground, elbows and knees swinging wide like a lizard, the profile flat so no part of the anatomy rose above eighteen inches, lest it be shot through by an enemy bullet, or trampled by a friendly — friendly? — boot. He kept tripping over the loose folds. But the sergeant's voluble encouragement kept him going faster than he would have thought possible.

Williams was way out in front, the first to reach the cans a hundred-fifty feet away. Tom and Hank were far behind. Tony stopped and lay there, not daring to get up until instructed to do so. He gasped for air.

Wally sidled up alongside, rested his head on his rifle. "Is this what they mean when they say an army lives on its stomach?"

****

"Okay, men, listen up," Lieutenant Wakefield bellowed. His eyes, as well as everyone else's, were on Corporal Mead and the heavy mailbag slung over his shoulder.

Tony was almost too tired to listen. When the buses had failed to show up at the rifle range at the appointed time, the entire company force-marched back to the barracks. This meant ten minutes running followed by five minutes walking. Tony was still out of breath, but Sergeant Hawkins hardly showed the strain. The lieutenant had ridden back in a jeep.

Mike Farnsworth had dropped out early in the march, and still had not put in his appearance.

"We've got army business to conduct before mail call. The forms that are being circulated among you are authorizations for savings bond purchases to be automatically deducted from your pay. It has been the policy of this company to urge every man to buy United States savings bonds. This will benefit you as well as your country. You will be building a future for yourself with funds that are redeemable at a later date when you really need them, and it will help your government by putting back into it some of the revenues it so desperately needs."

"This guy's a regular salesman," Wally quipped quietly. "I wonder if he ever sold used cars."

"The way it works is like this. Every month, before you get your pay voucher, six dollars and twenty-five cents will be put into the savings bond program for you. At the end of three months you will be credited with the purchase of a twenty-five dollar savings bond, for which you will only have paid eighteen dollars and seventy-five cents. If you want, of course, you may have the full eighteen-seventy-five deducted from each pay. That means that you will purchase a twenty-five dollar savings bond each and every month."

"This guy's a real mathematician. They're paying us chicken feed and they want us to feed the chickens."

"Let me repeat, it is the policy of this company that *every* man buys a bond. This company has always been the leader of the high standards set by this post, and we want to continue to be the leader. Every man *will* sign the form. Do I make myself clear?"

Wally's was the only reply. "No more Mister Nice Guy."

After a moment, the lieutenant shouted, "I can't hear you."

"Yes, sir," said more than two hundred men.

"I can't hear you!"

"Yes, sir."

"I CAN'T HEAR YOU!"

"YES, SIR."

"That's better."

Wally: "The fact that he's deaf is mitigated only by the fact that he can only count to three." When the clipboard reached him, he shuffled through the papers as if looking for a blank, made an exaggerated pretense of signing it, and passed it on to Tony. "No thanks, man.

I'm old enough to handle my own finances."

The pay scale for an E-1 was eighty-six dollars and fifty cents a month, not counting deductions: income tax, social security, G.I. life insurance, and laundry expenses. (First they made you crawl in the mud, then they made you pay to have your fatigues cleaned and starched.)

"I've still got bonds from when I was in primary school. Used to buy ten-cent savings stamps at the post office and paste them in a book." Tony passed on the clipboard. "I don't think it's practical for me to take another deduction."

****

"How many did you get this time?" Tom wanted to know, after Wally had trotted back from the mail clerk. "I counted five trips so far. Were any of them doubles?"

Wally smiled magnanimously. "Just one."

"Six letters. Ah don't believe it."

"Don't you get tired running up there all the time?" Tony teased.

Tom tilted his head and winked. "Hey, Wally. How many of those letters are from girls?"

"None."

"What's the matter? Don't you go out with girls?"

"Not since I was a boy. Now I only go out with women."

"All right, how many of those letters are from human beings of the female gender?"

"Including my mother?"

"Let me refine it to legally sexually eligible females."

"None of your fucking business," Wally snapped.

"Whoa, no need to get up tight about it."

"Well, it just so happens that, one, I have a lot of friends; two, they are all educated, sophisticated, and caring, so they write a lot; and three, half the people in the world are women and so, statistically, are my friends. *And*, eligibility is a mental and moral frame of reference — the legality is added by those too ignorant to understand this."

"Let me be even more definitive — how many are you screwing?"

Wally's face turned bright red, his eyes burned with solar flare intensity. He reached over and grabbed a handful of shirt, twisted it around Tom's neck. "I said, it's none of your fucking business. Now knock it off."

Tom knocked it off.

Later, in the barrack, Tom approached Wally unctuously. "Hey, Wally, I — I was just breaking up the day with — a little levity. I'm sorry if I got too personal."

Wally took it in stride. "That's all right, man. I'm sorry I blew up at you. I just don't like the insinuation that women are slaves, or menials, or puppets, to be looked upon as objects. Women are people. They think, and they have feelings — just like I do. I like them for that — I need them for that. I'm not as independent as you — I need people. I love people. I love humanity. I even love you."

Tom laughed, and backed off with mock fear. "Hey, let's not get carried away, now."

Then Wally laughed out loud, lunged for Tom, threw his arm around him, and made mock kissing noises.

Tony watched the antics from his bunk. Out of the corner of his eye he saw a short, red haired, fair skinned lad watching the whole affair with evident interest.

****

Dear Tony,

I don't understand why you haven't written yet, as I am dying to hear from you. Daddy told me he had already gotten two letters, and that you said you were very busy. But I hope you can find time to write, even if it's only a postcard. I guess you might still be upset about that little incident the night you left, but that's all over and forgotten. Frank was saying just the other day that he wished you would call, or something. We long to hear from you. All is forgiven here, so if you can find the time drop us a line and let us know how you are, and we will rest easier.

A letter came for you from the union last week and I took the liberty of opening it in case it was important, that you should know. It seems like you did all right on your tests, although they did not give your actual scores, and they want you to come in for an interview next week. Frank called them up and explained the situation. I don't know what he told them, but I guess it's alright.

Robby's been wondering why you haven't been around lately, and I've had a hard time trying to explain where you are. He's too young to understand. Maybe you can send him a little note. He'd like that.

Frank got two more jobs and it seems that some others will be breaking ground soon. He got some other apartment buildings for Santoni, in Andalusia, which is right outside the city, and some houses in Gwennyd. The houses are all singles with big lots, Frank took me out there to see them yesterday, and they're all going to be custom built, so that means he'll get lots of extras. The job will last several years, but the money is good because it's a bank job.

We've been telling everybody that you're in the army. It happened so fast that Frank's brothers didn't find out til after you left. But he told them all down the taproom that you got drafted before you could get your deferment from the union, which was too bad.

I'm glad you wrote to Mother and Daddy. Daddy hasn't been feeling well lately, and has had to go to the doctor to have some tests. They can't seem to find anything wrong with him, he just gets tired so easy that he can't get up in the morning and go to work. But Mother says he's in good spirits, and it really cheers him up to get a letter from you, so write to him often.

I'd very much like to know how things are with you. Please call or write if you need anything, like money or clothes or anything. All your things are just as you left them, and I haven't touched anything in your room except to clean around them. With you not here I have to get used to cleaning your room myself. But at least it's neat, not like Frank's desk. We've got some money put aside for emergencies, so let us know if you need any. We can send it by wire and you'll get it the next day. If there's anything else you need, let us know.

Well, guess I better go now. Hope things are well with you, and hope to hear from you soon.

Love,

Mom and Dad (and Robby)

Chapter 45

"If this don't beat all," Hank said.

At one extreme the obstacle course could be called an oversized playground; at the other it was a devastating collection of sand pits, water troughs, barbed wire, swinging logs, wooden walls for scaling, and rope slides. To some it was an amusement center, to others a torture chamber.

"It beats PT," Tony replied. "Especially in this heat."

The grove consisted mostly of forty-foot-tall Virginia pines, with a few red cedars for color. Standing like tall sentinels, half a dozen short-leaf pines stretched a hundred feet toward the blue Georgia sky, and offered some relief from the sun that the puffy, white cirro-nimbulus clouds, floating aimlessly, did not offer.

Tom puffed on a cigarette. "I've been through this before. There's nothing to it."

"I guess not, man, if you survived it."

Tom gave Wally a playful punch on the shoulder. Wally grinned back.

Mike Farnsworth hung back from the group, looking pretty haggard since he had lost over thirty pounds. Tony dragged him over, trying to include him. In his hand he was carrying notes from classes on ballistics theory, chain of command, identification of rank, and military occupational specialties, known in the business as MOS. No one in the whole company was trying harder than Mike to be the model soldier.

"What do you think, Mike?" Tony said conversationally.

"Well, I never been through anything like this before. I don't know."

Tom slapped him on the back. "Don't worry. Just stick with us and we'll all go through it together."

Mike still had not made it past the third parallel bar.

Sergeant Hawkins gathered the men around him, somewhat informally. He pointed to a field of barbed wire. "Awright, I guess I don't have to tell you how this is done. You all seen it in the movies. The first man jumps on the wires and holds it down with his chest, while the rest use him as a platform to get across. But there are a few tricks to it that you gotta know so you don't hurt the man on the bottom an' so you don't trip up the men if you're the one holding down the wire. I need a volunteer. Farnsworth, git up here."

Mike stepped forward unhesitatingly. He was almost a head taller than Sergeant Hawkins.

"Now pay attention, 'cause if you don't do this right, as big as this man is, he might get hurt." He led Mike to the wire fence and instructed him to get down on his knees, facing the wire. "You'll notice this part of the fence ain't got no barbs on it. That's because you're supposed to have a rifle under you when you do this, otherwise you get barbs in your chest." To Mike, he said, "Now, I want you to put your hands over your head an' fall forward."

So heavy was Mike that the wires stretched nearly to the ground, and warped the fence posts on both sides. The three strands gathered as one.

"Good, now you just stay there. Now, men, what you gotta do is run up here, gently place your foot between the shoulders, an' step over his head. Farnsworth, you gotta duck your noggin so's it don't get kicked, or so's someone don't trip over your skull. Now, men, remember that he ain't a diving board — you don't jump on him, an' you don't push off. You make believe you're stepping on a carton of eggs an' you want to swing your other leg past him. An' you gotta keep your foot up high — if you catch him below the shoulder you can knock the wind outa him, an' if you land too hard you can break his back. Everybody got that? Okay, now, I'll go first an' show you how it's done."

Wally whispered, "Poor Mike."

Sergeant Hawkins got far enough back so he could build up some speed. "Okay, keep your head down an' make sure you don't move." He charged forward like a bull, placed a combat boot precisely between Mike's shoulder blades, and leaped over the wire with the grace of a ballet dancer. So lightly had he touched Mike's back that the wire barely quivered.

"Notice I didn't put any weight down on him, I just used his back for a touching off point. Awright, git in line and try it." He knelt down beside Mike and half supported one shoulder with a huge, black hand. "Keep your head down, you be okay. Awright, let's go. An' remember, between the shoulder blades — gently."

Tony was the first to go across, and found it surprisingly simple. When done properly, there was very little actual weight put down — he sort of skipped across rather than pounded down.

One by one, the members of the platoon planted a foot on Mike's broad back and leaped across the wire fence. A big man named Jackson, from New York City, pounded his foot too close to Mike's neck, and too hard to be unintentional. Sergeant Hawkins reached out and grabbed his leg, tripping him in the air. Jackson tried to regain his balance but could not get his foot back in time. He did a half turn, sailed about eight feet, and landed heavily on his shoulder. The next man practically landed on top of him, but did a sidestep in midair and got away with only kicking him in the shin. The line of charging men screeched to a halt.

"*Jackson, git up here!*" Then, to the rest of the men, "Come on, jump across. What're you waitin' for?"

Jackson rolled out of the way, rubbing his shoulder. When everyone had jumped across the wire fence, Sergeant Hawkins helped Mike up. "Good work, Farnsworth. *You!*" — pointing to Jackson — "Git over here."

"Gee, sarge, I didn't mean any — " Before he could finish he was roughly thrown to the ground and flattened across the wire.

"Awright, men, let's try it again. But first, let me give you another example."

Wally said softly, "I think this guy Jackson has an attitude problem."

Tom tipped back his cap and wiped off sweat. "His problem is geographic. He's a fucking New Yorker."

Sergeant Hawkins charged the wire fence and leaped onto Jackson's back: his foot went down hard and low. Jackson woofed, and his forehead banged against the ground. The sergeant's boot managed to clip him behind the ear and knock off his hat. Jackson lay still.

"That's how *not* to do it. Now, Jackson, come over here an' help me demonstrate the log swing."

The twelve-inch-diameter log was suspended by ropes at either end. When it became his turn, Tony caught the swinging log in the pit of the stomach just as the log reached the apex of its arc, sailed over the mud pit, then flipped over the top and landed on his feet on the other

side of the pendulum. He landed right next to Jackson, who was covered with mud.

Tony sidled over to Tom. "1 think the sarge pulled his arm when he pushed him across, made him slip."

"Serves him right, the bastard."

"Listen, I know he's a loud mouth, but he's not in our squad. So what do you have against him? You hardly know him."

"The train from Bahston picked up all the riffraff from New York on the way down. You should have seen him, all dressed up in fancy clothes, bragging about his Corvette. I hate that kind of ostentation."

Wally approached, brushing dirt off his trousers. "He's a product of his environment. Population density has a pronounced effect on people."

Scaling the twenty-foot walls was fun for Tony, reminding him of Bowman's Tower. He scampered up one side like a squirrel, swung his legs over the top, and scampered down. The one that was erected like an isosceles triangle was more difficult. It would have been easier to run up the forty-five-degree-angle slope on curved logs, then run down. But the aim was to crawl, keeping a low profile. Climbing down resulted in barked shins and scraped elbows.

Wally picked up the conversation as if it had never been interrupted. "Now you take these Puerto Ricans, chattering along in Spanish like a high-pitched chain saw. They're as happy as little children, and have about as many worries. Basic training is a game, the army a welcome diversion in less opulent lives. They've probably eaten better in the past three weeks than they have all their lives. Notice how they laugh when the sarge drops them for push-ups, or makes them low-crawl around the formation. Does it stop them from talking? You'd think they were playing Monopoly and drew a Community Chest card that said 'Go directly to jail. Do not pass Go. Do not collect $200.' Shit, man, they're ready to roll the dice for doubles."

The water trough was thirty feet long. Logs — tamped down like piles almost even with the muddy, film covered, mosquito infected water — provided circular platforms for running troops. Jackson proved why it was necessary to have dry boots when navigating this obstacle, when Sergeant Hawkins made him walk through a mud puddle first.

"But take a crowded city, where a person is nothing more than a speck among the masses. There's a loss of individuality which makes people act in strange ways. Radical personality is an expressionism that keeps a person noticed, and sane. It leads to a cancerous outgrowth of paranoia, gnawing away at minds that are socially inbred."

The best was saved for last: the rope slide. The take-off platform was atop a forty-foot-high log tower. From there a rope slanted down toward the ground a hundred twenty feet away; a one-in-three ratio, thirty degrees. Tony grabbed hold of the hook that was suspended from the pulley wheel, and looked uncertainly down at the sawdust pile below him.

"They live on the edge of emotional trauma, and are constantly on the verge of outrage. They speak in guttural accents and clipped sentences with an abruptness that is difficult to follow. And they fly into a rage if you don't understand their speech and say, 'What?' They show no respect for the property or personal spaces of others, but they protect their own with a show of territoriality that is fiercesomely atavistic: snarling and baring teeth, and a show of fists. They surround themselves with imaginary lines, like a wolf's urine trail, that cordon off their domains. Everyone is a potential enemy, trying to take something away from them."

"*Wally!* Would you cut it out, please?" Tony rubbed his palms over his thighs, wiping off sweat. "I'm about to jump off a cliff, and you're giving me a course in sociology."

Wally's face twisted in mock anger. "Well, I'm sorry. I thought you were interested. After all, my master's thesis was 'Political Hierarchy and Personal Motivations in Dense Urban Populations.'"

Tony scowled, and grabbed hold of the hook again. His hands still felt wet; his heart was still in this throat. He took a deep breath, closed his eyes, and lifted his feet off the platform. About half way down he remembered to open his eyes, stretch out his legs, and brace for impact.

The rope was held high at the other end so that the lowest part of the curve ran about ten feet above the ground. With his arms extended below the hook, he had only two feet to drop into a running fall. But his arms, thrust out in front of him, overbalanced him. He went into a roll on the soft sawdust. Unhurt, he got up and brushed himself off.

"Nice going." Sergeant Hawkins gave the order to pull up the pulley for the next man.

A couple minutes later, Hank alighted on his feet beside Tony. Expressionlessly, he continued, "Crowding tends to heighten the feelings of threat, to intensify insecurity, to increase aggressive tendencies, to aggravate — "

"Wally, that's enough." Tony walked away, back to the tower where the water dispenser stood. He popped a couple of salt tablets into his mouth, drank several cups of water, and refilled his canteen.

Nearby gathered a disturbed group of men: those who were climbing back down the tower

after seeing the jump from the top, those who started to make the climb and found they were unable, those who refused to even touch the tower.

"Come on, you candy asses. What are you, a bunch of pussies? Git up there. You're supposed to be men, training to be soldiers. This ain't no kindergarten class. Git up there."

Sergeant Hawkins' intimidation was taking little effect. Already, some men were doing pushups for insubordination, others were low-crawling through mud puddles: anything rather than to climb that tower and jump off into space.

Mike Farnsworth looked up at the rope swing for a long time. His face was covered with sweat, his fatigues soaked. He rubbed his hands on his buttocks, stepped up to the base, and started his ascent.

Sergeant Hawkins dashed to the tower and put a hand on Mike's perspiring shoulder. "Son, this ain't for you."

****

"Hep, haw. Hep, haw. Hep, haw. Hep, haw."

The sun was hot. The road was hot. The air was hot. Tony was hot.

It was too hot to double time, but that was what they were doing. Long sleeves, long pants, caps worn at all times when out of doors — all paid due to the army motto: uniformity despite discomfort.

So they sweated.

But if Tony sweated, so did Sergeant Hawkins. He swung his beer gut as if it were a sack of feathers. He kept up the cadence, turned around and jogged backward, raced ahead and raced behind, and sang senseless ditties that were repeated in chorus by the troops. Tony never saw him take a drink of water.

"Hep, haw. Hep, haw. Hep haw," ad infinitum, ad nauseam.

Tony was ready to collapse from heat and exhaustion. He did not know if it was his built-in stamina, the three weeks of conditioning, or just plain fear of the consequences, that kept him from dropping out. "It's the mind that gives up," Sergeant Hawkins had said. "Not the body." If you keep telling yourself you can do it, then you can.

Mike Farnsworth was dropping behind. He ran with his eyes tightly shut, his face screwed up, his great, gasping lungs laboring like an ailing compressor. His chest heaved, his legs pounded, his arms swung — but his stride shortened and he fell behind. If his mind could make it, his body did not believe it.

Tony dropped back and kept abreast of him. "Mike, don't stop now — we're almost there," he lied. He thought he saw a movement of the head that resembled a nod.

"What's the matter, man?" Wally dropped back to the other side of him.

If Mike heard him, he made no comment. He just plugged along, picking up his elephantine legs and putting them down on the black, reflective macadam.

"Don't stop, Mike," Tony gasped. "Just another . . . couple blocks." Sweat trickled down his face, stung his eyes. He wiped, squinted, wiped again. If *he* could barely keep going, how could Mike? They were twenty feet behind the last man, then thirty feet, then forty.

At the head of the platoon, Sergeant Hawkins was still singing and calling cadence. "Close them ranks."

Others were starting to lag behind. The formation was stretching out, falling apart. The sun and the road and the air were eating them alive.

Mike stumbled. Tony grabbed his elbow and braced him. He stumbled again. He was still jogging, still picking up his feet and setting them down, but at such a slow pace that a short woman in a tight dress could have walked faster. He kept up the motion, his head thrown back so that he appeared to be screaming silently at the sky. His body moved in uncoordinated jerks.

"Mike, do you feel all right?" Tony could breath easier at this pace. "Do you have heat cramps?" His own calves were beginning to tighten up, and he could feel a vague, annoying pain in his side: dehydration and salt deficiency.

Mike loped along. He was not even sweating.

Tony squeezed his hands into fists, and repeated by rote: "Nausea, vomiting, dizziness, headache, unconsciousness."

Wally grabbed Mike's hand, and squeezed. "Shit, man. He's dry."

Tony struggled to remember what the sergeant had said in class about the body running out of water, about not being able to cool itself. *Coma. Without water the brain can fry.* "Mike, I think you've had enough."

Mike moved mechanically, stumbling, catching himself.

Tony grabbed him by the elbow, held him back. "Stop it, Mike."

"It's heat stroke!" Wally threw himself in front of Mike and absorbed the tanklike momentum as Mike fell against him, then encircled the plump waist with his reedlike arms and wrestled him to a halt. Tony swung behind and slid his arms under limp shoulders. Together they let him down to the road. Mike mumbled incoherently.

"Fan him, man. Fan him." Wally waved his

cap in Mike's face. As soon as Tony started fanning, Wally took out his canteen and poured what little water was left in it over Mike's pale face. Then he loosened his belt, unbuttoned his shirt, and crouched so that his body blocked the sun. "Keep fannin, man. Keep fanning."

A jeep screeched to a halt and two men leaped out. Captain Maxwell bent on one knee, and pulled down Mike's eyelid. "We've got to get this man to the hospital."

Lieutenant Wakefield pushed Tony aside. "Grab his legs, mister." While Tony and Wally got into position, the two officers pulled up on Mike's arms. Then Corporal Mead was there, holding up the limp head. The five of them carried the unconscious body to the back seat.

Captain Maxwell said, "Let's go, Mead. To the hospital."

The corporal jumped behind the wheel and ground the clutch. The jeep clanked off in jerky motions.

Lieutenant Wakefield called back imperiously, "You men get back to your platoon."

****

"Compan-ee-ee-eep, fall in!"

Most of the men lounged in the shade of the barracks or hid under the few, widely separated trees. In the afternoon heat, lethargy was in charge.

"You better *move* when I say fall in!" Lieutenant Wakefield's face was cherry red, like a cartoon character ready to boil over. Like everyone else, Tony dragged his feet in forming up and dressing off. "You're too slow. Fall out and we'll try it again."

With groans and curses the company separated into its component parts. Tony was tired of the game, but knew that he had to play along with it.

"Compan-ee-ee-eep, fall in!" This time there was more of a scramble as the men dressed-right-dress to the proper distance and stood solemnly at attention.

"No sense rushing, man. You know he's going to make us do it three times."

"You're still too slow! Now, fall out. And we're going to do this until you get it right."

Tony did not stray far. He joined the rest of the men in milling formation. "Compan-ee-ee-eep, fall in!"

Tony was certain that they were not any faster this time, but the lieutenant seemed satisfied.

"You men better shape up. You're getting lazy. When I say fall in I mean right now, not when you feel like it. I don't care if we have to stand out here all night practicing. If that's what it takes to make you men shape up, then that's the way we'll do it."

He pursued his normal pacing in front of the

formation: hands behind his back, Smokey-the-Bear hat peaked down, face set grimly. The four platoon sergeants prowled around the edges.

"Can everybody hear me?"

"Yes, sir."

After the usual two repetitions, he went on. "All right, I can assume then that there is no physical impairment to your hearing. Anybody who misses his cue now is going against a direct order. Do I make myself clear?" Three answers later, he continued. "All right, what I'm talking about is bonds. Savings bonds. So that there are no misunderstandings, I will now make it a command. Every man in this company *will* take out a bond. Do you hear me?"

"Yes, sir." "*Yes, sir!*" "YES, SIR!"

"Good. Now I know I'll get one hundred percent participation, because anyone who fails to comply with a direct order is liable for an Article Fifteen."

The clipboard shot around the formation. Judging from the number of times it stopped, Tony was certain that the original turnout had been small.

"He can take his bond and shove it up his ass." Wally passed the clipboard to Tony. "You do what you want, man."

Sergeant Hawkins stood at the side of the formation. Tony returned his arrogant stare. He shuffled through the top sheets, made signing motions, and passed on the clipboard.

"You're right. Now, where's the mail?"

****

Dear Tony,

Sorry for not writing sooner but I was sick last week. I woke up in the morning feeling sick to my stomach and I had awful cramps, but went to school anyway. Then the next day, Friday, I threw up in the morning and my grandmother made me stay home. I was glad, cause I wanted to get better before the weekend so I could go down the shore with Kathy. But she made me go see a doctor and I had to wait three hours in the office before I could get in to see him. He examined me and said there was nothing to worry about, that I probably had the summer grip, and that I would be better after a few days in bed. But he poked my finger to get some blood for a test. I almost passed out when he stabbed me with the pin, and I thought that was going to make me sick. Anyway he gave me some pills to take and my grandmother made me stay in, even though I felt good enough to go out. So I didn't get to go to the shore after all, and by Monday I was feeling good enough to go to school, although I still wasn't feeling perfect. Your letter did a lot to cheer me up, and so did Kathy cause she came to visit me on Saturday and told me she wasn't

going to the shore by herself and was going to a party instead. So now I'm feeling alright, although I still don't feel too strong.

Not much else is happening. Graduation is coming up and I'm getting kind of scared. I don't know what I'm going to do after I graduate, and I don't want to go work in a stuffy old restaurant with my Mom. I want to spend the summer down the shore, but not working, just playing and having fun. I think I've earned it, going to school all this time. Maybe I'll pick up a part time job around Shipbottom so I'll have some spending money. Kathy's already got a job lined up as a secretary, so she'll only be able to come down on weekends. Marion said she might come down too, but she's funny. She's going to go to night school and work during the day. It sounds awful, using all your time that way when you could be out having fun. But that's what she wants to do. Kate is taking the whole summer off because she's decided to go to college next fall. I don't know what she's taking up, I think its liberal arts. Her parents have a house in Wildwood. Ben's signing up for summer classes but I think he's crazy. Who wants to go to school in the summer. There's a rumor going around that Ben and Kate might get engaged, but I think Kate is spreading the rumor so its prob'ly not true. Anyway, why would she go to college if she's going to get married. Then she doesn't have to work or anything. I think mostly her parents want her to go.

My Mom says she can't afford to get me a TV for graduation. She didn't know how much they cost till she went looking. So she's going to get me something else and owe it to me. Maybe I'll get it for my birthday or something. That means I'll still have to watch TV with my rotten grandmother.

Write to me right away. I like getting letters. I even go through my grandmother's junk mail she throws out because its fun to read.

Sincerely,

Patty

****

How's the army treating you? I guess I'll hardly recognize you with no hair. Will it grow back curly? I'm thinking of getting mine cut short, too. I never had mine shaggy like Ben or George, but now it's getting long and Marion says she knows how to cut hair. She cuts her dad's. So she's going to give me a trim. And since I'm saving the barber's fees I'm going to take her to the movies.

Teddy's been showing us your letters (that's alright, isn't it? I've been showing everybody yours. The one you sent me that first week.) Anyway, we've been pretty much keeping up on what's happening with you. I understand you're doing pretty good with the guns. It must be fun shooting on the range all day long. You know, my brother goes to a shooting range out in the country where you have to pay to shoot, and buy your own guns and ammo besides, so you're getting something for nothing. Maybe that don't make you feel any better about the army, but if you gotta do it you might as well like it.

Don't worry about being on KP so much. My brother was in the marines and he just about had a bunk in the kitchen, he was on KP so much. It's just the military way of getting things done and keeping you under their thumb, too. But if I know you, you ain't gonna knuckle under nobody.

Well, I don't want to make you feel bad and tell you how much of a good time we're having, but the truth is that it ain't the same without you. I mean, we're still hotrodding it around in the Black Stallion, getting kicked out of Decatur Road and all, but I wish you were here. (There ain't been any more of them big raids like that time only our car got away and we almost ran over that cop.) Anyway, we got nobody to tell us why the stars come out at night and why birds fly south in the winter (other than it's easier than walking) and why locusts only come out every seven years and all that other science stuff. You could tell it better than any teacher ever could, and make it interesting besides. Hey, did you ever think of becoming a teacher when you get out? We could use somebody like you in school, except you couldn't work there unless you were a priest. That's a laugh — you a priest.

You'll be happy to know that your car passed inspection with flying colors. I took it in the garage and did it myself. The boss said I could fix it up on my own time and he would give me the parts at cost. (I explained how you had been drafted and I was watching your car for you while you were gone.) But it didn't need any parts. All I did was adjust the brakes and give it a lube. Teddy already helped me change the oil, so it's already for you when you get home for leave.

I was talking to Mrs. Clark and she said to tell you your stuff is alright. She got your letter but hasn't had a chance to write back yet, but she'll be doing it this week. She got a letter from Joey in Germany, and she says he's on 24 hour alert, but wasn't allowed to say anything more about it. He doesn't like it over there cause he never gets to fly. He's tied up with those bombers and all they do is sit around on call — and there's never any trouble. He goes up once a month to get his flight time and that's it.

The parties all set. As soon as you get home we're all heading for the shore — Kate's place

in Wildwood. Her folks have already given the okay, cause they know you're in the army. Her folks are really cool. Okay, gotta go. If you run outa pencils let me know and I'll send you a gross. But you don't have to write to me in particular — we all read your letters anyway. Just so long as you write to somebody your mail will get around. I'll try to get the other guys to write, but they are all too lazy. You know how it is. See you the 4th of July. Don't let your meat loaf, don't let your pork roll, and don't take no shit.

Your pal,
Petey

Chapter 46

"The steel pot is the soldier's most valuable tool, (the rifle being a weapon.) It serves as a seat, a container, a canteen, and a sink. It can be used to carry brass off the firing range or trash off the parade grounds. Filled with water, you can drink from it, brush your teeth in it, wash your face and hands in it, and clean your mess kit in it. In the absence of an entrenching tool, you can fill sandbags with it, or dig a sanitary pit. Fitted with a fiberglass helmet liner, you wear it on your head — and when a grenade goes off nearby, you *never* put your hands on top of it like they do in the movies. Unless you want your hands manicured with shrapnel."

Wally breathed out of the corner of his mouth. "This guy's humor is cold enough to freeze the nuts off an iron bridge. Why doesn't he just give up trying to be a comedian?"

Tony adjusted the leather sweatband and plopped it back on his head. He felt as if he would never get used to the weight. "I feel like I'm inside a turtle shell ballasted with bricks."

"Yeah, well, just be glad they're in such short supply or we'd have been wearing them weeks ago."

Lieutenant Wakefield motioned to the platoon sergeants. "Okay, get them back to the range. Charlie Company is moving out. And men, the steel pot will be worn from now on at all times."

The steel pot proved to be a sweatbox on the firing line. Heat waves across the sandy rifle range shimmered with such intensity that the targets — man-sized and man-shaped — appeared to be doing the Watusi. Sand clung to Tony's drenched fatigues.

One by one the targets were pulled up. One by one Tony shot them down. If they were close, he shot low. If they were far out, he aimed high. Days of repetition had turned him into an accurate marksman. At four hundred fifty meters he was hitting three out of four silhouettes; closer than that he never missed.

"I'll be glad to get back into those bleachers,

under the shade of the old pine trees," Wally sang.

"A few minutes ago you were complaining that the benches were too hard."

"Yeah but, man, it was cool. I could listen to Lieuy Wakefield talk all day about self-defense, chemical warfare, and first aid. Just get me out of this sun — and this goddamn helmet."

Tony rolled over and relaxed behind his weapon. "Just be glad we won't be here this afternoon."

"I'm so happy I won't even complain when they make us double time to the clinic so we can wait in line for an hour for more shots."

"Is that what you expect?"

"Expectations are reserved for officers and civilians. Me, I'm rolling with the punches. But I'd like to hand out a few, too."

****

"Are you back again?" Sergeant Breneke showed a mouthful of stained teeth. "What did you do this time?"

"I forgot to ask. What do you want me to do?"

The mess sergeant scratched his head. With the number of men he was getting for detail, he must surely be running out of work for them. "Well, that wall needs painting."

"Again! But sarge, I just — " Tony saw that leprechauns had been at work — the wall was black again. And he realized that if he did not paint the wall, he would end up scrubbing the floor — or worse. "Never mind. I know where the paint is."

He also knew where the cherries were kept.

****

Lieutenant Wakefield strode out onto the parade ground like a toy soldier, executed a sharp right face, and glared at the troops. He played the strict martinet right to the end. "Dis-*missed*!"

There was a moment's hesitation, men glancing around uncertainly, then wild shouts and pandemonium. Then the formation broke ranks and each man ran — *ran* — for the barracks.

"Haw haw haw haw haw. The first thin' Ah'm gonna do is take me a nice cool shower. Then Ah'm gonna lay around in ma shorts till supper time an' *relax*. Haw haw haw haw haw."

The human tide swept into the half-opened double-door, and split at the stairs. Tom was the first to reach his bunk. "I've got something a little less sensual in mind."

"What's that, man? Polishing your boots, or checking out your rifle so you can oil it down?"

Tom ignored Wally's innuendo. "I'm going to sit down and write a nice long letter to my girl."

"Why don't you write to the whole harem?"

"Because I'd need a week to do it. And if we get base passes tomorrow, I'm not hanging around here."

"All right, hot stuff. But you'd better put an ice cube under your pen so the paper doesn't catch fire."

Hank put one foot on Tony's bunk and leaped up. A dull thud was followed by, "Dayam." Hank rubbed his head, squinting. "Ah hit that doggone beam again."

Tony unbuttoned his fatigue jacket. He was still sweating from afternoon PT. His clothes were covered with dust and grime. "You don't know your own strength."

"That's the third time this week." He tried again with less effort, but fell back down. Finally, he placed one foot against the metal headboard and levered himself up. He rolled over and lay flat on his back.

Tom executed a perfect backward jump into his bunk. "Hey, I thought you were going to take a nice, cool shower."

"Well, I have to rest myself up first." Hank's arms hung out over the sides. "I don't want to get cleaned up till I stop perspirin'."

"You never stop." Wally took a huge stack of letters out of his footlocker, carried them to his bunk, lay down, and methodically started going through them.

"You know, I just thought of something." Sweat still beaded on Tony's brow. "Hey, Wally. If we have tomorrow off, you won't have to go to church to get out of police detail."

"Hallelujah. I'm for the base pool and a suntan. Hanging around in these olive drabs is for the birds. I'm down here in the land of sunshine and I look like I've been kept in a cave."

"Ah'm for the beer halls to git me some o' that three-point-two."

Tom stopped in the middle of a sit-up. "You can't get drunk on that stuff — it doesn't have enough alcohol in it."

Hank licked his lips loudly. "Ah sure hope they sell it by the keg, else Ah'm likely to wear maself out openin' cans."

Tony put his head on his pillow. "I think I'll just write letters, and read. I'm getting behind in my studies."

"What the hell are you studying, man? Military etiquette?"

"Well, I like to keep up with National Geographic and Scientific American. The base library should have the most recent issues."

"I'm going to the movies and I don't care what's playing," Tom said, sitting on the edge of the bunk.

"Hey, man, watch the feet."

Tom stopped kicking, and held his legs straight out in front of him, grimacing with the strain. "I hear they've got a pretty good military museum on base, too. I'd like to take in the weapon displays and get the feel of them."

"Ah'd like to get the feel of something, but it sure ain't a M-14. Ah don't know about you fellers, but after four weeks o' humpin' the roads between here an' the shootin' range, Ah'd like ta hump something a little softer. Ah'm horny. Haw haw haw haw haw."

"I'll second the motion." Tom hit the waxed floor and started undressing. "But for right now I'll stick to guns. They're a lot more predictable — you always know when they're going off, and which way they're pointing."

Tony dropped out of the repartee: it felt so good to simply rest, with no one shouting at him. Hank started snoring — his shower was going to have to wait.

"Hi, fellas," a deep voice said in Tony's head. He had trouble opening his eyes, realized that he had fallen asleep. He craned his neck and peered through heavy lids.

"Mike! When did you get back? Hey, guys, Mike's back."

"I got out this morning," he said laconically. "They told me to take it easy for a day or two."

"You're in luck, man. We've been given the rest of the weekend off." Tony rolled to a sitting position. "Gee, you're looking pretty good. They must have treated you right in the hospital."

Tom padded up the stairs in his shower shoes, wearing a towel that was draped around his middle. He took off the towel and started rubbing down. "Welcome back, Mike. Hank, wake up and welcome our friend back."

Hank stopped snoring, rolled over onto his side, and half opened his eyes. "What y'all doin' paradin' around with no clothes on?"

"I'm wearing a smile."

Wally tucked his letters under the pillow. "Yeah, man, well bend over the other way and aim that vertical smile at somebody else."

Tony dug his fists into his eyes. "So tell us all about it. What did they do to you?"

"Well, they were pretty nice to me. They carried me in on a stretcher —"

Tom leaned against the window sill and pulled on a clean pair of boxer shorts. "I'll bet it took four men."

" — and they took me right into the emergency room, ahead of everybody. I was so dizzy I couldn't even sit up on the examining table, so I just laid there while they put ice packs on me and gave me a shot of saline solution. I didn't know all this at the time — they told me about it later." He held his pudgy hands about a foot apart. "The needle was this long. They stuck it right in my behind, and boy did it

hurt. But I was too sick to care. Then they helped me up and walked me to a bathroom and put me in a tub of cold water. After a while, an orderly helped me take my clothes off."

"Y'all mean you took a bath with your uniform on?"

"Yes, but when they gave it back to me it was all clean and pressed." Mike tugged at the fatigue jacket. "Well, anyway, they gave me a pair of pajamas and put me in a room with about twenty other guys, what they called a ward, and gave me a bed with a curtain that could be pulled all the way around it. Then some nurses came in — "

"Gurls?" Hank was suddenly wide awake.

"Yes, girls. And they gave me a lot to drink — mostly fruit juice. And lots of ice cream, too. Then one of them gave me a back rub."

"Shit, man, if I'd known you were going to get that kind of treatment, I'd have lain down with you."

Mike laughed, and stared down at the floor, his face red. "Captain Maxwell stayed right there in the hospital, too, till the doctor said I would be all right. Even winked at me when the nurses came in. And he told me not to worry about missing classes, or workshops, or anything. He said he would take care of everything for me. And I thought he was going to be mad at me, you know, for not keeping up."

"That's our Maxy," Wally said.

"Were them nurses purty?" Hank wanted to know.

Mike grinned shyly. "Yes, they were pretty good looking. But they were, you know, nurses. Some of the guys tried to kid around with them, but they weren't going for it. But they treated me all right. Kept me supplied with plenty to drink, gave me lots of food. You know, it wasn't that bad."

Wally shook his head. "Bad? It sounds like you had a fucking holiday."

Tony pounded Mike on the shoulder. "Anyway, we're glad to have you back."

"Well, thanks." Mike looked briefly around, then resumed studying the tongue-and-groove pattern of the floor. "Uh, did the sarge say anything — I mean, was he mad about me dropping behind, or anything?"

"The bastard never even told us you were alive," Wally said.

"Well, did I miss much?"

Tony shrugged. "Same old stuff: rifle range, classes on self-defense. Oh, and we were issued bayonets."

"Ah got to shoot a M-14 that was fully automatic. It's jus' like our own cept'n it's got a selector switch that changes it from semiautomatic to fully automatic, so it works like a machine gun. It sure is a mean piece."

Tom said, "I could use a mean piece."

"You should have seen him. He was shooting the bark off a tree at twenty-five meters, and the gun was drilling him backward along the ground. He ended up three feet back from where he started."

"An' ma shoulder feels like somebody took a jack hammer to it."

"Well, I guess I didn't miss nothing important. I guess I'd better take another salt tablet and have a drink of water. They told me to build myself up."

As he started to move away, Tony called out, "Hey, Mike, they're letting us go to supper whenever we want, and no time limit. Why don't we all go together?"

"Okay."

"And no overhead bars."

****

Wally twisted the map around so it was aligned with the intersection. He glanced around at the buildings, searching for a landmark. Then, holding the map in place, he walked around it until he was facing the print.

"Come on, Wally, you can do better than that." Tony lifted his cap and wiped sweat off his brow.

"Look, man, as long as I'm doing it that's all that matters." He scratched his chin and squinted at a low structure. "It looks to me like Building 407 is that one over there."

"Which one?"

"The beige one."

"They're all beige."

"All right, man, the beige one with the two windows and a door and the car parked in front of it."

"Okay, let's go check it out." Tony waited for a truck to pass, then stepped off the curb and walked diagonally across the intersection. "What kind of detail do you think this is?"

"To differentiate between ignorance and apathy, I don't know and I don't care. What pisses me off is that the rest of the gang is lounging by the pool while we're working."

"Sergeant Hawkins knows what's going on. He seemed to think it was pretty funny. What do you think it is?"

"I don't feel like playing Sherlock Holmes. Why don't we just wait till we get there?"

"What did you do, get up on the wrong side of the bunk?"

"As long as it's an army bunk, both sides are the wrong side. The army tells us what we *need* to know, not what we *want* to know. And in a couple minutes we'll probably wish we *didn't* know."

Tony stopped by the four-door '62 Plymouth. It was olive drab with no chrome. "Wally, I've seen this car before."

"Man, you've been out in the sun too long."

"No, I recognize it."

"They all have U.S. Army stenciled on the doors."

"But the number — Wally, you remember the day we spent practicing standing at attention, just the two of us?"

"You think I'm a moron? How could I forget?"

"Well, this car passed us three times that day. I remember reading the number."

"So what's the mystery? The guy just uses the road in our compound to get to his office. Let's just report in and get it over with."

Tony could hear a compressor: the building was air-conditioned. "At least we'll be working some place cool."

The waiting room was less than lavishly furnished. A black telephone sat on the oak desk, the swivel chair was unpadded, and the four folding chairs were battered and worn. A map of the base covered the back wall.

Wally took a seat and stretched out. "Feels good."

Tony's voice echoed. "Hello. Anyone here?"

Boots scuffled in the next room. A PFC appeared in immaculately pressed summer dress and spit shined shoes. "Can I help you?"

"Yes, we were sent here for duty assignment. D-6-2, Captain Maxwell."

"Oh? I don't know anything about it."

"Is this Building 407?"

"That's right."

"Well, there's supposed to be somebody here who knows what this is all about. We were just told to report in."

"Sundays are usually pretty quiet around here — just me and the Colonel. And he's over in 406 conferring with Colonel Dunbrad. I could call him."

"Don't go out of your way on our account, man. We'll just wait for him."

"What outfit did you say you were from?"

Tony removed his cover. "Delta Company, Sixth Brigade, Second Division."

The PFC pursed his lips, nodding. "Okay, go ahead and make yourself comfortable. Things are pretty leisurely around here on weekends."

"Thanks."

Tony sat down, but Wally jumped up and paced the room like a caged tiger. "Just think, right now the rest of the guys are back at the barracks, taking it easy, catching a few extra zees, going to the movies, and lying around the pool. And here we are hanging around for some nitwit colonel. Oh, well, I guess it's all wasted time anyway. Who'd have thought I'd be spending two years of my life taking orders from short-haired ignoramuses?"

"Are you sure the plural isn't ignorami?"

Wally sat on the edge of the desk. "This is really a joke. I have no business being here. With my education I should be running for governor instead of toting a gun in some flea bitten army post. I represent the youth of today, the leaders of tomorrow, the great hope of society."

"Don't sell yourself short."

"Shit, man, this is really the doldrums."

The front door opened and a gold-braided colonel walked in briskly. "Tensh-*hut!*"

Tony vaulted out of the chair as if a spring had uncoiled beneath him. Wally scrambled off the desk with a clatter, knocking the telephone receiver off its cradle. He replaced it, and stood at attention. Recognition caused a knot of apprehension in Tony's stomach.

The colonel nodded grimly. "Still the same two jokers. Well, if you can't learn respect, I'll have to give you a job that will teach you. Follow me."

He passed between them and walked into the room where the PFC sat calmly behind his desk. The colonel sat behind his own workstation, leaned back in his seat, the wood creaking, and put his hands behind his head. "You're going to change my whole outlook on life by turning that brown outside my window into green. Watkins!"

"Sir?"

"Escort these men to the tool shed and fit them out with shovels, hoes, and rakes. They're going to be doing a little gardening today."

"Yes, sir." He motioned for them to follow him. The blast of hot air hit Tony like flames from a coal furnace. "I don't know what you guys did to deserve this, but it really must have been something."

"I marched on the White House," Wally recalled.

"I dropped out of college."

Watkins took them to a shed about the size of a single-seat outhouse. He took a key from an overstuffed ring, opened the heavy, brass lock, and flung back the hasp.

"Well, whatever it is, you sure picked the wrong day to work outside."

"I don't remember picking this day. Wally, did you pick this day?"

"Not a chance, man."

"Look, whatever you do, don't clown around when the colonel's around. He can be a real bastard when he wants to be."

"So I've noticed."

Watkins passed out the tools. "Look, I happen to know he'll be going out with his wife in a little while, so he won't be able to watch you all day. We've got a refrigerator inside stocked with juice and cans of pop, so I'll let you know when the coast is clear and you can come in and beat the heat."

"Thanks, man."

"Yes, thanks a lot. That's really decent of you. But tell me, when did this hothead become a colonel? When we ran into him a few weeks ago in the PX, he was a major."

"He got promoted last week, and it went straight to his head."

"Shit, man, being a major had already gone to his head. I didn't think there was room in there for anything else."

Watkins laughed with affectation. "Yeah, I know what you mean."

Colonel Cunningham, the base adjutant, stepped out the back door and pointed glowingly to six hefty sacks leaning against the back wall of the building. "This is three hundred pounds of grass seed, the best that military money can buy. Now, one of the things I want to do for this base is to beautify it, and I'm going to start right outside my own office. I want all the ground between the shed and this building, and that tree and 406, broken up and sown with grass. And just to make sure it doesn't get washed away by rain pouring off the roof, I want a ditch, twelve inches deep, running all the way around the back and side of this building so it will drain into the street. Now, get to it."

When they were alone, Wally sized up his tools. "Shit, man, I'm not a farmer. I don't know how to plant anything but a ski pole. Pick and shovel work isn't my style."

Tony sighed, and picked up the hoe. "Just follow my lead. I'll show you how it's done."

"This isn't exactly my idea of sowing wild oats."

Chapter 47

A tingling sensation on Tony's forehead was his first awareness of return to consciousness. The feeling ran through his scalp, across his neck, over his shoulder, then vanished as someone grasped his arm and stroked him gently.

"Tony, wake up. Wake up, Tony."

"Huhn?" He raised his eyelids enough to expose a millimeter-wide slit, and saw the dim glow of a flashlight pointed away from him. "What?"

"You're Tony Giovanni, aren't you?"

"Uh, yes."

"Well, you're on KP today. You have to get up."

"Oh, yes." The clouds were beginning to disperse from his mind. "What time is it?"

"Three-twenty. And they want you at the mess hall in ten minutes. Okay?"

"Okay." To prove his sincerity he swung his feet out of the bunk and sat up. The figure with the flashlight retreated into the darkness. Still drowsy, Tony wondered if it had all been a dream. No, he had felt that tender skin on his.

He shook himself awake, got dressed, and tightened up his bedding in the dark. He staggered toward the day room and the eye-cringing brightness. Had he done anything wrong this time? No, this was normal KP, his turn in rotation.

"Giovanni, checking out for KP."

Reds pushed his comic books and muscle magazines aside and smiled prettily. In his curious, high-pitched voice, he said, "Hi, Tony."

"Hi. Was that you who woke me up?"

Reds had carrot colored hair atop a face that was smooth and which had never felt the edge of a razor. A crop of freckles grew across his bright cheeks. He did not look more than sixteen, and was often the brunt of humiliating jokes. But he seemed to thrive on attention.

"I feel sorry for you." He had white, even teeth and thin, red lips. "I had KP last week and almost died from exhaustion — had to go on sick call the next day to make up for it. Watch out for that Sergeant Breneke."

"We've already met."

"Well, if you play up to him he's not so bad. And you better button up your pants because he holds inspection first thing."

"Thanks." Tony took care of the missed button. "Well, I'd better get going. See you later."

"Bye-bye," he sing-songed.

Outside it was a clear night: the deep purple sky was studded with twinkling stars. Light glowed through the mess hall windows, the only sign of life in this part of the base. The quiet was interrupted by the chirping of crickets — the birds were not yet awake.

At the mess hall door, Tony stopped and rubbed the tops of his boots on the back of his pants, wiping off stray dust. From the utter peacefulness of the outdoors, he stepped into the din and brilliance of the kitchen.

"You sure took your time gettin' here."

Tony could see that the other KPs were already working. "Hi, sarge, I — "

"Stand at attention."

Tony clicked his heels and squared his shoulders. The sergeant seemed not to recognize him.

"When I say KPs will report at three-thirty, I mean three thirty, and not three-thirty-one. Right away you're on my shit list for the day. Now listen up if you don't wanna get lower on that list."

Sergeant Breneke walked around and inspected Tony from every angle. "You'll do, but just barely. That belt buckle should shine like gold so you can see your face in it. I'll let it go this time. Now, I expect you to work hard, work fast, an' work well. If you wanna make this job easy, it'll be easy. If you wanna make it tough,

I can be tough. Right now you're makin' it difficult 'cause I have to repeat this for your benefit. We got a big responsibility here. We gotta feed two hundred an' fifty men, three times, an' we gotta be on time. If you do your duty everything will go all right; if you try to slack off, it'll go hard — for you. An' if I think you're not doin' your job, you'll be in front of the CO so fast it'll make your head spin. Do I make myself clear?"

"Yes, sergeant."

"Okay, then let's get to it. We got two hours till breakfast an' a lotta work ta do." He turned and motioned for Tony to follow. "The first rule for men working with food is sanitation, so wash your hands with soap an' water an' come back."

After Tony disinfected his hands, Sergeant Breneke examined the whorls in his palm and inspected his fingernails. "Okay, you can start by breakin' eggs."

From the huge walk-in refrigerator, Tony brought out forty-five *dozen* eggs and started cracking them into a stainless steel bowl the size of a small trash can. Then he mixed them with a blender that was hooked over the curled lip; it reminded him of a small outboard motor in a test tank.

Tony helped the other four KPs handle a multitude of tasks. Water was heated in a percolator the size of a *large* trash can, while five-pound bags of coffee beans were ground and added. Several crates of fresh oranges, delivered that morning, were sliced in half and thrown into a press. Seventy pounds of sausage links were laid out on thin metal pans and stacked in the ovens. Two fifty-pound bags of potatoes were peeled in an automatic peeling machine, run through a slicer, and dumped into vats of hot oil. Twenty gallons of milk were poured into a dispenser, and glasses were stacked for self-service. Bread was laid out on trays. The tables in the dining room were set with napkins and dispensers, salt and pepper shakers, ketchup bottles, and butter dishes.

By the time the men started coming in for breakfast, Tony was almost awake, and already tired. He was hardly aware of the noise and bustle of food being served; he was hunched over the sink scrubbing pots and pans and scraping sausage trays. He beat the soap out of a full box of Brillo pads. After two hours, his arms were as limp as the dishrag he was using.

"Okay, men, wash up and get ready to eat." Tony picked up a tray and helped himself to whatever was leftover. "Take as much as you want, and you got a half hour to eat it."

Four hours of weariness ached in his legs as Tony stuffed himself with eggs, orange juice, and coffee. He had barely noticed the other men on duty, and had hardly said a word to any of them. There just had not been any time. Now, Sergeant Breneke sat down with them and ate his own breakfast.

"When I joined this man's army there wasn't no war. Everybody minded his own business an' did his job an' nothin' was said about it. But when the fightin' started over there in Asia everybody got up tight. They was lookin' for excuses to send ya ta the front. Ya fuck up, ya go to 'Nam. Now I happen to like the army. It gives me three meals a day an' a place ta sleep an' some spendin' money, an' sometimes the time to spend it. An' I like bein' stateside. So I keep a low profile, I don't start no trouble, an' nobody notices me. I run my kitchen smooth, I don't make no waves with the old man, an' he let's me stay here till this little conflict is over. I aim ta keep it that way, an' I ain't gonna let no raw recruit fuck things up for me. Ya just do as you're told an' make me look good so's I can keep the old man happy, an' I'll be happy. But if ya make me look bad I'll throw ya ta the dogs. I don't care about none a ya guys, only ma own skin. So take my advice an' keep a low profile an' don't start no trouble, an' maybe nobody'll notice ya."

When they finished eating, and the leftover food was dumped in the garbage to be hauled away as slop to fatten the local pigs, the jobs were rotated. Tony loaded silverware and glasses into the dishwashers, scraped and rinsed the plastic trays and stacked them on end in the tray washer. He helped clean the tables, then upturned the chairs on them while the floor was mopped, waxed, and buffed. He scoured ovens and ranges, and helped wipe down every machine with grease cutter and cleanser.

Lying on the floor, cleaning the bottoms of the counters, the legs and stanchions, and the stainless steel bolts that stopped the equipment from moving, Tony fell asleep. A kick from the mess sergeant jolted him. He started moving his arms in a scrubbing motion, and the sergeant left.

Hours later, just as they finished cleaning up from breakfast, it was time to start lunch. Tony set to shaping a hundred pounds of ground beef into patties, while more potatoes were peeled and sliced. The ovens ran full time, adding insufferable heat to the already hot kitchen. Pots and pans had to be scrubbed, more dishes and glassware washed, endless amounts of kitchen equipment disinfected.

Lunch came and went. Tony's back was sore from the constant bent-over position. The kitchen enveloped him, became his whole world. All he knew from outside was that dirty dishes were piling up on the counter. A delivery truck brought hundreds of pounds of food —

boxes, packages, crates, baskets, and cans — that had to be stored immediately, especially the perishables. Then it was back to the sink.

"Now hear this," Sergeant Breneke intoned. "Captain Maxwell may stop in this afternoon for a spot inspection. My kitchen has never failed an inspection before — it's not going to fail now. You've got to work harder to make this kitchen shine. Now get to it."

Tony swallowed a hasty lunch on the fly.

"Giovanni, run that steel wool in straight even lines. I don't want these pans looking ragged."

Hours later, when it became apparent that the inspection was not going to occur, they stopped cleaning and started preparing the evening meal. One hundred twenty pounds of ham cooked slowly in the ovens. The potatoes were baked on trays. Cabbages boiled away in huge pots that sat above the gas flames. Tony was put back on pots and pans. He splashed water on his face to keep from falling asleep. He had already put in a day and a half of work and there were still another six hours to go.

There was no sitting down for dinner. In fact, Tony was not sure exactly when dinner had happened. He just kept working, and eating the scraps before they got dumped in the garbage. At least the nongrease meal was easy to clean up after.

"You got done so fast I'll let you clean out the freezer."

Tony dried his hands on a once-white towel. His skin was shrunken and shriveled, like those of an octogenarian.

"I want all the shelves cleaned with soap an' water, an' the floor swept and mopped. An' keep outa the pantry. Jars a cherries been disappearin', an' if I find out who's been disappearin' 'em, he's gonna be in deep shit."

"Okay, sarge."

What the mess sergeant called a freezer was really a refrigerator, kept just above freezing temperature. Tony opened the vaultlike door and climbed into the ten by ten enclosure. Filled with that afternoon's delivery, there was hardly room to step inside. The only part of the floor that was visible was the spot where he was standing.

Tony started with the crates on the floor, piling them up in the hallway outside the door. Oranges, grapefruits, apples, and peaches he piled as high as he dared, balancing the crates and baskets head high. Cardboard packages of meat, still frozen like rocks, he laid on the floor. Pork roll, roasting chickens, and giant roasts were the bill of fare for the next day. On top of this he stacked twenty-five pound blocks of cheese and large wooden crates of eggs. Ten-pound squares of butter went on top of that.

The items stored on the shelves were packed loosely. Tony carried out armful after armful of grapes, turnips, cucumbers, squashes, and cantaloupes; separate cartons of eggs; loose potatoes; bottles of ketchup and steak sauce; bags of flour. He hauled out the last of the vegetables, and was standing knee deep in red tomatoes, when he heard a murderous, spine tingling shout.

"What the hell are you doing with my food?"

Sergeant Breneke's face was twisted in anguish — or abject terror. His arms were outstretched as if he wanted to strangle Tony, but a barrier of meat, cheese, eggs, vegetables, and potatoes kept them apart.

"I'm cleaning the freezer, like you told me, sarge."

"Put that stuff back before it spoils."

"But I haven't had time to — "

"Put it back."

"But, sarge, it won't go bad in — "

"PUT IT BACK."

"But — "

"NOW!"

Tony grimaced, and shrugged his shoulders. "Okay, but how am I supposed to clean the shelves?"

"One at a time."

"Oh." He started cramming everything back into the freezer.

"Faster. Faster." Sergeant Breneke did not help, but he watched Tony's every movement until every shelf was packed, until the floor was filled and the hallway cleared. "An' keep that door closed. If any of that food spoils, I'll have your hide."

Tony started the laborious task of clearing each shelf, washing it (and the wall behind it), then restocking it before going on to the next shelf. It was so cold inside that every few minutes he had to step into the hallway to get warm.

"Hey, you know where the paint is?"

Tony looked up at the tall Negro. "Are you on extra detail?"

"Yeah. Mothafucka got me smokin' in the armory."

"Too bad." Tony pointed to the pantry. "It's in the right hand corner, on the floor."

"Thanks." He bent to pick up the brushes and cans.

"What are you painting?"

"Wall behind the stoves."

"Did he say what color?"

"Said black."

Tony realized that Sergeant Breneke's madness was not without its irony. The color scheme was simplicity plus: black men painted the wall black, white men painted it white. "It's a good thing there aren't any American Indians

in this outfit."

"Whassat?"

"Nothing."

Only physical labor and the cold of the freezer kept Tony awake. After he was finished with the shelves, he divided the space in half, and took all the food from one half and piled it on the other half. Then he lifted the wooden palates and cleaned the floor underneath. He had just finished reversing the procedure when the door opened and Sergeant Breneke stuck in his head and made a cursory inspection.

"All right, it'll do. Now get outa here. An' if I have to throw out any o' this food, I'll have it taken outa your pay. Now get."

Tony got. He staggered across the street, the last of the KPs to leave the mess hall. After nineteen hours of continuous work, he hardly had the energy to lift his feet. The snores of his bunkmates directed him through the darkness. Too tired to shower, or even to brush his teeth, he lay down fully dressed and closed his eyes. A voice from overhead sounded like a call from heaven.

"Tony, Ah picked up your mail for you an' put it under your pillow."

The entire day had passed without his ever once seeing the light. The mail would just have to wait.

Chapter 48

The firing range was a sea of mud and, in his Grandmother's vernacular, it was raining pitchforks and hoe handles. Tony stumbled off the firing line, leaned against a convenient tree, and pulled his poncho hood farther over his steel pot. He spread out the bottom of the poncho like a hoop skirt, and slid down to the ground, resting his forehead on his knees. Instantly, he was asleep.

Something slammed into his leg. Sergeant Hawkins' ebony face towered above him. "Whaddaya think you're doin'?" Water poured off the brim of his hat like a miniature waterfall, and plopped onto Tony's poncho.

"Just resting, sarge."

"You do your restin' at night. Now git on your feet — nobody sits down in the army."

Tony was too tired to argue. "Yes, sergeant." He stood up, but continued to use the tree as a back brace.

"Maybe you need some extra detail."

Tony tried hard to focus his eyes. *Giving more work to someone who is tired is like giving another drink to a drunk.* "I think what I need is more sleep."

"This ain't no holiday, an' you didn't come to Fort Gordon for a rest. You here to learn how to save your ass. When you git to Vietnam, they ain't gonna be nobody around to save it for you. You on your own."

"But, sarge, shouldn't we be in a classroom today, and pick a nicer day for the rifle range?"

"Wars don't wait for good weather. Now git over there an' grab some chow before the next platoon is called in."

A line of green ponchos stretched behind a canvas-covered deuce-and-a-half, from the back of which Sergeant Breneke and two servers dished out lunch.

"We're eating in the rain?"

"It never rains *in* the army, it only rains *on* the army."

Tony waded mindlessly through the growing puddles; his boots and pants were already soaked. He shook from cold and dampness.

"Man, you look like death warmed over. Where did you get to?"

Peering through half opened eyes, Tony tried to stop wavering. "I can hardly keep my eyes open from squinting through the sights. They kept clogging up with water."

Wally drew the drawstrings tight and his hood shrunk around his face. "Maybe some good army chow will wake you up. Turn around and I'll get your mess kit."

Tony presented his back. Wally lifted his poncho, unstrapped the fanny pack, and removed the utensils and mess kit. Tony pulled his metal canteen out of the pouch; with it came the canteen cup.

"Now you can do the same for me."

No one was in line by the time they arrived. One server ladled soup into Tony's canteen cup while the other piled French fries on the metal plate.

"Hey, what platoon you men from?" Sergeant Breneke inquired brashly.

"Second," Wally answered.

"Two platoon's been through already. You tryin' ta sneak seconds?"

"No, sarge. We were out on detail and just got back."

The mess sergeant eyed them suspiciously, and slowly placed a hamburger and two slices of bread in each plate.

"Hey, y'all, come over here."

The rain pattered down on Tony's hood like machine gun bullets, drowning out the direction of sound.

"This way, man."

Hank and Tom and Mike hunched under a tree out of the main deluge, but far from dry. Tony crooked his arm to hold the mess kit while he alternately sipped his soup or took a bite out of a soggy sandwich. "What did I miss yesterday?"

Tom chewed while he talked. "Lieutenant Wakefield was showing us some judo. He threw a couple guys over his shoulder for ef-

fect, but he really doesn't know what he's doing. In a real match he'd be flat on his ass in about two seconds."

"What makes you the expert, man?"

"I had judo — and karate — in college. I was even on the self-defense team. — "

"When you weren't playing football."

" — This stuff he's showing us is elementary. You need hours and hours of practice to be any good at it. All we'll get is enough to show us the moves, but we'll never get the proficiency to use it instinctively. And if it's not second nature to you, it has no value."

"Like sex."

"Haw haw haw haw haw."

"All right, you guys, make fun. This lieutenant may look like a tough guy, but I'll bet I could throw him."

"Don't talk too loud, man, or you may get the chance to prove it."

"Haw haw haw haw haw."

"All right, just wait till our next class. When he picks me, I'll show him what I know."

"Come on, man, he'll flip you like a pancake on a greasy grill. Tony, you should have seen me. One minute I was facing him, waiting to see what he was going to do; the next I was watching the ceiling, wondering how it got in front of me. He's fast, man. Shit, the only one he couldn't throw was Mike."

Mike grinned sheepishly, but let Wally tell the story.

"He went into this spiel about how you use your opponents weight against him, and how the smaller man is lower to the ground and has better leverage, and how the bigger they are the easier they are to trip up. Well, Mike really stuffed him into a cocked hat. He reached out and grabbed Mike's hand, like he did mine, stooped under him and got his shoulder under his belly, and Mike just picked up his feet. Fell right on top of him and flattened him like a steamroller over a pat of butter. Knocked the wind right out of him. You should have heard the men roar."

Hank's Mule Skinner yodel was joined by the others' laughter. Tony spit out a mouthful of cold soup.

"Hey, what're you men laughin' at?" Sergeant Hawkins approached and stabbed the group with dark eyes. When no one answered, he said, "Finish your food, an' don't throw any of it away. You got five minutes till we move out." He stalked off.

Wally peered into his canteen cup. "I'll never finish this soup in this rain: I can't keep up with it. It just keeps getting thinner and thinner."

****

Tony had just closed his eyes when a hand roughly shook his shoulder. "Pssst. Up and at 'em, Tony. You're next."

He did not move, or open his eyes. "What time is it?"

"Three o'clock."

"Okay. I'm up."

"You gotta sign me out." Ernie Holloway shoved a clipboard under his nose and handed him a pen. Tony rolled over, freed his hand from the sheet, and scratched his signature on the dotted line.

"How's that?"

"Great. Here's the watch and the flashlight. Don't keep it on too long, the batteries are going bad."

Tony thumbed off the switch and lay back down. A moment later his eyes jerked wide. He fumbled with the flashlight, peered at the watch. It was three twenty-four. He tossed off the sheet, grabbed the clipboard, and ran for the day room. The duty roster was on the wall. "Uh, oh." He raced downstairs and ran the flashlight along the heads of the bunks, reading each nametag. "Diment, I hate to do this to you, but you have to get up for KP."

Diment woke up easily, yawning. "Thanks, buddy."

"Listen, I wasn't paying attention so I didn't get you up when I should. You only have five minutes to get there. And Breneke's a bear if you show up late. I know, I was on KP yesterday."

"That's all right, I needed the extra sleep." Diment slipped into his clothes and boots, and signed out.

As long as he was downstairs, Tony stopped in the latrine and threw cold water on his face. Now he was alone with the dead, like a caretaker in a mortuary. The only sounds he heard were the creaking of bedsprings and discordant snoring. His eyelids still felt like lead.

He walked around, stared out the windows, threw more water on his face — twice. He leaned up against a column, and closed his eyes. He woke up falling. He threw more water in his face. He stood out on the front steps and listened to the crickets. He threw more water on his face. He dozed off.

What are they afraid of? That someone might break into the barrack and steal the toilet paper? At three forty-five, he advanced the watch hands fifteen minutes, and woke up his relief.

****

Lieutenant Wakefield stood in front of the bleachers with his legs spread wide and his hands behind his back in parade rest position. He peered out from under the brim of his Smokey-the-Bear hat with the demeanor of a mischievous boy dressed up in his older brother's Boy Scout uniform.

"Today we're going to go one step further in the art of armed combat. I'm going to teach you how to kill with a bayonet."

He took up his familiar pacing, from side to side, in front of the platoon. He stopped suddenly, whipped around with a loud shout, dropped into a crouch, and from his belt pulled out a foot long blade which he shoved against the neck of a Puerto Rican in the front row.

"This man is dead." He squirmed in the lieutenant's iron grip, but not too much: one good swallow would have cored his Adam's apple. "Next to your rifle, the bayonet is the best weapon you have. With it you can jab, stab, eviscerate, or skin a man alive — in that capacity it can be used as an effective counter intelligence tool to make a reluctant prisoner talk. Fixed onto the barrel of your rifle, it will extend your sphere of influence by three feet — you can kill a man on the ground without ever stooping over. Used as a tool, you can probe for mines, cut bandages, clean your nails, and pick your teeth. And if you keep the blade sharp, you can even shave with it."

He relaxed his hold on the statuesque trainee and stepped back. He ignored the hapless man, now folded limply on the bench, and strode across the front of the platoon. With exaggerated histrionics he spit on his arm, aligned the blade carefully at an acute angle, and gave a practical demonstration of how sharp he kept his blade. Blond hair accumulated on the edge of the knife.

"In a couple of years he'll be able to shave his upper lip, too." Tony shushed Wally with an elbow.

"It goes on the end of your rifle like so." Like a well-rehearsed thespian, he stopped his rambling gait and held out his right hand. Sergeant Hawkins slapped an M-14 into it, as a nurse would hand a scalpel to a doctor. Without looking down, he snapped the bayonet onto the tip of the barrel and locked it into place. "Now you are ready to kill."

He let out a bellow and made a lunge — this time away from the men in the front row. He held his pose for two seconds, yelled again, and jerked back to a half-crouched self-defense position.

"Always hold your weapon with two hands — it's important that you have it under control at all times. If you lose your grip you can find yourself in real trouble."

"Ah sure hope Gonzalez knows what weapon he's talkin' 'bout."

Tony put his other elbow to work — he did not need jokesters on both sides.

"Even without ammunition, the rifle can be a deadly weapon, as you learned with the pugil sticks. But with a fixed bayonet it becomes a psychological weapon, with great powers of persuasion. When you start waving this ten inch blade, people start getting out of your way."

Without warning he let out another bellow and charged toward the bleachers and the tight knot of men, slashing as he came. Tony was bowled over as those in the way lurched backward and sideways, toppling men like dominoes. The ground beneath the stands was littered with crawling bodies, adding truth to Lieutenant Wakefield's prophecy.

He calmly stepped back and tossed the rifle to Sergeant Hawkins, then turned and resumed lecturing. The men squiggled back to their seats.

"You'll notice that when I attacked, I acted decisively. In the use of the bayonet, as in every other military tactic, the best defense is a good offense. You must push forward your attack as if you meant it. Sergeant." Hawkins stood alongside the lieutenant and demonstrated as he called out directions. "Stand on guard with one foot forward. Then swing the other foot around while extending your weapon. After the blade has entered the body, jerk it back before your opponent falls down and drags your weapon with him. Then return to the ready position."

Sergeant Hawkins humphed at each movement.

"High thrust. Low thrust. Slash and parry. Down stab. When a man is on the ground you lean your weight into the butt, twist after it goes in, then place a foot against the chest and yank it back out. Always try for a gut shot because the blade will go in easily, and come out easily. The twisting motion increases damage to organs. Avoid hitting bones because they can either snap off the blade or make it difficult to retrieve. The worst thing you can do is get the bayonet wedged in the rib cage. Not only will a lung wound not kill as quickly as a gut wound, but your opponent may walk away with your weapon. If it does get stuck in the ribs, and you still have ammunition, you can pull the trigger and blow out the bottom rib. Then it will come right out."

"Shit, man, if I still had ammo, I sure as hell wouldn't let any gooks get that close to me. Or lieutenants, either."

"Unless you have to carve your opponent's face to gain psychological advantage, you should be aiming at his gut. A good slash can disembowel him in an instant." He paused dramatically for a moment, then continued, "Now, what is the purpose of the bayonet?"

After a month, they all knew the answer to that one. "To kill," the men shouted, as one.

"I can't hear you."

"Kill."

"I can't hear you."

"KILL!"

"And what is the purpose of a soldier?"

"To kill!"

"I can't hear you!"

"Kill."

"I *still* can't hear you!"

"KILL!"

"And don't you forget it, because if you don't try to kill your enemy, he'll try to kill you. It's you or him. And remember the two most important elements in the art of killing: surprise, and aggression.

Sergeant Hawkins, standing a good fifteen feet away, tossed the rifle across the platform. It traveled in a low arc, like a fastball. Lieutenant Wakefield plucked it out of the air and leaped forward all in one deft motion, charging into the stands. There was instantaneous pandemonium as the bleacher vacated, and men scrambled and jumped for their lives. The lieutenant slashed his way right up to the highest tier. There was not a man left on the elevated benches. He was king of the mountain.

"Take a break."

Wally low crawled out from under the stands, peered at Tony from under a dislodged helmet liner. "He sure knows how to get his point across."

****

"Com-pan-ee-ee-eep, fall in."

The parade ground erupted into olive drab as trainees poured out from under the trees and dressed-right-dressed in company formation.

Lieutenant Wakefield waited until the last man stopped moving. "Very good."

"Uh, oh. Our lieuy's gone blooey, man."

"We ain't never done anythin' right the fust time."

"What do you mean? We've never done anything right."

"Maybe he's sick."

The lieutenant stood as erect as always. "Captain Maxwell, as commanding officer of this company, is happy with your progress. Therefore, he has seen fit to allow (against my recommendation, I might add) — " He paused, as if it hurt him to say it. " — weekend privileges."

He was almost bowled over by the loud cheer, and it was several minutes before he regained control of his men.

"He has ordered that forty-eight hour passes should be issued, commencing Friday at sixteen hundred hours, to those deserving of such privileges. But — " He paused again and surveyed the troops. "There are certain restrictions that will be imposed, and certain obligations that must be met."

"The army don't never give nuthin' away for

nuthin'."

"Anyone already assigned for either KP or orderly room duty must be here to perform that duty." Several groans sounded out in the crowd. "Secondly, every one of you *will* look and behave like soldiers. Dress uniforms *will* be worn, shoes and brass *will* be shined, barrack and personal inspections *will* be performed. Haircuts *will* be given." Now everyone groaned. Tony thought about the black stubs that were just beginning to curl. "And thirdly, no one, I repeat, no one will get off-base privileges unless every man in this company has signed the bond withdrawal form. Right now we have ninety-five percent compliance, and I want to thank you men for your patriotism. But some of you out there have refused to back their country. So, if there is so much as one man among you who does not sign up for a bond, this entire company *will* forfeit their passes."

The resultant groans were coupled with dirty looks. Tony chewed his lip with a pang of guilt. He stared straight ahead, and kept quiet.

Lieutenant Wakefield, however, added corporeality to his guilt. "The following names are those whose signatures have not been recorded — " Of the fifteen names that he read, in full, only Tony's and Wally's were from the Second Platoon. The men standing around them made threatening grunts and gestures. "Now, I'm going to give you a ten-minute break. During that time I expect all you men who want passes to convince those who are responsible for preventing them, of the error of their ways. Remember, this is not just for the good of your country, it's for your own good as well. Fall out."

Jackson was the first to speak his mind. "All right, Giovanni, are you gonna sign up, or am I gonna hafta break both your arms?"

"You and whose army?"

"Me and my army."

Tony swallowed as some of his cronies crowded around.

Wally stepped closer and glared right into his face. "When you're talking to my friend, you're talking to me."

"And when you're talkin' to me, you're talkin' to *my* friends." Jackson glanced around at his entourage.

Tony said in a hushed voice, "Uh, Wally, I think things are getting out of hand."

But Tom cut in between Wally and Jackson. "Hey, cut the small talk. We can't solve anything by acting like animals. Look guys, I know you don't want any bonds, and that's okay with me. And I think you should do what you want. But we're supposed to be part of a team, and if you don't play ball with the lieutenant, we're all going to suffer. So how about taking out the

bond — just to keep peace in the family?"

"How about a black eye?" Jackson said in a gritty voice.

"Y'all want to go on pass your own selves, doncha?" said Hank.

"Wait a minute, man. Wait a minute. Don't think you can hold me responsible because that jerk of a lieutenant made up some stupid rules. My not taking a bond has nothing to do with keeping you from getting that pass. It's his twisting the conditions around to suit himself. Put the blame where it belongs."

"That's right," Tony agreed. "Can't you see that you're being used?"

Logic was in short demand. "It's all your fault."

"What are we supposed to do? Go tell the lieutenant to shove it up his ass?"

"Yeah."

"Ain't nobody gon' getta passes lessen you smarten up."

"I t'ink it best for we if you signature paper."

"We all gotta stick together, that's what brotherhood's all about."

"Yeah."

"What the hell, is six dollars and seventy-five cents gonna kill ya?"

"Yeah."

"Hold it. Hold it. *Hold it.* HOLD IT." Wally threw his hands up over his head; his face was twisted into a wreath of anger. His outburst cowed even the outspoken Jackson for a second, and Wally plunged right into the silent opening with the speed and spike of a lancer. "You guys better just cut it the fuck out. I'm going to say this once and for all, loud enough so you can hear it, and simple enough so you can understand it. I don't want a bond, I don't need a bond, and I am not — repeat — *not* going to buy a bond, under any kind of threat. And if you want to know why, it's because that's my choice. If you aren't smart enough to figure out that this half-assed second lieuy is pulling your strings like a Howdy Doody doll, then you have no business carrying around that dead weight called gray matter. Now you may as well just shut the fuck up because I . . . am . . . not . . . buying . . . a . . . bond."

He pushed his way through the throng of angry men, showing no fear of them, the lieutenant, or the consequences.

Jackson stabbed a thick finger at Tony. "What're you gonna do, punk?"

Wally was a tough act to follow. Tony squared his shoulders and did his best to make an impressive exit. "Well, I'll think about it."

****

The bulk of Mike Farnsworth threw a shadow across Tony's letter. He knew something was wrong as soon as he saw the round, perturbed face. "Hey, Mike, what's the matter?"

Mike just stood there, twisting his cap in his hand. He had just come from Sergeant Hawkins' room.

Hank leaned over the edge of his bunk. "The ole sarge chew yore ass out?"

Mike pursed his lips once or twice. "No, he said I got new orders."

Tony swung his feet onto the floor. "What do you mean, new orders? What kind of orders?"

"He says I'll be leavin' in the morning."

"What?"

He jerked his head to the side with every pause. "He says I gotta go . . . to a special training outfit . . . 'cause I can't keep up . . . you know . . . with the rest of the guys."

Tony tried to find something to say, but could not.

"Shit, man, if that isn't a kick in the butt."

Tom tucked his T-shirt into his boxer shorts, smoothed out the material. "Actually, it's the best thing for him. He's just not cut out for the regular army."

"Stop putting him down!" Tony yelled, losing his temper. "At least he tried."

"I wasn't putting him down. I didn't mean it that way, Mike. It's just that you'll be better off if you, you know, can go along at your own speed. Here you'll only be a hindrance."

Wally jumped up and poked a stiff finger into Tom's chest. "It's easy for you to be smug because you think you're a big shot. All your life someone's been telling you how great you were. Well, you're nothing but a big phony."

"Hey, take it easy." Tom backed away, glaring from one to the other. "There's no sense getting steamed up over it."

Wally's hands were balled into fists, his eyes locked on Tom's.

"Listen, I . . . I better go pack my things. I . . . I'm leaving in the morning."

"Mike, do you want some help?" Tony said.

"No, I can do it myself. Thanks. I'll see you later." Mike wandered down the aisle to his bunk, head drooping. Tony watched him go, his letters forgotten.

Dimly, from the other end of the barrack, Tony heard, "What's the matter, Mikey? Can't make the grade? What's the old man gonna do, send you to the circus for the elephant act? Why don't you take that little red headed queer with you?"

Wally was galloping down the aisle in a flash. Tony trailed after him. "Hey, man, you got something on your mind besides the top of your skull?"

Jackson eyed him warily, running his tongue over his teeth and under his upper lip. "Hoppy the happy hippo here is leavin' us. Goin' to a special place for special people. F Troop, I

think they call it."

Wally's face was red, his mouth a sneer. "How about laying off him and minding your own fucking business?"

Jackson plugged a cigarette into his mouth, drew deeply, and blew smoke toward Wally. "How about you takin' your own advice, shorty?"

Wally's hand swept up from the waist and slapped the cigarette out of Jackson's mouth. He looked startled for one fraction of a second, then reached out and shoved Wally hard in the chest. Wally took a step backward, caught himself, and brought up his other hand tightened into a fist. It contacted resoundingly with Jackson's cheek. His head had hardly been knocked backward when another fist buried itself in his belly. He bent forward with a woof.

Wally wrapped his arms about Jackson's neck in a headlock that stifled the grunt in his throat. With pressure on the windpipe, Wally throttled him from side to side, slamming him first into one bunk and then into the other. After the fifth or sixth collision, Jackson's knees buckled. Wally pushed him away. He crashed to the floor, sprawling, and worked his mouth silently like a fish out of water.

The knot of men who had rushed to see the excitement was cut apart by a burly black apparition. Sergeant Hawkins stared for a moment, nodded faintly. "I don't know what's goin' on here, but I want it broken up. You men have any differences, I'll take care of 'em. There ain't no fightin' allowed in the army."

After he left, there was a faint glimmer of a smile on his protruding lips.

Jackson started to make gasping sounds as he began to suck air into his tortured lungs. Wally stood on the balls of his feet, fists clenched, his hair raised like an angry dog's. When he turned to walk back to his bunk, the throng split apart like magic, opening a path that allowed plenty of room.

"Mike, are you all right? Do you need any help?"

"I'm helping him, Tony." Mike's bunkmate, Reds, put a soft hand on Mike's arm.

Mike said simply, "Thanks, we can manage."

The barrack hummed with word of the big fight, and several men ran downstairs to relay the news.

"Ah don't think Sergeant Hawkins likes that boy Jackson. Haw haw haw haw haw."

Wally lay on his back, hands behind his head, staring sightlessly at the bottom of Tom's mattress. "I know I don't like him."

Tom dusted off his hands. "That's what I'd have done to him if I had gotten to him first."

"You take a bunch of guys who don't want to

be taken, you put them in a place where they don't want to be, you make them learn something they don't want to know, you work them half to death, starve them, treat them like dirt, rough them up whenever you feel like it, then cram them into a room with thirty other guys, and expect them to get along like bosom buddies. That's like dumping a bunch of half crazed cats into a canvas sack, throwing them into the river, and expecting them to purr at each other. That's funny. What the hell are we in the army for if it isn't to fight? That's really funny."

Tom said, "It's not just funny, it's fucking ridiculous.

****

Tony stood firmly at ease, with elbows bent and hands dug into the small of his back, feeling slightly uncomfortable in his overstarched fatigues. His right foot barely touched his open footlocker. He hazarded a downward glance for the tenth time in two minutes, just to make certain that everything was properly displayed. Light shone through crystal clear windows. On this barrack inspection depended the weekend passes.

"Ten-*hut!*" Sergeant Hawkins came to rigid attention. Every man in the room stiffened with him. Tony stared straight ahead. Nowhere could he see even a speck of dust.

Lieutenant Wakefield swept across the dazzling, highly buffed floor and straight down the aisle. He did not look left or right, he did not inspect a single bunk. He stopped precisely in the middle of the room, executed a sharp left turn, removed the tray and closed the lid of the closest footlocker, and stepped on top of it. On his right hand he wore a white glove, the index finger of which he ran across the top of the rafter.

"Dirt," he said, and left.

****

Tony and Wally and four others reclined on wooden chairs in the orderly room.

"I can't believe they're making such a big fucking deal about a lousy bond. It's not like the country's going bankrupt."

"Yeah, you'd think they have to pay out of their own pocket what we don't buy."

"Quiet over there," First Sergeant Abrams called out. "You'll get your chance to talk when you go in to see the CO."

Tony shuffled in his seat. The minutes dragged on. Captain Maxwell's door opened and Private Benson, licking his lips and glancing sideways, emerged. He walked by without a word, and went out the screen door.

"Giovanni," the sergeant said gruffly. Tony jumped to his feet. "Do you know how to report?"

"Yes, sir. I mean, yes, sergeant."

"Then do it and make it snappy. You're keeping the captain waiting."

Tony knocked delicately on the wooden door. "Permission to enter."

A muffled voice said, "Come in."

Tony opened the door, stepped inside, and closed it smoothly behind him. He swallowed hard. "Private Giovanni reporting, sir."

"Stand at ease." Captain Maxwell pushed some papers around on his desk, then leaned back comfortably in his swivel chair. "Giovanni, I've taken the time to look up your records, and I don't mind saying that I like what I see. You've got one of the highest scores in the aptitude test, you've got excellent grades in class, you're one of our best marksmen, and your preliminary PT scores are — well, you're in good shape. Aside from that — little incident — after your arrival, you appear to be behaving well. Sergeant Hawkins recommends you highly."

Tony shifted uncomfortably.

"What I'm leading up to is that you show promise, both for yourself and for the army. The army needs men like you. The army needs officers like you. A man who is strong, smart, and responsible is the kind of man we want at OCS." He paused for effect. Tony stared blankly. "But for right now you're still a trainee. You still have things to learn, about the military, and about yourself. And one of the most important things you must learn is that you're part of a system — a vast, complicated, almost incomprehensible system. And while you may not grasp it all now, there is a rhyme and reason for everything. Do you understand what I'm saying?"

Tony swallowed again, tried hard not to let his eyes wander. "No, sir. I don't think I do."

The captain leaned forward and placed his elbows on the desk. His expression never changed, his eyes never moved. "Well, let me put it another way. When you leave here, when you are assigned to your final duty station, whether it be stateside, or Germany, or Vietnam, you'll find that the army has a certain way of doing things. And no matter where you go, those things will be done the same way. It's what we call uniformity. The military system may not be the best, but it has a record for effectiveness.

"By the same token, when you're in the field, under fire, as you may be, you might be given orders which will not seem to make much sense. But if they don't make sense to *you*, they *will* make sense to someone higher up, someone with an overview of the situation. You may question those orders in your own mind — *but you will still carry them out*. Your understanding is not necessary to an operation's success; indeed, you may not even know what constitutes success. But your performance *is* necessary. Your only responsibility is that you obey a command, immediately and without question, otherwise the object of that command will fail. Is *that* much clear?"

"Uh, yes, sir."

"Good. Now, how does this affect you and me, here and now? You are here as a trainee, to learn the military way. Part of what we are trying to teach you is to accept orders. And if you are to become an officer, the first thing you must learn is that taking orders is as important as giving them and having them obeyed. One of the orders of this post is that every man takes out a savings bond. There are many reasons for this order, none of which might make much sense to you, or even to me for that matter. But it's something that has to be done, an order which, for the sake of command and uniformity, must be carried out. I need to have one hundred percent participation so I can show my superiors that I am doing my job — and that way I get to keep *my* job. I can't afford to let a handful of men make waves that may reach the wrong shore. I need your cooperation. And if I don't get it, I will have to use force. Now, do you understand?"

By the very premise of his prattle, Tony could not understand it. But one thing was abundantly clear: he was about to get splashed by his own wave. "Yes sir."

"Good. Then all you have to do is sign this form and go about your business." Captain Maxwell pushed a sheet of paper across the desk. A pen lay on top of it. "Not only will I personally see to it that you get your pass, but I'll make sure that you are taken off any special duty for this weekend. That way you can go to town and have a good time. That's worth it, isn't it?"

My God, he's bribing me. "Yes, sir."

"Then you do understand that your signature can get us both out of a bind? You get your pass, I get off the hook. *Your* superior is happy, *my* superior is happy. And everyone comes out on top."

Tony picked up the pen and signed. He felt as if he were signing away his life.

****

"Hey, Tony. Shake a leg if you want to catch that five o'clock bus." Wally waited impatiently at the top of the stairs, urging Tony with his hands. They were practically alone in the barrack.

Tony tucked in his shirttail and adjusted his belt so that the brass tip barely protruded through the buckle. "The line out there's a mile long, and can't get any longer. You go ahead. I'll catch up with you."

"Okay, man, but hurry. I don't want to have

to run for that bus in this heat. The last thing I want to do once I'm out of this god forsaken hole is to work up a good sweat."

"I'll be right behind you." He sat down on his footlocker.

Wally descended the stairs two at a time.

Tying his shoes, besides making sure that the loops and laces were the same length, Tony was careful not to scuff the floor. The linoleum was as slick as a skating rink. An impromptu sliding contest had resulted in sending the winner, Jorgenson, thirty-three feet from the starting line. He would have gone farther had he not disappeared down the stairs, bumping on his buttocks all the way. The only injuries were split sides from howls of laughter.

"What's your problem, Giovanni?"

Sergeant Hawkins had never looked so resplendent. His full dress uniform glittered with brass buttons, badges, and battle ribbons. The black brim of his hat looked like patent leather.

"Well, uh, I'm having trouble with this tie, sarge. Never was any good with knots. I always wear the kind you just clip onto your collar. Could you, uh, give me a hand?"

Deep, ebony eyes stabbed at Tony like icicles. He practically shivered in the cold. But in a moment they softened and melted. "If I find out you're pullin' my leg, son, you'll live to regret it." He took the black material in his hand and gave it a yank. "I'm only gonna show you this once."

"Yes, sergeant." Well, he did say he was going to be his mother.

Sergeant Hawkins flipped the material through his fingers, and drew the tie tight around Tony's neck. "And take that hat off. The order of the day is for cunt caps. Only officers and NCOs can wear dress hats."

"Thanks, sarge." Tony put his brimmed dress hat back into his footlocker and took out the soft felt cap. Like an envelope, he split it down the middle and fitted it snugly on his newly shaven head.

"Now git the hell outa here. An' don't forget to run when you hit the dirt."

"Right, sarge." Tony started for the stairs. "And thanks." He ran smack into Wally. "Oh, sorry I took so long, I — "

"Never mind," he panted, his uniform already wet with perspiration. "The bastard wouldn't let me have my pass because he said I had the wrong headgear. Can you believe this chicken shit?"

He rebounded off Sergeant Hawkins' barrel belly and almost fell down. He recovered himself and looked up at his platoon sergeant. "Hey, sarge, you'd better change your hat or you're not going to get your pass."

Chapter 49

The air in Augusta was pure, hot, and humid, but the atmosphere was slow and thick: the personification of the south, where people lived slowly, easily, happily, and more assuredly. Despite the influx of khaki-clad soldiers, outnumbering the civilians four to one, the town remained peaceful and backwater.

"Haw haw haw haw haw." Hank took a bite out of a sandwich that practically demolished it. "This is the best gol-durn hotdog I ever did have. Haw haw haw haw haw."

Tony wiped mustard off his lips with a napkin. "That's what you said about the other two."

"An' Ah 'spect Ah'll say the same about the next."

Tom nodded and smiled with true southern hospitality at the good citizens making their way unobtrusively through the military mob. "You can't possibly eat another one, can you?"

"Man, you're going to be one sick honcho tomorrow." Slurping loudly, Wally drained the soda from the bottom of the plastic cup, then took out the straw and started munching ice.

"Y'all ain't seen nuthin' yet," Hank burped. "Onct Ah git ma stomach satisfied, Ah'm gonna start in on the beer an' throw me a real zinger. An' none o' that watered down three-point-two, neither. Ah'm goin' for the real stuff."

"Don't start howling until we find a place to sleep it off, man." Wally veered to a trashcan and dropped in the empty cup. "I don't think the MPs would appreciate us carrying a drunken rebel through the gate."

The tree-lined street swarmed with more than one training company that was out on its first weekend pass: thronging into five-and-ten-cent stores, clambering into diners, forcing money into soda machines, doing, acting out, having fun, and in many cases, creating a public nuisance.

"Hey, how about this place?" Tony pointed at the unpretentious sign hanging above the revolving door: Augusta Town House. The only adornment on the eight-story stone and brick building was a projecting scalloped roof.

Hank crumpled the mustard-covered cellophane in his hand and stuffed it into a pocket. "Don't look like much of a *hotel* to me."

Tony shrugged. "Well, I don't know. I've never stayed in a hotel before."

"One's as good as another as far as I'm concerned," Wally said.

"What the hell." Tom tossed the remains of his Coke at a nearby trashcan. It missed, bounced off the tree to which it was braced, and spilled ice on the patch of grass along the curb. He headed for the door. "Let's go in."

Tony circulated through the glass door into a small lobby that was deliciously cool. The red motif included a tiled floor, carpeted stairs, velvet papered walls, and lacy drapes. The desk clerk was dressed in a red uniform.

"Can I help you gentlemen?"

Hank eyed the colonnaded archway separating the lounge and bar, where soft lighting masked milling patrons. "Ah think Ah'm gonna like this place."

"At least we won't have to carry you far." Wally stepped up to the front desk. "Yes, do you have any vacancies?"

"For the four of you?"

"Yes."

"Well, a single room would be twelve dollars. But you can have a double for sixteen, and for twenty-two you can have a room with two double beds." Looks were exchanged, shoulders shrugged. "We're being paid peanuts, so I guess we'll live like sardines." Wally shelled out five-fifty.

Tom put six dollars on the counter, picked up the two quarters. "We've been sleeping together for a month. I guess another night isn't going to hurt."

Tony and Hank added their share.

The clerk smiled at Tom. Middle-aged wrinkles furrowed his brow. "Are you from Boston?"

"Cambridge, to be exact."

"I was up there once visiting my daughter and son-in-law." He scooped up the money and put it in a drawer. "They all talk like that up there, except my daughter, born and bred in Tennessee. But the grandchildren have a New England accent that can't be broken."

"Uh, where do we sign in?" Tony asked.

"No need." The clerk took a key ring off the pegboard. "Now, gentlemen, I only have two keys so you'll have to share them. If one of you gets locked out, come and let me know and I can lend you a spare, but you'll have to bring it right back. If you need more towels and wash-cloths, just let me know and I'll have a maid send them right up. Enjoy your stay."

The self-service elevator was waiting to whisk them to the seventh floor.

Their room was at the end of a long, broad hallway, thickly carpeted and gaily papered with springtime flowers.

"Lardy mercy." Hank was first to enter the finely furnished room. "Damn if we ain't got our own air conditioner." He wasted no time in turning it on full blast.

"What did you expect, man? This is civilization, not an army barrack." Wally cut short his exploration at the first bed and flopped onto it like a plastic mannequin, lower legs hanging over the edge. His muffled voice spoke through the quilted bedspread. "Jesus Christ, is this comfy."

"Hey, we even have a television set." Tom switched it on right away, then started undressing.

While the tubes were warming, Tony checked out the latrine — er, bathroom — found plenty of bright, fluffy, folded linen, and complimentary soap. The built-in tub had glass shower doors.

"Privacy. I don't believe it." With pure delight, Tony sank into the cushion of an over-stuffed chair. He laid his overseas hat across the arm like a doily, loosened his tie, and opened the top button of his shirt.

Hank stretched out against the mahogany headboard. "Turn that dayam thing off. Ain't nothing but commercials anyhow."

Tom spun the dial and caught a game show in progress. The woman on the screen was cheering and laughing and jumping up and down. "Dumb broad." The news was only local, so finally he switched off the set.

Wally moved to the window and parted the curtain. "Hey, we're in luck. We've got a movie theater right across the street."

"What's playing?" Tom peered out another window, now wearing only his skivvies.

"I can't quite make it out."

"Listen to that banshee saw wood." Tony tossed his hat, landing it squarely on Hank's belly. He made no notice. "I thought you said it was right across the street."

Tom let go of the curtain and plopped onto the flower print sofa. "It's about a hundred meters down."

"Will you stop with the metric bullshit? There's no one to impress around here." Wally perched like a bird on the sofa arm and removed his shoes. "That's three hundred thirty feet," Tony calculated.

"I can see that. I got eyes. But how the hell do you figure it out so fast?"

"It's easy." Tony sauntered toward the window. "A yard is thirty-six inches, right? Well, a meter is thirty-nine point three seven — almost forty. That's pretty close to ten percent more than a yard. So, a hundred meters is a hundred yards plus ten, which you get by moving the decimal point over one place and adding the two. Multiply by three and you have three hundred thirty feet. Or, you can convert a hundred yards to three hundred feet first, and add thirty. You can also reverse the process by subtracting ten percent, although there's a slight error there. But ten percent is close enough and you can do it in your head. And the movie is *In Harm's Way*, starring John Wayne and Kirk Douglas."

"Great. Not only a goddamn war picture, but a year old at that."

A knock on the door was followed by a high-pitched voice. "Maid service."

"I'll get it." Tony raced for the door.

"Omigod." Tom scooped up his clothes and dashed into the bathroom, slamming the door behind him.

Four men from their own platoon poured into the room, laughing, followed by three others from other platoons in the company: they had been on the train from Philadelphia. Holloway and Farley leaped onto the bed, landing on either side of Hank, and jounced him until he opened his eyes.

"We got a couple of rooms right down the hall," said Paulson.

Tom pranced out of the bathroom with his pants and shirt back on. "If I'd known there was going to be a party I would have dressed for the occasion."

"Then you better don your duds," said Albright. " 'Cause we're gonna blast this berg an' try an' drown our sorrows in beer."

"Haw haw haw haw haw. Lead me to the trough, Ah'm a thirsty cowboy."

Wally stretched out on the sofa, propped a pillow under his head. "I can see nothing manly or rewarding in surrounding myself with animals bereft of their reason, and making myself insensate. Leave me out of your bacchanalian brawl."

"Aaagghh, you're just too damn cheap. Why don't you spend some of that bond money you cheated the government out of?" Tom pulled on his socks and shoes, and knotted his tie. "Hey, Tony, how about you?"

"No thanks. I don't like being out of control."

Tom disappeared out of the door after the others. "You're on your own, then."

After several minutes of quietude, Tony said, "So what are you going to do tonight?"

"Well, I noticed a phone booth in the lounge, so I thought I'd make a few calls to the home front. Then, I don't know. I guess I'll just take it easy. How about you?"

"Well, I was kind of hoping to go to the movies."

"If you're asking me, it's a date. As much as I hate to admit it, I like John Wayne. But I've got to make those phone calls first."

Wally got five dollars worth of change and camped out in the phone booth. Tony turned in one of the keys. "Our friends went out and forgot it, and Wally and I will be together." The clerk accepted it with a smile and put it on the board. "And I noticed a candy machine in the lounge. Will it give change for a quarter?"

"No, you have to use dimes."

Tony handed him a dollar bill; the clerk

counted out ten dimes. The first Almond Joy tasted so good that he bought another. It seemed ages since he had eaten chocolate. By the time Wally finished inflating the stock in Bell Telephone, Tony had gone through two more candy bars — and had three more in his pocket.

"How's home?"

"Still there. Can you beat this?" Wally held up an issue of *Time Magazine*. On the cover was a crude bust of General William C. Westmoreland, and a diagonal banner with the proclamation "Man of the Year." "I found it in the lounge."

Tony flipped through the pages until he saw a photograph captioned "US. Marines in Action in Vietnam." An open rice paddy stretched beneath a limitless blue sky, while jungle-fatigued marines, crouched behind a dike, peered over bayoneted M-14's.

"This is the real thing, man. No script, and no take two. And these aren't exactly your John Wayne types, either."

Tony expected to see rough, rugged, bearded soldiers. Instead, the photographs showed kids: gaunt, fair-skinned, hollow-cheeked, and scared. These soldiers fought real battles, showed real fear, shot real bullets, bled real blood, died with unremitting finality. Winner takes all, the loser . . . loses. They had nothing to gain by their action, their valor, their privation, their struggle, their caring. They were not heroes — they were boys in the act of becoming men. That was their only reward.

"I guess Westmoreland's doing a pretty good job," Tony commented dryly.

"So was Hitler when he was *Time's* "Man of the Year" in '39."

****

"Is he alive?"

Hank lay on the bathroom floor in a pool of vomit and urine. His shirtfront was covered with crusty puke. And there was a lump and a dab of blood on his forehead where he had ricocheted off the toilet bowl.

Tony rolled him over onto his back, and started undoing his clothes. "Barely." With some difficulty he removed the shirt and pants and threw them into the tub with hot, soapy water. He used a wet towel to soak up the mess on the tiled floor.

Wally hung back by the door, holding his mouth. "Man, he was really riding the china chalice last night. Sounded like a cross between a diesel truck and a fog horn."

"Yeah, he woke me up, too." Tony slipped a wadded towel under his head, and threw a sheet over him. "He's too heavy to move. We'll have to leave him here."

"I'm sure glad you know what to do. If it had

been me, man, I'd have had to let him wallow in his own filth. Shit, I almost threw up watching you."

Tony snickered, and washed his hands in the sink. "Well, I've got a friend at home who tips a few too many every once in a while."

"Why do people do that to themselves?"

"I don't know. I've never understood it."

Wally tucked in his shirt and tightened his belt. "And the worst of it is, he'll probably brag about it later."

"When he should be ashamed of himself."

"Ashamed? He ought to be downright humiliated. He made a goddamn ass out of himself, man. And we don't know what went on *before* he got in."

"Maybe Tom can tell us."

"If we ever find him." Wally opened the door and almost tripped over Tom. He sprawled across half the hallway, flat on his back. "Well, at least his clothes are clean."

They each grabbed a leg and dragged him into the room. Tom's snores never missed a beat. Tony threw a sheet over him, and closed the door behind him. "Peas in a pod."

****

Tony lay on his back on the tall, green grass along the tranquil levee of the Savannah River, inhaling the fragrance of the flowers with each deep breath, and watching white lazy clouds drift across the blue sky. A cool breeze wafted through the leaves of elms and beeches, crinkling, and in the treetops, unseen birds chirped gaily as they flitted lightninglike from branch to branch as if in answer to some secret rite.

"You know something, man? I just figured out something about you."

"Oh? What's that?"

"You're too damned quiet. You don't talk about things. You never sit in on bull sessions and chew the fat."

"I'm not a cow."

"But you don't initiate conversation. You never give your opinion. You don't participate. You just sit and listen."

Tony laughed out loud. "I found out a long time ago that I can't learn anything by talking because I already know everything I have to say."

Wally was silent for a full two minutes. "But don't you think about things?"

Tony watched the clouds in the sky and fancied sculptures out of them. He tried to let his mind run free — as free as the broad Savannah sweeping timelessly past his bare feet. It neither knew nor cared about the bank it flowed past. It just moved relentlessly onward, toward the vast sea: never stopping, never slowing, never minding.

"Sure."

A dozen clouds floated past.

"Don't you ever feel a . . . need . . . to talk about what you feel?"

Tony rolled over onto his side and scrunched his hips into a comfortable dent. Tiny black ants scurried haphazardly across the brown dirt, zigging and zagging and touching antennae as if they were all part of a miniature demolition derby.

"No."

He took out another Almond Joy: his supply of dimes had dwindled at the same rate that his sugar intake had risen. He tore off the wrapper and placed it on the ground. The candy bar did not last long.

"Have you ever heard of feedback training?"

It was not long before an ant discovered the plastic wrapper and climbed onto it. Delicately, it approached a dark smear of melted chocolate, probing with its tongue.

"No."

"Well, let's say you have this thought, or idea, rolling around in your mind. It may have come from something you read, or picked up in conversation, or it may have just popped into your head all of a sudden, like a clear moment of insight. It's not true or false, or right or wrong, or up or down — it's just a naked idea, without form or direction. Outside your own mind it doesn't even exist. Now, if you don't do anything with that idea, if you just let it sit idle, it never becomes anything. It exists in its original form — half grown, incomplete, with little chinks out of it that need smoothing over. It never reaches a state of true enlightenment. It may even be forgotten. But, if you talk about that idea with other people, they can give you their thoughts and opinions about it. You can observe it from different angles, see it in a different light, study it from different points of view. Now, not only does the original thought exist in more than one mind, but you can change it, reformulate it, understand all its dimensions. This is called feedback."

The lone ant lapped at the brown pool of sweetness, seemingly mesmerized by it. Its legs were still, its antennae unmoving. Only its tongue lapped at the puddle, taking solitary nourishment.

"Facts are immutable."

"I'm not talking about facts, man. I'm talking about ideas. An idea is something that is created in the human mind, and therefore must have all the inconsistencies and misconceptions and frailties of that mind. Ideas don't arise fully formed, any more than a man is born fully mature and all knowing. An idea needs to ripen. It is only the seed of something larger. Take a handful of snow, pack it tight with your hands, roll it down a hill. It gathers more and more snow, increases its dimensions, and when it gets to the bottom of the hill, you have a much larger idea, a more rounded idea, a more perfectly formed idea. But the hill of human experience has no bottom — it goes on and on, forever, as long as there are people to pass the idea along. And as it grows, it's in a constant state of change and refinement. But if you never talk about your ideas, they never have the opportunity to become more fully formed. An idea is a living thing; it needs to be nurtured, and fed; otherwise it becomes stunted, or warped, and you end up with an idea that is no longer valid except in the dream world in which it was imagined. It has no permanence, no existence in reality. That's why you have to talk about things — all things. Discussion means growth. And if you don't continue to grow, you stagnate and die."

The ant backed away from its food, started walking slowly across the plastic wrapper. While two of its fellows walked in slow circles over the ground, it retreated the way it had come.

"Well, I think I'm still in the learning process. I feel that I need to know a whole lot more before I go around shooting off my mouth. After all, common sense is based on experience. The more experience you have, the more common sense you have, and the better equipped you are to deal with the world."

"No, man, because you'll always be in the learning process, throughout your whole life. You'll never reach this imaginary plateau where all of a sudden you know everything there is to know. Exchanging ideas is a process of learning, not the final product. Take me, for example. I like to talk. I like to think I have things to say. And I enjoy feedback. I want people to know what I'm thinking because it may be important to them as well as to me."

The solitary ant found its brothers. They engaged in a strange dance, touching each other with their antennae, stroking, tasting, passing messages, communicating.

"But there are times when it pays to keep quiet."

"It may seem that way when you get a negative response. But you still have to say what's on your mind. How else are you going to tell people who you are? And how else are you going to learn who *they* are?"

"But some people just don't care."

"Ignore them. If they are so wrapped up in themselves, they don't have the time for sharing and human understanding. It's their loss. Keep away from people who try to tell you how to live your life when their own is fucked up. And run from those bastards who can't wait to find fault with you so they can look good by comparison. Those are the jerks who talk the most and have the least to say — a diarrhea of words and a constipation of ideas."

"Present company excepted."

Wally ignored him. "I mean the people who talk about what's wrong with the world, but are afraid to do anything to change it. The paranoids who believe in this mysterious 'they' who control their lives. *They* raised the price of bread. *They* flunked me out of school. *They* gave me a ticket for going through a red light. *They* passed laws, *they* caused inflation, *they* are polluting the atmosphere, *they* are causing smog, radiation, and power shortages. It's always *they*, and never I or we. Well, listen, man, *we* are in control of our destiny, each and every one of us. *We* have to do something about this world of ours, because *we* want to live in it. And *I* am going to be a part of that *we*. *I* am going to accomplish something. I want to be a part of that great gestalt that does something to right the wrongs, to correct the mistakes, to educate society."

"To bend steel in his bare hands, to change the course of mighty rivers, to leap tall buildings in a single bound."

"That's right. I want to be a part of changing the river of humanity. I want to see it flow along with as little resistance as possible. I want to see people treated as decent human beings, I want to see an end of war, of hunger, of strife, of bloodshed, of ignorance, of aggression. I want to be a part of all that."

"And how do you expect to change something you know nothing about?"

"What's that supposed to mean, man?"

"Look, Wally, I know you're older than I am, but you're not exactly the old man and the sea. Granted, you're educated and well read. But everything you know has been learned vicariously. How much of life have you actually *seen*? You haven't traveled around the world, or even across the country. Your whole life has been spent in school, in one tiny, insignificant corner of the universe. Books may bring the world to you, but they don't take you out into the world. How much do you really know about other countries, other peoples? Our society represents only one tenth of the population of the planet — "

"One fifteenth."

"Whatever. The point I'm making is that maybe you should encounter more of the world before you make judgments about it. Now, I'm not saying I agree with everything that's being done in this country, but I will allow that our elected political figures have access to more information than we have, and therefore should be able to make more rational evaluations."

"That is pure, unadulterated, dyed-in-the-wool turkey turds. You've been brainwashed by Establishment dribble. Your beliefs are exactly what they want you to believe. Don't let them lead you around like a blind man — "

"Now who's being paranoid?"

" — You're not a kid any more. That's the first thing they told us at the induction center, remember? You're a man now, and as a man it's up to you to make your own decisions, and stand by them. You do what you think is right, not what somebody else tells you is right. Come to your own conclusions."

"Conclusions are based on facts. What you're expressing are opinions based on emotion. You should have more faith in a system that's worked for almost two hundred years."

"I've heard it all before, man, so don't rap it back at me. If those jerks in the big white shack can't make better decisions than they've been making, they should move over and let the younger generation take over. Let's face it, man, we couldn't fuck it up any more than they already have — "

"There's that 'they' again."

"You don't have to be as old as Methuselah and hitchhike all over the goddamn country to know something's wrong. I can see that from right here. If they were running things right, I wouldn't be a fucking E-1 in the goddamn army paying for their fucking mistakes."

"Okay, so maybe everything's not hunky-dory. But life is an experience, even military life. And it just may be that, even if you don't like it, you might learn something by it."

"This is insanity, man. Use your intellect. You don't have to jump off a thousand-foot cliff to find out what's going to happen when you hit the ground."

"Maybe not, but think of the geological strata you'll see on the way down."

Tony found himself surrounded by scores of ants, streaming back and forth in a row between the candy wrapper and a nearby anthill. Every time two ants met, they paused to shake antennae at each other. Where one ant had found a single puddle of chocolate, and carried the scent home, others had discovered that the wrapper had many, many puddles.

Chapter 50

"GAS!"

The gas mask case hung at Tony's side, suspended from his neck by a canvas strap. With his left hand he ripped open the three snaps, while with the right he reached in and jerked out the mask, folded in half down the line of the nose. He flipped it open, grabbed the straps, and drew the cumbersome contraption over his face. He inhaled. Air percolated through the chemical canister in the nose, but at so slow a rate that the mask sucked in- and sealed around his face.

"Mask!" Tony was ready for the attack. Many others were not.

"Too slow," Sergeant Hawkins bellowed, hands on hips. He leered over the stopwatch in his huge, black hand. "Seven seconds. Most of you are dead by now. You gotta do this in three seconds flat, an' we're gonna stand here all day till you do. Take 'em off."

Wearily, for the tenth time, Tony removed his mask, folded the straps inside, and crammed it into the case.

"Pssst." Tom pointed to his mask case. "Leave two snaps undone, and the straps hanging out."

"GAS!"

Tony yanked out the mask, fitted it to his face, and yelled, "Mask!"

"Too slow. Take 'em off."

He had it only half way into the case when the sergeant yelled, "GAS!"

The surprise move caught Tony off guard. The straps tangled and he almost dropped the mask. He made worse time than if he had started from scratch. By the time he donned the mask, the order had already been issued to remove them.

"Listen up, men. It don't matter to me if we stay here till midnight. I ain't got anywhere ta go. But you're the ones goin' to Vietnam. You wanna live, you better be able to do this in three seconds. An' if you wanna have an afternoon break, you better do it soon. Okay, we'll do it by the book. On your mark. Get ready — "

Tony licked parched lips. His life he could save later; right now he needed a drink.

"GAS!"

In one swift, deft motion the mask leaped out of its case and jumped onto his head. The rest of the men were so in tune that "mask" came out as a liturgical response.

Sergeant Hawkins charged through the front rank like a tank through a hedgerow, knocking men aside like tenpins. He caught a man in the third row, grabbed his mask by the protruding nose canister, and tore it off his face. The straps pulled loose, but not before pulling the man forward into the sergeant's fist. While he doubled over, hands on solar plexus, Sergeant Hawkins slammed the mask on the ground. Dry dust billowed from the impact.

"Don't you dare say 'mask' till those straps are cinched in place and you take a breath to check the seals. Now git down an' give me twenty."

Despite the fact that Jefferson had not yet restarted his inhalation cycle, he fell to his knees and got into the ready position. It was a full minute before he started a controlled breathing, and another before he slowly began to do pushups, counting off each one.

"Now let that be a lesson to you. You men aren't here to play games, you're here to learn how to save your own ass. S-Y-O-A. When poison gas is dropped on you, all the cheatin' in the world ain't gonna git that mask on in time. Only practice will. *Jefferson, I can't here you.* This ain't no high school. You don't write ponies on your hand an' laugh behind the teacher's back. You don't learn what I teach you, they ship you home in a pine box. The stakes in this game are life. An' when you lose, you lose for good. Okay, take 'em off. An' you git ta your feet an' no more funny business. Now let's see if we can git this straight before I have to send out for sleepin' bags."

Sweat poured down Tony's face, but he made no attempt to wipe it off. Every muscle was geared for —

"GAS!"

Open pouch, remove mask, pull over head. "Mask!"

Sergeant Hawkins' face remained expressionless as he glanced at the stopwatch. He walked through the platoon, tugging on straps, checking seals. Sweat beaded under the rubber and dripped down into Tony's eyes, stung cracked lips, pooled under his chin. Absently he tried to wipe it off — his hand ricocheted off plastic lenses.

"All right, take 'em off. But from now on, somebody yells 'gas,' you better git your face in that mask. All right, take ten."

The formation broke, raced for the beloved shade of the trees, and queued up in front of the water bucket. Canteen cups came out faster than any gas mask ever did. The water was warm and unflavored, but no one complained. Suffering, after all, was part of the training.

"Ah thought poison gas was outlawed by the Geneva Convention." Hank swilled water around the inside of his mouth, let some seep out between his lips, and poured a little into his hand and splashed it on his face. "How come we gotta have gas masks?"

Tom soaked up his water like a camel. "Because we're fighting an enemy that doesn't abide by the rules. They have no scruples against using gas, dumdums, punji stakes — "

"Napalm, flame throwers, saturation bombing."

" — torture, mutilation, dismemberment."

"You've been reading too much propaganda, man. That's all bullshit to scare the public and encourage enmity. You fight with what you have, and — "

"What's 'enmity'?" Hank interrupted.

"Feelings of hostility."

"And what are dumdums?" Tony wanted to

know.

"It's a bullet made outa soft lead," Hank explained, "so it flattens out when it hits something."

Tom added, "It makes a hole the size of a dime going in, and the size of a bucket going out. Geneva Convention rules require that all bullets used in warfare be steel jacketed."

"Makes a helluva mess outa your insides. We use 'em squirrel huntin', an' it sure blows them critters to kingdom come."

Tony squinted. "Doesn't that destroy the animal so there's nothing left to eat?"

"Who eats 'em? Ah jus' like ta blow 'em apart an' watch the fur fly."

"Hank, that's disgust — "

"GAS!"

Wally choked and spit water. "Shit, man, who's the fucking wise guy?"

"All right, men. Fall in," Sergeant Hawkins bellowed. "*Now!*" Metal clattered as canteen cups were stowed. "What the hell did you think, that gas attacks were only scheduled when you were standin' around with your hand on your mask? This is war, men. Things happen when you least expect it. You gotta be ready for an emergency any time, any place. An' you ain't got time to think, only to act. Now I gotta do something to make you remember. Tensh-*hut*! Right *face*! Double ti-i-i-me, *harch*!"

The platoon pealed out and started jogging along the unpaved road, gas mask cases bouncing. The sun beat down relentlessly.

"That just doesn't make sense, man."

Three miles, a cloud of dust, and a hundred degrees later, very little made sense.

"He would have found another excuse to get us running," Tom said.

"No, I mean the Geneva Convention."

"Well, that's what they call civilized warfare."

"That's a contradiction in terms, like military intelligence. What the hell's the sense of having rules for murder? If people want to be civilized, why don't they just pass a law against war?"

Tony said, "For the same reason they can't repeal the law of gravity."

"There is no gravity, man. The world sucks."
****

A rare, early evening coolness prowled the barrack, a welcome intruder, bringing with it the faint fragrance of new-mown grass. Intermittent coughing throughout the room was tangible evidence of the allergic reactions that some of the men were fighting.

"Dayam, Ah still have a headache from yestidy."

"It's called a hangover, man, and you should have a doozy." Wally's tone was unsympathetic. "You drank enough to drown a battalion."

Hank buried his head in his hands. "Shee-it. Ah didn't do nuthin' nobody else didn't do."

"Except that you did it better. And two nights in a row." Tony scratched his chin with the eraser of his pencil. "If Tom hadn't found a Laundromat, you'd have had to come back to the base naked."

"You're lucky we found you sleeping it off in that park, man."

"There you were, out like a light, under this statue of a civil war soldier. And the inscription on the monument said 'to the Confederate dead'."

"Talk about Confederate dead, man, you were as stoned as that statue and only half as alive."

Tony and Wally roared, but Hank kept hugging his temples. "Ah remember standin' under that statue, readin' the plaque, an' lookin' up at the man. Seems like Ah looked up too high, 'cause Ah fell over backwards. Ah hit the ground like a turd from a tall cow's ass, an' then Ah don't remember nuthin' till you fellers picked me up an' drug me off."

"At least you didn't start puking until we got your uniform off," Tony laughed.

"Man, you had your head so far into the toilet bowl I had to hold onto your legs so you wouldn't fall in."

"Y'all didn't hafta put the seat down on me."

Tom clap-clapped between the bunks in shorts and shower shoes. "Hey, you guys are missing the action. There's some hot stuff at the other end of the barrack."

Wally stuffed a pillow under his head. "Are you fooling around with Reds again?"

Tom leaped up onto his bunk and kicked off his footgear. "How did you guess?"

"How the hell can you keep a secret when we all live in a one-room pad? Why don't you leave the poor kid alone?"

"Aw, we're just having some fun. Besides, he likes the attention."

"Hey, he's not really, uh, homosexual, is he?" Tony sat up in his bunk.

"You want proof? Hey. Hey, Reds. Come here."

"Come on, man. Shut the fuck up and leave the kid alone."

Reds approached daintily, swiveling his hips and holding his hands up high and to the side. He smiled with uplifted cheeks, and his tongue darted past thin lips. His fatigues drooped sadly from his slender body, the tucked-in shirt hung out in billows. The belt was drawn tight around a waspish waist. "Hello, there. Did you call me?"

Tom jerked a thumb in Tony's direction. "Tony here doesn't believe you're really queer."

Reds ran his eyes up and down Tony's body. "Oh, yes, it's true. I like boys. They — do things to me. And I like doing things to them. You know, it's kind of fun being surrounded by so many husky, good looking men." His voice was sweet, and rang with melodic cadence. "I've watched you — sleeping. I've often thought of getting in bed with you some night — just to cuddle."

Tony's flesh crawled, his fists clenched. He suddenly had the urge to punch Reds in the face, to beat him to a pulp. But the thought of touching him made him cringe.

"Tell us about your boyfriend."

"Oh, *him*. I don't like him any more. He's too bossy. Wouldn't let me go out with other guys, like he owned me or something. He used to beat me up if he caught me making eyes at other boys. And he would keep me in the house for days. But I fixed him. I sneaked out one night, stayed with a friend who was real nice to me, then went and joined the army so he couldn't come after me. Now I've got men all around me."

Tony swallowed hard. "I — you're putting us on, aren't you?"

Reds grinned devilishly.

"Prove it to him, Reds," Tom taunted. "Prove you're a real queer."

"Don't you believe me?" Reds pouted. He curled his lower lip.

"I — I — all right — I believe you."

"He doesn't believe you. You'll have to prove it to him."

"How can I prove it?"

"Come over here and kiss my prick." Tom hung his penis through the hole in his shorts and dangled it between two fingers.

"In front of everybody?"

"Why not? You said you liked it."

"Well, I don't know." Reds slowly moved closer to Tom, gaze intent.

"Hey, man, leave the damn kid alone." Wally uncoiled off his bunk to full height. "Reds, don't let this joker make a fool out of you. He's just having fun at your expense."

Tony was speechless. He became aware of the abnormal stillness in the barrack. Others were watching the tableau unfold.

"Y'all let him make up his own mind."

"Come on, Reds, show us you're no liar. Come over here and kiss it." Tom twitched his penis.

Reds glanced around at the expectant throng, the corners of his mouth quivering. "Well, maybe just a little peck."

Tony was fascinated and terrified at the same time, the way he would feel at a car crash: drawn to the spectacle of blood and bodies but hoping inwardly that no one was hurt. Wally

closed his eyes and pushed his forehead against the metal frame of the bunk, muttering "Jesus Christ" over and over.

Tom scooted closer to the edge, waving his penis like a flag. "Come on, Reds. Just a little peck on the pecker. Then we'll all know you're telling the truth."

Reds' eyes were transfixed on Tom's organ. He put both hands on the mattress and pulled himself closer. He wet his lips, glanced around at the spectators, leaned close, and with a gentle pecking motion, barely a brush, he kissed it.

"Haw haw haw haw haw." The barrack burst into a wild cheer and a round of applause. Reds turned redder than his normal color, shrieked, and ran down the aisle. Jackson grabbed him by the neck as he went past, performed a 'rear take down and hold' (another class that Tony missed because he was on KP duty that day), and shoved a hand into his crotch.

"Hey, the little faggot's got a hard on. He really is queer."

Reds had learned some unarmed combat from Lieutenant Wakefield, too, and immediately went into the defensive maneuver for that hold. He let out a yell, trod heavily on Jackson's instep, stepped aside, and shoved an elbow into Jackson's solar plexus. As Jackson staggered away, Reds planted a side kick into Jackson's stomach, and he crumpled in half. Reds stood there in the ready position: legs spread apart, one toe pointed forward, the other sideways, one balled fist thrust forward in a straight-arm, the other cocked and knuckled. No one approached him.

"What the fuck is going on here?"

Sergeant Hawkins' roar of rage was followed by tomblike silence. Every man in the barrack froze, as if captured on one frame of a motion picture film that was jammed in the projector. Black, beady eyes took in the situation at a glance. "Farley, git back to your bunk. Move!"

The karate fighter melted into the slump-shouldered, pimple-faced, girlish teenager. Reds scampered to his bunk and threw himself into the covers, wailing like a lost child. The rest of the men were mannequins.

The sergeant took a deep breath, his potbelly expanded. "You men ought to be ashamed of yourself. You're supposed to be men, not children screamin' 'cootie' at some poor kid. You all know Farley's got a problem — an' I want you to leave him alone. The next man I catch foolin' around with him is gonna be rakin' the ground from six feet under. Do I make myself clear?"

Not a soul moved or uttered a sound. Somewhere a board creaked, a bedspring sprung.

"Good. An' don't forget it." He stalked into his room and slammed the door behind him.

Hank scratched his bony head. "Don't that poor Jackson never win *no* fights?"

****

Dear Tony,

I don't have much time to write, but I wanted to let you know that Daddy is in the hospital. He took sick the day before yesterday — Tuesday — and had to be rushed to Peninsular General by ambulance. He was having trouble breathing, and complained of having pains in his chest. They took him right into the emergency room, then transferred him to a private ward. I don't know how long they'll keep him in. I went down by bus and stayed with Mother, as she was very upset. When I went to see Daddy he didn't recognize me at first because they had given him some kind of pain medicine. He looks so weak and pale. I'm going to stay here until he comes home — I don't know when that will be. He's delirious most of the time, and asks for you constantly. He wants to know why you haven't been in to see him. I think he's forgotten you're in the army. . . .

****

Tony tapped ever so lightly on Sergeant Hawkins' door. It jerked open so quickly that it caught him off guard. The sergeant wore socks and shorts, and a T-shirt that was stretched wide over his ample paunch. On the television at the foot of the single bed, an announcer extolled the virtues of a new color portable, the demonstration being lost on the black and white screen.

"Giovanni, whaddaya want?"

"Well, sarge, I was wondering, uh, if you can make outgoing calls from the, uh, company phone?"

Beady eyes narrowed. "What company phone?"

"Well, you know, the one in the orderly room."

"Only official business goes out over that phone. You got official business?"

"Uh, well, not exactly. But something has come up and I've got to call home. Uh, if I can't use that phone, how about — I mean — is it all right if I slip out to the pay phone at the PX? I'll only be a couple minutes."

"Nobody leaves this building less he's got extra duty. You got extra duty?"

"Uh, no, but — "

"You want extra duty?"

"No, but I've got —

"Then you don't leave this building."

"But, sarge — "

"I said nobody, an' that means you. An' don't let me catch you tryin' ta sneak out." He slammed the door and creaked back to the bed.

Tony returned to his bunk and crawled under the single sheet. He rolled over and stared at the wall until lights-out. Much later, when the barrack simmered down to the random sounds of crinkling sheets, squeaking springs, halting snores, and bodies twisting in the heat, he rose softly from his bed. Quietly, he donned pants and shirt. He eased open the footlocker, removed the inspection tray, and scooped up all his loose change. He carried his boots in his hand.

If anyone but Jackson had been on guard duty, he would have announced his mission and gone out the front door. But with the New York bully in the day room, Tony changed his tactics. He tiptoed down the aisle past rows of sleeping recruits, to the fire escape at the back of the barrack.

The door was not locked — even the army would not lock a fire escape — but neither had it been opened very often. The wood was swelled into place by the constant humidity, and it took a considerable jar to free it. It came loose with a wrench followed by the creak of unoiled hinges.

The amount of movement picked up, several men rolling over or punching new holes in their pillows. He stepped outside and pulled the door partway closed, but did not latch it. From the railed, wooden platform he climbed through a trap opening and down the ladder rungs nailed to the outer wall. The stars were the parade ground's only lights, shining down like miniature beacons. The street was quiet and without traffic. Tony broke cover and raced for the nearest tree, melted with the dark trunk. All around him the post seemed deserted. He put his hands in his pockets, stepped out onto the sidewalk, and sauntered along as if he had a right to be there.

Because all the troops were already in bed, he encountered no one on his way to the PX. He spread his change on the metal counter, dropped a dime into the slot, and dialed O. "Hello, operator? I want to make a long distance call to Salisbury, Maryland. The number is PI-9-6506."

"That will be fifty-five cents for the first three minutes, please." The four coins clanked through the slots, followed by the distant ringing of a phone. After ten rings the operator cut in, "Your party does not seem to be — "

"Hello."

"Grandmom!" Tony screamed, forgetting the operator. "Wow, I'm sorry if I woke you up, but I couldn't get away any sooner. They keep a pretty sharp eye on us here."

"Well, land sakes, Tony, it sure is strange hearing your voice. I thought you were down in Georgia or some such place."

"I *am* in Georgia. Fort Gordon. It's right outside Augusta."

"And you're calling all that way? At this time a night?"

"I guess it's pretty late, isn't it?"

"Purty near midnight, I s'pose. But I wasn't sleeping. I was just sitting up with your grandfather, giving him his medicine."

"He's home already?"

"Day before yesterday. Didn't your mother write you?"

"Well, sure, that's how I knew he was in the hospital. But it takes a while for the mail to go through the army postal system. And then they don't let us read it until night time."

"Well, that doesn't seem right. I'd think you'd be a might anxious to read your letters."

"Yes, well, they keep telling us it's part of the training."

"Your Uncle Elmer used to say the same thing. He was in the army during the War, an' it was all he *could* do to get to a telephone or a mailbox. He used to call at the strangest hours, whenever he got the chance. An' anyhow, the phones we had in those days wasn't like the ones we have today. You couldn't hardly get through because the lines were always so busy, although I never did understand how those lines worked . . . "

"Grandmom, can you tell me about Grandpop? How — how's he doing? My mother just said he was sick and had to go to the hospital, but she didn't say what was wrong with him. How — is he going to be all right?"

"Well, Honey, he's got me pretty worried. It's not like your grandfather bein' sick. Why, he's never been sick a day in his life, 'ceptin for colds, an' an occasional flu. An' it pains me to see him hurtin' so bad. Now, the doctors say he should be up and around in a few weeks, an' they ought to know what with all that schoolin', but they say he cain't work no more 'cause he'll always be weak. It's a cryin' shame to see how weak he is. I got to feed him with a spoon an' wipe his chin, an' he's in awful pain only he keeps it all to hisself an' just real quiet like 'cept when it's time for his pills."

Grandmom sobbed for a few moments. When she came back on the line her voice was noticeably weaker. "Now them pills of his make him feel a whole lot better, but they make him so drowsy that he cain't hardly keep his head up to read the paper. I'm afraid his workin' days is over, lessen he can do odd jobs ever' now an' then. But the doctors say if he takes it real easy he's got quite a few days left to enjoy his retirement."

Tony wiped his eyes with his sleeves, and gulped his words. "I — I'm glad to hear that. He should have retired years ago, so I guess it's time he took it easy. But I still don't understand what's wrong with him. My mother didn't say

anything other than he'd been taken to the hospital in an ambulance. What exactly is wrong with him?"

"Well, Honey, I don't rightly know. He just started havin' trouble with his breathin', an' he got kinda pains in his chest ever' now an' again. Then one night he start to complainin' how he couldn't hardly breathe no more. Well, sir, I didn't know what to do other than to call the *po*-lice, an' they sent a right pert young man lickety split an' he took one look at your grandfather an' says he oughta be taken to the hospital right away, an' they come an' took him. Well, I was scared so bad I couldn't hardly stand up, so that nice young man stayed with me till I was feelin' better, then he took me to the hospital in his police car, an' brought me home afterwards, after I saw your grandfather was in good hands, an' they wanted to keep him there for some tests. Well, I went to see him ever' day till they said he was over the worst of it an' it was all right to bring him home. So your cousin Bobby picked him up an' brought him home, with all his medicine an' instructions on what I was supposed to do for him. So now I just have to be real careful an' give him his pills on time an' make sure he gets enough to drink. He's always got to drink, so I got to make him fruit juice fresh squeezed from oranges and grapefruits, an' give him Kool-Aid whenever he gets tired of havin' juice."

"Gee, it sounds like pneumonia."

"No, the doctors say it's not pneumonia."

"It's not his heart?"

"No, it don't seem to be his heart, neither. He says the pain is just an all around chest pain. An' he gets outa breath easy. Why, just walkin' to the bathroom gets him plum tuckered out."

"Is it emphysema?"

"No, I don't remember them usin' that word a-tall."

The operator interrupted in a deadpan voice. "You're initial time is up. Please deposit forty-five cents for an additional three minutes."

Tony counted out his remaining change, and dropped in the coins.

"That's only twenty-five cents, sir. Please deposit another twenty cents for an additional three minutes."

"Operator, I don't have any more change." He remembered the dime he had used to call the operator, and took it out of the coin return. "Oh, wait a minute. There, that's my last dime."

"Please deposit another ten cents for an additional three minutes."

"Operator, I just told you I don't have any more change. I've put in thirty-five cents, so I should get something for it."

"You now have two additional minutes."

Of which one was already used.

"Honey, are you still there?"

"Yes, I'm here, Grandmom. Listen, I don't have any more change so we'd better make it short. When do you think would be the best time to call so I can talk with Grandpop?"

"Well, Honey, I don't rightly know. He doesn't much like to be bothered during the day, he's in so much pain, even though he doesn't let on. Now, he's been havin' some company in the afternoon an' that plumb tuckers him out. An' he goes to sleep right early — just after supper — when I give him his pills. An' even when he's got company here he don't feel much like talkin'. An' you know something, Tony, we don't have a telephone in the bedroom, an' the doctors say he should stay in bed till the end of the week, or the beginnin' of next, so I don't know how he can get to the telephone."

"All right, Grandmom, just listen to me. I want you to tell Grandpop that I called. Tell him that I just found out about his . . . illness. Make sure he understands that I only found out about it today. I'll call again as soon as I get a chance, just to find out how he's — "

"Please deposit forty-five cents for an additional three minutes."

"Grandmom, I have to go. Just remember what I said — "

"All right, Honey."

" — and make sure you tell him I called, and that I'll call again as soon as I can —"

"I'll tell him, Honey."

" — to find out how he's coming along. Okay? Just tell him. And Grandmom, I love you. And tell Grandpop I love him, too. Okay? Okay? Grandmom?"

The phone was dead. Tony stared at it for a moment, then dropped the receiver into the cradle. He felt a dullness in his chest, like a pang of hunger. He leaned against the glass partition, listening to his own breath, seeing hazily the approaching headlights.

The car swung around and stopped with the high beams shining into the booth. Tony rubbed his eyes as he opened the door. "How about turning off the lights, pal?"

"How about showing me some identification, soldier." A uniformed figure stepped out on the passenger side, the letters "MP" stamped on his plastic helmet liner.

"Uh, well, I don't have my wallet with me. I was just out making a phone call. My company's right down the street."

"This is a training area, soldier. Are you a trainee?"

"Yes. D-6-2."

"How about getting in the car and we'll drive you back."

****

Knock, knock, knock.

"Permission to enter, sir."

"Come in."

Tony slipped through the half-opened door, closed it gently behind him, stood stiffly at attention in front of Captain Maxwell's oaken desk, and saluted briskly. Before he had the chance to announce himself, the captain said, "At ease, Giovanni."

"Uh, thank you, sir."

The captain leaned back in his chair with his usual nonchalance, but his eyes jabbed out with the thrust of a foil. Tony wilted under the visual assault. After an uncomfortable silence, Captain Maxwell said, "I'll come right to the point. You have committed a court-martial offense, and I have half a mind to follow up on it."

It was not framed as a question, but the length of the pause indicated an acknowledgment. "Yes, sir, I realize that."

"And do you realize what a court-martial would look like on your record?"

Tony did not. "Yes, sir."

"And do you know what happens to trouble makers?"

"Uh, no, sir."

Captain Maxwell's eyes continued to stab. "The ones who don't get put in the stockade, end up in a special training outfit. Now, wouldn't that be a shame for a man with your education, intelligence, and ability, winding up with a bunch of dolts and misfits and nonconformists and hooligans?" He paused again, but Tony could think of no suitable reply. The captain blurted out loudly, "What the hell got into you last night?"

"Well, sir, I didn't think — "

"You didn't think!" The chair creaked as he leaned forward on his elbows. "Then maybe you'd better *start* thinking. There's a proper way of doing things in the army, and one of the first things you learned here was the chain of command. You do *not* go off and do things on your own."

"But, sir, I asked Sergeant Hawkins to let me use the — "

"And what did Sergeant Hawkins say?" After a long and uncomfortable silence, "Well, what did he say?"

"He said I couldn't use the phone."

"And when he says it, he means it."

"But, sir, it was important — "

"It was *not* important. Nothing about you is important. You are a small cog in a big wheel, and for the next two years that's all you are. You are insignificant and meaningless. You have no life outside the army, you have no personal problems, you exist only for the benefit of Uncle Sam."

"But, sir, I — "

"Don't interrupt me, private! You are not a civilian. You are a subordinate member of the United States Army, and as of this time you are an insubordinate member. Your only purpose here is to please me."

"But, sir — "

"*Shut up!* Giovanni, the army is not going to cater to your individual whims. An army cannot allow every young whippersnapper to go running off on his own whenever he feels like it. You do what you're told, when you're told, and how you're told — nothing more, nothing less. And you had better learn it now because whether you like it or not, you're going to have to live with it for the next two years. Is that understood?"

Tony gritted his teeth. "Yes, sir."

"Good. Now straighten the hell up. You're not a whimpering sissy. You're a soldier, so act like one. Dismissed."

****

"All right, men. Attention." Second Platoon matched Sergeant Hawkins' casualness and raised him one. "Now, listen up, men. In case you haven't noticed, Private Farley is out on sick call today, so while he's not here I want to make something clear to you all: Farley is a sick man. He's sick in the head. An' all of you are smart enough to know what that means. Farley has a problem, an' the doctors are going to see what they can do for him. An' you don't help none by messin' around with him. What happened in the barrack last night is something I would expect from a bunch o' Cub Scouts."

Dark, piercing eyes surveyed the troops. "What I want is for you to leave him alone. I don't want you makin' fun of him — and the first one that does goes straight to Lieutenant Wakefield for a personal interview. Now, Farley's prob'ly goin' to be transferred out o' here, but till he does I want everyone to stop messin' with him. He's sick enough without needin' encouragement. So just leave him alone. Do I make myself clear?"

The "yes, sergeant" came out staggered, but he merely nodded.

"Good. Now, listen up. If you men want passes tomorrow you better have that barrack shinin' like a mirror. There's goin' to be an inspection durin' chow so that gives you — " He brought his arm up to his face. " — one hour to make it look shipshape. Now, get to it."

Tom conferred with the other squad leaders, and assigned jobs to his men. Then he moved to the window behind his bunk.

With a mop and a bucket of water, Wally started swabbing the floor. "So what did the old man say to you?"

Hank climbed on top of his footlocker and rubbed a damp cloth across the top of the beam. "Ah'll bet he really reamed yo' ass out."

"Oh, I wasn't worried about Captain Maxwell. Not after what I went through with the MPs."

"Treat you pretty rough, did they?"

"No, they didn't get physical." Tony washed the wall with a wet sponge. "But they sure threw a scare into me. They kept saying how much trouble I was in, for breaking out of my company area against a direct order. They said I was going to have to be locked up in the stockade for the night. They said they were going to call my platoon sergeant to come and get me out — and, boy, that sure scared me."

"And I guess you believed them, man?"

"Of course I believed them. How do I know what they can or can't do?"

"Man, don't you know by now that there's nothing anybody can do to you? The worst has already happened. You can't be drafted more than once."

"Sure, but I could still get into trouble."

"Man, you're in the army for the duration. You've already been sentenced, now it's just a matter of putting in your time. What difference does it make if you spend the next two years in jail or on some army base? It's all the same thing. All right, maybe they can slap a fine on you — an Article Fifteen. Or maybe they can take away some minor privilege, but other than that they can't do anything to you that's going to make any difference to the rest of your life."

"Well, I — I guess you're right. I'm just not used to being in trouble with authority. I don't like it."

"Bullshit. Sometimes that's what you have to do to get what you want, or say what you want to say. It's the principle that counts."

"Ma pappy always said 'if you're right, fight; but if you're wrong, admit it.' Sounds to me like you gotta fight, else how're you gonna find out 'bout your gran'daddy?"

With the floor done, Wally pushed the bucket aside and started checking his bedding. "Why the hell doesn't the army have fitted sheets? So what did the old man have to say about all this?"

Tony threw down the sponge and leaned against his bunk. "Well, he didn't really say anything — he just yelled and made a lot of threats. And he wouldn't listen at all to my side of the story."

"Prob'ly don't have a gran'daddy hisself." Hank finished with the beams; he pushed the footlocker back into place. "Guess he don't know what they mean to folks that grew up with them. Stupid bastard."

"Yes, and up until now I thought he was a pretty nice guy."

"Are you out of your fucking mind?" Wally screamed. "How can you say that about an officer? That guy's a prick from the toes up. He's so low down that an earthworm could crawl over him without touching him. He's got so many — "

"All right, already. I'm sorry I mentioned it. I admit he has his bad points — "

"Shit, man, he's got as many bad points as a mad porcupine."

"All right, I said. As a person he has his character flaws. But he *is* an officer, and he's got a duty to perform. I'm sure from his point of view, what I did was an egregious breach of military protocol — "

"There y'all go with them big words again."

"Man, you've been reading too much Emily Post."

"Well, look at the bright side. At least he didn't court-martial me."

"Yet."

"He didn't give out no passes yet, neither."

"Well, let's wait and see what happens before we pass judgment against him. He's just doing things by the book."

"Yeah, well, I'd like to rewrite a few chapters, man. I passed judgment on him a long time ago, when that son-of-a-bitch made us stand out in the sun for five fucking hours because he was afraid of some jerkwater adjutant. If he had any backbone he'd — Hey, man, what's the matter with you?"

Tom Gelbert stood slump shouldered, a letter dangling from his drooping hand. His eyes were full of tears.

Tony took a hesitant step closer. "What . . . what . . . Tom, what's wrong?" He put a hand on Tom's shoulder. "What is it?"

The tears poured down his cheek to a quivering lip. He held up the letter. "She sent it back to me. She sent it back."

Tony looked down, saw the letter, saw the glittering gold object in the palm of his hand.

"She sent back my ring." One ex-BMOC cried inconsolably for the rest of the night.

Chapter 51

"It's that big building up on the hill," the cabbie said.

Hank peered out the cab window, breathing on the glass. "Will ya git a load o' this?"

Tony followed his gaze. That big building was more like a mansion than anything he had ever seen before. The hill alone dominated the town of Augusta, but the seven-story ell-shaped hotel stood high above the trees that surrounded it, making it eminently visible. Six or seven hundred feet of frontage was painted white, with contrasting red eaves, in simple, modern design. "Now I'm glad the Augusta Town House was full."

The Bon Air Retirement Club slipped out of view as the cab veered onto a tree-lined driveway angling upward. Leafy magnolias and tall elms arched from both sides of the macadam, forming a shaded canopy. The cab reentered the sun for only a moment before coming to a halt under the arched breezeway.

"You'll like this place, boys." The bald-headed cabbie inflected his drawl with Southern niceties. "Ain't no guns here, but it's nice and quiet like — an' nobody to tell you what to do."

"You are a man with insight." Wally peeled off enough bills to include a healthy tip.

Hank surveyed the grounds. "Whaddaya say, Tom? This is a helluva place." Tom merely shrugged.

Tony tossed off a salute to three old men sitting on a paisley couch by the entrance. They eyed him noncommittally. In the lobby stood a front desk that was a room in itself. A floor-to-ceiling wall of mail slots stood adjacent to a giant pegboard full of keys for hundreds of rooms.

"How do you do?" The matronly woman spoke with a cute southern drawl and flashed a pert, disarming smile. Her gimlet eyes were undoubtedly due to the weight of her elongated false eyelashes. Platinum blonde hair, rouged cheeks, and cherry red lips completed the imagery. In her younger days, without the war paint, she must have been a sensuous woman. "My name is Phyllis. What can I do for you?"

Wally met her level gaze. "Hi. We heard in town that you have rooms available."

"That's right," she cooed. "We have plenty of accommodations. How many rooms would you like?"

"About twenty," Wally said evenly.

Her dimples drooped. "No, really. How many?" Wally gestured toward the door, where more cabs were pulling up. Her smile faded into dismay. "Oh, my."

"We brought most of Delta Company with us," he exaggerated. "Can you put us all up?"

She hesitated for a moment, then put the smile halfway back on her face. "Well, I suppose we can. Yes," she said, with more confidence. "You've come to the right place."

"How much are the rooms?"

"Eight dollars per night."

"Per person?"

"No, per room. Each room comes with twin beds."

"All right," Wally said enthusiastically, his smile matching hers in brightness. "That's cheaper than in town. We'll take two rooms before the mob arrives."

They each laid four dollars on the counter,

received a key, and grabbed the waiting elevator as the outer glass doors opened and bedlam arrived.

"What floor?" The operator was a slender black youth of high school age. His features were round and smooth, his hair cropped short like a Brillo pad, his skin glistened with just a hint of perspiration.

Tony read the operator's nametag. "Four, Barney."

He closed the outer door by hand, then pulled an accordion screen that prevented contact with the moving brick wall. He punched the button with a bent finger. The car crept along slowly, with creaks and groans.

"Excuse me, Barney. But, why do they need an operator for an automatic elevator?"

Barney flashed the quickest smile Tony had ever seen — it was gone almost before it had begun. " 'Cause o' the ole fokes."

"What ole folks is that?" Hank said.

"The ole fokes that lives here." Tony caught a glimpse of teeth before Barney launched into explanation, as if he were a tour guide. "This here is a retirement home for the aged. We got some sick people here, an' most ov 'em don't get aroun' none too good. Some never get outa bed, some get aroun' in wheelchairs, an' some ov the ones who can walk ain't right in the haid an' keep gettin' lost."

"The place ain't that big," Hank said, with a guffaw.

"Ain't the size, it's the mine. Some ov these fokes cain't remember their own names — I gotta remine 'em myself. Sometimes I hafta walk 'em down the hall an put 'em in their rooms an' close the door, else they'll go wanderin' off an' never fine it."

"Well, how do you know where they belong?"

"Aw, I got 'em all memmerized. I know where ever'body lives. Got one ole codger lives on the first floor, out'n the wing. Ever' day he gets on the elevator to go eat, 'cause he thinks he lives upstairs. I take 'im up an' bring 'im back down an' point him to the dinin' room, an' he's never the wiser. Gives me an argument if I tell 'im he don't need no elevator — complains he cain't climb stairs no more. So I take 'im for a ride an' keep 'im happy."

Wally snorted. "Senility is such sweet sorrow."

"You don't hafta worry none, though. They all harmless, an' won't bother you none. Well, here we are."

"Man, those oldsters sure don't have to worry about vertigo on this lift." Hank rubbed his hand over his face. "Ah need another shave already."

"Listen, is there a stairwell around here, in

case we have to leave before Christmas?" Tony asked.

"Fire escape bofe ends o' the buildin'." Barney pushed open the doors and pointed. "An' yo' room's down thataway."

"Thanks, man."

The hallway seemed endless. Every door was open, and every bed was made. Tony and Wally found the number that matched the key, and walked into a spacious room with a full wall of windows looking down on the town of Augusta.

"Man, this place is all right. We can have football games in here."

"And look at that view." Outside the city complex and its array of tall buildings, mile after mile of rolling forest spread like a green carpet below the fading pale blue of the sky. "We can almost see Fort Gordon from here."

"Let's get a basement room."

"I never knew Georgia was this pretty."

"It looks different when your nose is pressed into it doing a low-crawl."

"Hey, y'all." Hank peered out the bathroom door.

"How did you get there?"

"'Pears to me we're sharin' the same facilities."

Tony threw on a mock scowl. "Oh, great. I was hoping you could have your own bathroom to throw up in."

"No, sir. I'm on the wagon this time. I ain't gonna do nothin' but relax in the sun an' take her easy."

Wally said, "Dipsomania is an incurable disease."

"Well, Ah don't know 'bout no dippy manias, but somebody's gotta keep an eye on ole Tom, here. He's feelin' lower 'an a hoag on auction day."

"I'm sure we can find something to take his mind off things."

"Ah sure hope so. Ah hate the idee o' spendin' the weekend with a corpse."

****

Billiard balls crashed like the clatter of loose bones, and spread like a nuclear chain reaction: bouncing off each other and ricocheting off padded sidewalls; dark pockets swallowed up two striped balls.

"Haw haw haw haw haw." Hank tossed his hands into the air. "Way to go, pardner."

Smith and Calahan groaned in despair: if they lost this game they forfeited the tournament.

After the successful break, Tom Gelbert cued up for another shot. Cap cocked at a rakish angle, sleeves rolled up above the elbow, tie loosened with the top button opened, and a cigarette stemming loosely out of the side of his mouth, he studied the terrain. He squinted imperiously down the stick, made three or four practice motions, stopped, chalked the tip, eyed up again from a different angle, pumped the stick several more times, stabbed, and slammed the cue ball with the force of a ramrod. It smashed into a purple striped ball with a crack like a rifle shot. The white ball stopped dead and spun dizzily, while the striped one careened into the sidewall, rebounded in the other direction, narrowly missing two solid balls, and sank from sight into a corner pocket.

Tom let out a scream and spun three hundred sixty degrees on his heel, almost smashing the expensive looking Tiffany chandelier, which hung over the pool table, with his cue stick. Cheers erupted from the covey of half-uniformed rooters lining the walls of the tiny room, adding to an atmosphere thick with smoke, sweat, and four-lettered chatter.

Wally placed his lips close to Tony's ear, and yelled, "Let's get the hell out of here. The excitement is killing me."

The smoke was like acid in Tony's eyes. "I'm with you."

Several nurses still roamed the tomblike corridors, tending to the midnight needs of their patients. On an earlier tour, Tony had seen the inmates of the lower halls, with their sunken eyes and parchmentlike skin. He was filled with sadness not because they were old and dying, but because they were forlorn and forgotten. What lives they must have led? What experiences they must have had? What wars they must have fought? It was all a chimera as they waited vaingloriously for the ultimate obscurity of death.

"This place gives me the creeps." Wally took a seat in the library, out of the noise and confusion of the poolroom and the central meeting hall. Next door, the rest of Delta Company played poker and blackjack beneath beautifully wrought brass chandeliers, and drank amid the sixteen-foot-high plaster columns.

Tony scanned the shelves for reading material. "You should feel good. These people here have lost the most essential quality of life: initiative, challenge, and anticipation of the future."

"What future do we have?"

"Any one we want. No matter how bleak and dismal the present may be, we have the opportunity of working toward changing it."

"Tell that to Sergeant Hawkins." Wally laid back his head and closed his eyes. "Hey, did you ever get through to your family?"

Tony found a book on Brazilian exploration, and settled into a comfortable reading chair. "No. Still no answer."

****

There was something about spiral staircases that had always given Tony a creepy feeling. Without being able to see around the curving perimeter, it was too easy to let the imagination run wild.

The fire tower of the Bon Air Retirement Club was not actually a spiral, but the triple landings — which were squared off between floors — gave the same effect.

From the sixth floor Hank leaned over the iron railing, cleared his throat, and spat. A thimbleful of saliva floated down soundlessly to the cement landing on the first floor. "Hot, dayam. A bull's eye."

"Hey, man, this is a public building, not an outhouse."

"Still got chlorine on ma lips from the swimmin' pool."

"You spent more time in the chaise longue than you did in the water."

"That sun felt good on my nekkid skin."

Tony led the way up the last flight of stairs, enclosed by cement walls. Without bulbs, it was like entering a dark foreboding tunnel, seething in dusty cobwebs and purgative odors.

"What's that shitty smell?" Tom asked.

"Hank's sense of humor, man."

The fifth and sixth floors had been totally deserted, devoid of furnishings. A thick layer of dust had covered the carpeted floor, like miniature tumbleweeds. But at least there had been nightlights to lead the way.

Tony stubbed his toe as the steps turned ninety degrees. "Hey, Tom, flick on your lighter." In the tiny, wavering flame, Tony's shadow was cast ahead against the dingy walls, like some monstrous caricature. The flame danced sinuously in an otherwise imperceptible current, exaggerating his motions. Cool air blew in from a window opening from which the glass had long since departed. He caught a glimpse of the tall stack of the hotel's generating station, silhouetted against a purplish-black sky full of twinkling stars.

The steps were covered with a strange, mottled paint that was silky white and grayish black. Uneven encrustations lined the outer edges, while strands of straw, or grass, lay scattered about. Then came a sound, like newspapers fluttering in the breeze.

The darkness exploded with the flapping of hundreds of wings and a cacophony of high-pitched squawks. Tony ducked as things flew past his ears, touched his face. "Bats!" Tom yelled, dropping the lighter and extinguishing the flame. The animals funneled through the open window. Behind him, his companions screamed and cursed, and fell over each other.

"Shit," Wally said distinctly when the noise had abated.

"Anybody see the lighter?" Tony walked down a couple steps to where he had heard the clattering metal. He felt around in the cozy debris, located it, and brought the light to bear. Three haggard faces stared back at him.

"So this is what you do for fun at home? Man, you are one sick dude. Have you ever thought of bowling?"

Coo.

Wally used the roughcast walls to wipe the sticky excrescence off of his hand. "What did you say?"

Coo.

"I didn't say anything," Tony replied.

Coo.

Hank grinned in the light of the yellow flame, grasping a squirmy and feathery object that struggled for release. He tucked it into his armpit and petted its head and back. "It's a dove."

Wally shrugged loose from Tom's strangle hold. "So it's pigeon poop instead of bat guano. It still stinks. Hey, man, let go of me."

"Sorry." Tom leaned against the wall. "Damn, they scared the shit out of me."

"Add it to the pile. Hey, Tony, can we cut this crap and go back downstairs now?"

"Come on, Wally. We're almost there." Tony forged ahead, to where a narrow hallway led to a steel fire door. He pushed against the handle. The door was stuck, but a sharp shove with his shoulder dislodged it suddenly. He stepped out onto the roof.

Coo.

The seventh floor was the penthouse, inset so that it extended only a hundred feet on either side of the elevator shaft. The rest of what would have been the floor was the tarred roof above the sixth.

Imagined apprehensions faded in the pale moonlight. From the chest-high parapet, Tony looked down upon the brilliantly lighted town of Augusta. "It's beautiful." Stores, houses, office buildings, sidewalks, all were aglow with incandescence. Car beams moved in long chains, adding fluidity and life. The horizon was dotted with tiny points of light that flickered in the heat waves like stars on a still summer's night. Tony was reminded of the night they climbed Bowman's Tower — was it only two months ago?

Coo.

Tony edged along the parapet until he reached the wall of the seventh floor, found the door in the middle. He grasped the handle and pulled, the door flung wide. Inside was inky blackness. "Hey, come get a load of this."

Wally peered inside, his toe jammed against the sill. "This is crazy, man. I'm not going in there."

"Y'all scared o' the dark?" Hank walked right in, was swallowed up as if he had never existed. He scratched the wall along both sides of the doors. "Must have the power turned off. This switch don't work."

Coo.

Tom hung back. "I'm not going in there without the lighter."

Tony handed it to him, and gestured with a sweep of the hand. "Be my guest."

"I'll go last."

"Hell, there's nothing to be afraid of." Wally walked into the black hallway. "Hey, get in here with that lighter."

Tony stepped over the threshold, and Tom followed. The door squeaked like chalk across a blackboard, and hit the molding with a bang. "Just like in a horror film."

"Thanks, man, but I don't need any encouragement."

Except for the tiny flame, the blackness inside was absolute. At the far end, a couple hundred feet away, the faint glow of moonlight shone through the glass. Tony felt as if he were inside a telescope, looking up the tube.

"Weird, man. Way out."

Coo.

From door to door they played the feeble light. The entire floor seemed to be used for storage. The rooms were crammed with tables, chairs, and bureaus; others were piled from floor to ceiling with mattresses and bedsprings. One room contained nothing but lamps.

Tony blew thick dust off a mahogany surface. "Now we know why the fifth and sixth floors are empty. I guess with the old folks occupying the first three floors, they only need one floor for guests."

Hank pulled open a drawer, revealing solid wood instead of veneer. "Musta been a exclusive place at one time."

"It still makes my skin crawl," Tom said. "Let's go downstairs. I could use a drink."

"I'll second that," Wally said.

"You don't drink. Besides, as long as we're here, we might as well see what else there is." Tony moved on ahead, without the aid of the lighter. Wally stuck close. As they approached the elevator landing, the indicator light from the button panel illuminated their way. Opposite it, they stepped into a room suffused with moonlight. Furniture overlaid with cloth practically filled the suite.

"Hey, where'd y'all get to?"

Tony placed a hand over Wally's mouth, kept him motionless.

Tom extinguished the lighter. "You want to play games, we'll play games."

There were no shadows, no silhouettes, visible in the coal-black hallway. Scuffling sounds of shoes on carpet, and rubbing pant legs, gave away their position. The indicator light disappeared for a moment.

"I don't know about you, Hank, but I'm getting out of here." The annunciator light glared in the darkness.

"Why'd y'all do that? We ain't supposed to be here."

"Damn, I forgot about Barney."

They scurried down the hall, into an adjacent chamber. Tony allowed Wally to breath, pushed him farther into the room and out of sight of the elevator. In the deathly silence, the elevator motor was clearly discernable as the cables whined into action. Agonizing moments went by as the car climbed up from the ground floor. The loud *ding* was accompanied by a red light above the cage entrance. The door slid open and flooded the corridor with glaring, unearthly radiance.

There was no movement, and the silence was stifling. A dark head appeared, eyes darting nervously. The whites were highlighted as the black orbs rolled from side to side. One leg stretched out into the hallway. "Who there?" His voice was the merest croak.

Hesitantly, Barney stepped fully into the recessed vestibule. It was many seconds before he was far enough to have an unobstructed view down both sides of the corridor. "Hello?" His eyes continued to roll in their sockets. His body leaned forward, as if his feet did not want to leave the security of the elevator car.

Tony, still as a church mouse, wondered what might be going through his mind: shorted wires, crossed relays, stuck button — *ghosts!*

Coo.

Something fell with a crash, wings flapped madly into the hallway.

Coo. Coo. Coo.

"Aaaaggghhh!" Barney's eyeballs doubled in size. He spun on his heel and raced for the elevator, smashed into the back wall, ricocheted to the front, stabbed at buttons on the control panel — and kept stabbing. "Aaaaggghhh!" He wrestled with the door, slipped and fell, pulled it closed from the floor. He kept screaming.

The elevator slowly descended to the ground floor. They never saw Barney again.

****

The palm trees lining the drive seemed distinctly out of place, but the shade they offered was more than welcome. Tony leaned back in the lawn chair, reading a book, and listened to the playful banter of the forty or so men from Delta Company as they splashed in the pool, a hotel service that was lost on the elderly residents.

"Haw haw haw haw haw!" Hank screamed, in his best country western imitation. He did a cannonball off the diving board, hit the water like a ton of bricks, and sank to the bottom while a column of water erupted twenty feet into the air and clapped over his head like a peal of thunder, causing waves that cascaded over the sides of the pool.

"This place will never be the same," Wally observed. He lay back in the chaise longue, eyes closed.

"Did you get a load of the game room this morning?" Tony adjusted the towel over his legs, and hiked up his swimming trunks.

Wally nodded. "Some of these guys never went to sleep last night."

Many of them were asleep now, lying on the fresh-cropped lawn, or sprawled on hotel towels under the trees. Earlier, Tony had gotten a group of recruits to play stickball, or half ball: a game that was played in the narrow streets of South Philly. He bought a rubber pimple ball, cut it in half, and taught the men how to throw the half ball like a Frisbee, but overhand. For a bat, he cut the handle off a broom. Now, after a game in the hot sun, most of the men were either soaking in the pool or cooling off in the shade.

"How was that one?" Hank lumbered out of the pool and strolled to where Tony and Wally sat.

"Great. You even got *me* wet, way up here," Tony laughed.

"Man, that teddy bear body of yours is as red as a lobster after twenty minutes in the pot. Come in out of the sun."

Hank shook himself dry. "Where Ah come from we live in the sun, day an' night. Not like you city slickers, hidin' in the shade readin' books. You fellers are as white as a ghost." He picked a spot in the sun, stretched out on the grass, and worked his belly into the ground. "Why don't y'all go for a swim?"

Wally still lay in the same position; only his lips moved. I'm going to need all the rest I can get. Don't forget, we leave at five a.m. for bivouac."

"Guess I can stand a little hikin' through the woods."

"What do you say we go to town early and grab a nice dinner? We'll be eating c-rations for the next week."

Tony said enthusiastically, "How about if I call that Italian restaurant we went to last week, and make reservations for the four of us?"

Hank reached over and shook Tony's chair. He rolled onto his side and pointed across the pool. Tom and Phyllis, the hotel clerk, were walking hand in hand toward the lobby. Her buxom body filled out her bathing suit in a way that had captured the gaze of forty pairs of eyeballs. "Better make it for three."

Chapter 52

"Com-pan-eee-eep, halt!"

The two-hundred-odd segmented caterpillar accordioned to a stop as the platoon sergeants repeated Lieutenant Wakefield's cry. Decades of jeeps, trucks, tanks, and boots had ground the surface of the dirt road to fine dust that defied gravity at the slightest touch. It rose like a mist to clog eyes, nostrils, and throats, to congeal on perspiring pores, to sift into pockets and gun barrels. Dampened by sweat, it turned into mud on the palms.

"These shorts are killing me." Sweat from the groin caused the legs to cling and rise with every step until they were jammed tightly in the crotch. Tony pinched the rear of his fatigue pants and stretched them down, pulling the underwear at the same time.

Wally unbuttoned his fly, reached inside, and pulled down both legs. "Boxer shorts just weren't meant for this kind of use. Damn things nearly strangled me."

Sergeant Hawkins charged brusquely past the platoon. "All right, men, fall off to the side of the road an' take ten. Squads one an' three on the left, two an' four on the right. Buddy teams, one man on alert at all times. Break out your canteens if you want, but don't take more 'an a swallow. We got a long way to go."

Tony stumbled into the bushes and relieved himself. Wally sat down and licked his lips. Shade was at a premium, and already, at eight a.m., the sun was searing.

"Ma doags 're tired." Hank sat cross-legged and started unlacing his boots.

Tony followed Wally's example and resituated his shorts, then buttoned up his pants. "How's your sunburn?"

"Purty bad, but not nearly so bad as ma feet."

"I thought you southerners were outdoorsmen." Wally shrugged off his pistol belt and sat on the pack containing his blanket roll, poncho, shelter half, and entrenching tool. "How come you can't take a little constitutional?"

"It's these gol-durn boots. They ain't meant for walkin', jus' polishin'." He worked the socks off swollen feet and bent them back for a better look at the growing blisters. "How fer you think we done come so fer?"

Puffing smoke, Tom eyed his rifle, took a cloth out of his shirt pocket, and methodically wiped down his barrel, flecking off minute particles of dust. "Well, if we're marching according to army specs, we should be making three miles per hour. That's based on a fifty-minute walk and a ten-minute rest stop. Puts us at around the nine mile mark — half way."

Wally took off his steel pot and wiped sweat off his forehead. "What's that in kilometers?"

Tony pulled out his canteen, took one short swig, decided it was not enough, took two more, then another, and another. Except for the killing pace, the first two hours before sunrise had been easy. But the dawn had brought heat, and heat had soon turned to pain. He played with the cap of his canteen, finally took one last swig, swilled it in his mouth, and offered the metal container to Wally. He shook his head.

"*Hey!* Who told you to smoke? You wanta give our position away?" Sergeant Hawkins noticed Hank's naked feet. "An' git those boots on, soldier, this ain't no picnic. What're you gonna do if we get attacked now?" Without waiting for an answer he charged through the platoon, nitpicking all the way.

Tom crushed his cigarette in the dirt and took a long draft from his canteen. "I should give these up, anyway."

Too soon, Lieutenant Wakefield passed the order to his platoon sergeants. "Okay, men. On your feet."

Hank pulled on sodden socks and boots. He hunched his shoulders, and adjusted the harness straps over his sunburned back. "Lord a mercy. It's gonna be a long day."

Hours later they came upon a wood. The sergeants gathered around Lieutenant Wakefield, who knelt over a map and compass.

"I'll give these guys credit." Wally nodded toward the lone officer and his noncoms. "They marched every foot of the way."

When Tony removed his harness and pack, he felt as if he would float off the ground from the absence of weight. "With Sergeant Hawkins beating cadence."

"Ah sure am glad Ah ain't no cadent. Ah'm beat enough as it is."

Tom took out a cigarette, stared at it, stubbed it into the ground without lighting it. He drank some water instead of smoking. "You think this is the end of the trail?"

"Man, if it isn't, they'd better bring us food and water."

"Wally, that's the first time I've ever heard you complain about nutritional requirements," Tony said.

"Eighteen miles on a quart of water is more than I can handle."

"They 'bout twenty guys couldn't handle it."

"Yeah, and Jackson's one of them. I hope they don't find him."

A pickup truck led a cloud of dust into the pine grove. A PFC hopped out and saluted Lieutenant Wakefield. He emptied the first of several five-gallon gerry jugs into a large basin. The green liquid looked like warm lemonade. Tony drooled at the prospect of a drink.

"Listen up, men," the lieutenant shouted. "We're going to set up a tactical perimeter, with this point being the central locus. Your platoon sergeants will designate defense positions, and assign tent locations. I want you men to be alert, and on your feet at all times. Now, as soon as you get your tents pitched, we'll be moving out to the rifle range — " He ignored the chorus of groans. " — where we will take a preliminary marksmanship test. This will be your only chance to practice for the big test next week, so make the most of it."

The PFC at the water truck was making a lot of noise. One by one he opened the jerry cans, tasted the contents, and shook his head. He motioned to Sergeant Hawkins, who took a ladle and drank, stopped, spat, cursed, and stomped away. He whispered something into the lieutenant's ear.

The officer announced, "Second Platoon will have first crack at the water. However, I must warn you that the cook has made a mistake and added salt to the lemonade instead of sugar. Drink accordingly. Dismissed."

Tony suspected that this was just another military ruse, but when he carefully tasted what was poured into his canteen cup, he knew it was not. The drink was ten times as salty as seawater, and burned his chapped lips.

Wally complained in an intentionally loud voice. "They have a lot of fucking guts giving us this shit."

Lieutenant Wakefield pulled him around by the shoulder, and beamed daggers at him. "If you don't want it, soldier, pour it out. But keep your complaints to yourself."

Wally returned his icy stare, degree for degree, and accented his statement in true military parlance. "I *will* speak my mind when I have something to say."

The lieutenant blinked. "You *will* — " He stopped as the repetition of inflection became obvious. In a civilian, though not civilized, tone, he went on, "You will remember that you are a private and I am an officer. Your college witticisms have no meaning in this man's army. And you had better learn your place, son, or I'll heave your ass in the stockade."

Wally poured his so-called lemonade on the ground, and gritted his teeth. "If you'll excuse me for saying so, this man's army sucks."

Wakefield's ears turned an even darker shade of red than their already Georgia-burned hue. The veins in his throat and forehead stood out like strands of spaghetti covered with tomato sauce. With great constraint, he pronounced his words. "You'll regret that statement someday."

"I regret it already."

It was not until long after the lieutenant had left that Hank sidled up to Wally. "Y'all may've won the battle, but you're bound to lose the war."

****

"This looks like a good spot." Tony dropped his harness to the ground, removed his steel pot, and wiped sweat off his brow. The sheltered glade was surrounded by tall Virginia pines which had shed long, soft needles onto the level ground. They would make a bed that was comfortable as well as fragrant.

"Man, as long as they have room service, it's okay with me."

Hank and Tom walked past and found a suitable location some thirty feet farther on. The rest of the platoon spread out in the area that Sergeant Hawkins delineated.

Tony held up a wet finger and caught the direction of the wind. With the heel of his boot he inscribed a gash in the dirt as the axis on which he would place the pup tent for maximum ventilation. With his entrenching tool unfolded into a shovel, he started chopping down the sticks that marred the spot, then scraped pine needles into a pile and bared the ground to the approximate size of the tent. "Come on, Wally, I can't pitch this thing myself."

Wally unrolled his canvas shelter half, a leftover from World War Two, and threw it on the ground next to Tony's. "Hey, man, do you have the stakes?"

"Shelter halves don't come with stakes, we have to cut our own. And tent poles too."

Wally fingered the buttonholes that mated his shelter half to another. "Wouldn't you know it? We both have the same half — button holes with no buttons."

"Wait a minute, I'll see if I can trade with Hank or Tom."

"Ah was jus' gonna ask you the same thing." Hank stood there with his own half of a tent. "Ah've got a half with snaps, an' Tom's got a half with strings."

"Just like the fucking army, man. They got three kinds of shelter halves, all mixed up. I hope they don't run the war this way. That would be just great if we got out there and they had the wrong kind of bullets."

Tony just shrugged his head. "Why don't you start digging the drainage ditch while I go find someone to trade with?"

He and Hank started out through the milling troops. Men were walking around shouting "Snaps!" or "Buttons!" like marketers hawking their wares. There were inner snaps and outer snaps; and buttons and holes. Even the strings had overlap and underlap. Tony finally found someone with whom to trade, although Hank was not so lucky. But when they got back they found that Tom had gotten rid of his string tent to someone looking for a button tent, and got a snap tent in return.

"How did you do that?" Tony asked.

"Easy. I threw in a pack of cigarettes, too.

Without the temptation, I'll have a better chance of quitting."

Many men slept that night with jury rigged tents, overlapped and tied with T-shirts and bootlaces.

"You know something, man? I *still* haven't found anything in this army that makes sense."

****

Six men were taken to the hospital after that morning's forced march: four for heat exhaustion due to dehydration, and two who became sick after drinking the salted lemonade. Lieutenant Wakefield ordered that no one else was allowed to drink the contaminated water.

"That's an unusually astute decision for an officer," Tony commented dryly.

That afternoon, another truck was dispensed to the rifle range, carrying plain water and lunch. Hank said, "Ah thought they's gonna feed us c-rations."

Tony took out his mess kit. "Sergeant Hawkins said c-rations were too expensive. It's cheaper to make a hot meal and send it out to us."

After a hard day's shooting, and a course in personal camouflage, a hot evening meal was trucked out. Afterwards, the men were permitted to retire to their tent sites, and perimeter duty. At sunset, with very little else to do, the exhausted men who were not on guard duty were allowed to crawl into their tents.

Tony enjoyed the solitude of two o'clock watch, and paced back and forth with an empty rifle as he observed the quiet skies for meteors, listening to the unfamiliar night sounds: chirps, squeaks, and high-pitched twangs that could have been anything from crickets and frogs to squirrels and owls. Once he frightened a cottontail out of the brush. When the moon rose, he was able to read his mail by the pale light. Home was his only clutch on sanity in this topsy-turvy world.

After putting away his letters, he pondered the absurdity of army training. The recruits spent an inordinate amount of time in polishing boots and belt buckles in the evening, only to low-crawl across the dirt the first thing in the morning: immediately scraping and scratching off any semblance of polish. They practiced close-order drill for hours in the hot sun, then marched for miles along the streets while maintaining perfect formation in columns and rows. This led Wally to quip, "If I ever get into combat, I'll be able to dazzle the enemy by marching in step around them."

Many men missed essential classes or fieldwork because they were washing dishes in the kitchen or were assigned to some other duty.

Three Puerto Ricans were court-martialed and sent to the stockade to serve three-month sentences. Their crime: each had been caught leaving the rifle range with an empty cartridge as a souvenir. They could barely speak English, but had memorized the phrase "No brass or ammo, sir!" This catechism had to be repeated after every practice round. They didn't understand that keeping a single shell casing was a court-martial offense.

The ranks grew smaller at nearly every roll call. For six weeks men had been mysteriously disappearing. One day they were in the field — jogging, shooting, marching, drilling, eating, sweating, and swearing. Then came the shout: Private So-and-so, fall out. At the end of the day, another bunk was stripped of its bedding, another footlocker was emptied of its belongings, another name was scratched from the duty roster. The name was not called at the next formation, and the cadre never referred to the person again. Sick bay? Special training camp? Transfer? Stockade? Discharge? Death? The recruits seldom knew. They knew only that a man had been expunged from reality.

****

"All right, men, we all know what this is." Like a juggler, Lieutenant Wakefield tossed a fragmentation grenade from one hand to the other. His Adam's apple was synchronized with the rising and falling of the pineapple-shaped explosive. "You've been throwing them at target stakes for weeks, getting the feel of them. Accuracy at grenade throwing will count as one fifth of your final PT score. But today — " He paused dramatically, fingered the pin playfully, pulled it out, reinserted it, and resumed his tossing. "Today you're going to learn what it can really do. This is not a dummy."

"Oh, yes it is, said the grenade," Wally whispered.

The lieutenant put on his best John Wayne demeanor. He jerked out the pin, released the arming lever, and tossed the grenade into the middle of the company formation. Two hundred men stared at it, waiting for the rest of the instruction.

"*Jesus Christ!*" He turned bright red. "*Didn't you hear me say that grenade was alive?* When a grenade drops next to you, you have to react, and react fast, or you're a dead man." He stomped into the field and retrieved the one pound steel ball. "If this thing had gone off it would have killed every man within five meters — that's the kill zone. Anyone as close as ten meters would have been seriously injured. Even fifteen meters away you can be hit by shrapnel that can poke out an eye or take off a finger or rip out a testicle. Goddamn it, this is a dangerous weapon. From now on, if you see a grenade coming at you, you *do* something: duck, run, kick it down a hole, or swallow it if you're in a crowd. But do something."

By the end of his monologue he had regained his position at the head of the company. He spun quickly, pulled the pin, and tossed the grenade into the middle of the third platoon. It arced high in the air over the heads of the men in the front rank. One man jumped up and grabbed it like a fly ball, took a running leap forward, and tossed it back at the lieutenant. It churned the ground at his feet and rolled past. A rumble of laughter shook the rank and file.

The humor was lost on the officer. "Very good, son. But next time throw it in a different direction. Without leadership in the field, you'll never survive. But your reaction time was good. Remember that after you release the actuating lever you have only four-and-a-half to five seconds before it blows up. This is important to know when cooking it off — you throw it too soon and some gook'll throw it right back at you, too late and it'll turn you into mince meat. They'll ship the pieces home in a shoe box."

Lieutenant Wakefield called the company into the observation bunker: a hundred-foot-long chamber that was lined on one side with bulletproof glass, and roofed with concrete. From here they could observe the effects of hand grenades thrown into the adjacent firing range. He yelled into a microphone so the platoon sergeants outside the bunker could demonstrate the proper safety procedure and throwing technique.

Four dull green blobs arced out from the armored throwing bunkers, landed near the concrete posts that were the intended targets, and detonated with loud thumps that clapped in the air like thunder. Dust and sand spumed upward, but otherwise the explosions were disappointing. Metal pellets clattered on the roof, and pinged off the picture windows.

"Hand grenades are not designed to blow up houses and destroy buildings, like they do in the movies. They hurl steel fragments that can kill or maim."

It was a harrowing time for the platoon sergeants. One man pulled the pin, and froze. Sergeant Peterson had to reinsert the pin and pry the man's fingers apart. Third Platoon Sergeant Murphy had one recruit who dropped the grenade after pulling the pin. While the man screamed, the sergeant shoved the grenade down the sump hole, where it fell into a reinforced underground chamber that contained the explosion, and wrestled the man to the ground as steel and gas erupted from the opening like chain shot from the muzzle of a cannon.

"Giovanni, you gonna do what I tell you?" Sergeant Hawkins plowed his hands into the furrows of his hips.

"No problem, sarge."

"Okay. Now, here's what I want you to do." He slapped a grenade into Tony's hand, carefully folded the fingers over the arming lever. "You don't pull the pin with your teeth, or lob it over your head — you throw it just like a baseball from center field. Just like you been throwing them training grenades at the fence post. Understand?"

Tony nodded, staring at the one pound of explosives.

"You do exactly what the lieutenant tells you, when he tells you."

Tony was more afraid of making a mistake and incurring wrath than being blown up.

"And remember, you got only five seconds after you release the lever before that sonuva bitch goes off, so make sure you get rid of it fast."

"Okay, sarge." Tony got into the ready position: left leg extended forward, right leg bent so his weight was on the knee, aiming arm pointed down range, throwing arm bent at the elbow and hugging his chest. He looked through the sighting slot in the concrete bunker.

Lieutenant Wakefield shouted the orders over the loudspeaker. Sergeant Hawkins stayed close. Tony pulled back his aiming arm, crooked his index finger through the pin, pulled, extended, reached behind his head, and with all his might hurled the steel grenade over the parapet. It left his hand at the same time that his steel pot left his head. He tried to check the fall of his headgear, but it held back the follow-through of his arm.

"SHORT! *Get down!*"

Tony hit the ground, grappling for his steel pot, just as the sergeant's massive body landed on top of him. He was pinned as if by a hod of bricks. He crawled into the steel pot like a turtle retreating into its shell. Half an eternity later, four explosions went off in close order, much louder than from inside the observation bunker.

Sergeant Hawkins pushed himself off. "All right, Giovanni. All right. You done jus' fine."

****

They marched for an hour along dusty roads and dirty trails carved deeply with tank treads. The fine dust clogged ears, eyes, noses, and throats; sweat turned it into damp silt.

"GAS!"

Tony reacted instinctively. With one deft motion he whipped out his gas mask, knocked off his steel pot, seated the rubber, shouted, "Mask!"

Sergeant Hawkins pranced back and forth in front of the platoon, a big grin across his face. "That's the way I like to see it." He jerked a thumb over his shoulder, across the clearing.

"You see that tent over there? Well, Lieutenant Wakefield's gonna check you out with the real thing. That tent is full o' tear gas, an' if your mask is on right you won't even notice it. All you gotta do is walk up to the lieutenant, state your name, rank, and serial number, loud an' clear, an' walk out the other side. An' don't crowd the lieutenant, you'll all git your chance to speak. Let's go."

Still wearing masks, they walked off in single file behind the sergeant, like imprinted ducklings following their surrogate mother. They stopped in front of the closed canvas flap.

"No pushing or shoving. You gotta git through here in an orderly manner." He donned his own gas mask. Muffled, "Steel pots in your left hand. The lieutenant expects to be saluted. Okay, let's go."

The inside was dark, foggy, and thick with vapor. Tony inhaled, testing the chemical scrubber. His skin itched slightly. The sweat pouring into his eyes was a minor irritant compared to the stinging pain of tear gas when Sergeant Hawkins ripped off his mask.

"Did I forget to tell you that the lieutenant wants to see your face?"

It came so unexpectedly that Tony did not have time to clutch for his mask. He coughed as he involuntarily breathed the blinding, curling fumes. It was like inhaling nettles. He closed his mouth, breathed through his nose: cactus needles stabbed his nostrils. He covered his mouth with his hands, then with his collar. The tear gas was everywhere, there was no getting away from it. Gas filled the tent like a thick fog, and crawled over his skin like acid.

Sergeant Hawkins shoved the gas mask into Tony's hand. "Put it in the case an' stay calm. Remember to answer the lieutenant's questions."

His eyes felt as if red-hot brands had been shoved into them. Tiny, scalding needles penetrated his neck, his face, his throat. He coughed, gagged, tried to rid his chest of the liquid fire that flowed into it like lava. Tears poured down his cheeks. He dug knuckles into his eyes, but could not rub away the pain.

Wally crashed into his back, clawed past him, running his hands frantically over his face and neck, brushing away an imaginary army of red ants. He turned around and stared with bloodshot eyes. Tony steadied him as the man in front was given the go ahead, and ran out of the tent. Wally coughed out his name, rank, and serial number, none too clearly.

Lieutenant Wakefield moved a pencil across the clipboard in front of him, then stared up from his wooden chair. He glared at Wally through the large eye ports. "Please repeat that soldier. I couldn't understand you."

"Cough cough — Walter P. — cough — Gibson — cough cough cough — private — cough cough — US — cough — 52 — cough cough — 675 — cough cough — 191 — cough cough."

"I am an officer, son."

"Cough cough — sir — cough cough cough."

The lieutenant took his time locating his name on the list. "Your enunciation is not as clear today as it was when you said this army sucked. Perhaps you regret that statement now."

"Yes — cough cough — sir — cough cough — I — cough — regret — cough cough — it."

"I thought you would. And after this you *will* be certain you know how to don your gas mask, won't you?"

"Cough cough cough — yessir — cough cough."

"And you *will* show respect for your superior officers, won't you?"

"Cough cough yessir cough."

The lieutenant stared at him for several seconds. "I thought so. Okay, get out of here."

Tony stepped forward, threw a smart salute. His words came in a burst. "Anthony Giovanni, private, US52666498. Sir."

Lieutenant Wakefield shone a flashlight into Tony's eyes, held it for a second, then directed its beam on the roster. With the stub of a pencil he made a check mark. "Middle name?"

"Cough cough. John. Cough."

"John what?"

"John, sir. Cough."

"Next."

Tony was out of the tent in an instant, squinting in the brightness. He dropped his steel pot on the ground, yanked out has canteen, poured water over his neck and his face, and washed out his eyes. He coughed and spat, but the stinging persisted. He bumped into Wally in the shade of a nearby tree.

"Goddamn analretentive," Wally coughed.

****

On the fourth day of bivouac they learned how to use a compass.

They marched five miles to a location that was no different from the bivouac area except that it was five miles away. Sergeant Hawkins gave the instruction.

"For you dumb asses who don't know the difference, the shaded part of the needle is the end that points north. An' don't you forget it or you'll wind up goin' into Charlie country instead of out of it. Now, the thing that makes a compass work is magnetism. The Earth is one big, motherfuckin' magnet, an' that needle wants to crawl right up her snatch. All you gotta do is line up the needle with the N, an' you got her licked."

He paused, and held up a compass for every-one to see. "This is a lensatic compass, also known as a sighting compass. You open it so the cover with the hairline is perpendicular to the ground, unfold the lens to forty-five de-grees, bring it close to your eye, and hold it so the bubble is in the middle. Only thing you gotta remember is the needle is attracted to iron, so you can't be wearin' your steel pot, or have your rifle barrel too close. An' if you got fillings in your teeth, git rid of 'em. Okay, any questions? Good."

To each team he handed a slip of paper, on which was written six bearings and distances. Each pair started with one member counting off the distance while the other stayed put and sighted the compass. From the next point they leapfrogged a specified number of meters in a different direction. After repeating this process four more times, Tony and Wally, along with half the platoon, were back where they had started.

Sergeant Hawkins shouted to the men who were wandering in the clearing, or about to enter the woods. "You jerks out in left field git back here an' start over again. You got a sense o' direction like a cow with two short legs."

****

"Hey, Tony. What makes the stars jump around like that? Are they drunk or some-thing?"

From in front of his tent, Tony gazed up at the nearly black sky. The sun had already set, but the heat lingered on. "Atmospheric heat in-versions."

Hank said, "You mean like heat waves on a macadam road?"

"Exactly."

"Golly."

"Okay, men, on your feet."

Tony wearily stood up as Sergeant Hawkins approached. "What's up sarge?"

"After four days in the field, you men need showers."

Wally erupted from the tent. "All right, man, that's what I've been waiting for."

"Full web gear and weapons, soap, wash-cloth, and towel. Canteens if you want. Fall in by the clearin'." The sergeant disappeared through the trees, as light on his feet as a bird on the wing. Not a twig snapped nor a leaf rus-tled to indicate where he had gone.

"Well, if that don't beat all." Hank wiped sweat off his forehead. "Who the hell wants to go anywhere in this heat?"

Wally wasted no time gathering his gear. "I'll go anywhere for a shower."

"But we takin' our PT test tomorrow. It don't make no sense."

"This is the army, man. It doesn't have to make sense."

"It's all part of the training procedure," Tony said. "Destinations are just excuses to make us travel. Are you going to get Tom off guard?"

"But it's *hot*."

Tony quipped, "The army does not regulate its activities on personal comfort. It has aims and goals that operate on a completely different plane of existence."

Two hours later, and six miles down a dusty road, that plane of existence assumed a horrid semblance to reality. Tony's clothes were soaked with sweat, and his canteen was long since dry.

"Don't nobody drink the water in the show-ers," Sergeant Hawkins jerked a thumb in the darkness to a placid body of water which faint-ly reflected the light of the stars. "It's all sludge from the bottom of that lake, an' pure poison. Any man who gets sick still has to walk back, then he gets put on report for disobeyin' or-ders."

Tony filed into what looked like a concrete bunker in the middle of the forest, dimly light-ed by a couple of bare bulbs, and stripped out of his soggy clothes.

"This is the fucking pits, man." Wally stepped under a thin stream of water, fatigues and all, and proceeded to undress after his uni-form was completely doused. Then he brought out a bar of soap and lathered not only his body, but his clothes as well.

The tile floor was slimy underfoot. There were no hooks on which to hang clothes, so Tony stuffed them on top of his boots in a far corner. The water was shockingly cold at first, but he soon got used to it, then luxuriated in it. Like magic, it relieved his body of all pain and fatigue. Cool water ran over his pores, washing away days and nights of dirt, grime, and perspi-ration. "Hey, Wally. Don't drink that water."

After several more gulps, he said, "Why not? I'm thirsty."

"You heard what the sergeant said."

"I heard what he wants us to believe."

Tony dried himself off as best he could under such humid conditions. "Hank, your back is all blistered. Looks like you've got sun poison-ing."

"Ah know. But when Ah tried to go on sick call, the ole sarge tole me if Ah did, Ah'd get court-martialed for destroyin' gover'ment pro-pity."

Wally stroked off the water, wrung out his clothes, and donned them. "TAAA."

"Huhn?"

"Typical asinine army attitude."

Hank shook his head. "Y'all gonna git blis-ters on your feet wearin' them wet socks."

"I brought dry ones," Wally said smugly, pulling them on.

Tom lathered his face with white foam. "It sure feels good to shave with a mirror."

"Never tried it, man. Always used a razor."

"Ain't no gurls to look purty for out here. That Phyllis ain't gonna know whether your face is clean or not."

"She will next time I see her and rub it against her thighs."

They were hustled out of the building to allow the next platoon to take showers. Sergeant Hawkins formed them up on the edge of a dusty trail. Beady whites glistened in the rising moonlight. "All right, men, we gonna take a short cut back to camp."

Instead of taking the circuitous route along the winding roads, Second Platoon cut straight through the pine forest. They jumped over streams, climbed logs, fought through dense brush, and climbed steep hills. Sergeant Hawkins never once referred to a compass, but they arrived back at camp just like he said they would — an hour after everyone else.

"I hope you learned your lesson," he said.

Wally grumbled under his breath. "I'm as sweaty and dirty now as I was before we left."

****

Captain Maxwell strode confidently in front of the company, displaying spit-shined combat boots, trousers with a pressed crease that could scythe through wood, and a fatigue jacket that was so starched that it could have stood by itself. His gig line was mathematically straight. The only decorations he wore were the captain's bars on each shoulder, and a ranger patch on one sleeve. The brim of his baseball cap was pulled down appropriately; the early morning sun glinted off brass insignia.

"At ease," he said in a voice that was calm and controlled. He spoke affectionately, like an orator, and never kept his gaze in one place too long. "Well, good morning, men. I know you're all anxious to get on with the PT tests. This is where you find out how much stronger you've become in the past seven weeks under my command. And it's not just the constant exercise that did it — it's that good old army chow."

He paused as a snicker rippled through the formation. "Now, I know you fellows didn't get any breakfast this morning other than juice and chocolate rations, but I'm sure you'll find it's the best thing. You'll be lighter on your feet, less likely to get sick, and the sugar will give you extra energy. However, I've ordered the chef to have the lunch truck out here just as soon as the tests are over — and you can eat as much as you want."

He paused again, lending time for a chorus of 'yays.' "My purpose in being here it to en-courage you all to do your best. One of the things the army prides itself on is physical fitness. Each aim counts for a score of one hundred points. Out of a possible total of five hundred, I scored four sixty-two. Now, as you know, the man with the highest score in each company receives a trophy at graduation. As a further incentive, I'm going to add a twenty-dollar bill out of my own pocket. And for every man who gets a score higher than mine, I will relieve him of all extra duty for the duration of his stay with this company."

Hoots and howls went up from the peanut gallery.

"And, if this company comes out with the highest overall PT average of the ten competing companies, I'll see to it that you not only get a weekend pass, but that the weekly haircuts are discontinued. Now, go out there and do your best. I'll be rooting for you."

The cheering persisted as Captain Maxwell walked off the field to his waiting jeep. Lieutenant Wakefield hastened to take his place, and had to 'ten-*hut*' the troops twice before he got a response.

"Sergeants, take your men to their individual aims. And let me add some words of advice. Anyone who doesn't try his hardest *will* answer to me."

Tony had already gone through two cans of shoe polish due to continued practice, and prescribed punishment, of the low-crawl. This time Sergeant Hawkins followed the four-man heats down the twenty-five meter course, screaming invectives, and ready to wield his wooden paddle and thwack any rear end that stuck up too high. "Lessen you want your ass shot off, you better keep it down."

The run, dodge, and jump was a test of agility rather than speed. The fifty-meter course consisted of two sets of five poles, and a water filled sandpit two meters across. Tony shot around the poles and over the water trap like lightning, trying to keep up with Wally.

Six weeks of climbing the overhead bars to get into the mess hall had strengthened Tony's arms until they were wire taut. He raced along the bars with demon speed, far ahead of anyone else.

At the grenade toss he strove for accuracy, trying to hit the base of the wooden post within the highest rated concentric circles. Then he joined the rest of the platoon for the last event, the one-mile run.

"Hey, man, did you see that shot I made with the grenade?"

Tony jumped up and down, shook out his arms, and breathed deeply. "I wasn't watching."

"I bounced a grenade off the top of the pole

and hit the sarge square in the chest. Knocked the fucking wind right out of him. The bastard gave me a bull's eye score, too. He's some sport."

"Almost what you would call an all-right guy," Tony winked.

"Yeah," Wally said grudgingly. "How'd you do?"

"Years of playing football in the street gave me an edge. I couldn't miss. I was really hot."

"Ah'm hotter'n a toad on a fry pan." Hank poked a finger into his flabby belly. "Ah never run a mile in ma life till a month ago. Ah may not pass out, but Ah sure as hell ain't gonna break no records."

Tom grinned as he did deep knee bends. "If I can get a full hundred points, I'll beat Captain Maxwell's record."

"Yeah, well, don't go counting your money, man. Tony's going into this race with a perfect score. And into the valley of death rode the four hundred. If he crawls this mile he'll be number one."

Tom looked shocked. "How — how did you do it?"

"Quit smoking when I was three."

Captain Maxwell held a pistol at the starting line. "I want every man to finish, even if you have to walk. The biggest mistake most men make is they start out too fast. They burn themselves out in the first lap, then limp across the finish line. So, I'm going to pace you the first quarter mile. After that, you're on your own. And the man who winds up with the fastest time is relieved of all guard duty and clean-up detail. All right, let's hit it."

Tony took his place behind the chalk mark, wiped his sweating palms on his thighs. Nervous tension brought it right back again.

Captain Maxwell nodded to his executive officer, who took the pistol and held the stopwatch.

Lieutenant Wakefield fired the pistol. "Go!"

They went. The captain started out at a gait that felt far too slow for Tony, almost as if time did not matter. He and Wally were right on his heels, nudging him on, while behind, the rest of the platoon was bunched up, vying for foot space and room to swing arms. They leaned around the first bend and stretched out into the straightaway. Unbelievably, some men were already beginning to lag behind. Tony breathed deeply, smoothly, easily. He could run forever at this pace.

At the straightaway at the end of the first lap, the other three platoons cheered from the sidelines. As Sergeant Hawkins yelled encouragement, Lieutenant Wakefield called out the time. " . . . one-eighteen, one-nineteen, one-twenty . . . "

Tony calculated that the pace was five seconds too slow to make a five minute mile. As soon as Captain Maxwell veered off to the side, Wally charged ahead like a frustrated racehorse. Tony sped up, using Wally as a pacer — for about ten seconds. He could never finish at such a killing pace.

At the next bend be began to feel pain in his chest, a tightening in the calves. He kept close to the inside track, leaning inward. When he hit the second straightaway, Wally was already passing the starting line, with no sign of slowing down. Tony could hear Tom behind him, gasping as if he regretted every cigarette he had ever smoked.

" . . . two-thirty-nine, two-forty, two-forty-one . . . "

Tony started to fall apart. His legs were like leaden stumps, plodding methodically. His lungs were burning up. Even his arms hurt. He rounded the bend, and when he straightened out of it, Wally was a green, grasshopperlike blur entering the second bend, his legs pumping like pistons, his arms swinging like rocker arms. Tony tried to take his mind off the pain.

He took the curve at an angle and from across the track heard a cheer for Wally. But he could not pick up his head to look. By the time he reached the starting line, going into the last lap, he felt like chugging molasses. But he heard the cheers, caught a glimpse of Sergeant Hawkins waving, heard Captain Maxwell rallying him on.

" . . . three-fifty-eight, three-fifty-nine, *four*, four-oh-one ... "

Why was he running so slowly?

Tony threw a damp hand across his forehead and wiped away a gallon of sweat. His eyes were salty and stinging. He closed them, and erased everything from his mind except putting one foot in front of the other. His legs felt like stiffened telephone poles. His chest was in a vice.

Then there was someone in front of him, coming closer. Dazedly, he looked up — *when had he started looking down?* He lapped Jackson as if the man were standing still. He caught someone else at the curve, but did not glance up to see who it was. He passed him on the outside.

The pain!

He had to concentrate, to put everything but running out of his mind. He dragged air down his throat, swung his arms, let the momentum pull him along, and stretched out his legs as far as they would go.

Sergeant Hawkins was at his side, running. "Get that fuckin' ass movin'."

Tony's eyeballs rolled around in his head, pounding. He could not get enough air, was getting dizzy, was aching everywhere, but was not giving up. He watched the black stones pass underfoot as if the track were a treadmill going in reverse and he was standing still.

He heard the company cheer. Wally must have crossed the finish line. Then he heard his name. "Come on, Giovanni. Go go go." Not just one voice, but scores. They were all on the same team: recruits, cadre, and officers. They wanted him to make his score. How could he let them down?

Then Captain Maxwell was at his side, running step for step, shouting. "You can do it, Giovanni. You can do it. Don't give up now."

" . . . five-oh-eight, five-oh-nine . . . "

He was already too late, had lost his perfect score.

"Keep moving, Giovanni."

" . . . five-ten . . . "

The world moved in slow motion: every second was an era. Tony swam through space and time, floated from star to star, each step taking light years. *Don't be silly, a light year is a measure of distance, not of time.* His brain was starved for oxygen, his thinking processes deviant. He struggled to remember: light years, parsecs, astronomical units.

" . . . five-fifteen . . . "

Something hit him in the small of the back, exerted pressure. He accelerated effortlessly. His mind switched back to the world of reality. There was no sense in keeping up the pace, he had already lost.

" . . . five-sixteen, five-seventeen . . . "

Tony leaped ahead with the fleetness of a deer. Captain Maxwell propelled him along, his hand in the small of Tony's back, pushing. He wanted Tony to win. Tony sucked air, willed his legs forward, sucked more air.

" . . . five-eighteen, five-nineteen . . . "

It was like running downhill. He kept his feet moving as if his very life depended on it. Blood rushed past his eardrums, bringing with it the sound of cheering men. Lieutenant Wakefield never looked up from his watch.

" . . . five-twenty . . . "

"Nice going, Giovanni."

The pressure was gone. The lieutenant slipped behind. Captain Maxwell let him go. The men still cheered, even though Tony had let them down. He veered off the track like a drunk, barely able to stay on his feet. He had to keep moving, to keep breathing. He walked bent over, hands on hips, spitting phlegm. He had been so close.

Men clapped him on the back. "Nice going." "Great run." "Hot shit." "All right."

But Wally had won, and had made it in time. Pat *him* on the back. Saliva drooled out of his mouth. Everything spun around, as if he were on a merry-go-round. He felt as if he would pass out any second.

His goal. He had missed his goal. And he felt horrible about it. He could hardly live with himself. If only Captain Maxwell had not kept him back that first mile, perhaps . . .

Wally threw his arms around Tony, hugged him, ruffled his stubby hair. "Pretty fucking good, man." *His* breathing rate was already under control. He dragged Tony toward Sergeant Hawkins who, clipboard in hand, was writing down the times.

When Tony regained enough breath to talk, he shook his head. "You must have . . . broken the . . . record."

"Could have done better without long pants and combat boots."

Captain Maxwell beamed. "Congratulations, men. That was a good run."

Tony kept shaking his head. "But about thirty seconds too late."

"I don't think so. You got your perfect score."

"But how could I? I was supposed to run the mile in five minutes."

"Six minutes, Giovanni. Six minutes. Get your head out of the sand."

Chapter 53

"But, sarge, I'm not supposed to have any extra duty."

"Says who?"

"Says the commanding officer — the morning we took the PT test."

"I know what he said. I also know what he didn't say. He didn't say you could sneak off to make private phone calls during quiet hour. Now, you git your ass over there an' report to Sergeant Breneke. I already told him you're coming."

"But Captain Maxwell — "

"Captain Maxwell ain't here, an' when he ain't, I'm in charge. If you have a problem, you take it up with him tomorrow when he *is* here. But for now you git your ass over to the mess hall. Do I make myself clear?"

Tony sighed heavily. "I guess so — sergeant."

In the kitchen, Sergeant Breneke was in his glory, commanding a small task force of men who had allowed the permissive barrack restrictions to dictate their drinking habits. "Well, well, well. Welcome back, Giovanni. Are you just visiting, or have you come to make yourself useful?"

"Oh, I wasn't doing anything so I just thought I'd stop by to see if you needed any help."

"That's right neighborly of you. Whadja do this time?"

"Made the assumption that an officer's promise had meaning."

"Assume means make an 'ass' out of 'u' and 'me'." The sergeant's dental problems became obvious. "Well, I'm sure I can find something for you to do. Now, let me see — oh, yes, I'm overstocked on paint, so how's about doing that wall behind the stoves. White would look good."

"Again? Sarge, I've painted that wall three times in the past month. If it gets any thicker, you won't have any room left in the kitchen. And what about all the other guys who . . . "

"That's enough, Giovanni." The smile vanished like a switched off light. "I said that wall needs painting, and that's what you're gonna do. Now get started."

Tony rushed a little more than usual, drawing lines between the adjacent walls and the ceiling that were not as straight as he would have liked. The Negro who paints it black tomorrow can fix them, he thought. It still took him an hour.

Sergeant Breneke rubbed his hand over his mouth as he stared at the finished product. He glanced at his watch, then at the paint can. "Paint it again."

"But, sarge. You can't put a second coat on wet paint. It won't — "

"I said paint it again." He punctuated the close of conversation by showing Tony his back.

Tony fumed, but started over on the left side, where the paint was still tacky. The brush stuck to it whenever it was not sufficiently coated. As a result, he had to lay on a thick layer that had a tendency to run. The wall became a uniform mass of slowly sagging white on white, as if it were melting down into the ground.

"Well, what do you think?" Tony made a few touch-ups where long stringers of paint were dripping too close to the floor. The rest of the kitchen was a flurry of motion as men scrubbed floors, washed machinery, and polished counter space. "Can I go now?"

Sergeant Breneke cast a wistful glance into the paint can in Tony's hand. He had used only half the gallon. "You got paint leftover, an' I got no place to store it. Do it again."

A simple sentence that took no more energy than that expended by a fly walking across a leaf could result in countless hours of senseless labor, unnecessary toil, and useless activity. Tony was in a rage. He had already done the job his way — twice. Now he was going to do it the army way.

He laid the paint on as thickly as he could. He dunked the brush deep into the can, took it out dripping, and slapped it against the still wet wall. White paint ran in rivulets, but he did not care. He smeared it on until gravity became too large a force, let it pool along the bottom where the wall met the floor. Still, the paint was not being used up fast enough.

Holding the can next to the wall, near the ceiling, he *poured* it onto a surface already past the point of saturation. He slopped and slopped, but could not lose enough paint to empty the pail.

When the sergeant was distracted by some of the other workers, Tony meandered unobtrusively to the window for a breath of fresh air: the paint was going to his head. When no one was looking, he raised the screen and poured the rest of the paint onto the sand.

"Hey, sarge, I'm all done."

Sergeant Breneke surveyed the wall, looked into the can, and did a double take. Tony made a few ostentatious smoothing motions. The sergeant squeezed a finger up under his chef's hat, and scratched his head. "Well, I guess that's pretty good. I'll letcha go, but don't you go back to the barrack just yet. I don't want nobody knowin' I let you go early."

Tony made good his escape. On the way out the back door he slipped into the pantry, put away the tools, and grabbed a jar of cherries. He rationalized that since the army paid his room and board anyway, he was not actually stealing. Besides, in nearly two months of training, cherries had never once been served.

He slipped away from the company area and headed straight for the phone booth.

****

"Haw haw haw haw haw." Hank threw his arms around Tom and pranced about in a do-cee-do.

Tony cleared his rifle, slung it over his shoulder, and headed toward the dancing duo. "What do you suppose has gotten into those two?"

"Beats the shit out of me, man. The only thing to get excited about in this man's army is a discharge, seminal or otherwise."

Tony got within talking distance, but stayed out of range of flailing arms and legs. "Hey, what's all the ruckus about?"

"Y'all lookin' at a coupla winners," shouted Tom, doing his best to imitate Hank's drawl. The Bostonian accent did not do it justice. "We both scored a seventy, and that means we're taking the trophy."

"Yeah, the both of us." Hank kicked the dust with the toe of his boot. "They gonna hafta cut that there trophy in half, an' give us each a chunk."

"I knew that ROTC training would come in handy some day."

"Hell, where Ah come from, we learn ta shoot afore we learn ta walk. Ah could knock a fly off a melon at a hundred paces afore Ah was knee high to a toadstool."

"Hank, toadstools don't have knees — "

Wally cut Tony off. "Forget the toadstools, man, because I got a seventy, too."

Hank and Tom stopped their jig in midstep. Tom's face was crestfallen, as if his mother had just died. "You got a seventy-two?"

"No, no, no, man. Seventy, too, as in also. That trophy's got to be split three ways."

"Goddayam." Hank grabbed Wally and Tom and twirled them around in a pirouette. "Haw haw haw haw haw."

Wally pushed himself away and put on a sour expression. "Big fucking deal. It won't get me out of the army one day sooner."

"This is going to look great on my record," Tom said. "Charlie better watch out when he sees me coming."

****

"Giovanni! Gibson!"

Wally was still picking lunch out of his teeth with a makeshift toothpick. "Yo."

"Right here, sarge." Tony climbed to his feet, using the oak tree for support.

"Git over to the orderly room, the both of you. The old man wants to see you." Sergeant Hawkins glowered. "And *run*."

Tony arrived breathless at the orderly room door, and paused before entering. "What do you think it is this time?"

"I don't know, man, but don't sweat it. Just roll with the punches."

Tony nodded, shrugged, and opened the screen door. "After you."

"He said, going into the lion's den."

Two fans turned on pivots and kept a constant breeze going. Papers were held down with rocks and stones. Three men from other platoons already occupied the bench, but made room. Just as everyone got comfortable again, two more men came in. They all scrunched over. No one said a word.

First Sergeant Abrams picked up a stack of files from his desk, knocked on the captain's door, entered, and emerged a moment later. "Private Cunningham, the captain will see you now."

Cunningham went through the ritual of knocking, announcing, requesting permission to enter, waiting for acknowledgment, and entering with a sharp salute. The sergeant closed the door behind him.

Five minutes later he emerged, his shoulders a little straighter, his manner more assured. He walked past without looking right or left, donned his helmet liner at the outer door, pulled it down close over his eyes, stepped outside, executed a sharp left turn, and marched off.

Wally raised his eyebrows at Tony.

"Private Durham. Announce yourself."

Durham went in with a frown, but came out with a smile.

"Private Giovanni."

Tony swallowed hard, cleared his throat, and entered the captain's domain.

"Have a seat, Giovanni." Captain Maxwell gestured to the wooden chair in front of his desk. Tony sat on the edge of the seat. The captain studied a file laid out on the desk in front of him. After a minute, he said, "Giovanni, you've got a pretty good record here. In fact, it's a damn fine record. One of the best I've ever seen. You've won the trophy for the highest PT score, you came in second in marksmanship, and you have the second highest IQ in the company. In black and white, you are a model soldier — ideal material for Officers Candidate School."

Tony stared blankly.

Captain Maxwell sighed, reached out, and flipped the folder shut. He folded his hands in his lap and looked directly into Tony's eyes. "But I know that you are somewhat less than ideal. Since you've been under my command, you've been involved in numerous breaches of conduct. You've shown a firm lack of respect for authority. And you have a poor attitude toward military service. What do you have to say about all that?"

There was a long silence before Tony cleared his throat. "Well, sir, I — I — I don't think that's a fair evaluation."

"And why not?"

"Well, because it's not true."

The captain leaned forward, the chair screeching as the spring brought the back up behind him. He leaned his elbows on the desk. "Now look, I want you to understand that I hold no grudges against you. Personally, I think you have great potential. But you also have a disciplinary problem, and the army survives on discipline. You see, we have ways of doing things in the army, and for a very good reason — it works. You've been to college, you know how it is. You go to class, you attend lectures, you do your homework, you take tests. Why? Because that's the way it's done. If you don't like it, you can leave. But in the army, you can't leave. You're here for the duration. You have to conform. You have to go along with the crowd. So why not make the best of it? Accept the fact that you have to take orders whether you like them or not. You have to do as you're told, when you're told."

He leaned back in his chair; it squeaked. "Well, I'm getting a little far afield. Let me explain why I had you brought in here. The army is not run by men, it's run by officers. And officers are in short demand. So it's up to every training commander to interview each and every recruit who can be considered for OCS — the cream of the crop. It's done by the book: those with the best records, the highest scores, the most initiative, have the best chance of becoming officers. I must offer the opportunity to each man I think is fit for the job. But it's also up to me to turn away those I consider unfit, because only *I* can see the things that don't show up in the records. A poor recommendation shows up in *my* record as poor judgment. And as long as I don't recommend you, you'll never be able to prove that I was wrong. *I* am your only opportunity."

He lapsed into silence. Tony found a lump in his throat that prevented him from speaking.

"The best that I can recommend you for is military police school. They have very high standards, and I'm hoping that they will teach you the proper discipline you need to become a good soldier."

Tony cleared his throat once more, knowing that he had to say something. His silence almost outlasted his chances. Just when Captain Maxwell was about to speak, Tony found his voice.

"Sir, I don't think you're being fair. It's not so much that I don't like the army, I just don't like what I *see* in the army. The system might be efficient, but it isn't flexible. Are you training men, or machines?"

"We're training soldiers. And in order to be a soldier, you've got to think like a soldier. I'd rather have a soldier in the field who does exactly what he's told, when he's told, without compunction, without dissent — "

"Without thinking."

Captain Maxwell sighed. "You see, Giovanni, that's your problem. You're always arguing. You're always — " He shook his head. " — looking at the other side. Evaluating orders. That's not your job. You leave the 'why' to someone else; you just concentrate on the 'how.' And that's why I have to state in my report that you are not qualified to be a leader of men. Because to lead, you must know when to be led. And you will never know that." Very calmly, almost as an afterthought, he added, "Dismissed."

Tony rose, saluted, about faced, and left quietly. In the orderly room, he said to Wally, "Start rolling."

****

Just like that it was over.

The day dawned like any other: reveille at four-thirty, scrub down the barrack, early morning PT, the parallel bars and a rushed breakfast, practice formation in fatigues, parallel bars and lunch, then an afternoon graduation ceremony in dress uniform.

The footlockers were emptied, the duffel bags stuffed. Squad by squad the men were called to the orderly room where they were given written orders for AIT: advanced individual training. Wally was off to signal school, Hank was going into armor, Tom made the grade for airborne training and Ranger school. A week or so leave was squeezed in between departure from Fort Gordon and arrival at the next duty assignment.

Except for Tony. MP school was right there on base. For him there was no leave, no chance of skipping home to see family and friends, no opportunity to take care of unfinished personal business. Sergeant Hawkins' motto was 'the army is your business — your only business.'

"Fall in, men. Let's go, on the double. And bring your duffel." Sergeant Hawkins, resplendent in dress greens and ribbons, gave his final orders to Second Platoon. "And don't forget to *run*."

"Oh, man, when does this chicken shit stop?" Wally rolled off a bare mattress, all his bedding having been turned in.

"After your discharge." Tony did his best to cram all his clothes into the duffel bag. With difficulty he pulled the grommets together and forced them over the metal joiner. He threw the bag on his shoulder and joined the crowd that was jamming the stairs.

For the first time since his arrival, Tony did not run. He was already sweating in his khakis, and he did not want to get dust on his dress shoes. He hunched over under the weight of the duffel bag and walked past the waiting busses to the parade ground.

"Ten-*hut!*" Lieutenant Wakefield called out in his stentorian voice.

Wally whispered, "Shit, man, I thought we'd seen the last of this prick."

"All right, men, I'm glad to see you looking sharp. And I want you to stay sharp and pay attention. Don't think because this is your last day here we can't pull you off that bus and — "

"That's enough, Lieutenant. Thank you." Captain Maxwell motioned his executive officer aside. "Well, men, it's been a long hard haul, and I'm glad to see that you made it through. I told you eight weeks ago that we'd make soldiers out of you, and I think we've lived up to that promise. I'm proud of you — all of you. And I hope every one of you is proud of himself. You have every right to be. You've gone through some rigorous training. You've learned well. Now you're ready to go on to pursue your mission in the Army of the United States of America, and to serve your fellow countrymen standing behind you. I hope you'll remember your brief stay here — " Groans from the men were followed by a smile from the captain. " — and I wish you the best of success in your military career. Thank you."

Wally shook his head. "All that guy ever does is give speeches."

Then Lieutenant Wakefield took over. He paused dramatically for half a minute, surveying the troops, before he said for the last time, "Dis-*missed*!"

Delta Company, Sixth Battalion, Second Brigade, dissolved to pandemonium. Hats flew into the air, arms went around companions, dance steps pounded the red Georgia earth.

"Haw haw haw haw haw."

Wally put his hands on Tony's shoulders. "You never got your twenty bucks, did you?"

Tony shrugged.

"I knew the old dirtbag wouldn't come across. He told me the reason he wasn't recommending me for OCS was because I was the only holdout who never signed up for that fucking bond. Who the fuck wants to be an officer anyway? It means five more months of bullshit training before your two-year enlistment obligation commences." Wally tossed his duffel onto his left shoulder, thrust out his right hand. "Well, man, it was nice knowing you."

"Sure, same here."

Wally took back his hand, readjusted the weight of the bag. "See you in hell." He turned and boarded the waiting bus, bound for the train terminal in Augusta.

"So long."

Wally did not turn back.

"Y'all take 'er easy." Hank punched Tony lightly on the shoulder. "It's been real good knowin' ya. An' if y'all ever come to Winston-Salem after the war, stop in an' look me up."

"Thanks, Hank. And if you're ever in Philadelphia . . . "

"Will do." He squeezed his bearlike bulk through the door, pushing his overnight bag in front of him.

Tom gave Tony a backhand to the stomach, then held it out for a hearty shake. "The same goes for Bahston." He turned toward the bus.

"Thanks. And don't forget to write."

The door shut with a clang. Tony backed away to the shade of a tree and sat on the end of his upright duffel bag. The engine roared to life. The bus drove off the dusty parade ground. Arms stuck out the windows, waving.

Then they were gone; the parade grounds were deserted. Tony saw nothing but shimmering heat waves, heard nothing but the wind rustling through the trees. Off in the distance he heard the rumbling of running feet, the cadence of marching songs as another training company went through the motions.

He stood there long after the dust had settled. Then he shouldered his bag and started walking.

Chapter 54

"Who're you?"

"Uh, Private Giovanni."

"Whaddaya want?"

"I'm reporting in."

"For what?"

"For assignment." Tony pulled out his orders and dropped them on the desk. "I've been assigned here for MP school."

The sloe-eyed company clerk picked up the orders and stared at them as if they were written in some foreign language. Granted, military abbreviations were not the easiest code to decipher, but this was his job.

"Shit, you're not supposed to report in till twenty-two hundred hours Sunday."

"I'm early."

"By two days. Look, you're not supposed to be here yet."

Tony took back the orders, and glanced at them. "I think it says here that Sunday is the latest I can report in. It doesn't say anything about how early I can report in."

"Listen, I got enough things to do today processing out the last batch. Why don't you get lost for a couple days?"

"I have no place to go."

"Where did you come from?"

Tony returned the orders. "D-6-2. It's right down the road. But there's no one there now. They're either on their way home, or out on pass."

"Yeah, and I should be gone for the weekend, too. Look, I don't even have the new personnel roster. Why don't you catch a bus to town and stay in a hotel, or something?"

"I might consider doing that, but I'd like to leave my bags here."

"You can't leave them *here*."

"That's why I'd like to sign in."

"Look, there's nobody here who can authorize an off-base pass. Once you sign in you gotta stay here."

"Well, I can use my orders as proof that I'm allowed off base."

"If you sign in you gotta turn in these orders. Without orders you don't get off base."

"How about if I sign in, but hang onto the orders?"

"That ain't the way it's done. You wanta get off base, you don't sign in. You sign in, you gotta stay. Take it or leave it."

"Well, I'd like to have some place to sleep in case I decide not to go into town."

"The supply sergeant's gone, so I can't get you any bedding. Don't you understand I'm here alone?"

"I'm sure you have a key to the supply shack."

The clerk threw his hands into the air and

sighed loudly. "Jesus Christ, I wanta get the fuck outa here."

"Then the sooner you sign me in and issue my bedding, the sooner you can leave. Right?"

He sighed again, and stared with angry eyes. "All right, you win. But it's gonna take a while."

Tony shrugged, and suppressed a smile. "I guess I can wait. I've got nowhere to go. But I could sure use something to eat. Where's the mess hall?"

Wearily, "Mess hall's closed. Don't you listen to me? I'm the only one here."

"Well, how do I get something to eat?"

"Gotta go to the open mess down the road. But you need a meal ticket."

"Okay, how about a meal ticket?"

The clerk put down his pencil. "You can't get a meal ticket till after your processed."

Tony glanced at his watch. "How long will it take?"

"As long as it takes."

"Well, how long are they open?"

"I don't know. I'm not an information center."

"Hmmmn. Well, I wouldn't want to miss supper."

"Look, you think this is easy? I got a lot of work to do. I got a register book to make up. I got forms to find. I got papers to type. And if it wasn't for you, this wouldn't hafta be done till Sunday."

"Well, it doesn't make much difference whether you do it now or later."

"Except that I ain't on duty on Sunday."

Tony sat down on the nearest uncomfortable bench and pulled a paperback book out of his overnight bag. A couple chapters later, the clerk cleared his throat.

"All right, here you go. Sign the book and fill in the information under the appropriate columns: name, rank, serial number, date, time, order reference numbers, et cetera." He handed Tony a pencil and rummaged through his desk. "Shit, I don't have a placement sheet yet. I told you, you were too early. You can't be assigned to a platoon until I know where to put you."

"Can't I do that on Sunday?"

"I guess you'll have to," the clerk responded, with a snarl. He shoved a requisition sheet under the pencil. "Sign this, too."

"What's it for?"

"Your bedding."

"Where is it?"

"Just hold your pants on. I'm gonna get it for you just as soon as the paperwork's done."

Tony signed a few more forms, all of which the clerk stamped with a seal. When everything was in order, he took a key off the pegboard. "Get your duffel and follow me."

Tony signed more forms at the quartermaster's issuing shed, then received two sheets, one blanket, and one pillow case.

"Where do I sleep?"

The clerk gestured toward the four beige barracks. "Take your pick. Just don't mess nothing up."

"How about that meal ticket?"

"You know something? You are a royal pain in the ass."

****

Ring.

"Hello."

"Hi. Is Patty there?"

"Who's this?"

"Tony."

"Tony who."

"Giovanni."

"Who?"

"Tony Giovanni."

"What do you want?"

"I want to talk with Patty."

"What for?"

"Look, Mrs. O'Brien, could I please just talk with Patty? I'm calling long distance."

"Well, I'll see if she's here."

Muffled: "Patty, there's somebody on the phone for you. But keep it short. I don't want the phone tied up all night"

"Hello."

"Hi."

"Tony!"

"Hi, how are you?"

"All right, I guess."

"Good. Glad to hear it." Gap. "Well, how's everything at home?"

"About the same."

"Are you working hard?"

"No. Thank God the job fell through. I didn't want to work in a dingy old restaurant anyway."

"Well, what have you been doing with yourself?"

"Oh, nothing much."

"Come on, you must have done something. You don't just lie around in bed all day, do you?"

"Well, no, but it sure is nice to sleep late for a change."

"Well, how's the gang?"

"Okay, I guess. We're all going down to the shore tomorrow. Kate's parent's house in Wildwood."

"Yes, I'm sorry I won't be there with you."

"Oh, that's all right. It's a shame you can't make it, but I'm sure we'll have fun anyway, playing on the beach, walking on the boardwalk, eating cotton candy. The whole gang'll be there."

"Sounds like fun." Gap. "So, how are things

at home?"

Whispered: "My grandmother's been as bitchy as ever. She keeps making me do all these stupid errands for her, as if I don't already have enough things of my own to do."

"What do you mean?"

"Well, she makes me go to the store, just to pick up little things that she could do without. One day it's the hardware store, then it's the food store, then it's the drug store. She's always sending me to the drug store to pick up her stupid prescriptions."

"Is she sick?"

"Yeah, sick in the head."

"Yes, she wasn't very friendly to me on the phone just now."

"Well, she's not half as sick as I am."

"What's wrong with you?"

"Oh, nothing much. I'm just having woman problems. You know. I get cramps a lot, and I don't feel good all the time, like I'm sick to my stomach."

"Have you been to a doctor?"

"No, it's nothing that bad. I always get cramps anyway, every month. Besides, my grandmother wouldn't let me go unless I told her all about it, and I'm not gonna do that."

"Well, I certainly hope you're feeling better."

"Oh, I'll be okay."

Pause.

"Well, look, I guess I'd better be going. I — I just wanted to call and find out how you were."

"Okay."

"And — I can't wait to see you again." Pause. "I guess I'll be home for sure, in eight weeks."

"Okay. And keep writing. I like to hear — I mean, I like to get letters from you."

"Okay, Patty. I'll try. Uh, I guess I'd better say good-bye. I don't have that much change."

"Okay. 'Bye."

"I miss you."

Click.

****

"Hi, Grandpop."

"Well, hello there, Tony. How are you?"

"Oh, I'm just fine. The big question is, how are *you*?"

"Fair to middlin', I s'pose. I'm up an' around some, though I'm not winnin' any races. Your grandmother is takin' good care of me."

"I'm glad to hear that. Uh, did you get the phone moved to the bedroom, or are you in the dining room?"

"Oh, I'm sittin' in my favorite readin' chair. The doctors say it's good for me to get outa the prone position an' get a little exercise. So I walk around the house a bit, then rest in my chair an' read a book till I get too tired to hold my head up. Then I go an' lay down for a spell. I get tired pretty easy these days."

"Wow, I'm glad to hear you're getting better. I guess before you know it, you'll be playing ball on the back steps, and hitting homers."

"Well, I kinda think my ball playin' days are over, honey, but that won't stop me from watchin' you an' your dad play. When do you think you'll be comin' home?"

"Did you get my last letter — the one where I talked about going to MP school?"

"That must be the one that come yesterday. I keep all your letters right by the bed so's when I get lonesome for some company I read every one right through."

"Well, in that letter I said I was being assigned to MP school — that's military police. What I didn't know then was the school is right here in Fort Gordon, and it starts on Monday. So there was no time for me to come home. And even if there was, since my next assignment is on the same base, I wouldn't have gotten any travel allowance so I would have had to pay my own way home and back. Anyway, I guess it'll be another eight weeks before I get leave."

"My word, honey, what are they doin' keepin' you away for so long? Don't they know you got folks at home who care about you, an' want to see you?"

"Well, that's just the way it is, I guess."

"So how are they treatin' you? As bad as you thought?"

"Worse. No, only kidding. Actually, once you get used to the humiliation and make believe it's all a game, it's not so bad. Anyway, the worst is over. I guess they'll ease up on us now that we're out of basic."

"I'm sure glad about that. I see you shot expert. Second in your class, wasn't you?"

"Well, fourth actually. Three guys tied for first place."

"Nobody tied you in exercises, did they?"

"Well, no. I guess I was the winner there."

"I told you you could do anything if you set your mind to it. Now you just keep on tryin' your best. An' don't let nobody tell you different. You work as hard in the army as you did with them books in school an' you'll get by just fine."

"Well, the classroom work is the easiest part. Even the physical training is not too hard. The real killer is the heat. It's hotter here than it ever was in the watermelon fields."

"Just keep drinkin' a lot of water so's you don't get dried out. How are you makin' out with the food? Gettin' enough to eat?"

"Just barely. They always have plenty of food, but they only give us fifteen minutes to eat it. I always go out the door with a couple slices of bread in my pocket so I can sneak a snack later on."

"It's not good to bolt your food that way."

"I know, but I don't have any choice. And they don't let us have any seconds, either. They throw all the extra food away, and the local farmers come and haul it away for their pigs."

"Now that don't seem right."

"1 know, but that's the way it is."

"How are you makin' out with your money? You got enough?"

"I've got plenty because there's nothing to spend it on. I went into town a couple times and stayed in hotels, but other than that, the only thing I've bought are some meals and a few candy bars."

"How much are you gettin'?"

"Candy?"

"No, money."

"Oh. Well, I started out at eighty-six dollars a month, then got an increase to ninety-one. If you work that out on an hourly basis, using a forty-hour week, it comes to less than fifty cents an hour. But since we work sixteen hour days, it's really less than a quarter an hour."

"My word, that less'n I used to pay you for pickin' crab grass out'n the lawn — an' you was only a boy then."

"I know. A dollar an hour for picking watermelons seems incredible, now."

"It don't seem like very much money, no matter how little you spend. How are you payin' for this call?"

"Oh, I went to the PX and got a bunch of quarters."

"Well, from now on, when you call here you reverse the charges, you hear?"

"Aw, Grandpop, I don't want to do that."

"You just tell the operator I'll pay for the call. Just do it. Now listen, I think I hear your grandmother callin' me. An' I think I better go an' lie down for the evenin'. These ole bones can't stand to be up too long. But you call again real soon. An' you tell the operator to bill me. You hear?"

"Okay."

"Good. An' I'll write just as soon as I can. I know I haven't been too good about writin' — "

"But you've been sick."

"Well, maybe now I'm feelin' better I can do some writin'. But any time you want to talk — about anything — you just call. I can still talk on the phone. You hear?"

"Okay."

"Good. Then you take care of yourself. An' remember that your grandmother an' I love you, and wish you the best of health."

"Thanks, Grandpop."

"'Bye now."

"So long."

****

Clan! Clang! Clang! Clang!

"Wake up! Wake up! Everybody up! Outa them bunks! This ain't no fuckin' Boy Scout camp! I said WAKE UP!"

Tony barely opened his eyes when a vice squeezed his shoulder, picked him up, and propelled him out of the bunk and onto the floor. The sheet he had been using for a cover wrapped itself around him as he rolled into the adjacent bunk, and it took several seconds for him to disentangle himself. He was still squinting his eyes and shielding them from the bright lights when a body crashed onto the floor next to him.

"I said get outa bed, and that means you."

The man sat on the floor like a lump.

Tony must have been on the floor a moment too long, for the next thing he knew, he was picked up physically and placed on his feet. The sergeant's face was so close to his that the brim of his Smokey-the-Bear hat needled his forehead.

Bright blue eyes that could have been pools of Arctic water, but were as deep as Caribbean Blue Holes, stared from between a wrinkled brow and dancing crow's feet. A small mouth and thin lips grinned sardonically. Amid the wrinkles, a small nose flared like two miniature smoke stacks.

The sergeant raised the five-gallon pail to Tony's ear and beat the inside with a drumstick. "Get up, you dunderhead! Get up! On the double! NOW!"

Gone in a flash was the tranquility of the weekend, the peace and quiet of a lazy summer day, the serenity of an empty barrack. The room burst into life with the aimless precision of an anthill, with sheets and blankets flying, feet pounding, clothes donning. Those who were extremely fast got out of bed before they were thrown out. Tony was still draped in his blanket when the sergeant clanged back down the aisle.

"What're you looking at, fuck head?" Before he could think of an appropriate reply, Tony was dragged roughly to a closet and flung inside. "Pick up that bucket and mop and start swabbin' the deck."

"O — okay."

"WHAT!"

"I mean, yes, sergeant."

Padding along in his stocking feet, Tony skidded into the latrine and, while the bucket was filling from the utility faucet, splashed cold water onto his face. When he discovered that he was still wearing the sheet, he rolled it up and tucked it under his arm. Then he stumbled awkwardly back to his bunk with the full bucket, and started swabbing.

The barrack was in turmoil. The sergeant bellowed orders and shouted directions, and kicked those who were slow to respond. All the bunks were removed from the right side of the aisle to give clearance for mopping, waxing, and buffing. At the same time, men sponged down the walls, washed the windows, and dusted the rafters. Then all the bunks were removed from the left side to get at *that* side of the floor.

Another crew cleaned out the latrine: sterilizing the toilets, polishing the fixtures, washing down the tile, removing the showerheads and cleaning out the filters.

Outside, in the dark, the steps and sidewalk were swept. The windows were washed down with rubber glass scrapers like windshield wipers. The sand was diligently raked into neat, parallel rows. The rakers had only starlight to guide them.

After two hours, five o'clock formation was called, and the men were herded onto the parade ground. When they were dressed off, and standing rigidly at attention, the commanding officer made his appearance.

He was dressed in starched fatigues, helmet liner, and highly polished jump boots that matched the color of his face. "My name is Captain Johnson. I'm in charge of this training company, and for the next eight weeks you will do everything I say. You men are here to become military police — the pride of the United States Army. You must set an example as the strongest, the smartest, the neatest, the cleanest, the most dedicated — in a word, the best. And I'm going to see to it that you do. Anyone who falls below these standards will not remain under my command. You *will* do your best, or suffer the consequences. That is all."

Just like that he was gone. In the darkness, his black figure disappeared into the shadows. Then the blonde sergeant herded Tony and the rest of his platoon back into the barrack.

"I'm Sergeant Swansea, an' I'm a motherfucker. Anybody who gets outa line gets slapped up side the head. An' if that don't learn you to stay in line — there's worse. But you don't want to find out about it. Just do as I say, an' we'll get along fine. An' one thing you better get through your thick heads: there ain't no complaints in this outfit. You do what I say, when I say it. Or else you die."

****

Tony failed the first inspection. But then, so did everyone else, without exception.

He knew there was something wrong when he returned from breakfast and saw the pile of mattresses, sheets, blankets, clothing, and footlockers piled on the ground below each window. The second floor footlockers had not been thrown out with the rest, but their contents had

been, and the personal belongings of the second floor personnel was mingled with the first floor debris. Tony spent the entire morning separating his belongings from everyone else's.

Sergeant Swansea made them scrub down the barrack again before he permitted anything to be brought back inside. The moving-in procedure was complicated by the fact that he did not allow boots to be worn in the building, as the hard soles might scratch the newly buffed floor.

"Looks like a Japanese geisha house," one man commented.

Like everyone else, Tony took his turn at standing on the wooden steps, and shaking the sand out of his clothes and bedding. Toilet articles that had been used to pass many inspections in basic were bent, crushed, or just plain missing. Civilian items were not allowed in the barracks, and had to be stowed in the quartermaster shed, to be retrieved when training was completed. The only book allowed was the *Bible*.

"It could be worse," Tony laughed to his comrades. "It could be raining."

During the inspection that followed lunch, Tony stood by his bunk and watched as Sergeant Swansea tore the barrack apart, dumped the footlockers, and pulled down the bedding. Two hours later, Tony had all his clothes and his bunk put back together. It took Sergeant Swansea only a few minutes to destroy it again.

During the course of the afternoon there were also clothing inspections: one in fatigues, one in khakis, and one in dress greens (which Tony had never worn before). He said in aside, "My clothes are going to be worn out just from putting them on and taking them off."

After supper, the men spent until midnight preparing for morning inspection. Every stitch of clothing had to be pressed, and since only one iron was allotted per floor, this was a time-consuming task. Meanwhile, Tony polished brass buttons until they were slippery to the touch and glinted like gold. When he could see his reflection clearly enough on the toe of his boots to shave by it, he put away the polish.

At four thirty in the morning he was aroused by the tune of Sergeant Swansea's pail — and leaped out of bed before he could be thrown out. The practice barrack cleaning of the previous day was entertained in full earnest.

Every crack and crevice was scrubbed — with a toothbrush. The switch plates and receptacle covers were removed, and the spaces behind them cleaned — as well as the backs of the covers. The bunks were aligned with a string that was drawn across the room.

"This is bound to make me a better soldier."

In the latrine, the traps below the sinks were disassembled and scoured. The electrical fixtures were taken off the ceiling and washed out. The copper bases of the light bulbs, as well as the inside of the sockets, were shined with Brasso. The grout between the tiles in the shower stalls was touched up with white paint.

"Mister, is that toilet clean?" Sergeant Swansea pointed with rigid arm and finger.

The man who had just scrubbed it with disinfectant, for the third time, gulped. "Yes, sergeant."

The sergeant handed him a coffee mug. "Then drink it."

The man dipped the mug into the bowl, smelled it, and took a sip.

Tony sat mutely in the mess hall: no talking was allowed during meals. After he finished chugging his chow, he learned what the word 'strict' meant.

Captain Johnson marched stiffly into the barrack. Tony already stood at attention, but he got into more attention. Sergeant Swansea had rigged the string line so that the middle button on every man's chest was precisely the same distance from the center of the aisle.

The captain had two items in his hands: a three-foot carpenter's level, and a cardboard template. He held the level in front of each man, and plumbed his gig line. If anything was a hair out of alignment, or if the gig line was not perpendicular to the gravitational attraction of the earth, the man's clothes were ripped apart, buttons flying. The template was the size of the footlocker shelf, and it had cutouts that corresponded in size and shape of each toilet article. He dropped the cardboard into the shelf. If it did not fall flat so that the appropriate articles protruded through the openings without being touched, the platoon sergeant overturned the entire footlocker. Not one man passed inspection unscathed.

After that, it really got tough.

****

By the end of the week, Tony was getting used to having three inspections a day. Captain Johnson had set the standards, and Sergeant Swansea made sure they were upheld. He screamed constantly, ripped bunks apart, dumped footlockers, and tore off clothes.

"Military police are the finest, proudest men in this man's army. And they *better* look that way."

When he was not getting ready for inspection, or cleaning up after one, Tony read books, pamphlets, and bulletins on military courtesy, law, chain of command, obedience, and personal hygiene. He was given reading assignments, and was expected to study each night. He practiced on the firing range with the standard army

Colt .45 automatic pistol. And he drove a jeep and studied for his military driver's license.

It was not until Saturday that the army postal system caught up with his move and forwarded his mail.

****

Dear Tony,

I'm glad you called last night. I'm writing this from the shore. I was feeling kind of lonesome, and was watching TV and waiting for Kathy to come and pick me up. I didn't feel so good, but I wanted to get out of the house and away from my grandmother. She's been picking on me a lot lately, now that I'm out of school, and I would like to leave — for good. But I can't afford to. I don't have any money, and I have no place to go. My mother won't let me live with her because I may interfere with her love life. And my father — well, forget it. I don't remember the last time he came to see me. And ever since I turned eighteen he stopped sending checks, and my grandmother is really POed about that.

Well, anyway, Kathy and I went out and tried to have some fun, but I wasn't feeling too good. She knows all about it and thinks I should go and see a doctor. But I'm scared to go because I'm afraid my grandmother will find out. I'm afraid he'll call her and tell her what's wrong with me.

The problem is that I haven't had my friend for two months. Ever since you left. Of course, I've never been regular, but I never missed a month before. I'm scared. I don't know what to do. Please write and tell me what to do. I'm scared.

Yours truly,
Patty.

Chapter 55

"You ain't leavin' this base for nothing, I don't care if your mother just croaked."

"But, sarge, this is — "

"Who the fuck you callin' sarge? You call me sergeant, with respect."

"All right. Sergeant. Look, I've got to make a phone call. It's important. I — "

"There ain't nothing important to you other than doing what I say. As far as you're concerned, the rest of the world don't exist. *I'm* your world."

"But, sergeant — "

"That's all, Giovanni."

"But — "

"I said THAT'S ALL." Sergeant Swansea gritted his teeth and made feint motions with his fists. Blonde eyebrows pinched devilishly. "Now get back in there and get to work. And don't let me catch you sneakin' off, or I'll have your ass in front of the captain so fast it'll make your head spin. Now move."

Tony returned to his bunk, and reread his mail. The world *did* exist.

****

Sunday morning dawned with dress inspection. Shoes were buffed until they shone mirror bright. Brass buttons and buckles glittered with the luster of gold. Gig lines were mathematically straight; creases were scalpel sharp. Marksmanship badges, the only authorized insignia, gleamed silvery.

Military police were pious. As the entire company was marched to church, Tony spied a phone booth.

He paid little attention to the services. As the chaplain droned on about freedom and justice, Tony pushed through the crowd, turned off the anteroom, and ducked into the lavatory. He took a drink from the sink faucet, dried his hands, and stepped back into the anteroom.

Sergeant Swansea stood at the curb, about thirty feet from the arched doors, conversing with the other platoon sergeants. Tony stepped out onto the wooden landing. They took no notice. Soldiers from all over the base were attending. He leisurely walked down the steps, turned away from the gossiping sergeants, and passed around to the opposite side of the building. From there he veered at a diagonal, always keeping the church between himself and the NCOs. On the street he made a wide circuit that brought him to the phone booth.

Tony hailed three PFCs in fatigues. "Excuse me, but do any of you happen to have change for a dollar? I've got to make a phone call."

The tall one stuck his hand into his pocket. "I've got some. Let's see. Twenty-five, fifty, sixty, seventy, seventy-five, eighty-five. Nope, only eighty-five cents."

"That's close enough." Tony handed him a dollar bill and took the change."

Another was inspecting the coins in his hand. "Sixty cents here." Tony bought it with a bill.

"Only got a quarter," said the third. "But you can have it." Tony tried to give him a picture of Washington, but the PFC stuck his hands in his pockets. "I'm not gonna steal money off an E-2."

"Thanks. Hey, if I have any leftover you can have it back. They won't let us keep change in MP school because it rattles in our pockets."

"If you're an MP, I'm gettin' away from here."

"Thanks again." Tony shoved money into the coin slots, gave the number to the operator. His underarms were soaked, and his palms were covered with nervous sweat.

"Hello."

"Hello. Is Patty there?"

"Who's this?"

"Tony Giovanni."

"Well, she's not here. She went to mass."

"Do you know when she'll be back?"

"She's going out with her mother afterwards, so she may not be back till late."

"Oh." Pause. "Well, will you please tell her I called? And that I'll try to call her again when — as soon as I get a chance."

"Well, I guess so." *Click.*

Tony returned to the church, waited until the service was over, then mixed with the uniformed men as they emerged from the building.

****

"So what if it's Sunday night? I don't care if it's Christmas Eve, you ain't leavin' this barrack unless I get a direct order from the captain."

"All right, then let me see the captain."

"Nobody sees the captain unless I say so."

"Then say so."

"He ain't here. He's with his family on Sunday. And even if he was here, I'd still say no. He can't be bothered with insignificant details."

"All right, then just let me slip out for five minutes to make a phone call."

"You're gettin' on my nerves, Giovanni. I already said that's out of the question, and that's that. If I let every goddamn recruit out to make phone calls whenever they wanted to, this buildin'd be empty by now. You guys'd be roamin' all over this base. Now, the answer's no. And that's final. So don't pester me no more."

Sergeant Swansea slammed the door in Tony's face. Tony returned to his bunk, mumbling under his breath. "He's afflicted with incurable mental myopia."

"Don't take it so hard, buddy," Joe Gidley said. "They're just being tough on us because we're new. They want us to knuckle under. They'll ease up in a week or so."

Tony picked up a boot with a microscopic layer of dust on it, and gave it a few half-hearted swipes with the brush. "Yes, I guess you're right." He dropped the boot and brush, leaned back on his bunk, and stared at the ceiling.

A few minutes later, Sergeant Swansea made bed check. "You better be ready for inspection in the morning, Giovanni. I'm gonna be pissed if this platoon don't pass because of you."

"I'm ready right now."

The sergeant thrust out his pointed, clean-shaven chin. "Hmmph." He swaggered up and down the aisle, counting the men like a mother hen counting her chicks. He stopped at Tony's bunk on the way back. "And don't get any fancy ideas in your head about sneaking' out later. I'll be watchin' for you."

****

"What do you want, soldier?"

"I'd like to see Captain Johnson."

"Do you have an appointment?"

"Uh, no. Do I need one?"

"Of course. You think you can just walk in here and take up the captain's time?" The first sergeant narrowed his eyes. "Hey, who's your platoon sergeant?"

"Sergeant Swansea."

"Didn't he explain that to you?"

"About needing an appointment? Well, I don't think so."

"You're supposed to have classes in military etiquette. Or weren't you paying attention?"

"Well, I guess I just forgot. How about if I make an appointment now?"

"You don't make it here. You make it through your platoon sergeant. Then he makes it — if he thinks it's important."

"Oh."

****

"GIOVANNI!"

"Here, sergeant."

"Get your ass over here."

Tony stepped out of formation and jogged to where Sergeant Swansea stood, in the shade of a spreading magnolia tree, his Smokey-the-Bear hat pulled down close to knitted brows.

"Yes, sergeant?"

"Did you go into the orderly room this morning and make a request to see the captain?"

"Uh, yes — sergeant."

A shadow loomed out of the corner of Tony's eye. Then something as hard and as solid as an anvil crashed into the side of his head. His helmet liner flew off. He stumbled to the ground.

"Get on your feet."

Tony scrabbled to his knees, retrieved his helmet liner, and stood up shakily. He rubbed the side of his head, then donned the plastic liner. His face stung.

"Don't you ever go over my head again, you hear? The first thing you learned in basic is the chain of command. You got a problem, you come to me — and nobody else."

Tony tried hard to keep his hands at his side, to not rub his tingling face. "But sergeant, I did go to you. And you refused my request."

"And you know why? Because your request was groundless. That was my decision to make, and I made it. And once I make it, it stays made. You go over my head, and it shows you have no respect for my decision."

"It's not that, sergeant, it's — "

"Shut up when I'm talking. You better learn a lesson, boy. I'm in charge here. What I say, goes. And you don't do nothing unless I approve."

"Well, what do I have to do to get approval to make a simple phone call?"

"Don't get smart with me. You don't make phone calls, and that's final. You're in training, and part of that training is doing what you're told. And you better get that through your thick head. Now get inside and change that uniform. I want you looking spic-and-span and back in formation in five minutes."

"Yes, sergeant."

****

For the military police, the pride of the army, morning inspection was of paramount importance. Freshly starched fatigues were donned, bunks were made so tight that they could support a footlocker without sagging, the floors were scrubbed, waxed, and buffed. The latrine was as sterile as an operating room.

Captain Johnson marched in stiffly, accompanied by his executive officer and Sergeant Swansea. The XO carried a clipboard on which he made notations of everything: condition of the barracks, presentation of the men, and overall appearance. Demerits were given to each man for failure to comply with the strict rules of personal dress and deportment.

When the captain stopped in front of him, Tony snapped a proper salute. "Giovanni, Anthony J., private E-2, US52666498. Ready for inspection, *sir*." Captain Johnson scrutinized Tony's attire, looking for hair or dandruff on his shoulders, scratches on his belt buckle, dust on his combat boots. Then, without stooping or bending, he peered down into his footlocker: the tray had been removed and was sitting on the open lid, allowing a full view of all his possessions. The return salute was the signal that he had passed. Captain Johnson executed a left turn, but before he could step away to the next trainee, Tony said, "Excuse me, sir, but how can I get permission to make a phone call?"

Captain Johnson stopped as if he had run into a brick wall. His black face blanched. Tony became aware of a preternatural stillness in the barrack: the men had stopped breathing. The captain stared at Tony for a full minute before responding.

"Lieutenant, put this man on report. Extra duty plus ten demerits. Have him guard the motor pool tonight, and every night until he learns that privates do not talk to commanding officers unless instructed to do so."

****

The sergeant of the guard arrived for Tony in a canvas-covered stake-body truck, just as the sun was going down. After a whispered conversation with Sergeant Swansea, he motioned him into the back with half a dozen other men. Tony stared at his companions silently.

After a short but bumpy ride, the truck pulled off the side of the road and Sergeant Jordan, a three-striper with only a half serious demeanor, called Tony out.

"Look, mister, I'm supposed to see to it you don't make any phone calls, but I sure as hell ain't gonna spend the night baby sitting you. So I'll have to threaten you instead. First of all, there ain't a phone within a mile of this place, so don't go looking for one. Second of all, I pass by here about every thirty minutes, maybe not so you can see me — like, I may be patrolling across that field, but I'll be able to see if you're still here — so I'll be keeping tabs on you. And thirdly, if I come by here and you ain't here, and on the ball, you're ass is gonna be in a helluva lot more trouble than it already is. You get me?"

Tony nodded slowly. "It's all pretty clear, sarge."

"Good. You just do your duty and everything'll be all right. In the morning, I'll take you back to your company. Now, you walk up and down this fence, but stay off the grass. There's no walking on the grass. There's no resting, no stopping, and no smoking. Your rifle must be at parade arms at all times, but you can switch shoulders whenever you feel like it."

The sergeant reached into the cab and pulled out an M-14. He pulled back the bolt, checked the barrel, and handed it to Tony — empty.

Tony hefted the weapon. "Suppose I have to shoot someone?"

"Don't worry about it. Nobody's going to break into the motor pool at night. The gate's locked and the fence is covered with barbed wire."

"Then why bother guarding it?"

The sergeant stared at Tony in the half-light. "Now I see why they got you out here."

Tony let it go. "Am I just supposed to walk in front, or all the way around?"

"You just stay here by the street. You got three street lights along here — they'll come on as soon as it gets real dark — and anybody with any funny ideas will see you standing guard."

The sun set, the stars came out, the moon rose. Tony guarded, relentlessly. He inspected the hefty brass lock on the front gate, and quickly determined that it could not be picked with a hatpin. Besides, who would want to steal a deuce-and-a-half, or a tank? Where would you hide it? Where would you sell it? You could not file the serial numbers off a tank and unload it anonymously.

He was relieved at ten o'clock, and taken to the guardhouse where he was allowed to sleep under the brilliant incandescent lights until the midnight shift went out. At two a.m. he was picked up, trucked back to the guardhouse, and allowed to catch some more shuteye before being awakened for the four o'clock shift. At

six, Sergeant Jordan picked him up and drove him back to the company where he arrived in time for breakfast — and inspection.

Captain Johnson did not appear to be overjoyed to see him.

****

It was not until Wednesday that Tony figured out how to make his phone call. It was such a simple plan that he kicked himself for not thinking of it sooner. He went on sick call.

Sergeant Swansea glowered when he fell out along with half a dozen others. This was one thing, at least, that Tony did not need permission for. He signed for his pass in the orderly room. One man was selected as temporary squad leader; his job was to see that every man arrived at the clinic, and returned — together. They marched to the bus stop, two blocks away, and eventually arrived at the hospital on the other side of the base. Total travel time to the outpatient clinic was about an hour.

Tony then spent two more hours standing in line with some men who could barely stand. Some, of necessity, plopped on the linoleum floor and shuffled along on their knees as the line progressed with snaillike speed. Interns were seen on a first come, first served basis.

The medic perfunctorily took his temperature, pulse, and blood pressure. "What's wrong with you?"

"I think I'm going insane."

"What?"

"I wake up every morning in this strange building filled with naked men, and with this sergeant walking down the aisle beating a trash can with a stick. Then I've got to stand in the rain while someone reads my name off a clipboard, do a half hour of exercises, run for two miles, gulp down breakfast sweaty and gasping for air, stand in formation again, then raise my hand if someone asks me if I'm sick. That's not normal, is it?"

"Ha, ha, ha. You had me going there for a minute." The medic pushed back inch-long hair. "It may not be normal, but it's the army. So what's your problem?"

"I need a discharge."

"Don't we all. But you'll need to be a lot crazier than you are to get into the insane asylum."

"Who's trying to get into one? I'm trying to get out of it."

The medic laughed again. "Thanks. I can use a little humor in this job. But really, I've got some sick men out there. What's wrong with you?"

"Well, about five hours ago I had an upset stomach."

"All right, you win." The intern slapped a small plastic vial into Tony's hand. "Take two of these every four hours, get plenty of rest, and drink lots of fluids. Next!"

Tony pocketed the aspirins. "Thanks for the pep talk." While he waited for the rest of the men to receive their treatment, he sauntered toward a public phone and put through his call.

"Hello?"

"Hi. Patty? This is Tony."

"*Tony!* Where are you?"

"In the hospital."

"My God, what's wrong?"

"Oh, nothing, but it was the only way I could get to a phone booth."

"Why didn't you call me back on Sunday?"

"I couldn't. This is worse than basic training. They watch us here like prisoners. And after church we went straight to class. They're teaching us how to drive jeeps so we can get a military driver's license."

"Well, I waited around all day, expecting you to call. I was supposed to go out with Kathy. Instead, she hung around here. And you never called. She was really mad."

"Well, I'm sorry. I really didn't have much choice in the matter."

"You would have found some way if you really wanted to talk to me."

"Patty, I did want to, but I couldn't. We had class."

"Even on Sunday?"

"We have classes and PT and inspections every day — and night. I'm lucky I got the chance to call now. I was afraid after I finally got to a phone that you'd be away — at work, or something."

"I don't want to work like everybody else. I just want to get away from this house, and my bitchy grandmother."

"Well, I'm sorry. Anyway, how are you feeling?"

"Not too good. I sleep late every morning because I'm so tired. My grandmother keeps waking me up and nagging me all the time because I don't do anything. Look, I just got out of school after twelve years, and I need a rest. What the hell does she expect from me?"

"I don't know. Maybe she just wants you to, you know, pitch in around the house a little more. It must be a lot of work for her — she's pretty old."

"No, she's just being mean because my father stopped paying her money. I don't make any more money for her. I'm just another mouth to feed. She never really wanted me, just the money I brought in."

"Well, maybe you should figure some way of getting out and living on your own. You know, maybe you could get a job and move in with Kathy. You said she was getting her own apartment."

"But I don't have any money to pay for it. I'd have to pay for my own food. I don't have any money. I never had money like you had. The guys are always telling me that you always have money, so you don't know what it's like. But I never had any of my own."

"That's just because you never had a job. Now if you went to work — "

"But there's nothing I can do. I just got out of school, so what do I know about work? Besides, I don't feel good and I'm sick all the time, and soon I won't be able to work anyway. And what do I do when my grandmother finds out?" She started sniffing. "I'm entitled to a living just like everyone else. But nobody wants me. My mother won't let me move in with her. And my grandmother doesn't want me any more. What am I going to do?"

Patty broke down completely, sobbing uncontrollably. "What am I going to do?"

****

"Sergeant, I need to make an appointment to see Captain Johnson."

"Giovanni, how many times I gotta tell you? You can't see the captain."

"But this is important."

"Since when is making a phone call important?"

"Oh, this isn't about a phone call. I want an emergency leave."

"Are you outa your fucking mind? You can't get leave in the middle of AIT. Whaddaya think this is, some kinda kindergarten class, where you can go home crying for your mother every time something don't go your way?"

"But, sarge — I mean, sergeant. I have an emergency situation at home which requires my immediate presence."

"The only emergency that'll get you outa this program is a death in the family — your own. Now get your ass back in formation. And don't let me hear nothing else about leaves unless they're the kind that grow on trees."

****

"I'd like to see Captain Johnson, please."

"Do you have an appoint — " When the first sergeant looked up from his crossword puzzle and saw Tony, he changed his tune. "Hey, what do you want now?"

Tony enunciated with precision, "I would like to see Captain Johnson."

"Nobody sees the CO without an appointment. That's the rule."

"Well, guess what? It's time to change the rules, because I intend to see the captain."

The sergeant rose up out of his chair. "Just who the hell do you think you are?"

"Giovanni, Anthony J., private E-2, US52666498."

"Oh, a wise guy, eh?"

"I'm just answering your question, sergeant.

Also, I should like to mention that part of my training under this command has been in the legal aspects of the Unified Code of Military Justice. Under the USMJ, I am entitled to make an appointment with the commanding officer of my unit any time I have the need to discuss things of a personal nature."

"Okay, mister smart ass." The sergeant kicked his chair back against the wall. "You sit down right there and I'll see to it you get to see the captain."

Tony sat compliantly.

The sergeant stormed into the captain's office without knocking. He slammed the door behind him. Tony heard raised voices. The sergeant emerged a few seconds later with a smile on his face. "The captain will see you now."

"Thank you, sergeant."

Tony stopped at the sill and made his formal announcement. "Private Giovanni requesting permission to see the captain."

"Sergeant Baker informed me that you *demanded* to see me."

Tony stayed at the sill. He had not been given permission to enter. "Sir, I requested permission first. It was only after my continuous requests were refused that I was forced to make demands guaranteed by the Unified Code of Military Justice."

"So now you're a lawyer, are you? All right, Giovanni. Come in here."

Tony stepped into the office, remained at attention. "Sir, I am only repeating information I have learned during my attendance in class."

"It's nice to know you've learned something, even if it hasn't been respect for your superior officers."

"Sir, respect can only be earned, not enforced. I find it difficult to respect men who teach the Unified Code of Military Justice, but who choose not to abide by it. Speaking of which, I should like to mention that it is unlawful under that Code for a sergeant to physically abuse anyone under his command, under penalty of court-martial."

"And have you been so abused?"

Tony hesitated, feeling that he was being drawn into something beyond his control. "That is not my purpose in being here. Sir, I respectfully request an emergency leave of seven days in order to take care of some personal problems at home. I know this is out of the ordinary, but I did not receive the customary leave after basic training. And I'll gladly make up any classes I miss."

Captain Johnson grasped the arms of his straight-backed chair, his dark eyes unwavering. "For your information, it is not customary for recruits to receive leave after basic training. It is a military courtesy. One accrues leave at

the rate of thirty days per year, and until one puts in that year, one is entitled to nothing."

"That is essentially correct, sir, although adherence is not strict. However, if leave time is prorated on a daily basis it can be shown that for each day of service, approximately point-zero-eight-two-two days of leave time is accrued. Since I have been in service for ten and a half weeks, simple arithmetic will show that I have accrued six days leave time."

The captain studied him intensely for a moment. "Very well thought out, Giovanni, but it's not going to help you. As long as I'm the commanding officer of this outfit, we will do things my way. And I say you'd better get back to class and learn the rest of the Unified Code of Military Justice, because if you read far enough into it you'll find that I can court-martial you for insubordination."

"Sir, I'm not trying to be insubordinate. But this is an emergency. I've got this girl at home — "

Captain Johnson's voice was getting louder. "I don't want to hear about your personal problems, Giovanni. Every man in this outfit has a girl at home. Some of them have wives. Some even have children. But you don't see them in here complaining about it. They're out there in the field doing their duty, and that's what you should be concerned about. Think about your country for once, instead of yourself."

"But, sir, I — "

"I don't want to hear any more about it." He was shouting now. "You are staying in this company. You are going to attend classes and field exercises. And you are going to continue to pull guard duty until you learn that you can't buck the system. And that is all."

****

"Giovanni, get over here."

Tony left the formation and jogged to Sergeant Swansea's jeep. He noticed the pinched eyes, the balled fists. "Sergeant, it says in the Unified Code of Military Justice that it is unlawful for a superior officer, whether commissioned or noncommissioned, to physically assault his subordinates, whatever the provocation, under penalty of court-martial. Any misunderstandings must be taken to a higher authority for determination of cause."

The sergeant bit his lip, clenched his fists harder. He leaned forward and breathed into Tony's face. Tony did not blink. "Well, let me tell you something, mister smart ass. You gotta have witnesses to back you up, or else it's just your word against mine. So let me warn you, if you don't shape up, I'm going to invite you over to the orderly room some night and have a few words with you. Maybe we'll go for a little walk — in the dark. And maybe you won't feel so cocky afterwards. Do I make myself clear?"

"Your threats are perfectly understood, sergeant."

Sergeant Swansea's head jerked back as if he had been hit in the face with a poleax.

"And as long as we're having a discussion, I'd like to make an appointment with the chaplain."

"I'm warning you, Giovanni. Don't push me too far, or I'll beat your face to a pulp so your own mother wouldn't recognize you."

"I'm not intimidated by your overbearing and pugnacious manner, sergeant. May I remind you that the Unified Code of Military Justice assures every man the opportunity to see his chaplain if ordinary channels prove ineffective in aiding him? I am exercising my rights under that code. Now, may I please have that appointment?"

"Boy, you're in big trouble now."

****

The chaplain's office was nowhere near the church. It was tucked into an out-of-the-way corner of the administrative headquarters complex. The floor was worn and unvarnished, the once-white walls faded, the furniture chipped instead of Chippendale. It was as if no one really cared about the chaplain's office.

Captain Jonathan E. Marshall blended right into the room: he was short, thin, stoop shouldered, gray-haired, and still a captain despite his advancing years. "Please have a seat, uh, Tony." He motioned to a wooden chair which showed more oak than gray paint.

Tony rubbed his eyes, forcing them to stay open. "Thank you, sir."

"Yes, yes, of course." Captain Marshall slid delicately into his seat behind the oak desk. "You're eyes appear to be bloodshot. Are you sick?"

"No, I'm — I just haven't gotten much sleep lately. But that's not why I came to see you."

"Ah, yes, I understand you are having some kind of problems with your, ah, superiors?"

"My only problem is finding someone reasonable to deal with."

"Reasonable?"

"Yes. You know, someone who can hear what I'm saying."

"I don't think I follow you."

"Well, I can't seem to get through to anyone in my company. I try to explain, but they don't give me a chance. I get as far as saying that I have some personal problems — at home — and they go deaf on me. They tell me to shut up, that my personal problems don't exist. And they don't even know what they are. They're all solipsists, who think that reality ceases beyond their spheres of influence, or past their noses."

"Yes, well — Of course. Perhaps if you would explain it to me — "

"It's really very simple. There's a girl at home — in Philadelphia — who is pregnant. By me. And I want to go home and marry her."

"Ah." Eyebrows shot up, as if a bolt of insight had struck his brain. He glanced away with some embarrassment, and cleared his throat "How — how long have you known this girl?"

"Well, a few months, I guess — before I was drafted, that is."

"I see. How old is she?"

"Eighteen."

"And how old are you?"

"Nineteen now. My birthday was a couple of weeks ago.

"I see." Captain Marshall was silent for a moment. "Is there anything preventing you from getting married?"

"Only distance."

"And you have the girl's consent?"

"Well, I've talked with her on the phone, and we kind of talked about it. After all, she *is* pregnant . . . "

"With your child?"

"Yes. Anyway, it seems like the only solution. You see, she's living with her grandmother and they don't really get along. And if she found out she was going to have a baby, well — it would be best if she could get away from her. And if we could get married, I could take out an allotment and have the money sent directly to her, so she'd have enough to live on."

"I see." Pause. "You're in MP school?"

"Yes, sir."

"How long till graduation?"

"Six or seven weeks."

"I see." Captain Marshall scratched his nose with a long index finger. "Well, under the circumstances, and if you really have your mind set, and it seems like you do, and if the girl accepts your proposal, I would suggest that you go ahead with the marriage. It seems like the best and most honorable thing to do under the circumstances."

"That's what I want to do."

"Good. Well, I'm glad if my advice has been of some help to you."

"Wait a minute, sir."

"Is there anything else?" he said vacantly.

"Well, yes, there is. I'm talking about going home to get married, and you agree it's the best thing to do. What I need is someone to help me get an emergency leave."

"But, you'll be going home in less than two months — "

"I want to go home *now*. If I wait until AIT is over, she'll be four months pregnant. She'll have to live at home, with her grandmother, all that time. *And* I won't be able to take out an allotment for her."

"How much money is the allotment?"

"Well, if I have forty dollars taken out of my pay, the army will send her a check for ninety-five. But I need to show them the marriage certificate."

"Well, you can't leave in the middle of AIT."

"Why not?"

"Because it just isn't done."

"But why?"

"Because it just isn't. I don't know why. I guess it would cause a lot of clerical work. You'd have to get approval. You would miss classes. You might even have to be reassigned to the next training command so you could pick up your work. It's a lot of trouble."

Tony's voice was rising. "The world is in a lot of trouble, Captain, but we don't all stick our heads in a hole and wait for it to go away."

"Well, I just don't think that's the way things are done, that's all."

"It's not done because no one wants to take the trouble to do it. And that's what I want you to do."

"What?"

"Get me an emergency leave."

Captain Marshall sat up indignantly. "I can't do that. It's against army regulations."

Tony lost all control over his voice. "I thought it was your job to help soldiers in trouble. I thought you were empowered to — bend — regulations a little."

"Well, I'm here to help, but I can only do it within the framework of military jurisprudence. I can offer advice, I can offer comfort, I can offer understanding. But I can't go against army policy."

"Then what good are you?"

The chaplain's eyebrows shot up as if jerked by a string. His face reddened.

"Has the army bought out God, too? And all He stands for?" Tony knew that he was up against an immovable force, one that had been immovable all his life. The chaplain was completely without initiative. He had always floated along with the current, never making waves. His career had been spent without risk. True, one never gets into trouble by being cautious; but one never gets ahead, either. For Captain Marshall it was too late to start leading with his chin. "What kind of sinecure are you running here?"

"Really, I think you are quite out of line, Tony. I can't do the impossible. I can't go against army regulations."

Tony stopped beating his head against the wall. "All right, so what *can* you do?"

The chaplain spread his hands. "I'm afraid I can't do what you want me to do. I can't get

you leave."

"Well, how about going higher up the chain of command? How about getting me an appointment with the colonel of the brigade? Or a general?"

"Oh, that's something that's never done — except through your company commander."

"Well, *that's* not going to happen." Tony sat shaking his head. "Look, how about if you give it a try, anyway. At least make a phone call to brigade headquarters, or something. It can't take very long."

Spreading his hands was the chaplain's only movement. "I'll see what I can do."

****

What the hell do you mean by going over my head?" Captain Johnson's face was flushed, giving him the color of burnt sienna. He pounded his fist against the desk, shaking pens and pencils so they rolled over the edge, and upset the small brass lamp with crossed infantry rifles painted on the shade.

"Goddamn you, Giovanni, you've been nothing but trouble ever since you got here. You must be crazy, trying to make an appointment with a general. And even if you got to see him, he wouldn't do anything I wouldn't do."

"Excuse me for saying so, sir, but so far you've done nothing."

"You impudent little bastard. I could crush you with my bare hands. I didn't get to be captain of a military police training command by catering to trainees who think they can run this outfit any way they choose. I am in charge here, and I *will* have respect if I have to beat it out of you."

"Sir, if you would just look at the real problem instead of the one you've conjured up in your imagination — "

The captain leaped out of his chair and vaulted over the desk so fast that Tony did not have time to back away from the onslaught. Captain Johnson grabbed a fist full of shirt, and twisted it so hard that three buttons popped off. His breath was hot and foul. Beads of perspiration rose out of the skin of his forehead.

"You stupid son of a bitch. Don't you know that I control your life? I've got absolute power over your destiny." He stopped suddenly, his chest heaving. He slammed Tony against the door, then let go his shirt. He walked around his desk, picked up a handkerchief that was neatly folded next the blotter, and wiped his forehead. Still standing, staring out the window, he said in a strained voice, "I want you out of my office, Giovanni. I want you out, and I never want to see you in here again. Is that understood?"

Tony stared defiantly.

Captain Johnson turned. "Do you hear me?"

"I hear you. But I still think you're going

about this the wrong way. I'm not afraid of you, or of what you can do to me. I'm in this game for two years, and it doesn't much matter to me how I spend it. All I'm asking — "

"You will if you have to spend it in the stockade."

" — all I've ever asked for, is reason. No one in the army seems to understand that one simple word. Why can't you just act reasonably?"

"That's enough! Now get out!"

"Your ostrich outlook can't go on forever."

"Giovanni, I said that's enough!"

"I'm not playing a game of wills, I just want — "

"Sergeant, get this man out of here."

" — to be heard. You're so stuck up on power that you've forgotten how to act with compassion. You're so hung — "

"SERGEANT!"

" — up on manipulating people, on pushing them around to make yourself seem important, that you've lost all sense of basic humanity. You think you can pull — "

The door burst open and caught Tony in the back. He fell forward over the desk, groaning in pain. He looked up at the captain, gasped, and croaked, " — pull a few strings, and the whole world will dance. Well, your world is smaller than you think. You think — "

Rough hands grabbed Tony from behind, jerked him away from the desk, dragged him out the door.

" — you're in charge, but you're not. You're nothing but a puppet yourself. You can't even make one deviant decision on your own because you're afraid someone higher up the chain of — "

A thick arm wrapped around his throat, choking off any further communication. Suddenly, he was no longer in the orderly room. For an instant, the waxing yellow sun was in his eyes, then he saw the ground coming up at him. He hit with a terrible jolt, landing partially on one arm. Dust flew up into his face. He lay there for a time, feeling pain in his back, in his arm, in his throat, in his heart.

"Get up, mister."

Tony rolled over and saw First Sergeant Baker leering down at him. He looked like a lion about to pounce. Slowly, Tony climbed to his feet, rubbing his sores.

"Now get back to your barrack and get into a clean uniform."

Tony dusted himself off. He turned and walked nonchalantly toward the beige building. He heard a door crash behind him. Then something flew over his head, hit the ground about twenty feet away, and rolled into the steps. The fiberglass helmet liner was undamaged.

****

By the end of the week, the fatigue was catching up with him. He could hardly drag himself out of bed, and his head throbbed incessantly. He swallowed a couple of aspirins. But by mid afternoon he had more than a headache. His muscles ached all over, and faint nausea dwelled in his stomach.

Sergeant Swansea glowered. "Whaddaya mean you don't feel good?"

"Well, I think I might be coming down with something." He shaded his eyes with his hand, for the bright sun sent stabs of pain through his head like razor-sharp daggers. "Maybe if I could have the rest of the afternoon off, and lie down for a while, I'll feel better."

"Who're you trying to kid? This ain't no grammar school where you take the day off just because you feel like it. Now get back in formation before I kick you back. We got a class to go to."

"Sarge — I mean, sergeant, could I at least go back to the barrack to get some aspirin?"

"What're you, a privileged character or something?"

Tired, Tony responded, "No, I just want to get some aspirin."

The sergeant spoke with deliberate firmness. "The answer's no."

The rest of the afternoon classes were wasted on Tony. His headache intensified, his nausea worsened to the point where he was kept constantly on the verge of running out the door to vomit. His forehead was hot to the touch. *This is the army*, he thought. *Ignore it, and it will go away.*

He could not eat the evening meal. He approached Sergeant Swansea at the mess hall. "Sergeant, I think I'm going to have to go on sick call."

"Sick call is in the morning, Giovanni, you know that. You should have fallen out then — if you're really sick, that is."

Tony let the implication slide. "I know, but I wasn't that sick then."

"Too bad."

"I'm sorry that human pathology doesn't conform to military formality, but while a cold can be caught in the draft, it can't be controlled by anything more than a sniff."

"Don't try to get smart with me, mister, or I'll knock you up side the head."

"Sergeant, without going into polemics, just listen to what I am saying: I — am — sick. I'm not learning anything by sitting in some classroom trying to keep awake, or trying not to throw up. And I don't think I can wait until morning to go on sick call. So, may I please be excused for the afternoon?"

"You don't look sick to me?"

"What do you want me to do — bleed?"

"Another smart comment like that and you will. Now, I don't want to hear any more about you being sick."

"Sergeant, I —

"That's all, Giovanni."

Tony nodded weakly, and left. A cold drink of water from the cooler eased the scratchiness in his throat. He moved very slowly, and managed to get back to his bunk without collapsing. A few minutes later he was thrown out of bed when Sergeant Jordan arrived to pick him up for guard duty.

Tony dragged his feet with great effort along the worn path in front of the motor pool fence. Far away from the streetlights, he leaned up against the aluminum corner post and vomited. He felt better afterwards, but a drowsiness came over him that he could not fight off. Reluctantly, he lay down on the grass and fell fast asleep.

He awoke with a start when a beam of light briefly dazzled his eyes. An instant later he was on his feet, still not awake, but aware enough to know what he should appear to be doing. He started walking his post with his rifle on his shoulder.

The truck ground to a halt on the road next to him. "Okay, Giovanni. Here's your relief." As Sergeant Jordan shouted from the cab, a man leaped over the tailgate and took the rifle from Tony. Tony climbed gratefully into the back of the truck, slumped onto the rusting metal floor.

Back in the guardhouse, he chased aspirin down with water, crawled into an empty bunk, and tried to ignore the pounding in his temples and the nausea still tickling his stomach. He jammed a pillow over his head to drown out light and sound.

A touch on the shoulder brought him out of the nightmare world. "Your turn, Giovanni," Sergeant Jordan said quietly.

Tony rolled over dizzily, fought loose of the woolen blanket. Beads of perspiration dotted his face, soaked his clothes. He shivered uncontrollably. When he swung his feet onto the floor, waves of giddiness forced him to lie back down. He wrapped his fingers around the edge of the cot and hung on. He blinked at the gyrating ceiling.

He got up again, slower. The nausea hit him like a log. He lurched to his feet and raced for the latrine, barely reaching it before his stomach regurgitated his previous meal. He held onto the tank with both hands while he wretched. His knees threatened to stop their support. When the vomiting bout ended, he hobbled to the sink, rinsed out his mouth, and plunged cold water over his face. A grimy towel served to wipe away water, sweat, and tears.

Sergeant Jordan's bulk blocked the doorway. "What's the matter?"

"I guess I don't feel too well." Tony leaned back against the sink.

"Yeah? Well, you don't look too well, either."

Tony rolled his eyes, tried to focus them on the burly sergeant. "I've been pretty much under the weather all afternoon."

"If you were sick, why the hell didn't you go on sick call?"

"Sergeant Swansea said that sick call is only in the morning, and I didn't feel that bad this morning. Just tired."

"That Swansea's a jerk." Sergeant Jordan grabbed Tony by the arm, led him out of the latrine. "You can't work a man to death. You get back in that bunk, and I'll get someone to cover for you."

"I'll be all right, sarge. Honest. I can stand it for a few more hours."

"Like hell you will. I don't give a damn why they put you on this shit detail — you ain't no slacker. And you ain't gonna work when you're sick. At least, not while I'm in charge. Consider yourself relieved, and get some sleep. We'll talk about it in the morning."

Tony did not have the strength to argue. He nodded, managed a half-hearted smile, and limped back to his bunk. He curled up into a ball, covered himself with the blanket, and fitfully passed the rest of the night.

Another touch on the shoulder brought him out of his lethargy. "Come on, Giovanni. It's time to go." Tony climbed out of bed and followed Sergeant Jordan out the door. "Up front."

Tony sat in the front seat, shielding his eyes against the morning brightness, huddled against the chill. The truck bounced along an unfamiliar road.

"Hey, where are we going?"

"To the hospital."

"But I've got to report to my company first."

"You do that and it'll be hours before you get to the clinic. I just thought I'd shorten the process and bring you here direct."

"Can you do that?"

"I just did."

"But what will Sergeant Swansea say? Or Captain Johnson?"

"They ain't gonna say nothing. You're still in my detail till I let you go. And if I say you gotta go to the hospital, they can't do a thing about it." Sergeant Jordan pulled the truck to a halt in front of the hospital, helped him into the clinic. "Have a seat while I check with the staff."

Tony sat on a bench, eyes crammed onto fists, elbows on knees.

"Well, they said they'll have a medic right

out. Look, I'd like to stay with you, but — "

"Oh, that's all right, sarge. As long as I don't have to run a mile before the exam, I think I'll live."

Sergeant Jordan thrust out a hand. "Okay, you take care of yourself. See you 'round."

"Thanks." Tony made himself comfortable again, trying not to throw up. He lost track of time.

"You can't sleep here, mister." The white-clad orderly shook Tony roughly.

Tony protected his eyes, squinted through the pain. "I'm waiting to see a doctor. Is he here yet?"

"I'll check. Until he comes, you'll have to sit up."

"Right," Tony groaned. He passed some restless minutes trying to sleep in a sitting position, but his arm kept slipping off the armrest. His head lolled around like a child's top running out of spin. Finally, he gave up, and lay down.

The orderly shook him again. "Come with me." He escorted Tony to the examining room and turned him over to a medic.

"Well, I see you're back again."

Tony recognized the intern who had examined him several days previous. He smiled. "I think I'm *really* sick this time."

After the tests, the orderly handed Tony a piece of paper. "Okay, you better go see the doc. Here's an authorization slip. Just go down this hall to the third door on your left. Next."

After a half hour in another waiting room, a nurse ordered him onto an examination table, where she repeated the intern's tests. Then she wrote something on the authorization slip and left. Some time later a doctor arrived, looked at the slip, instructed Tony to open his mouth so he could probe his throat with a tongue depressor, felt his forehead, took his pulse, added a codicil to the authorization slip, grunted, and left. Tony waited.

Later, the orderly came back and glanced at the slip. "Follow me." They wound through corridors, up stairs, past nursing stations, and through doors, eventually arriving at a ward in an obscure wing of the hospital. The orderly turned the slip over to a white clad sergeant, and left.

"Well, Giovanni, how'd you like to stay with us for a couple days?"

"The way I feel, I'd like that just fine."

The sergeant puffed through chubby cheeks. "Good, because you're going to anyway."

"Does this mean I'm sick?"

"Nothing to be worried about. You've got a case of the grippe."

"The grip?"

"The grippe. The flu. Influenza. It's all the same."

"Oh." It was such an effort to stand. "Is it serious?"

"No. Plenty of rest, lots of liquids, some medication — only pills, no shots — you'll be okay in a couple days. A little weaker, is all." He smiled as he handed Tony a white bundle. "Go find an empty bed, change into these, and crawl in. I'll have an orderly come and take a blood sample. And I'll call down to the dispensary for your prescription. Then we'll see about getting you some breakfast."

"Thanks, but I think you can skip the breakfast part. I don't feel much like eating."

"Well, you do your best. Eat what you can, and try to drink all the juice."

The day passed in a stupor, punctuated by brief interludes of blood samplings, drinks, pills, drinks, meals, drinks, thermometers, and nurses trying to pour flavored water down his throat. He could have gotten more rest on a crowded elevator.

Just before lights out, the head nurse woke him up again. "Put on your robe. You're being transferred to another ward."

Two orderlies escorted him, each holding one arm, through darkened corridors quiet as a tomb. Tony did not speak, nor did they. After walking to a new wing, Tony was helped into a private room.

At least, he thought, there won't be any more disturbances. When the door clanged shut, he fell into a fitful sleep for the rest of the night. It was not until the morning rays of the sun broke through the barred window, throwing a meshed shadow against a door without handles, that he realized the walls were quilted.

Chapter 56

"Well, well, well. And how are you this morning?"

As the thick door swung open, a black, barrel-chested, white-clad orderly backed into the room. Two rows of white, even teeth formed the center post of a disarming smile. He pulled the stainless steel food cart in after him, leaving it so it blocked open the door. Plastic trays lay one above the other, resting on metal runners.

"I'm Corporal Miller."

"Tony Giovanni."

"Yes, I know. You were admitted last night." He took out the top tray and handed it to Tony. Steam rose from a plate that contained bacon and eggs, over light, and a generous portion of home fries. Surrounding this was a box of Rice Crispies, two slices of toast, cut diagonally and already buttered, two packets of jam, a container of milk, a plastic glass of orange juice, and a cup of coffee.

"Thanks. Oh, and good morning." Tony sat up and placed the tray on his lap. "Wow, this looks great."

"Feeling better, are you?" Corporal Miller looked down from his height of six-foot-four. His head was surprisingly small for one of his size.

"I must be. I'm famished."

"I hear tell you were a pretty sick dude when they brought you in here last night."

"Yes, the doctor told me I had the grippe, or the flu. Must have been the twenty-four hour variety, because I don't have anything now but a slight headache. And I'm weak. I'm so hungry I could eat a horse." Tony started stuffing toast into his mouth.

"Ha-ha-ha. Well, you just dig into them victuals. This food's guaranteed to help you get your strength back. Oh, and here, you gotta take two of these." He handed Tony a paper cup with two tiny tablets. "I gotta watch you take them." Miller was still smiling, but his attitude was insistent. Tony shrugged, and tossed them down his throat with a gulp of orange juice that drained the glass. "That's good. Now, you take your time with the chow, and I'll be back later for the tray. I got more hungry folks waitin' to be fed."

Just before the door closed, Tony blurted out, "Uh, corporal." The black face popped back into the room. "Why am I isolated like this — and in a locked room?"

"Ha-ha-ha. Don't you worry about a thing. The doc'll be in to explain it all."

"Well, do I have a contagious disease, or something?"

"Nothing that serious. You're just in for observation. Now you just take it easy and save all your questions for the doc. Okay?"

The door closed, the heavy lock fell in place. Corporal Miller peered in through the thick, six-inch-square glass, smiled, and disappeared.

Tony picked up the only utensil, a plastic spoon, and dug into the eggs. He ate every scrap of food, and drank all the liquids. When Corporal Miller returned a half hour later, Tony was calmly clutching the window grille and staring outside at a sky full of clouds not dark enough to be a forewarning of rain.

"You didn't leave enough food on that plate to feed a parakeet, I do declare."

"I told you I was hungry." Tony handed the tray to the corporal. "Do you think it would be possible to have another cup of coffee?"

"Cream and sugar?"

"Yes — one teaspoon."

Miller winked. "You got it." He closed and locked the door, but was back in a minute with a plastic cup.

"Thanks. Uh, corporal, what kind of observation am I under?"

"The doc'll explain everything," came the stock reply. "I'm just an orderly here, and I'm not allowed to say anything. But if you need something, you just push that button by your bed, and I'll come a runnin'."

"Wait a minute!" Tony grabbed the closing door. "Can I get washed up, and use the latrine?"

Corporal Miller winked. "There's a bedpan and a urinal under the bed." The door closed quietly.

The minutes passed like decades, the hours like centuries. Tony had nothing to do but sit on the bed, the only piece of furniture in the tiny room, and stare at the four walls, or out the window. Shadows passed the reinforced viewing port in the door, causing Tony to tense up each time. Time passed, and he waited patiently.

His stomach had been grumbling for an hour when Corporal Miller pushed open the door, and Tony smelled the hot lunch being wheeled in. The steak was chopped, and could be eaten with a spoon, and the potatoes were mashed. Tony gulped down the glass of water, and asked for more. Miller refilled the paper cup from a pitcher.

"Why don't you just leave the pitcher?"

"I can't do that?"

Tony winced. "I don't understand. Why not? If I can have as much as I want, why not just leave it?"

Corporal Miller smiled broadly. "Any time you want something, you just push that button on the wall."

About an hour after lunch, Tony pushed button.

A female voice answered, "Yes?"

"Uh, I was wondering if you could bring me something to read."

"I'm sorry, but you'll have to wait until the doctor sees you."

"Oh. Okay. Thanks."

Around mid afternoon, the lock rasped and Corporal Miller entered, bringing with him his wide smile and a short, four-legged stool. A tall, clean-shaven, meticulously coifed and manicured man followed him in. He wore an expensive wristwatch and carried a clipboard and a black medical kit.

"That'll be all, Miller. Thank you." His voice was an imperious monotone. He gathered his white smock around him, showing for a moment the khakis underneath, and pounced upon the stool. "Please sit down, Tony. On the edge of the bed."

Tony perched in front of the doctor. He opened the kit bag and took out a stethoscope.

"My name is Captain Daniels, and I'd like to ask you a few questions. Unbutton your shirt, please."

"Okay."

"First of all, how do you feel today?"

The stethoscope must have been kept in a freezer. Tony sucked in his breath as the cold diaphragm touched his skin. "Well, pretty good."

The doctor moved the cold disc across Tony's chest. "No more headaches, nausea, vomiting?"

"No, I feel fine. Well, pretty good, anyway."

Captain Daniels replaced the stethoscope with a sphygmomanometer, and wrapped it around Tony's upper arm. He increased the pressure, then released it slowly. "Well, you seem pretty healthy. How do you feel otherwise? Any — pressure? Anxiety?"

"No, I feel fine."

The doctor put away his instruments. "Do you know where you are?"

"It's not hard to figure out. This is the loony bin, the psycho ward, the crazy cradle."

The doctor did not smile. "Well, I wouldn't put it quite that harshly. Let's just say that this is a preliminary examining room, and that you are here for observation. All the precautions — " He gestured at the padded walls. " — are just to keep our more serious patients from injuring themselves. Until we know for certain that they're not hostile."

"And what would I have done to injure myself today that I wouldn't have done yesterday, or the day before, when I had the opportunity?"

"That's what I would like to find out." Captain Daniels glanced down at the chart on his clipboard, took a pencil out of his shirt pocket under the smock, and checked off some lines. "We don't like to put possibly hostile people in the open ward with the rest of the patients."

"And how do you find that out? By listening in on that hidden microphone?"

"Again, that's only a precaution to prevent patients from harming themselves. Now, according to a preliminary examination made yesterday, ah, morning, you had a temperature of one hundred three, blood pressure of ninety over sixty, rapid pulse, et cetera, et cetera. All indications of a true physiological ailment, and which was apparently treated successfully with — k" He glanced again at the chart. " — tetra-cycline."

"Does that mean I'm cured?"

"Of the flu, yes. Although several days of rest are recommended in order to prevent a relapse. But we've received a report from your company commander — " Chart. " — Captain Johnson. It says here that you have been acting strangely: flying into fits of rage, starting fights with the cadre, threatening bodily harm. He suspects that you are — troubled — in some way, and that you might need treatment of a —

psychiatric nature."

In the cold silence that followed, Tony felt a chill run up his spine. "I see."

"The reports state that you are generally uncommunicative, but that you occasionally, and without provocation, burst into 'tirades of verbal abuse.' Now, what I want to find out is why you do these things."

Tony shifted his weight, sat up a little straighter. "Wait a minute. Aren't you jumping the gun a little? You just stated that as if it were the gospel truth. What am I, guilty without a trial?"

"Come now, Tony, we won't get anywhere that way. If you want to get out of here, you're going to have to cooperate. It says right here in the report that all those incidents occurred. Are you trying to refute the word of an officer?"

"I don't know if this constitutes refuting, but I am calling him a liar."

Captain Daniels bristled. "That's a harsh accusation."

"No harsher than Captain Johnson's, and a darn sight more accurate."

"I can see already that we're going to have a difficult time with you." The doctor stood up and rapped at the door. It opened immediately. Miller reached in and grabbed the medical kit and the stool. "I'll come back when you're ready to talk some sense."

"I'm ready to talk sense right now. But you're not ready to listen."

"Not as long as you're going to spout slander against a fellow officer."

"Facts do not constitute slander."

"Let's leave personalities out of this. When you're willing to talk openly about your problems, I'll see about getting you out of this room. Until then, you are to remain here for observation."

"Is that treatment, or punishment?"

"It's a medical opinion."

"Well, if you're going to keep me locked up in solitary confinement, do you think you could get someone to bring me some reading material?"

"I'll see what I can do."

Tony raised his voice. "What do you mean, you'll see? You're the doctor, aren't you?"

"That's right, Tony. I'm the doctor."

He slammed the door behind him. Tony lay back on the bed, staring up at the ceiling. Several times he saw a darkening at the armored window, and twice caught Corporal Miller peeking in. Hours later, the corporal wheeled in his supper.

"Look here, Tony, you gotta keep the doc happy or you'll never get out of here. He's a tough man — and he don't let no one get away with anything. If you want to get out of here, you gotta sweet talk him."

"He's got the ego problem, not me. And I don't want to get out badly enough to prostitute myself."

"It can get awful lonesome in here."

"But not intolerable."

"Well, I'm only telling you for your own good. The doc just likes to be catered to. All you gotta do is show him some respect for his profession."

"All he's got to do is earn it."

"All right, but that isn't gonna get you out of here. And you got to do something besides staring at the walls. It isn't healthy."

"What do you want me to do — the Twist?"

"All right, now don't go taking it out on me. I'm just trying to give you some advice."

"Sorry."

"That's all right. But when you think you're getting his goat, you're just sealing your doom. When he talks to you next time, stay cool."

Tony grimaced. "From now, on I'm Nonchalant Lamont." He spent a lonely night practicing reserve.

He was already awake in the morning when Corporal Miller unlocked the door, bearing clean sheets and a breakfast tray. "Rise and shine, my boy, you got a big day ahead of you." Tony merely scowled. "No, I'm serious. You're going out into the big ward as soon as Molly checks you out. Molly is the head nurse — Lieutenant Tollman to her face, if you can stand to look at it. Come on, I'll give you a hand making the bed."

Tony brightened considerably. "Gee, thanks."

Miller whipped off the ruffled sheets and tossed them in a pile in the corner. He made the bed with expertise, pushing Tony aside whenever he tried to help.

"What else do I have to do?"

"Just stand there and look pretty when she comes — "

The door opened before he could finish. Lieutenant Molly Tollman was thirtyish and not bad looking; she was just plain, with features hardened by a bland expression. "Would you come with me, Private Giovanni? And bring your tray with you."

"Yes, ma'am." He winked at Miller when she turned her back, then followed her out carrying his breakfast. Miller took up the rear, with the used bedding and a half-filled urinal.

"General house rules are: no one's allowed in bed after eight hundred hours, or before twenty hundred hours. You have your own chair if you wish to sit, and there are more on the porch. Porch chairs are not allowed in the ward. You must make your own bed. House cleaning is done right after breakfast, super-

vised by Corporal Miller. You may read or watch television. And please, take a shower before the doctor arrives."

Lieutenant Tollman retreated to the armored nurses station, and locked herself in.

"Thank you, ma'am." Tony sat on the edge of his assigned bed, eating his breakfast, while he exchanged nods with the other patients in the ward. None were overly communicative.

Later, Corporal Miller gathered the trays and stashed the cart at the end of the hall, by the barred door. Out came buckets, mops, washcloths, and a floor buffer. Not so easily did the men come out to help.

One fellow refused to get out of bed and had to be dragged, screaming, by the bulky corporal. Then the man ran into a corner and faced the walls, crying. Others got out of bed reluctantly, moving like automatons. Told what to do, they did it; otherwise they stood and stared. Another patient with a long, stitched gash along his throat helped Tony mop the floor, while a man with slashed wrists — almost healed — washed down the woodwork.

Lieutenant Tollman shouted orders from her cage. The loudspeakers near the ceiling screeched with feedback. Corporal Miller had his hands full, but dealt with each patient delicately or forcefully, as the situation demanded.

Tony took control of the buffer and soon had the floor shining. When the chores were done to the lieutenant's satisfaction, he was allowed to take a shower.

"The soap is already in there, along with washcloths and towels," Miller explained. "If you don't have your own with you, you'll have to buy a toothbrush from Molly. And toothpaste, too. But you can't shave. No razors are allowed in the ward."

Tony authorized the purchases that he wished to make. Lieutenant Tollman removed the money from his wallet, put change in his pants pocket, and restored his possessions to the locker. The shower and the toothpaste washed out the signs and taste of sickness that still clung to him. Then he retreated to the porch and found a whole shelf of paperback books from which to choose. He sat on the sunny side, near the grate, lost in a mystery novel.

Most of the other patients gathered around the lone television, or sat and gazed catatonically into space. The situation was restful.

"Well, how do you feel today, Tony?"

Tony eyed Captain Daniels suspiciously. "Pretty well, doc."

"What are you reading?"

Still sitting, Tony showed him the cover. "It's a Perry Mason book, 'The Case of the Dangerous Dowager,' by Erle Stanley Gardner. I've read some of his other books and liked them a lot."

"Do you like to read?"

"Oh, sure. I read all the time."

Looking down from a height, "Mysteries."

"Well, mostly science fiction. Also natural science — any topic from biology to astronomy."

"Are you planning to be a scientist some day?"

"Well, I was majoring in geology in college. I'd like to go back to it when I get out."

"Tell me, how do you like MP school?"

"Well, it's not bad. It's a good learning experience, and the subject matter is fairly interesting. Although I think they're a little too strict. In fact, I think they're a lot too strict. But other than that it's a good school."

The doctor folded his arms across his chest; he acted gravely. "How are you getting along with your fellow trainees?"

"Well, to be honest, there isn't much time to get to know anyone. I mean, the training schedule is very structured, very rigid. It doesn't allow much time for fraternization."

"And how are you getting along with the cadre?"

"Not as well as I would like. There have been some misunderstandings between us. Sergeant Swansea is a very persuasive man and has difficulty accepting differing points of view. Captain Johnson displays aloofness to such a degree that he is unable to see his men as anything other than performance levels. We've bumped heads a couple times because I exercised my individuality."

"I see." Captain Daniels beetled his brow. "I guess this has caused you some anxiety?"

"I think frustration would be a better word for it."

"And what is it that frustrates you?"

Tony kept up his matter-of-fact tone. "Mainly, my attempt to reason with my superiors. It's rather like arguing with a child. I talk in terms of logic and get gibberish for an answer. When my reason is too well founded, they change the ground rules."

After a long silence, the doctor cleared his throat. "Do you think you could be more precise?"

"Oh, yes, of course. Well, you see, it all started because of this little problem I have at home, which needn't concern you. It was important for me to communicate with friends and family in order to straighten it out. I made a formal request with my platoon sergeant — that's Sergeant Swansea — about making a phone call. He not only turned me down, but forbade me to take my request to a higher authority. I did anyway, although the captain refused to see

me. When Sergeant Swansea found out about it, his response was to beat me up. Since I as unable to see the captain in his office, I approached him during one of our routine inspections. Instead of listening to the reasons for my request, he had me put on night guard duty.

"Meanwhile, the situation at home demanded my presence, forcing me to request emergency leave. Again, the chain of command offered no solace, so I went to see the chaplain. When Captain Johnson discovered I had continued to seek a solution to my problem, he leaped over his desk and forced me back against the wall, screaming in my face. The first sergeant came in and slammed the door into my back, grabbed me by the throat, and dragged me outside and threw me on the ground. These are grown men, mind you." Tony could not help the hint of derision in his voice. "Where I come from, this is not socially acceptable behavior.

"Now, coincidentally, due to the prolonged lack of sleep, I began to get sick. Sergeant Swansea refused to allow me to seek medical assistance. I not only had to remain with the company and attend classes for the rest of the day, but I still had to go on guard duty that night. When the fever and vomiting got to be too much for me, the sergeant of the guard relieved me of duty and brought me to the hospital. And here I am."

The captain's eyes had long since glazed over. "I see," he said perfunctorily. Then, after a few seconds, he focused on his clipboard and made a few notes. "Well, I think that's enough for today. I'll talk with you some more tomorrow and check your progress."

Tony kept to himself for the next twenty-four hours. He read two more mysteries (by Agatha Christie), got plenty of rest, continued to build up his body with good old army chow, and assisted in ward duties.

"Tony, I sure appreciate you helping me out with these patients." Corporal Miller rolled down his white sleeves and buttoned them. "But I don't think you belong here."

"In order for my CO to prove I'm crazy, he's got to prove that the army is sane."

"Tall order."

The following day's talk with Captain Daniels rambled on without any particular objective. The doctor seemed to be fishing for trivia, assigning subconscious motivations. Tony discussed everything with complete emotional detachment, as if he were talking about a character in a book. Not once did the doctor ask Tony to elucidate on his problems at home.

When Captain Daniels found him reading on the porch the following day, Tony opened the conversation. "Do you think I'm paranoid?"

The doctor refused to demonstrate surprise. He answered politically, "Do you know what it means?"

"It's a persecution complex, the world-is-out-to-get-me syndrome, a belief that someone is controlling your life, or wants to harm you. Sure, I know what it is. I've seen enough of it since I entered the service."

"It's a common malady."

"To you, perhaps. But because a car pulls into a service station with a faulty starter does not preclude that every other car in the world has the same problem."

Cautiously, the doctor said, "Why do you bring this up?"

"Because I was helping to tidy up the nursing station this morning and I saw that word on my chart."

"That's classified information."

Tony could not keep the rising inflection out of his voice. "Nothing about *me* is classified to *me*."

"Tony, why don't we forget the pretension and talk about what's troubling you?"

"Trouble is a state of mental distress so, according to that definition, I have no troubles."

"But you do admit that something is worrying you?"

"Worry is self-indulgent and counterproductive, something for which I have no time."

"You are unusually well informed."

"I had Psychology I and, while that doesn't make me a psychiatrist, it does acquaint me with the definitions as well as give me a basic understanding of motivation and the human psyche."

"I see."

"I will admit, however, that I have problems and concerns: a problem being something that can be solved, a concern being a method of working toward that solution."

Captain Daniels nodded slightly. "You're doing fine. Please continue."

"My problem is easily summarized: my girlfriend is pregnant. The solution is simple and straightforward: get married. *Voila!*"

Captain Daniels tucked the ever-present clipboard under his arm. "Tony, if you're trying to impress me with your mental gymnastics, you needn't bother. I've had enough practice in the field to enable me to see through simple play acting."

"When are you going to stop practicing and start doing your job?"

"There's no reason to be insolent."

Tony grumbled. "I'm sorry, doctor, and I apologize. But we seem to be working at cross-purposes. I do have a problem and, if you wanted to, you could help me solve it."

The doctor resumed his calm. "I'm here to help you, Tony, if you'll let me."

"All right, let me start out with a little story. Call it an analogy, or perhaps an allegory. Let's assume I'm a civilian, an average citizen of the United States, working on an average job, for an average boss. Some emergency at home comes up and I have to find out what's going on. So I say to the foreman, 'Hey, Boss, I gotta go make a phone call.' Now, this isn't the end of the world, and he, being an average guy, says, 'No problem.' On the other hand, maybe the job's running behind, or we have a quota to meet, and he's got to keep pushing. Then he might say, 'Okay, but I gotta dock you a half hour's pay.' Or, 'Okay, but hurry back.' No big deal, we just come to an understanding.

"Now, suppose I come back from the phone call and I say, 'Boss, something's come up and I gotta go home right away. I'll need about a week off.' He, being a normal human being, says, 'Gee, I'm sorry. I hope everything works out for you.' Or, on the other hand, the job needs to be finished right away, and he says, 'You'll have to get someone to cover for you.' Or, 'All right, but how about cutting it short, and when you get back, put in a little overtime to make up for it?' In any case, there's always room for compromise. We try to work out a solution together, one that benefits both parties.

"So, I take care of the emergency, and I'm right back on the job with as little loss as possible to anyone. That's the way responsible people respond. That's the way people should treat each other. That's the way I treat other people. And that's the way I expect to be treated. As one adult to another."

Captain Daniels ran his tongue over his teeth. "That's a very nice story, Tony, almost like a fairy tale. But it's hardly relevant to the issue at hand. You must learn to accept that you are now a member of the armed forces, and that you have certain duties and responsibilities to perform — "

Tony interrupted. "I never said I wasn't willing to perform such duties, only that I also have other responsibilities — as a person, not as a soldier — and that there must be room for both."

"This other so-called responsibility is now secondary to your prescribed purpose. You're in the army now, and you must work within the framework of that hierarchy."

"Do you think life stops with the draft? What you're saying is that a free citizen, once drafted, reverts to slavery, regardless of Constitutional guarantees."

"What I'm saying is that you must conform to the norm."

"And what constitutes the norm? The norm is nothing more than a statistical convenience describing the way most people react to a given situation. Well, of the two hundred million people living in this country, less than one percent are in the armed forces. That means that what takes place in the army is not the norm, but an aberrant reaction to abnormal conditions: according to definition, insane. And what I'm trying to do is to interject some civilized sanity into this Alice-in-Wonderland illusion."

"I think your attitudes are extremely selfish. I think — "

"Doctor, don't try to refute my arguments by attacking my character. Let's stick to logic."

"I'm trying to instruct you in logic," Captain Daniels said angrily. "I'm trying to get you to understand that the army has different rules and regulations, that it has its own set of standards. It allows for no mavericks in its ranks."

"Does it have its own sense of morality, too?"

"Forget morality. You're here to do what you're told, without thinking about it. If you recognize that fact, you'll get along well within the military infrastructure."

"Doctor, you're preaching tyranny, the very thing the army has been designated to prevent. How can the army fight for freedom when it operates on police-state principles?"

"Leave principles and morality for the politicians. You just do your job and don't think about what older and wiser men are paid to do."

"You mean, forget about what's right and wrong? From what I've seen, the army is not qualified to make those decisions. For me, or anyone else."

"What I'm saying is that you must see things in light of the situation, not in your own subjective reality."

"Reality can't be subjective. Your rationale on behavior is based on a false premise, like an impregnable stone fortress built on bamboo stilts. The strength of any argument is only as strong as its foundation. If we are to fight for the freedom of another country, we must first be free in our own. We can't — "

Captain Daniels sighed, and shook his head. "I can see that we're getting nowhere at all. I'm afraid that you have a very poor attitude toward government procedure — "

"So did John Hancock, and Thomas Paine, and Nathan Hale."

" — one that is going to affect your life significantly. In the army there is a place for every man, and every man must be in his place. Any other kind of system leads to chaos. And you'll just have to accept that."

"I don't have to accept anything. I happen to believe in the principles of this country, but I will not be browbeaten into bondage in order to gratify someone's warped ego. You and every other officer in this army may be satisfied with your role as puppets, as long as you have strings of your own to pull, but I'm not. You can't send slaves to fight for someone else's freedom. You can't dispense understanding unless you first have it yourself. And you can't stand up for someone else's principles unless you're willing to stand up for your own."

Captain Daniels worked his jaw, grinding his teeth together. He forced his words through pinched lips. "You're case is hopeless. I'm going to see to it that you are discharged back to your commanding officer. Perhaps he can make you see the way."

"Hey, doc, don't let it get you down. You and I are not going to affect the outcome of this conflict one way or another. And who knows? Maybe *I'm* the one who's crazy after all."

Chapter 57

"Well, Giovanni, I see you're all better now."

"Yes, sir. I am."

Captain Johnson nodded grimly, ruffled through the papers on his desk. "You've missed quite a few classes in the past week — too many for you to make up. Therefore, I've decided that you cannot continue with this command. I've had new orders cut, and you will be reassigned to another unit as soon as transportation can be arranged. Until then you are not to go to any classes, or to interact with the functions of this company. Sergeant Swansea will see to it that you have enough duties to keep you occupied."

He found the paper he was looking for, flung it across the desk. It landed face up in front of Tony.

"I'm sending you to infantry school. Maybe they can make a man out of you."

****

During his absence, and with the increase in classroom work, customary inspections had been reduced to once a day. Since he still occupied a bunk in the barrack, Tony stood rigidly at attention as Captain Johnson and the XO swept down the aisle.

After two days of orderly room duty, under the constant vigil of the first sergeant, Tony was eager to get out of MP school. He had just run back from washing the captain's jeep, but his footlocker was the neatest of anyone's.

"Giovanni, Anthony J., Private E-2, US52666498, reporting for inspection, sir."

Captain Johnson stopped in front of him in his immaculately pressed fatigues, polished brass, and undeviating gig line. When he looked down at Tony's footlocker his eyes widened, his dark skin changed color. He did not return the salute, but executed a left turn and stopped in front of the next man in line.

Tony's bags were packed. His footlocker

was empty. So was his victory.

****

The first sergeant handed Tony a thick manila folder, containing all of his army records, to hand-carry to his next duty station.

"And don't lose them or you'll be in real trouble, boy."

He was also given a carbon copy of his special orders assigning him to Fort Polk, Louisiana. That afternoon, he boarded a special bus that took him directly to the train station in Augusta. He was just in time to turn in his ticket and board the train for Atlanta. During the two-hour layover for the connection to New Orleans, he made a local phone call.

With his heavy duffel bag over his shoulder, his overnight case in one hand, and his army records clasped under one arm, he abandoned the train station. At street level he dashed along endless concrete corridors until he reached sunlight. He tossed his luggage in the first available taxi, and gave his destination to the cabbie.

"I have to be there by six. Do you think we can make it?"

The gray-haired man wasted no time in starting the car and pulling away from the curb. "It use'ly takes thirty or forty minutes, but this is rush hour. Friday night traffic's likely to be thick."

Tony glanced at his watch. He had close to an hour. "Do the best you can."

He settled into the rear seat, but could not relax. It seemed as if every car in the city was converging on the cab, intent on delaying him. Traffic signals turned red just as they neared intersections; pedestrians with their minds in the clouds lingered in the street long after the lights had changed. Traffic was so thick that lights flicked from red to green to red again, and never a car moved. Tony wished fervently that Ben was behind the wheel.

He kept one eye on his watch, one eye on the road ahead. Signs of their destination appeared; it was still several miles away. He had only ten minutes to his deadline. The cars crowded so close together that they seemed to be some weird metallic animal performing a ritualistic mating dance. They stopped dead. In the back seat, Tony sweated it out.

The cabbie stopped several hundred yards from the main entrance, waiting for the cars and trucks ahead to get out of the way. Tony could wait no longer. He thrust a handful of greenbacks over the seat back, and climbed out of the door, dragging his bags.

"Thanks for the ride. I'll walk from here."

He did not walk, he ran. Weaving through the crowds, groping for openings, taking in directional signs, he forced his way through the glass entrance and found the counter he was looking for.

"Am I — in time --- for the — six-oh-three?" Without waiting for an answer he dropped his bags and reached for his wallet.

The cheery blonde woman flashed white teeth. "You must be the soldier who called about the reservation."

Tony could only nod. He started counting out money and laying the crisp bills on the counter.

The clerk had a sweet touch of Southern accent. "Your ticket's already made up, and you will be able to travel military standby."

"That's great. Thank you." He stuffed change into a pocket. "Concourse B, Gate Six."

"Thanks," Tony yelled over his shoulder.

It seemed like a mile and a half to Concourse B, and another mile to Gate Six. His legs and shoulders were aching and his throat was full of phlegm by the time he reached the last counter and handed his ticket to a middle-aged man.

"Sally called ahead. You'd better hurry. They're already loaded and waiting for clearance.

"Is there time to get my bags aboard?"

The clerk smiled, and handed him two stubs. "You get going. I'll tag them and get them on the plane."

Tony was halfway to the door by the time he finished talking. He dashed across the concrete pad, boiling over with sweat. Two men in coveralls were pulling back the movable stairs.

"Hey, wait a minute. I've got to get on that plane."

Ten feet in the air, a stewardess peered through the glass port in the door. One of the men looked up. She nodded, and motioned with her hand. The powerful jet engines revved, drowning out the curses of the ground crew. The wind whipped past Tony, hurling dust and scraps of paper all over the airfield.

They rolled the stairs back in place, and the door heaved open. The stewardess smiled from the opening. Tony ran up the metal stairs on aching legs, clutching his orders to his chest.

She took his ticket. "Glad you made it."

"Glad to be here."

In the air-conditioned coolness of the plane, Tony realized that he was drenched with Georgia sweat. He wiped his forehead with his sleeve. Still breathing heavily, he crab-walked down the narrow aisle, picked out an empty seat, and sank into it gratefully as if he had just slid into home plate.

With engines whining, the jet taxied out onto the runway. Tony looked past a man in a mod gray business suit, saw the blacktop rolling past the window.

"You just about made it," the man said, smiling. "Where are you going in such a rush?"

Tony regained his breath. "Philadelphia."

Book Three
AUTUMN

Wise men speak and fools decide.

Anacharis, c. 600 BC

Of men who have a sense of honor, more come through alive than are slain, but from those who flee comes neither glory nor any help.

Homer, c. 850 BC

Chapter 58

Tony stepped off the subway at Snyder Avenue. At first glance, nothing of the old neighborhood seemed to have changed. The statue of William Penn still dominated City Hall; cars still edged through traffic lights turning yellow, then red; people still thronged along Broad Street, despite the late hour.

But as Tony approached Patty's house, he felt different. It was as if he had moved on while the city had remained stagnant.

He also looked out of place in his crisp, clean uniform. But the street was dark enough to act as a mask, and vacant enough to make obvious the two people sitting on the cement steps in front of Patty's house.

Tony stopped in front of them, deposited his duffel bag and overnight case on the sidewalk. "Hello, Patty. Hi, Kathy."

The duet gasp was followed by a stunned silence. For five, ten seconds no one said a word. Kathy was the first to recover. "Oh, my God. It's Tony."

"You were expecting the wicked witch of the west?"

Patty's eyes grew into saucers. "Tony, what are you doing here?"

"Well, I came to see you."

"But, I thought you were on your way — I mean, I just got your letter about Mississippi — "

"Louisiana. Yes, that's where I'm going. But I took a little detour and wound up here."

Patty stood up and took a hesitant step toward him, reaching out tentatively as if she did not believe what she was seeing. "I — I didn't think — you could do that."

You can do anything you want if you're will-

ing to suffer the consequences. "Sure, no problem." Tony held out his hands, and a moment later Patty was in his arms. She was trembling slightly.

"Look, uh, I think I'd better be going." Kathy stood up suddenly. "I'm sure you two have a lot to talk about. I'm glad you could get home, Tony. I think it's what Patty needs."

"Thanks, Kathy. Uh, I'm not chasing you away, am I?"

"No, I've got to get going anyway. I'll stop around tomorrow, Patty. 'Bye." Kathy walked hurriedly down the street, climbed into a maroon, '64 Buick, and drove away.

"Well, I'm glad I found you outside. I was afraid if I had to knock on the door, your grandmother would answer and chase me away. She's been acting strange to me on the phone."

"I told you, she's always that way. I'm not even supposed to be out here now. She doesn't like me being out after ten o'clock."

"But this is Friday night!"

"Well, if I ask her real nice, she lets me stay out till eleven on weekends."

"Patty, you're a big girl now. You're over eighteen and out of high school. You shouldn't be treated like a kid."

"Tell *her* that."

"I will."

"No, don't. She'll only get mad and take it out on me."

"You know, I used to think she was a pretty nice lady." Tony released his hold on Patty, and sat down on the steps where Kathy had been sitting. "Now she seems like a different person."

Patty sat close to Tony, her thigh touching

his. "That's because she thinks you're going to take me away from her."

Tony took a deep breath, then another. He swallowed hard and cleared his throat. "Well, I am. I came home to ask you to marry me."

Patty gasped. Her hand crawled over Tony's leg, and her fingers intertwined with his. She spoke with a tremor. "I'm glad."

A half grin split Tony's face. "Does that mean you want to get married?"

"Oh, yes. I do want to get married. Very much. But when? Do we have enough time — before you have to go back?"

"I'll make the time. I'm supposed to arrive at Fort Polk on Sunday night, but if I have to, I'll take a few extra days. Uh, have you said anything to your mother about — you know?"

She withdrew her hand and wrung it with the other. "No, I didn't want her to know anything until — well, until I talked to you. But I — I have a confession to make. I — I went to see your parents."

"You what?"

Patty inspected her palms. "I was scared. I didn't know what to do. So, one day I called up your mother and told her the story. We talked for a long time — about different things. The next day she met me on the Avenue — and we went shopping together. I didn't buy anything, I just talked. Then we went to her — to your house, and I stayed and had dinner. She was real nice."

Tony was stunned. "What about my father?"

Patty continued to stare at her hands, as she wrung them together. "I don't know if I can get along with him. He's always yelling: at your mother, at your brother, even at the cat. Oh, your brother's so cute. He looks a lot like you." She hazarded a sideways glance. "Anyway, I felt better about things after that."

Tony sighed. "Well, I guess that lets me off the hook about having to explain everything to them. I just can't believe you had the guts to go and see them."

"What else was I going to do? I'm all alone."

"Oh, Patty, you're not alone."

"You know what I mean. I don't have anybody to talk to."

"So how could you go and talk with perfect strangers?"

"Well, I just figured that since they're your parents, it was all right."

Tony shook his head.

"Well, anyway, now that you've let the cat out of the bag, I won't have to go and see them."

"Oh, but you should. They want to see you so much. At least, your mother does. You know, she was really hurt when you didn't go home to say goodbye. She told me so. And she cried."

"I can't imagine my mother crying."

"Well, she did. And you know what else? I think your father misses you, too. He's just too proud to admit it."

"Maybe, but I doubt it."

The front door squeaked and opened a crack. "Patty! You come in right now. Tell Kathy to come back tomorrow."

"All right."

The door shut with a bang.

"Great, now she thinks I'm Kathy."

Patty laughed. She kept her chin down, but peered through half-concealed eyes. "It's better that way. If she knew you were home, she wouldn't let me out to see you."

"Yes, maybe you're right." Tony hunched down to a lower step so his profile would not show should Mrs. O'Brien peek out the picture window. "Look, how about if I meet you some time tomorrow?"

"Okay. When?"

"Around twelve — at the frat house. We'll go out and have lunch, or something."

"Okay."

"You won't have any trouble getting away?"

"No, that'll be no problem during the day. I'll just tell her I'm going out with Kathy."

"Good." Tony stood up, and pulled Patty up with him. He swung her around so she was between him and the front door. "I guess — well, I don't have a ring, or anything."

"We can pick one up tomorrow." Suddenly she was in his arms, sobbing hysterically against his shoulder. "I'm — I'm scared, Tony."

He patted her on the back, kissed her neck. "Don't worry about a thing. Everything's going to be all right."

Patty shook her head against his shirt, smearing tears across her face. "Are you sure?"

Tony stroked her long hair, then held her head in place as he wiped away teardrops. "I'm sure." He kissed her on the forehead, on the tip of the nose, full on the mouth. She wrapped her arms around him and molded her body to his.

Long moments later, Tony gently pushed her back. "Look, you'd better get going before your grandmother comes out and yells again. She might see me the next time."

"All right."

"And cheer up that face. You don't want her to know you've been crying, do you?"

"No."

"And you don't want to crack any windows with that look."

Patty wiped away a stray tear with the back of her hand, and managed a weak smile. "I guess you're right."

"That's a girl. Now, just act as if nothing is wrong. "I'll see you tomorrow — the frat house at noon."

Tony melted into the shadows.

****

White Lightning was parked in front of Pete Robinson's house. It shone with a fresh coat of wax, gleaming white in the yellow glow of nearby street lamps. The chrome glimmered dazzlingly.

The steps of the Robinson house were cracked, and the brickwork needed pointing. Paint on the windows was faded and peeling. Inside, a nightlight threw garish illumination on worn furniture, threadbare rugs, and dull, papered walls.

Tony rapped gently. If Mr. Robinson was home from the bar, the faint sound would not wake him. But Mrs. Robinson might be up emptying her colostomy bag. A cricket stridulated from somewhere overhead. Cars roared by on the Avenue. Tony tapped on the pane of glass. A moment later a shape appeared on the steps, hugging the railing.

"All right. All right. You don't have to wake up the whole neighborhood." Petey, half asleep, fumbled with the dead bolt, threw open the door. His eyes widened. "Jesus Christ, Tony, what're *you* doin' here?"

"Well, I've been walking around for a couple of hours and thought I'd like to borrow the car for a while."

"That ain't what I meant. I thought you were on your way to Tiger Land."

"I am, but I'm taking the long way around."

"You ain't kiddin'." Pete pushed open the screen door and joined Tony on the landing. He wore nothing but jockey shorts. "Ain't nobody with you, is there?"

"No, I'm alone."

Pete punched Tony in the stomach, hard. "Gee, man, it's great to see you. You look like you're in pretty good shape."

"Yes, well, they have a steady exercise program for recruits."

"Yeah, I know. So what's the scoop? You gonna marry Patty?"

Tony sucked in his breath. "What makes you say that?"

"Hell, it don't take much figurin'. She's pregnant, you're AWOL. You ain't just passin' through."

"Pete, how did you know she was pregnant?"

"Everybody knows. What did you think, it was a big secret? You know the three best ways to spread news are telephone, telegraph, and tell a woman. Patty being a girl, everybody and their grandmother knows. Well, maybe not *her* grandmother."

"I don't believe this. How can everybody know?"

"Patty blabs to Kathy, Kathy blabs to Katie, Katie blabs to the world. It's as simple as that."

Tony digested that for a moment. "What about Marion?"

"Marion's as quiet as a mouse. She don't blab nothin' to nobody. She's a good kid, minds her own business."

"Still going out with her?"

"You bet."

"Well, I'm glad to hear that, anyway. You should stick with her. Listen, not to change the subject, but I've got to have the car keys. I've been walking around thinking about what I should do. I'm going to sneak into the frat house for the night, then go see my parents first thing in the morning."

"Mrs. Hart's been locking the back door lately, so you can't get in unless you knock. And you know she don't like nobody sleeping over. Look, why don't you spend the night here? You can sleep on the couch. My old man'll be sleepin' till noon, and my mom don't mind."

"Well, I don't know — "

"You can stay for breakfast, too."

"Well, I was going to get to my parents' house around breakfast time."

"All right, skip the breakfast. But at least stay here tonight. You shouldn't go wakin' Mrs. Clark up now."

"Well, I — "

"And no sleepin' in the car. Look, I'll give you the keys now, then you can leave whenever you want. Just don't wake me up when you go. But make sure you come back so we can talk."

Tony hesitated. "Thanks for understanding, Pete."

"Listen, I know you got things to do."

"All right. I'm meeting Patty at the garage at twelve. You want to tell the guys I'm home, and meet me there?"

"Sure thing. It'll be just like old times."

****

Tony felt like a burglar casing a joint.

He parked his car two streets over and wound through the narrow, smelly alleys. Rotting, wooden fences made the alley like a tunnel. Tufts of weeds, their spores carried into the city by the wind, struggled to maintain existence on patches of dirt that collected in cracks in the cement. He found his own back yard, and stared through a knothole until he saw movement across the windowpane.

He circled to the front of the house, picked up the morning paper, and used his key in the door. From the entry he glanced into the living room. When he walked into the kitchen, his mother was standing at the sink, frozen.

He tried to sound casual as he tossed the paper on the table. "Hi, mom."

She remained a statue for another five seconds, a coffee cup dangling from one hand, the other resting against the side of the sink. "I knew it was you. As soon as I heard the door open I knew it was you. What — what are you doing home?"

"I'm on travel time. I'm changing bases, so I thought I'd stop off and see how the home front was getting along without me."

"Well, you sure startled me, walking in like that at this hour of the morning." She broke out of her posture, put the cup in the sink. "Well, I hardly — know what to say. This is so unexpected. Well, sit down. The coffee will be ready in a minute. Uh, would you like anything else? Some toast, with jelly? We don't have much else. Since you left, I haven't bought any eggs — only cereal and milk for Robby."

Tony pulled out a chair and sat at his usual place. "Thanks, mom. Toast will be fine."

"When did you get in?"

"Late last night. I slept over at Pete's."

Elizabeth bustled around the kitchen, taking out plates, cups, saucers, and silverware. "That's nice. How long will you be — home?"

"A few days. Maybe a week."

"Well, it's nice to have you back. It seems like such a long time. And I haven't heard from you at all."

"I've been pretty busy."

The table was set, and she hovered around the coffee pot, waiting for it to perk. "Yes, I guess so."

"Well, everything looks pretty much the same. Hey, where's Kitty?"

As the coffee perked Elizabeth turned down the electric burner a notch. "Oh, she's probably around here somewhere."

Tony started making kissing noises, and calling, "Kitty, kitty, kitty." After only a few seconds, he heard the familiar click of her half-extended claws on the pantry floor. Then a little furred head peeped around the corner, whiskers askew. Green eyes twinkled in instant recognition. One more "Kitty" and she bounded across the linoleum and leaped into his lap, atop the hand that had been patting his leg.

A buffalo thumped down the steps, through the living room and dining room. "Oh, it's you. I was wondering who was calling the cat. When'd you get here?"

"Hi, dad. Just a few minutes ago. I thought I'd stop in for breakfast."

Frank started to nod, but instead bent over and went into a coughing spasm. He sat down when it stopped, pushed the table clear in front of him, and took out a cigarette. "Is that coffee ready yet?"

Elizabeth replied testily, "Yes, Frank, just as soon as I can get it out of the pot."

Frank unfolded the paper and stared at the headlines. The toast popped up. Elizabeth put two hot slices on a plate and handed it to Tony. She restocked the toaster, then took the butter out of the refrigerator and put it on the table.

"You look nice in uniform."

Tony started buttering the toast while it was still hot. "Thanks."

"Do they feed you all right? You don't look like you lost any weight."

Kitty purred in his lap. "Oh, sure, the food's fine. Most of the guys complain, but I think it's pretty good."

"Frank always used to say that army food was the worst in the world."

Frank seemed not to notice the mention of his name.

"No, it's all right. The only thing is they don't give us enough of it — or enough time to eat what they give us." Tony had not realized how hungry he was until he tasted the toast. He was already wolfing down the second slice.

"You want more?"

"Yes, please." He rubbed Kitty with both hands while she put two more slices in front of him. "How about you, Kitty. Have you had your breakfast yet?"

"You'll have to open a new can. She doesn't have any more in the refrigerator."

Tony ladled out a generous helping of smelly cat food.

"Where's the cream and sugar? Do I have to ask for everything around here?"

"Hold your pants on and I'll get it."

"You on leave?"

Tony sat down behind his toast. "Yes."

"How long?"

"A week. I'm being transferred to Fort Polk, Louisiana. Jungle warfare training."

Frank loaded his coffee with sugar and cream, slopping it onto the saucer while he stirred. "What happened to MP school?"

"I don't know. I guess I wasn't cut out to be a cop."

"So why'd you pick the infantry? That's where they dump all the jerks that can't do anything else."

"I didn't exactly pick it — it was picked for me. And besides, most men end up there anyway. There's a big demand for infantrymen."

Frank humphed, and coughed again. He tasted his coffee with a spoon, then sipped it between puffs on his cigarette. He turned to the second page.

"More toast?"

Tony stared at his empty plate. Other than a light snack on the plane, he had not eaten since lunch the day before. "Yes, I guess so. I'm pretty hungry this morning."

Kitty finished her food and rested on a throw

rug in the corner of the kitchen, licking her chops viciously.

"Tonwy."

"Robby!"

Tony's brother walked stiffly across the floor in his footed pajamas, carrying a ragged teddy bear held carelessly by one arm. In baby talk, he said, "You din' tell me you were home."

Tony laughed. "Well, I didn't want to wake you."

Robby climbed into his lap and placed his lips against his cheek — his version of a kiss, without the pucker. "I mist chu."

"I missed you, too." Not to be left out of the action, Kitty clicked across the floor and sat at the foot of the chair, looking up. She swiveled her hips, preparing to jump. Tony shifted Robby aside, made room on his leg, and patted. Robby scooped up the toast and crunched into it. Kitty landed on Tony's leg, and balanced there, sniffing at the toast.

"Get that damn cat down!" Frank yelled. Kitty cringed, but did not jump down. She stared at Frank for a moment, then curled up on Tony's leg and ignored him.

"What happened to your hair?" Robby ran his free hand over the black stubs. "You look funny."

"That's why they cut it all off. To make us look funny."

Frank pushed the paper aside, clattering plates and silverware. "Hey, get that damn cat down where she belongs and tell me what the hell's going on."

****

Tony's stomach contracted into a knot when he saw how thin and emaciated his grandfather had become. Gone were the ruddy cheeks, the firm forearms, the slight paunch that added more character than unsightliness. Now his cheeks were pale and ashen, his paunch sunken. His skin hung in loose folds about arms that were skeletal. He did not have the strength to lift himself from the bed.

"You'll have to pardon me for not gettin' up to greet you, Tony, but the fact is, I'm not feelin' too good today." He managed a wan smile, but took a couple of deep breaths before continuing. "I have my good days and my bad days, an' I guess this ain't one of the good ones. But my, Honey, you sure are lookin' like the picture of health."

"Yes, well, one thing I have to say for the army is that we get plenty of sunshine and outdoor activity."

Grandpop laughed, but in a way that showed how it pained him. "I guess you get more activity than you want — even for a strappin' young man like yourself. But you sure got a nice tan, kinda like you were workin' in the watermelon fields."

Now it was Tony's turn to laugh. He held up his arms. "Yes, but it ends at the neck and wrists. They won't even let us roll our sleeves up, no matter how hot it gets."

"Army never was much on common sense — guess it runs on momentum more'n anything else."

"How long's the phone been next to the bed?"

Grandpop squeezed his eyes shut, moved his body a little. He took several more deep breaths, then winked. "Ever since I got home. Didn't want to worry you none. They teach you how to shoot a gun?"

"Oh, yes, we had plenty of practice on the rifle range. I got to be a pretty good shot, too. Maybe almost as good as you."

"Aaagh. Always knew you could shoot better'n me, if you ever had a notion to pick up a gun and try. Still doesn't interest you much, does it?"

Tony shook his head.

Grandpop laughed. "That's all right, Tony. You were brought up in the city. It's a different life. When you're raised on a farm and you been huntin' with your dad ever' day since you were old enough to wrap your finger 'round a trigger, it just comes natural. Course, it was different when I was a boy. We depended on gettin' a few rabbits, some quail, even a deer, so's there'd be enough food on the table. Grew our own food, too. Now, you take this cornfield, here — "

He rolled his head on the pillow and nodded toward the window. Many a time Tony had sat upon the horse's back while Grandpop walked along behind with the plow. He took some more deep breaths.

"Now, I never really needed that corn, just grew it outa habit. It's all horse corn, and for our butter beans your grandmother'd go out and buy good sweet corn. But you know what I grew that corn for? To feed the horse come winter. Now, I needed the horse to plow the field for the corn, and I needed the corn to feed the horse. What did I get outa it? If I'd a got rid a the horse, I wouldn't a needed the corn. But I needed the horse and the corn. What for? Why, just because I liked doin' it, 'cause it reminded me of when I had to plow the field. You see, work ain't work when you like what you're doin'."

Grandmom bustled in then, wearing her ever-present apron and wagging her crooked index finger. "Tony, you're gonna plum tucker him out, talkin' a blue streak like that. You know the doctor said you're supposed to rest, an' you cain't be restin' when you're workin' that jaw like a buzz saw. Now, Walter, them pills have been settin' on that table for 'most a hour and you ain't touched 'em yet." Turning to Tony, she said, "You gotta watch him, or he'll forget ever' time to take his medicine. Now, I'll get you some fresh water an' you take them pills right now."

"Never heard tell of water goin' stale in a glass, Pauline," Grandpop snapped. "An' talkin' to my grandson's the best medicine there is. What did I just say, Tony. This ain't work. Talkin' with you is restful."

Grandmom returned with the water. "You stop talkin' nonsense, Walter, an' take them pills."

He grimaced as he put his hands under him. "I'm feelin' a might weak today. Tony, can you help me up?"

Tony ran around to the opposite side of the bed. With his hand under the pillow, he lifted his grandfather's head. Grandmom placed two pills in his mouth and held the glass close, but the bend in his neck prevented him from swallowing. Tony used both hands and cradled his grandfather's head while he lifted up his upper body; he was surprisingly light. He gulped down the pills and water without trouble. Tony eased him back down.

"Honey, I'd like to talk some more, but I've got to go to sleep now. You ain't leavin' right away, are you?"

"No. I'm going to stay over tonight and go home some time tomorrow."

"Good, then we can talk some later."

"Okay, I'll be here when you wake up."

A weak, calloused hand wrapped itself around Tony's, squeezed with the might of a child. "I love you, Tony."

Grandpop's eyes slowly closed, and he drifted off to sleep.

Chapter 59

The inside of the building was cold and damp, the result of a concrete floor which had not yet cured, and ongoing brickwork with its fresh mortar. The rear wall was in the process of being raised: a flurry of activity showed where laborers were mixing cement, and bricklayers were readjusting their string lines for the next tier.

Incessant banging was attributed to a handful of carpenters nailing studs together, and placing partitions where the roof was incomplete: two-by-sixteen joists only half covered with plywood. Plumbers were soldering pipes stubbed up through the floor, working in an area chalked out as a bathroom. Two laborers rushed past, pushing wheelbarrows piled high and awkwardly with trash and debris.

Tony recognized an electrician by the tools in his pouch. Except for his clothes, he did not look much different from a student on campus. His face was well hidden behind a year's growth of beard, dark and unkempt. His long hair curled down past a thin neck, and was held out of his eyes by a red handkerchief knotted on his forehead. He had a pipe bender in one hand and a ten-foot length of three-quarter-inch thinwall in the other. He placed the handle of the bender on the floor, shoved in the tubing, and aligned it on the mark. He pulled down sharply, eyed it suspiciously, and pulled down some more. When he flipped the tubing over to make the second bend for his offset, Tony approached cautiously, stepping over bundles of conduit and a stack of two-by-fours.

"Excuse me, can you tell me where to find Frank Giovanni?"

"Who wants to know?" A smile softened the words.

"I do. He's my father."

"Oh, you must be Tony. Glad to meet you. My name's Paul Maddox."

"Hi, Paul. Are you the foreman?"

"I wish. I'm nothing but a first year apprentice." Paul leaned over the pipe bender and scratched his scraggly hair. "I heard how you got shafted by the draft board."

Tony's eyes widened in surprise. "What?"

"Your dad was telling us how you dropped outa college to join the union, and got picked up before they could get you a deferment. I hear you're going to 'Nam now."

"Yes, well, I've got orders for infantry training, anyway."

"Yeah, well take it easy over there, man. It's some bad shit. I spent six months in-country back when nobody ever heard of the place. I was with the 9th Marine Expeditionary Brigade when they made the first landing at Da Nang. March of '65. Changed the name to III Marine Amphibious Force so it wouldn't scare the friendlies. Mostly we were there to defend the airbase. Things went great for a coupla months, until they sent us to Chu Lai to help the Seabees build the airbase. Then there was nothing but work all day and stand guard all night. Got in some crazy firefights when sappers tried to blow up the landing field."

"What's a sapper?"

Paul shrugged. "Infiltrators. Enemy demolition experts. They blew up a slew of choppers before we even knew they were inside the compound."

"Did anyone get hurt?"

"Only gooks. Blew five of them away while they were crawling under the wire."

"You did?"

"Naw, not me, man. I was too busy trying to crawl inside my helmet. I was locked up in a bunker with some crazy nigger from Georgia.

As soon as the mortars started coming in, he let loose with his M-14. Shot up more bushes than anybody else. Hell, we wasn't even on the same side of the field where the action was. But you couldn't tell old Matthew that. He was just trigger-happy. A great guy, too, when he wasn't scared."

Tony shifted his weight nervously. He just *had* to see his father right away, but what Paul Maddox had to say was fascinating. "Sounds like there was a lot of action."

"Not really. I never went out on any patrols, or nothing. Mostly it was just standing guard. What a joke that was. I spent most of my three years in the Marines guarding things that nobody would want, or could possibly take away. But I saw the guys coming back from the bush. They were always running into some shit and calling for support. Closest I got was one time when the sergeant comes around and rounds up a bunch of us taking a break. We were working in a hundred and ten degree heat — and in the sun, too — and could only stand thirty-minute shifts. So along comes this sergeant, and he grabs me and a bunch of other guys, and says, 'Come with me. You're going on patrol.' Hell, the bastard was serious. We went along and got our rifles and flak jackets and waited for a chopper to take us out. It never came, so finally we just went back to work. Hell, those Seabees were sure scared. Hadn't fired a gun since basic, and hardly knew which way to hold the barrel. Me, at least I got to shoot at shadows on guard duty. Mostly, I'd lob grenades from an M-79. We had a free fire zone where you could shoot at anything that moved. Helped keep me awake. The villagers, too. Hell, they never slept. There was always ordnance dropping in the ville."

Tony shifted awkwardly again. "How did you manage to get in the Marines?"

"Hell, I was so stupid I volunteered. I had it cool and easy when my old man got me in the union. Knocked around for a coupla years after high school before I entered. Then I got to thinking how dull it was working, so one day I up and joined the Marines. Had only been in the union for six months, just enough time to get clearance from the I.O. So I hitched up for three years and went for infantry because there wasn't any wars on, so I thought they didn't do anything but travel. Hell, was that a mistake. When you're not humping the boonies they got you cleaning equipment. I never knew that stuff had to be kept so clean. I cleaned my rifle so many times it was bored out enough to fire a mortar round through it. Anyway, I'm gettin' short, and I'm in Okinawa with six months to go, when orders come through for battalion landing teams to go on an exercise to set up a

perimeter around some airbase. So they ship us over and we make a beach landing, just like in the book. Hell, everybody and their mother knew we was coming. They even had welcome signs out for us — in English! So I stayed there till my time was up, then got the hell out of the Marines before the shit really hit the fan. When I came back, the union tells me I gotta start over again from scratch 'cause I didn't finish my first year. So now I'm a stinking first-year 'prentice again."

"Well, at least now you don't have to worry about rank."

"What are you, kidding? This is almost as bad as the fuckin' Marines. Everybody here thinks he's a fuckin' general. Hell, when I was in the Marines we'd a busted someone upside the head for some of the shit they get away with here. You're old man's all right, but most bosses would just as soon fire you for talking back. Here it's just me and Smitty. We work together, like a team. He even goes out and gets the coffee. But you get on a big job and a 'prentice ain't nothing but a gopher — go fer coffee, go fer tools, go fer wirenuts. Hell, I worked an office building downtown for eight months and didn't learn nothing but material handling and coffee getting.

"The Marines turns us into men, and the world turns us back into flunkies. I got in a fight with the foreman on the last job. Some young punk who started in the union right after high school, so by the time he's twenty two, twenty-three, he comes out a mechanic. I spend three years in the Corp, do a tour in 'Nam, and I gotta take orders from some kid who still don't know what a piece of ass is. He comes in one morning and says, 'Send the kid over for a coil of fourteen wire.' I says, 'Who the fuck you calling "kid"?' He looks at me and says, 'Got a bug up your ass?' I says, 'Yeah, and it's gonna be you. This "kid" is not only older than you, but he's seen more of the world than you'll *ever* see.' He says, 'Not likely.' I says, 'If you don't believe me, let's go outside and I'll prove it.' He says, 'You start any trouble on my job and I'll have you in front of the Examining Board.' I says, 'You do and you're ass is grass. And if you don't believe it, you just meet me at four-thirty. Come around to Harry's Tavern tonight and I'll show you some of my Marine training, punk.' So he just walks away, but he don't give me no more shit. And he damn sure don't call me kid no more.

"And that's not the worst of it. I get on another job and we're strapping pipe across a poured ceiling. I'm working with a mechanic with a Hilti gun. He puts a twenty-two shell in the gun, holds the pipe against the ceiling, marks the place for his clamps, and bangs in a stud with a pull of the trigger. I look at it and say, 'Hell, I can do that.' So I pick up the Hilti gun, load it, mark my spot, and the mechanic comes over and takes it away from me. I says, 'Whaddaryou doing?' He says, 'You're an apprentice.' I says, 'No shit. When'd you figure that out?' He says, 'Apprentices aren't allowed to use Hilti guns.' 'Says who?' 'Says the super.' 'He didn't say it to me,' I says. So we call him up — we're working on the eighteenth floor — and you know what he says? He says, 'The union won't allow 'prentices to use power actuated tools.' I says, 'Why not?' He says, 'Because they're dangerous.' I says, 'Hell, I've fired every weapon from automatic rifles to fifty calibers. Are you trying to tell me I can't use a fuckin' stud shooter? Hell, I never fired anything this *small.*' He says, 'Sorry, but they're the rules.' I says, 'What the fuck's the matter with you? I just got back from shooting real guns at *people*, and you're trying to tell me I can't shoot a toy at a lousy piece of concrete?' He says, 'Maddox, I know how you feel. But I can't let you use it or the union'll have my ass.' So you know what I gotta do? I gotta stand on a ladder and use a hammer and star drill, overhead, and chop them holes in by hand, and use lead cinches. Meanwhile, the mechanic just goes along laying five times as much pipe as me, shooting in studs as fast as he can pull the trigger. Hell, man, I didn't come back for this kinda chicken shit. You're old man, though, he don't care what I do, as long as I get the work done. 'You want to use the Hilti?', he says, 'Go right ahead. And if Smitty gives you any trouble, you tell him to see me.' Your old man's all right."

Tony cleared his throat. "Yes, well, I guess he figures he can make more money by paying an apprentice's wages and getting a mechanic's work out of him."

"Oh, sure, it's to his benefit, too. But I don't care. At least he treats me like a man."

"Yeah, I guess."

"Anyhow, he ain't here. Just checked up on us this morning, then left for parts unknown."

"Do you know where he went?"

"It ain't my turn to watch him."

"Well, thanks anyway, uh, Paul."

"Sure thing. And hey — kill a coupla gooks for me. And when you come back, maybe I'll let you be my 'prentice."

"Thanks."

****

Tony caught his father at the next job, an apartment complex, just as he was coming out of the builder's office trailer.

"Dad, I've got to talk with you for a minute."

Frank swung around sharply. "What are you doing here?"

"Mom said you either had to be here or at that office building. I already checked and you weren't there."

He kept on walking, and Tony had to run to keep up with him. "Well, don't hold me up. I gotta check on the men out in Gwennyd, and I got a meeting at two o'clock with the inspector. And I ain't had time to stop for lunch."

"Well, I'll only be a minute."

"Did you see Grandpop?"

"Yes, I just left this morning, around nine. Made it home in two and a half hours because it's a weekday and there wasn't any traffic."

Frank strode over the uneven ground. "Yeah, not like comin' home on a Sunday night in the summer, with all that shore traffic at Dover. That's when it's really bad — bumper to bumper for ten miles. A coupla weeks ago it took us almost four hours to get home, and we left late figurin' we'd miss most of it. You just never know. I can't understand why some people just don't stay home on the weekends instead of blockin' the roads."

"Uh, dad, can I get right to the point?"

"All right, but make it snappy. I told you I ain't got all day." He reached the Cadillac, now dull and dusty from airborne dirt at the unpaved job sites. He slipped inside and opened the electric window.

Tony glanced around, saw that no one was within hearing range. "Well, you know about me and Patty. I mean, you talked with her last week and she explained things."

"So?"

"Well, on the way down to Salisbury, I stopped at Elkton and picked up a marriage license. I made a few phone calls first, and found out that in the state of Pennsylvania you have to have blood tests, and I don't have time for all that — the results take several weeks. So, we decided to get married in Maryland. All you have to do there is wait forty-eight hours after getting the license."

"I think you're making a big mistake. You're too young to get married. You don't even have a trade yet. You gotta finish your hitch, then go through four years apprenticeship. I think you should wait."

"You got married while you were still in the army. And had me before you started your apprenticeship."

"That was different. Things were different in those days."

"And you were better, I suppose?"

"Don't get smart with me, or I'll knock you right on the ground."

"Great. And that'll solve everything, won't it?" Tony saw his father's hands tighten on the steering wheel. "Dad, just stop being belligerent for a minute and let's talk some sense. Now, here's the problem. According to some ridiculous regulation, the age of consent for girls is eighteen, but for guys it's twenty-one. I know it doesn't make any sense, but that's the way it is. That means Patty is free to get married any time she wants, but I've got to have parental consent. So, what you have to do is sign a consent form so when we go back to Elkton tomorrow there won't be any hassle."

"I don't have to do anything."

"What I mean is that you have to sign it so I can get married, not because anyone is making you."

"You ain't gonna make me do nothing I don't want to do. Since when do I gotta take orders from you?"

"Dad, would you just try to help me for once, instead of running me into the ground? I'm trying to reason with you."

"And I'm tryin' to help. That's why I ain't signin' no license."

"Dad — "

"Don't 'dad' me. Now, you listen. I got connections. I ain't been in business all these years without doing some favors, and havin' some friends in high places. You leave everything up to me and I can square it so you won't have to marry this girl. I can have her legs broke if she causes any trouble."

"Dad!" Tony shouted, rolling his head.

"And she can't do a thing about it."

"Dad, you don't understand. I *want* to marry her."

"What the hell do you know what you want? You're just a kid. Now you listen to me, you get your ass back to the army and leave everything up to me. I'll take care of it."

"Dad, besides wanting to get married, I *have* to — and soon. Before she starts showing."

"I got it all figgered out. This is gonna cost some money, maybe a grand, but I can handle it. All she's gotta do is go to New York for one day. She sees a doctor, he takes care of her, and she's on her way home a couple hours later. Then you don't hafta to marry her."

"You don't understand anything at all."

"I understand enough to know what's good for you."

"Look, why don't you stop trying to run my life for me? If you weren't always trying to manipulate things, I'd be in college right now and none of this would have happened."

"Yeah, and you'd become some pansy geographer. You gotta outgrow rock collecting some day."

"All right, so you took all that away from me. I hope you're proud of the way you ruined my career. But you're not going to take this away from me, too. I want this baby, and I want to get married. And one way or another, I'll do

it. With you, or without you."

Tony walked away with his fists clenched, before his father could have the satisfaction of driving off first.

****

Ben sprawled across his bed, the pillows stuffed under his left side. "So what's going to happen now?"

Tony heard the phone ringing downstairs, then Mrs. Clark's voice as she talked in low tones. "I don't know. There's nothing I can do unless he signs that paper. I talked it over with my mother, and I can't tell if she's on my side or not." Tony lay on his back, his head propped up against the headboard.

"Why don't you and Patty both go over there and have it out with them?"

"Are you kidding? Patty would break down and start crying the minute she walked in the door. You don't know how upset she is."

"Maybe crying is what you need to get to your parents' better side."

"They don't have a better side."

"Well, look, why don't you just go to City Hall and get the license here? Take the blood tests, and get married when you get back from Fort Polk."

"No, that won't make any difference. Pennsylvania has the same age of consent laws that Maryland has. All the states do — at least, the nearby ones."

"But that's stupid." Ben rolled back and stared up at the ceiling. "What makes them think a girl at eighteen has any more sense than a boy at eighteen?"

"The same kind of reasoning that makes you an adult at the movies but a child at the bar."

A shrill voice called from downstairs. "Ben. Tony. Dinner."

"Be right down, Mom," Ben shouted, but otherwise not moving. "So what are you going to do now?"

"Wait. And hope they change their minds."

"You can't wait too long. You can't stay AWOL forever."

Tony rolled off the bed, sat with his face in his hands. "I know. Well, let's not worry about it, huhn?" He pushed himself to his feet. "Let's eat, drink, and be merry, for tomorrow we die."

Ben said, "Yeah," as he followed Tony downstairs.

Mr. Clark was halfway through his first helping by the time Tony and Ben sat down at the table. "Hello, Ben, Tony. Dig in."

Mrs. Clark set two steaming bowls in front of them. She indicated Mr. Clark with her eyes. "And do it fast before *he* eats it all." They needed no second invitation. "I got a letter from Joey today. He says everything's fine in Germany, but he's getting tired of twenty-four hour standby and nothing but drills. He says it's been so long since he's taken the plane off the ground, he's afraid he's going to lose his flying status."

"Well, maybe he'll have the time to write more than once a month," Mr. Clark garbled, with a full mouth.

"And when was the last time you wrote to *him*?"

"Two weeks ago."

"And what about you, Ben?"

"Uh, I don't remember."

"Must have been pretty long ago, then."

"Well, I've been pretty busy with school."

"Not too busy to go gallivanting around with the gang every night instead of staying home and studying." Her tone was not as biting as her words. "Well, why don't you start thinking about what you're going to put down on paper tonight?"

"Aw, Mom, I have to go out tonight."

"You don't *have* to go out — you *want* to. Katie can wait. Your brother comes first. While your behind is warming a seat in a heated classroom, he's freezing his tail off by the Berlin Wall."

Ben kept shoving food in his mouth. "Mom, it's August in Germany, too."

"Beside the point." She looked at Tony. "How many times has he written to *you*?"

Tony stopped with the spoon in front of his lips. "Well, actually, I don't remember."

"Not very often, I'll bet. Right, Ben?"

"Aw, Mom, cut it out. I can't help it if I have a hectic schedule."

"The only hectic part about your schedule is your social life. Between campus rallies and drag racing, you never give a thought about who makes it all possible for you."

Ben placed his head in his hand and rolled his eyes. "Here we go again."

Mr. Clark came to his rescue at the end of a swallow. "At least he's not getting shot at. I'd rather have him in college than over there in that God forsaken jungle."

"Why?"

"Because he's my son."

"And all those other boys over there are son's. They all have families back here: mothers, fathers, brothers, sisters, wives, and children. I'd like to have them all back, not just because they're any relation to me, but because they're all out there fighting for us. And the reason there is so this schmuck can keep his nose in a book all day and in his girlfriend's neck all night."

"Mom," Ben said sternly.

"Somebody's got to lecture you once in a while, Ben, just so you don't forget to appreciate the world around you. Tony, you better eat

faster than that or these two bottomless pits will get it all."

Tony tilted his head. "Well, I guess I'm just not too hungry."

"You should be. That phone call a little while ago was from your mother. They'll sign."

****

Tony returned alone to his parents' house. Since there had been no formal invitation to dinner, he arrived at seven-thirty. Elizabeth was just putting Robby to bed, and hushed Tony down the stairs.

"I don't want you getting him excited seeing you, else I'll never get him to sleep."

Frank watched the news intently on the small black and white set in the kitchen. Tony eased into a chair and slipped the consent form across the table to him. He paid it no mind.

Kitty jumped into Tony's lap; he petted her as she nuzzled his face. From upstairs he could hear his brother howling, but Elizabeth dampened the noise by closing his door.

"Bring me them papers before you sit down," Frank commanded, as a commercial came on. He stirred his coffee, put the dripping spoon down on the table. He flashed a dark eye at Tony. "You gotta sign some papers, too."

Kitty purred as Tony ran his hand down her sleek fur. "What kind of papers?"

"Insurance papers. And something else, I want that car."

"What do you mean, you want that car? What car?"

"The white one, what the hell do you think!"

"But that's my car."

"It's in my name, ain't it?"

"Sure, but that's just for insurance purposes. I paid for it myself, and I pay for my share of the insurance."

"That don't mean nothing. As long as that car's in my name, I'm the one responsible for it. An' I don't want none of your friends joy riding in it 'cause if one of 'em gets in an accident, I'm the one who gets in trouble for it. An' I'm not gonna have my rates go up for nobody."

"But, Dad, Pete's taking care of it for me. He just inspected it at the station, he cleaned and waxed it, he starts it up once or twice a week — "

"You don't think I can start it up? What do you think, I'm some kinda dummy? Now you bring that car here before you leave, or I'll have the police bring it back. And anybody in it will be thrown in jail." To Elizabeth: "Where are those damn papers? I ain't got all night."

"I'm getting them, Frank, just hold your horses! The baby spilled some water on my blouse and I can't do two things at once."

"Well, shut him up."

Elizabeth left the room. The news came back

on. Tony scratched the cat and played with the pen. When his mother returned several minutes later, she flung the papers down on the table.

"Here are your damn papers. If you wanted them so damn bad you could have gotten out of your chair and gotten them yourself. You're not crippled, you know."

"I don't know where they are. You hide everything around here."

"They were on your desk, right where you put them."

Frank ignored her, spun the papers around and tossed them in front of Tony. "We're taking out a new policy on you."

Tony looked over the forms, deciphered the legalese. "This is for life insurance."

"What did you think, it was for your lousy stamp collection?"

"But, Dad, I already have life insurance. I've got a G.I. policy that only costs two dollars a month."

"This is different. This is a ten-thousand-dollar policy."

"That's what the G.I. policy is."

"Don't worry about it, it ain't gonna cost you a dime. I'm paying for it."

"I still don't need it."

Elizabeth sat down with a cup of coffee, stirred in some cream. "But we need it. You see, since you're going to go ahead and — marry this girl — you'll probably have her as the beneficiary. But we need to be protected, too."

"Protected from what? You're not dependent on me."

"No, but we would still have financial responsibilities to take care of. Funeral expenses, and what not. You wouldn't want to put that burden on you wife — or the baby — would you?"

Tony exploded with anger. "What are you talking about? You've got me dead and buried already."

Frank swung his eyes back to the television. Elizabeth stared into her coffee. "Well, it's not that. We don't expect anything to happen, but you never know. That's what insurance is for. Just in case."

"You think because I'm going into the infantry something is going to happen to me?"

"No, of course not. We just don't want to be caught short. And I'm not the one who picked the infantry."

"I didn't pick it either, but it's a job that has to be done. You people talk as if it's the scummiest job in the world."

Frank turned from the news broadcast, and gesticulated wildly with his arms. "Don't get smart, or I'll knock you right out of that chair."

"Frank, would you calm down?"

He slammed his fist on the table; the creamer jumped up and fell on its side, spilling its white liquid. "Jesus Christ, now see what you made me do?"

"Would you watch what the hell you're doing?" Elizabeth jumped up to get a dishtowel, started mopping up the mess. "Why can't you learn to talk with your mouth?"

"He makes me mad with his wise cracks." He pointed at Tony and managed to knock over the sugar bowl.

"Christ, Frank, you're worse than the baby."

He stabbed a finger at Tony. "I don't have to take any of his shit."

"Well, at least give him a chance to answer for himself. I don't know why the army doesn't let you make up your own mind about what you want to be."

"If you remember, I made up my mind a long time ago. I decided to become a geologist. But that decision was taken out of my hands, too."

Frank pounded his fist onto the papers. "Would you stick to the point? You think we don't already got insurance on you? We had a thousand dollar policy since you were a baby. But things have gone up since then. Everything cost more today."

Elizabeth made a semblance of orderliness out of the table. "Besides, it's like having money in the bank. Even though we're making the payments, the policy is in your name, and if some time you want to take it over, it will be cheaper since it was taken out when you were nineteen."

"And we'll give you the policy when you get out of the army. You can even cash it in if you want."

Eventually, Tony signed. Eventually, they signed, too.

"And don't forget. I want that car parked in front of the house before you go. And the keys and owner's card, too."

Chapter 60

"My, don't you look handsome on your wedding day. If I were a little younger I'd marry you myself."

Tony looked down at his black loafers. "Thanks, Mrs. Clark."

"You're getting to be such an adult, you're going to have to start calling me Frances."

"Gee, I don't think I could get used to that. You've been Mrs. Clark as long as I've known you." Tony glanced at the mirror and adjusted his tie, then buttoned the jacket of his sharkskin suit.

"Things change when you grow up. It's part of life." She clucked her tongue. "You look so confident. Where's that frightened little boy I used to know? On *my* wedding day, I was so scared I almost passed out walking down the aisle. Ben Senior was a lot like you: strong, self assured, good looking, and — loving."

Ben danced out of his room, light blue shirt-tail flapping. "Aw, Mom, what's wrong with this shirt? It matches the pants."

"You just do what I say and put on a white shirt. This isn't a costume party you're going to. It's a wedding. You wear those fancy clothes when you go out with Katie."

"Aw, Mo-o-om." Ben stomped back into his room.

Tony stretched his neck and pulled out the collar. "Well, I don't have to walk down the aisle. The office is barely big enough for the four of us and the JP."

Mrs. Clark lowered her voice as soon as Ben was out of sight. "Tony, have you thought this thing through?"

With his finger still as a spacer, Tony pinched his eyes at her. "What do you mean?"

"I mean, are you sure this is the right thing for you?"

He glanced at Ben's room. "Well, of course it's the right thing."

"For *you*?"

Tony shrugged. "Well, for everyone."

She pulled a handkerchief from her slacks, and dabbed her eyes. "Tony, I — " She pulled him close, and hugged him. When she backed away she dabbed her eyes again. "Sometimes — when you're in pain — even if you don't know you're in pain — it's difficult to make good decisions — to look ahead — to — like a child taking a test sitting on a chair full of tacks — his mind is so distracted he can't think right. Well, whatever happens, I hope it's for the best. I guess, under the circumstances, it *is* the best."

Mrs. Clark put her hands on Tony's shoulders, kissed his forehead. "May God bless you always."

****

Ben eased the Black Stallion between two parked cars in front of Katie's house. The '57 Chevy never shone so bright. He had cleaned and waxed it as soon as he heard of Tony's wedding plans, because he wanted to be chauffeur as well as best man.

"Never thought I'd see the day old Tone would be getting married."

Tony climbed out of the car and adjusted his jacket. "Just you wait. Some time your day will come."

"Isn't it 'some *day* your *time* will come'?"

"Whatever."

Ben slammed the door and wiped off an imaginary speck of dust. "Well, whether it's time or day, Katie and I are holding off till I'm out of college."

"Why wait if you're so sure?"

"The excuse is that Katie wants to save up some money so we can buy a house while I finish school and get a good job. But the *reason* is that I want to play around a little before I settle down. There are an awful lot of good looking chicks at Villanova."

Tony climbed the three cement steps and pushed the buzzer. "Ben, Katie's the only girl you've ever gone out with. You two must get along pretty well or it wouldn't have lasted this long."

"That's right, but maybe there's something better. I'll never know unless I shop around."

"Suppose Katie decides to do some shopping of her own?"

"She won't. She's too stuck on me."

The door burst open and Katie did her best to get stuck on Ben, wrapping herself around his body like a leech. "I thought you would never get here." She nuzzled his neck, kissed his cheeks, and broke free long enough to say, "Hi, Tony. Patty's inside, but she's not ready yet. You can go in anyway."

Patty was in the living room wearing a plain, white dress, her hair up in curlers. "Hi."

Tony gave her a peck on the cheek, sniffed in the fragrance of perfume. "Boy, you sure look different. How did you manage to get out of the house like that?"

"She didn't." Katie dragged Ben by the arm and closed the front door with a foot. "She got showered and dressed over here."

"Okay, let's cut the small talk," Ben said seriously. "I told you we'd be here at three o'clock. That meant you were supposed to be ready to go."

Katie pouted. "We'll only be a few more minutes."

"But it's going to take us an hour to get there, and they close at five."

"That gives us an hour to spare, doesn't it?"

"That's not the point," Ben persisted. "Suppose we have a flat tire or something on the way?"

Katie ushered Patty up the stairs. "Okay, so we'll hurry. We just have to put on the finishing touches."

Tony sat in a comfortable chair and waited nervously, while Ben chafed. Every five minutes he yelled up the stairs at Katie, and every time she answered that they were almost ready. It was a half hour before he hustled them out the door and into the car.

"Ben, why are we going in your car? Tony's car is bigger, and nicer."

While Tony held the door open for Patty, Ben forced Katie into the front seat. "Because my car's faster, and we need speed because thanks to you we're late. Besides, his car smells like a whorehouse."

"Why?"

"What do you think they've been doing at the river every night this week — talking?"

Katie gasped. Patty blushed. Tony merely smiled as Ben winked in the rearview mirror.

After an acceptable time, Katie threw her arm over the seat. "Aren't you excited?"

Patty smirked, and tilted her head. "Well, kinda. I guess, I never expected it to be this way. I always wanted a big church wedding. You know, with hundreds of guests, and a big cake, and a huge reception, and lots of presents. Getting married like this I won't get anything."

Tony nudged her with his elbow, saying with mock contempt, "Hey, you're getting me."

"You know what I mean. It's just not the same, sneaking off like this. What will everyone say?"

"Don't worry what everyone will say. It's not important."

"Not to you. But what happens when my grandmother finds out?"

"There's nothing she can do about it."

"That's easy for you to say. You don't have to live with her."

"Neither do you, any more, now that everything's set up with Kathy."

Katie fondled Ben's ear. "Yeah, but Ray isn't too happy about it."

Ben quickly veered through traffic. "Ray can stuff it. He'll just have to get used to it."

"Tony, are you going to give me some money before you go? I'll have to give Kathy half a month's rent."

"I'll give you my bank book so you can use whatever money you need for expenses."

"You mean I can buy clothes without having to beg my grandmother?"

"Sure. And when I get to Fort Polk, I'll have an allotment made out for you. Then the checks will come directly to you."

"Wow. For the first time in my life I'm going to be independent."

****

The ceremony was simple, direct, and to the point.

The Justice of the Peace was a soft-spoken, always-smiling, gray-haired old gent who boasted of having joined in matrimony upwards of fifty thousand couples in his three decades of service. Tony quickly calculated in his head that this was over one half of one percent of the total population of the United States. And after seeing how quickly the JP performed the deed, he could well understand how he could rack up such a score.

"Put more people together than the whole Catholic church," he bragged. With Ben and Katie acting as witnesses, he repeated the formula for the dozenth time that day. "Friday's are the busiest because people are trying to make it for the weekend."

Somehow he managed to make the hackneyed ritual sound fresh and alive and meaningful.

And just like that they were married.

Later, at a restaurant, Tony could hardly believe it had really happened. The girls went to the lady's room to powder their noses while he and Ben held the table.

"Tony, what's going to happen now?"

"I don't know, exactly. We've talked it over some, and I don't think it's going to work out as a permanent arrangement for Patty to live with Kathy. I guess eventually we'll have to get an apartment of our own."

"Do you have enough money for that?"

"I guess so. I've saved quite a lot over the years. And I don't really spend anything on myself. Besides, how can you spend money in the army? They pay my room and board, and give me a clothing allowance besides. At the end of the month, most of my money is leftover. If Patty could get a job — you know, temporary — until the baby is born, that would be a big help."

The waiter, immaculately dressed in a black tuxedo, brought four glasses of water. Ben took a sip. "What about Vietnam?"

"Oh. Well, that's why I think I'll have to get Patty set up on her own before I go over. And when I go, assuming I do, I'll get even more money. Combat pay is another sixty-five dollars a month. And everybody makes PFC as soon as he gets there, so that boosts my base pay up to a hundred twenty-five a month. With the allotment and combat pay, that comes to, uh, two forty-five. Not bad, considering."

"Yeah, considering being shot at. But forget about the money. I'm talking about Vietnam as an issue, not as a way of earning a living."

"Oh. Well, what about it?"

Ben leaned forward, putting his elbows on the white tablecloth. "Why do you think I'm going to Villanova?"

Tony raised his eyebrows. "To become an accountant."

"That's partly it. But also so I don't have to go to some backward hole-in-the-wall country to fight for something I don't believe in."

"You don't believe in democracy?"

"Hell, yes. I'd fight for democracy — in our own country. But you won't find me tramping around any damned jungle for a bunch of Stone Age peasants. I don't think we should be there in the first place. I don't think it's right for us to intrude into someone else's country and try to foist our own standards and ideals on them. I don't thing it's right for us to send troops over there to kill all those who don't think like we do."

Tony fingered his glass. "Sounds like a cop-out to me. What are you afraid of? Fighting, or giving up two years of your life."

"That's bullshit, and you know it. You know me better than that."

"I've found out that you never know people as well as you think you do."

"But we grew up together."

Tony took a long drink of water, and licked his lips. "So what do you think — that it's all right for the North Vietnamese to foist *their* ideals on the South Vietnamese? Do you think it's right for them to kill people because they're against communism? I mean, it's not like we're going over there to take over their country, or to have a big killing spree. We're just stepping in for the underdogs because they're not strong enough to fight for themselves."

"Or don't have the guts to fight for themselves."

"Or don't have the weapons to fight off a stronger opponent."

"Or who are ten thousand miles away and whatever happens to them can't affect us one way or the other."

"Ben, I went to college, too, you know. I've heard all those arguments before. Don't let that kind of narrow-mindedness get to you. You can't isolate yourself from the rest of the world. You stick your head in a hole, and just because you can't see what's happening doesn't relieve you of the responsibility of trying to do something about it. There are problems over there that can better be nipped in the bud than allowed to grow. It's easier to cut out a cancer when it's small than to wait until it has affected the whole body."

"And I've heard all *those* arguments before. You've been brainwashed by the army. I think it's about time we stopped trying to stick our noses into other people's business and mind our own for a change. If all of Southeast Asia fell into the sea tomorrow, it wouldn't make a damned bit of difference to us."

"That's right, but if it becomes communist it does. If all those people become the slaves of an overbearing aggressive nation, then we'd have to worry about them coming after us next. And by then they might be too strong to oppose. You want to wait until they're knocking on our own doors before we do something about it? No, we've got to fight aggression wherever we find it; we've got to seek it out and destroy it, to free all the subjugated peoples of the world, no matter where they live. They're all people, Ben. They're all human beings. They should have the same inalienable rights that your ancestors fought for in the past. Or have you forgotten that the only reason we

have those rights is because a couple centuries ago, someone got off his butt and went out and fought for them?"

"Now you sound like my mother."

Tony ignored him. "What did you ever do to earn your own freedom? You had the great fortune to have been born in a free country. And because those people live somewhere else, were born in a different part of this world, or have a different color skin and a different slant to their eyes, doesn't make them any less human. They're still people, and they're oppressed."

"You just go on believing that — propaganda. That's all it is. The opiate of the masses, made to keep people from thinking for themselves. We're not freeing anyone from anything, we're just killing off dissidents."

"You mean bandits? You mean guerrillas? You mean a group of outlaws that ransacks a village and takes all their food so the villagers have nothing to eat for themselves? You mean murderers and rapists? You'd think differently if it was Katie who was raped instead of some other eighteen-year-old you never met before. That's the way you have to think about it."

"I just happen to think that killing is wrong."

"Is being killed any better?"

"*I'm* not going to get killed because I don't plan to get involved in it. I'm going to stay in college until this whole bloody mess blows over. And I'm going to protest it all the way. I'm not going to let them turn me into a killer just to fight someone else's war, so some crooked politician can get rich with payoffs from the corporations that produce war materials. Don't you understand that's what this war is really about? It's an excuse for creating jobs for the unemployed, increasing productivity, bolstering our own economy. And people — Americans — are dying for that."

Tony took another long draft of water, draining the glass. "I'll admit there's a certain amount of that going on. It's inevitable with the kind of system we have. But I can't believe — I *won't* believe — that that's the prime reason for our involvement. America has always gotten involved where a weaker nation has been oppressed by a stronger one. Look at the Spanish-American War, the First World War, Korea. We started out in the wars without being attacked, and we fought them because the loss of freedom anywhere in the world is a potential threat to our own freedom. Do you think freedom comes free? Somewhere along the line, someone has to go out and fight for it, because if you don't, there's always someone out there willing to take it away from you. That's what our fathers fought for, and our grandfathers — "

"And look where it got us."

"Freedom is like a machine: if you don't maintain it properly, it eventually wears out and breaks down. In order for this country to remain free, and strong, we have to have allies who are free and strong."

"You can talk till you're blue in the face, but I'm not listening." Ben jabbed a finger into the table with an intensity that shook the silverware. "I'm staying here, and I'm staying in college — if I have to go for ten Ph.Ds."

"You're no better than George."

"You're wrong. George's trying to stay out of the service because he doesn't want to do anything, because he doesn't care about anybody but himself. I'm staying out because I have a set of ideals that tells me it's wrong to go and fight without conviction."

"You're just using that as an excuse."

"No, I'm not. I happen to believe it."

"Because you want to believe it. But you don't have any basis in fact for those beliefs."

"And you don't have any for yours."

Tony sighed. "All right, so I don't have all the answers." He threw his hands up in the air. "I don't even know all the questions. But — "

"If you two are talking politics, you can stop right now." Katie took a seat between them. "Vietnam is not an issue that interests me."

Tony jumped up and held the chair for Patty. She sat down and let him push it under her. "That's right. Let's talk about what's going to happen to me, not some dirty old foreign country a million miles away."

Tony took his own seat, and tried to keep his voice calm. "Patty, maybe you don't understand that I'll be going to that dirty old country in a few months."

"You don't know for sure."

"You don't take jungle warfare training to become an honor guard. Everyone leaving Fort Polk goes straight to Vietnam."

"Or Selma, Alabama," Ben said, with a laugh. Katie punched him under the table, and he let out a fake groan.

Patty twisted her napkin as she whined, "But I don't want you to go. I want you to stay here with me. Can't you get out of it if you're married?"

"That law was changed years ago."

"But I'm going to have a baby."

"Millions of women have babies every day. It's not a unique experience."

"This one is, because it's mine," Patty pouted.

Katie said, "Yes, Tony, you have responsibilities as a father, now. You can't just leave her all alone."

"You make it sound as if I'm going on vacation, or something. I'm not looking forward to this any more than you are."

"Well, even so. I don't like the idea of being by myself for the next two years."

"The tour of duty in Vietnam is only twelve months."

"And besides," Ben interjected. "You won't be by yourself. You'll have the baby."

"That's not what she means," Katie said, pinching her eyes at Ben.

"And she'll have all her friends. Just because I'm gone doesn't mean you'll be alone. Ben and Katie will keep an eye on you. And so will Pete and Marion, and Ray and Teddy."

"And Kathy," Katie added.

"And George," Ben said, with a laugh.

Tony added to the comedy. "And your grandmother."

"All right, cut it out," Patty said, none too happily. "But it's not going to be easy taking care of a baby all by myself. That's all I'm trying to say."

"No one said it was going to be easy. But it's been done before, and you can do it now." Tony leaned over and gave her a peck on the cheek. "I know you can."

****

Patty's mother lived in a small apartment that was actually one row home split in two, about a block from the Broad Street subway. But it was Bob who answered the door.

"Well, well, well. Look who we have here. Helen, we've got some company. Well, don't stand out there letting the cold air out. Come on in."

As Bob stepped back, Tony ushered Patty across the threshold. Despite the coolness inside, he continued to sweat.

"Patty, where have you been? Mother has me worried sick about you. She said you never came home last night and she's been calling all over for you."

Patty swallowed, and swiveled her eyes at Tony. He cleared his throat, and said, "She was with me."

"Well, that much I could figure. But where were *you*?" She went on before he could reply. "Do you know I've been calling all over? I called your uncles, your cousins, even your father — and I haven't done that in years."

"Yes, well, I'm sorry if we've — caused you any trouble. But we — uh — we spent the night at Kathy's. You see, we got married yesterday."

Helen stared in stunned silence, her jaw slack. Patty, whose eyes were already damp, burst into tears.

"Well, well, well. We should have known. Congratulations to both of you. Helen, I think this calls for a little celebration. The drinks are on the house. "You — "

Before Bob could pick up a glass or uncork a bottle, Helen charged ahead and threw her arms around her daughter. The two of them carried on like screaming cats, crying onto one another's shoulders. Tony stood aside awkwardly. Bob winked at him, then went about gathering four glasses and a bottle of brandy. He wrapped one huge hand around Helen's shoulder, pulled the two caterwauling women apart, and forced a glass into her hand. She emptied it without protest.

"Now, now, now. I know it's a happy time for you, Helen. For both of you." Bob refilled her glass. "Have another drink. I know it'll make you feel a whole lot better." He handed glasses out all the way around. Helen took another gulp. "Now, when my oldest boy eloped with his first wife, it was sure a shock to me and his mother, but after a couple — "

The two women started bawling again, wrapped together like nesting birds.

Bob shook his head, clanged his glass against Tony's. "I guess you didn't catch the game this afternoon? Well, the Phillies were really banging them out . . . "

****

When Tony parked his car in front of Patty's grandmother's house, Pete and Ray and Teddy were already there, dressed similarly in jeans, T-shirts, and sneakers.

Pete sauntered forward, his hands stuffed into his pockets. "How'd it go, man?"

Tony shrugged. "It went fine. We got her blessings, and a little money. She even offered to help us if we needed anything."

Ray puffed casually on a cigarette. "You got off easy, huhn?"

"So far." Tony indicated the O'Brien house with a jerk of his head. "The worst is yet to come."

"Aw, you don't have to be afraid of that old biddy." Teddy waved his hand as if at an imaginary fly. "You can take care of her with some of that judo you learned in basic."

"First of all, I didn't learn enough judo to throw anything but a slow moving bush. And second of all, I'm more afraid of her tongue than her fists."

"You can handle it, Tone."

Ray punched his brother in the arm. "Will you shut up, nitwit?"

"Ouch. Ray, leave me alone. And don't hit me in the arm or I won't be able to carry anything."

"I'd like to hit you in the jaw so you can't carry that big mouth."

"Yo, Ray, lay off." Pete stepped between them. "We got work to do."

"And we've got enough trouble as it is," Tony added.

"But he's such a pest, I'd like to exterminate him."

Teddy moved out of reach. "The reinforcements have arrived."

Kathy parked her car behind the White Lightning. Patty and Marion stepped out on the curb side, dressed in slacks and long-tailed blouses. Kathy wore skintight denims, and a flannel shirt tied in a knot in front, exposing her flat belly. "The boxes are in the trunk. We damn near cleaned out the supermarket."

Patty cast a nervous glance at the house. Tony took hold of her hands; they were damp and unsteady. "Don't worry about a thing. Just let me do the talking, okay?"

She nodded weakly.

Tony led the gang up to the cement steps, like Jason leading the Argonauts to attack the Hydra. The door opened as soon as he raised his hand to knock.

"What do you want?" Mrs. O'Brien asked belligerently.

Tony gulped. He was trying to think of what to say, and how to say it, when Kathy stepped up beside him. "Patty's moving out and we came to pick up her things."

Dark eyes stared out from deep-set, cavelike openings. "And what makes you think I'm going to let you?"

Tony at last found his voice. "Well, didn't Helen call and explain things to you?"

"I know all about you're running off behind my back. You young people today think you can do anything you want. Well, I won't stand for it. I'm not going to let you ruin my life by taking away my only granddaughter. I'm not going to let you ruin her."

"Excuse me, Mrs. O'Brien, but we just want to get Patty's things."

"This is my house, young man, and I'll decide what goes on in it."

"Please, Mrs. O'Brien, don't make things difficult for us. I'm sorry you feel the way you do, but you can't run Patty's life forever. She's old enough to make her own decisions. Now, we're married, and that's the way it is. Please let us get on with our work."

"No." Her thin body stood directly in the doorway. "Maybe you have stolen my granddaughter, but I'll see to it that her things stay where they belong."

"Mrs. O'Brien — "

"Coming through," Kathy called out. She brushed Mrs. O'Brien aside like an autumn leaf. "Come on, gang, let's get this road on the show."

While Mrs. O'Brien was choking on her tongue, Marion swept past her and followed Kathy up the stairs. Tony turned around and exchanged awestruck looks with the guys. Pete shrugged. Then Teddy launched himself through the door with an armful of boxes. Pete followed, then Ray. Mrs. O'Brien sputtered, but before she could form any more words of protest, Tony dragged Patty inside and raced for the stairs.

"You can't do this. This is my house. I'll call the police and have you arrested."

Kathy was already coming down the stairs with an armful of dresses. "The number's in the phone book."

Marion was right behind her, carrying shoe-boxes. "Or better yet, try directory assistance."

Then Teddy raced down with a boxful of cosmetics. "Yeah."

****

"I've never seen so many people moving in so many directions — and so fast," Patty said.

"And I've never seen so many men in uniform." Teddy stared at the beehive of military activity.

The Philadelphia Airport was full of soldiers, sailors, marines, and Air Force personnel, either coming, going, or transferring.

"The war's makin' the airlines rich," Pete commented.

"Watch out. Here comes another MP."

Ray punched his brother, hard. "Yo, Numb-nuts, you wanta make an announcement over the loudspeaker."

Teddy rubbed his shoulder. "They don't look so tough."

Tony ignored the sibling rivalry and kept walking through the masses. "Is everything all set with the car?"

Pete slapped his dungaree pocket. "I got the keys right here."

"Don't forget to tell my father the owner's card's in the glove compartment."

"Gotcha."

"Patty, you have the key to Kathy's apartment?"

She nodded silently.

"And I'm going to stop over tomorrow after school and get a couple extra copies made."

"Thanks, Ted. And keep an eye on Patty, will you? If she needs anything . . . "

"We can use my car again tomorrow," Marion offered.

"I appreciate it." Tony handed in his ticket, and watched his duffel bag roll along the conveyor belt. "Well, I guess this is it."

Marion wiped tears from her eyes. "Take care of yourself, Tony."

He nodded, gave her a peck on the cheek. "I'll try." He stuck out his hand. "Pete."

Teddy started to unbend from his stint under the duffel bag. "So long, Tone. Show those guys who's boss when you get there."

Tony shook his outstretched hand, then sought out Ray's. As the intercom announced immediate departure, he devoted his attention to his wife. "Now, remember, if you need anything, you've got friends to call on. "Okay?"

Patty nodded, dry-eyed. "I'll need a ride to the doctor's."

"I can take her," Marion said.

"Well, it seems like you're in good hands. I guess — I'll see you in a couple months." He kissed her on the mouth, stared into her eyes, held onto the warmth of her body, and remembered what it had been like those few precious nights in bed. He tried to memorize the sensations, to evoke the feelings. But they would not come back to him.

If they had, he never would have left.

Chapter 61

"While the performance of the individual soldier is a key factor in success in combat, a more important consideration is the close team-work and unity of effort of all elements of a division."

Captain Whale, commanding officer of Company D, Fifth Battalion, Third Training Brigade, managed to imbue a spark of informality into an otherwise orthodox definition. His fatigues were pressed enough for convention, but no more. His helmet liner kept his eyes shaded, not his nose and mouth. His poise was military without being stiff and pretentious. And his voice was a husky drawl that had been acquired rather than inbred. He was strict and casual at the same time.

"One of the things we're going to learn here, in addition to weaponry, is the tactics of rifle squads, platoons, and companies. Only by fighting as a unit, and by gaining superior fire-power over enemy forces, can battles be won. This must be predominant in your mind. While your buddy is relying on you, you must learn to rely on your buddy."

The bleachers groaned under the combined weight of some two hundred-odd men. The hundred foot profiles of spruce and pine kept most of them in a pleasant shade, while a light breeze, gusting strongly at times, swept dried needles along in little bunches and kept tumble-weeds rolling. The air offered a crispness that was invigorating. September in Louisiana was a far cry from August in Georgia.

Captain Whale glanced at his wristwatch. "Okay, men, let's have a break and be back in, say, fifteen minutes. Then we'll talk about the Matty Mattel' toys you picked up this morning. Dismissed."

In a clatter of rifles and helmet liners, the men scampered off the bleachers and headed for the trees. Those who had to urinate stood on the edge of a ditch and added to the rising flood that wallowed in its bottom. The rest sat on the ground and, if thirsty, sipped water from their canteens.

"Where did you come from?" asked a sandy-haired man who had introduced himself as Terry Kurtz. His handsome face was marred only by an ugly bruise below the right eye.

"My mother found me under a cabbage leaf."

"Oh, a comedian, huhn?" Terry flashed a smile. "We can use some humor around here. Let me try again. What city was this cabbage leaf in?"

"Philadelphia."

"I went there once," Terry said, imitating W.C. Fields, "but it was closed." Changing voices, he went on, "I'm from L.A., along with about half the goons here. We all took basic together. Fort Ord. Up the coast about two hundred and fifty miles."

Tony picked up a handful of triple-clustered pine needles and tossed them like little rocket ships. "Almost close enough to get home on weekends."

"What do you mean, almost? We *were* home on weekends. It's only four hours by car, hauling ass."

"Did they let you keep cars in basic?"

"Naw, I had mine parked in the back of a supermarket. Every Friday night I'd slip into town with about five other guys and hightail it for home."

"Didn't you have a fifty-mile limit on weekend passes?"

"What are you, a lawyer? You can't go by the rules. If you did, you'd never get anywhere in this world. Rules are made for people stupid enough to follow them. We kept civvies in the trunk, and as soon as we got there we'd change clothes, right there in the parking lot. Then we'd hit the highway and bomb it home. Besides, nobody gave a shit. The cadre were too busy picking up ass in Monterey. Even the Old Man was shacking up with some broad, and was she a looker. She used to stop by the compound on Friday nights to pick him up. She had tits like basketballs and an ass that should have been illegal. The Old Man was sure happy come Monday morning."

Terry slipped off his helmet liner and scratched the top of his nearly shaven head with the rim.

"Get your ass off the ground! And you, stop holding up that tree, it can stand by itself." About twenty yards away, two men did the sergeants bidding. "Now get those rifles up at port arms and try to look serious. As far as you're concerned, this is the Nam. And you better practice staying alive starting now, or you won't be in a couple of months." The sergeant stalked off.

Tony dropped his pine needles. "What was

that all about?"

Blue eyes twinkled as Terry shook his head. "Nothing to worry about. But that's the reason they call this place Tiger Land, 'cause the sergeants are carnivorous. Anytime we're on break, we're supposed to have guards posted, just like we were in the real war."

Tony cleared his throat, hugged his rifle a little closer. "How much else did I miss?"

"Nothing much, except work details and orientation. Guys were straggling in all week, but we didn't have any formal training until Friday. And mostly that was getting the payroll squared away and issuing passes. Wait till you see Leesville. It is some dead town. It's only got one main drag, with a couple of bars and a pizza parlor. All the local hicks hang out at the Laundromat. That's where I picked this up." Terry indicated the bruise.

"Did you get hit with a pizza crust, or a dryer door?"

"Neither. I was trying to pick up a chick by buying her a box of soap. You know, just to open the conversation. What the hell, if we'd have been in a bar I'd have bought her a drink. But she said no, she had to get her clothes done so she could go to work on Saturday. So I bought her a bag of peanuts and a coke from the machine. Well, I wasn't the only EM in there. Where the girls are, the enlisted men follow. I guess there were about five of us, two I didn't know. So two hicks stroll over and say leave her alone. Well, these guys are about my size, so I said beat it. Go get your own dates. Two of my buddies back me up. One of the hicks raised his hand to his ear and said 'What?', and before I could answer his hand comes down right across the bridge of Kozel's nose and the other one swings from the hip and catches me in the ribs. I fell back over a bench and missed most of the fight, which lasted about another ten seconds. The two EMs I don't know jump the hicks from the rear and they all go down in a scramble. By this time women are screaming and more hicks start pouring in the door like they were out there waiting for a signal. I threw a few punches and fought my way out, dragging Rangely with me. I don't know what happened to the rest of the guys, except Kozel showed up about an hour later with a broken nose and some fractured ribs. That's why you got his bunk. They say it'll be a few weeks before he's ready for duty. He's been dropped from the company roster."

"So how did you get the bruise on the eye?"

"Oh, on my way out the door, the girl hit me with a box of soap."

Tony could not help but laugh. "I'm sorry. I'm sure it wasn't funny at the time, but it's hysterical now."

Terry waved his hand. "I think it's pretty hysterical myself. Uh, oh, here comes mister tough guy." They wiped their faces clean, and sat up straight. Terry lowered his voice. "The only thing you have to remember is that this is Vietnam."

"Huhn?"

"That's what they told us on Friday. Part of the training is making believe we're in Vietnam. That's why Holtz reamed those two guys out. We have to make believe this whole training process is a real combat mission. That means we post guards every time we break, we carry our rifles everywhere we go. We have to be on the alert all the time. No big deal. It's just part of the game, so go along with it."

Tony clutched his rifle closer. "Sounds all right to me."

"It won't be when you have to walk guard duty around the barrack in the middle of the night. Weekends we're allowed to be off, but during the week we have to play it straight."

"For someone who likes bending the rules, you're awfully willing to play the game."

A smile broke out across a face bronzed by the California sun. "I only bend them when I can get away with it. So what's your excuse? You stroll in here this morning like you own the place. You oversleep, or what?"

Tony could not prevent the smirk from crawling over his face. "No, I was on my way from Fort Gordon when I got on the wrong plane. Somehow I ended up in Philadelphia, so as long as I was there I picked up my girlfriend and got married. It took me a week to get untangled."

"Ha, ha, ha. And I thought you were straight. Put it there." Terry thrust out his hand. "So what did you do to deserve the infantry?"

"Flunked out of MP school."

"No shit. They had you pegged for a cop?"

"At first. But I had a lot of trouble with the CO. We didn't see eye to eye on personal philosophy. One thing led to another, he relieved me of duty, and had my orders recut. So, here I am."

"Hey, bro, how you doin'?" A gangling Negro squatted on the sand. Terry made the introductions. "Alexander Hays, Tony Giovanni."

"Glad to meet you. Do they call you Alex, for short?"

"Call me Hays." Coal-black eyes glittered in the sun. "I heard the Old Man reaming you out this morning. I was only five minutes late and he sure laid into me. How late were you?"

"A week."

"Are you shittin' me? A week?"

Tony removed his helmet liner, fingered it, and put it back on his head. "The captain was

pretty easy on me, though."

"I'll be a son of a bitch. Here I'm five minutes late coming back from pass and I get holy hell. You come in a week late and get off scot-free."

"Well, I didn't exactly get away scot-free, but he didn't treat me like a criminal. Of course, he did revoke my pass privileges."

"A week? You coulda been court-martialed."

"I know, but I explained the circumstances about going home to get married, even asked him to help me set up an allotment for my wife, so he went pretty easy on me when he heard the story."

Terry said, "How did the MPs get you?"

"They didn't get me. I got them. The closest I could get by plane was Alexandria, then I had to take a bus. By the time I got in last night, it was almost midnight, and I didn't know where to go. There were a couple of MPs at the bus station in South Fort, so I asked them where I was supposed to go if I was AWOL. They pointed to the back of the car, and drove me to the station. Then they let me go to sleep while they tried to find out what to do with me. This morning they called the company, talked to the first sergeant, and brought me out."

Hays slapped his leg. "Door to door service. Dig it."

"One thing I'll say, you got balls," Terry commented.

"Well, I really didn't have much choice. I couldn't very well — "

"Fall in, men. Hop to it."

"Sergeant Holtz again," Hays groaned, climbing to his feet. The trio started toward the bleachers. "Hey, I almost forgot. We're havin' a sniffin' party tonight behind the barracks. You interested?"

"You can count me in," Terry said, without hesitation. "But I'm a little short at the moment. Couldn't get any stuff before I left home. But I'm expecting a shipment from a girl back in L.A. Can I bum some?"

"Natch. You're in. You can cough up later."

Terry jerked a thumb at Hays. "He's a head."

"A what?"

"A head. You know, goes in for it in a big way. So am I. Ever try it?"

"Well, actually not. I've always heard that sniffing glue can cause brain damage."

"Who's talking about glue? That's kid's stuff. We're talking about pot, grass, the big weed."

"Oh, marijuana."

"Yeah, it's called that, too. Ever try it?"

"Uh, no."

"You don't know what you're missing."

"Well, I'll take your word for it."

"Come on, man, don't be a square."

"I'm not — just slightly rectangular."

"Well, look, why don't you come around anyway. You don't have to smoke if you don't want to, just come along for the ride."

"Well, I don't know — "

"We need a straight man, anyway. You know, to keep an eye on things. Sometimes when you're high you forget."

"But what'll I do?"

"Just watch. And make sure we get back to our bunks."

"All right. I can handle that."

****

"At ease, men." Captain Whale jumped onto the wooden platform in front of the firing range: a huge field backed by tall pines in the distance. He held a book in front of him.

"Let me quote you from the manual. 'The M-16 is the new standard rifle of the United States Army, firing a lightweight, high velocity round which causes large exit wounds, leaves severe tissue damage, and affects blood vessels and muscle tissue out of the direct path of the bullet. Rapid fire capability increases the proportion of multiple wounds.' "

The captain placed the manual on the floor beside him. "Before we get on with the demonstration, I'd like to say that I think the M-16 is the finest light-arm weapon in the world, despite claims to the contrary about the superiority of the AK-47, which we'll talk about later. The M-16 supersedes the older M-14, which you've all trained with in boot camp. The M-16 is lighter and easier to carry, more accurate, and more damaging. By the time you leave here you will have gone through so much with your individual weapon that you'll feel naked without it. It will become a part of you — an extension of your hand. Now for a demonstration. Sergeant?"

Sergeant Holtz stood with ramrod straight posture, and a tanned face that was already dark with five o'clock shadow. His props were simple: a saw horse on which stood two number ten cans of tomato paste, and an eight foot sheet of plywood, painted white, as a backdrop.

He approached the firing line carrying an M-14, its wooden stock well oiled and polished, the bluing still predominant on the barrel. Observing safe procedures, he carried the barrel up while he cleared the chamber and shot the bolt. He then loaded a single bullet into the receiver, aimed downrange from a hard standing position, and drilled a neat hole through the can on the left. The bullet also burst through the plywood, leaving a red ring of tomato paste around the hole. The can was knocked to the ground by the impact.

"Thank you, sergeant." A corporal brought the wounded can to Captain Whale. He held it

aloft. "You'll notice the can has two holes in it with, uh, tomato paste dripping out." He pushed the can out to arm's length, and made a face that compelled the men to chuckle. "Now the M-16, Sergeant."

Holtz exchanged rifles. He cleared the M-16's chamber, inserted one bullet, aimed, and fired. The other tomato can was thrown straight back into the plywood, where it clattered to the ground, leaving a red splattered stain that could not be covered with a bath towel. Gobs of tomato paste dripped down the white board.

What was left of the can was brought to Captain Whale. He held it deftly between thumb and forefinger; only a little of the contents remained to pour out. The entire back of the can was gone, shredded as if a grenade had exploded inside it.

"As you can see, the bullet from the M-16 creates havoc. A hit like this, anywhere on the body, can be injurious to your health: it usually results in death. There are very few wounds with the M-16. If you hit someone in the arm, it can take the arm clean off. A bullet in the foot can remove the foot, or leave it so mangled that your victim dies within minutes from shock and loss of blood. A hit in the vital organs can leave gaping holes big enough to put a grapefruit into. So you can see that this weapon increases the size of your target. You don't have to hit someone in the head or chest for a kill, all you have to do is hit him."

The captain paused for a moment to let it sink in.

"Okay, the projectile is a 5.56 millimeter, smaller and lighter than the 7.62 of the M-14 and the AK-47. This also means that the shell is smaller, since it doesn't have to propel as large a bullet. In fact, the ammo pouches made to carry an M-14 clip can carry two twenty-round clips for the M-16. And the whole weapon itself weighs only seven and a half pounds, fully loaded, as opposed to over ten for the M-14. As you have seen, the tremendous muzzle velocity of 3,270 feet per second gives the bullet incredible striking power, as well as an accuracy up to four hundred fifty meters. And don't take stock in any rumors that the weapon is unreliable because it jams in field use. Like any tool, it needs to be properly maintained. You take care of your weapon, and your weapon will take care of you. And that goes for more than your weapon."

He waited for the laughter to die down. "The only drawback to the M-16 is that the plastic stock makes a poor weapon for hand-to-hand combat. If you hit someone on the chin with this rifle you're just as likely to break the stock instead of your enemy's jawbone. Let me make it clear now that we don't intend to teach you hand-to-hand combat here. Your MOS is 11B10, except for those of you who will become mortarmen. This is light-armed infantryman. We are going to teach you how to use weapons, not fists. Acting as a unit, and given enough firepower, you shouldn't ever get close enough to the enemy for hand-to-hand."

Captain Whale surveyed his troops as an experienced orator, his gaze passing slowly back and forth along the ranks. "The key word in today's war is firepower. If you can shoot more bullets than Charlie, he's either got to keep his head down or get it blown off. Uncle Sam can supply more ammunition, more bombs, more rockets, more mortars, more weapons and tanks and planes, than you'll ever need. Don't be afraid to use them.

"Now, I'm not telling you to waste ammunition. One of the things you'll be doing here is striving to increase your shooting proficiency. There's nothing better about using twenty bullets when one well-placed shot will do. But you'll be practicing the techniques of automatic weapons. Remember, the object of the infantryman is to kill the enemy at a reasonable distance. If Charlie ever gets too close for comfort, don't start swinging that plastic rifle at him; hit him with your entrenching tool."

The captain had the men right in his pocket: they were all ears. "Now, a word about the Chinese assault rifle, the AK-47. AK stands for automat kalashnikov, and it's a damn fine weapon. In experienced hands, it's accurate up to five hundred meters. It's heavier than the M-16, and not as reliable. The curved banana clip holds thirty rounds, but bullets frequently jam because of the curvature and the heavier weight of the bullet: the same 7.62 used in the M-14. It was designed that way so it could utilize captured ammunition. You men who will be taking mortar training will find that their mortars use an eighty-two millimeter round. This means that their tubes will fire our eighty-one millimeter mortars, but we can't fire theirs.

"Anyway, be glad they are using the AK-47. You've seen what the M-16 bullet did to that tomato can, and that's what makes it superior to the AK-47. The 5.56 projectile is not a mushroom round, or a dum-dum; it is not made of soft lead. But it *is* unbalanced. Only the increased rifling and the high muzzle velocity keep it spinning fast enough to maintain a good arc. But once it slows down it begins to wobble. Very close, this wobble is not noticeable. But the farther it goes, the more the wobble increases, which is why it's not more accurate than it is. But it doesn't have to be that accurate, since it's tearing action increases the lethal size of your target. As soon as the bullet hits something, its stability goes all to hell; it begins to tumble, especially if it hits something like bone or hard muscle. What it did to this tomato can, it can do to Charlie.

"So, when you're over there, be glad *they're* using an AK-47, and *you're* using an M-16. It could make all the difference in the world whether you live or die."

****

Hays strutted along the aisle, arms akimbo and cap askew. "Cadre's gone. Nobody here but the orderly."

Terry gave thumbs up, but Hays was already on his way. "Hey, Tony, you ready to roll?"

"Well, I don't know." Tony put down his book, peered over the edge. "I thought I'd just lie here and read."

"Come on, don't be a dead head." Terry plunked his feet into his boots. "You don't have to do anything, just watch. Besides, it'll give you a chance to meet the guys."

Tony sighed, and slipped a bookmark into place. "Well, maybe you're right. I guess I don't want to become a mole."

"That's the spirit."

Carefully, Tony swung his feet over the edge of the upper berth and dropped to the floor. He landed only inches away from the opposite bunk. Because of the upsurge in jungle warfare training, billeting at Tiger Land was at a premium. Two platoons were crammed into each barrack, one to a floor. Footlockers were lined up along the outer walls, edge to edge. And the bunks were so close together that if one jumped too far out of one bunk, he was likely to find himself landing in the adjoining bunk.

"It's not a matter of spirit, I just don't want to get into any more trouble than I'm already in."

"Bah. There's nothing to worry about. I've been through thick and thin with these guys back at Ord."

"Okay, but remember, I'm just here to watch. Don't try to pressure me into anything."

"Hey, nobody's going to push you. If you don't want to get high, that's cool. Like I said, it's nice to have a straight man along, in case we lose our way home."

Tony finished lacing his boots. "Since we're only going to be on the other side of that wall, that shouldn't be too much of a problem."

Terry smiled. "You never know."

Crickets chirped in the darkness between the barracks. Towering pines blotted out much of the light from the moonless sky. A boarded path, lined with logs, ran along the building and back to the fire escape.

"Hey, man, over here." It was Hays, whispering.

Terry led Tony to where Hays blended in with the blackness. "I thought we were meeting between the buildings?"

"Too much light from the windows. Go straight through here and across the road." He shoved the two in front of him. When they reached the clearing beside the macadam, they dashed across, hunched over, and entered a dark wood on the other side.

Beyond was nothing but dense forest and tank trails. Tony shuffled through ankle deep longleaf pine needles; the odor was sweet and pleasant. For a moment he was transported to Salisbury. Memories of walks through the autumn woods with his grandfather, accompanied by yelping dogs, flashed through his mind,

The dream was dispelled as they entered a small clearing. Twenty men huddled in a circle, talking and laughing in hushed tones.

"Hays, you got more shit? We're almost out." Tony recognized Richard Haiburn, known as Pops because he was married and had a little girl only six months old. He stood five-foot-four in elevator combat boots, a machinist becoming a machine gunner.

Tony recognized other men from the squad. Pete Gormley had been a beach bum along the California coast, living off the land, and off those women who found his charms irresistible. Ron Kitson had been slapping hamburgers on a grill while searching for truth, love, and sex, but not necessarily in that order. Mack Johnson, for all his size, was unusually docile. His attitude was that if he could stroll through life without hurting anyone, he would have done his part to advance humanity on its course toward social maturity. He also had the build to crush anyone who disagreed with him.

Terry intercepted a joint and explained the procedure before passing it on. "You have to hold the smoke in, see, in order to get the full effect. It's not like smoking tobacco, where you just blow it out and take another drag. You do that to keep the taste rolling over your tongue. What you want to do with grass is keep the smoke in your lungs so it can get absorbed into your bloodstream. You inhale, hold your breath, and pass the joint on to the next guy. That way you don't waste it. That's a nickel bag he's got in his hand, and that ain't cheap."

"Hey, man, you gonna smoke that joint or marry it?"

"Sorry." Terry put it to his lips, inhaled deeply, and passed it on. "Keep it comin'. Keep it comin'. I ain't high yet, an' I sure wanna be."

"You wanna bee? How's about an ant?"

"Or an uncle?"

"Ouch. Hey, anybody got a roach clip?"

"Wow, are these woods spooky."

"Give it here if it's too hot to handle."

"She-e-e-eet. You got enough left on here for another platoon."

"Goddamn it, I burnt my fingers."

"So hold it with your toes."

"With those lips of yours you can hold anything."

"Ain't got a clip, but here's a tweezers."

"Don't get sassy, whitey."

"Whaddaya use these for, pluckin' out eyebrows?"

"Don't bump me, damn it, I'm trying to roll another one."

"I got a hemostat around here somewhere."

"Cut me a break, will you?"

"Good, clip this joker's lips together."

"It's hot. I just burnt my throat."

"Well, don't swallow it, just suck on it."

"What're you, a first timer?"

"Oh, man, am I gettin' high. I can see stars between my feet."

"I been smokin' this stuff since before you was in diapers."

"That's 'cause you're layin' on your back like a dead cockroach."

"Somebody around here's got the exactlies."

"Shit, I just remembered. I left the hemostat in my other pants pocket."

"What's the exactlies?"

"Is that what you say to the whores when you can't get it up?"

"It's when your breath smells exactly like your farts."

"I ain't had trouble gettin' it up since I was twelve years old."

"Late comer, huhn?"

"Oh, yeah, when did you start jerking off?"

"Man, I's born with a hard on. They had to pry me outa my mamma's cunt."

Finally, Terry exhaled. "Simple, see?"

Three or four joints continued around the circle at the same time. When one died out, another was rolled and lighted. Each time a man took a puff, Tony got a glimpse of intense features made monstrous by the temporary red glow. Reaching hands, pursed lips, and passive faces were sprinkled black and white, like salt and pepper on a plate. Smoking pot was an integrated procedure: hallucination knew not the bounds of race.

Joints came and went. Terry huffed and puffed. Some men got loud, some got sullen, some got melancholy, and some showed no outward change at all, but appeared to be lost in a world of introspection.

Johnson continued his astronomical observations. Gormley hummed to himself, softly, in lullaby form. Hays kept repeating "She-e-e-eet" whenever someone called his attention to some insignificant event which had suddenly become of vast importance: the lines in his hand, the part of his hair.

"My face is stoned!" Pops pinched his

cheeks, laughing. "I can't feel it any more."

"I wish I didn't have to look at it."

Kitson lay on the grass, lighting matches and seemingly enthralled by the flame, like a fluttering moth.

Gormley put a leaf up to his ear. "Hey, can you hear that? The sap's still flowing through the veins. Wow."

"Man, am I high." Terry's strong features were visible only in outline. He sat cross-legged, staring into space. "This is great, really great. I've never been this high before. Like, wow. Like, I'm sitting right here on the ground — I can feel the dirt through my pores — but I'm soaring right through my mind. I'm in the middle of my brain, looking around at the folds. There are flashes of light all around me, and each one is a thought. Like, it's wild. I can't stay down. Gravity is falling apart and I'm lifting right through my skull. God, I'm ten feet in the air. I can look down at myself, sitting there on the ground. I can see everybody around me. We're all here. My eyes are closed, but I can see all of you. I'm seeing with my mind. I'm going higher. Everybody's getting smaller. I'm twenty feet up, thirty feet, fifty. Now I'm through the trees and going right up like a rocket, through the clouds. I can see the whole base laid out beneath me; now the whole state. I'm in space, and just like that I'm past the moon. I didn't even seen the planets go by. I'm surrounded by stars, and I can still breathe. I don't know how; maybe I've got my own envelope of air. Or maybe I don't need to breathe any more. This phase of consciousness is not dependent on air. All it does is see, and think. Like, wow. The stars are all different colors: greens, blues, and reds, and they're flashing on and off like neon signs. They're moving so fast that they're blurred. No, it's not the stars that are moving. It's me. I'm surfing right through hyperspace. Like, wow. I can explore the whole universe like this. Man, you gotta get into this. It's like, wow, man. I've never been this high. This is fantastic, simply fantastic. Tony are you with me? Tony are you with me? Tony are you with me?"

Tony coughed from the thick wisps of smoke coiling like snakes through the air. "I'm with your body on the ground, and I'm having trouble breathing."

Chapter 62

Four thirty seemed to come awfully early the next morning.

Sergeant Holtz switched on the lights and walked up and down the crowded aisle, shouting, "Up and at 'em, men. Formation in ten minutes. Come on, let's go."

Tony leaped out of bed, scrubbing sleep out

of his eyes. He shook Terry in his bunk. "Hey, how's the hangover?"

Terry tossed the covers aside, slowly rolled up to a sitting position. "You don't get hangovers from smoking pot."

"I wasn't sure after last night. You saw more of space and time than Olaf Stapledon."

The men quickly got dressed and raced down the stairs to the parade ground. On the way, Terry stopped at a small black oak tree that had intruded itself into the pine grove. He shook it violently, shouting, "Up and at 'em, you hear me? Up and at 'em."

Tony dragged him away. "What are you doing?"

"Waking up the birds. If we have to get up before the sun, so do they."

After everyone was found present and accounted for, the entire company formation hit the blacktop. Each platoon sergeant led his men on the four-mile tour along a macadam road that led nowhere, cut through woods and swamp, passed a few storage sheds, and returned along a parallel road.

Three quarters of an hour later, Sergeant Holtz appeared calm and unperturbed by the exercise. "Men, I have it on report that a number of you were out late last night, coming in just before bed check. I don't know who you are, or where you went, or what you did, but let me warn you that you are to remain in the barracks or within the company perimeter after dark. I won't threaten you; I just want to make myself clear. Okay?"

A few muttered voices said, "Yes, sergeant."

"Come on, you can do better than that."

"Yes, sergeant."

"Okay, that's better. Just don't forget it. I'm not going to get my ass in a sling because some of you jokers get the wanderlust. Next week you'll be given base privileges for the evenings. Okay, fall in for chow."

Tony found it strange that they were allowed to talk during breakfast. "That's about the easiest dressing down I've ever heard."

Terry choked down a mouthful of ham. "Holtz is an all right guy. He only acts tough when he has to. It's part of his job."

"Not only that, but he's the first sergeant I've ever met who isn't deaf and speaks English."

"Yeah, I know what you mean. You'd think they were either retarded or juvenile delinquents."

After checking their rifles out of the armory, they were loaded into cattle cars — huge tractor-trailers in which the men were packed pelvis to buttock — and trucked out to the rifle range.

"Yesterday you learned how to take the M-16 apart and put it back together again,"

Sergeant Holtz said. "Today you're going to learn how it fires. You already know from boot camp that in order to assure accuracy, you have to hold the rifle tight against your shoulder, breath slowly, aim, and fire. And if you don't hold it tight, you not only miss your target, but you get a black eye into the bargain. Let me show you a little trick of the M-16."

The sergeant took a rifle from a man in the front row, inspected it, cleared it, then picked up a full magazine and inserted it. He pulled the bolt back with two fingers. The spring in the clip pushed the top bullet into the receiver. When he released the bolt, the rifle was ready to fire.

"Now I want you to notice how hard this baby kicks."

He stood at the firing line, aiming downrange. With a smirk, he placed the butt of the rifle right in front of his crotch, touching the material of his fatigues. He pulled the trigger once, then again, then in a series of bursts. The barking of the rifle was followed by puffs of dust a couple hundred meters out in the field.

"If you did that with an M-14 you'd be a eunuch after the first round. Now step up to the firing line, men, and don't be afraid to shoulder that toy."

The men zeroed in their rifles within the hour, and by lunchtime they were engaging in regular target practice. Each man-sized target was operated by a tiny motor that was buried beneath it, and actuated from the fire control station. Captain Whale could raise whatever targets he wanted, at the desired distance, from a control panel at his fingertip.

"Now we're going to flip the selector switch and throw this baby on full automatic. You can empty the magazine in about three seconds, but the idea is to shoot in short bursts of three to five rounds, aiming at the lower left of your target. The rifling will bring the barrel up and to the right, effectively slicing your target diagonally."

That night, after a full day at the range, Sergeant Holtz issued cleaning rods, cloths, and lubricating oil. He pranced up and down the barrack floor while the men cleaned their weapons.

"Men, let me repeat some of what Captain Whale said. From now on your rifle is a part of you, a very important part. Your life will depend on it. Now, I'm not trying to scare you, but you should know the facts by this time. Everybody here is going to Vietnam. Make no mistake about it — the orders have already been cut. Most of you will be going to the same outfits. Over there, in the war, men are dying. Some of you are going to die. And I'm going to try my goddamnedest to see that you have the best possible chance of surviving. I'm going to hound you day and night, I'm going to show you and teach you every trick in the book that may someday save your life. I want you to pay attention, and when I say it's for your own good, I ain't just spitting apples. You're going to have as much training as we can cram into nine weeks, because that's all the army allows us to turn you into fighting machines.

"You have a duty to perform for your country, so you're being sent to Vietnam to do it. But you also have a duty to yourselves. That duty is to stay alive. There are no tests here, no passing or failing. Everyone goes. But when you get there, you will take the biggest test of your life. If you fail, you die. And I don't want any of your deaths on my conscience. So for God's sake listen to what I have to tell you. And if I get tough with you, just remember that I'll be the happiest man in the world if a year and a half from now, you walk back in here as civilians and spit in my face. I'll even shake your hand for it."

****

By the middle of the week, Sergeant Holtz knew everyone by name, without looking at nametags. And true to his word, he did not let up on them for a minute. He kept his platoon on the firing line long after the other sergeants had allowed their men a break. He offered encouragement when it was needed, gave individual instruction as required, and cajoled, coerced, and threatened as necessary. Tony learned to fear him with a strange kind of respect.

"If you're not sure of your distance, shoot low rather than high: you can tell by the dust kicking up how to adjust your aim, and there's a good chance your bullet will ricochet into your target."

They moved to a firing range that had motorized targets mounted on rails. When they rose out of the ground, they moved just like real soldiers. Tony learned how to lead the target to make a hit.

Concerning squad tactics, the sergeant said, "You'll find that radios and machine guns attract lead like a magnet attracts iron. That's because the first thing Charlie wants to do is knock out your communications and your greatest fire power."

On company patrols, he advised, "Once you're in the field, your uniforms will have no name tags or insignia of any kind. This is to protect your officers and noncoms. Whenever Charlie sees bars or stripes, he starts zeroing in on them. Remember, a company without a leader is like a chicken without a head: it's no longer a controlled fighting unit, just a bunch of armed men running around in circles. Battles aren't won by firepower alone, but by the intelligent direction of that firepower. When you lose your command people, you lose the ability to call in air strikes, artillery, mortars, and medevacs. When it comes to the CO, it's his job to support you as much as it's your job to support him."

On the enemy: "Make no mistake about it, the North Vietnamese Army — the NVA — are trained soldiers. Not draftees doing a twelve-month tour, but regulars with years of experience. Their uniforms are black pajamas. But the Viet Cong are local people: guerrillas who know the territory and can't be distinguished from your allies. They may be sympathizers who supply food for the enemy; it could be the laundry woman who plants booby traps outside your tent, or the whore with a razor blade up her cunt, or the farmer in the field who gives information about U.S. troop movements, or the baby sent into camp with a live grenade in his arms."

Hays raised a lanky arm. "Why're they called Charlies?"

"The radio code for VC is Victor Charlie. And since we're supposed to be the victors, we call *them* the Charlies."

"She-e-e-eet. They all gooks to me."

****

Friday afternoon, while Tony was cleaning his rifle in the shade of the barracks, Sergeant Holtz called him aside. "Giovanni, you're damned good with that weapon."

"Thank you, sarge."

"Fired expert on automatic, didn't you? Well, I have no complaints about you."

"Uh, thanks."

"Unfortunately, your name's on the shit list. This has nothing to do with me, or even the captain. It's procedure, a formality. You were AWOL, and they just don't give out passes to guys likely to go AWOL. You can't have a pass this weekend — or any weekend as long as you're with this outfit."

"You mean I have to stay in the barracks?"

"No, you're just restricted to base. This way the captain can avoid court-martial proceedings. He tells the adjutant you're being punished with extra duty."

"Well, as long as you put it that way . . . "

"You'll be working in the orderly room this weekend. Sorry, but that's the way it is."

Tony stayed in his fatigues while the rest of the men showered and donned khakis. Terry stood in their crowded bunk space and buttoned his shirt.

"What the hell's the sense of living unless you've got pazzaz in your life? I was bound for hell long before I got drafted. All Uncle Sam's doing is accelerating my progress. But I've got to make a few stops along the way, see?"

"I see," Tony replied. "But don't make one of them the Laundromat, will you? You were taken to the cleaners last week."

Terry readjusted his tie. "Hey, I never look for trouble. But I never hide from it, either. If these local yokels want to pick a fight, then I'm going to oblige them."

"Try to look at it from their point of view. This is their hometown; they've lived here all their lives. And they'll probably never leave it. Now, because of some conflict on the other side of the world, there's an influx of several thousand soldiers, all competing for the girls these guys want to marry. They're not doing anything but trying to protect their way of life."

"The girls in this town are free living souls — "

"I'm not saying they aren't. Just remember that you're encroaching on someone else's territory, so don't blame them when they're pushed into a sociological corner."

"All right, so maybe they've got a legitimate beef. What am I supposed to do, duck into a dark alley every time a pretty girl walks by?"

"No, just try to look at things from their point of view."

Terry ran a brush across his shoes, chucked it into his footlocker. "Point of view? You want to hear about point of view? You know what happened to a guy at Ord? They have these jeeps leftover from the War. They had so many parts replaced, the only thing original was the chassis. We pull detail to load them up onto flatbeds so they can haul them to a junkyard and crush them for scrap. They use us like Egyptian slaves. We sling beams under the jeeps, five men on each side, and we *carry* them onto the trucks. Riley notices a set of windshield wipers that'll fit his car, so he hocks them. Well, the sarge catches him and drags him in front of the provost marshal, and he gets court-martialed — for taking something they were throwing out in the first place. Tony, this world is fucked up."

"No sense making it worse."

"It's beyond saving. I only care about one thing — me. You only pass through this life once. But if you do it right, once is enough."

By eighteen hundred, mess had been served and the barracks were empty. Tony strolled across the tree-lined path to the orderly room.

"Pull up a chair and make yourself at home," said the Negro three-striper sitting behind the desk. "My name is Sergeant Brown, and I'm going to give you a one minute crash course in orderly room duty. All you gotta do is sit here and answer the phone. If it's for one of the men, you check the pass list to see if he's here. If he is, you go find him. Otherwise, take a message. If it's official business, write it down. And if it's something you can't handle, call this number."

Tony glanced at his watch. "That only took thirty seconds."

"You got time for questions."

"What do I do when the phone's not ringing?"

Sergeant Brown took a deck of cards out of the desk drawer. "I like solitaire, but you can do what you want. Stare out the window, look at dirty magazines, play with yourself." He turned around at the screen door. "Just don't fall asleep."

Tony wrote letters, read books, did crossword puzzles. It was an easy night: the phone never rang once.

****

Tony awoke to the sound of singing, badly out of key. Two long nights of orderly room duty had gotten him off his sleeping schedule.

Terry, Hays, Pops, and the rest wavered along the aisle, arms entangled like a couple of fighting octopi. It was the only thing that kept them from falling down. Several tunes were being sung at the same time, in different keys. They collapsed in a heap in front of Tony's bunk.

"Well, it looks like you guys had a good time."

Terry disentangled himself from his companions, and crawled half a body's length toward his bunk. "Baton Rouge. How should I ever forget Baton Rouge?" Gormley and Kitson crept away, dragging Johnson with them. Hays and Pops were singing the same song, but in different parts.

"You should have been there."

Hays broke off from his song. "The white meat sure was tasty. Hey, Tony, you shoulda come along. There was enough for all."

"Enough what?"

Terry winked from his position on the floor. "Women. See, Baton Rouge is the hot spot of Louisiana. And here we were led to believe that Fort Polk was in the uncivilized wilderness, while all the time love is right around the corner."

"I don't know about love," Pops slurred. "But there's something that makes up for it."

"Baton Rouge is a couple hundred miles away."

Hays pulled himself up to his bunk and rolled into it. "One hundred seventy-three point one, according to the taxi driver. One way."

"But you're not allowed that far from base. What were you doing there?"

"The question, my man, is what weren't we doing there?" Pops said. "I just hope my wife never finds out."

Terry held his head in his hands, pinching his eyes. "You wouldn't believe the women they have in this part of the country. And I thought all the good looking chicks were California beach girls."

Pops tried unsuccessfully to get into his upper berth, instead falling in with Hays. "How'd you like that white pussy, nigger?"

"It was fine. Real fine."

With great effort, Terry managed to climb into his bunk. "Last night I slept with the perfect picture of pulchritude — "

"While you white boys were sleepin', I was busy fuckin'."

"Yeah, like a rabbit," Pops said. "You weren't in there more than ten minutes."

"Long enough to get what I wanted."

Terry yelled into his pillow. "She knew more ways of making love than I thought were possible."

"Ain't but one that counts."

"And she could make it last longer than any woman I ever made love to."

"Fuckin' waste of time."

"Any time spent fucking is not wasted," Pops said.

"She-e-e-eet. You white boys're always makin' out like your way's better. Pussy's pussy. An' a whore don't rate no reviews."

"Tony, you shoulda been there," Terry lamented. "You really shoulda been there. The horizons of life are forever broadening in front of me."

Tony said quietly, "Just hope they don't get out of sight."

Chapter 63

"Ain't this the shit?"

Tony, resting on his elbow on a couple of sandbags, stared at Hays from under the muzzle of the machine gun. The bright sun beat down on his steel pot and cast a dark shadow across the darker face. His skin glistened like a wet bowling ball.

"What's the problem?"

Hays squinted over the mile-long sand pit. Not a single stalk of vegetation clung to the bomb craters. Along the ridge on both sides, gun positions nested in hollowed pits.

"I don' belong here. She-e-e- eet, I belong back home tending the ranch. My fambly's got a spread in the Pan Handle, and a couple of thousand haid."

Tony jerked a thumb toward the next mound, where Terry and Pops were arguing over the sight adjustment of their gun. "I thought you were from California, with those guys."

"She-e-e-eet, I ain't no hippy. I'm from the Lone Star state, an' proud of it."

"But the marijuana — "

"Ain't gotta be a hippy to smoke grass. Why, we grow our own out on the prairie." Hays pushed back his steel pot with a bent thumb, as if he were tilting a ten-gallon hat. "My pappy didn't know that, naturally. Me an' ma brothers usta ship it to the dealer in town whenever we went in to buy supplies — mebbe ever' other week."

"No kidding. You mean you live out in the boondocks on a big ranch?"

"Ten thousand acres, small as ranches go. Enough to keep us goin'."

Tony tilted back his own steel pot, wiped sweat off his forehead. "Sounds just like in the movies."

"Yeah, we have horses fer chasin' cattle outa the brakes, but mostly we use four-wheel drive pickups. We got a drift fence to keep strays from gettin' onto our neighbor's land."

"Do they still brand cows with a hot iron?"

"When they're calves. Only way to tell who they belong to."

"So, you're an honest to god cowboy. I thought you seemed pretty comfortable around guns."

"Been shootin' all ma life. Never at no people, though. Never thought I would, neither."

"What about rustlers?"

"Ain't no rustlers, not with airplanes an' helicopters to chase 'em, like the big ranchers got." Hays rubbed the barrel of the M-60, locked into its heavy steel tripod. "I don't wanta hurt nobody, but I sure do aim to stay alive. That's why I listen to everything the man says, do everything he does. Holtz is one smart dude. Ain't no room in this world for a one-legged cowboy."

A roar erupted to the right as Sergeant Holtz fired a burst. Half a mile down range, sparks and splinters flew out of an orange oil drum, and spouts of dust kicked up behind it. "Right on target. Very good."

The sergeant approached their position. "Good afternoon, men."

"Howdy, sarge."

He set down the ammunition box, unclamped the lid, and extracted the belted ammunition. He tore off five rounds and handed the truncated linkage to Tony. "Load her up."

Tony clamped the end bullet in the breech, and Hays slammed down the lid. Holtz put the binoculars to his eyes. "Give it a burst."

Hays touched the trigger. The receiver ate the bullets in less than a second; the barrel spat them across no-man's-land.

"Raise it up a couple clicks. I think you're underestimating the distance — about six hundred meters."

Tony adjusted the notches on the tripod. Sergeant Holtz handed him five more rounds. At the sergeant's nod, Hays pulled the trigger again. Out in the field they barely nicked the bottom of the drum, spitting sparks into the air as the bullets ate through metal.

"Raise it another notch." The sergeant moved on to the next machine gun nest.

Hays crawled up behind the gun and glued his eye to the sight. He rolled aside to let Tony take a look. "What do you think?"

"I don't think any of us belong here."

****

"Okay, men, listen up. Next week you'll be going on your first patrol. It's going to be short, simple, and safe. You won't have to worry about snipers, booby traps, mines, or punji stakes. That comes later, in the real war. But you *do* have to worry about other things, such as snakes and scorpions."

A few snickers coursed through the platoon.

"Okay, I know you think I'm trying to scare you into maintaining a sharp lookout. Well, I'm not. We lose a couple of men out of each training group. Now, I don't mean anyone has died — we've been pretty lucky so far. But we've had some pretty close calls. And it's what you learn here today, and in succeeding classes, that'll increase your chances of living through Tiger Land."

The snickers died down. Already men were casting furtive glances at the ground and the surrounding bush. Out of a rough wooden shed the size of an outhouse, Sergeant Holtz pulled several sheets of cardboard covered with vivid paintings of crawling reptiles, all in glowing color.

"Every venomous snake that inhabits the North American continent is found in the bayou country of Louisiana. This means rattlesnakes, copperheads, cottonmouths, and coral snakes. In addition to which we have scorpions, wasps, bees, and stinging ants. And that's to say nothing of wolves, wildcats, and boars. The cardinal rule of survival here is: if you see something you don't recognize, stay away from it."

Sergeant Holtz launched into a long discussion of the characteristics and identification of snakes.

"My advice to you is to stay away from all snakes, even if it doesn't have the triangular shaped head of most vipers. The coral snake is as deadly as it is lovely. As far as scorpions go, make sure you look where you sit down, especially in rocky areas. They like to hide in crevices — or boots, when you take them off at night. Swipe your feet over the ground before you sit down, and keep your eyes open for anything that moves. Even if it's not a scorpion, the ants that don't sting have a hell of a bite, and the wasps have been known to attack and kill small mice. And the mosquitoes are so tough they check your dog tags before biting, to see what type blood you have.

"Okay, in case somebody does get hurt, no

matter what the cause, I want you to see me immediately. I'm not carrying this first aid kit for my health. Well, maybe I am. But mostly it's for *your* health. Out in the swamp, even a tiny scratch can become infected.

"Another problem is your feet. When you get to Vietnam you'll be issued jungle boots. These have drain holes in the sides and canvas uppers that allow water to flow in and drain out. It's when water stays in the boot and stagnates that your real troubles begin. Immersion foot, better known as trenchfoot, has put as much as fifty percent of our men out of action in the Mekong Delta area. Now, you won't be walking through shit-filled rice paddies here, but we do have swamps and they're not all clean. The best thing you can do when we're out on overnight patrols is to put on dry socks every night. And if you get blisters, treat them right away. You don't want to have open sores on your feet.

"I've also got a snake bite kit with a tourniquet, lance, siphon, and disinfectant. If you're out on your own and your buddy gets bit, you can use your belt or T-shirt as a tourniquet, a knife or bayonet as a lance — Sterilize the cutting surface with a match but don't let it get black: carbon soot can cause infection — and either squeeze or suck out the blood. And don't swallow it or you'll poison yourself. Just spit it out."

Hays raised his hand and asked the inevitable question. "What happens if you get bit on the ass?"

"Then you're gonna die."

****

During the second week of weapons familiarization, the men were split into two groups: one learning mortars, the other continuing their proficiency in light arms: Colt .45 pistol, M-79 grenade launcher, M-72 antitank weapon, the M-18A1 antipersonnel directional mine. At night, Tony's ears were still ringing after eight hours firing the machine gun. When Bill Larson, the assigned platoon leader, flashed the lights as a ten-minute warning for bed check, half the bunks were empty. Tony folded his letters and put them away, pulled on his boots, and tied the laces loosely.

"Where do you think you're going?" Larson blocked the door with his body.

"Some of the guys are out catching a smoke. I'm going to haul them in."

"Leave them alone. I'll put them on report for missing bed check."

Tony shook his head and shoved past. "Why do that? I'll have them back here in five minutes."

"I know what they're smoking out there."

"So does everyone else. And so *is* everyone else. Be right back."

Tony ran across the hardtop and along the worn, narrow path that wound through the trees and brush. A murmur of voices blended with the wind that wafted through the pine needles. Thirty men sat in a tight circle, easing the conscience of the day's turmoil.

"Tell me how you got that shiner, Pops," came Terry's squeal.

"Go to hell."

"Come on, bro. Let's tell 'em about mortar school."

"Shut up before I give *you* a black eye."

"Ho, ho, ho. I guess you'd like to give me a fat lip, too?" In a hushed whisper: "Left his eye on the sight when Kitson pulled the lanyard. Right on target, both of 'em."

Tony sat down amid gales of laughter. "I hate to interrupt this intellectual tête-à-tête, but it's time to go nighty-night. Our illustrious squad leader would very much like to put every one you on report."

"Hey, perfessor, sit down an' have a sniff."

"I'm having one right now, just from your exhalations. Last night I practically floated back to the barracks."

"Imagine how I felt," Hays said.

"I'd rather not. Now let's get going, all of you. There's no sense getting put on report for being a couple minutes late."

"Tomorrow we'll have to start earlier."

****

"How the hell can we shoot machine guns at night?"

"By pushing the thumb trigger," Tony replied.

"Yeah, but how are we supposed to know if we hit anything?" Terry unbuttoned his shirt and shook in some cool air. Despite the darkness, the heat of the day lingered on. After ten hours on the firing range, the men were fairly well worn out.

"I think we might see sparks when the bullets hit the drums."

Terry scowled. "I'd still rather be back at the barracks having a smoke." A burst of fire to the right drew Tony's attention. Ten magnesium-coated rounds spat from the end of the barrel in less than three seconds. The percussion of exploding shell casings stopped before the first projectile reached its target, nearly a mile away. Then the flaming red steel bees ripped through the fifty-five gallon drums in a mute, fiery display as steel struck steel, and red-hot metal leaped randomly into the air.

"See. What did I tell you?"

"Yeah. And dig those tracers. Like, wow."

Sergeant Holtz moved toward their gun emplacement, a moving wraith in the night, his steel pot rattling. "Kurtz. Giovanni. All set?"

"I guess so."

"Good." The sergeant produced a small flashlight and crouched between them. "Take out your card and let me see it."

Tony took the three-by-five card out of his pocket and handed it to the sergeant. Sergeant Holtz compared it with the master list that he carried on a clipboard. "All right, set your coordinates for target number five."

With the card back in his hand, Tony read the numbers aloud while Terry adjusted the course correctors on the tripod. They could barely see in the glow from the flashlight.

"Ten rounds."

Tony counted out the bullets, broke apart the disintegrating belt, and slammed the breech down on the first round. "Ready."

"Go ahead and fire."

Tony depressed the trigger. Instantly, the night silence was broken with a loud rat tat-tat. Red-tipped projectiles flew out of the muzzle like tiny flaming darts. The slender stream of bullets arched high in the air, speeding out across the darkened field. The tongue of red flame touched the ground and was swallowed as if by a dark hole. Then blobs of metal broke off as the drum was ripped apart and hurled away. The noise of firing stopped, but the silent phantoms of the night continued to tear into the drum for another few seconds.

"Good work, men." Tony saw a momentary flash of teeth. "Giovanni, you make the corrections this time. Target number three." They reversed positions, and Terry read off the coordinates while Tony made the appropriate changes. "All right, just sit tight until the captain gives the word."

Sergeant Holtz moved on down the line. A machine gun from third platoon burst into action. For the next half hour they sat back and watched the intermittent fireworks. Stars low on the horizon twinkled through heat waves off the still-warm sand of the firing range. The moon had risen and was barely visible through the trees, casting long shadows.

"Okay men, this is it," Captain Whale's voice boomed from the observation tower. "Load up all remaining ammo."

Tony pulled the end of the ammunition belt out of the box and loaded it in the receiver. They had eighty rounds left. Terry grabbed the belt and stretched it out, ready to twist the linkage in case of a jam or a runaway gun.

"Ready on the right!" the captain's voice called over the loudspeaker.

Two sergeants shouted, "Ready!"

"Ready on the left!"

"Ready!"

In the long dramatic pause, Tony heard a lone cricket chirping from somewhere in the desolation of the range. He realized after a moment that he was holding his breath.

"*Fire!*"

The sky literally exploded with a deafening roar of sound and a pyrotechnic display that rivaled a Fourth of July fireworks finale. Hundreds of tiny bolts of lightning burst from scores of machine guns in a sustained fire that crisscrossed in wild disarray. A thousand meters away, steel-jacketed pellets ate through metal, ricocheted off the ground, and sped off again until their magnesium tips burned off and they became invisible.

With every gun hammering its deadly load into space, the drums disintegrated under the terrible onslaught. Tony, mesmerized by the awesome power that he held in his hands, forced the trigger with hardened fanaticism. Twice, against unbelievable odds, he saw bullets collide in the air as their trajectories crossed.

Then, as with the turning of a switch, the thirty-second burst of thunder ceased. For several more seconds, in utter silence, the tracers seemed to retreat to the other side of the field, like a pulsating web of fire. Just as the last drum was hit, as the last spark leaped mutely into the sky, a short burst of fire reverberated from down the firing line. Another stream of fiery pellets struck out across the field.

Then, except for the ringing in his ears, all was quiet. A long time later Terry found his voice.

"Holy fuck."

****

"Look what I got in the mail today." Terry handed him a plain, white envelope.

It bulged ominously in Tony's hand. "What is it?"

His mischievous expression spoke more than his words. "Take a look." Tony opened the flap and took out a pinch of shredded wheat that was dark green in color. "Marijuana?"

"And none of that Texas shit, either. This is straight from Mexico. An old girlfriend sent it to me."

"Yeah? How old is she? Fifty? Sixty?" Hays snapped the envelope out of Tony's hand and passed it under his flaring nostrils. "Hey, this does smell like some good shit."

"I'm not knocking your Texas weed, but this here's the real McCoy."

"Yeah, well, let's you an' me go out back an' give it a try."

"Listen, don't you think you'd better slack off on this stuff? I mean, you've been smoking it every night. When are you going to get serious about — well, about the war?"

"Later."

"Some other time."

Tony shook his head resignedly. "All right,

but I'd better go along to make sure you two can find your way back."

They stopped behind the fire door and, in the evening twilight, Hays produced a packet of cigarette paper, poured a healthy proportion of grass onto it, rolled it together, licked the seams, and pinched the ends. Terry lit a match and let him have the first puff.

"Not bad, bro. Not bad."

"I told you it was the best." Terry inhaled deeply, closed his eyes, and held his breath for a full minute. His eyes were glassy when he started to breathe again.

"How much more you got?"

"Only what's here, but there's more coming in a couple days."

"This'll pay back in spades for what you bummed."

"Listen, before you two get completely blown away, don't you think it's a little dangerous sending this stuff through the mail?"

Terry took another puff. "Naw, it's wrapped in cellophane."

"That isn't what I mean. I think it might be some kind of federal offense, or something."

"Don't worry about it, see. The girl sends it without a return address so it can't be traced. And I can't be held responsible if someone wants to play a joke and send me the stuff. See, I'm in the clear."

Tony thought for a moment. "I guess she doesn't send it insured, does she?"

"What're you, outa your fucking tree?"

"Bro, that's sure some fancy weed. I'm higher'n a kite already. But let's have another joint just to be sure."

"Hey, I thought we were going to the movies tonight," Tony protested. "We'd better hurry if we're going to catch the bus."

"You catch the bus, bro. We'll fly."

"Are you going to fly when you get into trouble in Vietnam, too?"

"Not a chance, bro. We gotta have all our fun now."

"Yeah. What's the matter, Tony? You having an attack of conscience? You're not smoking the stuff."

Patiently, Tony said, "For your own good, I think you should concentrate more on what you can learn here. You're going to need all the training you can get."

Hays sucked on the joint. "Maybe you got something there."

"Aw, he's just trying to spoil our fun. I say let's have a blast today, in case we get blasted away tomorrow."

"It might happen if you're not careful," Tony warned. "It just might happen."

Terry kept puffing. "If it does, I'll never know it. I'll be oblivious of oblivion."

"If you won't think of yourself, how about thinking of the guys who will be depending on you?"

"I told you before, I'm the only one who counts. Fuck the rest of them."

Chapter 64

"Sound off. SOUND OFF. One two. ONE TWO. One two three four, one-two — THREE FOUR."

Tony's boots hit the blacktop in time with some two hundred others, while Captain Whale sang the cadence for the troops to answer.

The barracks disappeared quickly, covered by wisps of mist that hung low to the ground, like wreaths. First the outline of the buildings went, then the yellow blobs that were incandescent lights. He could see nothing but the men ahead, the road under his feet, and the silhouettes of trees along the sides. Sound carried well in the water-laden air.

After a weekend sleeping and standing orderly room duty, Tony should have been well rested. Yet his mind was running rampant with thoughts of home; his concentration was weakened.

The fog grew thicker as they entered the swampy area. Strands of mist like frayed rope drifted through the platoons. Captain Whale was nothing more than a disembodied voice, chanting from another world. Sergeant Holtz was only a ghostly shade.

Patty's arrangements with Kathy were not working out. Two girls, the best of friends, did not necessarily make good housemates. Patty complained in her letters that the profusion of men visiting the apartment was distracting.

Tony felt a pain in his foot under the heel: a stone, or a knot of material. Without missing a step, he banged his toe on the ground to dislodge the stone into the hollow of his instep, or between his toes. But no amount of squirming had any effect. Holding his rifle in one hand, he reached down and made a grab for the sock. After several tries he got it pulled up, but the pain persisted.

Poor Teddy had a dislocated jaw because of his brother's hostility. Then, he had been mistaken for Patty's husband because he had accompanied her to the doctor's office. He had had to answer some embarrassing questions before he made good his escape.

A small stream passed through a concrete conduit under the road. Tony slipped out of formation without being seen, propped his rifle against a metal guardrail, and unlaced his boot. Third platoon plowed past only a few feet away, cloaked by the thick fog. They passed from sight as if a white, misty door had closed upon them. Faintly, he could still hear the pounding boots and the singing cadence.

The sock had rolled down and bunched under his heel. He pulled it taut, slipped the boot back on, and relaced it. By this time the entire company was not only out of sight, but out of hearing. He was all alone, with his thoughts. The trickle of water was the only sound.

Should he try to catch up with the company? Should he turn back? There was another stream on the parallel road, probably the same one. If he could cut through the woods and meet the company on the return . . .

Marion had gotten a full-time job as a secretary, and was taking night courses as well. Pete did not care for the arrangement since it cut into the time she had to spend with him. As a result, he decided to work on cars on the side — to take up time as well as to earn extra money.

Tony picked up his rifle and started picking his way along the bank of the creek. The woods were darker than pitch, but he could make out tall shapes that were thick boles. It was good to be alone, almost as if he were hunting rabbits with his grandfather.

Grandpop! He was sick — so sick, and weak. It was pitiful to see him, to think about him. But he was so proud of Tony, so happy that he had found a wife, so expectant to see his grandchild. Tony wiped away a tear, tried to shake free of his thoughts. He wanted to be home, to help, to comfort, to take his role in life and ongoing events.

The water was barely a trickle, just enough to follow by ear. It was his only signpost in this nether darkness. His boots sank deep into the muddy morass. Dank moss hung from the trees. Vines stretched along the ground. When the water broadened into a swamp, he had to retreat and circle. Maybe this was not such a good idea after all.

Ben had led a student demonstration, a sit-in which nearly got him expelled from Villanova. He was now on probation. Ray spent every spare moment hanging around Kathy, even though she often refused to see him. George was still fighting the draft, and losing the battle.

A horizontal line cut through the trees. Tony approached cautiously, trying to identify the supernatural appearance. It was as if a floating platform sat in the middle of the forest above the fetid water. From five feet away, the mist thinned enough for him to see that it was the road. Eagerly, he climbed onto the stony macadam. Then he crouched by another metal rail, and waited — lost in thought.

Faintly, he heard it in the distance. "Sound off."

It was as if he were in a large building, and several floors away, a sound was echoing up the stairwell. "One two."

The singing was coming closer, like angels descending from heaven. Tony did not want them to arrive. He enjoyed the solitude that the forest had brought him, the surcease from reality. He wished that he were carrying a fishing pole instead of a rifle.

"One two three four, one-two — *three four.*"

They were here, the first platoon plowing past like the spectral march of the dead. The road shook with the tramping of boots; steel pots clattered and material crinkled. Tony went unseen in the pre-dawn grayness.

When the second platoon came abreast, Tony lurched up from the ground, caught up with the last rank, and kept up the pace. Terry jogged along in a world of his own. Behind, the third platoon was a ghostly outline. His absence had not been noticed. He had gotten away with the scheme.

But his mind was still in turmoil.

Home.

****

"She-e-e-eet, back home in Texas I used to catch rattlers by the tail and whip them 'round my haid till they was so dizzy they couldn't stand up straight."

"You dumb nigger, snakes don't stand up."

"Listen here, whitey. Back home we got snakes that stand on their tail an' spit in your eye if you get nigh onto ten paces of 'em."

Terry shook his head. "Now I know what they mean when they say everything is bigger in Texas. That's the tallest tale I ever heard."

"Okay, bro, don't believe me. Just you come out there some day an' see for yourself."

Terry shrugged him off with a wave of the hand. "Forget it. But I think I got something here that will interest you." He dug into his pocket and took out a plastic bottle.

"Darvon?" Tony asked, reading the label.

"This is good stuff if you know how to take it. You go on sick call and they give this stuff away for anything from a headache to a hang-nail. These things will blast you out of your mind."

"She-e-e-eet, you California pill poppers know all the tricks, doncha? I bet you'd smoke a banana peel if they wasn't nothing else around."

"Don't knock it till you've tried it. Only two reasons for living in this world: getting laid and getting high."

****

At first glance, the M-79 grenade launcher seemed to be a caricature of a shotgun, sawed off as if for riot control. The wooden stock and the hinged barrel broke apart so that a forty-millimeter canister-type grenade could be inserted in the tube. The aluminum barrel was rifled to ensure accuracy.

"You got four kinds of grenades: high explosive, shrapnel, illumination, and signal flares. The effective range of this weapon is four hundred meters, while the minimum arming distance is fifty feet. This covers the distance between the longest hand grenade throw and the shortest mortar round — it fills in the gap. We had a guy got hit right in the chest with one of these babies. He was so close the grenade hadn't armed itself yet so all it did was crack a few ribs and knock him down. Oh, yeah, and it scared the shit out of him."

When the laughter died down, Sergeant Holtz continued. "Because of the weight of the grenade, it's got a low muzzle velocity. And it falls fast. So you aim high, sighting for windage, and arc it onto your target. Once you learn how to range it, you'll be surprised how accurate it is."

The launcher kicked slightly as the grenade whumped out of the tube. It was big enough and slow enough to follow with the naked eye until the practice grenades exploded with red smoke near the targets.

"You don't have to hit the bull's eye to make a kill. Shrapnel from a near miss can be devastating, to say nothing of the psychological damage."

After three days of practice, Tony could hit a mock-up hooch at maximum range, four times out of five. He then spent the rest of the week running compass courses.

"Come on, Terry, don't you want to know where we're going?"

Terry folded his compass, put it in his shirt pocket. "Naw, I know you'll get us back to camp. That's what buddies are for."

Tony kept one eye on the blackened tip of the needle, the other on the woods. He picked out a tree in the distance that was on their course, and walked straight for it, jumping over logs and meandering streams. "And what are you going to do when you get to Vietnam? You've got to know how to do this yourself, in case you get lost."

"I'll just get high enough to look down on the terrain."

"Getting high isn't the answer to everything. We're supposed to work as a unit, to rely on each other. Terry, I have to tell you this for your own good: you're unreliable."

"Yeah, and I like you, too."

"I mean it, Terry. This is serious business, and you and the rest of the guys better get used to it."

"I don't want to be a well-greased tooth in the meshed gears of the military machine."

Tony took a new sight, started out across an open field. "I don't want to be either, but I want to survive this ordeal. And if I have to depend on men like you for support, I might not."

"Don't worry about me, man. I'll take care of myself. You'd better learn to do the same."

"Yes, maybe I'd better."

Chapter 65

Terry squinted at the tree line a quarter mile away. "Can you make anything out?"

"All I see are a bunch of trees." Tony shifted the straps of his web gear. After two weeks of wearing full equipment, steel pots, and carrying a rifle, he was finally adjusting to the constant load. "They have to be kidding if they think we can see anyone over there wearing camouflage clothes and bushes in his hat."

"Yeah, if there's a guerrilla sniper sitting in the bushes, we're dead meat."

After five minutes, Sergeant Holtz said, "Okay, I'm going to signal them to move. Remember, this will be one quick and sudden motion, nothing else. You have to catch it right away." He popped a purple smoke grenade.

"I still don't see anything," Terry said in disgust.

Tony drew a stick figure on his control card. "I think I saw something."

"Where?"

"I can't tell you."

"Come on, cut the crap. Just give me a clue."

Hays joined them, pencil in hand. "Who's gonna help you in the Nam, bro?"

"Hey, what's gotten into you lately? It's only a game."

"Bro, I seen the light. I ain't aimin' to get my ass shot off. From here on out I'm playing it straight. Right, Tony?"

"Right."

"Aw, you guys are a pain in the ass."

"Get ready, men." The sergeant popped a green smoke grenade. "They're going to make a five second move. Look for slowly waving arms."

This time Tony saw three men for certain, and made the appropriate markings on his card.

"Hey, what do you think you're doing?"

Terry dropped down from tiptoes and stepped away from Pop's side. Sergeant Holtz grabbed him and swung him around, his face only inches away from Terry's. "Let me see that card." Without waiting, he ripped it out of Terry's hand, glanced at it. "He's wrong, and you're double wrong. How are you going to cheat when you're in Nam and Charlie's got a bead on you, huhn?" He put a firm hand on Terry's chest and pushed him away.

"Okay, men, gather around. And *you*, joker, listen up well. This is not just an exercise, it's not a test, there's no passing and failing. Not now, anyway. I've told you this before and I'm going to tell you again. The test is in Vietnam, and the stakes are your life. Can't you get that through your thick heads?"

He held up Terry's card. "Kurtz, here, is a fuck up. I know some of you men look up to him because he's a head. Now it's time you get your own heads out of your ass. This guy's so doped up on marijuana that he's seeing things. He's got four men on this card — and there were only three men out there. And he's got them all in the wrong place."

The men murmured and gasped in response to the sergeant's accusation. He surveyed the platoon with a jaundiced eye. "What, you jokers think I don't have a nose? You don't think I know what the shit smells like? Well, let me tell you something, brother: you're not fooling me. I know what goes on behind the barracks every night, and across the road. You fucking potheads are only fooling yourselves.

"Charlie is a formidable enemy. You're going to have enough trouble scratching your ass to stay one step ahead of him without being blown away on wacky weed. You got enough to fight without having to fight yourselves, or your buddies, too. And if you want men you can depend on, you've got to be dependable yourselves. You've got to be on the fucking ball if you want to come home in one piece, instead of as a telegram for your folks. Believe me, men, it's a fucked-up war you're getting into, and you've got to have your wits about you. Stay alert, and maybe you'll stay alive."

****

Tony rubbed black rouge on his face, then handed the stick to Terry. "Put a little more on your neck. Lower down, and under your collar."

Terry smeared the rouge around with his hand. "How do I look?"

"Like a minstrel."

Sergeant Holtz walked among the men as they sat in small groups on the sandy soil. "Now, you black folks may think you have the edge on the rest of us, but your skin is just as shiny and can give you away just as easily. You'll use this lighter, brown rouge to tone down your skin. For night patrols add a touch of red. And whatever you do, don't smile. And I'm not just spitting apples."

Terry watched Hays putting on the finishing touches. "Hey, you're beginning to look like Stepin Fetchet."

"Feets, don't leave me now."

"Aw, go pick a watermelon. And make sure you put two coats on that forehead or you'll be drawing bullets like shit draws flies."

"She-e-e-eet, you white honkies don't know." Hays dabbed some rouge under each eye. "I usta do this kinda shit back home on the range when I was deer huntin', only I jus' rubbed on a little clay and it did the trick."

Tony said, "Only now you're trying to fool an animal that's a little smarter than a deer."

Hays pursed his puffy lips, then dabbed on another layer. "Guess you're right."

When the platoon was finished applying paint, Sergeant Holtz inspected the troops. "You look like a bunch of mummers ready to march in the New Year's Day parade. But you're never going to make it with those polished boots and shiny buckles. Snipers'll see you so far off there'll be bamboo growing in their tracks by the time the survivors get to where they fired the shots. Remember, we're dealing with highly trained professionals — men who have spent their entire lives in the jungle. Those brass buckles will look like signal mirrors, and your boots like neon signs. The Vietnamese have been playing at guerrilla warfare for decades, their ancestors for centuries, and they're experts in the art of camouflage and how to detect it. They can move like the wind, flit like a bird, hit like an elephant, and melt into the jungle like they never existed. Never, never, never underestimate your enemy. All that propaganda bullshit they feed the public about U.S. troop superiority is a political placebo. American soldiers are outclassed in everything except firepower.

"Sure, you can call in a gunship for support, and artillery, and bomb strikes, but that won't save your ass while Charlie sits in his spider hole and picks you off one by one while you sit there wondering where the bullets are coming from. So, we're going to teach you how to slink through the jungle just like Charlie does. We're going to play his own game on him. Start rubbing sand on those boots and buckles. In five minutes, I don't want to see anything shining other than your wit."

****

"Some things in this army jus' don' make no sense at all."

"Only *some* things?" Tony put down his letter and cocked an eyebrow in Hays' direction.

He sat on the edge of his bunk with his chin in his hands, a picture of dejection. His black hair had grown in just enough so tiny Afro knots were beginning to curl.

"Yeah, like when we were tole in boot camp that a forty-five is a gun an' an M-14 is a rifle. Now they hand us an M-60 that's bigger and shoots bullets faster than anythin', an' they call it a machine gun. How the hell did we get back to a gun again?"

Tony laughed. "Reason and rationality are civilian concepts. You're confused with military logic where, instead of one plus one equaling two, it equals whatever they want. Just go along with it."

"I can't go along with somethin' that jus' don' make no sense."

Tony climbed down from his bunk and sat opposite Hays. "There are a lot of things that don't make sense. War doesn't make sense. Poverty doesn't make sense. Religion doesn't make sense. Unemployment doesn't make sense. Starving children don't make sense. Death doesn't make sense. I'm beginning to think that *life* doesn't even make sense."

Hays transfixed Tony with dark, doleful eyes. "Whatchu talkin' 'bout, bro?"

"I'm talking about this conflict we're all involved in."

"Now that's the biggest ball o' nonsense I ever did hear. I been reading the papers lately, an' I can't figger it out. Here's this poor guy growing rice for his fambly. Along comes the VC, they take his rice, an' we call it extortion. But when the government takes their percentage, they call it taxation. What the hell's the difference?"

"That's like asking the difference between unionism and communism."

"What *is* the difference?"

"Scale. If you organize a trade, it's unionism. If you organize a country, it's communism."

Hays' eyes brightened. "I getchu. It's like if a bunch of college students protest the war, it's a minority. But if the president is for it, it's a majority."

"Right! That's it exactly. The president's supposed to represent the people, but actually he represents his own self-interests, or those interests which got him into office. That's the real conflict. Instead of doing what's right, he's doing what will make him popular and win more votes."

"An' he don' never ask whether it's right to drop bombs on villages, or napalm on refugees, or gun down citizens. He wants us to go out there an' do it, but he don' want to tell us why it's right."

Tony threw his hands wildly into the air. "And don't you think any soldier would fight better if he believed in the cause, if he had a sense of moral obligation and the strength of his convictions as an incentive? No one in the army has ever said anything about *why* we're going to Vietnam. They're training us to fight, but not to understand. Like mercenaries instead of compatriots."

Hays held out his hand, palm up. "Put her there, bro. You an' me kinda think the same way. Not that I understand everything you said, but deep down inside, if you know what I'm talkin' 'bout, I think I know something's wrong

somewhere. I jus' have a feelin', an' I think you made me see the light."

Tony slapped his hand. "I hope I didn't blind you, because that's how I feel — blinded by a light too bright to look at."

Hays held onto Tony's hand, squeezed tight. "I don' know about that. But I do know one thing: I'm gonna live through this whole mess if it kills me. I guess that's what's been gain' through my mind lately. I'm startin' to listen to the good sergeant, and what he says makes sense. I know I ain't the smartest son-of--a-bitch in the worl', but I ain't the dumbest, either. I don' know about all that gover'ment stuff, communism an' whatnot. But I know I got a mammy an' a pappy an' brothers an' sisters who need me. I'm takin' the only good advice I ever heard in the army: I aim to take care of myself. I'm gonna listen to ever'thin' the good sergeant says, an' I'm gonna learn ever'thin' he has to teach. An' I'm stayin' away from that shit that fucks up your brain, 'cause there ain't no room for it now."

****

"The first guy who calls this a bazooka will walk back to camp tonight — backwards. And when I say it's the law, I mean it."

Captain Whale issued his instructions from a sandy hillock the size of a pitcher's mound, but which was built up by sandbags to a height of five feet. This was the only high ground anywhere around the firing range. The range itself was strange in that it was dotted with trees, mostly reddish barked swamp oaks, and what appeared to be billboards.

"The bazooka is an old World War Two weapon and not in use any more. The only place you're going to see it is in the movies. What you see here — " He held up something that looked like a fat mailing tube. " — is a recoilless rifle, a Light Antitank Weapon, abbreviated LAW. It fires a sixty-six millimeter high-explosive rocket with an effective range of two hundred and fifty meters. As you can see, the M-72 is open at both ends. The rocket comes out the front, the exhaust out the back, which is why there's no recoil. It's fired from the shoulder from either a standing or kneeling position. It's not a good idea to fire it from the prone position, because the rocket exhaust flames back about five feet and you're likely to give yourself a hotfoot."

He paused while a few chuckles and one or two guffaws filled the air. He pulled the rocket out of the tube and held it aloft; it looked like a stylized rocket ship, complete with landing vanes. "The nose is armor piercing and will go through any normally armored tank — and explode inside. During the firing procedure you will have a buddy who will tell you when to fire. It's up to him to make sure no one walks behind you, that you yourself are clear, and that the exhaust is not aimed at anything dangerous, such as dry grass or other rockets and ammunition, since the heat is intense."

He tossed the rocket to Sergeant Holtz, then held up the tube again. "The sights are collapsible and already aligned with the tube, so there are only calibrations for elevation. To arm it you pull this release, to fire it you pull the trigger. After firing, you break the cardboard tube in half, crush the plastic sights and trigger mechanism under your boot, and bury the remains."

Tony whispered to Terry, "Now I've heard of everything: disposable weapons. Shoot it once and throw it away."

"The epitome of modern technology."

"What we need now is a disposable war. Then we could all stay home and watch it on television."

After Sergeant Holtz demonstrated the correct firing procedure, the formation separated into buddy teams. Tony picked up the LAW, removed the plastic endcaps, and nestled the tube comfortably between his neck and collarbone. The five-pound rocket launcher was well balanced.

"First we'll fire it from the kneeling position. That's so you can pray the rocket doesn't blow up in the tube." He stood by Tony's side as he raised the front sight a notch. "It's foolproof, but not idiot proof. That's why you don't fire until your buddy gives you the all clear with a tap on the helmet."

He nodded, Terry tapped, and Tony fired. The rocket rode a tail of fire over the trees and arced down right through the middle of the paper billboard.

"Beginner's luck," Sergeant Holtz said, shaking his head.

But Tony's luck carried him through another week of weapons training with the M-67, a ninety-millimeter recoilless rifle, and the M—2, an eighty-pound fifty-caliber machine gun that could fire five hundred rounds per minute — nine bullets per *second* — and was accurate up to a mile.

"This bullet could knock you down if I just tossed it at you," Terry said. Tony confidently slapped in the belt of ammunition. "Watch me tear that tree apart."

"What tree?" Terry shaded his eyes, looked out over the immense firing range.

"That sapling at the other end of the field."

Tony aligned the sights and pulled the trigger. When the smoke cleared, the tree was gone.

Chapter 66

When individual weapons familiarization was completed, and Hays, Pops, and the other mortarmen rejoined the company, small unit tactical maneuvers were begun.

The morning started out like any other: reveille at four-thirty, barracks scrub-down, the four-mile run, a hearty breakfast, and company formation. Tony collected his rifle from the armory and joined his platoon. Sergeant Holtz led them on a cross-country compass course.

Strictly speaking, he did not lead. He rotated the men, letting each take the compass for thirty minutes at a time. And from this point in their training, each man got to be squad leader for a day.

"This is to instill confidence, and to give everyone the opportunity of command. The well-rounded soldier is one who can take any position, at any time."

Two hours passed before they arrived at the position that Sergeant Holtz indicated on the map. A sixty-foot-wide ravine cut through the swamp, and a series of ropes had been strung across the ravine. Tony buttoned his collar and tucked in his shirt where it had slipped out; clouds hid the sun, and a chilly breeze added a bite to the air. It was the first sign of autumn although, among the predominantly evergreen forest, there was very little color change. Pine needles fell in clusters, blowing around on the ground and crinkling underfoot.

"Squad leaders, set out your guards." Four men were picked and set in position close to the trees. "Now, the rest of you line up along the edge and point your guns across the ravine. Kurtz, sling your weapon and get ready to cross."

Terry shook his head, and appealed to Tony. "All he does is pick on me."

"I think he wants you to go straight."

"Yeah, straight to hell." Terry looked down. The drop was only twenty feet to the muddy water, but along the edges, thick, black muck choked the banks. The triple-rope cross was simple, with one rope to walk on and two to hold onto. Still, Terry trembled enough during his traverse to vibrate the manila hawsers. He walked across slowly, without looking down. Tony followed him, then Hays.

"A piece of cake," Tony commented.

"Yeah, but I'm afraid of heights."

Hays made smoking mimes with two fingers. "She-e-e-eet, you been a lot higher than this an' it never bothered you before."

After Sergeant Holtz crossed, he had the men guard the opposite bank while the rear guards were called in and made their crossing. When they were all grouped around the lone pine that acted as the stanchion for the ropes, he said,

"Now, we're going to discontinue the tactics for a while. I want you all to leave your rifles here in case someone drops one in the drink. The other two crossings aren't so easy."

The rifles were stacked in circles, leaning against each other. Tony sidled over the two-rope cross with the bottom rope notched under the heel of his boot. He let the top rope slide through his hands until he reached the other side. Pops, being only five-feet-two, had to stretch. In the middle, where the sag was the greatest, the bottom rope sprung out from under his outstretched arms. The top rope sank with his weight, but he maintained his grip. With the strength of a great ape, he climbed hand-over-hand to the opposite bank. The men cheered.

"Way to go, Pops."

"Nice going, short stuff."

After Sergeant Holtz tightened the turnbuckle, Tony volunteered to be first to tackle the single-rope cross. Following the sergeant's explanation, he lay down with one arm extended and the other under his stomach, one leg bent and the other one stretched out. Balanced on his thigh, he pushed forward with his ankles while pulling with his arms, caterpillaring across the ravine. He was barely a third of the way across when Sergeant Holtz put Terry on the line.

Terry's fear was transmitted through the rope by the vibration. Tony clung tightly as the line start to shake. But when he heard the sergeant call out to Pops, and felt the resultant sag as his weight was added to the rope, he threw balance to the wind and slithered forward as fast as he could. With three men moving together, the rope heterodyned sickeningly.

Tony stared down at the mud bank below, then up at the edge of the ravine a couple body lengths away. The rope swung crazily, and his equilibrium faltered. He ducked his head and saw Terry, from upside down, where he had stopped in the middle of the crossing.

"Move it, man. Move it," Pops screamed.

Terry moved — and rolled right off the rope. The jarring motion knocked Tony off his perch. He tightened his grip as his legs slipped off; then he was hanging by his hands, swinging freely. As soon as the rope stopped gyrating up and down, he raced hand-over-hand for the ledge, and dropped off onto the grass-covered slope.

Breathing hard, he watched as Terry swung his legs wildly in an attempt to get them back over the rope. Pops executed the maneuver without difficulty, and hung there like a calf tied to a spit, shouting imprecations. Terry did not appear to have either the strength or the agility to follow his example. He dangled and kicked like a man being hung, slower and slow-er, until his strength gave way and his fingers plunked off the rope one by one.

He shot downward with his arms still over his head, like the victim in a stickup. He knifed into the water and disappeared. The sudden loss of weight caused the rope to spring upward like a released bowstring, ripping it right out of Pop's hands and feet. Like a cartoon figure, he seemed to float in the air for a moment until he realized that he was no longer holding onto anything. Then he plummeted like a long sack of potatoes, narrowly missed the water, and sank with a dull thud into the mud.

Terry bobbed up screaming, "I can't swim. I can't swim."

Sergeant Holtz tossed one end of the safety rope across Terry's head. He grabbed for it frantically, and clung to it while the sergeant and several men pulled him ashore. He waded through knee-deep mud, was pulled forward onto his face, and finally reached the rocky ledge at the bottom of the ravine. He refused to let go of the rope.

"The next time," Sergeant Holtz bellowed, "take your steel pot off or it'll drown you."

If Terry heard, he made no reply.

Pops still lay lengthwise in the mud, arms straight out like a cardboard cutout. He made frantic attempts to roll over, but the suction held him in place. "Get me outa here, goddamn it. Help me. I'm stuck."

The men were laughing too hard to attempt a rescue. Even Sergeant Holtz stared down with a broad grin, the rope hanging limp in his hands. Eventually, he coerced Terry into letting go the end, and tossed it to where Pops struggled like a fly caught in a web. With a firm grip he pulled himself erect, leaving a gingerbread imprint (a mud angel rather than a snow angel), then sloshed to a spot where the bank was more solid. He followed Terry as he climbed the rocks to the top of the ledges.

Pops threw a punch that knocked Terry flat. After a moment, Terry sat up rubbing his chin, locked eyes with Pops, then leaped to his feet and started swinging.

"Hey, no fighting." But the sergeant's admonition went unheeded.

Pops ran like a football receiver, twisting and turning through the throng of riotous troops, with Terry close on his heels. Pops broke into the open and raced for the cover of the trees. Terry gave up the chase at the edge of the pine forest, shaking his fist.

"All right, men," said Sergeant Holtz, after the excitement died down. "Let's walk around and pick up our weapons. If we hurry, we can be back at camp in time for lunch."

Tony pulled his rifle out of the pile, handed another to Hays. "I think the lesson is: only one

man should be on the rope at a time."
****

The armored personnel carrier was quite a machine: forty tons of green steel that could cross a ten-foot wide ditch on cleated treads; climb a forty-five degree rocky slope; travel up to thirty miles per hour through sand, mud, and swamp; and, with hatches sealed, could float on water and buck a five knot current. It looked like a cross between a rectangular breadbox and a tank with the turret missing.

Unlike the tank, which was a mobile gun platform, the primary use of the APC was to assist the rifle squad to reach areas that were otherwise too hot for comfort. It was impervious to mortars, grenades, and small arms fire, and, in the land of booby traps, it could stalk unharmed through punji stakes and antipersonnel mines. It was a suit of armor worn by eight men simultaneously.

The M-113 also had its disadvantages. Large antitank mines, that a foot soldier could step on and walk away from, were triggered by the weight of the APC. The soft underbelly lacked the thickness of tank armor, so a ground explosion would split it open like a can of sardines. The bulkheads could also be breached by Viet-Cong recoilless rifles and well aimed RPGs — rocket propelled grenades. An internal explosion could detonate the fuel tanks, converting the machine into an eight-man coffin.

Tony watched as sand spit out from under the treads, and the operator showed off his skill. The APC lurched over a ditch and through a bog on the other side. It bucked like a wild bronco as it crashed over sunken tree trunks, and skewered through ooze at the edge of a placid pond. With the tracks spun in opposite directions, the machine pivoted in its own length, charged up a hill, spun again on the ridge line, and raced down at breakneck speed, splashing into the pond with such force that water spouted from three sides in thick sheets that rose twenty feet high; two foot waves washed over the shore. It cruised slowly and quietly, its engine noise effectively muffled by water, until it reached the opposite shore. Then it climbed out over stumps and potholes, and mowed down small trees like ten pins.

"I sure wish I had one of them on the Schuylkill Expressway," Tony said.

"It sure is hell on tracks," Pops commented dryly.

Terry stepped back as the machine ground to a halt in front of him, water pouring off its upper works. "I wonder what he does for an encore."

The driver sat placidly in his seat, with only his helmet and eyes visible through the slit. The gunner sat behind the sole offensive armament,

a mean looking fifty-caliber machine gun with a belt of ammunition draped into the cab.

"That thin' sure would be great for chasin' cattle outa the arroyos."

Sergeant Holtz waited until the comments died down. "Okay, remember what we went over in class this morning. As soon as you get out of the track, you get into position and hit the dirt, and I mean hit it. That man up there's going to be shooting live rounds over your head, and anyone who gets his steel pot nicked has to pay for damages."

Tony was locked into the steel chamber with the rest of the rifle squad. The gunner used a pulley to crank up the rear door and lock it in place; a rubber gasket sealed out water. A little bit of light entered through the gunner's opening. The side benches held four men each, their knees touching across the narrow aisle. Tony clutched the leather strap overhead.

The driver dropped the clutch and the APC leaped forward. As close as they were inside, they suddenly got closer, piling up against the rear door and crushing Hays and Kitson. The ride that started out rough, got rougher. The machine careened from side to side as if it were passing through a boulder field. Tony was bounced around like a ping-pong ball: front to back, man to man, seat to ceiling. His steel pot repeatedly clanged off the roof.

When the going *really* got rough, he jammed his back against the outer bulkhead and his feet against the solid base of the opposite bench. Pops, because of his stature, practically had to lie down to make the two-point contact. Soon everyone was doing it, until they had a cat's cradle of intertwined legs.

After the APC came to a screeching halt, they all piled up at the forward end of the compartment. The gunner tripped the door lever and the massive tailgate dropped with a crash; he opened up with the fifty-caliber. "Get out! Get out! Everybody out!"

Galvanized into action, Hays and Kitson tumbled out of the opening and onto the muddy field. Tony's legs and rifle were tangled with Johnson's; and a moment passed before they were loose. He jumped out and charged along the side of the machine through knee-high brush covering a rising hill that was a sea of mud from yesterday's rain.

Tony ducked instinctively as the gunner poured bursts of hot lead not much higher than bush-top level, the tracers flaring like small rockets. When the gunner yelled, "Hit the ground!" Tony hit it — right into a mud-filled puddle. From the prone position only his upper body, leaning on elbows and aiming his rifle, stayed dry. He was lying in water from the waist down.

Tracers raked dirt and damp leaves like a threshing machine. As soon as the squad was fanned out, the gunner gave the order to advance. Cautiously, Tony drew his legs under him, without raising the level of his head. The deadly sparks seemed to be getting closer, the booming louder. They advanced slowly, no one too eager to be the first to reach the top of the hill.

Hays, who was squad leader of the day, tried to keep them in an even line. The APC crawled up behind them, maintaining a twenty-foot distance, and spreading ruin and destruction in front of the squad. As they gained the top of the hill, the gunner silenced his weapon. The hilltop was plowed with deep furrows.

"Well done, men," Sergeant Holtz said, approaching. "But next time, remember to glance right and left to make sure you stay on line with your buddies. Okay, go take a break while the other squads get a chance."

Wet, slimy, and muddy, Tony retreated to the security of the pine forest and did his best to clean up, using clusters of needles as washcloths. "I wonder if they have one of these rides at Coney Island."

****

"Look, I don't do anything but type up what they give me." Corporal Velden turned his acned face away and jerked a thumb over his shoulder. "You got a problem, take it up with the Old Man."

Tony turned to First Sergeant Moberly, a tall stocky man with graying hair, and plenty of it. "Giovanni. Giovanni. Seems to me I've heard that name before." He shuffled through some paper on his desk. "Oh, yes, you were the one who was a week late getting here because you had to, uh, get married." Bushy eyebrows shot up.

Tony shuffled his feet. "I'm the one."

"Yes, and your name keeps cropping up on the duty roster, doesn't it?"

"Yes, I've been pulling orderly room duty every weekend."

The eyebrows sagged, the corners of the mouth turned up. "Well, I haven't heard any complaints about your work. Now, what seems to be the problem?"

"Well, I applied for an allotment for my wife as soon as I got here. In fact, Captain Whale got the forms for me. But there was no deduction made for it in my pay."

"Oh, sometimes these things take a month or two to go through channels."

"Yes, but in the meantime I lose sixty-five dollars."

Sergeant Moberly ran a hand through wavy locks. "Oh, it doesn't mean you're losing it. It's just that you're not getting it."

"It amounts to the same thing — I still end up without it."

"Yes, I guess that's true. But I don't know what else you can do about it. Maybe it'll be in next month's pay."

"But I don't want to wait to find out."

The sergeant rubbed a pudgy hand over his chin. "Well, you could file another form. If the first one goes through, it won't matter. But just in case it's been lost or misfiled, you'll be covered."

"Can it be made retroactive? After all, I signed up for it a month ago. It should take effect from the time I sign up for it, not when it gets processed."

"Hmmn, I've never heard of anything being done retroactively before. Why don't you just make a notation on the form that this is your second request? Corporal, bring me an allotment form."

Corporal Velden slammed a couple drawers, leafed through some files, and finally found the proper form in a stack of papers. Tony sat down and filled them out — in triplicate.

"Do you have any carbon paper?"

"No. And you can't use it anyway. Each copy has to be an original."

"Then it's not a copy, is it?"

The corporal scowled.

When Tony finished, he said, "I'd like to have a receipt this time. You know, in case this one gets lost, too."

"This ain't no department store."

"I know, but how do I prove I've filled out this form if it gets lost again?"

"It's not going to get lost," Corporal Velden said harshly.

Sergeant Moberly cleared his throat. "Corporal, just stick in an extra carbon when you type it up."

"You mean, after I just filled out this form in triplicate, you still have to type it?"

"In triplicate," Velden said, as if it entailed extra work.

Tony just shook his head. "Never mind, I won't even ask. I'll stop in later for the extra copy." He got up to go when Sergeant Moberly called him back.

"You know, I just remembered why your name was on the tip of my tongue. The captain asked me to write up the weekend duty roster and your name was on it. We've got some special details coming up, before bivouac. Nothing personal, you understand. But at least you'll be getting off base for the weekend."

****

"All right, men, fall in. Let's go let's go let's go."

The men scrambled into formation, but not fast enough for Sergeant Waltham. He unscrambled them.

"Just like basic. Don't they ever get tired of playing their silly games?" Terry huffed, leaning against a tree.

Pops sprawled out as if he were going to take a nap: one hand under his head, one over his eyes, his steel pot pushed back. "What the fuck else they got to do? It don't cost *him* nothing."

Terry peeled bark off the tree. "I'd like to plant one of those claymores in his back pocket. It would give me a great deal of pleasure to blow his ass away."

"You're gonna hafta knock me out to do it," Pops said, without opening his eyes. "Soon as I get the chance, I'm gonna drop a mortar down his throat. Why'd you think I'm practicing so hard with those sights?"

"Another black eye?"

"She-e-e-eet, I thought all you wanted to do was kill gooks."

"I don't want to kill nobody, except maybe that smart ass sergeant."

Tony squatted Indian fashion on the cool ground. "Hey, why are you guys so down on Sergeant Waltham?"

"Yeah, you got a bug up your ass?" Hays added.

"I don't like him because he's a sergeant," Terry said.

Pops opened his eyes for a moment. "And I don't like him because he's . . . he's . . . well, I just don't like him on principle."

"Well, maybe he's not as good as Sergeant Holtz — " Tony started.

"When did you fall in love with Holtz?" Terry wanted to know. "He's put you on extra duty every weekend since you got here. Shit, you haven't had one fucking pass."

"Yes, but he's always so *apologetic* about it. And besides, it's not his fault."

"Yeah, it's that mealy-mouthed Whale."

"No, I don't blame him, either. He's just doing what he has to do to placate the higher-ups who would just as soon have me court-martialed."

"That doesn't make him a goody-two-shoes. After all, he *could* just *tell* them he was coming down on you without actually doing it."

Hays kicked a little sand around with his boots. "You guys are just impossible to please. They go outa their way to teach us what we need to know, an' you're still bitchin'. Look, I got Waltham for three weeks on mortars, an' he weren't that bad."

As if in answer to his name, the sergeant bellowed, "All right, men, fall in. Last five men get detail."

Tony was polishing the sergeant's buttons with his breath before he was halfway through his speech. Even so, there were twenty men

ahead of him.

"You. Up front." Even without looking, Tony knew that Sergeant Waltham was pointing at Terry and Pops. "And you. And you. And you. That's right, the one with the dancing eyes. Up front." Most of Tony's squad stood before the sergeant. "All right, you men are gonna be servers. Get over there and help Corporal Velden."

The pimple-faced corporal was standing on the bed of a canvas-covered deuce-and-a-half, along with the green, insulated slop containers that held lunch.

"At ease, men, but keep your eyes up front. Anyone who is interested in chow can help serve it. We got business first." Sergeant Waltham walked slowly back and forth across the front of the formation. "The captain's not too happy about your claymore placement. We walked down that trail and saw more mines than you could shake a stick at. We ain't hiding Easter eggs here. What the captain can see, Charlie can see. Only difference is, the captain ain't gonna shoot you for it — he's just gonna let me chew your ass out.

"So listen up, and listen up good. We're gonna give you another chance this afternoon. First thing, we're gonna take down all the claymores we laid out this morning. Then we're gonna find another place to set them up. And if the captain sees so much as one claymore exposed, we'll do it over again, even if we hafta spend the night here. Now go collect your mines, then we'll think about having chow."

Earlier that morning, Captain Whale had said, "The M18A1 antipersonnel mine is a directional, fixed fragmentation mine that is used primarily for defense of bivouac areas and outposts, and against infiltrators. It is also effective against thin-skinned vehicles such as jeeps, automobiles, and trucks, readily perforating the outer body and injuring or killing the occupants. The fragments will also puncture tires, gas tanks, crankcases, radiators, and engine accessories. When detonated, a fan-shaped sheaf of several thousand spherical steel pellets is projected in a sixty-degree horizontal arc covering a casualty area of fifty meters to a height of two meters."

It could also be used to form an ambush. Tony had set the collapsible wire legs behind a log, and laid a blanket of leaves and needles between it and the trail. The detonation wire ran back fifty feet to where he would be protected from the backlash by a depression in the ground.

"I know they didn't find my claymore," Hays said casually, beating through the brush. "I hid it so good, *I* can't even find it."

Tony helped him, and five minutes later they

detected it artfully decorated with sticks and dirt. With the smell of hot food in the air, they rushed back to the formation area. Sergeant Waltham was reading from a list.

"After chow the following men will fall out and accompany Corporal Velden back to base for special detail. Beltz. Duncan. Giovanni. Stoker. Walker."

****

At the armory, Corporal Velden passed out bayonets and magazines of blanks.

"Hey, how about some real ammo?" Walker said.

"You're not supposed to kill anybody."

"How long's our shift?" Duncan asked.

"The lieutenant told you to pack your blanket roll because you'll be sleeping over."

Beltz tightened the straps holding his poncho in place. "But bivouac starts Sunday night. Don't we get a break before staying out in the woods for a week?"

"You're gonna go right from guard duty to bivouac."

"But we hafta come back an' get cleaned up. Otherwise we'll be out for ten days straight."

"You don't hafta get nothin'. You guys are on the shit list."

Tony buckled on his pistol belt, and moved the bayonet so that it did not stab him in the leg when he walked. "Excuse me, corporal, but will I be able to call my wife some time?"

"Where you guys are goin' there ain't no telephones, there ain't no room service, and there ain't no roads. For the next two days and two nights, you'll be livin' with snakes an' wild hogs."

"You takin' us to the officer's billet?"

"No, I'm packin' you all in the back of a jeep and drivin' you forty-five miles off base."

Stoker snorted. "What the hell's out there? Fort Polk is in the middle of nowhere."

Corporal Velden smiled as he stalked off to get the jeep. "If you think this is the boondocks, wait till you get in the bayou."

Walker shook his head. "Don't let him scare you. He's just scared himself, and trying to pass it on."

"Doin' a good job, too."

Chapter 67

The jeep bumped to a halt in front of two forty-foot-long, olive drab command tents. Sitting side by side so close together that their guy ropes intertwined, they were backed up to thick vegetation that passed for forest in the bayou. On the other side of the dirt trail stretched a huge expanse of rolling grassland that seemed completely incongruous to Tony's conception of Louisiana.

"Giovanni, hop out. It's the end of the line

for you."

Tony jumped over the rear fender, dragging his pack and rifle with him. Corporal Velden kicked a case of c-rations off the passenger seat. It collided with the ground in a puff of dust.

The corporal tossed out a waxed cardboard container. "All I gots for you to drink is a quart of milk."

Tony dropped his pack and made a grab for the milk carton. "How long am I going to be here?"

"The whole weekend."

"But I only have one canteen with me."

"It'll have to do. If I get the chanct, I'll drop over tomorrow night and resupply you. But no guarantees. You're on your own."

Tony looked around at the desolate country, buttoned his collar against the October chill. "But, what am I supposed to do?"

Corporal Velden smiled maliciously, nodding with his chin. "Ya see them two tents? Guard them — with your life."

He popped the clutch a little too hard. The jeep coughed and jerked away, spitting sand from all four tires. In a few seconds the whining engine noise was swallowed by lacy foliage, and Tony was left with the sounds and solitude of the wilderness.

The view in front of the tent site would have fattened the wallet of any condominium entrepreneur. A gently undulating plain that was thousands of yards wide and miles in depth dipped into a treeless valley and rose up into a forest so far away that the trees looked like shrubbery. Nothing grew on the little hillocks but ankle high grass. Rocky outcrops — overgrown with green, orange, red, and brown moss — added relief as well as color.

Tony carried his supplies into the tent that seemed to be in the best condition. The zippered flap opened from the bottom, but most of it was torn away. Inside, the musty smell of mildew was thick, choking. He could see light through rents in the canopy, but found a corner which looked as if it might stay reasonably dry in case of rain.

He tied back the rear flaps as well as the front, and let the cool air ventilate his sleeping quarters. Except for tree limbs, stripped and pointed as extra poles, the tent was empty. During a check of the stakes and guy lines, Tony tightened anything that was loose. The only thing the adjacent tent had to offer was a better view of the sky.

Outside of the natural clearing, the loamy soil slurped at his boots at every step as he collected materials. With his entrenching tool he scraped an area clear of grass and brush, dug a small pit in the middle, and built a little wall with the dirt. He laid a bed of pine needles on the bottom for tinder, then some dry twigs and strips of bark for the next layer. When he had a pyramid built, he struck a match from a c-ration sundry pack. As soon as the kindling was ablaze, he added sticks, then logs, until he had a roaring fire that sent sparks shooting skyward in the updraft.

As darkness fell, and the mosquitoes accumulated in droves, he laid dried moss on the fire. The black smoke made a fairly efficient smudge pot. Without an axe, he resorted to the old Indian trick of arranging long logs around the fire like the spokes of a wheel. As the ends burned off, he shoved them in a little farther.

With twelve c-ration meals he could afford to be selective. He chose whatever he wanted to eat, heated the cans over the open fire, and ate to his heart's — and his stomach's — content. Then he sat and stared at the fire, mesmerized by the flickering tongues of flame, and warmed by the cherry red embers.

He made his bedroll under the stars, close enough to the fire so he could waken every hour and push in the logs. After the confusion of the barracks and the constant harassment of army life, it was good to be alone. Instead of snoring, sleep talking, and creaky bedsprings, Tony's ears were filled with nature's concerto: burping tree frogs, hooting owls, and scratching rodents.

The solitude that would be unendurable loneliness to most people was a soporific to Tony. He slept peacefully until long after daybreak.

By morning his muscles were stiff and raw from the cold that seeped up from the hard ground and through his bed of pine needles. The single blanket was woefully inadequate. He did a fast thirty pushups to increase the circulation of his blood, then shook out his boots and pulled them on.

The sky was gray, the grass wet. There had been no dawn, just a gradual lessening of darkness. But near the horizon he could see patches of blue.

He rejuvenated the fire and boiled water in his canteen cup. Over coffee, he scavenged through the case of c-rations and pulled out all the cans of fruit. Their liquid content would help in case Velden did not show up with more water. Later, deep in the woods, he dug a hole in the thick moss in which to stash the call of nature. Then he washed his face and hands in a trickle of water; the stinging iciness brought him to full wakefulness.

Because of the incipient cold, he decided to keep on the move. He ventured across the jeep trail onto the wide prairie, scouting for signs of animal life. He found nothing but cow dung, distinctly out of place. After lunch, the sun played hide and seek with the clouds, bringing little additional warmth.

He tramped into the lush jungle and found, to his surprise, that a few hundred yards away the ground elevated and dried off. In the thinner pine forest he chased scurrying lizards, listened to the songs of unidentified birds, swatted insects, and caught a glimpse of several prehistoric-looking armadillos as they receded into their holes at his approach. For most of the day he read; he had had enough forethought to stuff some paperbacks in his pack.

That evening he made hot chocolate and sat by the fire, watching the bright orange ball of the sun project its last shimmering glow across the hazy sky. When it slipped quietly away, and twilight melted into night, the clouds won possession of the sky. With the first patter of rain, he picked up handfuls of his bed and transferred it to the inner gloom of the tent, then closed the flaps.

He had another long sleep.

A deep-throated rumble brought him to consciousness. It could have been a foghorn, or a tugboat. He rubbed his eyes and saw sun streaming in through the rents and buckshot holes that peppered the canvas. Then he felt the ground vibrate, heard the crunching of wood and underbrush. He parted the flap.

Ten feet away, on the far side of the fire pit, a fat cow eyed him curiously. She was either munching or chewing her cud.

A stentorian moo caused him to look to the left. He saw not just another cow, but an entire herd of cattle — fifteen animals altogether. Some stamped down the dirt road, others grazed in the clearing. As he slipped out of the tent, several massive heads turned in his direction, and large, dark eyes scrutinized him suspiciously.

Tony plucked a tuft of grass and held it out in front of him. "Here, cow. Here, cow. Nice cow."

The general direction of the herd changed a few degrees.

"Come on, cows, I'm not going to hurt you."

The tempo of mooing increased as they veered more sharply toward the open pasture. Only a few continued to graze. Tony stood still until they stopped retreating, then he advanced on them a step at a time. The myopic cattle put their hooves in motion and sauntered away.

Tony picked up the pace, heading straight toward the milling cattle. He did not get much closer before they moved out of reach as one connected mass of flesh. When Tony ran, they ran, like rocking horses: stiff-backed and rigid-legged. They displayed a surprising agility for creatures so immense.

They slowed to a halt about a hundred yards away. A disconcerted mob, the frightened cows had instinctively closed ranks until they were a tight bundle of beef. Several mooed forlornly. Tony stood his ground, neither advancing nor retreating, and gradually some of them returned to grazing.

As soon as they seemed to have settled down, Tony started an oblique approach. As he walked from side to side, he closed ranks with them. By now they were wary of him, and showed signs of distress. Huge heads swung, and dark eyes, the size of silver dollars, ogled.

Suddenly, Tony let out a bloodthirsty scream, and charged. The herd stampeded into action, racing across the grassland like a bunch of scared rabbits running from a pack of hounds. Legs pushed at the ground like pile drivers, throats mooed like bulldozers.

Experiencing racial déjà vu, Tony became an Indian hunting bison. In the thrill of the chase he shouted atavistically, galloping across the veldt in pursuit of food, lusting after meat on the hoof, forcing the dimwitted animals to their deaths over a sheer cliff face, hacking flesh off bone with a stone knife, gorging on blood and warm meat, cutting out a still-beating heart and feeling its superstitious power.

He laughed out loud at the incongruity of a one hundred seventy pound man putting to rout beasts that weighed over a thousand pounds each: nearly ten tons of hulking protoplasm. Yet, as fast as he could keep his feet moving, he could not catch the lumbering but limber beasts.

With his lungs screaming for air and his legs aching, he finally had to concede the race. "I only wanted to pet you, you stupid cows."

Several hundred yards away, the herd slowed to a standstill, mooing and milling. Condensation masked their faces as massive lungs labored. Tails switched back and forth like twisted cables.

Still panting, and having had enough morning exercise, Tony headed back toward camp for breakfast. The episode had brought him over half a mile across the sloping field. But he had not gone far before he heard the ground rumble, as if an armored personnel carrier were chewing the ground. He scanned the road to the left and right, but saw nothing. Yet, the sound was becoming louder — he could feel it through the soles of his boots.

Some hidden sense warned him to turn around. His eyes widened as he saw an enraged bull charging toward him like a speeding freight train. Staring unbelievingly, he momentarily stopped dead in his tracks. The bull skidded to a halt a scant fifty feet away, his dark mane raised in terrifying profile, and steam

shooting from his nostrils like a fire-breathing dragon. The bull dug his hooves into the ground, first one, then the other, and kicked back clods of dirt and grass. With each pawing motion came a snort like the thump of a mortar round.

"I thought they only did that in cartoons," Tony breathed.

As soon as he realized his predicament, he turned and ran like the wind. And as soon as *he* ran, the bull ran. The tent was in sight, but how much protection did a thin layer of rotting canvas offer? Perhaps the forest beyond —

Tony glanced over his shoulder, saw the bull gaining on him. If he could only reach his rifle, perhaps the noise of exploding blanks could scare off the bull. Tony tripped, and went down headlong. He spun around and faced the beast, sitting.

As if he had run into an invisible force field, the mad bull skidded to a halt. Again he snorted and pawed viciously at the ground.

Tony swallowed hard. Without taking his eyes off the animal, he pushed himself to his feet. Still, the bull did not charge. Tony stared. The bull stared back. Tony took a step forward. The bull snorted, but backed half a step, and kicked up huge clods of earth. A broad smile broke out on Tony's face.

He turned his body, but kept an eye on the bull. He moved slowly toward the tent. The bull followed — but only when Tony was not looking. He started walking briskly. The bull picked up speed. He stopped and turned. Half a ton of destructive power came to a thundering halt.

Tony spun on his heel and raced full bore for camp. The bull took up the charge. Tony waited until the animal was racing at top speed, then he stopped short and whipped around, let out a banshee yell, and charged toward the bull.

The bull jerked back like a dog on an anchored leash. As Tony continued to run toward him, the bull pivoted on all four hooves, digging at the ground to get his momentum going. Tony kept shouting and running. The bull kept going — all the way down into the valley until he reached the safety of his harem. He hid among the milling cows, never offering a backward glance.

Tony remembered the word of Sergeant Hawkins. "Aggression."

Chapter 68

"How'd you enjoy your weekend?" Terry said, with mock sarcasm.

"What are you, a wise guy?" Tony threw his pack and web gear on the ground. "I spent two days and three nights out in the woods guarding two tents that had been sitting there since the time of Moses, and were so full of buckshot I had to sweep the lead off the ground. They've got cattle ranches out there, and the local cowboys use our bivouac areas for target practice. The only good thing I can say is, I got lots of rest."

"Wish I could say the same." Terry shifted his steel pot and rubbed his head. "I think I had a good time, but I don't remember too much about it. One thing for sure — I was feeling no pain."

"You wasn't feelin' nuthin'." Hays kneeled on the ground, rolling up his blanket and poncho. "She-e-e-eet, you was blasted away and unconscious for two days straight. You didn't know if you was comin', goin', or standin' still."

"Yeah, it was great."

"You may think it's great now, pardner, but when you wake up in the Nam, you won't know which end o' the rifle to hold. Then your ass is gonna be in big trouble."

Terry waved Hays off. "I'm just trying to cram as much fun as possible into the next couple of months, in case there's no time to do it afterwards."

"You pay attention to what's goin' on now, an' you'll have a better chance of bein' aroun' later on. You gotta stay off them joints."

"I'll have you know that not one breath of foul air passed through these cherry lips since Thursday night."

"Then what the hell were you so high on?"

Terry reached under his shirt button flap and pulled out a plastic pill bottle. He poured the Darvons into his hand. The slender capsules were two-tone in color: red and white. "What you do is this. You break open the capsule and dump out the white powder — that's nothing but aspirin. What's left is this tiny bead, the pure Darvon, the real worker. Well, you pop about five or six of these, and in no time you're flying high enough to keep tabs on 707s."

Hays looked at Tony. "And without chu to keep an eye on 'em, I got stuck with the detail. Had to drag him and the rest of the weirdos home like a mother hen."

"You talk pretty highhanded for an ex-head yourself," Terry accused.

"Yeah, but I seen the light. I ain't goin' over there to get my black ass blown away. Soon's I do my time, I'm home, home on the range. Mebbe then I'll think about takin' up the weed, when I don't have to dodge nothin' but hailstones and cattle shit."

"Well, I'm not afraid of getting scratched. My motto is drink, fuck, and get high, for tomorrow we die."

Tony interrupted. "With an attitude like that, you're going to make things happen."

"You go ahead and play soldier boy if you want. But me, I'm gonna have the time of my life — here, there, and everywhere. And don't you try to stop me."

Terry stalked off and joined the other potheads.

"Well, if that don't beat all." Hays pushed a clawed hand under his steel pot and scratched his head.

"Don't give up, Hays. We've got to show these guys this is serious business."

"A guy like him I don't even want proddin' cattle outa the brakes, much less pokin' gooks out a spider hole."

"Hey, that reminds me. *You* know something about cows, and I've got this bull story to tell you . . ."

****

Tony walked cautiously through the minefield, alert for any unnatural mounds of dirt or evidence of recent digging. He scanned with his eyes, and felt with his feet. With each step forward, a tingle ran up the calf of his leg: would he hear that fateful click that meant a primer had been set?

The brown sidewalls of anthills rose several inches above the ground, and contrasted sharply against the pearly whiteness of the sand. A flurry of activity surrounded each tiny hill. Low bushes squatted haphazardly throughout the level expanse, their green foliage glittering in the heat of the afternoon sun.

"Mine!" he called out, loud and clear. The platoon froze like a frozen frame in a motion picture.

Sergeant Holtz stepped slowly behind him, his boots filling Tony's tracks. "Check it out." While Tony bent to inspect the trip wire, the sergeant said louder, to the platoon, "Don't move around, but check out your area."

Tony studied the ground before he laid down his rifle. Then he got down to his knees and crouched before the taut piano wire. It was suspended about half an inch above the ground, running from bush to bush. He carefully lifted the stems and saw where the wire was tied to the woody base. Even more carefully, he followed the other end where the wire went through a grooved notch on the adjacent bush, angled down, and disappeared into the sand.

"Careful," Sergeant Holtz breathed.

Tony wiped sweat off his brow. Solidly planted on both knees, and poised forward, he studied the situation while he pulled the bayonet out of its sheath. Delicately, he prodded with the sharp point, feeling for a metallic contact. After several minutes of poking, he determined that the mine was twelve inches in diameter and less than an inch underground. He gently fanned the sand off it.

It took several more minutes of slow work to uncover the top and expose the triggering mechanism. The final touches he made by blowing across the rusting, iron surface. The platoon watched silently, the only sound being that of Tony's own forced breathing. Sergeant Holtz moved so that his shadow did not obscure the precision work. The mine was smooth on top, and tapered down toward the edges like an inverted dinner bowl.

Tony laid down the bayonet, wiped both hands on his pants until they were devoid of sweat and sand. With thumb and forefinger, he grasped the plunger where it was attached to the trip wire, and squeezed. As long as he held it, the spring release was immobilized. Then he unscrewed the detonator, and the mine was disarmed.

Sergeant Holtz was right behind him. "Remember, Charlie is one smart son of a bitch."

Picking up the bayonet again, Tony poked it gently under the mine, in case it had been booby-trapped with another. After a thorough examination, he cast a glance at the sergeant for approval. The sergeant jerked his chin down once. With shaking hands, Tony lifted the mine out of its hole. Nothing happened. He started to breath again.

"Good work. Okay, men, move out."

****

"She-e-e-eet, you jumped two feet in the air when you tripped that mine."

Terry chugged water from his canteen. "What the hell did you expect? The damn thing went off practically in my ear. Why the hell do they put blasting caps in the primers?"

"They gotta have some way o' lettin' you know you fucked up."

"All right, already, so I made a mistake. They don't have to scare the shit out of me."

Hays unfolded his entrenching tool and tightened the nut. "If they scared all the shit outa you, they could carry you away in a ammo can."

"Yeah, well, how'd I know the damn thing was going to be so slippery?"

"If you'd a been in class the day we studied 'em, instead o' runnin' off on sick call to get more o' them pills, you'd have known."

Tony threw another shovel full of dirt out of his foxhole. "Hey, can you guys work while you reminisce? The sergeant's going to be coming along any minute, and you'd better be four feet underground by the time he does."

"That nigger's going to be six feet under if he doesn't shut his fucking mouth."

"I like you, too, whitey." Hays turned his attention to Tony. "I hit a fuckin' root. Maybe I'll jus' dig down three feet an' crouch all night." He swung the entrenching tool like an axe, and

hacked away at the thick root. When it separated, he tossed it over his shoulder into Terry's hole.

"Hey, watch what you're doing."

"Don't get mad. I was jus' rootin' for ya."

"Yeah, well, you damn near killed me — with the pun, not the root."

"Hey, ain't you guys done yet?" The squeaky voice belonged to Pops. He stood with hands on hips, looking less than resplendent in his baggy fatigues. Terry leaned against the side of his foxhole. "What're you, a mole?"

"When you're short, you don't have so far to go." Pops demonstrated with his hand. "Just like the good sergeant said: chest high in the hole, chin high with the dirt."

"The world is full of comedians," Terry complained. "But why, dear lord, do they all have to be in my squad? Hey, make yourself useful and punch some of these ants in the kneecaps, will you?"

Pops ignored him. "Listen, as long as you guys are in those holes and I'm up here, I'm taller than you. So I aim to stay here and enjoy it."

"Yeah, but you're still the only guy I know who can swing from tree roots without getting his feet dirty."

"When I want noise out of you I'll rattle your cage."

"But you have to stand on your toes to be even with the ground."

Pops ignored him and wandered to Hays' foxhole. "What're you doing, praying?"

His dark head popped up a few seconds later. "I'm trying to ignore you two idgits by diggin' a sump hole. Or did you forget that?"

Terry shouted, "Come on, baby, nobody's going to throw grenades at us. This is only practice. Save the crap for the real war. And listen, I got something that'll brighten up your pearly whites: the chow wagon is on the way. We get to eat real food tonight."

Hays salaamed from inside his hole. "Hallelujah."

"Thank god," Pops said.

"Hey, what're you guys complaining about?" Tony threw another load of dirt in front, and packed it down. "You act as if you've been on C's for a month. You only had them for lunch today. I've been eating them for three days."

"I'll try anything once." Terry climbed out of his hole and threw down his entrenching tool. He took Pops by the arm. "But once was enough. What say you and me go rest under a tree till the mess truck gets here?"

Tony scraped the sidewalls smooth, and made sure his sump hole was wide enough and deep enough to swallow a grenade before pronouncing his work complete. After supper, Sergeant Holtz made an inspection of the hill and their defensive positions.

"You're looking good, men, but I notice that some of you did not dig sump holes, so I'm going to ream you for it. Get in the habit now of doing the right thing, so you won't forget when the time comes. That's the purpose of training. Now, after dark, we will go on fifty percent alert — I want a man in every other fighting hole. Two hour shifts. When you're not on duty, you can wander around as long as you stay within the company perimeter. But I'll be checking — and smelling."

While the rest of the men were making the additions to their holes, Hays ran around chanting, "I tole you so. I tole you so. I tole you so."

****

"Okay, first let's go over what we learned yesterday about mines." The platoon gathered around Sergeant Holtz. It was another hot day, and he let them remove their steel pots while he lectured.

"Antipersonnel mines are designed to injure, not to kill. A man killed is only one man out of action, but a man injured means at least three are taken out — two to carry him away, maybe a medic to take care of him. A wounded man also means a vast and complicated backup organization such as medical evacuation helicopters, first aid stations, field hospitals, surgical facilities, and medical supplies. It means doctors, nurses, and orderlies. And while an injured man is recuperating it means other side effects at home: convalescent clinics, the financial drain on the country, and an emotional drain on friends and relatives. *And*, equally as important, the continuing psychological effect of fear. A dead man just means a body bag and a telegram, soon forgotten. Charlie's not out there to get you, he just wants to win the war — any way he can. He doesn't have to kill you to stop you from fighting; he can accomplish the same thing by blowing your little pinky off. And he knows it."

Sergeant Holtz paused for a breath. "Now, so far we've learned about the different types of mines, how to detect them, how to disarm them. Anyone who set off the blasting cap by stumbling over it, or failing to disarm it, has flunked. Okay, so you get a demerit. But the next time you make a mistake, you lose an arm, or a leg, or your balls. Today, we're going to learn about booby traps. The same rules for mines apply here. Their main purpose is to maim and maul, and cause morale problems.

"Now, most booby traps are homemade, usually by the innocent looking mamasan grinning toothlessly at you as you walk through her rice paddy, or by the papasan who doesn't bother to look up as you tramp through his village. The most easily obtainable material to the VC is bamboo. They use it for all sorts of things: walls, fences, matting, carts, and punji stakes. The punji stake is usually used as a defense around the villages and hamlets, just like stone walls and moats were used around castles. When they're shaved to a point and facing out, they're worse than barbed wire. You can't go over them or through them — you have to go around. And that's just what they want — to channel you onto a path loaded with booby traps, or backed up by a machine gun.

"But most punji stakes are hidden. They're set in holes and covered with leaves or shrubbery or loose sand, or even water. If you step on one it can go through your boot and your foot. It can sever tendons, cut nerves and blood vessels, and break bones. It won't kill, it just takes the man out of action. And to make sure he stays out of action, they smear human feces on the points so the wound becomes infected. And to make matters worse, sometimes they have barbs carved into them so it can't be pulled out — it has to go all the way through. And don't think that the jungle boots with the steel shanks are going to protect you — in most cases, unless you step on it lightly, they won't. Well, no one said war was all fun and games. This isn't a John Wayne movie where the bad guys drop dead from a shoulder wound and the hero lives long enough to smoke a cigarette and say some last words for his wife and repeat the Lord's Prayer. This is the real war, where men don't die clean. They die violently and explosively. Men lose arms and legs and fingers and eyes and faces, and chunks of flesh that never grow back. And I'm not just whistling Dixie. I'm trying to scare you, because the more scared you are, the more careful you'll be, and the better chance you have of coming back in one piece."

****

The mock village loomed eerily out of the forest. Bamboo shoots and leafy foliage mingled with morning mist to form a realistic vision that blended together like a fading watercolor. The aroma of boiling rice added a touch of verisimilitude that was broken only by the shrill call of itinerant swifts flitting through the trees. If one could imagine that they were a troop of monkeys, the illusion would have been complete.

"Hold up, men, and cut the chatter. This isn't a Sunday picnic."

As winter was approaching, each morning seemed to dawn a little colder, and the matting of long pine needles grew thicker. But an hour's hard walk warmed Tony's stiff muscles and dampened his clothes. He studied the impenetrable bamboo fence, each pole leaning out at a forty-five degree angle, and honed to razor sharpness.

Sergeant Holtz faced his platoon. "Okay, now, we're going to go single file along the path and we'll regroup inside. Now, I want you to look carefully along the sides of the trail and you'll see what we were talking about yesterday: punji stakes, trip wires, pitfalls, and sprung trees loaded with spikes. Of course, in the real war they'd be hidden as well as your claymores. And whatever you do, don't touch anything — just observe. Now, follow me — slowly."

Tony rushed to be in front, along with Hays, so he could better observe the booby traps as the sergeant pointed them out. The weird contrivances that huddled in profusion in the trees and shrubbery that lined the path were as ingenious as they were devilish: spikes, stakes, pieces of sharpened metal, and shards of glass. The human body could be ripped, torn, shredded, and severed a hundred different ways, with hidden knives, swinging blades, and leveled crossbows. There was no need for a live enemy.

After viewing the VC arsenal of snares and ambushes, they entered the village proper. Several corporals minded the village, dressed in traditional black pajamas but wearing U.S. combat boots. They cooked rice in the center square that was flanked by thatched huts.

"Now we're going to get into the shit," Sergeant Holtz said. "And I don't mean that stuff you guys have been smoking behind the barracks, either. This place has more booby traps than the whole Mekong Delta. They're loaded with blasting caps so you'll know when you trip one, and so I'll know you're not paying attention. Now, we're going through this village with a fine-toothed comb, and find every booby trap there is. Use the methods I showed you, take your time, and expect the unexpected. And remember, this ain't no Easter egg hunt. You got any questions, ask me. If you see anything suspicious, bring it to my attention. Okay, split up into squads and take on a hooch. The corporals'll be keeping score."

Approaching the nearest hut, Tony looked for the obvious things such as trip wires and primer buttons, while Hays inspected the bushes that grew along the front wall. The rest of the squad surrounded the bamboo building and leveled their rifles.

Tony shrugged his shoulders, Hays tilted his head. Tony took hold of the rope loop that served as a handle, inched it out, and ran his hand along the inner edge. Almost immediately he felt the trip wire at the top — one that would have triggered an explosion if he had jerked open the door. He called out to the cor-

poral, who made a notation in his pad. Then he disengaged the wire loop and eased open the door.

A blasting cap detonated slightly above the bottom hinge. Sheepishly, Tony crouched down and studied the leather thong that acted as a pivot, and saw the primer button that had been released when the door had been opened. A c-ration can had been used for the makeshift bomb.

"You're dead, Giovanni."

"I know, sarge."

"Okay, check it out and see where you went wrong. Remember, whatever you don't learn here, you learn over there."

****

"Did ya hear? A coupla guys in Company A got bit by a snake." Hays had no reason to raise his voice above a whisper because he and Tony were shoulder to shoulder, sharing the same foxhole.

"No, where'd you hear that?"

"Heard the mess sergeant tell Sergeant Waltham. Weren't none too concerned about it, neither. Thought it was a joke. Fuckin' nigger."

Tony slid down until his kneecaps jammed against the front of the hole.

"Hey, don't go talking about your own kind that way."

"Sergeant Williams may be black as pitch, but he ain't my kind. He's a real bastard. I know, I had him for KP last week. Jus' loves orderin' people around. Do this, do that, do this, do that. All day long, with no let up."

"Sounds like any other sergeant."

"Wait till you get KP. You'll find out."

Leaves rustled behind them, and Tony spun quickly. "Halt. Who's there?" A shadow separated itself from the trees. "Captain Whale. Persimmons."

Tony recognized the password. "Advance."

"At ease, men," the captain said casually, returning their salute. He crouched beside them and said in a mild voice, "We're going to have some psychological warfare training in a little while. Make sure you stay in your positions."

Then he was gone, moving along the line of foxholes.

"Now, what the hell is that all about?"

"I don't know, but if you wait you'll find out. Anyway, now you know why we're on hundred percent alert."

"She-e-e-eet, I'm always on hundred percent alert. An' I aim to stay that way. Ain't no sappers gonna sneak up on ole Hays."

After a long silence, Tony whispered, "Were they venomous snakes?"

"Nah."

Tony stared at the shapes of tall pines that were silhouetted against the dark sky. Without heat inversions, the stars appeared bright and untwinkling above them. A little while later, the trees began to sing.

Hays jumped up to his full height. "What the hell is that?"

Tony nostalgically identified the musical sounds of Glenn Miller. "Moonlight Serenade."

"That's not what I meant."

"That's what you asked."

Out of the darkness to the left, Terry called out from the foxhole that he shared with Pops. "Hey, you guys. What's going on?"

Tony saw the glow of a butt, strictly prohibited. "It's a USO show."

"Everybody's a fucking comedian."

A medley of Glenn Miller tunes continued for about ten minutes, then ended when a smooth, female voice called out from the trees.

"Hello, boys, this is Tokyo Rose with evening entertainment for all you GIs so far away from home on this dark, lonely night. I know how you must feel, out there in the jungle, missing your loved ones, aching to be with your family by a nice, cozy fire. Don't you wish this war were over, so you could go back to your wives and sweethearts, mothers and fathers, brothers and sisters? Wouldn't you like to be home right now?"

Nostalgia became a hollow ache in the middle of Tony's chest. The lovely, plaintive voice evoked emotions from within that he had thought were under control.

"Who is this fuckin' bitch?" Hays nearly screamed.

As if in answer to his question, the melancholy voice of Tokyo Rose droned on. "I know how lonely you boys are, sitting in the dark, in those ditches and foxholes, watching the stars. Don't you wish you could see the stars from your own back yard? Don't you wish you were there with the people you love?"

"What the fuck is she talkin' 'bout?" Hays' outburst was accompanied by shouts of derision from the men on both sides.

Catcalls rang out all along the perimeter: "Shut up, you bitch." "Pull the plug on that slut." "Goddamn it, someone give me some real bullets."

Tony slunk down in the narrow foxhole while visions of home ran through his head. He pictured his grandfather sick in bed, Patty getting fat with his child, his brother forlornly crying for attention, the smiling faces of Pete, Ben, Ray and Teddy, Katie, Marion, and Kathy. He had difficulty swallowing.

But Tokyo Rose did not let up. "And do you know what the saddest thing is about those people at home? They've forgotten all about you. They've forgotten how to care about you. They're so busy with their own lives, with having fun, with going out and having a good time, that they have forgotten that you're out here fighting for them. While you're out here all alone, your wives and girlfriends are busy going out with your friends, having a drink, eating together, making love. And there's nothing you can do about it because you're so far away from home, and so forgotten."

Tony could hardly hear the voice over the loudspeaker, now, for the screaming men. They were throwing rocks and sticks and anything they could get their hands on. All their missiles fell short, but they followed them up with oaths and curses. Several men climbed out of their holes. A riot was forming.

Abruptly, the voice stopped; the background static ceased: the transmission had been switched off. Gradually, the men calmed down. Eventually, silence returned, punctuated by stridulating crickets, the stray hooting of an owl. And with the return to reality, Tony felt a longing, a loneliness, that he had never felt before. At that moment, more than anything, he wanted to be home with his friends, with his grandfather, with his wife at the time of birth. He was filled with fear that the world would go on without him, that he would be a stranger upon his return.

He felt a hand on his shoulder. He had not realized that he was staring down into the blackness of the foxhole. He looked up, saw Hays through wavering sheets of water, felt the tears trickle down his cheeks.

"It's all right, bro. We gonna get outa this. You jus' hang in there. We all gonna be back in the saddle some day."

****

"Are you crazy? They got fucking alligators in that swamp. And the sarge is taking us out on a night patrol? Not me, brother."

"Terry, you're more likely to get bit by a mosquito than an alligator. They live in Florida, not Louisiana."

"Look at me, will you? I got so many welts, my face looks like a pimple ball. And the 'gators are too stupid to know they're not supposed to be here — they don't read the same books you do. I'm telling you, man, I'm getting out — and now."

He took a bottle of pills out of his pocket and, before Tony could stop him, uncorked the lid and swallowed them all.

"You idiot," Tony screamed. "You'll kill yourself." He grabbed the empty container, looked for a label. "What are these?"

Terry took out his canteen and drank some water. "Don't worry about what they are — all they'll do is make me sick. Now, you want to do me a favor, go get the sarge and tell him I'm sick. I will be by the time you get back here."

"Listen, stick your finger down your throat before they kill you."

"I'm telling you, it won't kill me. Now go get the sarge. And tell him to get my chauffeur ready." Terry sat down on the edge of his hole and stared out at the trees.

"Hays, do something."

"Ain't my province to stop someone from doin' what he wants, long's it don't hurt me none."

Tony shook his head, then went for help.

Sergeant Holtz put his hand on Terry's head. "Okay, he's got a fever. Get your things together and get over to the command tent. I'll get Corporal Velden to take you to the clinic."

A few minutes later, Tony and Hays helped load the stretcher into the back compartment of the ambulance truck.

Terry winked mischievously "See you in a couple days."

****

The air was thick and humid. A cloud cover had rolled in around sunset, obscuring the stars and making the darkness absolute.

"Okay, now, for night patrols we don't use the wedge formation or point men. Walk in single file, stay with your squad, and keep the man in front of you in sight at all times. Make sure your gear is tied down — we don't want any unnecessary noise. Squad leaders, I'll expect you to be responsible for your own men. Okay, let's go."

Bill Larson, acting squad leader, held them back until the other three squads went by.

"Hey, we got time for a smoke?" Pops wanted to know.

Larson watched the men streaming by. "No. And I don't want any joints pulled out, either."

"Hey, who the hell are you?"

"Yeah, give a guy a coupla temporary stripes, an' they crawl up his sleeve an' git into his head."

"I only asked a simple goddamn question, you don't have to jump down my throat."

Larson ignored their protests. "All right, everyone follow me. And stay close."

"That's one thing I'm *gonna* do."

"I got enough grass in my pocket to start a lawn."

"An' I got enough IOUs to start a bank. Got more than I can smoke in a month o' Sundays."

"Hey, you hear Terry's girl sent him some loose seeds Scotch-taped to the back of a postcard? Did it as a joke."

"Won't be no joke when they come an' take 'im away."

Hays cut through the banter. "Hey, will you guys stay close an' keep movin'?"

"What're you, afraid of getting lost?"

"She-e-eet, I ain't gonna get lost. But this is a patrol, goddamn it, an' I want to learn somethin' on it."

"The only thing you'll learn is — "

"Hey!" Larson shouted. "Keep it down, will ya, or the sergeant'll be on my ass."

Someone muttered under his breath, "Good for you."

The pine forest gradually yielded to a soggy moss that squished with every step. The route led down into a narrow ravine with sides slippery enough to send several men onto their fatigue bottoms. Moisture soaked into material, muddy water drowned boots.

"Tony, you with me?"

"Right on your exaggerated lumbar curve and protruding buttocks."

"Shut up back there," Larson cursed. "You wanta wake up the dead?"

Vines and brush swatted Tony's face. The swampy lowlands were thickly overgrown, dark and dank, and densely inhabited by mosquitoes. He slapped at them constantly, and waved his hands wildly as they buzzed around his ears. Sweat collected on his forehead. He kept bumping into trees.

For an hour they squished through putrid water, climbed over rotted logs, pushed through bushes as strong as wire fences, swatted, scratched, wiped, and cursed. A steady stream of perspiration dripped down from Tony's sweatband. His rifle kept tangling in the undergrowth. Branches lapped his face and poked him in the eyes. Mosquitoes grew thicker, louder, larger, bolder. There were no rest stops.

"Ouch!" Tony backed away, rubbing his forehead.

"What's up, bro?"

"I ran into your rifle. Why'd you stop?"

Larson's voice sounded preternaturally loud in the Stygian blackness. "Keep it down back there."

Hays was a phantom, dimly visible. "Sounds like they're crossin' a crick."

When the splashing stopped, Tony could hear Sergeant Holtz call out for the next man to cross. Hays took two steps forward and was immediately enveloped by the infernal blackness. Tony stood where he was and kept swatting mosquitoes.

"Come toward me. That's it, keep coming. Good, now go straight ahead and keep your rifle held high. No, over your head. That's right. Next."

Tony fought the suction of the mud and slurped ahead. Pungent odors arose from the turbid water. The mosquitoes took advantage of his predicament. He could see nothing but indistinct shapes: solid masses that turned out to be trees, invisible creatures that touched his cheek and became sticks or vines. He jumped back, startled, when one crazily branched tree trunk spoke to him.

"You're doing fine, but keep your rifle over your head," Sergeant Holtz murmured. His hand gripped Tony's elbow firmly and guided him along. "Keep going this way, to the left of that tree. Larson will guide you from there."

Two steps more and he was knee deep in water. The sergeant ordered the next man on. Tony held his rifle on level with his chin, where he could use it to swipe branches out of his way, and where he could wipe his forearm along his face to brush off mosquitoes.

By the time he reached the tree that Sergeant Holtz had pointed out, the water was mid way up his thighs. Leaning against the peeling trunk, he took a moment to transfer his wallet to his shirt pocket, and made sure the flap was buttoned securely.

The water was so warm that he could hardly feel it. But at the next step he sank in to his waist and almost became nauseated by the stench. He clung to some vines for support, and kept moving.

A voice called out of the darkness, "I hear you, but I can't see you. Follow my voice."

Tony homed in on the sound, turning sharply to the right. He waded for several more yards before the ground — thankfully — began to rise. He heard a rifle clatter, then a splash.

"Shit!" It was Larson's voice. Tony could see him now. When Tony reached water that rose only as high as his knees, he was standing beside the squad leader, who was wiping the butt of his rifle on his shirt. "Okay, just move along so there's room for the other guys."

He walked on a little farther, and found Hays standing high and dry on a mossy hillock. Tony slurped out of the water and stood beside him. About ten feet away, men from the other squads were wringing out wet clothes. Pops joined them in a moment, pouring water out of his steel pot.

"Water too deep for ya, short stuff?" Hays said.

"Smile when you say that so I'll know where to send my knuckles."

"Looks like half-pint got a couple quarts."

"Show some sympathy for your betters. Is it my fault Larson touched me and scared the shit outa me? I jumped away and fell down. Would've screamed if my mouth hadn't been underwater."

"Hey, shut up you guys," Larson yelled. "This is a patrol."

"Sorry." In a lower voice, "Man, if we live through this, we can live through anything."

After some more splashing, the whole squad was together. Sergeant Holtz dashed past and again took the lead. The platoon moved out.

"Come on, men," Larson urged. "We don't wanta get behind."

Pops lashed his steel pot on his head. "Did you hear about the butcher who backed into the meat grinder and got a little behind in his work?"

Everyone laughed except Larson. "Cut the comedy and get moving."

Hays said, "You been takin' voice lessons from Sergeant Waltham?"

Tony could practically *feel* Larson's eyes glaring as he plummeted through the underbrush. The ground started to rise, and the moss that they had been sliding down before, they now found themselves scampering up. The loose moss came out by the handful as Tony clawed up the steep slope. Soon, they were back in level, open pine forest, where the footing was easier. The clouds soon dissipated, letting the moon cast a garish white light on the land.

"Hey, Larson," Tony said. "Where are we going?"

"We're following the other squad, dumbo."

"Well, I don't hear them."

The men stopped immediately, and listened. The only sound that Tony heard was that of crickets rubbing their legs together. The mosquitoes had been left behind in the marsh.

"I heard them a little while ago," Larson said tentatively.

Tony dropped down to one knee. "There aren't any footprints, either."

"I know I heard them."

The men huddled together like grapes in a bunch, and buzzed like homeless bees.

"They can't be up front or the crickets wouldn't be chirping up there."

Larson spun around, once, twice. "Where the hell . . . "

He stepped to an opening in the trees. "This must be the path."

"Hey, where the hell you going?" Tony breathed a sigh of relief at the sergeant's unmistakable voice.

Faltering, Larson said, "Gee, sarge, we were following the other squad . . . "

"Well, you weren't doing a very good job of it. I heard what Giovanni said about the crickets. You got all your men here?"

"Uh, yeah. Sure."

Sergeant Holtz grinned in the moonlight. "Would you count them, just to humor me?" After the count, the sergeant said, "Okay, now follow me. And keep it tight."

Under his breath, Hays said, "You an' me got the same shadow, bro."

In short order they rejoined the rest of the platoon, on a dry knoll that protruded above the tops of the trees in the swamp. Sergeant Holtz led them through the woods with uncanny ability, and fifteen minutes later they arrived at the perimeter of their camp.

"Okay, go back to your fighting holes and don't worry about mounting a guard. Just get some sleep."

"Hey, sarge," Hays interrupted. "Is Vietnam really gonna be like this?"

"No, it'll be worse, 'cause somebody'll be shooting at you."

Chapter 69

"Okay, men, here's what we're doing."

Sergeant Holtz sat in a crouch with the platoon gathered around him in a semicircle. He doodled in the sand with a stick.

"We're going out on a simulated combat patrol. This means we'll be walking in a staggered V formation with point men front and rear. The most important thing on any patrol is silence: all straps are cinched down tight, no loose change in your pockets, canteens either full or empty so they don't slosh. Rifle slings are taut: you carry the weapon in your hand, not on your shoulder. You never know when you'll receive sniper fire, and there's nothing worse than being shot down with your rifle still on your back."

Tony shifted his web gear and tightened his pistol belt so he could swing his arms freely. The load did not feel heavy as long as the weight was distributed properly.

"Okay, we'll have First Squad on the right, Second Squad on the left, Third and Fourth behind. Eberly walk point, Lemle take left rear guard, Norton right rear guard. Make sure you know whether you're odd or even, and if anything happens and I call for a split, make sure you stay with your squad. Okay, since this is your first full-fledged daytime patrol, we're not going to do anything difficult. We'll go three or four miles and take our time. The terrain is flat and heavily forested, so make sure you always have the man in front of you in sight — if you get lost, everyone behind you gets lost. But keep your distance, too — no closer than five meters — so a grenade won't get more than one or two. Okay, let's form up and move out."

They headed south like a flock of migrating geese. Sergeant Holtz occupied a position in the middle of the formation from which he would shout instructions. "A little tighter on the left. Don't crowd the point man. Don't look at me, you're supposed to be looking for snipers and booby traps."

The sun peered down through the deep blue sky, just enough to make travel comfortable. Birds chirped merrily and flitted in the treetops. Tony recognized a mockingbird, and heard a blue jay, but the rest were too fast to identify, and their songs were unfamiliar.

The patrol went through forest and glade, veering as Sergeant Holtz called changes in direction. Tiny rivulets carved narrow grooves in the sandy soil. Nests of berry-sized black droppings attested to the prevalence of cottontail rabbits. For Tony, it was a pleasant stroll in the woods — carrying a rifle instead of a fishing rod.

After two hours, the sergeant referred once again to his compass, ordered a change in course. A half hour later they left the forest for broken, uneven land that was dotted with sagebrush, and that was deeply rutted from run off. Dirt mounds and foxholes, half filled in, lay scattered in an uneven pattern: the remnant of some previous patrol exercise.

"Okay, men, gather round." In a louder voice, "And pull in those point men. We're having instruction." While the familiar semicircle was forming, he said, "And check the ground for scorpions before you sit down."

Loose stones and sticks were kicked away.

"Okay, in case you guys don't think I know where we are, I'm going to give you a course in map reading. By now you should know the fundamentals of using a compass. If you missed it in boot camp, you can pick it up along the way. Team up with someone who knows when we start doing the exercises. For now, take a look at these maps while I explain how to use them."

Each pair received a topographic map, tinted green, and full of squiggly lines.

"Okay, let's go over some basics. All that green you see is forest, the blue is water, the blue with the funny looking bushes in it is swamp or marsh, and the white zones are clearings, like the one we're in now. Now, how can you tell this clearing from any other? Well, the most important thing about map reading is to never allow yourself to become lost. Always keep an eye open for landmarks — that way you're constantly checking yourself. But, if you do get turned around, you can always find yourself by studying those brown lines. They're contour intervals, and each one represents an elevation change of twenty feet . . . "

For the next hour, the sergeant droned on about the intricacies of map reading, and how to translate what was on the map into what they were seeing, and vice versa. They learned how to recognize hills and valleys, rivers and ponds and streams, roads and trails, buildings, boundaries, levees, power transmission lines, telephone lines, and pipe lines. They learned about benchmarks, and the idiosyncrasies of magnetic declination.

"Okay, men, take an hour for lunch. I want guards posted at all times, to be rotated every fifteen minutes. Stay within the perimeter, and don't get farther away than arm's reach from your rifle. Squad leaders, assign your men."

Larson was squad leader again; he had not earned any endearment from the men. "Hays and Haiburn, up first. You know the rules. Gormley and Kitson next. Johnson and Jordon. Giovanni and Kurtz."

As they retreated to the shade of a tree, Terry muttered, "If this gets any harder, I'm going to take some more pills and miss a few more days."

"You take too many and you'll be missing the rest of your life." Tony heard squirrels chattering overhead, angry at the encroachment. He could not see them; only madly swinging tree limbs gave away their location. "Be careful."

Terry leaned against the tree. He looked down sharply, kicking savagely at the ground. "Scorpions?"

It was already too late. "Sap."

"Who's a sap?"

Tony pulled Terry's shoulder away from the tree. Sap oozed through the damaged bark, and stuck to the back of his shirt.

"Shit." He tried to wipe it off, but succeeded only in smearing the sticky substance on his hands. "Goddamn."

Smiling softly, Tony sat down with his rifle across his lap and took out a box of c-rations. He opened a can and started to eat.

"This is the pits. This just isn't for me."

With a mouthful of beef and potatoes: "What isn't?"

Terry gave up on the shirt, sat down, and tore open a box of C's. "I'm not cut out for this shit: traipsing through the woods, eating out of cans, dodging wild animals and poisonous snakes and giant man-eating mosquitoes. It's frightening."

"Don't tell me you're scared."

"Of course not. It's just frightening, that's all."

"Terry, what's there to be afraid of? Rabbits and squirrels? Birds and frogs? A few armadillos?"

Terry dug a spoon into chicken and rice. "You forgot to mention snakes. Poisonous snakes."

Tony did not mention the two men in Alpha Company. "Come on, we haven't seen a snake yet. And chances are they're more afraid of you than you are of them.

"That remains to be seen."

"And if we do come across any snakes, they'll run away as soon as they hear us coming."

"Snakes can't run. They don't have feet."

"How can you be afraid, with the things you do?"

"But that stuff's normal, see. I'm used to the city threats: freeways, bars, brawls, knife fights, smoking pot, dropping acid."

Tony opened a can of fruit. "Statistically speaking, you have a better chance of getting killed on the highway than you do in Vietnam."

"Not when your MOS is 11B10. Bullets travel both ways, you know. And the woods are for the birds. I'm from California, see. We're civilized out there. We're progressive. We know where it's at."

"Do you know where Vietnam is 'at'?"

"Hell, it's so far away it doesn't matter. The only thing you know about it is what the high-hats want you to believe. And the only thing the gooks know is what *their* government wants *them* to believe. Hell, they were better off under the French. Now they decide they — "

Tony had heard it all before — and in almost identical words. "And Hitler thought you'd be better off as a Nazi."

" — made a mistake and they want us to come save their ass for them. And don't give me any more of that communist domino bullshit. I've heard it all already. That's a civil war over there and we have no business sticking our noses in it."

"We always stick our noses into world affairs, fighting for the underdog."

"Maybe your 'we' does, but not my 'we'. I'd have been better off staying a protester. If I live through this shit, I might just change my name and disappear for a while, until this scene blows over."

Tony shook his head. "You'll only get into more trouble, then."

"I'm not worried about getting into trouble. I'm used to it. I'm worried about getting my legs blown off by some goddamn fucking mine. What's a few years in the slammer compared to a lifetime of paraplegia?"

"But if you learn how to be careful — "

"Hey! Where's the goddamn sentry?" Sergeant Holtz strode to where Larson was casually finishing his meal. "Where the hell is he? Larson, you're supposed to have a man posted at all times."

"Uh, gee, sarge, I told Haiburn what to do — "

"You *told* him? You're supposed to check up on your men when you're in charge. Now, where the hell is he?"

Pops was running through the trees toward the ruckus, hiking up his pants. "Here I am, sarge. Here I am."

"What the hell do you think you're doing?"

"Nothing, sarge. I was just taking a shit."

"And where were you taking it? To Charlie's back yard? This is supposed to be a reconnaissance patrol in enemy territory, or weren't you listening? You don't know who's out there.

There could be VC behind every bush, and you'd have your ass blown off by now so you wouldn't have to wipe it."

"Sarge, I was only — "

"Shut up, soldier. This isn't any game we're playing. Your life is at stake. And every time you do something stupid, you endanger the life of every other man in the outfit. So start getting used to the fact that we act as a unit. We do everything together. We eat together, we sleep together, we shit together, and maybe we'll come out of this alive together. Do I make myself clear?"

Pops swallowed visibly, thoroughly cowed. "I'm sorry, sarge. I guess I just wasn't thinking. It won't happen again."

"If it does, it may be the last time."

****

"What's it say next, bro?"

"Two hundred sixty-seven degrees, two hundred twenty yards." Five metal flags were nailed to a stout wooden pole, pointing in different directions like road signs. The number on one of them coincided with the number on the card that Sergeant Holtz had given to Tony. "That's almost due west."

"Good. Then all we hafta do is follow the sun. It's afternoon, so it's going our way."

"It's not that simple." Tony wrote the numbers on the card. "You see, because of the inclination of the Earth — twenty three and a half degrees — the sun never rises exactly in the east or sets exactly in the west, unless you're on the equator — "

"Spare me the astronomy lesson. I just wanna know how to get to the next pole."

Tony held the compass to his cheek. Looking down through the half-folded lens until he found the degree marking, he aligned the vertical sighting wire with a distant tree. He carefully counted his paces until he reached it.

Pops tramped out of the woods, his eyes glued to the compass instead of where he was going. His short legs made him appear like a circus clown because his long pants bloused so large above his boots. Behind him, Terry stared into the trees like a bird watcher.

"Hey. Where're you going?" Tony shouted.

"Hey, bro. What's happening?"

"Goddamn it, you made me lose count," Pops said caustically.

"With them short legs it should be up aroun' a million and a half."

Tony shook his head. "That's not the way you're supposed to do it."

"Yeah," Hays added, as they came closer. "You're supposed to pick out a target an' aim for it."

The two men halted, Terry cradling his rifle as if he were holding a baby. "Well, we could-n't find anything going across that field, so what're we supposed to do?"

"One of you watches the compass and the other goes out and becomes the target," Tony said. "That's how Hays and I did it."

Pops slapped his forehead with the palm of his hand. "Now I remember. I couldn't figure it out before."

Terry said, "What's wrong with this way?"

"Too much deviation. You can't follow a perfectly straight line just by watching the needle."

"It's going to take more than a compass to make me go straight."

Pops shrugged his shoulders. "It doesn't matter anyway. According to my count we're about a hundred paces past where our third post is supposed to be."

"Hey, you got any water?" Terry said. "We've been wandering around out here for hours. I'll be glad to get back to the barracks."

Tony handed him a canteen. "I suggest you shoot a back azimuth and start over."

Terry took a long drink and passed the canteen to Pops. "Thanks. Come on, Shorty. Let's go back to that last pole."

Gurgling: "Think you can find it?"

"Nah. But if we don't we'll just wander around until we come across it."

Pops snapped the compass shut, returned the canteen, and the pair turned and headed back into the woods.

When they were gone, Hays said, "Are those two really going to Vietnam?"

****

Tony and Hays were the first men back from the compass course. Others straggled in over the course of the next two hours. When the last of the stray lambs arrived, Sergeant Holtz gathered them around as a sheep dog gathers his flock.

"Okay, men, listen up. Now, I'm not going to yell at you fellows that fucked up today. But I do want it to be a lesson to you — if you get lost in Charlie's territory you may not be so lucky. Tomorrow we're going to come out here and try it again — not as punishment, just for practice. And for those of you who seemed a little confused, I'm going to team you up with someone who knows which end of the needle points north. And I don't want you to just follow him around. You have to take an active part in learning, for your own good.

"Let me give you some simple statistics. A year ago in July, President Johnson announced that U.S. forces in Vietnam would be raised from 75,000 to 125,000. People squawked, but they still went. A month ago, U.S. military strength rose to 300,000. People are still squawking, but soldiers are still going. In another year there may be as many as half a million of our men fighting over there. And you're going to be one of them. So pay attention. The life you save may be your own."

Groans accompanied his next set of statistics.

"Now, we're due back at the barracks at seventeen hundred. Because some of you jokers extended your walk in the woods, we're running behind schedule. That means that we're going to have to run in order to make formation. So let's hit it."

The first half-mile took them through the woods and over some very difficult terrain. They dodged trees, jumped over logs and small streams, tore through brambles, and climbed hills. Tony was breathing pretty hard, and his shoulders ached from the weight of the pack and from holding the rifle at port arms.

They emerged onto a tank trail and the going got rougher. The loamy soil had been ground to fine sand that sucked at his boots, making every step pure torture. Without a steady purchase for the launching foot, he felt as if he were sliding backward with each forward lunge. And once out of the protection of the forest, shade was at a premium. His throat was as dry as his canteen.

After twenty minutes, the tank trail merged with a macadam road. Without a break, they jogged along in late afternoon heat. Sergeant Holtz began singing cadence, the men adding the chorus. Tony popped a smooth pebble into his mouth and clamped it shut, sucking at the saliva.

Larson tapped him on the shoulder. "What's the matter, the songs not good enough for you?"

Tony pointed up to the sun, wiped sweat off his brow, and stabbed a finger at his mouth.

Larson jabbed the barrel of his rifle in Tony's ribs. "Start singing."

To make him understand, Tony removed the pebble and held it out for him to see. "If you keep your mouth shut it'll keep the dust out, and the stone causes salivation. It's an old Boy Scout trick."

A moment later, a rifle crashed against Tony's rib cage, knocking him aside. "Hey, what's the matter with you?"

"I said sing."

"Why don't you mind your own business?"

Larson intimidated him with his rifle. "Everybody in my squad sings."

"Look, I don't feel like singing, all right?"

"Leave him alone," Terry called back.

"Eyes up front, up there. This is none of your business," Larson shouted.

"You better watch who the fuck you're talkin' to, bro."

"I said turn around, or you'll end up on report with your buddy."

"You gonna end up dead, you keep this shit up."

For a long moment no one at the back of the formation was singing. No one said a word, they just breathed at each other. Then Sergeant Holtz dropped back, stared at the belligerents. Everyone joined the chorus until they rounded the final bend in the road and the pace increased to a trot. The rest of the company was already in formation.

"Fall right in, men," the sergeant called out.

Huffing and puffing, Tony bent over with hands on hips and tried to get back his breath. Captain Whale addressed the company.

"Men, I want you to know that I'm proud of the progress you've made in your first month of training. You've worked well together: as squads, as platoons, and as a company. Next week we're going to put some of what you've learned to a test — we're going on a five-day bivouac, this one a simulated patrol into enemy territory, and along the way we'll inspect more simulated Vietnamese villages, learn infiltration techniques, and find out how to — "

Without warning, something struck Tony in the jaw with the force of a hurled brick. He staggered out of rank, his right leg crumpled under him, and he hit the dirt with out-flung hands. His rifle clattered to the ground. He groveled on his hands and knees until two pairs of arms lifted him bodily and set him back on his feet. Groggily, he noticed that Terry and Hays were holding onto him.

"What happened?" he said.

Out of the corner of his eye he saw Sergeant Holtz approaching quickly. Hays thrust his rifle into his hands.

"What's going on here?" the sergeant demanded.

Several men looked around in stupefaction, as if nothing were wrong. Tony licked the inside of his mouth, swallowed blood. He was careful not to let any seep through clenched lips. After a while, and with many a backward glance, the sergeant ambled off.

Tony turned around and saw Larson smiling smugly, rubbing the knuckles of his right hand. The numbness in Tony's face made it difficult to speak. "Tonight. Behind the barracks. Eight o'clock."

****

Tension gripped the barrack air with the bristling, hair-raising tingle of a static discharge. The cadre were gone for the night, a lone orderly sat at the orderly room desk, the men were left to their own devices.

"Hold 'em up higher, bro. No, higher. That's it, but keep one close to your chest."

Tony did as he was told. "Like this?"

"That's good, but keep your guard lower." Hays positioned Tony's hand, threw a mock punch at his midriff. Tony blocked instinctively. "That's it. That's it. Now you're cookin'."

On his bunk, Terry folded a plastic bag full of grass. "And don't worry about a thing. If he starts to get the upper hand, I'll just step in from behind and lay him flat with a two-by-four."

"But that wouldn't be fair."

"Hey, bro, it ain't how you play the game, it's whether you win or lose."

"And how fair was he when he hit you from behind?"

The sudden surge of anger that Tony had felt at the time of the sneak attack had blended with the slow awakening of fear that he had acted rashly. His opponent not only had him by weight, but by experience.

"An' if you really get in trouble, kick him in the balls."

"But if I don't fight fair, he won't either. Then I'll be worse off than I was before."

"Not if you don't fight fair first," Terry said. Then as an afterthought, "Hey, I thought South Philly was a tough town, full of gangs and street fights. What happened to you?"

"That's just a stereotype, like blacks chucking spears."

"Bro, I can part your hair from fifty paces, an' give you a pompadour from twenty-five. You jus' do what I tole you an' you'll be all right. Get in there right away an' start throwin' punches. Don't worry 'bout hittin' him at first, just dazzle 'im with your handy-work. You don't win a fight by studyin' the situation — you win by hittin' him more'n he hits you. So git in there an' jus' keep punchin'."

Tony was still unsure of himself. "Suppose he does the same thing?"

"He won't. I watched him. He relies on his size, not speed. You're smaller so you got all the advantages."

Tony failed to see the logic in that.

"Besides, I started a rumor that you were a middle weight champion in college." Terry smirked as he twirled the joint in his fingers.

"An' if he beats you up, we gonna gang up on him later. Turn his face into meatloaf."

"Or Swiss steak."

"It's nice to know you'll be avenging my death. I wish I could be here to enjoy it."

"Don't be melodramatic." Terry looked at his watch, rolled out of his bunk. "Well, it's time to go. Ready?"

Tony's stomach was in knots, and his legs were shaking as he led them down the aisle past smiling faces and thumbs-up gestures. "As ready as I'll ever be."

"That's the spirit, bro. Jus' don't let him back you up. Clench him instead, and gut punch 'im. Do that an' you can't lose. Besides, it wouldn't look good on my record. As a fight manager I never lost a fight yet."

"How many fights have you managed?"

"You're the first."

"Great. That makes me feel good."

Outside, the light from the barrack windows cast an eerie yellow glow on the multitude of faces that formed the makeshift ring. Terry made way for Tony and his manager, pushing through the noisy throng.

"Do some limberin' up exercises, bro."

"But everybody's looking at me." Tony was more cowed now by the sea of men than by the prospect of getting thrashed.

"Never mind, here he comes."

Tony could see Larson's head above most of the others as he waded through the crowd. He had never quite realized how big his opponent was until now.

"All right, bro, get ready."

"He's not here yet."

"Don't give him a chance. As soon as he steps in the open, go after him." Twenty feet away, on the other side of the crude circle, two men parted.

Larson's features were hidden in the shade of his cap, but the breadth of his shoulders was not.

"Go get 'im."

Hays shoved Tony so hard that he stumbled the first few feet. When he regained his balance he knew there was nothing to do but continue forward. Larson glared down at him and started to open his mouth. Then Tony was on him, his left fist chalking up a body blow, his right partially deflected by Larson's upthrust arm.

"Wait a minute — "

Larson backed up at Tony's aggressive assault. He tried to ward off the blows that rained on him with thudding accuracy. Tony's tunnel vision prevented him from seeing anything but that stunned face, the craggy features, the thick arms moving defensively. When Larson crashed into the jeering crowd and could retreat no further, he threw his arms around Tony and wrestled with him.

"Will you listen — ?"

His grip was like two steel bands, pinioning Tony's arms to his side. He could barely struggle. He stuck one foot between Larson's outspread legs and twisted. They crashed on their sides, and Tony rolled away and was up on his feet in a flash.

"Kick 'im!"

"Crush the bastard!"

"Bash his face in!"

Tony assumed the defensive stance, fists

ready.

Slowly, Larson rolled up to his knees, breast heaving, lips and nose bleeding. "Will you listen for a minute?"

"Watch out, bro. It's a trick."

"Get him while he's down."

Tony never took his eyes off Larson's steely grays. "Come on, big mouth. Get up."

Larson blinked slowly, climbed to his feet. "Giovanni, I'm sorry. I don't want to fight."

Tony's tensed arms did not waver. He bent into a half crouch.

"Don't listen to him, it's a trick."

Blood trickled from the corner of Larson's mouth. He licked his cracked lips, wiped the blood off his nose with his sleeve.

"Listen, I just had some things on my mind. I shouldn't have hit you."

Tony ran his tongue around the inside of his mouth. "That's not going to reduce the swelling."

"I said I'm sorry. I — I know I was wrong. I don't want to make it any worse. I don't want — any trouble. I'm sorry."

The great head drooped, the eyes faltered, and Larson turned and pushed his way through the mocking hordes of faces and leering fists. Very slowly, Tony dropped his hands to his sides, almost refusing to believe the fight was over.

"Fucking bastard," Terry said. "He knew he was going to get his ass kicked."

Chapter 70

"How do you feel?"

"Like a piece of macadam that had been jackhammered for a day and a half."

"Imagine what it would be like if you lost."

Tony inspected the mirror. As a result of Larson's sucker punch, his cheek was puffed out as if a golf ball had invaded his mouth. "I'd rather not."

"I got something for you." Terry flushed the toilet, approached the sink with a swagger, rinsed off his hands, and emptied a bottle of pills onto his palm.

Tony eyed him suspiciously. They looked like tiny white ant eggs. "No thanks. I don't think getting high is going to solve anything."

"It's only penicillin."

"Where'd you get them?"

"From the dispensary, when I got bit by that wasp last week."

"Wasps don't bite, they sting. And we had bivouac last week."

"Okay, so it was the week before. It's not a jar of mayonnaise that'll go bad in the sun. It's just for infection."

Tony scowled, but took one of the tablets, grabbed a handful of water from the tap, and washed it down. "Antibiotics I can handle. Thanks."

"Take 'em all. I'm going on sick call in the morning so I can get some more tomorrow."

"What are you going for this time?"

"I don't know, but I'll think of something."

"Terry, I really don't think you should miss tomorrow's exercise. You need some more practice in compass and map reading."

"You gonna teach me?"

"I can't. I have KP. But Hays can help you. He was brought up finding his way through the woods."

"No thanks. I need a day off."

"You know, sooner or later Sergeant Holtz is going to get wise to your frequent trips to the clinic."

"So what? What's he going to do to me? Give me a demerit? Slap my hand? Put me on extra duty? Send me to Vietnam? What the hell, he can't do any more to me than is already going to happen. He can't hurt me."

"That's not the point. Why get into trouble when you don't have to?"

Terry rolled his eyes at the ceiling. "Tony, you've got to get it out of your head that you have to do everything you're told. Hey, if somebody tells you to jump off a bridge, are you going to do it? Then what makes you so eager to obey every rule, no matter how ridiculous, just because it's given by the army, or the government? Hell, the only reason I'm in the army is because it's the lesser of two evils. The alternative to the draft is five years in prison. Does that sound like freedom to you? What kind of freedom does a person have if his government can lock him up for no reason at all? Freedom in this country is bullshit. We'd be better off without any government at all, if that government has the arbitrary power to enslave its citizens."

"Given the present state of human nature, anarchy just doesn't work. Society needs a legal framework, and the individual has to live within the system. You've got to have some respect for authority or else — "

"Fuck authority. Authority is someone telling you that you can't do something you want to. Authority is someone telling you how to live your life. Authority is someone telling you that he has more control over your life than you do. Authority is someone telling you to go get killed in some goddamn country you never even heard of because some political do-gooder wants an epitaph on his tombstone and a page in the history books. Nobody has the right to tell you what to do, any more than you have the right to tell somebody else what to do. Christ, if everybody would just mind his own goddamn business instead of minding everybody else's, I'd be a civilian and we wouldn't have half the trouble we have in the world."

"But that's the whole idea behind this conflict. There are some nations that would like to subjugate other nations, weaker nations. And all we are doing is sticking up for the underdog."

"Bullshit. Let those people fight their own wars and let me fight mine."

"But they're not strong enough to fight on their own."

"Then maybe they don't deserve to live on their own."

Tony stared, his eyes pinched. "That's pretty cynical, don't you think?"

"Hell, no. It's realistic. It's survival of the fittest, and may the best man win, and all that. I have my own life to live, I don't have time to save the world."

"No one's asking you to save the world. All I'm saying is that you should share a little of the freedom you happen to have been born into. No one asked those people to be born in Vietnam; it's just an accident of birth."

"Yeah, sure. The next thing you know, you'll be talking about 'civic responsibility,' or some such nonsense."

Tony sighed deeply. "Terry, the world just wouldn't work if everyone just did as he pleased. You need some set of principles to make things run smoothly. And once you have them, you have to uphold them, or it doesn't make any sense. If you change your principles when they become uncomfortable, you really don't have any. Laws and codes and ethics are necessary to maintaining rationale in the world. If you start breaking them, the world begins to fall apart."

"You goddamn Catholics are all alike: God, home, and country, and never yourself. You treat law like the *Bible*. Laws are not immutable, like the law of gravity. They have to change with the times, and be flexible enough to suit circumstances. What're you going to do if you're taking your wife to the hospital in an emergency and you stop for a traffic light? Let her die while you're waiting for it to turn green, so you can say you observed the law?"

"That's being a bit simplistic. Besides, you're talking about ethics now, not law."

"But laws were made for people who either don't have or don't understand ethics. Laws are nothing more than a method of standardization, so you don't have to take the time to think about whether or not something's right or wrong; it's already been decided — by someone else. And besides, ethics change from country to country — even county to county. There are a lot of things you can do in this country that would get you locked up for life in another country."

"Exactly!" Tony triumphed. "And that's why we're fighting in Vietnam. We're trying to standardize our ethics, not just nationwide, but worldwide."

"Now you're being idealistic."

"I am not. I'm just looking at the big picture, treating the world as an extension of my family instead of a storehouse to plunder."

"Then, baby, you'd better start thinking more about yourself and less about the world, because you can't change it no matter how hard you try."

"I'm not trying to change the world, just my little corner of it. And if I have some excess humanity, I can afford to share it."

"I'm telling you, Tony, you have to start thinking more about number one. You want to help somebody else, donate to charity — but don't die for them, because they'll never appreciate it. The first thing you have to learn about right and wrong is what's right for you. That is the foundation of life. Everything else devolves from that. Fuck the rest of the world. It got along without you before, it'll get along without you after you're gone. And you're a fool if you think otherwise."

****
****

"You late, Giovanni."

His puffy, nearly immobile jaw was compounded by a throbbing headache that had kept him awake half the night. "I guess I'm feeling a little slow this morning, sarge."

"Well, I got just the thing to perk you up." In the heat of the kitchen, tiny droplets of perspiration glistened off ebony skin as if Sergeant Williams had just stepped out of the shower. "Git over there on them pots an' pans an' start scrubbin'. You already behind."

"Sure thing, sarge."

The sink was piled high with trays, saucepans, platters, and skillets. Tony remembered his bruised knuckles as soon as he plunged his hands into the hot soapy water. After his wounds were cauterized, he picked up a steel wool pad and worked with mechanical languor. Time passed painfully.

"Ain'tchu done with them trays?"

Tony must have been daydreaming, for he opened his eyes suddenly and found that he had been scouring a pot unawares. "I can't get down to them, sarge. They're too many things piled on top."

"So whatchu gonna do, leave 'em there all day?"

"Well, I hadn't really thought about it."

"Then start thinkin'. I need 'em right away."

Tony closed his eyes for a second, willed away the pain in his temples. "Okay, I'll get right on them."

"You better perk up, boy. You gots a lot more comin', so hop to it."

When he was gone, Tony sneaked the trays out from under the growing pile, and soaked them in the warm water. He seemed to be stuck in low gear; the sore jaw and aching temples held him back, like reins. Vaguely, he was aware of chow being served. He maintained his station and nursed a cup of coffee. By the time breakfast was over, he was entertaining a pile of ironmongery that was almost beyond reach. Before the delicately stacked kitchenware tumbled over like a fallen tree, he removed those pieces that were most unstable and started another pile at his feet.

"What the hell're you doin'?"

Tony put both wet hands in the small of his back and eased himself upright, groaning. "Washing pots and pans."

"Git that stuff off the floor. Nuthin' my men eat outa goes on the floor."

"But sarge, I'm running out of room. There's no other place — "

'I said git it off the floor an' I mean now."

"But, sarge — "

"Did you hear me?"

Tony bit his tongue. "Where do you want me to put them?"

"I don't care, jus' git 'em off the floor." Sergeant Williams stalked off, adding as a parting shot, "An' you better start workin', boy."

Wearily, he dragged two stools close to the stainless steel sink, and used them as a bench. He piled uncleaned kitchenware on them, then took some time to dash around and replace some items that were already washed. By the time he returned, more egg-splattered and greasy pans had been added to the tottering collection, and the pile was again on the brink of toppling over.

He had barely started to lower the stack when Sergeant Williams put in another appearance. "What's this?" he shouted, practically in Tony's ear.

He squinted through pounding eyes at the spot where the curled, black finger was pointing. On the lip of a ten-gallon steamer he saw a microscopic brown speck, and flicked it off with a water-softened fingernail.

"It's nothing."

"It's dirt!" The sergeant hurled the pot back into the sink, splashing hot water all over. "Now clean it again an' make sure it got no dirt on it."

Tony held onto the edge of the sink with both hands, his head drooping. He was sick, he was in pain, and he was quickly losing patience with the sergeant's demands. He took a few deep breaths, rinsed off the pot, dried it, and stored it. A little while later the sergeant returned.

"I need those two trays. Get 'em done. Now."

Sinking into a deeper lethargy, Tony realized that hurrying was not going to help. He was going to be here the entire day, no matter what. Meticulously, he cleared off the top layers of pans to get to the indicated trays. With slow, machinelike precision he washed, rinsed, and stored one item at a time. He hummed little tunes in his head to help pass the time of day.

"What did I tell you about doin' things right?"

Tony turned around and wiped sweat off his brow. "What's the beef this time?"

"There's dirt on this pot, an' I want it off! Now you clean it again."

"Sarge, how about if I just clean the dirty spot instead of the whole pot? It will help speed things up a bit."

He dropped it into the sink. "You'll do it all over again until you learn to do it right."

Tony picked up the pot and held it in the light. "You know, I don't see anything on here. Are you sure there's a dirty spot?"

"Look here, boy. I been a mess sergeant for twenty year, an' I know a dirty pot when I see one." He made jabbing motions with his right hand, poking Tony sharply in the chest. "An' just to show I mean business, you can clean 'em all over again. Everyone one of 'em."

Tony matched him decibel for decibel "Yeah, well, if you think you can do better, you wash them."

Tony whipped the dirty dishrag out of the sink and slapped it down hard onto the still outstretched hand. It hit with a splash that tossed drops of soapy water up into the mess sergeant's face. In the stunned silence that followed, Sergeant Williams stood with mouth agape, lower lip quivering. He paled to a lighter shade of brown.

When he started to recover, Tony grabbed a black iron frying pan by the handle and held it up threateningly. Sergeant Williams took one look at it, fell backward, and charged out of the kitchen. He hit the screen door without opening it, ripping out the latch and the lower hinge. It swung back at a drunken angle. Unintelligible obscenities filled the air.

After casting a baleful eye at his fellow KPs, Tony calmly turned back to the sink and resumed his work.

Five minutes later, Corporal Velden ducked under the torn door. "Giovanni, the captain would like to see you in his office."

Innocently, "Why, is something wrong?"

The corporal grinned broadly. "It sure looks that way."

With exaggerated slowness, Tony put down his steel wool, dried off his hands, tucked in his shirt, and made a pretense of combing his short hair with his hands. When he entered the orderly room, he saw Sergeant Williams babbling incoherently and gesticulating wildly. The first sergeant was trying to calm him down. Lieutenant Satterlee looked on from the security of his office, standing on the sill as if he was afraid to come out.

Corporal Velden indicated the captain's office. The door was open, so Tony knocked on the frame and announced himself. A hand waved him in. "You wanted to see me, sir?"

Captain Whale leaned on one elbow, palm covering his mouth. He wiped his hand down over his chin. With eyes narrowed and locked onto Tony's, he pursed his lips several times before speaking. "Giovanni, I understand you've had a little, uh, altercation, with Sergeant Williams?"

"Yes, sir. That's right."

The captain cleared his throat. "Would you like to tell me what it was all about?"

Tony thought about it for a moment. "No."

As if a board had hit him on the forehead, Captain Whale jerked back. "And why not?"

"Because it wouldn't do any good. He's a sergeant and I'm a private, and in the army that's the difference between right and wrong."

The captain took a deep breath, lurched up out of his chair. He paced for a moment behind his desk. "It's true that Sergeant Williams has the advantage of rank. And he's been with the company a good while. Served good food. I'm willing to admit, however, that at times he is a little on the ornery side . . . "

"*A little?*" For a moment Tony forgot his place. "Sorry, sir."

Captain Whale stopped short. "Under the circumstances I'll let it pass. But I want you to understand something. For the past month and a half we have been preaching cooperation, teaching you to act as a unit, working together. Naturally, there's always someone in charge, a noncom or an officer. That is military hierarchy. But out there in the field, things are different. The only real authority an officer has is what is ingrained into his men. They have to believe in him. They also have to accept his, let us say, personality. You don't have to like him, just accept him. As long as he does his job, you put up with his attitude. This is the way I treat Sergeant Williams, and it's the way I would like you to treat him. You have to take the good with the bad. So get back to work, do your best, and just try to stay out of his way."

A smirk spread across the captain's face. "And I'm sure he'll be staying out of yours."

****

Stars shone down from the midnight sky with a diffused brilliance, transforming the open field with its spotted shrubbery and tall trees into an alien landscape, like the surrealistic painting of another world.

"I thought you said there was going to be a moon tonight." Terry clenched his rifle between his legs as he straightened out his web gear. The engine sounds of the deuce-and-a-half, which had just deposited them in a secluded section of bayou, faded in the distance.

"There will be, but it won't be up for another — " Tony held his watch close to his face. " — thirty-five minutes."

Hays jumped around testily, as if warming up for a race. "How'd you know that?"

The rest of the men — except for Jordan, who was sick with a mild fever from a snake bite — huddled within ten feet of the drop-off point on the sandy trail. It was no accident that Tony had been selected as squad leader for their first solo night reconnaissance patrol.

"I noted the time the last night of bivouac, when it was on the wane."

"What's that mean? I'm a bit rusty on my 'stronomy. All's I can remember's when the moon's full it comes up at the same time the sun goes down."

"An old range rider like you? Well, when it wanes it gets smaller, and rises fifty minutes later each night. Tonight it's not due to rise until twelve thirty-five, and it'll be only a quarter moon."

"Hey, somebody help me with this buckle." Pops held his pistol belt apart. "And lay off about the moon. Sometimes you scare me, I think you know what you're talking about."

Gormley helped Pops snap the belt together while the rest of the men performed last minute checks. Tony checked the luminescent compass dial, aligned the bezel for their first course.

"I sure wish Sergeant Holtz were here," Terry lamented.

"She-e-e-eet, you don't even like the man."

"No, but I'd feel a whole lot safer with him."

Tony gripped his rifle by the sight; the sling had been removed. "What's the matter, don't you trust me?"

"It's not that, it's just that I trust the sergeant more. I still can't figure how he got us out of that swamp last week."

"He paid attention to where he was going. Now, let's remember, this is supposed to be a combat patrol in enemy territory, with VC and NVA all around. So let's keep the noise down and make believe it's real."

"Fuck all that simulation bullshit and let's get on with it," Terry fumbled in his pockets, brought out a plastic bag and some wrapping paper. "I've got a date with my bunk sometime tonight and I don't want to miss it."

"Bro, you better listen to what the man says, 'cause someday you may be doin' this on your own. Then you'll be sorry."

"Cut the crap and give me a match."

Not too loud, but very clearly, Tony said, "No smoking tonight."

Several seconds passed in stunned silence. "What — who — what are you talking about?"

"Terry, I don't want to pick on you. This is really for everyone. I — I don't — want to sound — authoritarian, *but*, there's a time and a place for that stuff. I mean, there's nothing wrong with having a little fun, but sometimes we have to knuckle down to serious business. And tonight, just for this once, I'd like to have you all play along with the game — just to humor me. And maybe for your own good."

"Jesus Christ, you sound like my old man."

"Hey, who made you king for a day?"

"Boy, give a guy a stripe and he tries to beat you with it."

"You're worse'n Larson here."

"You buckin' for sergeant?"

Tony waved them down. "Listen, I'm just — will you pipe down and give me a chance? All right, now, I just want to have some cooperation. If we do this exercise right, we'll be out of here in no time. But if you start smoking pot and getting high, if you get separated, we'll be out here all night. So let's just do the job and have our fun later."

"You've got a lot of nerve — "

"Bro, you better listen to the man. An' you most of all."

"Hey, what're you — "

"I'm standin' by what he says, not because he's the squad leader, but 'cause what he says is right. Now, we all in this together, so listen to the man."

Terry glared out from under his steel pot. "Okay, so talk."

"Well, I've already said my piece. Let's just get going. And you can help by counting your steps." Tony nodded to Hays, and started out in front, leading them along in single file like quacking ducklings.

"Hey, mister squad leader," Pops said, halfway between jest and jeer. "What're the chances of us meeting some of the other squads out here?"

"Probably none. They're all being dropped off at different locations, and at different times. We won't see them until we converge on the objective."

"You mean the truck that's supposed to be waiting for us?" asked Gormley.

"That's right."

"*If* we ever see it," Kitson said.

Larson spoke for the first time. "I think part of this exercise is to instill self-confidence, which means starting out with a positive attitude."

"Who rattled your cage?" Johnson chided.

"Hey, bro, how's about gettin' into the spirit? We gotta act as a team, an' Larson's part o' that team. Ain't that right?"

"Thanks, Hays."

Pops said in his tinny voice, "Yeah, well, maybe we don't want him on our team."

"Listen, I know you guys don't like me, and I really don't give a shit. But let's see if we can get along until this thing is over."

The terrain sloped downward and the ground became wetter. After another quarter mile, they were walking through a marsh that was intersticed with winding narrow brooks that bubbled around clumps of weeds that looked like shaggy mops.

Terry stumbled over a clod of cattails, and crashed into Larson, who held him up. "Thanks." His voice was without tone; he jerked his arm away.

"What's it look like, bro?"

Tony slowly shook his head. "Without the moon we can't see what's ahead. And without a map we can't check it out. It may get worse."

"Those bastards're trying to drown us," Johnson said gruffly.

"No, we can probably get through, but I think it might be better if we went around. There's bound to be some high ground around here."

"It gonna throw our calcalations off, bro."

"Yeah, how are you going to keep track of the distance?"

"Terry, we're *all* supposed to be keeping track of distance, not just me. And the way we'll do it is to interpolate."

Hays said, "What's that mean?"

"It just means that if we veer off at an angle for a hundred paces, we have to veer back the same amount, then do a little geometry to figure out the straight-line distance."

"Right on, bro."

"Yeah, can you do that in your head?" Terry wanted to know.

"Sure."

Pops squished his boots in the muddy water. "I think we're going to get lost. Aaaaggghhh." As he screamed, he practically jumped into Terry's arms.

"What the hell's the matter with you?" Terry pushed him off and regained his footing. "You scared the shit out of me."

"Something ran out from behind that bush."

"Weren't nothin' but a rabbit," Hays said, scowling.

Tony laughed. "Come on, Pops, you're not afraid of a little cotton tail, are you?"

"I ain't afraid of no tail, but how the hell was I supposed to know what it was? Why'd it have to run out like that?"

"What do you expect it to do, sit there and get trampled by eight pairs of combat boots? Come on, let's get going. Hays, are you still keeping count?"

"Five twenty-five."

"Good. I've got five hundred even. That's pretty close for terrain like this."

"Your terpolatin's prob'ly better'n mine. An' your calcalatin's right on time."

The moon crept above the surrounding forest. Tony could now see that the land ahead was an immense bog that was dotted with bushes on little islands. "Let's go more to the right where the marsh narrows by the woods. There'll be less water to cross."

The squad struck out through the wetlands, but avoided the streams that meandered like jumbled ropes, crisscrossing their path. Tony and Hays led the squad, while Larson kept a rear guard. The others in the middle huddled like baby birds in a covey, and cackled just as loudly. One thousand two hundred twenty-three paces later, according to Tony's count, he brought them to a halt by a wide trough of muddy water, its banks overgrown with thickets and brambles.

"Uh, oh," said Pops.

"Now what do we do?" Terry whined.

"No problem." Tony turned and started walking up the gradual rise. "Let's just walk upstream until it narrows enough to cross."

He tramped close to two hundred yards before he forced an opening through the bushes and found a bank that sank to the water's edge. A log bridged half the gap to the other side.

"I'll go first." Tony used his rifle as a cane, stepped out onto the sloping log. "Be careful, it's slippery." He dug his boots into the rotten wood. When he reached the point where the water covered the dead trunk, he measured the distance mentally and took a flying leap. He grabbed a handful of limbs as his feet sank into mud, then scrambled up the three-foot-high ledge onto the wet grass. "Okay, come on."

"Bro, back out the way." In one lithe motion Hays raced down the log and leaped high, landing on both feet next to Tony.

"Hey, I ain't got long legs like you."

"Don't worry, Pops. You light enough to climb acrost a spider web." Pops landed with a splash, then scrambled into Tony's and Hays' arms. They pulled him up. "Man, I don't like this at all."

"Jus' be glad it's too cold for skeeters."

"Always a bright side," said Tony.

"You guys are too much." Pops readjusted his web gear. "Hey, Terry, it's a walk in the park."

Just then Terry slipped off the log and fell headlong into the water. He came up an instant later, sputtering. "You fucking asshole. Who pushed me?" Laughter burst from the opposite bank while he splashed ashore. He ripped out handfuls of branches in his scramble, then slipped on the mud and slid right back in. "Why the fuck didn't you grab me?"

"My hand was out all the time," Hays said.

"How'm I supposed to see a black hand on a night like this?" He was halfway up the ledge the second time before he let out a scream. "Oh, Jesus Christ, I dropped my gun."

"Isn't it attached?" laughed Pops.

"Listen, half pint, if you weren't so short already I'd cut you down to size. Goddamn it, man, I dropped my gun in the crick."

"Here it is." Larson held a long branch in his hand and dragged it through the water. A moment later he pulled it out, dripping and muddy. "Can you catch it?"

"Yeah, I guess so." Larson threw it high, and Terry caught it with one hand. He aimed it down and poured water out of the barrel. "It's gonna take me a week to get this fucker clean."

Kitson yelled over, "It'd take you a year to pay for it."

"Always a bright side," Tony repeated.

Larson jumped across, then acted as an anchor for the others. One by one he caught them as they leaped onto the tree-lined, muddy bank.

Terry wrung out his clothes, hunched forward like an aged gnome. "I don't need any words of wisdom. Shit, I'm freezing."

"Then let's get moving."

"You want to go back down the creek to where we had to turn aside?" Larson asked.

"Yes, then we'll pick up our compass course again. We've still got a couple miles to go."

"Hey, I'm freezing. Can we talk while we walk?"

They proceeded through the marsh, taking a winding route that avoided any more stream crossings. The moon helped light the way until they entered a pine forest. That lasted only for half a mile, then they broke out from the fresh scent of pine into another open area that was suffused with the chemical odor of methane.

"Marsh gas," Tony said quietly. "One match would blow us all up."

The dank odor was visible in the form of white fog that clung to the ground. Swirling, crazy patterns looked like wraiths in the scattered moonlight. Shrubbery and clumps of grass took on weird, fantastic shapes that seemed to undulate as a gentle breeze made them sway.

"This is spooky," Terry whispered, through chattering teeth.

Hays surged ahead, but stopped when his boots sank into the dense plant growth, and water welled up out of the ground. Larson went farther. Tony could hear mud sucking at each step. He stopped and looked back.

"I ain't going through that shit," Pops said.

"Whatcha say, bro?" Hays looked at Tony expectantly.

"I say we should vector over to high ground and circle around this stuff. It means a longer hike mileage wise, but I think it'll take less time."

Terry was shivering, trying to warm up by hugging his chest and rubbing his arms. "Shit, anything's better than that fucking mess out there. And as long as we can move fast, I can stay warm."

"Lead on, o fearless squad leader," Pops said.

Tony led the way out of the morass, and stuck to the sparse pine forest. He made mental calculations as he counted steps over the undulating, pine needle covered ground. As the moon rose higher, it shone through the trees with eerie silence. Thirty minutes later they stepped out of a line of trees, on the farther edge of the fetid bog, from where a long, grassy, but dry swath cut through the trees.

"You is all right."

"Fucking A."

"I never doubted you for a minute. Well, maybe for a couple of seconds."

Tony tried to control his smile. "Look, we're not out of the woods yet. We still have the longest leg to do: three kilometers at thirty-two degrees. That's where we'll find the truck."

"Then let's get truckin'."

"I can smell the sheets already."

The field was as open as a golf green for the first mile. Tony put away the compass and, by keeping the moon on his shoulder, plotted the course by dead reckoning. He entered a wide stand of trees, but kept going forward. When he broke out to another open area, he held up his hand.

"Wait a minute. Listen."

After a strained silence, Terry said in a hoarse whisper. "What the hell's that?"

The men stood stock still, and when their clothes had stopped rustling, Tony smiled. "It's a generator."

"It's the truck!" Pops shouted. "We're saved."

"Hallelujah!" yelled Hays.

As they got closer, a faint light shone through the forest, and when they climbed out of the last stand of trees, a brilliant beacon was visible across a broad, open field. In a sudden splurge of energy, the men charged the last quarter mile. When they got to the truck, Cap-tain Whale and Sergeant Holtz were calmly sipping coffee on the tailgate.

The captain stared at his watch, frowning. "I don't know how you got here so fast. We weren't expecting anyone for hours."

Chapter 71

Not everyone located the truck that night. For some, the compass course was a miserable, grueling odyssey: a night of wandering, of loneliness, of hunger and thirst. Throughout the day they arrived by ones, by twos, and by squads, harried and haggard.

Of those who missed the collection point, some were found along the desolate dirt roads by rescue patrols; some were found by local farmers and cattle ranchers on their way to the fields and ranges; some hitchhiked into town and obtained transportation to the base by bus. One arrived in a taxi — two days after he was posted missing. Some arrived smiling, others scowling. One arrived in tears.

No retrials were permitted, and there were no dropouts from training. Performance was not graded. The men had to move on to other subjects. Communications classes included learning the language of the airwaves, stringing wires for radiotelephones, and using the handie-talkie. Demolition courses were followed by exercises with dynamite, blasting caps, and primacord.

Further inoculations were given against typhus, typhoid, tetanus, yellow fever, cholera, smallpox, and a dozen other diseases of which Tony had never heard.

The one-hour lecture on the Vietnamese people was not very informative — the army did not seem to know much about them.

****

Dear Tony,

Things have been kind of slow around here lately. School is a drag, although I'm doing well. Ray is pissed off because Mom keeps saying to him, "How come you never got grades like that?" All he ever got was detentions. So I get to laugh at him a lot, but only when Mom's around. Anyway, he's been spending so much time at Kathy's that I hardly ever see him. He even stays over some nights, when they aren't fighting.

Pete and Marion are officially going steady. She's going to Temple now, full time, and working nights as a waitress. On Saturday's she does some kind of volunteer work, I'm not sure what kind. Ben and Katie are talking about getting married (aren't they always) but not until after Ben graduates. Katie's getting involved with something having to do with computers, but she doesn't talk about it much. The big news is that George might finally be getting a job. His dad is going to put him to work in one of his tire plants. He was around the other week to visit Mrs. Hart. I think she's asking for more money and is threatening to take him to court. That's why he gave George the job.

Well, I guess you want to hear mostly about Patty. Well, she's really getting plump — with the baby, I mean. She let me feel her stomach because she says you can feel it, and sure enough I cold feel something moving around in there. (I hope you don't mind.) It's really scary, having something alive inside you, but she doesn't seem to mind at all. Bets are being made about whether it's going to be a boy or a girl. Patty says that since it started moving so early it means it's going to be a boy. That's what her Mom told her. I don't know about that, but I think it's going to be a boy anyway. I never asked you — what do you want, a girl or a boy? Well, other than Patty being tired a lot of the time, she's doing okay. She says it's the extra weight, and the baby taking some of the food. I guess that's the way it is when you have a baby. I don't know. Well, anyway, I guess you'll be home in a few weeks. I can't wait to hear all about Fort Polk. I hear it's a really far out place, with jungles and swamps and things. Has anyone died while you were there? Mr. Clark said that when he was in the war President Roosevelt made an announcement praying for all the men fighting in Europe and the South Pacific, and for all the men training in Camp Polk. Is that true? Well, we're all looking forward to seeing you. Are you going to fly this time, too? If so, let us know so we can meet you at the airport. Oh, and can you bring me any c-rations? I'd like to try them out. See you soon. Teddy.

****

"Put a little more rouge under your eyes." Before Tony had the chance to comply, Sergeant Holtz took the black stick himself and painted dark splotches on his cheekbones. "Now remember what I told you — keep quiet, keep near cover, and keep moving. And good luck."

"Thanks, sarge." He blinked in the light of the bare incandescent bulb. Shuffling away from the men in the lean-to, he stepped through deep piles of longleaf needles, and blended into the dark pine forest.

With no steel pot, no pistol belt, and no web gear, he ran quickly and lightly, free as the wind. A hundred yards into the woods, red flags had been nailed onto the peeling trunks, marking the beginning of the Escape and Evasion course. Heeding instructions, he crouched behind a bush for ten minutes while his night vision developed.

Just as he was about to depart, a distinctive voice called from the nearby shrubbery. "Pssst. Hey, Tony. Over here."

"Terry, what are you doing here?" Tony ran in a crouch and joined him, squatting. Under his baseball cap, his face was thickly covered with cosmetics. "I thought you left a half hour ago."

"Didn't you get the word? We're all meeting here and going through as a group. Anybody gives us any shit, we can tell them to go fuck off."

"You're supposed to do it alone."

"Bullshit. I'm not about to get picked up by some stupid referee and spend the night in a mock prison camp. That's for idiots and ass-holes."

Tony shook his head, forgetting that Terry could not see it in the dark. "Well, I think I can make it better on my own."

"You do what you want, but I'm waiting right here for the rest of the guys. We've got a better chance if we stick together."

"I'm glad you're finally realizing that." Tony stood up and looked around. "Look, I'm going to avoid the crowd. See you back at camp."

Just as he ducked under the flag into "enemy" territory, Terry called, "Good luck, you idealistic fool."

Tony did not answer, for a referee could be hiding by the next tree. Somewhere in this two-mile expanse, an unknown number of privates and corporals — gathered from the neighboring training companies — were acting as enemy guerrillas. Their task was to capture as many trainees as they could.

They were allowed to deploy non-injuring traps, such as strings with noisemakers attached to simulate mines and booby traps; they were allowed to hide in the bushes, in the trees, or disguised as other trainees.

Meanwhile, men were dribbled into the woods one at a time. They had no provisions, maps, or compasses, and were strictly on their own, playing the role of escaped prisoners of war.

The object, of course, was to avoid capture.

Tony crouched close to the ground, next to a bush, listening intently for any sound that might give away someone lying in ambush. Hearing nothing, he advanced slowly, still crouched, to another bush. He kneeled, and listened again.

The slight rustling he thought at first to be a stray breeze, turned out to be a hungry rabbit out for its nightly forage. Tony listened, ran, crouched; listened, ran, crouched. Each time he stopped, he surveyed the dark shadows closely, not just in front but all around.

He came upon a wide separation in the trees, where star glow was certain to give away anyone passing. He was positive that one of the referees would have the same thought. With careful strides, he worked his way along the tree line until he found a dry streambed: too obvious. He skirted past it to where tall grass offered concealment, then got down on his belly, and low-crawled across the opening. He figured he was about halfway home.

He rested under a bush, listening. This time, the rustling he heard was not a rabbit. Someone was walking openly through the trees, crushing twigs and pine needles underfoot without heed, and right toward Tony. He held his breath as the figure halted on the other side of the bush, so close that Tony could have reached out and untied his bootlaces. He swore his pounding heart would give him away. For several seconds the boots faced him; he could imagine their owner staring over the top of the bush. Then he crouched so that his knee almost hit Tony in the head, turned abruptly, and jogged off.

Something erupted from the grass. "Hold it, you!"

Tony recognized Larson when he froze at the command.

A vaguely familiar voice said, "Okay, you're captured. Come with me, big boy."

Larson did not move, but stood facing the referee, who walked up and formally placed a hand on his shoulder. "Don't you know any better than to stand out in the open, you dumb ox?"

Larson never said a word. But his huge fist came up from the ground and caught the referee on the side of the face, knocking him completely off his feet. Before he hit the ground, Larson was off and running, and was soon swallowed up by the darkness. The man on the ground did not move.

Tony crept closer. Corporal Velden was out cold, but alive. Tony had no water to splash in his face, so he chafed his wrists and slapped his good cheek until he responded. "Hey, are you all right?"

The corporal's eyes flicked open. He stared up at the sky for a full minute before the glaze left them. "Who was that bastard?"

"It was too dark to tell. Are you okay?"

A hand went up and touched the side of his face, and a creaky voice said, "I think he broke my jaw."

"I doubt if it's that bad. Do you think you can stand?"

"No."

Tony put an arm under his back and helped him to his feet. "How do you feel?"

He stared ahead like a zombie. "Dizzy as hell. You'll have to help me back."

"I can't. I've still got to avoid capture."

"Not any more. You're my prisoner."

"No, that was the guy who hit you. I just stopped to see if you needed help."

His speech was getting clearer. "And now you're my prisoner."

"Wait a minute, that isn't fair."

"That's your tough luck, kid. I gotta have a prisoner or the Old Man'll have my ass. Now get movin'."

Tony moved. He planted an elbow hard into Velden's midriff and ran like the devil. He saw the corporal buckle over, stumble, and fall backward to where he had first picked him up. He beat Larson to the safety zone by a good ten minutes.

****

Autumn winds rattled the barrack windows, and swept foot-long clumps of pine needles into drifts against the building. Sunbeams played tag with dust motes churned by currents sneaking around the edges of loose-fitting glass.

Tony stuck his head out from under his blankets like a turtle from its shell, and breathed in the cool air. "Hey, is anyone awake?"

Twisting bodies wrapped themselves into their covers, cocoonlike. Deep-throated groans were the only reply.

Five minutes later, Hays, with a coarse timber in his voice, croaked, "I'm awake, but I ain't alive."

"What time did you guys get in?"

The reply was muffled by two layers of wool. " 'Bout dawn."

"How come so late?"

"We had to wait fer ever'body to get together. They's comfort in company."

"You mean, you didn't run the course yourself?"

"Tha's right."

"But Hays, I thought you were serious about this training."

"I'm a whole sight more serious 'bout not gettin' captured by no smart ass sergeant and spendin' the night in — in — incarcerated."

A squeaky voice from Pops' bunk said, "What's with the big words, cowboy?"

Terry rolled over and stuck out a nose. "And if you have to use any words at all, can you keep them down to about a decibel and a half?"

The ensuing silence lasted ten minutes. Hays finally stretched out his arms, and yawned cavernously. "Some guy from fourth platoon ended up in the hospital. Got bit by a snake."

"Poisonous?"

"Don't know, don't matter. He's still in the hospital."

"Jordan's in the hospital, too," Pops added.

"What did he do, trip over his shoelaces?"

Now the men started waking up.

"Tony, you're a regular comedian."

"No, he got captured."

"What'd they do to him?"

"Beat him up so bad you wouldn't recognize him."

"No shit?"

"Think he got a broken arm."

"Did you see that guy they had locked up in the bamboo cage? It was so small he couldn't sit or stand. They ran canes along the pickets to rattle his brain, and they poked him with burning sticks."

"How about those two guys from first platoon that nearly drowned from Chinese water torture? They tied 'em down and poured water into their mouths till they passed out."

"Yeah, they were vomiting all over the place."

"Shit, that ain't nothing. One guy from the third was crucified."

That caused a few heads to pop out of their blankets.

"Yeah, I seen it myself. I was one of the last ones in, and they stopped by the POW compound to pick up some referees. They didn't use nails, but they had him stripped naked and tied to a pole. They were teasing him like they were gonna cut his balls off."

"I saw it too. And did you see that other guy they had hangin' by the wrists? If he stretched, he could touch his toes to the ground. Then when he got tired, he hung until the straps cut off the circulation in his hands. Then he had to try standin' again. He was crying real tears, too."

"Hey, don't you know they took all the trucks past the compound just to show you guys what it's like if you get captured?"

"What I saw was enough to make me damn sure I'd kill myself before I'd give myself up to those gooks."

"They had one brother buried up to his neck, and they were pouring honey on his head and waiting for the ants to come and eat it off."

"They had another guy bent over backwards on a board, with ropes tied to his hands and feet, and they were pulling him apart. You could hear him scream half a mile away."

"Those fucking sergeants were laughing the whole time, too."

Tony sat up with the blankets still wrapped around him, and noticed the number of empty bunks. It was not until later in the afternoon that the missing men appeared. They arrived on foot with their hands cuffed behind their backs and their legs manacled. Rough sisal ropes bound tightly around their necks were connected to a chain that connected them all together. They wore no clothing other than boxer shorts. They shivered in the cold.

The captured escapees were herded onto the parade ground, wincing in pain as they stepped on sharp stones with bare feet. Scars, bruises, and chafed skin made them look like real prisoners of war. And they were the lucky ones, for all those who did not answer the role call were receiving medical attention.

Captain Whale addressed the company. "Men, I'm truly sorry for those of you who are suffering, but it has been my contention that a soldier who knows what he is up against will make a better soldier. This is what could happen to you should you have the misfortune of surrendering to the enemy. He is ruthless, he is corrupt, he is without feeling. And those of you who still believe in Santa Claus and the Geneva Convention better get your heads out of the chimney."

Chapter 72

Eighth-week bivouac was a base camp gouged out of a slight rise that overlooked primeval pine forest that looked like a page out of a paleontology magazine. Machine gun emplacements commanded wide fields of view, foxholes stretched like a string of loose beads along the uneven pattern of the hill, real blanks had been issued — and real flash suppressors so that no one would get hurt by an overeager defender.

For three days they sat — and watched — and waited.

"If this is what it's like in the Nam, I'm sure gonna love it." Hays chewed thoughtfully on a twig.

They had dug holes, filled sandbags, built a command bunker and ammunition dump, and constantly refortified their position. But guard duty was a time to relax.

"Don't get too complacent." Tony surveyed the trees that grew on the other side of the clearing fifty feet from their position. "I'm sure they're cooking something up for us. We're not on fifty percent alert for nothing."

Hays was silent for a moment. "You know, you're right. Captain Whale got something up his sleeve. I kept thinkin' all night they was gonna have a raid agin us. What about you?"

Tony readjusted the blanket over his legs. "I don't know. I spent all night shivering — I didn't have the energy for thinking."

"I know what chu mean. The ground's so cold it'd make Pops a Popsicle. This don't make no sense. We had sleeping bags in boot camp, in the middle of August. Now we almost into November, an' they don't give us more'n a blanket. This simulatin's gone too fer."

Tony tried to unclench his teeth for a laugh. "How about letting me have more of that blanket?"

"Sure thing, bro. I'm finally gettin' warm,

settin' here in the sun."

"Hey, fellas, cheer up." Terry approached with his hands full. "I got breakfast for you."

"Is it thawed?"

"It's even heated. They trucked it out this morning and it was sitting on the transmission the whole way. Now, what is your delight: ham and eggs, chopped, with a B-1A unit; spaghetti with ground meat, and a B-2; or chicken and noodles with a B-1A?"

"I'll go for the ham and eggs, if no one else wants it," Tony said.

"I sure don't want spaghetti for breakfast," Hays scowled.

Terry handed out the packages. "Chicken and noodles it is." He ripped open the remaining box, produced a P-38 can opener, and passed it around. "Did you hear about the guy in fourth platoon? Got bit by a scorpion."

"Scorpions don't bite, they sting," Tony emphasized.

"Whatever the hell they do, he got it. Can you believe, he actually took his boots off when he crawled into his sack last night? Well, when he got up this morning he remembered he was supposed to shake them out before putting them on. Only thing is, he shook them out over his feet, the dumb bastard. The scorpion fell out and got him on the foot."

"Is he gonna live?" Hays asked, with a spoon in his mouth.

"They took him away in the ambulance truck, and he was one sick dude." Terry shoveled a forkful of spaghetti into his mouth; he seemed to be enjoying it as much as the story.

"He'll probably be all right. North American scorpions are not deadly — unless you happen to be allergic to the venom."

"Yeah, well, his foot was swelled up like a football, and he was sure screaming bloody murder."

Tony spoke matter-of-factly. "Oh, I'm sure he'll be sick. Probably have a fever for a couple days."

"This place gives me the creeps. I'm telling you, I don't know how much more of this shit I can take. It's frightening."

"Don't seem to have hurt your appetite none. How can you eat that shit for breakfast?"

"One can of shit tastes just like any other. Besides, you should see what I left behind. I just grabbed these before that bastard Holtz came around and caught me picking the crud of the crop."

"Whatchu got agin the good sarge?"

"What is there to have *for* him? The prick made me carry that ammo can for five fucking miles, and there was nothing in it but twenty pounds of sand."

Tony reached for the can opener. "That's be-cause you forced him into it. You purposely do things to make him mad. Instead of blaming him for your character faults, why don't you try to grow up a little?"

"Hey, what makes you so fucking holy you can pass out judgments? I didn't ask to be draft-ed into this fucking army. I don't like being treated like a baby, and told what I can and can't do. I have rights, and I have reasons, and they're just as valid as yours. I don't like this outfit, and I don't like the way it's run. I don't like getting up in the dark, or running till my ass falls off, or eating army slop. I don't like being told when to stand, when to sit, when to salute, when to breathe, and when to wipe my ass. I want to run my own fucking life, and no-body's going to tell me how to do it."

"Terry, I only meant — "

"I don't care what you meant. I'm telling you like it is."

"Then let me tell you like it is. Uncle Sam may be running part of your life, but if we don't fight for our freedom, some other country would like to run *all* of it."

"Man, are you brainwashed."

"I'm just seeing reason. As long as there's no freedom for everyone, there's no freedom for anyone. If we don't keep Vietnam free, we lose that much of our freedom ourselves, and the ag-gressors of the world come that much closer to taking our own away. That's the reason."

Terry stuffed his empty cans into the card-board c-ration box. "You've got a hang up about reasons. You think that just because you invent a reason for doing something, that makes it all right to go ahead and do it. Well, I don't think that way. Not when somebody else is making up the reasons. I want to make up my own. And one reason I have is that I want to live. I have a right to that, no matter what any-body else says. I come first, the rest of the world comes somewhere else along the line."

He tramped off in a huff, and tossed the half-full can of spaghetti against a tree, spilling the contents.

Tony opened another can, and munched on crackers and peanut butter. After rinsing his mouth with water from his canteen, he said, "Hays, do you think I'm too judgmental?"

Hays finished eating, lit up a cigarette from the sundry pack, and stared at the blue, cloud-less sky. The sun was warming up the air.

"Well, I guess we all got to make judgments. An' there are plenty of people ready to judge us, right or wrong. Mostly, we got to judge our-selves. Me, I kinda roll along with the punches. I don't make no judgments, I don't listen to none. Some folks got to strike back, hard, 'cause they want to hurt what they can't under-stand. But all folks, no matter who they are, got to learn to get along with other folks. That's the only way to end all this nonsense. We gotta get along."

****

That night, Tony shivered between a poncho and two woolen blankets, one of which belonged to Hays.

Hays woke him for watch. "Your turn, bro."

In the light of the moon, Tony saw him stooping, silhouetted against the purple sky. His right side was stiff where it had lain on the cold, hard ground. He uncurled from the fetal position. His hands were like ice, despite the fact that he had sandwiched them between his legs.

"I feel like I just got in here," his voice trembled. "I didn't sleep a wink. It's too cold."

"I know whatchu mean — I been shakin' the shit outa that foxhole."

It took every ounce of willpower, and then some, for Tony to fling back the covers. The icy air hit him like a snowball. "Even my goose bumps have goose bumps."

"No field jackets, no sleeping bags, not even long underwear. Don't they know that November in Loosiana is cold? It ain't gonna be like this in the Nam, why they gotta make us suffer?"

Tony got onto his knees, then pushed himself semi erect. His joints did not want to cooperate. "Part of the simulation — carry only the gear you would carry over there."

"But this is insane."

"So is war."

Hays crawled under the covers, huddled into a ball. "Goddamn, it ain't no warmer in here."

"What did you expect? I'm a living icicle." Tony tried to laugh, but his cracked lips caused him too much pain. "Keep the sides tucked in and don't move around. That'll trap as much warm air as possible."

"I can't move if I'm frozen solid, can I?" As Tony started to walk away, Hays called out, "And, hey, shake that canteen every onct in a while, else the water freezes 'round the lip."

Tony laid his rifle on the ground and did some quick calisthenics; the bitter air immediately convected away any heat that he produced. It was even colder in the foxhole, surrounded by cold earth. Very soon he was shaking so violently that he bounced back and forth, ricocheting like a billiard ball from front wall to back.

Moonlight bathed the open space with a suffused glow, as cirrus clouds raced across the sky, leaving tendrils of ghostlike mists across its white face.

Tony's teeth chattered so loud that someone two foxholes away whispered, "Stop bangin' those sticks." To deaden the sound he placed a piece of cardboard in his mouth. Then he pulled a pair of dirty socks over his hands.

Something moved out around the tree line. It was short, and close to the ground — a sergeant sneaking up to see if he was awake? In quick, jerky motions the figure crept across the rocky terrain and passed behind the trunks of trees. Tony heard a noise, like a snort. He thumbed the safety.

If anyone along the perimeter of defense had been asleep, the rattling of metal on metal could not have failed to bring him to attention. Whoever was out there had bumped into the string that was rigged with empty c-ration cans.

"Halt, who goes there?" came a voice to the left — Gormley's.

In answer came a recognizable snort, deep and nasal. Someone was trying to pass himself off as an animal, Tony thought. But then the cans rattled again, and he knew that no one could be stupid enough to make the same mistake twice.

The wraiths moved away from the moon for an instant. Tony breathed to the side so that the condensation did not form in front of his face. He saw the shape more clearly: a wild boar, rooting and sniffing along the ground and, in the dimness, blundering into the signal wire.

"Halt, who goes there?" Gormley's voice trembled.

Tony almost spit out the cardboard as he stifled a laugh. He released his grip on the rifle.

With fear, "Halt or I'll shoot."

Crash went the cans.

Pow, pow, pow, pow, pow. Gormley's rifle blasted the silence as red darts licked out toward the unsuspecting boar. Squealing and spinning, the tusked animal beat a hasty retreat into the woods.

Moments later, Tony heard Sergeant Holtz's voice. "Who fired that weapon?"

"I don't know. I just saw something move. When it didn't answer my challenge, I fired. Whoever it was ran away."

"Probably an animal. All right, just keep your eyes open. But next time, know what you're shooting at."

"Right, sarge. But you said someone might try to sneak up on us."

"Not tonight. It's too cold. Just stay alert." The sergeant scrambled across the intervening hillocks. "Giovanni, you see anything?"

Tony stifled a snicker. "Just a shape. I couldn't tell what it was."

"All right, I guess it was an animal."

"I guess so."

****

"Praise the lord, here comes the sun." Hays raised his hands toward the eternal sky like some sun worshipping African native.

The sun was small and dull, and sent a white light through the trees that was not at all warm or comforting. Hays and Tony sat on the back edge of their foxhole, arms interlocked and legs touching. Both blankets and ponchos were draped over their shoulders and tucked under their legs. Hays, too, was wearing socks on his hands. Tony had black and blue marks on his chest and back, caused by his violent shaking against the hardened dirt.

"Hello-o o. Lovely weather we're having, isn't it?" Terry hardly ever suffered from lack of sleep.

"If you're a polar bear," Tony said, through gritted teeth. The camp slowly came to life. Along with the rustling of men crawling out of their blankets, or climbing out of frigid fox-holes, or chafing for warmth, birds flitted in the trees and chirped merrily.

"Hey, look at this." Terry pointed down into the hole.

"I've got to move around anyway," Tony said. He stood up stiffly and hobbled on numbed feet to Terry's foxhole. At the bottom, a steel pot lay over a lumpy blanket. "What is it?"

"It's the Baton Rouge gigolo."

"Are you kidding?" Tony poked the brown wool. "Hey, Pops, are you down there?"

After a long silence, the blanket groaned and seemed to be imbued with life, as it rippled in an unlikely manner. The steel pot rose into the air, dragging the blanket behind it. When it reached ground level, half-closed eyes peered out from the helmet rim.

"Is it time to go home?" Pops wore the blanket on his head, tucked into the steel pot like an Arabian sheik wearing desert garb.

"Two more days yet, bright eyes," Terry chided.

Pops groaned and sank back to the bottom of the hole. "Wake me when it's over."

"This is no time for the Cowardly Lion act," Tony said. "It's warmer out here, so come out and catch a few rays."

"How about putting some in a can and sending them down. I need some sleep."

"You've been sleeping all night," Terry said.

"Bullshit. One hour on and one hour off don't mean you sleep all night. Especially when it's in a refrigerator."

"Oh, I don't know. Things weren't too bad until that idiot started strafing the neighborhood. Who the hell was that?"

"Gormley," Tony said.

Hays hopped by doing his imitation of an Indian sun dance. "What was he shootin' at?"

"A pig."

"There ain't no pigs out here," Pops muttered. "They're all in Baton Rouge."

"This was a real pig. A wild boar. With tusks."

"No shit?"

"I saw it. It walked into the signal wire and Gormley started talking to it. 'Halt, who goes there?' he said. When the pig didn't answer, he told it to halt or he would shoot. When he did, the pig took off as if real bullets were chasing it."

In minutes, the whole camp heard the story and Gormley, good naturedly, laughed with the rest of them.

"Shit, how can anyone tell the difference between a sergeant and a pig?"

****

"I don't believe they're wastin' our time this way."

Tony stared out into the woods, hugged his chest a little closer. The afternoon was only slightly warmer than the morning. "How are we wasting our time?"

"She-e-e-eet, we been here five days an' ain't done a lick o' work 'ceptin' to go out on patrols an' set up ambushes. The rest o' time we're sittin' here twiddling our thumbs."

"Not me, my thumbs are too cold to twiddle. Besides, what do you expect them to do, stage a big battle just for your benefit? This is probably what they do in the field. And we've been through that village a few more times, picking up a few more pointers."

Hays grabbed a pine needle and stuck it between his bright teeth. "I can walk through that village blindfolded an' still find all the traps. She-e-e-eet. The only excitement's been when Sergeant Holtz snuck up on Johnson an' turned his machine gun around on 'im."

"He shouldn't have fired it though. Those powder burns could have blinded him."

Hays laughed right out loud. "You're right, bro, but he sure scrambled outa that hole lickety split. I was watchin' him."

"Yes, I guess he'll stay awake the next time."

"If there is a next time. This is almost over."

Tony stretched his arms, balancing his rifle on his lap. "Just one more day of freezing boredom."

"I don't mean bivouac, I mean the whole damn shebang. Two weeks from now we could be sittin' in some rice paddy, waitin' for the real Charlies to attack."

The realization dawned slowly on Tony. He was still a trainee — still felt like a trainee. Could it be true that he would soon be shooting real bullets, going on real patrols, fighting an enemy that was not imaginary? He sat a little straighter, watched the woods with more attention. When did the game end and reality begin?

"It doesn't seem possible, does it? I mean, I don't *feel* like a soldier."

"I know whatchu mean. I guess you ain't a real soldier till somebody pops a grenade in your lap, or burps a AK at chu — or you kill somebody."

The birds still chirped overhead, oblivious of the men below. A light wind rustled the pine needles.

"Now Charlie, he's born into it. From the time they's babies they don't know nuthin' but fightin'. Seems like somebody's always tryin' to take their country away. He's born in the bush, he lives in the bush, an' ain't nobody gonna get 'im *outa* the bush. No amount o' bombs or bullets. 'Cause he ain't got nuthin' to live for *except* the bush."

Tony shifted uncomfortably. "You sound as if you think we can't win this conflict."

"There ain't never been an invader who's won against a guerrilla army. 'Specially when you fightin' amateurs."

"You mean like us?"

"Exactly. Like you jus' said, trainin' don't make you a soldier, it jus' gets you ready to *be* one. An' by the time we get to be real soldiers, we'll be rotatin' home — an' Charlie'll still be sittin' there in the bush, ready to take on the next bunch. He gots to, 'cause that's his home. He got nowhere else to go, so he'll stay there an' fight till he dies. Ain't no discharge for Charlie, an' the only pension he'll get is the chance to fight agin."

Chapter 73

"I'm gonna miss you, bro."

Tony managed a half grin. "I'm going to miss you to."

"Ain't never had a buddy like you. You taught me a lot. I feel like we was, well, like real brothers. I — "

The gap was awkward for both of them. Tony tried to think of something to fill the silence. "It seems like it's ending too fast, as if we just got to know each other. I mean, the training is so rushed, there's so much to do, I didn't have time to think — "

"You gotta think about these things, bro. People are the mos' important thing in the world. They's a part of us in everyone you meet. That's why you can always find somethin' to like in ever'body — even if it's only a little bit. Most fokes today don't care 'bout nuthin' ceptin' how many cars they got, an' how big a house they live in, an' where to get the money to go on vacations. They ain't no togetherness in the country; people are jus' out for a good time. An' that's sad, 'cause when people don't look out for each other, they start driftin' apart."

The cool November breeze played briskly with Tony's hair, which had been allowed to grow to almost half an inch on top. Hays threw his arms around Tony, squeezed him as a mother bear would hug her cub.

Tony backed away, stared into coal black eyes that were deep pools which he realized he did not fully understand. "That's why I find it hard saying goodbye."

"This ain't goodbye, bro, it's only so long. We all been assigned to the 25th. We'll meet again — over there."

"Yes, I guess."

Pearly white teeth flashed. "An' if we don't meet again in this world, we'll meet in the next."

Tony's lack of faith in *this* world was shaking his belief in any other. "Sure."

"Hey, when you sentimental fools are done with the Casablanca scene, you can put your addresses in this book." Terry handed the pencil and tablet to Tony. "What bus are you on?"

"I'm headed for New Orleans, but it won't be here for another hour."

"That's the fucking army for you. Wait, wait, until it's too late."

Tony handed the writing materials to Hays, who inscribed it with large, flowery letters. "This don't make no difference. I'm on the Shreveport bus witchu."

"Yeah, but once we get started — you know — I'll probably forget everything. Maybe even my name."

"You get high enough on that shit an' you can fly home without the plane."

"How about getting off my fucking back, nigger?"

"Hey, Terry, that's uncalled for. He was only joking."

"Fuck you, too, Tony, and spare me the sentimentality. It's been fun, swell, and razzmatazz, but I've got places to go, people to see, and things to do. And none of it involves either of you. It's been great, but now it's over, and I'm California bound."

So saying, Terry still stuck out his hand, smiling. His handclasp was warm and firm, belying his roguish manner.

Hays handed back the tablet and pencil. "You break up with your girlfriends that way, too?"

"Hell, no. I just leave one day and don't come back."

The horn beeped, and Tony accompanied them to their bus. "You know, I just figured out what I hate the worst about the army — it's the constant goodbyes."

Terry boarded without a backward glance. "What I hate are the greetings."

Hays stuck out his hand. "Luck, bro."

"Luck."

"See you in the Nam."

Book Four
WINTER

He who is wise tries everything but arms.
Publius Terentius Afer, c.190 — 159 BC

We will either find a way or make one.
Hannibal, 247? — 183 BC

Chapter 74

November in Philadelphia was cold, drab, and inhospitable, made worse by nighttime winds. Tony shivered in short-sleeved khakis, and wished that he had been allowed to wear his dress greens instead. But military regulations were strict on that point: the army dictated when a soldier could change his clothing, not the weather.

No lights shone through the heavy curtains as he tapped on the front door of the brownstone. It took several knocks before a rustling within presaged the shooting of the bolt. The oak door opened to the length of a retaining chain, and a suffused light from the living room worked through the slender crack.

"What do you want?" said a throaty voice. She stood to one side so that only her head and long black tresses were silhouetted.

"Hi, Kathy. It's me, Tony."

The pause that followed was overlong. "Uh, Patty's not here."

"Oh? Where is she?"

"She's visiting — your parents."

"*What*? But I called from New Orleans and told her I'd be home tonight."

"I don't know. I didn't talk to her today."

Tony threw down the heavy duffel bag, rubbed his sore shoulder. Sighing, "Look, why don't we discuss it inside. I'm freezing out here."

Springs creaked in the background. "Well, I've got company."

"Ray? Is Ray here?"

"No."

"Oh," Tony said, with disappointment. "Who is it?"

'It's none of your business. Why don't you go home and talk to Patty?"

"Hey, what kind of a reception is this? This is Patty's home, and I'm paying half the rent, remember?"

The dark hair shook. "But this is my night, and Patty has to stay out."

"Listen, Kathy, I don't know what's going on here, and I don't care. But I'm not going to stay out here and argue with you. Now, I'll go to my parents' house and leave you alone, but I'm not going to drag all this luggage with me. So open the door and let me bring it in."

Another pause. Finally, the door closed. It was a full minute before the chain rattled. Tony was about to knock again when the door opened. The nightlight had been switched off. Kathy drew the black robe tight about her body as the wintry wind blew in. Her bare feet stood on varnished wood.

"Thanks." Tony took the duffel bag by the strap, and towed it in after him. He threw his overnight case on a threadbare chair. He had never seen Kathy's apartment, and he could not see it now. But he smelled the distinctive flavor of cigar smoke. He left slightly miffed, and without saying goodbye.

He passed by the frat house on the way, but its lights were out and the door was locked. He did not bother to knock, even though he could see movement upstairs. When he was only half a block from the Murphys' house, he turned up their street.

"Tony!" Teddy practically leaped out of the door after he answered Tony's knock. He pumped Tony's hand furiously, and slapped his shoulder with stinging blows. "When did you get back? I've been expecting you all day."

"Had a little trouble at the airport — " Tony started, with Teddy dragging him inside.

"Mom! Ray! Look who's here. Wow, it's great to see you. And look at those arms. You look like you've been doing some exercise.

Ray and I were just talking about you."

"Is Ray here?"

"Of course I'm here." Ray appeared laconic, with a cigarette stuck in the corner of his mouth. "Where the hell else would I be on Saturday night?"

"Teddy! Shut the door this instant." Mrs. Murphy's voice had the clear tones of an opera singer; her face had the looks of a model: a most elegant widow in her satin dress and swept up, pitch black, silky hair.

Tony held Ray's limp hand for a weak shake. "Hello, Mrs. Murphy."

"Hi, Tony. The boys told me you were coming home." She padded across the deep piled carpet in slender high heels, the mark of a smart businesswoman. "My, don't you look sharp in that uniform."

"Cold, too. It was seventy degrees when I left Louisiana."

"I've got some fresh coffee on the stove. Would you like some?"

"I'd love it."

Still smiling broadly at Tony, she said, "Ray, get him a cup of coffee, please."

"Yo, Teddy, you know where the cups are." Ray pointed with his cigarette. "Go get 'em."

"Mom said for you to get it." Ray cast a glaring eye at Teddy while Mrs. Murphy smiled obliviously. "Aw, all right."

After Teddy ducked into the kitchen, Mrs. Murphy swept her hand toward a blue velvet chair. "Please have a seat. And Ray, turn the television off while we've got a guest."

"Thanks." Tony sat down next to a glass-topped coffee table that was covered tastefully with artistic heirlooms.

"You look tired."

"Well, I've been on the go for almost twenty-four hours. Took a bus from Fort Polk, then a midnight plane from New Orleans. I should have known something was wrong when I saw that black liquid pouring off the wing. Then I *did* know something was wrong when the engine burst into flames."

"No shit! The plane caught fire?"

"*Ray!*" Mrs. Murphy looked sharply at her son. Ray rolled his eyes at her.

"We kept right on banking with the pilot announcing calmly over the loudspeaker, 'We are experiencing technical difficulties and will be returning to the airport.' Just like they say on television."

Teddy burst into the parlor carrying a steaming cup. "Did he talk with a Southern accent, too?"

"As a matter of fact, he did have a kind of a drawl. Anyway, since I was traveling military standby, I almost didn't get on the next flight. Slept on a bench until morning, then had to take

a local that made half a dozen stops. They made me get off at D.C. when a colonel came aboard, but then found they had an extra seat and let me get back on. Then, to top it all off, I went to Patty's apartment — I mean, Kathy's apartment — and she told me that Patty was at my parents' house. So, on the way — "

"Who told you?"

Tony held the cup in both hands, warming his palms. He looked at Ray over the steam. "Kathy told me."

Teddy started, "You mean you haven't even seen — "

"*Shut up*, pea brain. Who told you Patty wasn't home?"

Mrs. Murphy pouted. "Ray, please don't be rude."

He ignored her. "Did you see Kathy?"

"Yes."

"Where?"

"At her apartment. She told me — "

"That bitch." Ray leaped out of his chair and slapped a fist into his palm. The veins on his neck popped out with each syllable. "She told me she was going down the shore this weekend. And she's been there all this time, not answering the phone. I'll kill her — "

"Ray — "

He was already out the door, necktie flapping, and without his jacket. After a long silence, Mrs. Murphy stood up and gently closed the door. "Teddy, why don't you take Tony home in my car? I think he would like to see his wife some time tonight."

"Sure thing, Mom. Thanks." He grabbed the keys off the silent television. "Come on, Tony. Let's go."

Tony gulped his coffee. "Thanks a lot, Mrs. Murphy. I really appreciate it."

"Think nothing of it. It's good to have you back. I'll see you again before you leave."

Outside, Tony climbed into the pink Ninety-Eight, thinking that it must be the only one of that color that Oldsmobile had ever made.

"Now that I have my license I can be part of the gang," Teddy said proudly. He took off with full acceleration. "Mom let's me have the car on weekends, and sometimes to go to the store at night, as long as I'm not out after midnight."

"Even with a junior license you can drive after twelve if you have someone with a senior license with you."

"Oh, not because of the law, because of my Mom. She doesn't want me out too late." Teddy patted the plush dashboard fondly. "I call her the Pink Panther. It's got a four-twenty-five with a quad, and you should see this baby haul."

Tony quelled the butterflies in his stomach. "I can see that already. Don't you think you should slow down a bit?"

"Aw, gee, I can handle this machine as good as you — or Ben. I took driver's ed. Got cheaper insurance rates, too."

The car veered dangerously close to cars parked along the narrow city street. Tony cringed with the muffled roar of each passing. "How come Ray never got a license?"

"He'd rather let someone else do the driving, I guess."

"What's he do when he goes out with Kathy? Let her drive?"

"Yeah, unless they just stay in the apartment."

"I don't understand. What's with her? I thought they were supposed to be going steady."

"So does Ray. But Kathy has other ideas. She wants to, you know, play the field, and Ray doesn't want her to."

"So what's he going to do, beat her door down?"

Tires squealed as the Oldsmobile took a corner, barely nipping cars that were parked too close to the intersection. "I don't know. This isn't the first time she's lied to him. The problem is, if she tells him the truth, he gets mad. And I mean really mad. If I were Ray, I'd just forget about her."

Tony was no longer thinking about the cold. "That's not always easy to do. Hey, you're going to pass it."

Teddy slammed on the brakes and the car screeched to a halt. Then he threw the automatic transmission into reverse, and laid rubber as he backed to the right set of marble steps.

"I was trying to sneak in unannounced."

"Oh. Sorry."

Tony grinned as he got out of the car. "That's all right. And thanks for the ride. You have Coney Island beat by a mile."

Teddy rolled his head sheepishly. "I just wanted to show you what she cold do. I'll stop over tomorrow. Say hello to Patty for me." He did not burn rubber as he left, but squealed around the corner at the end of the block.

Tony searched through his keys until he found the one that he had not used in such a long time. In the living room, the television was switched on, but no one was watching it. "Anybody home?"

The only answer was the familiar clicking of claws on the linoleum floor. "Kitty." She looked up warily, her eyes bouncing slightly from side to side. "Kitty, it's me." Tony got down on one knee and made kissing noises. She stayed put. Slowly, he crawled toward her, calling all the while. He held out his hand. From a crouch she sniffed the fingers. When he had her confidence, he petted her head, then picked her up and cradled her in his arms like a baby.

Footsteps on the stairs stopped suddenly. "Tony, you scared the living daylights out of me."

"Hi, Mom. There was no one here when I came in."

She descended the rest of the way. Her hair had been recently coifed, and stood up on her head like a beehive. "I was waiting for you to call."

"I thought I'd surprise you."

"Well, you certainly did that." Another step sounded at the top of the stairs. "We were just going through some old pictures in your room."

"Tony!"

He looked up, smiling. He put Kitty on the floor as Patty raced into his arms. Tony hugged her, kissed her, and hugged her again. "Tony, don't squeeze me so hard. You'll hurt the baby."

He pushed her away, and gazed up and down at her body. "Boy, look how — big — you've gotten. But it looks good on you."

"What took you so long getting home? I expected you hours ago."

"Oh, there was some trouble with the planes. I — "

Elizabeth interrupted. "Tony, I've already missed the news, but I want to see the weather. I have a hairdresser's appointment tomorrow, and I don't want to go out if it's going to be windy."

"Uh, well, I — "

Patty interrupted. "Tony, let's go up to your room and talk. We were just looking through some of your baby pictures."

"Oh, sure. That's fine."

Elizabeth switched channels and grew absorbed. Tony and Patty ascended the stairs. He paused at the threshold, staring into the room that used to be his. Not a thing had been changed. Even his schoolbooks still sat on the desk, long abandoned. His models were all on their shelves, his hanging of the solar system was still on the wall. His star chart and geological time scale was still thumbtacked to the closet door.

Tony sat on the bed, experiencing the déjà vu of a traveler in a place he could never have been. "I went to the apartment first."

Coyly, Patty walked around and sat next to him. Her belly bulged out as if she had hidden a small watermelon under her dress. "Kathy wanted to be alone tonight."

"She wasn't alone."

"Well, you know what I mean. Hey, I've got something I want you to see." She took his hand and placed it against her bulge, moved it around, then pressed it flat. "Wait a minute."

Tony stared into her eyes, squinting. Suddenly, her belly rippled spasmodically, like a muscle contraction, but alien and scary. He jerked his hand away. "What was that?"

Patty grinned mischievously. "What was what?"

"I felt something — *move.*"

"That's the baby kicking. It's been doing that for almost a month."

"Wow, why didn't you tell me?"

"Well, you just got home. I haven't had time to tell you anything, yet"

"But, you could have said so in a letter."

She shrugged. "I guess I didn't think of it. I mean, I thought of it, but I guess I forgot to think of it when I was writing. The doctor says it's normal. It's just a foot or a fist. I guess it's practicing."

"Wow, that's really neat. Can I feel it again?" He placed his hand back to where he had felt movement. The tiny kicks foretold of the life that was to come. "Wow, I can't believe this. I can't believe I'm going to be a father."

Even as he demonstrated his excitement, the smile faded from Patty's face. "Tony, I'm — I'm scared."

"Honey, what's wrong?"

Her breathing came in short gasps, her shoulders sagged. "I never had a baby before, and I don't know what's going to happen to me."

"What do you mean, you don't know what's going to happen to you? What *could* happen?"

She cried quietly. "I don't want — to be — a mother by myself."

Tony shook his head. "I don't understand."

After half a dozen stifled sobs, "I don't want to be alone."

"Honey, you won't be alone. Someone will be with you all the time."

"I don't want just someone. I want you."

"Well, I'm here."

"No, I mean, I want you when the baby is born."

"Well, I'm doing everything I can." Tony wiped the tears off her face with his pinky, but more took their place. "I want to be here, too, you know. I've filled out some forms for a compassionate reassignment, and it should be waiting for me when I report to Fort Dix."

"But, what if you don't get it?"

"Don't worry about it. I'll get it. It's no big deal. I'm just asking to be held back from my tour of duty until after the baby's born. It's not like I'm asking for the world. It's standard operating procedure."

Patty stopped sobbing. She rubbed her face on the loose folds of her maternity dress. "I know, but I'm still scared. I want to have you around — all the time."

Tony kissed her cheeks and sucked away the saltiness. "Don't you worry about a thing. Eventually, all this confusion will end, and we can get a place all our own — just you and me, and the baby."

"You mean a house?"

"If that's what you want."

"Oh, I do. I want a house all my own, where I won't have to take any orders from anybody. I'm tired of living in other people's houses. I mean, Kathy's okay, but — "

"I know. I know." He kissed her cheek again. His hand drifted across her belly, feeling for another reassuring kick from the bundle of love inside. "Everything will turn out all right."

A hinge creaked, the door burst open, and a narrow shaft of light pierced the room. Patty gasped, then shrieked when the bed bounced.

"It's all right, Patty. It's only Kitty." Tony petted them both.

"Get it away from me."

Kitty curled next to Tony and started licking his hand. He scratched her behind the ears. "You miss me, too, don't you, Kitty?"

"What's it doing here?"

"She lives here."

"Well, I don't like cats. Get it out of here."

"Oh, Patty, stop being silly. Kitty's been coming in here and sleeping with me for ten years."

"I don't care. I don't like animals."

Tony stood up, taking Kitty with him. "Well, this is one animal you'll have to learn to like." He nestled in her fur, planted a kiss on her soft sides.

Patty was not appeased.

"Come on, I think we'd better go."

"But this is your room. Don't you want to look around a little?"

Still holding the cat, Tony glanced quickly at the walls, the furniture, the floor. He touched the half completed model of an antique, horse-drawn fire wagon that perched on the bureau. A partially used tube of glue sat at its base, along with the forgotten decals. "No," he said wistfully. "It's not my room any more."

Chapter 75

The next day, while Patty still slept, Tony threw his fatigue jacket over civvies and caught a trolley to his former residence. He smelled coffee brewing in the kitchen, saw his father glued to the morning paper.

"Hi, Dad."

Whiskers bristled darkly, and hair that had once been thick and wavy now was thinning and straight, and stuck out in all directions. "Oh, you finally made it. I thought you were coming in yesterday."

Tony helped himself to a cup of coffee and

took a seat opposite his father. "Well, I had a few problems making plane connections."

"If you got in late you shoulda stopped at the taproom. Everybody was asking for you last night."

"Really? Who's everybody?"

"Your Uncle Richard, P.J., Dizzy Dom, Hunks, the Gimme. And Aunt Rosie."

"Aunt Rosie was at the bar?"

Frank kept one eye on the paper while he talked. "No. Afterwards we went back to Richard's house, and she was asking for you. I told her you were going to Vietnam."

"I've got two weeks leave. I'll stop over and see them."

A thick finger pounded the paper as Frank twisted it around. "They're really going after 'em with Operation Thayer."

"Oh? What's that?"

"Don't you read the papers down there? You're going to Vietnam and you don't even know what the hell's going on over there?"

"We didn't get much in the way of politics," Tony said evenly.

"It's been going on since September — biggest battle going. Got the whole 1st Air Cav involved, and part of the 25th Division."

"Hey, that's the outfit I've been assigned to."

"Then you better pay attention, 'cause they're right in the thick of it. They're fightin' the 18th Regiment of the NVA. We'd be losing without Arc Light."

"What's an arc light?"

"Don't they teach you nothing? You're going to Vietnam and you don't know what Arc Light is?"

"Our training was mostly in light arms and small unit tactics. We didn't go into special weapons, or battalion operations."

"Yeah, well, you better pay more attention to what's going on if you want to know what you're getting into."

After a long pause, Tony said, "So what's an arc light?"

Frank looked up from the paper. "They're B-52 raids. They send out eight or ten Strato-fortresses at a time, each one with twenty-five tons of bombs. The jets are flying at thirty-five thousand feet. The Vietcong don't even hear 'em comin'. They show it on television all the time."

"Well, we didn't really have much time to watch television. They kept us pretty busy with other things."

"You prob'ly weren't payin' attention. They got this thing going now so they can pick out one little village and drop every bomb on it with pinpoint accuracy."

"Sounds like they don't need an infantry."

"This country's got something better than the infantry. They got technology. They got listening devices they can drop out of helicopters so they can hear troop movements. They got cameras in satellites that can see trucks moving on the Ho Chi Minh Trail. Sees the heat of the exhaust. And radar! They can pick up a tank five miles away — and home in artillery shells on it. We didn't have this stuff when I was in the army. They got it easy today. We didn't have no helicopters to fly us in and pick us up. We had to walk everywhere, and carry everything on our backs: food, ammo, everything. There was no picking up the phone and saying, 'Bring us some hot chow.' We learned how to live off the land, to improvise."

"But, Dad, you never went overseas."

"Well, that don't make no difference. I was still training to go. I hiked as far as anybody else. We were a tough outfit on maneuvers, and I kept up with all of 'em. They never had to wait up for me. We were tough. Didn't have helicopters, and jeeps, and trucks to carry us around."

"Speaking of vehicles, that's the reason I came over here. Mom couldn't find the keys to my car, so we had to walk home last night because the trolleys had already stopped running."

Frank's face clouded over. "You should be used to walking."

"I am. But it was hard on Patty. Anyway, I'd like to have the keys, since I'll be home for a couple weeks."

"They're on the desk, where the hell did you think they'd be?"

****

"What's the idea of walking right by our house and not stopping in?" Mrs. Clark pointed her finger with mock anger. "If you needed a ride home, Ben could have taken you."

Tony exchanged looks with Ben and Patty, raised his eyebrows. "Well, uh, I didn't see Ben's car, and, uh, — "

"Ben was out gallivanting with his girl-friend, but Jack was sitting here doing nothing. And where's your uniform? I expect to see you dressed like a soldier."

"Gee, well, I never thought that Mr. Clark would, uh . . . Besides, I didn't know if I should . . . And my uniform was kind of rumpled because I had to sleep in it — "

"Excuses! Excuses! And lame ones at that."

"Hold on just a minute," Ben shouted. "Mom, I was not out gallivanting. We went to the movies, and that does not constitute galli-vanting."

"Don't try to talk your way out of it, young man. You didn't come home with a neck full of hickies from the movies. I know you were parking down by the river."

Ben shrank a little deeper into his turtleneck.

"Mrs. Clark, I'm sorry I didn't stop in last night. But it was late and I was tired and I wanted to get Patty home and I figured we could talk later."

"Are you implying that I'm a garrulous old woman?"

"No, of course not. It's just that I know that when we're together — we have so much to talk about. I mean, there's so much I want to tell you — "

"You got out of that one pretty good. All right, I'll accept that as an excuse, but don't let it happen again. And you, young man, should know by now that you can't hide your love wounds from me. I got wise to that sweater trick a long time ago. And Patty, I must say you're looking fine. You look charming in maternity clothes, and that outfit is very chic."

"Thank you, Mrs. Clark. I picked it out myself."

Mrs. Clark ushered them through the living room. "Now, you better get in the kitchen and make yourself a sandwich before Jack eats it all up. We want that baby to be strong and healthy, now, don't we?"

Mr. Clark was already attacking the layout of lunchmeats and cheeses. He nodded in his usual, reserved manner, without slowing down his intake.

A knock at the front door was followed by a shrill voice. "Hello, anybody home?" A moment later Katie walked in, still wearing her church clothes, a stylish, wide-brimmed hat, and high heeled shoes in which she walked rather awkwardly. She greeted them with a roll call, and gave Ben a peck on the cheek.

"Katie, you'd better watch out. Ben's got some contagious disease: red splotches all around his neck."

Her pearly white face darkened to a bright scarlet. Ben laughed out loud, and handed her a pickle. "Don't just stand there with your mouth open, put something in it."

Katie slowly regained her composure. "Mrs. Clark, sometimes I don't know when you're serious or just pulling my leg."

"I wouldn't think of pulling your leg. Ben does enough of that."

Amid the confusion of laughter, Jack Clark said, "Frances, why don't you leave the kids alone? You're always heckling them."

"Oh, Jack, you're just an old fart. You're just jealous because I'm a bridge across the generation gap."

"No, I just don't want to pay the toll."

Ben screamed and jumped up and down. "Whoo-oo-ee-ee-ee. Score one for Dad."

Mrs. Clark waited for the chuckles to dip down. "Okay, grandpaw, you just sit there and rub your rheumatism. But I'll still be around when you climb in your coffin."

The front door opened and closed. Pete, Marion, and Teddy pushed through the swinging door into the kitchen.

"Hey, man, you're lookin' good." Pete shook Tony's hand so quickly that he had not had time to wipe the mustard off the palm. "I was beginning to worry about you. When we didn't hear from you Friday night, I was gonna send the MPs out after you. Figured you got waylaid along the way."

Tony managed to extricate his hand in one piece. "I don't need any help from *them*."

Marion planted a sisterly kiss on his cheek. "Glad to have you home, Tony."

"Thanks. It's good to be home. And thanks for all the letters. It really helped to keep up my spirits knowing that — people at home — were still thinking about me."

Marion glowed radiantly, her red hair aflame and the freckles standing out against her tanned face.

"Where're Ray and Kathy?"

Teddy wasted no time with the food: he already had a mouthful of potato salad. "We have to pick them up, yet. She had some things to do after church."

"And Ray didn't want to let her out of his sight," Ben added.

"Ben-n-n-n," Katie whined.

"If the foo shits, wear it. Boy, would I like to hear *her* confession. If I had a week to spare."

"Ben!" Mrs. Clark was more emphatic.

Tony picked up a paper plate and started piling coleslaw on it. "What about George?"

Ben hit himself on the forehead with the flat of his hand. "Oh, no. I must have forgotten to call him."

"Don't bother to remember now," Pete said, swilling Coke.

"What is the matter with you boys lately?" Mrs. Clark pinched her eyebrows in real concern. "Now you get on that phone and tell him to come over here right away."

"Aw, Mom."

"Don't 'aw Mom' me. You call him up this instant."

"But, Mom, he — "

This time Mr. Clark interrupted. "Ben, you do what your mother said, and don't give her any back talk about it."

Mrs. Clark smiled and wiggled her finger at Ben. "You may be taller than me, but I can still take your car keys away."

"Okay," Ben whined, with poor grace. He slumped into the living room to make the call. He came back several minutes later with a broad grin on his face. "We're in luck. He can't make it anyway."

"What did you do, try to talk him out of it?" Mrs. Clark said.

"No, he said his father was coming over this afternoon."

"Something must be wrong," Pete scowled. "The old man never visits unless there's a crisis. Is one of 'em dyin', or did Mrs. Hart flip her wig again?"

Ben got back into the sandwich makings. "I don't know. He wouldn't tell me. My guess is that it has something to do with his father's tire plant."

Tony leaned against the flowered wallpaper, plate in hand. "I thought he had already started working. Somebody, Teddy I think, told me in a letter."

"It wasn't Ben who told you," Mrs. Clark chided, "because he never writes."

"I spend two hours a day writing term papers. Isn't that enough?"

"But you don't write a goddamn word to your brother in Germany, do you?"

"Frances, stop picking on the boy."

While Mrs. Clark glowered, Marion said, "I think he's going to work in one of the out of town plants."

"Isn't that a shame?" Pete pouted. "That'll mean the bastard'll have to move away."

Mrs. Clark treated all of them as if they were her own sons. "You keep a civil tongue in your head and a civil tone in your voice. I can still spank *your* behind, too."

"Sorry, Mrs. Clark."

Tony finished his sandwich, and cleared his throat. "Listen, while you guys are going over to pick up Ray and Kathy, I think I'll stop over and have a talk with George."

"Good for you, Tony," Mrs. Clark beamed. "I'm sure he'd like to see you."

****

Mrs. Hart answered the door, wearing a bright green housecoat and matching slippers, neither being quite new. Her eyelashes were dark with mascara, her cheeks thickly rouged. She was as tiny as a painted doll.

"Hello, Tony." The corners of her mouth turned up into a quixotic smile, but her voice was flat and her blue eyes unemotional. She glanced over her shoulder. "George's in his darkroom. Why don't you come in and I'll call him."

"Thanks, Mrs. Hart." Tony stepped over the cracked sill onto the worn, wooden floor. The old furniture in the living room was made more dingy by the drawn purple curtains that did not hide the threadbare area rugs and their frayed material. "I knocked downstairs, but didn't get an answer."

She stepped back and closed the door behind him. "Oh, he probably has the radio on. I'll get him."

The black and white television screen was the only illumination in the room. Sitting in front of it, quiet as church mice, were George's brother and sister. Lonnie was fifteen, tall and lanky for his age; Susie was twelve. They were both hypnotized by a western shoot-'em-up: Indians howling, guns firing, and trumpets blaring. Neither acknowledged Tony's presence.

Mrs. Hart returned in a moment, with two buttons of her housecoat somehow loosened, revealing her chest almost down to her navel. She wore no brassiere, and the inner bulges of her ample breasts were visible to Tony — and distracting.

"He said he'll be out in a few minutes. He's in the middle of making some prints, I think, and can't open the door till he's done."

Tony stood awkwardly, tried hard to glance away. "Oh. Okay. Is it all right if I wait?"

"Oh, sure." She moved closer, right under him. "I hear you're a married man, now."

"Yes, that's right."

"My, you boys sure do grow up fast. I can remember when you wouldn't even look at a girl, much less think about — marrying one."

Tony forced a smile. "I guess things change as you get older."

Mrs. Hart parted the drapes so the sun shone full upon her tanned body. Lonnie and Susie wailed simultaneously as the light cut down their viewing. "Hush!" Mrs. Hart continued to stand in the sunlight, half turned so that more of her left breast was revealed. She flashed a smile at Tony, showing even teeth and a mouthful of solder.

"Uh, maybe I can wait for him downstairs. In the garage. There are some books I want to look for, anyway."

She nodded faintly, stepping so close that Tony could smell her breath. When the front of her housecoat rubbed his sleeve, he could smell the fragrance of recently permed hair. She bent way over, still in the rays of the sun, and picked up some magazines from the scratched coffee table. "Would you take these down with you?"

"Sure."

Her long nails raked the back of his hand. "Thank you so much. I hope you'll stop in and see me again — before you go."

Tony stumbled across the living room toward the cellar steps that went down from the kitchen. He spread his lips. "We're going for a ride today, but maybe some other time." Then he was out of her sight and in the basement. He placed the magazines on the shelf with hundreds of others: *Cosmopolitan*, *Mademoiselle*, *Ladies' Home Journal*, and *Harper's Bazaar*. The rest of the basement was full of boxes, newspapers, dirty clothes, and a washer and dryer. At one end, adjacent to the outside door, was a plywood barrier wrapped in black plastic.

Tony knocked lightly. "George, it's Tony."

Muffled, "Okay, I'll be out in a minute."

"I'll be in the garage." Tony ducked under the drainpipe and entered the frat house. It looked and smelled much the same as when he had last seen it: the mildew covered rugs, the wobbly furniture, the paisley sofa. Yet it seemed so — odd, part of another world, another life. He rummaged around and found his books in a drawer, and leafed through them as he waited.

"Hi. What do you want?"

Tony looked up. "Well, that's a fine how-do-you-do." Tony tucked the books under his arm, and stuck out his right hand. "I haven't seen you for a few months so I thought I'd stop by and see how you were doing."

George took the hand for the barest second. "I'm doing all right."

"Still working on your photography, I see."

"Um hum."

"Well, can I talk you into taking the afternoon off and going for a ride? We're going to the Poconos."

Sloe eyes peered through dirty blonde bangs. "Thanks, but I'm pretty busy. Besides, my father's coming over later."

"Yes, I heard you were going to work in one of his tire plants. Congratulations."

George nodded.

"What kind of work will you be doing?"

George plopped down in a soft chair, sank right through the worn springs until his knees were even with his chest. "I don't know. I guess I'll start out mounting tires and putting in studs."

Tony sat cross-legged on the sofa. "So, you're going to learn the business from the ground up?"

George scowled, picked up a dart, and tossed it. It reached the bottom edge of the board. "Um hum."

"Well, do you know where you'll be working? I mean, it's kind of far to that plant out in the Main Line. Besides, I heard you might start out in another city."

"I don't know. Maybe Denver, maybe Toronto. I don't know."

"Why so far away?"

George picked up another dart, but did not toss it. He played with the loose threads on the chair cover with the point. "I don't know. I guess it won't be so obvious I'm the boss's son if I'm somewhere else."

"Not only that, but you won't have to worry about having your father around all the time. I always had problems working for my father."

"Urn hum."

"Some of the men resented me, and called me a stool pigeon. And my father was always pushing me around." Tony pushed himself up and perched on the edge of the sofa where the wood showed through the material. All the fraternity furniture had been obtained by trash picking. "Well, it sounds pretty interesting, anyway, going to another city for a while. I guess it's better than being stuck in South Philly all your life."

"Um hum."

"Maybe with the extra money you can take some photography courses, too."

George did not answer, but finally threw the dart at the board.

"Maybe you could even get some part time work as a photographer. You know, to break into it, if that's what you really want to do."

"If I want to, I will."

"Well, you don't have to act so huffy about it. I just thought that's what you wanted."

"Maybe I do, maybe I don't. In any case, it's none of your business."

"George, if you've got something on your chest, get it off right now."

"I don't have anything on my chest, I just have you on my back. So lay off, okay?"

"What's eating you? You act as if I came over here to make fun of you, or something."

George looked up sharply. "Well, didn't you?"

"No, I came to see if you wanted to go for a ride with us, with the gang."

"Well, I don't need the gang. And I don't need you."

"Hey, no one said you needed anything. I just thought you might want to come along."

"Why, so the guys can make fun of me? Well, no thanks. I don't need it. I don't need *it*, I don't need *you*, I don't need the *gang*, I don't need nobody. So just get the hell out of here and leave me alone."

Tony stood up with his books. "You want it, you got it."

****

The day was bleak and blustery, the sky darkened with low, threatening clouds. Autumn had come and gone, in all its pageantry, and already the great oak trees stood naked. Grandmom's garden, recently gay and colorful, was now a tawny patch of flowerless sticks and leafless bushes. The birdhouses were choked with straw and corn silk, carried in by sparrows during the hatching season; their families raised, the birds had long since flown south for the winter.

The two story house appeared careworn: paint was peeling from window sills and door ledges; whitewashed walls showed thin in spots; several roof shingles had been blown away, leaving the tar paper exposed; the grass was long overdue for its final cutting before snow fell.

"This isn't how I imagined it. It's so dull and drab — and lonely looking."

Pebbles crunched under the tires as Tony turned the Ford into the driveway. "It's different in the spring when the flowers are in bloom and the trees are covered with green leaves — and later, when the field is filled with rows of yellow corn."

Patty slowly shook her head. "I don't like it. It's too — open. There aren't any houses around, no neighbors to talk to. Nothing but dirt and trees."

"That's the way farm houses are. But wait until you see the inside. It's nice and homey, with old-fashioned furniture and a red brick fireplace."

She seemed not to have heard. "How long do we have to stay?"

Tony turned off the engine. "We haven't even gotten here yet and already you're asking when we're going to leave."

Patty shrugged, a look of self-pity on her face. "It's not that, it's just that I don't have any friends here."

"Now, come on. Cheer up." Tony leaned over and kissed her on the cheek. "I don't want you looking so gloomy when I introduce you to Grandmom and Grandpop." He tickled her leg just above the knee. She pushed his hand away, but smiled. "That's better. And your face didn't even crack, see?"

He got out and walked around to open the door for her, then took a suitcase and a shoulder bag from the back seat. He led the way to the back door.

"See this?" Tony pointed to a wooden thread spool that was screwed to the screen door through the hole in the middle. "Grandpop put that there when I was a baby, because I wasn't tall enough to reach the door knob."

"Oh, that's cute." Patty laughed.

Inside, the kitchen smelled of frying chicken, simmering butter beans and corn, and baking corn pone. The room was not only warm, but delicious. Several pots steamed merrily on the gas range. Tony put the luggage next to the tall-backed rocking chair, and went to look for Grandmom.

"Hello, is anyone — " He practically ran her down as he stepped into the dining room.

"Why, Honey, you nearly scared the skin off'n me." She jumped back holding her delicate hands to her slender chest. She wore a simple print dress and black, low-heeled shoes. Her silvery hair glinted in the incandescent light, and sparkles reflected off her glasses.

"What takes you here so early?"

He put his arms around her and squeezed gently. When he pulled back they exchanged kisses. "Well, we had nothing planned for the day, so I thought we'd leave in the morning and drive leisurely, so I could show Patty the sights along the way. She's never been south before."

"Land sakes, you must be starved, and dinner won't be ready for hours."

"Oh, that's all right. We had lunch on the way — at English's." He ushered his grandmother into the kitchen. "Grandmom, this is Patty. Patty, my grandmother."

Patty smiled genuinely. "How do you do?"

"I'm doin' tolerable well, myself. An' I've heard so much about you, I can't tell you how much I've been looking forward to meeting you. Why, as soon as Tony said he was bringing his wife home I said to Walter, 'Walter, now you better get yourself well, an' do it quick, 'cause Tony's bringing his bride to meet you.' Well sir, he 'most sat up in bed when he heard that. 'Bring me some lunch,' he says. 'I got to get my strength up before he gets here.' Lord o' mercy, I just remembered, I was coming out to get a snack for him."

Grandmom bustled to the stove and removed the frying pan. "I'm frying him one or two pieces of chicken, just the way he likes it. Only thing, the doctor says I got to take the skin off'n it before I give it to him, an' he likes the skin so much."

Tony watched her pour the grease into a jar. "How is he? I mean, is it all right to go in and see him?"

She put the two chicken legs on a paper towel to drain the remaining grease. "Oh, he's awake all right, an' complaining too if I don't bring him something the minute he wants it. Honey, why don't you go in an' keep him company whilst I heat up this milk. He'll be tickled pink to see you. And your wife, too."

"Okay." Tony held his hand out to Patty. He took her through the dining room, and stopped just outside the bedroom door. "We haven't told him about the baby. He's got enough on his mind, just finding out about us being married. And the doctors don't want him to get too excited."

Patty nodded silently. Tony tapped lightly on the shellacked door, pushed it open, and peered in.

A strange man lay in the bed: an old, wrinkled, withered husk of a man. He lay flat on his back, the pillows pushed to the headboard, and stared vacantly at the ceiling. He might have been asleep, except that his eyes were open. He was breathing slowly, too slowly, rasping with each inhale and exhale. Tony hardly recognized him.

"Grandpop?"

The bald head rolled sideways. Tony saw sunken eyes, shallow cheeks, sagging skin. But a smile touched the corners of the bloodless mouth and spread slowly, coming to life like a dying fire fed oxygen with a bellows.

A voice crackled like radio static. "I've been waiting for you, Tony."

He stepped fully into the bedroom and walked to his grandfather's side. A hand worked its way out from under the covers, as if it took all his energy to move a few ounces of cloth. Tony took the hand, bent down, and kissed his grandfather on the cheek.

"Hi, Grandpop. It's good to see you."

The weak smile seemed to require a gathering of strength. "I'm glad you could come and see me. I've been praying you would come, and the Lord has answered my prayers. But I'm not feeling my best today." It seemed to take him forever to say this. Then, he paused twice as long before continuing. "I have my good days and my bad days."

Tony squeezed his hand. The pressure he returned was the ineffectual quivering of a newborn babe. "I'm glad to see you're all right, Grandpop."

Tony saw a movement that he took for a nod. Looking past Tony, he said, "Is that your wife back there? Tell her to come in where I can see her."

Tony gestured to Patty. Reluctantly, she stepped into the room, came to the edge of the bed. Grimacing, with her hands clasped behind her back, she whispered in a voice almost as inaudible as his. "Hello."

Grandpop forced another smile. "My, my, my, you sure do know how to pick 'em. She's a fine looking girl."

Tony smiled. "Her name is Patty."

His words came slowly, carefully chosen. "Well, Patty, I'm right happy to have you here. You've got a strapping young man here. A fine young man."

Patty hung back, out of reach, her smile fading.

Grandmom rushed into the room, carrying a tray with a glass of milk and a pie plate with only half a dozen finely chopped pieces of chicken. "You children are going to have to excuse me while I feed your grandfather." She tossed open a cloth napkin and tucked it in under his nightshirt. "Tony, would you help me get these pillows under him so he can swallow without choking on his food?"

Grandpop struggled to get into a sitting position, but did not have the strength to get his elbows back under him. Tony jumped to help him up. His body was a mere bag of bones, weighing no more than a child. While Tony held him up, Grandmom shoved the pillows under him. He relaxed against their downy softness. Then Tony stood back and watched, helpless, as Grandmom spoon-fed him.

After several bites, and a couple swallows of milk, he sank back, seeming to crumple into the pillows. "Let me rest a while," he whispered. Rolling his eyes toward Tony, "I don't have the strength I used to have."

His eyes closed. He drifted off to sleep.

"Honey, let's let him get his nap out."

When Tony turned to leave, he noticed that Patty was no longer in the room. Grandmom closed the door behind her, said something about checking on the butter beans and corn, and headed for the kitchen. Tony found Patty in the living room, staring out the front window.

"What's wrong, Patty?" Tony stood behind her, snaked his arm around her waist, and pulled her close.

"I don't like it here."

"Well, I realize these aren't the best of circumstances, but that has nothing to do with the place. You'll get used to it."

"No, I won't. I don't like this place, and I'm not going to like it — ever."

"But, why?"

"Because I don't like old people. And I don't like sick people. They give me the creeps."

"Patty, you're talking about my grandparents. These are people I love."

She continued to stare out the window for a long time. Finally, she said, "I want to go home."

"But, Patty, we just got here."

"I don't care. I don't like it here, and want to go home."

Tony heard his grandfather cry out in anguish: a fearful, desperate cry of pain. He started to run to him, but Grandmom stopped him in the hallway. She had a glass of water in one hand, two white tablets in the other.

"Don't go in there. He — he doesn't like people to see him — in pain."

"But, can't you do something for him?"

She held up the hand with the pills. "This'll take the edge off'n it, an' make him sleep. But the doctors say it's mostly up to God after that."

Chapter 76

The '57 Chevy fishtailed severely on the dry cinder road, swerving so far out of the direction of travel at each outward swing that it was at times rushing ahead sideways.

"Jesus Christ!" Ray screamed. He jammed his hands into the aged and cracked dashboard.

Ben, completely in control despite not having his hands on the wheel, laughed maniacally. The steering wheel spun of its own accord, banging to the limit of travel just as the car was facing perpendicular to the road, and spinning back so that the Black Stallion rotated one hundred eighty degrees; then the wheel banged on the other side of its travel limit and started the gyration over again.

In the back seat, Tony was alternately crushing Teddy and Pete against the right door, and being crushed by them against the left door. Teddy, sitting in the middle, got crushed both ways.

"Stop the goddamn car!"

Still laughing, Ben took his foot off the accelerator and let the car decelerate. A hundred yards farther along the road, when the spokes on the steering wheel were circling slowly enough to see, he took hold of it and brought the car to a halt where the cinder road narrowed, under the spreading branches of a sycamore tree. The car was silent, as if all sound had been siphoned off and shunted to an alternate universe.

"You — are — crazy," Ray said, when he found his voice. "You are out of your ever loving, numskull, pea-picking brain. What the hell are you trying to do, kill us all?"

Softly, with a sardonic grin, Ben said, "Honestly, Ray. Sometimes I think you don't trust me."

"I trust you to send me to hell and back."

"As long as you get back there's no sweat."

Tony shifted to a more comfortable position near the door. "I see you haven't lost the old touch, Ben."

Pete chimed in, "Yeah, way to go."

"That was great, Ben. That was really great. You really know how to handle a car."

"Shut up, pipsqueak." Ray reached over the back of the seat to give Teddy a punch, but Pete deflected it with his forearm.

"Stop picking on him, will ya? Just because you were scared and he wasn't."

"Who was scared?"

"You were scared. I could tell because you left out the aitch."

"What the hell are you talking about?"

"Ray, you always say Jesus *H.* Christ, except when you're scared."

"You're full of shit."

Teddy wagged a finger. "He's right, Ray. You always say aitch."

"You keep out of this, flea brain."

Mockingly, Tony said, "Honestly, Ray, I don't think the experience warrants that kind of outburst."

"But you're lucky; you haven't been driving with this maniac all summer. A hundred and twenty on the Parkway if he was going an inch. He's a madman, I tell you."

"Ray, a mile-per-hour is a unit of time, and an inch is a unit of measurement. You can't mix

the two in a comparison."

"Did they teach you anything other than sarcasm in the army?"

"I hate to interrupt this conversation, fellas, but there's a car coming our way."

They all craned their necks to see where Pete was looking. Several hundred yards away, two headlights were bobbing on the uneven surface, approaching fast.

Ben doused the lights. "Hang on. I'm going to hide the car."

He eased the Black Stallion forward a hundred feet without touching the brake pedal, so the signal light would not flash on, swept the car in an arc between two trees, cruised through fender-high grass, and let the car roll to a stop. "Katie and I park here all the time, and no one's found us yet."

"Where the hell are we?" Ray whispered.

"Right by the Torresdale Filter Plant. Come on, let's go for a walk. I'll show you something."

Tony held back. "I really don't want to go. I'll wait here."

"Hey, what's the matter with you, man?" Pete dragged him out by the arm. "You didn't even want to come out tonight."

"I don't know. This kind of thing just doesn't seem like fun any more."

"Don't be a stick in the mud."

"Whaddaya want, someone to order you to do it?"

"It's just another adventure, like Bowman's Tower. Remember?"

Tony scowled, but let himself be led through bushes and over rotting tree trunks, up a hill, and onto a cobblestone road. "What is this?"

"I don't know, but it's old," Ben said, in a low voice. "They haven't made roads out of cobblestone for fifty years."

A few minutes later, four red brick buildings came into view. Each measured a couple hundred feet in length, and was indented periodically with doorways that were boarded up with joists and two-by-fours.

"Man, this is weird." Pete kicked a loose board on the ground. "What is this place?"

Ben took them between two of the buildings. "Don't know. Katie and I found it a few weeks ago when we came out here to fly my radioplane. You can see through the cracks, and it looks empty inside. It's been abandoned for a while."

Teddy stuck his nose close to a loose board, squinted. "Hey, I didn't know you had a radioplane."

"Shut up, Numskull. We're not talking about planes."

"Think it could have anything to do with the House of Correction?" Pete pulled out the bottom of the board. Blackness leaked out from inside. "Hey, Ray, toss a match in there."

"What do you want to do, burn the place down?"

"No, I just want to see what's in there. Why don't you — "

Pete was interrupted by Ben's whispered shout. "Holy shit, man, what's that?"

The unmistakable sound of a car motor was getting louder. The tires made hollow thumping sounds as they rolled over cobblestone. Then twin headlights soared around the corner and speared the first building.

"Jesus Christ, it's the cops," Ray screamed.

"Run for cover," yelled Pete.

They scattered in different directions: in doorways, behind brick protrusions, in back of a pile of trash. Ray raced down the middle of the road that separated the two buildings. He was still in the open as the car — with a flashing bubble gum machine on the roof — swung into the drive behind its high beams. His spindly stick figure bobbed in the white light. The police car crawled behind him. Ray ran to the end of the drive, into another police car. Two uniformed men jumped out, wielding flashlights.

Ray threw his hands over his head. *"Don't shoot! Don't shoot!"*

The car that had been chasing him stopped, and two more policemen got out. While the four patrolmen converged on him, he turned around and around, repeating his request.

"You can put your hands down, son. We're not going to shoot." None of the officers had even drawn a gun.

They had him penned like four hound dogs on a rabbit. Hesitantly, Ray lowered his arms.

"Okay, son, where are the rest of 'em?"

"I d-d-d-on't know."

"I saw two others."

"I saw three," another added.

From his darkened doorway, Tony knew the jig was up. Ray had already admitted, under threat of flashlight beam, that there were in fact others. "Over here." He stood out waving his arms, and walked directly into the crossed beams.

Groaning, Pete and Ben emerged from concealment, walking nonchalantly. "That's four of 'em. Are there any others?"

Tony glanced around, saw no other movement around the buildings. "No, just us."

The lead patrolman nodded, walked back to his car. Leaning into the open door, he picked up the microphone. "Sir, we've got 'em up here. Four of 'em." The radio crackled. "Okay, we'll be right down." He walked back to the group. "Anybody here own a black '57 Chevy?"

"Yeah, I do."

"Okay, you two get in that car. You two come with me."

"Hey, w-w-w-wait a minute," Ray stuttered. "Where you taking us? We didn't do nothing."

"We're just taking you back to your car. The lieutenant wants to talk to you."

After a short, silent ride, they poured out of the cars and were paraded in front of an officer and his driver. They had another police car parked behind the Black Stallion. The doors of the Chevy were open, proof that they had already examined the interior.

The lieutenant peered out from under a peaked cap that was pulled down so far that his eyebrows were concealed. "Do you fellows mind telling me what you were doing up there?"

"Exploring," Tony volunteered.

"Exploring? Exploring what?"

"If you're really exploring, you don't know what. Otherwise, it wouldn't be exploring."

During a long pause, the lieutenant eyed each one of them, then came back to Tony. "Did you ever think of doing your exploring in the day time?"

Tony shrugged. "It's not as exciting."

The police lieutenant nodded noncommittally. "How about if you guys show me some identification."

They all pulled out their wallets, except Ray. "I don't have any."

"Why not?"

"I left my wallet home because I don't have any money."

The lieutenant leafed through the three wallets, then handed them to his subordinate. "Write them up."

"B-b-b-but, we didn't do anything."

"I only want your names and addresses. Which one's Tony?"

"I am."

"You got a military ID. You in the army?"

"Yes."

"What're you doing *here*?"

"I'm on leave."

"Got any papers to prove it?"

"Not on me."

"You know I can take you right to jail and call the MPs to verify that?"

"No, I didn't."

"I can. And I just might."

"You can't do nothin' to him," Pete said. "He's goin' to Nam in a couple weeks."

The lieutenant stared long and hard at Pete. "I can do anything I want, son, and I don't need any advice from juvenile delinquents. All right, you," he turned to Ray. "You know you're supposed to carry a draft card at all times?"

"N-n-n-no, sir."

"You're in big trouble, too. I can lock you up and call the FBI. It's a federal offense to be without your draft card.

"L-1-1-l-look, officer, er, lieutenant, sir. I d-d-d-d-didn't know. I'll make sure I carry it with me from now on."

"Get his name." When Ray finished stammering his name and address, the lieutenant said, "Now, you kids listen to me. I don't care if you're in the army or not, going to Vietnam or not. When you're in my jurisdiction you're nothing but punks, see? You're not even wet behind the ears, yet, as far as I'm concerned. Now, I'm letting you off the hook this time, but don't let me catch any of you South Philly hoods out here in the Northeast again, or I'll throw you all in the slammer. And then I'll call the proper authorities. You got me?"

Four heads nodded silently. He handed back the wallets. "Now get the hell out of here."

In the car, Ben started the engine, and waited for the police car that had blocked him in to get under way. "Whew, that was a close call."

"They couldn't do nothin'," Pete said.

"You and your big mouth," Ray screamed. "You almost got our ass cooked."

"What the hell're *you* talkin' about. *You're* the one who stood in the middle of the road and waved his hands. Shit, we'd a got away if it hadn't been for you."

"I didn't want to come here in the first place. It was *his* idea." Ray stabbed a thumb in Ben's direction.

"You were the one who was running like a scared rabbit. Right down the middle of the road, too stupid to get out of the way."

"Look, don't start picking on me. It wasn't my fault."

Tony interrupted. "Listen, it doesn't matter what happened up there, they would have caught us anyway. All they had to do was sit by the car until we showed up."

"Yeah, he's right," Pete admitted.

Ben added grimly, "And right now we better worry about finding Teddy."

"What happened to the little twirp?"

Pete leaned forward until he was right in Ray's face. "He got away. Like we all would have if you hadn't started advertising for us."

"Look, it wasn't my fault."

"Hey, let's stop the bickering and just keep a lookout for Teddy," Tony said.

Ben coaxed the car back out of the weeds and onto the cinder roadway. "How come *you* gave up so easily? You didn't even try to make an excuse." Tony shrugged. "I'm just not in the mood for games."

Ben drove slowly while they looked for movement in the shadows. "I don't understand what's come over you."

"Pay attention, will ya?" Ray yelled. "And keep your eyes peeled. I hope to hell Migraine's all right, 'cause if he gets hurt my mother'll kill me."

"Are you worried about his ass, or your own?" Pete said.

Ray did not answer. A couple minutes later, Ben stopped the car at the first intersection, where cinders became macadam. "Well, what do we do now?"

Before anyone could think up an answer a shadow detached itself from the weeds and ran crouched toward the car. "Hi, fellas. How'd everything go?"

"Where the hell have you been?" Ray yelled, as his brother slid into the back seat.

"Well, I wasn't going to wait around and get picked up by the cops," Teddy said matter-of-factly. "I climbed up the wall and hid on the roof until they took you all away. Then I ran over here to wait for you. Ray, you really looked funny, standing out there with you hands up yelling, 'Don't shoot. Don't shoot.'"

"I didn't say, 'Don't shoot.'"

"You did too. I heard you."

"Did not."

Ben carefully signaled his turn, looked both ways, and pulled slowly onto the paved road. "Ray, did anyone ever tell you that you were a jerk off?"

****

After Tony completed his transactions at the bank, he hoisted his collar over his neck and pushed through the swinging glass doors into the rainstorm. He ran halfway down the block, dodging people and puddles, dashed between two parked cars, and crossed the street to where Patty sat waiting in the White Lightning.

"All right, here's what I did," he said gruffly, wiping his wet hands on the front of his pants legs. "I cashed in one of my savings bonds and deposited the money in the savings account. That should give us enough until the allotment comes through. But just because there's money in the account doesn't mean you have to go out tomorrow and spend it all."

"Can I help it if I need money?" Patty pouted.

"You don't *need* money, you just like to spend it."

"Tony, husbands are supposed to make money, and wives are supposed to spend it. That's the way it is."

"It may be the way you want it, but it's not the way it's going to be. Not in this family, anyway. Do you know you squandered practically my entire life savings in just two months?"

Patty stared out the rain-spattered windshield. "Can I help it if I never had a lot of things? You knew I was poor when you married me. Besides, you have a lot more than what's in the savings account. You've got all those bonds, and things."

"That's no excuse for going on a spending spree just as soon as you got my bank book. And you don't even know what you spent it on."

"I told you, I had to buy things for the baby. And I had to have new clothes because I didn't fit in any of my old ones. And besides, I didn't want to wear any of them because they remind me of my grandmother. And there were doctor bills, too. And rent. And food."

"But, Patty, we're talking about thousands of dollars. And you don't even have anything to show for it. Things for the baby amounts to a blanket, a rattle, and a pair of shoes."

"But you didn't send me any money like you were supposed to."

"I told you, I made out the allotment forms, they just haven't started yet. The army doesn't do things overnight. It takes time. And I only make a hundred dollars a month, anyway. You're spending ten times that."

"Well, I can't help it. I don't know where all the money went, but I know I needed the things I bought."

"Then what *are* the things you bought? Show them to me."

Patty lapsed into silence, her eyes dropping from the windshield to her lap. She folded and unfolded her hands, playing with her fingers. "All right, I'm sorry. What else do you want me to say?"

"Saying you're sorry won't bring the money back. And I don't have that much more for you to throw around. So, what I want you to do is learn how to handle it. And you could try cleaning up the apartment a little. It's a mess."

The side windows fogged, and water streaming over the windshield made the world look like a distorted, shimmering caricature seen through isinglass.

"It's half Kathy's, too, you know. And besides, I don't always feel like doing work. I have a baby to carry around, you know."

Tony gripped the steering wheel fiercely. "Look, a lot of women in this world have babies, but I've never heard any of them make as many complaints as you do. It happens to be a normal female function. Now, I don't mean to say it's easy, but it surely shouldn't prevent you from doing *anything*. You know, the women in Vietnam work in the rice paddies right up until an hour before they have their babies — right through labor. Then, when they feel they're getting pretty close, they step into a nearby hooch, have the baby, clean it up, put it in a pouch, and an hour later they're right back out in the paddies picking rice. They carry them in

a sling so they can feed them while they work."

"Well, I'm sorry, I'm just not as strong as a Vietnamese woman. Besides, you're probably just making that up."

"No, I'm not. When I had weekends off at Fort Polk, since I wasn't allowed to leave the base, I used to go to the base library and read up on Vietnam."

"Why would anybody want to do that?"

"Because the army didn't teach us about the people."

"So who cares about them?"

Tony's fists clenched and unclenched around the plastic steering wheel. "Did you forget that I'm going to spend a year there? And the reason is so I can protect those people. So, I want to know about who I'm going to be fighting for. I want to understand their habits, their life styles, their ideologies."

"But what difference does it make — they're all so backward."

"The difference is that they're people, just like you and me. The fact that they don't have running water and air-conditioning doesn't make them any less human."

Patty started choking. "All I know is because of this stupid war they're taking my husband away for a year, and leaving me all alone. And I'm going to have a baby and I want my husband around when it happens."

She cried uncontrollably for a minute. Tony, powerless to help her, gripped the wheel and stared out the window.

"I need you, you know."

Tony stared at her, watched the tears roll down her cheek. "Sure, I know you do. And I need you, too." He put his arm around her; she tucked her head into his neck. He felt the wetness of her tears. "But you've got to learn to handle money. You have to get along with what we have. Okay?" After a long pause, while she continued to sob, he repeated, "Okay?"

He felt her head nodding faintly against his throat. "I - I - I'll try."

"Good. That's all I ask — that you keep trying."

****

Helen MacDonald wore a colorful, loose-fitting blouse, and no brassiere. When she bent over to light the candles, her breasts, nipples protruding, were clearly visible. "There we are. Now I'll just turn off the lights, like so, and we can have a nice candlelight dinner. Bob, would you start passing the plates, please?"

Bob Windsor was decidedly pleased. "Anything for you, Honey." He picked up a plate of mashed potatoes, took a spoonful, and passed the plate to Patty.

"Mom, could I have a glass of milk, please?"

"It's on the table already. But I thought we'd

start out with a little wine. Bob, do you mind if I pour?"

"No, go right ahead."

Patty placed a napkin on the lap of her new maternity dress. "I don't want any."

"Oh, but you have to." Helen poured wine all around as the plates quickly filled. "We're going to have a toast."

Bob took an extra helping of lamb, and covered it with mint jelly. "You know, if you weren't such a good waitress — "

"Hostess."

" — hostess, I'd make you a cook."

Helen replaced the wine bottle in the ice bucket. "You've already got a great cook in that restaurant. Why would you want me?"

Bob ran his hand over her thigh, and kissed her on the white softness of the neck. "Because he's short, fat, and dumpy, and you're exquisitely beautiful."

"Oh, Bob, don't get sexy in front of the kids."

"It's all right, they're married now."

Playfully, she pushed him away. "Now keep your hands to yourself and your mind on your food."

"Hey, don't let us stop you," Tony said, winking. "Maybe we can learn something."

"Cut it out." Patty pushed Tony's hand off her leg.

"Ha, ha, ha. Maybe I can learn something from *you*."

"Oh, Bob, sometimes you're impossible." Helen fought off his attentions. "Now you start eating your food, because you'll need all your energy for later."

"Now, that sounds like an offer." Bob attacked his plate without further ado. He directed his gaze at Tony. "When you're in a lady's apartment and she says something like that, you sure better listen, or there won't be any dessert. Ha, ha, ha. So, tell me, did you get your car straightened out?"

Tony charged into his meal. "Mechanically. The bumper and fender are still bent out of shape."

"How'd it happen?"

"Well, my father didn't want to mess up his Cadillac on some of the jobs because of the dirt and potholes. So he's been using mine. And he ran it into a ditch that had just been filled in with loose dirt."

"How'd he do that?"

"Well, it had just been backfilled so it looked like level ground. But with the weight of the car it just sank right down. Of course, if he hadn't been going so fast there probably wouldn't have been much damage."

"What did it do?"

"Bent a tie rod, broke one spring, and snapped a brake line. The gas station fixed all that, he said, but not the body damage. My father said since the car's old, it's not worth fixing, so he's just going to keep the insurance money and let it go."

"But it's not his car."

"I know, but there's not much I can do about it. It's in his name, he put in the claim since he was driving, and I don't have the time to argue about it."

Helen raised her wine glass and waved the others to do the same. "You know, that surprises me. He seems to be such an — honest man. He must have a good reason for doing it, I'm sure. Now, before this meal goes on any further, let's have a toast. Prosperity, sincerity, and love."

The glasses clinked all around. Helen and Bob drained theirs, Tony and Patty took only token sips. The meal went well, but later, over brandy in the living room, Bob turned on the tube.

"You know, this war on television's really getting out of hand."

Tony stuffed his mouth with apple pie. "The stations going at each other?"

"No, this Vietnam thing. They show it every night."

"I don't like war movies," Patty said. "I usually turn it off, or watch something else."

"Wait a minute. I don't understand. I must have missed something." Tony pushed away the pie plate. "Are you talking about a television production, or something?"

Helen laughed, and emptied her third glass of brandy. "No, dear, he's talking about the six o'clock news. It's just awful what they show on television today. I wouldn't think the FCC would allow that kind of violence."

Tony pinched his eyes, still confused.

Bob said, "It's like a war movie, only worse."

"Yes, there's all this shooting, and bombing, and those people are forever having their villages burned down. I wouldn't live in Saigon for the world. I don't think they should show that kind of stuff when the children are still up."

Tony did his best to control the tremor in his voice. "What are you afraid of, that they might see the world as it really is?"

With a second slice of pie on his plate, Bob kept forking it in. "It's not that. It's just that they shouldn't show all the violence."

"But war is violent."

"I know, but they don't have to show it on television. Besides, it's irrelevant. I would rather see news that's closer to home, something we're involved in."

"But, we're all involved in this conflict."

"Well, I know being in the army involves *you*, but I'm involved in running a restaurant. To me, the war's just something I see on the news. It's kind of like watching *Peyton Place*: every week there's a new situation, new characters, new places, and it never really ends. It's an entertainment. But, I've got my own problems to solve, my own life to live. When you come back you'll understand, because you'll be starting out fresh. You'll have a family to take care of, and that's enough for one man to do. You just do your job and let the rest of the world take care of itself."

"I'll change the channel," Helen said.

****

Kathy had long since gone to bed, this time alone. Tony and Patty lay side by side in the dingy surroundings, listening to traffic and the upstairs neighbors arguing.

"You know I'm going to miss you," Tony whispered. "I'm going to miss you very much."

A white beam from the streetlight found its way through a chink in the Venetian blinds, lay across the growing bulge of Patty's stomach. "Tony, I'm scared."

"Scared? Of what?"

"Well, suppose something happens to you — over there. Who's going to take care of me? I mean, what am I going to do if you get hurt, or something?"

"Oh, Patty, don't worry about that. Nothing's going to happen to me. That stuff you see on television is just a matter of statistics. There are almost half a million men over there, so when two or three get hurt they make a big showing out of it, but percentage wise the number is minimal. I'll be safer there than on the Long Island Expressway."

"But, I don't want to be left alone."

"Nobody's going to leave you alone. Your mother's going to stop over a couple times a week, and if you need a ride anywhere, either Ben or Teddy can take you. Marion said she would help out, too."

"That's not what I mean. I'm scared of — having a baby. I want you to be with me when it comes."

"Listen, I told you I've already applied for a temporary reassignment. Now, the papers are probably waiting for me as soon as I report in tomorrow. They won't send a man overseas if his wife is about to have a baby."

"Are — are you sure?"

"Sure. I asked about it down at Fort Polk. That's why I filled out the papers already — knowing where I was being assigned. So don't worry about it. Everything's going to be all right."

Sobbing, "You promise?"

"I promise."

****

The two-week leave had passed like lightning. It seemed as if only yesterday Tony got off the plane from Louisiana, and today an MP was waving him through the gate at Fort Dix. Ben stopped the Black Stallion and rolled down the window.

Tony leaned forward from the back seat. "I'm returning from leave. Can you tell me how to get to Overseas Processing?"

The face was a mask, the voice a monotone. "Straight ahead, second turn off the circle."

"Thanks."

Ben slammed the car into gear and drove under the lifted gate. "Boy, I can't imagine *you* standing there saluting all day like that asshole."

Katie slapped his arm. "Ben, watch your language."

"Is that what they wanted you to be?" Patty said.

"Yes, but the CO said I had a poor attitude toward military service, whatever that means. Ben, you'd better take your time through here. They're pretty strict about the speed limit."

"So what? I'm a civilian. They can't do anything to me."

"No, but they could make it tough on me."

"So what are they going to do, send you to Vietnam?"

Tony snickered. They passed a long row of decrepit barracks: bare wood scraped clean of paint, window frames hanging half out, glass missing. "Is that what you have to sleep in?" Patty said, aghast.

"Yes, along with about eighty other guys."

"Yeech. How can you put up with it?"

"It's simple. I don't have any choice."

"And you don't even have your own room?"

"We don't even have private stalls in the latrine. Not only that, we have sergeants who are as bad as your grandmother." After a moment, he added, "Well, almost."

"How do you feel going away like this?" Katie asked.

"I had a bigger sendoff when I went to basic training."

"I guess everyone's gotten used to you being away."

Ben said sharply, "Katie, you really know how to say the wrong thing at the wrong time."

After an uncomfortable silence, Tony tapped the glass. "There it is, Ben. Pull over into this parking lot." He glanced at his watch. "We made pretty good time. I've still got a half hour before I have to report in."

Katie twisted in her seat. "I don't think we can wait. My parents are expecting us for dinner."

"Katie, we'll be there in time, so will you

stop worrying about it?"

"Well, I'm sorry, Ben, but I promised we'd be there."

"We'll be there. If not, I'll take the blame."

"Well, it's not as if he's leaving for good. He said he's going to get some kind of reassignment."

"Compassionate reassignment," Tony offered.

"Yeah, well, if you have any compassion leftover, save it for Katie." Ben jerked a thumb at her. "She needs all she can get."

"Ben, I do not like being talked to that way. I've — "

"Katie, will you shut up!"

After sixty seconds of silence, Tony said, "Well, uh, we've pretty much said all our good-byes. I'll call as soon as I get any news — about the reassignment."

Patty nodded, and swallowed hard.

Ben got out of the car and unlocked the trunk, while Tony held the door for Patty. Katie pouted in the front seat.

Tony held out his hand. "Thanks for everything, Ben."

"Have a good time, and don't forget to write."

"That's what I should be saying to you."

"Touché."

Tony threw his arms around Patty. "Now, don't you worry about a thing. It's all going to work out. Okay?"

She mumbled an acknowledgement. Tony kissed her lightly, then shouldered his duffel bag, picked up his overnight case, and marched off toward the Overseas Processing Center. He looked back once, and they were still there, waving frantically. He could not wave because of his bags. When he reached the dilapidated, one-story building they were still waving. He ducked inside.

"Hey, get those bags out of here. Can't you read?" The husky sergeant glowered from behind his desk, mustache bristling.

"Uh, sorry, sergeant." Tony hurriedly backed out the door and put his baggage on the ground next to the sign that he had failed to notice. He looked back just in time to see the '57 Chevy turning a far corner. This time he waved, but there was no answering movement. Sighing, he went back inside.

"That's better." The man behind the name plaque was short and stout in pressed fatigues, with a dark face and a brush haircut. "They put signs up to read, soldier."

"I'm sorry, Sergeant Mendez. I wasn't paying attention."

"You better pay attention now. Sign in here and leave your orders with me. Here's a bedding slip. The issuing office is right around the back of this building. You're assigned to Barrack B, which is right across the parade ground. Chow's at seventeen hundred. You wanna eat, be there. Otherwise, don't leave the barrack. Lights out at twenty-two hundred, reveille's at oh-six hundred. Now get outa here."

Welcome back to army life.

Chapter 77

The next morning started like any other army morning: up at dawn, clean the barracks, outdoor formation (shivering from the cold), general inspection, and march to the mess hall. After all the hustle and bustle, there was nothing to do but — wait.

Names were called out three times a day, during formation, as seats were allocated on the planes. Shipping out time could be anywhere from two days to a week; with luck, longer. The first thing Tony did after breakfast was to inquire of the barrack sergeant the proper procedure for settling personal problems.

"Go see Sergeant Mendez in the orderly room."

Tony was not the only soldier with problems. It seemed as if half the U.S. military force was packed in the office. The line extended right out the door, down the wooden steps, and across the yard. "What are they doing, giving out discharges?" Tony took his place at the end of the line, stamping his feet along with many others who were trying to keep warm.

A steady flow of uniformed men moved through the orderly room doors, all imbued with a haste that added to the frenetic level of activity inside. It was not until nine-thirty, when Tony stepped over the splintered sill and reveled in the inner warmth, that he came to understand the pandemonium.

The single room measured forty feet in length, and was half as wide. Benches lined the center aisle, but precious few found a place to sit. Along both sides, beat-up desks were occupied by PFCs and corporals who clacked away at typewriters, rummaged through filing cabinets, and filled out forms for those who needed help. Added to this were jingling telephones, men running and shouting, chairs and feet scuffling, and papers flying. It was complete and utter bedlam. But at least it was warm bedlam.

Another hour passed before Tony stood in front of the cluttered pine desk of the harried processing sergeant. He was doing five things at once: answering questions from a corporal pointing at blanks on a form, talking on the telephone, writing notes, signing papers, and out of one ear listening to a sob story from the recruit in front of him who wanted to get a message through the Red Cross to his mother before he shipped out.

Sergeant Mendez attached him to the corporal who was presently pestering him, and told him to take care of it. The corporal scowled and walked away, the private following him uncertainly. Tony waited for a short respite in the sergeant's demands before blurting out his dilemma in a rush of words.

"My wife is pregnant and I've filed for compassionate reassignment until after the baby is born."

About a minute passed, during which the sergeant vigorously wrote two memorandums and answered one phone call. "So whaddaya want me to do about it?" Before Tony could think of an appropriate reply, the phone rang again and a corporal approached in haste with a sheaf of papers and half a dozen questions. "Read the form. Read the form," the sergeant shouted gruffly, waving him off. Into the phone, "Tell him I'll call him back." *Slam.*

After another minute the sergeant looked up. "Are you still here?"

"I want to know if the papers have arrived yet."

"What papers?"

"For my reassignment."

"Mister, I don't even know who you are."

"Giovanni, Anthony J., private E-2, US52666498."

The sergeant's tongue flicked out and brushed the bottom of his bristly mustache. "Mister, this is a transient processing center. We don't handle change-of-order requests. You'll have to wait till you get to your final duty station for that."

Above the noise, Tony said, "But that'll be too late. Once I get to Vietnam, they're certainly not going to send me back here until the baby is born."

"What baby?"

"My wife's baby."

"What the hell are you talking about?"

"I've put in for compassionate reassignment until the baby is born."

"We don't handle reassignments, I told you."

"No, you don't understand. I've already applied — at Fort Polk. They told me the paperwork would have to be forwarded, so I'd like to find out if it has arrived."

"Any paperwork from your last duty station would be sent directly to your next duty station. Not here."

"That's not what they told me."

"That's what *I'm* telling you. There's nothing I can do about it. Now move on."

"Wait a minute." Tony clung to the desk as the man behind started to shove him out of the way. "I'm not done." To the sergeant, "The change of orders is supposed to be a temporary reassignment *before* I get to my next duty sta-

tion, otherwise it doesn't do any good. So, how do I find out about the change of orders *now*?"

"I told you, I don't know."

"Then please direct me to someone who does know."

Sergeant Mendez slammed his fist on the desk with enough force to bounce papers onto the floor, and loud enough to turn faces in his direction. "All we do here is process men through. If it's in your orders, we can handle it. But we don't make changes. Do you understand that?"

"I understand, but — "

"Then get the hell out of here. Everything will be taken care of when you get to your next duty assignment. There's nothing more I can do."

"What do you mean there's nothing *more* you can do. You haven't done *anything* yet. Now, my papers are supposed to be forwarded here from Fort Polk. They can't already be in my hand-carried orders because I filed the forms just before I left, and they didn't have time to be processed. They're supposed to reach me here."

"And I'm telling you they're not here!" The sergeant's ruddy complexion darkened.

"How do you know? You haven't even looked yet."

The sergeant came right up out of his seat, and gritted his teeth. "Get this through your fat fuckin' skull. We don't do anything here but process orders. You got a problem, you take it to your commanding officer when you get to your final duty station."

Without waiting a second or batting an eyelash, Tony said, "My orders say to report here, so for the time being my commanding officer is right here. Now, if he's the man I have to see, I'll see him. Otherwise, tell me how to go about getting the information I need."

By this time Sergeant Mendez was apoplectic. He leaned forward on balled fists, breathing hard. "Get him outa here before I tear him apart."

A ringing phone sounded unduly loud in the sudden stillness of the orderly room. Tony glanced around and saw that every eye was on him.

"Uh, sergeant, maybe I can take care of him," said a short, corporal who stepped to the edge of the desk.

"I said get him outa here."

The corporal motioned with his finger. Still glaring at the sergeant, Tony followed the corporal as he weaved through a warren of small desks to a cubbyhole in the corner of the room. Gradually, the hubbub recuperated, the sergeant resumed his seat, another corporal put a cup of coffee on his desk, and the sergeant continued to answer the phone and write an endless stream of notes.

Corporal Ringgold hunched into a chair, the legs squeaking on the rubbed, wooden floor. "What the hell did you want to get the sergeant riled up like that for?"

Tony saw no other chairs, so he remained standing. "The sergeant got himself riled up. I had nothing to do with it."

"Yeah, well, listen buddy, we got enough troubles without you stirring up more. We gotta work with him all day — every day."

"I feel sorry for you, but I have problems of my own." Tony gave a short recounting of the situation.

The corporal was unimpressed. "Well, there's nothing I can do about it."

"You can check to see if the forms have been forwarded to this base."

"Nothing gets forwarded to this base, this is only a processing center."

"Then how are they supposed to catch up with me?"

"I don't know. You should. have had them processed before you left Fort Polk, and hand-carried them with you."

"But they weren't done yet."

The corporal shrugged his shoulders. "I can't help that."

"So what do you suggest?"

He shook his head. "I don't know."

"There must be someone I can see, someone who can do something."

"The sarge's the only one who can do anything."

"But he doesn't *want* to help."

"Well, maybe the Old Man can do something, but I doubt it."

Tony sighed. "And how do I go about seeing him?"

"You have to make an appointment — with the sergeant."

"Oh, great." Tony stopped twirling his hat around in his hands, and put it against his heart, as if it would protect him. "Well, here goes nothing."

"Hey, wait a minute," Corporal Ringgold called out. "You can't just go up there now. You have to get in line."

"I've been in line already. I spent the whole morning in line." Tony did not give him time for further protest. He threaded his way through the forest of desks, filing cabinets, and clerks, stopped in front of Sergeant Mendez, and waited for him to look up. "Sergeant, I would like to see the CO."

For a moment the sergeant was speechless. Then he grimaced, "There's no butting in. Go get at the end of the line."

"Sergeant, I've already been in — "

Shouting, "I said go get at the end of the line."

"But all I want — "

"I don't care what you want, mister. All these other men want something, too. Now you get out of here and come in in the proper order, or I'll have you thrown out. Understand?"

"Sergeant, these silly delaying tactics are — "

"Get the hell out of here!"

Tony shook his head in disgust, making sure the sergeant saw him. Then, he turned and went back to the barrack. It was almost noon, so he went to lunch. Afterward, names were announced and men fell out of formation to retrieve their duffel and board the bus to adjacent Maguire Air Force Base. Tony was volunteered for police detail.

As protest was useless, Tony ducked behind a barrack as the selected squad leader marched the men away. He waited until they were out of sight, then ran to the orderly room. The line was longer than it had been that morning. Three hours later, he stood before Sergeant Mendez' desk.

"You again."

"Yes, sergeant. The corporal was not able to solve my problem and he suggested that I see the CO to get it straightened out."

"Oh, he did, did he?"

"Yes, sergeant."

Sergeant Mendez jerked a fat thumb over his shoulder, at a sign on the door that said Captain Pierson. "And do you think everyone who comes in asking to see the Old Man just goes right past this desk and sees him?"

"I wouldn't know that, sergeant. But I need to see him."

"Well, the captain's too busy today. Come back tomorrow and I'll see what I can do."

"Thank you, sergeant. What time is my appointment?"

"Come back tomorrow and we'll see if he has any time in his schedule."

Offhandedly, Tony said, "Actually, I think it would be more efficient if I just made the appointment now. You see, I don't know when my name might be called out for a flight, and that would add further complications to — "

"Mister, you're beginning to get on my nerves. Now let me tell you something. The Old Man doesn't have me sitting here so I can let every man jack in to see him. He has to go through me first, because the captain's a busy man. And I'm telling you to come back tomorrow and we'll see what we can do. *Now get your ass outa here."*

****

At evening formation, names were announced for nighttime flights. Those men who were called were hastily marched to the mess hall for their last meal.

After dinner, base privileges extended to the PX, snack bar, beer hall, and movie theater. Most of those who chose to remain in the barrack gathered in small pockets under bare bulbs, and played cards, rolled dice, or engaged in bull sessions. The smoke was as dense as that of a pool hall on Saturday night. The camaraderie was the optimism of a temporary stay of execution.

In the morning, Tony played maverick and skipped breakfast call. He went directly to the orderly room. He was not the first one in line, but his forward progress was faster than it had been the previous day. An hour and a half after his arrival, he stood in front of the despotic sergeant.

"Well, Giovanni, I got some bad news for you. The captain ain't coming in today. So just shuffle outa here and come back tomorrow."

"But, sergeant, I may not be here tomorrow. My name — "

"That's what I'm hoping."

" — could be called any minute if I don't get those reassignment papers."

"That's your problem, mister, not mine."

Tony thought about it for ten long seconds, with the sergeant leering at him. "All right, then who can I see who can give me immediate action?"

"There ain't nothing immediate in this man's army."

"Starting at this desk," Tony mumbled. *Why not go all the way to the top?* "In that case, I'd like to make an appointment with the base commander."

The sergeant's jaw dropped slightly, then he took up the slack and slapped it shut. "I don't know what shenanigans you're trying to pull, but it ain't gonna work. Now you just get the hell outa my office before I have you drug out."

"Sergeant, it sounds as if you are purposely trying to hinder me."

His words came out as a hiss. "Mister, I'm warning you."

"I don't understand what you hope to gain by it. I would think if you took any real pride in your job you would want to help people."

Instantly he was on his feet. He reached over the desk and grabbed Tony's tie, applying a twisting motion that snapped him closer. Tony smelled stale tobacco on his breath. "You get outa my office and don't ever come back, or I might reassign you to the hospital." He released Tony with a shove that pushed him back five feet. "Now, get out."

Tony made a tactical retreat. He was mulling over the situation on the outer steps when someone yelled, "Ten-*hut!*" Automatically, he jerked to attention. An officer approached and returned a hasty salute. As the captain passed through the door, Tony noticed his nametag: Pierson. The sergeant had deliberately lied to him.

He punched his left hand with his fist, ducked inside. The captain was already entering his private office behind the sergeant's desk. After six months of experience, Tony had learned different ideas about circumventing military protocol.

He ran around the building, glancing up into windows. He found some cinder blocks and two-by-fours that had been thrown under the flooring, dragged them out, and made a platform so he could see inside. He knocked on the pane ever so lightly.

The captain was sitting at his desk, drinking a cup of coffee and eating a doughnut. Very slowly he turned, and squinted. Tony tossed off a salute, cupped his mouth and put it to the glass. "Sir, the desk sergeant won't let me see you, and I have something urgent to discuss."

Captain Pierson's face remained blank for several seconds, then slowly dissolved through a series of expressions, ending in anger. He came right up out of his seat, took one faltering step toward Tony, then spun on his heel, ran, and yanked open his office door.

Tony did not wait to hear what he was saying. He jumped down from his board and ran across the lawn to a neighboring building, and ducked behind it. As he spun around the corner, he caught a glimpse of two men lighting out after him. He charged across a parade ground to another building, a barrack, ran in the front door and right into the latrine, stepped up to a toilet and dropped his pants, sat down, and tried to control his breathing.

He looked up wearily when the two corporals peeked into the room. He waited five minutes before pulling up his pants and moseying to the mess hall for a belated breakfast. He took his time eating.

****

Because of the constant flow of men through the Overseas Processing Center, it was virtually impossible to keep an accurate muster roll. Tony found it amazingly simple to skip out whenever he wanted.

"Well, I don't know what I can do," said the sandy-haired chaplain."

"You can call the CO and make an appointment for me."

"Well, I don't know if I can do that."

"Sure you can, sir." Tony pointed at the instrument on his desk. "Modern technology. You've got a phone, he's got a phone."

Middle-aged wrinkles formed under faded blue eyes. "Well, I didn't mean that. I meant that strictly as a matter of protocol, I'm not supposed to intercede in the chain of command."

"Then please tell me, sir, what a chaplain *is* supposed to do?" Tony ignored the raised eyebrows. "Explain to me how *you* view your job. Aren't you supposed to help when normal military procedure is causing a problem? Aren't you some kind of — wild card — in the deck, to fill a hand?"

The chaplain laughed at Tony's analogy, his double chin wobbling like a turkey's. "I guess our duties are rather nebulous. You could say that we're here more for moral support than anything else. Of course, under the circumstances I *can*, let us say, make suggestions to proper authorities."

"Well, sir, I don't need any moral support. What I need is to find someone, one single person, who is willing to stick his neck out to help. This entire army is mobilized in order to help other people in other countries, why can't it also help those who are doing the helping? Is it because we're not worth saving, but the Vietnamese are? I mean, what's the point of brutalizing our own people for the sake of another?"

The chaplain's eyes dropped to his shiny desktop. Gravely, he said, "A great many things in this world don't seem to make sense, especially when you're as young as you are. But as you get older, and more world wise, you come to understand that life isn't fair, doesn't have to be fair. Only people can be fair. And sometimes there's just not room for fairness."

"But, sir, I'm supposed to be a free citizen of this country — not a slave bent to someone else's will. Fighting for the freedom of an oppressed people is fine and noble, but I'm beginning to wonder if it's worth the price of our own freedom. Don't we first have to find peace in our own house before we can look for it in others?"

Slowly, the chaplain nodded. "Yes, I suppose you're right — although I'm not sure I understand it all myself."

"But you *are* in a position to help."

"Yes. Yes, I guess I am." He reached for the telephone and dialed a number. "Captain Pierson, please. This is Captain Hunley. . . . Yes, I'll wait. . . . . Hello, Captain? This is Captain Hunley. . . . Yes, very well, thank you. And you? . . . Glad to hear it. Captain, I've got a boy over here name of Giovanni. He's got a problem that's more in your department than mine. Some of his paperwork was to be forwarded here, and it hasn't arrived yet. Or if it has, it hasn't been located. I was wondering if you could help him with it. . . . No, it's about reassignment, a temporary reassignment. He's got a baby on the way and . . . No, he filled it out one or two months ago, but you know how these

things get held up sometimes. . . . Yes. . . . Yes. . . . Yes, that would be fine. How about if I send him over and he can explain it to you? . . . That would be fine. . . . Thank you, Captain. . . . You, too."

The receiver clicked in its black cradle. "Captain Pierson will see you this afternoon. What he's going to do is have you fill out another form, just as a follow up. You'll have to write in that you've already filled out these forms, and when."

"But, will he see to it that my name's not called out in the mean time? I mean, I could be called this afternoon. That would really complicate things."

"Well, that's up to him."

"But can't you — "

"I've done all I can do. I have no real power over any of this. Now you just wait and talk it over with Captain Pierson. He'll take care of everything."

****

"Excuse me, sergeant, but I have an appointment with Captain Pierson." The orderly room was full of noise: typewriters clattering, filing drawers slamming, chairs scraping, men talking. "Excuse me, sir — "

"I heard you the first time, mister." Sergeant Mendez stopped writing and pushed the pad aside. "And nobody has an appointment with the Old Man unless he gets it through me."

"The chaplain, Captain Hunley, has already arranged — "

"And nobody gets to talk to me unless he comes through that line."

"But, sergeant, my appointment has already been set up. I just — " Sergeant Mendez smiled smugly. "I don't care what's been set up, you're not getting past this desk unless you get in line like everyone else."

Tony had nothing planned for the afternoon anyway, so he got in line — outside. It moved quickly today, and in only an hour and a half he was standing before the grim-faced sergeant.

"Sergeant, I have an appointment with Captain Pierson."

The sergeant scribbled out a form without looking up. "I don't remember making any appointments for anybody today."

"You didn't make it. The chaplain did."

"Oh, yeah. And why was that?" He pushed away his paperwork and glowered.

"Because he thought Captain Pierson should look into my problem."

Sergeant Mendez stared for several seconds. His cheek muscles pulsed as he ground his teeth together. The phone rang, he answered it, talked for a couple minutes, and hung up. "Take a seat and I'll let you know when the Old Man's free."

"Thank you. The name's Giovanni."

"I know who you are, mister. Now just take a seat and shut up."

Tony grimaced, but did not answer. Fifteen minutes later, a private stood up from the crowded bench in answer to a call by one of the clerks. Tony squeezed into the narrow slot and tried to make himself comfortable. He could not stretch out his legs without tripping someone, so he tucked them under the bench. He could not make a move without causing everyone else on the bench to move.

He kept a sharp eye on Sergeant Mendez, and listened to him talk on the phone, give orders, and shout at men seeking aid. During a lull, when one of the corporals put a cup of coffee in front of him, Tony approached his desk.

"Sergeant, have you told the captain I'm here?"

"Mister, are you trying to tell me how to do my job? I got more important things to do than sit and listen to whiners all day. Now go and sit down until I call you. Understand?"

"But I haven't heard you tell him I'm here."

"What're you doing, spying on me?" At that moment the sergeant's face could have stopped a freight train. "I keep the Old Man's book and I know when he's got time. Now get the hell outa my hair."

Tony sat down. About an hour later, while he was dozing, someone yelled, "Attention!", and he was momentarily left sitting alone. He jumped up in a rigid pose, not sure what was happening, and just caught a glimpse of Captain Pierson going out the door. After the men sat down, he ran to the sergeant's desk.

"Sergeant, what time is my appointment?"

Sergeant Gonzales was grinning from ear to ear. "Mister, the Old Man has left for the day. Why don't you try again tomorrow?"

Tony was fuming. His fists clenched and unclenched as he returned the sergeant's gaze. He spun on his heel and charged through the door, slamming it against the railing. He walked around in the cool air for a few minutes, then double-timed to the chaplain's office.

"Sir, that desk sergeant won't let me see the captain, even though I had an appointment. He refused to let him know I was even waiting. Now he's gone, and the sergeant just said come back tomorrow."

"Well, if he's gone for the day there's nothing I can do about it. You have to understand that a commanding officer has a great many things on his mind. He's got a big operation to run, and you're just a small part of his duties. Why don't you just calm yourself down and see him tomorrow?"

"But the sergeant won't announce me. He's still a barrier I can't get through."

"Well, it wouldn't be wise for me to pester Captain Pierson. That would only make him angry. Why don't you go in tomorrow, early, and try again."

Tony stalked out of the chaplain's office and kicked down a trashcan outside. He walked around until it was almost time for supper, then returned to his barrack.

"Hey, is your name Giovanni?" said a nearby bunkmate.

"Yes. Why?"

"Well, I think they called your name at the noon formation. You better check with the sarge."

"Thanks." The barrack sergeant was in the day room opposite the latrine. Tony knocked on the door jam (there was no door), leaned in, and said, "Sergeant, one of the men said my name was called this afternoon."

"Who're you?"

"Giovanni, Anthony. Uh, I didn't hear it myself, but I thought I'd better check up on it."

"Were you there?"

"Yes," Tony lied.

"Hmmmn." The young three-striper pulled a clipboard off its nail and ran a finger down the list. "Don't see nothing — oh, wait, here it is."

Tony felt a sinking sensation in the pit of his stomach.

"No, that ain't you. This is Giocomo, Philip R. There ain't no Giovanni."

Tony breathed a deep sigh of relief. "Thanks, sarge."

****

Sergeant Mendez was happy again. "The Old Man ain't in today, so I guess you'll have to come back tomorrow."

"I guess I will. But in the mean time, I'd like to fill out the reassignment form that the captain is going to have me fill out."

"I don't know nothing about that."

"But I do. He mentioned it on the phone when he was talking with Captain Hunley. It would save a lot of time if I had it already filled out for him. One of your men can help me with it, I'm sure."

"You're very persistent, aren't you?"

"I'm just trying to do things by the book."

The sergeant's smiled faded into a grimace. Still staring hard at Tony, he said, "Pappernick, take care of this man. And make sure the paperwork is on my desk before you leave. I want to take care of this personally."

****

The next morning, Tony appeared bright and early, and was again at the head of the line. He was standing in front of Sergeant Mendez before he had finished drinking his first cup of coffee.

Tony offered a disarming smile. "If the captain's not in yet, I'll wait."

"Giovanni, you're beginning to piss me off."

"And I thought I'd fill out another set of re-assignment forms. You know, just in case the others got somehow — misplaced."

The sergeant rose slowly to his feet. "Now you get this and you get it straight. I don't want you hanging around my office all day. The captain will see you if and when he gets the time. Now you just go back to your barrack and wait till I call you."

"I think I'll stop over and see the chaplain again."

****

Tony crossed the parade ground in the dark and walked imperiously into the orderly room, blinking at the bright lights within. "Private Giovanni reporting, sergeant."

Sergeant Mendez, alone in the building, looked up from his crossword puzzle, his beetle eyes squinting. The desk lamp by his chin gave his features a more garish look than usual. The normal pandemonium had ended hours ago.

"Well, well, well. Come in, Giovanni."

Since he was already in, Tony stood uncomfortably for several seconds. "The orderly said you wanted to see me."

His eyes twinkled like tiny fires, ready to reach out and burn someone. "Yes, I wanted to see you, you lucky son of a bitch. I was hoping to get rid of you permanently, but it looks as if your luck has held out. And there's nothing I can do about it."

Tony began to relax, but he refrained from smiling triumphantly.

"We got a telegram from the Red Cross asking for emergency leave for you. If it had been up to me, I'd have thrown it out and said we never got it. Then I'd have you on a plane tomorrow. But it came straight from battalion HQ."

The sergeant flung the brown parchment over the top of his puzzle. Tony cringed inwardly as he bent to pick it up. In the subdued light he read the curt message, a single sentence. His vision blurred, the telegram shook in his hand. He could no longer see the writing. He could not even see the desk except as a wavy dollop of light going round and round. He felt weak, ready to collapse.

"I don't know how you timed it this way, Giovanni, but I'll tell you this: if you're not back here by Friday midnight, I'll have your ass in front of a court-martial board. You got that?"

Despite the stabs of pain that were wrenching his heart, Tony wanted to smash his fist into the sergeant's mocking face, and knock every one of those gleaming, flaunting teeth down his

bulging throat. But before his tear-stricken face became apparent, he turned and ran out of the office in which so many men had met their nemesis.

Out into the blackness and the all-forgiving night, he ran with creeping horror, across the wide parade ground, until he fell into a heap under a crouching oak, there to sob out the pain and loneliness brought by the message that he clutched tightly in his fist. But darkness could not hide, nor crying subside, the meaning of that hated sentence.

"Request seven day emergency leave for Pvt. Anthony Giovanni, US52666498, because of grandfather's death."

Chapter 78

Dark gray clouds filled the morning sky. A brisk breeze swept dry and crumbling leaves across the cemetery, like children playing tag among the tombstones. The chill in the air was made more biting by the sprinkle of rain.

"Yea, though I walk through the valley of the shadow of death, I shall fear no evil, for thou art with me. . . "

As the Baptist preacher droned, the pall bearers loosened their grips on the ropes and slowly lowered the casket into the ground. Pauline and Elizabeth held their handkerchiefs to tear-strewn faces. Frank stood stoically, with a somewhat bored expression on his face. Patty, standing by Tony's side and holding his hand, was unmoved by the procession. Robby stared blankly, his childish lack of awareness of events protecting him from feelings of pain, of loss, of emptiness. Tony wept quietly, sniffling because he had no handkerchief in his uniform pocket.

" . . . and I will dwell in the house of the Lord forever."

The casket came to rest on the hard-packed dirt at the bottom of the hole; the ropes were withdrawn. People in the rear of the crowd started peeling away. The grave was still open as the family departed, later to have a cement vault lowered into it before the dirt was shoveled on top.

The mourners bent against the wind, and held tightly onto their umbrellas. Car doors opened and closed. The weeping continued in the tiny, separate environments. Robby climbed into the limousine, too awed to talk or ask questions. Tony could see that his brother knew that his grandfather was dead, but suspected that he did not comprehend that he would never see his grandfather again, or that there was a quality of life that he would grow up without ever knowing.

But Tony understood it all, and had to live with that understanding.

****

The last of the guests had gone. Darkness had descended, and at last the long, hectic day was nearing its end. Grandmom was busily scraping dishes, and wrapping leftovers from the buffet in cellophane.

"Can I help, Grandmom?" Tony carried dishes and plates to the sink, put them under the faucet.

"I got most ever'thing washed cept'n the platters, Honey. You can rinse them off an' help me put the cold cuts in the ice box."

"Okay." Tony tore off a sheet of cellophane and began neatly packaging the extra ham, turkey loaf, and cheese. Grandmom resumed her position at the sink and started running hot water into the basin. She bowed her gray head forward, reached behind her and retied the strings of her apron. She had been doing that for nearly fifty years: a habit which she was unlikely to change.

"I don't know what I'm gonna do with all this food." The basin was filled. With her hands immersed in the soapy water, she started washing the meat platters. "With your grandfather not needin' any lunches, I'll be a month o' Sundays eatin' it all. Why don't you ask your mother if she wouldn't like to take some of it home?"

Zombie like, Tony said, "Okay."

"You can take some yourself, if you need it. When is it you have to go back to the army?"

"Well, I don't have to report in until Friday."

Scrubbing and rinsing, she nodded. "Honey, I got a passel of things left undone, and with your grandfather not here to help me, I don't think I can do it all. Do you think you can you stay a day or so an' help me put things away?"

"Sure, Grandmom. I want to stay anyway. And I've got my car so I don't have to go home with Mom and Dad."

Dishwashing completed, she poured the dirty water down the drain and began rinsing. "Well, I certainly 'preciate it."

Elizabeth entered the room carrying a bundle of clothes. "Mother, what do you want to do with these things of Daddy's?"

" 'Spect I'll just give 'em away to the Good Will, and let some poor colored folk have the use of 'em. God knows I don't need 'em no more. Just put them aside and I'll get a box for 'em. And Bethy, do you want to take some of that lunchmeat home with you? Maybe Frank can take it for his lunch."

"All right." Elizabeth dropped the clothes onto Grandpop's favorite rocking chair. "Do you want me to put them in a bag?"

"No, I got some boxes in the basement. I'll get 'em later. Bethy, when are you an' Frank plannin' to go back?"

"Oh, I don't know. I'll have to ask him. He says he's got some job to check up on, but I don't know why it can't wait another day." She turned and stepped to the kitchen doorway, and called out loud, "Frank, when do you want to get ready?"

The television blared from the living room. Patty looked up, but Frank ignored her.

"Frank, answer me."

"What?"

"I said, when do you want to start getting ready?"

"I told you, I got a meeting tomorrow. We gotta leave first thing in the morning so I don't lose the afternoon."

Elizabeth shook her head. "I guess we'll go right after breakfast."

"Mom, I'm going to stay a day or so and help Grandmom out."

'I got some things that need movin', an' some chores I just can't handle by myself."

"You may as well stay and help, then," Elizabeth said. "You don't have anything to do at home anyway."

****

Tony did a variety of tasks, from cleaning the attic and going through decades of old memorabilia, to replacing some missing shingles on the roof and organizing the garage, tool shed, and basement. Items for which his grandmother no longer had any use were separated into lots, to be given to those relatives who would get the most out of them.

Smelling of musk, his clothes covered with dust and cobwebs, Tony sank down wearily beside Patty in front of the television. He rubbed her tummy thoughtfully, never getting enough of the movement that was life. During a commercial, she asked, "Tony, when can we go home?"

He lay back on the floor and closed his eyes. "Oh, I don't know. I'll have to ask Grandmom what else needs to be done."

"I'm tired of being here."

"How can you be tired? Grandmom and I have done all the work."

"That's not what I mean. I just don't like being stuck way out in the country."

Tony managed a weak laugh. "Yes, I guess for a died-in-the-wool city slicker like you, it must be different."

"That's not what I mean. I don't have anything to do."

"You could help out."

"I didn't mean work."

He opened his eyes and rolled them in her direction. "Well, it doesn't matter. I need the work. I need to be here, in this house, with Grandmom, because of the memories. I feel comfortable here, and I don't want to leave.

I'm afraid it won't be here when I get back. Besides, you can watch television here just as easily as you can at home."

"But they have only one channel here, and they keep switching from one network to another. There's no way of telling what's coming on."

Tony closed his eyes again, drifting off. "Life is full of problems."

****

"Well, Honey, I want to thank you for all the work you did." Grandmom twitched her lips into the semblance of a smile. She pulled her shawl tighter over her narrow shoulders with thin, veined hands.

"Oh, that's all right, Grandmom. I was glad I could help. I — I'm glad I got to stay around for a while. I needed to, just for myself."

She bent over and peered into the car. "Now, you take god care o' that baby of yours, Patty. We want to see it grow up big and strong."

Patty half smiled. "I will."

Tony stood by the open door for a moment, pulled his grandmother close and kissed her on the cheek. "Will you be all right?"

"Don't you worry 'bout me none. I got plenty o' people as can come an' help me if need be." She kissed him again, then pushed him away and held him at arms length. "Tony, I almost forgot." She fumbled in the pocket of her faded print apron, brought out something that gleamed gold in the sun. "Your grandfather told me he wanted you to have this." She pressed the Waltham pocket watch against his palm. He could feel it ticking. "He said he knew you would take good care of it."

Tony swallowed hard, blinking away tears. "Thanks," he croaked. After one final embrace, he pocketed the watch, climbed into the car, and pulled the door shut. "Bye, Grandmom."

"Bye, Honey."

As he backed down the stone driveway, she stood there alone: a frail and pathetic figure. She had nothing behind her but an empty house, nothing ahead of her but a lonely and directionless life. Her silver hair sparkled in the sun, her eyes glinted. She smiled, but as she did, a small tear rolled down her cheek, off her jaw, and onto the ground, where it was instantly swallowed by the dry and thirsty earth.

Tony did not want to abandon her. He wanted to stay forever, with her, with his memories. But the world was pressing in on him, and he had things to do. He wiped his eyes so he could see the road, but his thoughts would not leave him any peace.

They would never leave him.

Chapter 79

Tony's pass expired at midnight; he checked in with only minutes to spare. "I'm returning from emergency leave."

The unfamiliar desk sergeant glanced at his papers, pushed around the sign-in book. "Where you headed?"

Tony scrawled his name with the pencil stub. "Well, I'm supposed to be waiting for reassignment papers until after my wife has a baby."

"Guess you belong in Holding Company, then. Give this to the barrack sergeant." The sergeant handed him a slip of paper. "Go out to the street and turn right. It's that barrack in the next block. You can't get bedding till morning, but they prob'ly got a few spare blankets."

"Thanks." Tony shouldered his duffel bag and carried his overnight bag through the chill night air. He was more than happy to get into the dilapidated building. "Just got in from leave."

The three-striper had been leaning back on a flimsy wooden chair, barely awake, but Tony's entrance brought him to full awareness. He looked at the chit, pulled a clipboard off a nail, and entered Tony's name. "Grab a bunk with some blankets on it and sack out. And keep the noise down."

"Thanks." The room was in darkness, but he was able to find an empty bunk without too much stumbling around. He spread out the blanket, as well as one from the neighboring bunk, and wrapped them around him cocoon-like. He was too tired for the mattress buttons to bother him.

When he opened his eyes, the sun was unusually high. A glance at his watch told him that the time was after seven. He sat bolt upright, noticing that the dozen or so men in the room still slept.

"Don't start worrying," said the sleepy-eyed man in the bunk next to him. "We don't go to breakfast till seven thirty."

"How come?"

The man pulled the covers over his head. "Been that way as long as I been here."

Twenty minutes later, the barrack sergeant entered the room and switched on the lights. "Anyone for breakfast, follow me."

Tony threw on his clothes, but half the others simply rolled over and ignored the wake-up call. Over a second cup of coffee, Chapman, the bunk mate, explained that Holding Company was a dumping ground for those who were awaiting reassignment, change of orders, court-martial, Article 15, or were held over for medical reasons. One man had sprained his ankle and the doctors did not want him shipped to Vietnam until the cast was removed.

"I got a sure fire method," Chapman explained. "Most guys hand-carry their orders during transfer. But sometimes, like when a whole outfit is being shipped over, they send the orders by courier. The thing is, at the receiving station they never know how the orders are coming. So, when I got my orders, I dropped the whole envelope in a trashcan and burned them up. When I got here, I told 'em they'd been sent ahead. They waited a while for 'em to show up. After a couple of weeks, there was nothing they could do but requisition a duplicate set. The whole process takes three months. When HQ called me in and gave me the new set, and told me to go to Overseas Processing, I did it all over again. Not a damn thing they can do to me, so I gotta wait till they get another duplicate set made up. The sergeant'd love to get rid of me, but he can't do a thing without orders. If I can keep it up long enough, I figure I'll be up for discharge before I get sent to Nam."

Although Tony realized that the night-shift sergeant had made an error in sending him to Holding Company, he took Chapman's advice and kept a low profile. As soon as he learned the ropes of his new position, he took advantage of the situation.

****

When Tony walked into the garage, the heated discussion that was in progress promptly broke up. "Hi. Mind if I come in?"

"Tony!" Teddy leaped across the floor and grabbed his hand, pumping it violently.

"What're you doing home?" Ray said, with less enthusiasm.

"Well, I managed to get away for the night. They didn't need me."

"Man, you're just like a bad penny — you keep coming back." Pete gave him a shot on the shoulder which nearly knocked him over.

Ben swept long blond hair out of his face. "Yeah, but I'm the one who's got to keep taking you back all the time."

"Not this time. I'm going to take my car with me so I can commute." Tony was instantly hammered with questions. He hushed them with a papal wave of the hands. "I'm in a Holding Company, and I'm supposed to wait there until further orders. It's great because every day they assign a new group of guards to keep an eye on us, but they're just regular guys on their way to Vietnam, so they're pretty lax about things. All I did was sneak away after chow, get a bus in Wrightsville, a little town that's actually inside the base, and as long as I'm back for morning roll call, everything's groovy."

"You are one smooth son of a gun," Pete said.

"All I do all day long is read. I lie in my bunk until I get uncomfortable, then I sit in a chair for a while. The guards take turns going to the

PX, and they don't mind us tagging along. I'm telling you, it's really great."

Ray smoothed his slacks and reached for his overcoat. "Hey, let's celebrate. We'll go out and get a hamburger."

Ben scowled. "You go out and get a hamburger every night — that is, if you can get someone to drive you."

"Yes, but we have to take Tony home."

"Ray, you're as transparent as that jewelry you sell. All you want to do is to check up on Kathy."

"You watch your goddamn mouth." Ray stabbed a finger in Ben's chest. "I don't need any grief from *you*."

"Yeah, well maybe — "

"Hey, yo. Guys. Do you mind if we cut out the fighting? I don't have much time. And I would like to see my wife sometime tonight."

For a while it seemed like old times: the jokes, the gags, the screaming out the car window, the French fry fights. But only for a while.

****

When the alarm went off at five a.m., Tony reached out of bed and punched it before its rattling woke up Kathy in the adjoining room. Patty stirred, but kept her eyes closed. She snuggled close to Tony under the covers.

Tony disentangled himself from her, climbed out of the warmth of the bed, and switched on the closet light. He kept the door partially closed, and got dressed in the thin shaft of light that shone through. He buttoned the dress green jacket, but left his tie hanging loose from his neck. Then he kneeled by the bed and kissed Patty on the cheek. "I have to go now."

She smiled, and half opened her eyes. Her arms came out from under the blankets and surrounded him. She pulled him close and kissed him on the lips. "Will you be able to come home tonight?"

"I don't see why not. But if I can't, I'll call."

"Okay."

Tony gave her another peck on the cheek, and patted her bulbous tummy. She released him. He crept out of the room into the crisp predawn. He let the car warm up before driving to camp. An hour later he stepped jauntily into the barrack, swinging his overnight bag. "Hi."

The guard had been sitting with his chin against his chest, and breathing sonorously. His head jerked up with a start, and his eyes blinked in the dim light. "Hey, where the hell have you been?"

"I had an emergency at home."

"Well, Jesus Christ, man, don't sneak off like that. I'm responsible for all you guys if you aren't here for roll call."

"Gee, I'm sorry. I didn't mean to get you into any trouble. But I figured you wouldn't let me go if I just asked. Would you?"

"Yeah, well, I guess not. I don't really care what you guys do, you know, it's just that I gotta turn in a report after you're mustered in. You live around here?"

"Philly. Only took an hour to get here. There isn't much traffic this time in the morning."

"I guess not."

"Well, if you don't mind, I'll catch another hour's sleep before chow."

And so the days passed. Tony remained inconspicuous. During the day he read and slept; during the night he hung out with the gang or spent time with Patty. In the barrack, men came and went. And every morning he surprised the neophyte guards who had thought he was missing. They were always so pleased to have him back that they never gave a thought about reporting his nocturnal activities. It was an idyllic, almost happy life.

Until the surprise barrack inspection just before Christmas.

****

The first snow flurries of the year swept across the ground: large white flakes that were too dry to stick. The wind whipped them along so fast that they did not have time to settle, except where they accumulated against curbs and leafless trees and buildings.

Holding Company did not have central heat, so the men either slumbered in their bunks under a pile of wool blankets, or gathered around the lone kerosene heater. At the far end of the room, condensation on the windows had long since formed into a glistening pattern of interlocking crystals. No one ever ventured to the second floor.

Sergeant Mendez entered without a flourish. He stamped his feet on the creaking wooden floor: his spit shined shoes were covered with cold, white dandruff that quickly melted. His face was a barren plain, pockmarked like the face of the moon — and just as cold and foreboding. Only his eyes were alive, stabbing out from under darkened brows with steely radiance.

"You men better stand at attention when I come in here."

For about five seconds no one moved. Then the corporal in charge for the day dropped his cards and yelled, "Attention!" falling back over his chair. The men burst into activity. Loungers jumped off their seats, blankets flew off men lying in their bunks, a poker game was abandoned with loose change jingling to the floor, comic books and magazines were dropped, conversation was halted. Like a call to arms, every man scrambled back to his bunk and stood rigidly at attention.

After the noise died down and the last boot shuffled, Sergeant Mendez strutted slowly along the aisle. He cast a dirty look at the table that was placed near the heater.

"Guards! You let these men play cards in a military barrack during duty hours."

The corporal stumbled forward. "Sergeant, I didn't think there was anything wrong — "

"There will be no more card playing during duty hours," the sergeant boomed. The guard wilted like an overcooked strand of spaghetti. "These beds *will* be made every morning, and not slept in except at night. This floor *will* be waxed and polished."

"But sergeant, the water pipes are frozen, and we can barely flush the — "

"No excuses." He stopped in front of Chapman. "Ties *will* be worn. And you, take off that jacket!"

Tony fumbled with the zipper. "It's pretty cold in here, sarge, and — "

"Field jackets are not worn over dress uniform, is that understood?" Tony dropped it on the bunk behind him. "Yes, sergeant."

The sergeant walked slowly back along the aisle, and stopped in front of the corporal of the guards. "Mister, I want this place cleaned up and everything looking like a military showcase by seventeen hundred hours. That means everything from dusting the attic to polishing shoes. And you — " The finger pointed directly at Tony. "Report to my office."

****

The Overseas Processing Center was just as crowded, just as noisy, and just as chaotic as always. And the line to get inside was just as long.

Tony swung his arms amid the swirling snow in a vain attempt to keep from freezing. Dress greens were the only allowable uniform, and the thin jacket was woefully inadequate. Without gloves, earmuffs, long underwear, and an overcoat, the cold was intensely painful. But Tony had never been issued any of these items. He stood outside for over an hour before reaching the door and the welcome warmth inside.

Amid the typing, filing, and screaming, pandemonium reigned. Tony had not yet stopped shaking from the cold when Sergeant Mendez, his desk still thirty feet away, spotted him.

"Where have you been, mister?"

"Standing in line, sergeant."

"Get up here and stop stalling around."

As Tony approached the sergeant's desk, he cast apologizing expressions to the men who were waiting in line. "I wouldn't want to butt in front of all these men, sarge."

Sergeant Mendez had the look of a hungry bear. "What kinda game are you playing, Giovanni?"

"Sarge, I know how you don't like it when

men buck the line, so — "

"Don't get cute with me."

"Sarge?"

"You were supposed to be outa here a month ago. Now I find you slinking around in Holding Company where you have no business being."

"Sergeant, don't you remember that I applied for a compassionate reassignment? Now, the baby's due in a few weeks — " It never hurt to stretch a point.

"I don't remember nothing about you being given a reassignment — of any kind. I only remember you playing footsie and hiding behind dead relatives so you could stay stateside while all your buddies are fighting the war for you. Now, before you get any bright ideas, I've already talked this over with the Old Man. We can't find your records because they've already been sent to your unit, where *you* should have been sent a long time ago. But one thing I do know: there ain't any reassignment papers to keep you here."

"But, sergeant, I've filled out the forms more than once, even right here in this office — "

"We don't have any record of it."

"Then you can't say they haven't been approved unless you have specific orders disapproving my reassignment. Now, the baby's going to be here any day now, and all I need — "

"There are thousands of babies born in this country every day, and everyone is born without the father's help. Yours is no different. I've seen a lot of you malingerers come through here trying to shirk your duty. And it's my job to see to it that you guys get to where you're going. They need you over there. I've heard a million excuses, and that's all they ever are — excuses."

"But, sarge, I'm not trying to get out of anything. I just need a little time — "

"That's enough!" He jumped to his feet and at the same time slammed his fist on the desk. An unearthly silence took control of the room: not a loose sheet of paper shuffled.

"It's not enough!" Tony shouted, then stepped back immediately as a fist shot across the desk. The sergeant made a grab for his jacket, but missed. "I told you I only wanted to be held back long enough — "

Sergeant Mendez regained his balance, if not his composure. "You don't tell me nothing, mister. I give the orders around here. And right now I'm gonna see to it that you're on the next plane outa here."

Controlling his voice, Tony said, "I'm not leaving until I know my wife is all right."

The sergeant was breathing like a bull in heat. "Mister, you better listen and listen good. I'm telling you to get back to your barrack and pack your bags. I want you back here in ten minutes, or I'll come looking for you. I'm putting you some place where I can keep an eye on you until I cut your orders. Now get moving."

Tony got moving, all the way. Ten minutes later, he eased the white Ford Galaxie through the west gate.

Chapter 80

Patty's eyes were filled with tears; her auburn hair framed her now pudgy face like a picture of sorrow. Lying in bed, she was propped up against the antique headboard with a pillow supporting her lower back. Her belly arched with life under the soft, pink blanket.

"I don't understand. How can they do this?"

Tony sat on the edge of the bed and shrugged his shoulders. "I don't know. I don't know if the reassignment was turned down, or if it was never put through, or if the sergeant just threw it out."

"But didn't you tell him — "

"There's no telling a sergeant." He stared down at his hands, balled into fists of frustration. He was shaking slightly. "He just wouldn't listen. He doesn't even care. No one cares."

Patty reached out and placed her warm hand on his thigh. Her lower lip trembled. "You're not going back, are you? They'll just send you away. I need you here."

Tony breathed deeply and looked into her watery eyes. "No, I'll stay here with you. Now that I've taken the big step, I intend to see it through. After all, I did everything I could — filled out the forms, twice; tried to see the CO. It's their fault, not mine. If they only would have listened . . . "

****

"Jesus Christ, man, won't you get into trouble?" Pete barked.

"Of course I'll get into trouble. But what can they do, send me to Vietnam?"

"Shit, that ain't very smart."

"Neither is getting drafted," Ben bristled. He ran his hand through his hair where it was touching his collar. "Now you know why I'm against all that. This whole Vietnam scene is a load of crap."

"Ben, this has nothing to do with the moral implications of the war."

"It has *everything* to do with it, because it's not our war. And it's causing all this — strife — when we should be minding our own — "

"Hey, man, lay off, will ya?" Pete cried. "It don't matter whether the war's right or wrong, we're in it."

"That's where you're wrong. You're deluded. There's more fighting and contention *here* than there is in the jungle. The major conflict is right here, in our own country, because people don't believe in this war."

"People?" Pete screamed. "What people? Kids? College jerks hiding behind their books to stay out of the draft?"

"I don't see you running off to the recruiting office," Ben retorted smugly.

"Yo! Guys! Hold up!" Tony stepped between the two before they came to blows. "We don't need another fight."

The two glared at each other. Ben, a head taller, peered down his long nose in silent fury. He moved aside and sat on the tattered cushion of a springless chair in the corner of the garage. He stared broodingly at the ceiling.

"Sorry, Tone," Pete said.

"That's all right."

"So what're you gonna do?"

Tony paced back and forth across the three-layered carpet. "I don't know. I haven't figured it out yet."

"Haven't figured what out yet?" Ray ducked under the drainpipe, pulling in the sleeves of his blue serge coat. The crease on his pants was knife-edge sharp.

Teddy marched in behind him, wearing a beige CPO jacket. "Hi, Tone." His smile faded as soon as he saw the roomful of long faces. "Hey, what's wrong?"

Ray brushed snow off his overcoat and hung it up neatly on a hanger. His dark blue suit was immaculate. "What's the matter? Somebody die?"

"Worse than that. I'm AWOL."

Ray let out a little snicker. "Well, it's not the first time, is it?"

"No, but this time it's bad, because it's permanent."

Ray shrugged, picked up a handful of darts, moved to the opposite side of the garage, and started shooting at the well-worn corkboard.

Teddy reached his hands out imploringly. "What do you mean? You're not going back?"

"It's that Sergeant Mendez again. He found out I was in Holding Company and told me to get ready to ship out. I tried to tell him I couldn't go yet, but it seems that once you get drafted you give up all rights of being a citizen."

The feathered darts thudded into the cork as Ray, with his back to Tony, appeared to pay little attention.

"I only want to stay until after the baby is born, but they won't listen. So, since I couldn't do things the right way by getting the temporary reassignment, I had to take matters in my own hands. I'm not going back — at least, not until after I'm sure Patty and the baby are all right."

"Tone, they can't do that to you," Teddy said.

Ben shifted his weight in the chair, the aged wood groaning. "Oh, yes they can."

"But that's not fair. You've got a family to take care of."

"Doesn't mean anything to the army," Tony said.

"But, what's going to happen to you?"

"Well, I guess when I turn myself in, I'll be court-martialed. I might have to go to jail."

Still intent on his game, Ray pulled the darts out of the board. "You gotta do what you gotta do."

Ben shook his head. "You're a big help."

"Hey, Tone," Pete said, brows beetling. "What're you gonna tell your folks?"

"Yeah, your old man's not going to like it," Ben said.

Tony thought before answering. "Well, I guess I'll just have to make them believe I'm still going to the base every day, even if I don't. There's no way he can find out otherwise."

Pete whistled. "Boy, are you gonna be in trouble when he does."

"And suppose the MPs come checking around your house," Ben said.

"Yeah, that's how my brother got caught." Pete perched on the end of the sofa, his sneakers on the torn cushions. "He was coming home unofficially when he got picked up at the airport by MPs checkin' passes."

"Do they really do that?" Tony wondered.

"Yeah, they locked him up right on the spot, handcuffs and all. And if you desert, they'll send the FBI to your house."

"What constitutes desertion?"

"Anything more'n thirty days AWOL."

"Oh, great."

Ben picked up a half inflated football and tossed it in the air, bouncing it off the ceiling. "Well, look at the good side of things. At least you'll be home for Christmas. And you'll get to see my brother."

"Joey's coming home? Wow, that's great."

"Yeah," Ben said tonelessly.

"Don't get too excited. It's only been a year."

The football took a wrong bounce and sailed across the room, hitting Ray in the leg. "Yeah. The stupid bastard's only got six months to go, so what does he do? Extends so he can apply for combat duty. The son of a bitch wants to be a fighter pilot in Vietnam."

"You gotta do what you gotta do."

****

Tony accompanied Patty to Wanamaker's, as much to be with her and carry her packages as to prevent her from spending too much money on Christmas presents. But he refused to enter the lingerie department until circumstances forced him.

"Patty, you're not going to believe what just happened. There were two kids out there, grade school kids, and they called me a killer. And the people who heard it looked at me as if it were true."

She held up a sheer negligee to the light. "Anybody you know?"

He twirled his army hat in his hand. "No. I don't think so. It must have been the uniform."

"Then don't worry about it. Look, what do you think of these?" She handed him the stockings that were draped over her arm. "They're on sale, one third off. And I need stockings."

"Patty, you don't understand. They called me a killer — a baby killer. Now, where do you suppose they picked up something like that?"

"They're just kids. You know, the price is so cheap I think I'll buy a dozen."

"I thought we came here to get a gift for your mother?"

"I need some things, too."

"But why would they say something like that? It doesn't make any sense." Patty started looking around for a sales girl. "Let me have some money." Tony ran after her. "Patty, you're not listening to me."

She stopped in the middle of the aisle. "I heard you the first time. But what do you want me to do about it? Now, give me some money so we can get out of here."

****

"Are you sure this is the right address?"

Tony opened the car door and gave Patty a hand. She squirmed her body around and let him pull her onto the sidewalk. He stared down the row of brick homes. "She said the corner house, with the lights on. The corners are always duplexes."

"All right, but we can't stay long. My mother's expecting us to go shopping with her and Bob."

"We just got back from shopping. And here your girlfriend gets her own apartment and you don't even want to stop in and see it. Besides, she's probably got a Christmas present for the baby, or something, if I know her."

"But, Tony, I haven't bought anything for her. You're so stingy with the money, I couldn't get her anything."

"That's not the way presents work. Some people just like to give."

They passed under the streetlight, it's bulb spreading a yellowish glow to the snow that still clung to the walkways. A narrow path had been cleared on the pavement, and the stone steps had been swept clean.

"She lives in the downstairs." Tony pushed the lower doorbell button. "It's a good thing for Pete she decided to get a place of her own. Now he can come here when he gets dr — when he drinks too much, and doesn't want to face his parents."

The lock snapped and the inner door opened. Through the glass panes, Tony saw Marion

backlighted by incandescent lamps, her red hair sparkling like a solar corona. Then the outer door squeaked open on rusty hinges.

"Tony. Patty. I'm glad you could come. Please come in."

Tony pushed his wife in front of him. Marion gave her a quick embrace, and Tony a friendly peck on the cheek. Tony said, "Trying to drag her out of a department store is like pulling teeth from a lion."

"We can only stay for a couple — "

"*Surprise!*"

Patty stopped dead in her tracks, with one hand in Marion's and the other against the doorjamb. The chorus of voices came from more than twenty women inside, all decked out in lovely party dresses. Some were standing, some were sitting, many were stretched on the floor. Marion did not yet have much furniture.

Tony pushed Patty into the room. "Humph. Looks like a surprise baby shower."

Patty turned a bright shade of red, like cherry blossoms in spring. "Did you know about this?"

He smiled, pointing, "Why don't you ask your mother?"

****

The college campus was not as he remembered it: the spring flowers were gone, the trees were barren of their leaves, the sidewalks were cold and empty, and the grass where so many students had lain was brown and withered. Only the ivy-covered walls remained the same. The chill in the air was made evident by an occasional passerby bundled like some winter gnome. Tony walked against the wind, hunched over with his hands in the pockets of his dress greens.

From the direction of the dormitories exuded a sound that floated in the crisp air like a weird cabalistic chanting, or a secret voodoo ceremony deep in Jamaican jungles. At first the chant was muffled by the fragrant gusts. As he got closer he could make out the words — faintly, but all too distinctly.

"Hey! Hey! L.B.J.! How many kids did you kill today?"

When he rounded the corner of the main lecture hall and entered the Mall, he saw several hundred students, clothed in a wide array of jackets and overcoats but for the most part hatless, swinging placards in the air as they shouted their requiem. Several fifty-five gallon drums blazed with fires that were kept alive with rolled newspapers and scraps of wood. From one of the drums sprouted a stuffed, rubber-masked scarecrow nailed to a cross, in effigy of President Johnson. Cheers arose as the ragged feet caught fire. In seconds, the entire straw sculpture was engulfed in flames that soared twenty feet into the air.

"Hey! Hey! L.B.J.! How many kids did you kill today?"

Tony saw no teachers or proctors; they were being smart and staying out of the way. This activity was beyond faculty control, anyway.

A group of young men surrounded another drum. One by one, ceremoniously, and to the cheers of the crowd, they held tiny slips of paper high in the air, approached the blaze, yelled out, "Up yours, Johnson!" They deposited their draft cards in the cauldron of fire.

Above it all arose the chant, "Hey! Hey! L.B.J.! How many kids did you kill today?" The students were intent on their antiwar ritual with a fervor borne only by crowds out of control.

Even though he hung back behind the fringes, soon someone noticed him. "Hey! G.I. Joe! You gotta lotta guts coming around here."

Gradually, they began to take notice of his uniform. It was like waving a red cape in front of an angry bull. Most of them just stared, unbelievingly, but some called out, some sneered, and some made obscene gestures with extended digits. Tony heard language from fuzzy-haired girls that he had thought only came out of the mouths of sergeants.

"Get a load of the ROTC man."

"Who the fuck invited him?"

"Why don't you stick those ribbons up your ass?"

"Hey, cock sucker, you're not gonna get my pussy."

Tony stood speechless. Now the crowd gathered around him, and he began to feel like a clown between acts in a three-ring circus. Two people broke from the encircling throng, advancing purposely. The girl wore a thick, woolen rag coat with an attached hood that was pulled down to reveal an even more ragged mop of dark, curly hair. Large brown eyes bulged from a flat, featureless face.

"Gail?" Tony said cautiously.

The other was thickly bearded, and wore skintight jeans and a worn leather jacket. Quick, birdlike eyes peered through rimless glasses. "Dennis?"

"As a joke it's in poor taste." Dennis Kravetz responded with a savagery that Tony had never seen before.

Tony looked from one to the other, trying to envision his long-time classmates through the sadistic anger that marred their faces. "What are you talking about?"

"The uniform. Even the ROTC boys know better than to wear their clown suits to a rally. Are you looking for trouble?"

Tony did his best to ignore the gang that was closing in from behind. "No. But I'm supposed to wear it. I'm in the army, you know."

Gail Levy scowled. "Oh, no. Not you."

"So *that's* why you quit?"

"No, it isn't. I had — other problems. I just got caught in the draft."

"Very funny," someone jeered, elbowing his way between Gail and Dennis. The tall youth wore a bright red jacket that was snapped tightly to his neck. With his collar turned up, his face loomed like an inflated balloon above it. Long blond hair was tied back in a ponytail. "You know this joker?"

"Well, we used to," Gail said hesitantly. "We — we had some classes together."

"He's no friend of mine," Dennis said through clenched teeth.

"What do all these fancy badges mean, Mr. G.I.? What're they, merit badges for each baby you killed?"

Tony was shaking now, but not from the cold. He kept his hands tucked tightly in his pockets. His ears were beginning to burn from the cold. "Listen, I only just got out of training. I'm on — leave — so I thought I'd stop by to see the old school."

"Yeah, well, we don't want to see any of the likes of you."

Tony could feel people moving behind him. The condensation from their combined breaths was whipped past him in the breeze. "Look, I didn't come here for any trouble, just to see how things were."

"Yeah, well, now that you've seen, you can get the fuck out." The last four words were taken up and repeated over and over by his supporters. "Get the fuck out! Get the fuck out! Get the fuck out!"

Attention was temporarily diverted as the burning effigy collapsed when the base of the cross burned through. Girls screamed and boys yelled warnings. The crowd surged away from the flaming debris as it crashed onto the cement walkway.

"Hey! Hey! L.B.J.! How many kids did you kill today?"

The students closest to the fire fed the fallen, still burning effigy with more wood. Tony recognized broken armchairs from the lecture hall, and desk legs. A wooden chair seat flew high into the air and crashed to the ground next to where Tony was standing. It was followed closely by a cross member, with one leg still attached. It splintered apart on contact with the cement; one piece ricocheted sideways and hit his leg. Gail and Dennis stayed still, but the crowd surged past them. Tony did not move, but slowly took his hands out of his pockets.

"Go back to where you came from," the tall, pony-tailed youth grimaced. "We don't want your kind around here."

"Does your mother know what you are?"

"Murderer! Murderer!"

"Kill the mother fucker!"

"Toss him in the barrel."

A pair of hefty arms shoved at his back, and Tony lurched forward into the tall youth, who shoved him back again. He put up his arms to ward off blows that were coming in quick succession: at his face, his body, his groin. In a moment he was battered down to his knees. A foot lashed out and sent him sprawling on all fours. The word "Peace" appeared in front of his eyes, then the placard and the fat girl holding it fell on top of him. The crowd pushed in, two more people tripped over him. He curled up on the ground as shoes and sneakers pummeled his body.

There were too many to fight, and no way to win. All he wanted was to get out of there. He grabbed a leg and twisted. The scream was followed by the thud of a falling body. Tony jumped up and lashed out with open palms, trying to clear a circle around him. They grabbed at his clothes, his skin; they punched, slapped, knocked him about, from one to another, like a volleyball.

He lowered his head like a linesman and plunged into his tormentors, slamming into bodies left and right. Those who, a moment before, had been shouting and swinging fists at an unresisting figure, dodged out of the way. Tony kept swinging wildly with his open hands. Someone tackled him, and he fell heavily against one of the drums. The heat from the rusty metal burned through his uniform. His hat was plucked from his head and chucked into the conflagration. His tie was grabbed, choking him. The buttons of his jacket were yanked off, his shirttail pulled out.

To the sound of Dopplering sirens, Tony crawled away from the flames, slapping at the burning shirttail. He scrambled to his feet and charged into the mob, away from the oncoming police. He knocked several people down during his mad egress. Then he was in the open, running for the touchdown, in the clear.

"Hey! Hey! L.B.J.! How many kids did you kill today?"

****

Professor Dean must have watched the whole scene from his office window, for he called to Tony as he jogged drunkenly past the Administration Building. When Tony slowed down, the professor took him forcibly by the arm and dragged him up two flights of stairs. He stopped along the way to pick up some paper towels, which he dampened in a drinking fountain. He pushed Tony into the tiny, cluttered cubicle that was his office.

"Mr. Giovanni, you ought to have more sense than to appear in uniform on a troubled campus."

He touched portions of Tony's forehead with the soaked towels. Tony winced as they came away red.

"I didn't know this was a troubled campus."

"Where have you been for the past six months? Don't you read the newspapers?"

"Well, actually, I've been away. I got drafted, you know."

"You never should have left school."

"I know that now, but I didn't have much choice about it. My father had other ideas about my future."

"Was one of them sending his son to fight some senseless and immoral war?"

Tony cringed from the stinging pain of Mercurochrome. "Since when did *you* become a pacifist?"

"I'm not a pacifist. I'm a realist. And right now I'm a very confused realist."

"I never thought you were confused about anything."

The professor put down the bottle of Mercurochrome. Out of the same drawer came a box of bandages. He selected one of the proper size, taped it across the gash made by the knife-like edge of the cardboard placard, then took Tony by the shoulder and led him to the window that overlooked the courtyard.

A line of policemen brandishing billy clubs forced the students back from the flaming drums. The police made no attempt to do anything more than threaten the protesters with their wooden weapons. The students showed no qualms against hurling flaming brands at the men in blue, who did their best to dodge the flying debris, while still moving forward and forcing the aroused students away from the fires.

A fire engine entered the Mall and drove over sidewalk and lawn. Firemen in traditional uniforms of rear-peaked helmets, protective overcoats, and rubber boots pulled hoses out of the fire truck and sprayed the fires, which were soon extinguished. The students were scattered by the police, although a few lingered to taunt the constabulary with curses and obscene gestures.

Professor Dean pointed with his nose. "That's why I'm confused. Look at those kids. Most of them are immature, uneducated as yet, acting emotionally instead of rationally, and yet they have some innate perception that something is wrong. They don't know what, and they don't have any answers, but they have a gut feeling that their elders, their government officials, are misleading them.

"Can so many people be wrong? Of course," he said, answering his own question. "Can so many people be misguided? Yes. But can so many people be ignored? Definitely not. They thrive on the wisdom of innocence. They feel something that we in our antiquity are overlooking. Which is not to say that they are right, only that they are to be heard. Youth has one thing that their elders have not: flexibility. They are not set in their ways, they do not accept everything on faith. They are constantly questioning, constantly discovering. And still they are deluded."

Tony tucked the half-burned shirttail into his pants, readjusted his jacket. "I guess I never looked at it that way."

"Don't! They are fools, all of them. They don't have all the facts and figures in front of them. They're reacting purely emotionally. They think that because they are dissenters, that will make them more admirable in the eyes of their peers. Their dissent is for selfish reasons only.

"They are nothing more than a group of seventeenth-century witch hunters looking for victims. They damn your uniform because of what it represents. They cannot fight Washington, so they pick on the soldier instead. They single you out as the personification of all their pent up anger and hostility, anguish and discord."

"But I'm just a cog in the wheel." Tony raised his hand to his scalp wound. The growing lump was stretching the bandage. "I didn't ask to be drafted, I just was."

"Wrong, wrong, *wrong*. In a truly free country one has control over his own destiny."

"But someone has to do the fighting. You said yourself that freedom doesn't come for free, it has to be maintained."

"That is an idealistic assumption based on crude concepts of morality. Before you start thinking about saving the country, think of saving yourself." Professor Dean gestured toward the declining group of students, the milling policemen, the firefighters clambering onto their truck. "Those people out there aren't thinking about you, nor are they going to stick up for your rights. Each one of them is out for himself, and the sooner you learn that lesson, the better off you will be."

"But what about the country — the community?"

"Mr. Giovanni, you are too ethical for your own good. Do not try to understand what I am saying — you will only go crazy if you do. Just recognize the fact that those people out there have no idea what this conflict is all about. And most of them do not care. They just want to be part of the crowd. Morality is not the issue. It is acceptance that they are after."

The firefighters gathered their hoses. The police knotted together, drinking hot coffee from Styrofoam cups. The few students that remained, talked in small groups.

"Mr. Giovanni, believe me when I say this. Your first duty is to yourself. Life is a long and lonely conflict, and what you do with it is up to you. And *only* you. Do not let anyone else make your decisions for you — because when it is all over, you have only yourself to answer to. Society can make the rules, but you have to decide which of those rules are best for you under the circumstances of the moment. It is *your* conscience that you have to live with for the rest of your life."

Chapter 81

"Ho, ho, ho," Bob laughed expansively in his best Santa Claus imitation. "I'm glad to see you could make it."

Patty and Tony entered the plush restaurant with some trepidation. She was feeling uncomfortable in her later stages of pregnancy, and he felt awkward in his suit. He had worn it on only one occasion: in high school when he walked down the auditorium aisle to the tune of Elgar's *Pomp and Circumstance*. After months of army physical training, the gray sharkskin fit snugly across the shoulders.

"Here, let me take that." Bob helped Patty out of her new woolen overcoat. He handed it to the hatcheck girl, dressed in the holiday spirit in a white ruffled blouse and red vest and skirt, and handed the ticket to Tony. As he ushered them past the cashier, also in uniform, he took two menus from the maitre d'. "Nancy's taking over for your mother. And I've picked out a special table for us — my favorite."

In a darkened corner of the room, sequestered behind two tall panels which gave it the aspect of a booth, sat a table surrounded on three sides with wraparound brown leather seats. Once inside, the panels acted as soundproofing, although the restaurant was already fairly quiet with only murmurs from the few early patrons.

Bob placed the menus in front of them. "Helen's getting changed for dinner. She didn't want to dine in her hostess outfit. I'll go and tell her you're here."

The booth was lighted demurely by a tall, candy-cane-striped candle. Tony whispered as if in church. "I never realized his restaurant was so luxurious."

"Yes, isn't this wonderful? I love eating in places like this."

"You make it sound as if you do it all the time."

"No, but I could get used to it."

The red crushed velvet wallpaper contrasted thematically with the white linen tablecloth and red napkins. A wine steward appeared bearing a bucket of ice and a bottle of champagne. His red tuxedo jacket covered a white ruffled blouse identical to those the women wore, but somehow it did not seem feminine on him. His red slacks were creased sharply, almost militarily.

"Mr. Windsor said you would like this now," he enunciated clearly, in half question. He turned over the long-stemmed glasses, went through the ritual of showing Tony the label, waited for him to nod, opened the bottle with exaggerated flourish, and poured a little into his glass. Tony had seen enough television to know what to do, took a tiny sip, and lent his approval. The steward filled all four glasses halfway, and left the bottle in the ice bucket on a collapsible wooden table within reach of the booth. "Enjoy your meal."

After he stepped out of hearing range, Tony whispered, "Would it be to gauche to order a Coke?"

"I don't think so. I'm just going to drink water."

"Good idea." Then, opening the menu, "Would you get a load of these prices?" Patty nodded. "And you had a chance to work here?"

"I'd rather be served than on the serving end."

"It's not such a bad job. Your mother seems to make pretty good money at it. With these kinds of prices, the tips must be pretty heavy."

"*Oh*, they have snapper soup. I've always wanted to try that. And Mom raves about the beef Wellington. And they have fresh broccoli. Where do they get fresh broccoli in the middle of winter?"

"Winter only started officially three days ago. And they probably grow it in greenhouses."

"Well, hello Patty. Tony. Merry Christmas." Helen looked resplendent in her sheer evening gown. Her hair was coifed atop her head, and her face was fastidiously painted with makeup. Tony made a half attempt to crawl out of the booth to stand, but she waved him down with a quick, "Don't bother," and slid in next to him. Bob pushed in close to Patty.

"Ha, ha, ha. I see you've already tasted the champagne."

Helen took a less than delicate sip from the glass in front of her. "Oh, Bob, this is delicious."

"I've been saving it for a special occasion. And having the family together at this time of year was special enough to bring it out."

"Mom, I love your dress."

"Do you like it? Bob just bought it for me. It's supposed to be a Christmas present, but I told him I wanted to wear it tonight."

"I told her she could put it on as long as I

could take it off. Ha, ha, ha."

"After dinner I've got to change back into my work clothes."

"No rest for the weary. And we'll be hustling later on. Say, are you going to be around this week, or do you still have to report in every day?"

Tony had already prepared his story. "I couldn't get any leave, but I don't have to report in every day. At least, not Christmas and New Year's."

"Oh, that's awful." Helen polished off the rest of her champagne and Bob, ever attentive, filled it immediately — right to the top. "Thank you. I think soldiers should be allowed to go home for Christmas."

Tony waved the bottle away from his glass. "It sure would be nice, but you can't run a war that way. They don't stop for holidays."

Bob screwed the bottle into the ice. "How right you are."

"Well, it's still a shame," Helen slid.

"I'm sure all my cooks and waitresses and busboys would rather be home tonight than working. But I've got a living to make, and this is a big profit night. So is tomorrow. Of course, I put something a little extra in their envelopes this week. And they all get a nice big turkey — even the clean-up men. I always say happy help is good help."

Helen took another drink. "Well, anyway, Tony, I'm glad you're home. I say the hell with the army, interfering with people's lives that way. Married men with families on the way shouldn't have to serve military duty. You should be out working, and coming home to your wife."

"That day will come," Tony said.

"But it shouldn't be allowed, not when you're an expectant father. Oh, my God." Helen put a hand to her mouth. "I just realized, that's going to make me a grandmother."

"Ha, ha, ha. But she still acts like a teenager in bed."

"Oh, Bob. Not in front of the children."

"What children? They're about to have a child of their own. Anyway, we're glad you could be with us today."

"Are you still going to the Clark's tonight?" Helen asked.

"Yes, and midnight mass, too," Tony replied.

"When are we going to exchange presents? You're going to Frank and Bethy's in the morning, and we've both got to work all afternoon and evening."

"Helen, stop being serious." Bob raised his glass ceremoniously, waving the others to follow suit. "For now, I propose that we eat, drink, and be merry. We'll handle tomorrow when it gets here."

****

"Tony, long time no see."

Tony had not seen Joey Clark since he had joined the Air Force. He looked much older than Tony remembered him. "Yes, good to see you, Joey." Tony took the outstretched hand. "Oh, and this is my wife, Patty."

"I heard you got married. How do you do, Patty?"

"Fine, thank you. We've never met, but I've heard so much about you."

"Uh-oh. I hope it wasn't all bad." When Joey laughed, his round, fleshy face jiggled, but a touch of seriousness remained. His skin was splotchy: not quite freckled, but off colored. "Well, come on in the living room." He pointed to her belly. "I've heard a lot about you, too. When's the little one due?"

Patty's face flushed as she took off her new coat and handed it to Joey. "Five or six weeks. Sometime around the beginning of February. Oh, your tree looks so nice. We — we couldn't afford one. Who did the decorating?"

Joey took Tony's coat and hung them both in the closet. While the guests took seats, Joey leaned on the arm of a nearby chair and dug his hands into a bowl of pretzels. "It was a family affair. I did the tinsel, Ben did the balls, Mom did the candy canes and lights, and Dad supervised and stuck in the plug."

"You've got lots of presents, too."

"I brought some stuff home from Germany: things that are very cheap over there, but very expensive to import. And Mom, she roots around the house and wraps up everything she doesn't need and uses them as presents for her friends."

Tony laughed. "That's a practical way of getting rid of things you don't want."

"Until they start coming back again a couple years later. You know, Tony, I don't remember you being so tall, or filled out. I have to look up to you now."

Snickering, Tony reached for the pretzels. "I thought it was strange looking down at you. Have you shrunk?"

"Not according to my medical records. But you've been growing the past couple years." Joey punched his slightly bulging midriff. "Of course, I have, too. Too much good living."

"You look older than I expected," Patty said.

"That happens when you're over twenty."

"I think the uniform does it. Tony does, too."

Joey polished the captain's bar on his collar with the sleeve of his blue jacket. "I didn't want to wear it for the party, but Mom insisted. She wants to show me off, so I'm catering to her whims."

"And she usually gets her way," Tony laughed.

"How come you're not wearing your army duds?"

"Well, I've had some — trouble — wearing it around the city." He fingered the scar on his forehead. "It seems like soldiers aren't liked too much these days. Anyway, I feel more comfortable in civilian clothes."

"Yeah, I know what you mean. I don't get the respect I deserve, either. Some people just don't realize what we're doing for them. Hey, how about a drink? Mom's mixing up some punch with a punch."

"I'm not really a drinker, but I'll try some."

"Patty?"

She rubbed her belly significantly. "The doctor said I should stay away from it."

"Sure. How about a soda?"

"Seven up, with ice."

Joey shoved a pretzel in his mouth and jumped away like a tightly compressed spring looking for the chance to expand.

Tony followed him. "I'll come with you." Turning, "Will you be all right for a few minutes?"

Patty nodded.

In the kitchen, Mrs. Clark was trying to get the lid off a can of Sterno. "Hi, Tony. Heard you come in. Joey, would you get this thing going for me? Jack's down in the basement puttering as usual, and Ben's gone after Katie. I don't know what takes him so long, she only lives a few blocks away."

"You know Katie's never on time," Tony said.

"Yes, you're right. And neither am I. Joey, answer the door if anyone knocks, okay? I'll be upstairs." She bustled out.

Using a spoon, Joey pried the lid off the Sterno can, placed it in a holder under a stainless steel bowl full of Swedish meatballs, and lit it with a wooden kitchen match. With a ladle, Tony scooped out two cupfuls of lavender punch, and handed one to Joey as he shook out the match and dropped it in the sink, sizzling in a streak of water.

Joey held the plastic cup high in the air. "Cheers."

"Cheers." Tony took a small sip, wincing at the slightly sour, biting taste.

Joey gulped his right down and refilled his cup. "Ah, that's good. A little strong for me, but Pete'll love it,"

Tony's voice crackled. "Why? Does Pete drink?"

Without sarcasm, "Every now and then."

"Yeah, like every marine. Ben said he's talking about joining up."

"He is? He didn't say anything to me about it."

"Apparently it's *because* of you he's talking

about it. That and the fact that his father and brother were both in the marines."

"What do I have to do with it?"

Joey took another swig, this time downing only half the cup. "I guess it's all your stories about jungle warfare training. I understand you were in Camp Polk?"

"Fort Polk."

"Yeah. Well, I can't say I envy you that, but apparently Pete does. Ben says he's done nothing but rave about your good times."

Tony forced a half smile. "I wouldn't classify them as good times. It was just something I had to do because I had no choice."

"Yeah, I guess one man's meat is another man's poison." Joey absently stirred the meatballs. "And Pete's a pretty tough egg. Always was, even as a kid. Kind of earthy, if you know what I mean."

Tony put the cup on the table after another tiny sip. "No, I don't think I do."

"Yeah, now take me for example. I'm going to Vietnam in style. I'll have private quarters, decent working conditions, good pay, no nonsense. While the hacks take care of my plane, all I have to do is get in and take off. I'll be up there in the clean, clear sky without a worry in the world. I can drop bombs, shoot rockets, lay a blanket of napalm, maybe kill hundreds of gooks at a time. And they can't shoot back because they don't have anything that can knock me down. When I'm out of ammo, I just cruise back to base and let the hacks take care of my plane while I lounge around the pool waiting for the next mission.

"Now Pete's different. He wants to be there in the mud, trudging along with those crummy people and blasting away with a machine gun, mowing them down like stalks of corn. He wants to do the same thing I want to do, but he wants to be there and see it all happen."

Tony decided he needed a drink. It was bitter in his mouth. "That sounds pretty cynical to me."

"Why? What are you in it for?"

"I'm in it because I was drafted into it. Not that I think there's anything wrong with it. I mean, I understand about freedom and democracy and all that, but I don't think it necessarily implies that someone with a different way of thinking deserves to die. At the same time, I went through all the motions, learning how to shoot a gun and throw a grenade. I wanted to do the best I could. But I don't really want to kill people. I guess if I have to, I will. But I want to make sure that the guy on the other end of my sights is really the enemy."

Joey shook his head, crunched on an ice cube. "Let me tell you, you're in for a tough time, because you'll never know who the enemy is. You're not in a position to know. Look at it this way: somebody comes up with an intelligence report that a certain village is communist controlled. You don't know any different. You have to assume they know what they're talking about, and go in there and blow them away. You think I'm going to know any better when I get orders to drop a load of high explosives on VC suspects? The decision is made higher up, and if there's a mistake, it's not your fault. You'd still be doing your job to the best of your ability. It's up to someone else to say 'kill.' It's up to you to do the killing."

"What you mean is, you're willing to let someone else do your thinking for you, to make your decisions for you, to tell you what's right and wrong? Well, I don't accept that. I'd rather use my own judgment."

"Forget it. You'll only get yourself in trouble if you do. Leave the moralizing to someone else. If you worried about whether every little thing you did was right or wrong, you'd go crazy."

Tony took another sip, longer. "I don't think I can act that — unconscionable. At least, I hope not."

"Forget about conscience. Just do what you're told, and you'll get along just fine, whether you're a grunt in the field or an officer in the air. You think I'm going to refuse to support a rifle company because from ten thousand feet I can't see uniforms on the people they're fighting? How would you like it if you were down there being overrun and I had an attack of conscience? Hey, somebody's got to make the decision, and somebody else has to abide by it. We can't all be moralizers. No, if somebody says spread your napalm on a certain hamlet, I'm going to do it. I *have* to do it. And if there *is* a mistake, I'm not the one responsible for it."

"You're wrong. You're always responsible for your own actions. Now, maybe it's different for a B-52 bomber dropping his load from thirty thousand feet, but for a man in the field, the ultimate moral obligation lies with him."

"Is that what they taught you in the army?"

"No, that's what they taught me in church."

Joey looked thoughtful for a moment, grimaced. "Yeah." He stared over his cup for a long time. "I think I'll go to midnight mass with you guys tonight. And I'll pray to the Lord that he makes the right decisions for me. I'm not saying you're right, I'm just saying you might not be all wrong. And in case I make any mistakes over there, I want to have all my bases covered. A little preconfession wouldn't hurt."

****

The church was full to overflowing. Even the stairs to the second tier were jammed with people — and a hundred more lined the stone steps outside and the sidewalk for thirty feet in either direction. Most of them could not hear a word of the ceremony, but would pray and kneel and repeat catechisms by mimicking others, like a human telegraph system. The fraternity gang, along with Mr. and Mrs. Clark and Joey and the girls, were pressed together in the rear corner. Pete and Teddy and Tony formed a barrier around Patty so the crowd did not press too tightly against her. Only George was missing.

"He's probably having a private mass in his darkroom," Pete quipped.

"Or packing his suitcase," Ben said, out of the corner of his mouth. "He's got to start work before Uncle Sam catches up with him."

Tony whispered, "Will that job make him ineligible for the draft?"

"It will if it's in Toronto."

"Hush up, boys," Mrs. Clark admonished, "and pay attention to the sermon. And don't talk about your friends that way — especially on Christmas."

When the service was over, everyone held hands in fellowship and squeezed through the church doors into the chilly air. The night was crisp and clear, the stars shining down brilliantly the way they must have shone nearly two thousand years before, lighting the way for three wise men seeking the goal which was still being celebrated today.

Separated from the throng, Tony dragged Ben out of his mother's hearing. "What's this about George going to Toronto? Is he taking that job with his father's company?"

"Sure, but he ain't goin' there to work," came Pete's sarcastic comment. "You can bet your ass on that."

"Pete!" Marion shouted, in a hushed tone.

"Sorry 'bout that. You can bet your buttocks on that. He's headin' north to keep out of the cold."

Ben scowled. "Avoiding the draft."

"Will you stop talking about George?" Katie whined. "I don't like him, and I don't want to talk about him on Christmas."

"You're not talking about him. *We* are."

"Well, I don't want to hear about him."

"So shut your ears."

"You talk to me in a civil tone or I'll box your ears."

"An' wrap 'em up and put 'em under the tree," Pete completed.

Teddy pushed his way between the contenders. "Hey, whatever happened to peace on Earth and good will toward men?"

"Who asked *you*, Stringbean?" Ray disengaged his arm from Kathy's, gave Teddy a thump.

Kathy walked away.

"Hey, where you going? Kathy! Come back here. Kathy!" Ray ran after her, mumbling, "That bitch."

"There they go again," Pete said. "He's losin' his piece."

"Pete!" Marion said, louder.

Wobbling unsteadily, Pete pointed to Tony's head wound. "Look at him. He got peaced and good-willed over the head."

"Pete, you're drunk."

"But not enough."

Tony grabbed Ben's suit coat to get his attention. "Can we quit the clowning around for a minute? I want to know about George."

Ben stared straight into his eyes. "Don't you understand? He's going to Canada so he can stay out of the army."

"But — but — that's draft evasion."

"Now you're getting the picture."

"On a wide angle screen, in glowing Technicolor. Do we hafta make it any plainer?"

Tony was speechless for a moment. "No. No, I guess you don't."

****

Grandmom was already up and busy in the kitchen when Tony and Patty let themselves into the house. He approached her from behind and gave her a peck on the cheek. "Merry Christmas, Grandmom. What are you doing?"

She jumped and half turned. "Land o' mercy, Honey, you startled me out o' half a year's growth, sneakin' up on me like that. You shouldn't be up this early, an' out when it's so cold. I wish I could get by on as little sleep as you youngins, but if'n I don't get to bed right early it just takes my strength away. Now, I got to get that turkey trimmed and stuffed so's it'll be ready to go in the oven. An' I got sweet potatoes to peel, an' an apple pie to bake, an' I think I got enough fixin's for a pumpkin pie if your mother remembered to pick up a can o' pie fillin'. Cain't make a fresh one, so a canned pie will have to do. An' merry Christmas your own self."

She stopped her rambling long enough to wipe her hands on her apron. She drew water from the faucet into the coffee pot and scooped grounds into the percolator. "Your father'll be wantin' some coffee soon's he gets up, I 'spect. Honey, how do you work this range? I never could get used to electric stoves."

Tony turned it on for her. "It'll take a minute for the elements to get hot."

Patty slumped into a chair, yawning. "How long will the coffee be?"

"Water ain't even started yet, and once it boils it's got to perk for five minutes before it's strong enough to taste. At least, that's what your grandfather always used to say."

Tony grabbed cups and saucers and started

setting the table. Patty shifted her enlarged abdomen to a more comfortable position, and rubbed sleep out of her eyes. "I don't like getting up this early, but I'm anxious to open my presents and see what I got."

"You'll have to wait until everyone else is up." The breadbox yielded its contents, and Tony plunked two slices into the toaster.

Pouting, "But I can't wait."

"Now, you just hold your horses an' this coffee'll be perkin' in two shakes of a lamb's tail." Grandmom wagged a spoon at her. "Them packages ain't goin' nowhere less'n the mice carry 'em off."

Tony caught a glimpse of Robby dashing into the living room from the stairs, heard his loud scream of delight. "Look what Santa brung me!"

"Uh, oh." Tony and his grandmother piled out of the kitchen after the little tot. Robby was already sitting on the red tricycle. It was a trifle too big for him, but he stretched his legs and touched his toes to the pedals.

Unfortunately, he pushed the wrong way, causing it to back into the wall. When he tried to go forward he turned the handle bar so that his feet slipped off the pedals, but the forward momentum carried him into a pile of colorfully wrapped packages. Tony barely caught them before they toppled over.

Robby straightened the handle bar, learning quickly how to slide forward off the seat so he could manage the pedals, and he was off like a shot. He almost ran Grandmom down as he tore through the dining room. He wheeled around the table and back into the living room, scraping the rear wheel along the material of the sofa.

"Hold on there, pardner." Tony laughed as he knelt in front of him and easily brought the rampaging trike to a halt.

Kitty peered from under the branches of the blue spruce, warily eying the proceedings. Patty, somewhat sourly, waddled in from the kitchen.

"I wanna wide. I wanna wide."

"Okay, Robby. All right. But you'll have to wait. You know we don't open presents until Mommy and Daddy are up."

"I don't wanna open pwesents. I wanna wide."

"I know you do, but you'll have to wait. If you make too much noise — " It was already too late. Thundering hooves pounded along the upstairs hallway and halfway down the stairs. Robby cringed instinctively.

"What the hell's all the noise about?" he shouted hoarsely. After a night of singing, dancing, and drinking, his voice was usually strained — and he was never at his best humor without enough sleep.

Tony plucked Robby off the tricycle and cradled him on his lap as he crouched on the floor. Kitty came forward and rubbed along his legs. "We just got a little carried away, Dad. That's all."

"Oh, my word. I can hear that coffee perkin' already. I got to go turn it down. It'll be ready soon, Frank."

"I don't want no coffee. I want to go back to sleep. And without any more noise." He stormed back up the stairs and into the bedroom.

Elizabeth was on her way down, but called up to him. "It's your own fault for staying out so late. Do you expect everybody to wait till noon to open their presents?" By that time he was already back in bed. "He makes me so mad I could spit nickels."

They diddled over breakfast for an hour, with Robby complaining the whole time. Finally, Elizabeth poured herself another cup of coffee. "Well, we're not going to wait any more. The grouch can open his presents by himself."

After trooping into the living room, Robby took charge of handing out the packages. He picked them up one at a time and took them to his mother. She read the name, and he handed the package to the recipient, pleading, "Can I open it?" Tony and Grandmom did not mind, and he took as much pleasure from ripping off the wrapping paper and opening the boxes as he did from getting toys for himself. Only Patty denied him.

Frank appeared about halfway through the procedure, hair sticking out in all directions. His face was gray and clouded as he thundered through the pile of torn paper and snatched a cup of coffee.

"Daddy, this is for you," Robby said proudly, handing him a box.

"Thanks." He did not open it, but kept it on his lap.

Elizabeth: "Oh, Frank, why did you get me another bottle of perfume? I've got more now than I could use in a month of Sundays."

Patty: "Oh, this is nice. It's just what I always wanted."

Grandmom: "What, another one for me? Land o' mercy, I never got so many presents in all my born days."

Elizabeth: "Now where am I supposed to put candle holders? As if I don't already have enough knick-knacks to dust around here. And I don't want wax dripping all over my clean table cloths."

Tony: "Thanks, Mom. I think this is something I can use."

Robby was not happy about receiving clothes. These were things that would have been provided anyway. But the cowboy spurs and holster set with plastic cap guns and the miniature ten-gallon hat were more to his liking.

Finally, Frank opened his presents: shirts, ties, pants, and cartons of cigarettes. He thanked each person named as the giver on the card, and put it back in the box.

Kitty played hard with a catnip mouse that Tony had bought for her, then ran madly through the piles of wrapping paper, chasing ardently after ribbons that Tony dragged through the mess.

"I plum forgot. I got to get that turkey in the oven, and get that corn bread started. I don't know what I'll do without Walter around to remind me of things."

****

Over the muzzle of a fifty-caliber machine gun, a fatigue-clad reporter, microphone in hand, talked briskly at the television camera. Behind him stretched an immense, pockmarked field, dry and barren of all but the skimpiest of vegetation. In the far distance, several thatched huts stood outlined against the tall green trees of the jungle barrier.

The camera panned to the left where a group of marines lounged in the protection of a roofless sandbag bunker. Some were shirtless in the bright sun, others had their sleeves rolled up to their shoulders, revealing dark, even tans or black, Negroid skin. None wore hats or helmets; headgear and flak jackets lay in a pile where rifles were stacked within each reach.

As the clean-shaven reporter droned on about the twenty-four hour holiday truce, the camera panned across him to the right, where another bunker stood with more serious intent. Two marines held their ears while a third casually dropped an eighty-one millimeter round into the tube. As he stepped back, a puff of smoke exploded with the *whump* of an escaping mortar. The reporter explained that it was nothing but the usual harassment and interdiction fire intended to let the VC know that the Americans were on their toes.

The camera returned to the first bunker. An upended mortar tube was being erected as the base for a mock Christmas tree, the hewn stump being fitted into the opening. The leafless, denuded tree had already been decorated with grenade pins, can lids, and cigarette pack linings stripped into tinsellike strands. The stump was topped with a white star painted on a piece of cardboard.

Ammunition boxes served as seats, and a wooden case of explosives became a table. A huge turkey, drumsticks upturned, was placed ceremoniously on the case, to be instantly surrounded by slashing bayonets.

When the camera zoomed in, it became obvious that the turkey was as fake as the tree. It had been molded out of clay by a marine with an artistic flair. As the camera zoomed out, packages were distributed from under the tree. They were undisguised boxes of c-rations. The *whump* of another mortar went unnoticed by the troops as can openers were brought out and each man peeked into the box to see which prize dinner he had drawn.

The camera shot close ups of each G.I.: bearded, sun-baked, and creased with endless days and nights of tension. Smiles seemed out of place on faces that were drawn and haggard. But through the disguise pervaded the sparkling eyes of youth.

Ten thousand miles away, months and months from their loved ones, years from their hopes and aspirations, these men made do with what they had. There was little to be joyous about, except the fact that they were still alive to talk about it.

For them, and many like them, there was no Christmas — just another day in the hot sun, or the rain forest, or the rice paddies.

And another day closer to coming home.

Chapter 82

For the first time in many months Decatur Road was back in business. It was reasoned that on New Year's Eve, the police would find better things to do with their time than harassing teenagers who were testing their road machines. Even so, the crowd was small because most people were thinking about parties and the warmth of cozy apartments rather than racing in subfreezing weather.

"Jesus H. Christ, it's cold." Ray hunched in his jacket like a fat gnome. Underneath, he wore a double-breasted suit, white shirt, and tie. His hands were buried in his pockets, but every once in a while one would dart out and relocate the cigarette from one corner of his mouth to the other.

"Ray, would you stop breathing this way?" Ben leaned over the radiator halfway into the engine compartment. He handled his tools easily, without gloves, but the flashlight in Pete's hand wavered as he shook with cold.

"It's the only way I know how to breathe."

"I mean in this direction. I can't see what I'm doing because of the condensation."

"Well, excuse me for condensating!"

Teddy nudged his toe on the air cleaner lying on the smooth macadam. "Can't stand his breath, can you, Ben?"

"Shut up, pea brain. If my hands weren't so cold I'd punch you." Ray danced from one foot to the other, making certain that his wing-tipped shoes stayed clear of any oil puddles. "I don't know why I came along with you guys anyway. I'm supposed to pick up Kathy in a couple hours."

"Because you don't have a car," Pete jibed, "and you have no other way of getting to the party."

Tony leaned against the fender for a moment, watching Ben work. "Need the screwdriver?"

"Yeah. Thanks. Ray, hand me that ratchet next to the tool box, will you?"

Ray cringed. "It's covered with grease."

"It's not going to hurt you." Ben tossed a rag onto the ground. "Use this, if you're so fussy."

"Why the hell don't you adjust your carburetor *before* a race?" He took the rag, holding it gingerly between thumb and forefinger, wrapped it around the ratchet handle, and proffered it to Ben.

"This *is* before the race."

Pete took the ratchet and held it until Ben was ready for it. "Hey, this's too small for a ratchet. It must be a mouse shit."

Teddy started laughing, but Tony cautioned him with a squeeze on the arm. "Don't look now, but I think we've got company."

Everyone looked. "Shit," Pete said.

"There's only one of them," Ben muttered.

The red police car stopped in the middle of the road, switched on its high beams. Two more appeared behind it, lights flashing. Sirens were wailing up Red Lion Road, still out of sight around the bend.

"Jesus Christ, it's a raid."

Within seconds, a dozen engines had started and the street was a demolition derby. Screaming girls, squealing tires, and whining engines split the night like a civil defense drill.

"More bubble gum machines coming this way," Pete commented, dryly.

Now the police cars slid sideways across the road, blocking any attempt at escape. Uniformed men, wearing long leather coats over their blue suits, jumped out of cars and waved billy sticks menacingly.

With the air filter off, hoses disconnected, and the carburetor linkage out of adjustment, the Black Stallion was not going anywhere, even without a police blockade. Ben stood stoically by his car, shooing off his friends. "Go on. Get out of here."

Ray opened the back door and jumped in. Tony backed over the curb. "Follow me. Come on."

"Where we goin'?"

Over his shoulder, Tony shouted, "Just follow me." He ran through tall weeds and shrub spread across uneven ground that was grooved by water run-off. A beam of light speared his flight just before he entered a stand of birches.

"Hey, you, come back here."

Tony dashed past peeling trunks and down a shallow gully that led to a gleaming metal fence that was cross-linked to seven feet in height and topped with a two-foot tray of outward-leaning barbed wire. Pete and Teddy were right behind him.

"Whadda we do now?" Pete said breathlessly, sliding to a halt.

Teddy was moving too fast. He put out his hands and used the springiness of the fence to stop himself. "Over the top?"

Tony shook his head. "No." Beams of light carved the air overhead as the police beat their way through the brush. "Quick, give me the flashlight."

"What?"

Tony wrestled it out of Pete's grip. "Keep close." He thumbed the switch and aimed the weak beam down to where the fence met the ground. The water had eroded furrows in the rocky soil.

"They're getting close," Teddy said, matter-of-factly.

Tubular metal poles were planted deep in the ground at ten-foot intervals, each made firm by a cement pot. Tony scampered from pole to pole, scarcely wondering how Pete and Teddy were making it in the dark. "We can get through here."

He took hold of the fence where it spanned a deep gully, and pulled it up as hard as he could, aiming the sharp points on the bottom cross-links upward. With another foot of space, Teddy unhesitatingly dropped to his stomach and slithered under the barbs. As soon as he was on the other side, Tony said, "Get going, Pete." Lying on his back, and pushing himself feet first, he squirmed through. His jacket got pushed up under him, almost shoving his face into the sharp points. He laid his head flat and kept going.

Tony released the wire and pushed it through to the other side. "Grab it and pull it up." Teddy grabbed it first, then Pete. In a jiffy, Tony low-crawled under the fence, jumped up, and started running. "Come on."

Within seconds they reached the bottom of a dry streambed. With flashlight held low, he dashed over the frozen rocks. Bushes and weeds on both sides kept the escapees out of view. After a hundred feet or so, he stopped, switched off the flashlight, and listened.

"Think we got away from them?" Teddy whispered.

"Don't know yet."

"What the hell did we run for in the first place? They weren't gonna do noth — " Before Pete could finish, Tony dropped to a crouch and yanked both of them down to the ground. "If they catch us now we're in trouble."

Tony spoke in a hushed tone. "Because they might ask for draft cards when they check IDs. Why do you think Ben told me to go ahead?"

"Gee, I never thought of that."

"Would they put you in jail?" Teddy asked.

"I don't know, but I don't want to find out. I just hope Ray has his wallet with him this time."

Pete glanced around in the darkness. "Well, where are we? And where the hell are we going?"

"Northeast Airport. I used to come out here on Saturdays to watch planes take off and land. If we can get to the other side, we can get the B bus on the Boulevard."

"Oh. Well, let's get moving before we freeze to death."

Tony led the way up the wall of the gully, and clambered through thick brush. They rustled through a forest of birch and maples, the ground littered with dry, crackling leaves.

"You think the cops are coming after us?" Pete asked.

"I doubt it." Tony saw no lights behind them. The trees ended suddenly, and he stood on the edge of what appeared to be a vast, mowed lawn. About two hundred feet away stretched a runway, lined with red and green lights. Half a mile to the left, the cluster of administration buildings were lit up like a miniature city. Atop the tallest, a great searchlight swept the sky, illuminating the low cloud layer with a white platter that looked like a flying saucer plying in lazy circles around the perimeter of the airport. "Get down!"

They lay flat in the grass as two great headlights bobbed down the runway. A moment later, a plane roared past, leaving the ground with the smooth, easy grace of mechanical precision.

"All right, let's go."

They dashed across the grass, over the runway, and onto the grass on the other side. Trees blotted the horizon like many-limbed phantoms. They had to fight through dense brush before reaching the relatively clear zone of the forest. A few minutes later, when the brush and trees ended and the ground became smooth and hard, Tony pushed the flashlight switch halfway and pressed the thumb button for an instant.

"What the hell's a road doing back here?" Pete said.

"Used to be Bluegrass Road, before they extended the airport. The road's been rerouted, and this piece of blacktop begins and ends nowhere. There are a couple of abandoned houses along here, too. I was going to bring you guys out here some day — or night — to do some exploring."

"Let's make it another time," Pete said.

"Yeah, and how come you know so much about this place?" Teddy wondered.

"My father did the electrical work. I was pretty small, used to collect soda bottles and take them to the supermarket for two cents apiece." Tony started marching along the dirt-covered macadam. About five hundred feet away, he stopped at a tree that was unusually full, as if the leaves had not had the sense to drop off. He aimed the flashlight, saying, "Now, that's strange."

The tree burst into a cacophony of rushing wings as the whole top of it lifted right up into the sky, followed by a squawking that paralyzed all three of them in their tracks.

"Pheasants," Tony said, when his heart had stopped racing. "But I've never seen them in trees before. They usually nest on the ground."

"They obviously never saw a flashlight before, either," Teddy said excitedly. "Wow, that was neat."

"Shit, man, they scared the shit outa me. One jumping outa the brush is enough to turn your hair gray, but a whole tree full of 'em will put you in your grave."

Walking ahead slowly, Tony explained, "The airport grounds is a natural refuge for wildlife: rabbits, squirrels, all kinds of birds. No one's allowed in here and the animals know it." Tony gave the light a couple seconds exposure in order to determine his position. "Pete, when was the last time Ben put batteries in this thing?"

"prob'ly when Christ was a corporal."

"I can't get it to come on."

"Give it to me. It's got a two switch mechanism like any other flashlight." Pete took the flashlight and rapped the base against his palm. A shaft of light shot into the air. Quickly, he turned it downward and handed it back. "Sorry, Tone. If it gives you any more trouble, just hit it."

"Thanks."

When the macadam road petered out and a rutted, dirt trail forked off to the right, Tony followed it until they reached another tall fence bordering the back lot of an industrial center. Mercury vapor lights turned the parking lots into daytime, and illuminated the patrol car prowling slowly along the road, searchlight stabbing. It turned into a driveway and parked.

"Now what?" Pete said.

"Now you're beginning to sound like Ray."

"Hey, I was just asking a question."

"All right. But remember, I didn't want to come out here tonight anyway. You guys dragged me out."

"Shit, we just want you to have some fun."

"Yeah, Tone," Teddy said. "We know it's

been tough on you. But that's no reason to get mad at us."

Tony grimaced in the dark. "All right, I'm sorry. But I have a lot of things on my mind, and I don't need this kind of excitement. All I want — " The patrol car backed out of the driveway, throwing his headlight beams across the fence. "Get down!"

They crouched in the tall weeds as the car cruised slowly past them.

Tony skittered away on knees and knuckles. The cold had almost numbed his fingers by this time. "Come on, but be careful." He held the flashlight beam close to the ground. "Wait a minute." He was standing on the edge of a cement curb that dropped off into blackness.

"What the hell is this?" Pete wanted to know.

Tony played the light around, then dropped down the nearly vertical wall, slipping and almost falling when he reached the bottom six feet below. "Careful. It's icy down here."

"Okay, so what the hell is it?"

"It's an old streambed that's been cemented in to prevent erosion. Further down it runs under the road. We can cross the boulevard without being spotted, and it'll be warm inside.

"Oh, wow, this is all *right*."

Pete said, "Ain't your mouth frozen yet?"

"Are you kidding? This is fun."

Tony shook his head, the movement hidden from the others by the darkness. He pointed the light so they could slide down the wall. Then they walked along the three-sided cement streambed until it appeared to be swallowed up by a black, abysmal maw.

"Holy shit. Are we going in *there*?"

"You have a better idea?" Dull *whumping* sounds called from the blackness. "Cars running over manholes. If we can get to the other side, we can crawl out through one of them."

"All *right*. This is really cool."

"Cool? I'm damn near frozen. And what happens if we poke our heads out when a car comes by."

"Stick a hand out and thumb a ride?" Tony attempt at humor went unappreciated by Pete. "I guess you'll just have to be careful."

"Me? Whaddaya mean me?"

"You're right, Tone. He *is* beginning to sound like my brother."

"Listen, I ain't sayin' I'm afraid. I just don't like the idea of crawling into a sewer and climbin' through shit."

"Pete, this is a storm drain. It only carries run-off from the streets. And besides, it's big enough to walk through. See?" They reached the opening, and Tony pointed to the ceiling a couple inches over his head.

Pete shrugged. "If you say so. Lead the way."

"Boy, this is neat."

Water made hushed gurgling sounds as it trickled over a two-inch drop. Inside, sand was piled a foot deep on one side, swept there during summer thunderstorms, and in the middle, where most of the water flowed, rocks and basketball-sized boulders sat on bare concrete.

"Well, you were right about the temperature." Pete worked his fingers in and out. "I can feel my hands again."

"This is neat."

"Yeah, it's neat. I just hope to hell you know where you're going."

Crouching, Tony shone the light around the inside of the rectangular enclosure. He spoke in a low hush which they all heard in echo. "That's funny. It's shorter than the last time I was in here. It must have shrunk."

The walls and ceiling were wet with condensation, and the humidity stood at nearly nearly one hundred percent. They walked on the sand to avoid getting their shoes wet.

"Holy shit, what's that?" Pete's voice echoed loudly in the narrow confines of the concrete room. About fifteen feet away, a small rat scrambled along the wall and disappeared into a side passage, a tube no more than six inches in diameter.

"Don't worry about the rats. They're more scared than you are."

"You wanna make a bet?"

"Wow, this is really sharp."

"You know, I'm beginning to think your brother's right about you. You *are* a goofball. How far we gotta go through this?"

They sloshed along through the shallow water. Here and there, small conduits entered the main thoroughfare, each transporting mineral-laden water that stained the walls red, and left calcium deposits like miniature cave formations.

"Hey, Tone, is it getting darker in here?" Teddy said.

"You're glasses are steamed."

Tony shook the flashlight. "No, he's right. The batteries are dying."

"Wha — what happens if the light goes out?"

"We walk in the dark." Tony switched off the flashlight. The blackness exploded upon them.

"Quit fooling around," Pete said, a slight tremor in his voice.

"I'm not. I'm trying to conserve the batteries. I'll flash it on every couple of seconds, as we need it."

Teddy said, "Wow," but was cut off immediately by Pete.

"Don't say it."

"Keep one hand on the wall," Tony suggested.

"What'll we do if we fall into a side passage on another level?"

"There aren't any other levels."

"But these walls are covered with slime. Yeech."

"Just drag your finger, then. And stay close."

"If I get any closer I'll be wearin' your jacket."

Ahead, a pencil of light stabbed down from the roof, illuminating a cone on the sandy floor. It flickered off for fractions of a second at a time as cars drove over the manhole cover. When they reached it, Teddy climbed up the metal rungs that were sunk into the cement wall, and peered through the slotted cover.

"All *right*."

"Will you cut out with the 'all rights'?"

For another tenth of a mile they encountered nothing but sand and rocks and water — and a failing flashlight. Then they heard a strange moan, punctuated by short, crashing hums.

"I feel like saying another holy shit."

"They must be trucks. That means we're under the Boulevard." They passed under another cone of light, with Teddy taking another peak at the undercarriages passing only inches above his nose.

"Tony, this is really neat."

Pete groaned. "Now we're back to neat again. How long we gonna go through this thing?"

"Well, we don't want to climb out here. But on the other side of the Boulevard we'll get into some side streets where it should be safe."

The water started getting deeper. When it ran over the tops of Tony's shoes he flicked on the beam. It glowed for a moment, then faded rapidly to nothing. "Oh, great. It's dead."

Suddenly, a bright light flashed out from behind, and Pete almost jumped into Tony's pocket.

"Anyone for a match?" Teddy said calmly, walking past. He held the burning stick out in front of him.

"Where the hell'd you get that?"

"I've got a whole pack in my pocket. Ray's always losing his, and he gets mad at me if I don't have any. I was waiting until we really needed them."

Pete said angrily, "We really needed 'em about ten minutes ago."

"Hey, there's a big tunnel up here."

Tony caught up with Teddy. "Put out that match." In the utter darkness, he could see a faint glow of light emitting from the side passage. "Come on, this is the way out." He tiptoed through water and ducked into the round pipe. It was only four feet in diameter, and water trickled down the middle of the curved floor. Tony straddled the stream. "Come on in."

Teddy lit another match while Pete splashed through the water, cursing, and grabbed onto Tony's jacket tail. Suddenly he screamed, and crashed into Tony's back. "Goddamn spider."

The match went out and they were plunged into darkness again. Tony led the way while Teddy lit another match from the rear. "Hey, you feel the air getting colder?"

"Yeah."

"We must be near a big opening. Hey, I think I can see a light up ahead."

"Hallelujah."

Another match died out. "Hey, I can see it, too. Boy, this is really neat."

Tony slurped through mud toward a circle of light. All of a sudden he was outside, surrounded by trees and bushes. The mud was solid underfoot, the air was crisp, and he heard cars whooshing past nearby. "How about that. There's a stream coming in from the woods."

"That wasn't so bad," Pete breathed. "But I was never so glad to see the world again."

"Tony, that was really neat. When can we do it again?"

Tony clambered up a weed- and log-covered slope, through an aged fence, and stood on the sidewalk. "We're just in time. Here comes the bus."

****

"Omigod! Omigod! What's going to happen to my Ben? Will he have to spend the night in jail? Is he going to have a record? Will they kick him out of school? And what will his parents say? Omigod!"

The loud party music drowned out Katie's rambling to all but those closest to her. Marion and Kathy did their best to calm her down. Tony had answered her questions at least three times. He made his way to the refreshment table, poured a Coke, and spotted George sulking in a corner with a soda, sandwich, and a plate full of potato salad. He worked his way through the dancing couples to George's hideaway.

"Hi, George. How's it going?"

George crouched forward on the wooden chair, staring idly at his feet as he toe-tapped in time with the music. His shirttail was pulled out of his pants, revealing a dirty T-shirt, and his hair was an unruly mess.

"Haven't seen you since before Christmas."

George's reply was almost inaudible in the din. "I've been busy."

"I stopped at the house a couple times. Your mom said you were out." His whole upper body nodded. "I had some loose ends to tie up."

"Did you sell the newspaper stand?"

Was his head nodding, or keeping the rhythm?

Tony made conversation. "What do they do

at the Toronto plant?"

"Make tires."

"Gee, that's pretty far away. You won't be able to get home much."

"I won't be missing anything."

"Well, there's the fraternity."

"Not any more. As soon as I leave, my mom's going to rent it out to a guy who needs some storage space."

"What? She never said anything about it — to me, that is."

"That's her business. It won't be till the end of the month."

"You mean tonight?"

"January." What was it about his shoes that George found so fascinating? "You'll have plenty of time to get your junk out."

"But, George, what about the fraternity? Where will we meet?" Tony thought he detected a slight rumpling of the shoulders. "Is it a matter of money? Does she want more rent? Maybe we can — "

"She just doesn't want the hassle of having all kinds of people coming through the house all hours of the day and night."

"But, that's never been a problem before."

"That's because she had me to keep an eye on things. She could trust me." There was an extra emphasis on the 'me.'

"Oh, come on, George. She never had any reason to distrust us. You know that."

"It doesn't matter. It's already done."

Tony lapsed into silence for a moment. The album ended and another dropped into place on the record player. "It sounds as if you're not planning to come back right away."

George shrugged.

"George, you know this could be serious."

"You'll find some place else."

"That's not what I mean, and you know it. You're leaving the country. You're going to Canada to avoid the draft."

"What's it to you?"

Tony leaned closer, fighting the resonance of the speaker system that was turned to its highest volume. "It's not what it is to me, it's what it is to you. You'll be in big trouble."

"Look who's talking — a deserter!"

"My situation's different. I've got paperwork that just hasn't come through yet because of army inefficiency. When it does, I'll be cleared. But what you're doing is irrevocable. Once you leave the country you can never come back, because if you do they'll put you in jail. You'll be exiled."

"I don't believe in fighting."

"Yeah? Well, I don't think you believe in anything."

Now George looked up, his lower lip quivering.

"George, don't do it. You're only making it worse for yourself. You'll be giving up your whole life, just to avoid a couple years of military service."

"I'm not going to fight. And I don't need any advice from you. My father thinks it's all right. Now get off my back."

The album ended just in time for George's last comment to blare out during a moment of awkward silence. Every eye in the room turned. George looked up, stared vacuously for a moment, then lurched up out of his chair. His sudden movement pushed Tony backward, sprinkled potato chips over his jacket, and caused him to spill some of his soda on the floor. George forced his way through the gawking crowd and raced out the back door, slamming it behind him.

Katie hastily threw another record on the turntable. Not bothering with the delicate counter balance, she scratched the needle onto the rotating plastic disc and flooded the room with music. Gradually, people took up the beat and returned to their dancing. The episode was nothing more than a normal party confrontation.

Marion appeared with a handful of napkins and started to soak up the soda. "What's the matter with George?"

Picking up crumbs, Tony scowled. "Oh, I was just trying to have a heart to heart talk."

"Only his father can have a Hart to Hart talk with him."

"You've been hanging around Pete too long — you're beginning to sound like him. You know, I just don't understand what's eating him."

"I don't think he likes sewers."

"I mean George. He seems to have a grudge against the whole world." Tony ran out of potato chips to pick up from the floor. "Anyway, I'm glad to see Pete's sticking to Coke."

Marion sopped up the last of the mess, and squinted. "Don't let Katie find out, but that's not Coke in that six pack he brought in. He refilled the empties with beer, and recapped them."

Standing, "I thought he was going to slow down his drinking habits?"

"He is. He's drinking a lot slower. But he makes up for it by drinking longer. So how's Patty?"

"Oh, she's all right. Just feeling a little tired, is all. That's why she decided not to come tonight. I'll have to leave early so I can be with her at midnight. Actually, I'm more worried about George."

Katie turned the volume up from its already ear shattering level to where it was painful. Marion brought her face close until her lips were only inches away from Tony's ear. Cheek to cheek, he could smell the sweetness of her perfume, feel the tickling of her wiry, red hair.

"Forget George. I'm more worried about you."

"Me? I think you'd better worry about Ben and Ray. They're the ones in trouble."

"That's not what I'm talking about. They're not in any real trouble — not anything that counts, anyway. I'm talking about you."

"Listen, Marion, I know it's not right, but it's just something I had to do. I mean, I didn't want it to happen this way. I followed all the procedures, I filed all the proper paperwork. It's just that — I don't know — nobody seems to care."

"I care." Despite the blaring music, her voice was a tender petal caressing his ears.

Tony backed away so he could look into her eyes. Her hair brushed his lips. "Thanks — for caring. And for saying it."

"I just wanted you to know that I think you're doing the right thing. I think it's great when someone stands up against authority for what he believes in. I think it takes a lot of courage."

Tony tilted his head. "That's what George's doing."

"No, he's just scared and selfish."

"Well, I'm pretty scared myself. And I'm not AWOL because I'm chasing a cause. My motives are pretty selfish."

"Everything we do is done with selfish motivation. When you help an old lady cross the street, you do it partly because it makes you feel good. When you stand by a friend in trouble, you expect him to do the same for you some day. When you love someone, it's because you expect to be loved in return. There's nothing wrong with any of that. It doesn't make you any less of a person. It's just racial instinct acting on a personal level."

Tony squinted his eyes. "Marion, you didn't pick that up from Catholic high school."

"I'm taking psychology courses at night," she smiled. "But that has nothing to do with it."

"Well, it's a little too deep for me. I think I'm just as scared as George. I really don't want to be separated from my friends, or my family — or my wife."

"There's nothing wrong with feeling that way."

"But sometimes it's worse than that. Sometimes I feel real fear about what I've gotten myself into."

"You've never been afraid, or you wouldn't be doing what you're doing."

"I don't know. I was pretty scared running from those cops tonight."

"That's not fear; that's recognition of consequences."

"And what about the consequences of being AWOL? I recognize that, but it didn't stop me."

"Because to you the consequences of going away and leaving your wife alone, and about to have a baby, are less frightful. Sometimes you have to act on your feelings, and be your own judge."

"If everyone were his own judge the jails would be empty, because every criminal would judge his acts as morally right." Tony shook his head. "No, the difference between right and wrong has to be absolute."

Marion, too, shook her head, pounding Tony's face with her hair. "Morality is not an absolute, it's a majority. And sometimes even the majority is wrong. In the sixteen hundreds, so many people believed in witchcraft that women were burned at the stake for it."

"And that was wrong, no matter how you look at it."

"The act was wrong, but not the people. They were acting on their beliefs, on what their society told them was true. That doesn't mean the people were bad, just that they were misdirected. None of those people would have done what they did on their own. They did it because their culture accepted it. We should have learned that by now. We each have to stand on our own."

Tony pursed his lips in anguish. "That's what scares me the most — standing out there on my own."

The smile that piqued Marion's lips was quixotic. "You're never really alone. Not as long as you carry people with you in your heart. And I'll always be with you."

The needle scratched, the music stopped, and Katie shouted, "Ben!" She ran through the halted dancers to where Ben and Ray were calmly, almost smugly, walking down the cellar steps. Katie threw her arms around Ben before he reached the bottom. "Are you all right? Did they beat you up? Did they hurt you? Are you all right?"

Tony put a hand on Marion's upper arm — her skin was soft and warm, and the muscles were firm — and pulled her along through the crowd. Pete and Teddy met them in the middle of the room. Together they piloted her to the stairs.

Ben grimaced and shook his head. "Katie, will you cut it out? I'm all right. They didn't beat us up, they just took us in with about fifty other guys."

"And gals," Ray added.

"It's no big deal. Of course, my dad and Ray's mom had to come and get us out."

Teddy snickered. "I'll bet my mom is mad."

"Shut up you little squirt!" Ray lunged for

his brother, but Teddy danced out of his way.

Ben ruffled Katie's hair. "Dad never said a word, but Mom sure laid into me when we got home." He shrugged, and smiled. "But she'll get over it. And Ray, next time carry a wallet with you, will ya, or the next time the cops grab you they'll take you away and throw away the key."

"There ain't gonna be no next time."

Pete took a long gulp from his Coke bottle. "There's always a next time, unless it's the last time."

"You can go to hell."

"Don't like your mother's cookin'."

Chapter 83

"Hi, Mom, Dad. Patty said you called." Tony noticed his mother was leaning against the sink sobbing quietly over a box of tissues. "Hey, what's the matter?"

"Get the baby outa here!" Frank flung out his arm and shoved Robby on his way. He ran as if he were being chased by ghosts. Kitty, startled by the shout, ran out too. Then Frank stabbed the table with his fist. "Look at this."

Tony stepped up behind his usual chair and put both hands on the back, keeping a wary eye on his father. Frank waved a sheet of paper in the air, then sailed it to Tony with a flick of the wrist. It came to rest in front of him. "Read that."

The letterhead caused him to swallow hard: it was from the United States Army. The form letter was single spaced, and filled the whole sheet. Blanks were underlined where appropriate material had been entered.

"It has been established by this command that Private E-2 Anthony Giovanni has been missing from his assigned duty post for a period exceeding thirty days . . . "

"There — there must be — some mistake," Tony stuttered. The lump in his throat made speech difficult. "I'll — I'll check it out tomorrow — "

"There ain't no mistake," Frank screamed furiously. "You been pulling the wool over our eyes long enough, but you can't lie your way outa this one. After the letter came I checked the mileage on your car. And tonight I went over to your apartment and checked it again. You ain't gone more then twenty-five miles since yesterday, so how do you explain that?"

Elizabeth pulled out a new tissue and blew her nose. "I didn't want to believe it was true."

"I knew something was funny when I asked him to buy me cigarettes from the PX and they had Pennsylvania tax stickers on 'em. I'm no dummy, you know. But would you listen? Bah!" Frank threw his hands up into the air.

"Look, Dad, I know it looks bad, but — "

"Looks bad! Looks bad! You'll end up going to jail for this. Whaddaya think, you can just walk out on the army any time you feel like it? And what am I supposed to tell everybody — that my own son's a deserter? How's that gonna sound?"

"Frank, stop worrying about yourself, and talk to him. I've never been able to talk to him."

"It's too late to talk. I'll be lucky if I can get him off with just a jail sentence. He might get a dishonorable discharge, too."

"Listen, Dad, I planned to go back right after the baby was born. I didn't want it this way, but they just wouldn't listen."

"The army don't have to take orders from you." Frank screamed and tossed his hands wildly in the air. "Whaddaya think, a baby's never been born without the father around? You don't gotta be there, you know?"

"I know I don't *have* to be — I *want* to be. And it would have worked out all right if there wasn't so much red tape. I made all the right applications, it's just that they didn't come through in time."

"I don't understand this new generation. When I was a kid we did what we were told, without asking no questions. The kids today think they're too smart for the gover'ment, like the politicians don't know what they're doing. Whaddaya think we got a gover'ment for, to sit up there and not know what's going on? These damn college kids think they're so smart they don't have to listen to nobody."

"Frank, will you stop it!" Elizabeth matched him decibel for decibel. "I don't need another lecture right now. What I'm worried about is what's going to happen to him."

"He's gotta go back, there ain't no way around it."

"Dad, I told you, I always planned to go back. But as long as I'm AWOL, a couple more days won't make any difference. Patty's home having contractions right now, so I can't leave just yet — "

"I don't want to hear no more excuses about the baby." Frank swung his hands so far behind him that he knocked the spice rack off the wall. It hit the floor with a crash of broken glassware. "You been lyin' to me all this time, makin' me think you were goin' back every day. You were makin' a fool outa me, right in my own house. You . . . "

Suddenly, Frank lunged across the table and made a grab for Tony's tie. Now the uniform seemed like a useless charade. He managed to snatch the shirtfront and rip off several buttons before Tony twisted away. He was almost strangled by the tie before Elizabeth leaped forward and beat down Frank's hands.

"Frank, don't make it any worse."

"I'll teach him to make a fool outa me." Now Frank was on his feet, trying to work his way around the table. But Elizabeth clung to his arms, slowing him down if not stopping him. Tony edged away from his enraged father.

"Everybody's gonna laugh at me when they find out he's been AWOL."

"Frank, would you please stop it."

Thick veins popped out across Frank's forehead and neck, and his voice was choked. Spittle flew out with each word. "You get outa my sight before I break every bone in your body."

****

Patty sat on the edge of the bed with a pained expression on her face. "So what did he say after that?"

"Never mind. How do you feel?"

"Well, I've been having the pains more frequently. I think it's about time."

"But, you've still got another week to go."

"I know," she whimpered. "But the pain's getting worse. That's what my mother said it would be like."

"Oh, boy." For the moment Tony forgot all about his father. "How much longer do you think it will be?"

She shrugged.

"Well, I picked up those things you wanted. I'll go out to the kitchen and put them away. What time's Kathy coming back?"

"I don't know."

"Well, do you feel like eating anything? I can make some soup."

Patty shook her head slowly.

"Well, why don't you just lie down." Outside, a car door slammed. "That must be her now. Is Ray staying over tonight?"

Tony walked to the front of the living room and parted the blinds as more doors slammed shut. Four uniformed men stood in the wet street. Windshields glistened with rain. "Uh-oh."

He scrambled back from the curtain and dashed into the bedroom, breathing fast. He grabbed his hat from the bureau and stared at Patty. She looked up, startled. "What is it?"

"MPs. My father must have called them."

"Oh, no. Not now." Her hand fell from her distended abdomen. Tony flung on the green dress jacket.

"What are you going to do?"

"I'm leaving." He peeked out the back window, into the tiny yard. It was dark, but he saw no movement in the shadows.

"But — what'll I do?" she whined, wringing her hands tightly.

There was a knock at the front door. "You hang around and have that baby."

She reached out imploringly. "But — "

"I'll be in touch."

"Tony — "

He went through the living room and into the kitchen, jiggled the door open, and dashed out onto the cement yard. The alley door was aged, hanging by rotted timbers; he almost pulled it off the hinges in his haste to get it open. He could hear the imperious knocking behind him.

"Hey you. Hold it."

Tony ignored the MP who was racing down the garbage-filled alley, and ran the other way. The man had wings on his feet, but Tony had desperation in his heart. The lead he started with grew larger. He just hoped they hadn't sent another MP to block the other end of the block. When he burst into the street he heard squealing brakes, but kept on going. He raced in front of the headlights and ducked into the alley on the other side. He knocked over three trashcans and scared the daylights out of two cats during his headlong flight to the next street. Then he struck out for the sidewalk and ran two blocks to the left. He ducked into another alley that bordered on several abandoned buildings, found a hole in the fence, and crawled through into a decrepit yard that was littered with lumber and packing crates.

He tried the back door, but it was locked. He felt his way along the crumbling brick wall until he reached the woodpile, crawled under a large section of flooring, and sat with his knees drawn up to his chest. It was no warmer in here, but at least the misting drizzle would not soak through his clothes. He felt sawdust and torn paper on the ground, and heard the squeal of rats.

When he regained his breath, he snuggled up as best he could, hands tucked into his armpits. Then he shivered throughout the long, wintry night. Later, pattering overhead attested to the recurrence of rain, heavy at times. The rats tried to reclaim their home, but Tony kept moving and shouting whenever they approached too close. He stayed dry, if not warm, in his niche.

There was no dawn, just a gradual lightening of the sky. Tony stretched muscles that were cold and cramped. Slowly, he crept out from under the woodpile, brushing dirt and droppings from his rumpled uniform.

The temperature had dropped in the early morning hours, and the rain had become sleet. He did calisthenics to restore his circulation, jogging in place with high, knee-kicking steps that helped to chase away the shivers. Still, his exposed hands wished for a pair of gloves. He jammed them deep into his pockets. His ears had long ago become numb.

He reentered the alley, walking on feet that were painful stubs that hardly seemed part of his body. His toes he could not feel at all. From the knees down, his pants were like stiff cardboard. Where they had gotten wet the night before they were now frozen solid, and moved with a cadence of their own.

The row homes of South Philly were alive with the yellow warmth of light, and chimneys spouted white smoke. Tony imagined people in all stages of life: some still slept peacefully, some were just getting out of bed, some were brushing teeth, some were eating breakfast, some were already warming their cars to go to work, or getting the kids out of bed and ready for school. The stereotypic American family was gearing up to face the trepidations of a new, February day.

Tony felt that he had somehow become an alien in this world. He was a stranger in his own neighborhood, an outcast from all levels of society. He was separated from his friends by distance, from his family by his actions. Without a wallet he had no money, no identification: which meant that he had no identity. He was a non-person.

He was no longer a member of society. And to the army he was nothing more than a number. When had the transfer taken place? When had he ceased to exist? Or had it happened so gradually that no one was aware that the change had been taking place?

Inside his mental chrysalis he had been changing. What would he be when he emerged?

Chapter 84

The waitress was a hatchet-faced matron in her late forties. She stared at Tony with a mien that could break mirrors, and scowled wordlessly.

"Coffee," Tony mumbled, after his third attempt to get his numbed lips to form the single word. In the blink of an eye, the waitress produced a mug, and filled it with steaming black brew from a glass pot. As she turned to walk away, he added, "And toast."

Tony groaned with pain as he wrapped his frozen fingers around the thick ceramic mug. The heat would have burned normal hands, but it merely took the stiffness out of his digits. The pain he felt was from thawing, not burning. When he tried to raise the mug to his lips, hot liquid spilled out: he could not control his shaking. Instead, he placed the mug on the counter, lowered his lips to the rim of the mug, and gratefully sipped the black brew.

As the circulation returned to his fingers and hands, he brushed off the snow that still clung to his trousers and uniform jacket. He sat hunched over like a gnome, his body racked with violent shivers, and luxuriated in the hot steam that rose into his face.

A moment later, a plate of toast appeared in front of him. Tony's mouth watered as he looked up and forced a broken smile. "Th — th — thanks." The stone-cold waitress walked away without replying.

Tony stared at the already buttered toast, but could not force himself to let go of his only source of warmth. He raised the mug several inches above the counter, succeeded in getting some coffee into his mouth. He gulped. Mechanically, his arms levered downward and deposited the mug somewhere on the counter.

After another minute of soaking up the heat, he took a third sip. The hot coffee had begun to take the chill out of him. With tingling fingers, he reached out for the triangular slices of toast. He gobbled down two slices greedily, then finished the coffee in one large draft. The rest of the toast soon disappeared.

He held onto the empty mug as if his life depended on it. It still radiated warmth. He was looking straight down when the waitress sauntered back with the pitcher in her hand.

"Want another cup?"

Tony searched for a soul in those dark, hardened eyes. He swallowed, his gaze straying between cup and waitress. "I haven't got any — that is, I forgot my wallet. I can't pay for it — now."

The waitress sighed audibly, rolling her eyes at the ceiling. As she was turning away with the coffee pot a dark shadow loomed behind Tony, a dollar bill fell onto the counter, and a gruff voice blurted out:

"Fill it up."

Tony twisted around on the stool, for the first time aware that the booths along the wall were filled with groups of people on their lunch break. At one table, four women gabbled incessantly; at another, two businessmen chatted quietly. The rest were evenly split between white-collar people in suits and overcoats, and construction workers.

The man who had tossed the paper dollar on the counter sported a face that had spent most of its time in the weather. It was darkly tanned, and deeply etched with lines that created a pattern all their own. The eyes were sharp points of blue ice; the hair that curled out from under the hood of his sweatshirt was a blonde lock. Much of the barrel chest was clothing, but Tony knew that there was bulk there, too. The hands were calloused from years of rough work.

The waitress stared for a moment, then turned wordlessly and refilled the cup.

"Thanks," Tony said perplexedly, to both waitress and his benefactor. The waitress just moved away. "Uh, my car — " Tony fumbled for the right words. "I'm stationed at Fort Dix.

My wife — just had a baby — I think."

The construction worker took it all in. Looking Tony up and down, he said, "Don't the army give you any better clothes than that?"

Tony shrugged. "This is regular issue. I've got orders for Vietnam, so I didn't get an overcoat."

"Yeah. The army ain't got any smarter since I was in. You want a lift?"

"Uh, well, thanks — but — well, it isn't open to visitors yet. I — I think I'd rather soak up some more coffee."

The man pulled on a pair of cotton gloves. "Okay." He turned his lips into a semi smile and joined his buddies who were paying at the cash register. "Hey," Tony called out. When the grizzled man turned, he said, "Thanks. I really — appreciate it."

"Sure thing." He paid his bill and left.

Tony wasted no time in downing the fresh cup of coffee. He had no sooner finished it than the waitress appeared with the glass pitcher in hand and refilled it without uttering a word.

"Will that dollar cover me for another order of toast?"

Neither batting an eye nor deeming to smile, she said in a deadpan voice, "It'll cover you for as long as you want to sit here and eat and drink. I'll get you some jam, too."

****

When Tony awoke, he only vaguely remembered leaving the stool by the counter and entering the booth near the heating duct. A half-filled mug sat in front of him, and a small plate of crumbs. It was the noise that had jarred him — the diner was filling up with the supper crowd.

He slid out from under the table, hardly remembering how stiff and numb his arms and legs had been when he had stumbled into the diner earlier. Looking around for the elderly, stern-faced waitress, he saw only a younger woman behind the counter.

"Uh, excuse me. Where's — " He realized he did not even know her name. " — the waitress who was here before?"

"You the soldier that came in half frozen?"

"Uh, I guess so."

"She went off at three. Said to give you more coffee if you needed it. Do you?"

"Well, no, I guess I've had enough."

She nodded, then crouched behind the counter and came up with a paper bag. Smiling, "Left this for you. Said it was already paid for."

Tony took the bag without protest, or question. "Thanks. And — I wanted to say thanks — to her. Could you tell her for me?"

"Sure thing."

He nodded, and left the diner gracefully. But as soon as he was out the door he ripped open

the bag and tore into one of the sandwiches that had been packed in waxed paper. He ignored the deep snow that drifted over the tops of his low dress shoes. By the time he reached the hospital, he had engulfed the other sandwich and the cold French fries, and left nothing but a meager apple core and a few seeds.

Opposite the well-lit building, Tony slinked into an indentation between two storefronts, hidden behind snow-covered trash barrels. Police came and went, but no MPs. Still, he did not know if his father had also alerted the local constabulary, so he waited for a lull in the traffic before venturing across the recently plowed street and into the lobby. He felt conspicuous in his now disreputable uniform as he walked hesitantly through the waiting room, full of people talking and reading magazines, and up to the nurse on duty.

"Can you tell me if someone has checked in? I mean, can you tell me what room number she would be in — if she's here?"

The elderly nurse put down the clipboard she had been studying, her perplexed expression adding wrinkles to those that already crowded her face.

"I mean, I'm looking for someone, but I'm not sure whether she's here or not. It's a maternity case."

"What's the name?"

"Patty — Giovanni." The last name he said in a hushed voice, looking around.

The nurse thumbed through a card file. "She's not on the morning roster."

"She might not have been admitted until today."

"Oh." She scanned a list of names on three stapled sheets of paper. "Yes, she's a late admission. She was assigned to room 403. That *is* the maternity ward."

"Do you know if she's had the baby yet?"

"No, but I can check the floor desk for you."

"Oh, that's all right. I'll go up myself anyway."

"Only members of the immediate family are allowed on the maternity floor, sir."

Tony flashed what he hoped was a casual smile. "That's all right. I'm her — brother. Uh, can you tell me how to get there?"

The nurse's gaze dropped from Tony's brown eyes to his disheveled uniform. After a perceptible pause, she said throatily, "Just take the elevator to the fourth floor and turn to your left."

"Thanks. And, uh, is there a men's room around?"

The flaccid face sank. "Right down this hallway, fourth door on your right."

"Thanks."

Tony spent a few minutes knocking the snow

out of his shoes, and getting cleaned up. His hair was so short that it did not need combing, and his beard was not dark enough to require shaving under any conditions other than strict army inspection. He washed most of the dirt off his face with soap and hot water.

Avoiding the elevators, he climbed the fire tower and peeked out the heavy, iron door into the immaculate hallway. Nurses scurried along the corridor, mothers waddled with still lingering pain, and a group of visitors was gathered around the elevator door. Tony recognized no one.

Outside room 403, the only voice he heard were those on the television. He peeked in, saw that the bed next to Patty's was vacant, and that she was alone. She lay on her back, staring up at the small screen, her profile a lot flatter than when he had seen her last.

"Hi, Patty."

Her face was blank for a second or two. "Tony!"

"Not so loud." He put a finger up to his lips and stepped into the room, and bent into her out-flung arms.

"Ouch." As Tony backed away she looked down at her breasts. "They're still a little sore yet. You'll have to be careful with me for a while."

Tony laughed. "How are you otherwise?"

"A lot sore."

"The baby. Is — it — all right?"

Tears rolled down into her ears. Tony kissed them away. "It's a boy. Seven pounds two ounces."

"Where is he?"

"In the pediatric room at the end of the hall."

"Can I see him?"

Patty nodded. Abruptly, she blurted, "He called the police, you know."

"I wasn't sure. Are they looking for me?"

"The MPs went back to Fort Dix. He went to the police station first, but they said they couldn't arrest you unless you had done something wrong. He tried to get them to come to the house and — detain is the word, I think — detain you. Then he called Fort Dix and they sent the MPs right away."

"Are they still out looking for me?"

She shrugged.

"I guess he's pretty mad, isn't he?"

Patty sniffed, and nodded.

"Well, I'd better hurry if I want to see the little tike."

She smiled. "He's so cute, just like I knew he would be. Even has curly hair like you."

Tony's military haircut left follicles too short to be curly. "I'll be right back." When he peered into the hallway, he saw a policeman lingering around the nurse's station in the middle of the floor. Instantly, his heart started thumping. "There's a cop outside."

Patty clutched the blanket to her throat. "What are you going to do?"

"Get out of here right away — without being seen." He went to the window and stared down at the circular driveway. A patch of grass harbored a clump of bushes. But there were no police cars in sight. The city was painted white.

"Can't you wait? I've got to feed him at nine."

"Where do you feed him?"

"The nurse brings him in here because they don't want me getting out of bed yet, except to go to the bathroom."

Tony stared out the window again. "Will you be alone for a minute?"

"Maybe."

"Do you think you can make it to the window without hurting yourself?"

Patty shrugged.

"All right, I'll wait outside until feeding time. I'll be right down there, by that big bush. When the nurse leaves, you bring him over to the window and hold him up. Can you do that?"

"I'll try."

He bent over and gave her a peck on the cheek. "Okay, you just do your best. If it doesn't work out, I'll understand. And I'll be back tomorrow. Okay?" Patty nodded.

"Good girl." Tony plucked an orange off the nightstand, and dropped it in his jacket pocket. "I'll be waiting. And I'll be here first thing in the morning."

"Be careful."

Tony kissed her again, squeezed her hand, and left. The policeman was still at the desk, but his back was turned toward Tony. Tony dashed across the hall and slipped into the stairwell. At the first floor he slowed his breathing, made sure the coast was clear, and calmly walked past the front desk and out the door. At the end of the driveway, he doubled back through the snowdrift and ducked into the cover of the bushes.

He waited with his hands in his pockets. Snow was falling again, but lightly, and the temperature hovered around the freezing mark. Without the dampness, he felt warmer than he had the night before.

Cars kept entering the driveway, their passengers totally unaware that he crouched in seclusion only a few feet away. The huge mountain laurel leaves, green and shiny and distinctly out of place in the concrete jungle, kept him well hidden. The blanket of snow acted as insulation.

It seemed as if hours dragged by as Tony waited in the bush. He did deep knee bends to keep warm. Large, white flakes fell straight down from the windless sky, damping the sound of cars on the street. The occasional wail of an ambulance siren cut through the quiet as the slippery roads brought a rash of minor automobile crashes.

Finally, he saw a silhouette in the fourth floor window. He clambered out of his leafy concealment, shaking white fluff from his shoulders. The driveway lights reflected off the snow with daytime brilliance. Tony waved both arms over his head, saw a wave in return. Patty held to her side a tiny bundle wrapped in a blanket, hardly recognizable as a baby from four floors away.

But Tony knew that this was his child, his son. At that moment his heart swelled with pride. Nothing mattered to him other than that he was this boy's father, that this was the ultimate that life had to offer in fulfillment. And he knew that we would gladly go through those months of agony all over again to be here for this momentous occasion.

He was filled with happiness.

****

"Oh, my God. Look at you," Helen gasped, staring open-mouthed at Tony curled up in the foam-padded chair.

His uniform was wrinkled almost beyond recognition, his face had not been shaved in three days, his lips were cracked and painful, his hands had not been washed, and dirt was caked under his fingernails.

Bob said, "Are you going to let your wife see you looking like that?"

As Tony climbed to his feet, Helen put her hands on his shoulders and hugged him. "Where've you been these last two days? We've all been worried sick about you. Are you all right?"

"Oh, I've been hanging around — you know, staying out of sight. Uh, are there any cops around?"

"Ha, ha, ha. Don't you worry about them."

"But my father . . . "

"He was just bluffing you. The local police have no jurisdiction over military personnel."

Helen kept her hands on his shoulders. "I talked with him last night. He's really trying to do the best for you, and — doesn't want to see his son get into any worse trouble."

"But I told him I would turn myself in — as soon as the baby was born. I mean, at this point what's a couple more days?"

"Well, your father's just a little impatient, that's all." Helen turned to Bob. "Take him to the men's room and help him get cleaned up. I'll go up and talk to Patty and tell her everything is all right."

"Ha, ha, ha. She's right. They won't even let you on the ward in that condition. You have to

be damn near sterile to get near the tots. Which doesn't make sense in a way. Ha, ha, ha."

Later, in the maternity ward, Tony stood in front of a large, plate glass window. On the other side, a roomful of cribs held doll-like infants, some sleeping, some crying. They were so tiny that to Tony they seemed more like animated toys than living babies.

He located the crib with his surname scrawled on it. The baby in it looked no more recognizable to him than any of the others — except, perhaps, for the crown of thick, dark hair. The dwarfish hands clenched and unclenched, the legs gyrated in a bicycle pattern.

The young policeman who had been there the night before stood next to Tony. He stared down at an adjacent crib, and made waving motions with his fingers. Tony smiled, and nodded. The policeman did the same. Both fathers stood silently and admired their progenies. Later, they even got to hold them, and carry them to their mothers.

Tony's son was named David.

****

"I don't think it's going to work out." Kathy paced the small living room in her apartment. "It's too crowded as it is, and with a baby here — I just can't stand all the noise. I moved away from my parents so I could be alone."

"So what am I supposed to tell her when I bring her home tonight? That you don't want us around? And I'll be leaving tomorrow, so you won't have me to worry about."

Ray jumped up and smoothed out his vest. "That's not the point. It's just that we want some place where we can be alone — "

"*I* want someplace where *I* can be alone." Kathy stabbed Ray with a cold stare. "I have my own business to attend to and — "

"You listen to me, you stupid bitch. I don't want you running around with — " He clamped his mouth shut as someone knocked at the door.

Tony said, "I'll get it."

The two men standing on the stoop were in their middle thirties. They wore suits, overcoats, and hats. The nearest one held out a leather wallet and exposed his identification badge. "We're from the FBI."

Tony gulped, and took a faltering step backward. His spine tingled, and instantly he could feel the sweat dripping down his armpits, beading on his forehead. "I — I — "

While one man guarded the doorway, the other strode in confidently. Tony waited limply. The man walked past Tony, put a hand on Ray's shoulder. "Raymond Alan Murphy, I hereby place you under arrest for draft evasion."

****

When they arrived at the house, Frank was inevitably reading the newspaper and sipping coffee. At first he merely raised his dark eyes, registering no emotion. But when he saw the baby in Patty's arms, his olive skin assumed a slightly reddish color.

Frank stood and parted the blankets with a calloused hand. "Well, hello there, Davey. Gitchie gitchie goo."

A dimple appeared on the smooth skin, then the face wrinkled up like the clouds of a storm. Davey began to cry.

"What did I do?"

Elizabeth scowled. "You scared him. Don't be so rough with him. He's just a baby."

Soon Davey was wailing like a siren. Patty cradled him in her arms and gently rocked him back and forth. "He's not used to the bright lights. It wasn't anything you did. He'll be all right. Won't you?"

"Do you think it's time for a feeding? I can heat up some water for the bottle." Without waiting for an answer, Elizabeth put a pan of water on the stove.

"Thanks, Mom," Patty said, over the crying baby.

Robby skidded into the kitchen, mouth agape. "Is 'at my new brother?"

Tony laughed. "No, Robby, he's your nephew. You're an uncle."

"Uncle?" he mimicked, wrinkling his nose.

"Yes. You know, like Uncle Harry and Uncle Sammy."

"I an uncle?"

Patty said, "I think he needs a diaper change."

"We can do that on the dining room table. Frank, keep an eye on the water and let me know when it boils."

Robby tagged along after Patty, but before Elizabeth could leave, Frank said, "I want to know when he's going back."

"Oh, Frank, give him time to sit down, at least. He just walked in the door and already you're picking on him."

"I'm not picking on him. I just asked him a simple question."

Tony fidgeted. "Well, I thought I'd go back first thing in the morning." Frank's face plunged into a whirlpool of anger. "You know what they can do to you for desertion? In time of war? They can shoot you."

"Frank, stop trying to scare him."

"I'm not trying to scare him. I'm telling him the way it is."

"Well, this isn't a war — it's a conflict. They say it every night on the news. Nothing's been declared."

"Would you keep out of this?" To Tony, "You're in deep shit no matter what they call it. Even if they don't shoot you they can lock you up and throw away the key. You stupid bastard,

I had them convinced you wanted to turn yourself in, and you had to go and louse it up by running away. You made me look bad."

Tony stopped fidgeting and straightened up. "Well, I think it was a rotten thing to do."

Frank half rose from his chair, fists clenched. "Who do you think you are, talking to me like that?"

Tony refused to back away. "Will you sit down and listen? You want to talk this over with minds or fists? I'll accommodate you either way. We're not going to accomplish anything by arguing over it. I did what I did and that's all there is to it. I knew what the consequences were. And they don't shoot anyone for going AWOL."

Frank, frozen half out of his chair, slowly eased back down. "You'll still get court-martialed, and that'll go on your record."

"Okay, so I get court-martialed. I didn't do anything criminal, all I did was quit my job for a couple months."

"And that makes you a deserter."

"Only by a legal technicality."

"They can still hang you on a technicality."

"They're not going to hang anyone for going AWOL. Besides, I have the paperwork to prove that I requested a reassignment. They'll have to take that into consideration."

"The reason don't matter to the army."

"But it matters to me, and that's what counts." Tony took a deep breath. "Look, if you really want to help me, you can. I need a ride back to base. Will you take me?"

Frank threw his hands into the air. "I ain't got time to go gallivantin' all over Jersey."

"Oh, it's all right to call them up on the phone to come and get me, but you don't want to go out of your way. Is that it?"

"I got a meeting in the morning."

Elizabeth moved the boiling pot off the hot burner, shouting, "Frank, what's more important, some stupid meeting, or taking your son back to — wherever he's got to go?"

"What am I supposed to do, go out of business just because he goes AWOL?"

"Well, you ought to do *something*. You never have before."

Chapter 85

The army called it a stockade.

The term was leftover from cavalry days during the taming of the west, when forts were built by driving a barrier of wooden stakes into the ground. Even though they were now made out of stone and brick and barbed wire, even though the original purpose of protecting those within from those without had been reversed, the name stuck. And while four walls may not a prison make, those inside could seldom be convinced of this.

All the inmates were prisoners. But not all the prisoners were convicts. And hardly any of the convicts would have been found criminal in a civilian court of law. At least three-quarters of the men who were confined to the Fort Dix stockade were guilty of the same infraction against the Uniformed Code of Military Justice: absence without official leave. And most of *them* were still awaiting trial. According to the Constitution of the United States, those men were technically innocent until proven guilty in a court of law. But they all shared the same quarters, washed in the same sinks, and used the same toilets as the murderers, rapists, thieves, muggers, and forgers, and were treated with the same cold indifference.

"What're you, afraid of a little ink?" The gruff sergeant pushed Tony's fingers roughly onto the blue-stained pad one at a time, and pressed them on a white form sheet. "Now, that didn't hurt at all. Get over there an' have your picture took."

Tony's uniform was stripped off of him. He was given a set of fatigues without insignia or nametag. His personal possessions were locked up, and he was issued a toothbrush, toothpaste, a washcloth and towel, and an extra change of underwear. The hair that had been growing in thick and black was neatly shorn off. Then the barber stood watch as he shaved. Afterwards, the razor was taken from him. Then he was let loose with the inmates and assigned to a bunk. Gradually, he was introduced to those around him.

Alexander Fossick had gone AWOL because the army had ruined his career in an advertising firm. He was twenty-five years old, three years out of college, and well on the way up the organizational totem pole when his "greeting" arrived from Uncle Sam. Instead of reporting to his recruiting station on the designated day, he had moved from his apartment in New York City to another not far away, under an assumed name. He continued work as if nothing had happened. For a year he had kept up the deception, seemingly oblivious of the eventual and inevitable outcome of his action. The FBI had finally traced him to his place of employment through his social security number. They walked in one morning during his coffee break, asked for him by name, and walked out with him less than two minutes later. He had been allowed to don his coat and hat. He now had an apartment on which the rent was overdue and the utilities unpaid, and his car left on a street with no overnight parking. The number of tickets that must have piled up by now could lead to serious difficulties with the Department of Transportation — should he be so lucky to have

that as his only problem. He now faced a possible five-year sentence for draft evasion. The money he had saved during that year was being used to engage the best civilian lawyers.

Robert Connell had been stationed at Fort Dix with the Signal Corp. He had gone home to Passaic, New Jersey, on a routine weekend pass when the local police came to his parents' house and arrested him. The charge was statutory rape. His girlfriend's father, who had never liked him, had taken it upon himself to invade the privacy of her diaries, to which she had confessed their lovemaking in glowing and intimate terms. Connell was eighteen years old, having joined the army directly after high school. His girlfriend was a lower-grade classmate only sixteen years old, and therefore underage in the eyes of the law. Although she had been a willing participant, her father had insisted that jurisprudence be maintained. Connell had sat in a civilian jail for two months awaiting trial. When his case had come up for hearing, he had been found not guilty: the girl testified that her diary contained nothing but fantasies of what she dreamt would happen after her marriage. His troubles did not end there, however, for the army had been carrying him on the books as AWOL. Instead of being released from prison on the day of his acquittal, he had been held in custody until the MPs could be sent to transfer him to his present address. Now he was awaiting court-martial for desertion.

Leroy Johnson had been a street fighter in Harlem long before he had been drafted into the army. He was the kind who took gruff from no one. He was prize material for the infantry, for he was utterly fearless. But his huge size and unruly disposition got him started fighting before he could reach the combat arena. During bayonet training with pugil sticks, he had been delivered an underhanded blow by an overzealous sergeant. Johnson drove in with a passion, using techniques he had picked up on the streets. After cudgeling the sergeant soundly, he ripped off his helmet and broke his jaw with one well-placed fist. He had then been charged and tried for assault and battery, and sentenced to one year at hard labor — and a dishonorable discharge. It seemed that the army did not like hard-fisted men who fought too well. Soon he was to be shipped to the army prison at Fort Leavenworth where he would complete his sentence.

Derwood Mason, known as Woody, was a rebel from the deep South who had signed one paycheck too many — and got caught at it. As a clerk in the payroll department, he had a penchant for forging names, and had successfully stolen several thousand dollars before an investigation was initiated because the books were not balancing after several men had complained of not receiving their pay. Since he was in the Air Force, stationed at Maguire Air Force Base, he was sent to the adjacent Fort Dix stockade. The Air Force had none of its own. He had been duly tried and found guilty. His sentence was to work in the stockade without pay until all the embezzled money was returned, at which time he would be returned to service to finish his time — the Air Force did not like to besmirch its records with dishonorable discharges. He was presently working under minimum security, drafting signs and doing artwork. It seemed the best way of taking advantage of his wild talent.

Then there was Casey Adams, another New Yorker who had won competitions as a body builder. He found that the army training methods were substandard. They did not coincide with his ideas of proper nutrition, strenuous weight lifting, and sufficient rest. After a month of basic training, he had left base on a weekend pass and forgot to come back. He had decided to go to California to stay with his older brother, but had been picked up at the airport by MPs making routine checks of all men with short hair wearing civilian clothing.

Those who Tony tried to stay away from were the men with long criminal records, both civilian and military. These were the ones who were just as likely to break your jaw if you did not bestow a free cigarette, as they were to set fire to the mess hall if they did not get enough to eat. There were a lot of fights that never reached the attention of the guards — ratting could be less healthy than suffering.

****

"Private Anthony Giovanni, US52666498? I'm Captain Ralph Masters, and I've been appointed by the court to present your case."

The trim looking officer held a briefcase in one hand and a gold braided hat in the other. He placed them on the table and took the seat opposite Tony. He was in his late twenties, had regulation inch-long dirty blond hair (parted neatly), dainty eyebrows, and a fair but uncompromising face. He was straight-shouldered and strictly professional.

Tony had been in the stockade a week, and sitting at that table for two hours. He remained silent.

The captain snapped open the briefcase, took out a folder, and thumbed through a sheaf of papers. "According to my records you have been absent without leave for a period of — " A rueful eye scanned the page above his neatly filed index finger. " — sixty-seven days."

"Is that how long it was?" Tony said ingenuously. Then, after a moment, during which

Captain Masters transfixed him with a baleful stare, he hastily added, "sir."

"Don't you know the length of your own crime?"

Tony cleared his throat. "Well, sir, I never really counted it up."

Captain Masters leaned forward on his elbows. "Private Giovanni, as an officer I must admonish you not to be flippant with the Unified Code of Military Justice. As an attorney, I advice you to take a more serious attitude toward your offense. And as a member of the court I think you had better treat me with more respect."

"Sir, I didn't mean any disrespect, and I wasn't being flippant. But I don't know when you're counting the period of AWOL. I left just before Christmas, and that's not more than six or seven weeks. What starting date are you using?"

"According to this report, you were assigned to the 25th Infantry Division in Vietnam, were awaiting transportation at Overseas Processing — hmmn, I see that your grandmother died and you were granted a seven day emergency leave — "

"It was my grand*father* who died."

Again came the icy stare. "Your grand*father*, then. In any case, you never reported back from that leave. You really took advantage of the situation, didn't you?"

"Sir, I did report in. I signed the register and was sent to Holding Company to wait for a change in orders. I had put in for a compassionate reassignment because my wife was due to have a baby soon."

"I see nothing about a change of orders here," the captain stated flatly.

"Well, the paperwork hasn't caught up with me yet. It's been lost in military red tape somewhere between Fort Polk and here. You see, I had some trouble with the clerk down there. He didn't like me and I suspect he threw out my forms. But I have a carbon copy. It's all because of him — "

"'If what you say is true, why didn't you take this up with the commanding officer at Overseas Processing?"

"I tried to see the CO, but the first sergeant wouldn't let me. I even had the chaplain make a special appointment for me, but Sergeant Mendez — "

"Oh, yes, I have a special report from him." Captain Masters shuffled through more papers. "According to him you did some rather unorthodox things that completely obviated the chain of command, started fights in the orderly room, tried to break in through the back window — "

"That's a lie. The sergeant wouldn't let me

see the CO. He purposely blocked all my efforts — ”

“I'm not here to listen to excuses.” The captain pulled out a carefully typed letter with a blank line at the bottom. He flipped it around and slid it in front of Tony. Then he took a pen out of his breast pocket and placed it on top of the paper. “If you'll just sign here we can get this case out of the way.”

“What is it?”

“A confession. It will save time for both you and the court.”

Tony looked up sharply. “You mean, by signing it I'll be saying I'm guilty?”

“Of course. It's all cut and dried, Giovanni. You were apprehended by the military police on this base — ”

“Now wait just a minute. My father drove me here and I turned myself in.”

“It doesn't matter. Just sign it and I'll get it processed as soon as possible — say, a couple weeks.”

“Don't I even get a trial?”

“Of course you'll get a trial. But that's merely perfunctory. There's no contradictory evidence to be submitted.”

“But I wasn't AWOL that long. I was in Holding Company for a month. And what about mitigating circumstances? I want to plead for leniency.”

“On what possible grounds?” Anger was rising in the lawyer's voice.

“On the grounds that my wife was expecting a baby, and that I was waiting for orders for a temporary reassignment.”

Captain Masters sighed heavily. “That has no bearing on this case. The records prove that you were absent without leave. You refused to fulfill your military obligations. You should have thought of that before taking the action you did.”

“Well, sir, maybe the army should think about me for once instead of their precious protocol. I'm not to blame because you people are so inefficient that you can't process a simple reassignment form in less than three months. And as long as I'm a citizen of this country, I expect to be given a fair and impartial trial.”

“You are a member of the United States Army, and as such are bound by the laws set forth in the Uniform Code of Military Justice, *not* the law of the civilian land. You've been in the army long enough to know that. Now, will you please sign the confession so I can get out of here? I have more important things to do than explain regulations you should have learned in basic training.”

Tony, quite simply, said, “No.”

The captain's face slowly reddened. “What do you mean, no?”

“I mean that I think it's extremely poor advice for an attorney to try to get his client to plead guilty when he is innocent.”

“Who said anything about being your attorney? I'm an official for the board of courts-martial.”

“But, I thought you were my lawyer.”

“What do *you* need a lawyer for? I already told you, your guilt is right in the records. You should count yourself lucky that we're giving you a summary court-martial, instead of a general. Desertion is a serious offense.”

“I didn't desert. I came back, didn't I? And besides, I was in Holding Company where I should have been anyway if my new orders had been processed on time.”

“Giovanni, there's nothing in your records about new orders, so forget about it. Now, just please sign the affidavit.”

Tony stared into the captain's blue eyes, and said evenly, “I want a defense attorney who is willing to present my case — someone who will be on *my* side.”

Captain Masters turned violent purple. In a huff he pulled back the confession, gathered the papers, and stuffed them into the briefcase.

“All you young punks are alike. You think you can remake the laws to please yourselves.” He snapped down the case, stood, and donned his hat. He peered down his nose at Tony from his height of six-foot-two. “All you're going to do is make things more difficult for yourself. The board of courts-martial will view your uncooperativeness in an unfavorable light. You may have just lost your chance for a summary court-martial and gained a general after all.” He glanced hurriedly at his wristwatch. “Well, have it your own way, Giovanni, but I have important things to do.”

He stormed out the door. Tony sat at the table, waiting to be told to return to his barrack. But through the closed door he could hear the captain shouting into the telephone.

“I'm sorry, June, but I've run into a little snag. I'm going to be a little late for our date.”

****

On Sunday morning, a chaplain was brought into the compound, and services were held in the large, communal room, with the men sitting on uncomfortable folding chairs that were aligned in rows. Afterward, the chairs were turned and arranged in pairs or triplets, facing each other. Sunday afternoon was visiting time.

“All right, you guys. File in one at a time, and no pushing. First one gets outa line, his folks are sent home.”

Along with some fifty other men, Tony entered the under-heated room, his heart beating quickly. He glanced around for a familiar face, saw Teddy standing and waving frantically with both hands. Tony could not contain his smile as he wound through the roomful of visitors. He had only one person in sight.

Patty stood and gave him a hug and a kiss as he drew near. "Oh, Tony, I thought they would never let you come in."

"Just usual military hurry-up-and-wait. It's good to see you, Honey. How is everything?"

Before she could answer, Teddy grabbed his hand and pumped it furiously. "Good to see you, Tony. Everything's fine in Philly. How's prison life treating you?"

Tony still had his arms wrapped around his wife. Slowly, they disengaged, and took their seats. "Well, not too bad, although they don't feed us too well. Won't even let us have an extra slice of bread. I had to sneak some out in my shirt because we only get fifteen minutes to shove down our food. And get this: prisoners don't have any privileges, even if you're not convicted yet. It's a case of being guilty until proven innocent. So, we don't have the right to salute officers." Tony laughed. "I always thought that was something we were forced to do, not privileged. Anyway, how's little Davey?"

"Oh, he's doing just fine. He doesn't give me any trouble at all, except for the two a.m. feeding. But even then he's good. I just give him his bottle and he goes right back to sleep."

Teddy was enthusiastic. "Yeah, and you should see him go on that bottle. He empties it like there was no tomorrow."

Tony laughed. "Where is he now?"

"He's outside, with my mother. They wouldn't let me bring him in."

"How's everything else — at home?"

Patty shrugged. Her shoulder length tresses lay limply on her gaily-printed blouse. His hands lay in the lap of a new skirt. "Okay, I guess. But Kathy's complaining that the baby is too noisy, and that his diapers smell, and that I'm not keeping up my half of the housework. But I'm so *tired* all the time. She doesn't know what it's like."

"Does she still want you to move out?"

Patty nodded, her chin barely leaving her chest.

To Teddy, "Hear any word from Ray?"

With his cheerfulness fading, Teddy shook his head. "They've got him locked up downtown, in a detention center. He's not allowed to have any visitors, but my mom got a lawyer for him."

To Patty, "What about the allotment?"

"I haven't gotten any checks yet."

Tony sighed. "I can't believe it could take so long. It seems as if the army can't do anything right." He slammed his fist onto his knee. "Well, I'll see if I can talk with someone about it, but it's awfully hard to make appointments around here. They always think you're making excuses to get out of detail, or something. I swear, if I rake the ground one more time I'll throw up. And the buildings have so many coats of paint that the wood could completely rot away and the walls still couldn't fall down. I mean, this place is worse than basic training."

"Hey, speaking of basic," Teddy said, perking up. "Did you hear about Pete?"

"No, the phone's been busy."

"Well, he joined the marines."

"He *what*? When did he go?"

"The day after George left."

"Left for where?"

"You know, Toronto. Monday, I guess. He tried to get in touch with you, but didn't know how. Pete, that is, not George. George never said goodbye, just got in the old Green Lantern and took off. The next day the garage was locked, and Mrs. Hart said we couldn't come in any more, except to take out all our junk. Well, the next day Pete went down to the recruiter's office and enlisted. He was mad 'cause George was running out on his country. He's leaving next week. They have a special two-year hitch, except that you don't have a choice of jobs."

"But they'll slap him right in the infantry."

"He knows that, but he doesn't care. He says he wants to get where the fighting is. He says if he's going to leave the country, he's going to do it the right way. Anyway, he's already got his bags packed for Parris Island. He's still working part time at the auto shop, and giving the money to Marion so she can go to school."

"Are they planning to get married?"

"Naw, he says he's not ready to get hitched yet, but maybe when he gets out. Marion's taking it pretty hard, but doesn't mind waiting."

"Tony, you've got to get that allotment for me. I want to be able to get a place of my own."

"Can you cash another bond? I still have a couple left, don't I?"

"Not without your signature."

"Bring it with you next week. In the meantime, try to get along with Kathy."

"But, she's always bringing these strange men home, and they smoke and drink and get rowdy. There are all these strange noises coming from her bedroom — "

"So, why don't you move in with your mother?"

"She doesn't want me around all the time, I told you that. It interferes with her social life."

"Well, can't she spend time at Bob's house if they want to be alone?"

"She doesn't always go out with Bob."

"What are you talking about? I thought they were going steady, or whatever older people call it when they're seeing each other."

"Bob is, but not my mother. She still goes out with other men, only Bob doesn't know about it."

"But, Bob's such a nice guy. Why would she want to go out with anyone else?"

"I don't know, that's just the way she is. Bob's all right, I guess, he just thinks he owns my mother."

Teddy interrupted, "Yeah, Bob's a neat guy. If it hadn't been for him, we wouldn't have known about visiting hours today. He's the one who called the MP station and asked about you."

A firm hand squeezed Tony's shoulder. "Time's up, mister."

Tony looked up at the sergeant, then around at the scores of people scraping their chairs and making their exit. "But, I'm not through. I've got more questions that need — "

"I said, time's up. Another word, and this'll be your last visitor."

Chapter 86

Another week passed before Tony was permitted to meet his newly assigned defense attorney. First Lieutenant Granger Roberts spoke in a voice that still carried the high baritone of youth.

"Now, uh, it says here, Tony — may I call you Tony — that you were absent without leave for sixty-seven days. Is that correct?"

Tony sat on the scratched oaken chair on the other side of the wobbly table. He considered asking for clarification of the question: did the lieutenant want him to confirm what was written on the paper, or did he want to confirm that the facts were correct? Instead, he said simply, "Essentially."

Large, quickly darting eyes shared their time between Tony and the desk. "I also understand, from Captain Masters, that you had put in a request for compassionate reassignment, uh — " He thumbed through the sheaf of papers in front of him.

"I did that at Fort Polk — back in September. And again in November. At the time, I was told that the first one might have been misplaced."

"Yes, I quite understand." The lieutenant did not look up. He thumbed through several more sheets of paper. Arching his narrow neck, he squinted at Tony through wire-rimmed glasses. "You understand that it makes no difference in this case, since the purpose for which you made such a request did not comply with regulations. It would have been turned down because at that time your wife was not six months pregnant."

"No one told me that."

"That does not change the regulations. No matter what you were told, that is the rule. So you see, you have no defense on that score."

"But I tried to file another reassignment request when I got to Fort Dix, only the sergeant wouldn't let me have the papers. And he prevented me from seeing the CO, who could have authorized it."

"Again, that would have made no difference. Once you have officially been assigned, you cannot afterwards be reassigned. That, too, is the rule. Any requests for reassignment must be made before the fact."

Tony stabbed the table with his finger. "Now wait a minute. How would I know before hand I would want my orders changed if I didn't know what they were in the first place?"

Lieutenant Roberts remained unflustered by Tony's logic. "You must understand that operating an army of some two million men is a complicated task. It takes a great amount of order and discipline, otherwise we would have total chaos. The army is not geared to suit the needs of the individual. So, we have certain rules, and we must abide by them."

"Even when they're wrong? Even when they make no sense? Even when they cause more harm than good?"

"I am not here to argue politics or philosophy. I'm simply trying to explain the reason for having rules, and why you, as a rule breaker, must pay the penalty."

Tony leaned forward in his chair. It creaked ominously. "Just whose side are you on, anyway? Aren't you supposed to help me present my side of the case, instead of telling me that I'm already guilty before I walk into the court room?"

The lieutenant slowly removed his glasses, and tapped them against the manila file folder. "I will represent you to the best of my ability. But I can only state the facts of the case."

"Then how about stating that I am not sixty-seven days AWOL because I was sitting in Holding Company for a month — my signature can be found on the sign-in roster? And how about mentioning the fact that I have a carbon copy of the reassignment forms I submitted in November — *after* my wife was in her sixth month of pregnancy? And how about stating the fact that it does no good to put in reassignment papers if it takes the army over three months to process them? On one hand you're saying I can't request a reassignment until my wife is in her sixth month, while on the other hand you're saying that once I wait until that time and it takes more than three months to process the forms, they don't do any good. The army doesn't have overnight processing. And if, in the mean time, an assignment comes through, it can't be changed by a reassignment request. None of this makes any sense to a normal, sane person."

"If you think — "

"What I think is that I have a reason for breaking the rules, because those rules are stupid and useless. And if you can understand that, and still choose to go along with it, than you fall into the same category. And that is the point I want to get across — to you as well as to the court-martial board. I may not be able to beat the charges conjured up against me, but I want it known that it was the ridiculous and antiquated military regulations that made my actions necessary."

Lieutenant Roberts was red in the face, and his cheek muscles were twitching.

"So, what I want to know right now, before we go any farther, is: are you going to defend me, or just spout army regulations? Because if that's all you're going to do, I'd just as soon defend myself. The court has already assigned one prosecuting attorney — I don't need another."

****

Two weeks later, Tony was escorted out of the stockade by two burly MPs, and locked into the back of an olive drab '65 Plymouth. They did not talk, and he was separated from them by a steel grating. After delivering him to a nondescript, beige clapboard building, he was turned over to an officer of the court, and put into a tiny room that contained nothing but three chairs. Tony sat in one and tried to make himself comfortable.

Lieutenant Roberts entered, briefcase in hand. He blinked continually from behind his wire-rimmed glasses, and wasted no time on protocol. "As I explained before, this court-martial is purely perfunctory. The prosecutor and I have submitted our evidence, which the three judges will have read in advance. There are no witnesses to be called, and no other matters are to be brought before the board. It is simply a matter of passing sentence."

Tony climbed to his feet and leveled his gaze with the lieutenant's. "You mean that I've already been judged guilty."

Without blinking his large, cowlike eyes, Lieutenant Roberts said evenly. "It is not a matter of judgment, merely meting out punishment requisite with the situation. They already have the necessary evidence."

"Then why bother with this mockery of a trial?"

The lieutenant stifled a gasp. "Because things must be done formally, and you must receive sentencing in person. Look, your case is no different from thousands of others. It's a cut-and-dried case of absence without leave, and you can't get out of it."

"I'm not trying to get out of anything. All I want is justice — true justice, not your kind,

based on some idiotic rules that don't allow for flexibility due to circumstances. I want it known that I tried first to do things the right way. It's not my fault that my paperwork was mislaid, or that all my personal belongings in Holding Company were stolen. I'll bet that Sergeant Mendez did it on purpose. But even without that carbon copy, the forms were filed. And a simple phone call to my company commander in Fort Polk will verify it."

"Tony, we can't take the time to investigate this case as if it were more important than it is. No matter how many excuses you have, you were still absent without leave — "

"But not for the time you've got me down for."

"It doesn't matter. You still — "

"I'm still being treated like a common criminal, for missing a few days work I should have been given off in the first place."

****

The courtroom was unpretentious: twenty feet by forty, a door at either end, an aisle lined by three rows of rough wooden chairs on either side, a broad desk on an upraised floor where the judges sat. Fluorescent fixtures cast an even, white light. The silence was so pronounced that every rustle of clothing sounded like scraping sandpaper. And winter cold seeped in without hindrance.

Three officers sat behind the judge's bench: a colonel flanked by two majors. None looked up from their papers as Tony and Lieutenant Roberts entered. Captain Masters nodded obliquely to the lieutenant from where he sat. Roberts motioned Tony to the opposite side of the aisle.

Without preamble, the prim looking colonel glanced up and intoned in a businesslike manner, "Private E-2 Anthony Giovanni, US52666498, versus the United States Army. He is charged with being absent without leave for a period of sixty-seven days. Now, we've all read the brief submitted by attorneys for the defense and prosecution. Captain Masters, do you have anything to add?"

He rose to his feet and stood stiffly. "No, sir."

"Lieutenant Roberts?"

The lieutenant rose as the captain sat down. He glanced nervously at the superior attorney, then cleared his voice and, with more tremor than timber, said, "Sir, on behalf of my client I would like to remind the court that he was under extreme mental stress due to his wife's pregnancy, and that he had in accordance with regulations submitted on more than one occasion a request for temporary reassignment until after the birth."

Captain Masters was on his feet in an instant.

"Your honors, I submit that any requests for reassignment under pregnancy clauses are invalidated since the wife of the defendant was not six months pregnant at the time such a request was allegedly made. According to the law, six months pregnancy means that she had to have been in her seventh month at the time of the request for reassignment. Even supposing there *was* such a request made in November, by that time she would have been only five months and three weeks — "

The captain was cut short by a wave of the hand. "There's no need to go into the mathematics any further, Captain. The records are all in order, and as I said we've all read both briefs. We can dispense with any further argument. This board of court-martial finds the defendant guilty as charged. He is sentenced to three months hard labor, starting from the day he first entered prison. He shall further forfeit all pay that might have accumulated during the period of absence, as well as time spent in prison, all of which will count as bad time and not toward the fulfillment of his military obligation. He will not be reduced in rank, but we recommend that he not be advanced in rank for six months after his release. That is all. Thank you, gentlemen."

Both attorneys saluted.

Tony jumped up angrily, his face contorted. "Now wait just a minute. I didn't have a chance to say anything."

The colonel, who up until now had been calm and deliberate, tensed up. His head jerked back as if he had been punched in the face. The two majors stared, aghast.

"This outburst is outrageous. Must I remind you that as a prisoner you have no right to speak? You forfeited that right when you committed an act against the Uniform Code of Military Justice."

Tony was not to be intimidated. Louder, and with more confidence, he said, "It also seems to me that when I got drafted I forfeited the rights guaranteed to me under the Constitution of the United States, including the freedom of speech."

All five officers were stunned. In the lag between one sentence and the next, the only sound was a collective, startled intake of breath.

"Ever since I've been in this army I've been poked and prodded, pushed and pulled, screamed at like some dumb draft animal, but never listened to. Now I've got something to say, and I'm going to say it. I think this whole rotten system stinks. When a simple request like a man wanting to be with his wife during the time of birth becomes a major crime, it's time for something to be done about it. I have

tried to follow this insane set of rules by doing things by the book, but I've met with nothing but ridicule and abuse. I was forced to take matters into my own hands because there was not one idiot with the sense or the sensitivity of a flea who would help me. I have done nothing morally wrong, and nothing I'm ashamed of, and if this kangaroo court thinks otherwise, it is nothing more than a mockery of all we've fought for since the Revolutionary War."

Tony found himself shaking all over. His anger died down, and fright took its place. But that fright was tempered by satisfaction: he would have felt much worse had he remind silent.

Judges and attorneys exchanged frantic looks with each other. Only the colonel's eyes never left Tony's; they seemed locked in some intimate embrace, like two mountain goats who had locked horns during a duel.

"Young man, I don't know who you think you are to speak to this council in this manner, but I assure you that you have only further harmed your case, and lost any chance of clemency. You are no longer a civilian, and are no longer bound by the laws of civilian courts. You are a soldier, and you will abide by military rules and regulations. The slightest infraction of those rules would result in chaos. That is why adherence is applied stringently, and punishment meted accordingly. You should feel grateful that you got off as lightly as you did. In fact, I may later decide to extend your sentence because of your insubordination."

Tony stepped into the aisle and approached the bench. "Well, as long as I have nothing to lose, let me make my point abundantly clear. I am a *citizen* of this country, and I refuse to give up my rights of citizenship just to fatten your precious ego. Instead of sitting — "

"Guards!"

" — up there on your high horse, you should be performing a useful function. You've got an army here that is treated like dirt, and you expect them to fight with the highest morale. You can't fight slavery with slaves. You need free men — "

"Remove this man and escort him to the stockade."

" — who have faith in the system they're supposed to be fighting for. How can you expect — "

A hand clamped over Tony's mouth, both arms were gripped firmly, he was dragged out the door on his heels. Still, he returned defiantly the colonel's gaze.

"Of all the impudence."

****

Tony resumed stockade life as if the trial had never taken place. He was treated no differently than before being found guilty, and the hard labor turned out to be a continuation of the endless and mindless chores he was already used to. He and Rodney Englewood scraped many dollars worth of stainless steel off kitchen hardware.

Like the Puerto Ricans in Tony's basic training company, Englewood had been apprehended during rifle training, leaving the firing range with two expended brass cartridges in his pocket. He had been court-martialed and sentenced to six months — long enough to serve as an example, but short enough so he did not have to be transported to Leavenworth. When his jail term was served, he had to take basic training all over, and then fulfill the three-year term of his enlistment.

While hundreds of dollars of leftover food was dumped into the stockade garbage pail every day (prisoners could not have second helpings), while thousands of dollars worth of building materials were being used for unnecessary maintenance, while millions of dollars worth of used equipment was discarded or abandoned to make room for new materiel, one soldier was being jailed for stealing a few pennies worth of used brass. Those were the rules: arbitrary, but immutable.

Then there was the strange case of William Bates and Charles Fenshaw, pre-draft buddies who had swapped enlistment papers in the induction center, each signing the other's. They had gotten all the way through basic training and were on their way to AIT before an astute company clerk discovered the deception.

Since neither one had been properly inducted, the army was trying to figure out their exact status. Were they still civilians, or soldiers bound by military obligation? Were they under the jurisdiction of the FBI, or the army? They had to be court-martialed for something, but what? Forgery? Fraud? In civilian court, or military?

For Tony, weary weeks passed. A heavy snow blizzard swept across the base, and the men spent long hours standing in formation, hands in pockets, faces turned from the freezing wind, while their names were called out over the howling of winter storms. Every day, without fail, they stood through roll call seven times: before and after each meal, and again at bed check. When there were not enough work details to go around, they huddled in their bunks without books, cards, or any way of passing the time other than talking — and fighting.

During lighter moments in clement weather, they marched in formation to the cadence of the Stockade Shuffle: left, right, left, drag the right boot along the dirt; left, right, left, drag. The scraping sound of the dragging boot was amplified a hundred times. The cadre threatened the prisoners with repercussions, but there was not much they could do to a man who had nowhere lower to go, and who existed without hope.

Tony lived for Sundays when he could expect to have short visits from Patty and Teddy, or Bob and Helen. Two visitors at a time was the limit. He longed to see his little son, Davey, but babies were not allowed in the visitor's auditorium.

"Well, Marion, if this isn't a pleasant surprise." He kissed and hugged his wife, then exchanged pecks on the cheek with the redhead. "How did Teddy allow you to steal his place?"

Marion smiled, glancing around at the crowd. She raised her voice against the din. "He's in the waiting room taking care of Davey." Her red hair was just as wild as he remembered it, and her freckled face was almost white. Next to Patty, who had not yet shed the excess weight of pregnancy, she appeared prim and shapely.

"And right now he's not too happy about it," Patty laughed. "Davey just wet his diaper before we came in, and Teddy got stuck with changing him."

Marion added, "He complains, but he really doesn't mind."

"He's so cute sometimes — Teddy, I mean. Last week he took me and Davey to the pediatrician, and he was so embarrassed sitting in the waiting room full of women that he hid his face behind a magazine the whole time. I heard one woman say under her breath that he looked so young to be a father. Teddy heard it, too, and turned red as a beet. You should have seen him."

"That's funny. And how's Pete doing?"

Marion pulled her dress down over her knees. "Well, he seems to like it, even though he lost half a tooth."

"What? How did that happen?"

"Some sergeant punched him for moving his eyes during formation. He said they put a cap on it so you can hardly tell. And he put in for armor school. I don't understand; they don't wear armor any more, do they?"

Tony laughed. "No, that means tanks and armored personnel carriers. He'll probably be a driver, or a gunner — or maybe maintenance. With what he knows about mechanics and engines, that would be the best place for him. What's this rumor I hear about Ben and Katie —"

Patty interrupted. "Can we stop talking about the gang for a minute? Kathy really wants me to move out, and I've got to have some money."

"Patty, I've put in two tracers since I've been

here, and submitted a voucher for back pay that was coming to me before I — went AWOL. They say my records were sent ahead, to Vietnam, and it's difficult to track them down."

"But I need some money, and I can't get into your bank account."

"Didn't you ask if they had some form I could fill out that would allow you to make withdrawals?"

"Yes, but you have to go to the bank to sign it. They won't give it to me and let me bring it here because it has to be no — notar — "

"Notarized," Marion supplied.

"What about the savings bonds? I keep asking you to bring one so I can sign it over."

"I know, but it's at your house, and I don't want to go over there to ask your parents for it. It's too — humiliating. Your mother hardly ever calls to ask about the baby."

"Did you ever think of just stopping over there for a visit?"

"I can't do that. They don't like me. That's why I need you to do something."

"Well, Patty, someday you're going to have to learn to do something on your own."

****

In his bunk, Tony looked at the picture that Marion had given him. She had taken it with her new camera and flash. Davey had lost some of the dark, curly hair he had been born with, but Tony thought that he could see Patty's rounded chin, her squat nose, his own brown eyes.

Lying in the crib he seemed so helpless, so — fragile. He had the appearance of a doll, but one that lived and moved. In six weeks he seemed to have grown so — how much would he change in six months, a year? Eagerly, Tony looked forward to the following Sunday. Marion had shot another roll of film, and promised to have them developed during the week.

On Thursday morning, his name was called out for special appointment. He was directed to go to Headquarters and await further orders. He was hoping that it had something to do with his request for an updated pay voucher, or the allotment tracer.

After waiting for an hour, he was called into the CO's office. The swarthy-faced captain did not allow Tony to stand at ease, but launched right into the subject.

"Your sentence has been suspended as of today, in compliance with outstanding orders that you be delivered to your next duty station. Turn in your bedding, Giovanni. You're going to Vietnam."

Chapter 87

"But, sir, I can't just pick up and go. I've got to let my family know I'm going. I've — I've got to see them before I leave. And I have to make some financial arrangements — for my wife and baby.

Major Pinchot's bushy eyebrows shot upward, as if he could not believe what he was hearing. "For a prisoner you have an awful lot of wants. You should be grateful we're letting you out of here early. You'll have less bad time on your record, you'll be able to catch up with your unit, and you'll be doing your country a favor. They need men in Vietnam, especially in the 25th. They're taking heavy casualties and need every replacement they can get."

"But, sir, I'm not objecting to going. I just have some unfinished business to take care of. A two-day pass is all I need — "

"A *pass!*" The major lurched upright in his chair. "You must be crazy. You're still a prisoner, and don't make any mistake about it. Prisoners don't get passes."

"But, sir, you said I'm being released, and — "

"Your release is not effective until you enter the war zone. Until then you are a prisoner and will be treated as such. You will be escorted to the airport and placed aboard a plane, and that's all there is to it."

"But, sir, I can't just take off without telling my wife I'm going. She'll be worried about me."

"Send her a postcard. Now, get out of here and start packing."

"But, sir — "

"*Stop but-sirring me!* Just get out. Clean up your bunk, turn in your linen, and pick up your duffel. There's an escort on the way, and when he gets here you better be wearing dress greens. Now, that's all."

Tony wilted like a dying flower. He tossed off a half-hearted salute, despite the fact that as a prisoner his saluting privileges had been revoked. "Yes, sir." The major did not seem to notice. Tony did an about face and slumped out the door — but not before he saw the major pull a crossword puzzle book out of his desk drawer, and pick up a pencil.

****

"Where's the rest of my stuff?"

The desk sergeant glanced at the list on his clipboard. "You Giovanni, Anthony J.?"

"Yes."

"Then that's all there is."

Standing in his skivvies, Tony dumped out the half empty duffel bag. He was in a hurry to get dressed because of the cold, but only his uniforms were in the bag: all his underwear and personal belongings, including his overnight case, was missing. "I thought he only took my papers."

"Them boys that broke into your locker prob'ly took anything of value. When you go

AWOL, there's no way they can get caught, is there?"

"I wouldn't be surprised if Sergeant Mendez himself stole my stuff." Tony stuffed the summer uniform and fatigues back in his bag, and unwrapped the package that held his dress greens. They had been taken from him upon his entrance to the stockade, and had not yet been laundered, or even properly folded. "Boy, they're going to love me on that plane."

He waited another hour before his transportation arrived. Sergeant Mattwell was a broad chested three-striper who exuded muscular strength with every movement. But his ebony face seemed complacent when he returned Tony's nod.

"Just see that he gets there," the desk sergeant cautioned after the sergeant signed for his charge.

Side by side they walked out the gate. Sergeant Mattwell opened the rear door of the Plymouth and tilted his head. "Throw your duffel in there. You can sit up front."

The heater was going full blast, and Tony rubbed his hands under the hot air. "I don't see any MP insignia on you." He saw no gun, either.

"I'm not an MP. This is just temporary NCO duty. What're you in for — AWOL?"

Tony nodded.

The sergeant kept his eyes on the road. He was so tall that he had to duck his head in order to see out the windshield. Little piles of snow lay encrusted on the sides of the road where it had been plowed. The white purity had long since been blackened with exhaust soot.

"Going to Vietnam?"

"Yes."

"That why you went AWOL?"

"No."

Sergeant Mattwell drove for a full minute before speaking again. "I'm trying to get back there myself."

Another minute passed. The road reeled under the car like a long, black conveyor belt. The sky was partially overcast, but clearing. Leafless trees lined the road like lonely, naked sentinels.

"Just got back from my second tour. I put in for a transfer right away, but the army wants to stick me in a training command. Because of my experience, they say. Meanwhile, I'm doing temporary escort duty. Imagine, *me* an escort." He shook his head slowly from side to side. "Most of the time I drive majors and colonels. You're the first private I've had."

Tony could not help but smile. "You should feel honored. So, how come you want to go back?"

"I don't know. I guess it's the excitement."

"Excitement?"

Sergeant Mattwell let half a minute pass. "Yes, excitement is the right word for it. The excitement of going into battle — not to kill, not to maim, but just to be there, against the odds, to fight your way through, to survive. At first you know nothing but fear. You jump at every rifle crack, every rocket assault, every mortar attack. But you get used to it. The fear dies down and you find yourself — thriving on it, looking forward to the next firefight, the next barrage of incoming. Each time you find yourself more alive than the last because you have lived — *lived* through something remarkable. Excitement becomes a drug, and you become addicted to it."

They drove past the entrance sign to Maguire Air Force Base. Sergeant Mattwell swung the car toward the airfield. Gigantic hangars were visible, as well as the large administration building. A jet was streaming gray smoke as it angled skyward, soon to disappear into the clouds.

"I — I don't think I understand that," Tony stammered, wincing. "I'm not sure I want to."

The sergeant laughed grimly. "No, I don't suppose you can. But you will in about three months. You going into the bush?"

"I guess so. My MOS is 11B10."

"Infantry, huhn? Well, make that a month. Then you'll know what I'm talking about."

The airport terminal was a beehive of activity. Cars jockeyed for parking space, buses disgorged soldiers in dress green, civilians either wandered around or were directed by MPs toward appropriate doors. Inside was a madhouse. Throngs of people clustered in front of ticket counters, plagued information booths, mobbed the cafeteria for a last minute bite, or simply stood around in groups. Officers, enlisted men, and civilians bustled in all directions along the concourse, walking around knots of soldiers, hugging couples, families saying their goodbyes.

"This is worse than Grand Central Station."

Sergeant Mattwell led the way with confidence. "Just follow me. I know where we're going." Tony followed the burly sergeant as he line-backed through the crowd. "Put your bag down. I'll get your ticket squared away."

"Mind if I make a phone call? No one at home knows I'm leaving. My wife — " Tony trailed off with a shrug.

The sergeant glanced around the mobbed terminal. "As long as you don't get out of sight. You can use that one over there."

"Hey, thanks, sarge."

Tony fished a dime out of his pocket and made for the phone. His finger was shaking as he dialed the operator to call collect.

"Is that you, Tony? I can hardly hear you. Where are you?"

"Patty, I'm at the airport — Maguire Air Force Base."

"What — what are you doing there? How did you get out of the stockade?"

"My sentence has been suspended — " Tony paused while he fished for the right words. " — on condition that I be sent immediately to my duty assignment. I'm leaving for Vietnam on the next plane."

"Oh, no," Patty cried, bursting into tears.

Tony stared nervously at the crowd. All around him people rushed around, oblivious of his conversation. Sergeant Mattwell had his back turned, lifting the duffel bag through the counter.

"Patty, Honey, listen to me. It's all right. Everything's going to be okay."

"Tony, you can't just take off without saying goodbye."

"I *am* saying goodbye."

"That's not what I mean. You can't just — leave. Kathy wants me to move out by this weekend. And Davey's sick. He won't drink anything. I just called the doctor, and he wants me to bring him over right away. He said it might be infantile botulism."

"I've never heard of it. Is it bad?"

"Tony, he might *die*." Patty continued to wail into the mouthpiece. "I'm — I'm scared. I need you. Please, Tony, you've got to come home."

"Honey, I can't. They've already got me booked on a flight. I can't get out of it now."

"You've got to do something. Doesn't your son's life mean anything to you?"

"Of course it does, but I don't know what I can do about it." Tony was soaking wet under his uniform. Beads of perspiration dripped down his forehead, but his hands were stone cold. "Patty, stop crying for a minute and listen. Patty? Patty, are you listening?" Her reply was little more than a sob. Sergeant Mattwell finished his business at the counter and strode purposely toward Tony. "Patty, I've got to go now. I'll call you later."

"Tony!"

"Bye." Tony leaned against the wall, unmoving, staring blankly.

A hand fell on his shoulder. "Hey, buddy, are you okay? You're as white as a ghost."

Tony turned slowly and faced the sergeant. "I — I — I don't — feel well. You know, they made us stand in formation without jackets. I think — uh, is there a men's room around here?"

"Sure, right over there."

"Thanks." Tony followed the pointing finger. "Uh, I'll just be a minute." He staggered off, pushed through the steel door. A moment later he crashed against a stall partition, fell to his knees, and sprawled across the floor. He lay with his eyes closed, but heard the outer door open and felt rough hands roll him over.

The sergeant's voice was thick, and commanding. "Go call for an ambulance. We've got to get this man to the hospital."

****

That night found Tony back in Holding Company, under guard. This was a different barrack than the one to which he had been assigned before, but it was just as ramshackle and twice as cold. It was intended for overnight transients who did not require jailing, but who needed supervision. The guards themselves were transients who were caught between flights.

Without heat there could be no water; the pipes had long since frozen. Therefore, all soldiers under temporary restraint had to be escorted to an adjacent barrack for latrine necessities.

"I hate to disturb your rest, but I've got to go."

The guard looked up with weary eyes. His fatigues, recently retrieved from his duffel bag, were faded and creased like a used road map. His shirt had pulled out in the back. His boots sported a chalky layer of dust which accentuated the cracked leather uppers.

"Again?" The sloe-eyes widened half a millimeter.

"What do you mean, again? This is my first time."

The guard remained seated on the oaken chair, leaning back on two creaky legs to an angle that was barely beyond the balance point, so that the upper back support rested against the barrack wall. Paint chips on the floor attested to the gouged holes in the wooden partition. He kept his eyes at half-mast.

"So whaddaya want me to do, hold it for you?"

Tony saw a man flying a holding pattern until he was transported from the aseptic cities of America to the rotting jungles of Vietnam; from civilization to animalism; from life, possibly, to death. And when he was gone, he would briefly become a weekly statistic before being swallowed by the gaping maw of anonymity.

"You're supposed to follow me over there."

The chair hit the floor with a thud, the man's crossed legs unfolded, he hit the floor with both feet, and he rose with one fluid, practiced motion: an amazing display of coordinated laziness. He tossed the nudie magazine to the side. "All you guys ever do is eat, sleep, and shit."

"The doctor says it's good for me."

"Wasn't no army doctor. He'd a told you to

take two aspirins and get back to work." The guard laughed at his own hackneyed wit. He hitched up the pistol belt and realigned the forty-five in its holster. "Come on, let's get it over with."

The guard pulled on his cap. Tony, in keeping with the mandates of the detention barrack, was uncovered. If anyone ran away, he could be easily spotted by his bare head.

The last time Tony had looked outside, the sun had been a dull, orange ball, partially obscured by dirty white clouds that looked like slush on a street after three days of exhaust fumes. Now it was gone, and only dim starlight peeked through the overcast, silhouetting the army compound like a dismal, tractless boardinghouse of lost souls bound for the gates of Hell.

The latrine barrack had heat and water, but little else. Armored cables hung loosely from the ceiling connected to two bare bulbs. The floor was a concrete pad without tiles, so the swirls of the mason's trowel were left on the uneven surface. The paint did not fall off in chips; it peeled off in sheets.

One wall was adorned with a porcelain pit trough that served as a sink: little piles of dust and plaster coated the chipped, chromed fixtures, while a green patina grew around the knurled nuts. The adjacent wall had a similar trough at knee level, and a dirty copper pipe that fed water for flushing. The urinal was choked with butts and filters and chewing gum wrappers, and except for the row of broken flushing handles, the major distinguishing feature between it and the sink was the height. On the blue-tinted, moldy wall someone had scrawled with white chalk, "don't eat the mints." The macabre sense of humor was surpassed by the legions of powder room poets who had left their four-line witticisms on the partitions of the toilet stalls.

The porcelain bowls were separated by plywood boards, unpainted, but the stalls had no doors for privacy. Most of them were uninhabitable because of the filth — two were unflushed and reeked of previous deposits. Tony settled in the one closest to the door — not because of its cleanliness, but because of its value as a piece of real estate — location. And although he dropped his drawers to the floor and sat upon the frigid, encrusted wooden seat, he did nothing more than cogitate.

While Tony planned his campaign, the guard fell right into place by deciding to mix pleasure with business. He sat in the corner stall farthest away from the door because of the obvious advantages: warmth, a modicum of cleanliness, and toilet paper. No sooner had he acquired his seat than he cursed and stormed out, holding his pants up with one hand. He swiped some dry paper from a less well-kept stall to replace the soggy mess that sagged from the roller in his hand.

Taking advantage of the guard's predicament and physical needs, Tony hunched over and pressed his head between his knees. From this awkward position he could see under the partitions all the way to the unlighted end where the guard was perched delicately, arching his feet on his toes so that his pants did not drag on the dirty, moist floor.

As soon as he heard grunting, Tony flushed his toilet, pulled up and zipped his pants, and stepped to the sink. Keeping an eye on the guard, he ran water into the scummy sink, closed the tap, and walked softly and casually to the latrine door. He leaned against the jamb nonchalantly, crossed one foot over the other, and rested it on its toe. He stared out into the gathering darkness.

The grunts and groans emanating from the corner sounded like a bull elk in rut, and every once in a while there burst forth a sound like the tooting of a trumpet. Tony surmised that the guard was temporarily out of order. Glancing in the direction of the caterwauling, all he could see were combat boots surrounded by folds of olive drab. He took a casual step out the door and onto the worn gravel. The guard, caught up in problems of his own, did not protest.

The athletic field was a worn patch of no-man's-land, assaulted by decades of soldiers doing close order drill. Here and there, tufts of grass struggled to survive the almost daily beating it received at the business end of those hordes of spit-shined boots. The only people visible in the dim afterglow of the nearby streetlights were stick figures on the far side, unconcerned about a lone soldier a hundred yards away.

Tony reached inside his green jacket, unbuttoned his shirt, and pulled out his flattened overseas cap. He separated the folds and stuck his head inside. Once covered, he dashed around the back of the latrine and lit out across the lot between two abandoned barracks.

He peered around the corner of the building: the coast was clear, the road deserted. On the other side, a hedgerow lined the road for several blocks in either direction. Tony took one last look at the latrine, saw no untoward motion, dashed across the street, and climbed through a break in the bushes. He was nothing more than a fleeting shadow in the night. He then ran along the unclipped and unkempt hedgerow for a tenth of a mile, towards the traffic circle that served as an intersection.

He found a spot where he could lie on the frigid ground and watch cars approaching from both directions, and from where he could make a quick escape if he was detected.

Then, shaking with cold, he waited.

Chapter 88

After what seemed like hours, a squarish looking black car drifted slowly through the yellow beam of a distant streetlight. Tony, crouching in the bushes, hesitated to rush out until he was certain that it was the Black Stallion.

As the smooth-firing engine brought the car closer, Tony leaped from concealment, waving one nearly frozen arm to attract attention. The car screeched to a halt. Tony ran around the back and, using both hands and ten stiff fingers, wrenched open the door.

"What kept you? You stop on the way for a hamburger, or something?"

Ben brushed long blond hair out of his eyes. "I ran out of gas and had to jog a mile and a half back to a gas station. Then I had to walk back with a five-gallon can in my arms. You know how much that weighs?"

"At seven pounds per gallon, thirty five pounds — not counting the weight of the can."

"Yeah, and there's not much traffic on these Jersey back roads."

"All right, I'm sorry. Can you turn the heat up? I've metamorphosed into an icicle lying on the ground."

Ben turned the fan to high. "I was doing ninety miles an hour on the turnpike."

"All right, I said I was sorry."

The car moved forward slowly. "Where did you call me from?"

"The hospital. I faked a fainting spell and missed the flight. They put me in Holding Company for the night. Did you have any trouble getting by the gate?"

"The guard looked in the back seat with his flashlight, and asked me what I was doing."

"What did you tell him?"

"I said I was meeting a friend going to Vietnam."

"And he let you through?"

"No problem." The car hummed along the darkened road with scarcely a sound. "Now, would you mind telling me what the hell is going on?"

With his hands under the heating duct, Tony squeezed his fingers but could not make a fist. "Didn't Patty tell you?"

"No one was home. So what's this about you leaving all of a sudden? And how did you get out of the stockade? And what kind of trouble is this going to get you in? Christ, Tony, tell me *something*, will you?"

The long, black ribbon of road was nearing a concentration of lights. As closing time approached, the PX became more crowded with last minute shoppers and soldiers buying beer.

"Just don't do anything conspicuous. We can't afford an inspection."

"What can they do to us?"

"To you, nothing. To me, plenty. Just don't make any U-turns. We'll follow the street to the next circle and head back for the gate."

"Suppose we get stopped."

"They don't usually stop people leaving, only entering."

"And if they do?"

"We'll crash that gate when we come to it."

"So how come you're not back in the stockade?"

"For one thing, by the time I left the hospital the stockade admissions office was closed. And anyway, officially I've been released. That means technically I'm not a prisoner any more. So they just rescheduled my flight and put me to bed for the night."

Ben slowly shook his head. "Boy, you're a wild one. I wouldn't have the guts to do what you did."

"What do you mean? I'm scared to death. I just don't have any choice."

The silhouette of a car loomed out of a half-concealed parking space. Headlights flashed on and stabbed through the passenger window at the same moment that Tony ducked under the dashboard. He whispered, "Did they see me?"

Ben kept the car going at an even pace. "I don't know. But I don't think they can hear you."

Tony crept up the back of the seat and sneaked a look out the rear window. The headlights dimmed for a moment, then came back to full brightness. It eased into the street and turned in their direction. Tony could not help but whisper. "I think they're coming after us."

"Maybe not." Ben stole a glance at the rearview mirror. "It could be a coincidence."

"Was it a Plymouth?"

"I couldn't tell. Why?"

"The army uses Plymouths."

"It was too dark."

"All right. Just go slowly and let's see what they do."

"What if they pull me over?"

Tony did not answer. He tried to remember the Plymouth's headlight configuration. Then they burst into the light of the Post Exchange, where soldiers were still drinking beer and making last minute purchases.

"Quick. Pull into the PX."

Ben jammed on the brakes and grappled with the wheel. The tires squealed momentarily before the car turned to the right and hit the low curb, missing the driveway. It bounced over the concrete ridge on heavy-duty shocks, headlights bobbing.

"I said don't do anything conspicuous."

"Next time give me a little warning."

At five miles per hour, Ben wound through the parked cars and carousing enlisted men. Closer to the front door, several women in civvies stood out among the uniforms. Ben stopped the car to let one woman and her husband, a captain, walk by. Then he moved forward at a crawl.

"Go past the canteen and around the back."

One straight-backed sergeant, limned in the lights of the glass-fronted building, gave them a passing glance as they cruised by. Tony realized that having only his head showing could attract attention, so he pulled himself up in the seat. Only then did he recognize the man staring awkwardly after them.

"Oh, no. It's Sergeant Mendez. Don't stop now."

Ben halted the car as a throng of rabble-rousing troops poured out of the door of the canteen and blocked his path. "I can't run them over."

One soldier, who had obviously had too much three-point-two, tapped a tune on the hood of the Chevy as he swept past. His buddies laughed and sang horrible choruses out of tune. The strange car that had been following them turned into the parking lot, and in the cone of light Tony could see the military police insignia emblazoned on the side panel. Now Sergeant Mendez was reaching out to put his hand on the door handle.

"Ben! Move it!"

Ben raced the engine, dropped the clutch, and the car lurched forward expertly, without squealing tires. He turned sharply around the building. "What'll I do?"

"Keep going right on around, but take it easy." Tony stared out the rear window. "We may be able to convince the MPs there's nothing wrong, but we'll never convince the sergeant."

"Oh, great. Before you know it we'll have the whole army out after us."

"Quit complaining. Just get back on the street."

Ben tooled the car completely around the building and headed for the entrance. The MP car had stopped for the gesticulating sergeant.

"They're definitely on to us."

The car hit the road and turned back the way they had come. "So what'll we do?"

"Don't speed yet, until we're sure. Just head back to the circle."

"Tony, I don't know why I'm doing this."

"Because you're my friend."

Ben shook his head, collar length hair bobbing loosely. "I'm already in trouble for that demonstration last week. I'm on suspension."

"Don't worry. You're not in the army so they can't do anything to you. This isn't a civilian matter. They can't even give you a ticket. Just get to the gate and you're in the clear."

"Goddamn it, they can call the Stateys. If this goes on my record and I get kicked out of school, my old man'll kill me."

The police car hit the road and began accelerating rapidly. Tony groaned. "All right, then let's not get caught. They'll hang us both."

"If I stopped now, can they get me for aiding and abetting an escaped convict? I mean, I don't know you're AWOL."

"Ben, I'm not an escaped convict. I didn't do anything criminal."

"It's not just that, Tony. I don't want to have anything to do with this conflict. It's not my fight, and I don't want to help kill people. I just want to live my own life and let other people live theirs."

"This is a heck of a time to have a philosophical discussion."

"Look, I want to help you, but I don't want to get into trouble with the army. Don't you think they can have my classification changed faster than you can snap your fingers? And I can't afford to get drafted. I need that degree. Katie and I have our own life to live and — "

"So what are you doing getting involved in student protests?" Tony was practically screaming now. "You're not making any sense."

"But that's safe. All right, this time they took down names and some of us got suspended. I'll be more careful next time. But — "

Flashing high beams illuminated the car. Ben took his foot off the gas and applied pressure to the brake pedal.

"Ben, what are you doing?"

"I've got to stop," he said, as if it were the most natural thing in the world. "I don't want any trouble."

"You hypocrite! You're afraid to stick your neck out, aren't you? Your convictions are only as strong as your safety." Tony stared out the rear window. "If Sergeant Mendez told them who I am, they'll take me back to the guard house and lock me up. And I've got to get home — to see Patty, and Davey. I've got business to take care of."

Ben eased the car off the road and brought it to a halt. In the utter darkness, only the two sets of headlights illuminated the oak trees and the snowdrifts on this otherwise deserted stretch of road. Ben stared sightlessly out the windshield, grim-faced.

Behind them, the police car stopped.

Ben's hand rested lightly on the gearshift. The Black Stallion hummed with a barely perceptible ping. "I think I could use a quart of oil."

"I think you need your head examined. What happened to friendship? Are you just going to let them take me in? Is that what you're going to tell Patty — and Katie — and the guys? That you sat there and let them take me away?"

Two car doors slammed like thunderclaps. A storm was brewing.

Tony took a handful of jacket and jerked Ben around. "Where's your nerve, Ben? Have you lost it? Where's the stunt driver who raced the cops through a cornfield? Where's the racer who does seventy miles an hour on Broad Street? Where's the guy who laughs every time he passes a cop? Where is he now, Ben? Huhn? Where is he?"

Mechanical steps approached, crunching crystals of snow on the macadam hardtop. A flashlight beam sprayed through the windows, dousing the two in stark, white light.

"Thanks a lot, Ben." Tony slouched back in resignation, stared grimly to the side.

The flashlight came closer, and a hand rested on the door. At the same time, there was a loud roar and a terrible pressure that drove Tony back against the seat. One MP let out a stentorian shout, the other jumped back. Both were engulfed in a cloud of dust and a clatter of stones. The high-pitched whine of the straining engine matched the squealing tires, until the fraction of a second thump denoted the slamming into second gear. The tires chirped again as the Chevy burned rubber.

"I guess you're right," Ben said, through gritted teeth. Then he turned to Tony, and smiled. "Just for old times' sake."

By the time he hit third gear, the four-barrel carburetor was spitting gas to the engine with the force of a fire nozzle. The car roared like a maimed lion, and raced like the wind. Far, far behind, the MPs were just recovering from their shock and dashing back to their car.

At eighty miles per hour, the trees rushed by like fence posts. The engine ping was drowned out by wind and whine. The speedometer needle touched ninety, then ninety-five, and hovered.

Tony straight-armed the dashboard. "The circle's right up ahead."

Ben started braking, and monitoring the rearview mirror. "Holy cow, I think we've got a tiger by the tail. Those bastards are catching up to us. What've they got in that thing, a three-eighty-three?"

"*Slow down, Ben.* The circle's coming up."

Ben pumped the brakes as the rotary approached rapidly. The smell of burning rubber warned that the brake shoes were warming up.

"Ben, watch out for the circle." His own foot automatically went to the floorboards, stamp-

ing a nonexistent pedal. Too late he started fumbling for his seat belt.

The Chevy was still going fifty miles per hour when it entered the rotary. Ben swung the car to the right and creased the edge of the gravel shoulder. Branches from a nearby oak swept across the windshield and roof. Once clear, he turned the wheel harder so the car swerved sharply and tilted over, lifting the two right tires off the road. Tony dropped the loose seat belt and pinned himself in the corner between the dashboard and the seat. His eyes were as big as quarters.

Almost instantly, Ben spun the wheel the other way. The car straightened out for a moment, sat flat on the road, then tilted to the passenger side. Black smoke and the smell of rubber permeated the air as the car screamed around the circle counterclockwise.

With an unmilitary flash of insight, the MP driver anticipated the Chevy's flight pattern, and took a different tack. Plundering into the rotary right behind them, with brakes burning and tires screeching, the Plymouth cut to the left against the normal traffic flow and spun around the circle in the opposite direction. But they were going too fast for the maneuver. What would have been a cut-'em-off-at the-pass turned into a rout, as the heavy car skidded sideways off the macadam and onto the dirt track in the middle of the circle, plowing through a snow drift and kicking up great clouds of brown dust and clumps of grass. The Plymouth spun out. It traveled sideways completely across the circles, and bounced over the low curb. When the tires hit the macadam, they grabbed and sent the car gyrating out of control.

"*Watch out!*" Tony screamed, as the bulk of the Plymouth loomed directly in front of them — and heading toward them at an angle.

Ben gripped the wheel with fingers of steel. Using all the skill of his back-road racing days, he stomped the accelerator and turned into the inner circumference of the circle. Vectoring sideways, the Chevy missed the Plymouth by the thickness of a layer of paint. Tires screaming, it kept right on going around the circle, just outside the inner perimeter, and missing the road that led to the gate.

"Head for Wrightstown." Tony let go the dashboard with one hand long enough to point the direction and pound the seat in his excitement. Then he retained his grip. "*Go for it!*"

Ben took the Black Stallion all the way around the circle again, tires screaming as he maintained speed in a long, controlled skid. The Plymouth seemed to have stalled out after the spin, and slammed against a hedgerow. The Chevy completed its circuit and spat out of the rotary like an electron from a particle accelerator.

"There's another circle half a mile ahead." Tony breathed easier once they were on the straightaway, and their pursuers were temporarily out of action. "From there we can get to Wrightstown and out the north gate."

Ben downshifted and floored it. A sardonic grin spread across his face. "Just like old times, huhn, Tony? Decatur Road all over again."

Tony wiped sweat off his forehead with his jacket sleeve. He had no more thoughts of cold. He stared back incredulously. In perfect synchronization, Ben slammed the column-mounted shifter into third gear. The car jerked and tires squealed because he never let off the gas. The engine whined as if it were getting ready to throw a rod.

"Uh, oh."

Tony jerked around and saw headlights in the distance. The Plymouth was on their tail again. "They must have a souped-up engine."

"I can't take them on a straightaway."

Tony kept his eye on the military police car, closing the distance. "The road to Wrightsville is too long. At that speed they'll catch up with us."

Ben nodded grimly. He took his foot off the pedal and let the car slow down naturally. "I've got a plan." The Plymouth was catching up rapidly. The Chevy hit the next circle at a leisurely pace, swung right, and hugged the inner perimeter slowly enough so that the tires did not squeal.

The MP car was moving so fast that the driver was forced to jam on the brakes. With a wild screech, the Plymouth skewered sideways and came to an abrupt halt just inside the circle entrance. Ben was still coming around the other way when the driver started backing around the circle on an intersecting course with the Chevy.

"Watch out! He's trying to ram us."

With tires spinning in reverse, the Plymouth gathered momentum, but Ben had plenty of time to avoid a collision. He cut sharply to the left and plowed over the grass of the inner circle while the MP car shot straight back and braced for impact. They scraped bumpers just before the Chevy cut diagonally across the circle, tires digging two deep grooves through the snow and the withered, brown grass underneath.

With the wheel still turned, the car came out sideways between two spokes radiating out from the circle. Ben kept the steering wheel hauled tight. He floored the pedal so the car continued around the circle for the second time.

The MP driver jammed on his brakes and spun tires getting his gearshift into forward. The transmission screamed at the sudden change of direction, and threatened to tear itself apart. The rear wheels started going, but the momentum kept carrying the car backward at a maddening pace — right into the trunk of a sturdy oak.

As the bumper bit bark and wrapped itself around the thick bole, the trunk lid popped up into the air with a resounding crash. Both hinges snapped. The lid flew upward, describing an arc, and landed in the cavity of the open trunk.

By this time the Chevy was halfway around the circle again. Tony was plastered up against the door by the terrific centrifugal force. Ben held himself in place with an iron grip on the wheel. So tight was the turn that the car was literally going around on two wheels. They passed the MP car like a flash, and dashed off the circle back the way they had come.

When second gear cried for mercy, Ben shifted into third. The air was full of chemical odors: burning rubber, burning brake shoes, burning transmission fluid. Tires lost no more tread on that trip — just a lot of sidewall.

While the Plymouth was trying to extricate itself, the Chevy straightened out at high rpms, and moments later bore down on the first rotary. As there was yet no pursuit, Ben decelerated in plenty of time to make the quarter turn. But another car entered the circle from the other side and was going around, temporarily blocking the path.

Ben jammed on the brakes when collision became imminent. Everything would have gone fine if the other driver had not done the same thing, and reduced speed at the same rate. Legally, the vehicle already in the circle had the right of way, and had he taken it without hesitation there would have been no confrontation. The Chevy started fishtailing in a protest of rubber. When the headlights struck the other car, Tony could see the driver of the beat up, fifty-five Dodge, his mouth open wide, his face frozen.

For a drawn out moment, the two cars paralleled each other, side by side. Ben could have reached out and touched it as they drifted along together. In the crystal clarity of that isolated moment in time, Tony studied the terrified features of Sergeant Mendez.

Then Ben hit second gear and surged ahead, taking the right-hand road wide. This forced the sergeant's unkempt vehicle further out of line. He missed the road and veered off the rotary between two leering maples, bowled down a clump of bushes, and screeched to a standstill in a ditch beyond, tires spinning.

Not until the speedometer needle had passed sixty did Ben shift into third. The car was performing at peak efficiency, and Ben was as one with his machine. By the time they saw the lights of the entrance gate, a mile and a half down the straightaway, they were traveling over a hundred miles per hour. Tony cast a glance over the rear seat and saw headlights swerve onto the road in a wide arc.

"I don't believe those guys. They never give up."

Ben nodded grimly, but kept staring straight ahead. "Oh, my God."

Tony swung around, and saw what Ben saw. "They've got the gate down." The simple railroad gate was one board thick, the short end being equalized with a counterweight so it could be raised and lowered by one man.

Ben touched the brake, but the effect was negligible, and he could not downshift without blowing up the transmission. He started pumping the pedal.

Then Tony kicked his foot aside and jammed his own down on the accelerator, pressing it to the floor. All four barrels caught hold with a quiet surge. "Crash it. It's our only chance."

"You're crazy." Ben struggled for control. Sitting side by side, the two of them held onto the wheel for support. One foot was on the brake, the other on the accelerator. Tony's heart pumped like a steam locomotive.

The guard stopped waving his hands and leaped out of the way into the guard shack. At better than eighty miles per hour, the low gate struck the Chevy's grill. The car jolted imperceptibly. A shower of wooden splinters cascaded into the air while the Black Stallion bounced over tumbling boards. Tony lost his grip and slipped sideways and off the seat. He came to rest crumpled on the floor.

Ben's demonic grin spread from ear to ear. "I guess we showed them, didn't we?"

Tony clawed his way out from under the dashboard. His hat had been shoved so far down over his head that it half covered his ears. Completely disheveled, he shook his head in disbelief. Then he saw the lights sneaking up behind them.

"They're still after us!"

Ben chanced a look through the rearview mirror, and merely nodded. On the back street drag strips, there were few drivers who had the guts to beat him up the narrow, crowded lanes between traffic signals. But in the long haul, the larger engine of the Plymouth could overtake the '57 Chevy.

The road leading out of Fort Dix was perfectly flat and straight as an arrow. In daylight one could see literally for miles ahead. At the top of occasional hills one could also look over tens of square miles of pine barrens and marshland. Now, at night, the only object in view was a traffic signal ahead, lost in perspective.

"You'd better start slowing down," Tony warned.

The speedometer needle was bouncing radically, and the car seemed to float in some dreamlike trance inches above the macadam. With the windows rolled up tightly, they seemed to be traveling through a vacuum.

The traffic signal turned green, but did not appear to be getting any closer. "Ben, it'll be red before we get there."

Ben was mute, and his foot stayed close to the floor. The needle now fluctuated wildly, bouncing off the one hundred twenty mark that was the last number on the circular dial.

"Start — slowing — down." Even as Tony spoke, the light turned red.

They were close enough to see cars and trucks moving across the intersection.

Ben seemed hypnotized. His body did not flinch at Tony's words, and his face had a blind, moronic stare as if his mind were a million miles away.

"Ben, for God's sake, slow down."

Like a pair of railroad tracks coming together in the distance, the tree line merged to a point at the intersection. Tony felt as if he were speeding down a long, black tube, helplessly falling, nearing the crunching jaws of death.

"Ben — please — stop — the — car. You want to kill us both?"

Vehicles of all dimensions streamed along the crossroad like snails in a hurry to go nowhere. Tony slid across the sat and screamed in Ben's ear. Now the tables were reversed as he tried to kick Ben's foot off the accelerator and get his own on the brake pedal. But he could not get around Ben's leg. The accelerator pedal was part of the floorboard.

Tony froze with one hand on the dashboard and one hand on Ben's shoulder. His throat was parched and he could do nothing but watch the inevitable doom. The trees were a blur. The busy intersection was jumping into the front seat with amazing celerity. The speedometer had left the domain of reality, buried against the peg as if it had died there.

Then the cars were slowing down. The red light was almost overhead. A momentary hole appeared in the line of vehicles — an empty slot in a funeral procession. A Mack truck hauling a gleaming silver trailer honked to a stop. A blue, '65 Galaxy edged slowly past the white line, then halted.

A flash of green reflected off the windshield just as the Chevy reached the crossroad. With the speed of a high-powered bullet, they shot across the single lane highway so fast that if any of the waiting drivers had blinked they would not have seen the Black Stallion pass at all.

For an instant the interior was bathed in crisscrossing headlight beams. Then the darkness of the surrounding forest closed in on them. Finally, Ben pulled back his foot and allowed the car to slow down on its own.

Tony melted to the side, a quivering mass of protoplasmic jelly. His heart was pounding so hard that it threatened to fracture his ribs. Sometime later, he remembered to breath. Every muscle in his body ached from the terrible tension.

In a clear, crisp voice, Ben said, "I thought I had it timed right." The corners of his mouth perked up into the caricature of a smile.

For several seconds Tony said not a word. Then, catching his breath, he finally blurted, "And suppose some joker had run the light?"

Ben's smile broadened. "I figured they were all law abiding citizens."

As they approached a curve, the Black Stallion slowed its charge to about eighty miles per hour. The pine trees gave way to open fields: broad expanses of land on both sides that were waiting for spring tractors to plow them into long, even furrows.

"Damn." The Chevy jounced abruptly over a frost heave. Ben punched the accelerator. "That lousy bastard is still behind us."

As Tony spun around, Ben slammed on the brakes. The car pulled to the left, throwing Tony against the door and pinning him there. Ben clutched the wheel and let it slide. Tony rolled his head as he felt the car tilt over. Instead of overbalancing, it spun completely around on its low center of gravity until it was facing the way they had come. The stench of burned rubber and smoking brake drums was thick.

For a split second the engine idled quietly, except for a loud ping. Then Ben shifted into first and floored the accelerator, peeling rubber for a good ten seconds before he let up on it. At breakneck speed, they approached the curve just as the military police car came speeding toward them in the adjacent lane.

Ben grinned maliciously as he flashed on his high beams — and left them on. The Plymouth's headlights switched to high, then low. Still wearing his grin, Ben turned on the dome light just as the other car passed. An instant later brake lights flashed on.

But the policeman had not figured on the curve. With the brakes locked, the olive drab Plymouth kept its forward momentum and direction of travel. In a cloud of smoke, the car flew off the road onto the soft, sandy shoulder. A moment later it was engulfed in a cloud of dust and dirt as it continued on its course through the frozen field, plowing four diagonal furrows into the farmer's carefully planned design.

Tony heard splintering glass, rending metal, the hiss of a disintegrating radiator, and the roar of an unmuffled engine as the exhaust system was scraped off and scattered across the clearing. The lights went out. In the star glow, he saw two silhouettes fall out of the doors. The MPs had a long walk back to base — and a lot of explaining to do when they got there.

Ben was laughing maniacally now, banging his palms against the steering wheel and whooping like a Cherokee warrior. He laughed even louder when an oncoming car blinked its lights; Ben started flashing his high beams continuously. "Take that, you bastard."

"That's Sergeant Mendez."

Tony no sooner spoke than the old Dodge struck the frost heave, and its headlights speared a madly spinning trunk lid — obviously bounced out of the Plymouth's trunk when the Plymouth struck the frost heave. The sergeant's car crashed into the trunk lid just as the Black Stallion passed by the spot. Tony caught a glimpse of the lid burying itself in the Dodge's grill, heard the resounding crash. The heavy car made at least five revolutions before slid to a stop, steam gasping from its burst radiator.

Ben laughed raucously. "I bet that'll make the old sarge dizzy."

The Chevy zoomed toward the crossroad again. Tony grabbed Ben by the shoulder. "Forget about the sergeant. How about stopping this car?"

Ben laughed again. The light turned yellow, and traffic on both sides started edging into the intersection. The Chevy was still going sixty miles per hour, and hardly decelerating.

"Come on, Ben, slow down."

The car never slackened its pace.

"Ben, would you slow down!"

Ben stopped grinning. With both hands on the wheel he refused to be distracted. His lips were set tight.

"BEN! STEP ON THE BRAKES!"

Very calmly, almost casually, Ben said, "I've been standing on them for the last thirty seconds."

The light turned green for opposing traffic. Ben downshifted into second as a solid black Cadillac and a large, stake-body truck moved into the intersection from opposite sides. They slowly passed through, and behind them a line of vehicles crept forward like the body of an iron centipede.

Ben was as rigid as a corpse in rigor mortis. The car continued to glide. When Tony saw his ashen face, he knew that Ben was no longer in control of his vehicle. Without thinking, he pushed down the door lock, and again fumbled for the seat belt.

Ben leaned on the horn for five unendurable seconds, then started tooting short blasts. Cars continued to move across the road, their drivers oblivious to impending disaster. Ben took his foot off the brake, turned the steering wheel to the right, and jammed the brake pedal hard. It sank sickeningly to the floor, with barely enough grab to send the Chevy into a skid on the loose cinders and sand that had been used to cover the snow.

The Black Stallion slid sideways at forty miles per hour through the space between the rear bumper of the stake-body truck and the tractor-trailer that was struggling to get out of first gear. After passing an oncoming GTO nose to nose, the Chevy careened off the road and onto the sandy shoulder. Great clouds of snow and dirt spumed into the cool, night air. Several small trees thumped into the undercarriage as they were scythed down like stalks of wheat.

Ben hit the accelerator and gave the car forward momentum. The Chevy pulled out of its glide just before contacting the dense pine forest broadside. Spitting gravel from the rear tires, it raced along the shoulder, fishtailed once or twice, passed several oncoming cars, then jumped back onto the road in front of the stake-body truck. He oversteered and briefly touched the shoulder on the other side of the road before bringing the car back into line.

Plucking through the gears, Ben took off as if all the hounds of hell were after him. Ten minutes, and fifteen miles later, the battered Chevy wheezed and coughed. The engine conked out, caught, conked out again, then alternately started and died while Ben frantically twisted the key and popped the clutch.

"I think we're out of gas."

The engine died for the last time. Ben depressed the clutch and let the car roll. A hundred yards away, a small, lighted sign advertised gasoline prices. With barely enough momentum, the car rolled into the drive and coasted to the pump, completely spent.

Neither Ben nor Tony moved. After a few seconds, Tony emitted a deep sigh of relief. He stared at Ben wordlessly.

The gas station attendant approached, his grizzled face smiling. "Howdy there. I was wonderin' when you was gonna bring back that gas can."

****

Tony formed a half smile that was more a grimace as he waved goodbye to Teddy, who was sitting proudly in his mother's pink Oldsmobile. Teddy waved back gladly. Tony turned and waded through the door of the military police station as if his shoes were weighted with lead.

"Sergeant Mattwell! What are you doing here?"

The sergeant sat serenely on the back legs of a chair, reading a gun magazine. When he looked up, his face grew grim with an expression that would have stopped a truck. "The question is, what are *you* doing here?"

Fighting down the goose bumps that were crawling along his spine, Tony tried to act nonchalant. "I've got to catch a plane."

"Giovanni!" shouted the desk sergeant, scrutinizing Tony's plastic nametag. "You're ass is in big trouble. Where the hell have you been?"

Tony met the enraged sergeant's gaze levelly. "I've been waiting for my plane, but no one came to pick me up."

"Waiting *where*? I've got you listed as AWOL. The barrack guard reported you missing from morning formation."

"*What?* Sarge, there must be some mistake. I mean, I know I missed breakfast and lunch, but I didn't think it mattered. Some friends stopped by to say so long, and — "

"Now, look here, soldier. If you think — "

Sergeant Mattwell leaped out of his chair and stepped between the two. "Hold on, Tom." He put a restraining hand on the desk sergeant's broad chest. "Let me take care of this."

"Whaddaya mean, take care of it. This man's in trouble whether he knows it or not." Sergeant Thomas Chadwick shifted his gaze. "And I'm gonna see to it that he pays for it. When you're under my command, you damn well stay in line, or suffer the consequences."

Sergeant Mattwell drew attention to his watch. "Tom, what can you do to him worse than sending him to Vietnam?"

"*What can I do?* Why, I can — that is, if I only had him — he'll be sorry he ever — "

"Let's be reasonable. I know things look a little unorthodox. But if we hurry, we can get to the airport in plenty of time. His duffel has already been sent ahead, and his unit's waiting for him."

Sergeant Chadwick put his hands on his hips. "Why you old son-of-a-bitch, what're you stickin' up for him for?"

"I'm not sticking up for him. All I'm saying is the man's here, and another plane is leaving in an hour. What do you prove by keeping him off it?"

"I prove that no stinkin' private is goin' to run this man's army his own way. We got rules and regulations — "

"And we've got units in the bush who need every man they can get. And we both know you're not as worried about the rules as you are about your authority. You can't buffalo me, Tom. I know you too well. So maybe his actions are a little — irregular. But since he's here now, we can still get him on that plane. Now on the big scale, what's more important?"

The desk sergeant chafed at Mattwell's logic. Harrumphing in bass tones, he said, "I don't like it. I don't like it a bit." Stabbing a thick finger at Tony, he said, "And *you* make sure you get on that plane. I don't want you gettin' sick or nothin'. Ya hear?"

"Yes, *sergeant.*"

Sergeant Chadwick shook his head as he took a set of keys off the pegboard, and tossed them to Sergeant Mattwell. "Go on, get out o' here, before I change my mind."

Sergeant Mattwell smiled. He took Tony by the shoulder and ushered him out the door and into the car.

Tony settled into the seat. "Is my flight still confirmed?"

The engine coughed and started slowly in the cold. "As far as I know. Last call is held at the airport, and anyone who doesn't answer has his spot taken by a standby."

"Then let's make it this time."

The sergeant revved the engine and backed out of the parking spot. "If you miss two planes in a row, the President of the United States won't be able to help you. Now, are you feeling all right this time?"

Tony blushed. "Yes, I think so. And, uh, thanks for helping me out back there. I wasn't sure what was going to happen. I mean — "

"No more phone calls?"

"No. Everything is okay. My son's got dehydration, and — "

"I don't want to hear about it. The less I know, the less I can tell. What you got there?"

Tony had pulled a small, silver medallion out of his pocket, and fingered it unconsciously. "It's a Saint Christopher's medal." He coiled the slender chain in the palm of his hand. "He's the patron saint of travelers. Marion — " He slipped the chain over his head and tucked the

medal under his khaki collar, felt the cold metal against his bare chest. "My dog tags were stolen along with the rest of my belongings, so this'll have to do."

"I'm a Protestant myself. But let me give you a word of advice: get a new set of dog tags. If something happens to you in the bush, you'll need them for identification, blood type, that kind of stuff."

"Sure, I'll do that."

At the reservation counter, the sergeant explained the situation to a harried receptionist. She rifled through a drawer under the counter, and brought out an envelope. "Yes, it's here, but this plane's already loaded and ready for takeoff. They've probably called for standbys long ago."

"Honey, you better tell them to hold it up, 'cause Uncle Sam's gonna be awful mad if this man misses his plane again."

She nodded her matronly head. "Well, I'll call and tell them you're on the way."

The sergeant whipped the ticket out of her hand. "Thanks." He led the way through the crowded concourse, pushing people gently aside like an apologetic football blocker. Tony followed in his wake. When they reached the proper gate, the sergeant waved the ticket and rushed past an astonished clerk.

The moveable stairs waited for them. At the top, in the doorway of the Boeing 707, a pretty stewardess was receiving instructions from the pilot's cabin.

Sergeant Mattwell handed her the ticket. "This here is Giovanni."

"Oh, yes. We've been expecting you."

Turning, the sergeant looked down at Tony. "Well, Giovanni, this is where the chickenshit ends. Now you got to face VC guerrillas instead of mealy-mouthed drill sergeants."

Tony shook the outthrust hand. "This time, I'm ready for it."

Book Five
SPRING

Only the dead have seen the end of war.

Plato, 427? - 347? BC

Peace is better than war, for in peace the sons bury the fathers, while in war the fathers bury the sons.

Croesus, died 546 BC

Chapter 89

As suddenly as it began, the jungle ended.

Stretching as far as the eye could see, a patchwork quilt of paddies was stitched together by low dikes. Vietnamese peasants toiled in the fields, ankle deep in muddy water, up to their knees in green shoots that swayed in the Huey's downdraft.

The flight became a newsreel montage: green, verdant paddies stretched limitlessly in all directions. Throngs of girls and old women, wearing conical straw sunhats and bent over like sawhorses, plucked the drowned, ripe rice. Bearded old men danced along grassy dikes balancing shoulder boards from which dangled baskets of fertilizer, firewood, or fresh produce. Water buffalo grazed languidly, munching vegetation along the hedgerows. Dogs and chickens roamed freely within the bamboo fences of the hamlets, while children huddled close to thatched-roof huts and animal pens. It was an overall vision of beauty and simplicity, ceaseless toil, and apparent unconcern.

In this timeless, aboriginal land, the helicopter was a technological anachronism, gliding across the clear, azure sky on a cloud of thunder — ready at a moment's notice, or at the slip of an overzealous finger, to spew forth the wrath of American gods, to strike down man, woman, and child: friend and foe alike.

If the local peasants were aware of this strange dichotomy, they did not show it. They neither looked up in curiosity, nor away in fear. They simply ignored. The Huey proceeded on its way without eliciting response of any kind.

The people went about their business. They demonstrated no evil, no intent to harm — just a desire to live. From the air this did not seem to be a war-torn country — until a bomb crater made itself evident in an abandoned paddy; until a scarred patch of jungle gave mute testimony of chemical defoliants; until a burned-out hamlet showed the ravages of recent conflict; until fields that were flooded with stagnant water bore noxious odors into the air, and crawled with the disease of spawning larvae.

The engine whine diminished, the ground slowed. The paddies dried out until they were either overgrown bogs or clumps of baked clay. The Huey hovered over a jagged perimeter that was a four-foot wall of sand punctuated by sandbag bunkers. Mesh tents were pitched haphazardly within the fifty-meter diameter circle. Soldiers sat or crouched or milled in small groups near the improvised bunkers.

By the time the Huey settled down to the ground, the crew chief already had the cargo untied. He shouted for the three passengers to disembark. As they jumped to the ground, they were met by half a dozen men in wrinkled combat fatigues, sleeves rolled up past the elbow. They were swarthy, suntanned, unshaven, and full of smiles.

"I thought you guys would never get here," one of them shouted over the noise of the Huey's blades and engine. "I can use a hot breakfast."

Tony offloaded one of the heavy crates. "We brought ammo, too."

"Fuck the ammo, just give us the food."

The Huey shot upward at a forty-five degree angle, swung around to the south just barely clearing the nearby trees, and raced out of sight. The sudden, numbing silence was welcome.

A short, lithe man joined the laboring grunts where they were putting down their loads. "Whatcha got there?"

"Two cases of grenades, one case of flares, and two boxes of M-60 ammo. And I'm a new replacement."

"First time in the bush?"

"Yes."

"Glad to have you. Henderson, glad to see you made it back without getting any social diseases."

White, even teeth contrasted sharply against coal-black skin. "I tried, sarge. Honest I did."

"I'll bet you did. Pepper, try to watch where you're takin' a shit next time, will you? You're likely to get your balls blown off — and that would ruin your whole afternoon. Now get this stuff to the dump, then go back to your squads. You — what did you say your name was?"

"Giovanni."

"Okay, Giovanni. I'm Sergeant Miller. You come with me."

Henderson and Pepper started humping the explosives to the heavily sandbagged ammunition dump. Tony carried his M-16 by the rear sight grip, and chased after the sergeant, web gear clattering.

What had once been a command tent occupied the center of a small perimeter bounded by double-layered sandbags. The sides of the tent had been slit and rolled up, offering an unobstructed view of the camp. Several men lounged among metal ammunition cans, wooden crates used as seats, radio sets, gerry cans full of water, and several large piles of c-ration cases: perhaps three or four hundred individual meals, little more than a day's supply for the company.

None of the men wore rank or insignia of any kind.

"Cap'n, we got those grenades you asked for — and the flares. Henderson and Pepper are back, and we got one new recruit."

"Good, we can use the manpower," said the youngest looking man in the group. The captain wore a Colt .45 on one hip and a bayonet in its sheath on the other. He finished shaving out of his steel pot, and dumped the dirty, lather-filled water on the ground: the dry sand soaked it up like a sponge. His hair, close cropped and short, was a dirty blond, and his face was bronzed by the equatorial sun. His eyes shone with a bright, blue intensity and were surrounded by creases that hinted of hardship and responsibility. "What's your name, soldier?"

Tony stepped forward and tossed off a snappy salute. "Private Anthony Giovanni, sir."

"Nice to have you with us, Giovanni. I'm Captain Collins. You can call me sir, but as long as we're in the bush, don't you ever salute me. It attracts too much VC ore."

"Uh, yes, sir. Sorry."

"That's all right, just as long as I don't have

to tell you again. And from now on you're a PFC."

"*Thank* you, sir."

"It's SOP." The captain dried his face on a green, camouflaged towel, and hung it on a nail to dry. He picked up two maps, folded them neatly, and shoved them in the oversized pockets of his jungle fatigue jacket. Four other men arrived with mess kits full of bacon and eggs, oatmeal, toast, and black coffee. Collins took one. "Thanks, Yates. Blake, since you only have two squads left you can have him."

A man with his back to Tony sat hunched over another map. "We can use him. Miller, do you want him?"

"Yates's got less men than I have. Put him in C squad."

Captain Collins swilled his coffee. "Corporal, I want him and the other two men — "

"Henderson and Pepper."

" — to hang back today. We're pulling out right after chow, and we've got a short patrol. We'll be back early. Let them guard camp, and you can break Giovanni in tonight."

"Right, sir." Turning to Tony, Yates said, "You look like you're dressed to kill."

"I feel like it, too."

"Okay, let's check in with the squad." They strolled across the camp toward the southern border. Yates was several inches taller than Tony, much broader, and almost too handsome. His blue eyes seemed to smile even when his movie star face showed no expression. "So what did you do to deserve us?"

"Guess I got up on the wrong side of the cot this morning."

"That's two counts in your favor. The first is that you got up at all, the second is that you slept on a cot. Tonight, what little sleep you get will be on a bed of hard sand crawling with ants."

"Sounds inviting."

"It's not much, but we call it home. Well, here we are."

They stood before a cubelike structure that stood less than head high. It was roofed with heavy planks and three layers of sandbags. A narrow vertical opening served as an entrance, while a horizontal slit commanded a field of view across the dry, forsaken paddies that extended several hundred meters to the tree line to the south. One soldier sat cross-legged on the roof, staring outward.

"Hey, Wallace. Come on down for chow. We got a new man." Aside, Yates added, "you can drop your gear anywhere."

Thankful to be getting rid of his burden, Tony climbed out of the bandoliers and two hundred rounds of ammunition, the web gear with its two canteens, bayonet, extra ammunition pouches with another eighty rounds, fanny pack with entrenching tool strapped on the outside, and his poncho, spare socks, a towel, and a few meager personal possessions packed inside. He placed his rifle on the sand and rested the barrel on his pack. Then he rummaged through the pack and found his mess kit and utensils.

Wallace was a giant of a Negro with the well-proportioned body of a Roman statue, the face of a bronze bust, and the voice of an opera singer — a soprano. "She-ee-et. Why couldn't he a been here last night? Then I wouldn't a had to stand a double shift." Lanky legs unlimbered as he sidled off the bunker roof, slinging his rifle over his left shoulder and stretching out an impossibly long arm. "Glad to meetcha."

"Same here." Tony looked way up into pitch-black eyes under a furrowed brow. Slowly, the rest of the squad gathered round.

"Giovanni, this is Burns, our machine gunner."

"Welcome aboard." Burns was about Tony's height, but larger boned and heavier, most of the extra weight being concentrated in a paunch that was evident even under the loose fitting fatigues.

Yates explained, "Burns used to be a sailor in civilian life. He raced yachts for the Bermuda cup — but never won."

"Why didn't you join the Navy?"

"Because they don't sail in the Navy."

Yates laughed at Burns's stock answer. "The midget over there is Rodriguiz, our token Puerto Rican."

Rodriguiz stood only five-foot-two in his steel-shanked jungle boots. With sleeves rolled up past his elbows, the arms that were exposed were as thin as wires, braided with bulging veins. His mouselike face was a chestnut brown, frozen into a perpetual grimace.

"Don't let Mister Squad Leader fool you, amigo. I'm from New York." His accent was curiously clipped.

"Right around the corner in Philadelphia." Tony extended his hand. "We had quite a few Puerto Ricans in my basic training company, but they were straight from the old country. Hardly any of them spoke English."

"Rodriguiz spouts off in that slut Spanish of his when he gets riled," Burns said.

Not a muscle on his face cracked. "I use the mother lingo to confuse the Cong."

"The black dude over there is White, our grenadier. My advice to you is to never get between him and the chow line."

"Peace, bro." Tony was momentarily embarrassed when he tried to shake hands, and White grappled him into an upward facing handshake. White's forearm bulged like a weight lifter's,

his fingers gripped with hydraulic power. His ebony face was hewn granite.

"Likewise."

"Tait is the old man of the outfit."

The tall drink of water who ambled toward Tony was rolling up his sleeves in neat folds. He was only six foot one, but his leanness made him appear taller, until he stood next to Wallace and the difference became apparent. His shoulders were slightly hunched, his nose sharp and pointed, his face narrow, almost beady. He spoke with a controlled, Midwestern drawl. "How do?"

Tony tilted his head once. "Nice to meet you."

"All right, now that we're all friends — "

"Speak for yourself," said Burns.

" — let's go get some chow."

Mess kits were produced and White, licking his thick lips, led the group. The rest of the men staggered along. Yates stopped so suddenly that Tony almost blundered into him.

"The rifle goes with you." Tony realized that everyone carried an M-16 in one hand. The smooth voice continued. "First lesson is never be more than arm's reach from your weapon. It goes where you go: for food, for water, for a shit. Your rifle just became part of your arm."

"Okay. Thanks." Tony ran back and grabbed his rifle. He caught up with Yates as he was opening his mess kit.

Yates looked at him with his head shaking. With disciplined patience, he said. "It's got to be loaded."

"Uh, sorry." Tony ran back again, took a clip out of the bandolier, and snapped it in place. Aiming the rifle into the air, he pulled back the bolt and inserted a round, then made certain that the safety was on. By the time he rejoined the squad, they were being served.

"Back it up, men. Back it up," Yates was yelling. "You too, Burns. One mortar would get the lot of you." He was not satisfied until there was a three-meter interval between individuals. Even the servers were five meters apart. "I hear you, but if I don't get close to White, he'll get it all."

White took an extra helping of oatmeal. "You can lick my plate, Burns."

"And you can lick my ass, White."

"It's already white, less you forgot to clean it."

A pock-faced man stepped in front of White and forced a pill into his hand.

"Whatchu want me to do with this, bro?"

"Same thing you've been doing with it every day. Swallow it."

"Aw, man, you're worse 'n my mother." But he popped the pill into his mouth and gulped some coffee after it. "Coffee's already cold."

With all the food he could carry in one hand, he headed back to the bunker.

The pock-faced man continued to issue tablets to each man in line. Yates swallowed his pill dry. "Andrews, this is our new man, Giovanni. Giovanni, this is our platoon medic. Fortunately, you won't see too much of him, because he spends most of his time kissing Miller's ass."

"I'm assigned to A squad, but you'll see me at least every morning with your anti-malaria tablets."

"And every time we stop for a break, making sure you take your salt pills like a good little boy."

Tony downed the tiny, white pill. "Thanks."

From the front of the line, Wallace was complaining. "What, no O.J.? What's this army comin' to?"

"Hey, man, quick kickin'," said Burns. "Be glad it ain't c-rats. Remember, Charlie don't get nothin' but plain rats."

"She-ee-et. They got salt in the NVA."

"Hey, amigo, you wanna keep off my heels?"

"Sor-*ree*," Burns pouted.

"It's all right, amigo. Just don't get close."

Back at the bunker, Yates was the ever-efficient squad leader. "Wallace, you're still on guard."

"Right." There was no inflection in his voice. With his breakfast and rifle, he climbed atop the bunker, sat cross-legged, and watched the distant tree line.

Rodriguiz sat on his haunches, M-16 across his lap, back against the sandbags. Ever cautious, he chewed his food quietly. He was the only man in the whole outfit wearing a flak jacket. It was tattered and torn, but still retained its usefulness. Not regular army issue, Tony later learned, he had wrangled it out of an amtrak driver who needed greenbacks for a trip to Saigon, where real American money had more purchasing power than Military Payment Certificates — at least, for what *he* had wanted. Now, Rodriguiz never took it off. The flak jacket was as much a part of him as his skin.

Yates moved Tony a respectable distance from the rest of the squad. "We never want to get too many men concentrated in one spot, even in camp. Remember to keep your distance, especially from Rodriguiz — he's paranoid."

Tony scraped his plate clean. "So I've noticed. So what am I supposed to do today?"

Yates lit a heat tablet under his canteen cup and warmed his coffee. "That hamlet out there's deserted, but people may be moving through it on their way to the fields. That's okay, as long as they don't get too close. If any

of them wander too near the perimeter, fire a couple rounds over their heads and they'll scamper like scared rabbits. Stay in the bunker through the heat of the day, but keep on the alert. That's about it."

"What happens if they don't scamper?"

Yates tasted his coffee, decided it was acceptably warm, and covered the small flame with sand. He took a long draught, finishing the coffee with one swig. As if he were asking Tony to pass the salt, he said, "Shoot them."

****

"Move out."

Men grumbled and climbed to their feet. The clattering of mess kits and canteen cups could be heard all over the camp. C-rations were handed out for lunch and stuffed into packs. Toothbrushes were put away, letters were tucked into breast pockets, weapons were given a last-minute check.

Within minutes the men were armed and ready to go. Burns left his M-16 in the bunker, then threw the twenty-three-pound M-60 over his shoulder, barrel forward. He carried two belts of ammunition. Wallace carried four. Instead of a single shot M-79, White's M-16 bore an attached M-203 grenade launcher, slung under the rifle barrel. Except for the difference in the size of the barrels, the combination looked much like an over-and-under shotgun. He could fire three 40 millimeter grenades in succession, giving him rifle point fire as well as grenade area fire. His pack bulged with extra grenades.

Rodriguiz loved hand grenades, and carried a dozen of them in four rows clipped to the front straps of his web harness. Years of pitching in games of street ball made him deadly accurate, and in close-in fighting he would frag a gook rather than shoot him. Yates and Tait traveled with the normal compliment of 5.56 cartridges: three hundred sixty rounds distributed in pistol belt pouches and over-the-shoulder bandoliers. All carried at least two canteens, while some had in addition a two-liter clear plastic water bladder. Entrenching tools and ponchos were practically part of the pack.

Burns checked the bipod legs for ease of movement. "Take it easy, Giovanni."

"What he means is, don't fall asleep through boredom." Wallace looked impressive under four belts of ammunition. "It's gonna be a long day in this heat."

Tony wiped sweat off his brow. "I heard you've only got a short patrol."

Burns scowled. "That can mean anything shy of Hanoi."

They crossed the dry paddy to the west and entered the jungle a hundred meters away. In dribbles and drabs, the rest of the company melted into the foliage. Then he was alone.

Tony took a good look at his surroundings. The camp was an irregular square in the middle of a huge paddy field. The low dikes had been raised with much backbreaking work, using short-handled entrenching tools. To the east a series of untilled, lumpy mounds extended to a wooden railroad bridge. The tracks followed a twenty-foot-high bed running north–south. North of the camp was a water-filled area: once a working paddy, it was now a swamp that was an extension of a creek that entered from the west and exited east into the stream that carved its path through a culvert under the railroad bridge.

To the south, disused paddies reached a tree line which terminated before it reached the jungle. Mounds of hay started from this slot, and pimpled the terrain for thousands of meters. Peasants hunched over in the distance, attending to their daily chores.

After a walk around the perimeter, Tony heard voices breathing out of a bunker. He stopped a couple meters from the opening. "Anyone home?"

"Yeah, man, come on in."

Crouching low, he stepped into the narrow doorway. Henderson and Pepper were sprawled inside with their steel pots in their laps. Marijuana smoke hung heavily in the air. Half in and half out of the opening, Tony managed to stay out of the sun and still inhale clean air.

Pepper held out a butt. "Wanna drag?"

"No, thanks."

"It's okay, man. This is your last chance before we start goin' on patrol."

Henderson took the joint from his companion, sucked deeply. "Don't smoke no weed in the bush. Can't afford to be fucked up when Charlie's around."

"What do you call this?"

"Shit, man, nothin' ain't gonna happen here. Ain't a gook within five klicks o' this place, an' then they're dug in so deep you need a oil rig to find 'em."

"What's a click?"

"A kilometer, man."

Pepper reclaimed the joint. "You really new, ain't chu?" White teeth were visible in the dark interior of the bunker. "Well, don' worry 'bout nothin'. We don' get much contact, jus' snipers an' shit. Mostly they're in their spider holes durin' the day, when it's hot. An' we don' go out at night. Search a few villes, beat through some thicket, kill a few mamasans. We get into trouble, we call in artillery, or an air strike. What chu gotta watch out for mostly is mines an' booby traps."

Pepper was having trouble holding the roach. He let it drop. "Roll another one, man."

"Is that what happened to your foot?"

"No, that was a accident."

Henderson burst into gales of pot-induced laughter. "Accident, shit. Go ahead an' tell 'im the truth, man."

"Why you always on my ass, nigger?"

Henderson finished the newly rolled joint, took a puff, and handed it to Pepper. "Better me 'n a claymore."

Pepper took a long drag, held it for half a minute. "One night I got to take a shit, see. The claymores was already set out so I tells Polanski — he's on guard — I'm goin' out. He says okay, an' I go out to do my business. I ain't even got my entrenchin' tool out yet when the mothafucka gets relieved an' don' tell Doerner I'm out there. Doerner's new — ain' been inna bush more'n a week — so he don' know no better. He hears me diggin' an' burps off half a clip over my head. Mothafucka don' know Charlie can zero in on the muzzle flash. I start screamin' an' yellin', an' runnin' in with my pants half down — I think we're bein' attacked. He hears me comin' an' panics. Jus' as I'm comin' over the top, he sets off the claymores. A shrap from the backlash goes through my boot, steel shank 'n all. I go into a roll cursin' like crazy. Doerner damn near shoots me daid before that mothafuckin' Pollack gets to him an' knocks 'im down."

By this time Henderson was crying with laughter. Tony found it hard to restrain himself. Even Pepper managed a grin.

"Anyways, the shrap goes through my foot an' you can see it bulgin' under the skin on top. Cap'n says it ain't bad enough to send for a dustoff, so he makes me wait 'til mornin' an' sends me back with the chow wagon."

Henderson wiped tears from his face. "Man, you get in the strangest kindsa shit."

"Yeah, well, at least I got a week's R 'n R outa it."

"An' I'll bet you tole the nurse every time you lef' the room to go take a shit."

"Go ahead an' laugh, nigger. Some day you'll get yours — then *I'll* be laughin'."

"Next time yo wipe yo ass with sheet metal, hold onto yo balls so they don' get blowed off."

"Some day Charlie's gonna put a bullet through that big mouth o' yours. Got a target he can't hardly miss."

The joints kept passing back and forth, the stories kept getting wilder, the language more undecipherable. After they fell asleep, Tony wandered back to his own bunker. He was so thirsty that he downed a canteen in a matter of seconds. There were c-rations in a corner, so he ate while watching the peasants working in the field near the bales of straw.

Later, without knowing that he had fallen

asleep, he awoke drenched with sweat. The sun had turned the bunker into an oven — yet it was hotter outside. How were the men on patrol able to walk with their heavy loads in this heat? He emptied another canteen. The only sound he heard was snoring from across the perimeter.

Finally, in mid afternoon, he heard noises to the west. With heart thumping, he grabbed his rifle and crouched by his bunker. A shape strode out of the jungle, its olive drab uniform visible only because of its movement. In a cold sweat, Tony slipped off the safety.

Another shape detached itself from the foliage, then another and another. Where were Pepper and Henderson? What was he supposed to do? Suddenly the field was full of men, marching inexorably toward the camp. Tony's pulse was racing. He took aim.

"Hey, anybody awake?"

It was good old American English. Tony breathed a sigh of relief. He tasted salt as his own sweat dripped past parched lips. He wiped his forehead with his sleeve as he stepped out of the protection of the bunker and raised his rifle over his head, waving it slowly.

The men poured into camp. With shoulders sagging and the spring gone from their step, the bedraggled members of Bravo Company sought out the squad areas that they called home.

Yates dropped his web gear on the ground. "You didn't miss a thing. It was all pretty routine."

"Yeah, we didn't see nothin' today — not one stinkin' dink." Burns flung the machine gun on top of the bunker, retrieved his rifle.

"1 still think that ole mamasan had something in the bush when she saw us comin'," Wallace said. "White saw it, too."

"Yeah, man."

"Aw, she was just takin' a shit."

Equipment clattered to the ground like leaves from a tree in autumn.

Guns, grenades, and bullets — messengers of death — were kicked aside as useless impediments.

"Goddamn." Wallace dropped the last of the four belts of linked cartridges and tried to stand up straight. He arched his back and stared at the sky. "Carryin' all that shit for nothin'."

Burns put the M-60 on a tripod. "I'd rather carry it out an' bring it all back than not have it when we need it."

"You didn't have to carry it," White snickered.

"You think that gun's a Matty Mattel toy like that plastic pea shooter you're haulin' around?"

"How come when it's a pistol, it's a gun; but when it's a rifle, it's a weapon? Then when it's big enough to carry on your shoulder it's a gun again?"

"Another contradiction in terms, like military intelligence."

Yates interceded. "Would you guys quit acting like old women at a bargain basement sale?"

"Shit, man, we're gettin' paid to kill gooks, not to go on Sunday afternoon strolls," White said.

"Today ain't Sunday."

"How can you tell in this goddamn country?"

"Cause they don't *have* Sundays. That was invented by unions."

Wallace was still staring at the sky, fists dug into his back. "An' as soon's we knock off all the fuckin' gooks we can go home an' knock off some ass."

"When the hell're we gonna make contact? Alpha Company got the shit shot outa them last night. So where'd all them gooks get to, huhn?"

"Knock it off, Burns."

"We prob'ly walked right over 'em." Wallace bent forward at the waist, staring at the ground. "An' they just laughed at us bakin' in the sun while they cooled their heels in their air-conditioned holes."

"Okay, that's enough," Yates said, louder. "We'll make contact tomorrow."

"That's what you said yesterday."

"And the day before that."

"So what do you want me to do? Send them a written invitation?"

"I'd like them to stay the hell out in the open long enough so we know they exist."

"Alpha Company sure knows they exist."

"She-ee-et." Wallace stared back at the sky again. "I'm gettin' tired o' this shit. I wanna go home."

Tait spoke for the first time. "You and half a million other guys."

"That's easy for you to say — you're short."

"Nobody's short 'til he gets on the plane."

"Goddamn it, I said knock it off!"

"Aw, man . . . "

"*Now.*"

Twenty feet away, perched on his haunches, and staring out over the dry paddies, Rodriguiz kept his interval. Wallace called out to him, "Hey, Hispanole, don't you never complain about nothin'?"

Rodriguiz was silent, watchful.

Sergeant Miller joined the group. "Sorry to interrupt your act, but we got a sighting out there on those haystacks. Two men with a B.A.R."

"Who saw them?" Yates wanted to know.

"The lieutenant. With his binoculars. The Old Man wants a detail to take care of it."

Burns let out a howl. "Why do we gotta be

the favorite squad alla time?"

White chuckled. "Hey, man, weren't you jus' complainin' about not makin' any contact?"

Rodriguiz still stared out over the dike. "I seen something move out there, but I thought it was a dog."

"Ain't no dogs within a hundred miles o' here," Wallace said. "The gooks done et 'em all up."

Miller said, "Giovanni, you see anything out there today?"

"Well, sure. I saw peasants working. Although it was too far for me to tell what they were doing."

"Were they hangin' around those haystacks?"

"Well, I didn't really notice. But they were working in that general direction."

"All right, Yates. Get your men together and go check it out. Burn them haystacks down to the ground. I don't want anybody sneakin' up on us in the dark."

Yates took the order calmly. "All right, men. Let's go. Burns, leave the gun and grab your rifle. Rodriguiz, turn half those grenades in for flares. Burns and Wallace, second place. Tait and White, third. Giovanni, you walk point."

Within seconds the squad was moving out in a V formation, with Yates hanging back waiting for Rodriguiz to catch up with the flares. Tony was in the lead as they climbed over the berm, moving out slowly — so slowly — toward the tall stacks of hay.

"Are you sure this is the way to do this?"

"She-ee-et, we done this a hundred times if we done it onct," Wallace said. "It's the only way to draw fire."

"This shit is for the birds," Burns grumbled.

"You ain't gotta worry. They always get the point man first."

"Yeah, but I'll be the next in line."

"She-ee-et, with a B.A.R. they'll get us all in the first burst. When we hit the ground it'll be for good."

Rodriguiz caught up, and Yates took his place in the center of the V. "Hey, don't bunch up, up there. Give the lead man some room. We're supposed to be spaced out like a flock of geese."

White shifted his rifle uneasily. "I wish I *was* spaced out. Then I wouldn't be so scared."

"You're always scared," Burns called back. "You're the only man I ever seen who can fit inside his steel pot like a turtle."

Wallace said, "Hey, man, how you makin' it?"

"I feel more like a sitting duck than a lead goose." Tony squeaked so low that only Burns and Wallace heard him. They both started laughing much too loud for Yates.

"Hey, cut the chatter before you scare them off."

"Yates, we don' wanna lose a man on his first day inna bush," White said. "We ain't had a chance to ask him how are things back in The World."

"Yeah, when's LBJ gonna bomb the hell outa Hanoi?"

"Fuck Johnson. What's the latest cut by the Temps?"

"I said cut the chatter. And back off the lead man. Giovanni, can you walk a little faster?"

What started as a long V was turning short and fat. With each step Tony's pace get slower, while his heartbeat got faster. His sweaty palms had a death grip on the rifle. His legs were shaking, and his body felt like rubber. He barely noticed the water trickling through the drainage holes in his jungle boots.

"All right, let's move it out. We haven't got all day." Yates quickly walked up behind Tony as the first stack of hay loomed close. All eyes were intent, all rifles aimed. Rodriguiz hung back, but there was a grenade in his hand and the pin had already been pulled: he held it in his teeth.

A snake slithered out of the inch-deep paddy water, crossed Tony's boot, and dived into the green slime. A portion of Tony's brain was vaguely aware of it.

"Okay, hold it up." The formation halted instantly. Yates took the lead and walked completely around the haystack. "Okay, it looks like if there was anybody here they got away. Rodriguiz, torch it."

Rodriguiz reinserted the pin, and clipped the grenade to his belt. He grabbed a flare and ignited the pile of dry hay. It flared like kindling, bursting into flames that climbed ten meters in the air. The men backed away from the heat. He torched the other two haystacks that stood nearby.

Smoke billowed high overhead while the squad turned their backs on their handiwork and headed toward camp.

"Another wasta time."

****

When the purple haze of twilight deepened into a pervasive blackness, the men set about their nightly chores. Mess kits were rinsed in the water of a paddy just outside the northern perimeter, and face and hands were washed and teeth were brushed in the same water. Boxes and cans from the c-ration supper were buried in a vast hole in the middle of the camp. Claymores were set, their trip wires run through the rifle slit in the bunker and onto the roof. Mosquito mesh tents were pitched, and sleeves were rolled down for the night. The last cigarette was crushed out in the sandy soil.

Nowhere was there glint of steel or glow of butt.

"When they says lights out, mister, they means lights out."

Burns said, "Shut your mouth, Wallace, before the reflection of your teeth gives our position away."

Tait handed Tony half a dozen bamboo stakes and helped him with the unfamiliar mesh tent. "Keep your poncho with you in case it rains. You can change your socks, but put your boots back on. And make sure your rifle is within reach so you can find it in the dark."

It was a clear night, and the stars shone overhead in unfamiliar constellations. Shapes like phantoms moved throughout the camp. The men talked quietly. Those on early guard perched atop the bunkers, grenade launchers in hand.

Yates' distinctive voice echoed out of the darkness. "And make sure it's loaded." His face glowed like that of a disembodied ghost. He removed his steel pot for a moment to wipe sweat. Tapping the metal significantly with a thick finger, he added, "And keep this with you, too. You don't have to sleep in it unless you want to, but you'll want to know where it is."

"Are all these precautions neces — "

Tony broke off as he watched a strange phenomenon leap out of the blackened jungle. A stream of tiny red fireflies sailed silently over the camp, as if wafted on a westerly breeze. The vanguard of the swarm passed overhead no more than five meters high. The insects made not a sound.

"INCOMING!"

The rat-tat-tat of distant automatic weapons fire came at the same time as the frantic scream. There was only a moment's hesitation before the whole camp was in motion — running for the nearest bunker.

The seven men of C squad hit the opening at the same time. A flood of bodies crammed through the narrow doorway, including one man from another platoon who just happened to be passing by. They were packed inside like sardines in a can, breathing hard. Eyes peered through the rifle slit, toward the jungle to the right. From the western perimeter, a barrage of return fire from M-16s and M-60s poured into the trees, along with the occasional *whump* of a grenade launcher. A deadly swath of lead poured into the spot from where one burst of fire had erupted.

While Second Platoon emptied their weapons, the men of C squad waited in silence. Yates watched the tree line two hundred fifty meters to their front.

Tony was face to face with him, noses almost touching, inhaling each other's breath, staring, wondering, hardly daring to breath. But there was no attack from that direction.

The shooting gradually died down until only the grenade launcher harassed the enemy sniper. It seemed roomy inside a bunker that only that afternoon Tony thought was crowded as he sat in it alone. Now every breath could be heard, every armpit could be smelled. In the darkness someone was shaking, his steel pot making a curious scraping sound over his helmet liner. The vibration radiated through them all.

Finally, Yates broke the silence in a deep voice that was strangely calm and perfectly clear and controlled:

"Congratulations, Giovanni. You just earned your C.I.B."

Chapter 90

Bravo Company tramped in staggered double file along a dirt road that was dry and dusty and burnt by the sun. A hedgerow on one side held back the primeval jungle; opposite, hundreds of meters of abandoned rice paddy were sectioned off by crumbling dikes. Ahead, an intact artillery shell lay in the middle of the way.

It could be a dud, lying where it had dropped and failed to explode. It could have fallen from an ARVN supply truck bouncing over the rutted and unpaved surface. Or it could be a booby trap.

Did a sapper wait patiently in a distant treetop shelter with his hand on a command detonator, watching, waiting? Was it surrounded by hidden tripwires? Did its weight hold down a spring detonator?

No one would ever know, for the men of Bravo Company streamed off the road like two lines of ants. Some chopped through the jungle, hoping there were no wires or hidden punji stakes; others swept over the dry paddy, searching for antipersonnel mines. The next time they walked this road the shell would be gone. Where, no one would ever know. It would be only one more mystery never to be solved, and promptly forgotten.

With large clouds of buzzing insects the men converged on the road again, fifty meters beyond. They carried their rifles loosely, almost lackadaisically, either by the pistol grip or by the arched rear sight. The road to Dong Hoa village was an old one, and well traveled.

"All right, men. Split up."

The road led to a narrow, wooden bridge that was covered with sand and dung. It spanned a creek not more than ten meters wide. The banks had been built up to keep the water from flooding the paddies, and old dirt floodgates were visible where the creek had been used during planting season.

Somewhere in the middle of the double columns, the officers comprised a group unrecognizable from the NCOs and enlisted men. On a simple patrol like this, there was no reason for lieutenants to take charge. The platoon sergeants were well versed in their roles, and carried them out without direction. Sergeant Miller motioned left for his squad to spread out along the bank of the creek. Yates took his men to the right.

Yates nodded with his pronounced chin. "Giovanni, go about fifty meters upstream and look for a good place to cross. The rest of you guys keep your interval. You too, Rodriguiz."

Tony led the way, in front of Tait. "What's wrong with using the bridge?"

"It might be mined."

Willows and eucalyptus shared the bank with bamboo thickets. Frogs chirped and insects hummed. Colorful tropical birds twittered in the trees. Snakes slithered through the untrimmed grass.

An old footpath descended through the brush to the level of the water. The muddy landing at the bottom had served as a watering place for thirsty buffalo, and perhaps as a fishing spot for small boys with their hand lines.

"Does this look okay?"

Tait stared cautiously, not at the brush but at the far bank. After a moment, he nodded. "It'll do." He walked another ten meters to where he could see through the thicket, and crouched low with rifle poised.

Except for Yates, the rest of the squad hung back. "Burns, get over here with the -60."

Big Burns loped to the indicated spot with the machine gun, unfolded the bipod, and found a comfortable place to lie down. He took the half-belt of ammunition that was draped over his shoulder, and laid it out in a straight and orderly fashion on the grass. Wallace took a position to his left. White walked past the spot where Tait was stationed, and hid behind a tree. Rodriguiz crouched to the left of Wallace, ever vigilant.

"Ever made a river crossing before?"

Tony looked up at Yates' handsome face. "No."

"Got a wallet?"

"Sure. Why?"

"Put it in your shirt pocket or it's gonna get wet." While Tony fumbled with his buttons and effected the change of venue, Yates explained the procedure in his cool, deep voice. "Keep your rifle high over your head, and watch out for debris and mud on the bottom. When you get to the other side, check it out, then cover for us."

Tony nodded silently, took a deep breath, and slid down the dry embankment to the water's edge. Shaded by overlapping willows, the water was dull brown and murky, with no perceptible flow. It flooded his jungle boots, was absorbed by the padded socks. By the time he was knee deep, the initial sensation of coolness had worn off.

The bottom was oozy; at each step the mud sucked at the lug soles. Tony fought to keep his balance. By midstream the water was waist deep, then it started to get shallow. He brought the rifle down to a more comfortable position in front of his chest.

He heard a rustle in the bushes, saw a blur of movement. Came a frightened shout, "Hey, there's somebody over there."

A bullet popped close over Tony's head. He ducked so fast that water splashed onto his face. Somehow, he remembered to keep the M-16 thrust up high. His pulse rate jumped from eighty to one-forty as he lurched forward for the protection of the brush-shrouded bank.

Burns cut loose with the M-60 like there was a whole company of NVA coming over the ridge. Bullets tore through the foliage; leaves and bark were shredded and fell like confetti. After the half-belt was consumed, the air was rent with the burps of M-16s. Lying flat on his stomach, Tony craned upward and let loose with his rifle on full automatic.

"Wallace, gimme a belt! Gimme a belt! Gimme a fuckin' belt!"

"I'll give yo' a belt 'cross yo' goddamn mouth." Wallace crabbed across the ground behind the dike. He flipped a belt of ammunition over his head, separated the linkage, and snapped the end into the breech. Burns slammed the breech cover down.

"Cover me!" Yates slid on his buttocks down the embankment and hit the water with a splash. "I'm going across."

Tony slithered over the sandbar toward an undercut hollow where tree roots sprouted down in search of soil. He rolled over on his side and fumbled frantically with his ammunition pouch for another clip. His fingers were wet and muddy, and trembled epileptically. He kept trying to jam in a full clip without having first removed the empty one.

Two grenades went off, one right after the other, flinging shrapnel through the shrubbery. The machine gun came back on line. Burns stitched a double hem through the thicket, cutting bamboo like a scythe. The slender, ten-foot rods fell on Tony like Pick-Up sticks. He screamed when something grabbed his ankle. It was Yates' hand.

The squad leader crawled onto the sandy bank and flopped down next to him. Through the noise of gunfire he yelled into Tony's ear,

"You see anything?"

Tony could not find his voice, so he shook his head vehemently. When he figured out what he was doing wrong with the rifle, he removed the spent clip and dropped it. He started to jam in the new one, but it was full of water.

"Stay flat."

Tony did not need to be told. The machine gun was still barking, kicking up puffs of dirt in the rice paddy beyond the thicket.

Yates yelled, "Burns, cut it out. Burns, cut it out."

Just as the M-60 stopped, Rodriguiz flung another hand grenade across the creek. It hit the smooth trunk of a Japanese lilac and bounced back into the stream with a plop. A moment later the stream erupted with a roar, spraying both Yates and Tony — with water.

"*Cut it the fuck out.*"

White's rifle burped once more, then went silent. In the aftermath of shooting, Tony's ears rang as if his head had been used as a clangor inside a bronze bell. Leaves were still falling to the ground like green snow.

In a calmer voice, Yates said, "Did anybody see anything?"

Before anyone could answer, a peach-fuzzed face appeared above Burns. The figure in non-descript jungle fatigues was tall and gangly, like a loosely connected puppet. "Hey, what's all the ruckus about? What are you shooting at?"

Tony pushed off some bamboo rods and sat up. Yates stood, and wiped his muddy hands on his trousers. "Somebody saw something and opened fire."

"Who was it? What did you see?" There was a long silence, pregnant with guilt. After several breaths, the spindly man raised his voice. "Well, who started firing?"

Still, no one replied.

"Goddamn it, somebody must have fired first. What am I going to tell the captain?"

White took a tentative step forward. "I — I heard a rifle shot, sir. But I didn't see nothing."

"Great. Fucking great. You trigger-happy bozos have given away our position to every damn gook in the neighborhood. From now on, don't shoot unless you know what you're shooting at." He stalked off.

When he was out of earshot, Burns uttered under his breath, "Easy for him to say. He don't hafta stick his neck out."

Tony breathed a sigh of relief. "Who was that kid?"

"That kid," Yates said, as he snapped his safety back on, "was your platoon leader, Lieutenant Blake. He's got more time in-country than you — but not much." The smile he flashed was perfunctory.

Leaves rustled on the bank above. Tony scrambled, and aimed his empty rifle at the leering figure.

"Hey, if you guys are finished mowing the lawn, we got a company to get across this crick." Sergeant Miller stared down from the top of the dike with one hand on his hip and his rifle held casually at his side. Yates looked up, and sighed. Miller grinned broadly. "Breakin' in the newbie?"

He extended a hand and helped Yates scramble up the slippery embankment. Hoisting him aside, the sergeant reached down for Tony.

Yates scraped gobs of mud from his lower pants legs. "I think it was a false alarm."

"I *know* it was a false alarm. There ain't no footprints anywhere around — and one thing Charlie can't do is fly. You really got your ass chewed by the lieutenant, didn't you?"

"Wasn't the first time."

"Won't be the last, either. All right, get your men across and make a search. Then stand cover and take up the rear." Sergeant Miller marched back toward his own squad.

Yates shouted across the creek. "Burns, get over here and set up that gun. And don't shoot at anything that ain't human."

Burns grumbled unintelligibly. He loaded another belt into the M-60, slid down the embankment, and started wading across the creek.

"White, I know you fired first. I don't know what you saw, or what you *think* you saw, but from now on don't be so goddamn heavy in the finger."

"Man, why do I always get blamed for every — "

"Because you're a very responsible man. Every time something goes wrong, you're responsible. Now stow it. And Rodriguiz, watch where you're throwing the fucking grenades. We didn't come here to kill fish."

"Si, amigo."

"Giovanni, take a look through that thicket. We might have killed a pig, or something."

"Right." But before he moved, he poured the water out of the magazine and snapped it in place. He was soaked from head to foot. "Uh, by the way, my wallet's soaked."

Yates scowled. "As long as it ain't blood, it doesn't matter."

****

Dong Hoa was a typical Vietnamese hamlet. Surrounded by a wall of bamboo that was more effective than any manufactured fence, it was a fortress in miniature. The jungle layout within was interlaced with footpaths and shaded by tall coconut trees, the fruits of which provided food as well as fuel: after eating the pulp, the dried husks were burned.

The huts were simple affairs of thatched

walls and roofs made from waterpalm fronds. Horizontal and upright supports of areca wood were lashed together with vine which had to be replaced periodically. Sleeping areas were sectioned off with additional thatched partitions. The doors and windows were mere openings. The hard-packed dirt floor accumulated dust and debris which was constantly swept out of the doorways by energetic elderly women.

"Okay, mamasan, out o' the way." White ducked under the low sill and barged into the house. He flashed his M-16 around to show that he meant business.

Five wide-eyed children cowered in the corner next to a wooden cabinet. Like mother ducks, two young women squatted among them, hardly more than girls themselves. They wore traditional ao dais, black cloth pajamas that were loosely fitting and functional in the heat, and sandals. The children were barefoot, the two boys wearing shorts and the two girls wearing long tops that reached past the hips. The baby was nude, and would stay that way until toilet trained.

The old woman barring the door was pushed aside; she babbled in Vietnamese and supplicated with outstretched arms. White ignored her as he glanced around the room. Tony stood guard. The only other furnishings were a homemade table and several rough chairs. White stomped across the floor, ammunition belts clanking, and rifled through the cabinet behind the children. He dragged out a pile of tattered clothing, some wooden rice bowls and carved utensils, and a small stack of candles.

"Okay, mamasan, where you hidin' the menfolk?" The villagers did not understand a word he said. He picked up a brass incense burner from the top of the cabinet. It was the family ancestral altar.

Yates stuck his head through the doorway. "Put it back."

"I was only lookin'." He set it down with a thunk. The old woman continued to babble, still gesturing. "If these people are so poor, how come they got stuff like this?"

The incense burner was intricately carved, and probably very old.

"For the same reason people live in slums and drive Cadillacs. Now put it back."

"It's back. See?" He removed his hand to show that the piece was still there.

"Check the back door."

Tony walked through the room and peeked outside. Burns stood in the trees with the M-60 trained in his direction.

Wallace crouched his giant body a few meters to Burns' right. "No one come out this way."

Tony nodded and stepped back inside. Yates indicated a sack of rice in the corner of the room. "Check it out."

Tony stuck his hands inside the burlap. "Nothing but rice."

"Pour it out."

"All of it?"

"They might be hiding something in it."

Tony picked up the bag and upended it on the rickety table. White grains flowed around the oil lamp, some of it dropping through the slats and forming neat rows on the floor. He sifted through it with his hands, finding nothing.

White shoved him aside. "You gotta be more thorough than that." Beads of perspiration dripped from his black crown as he scattered the rice all over the room, knocking down the oil lamp in the process and breaking the glass globe.

"Watch it, will you?" Yates said angrily. "I don't want you to tear the place down."

"Jus' makin' sure. Remember Hanes."

"I remember. But that's no reason to break up the ville."

"Reason enough for me. These people are VC an' we all know it."

The old woman never ceased her chatter. The younger women and the children watched with wide, Oriental, dark brown eyes.

"Let's go."

Tony stepped out into the bright sunlight next to Yates. Tait and Rodriguiz watched from an adjacent doorway over a throng of women and children who were gathered in the open. Several old men stood among the group, white hair and flowing beards sparkling like snow.

White hung back a moment, then came out with the woman still screaming at him. He put a broad hand on her flat chest and shoved her brutally back through the doorway. She slipped and fell down, still jabbering. "Fuckin' mamasans."

"Okay, move on to the next one."

The men walked stealthily toward the next hooch. White stopped at the door with easy nonchalance. "We ain't gonna find nothing here. We never find anything here. Why don't we jus' blow 'em off the map and forget about it?"

"Just check it out and don't give me any grief."

"But there ain't nobody here. There ain't no men over the age o' ten. They all went off to join the NVA. Else they're hidin' out in the bush with the Vietcong."

"Just check it out."

Grumbling, White barged boldly into the hut. Tony started to follow him, but before he reached the opening, White was coming out.

"It's deserted, man. There's no one home."

Yates ducked in and scanned the room. "Okay, let's break for lunch." He waved the rest of the men inside, leaned his rifle against the bamboo wall, and wriggled out of his web gear. The rest of the men followed suit. The villagers remained in full view, going about their business as if the American soldiers were not even there.

After poking through the hedges all morning, the men of Bravo Company were tired, thirsty, and hungry. By noontime, Tony had drunk two canteens of water, and sweated out three. Salt tablets, distributed by the ever-present medic, were all that kept him on his feet.

Wallace unfolded the end of his flexible water bladder and held it over his head. He poured half the water over his black, wiry hair and let it dribble down his face and neck. Then he swallowed the rest in one huge gulp.

"Go easy on that," Burns warned, taking a sip from his own two-quart bladder. "Less you want to drink the poisoned stuff they got in these wells."

Wallace chirped in his high-strung, singsong voice. "She-ee-et, if I had a nickel for every quart o' well water I swallowed in-country, I'd own me a cotton mill by the time I got back to Jackson."

Mississippi born and bred, he had spent every summer he could remember helping his father pick cotton in their little patch of bayou. They had lived a hand-to-mouth existence, for it was the mill owners who reaped the biggest profit from the toils of their labor. But in the lean years, when the crops were sparse or the market poor, it was his mother and father and family of seven who suffered. His father's premature death had been the man's only salvation — the only way he could rid himself of the chains which had bound him to the earth. But for Wallace there had been another way out — Vietnam. He lived on only one third of his pay, the other two thirds being split between savings bonds and an allotment sent to his ailing mother.

On guard duty, during the march, and on breaks, there were only two topics of discussion: home, and the war. In less than a day, Tony had already heard scraps of earlier, distant lives, as if they were part of some other world; a fantasy as opposed to the reality of the jungle.

"Besides, there ain't nothin' wrong with well water. It's better than that paddy water we hadda drink when we got pinned down over by Cha Phat."

Burns meticulously sealed and folded the bladder, then cinched down the strap. "That's different. At least you know what kinda shit you're drinking there. The VC wouldn't think nothin' o' poisonin' a whole ville just to give dysentery to a few GIs."

Wallace put away his empty canteen. "You been readin' propaganda sheets again."

"That's not necessarily so," said Tait in a slow drawl. "If the villagers were American sympathizers, the VC would have no compunction against killing them. And we still have no direct evidence that this village is VC controlled."

"There was Hanes. Booby traps don't grow on trees." White added, "They put there."

Tait shrugged it off.

By this time, c-ration boxes were being taken out of waist packs and their contents greedily devoured. Kool-Aid packages were passed around; the flavored mix was all that made the perpetually warm water palatable once the initial thirst was slaked. Something was needed to force the men to drink.

Rodriguiz, flak jacket open in the front, ate standing up with his rifle over his shoulder. His dark eyes watched the Vietnamese go about their chores, watched the children play, watched the mamasans cook rice in an old iron pot over an open fire, watched papasans crouch in the shade fingering their rotten teeth. Village life went on as usual, despite GI intrusion.

White nudged Yates with a plastic spoon. "Tell me the truth, man. Was they jus' lookin' for an excuse to get us out there to burn those stacks down?"

"Could be. What difference does it make?"

" 'Cause it coulda saved us a lot o' gray hairs if they'd a tole us."

Tait shoved food into his mouth. "Someone must have been out there last night."

"They sure took care of his ass," Burns growled. "They must have poured a thousand rounds into those trees, not countin' the grenades."

"Don't mean shit. He'll be there tonight, waitin' for us," said Wallace.

"Don't say that. We gotta walk right past there on the way back."

"So look around. Maybe you'll see 'im."

White had already finished his meal. He pulled a candy bar out of his pack and stripped off the wrapper. The chocolate was melted, but he seemed not to notice. "I'll bet five seconds after he fired that burst he was twenty feet underground."

Yates laughed. "At least Giovanni got his Combat Infantryman's Badge out of it."

"That an' a quarter'll buy you a cup o' coffee," Burns quipped. "Back home. Out here, it won't buy you nothin'."

Sergeant Miller appeared from behind a hooch; he shoved his way through milling villagers. He yelled and flailed his arms if they did not move fast enough to suit him. "Hey, this is supposed to be a combat patrol. I can hear you guys arguing from a hundred meters away."

White loved to argue. "We been through this ville half a dozen times already an' we ain't found nothin' here yet."

"And the first time we do may be your last, you keep that attitude." He turned to Yates. "Keep these men quiet or you'll have the lieuy on your ass again. And twice in one day don't make it."

Yates ignored the rebuke. "Anybody else find anything?"

"Naw, course not. Like White said, we been through here enough times to know better. Fuckin' intelligence keeps saying there's an NVA outfit operating in these parts. What the fuck do I know? I just do what they tell me — and keep on the alert. Put your rats away and finish 'em later. We'll take another break in the afternoon, when it's hot."

The sergeant stalked off. Tony glanced around at the tired faces. "I thought it was hot at nine o'clock this morning."

"You don't know what hot is till you been humping the boonies in mid afternoon." White looked up at the sun, squinting. "You'll find out in a coupla hours."

Yates was the first to get to his feet. "Okay, men, you heard him. Let's get going."

****

Tait was the oldest man in the company, including the captain. He was drafted at the age of twenty-six, the upper limit, shortly after his divorce. "My ex-wife contacted the draft board as soon as she got the final papers. A couple weeks later I received a change of status in the mail."

His words faltered as he pushed his way through a bamboo thicket. The limber rods would bend, but not break. "I took my girlfriend with me to the recruiting station. She posed as my wife and told them it was all a mistake. But my ex had been thorough — sent them a copy of the divorce papers. They couldn't do anything to my girlfriend for lying, but the recruiter told me to start packing my bags, 'cause he was going to see to it personally that I got my notice."

Tony, tagging along close behind, kept one arm in front of his face to ward off springing shoots. "So why didn't you just marry her and get your deferment back?"

"Don't work that way." He broke into a glade with an old, stone-walled well in the middle. Several village paths spoked out in different directions, but there were no villagers around. He licked his lips as he picked up the bucket beside the watering hole. He lowered it on a frayed, mud-encrusted rope. "Once you're divorced you become 1A again. They sure didn't waste any time scooping me up."

Tony leaned his rifle against the side of the well, watching as Tait drew up the bucket of water. As he set the wooden pail on the crumbling rim, a frog leaped out of it. Tait ignored it, twisted off the cap of one of his canteens and, after dropping in two purification tablets, filled it with cool water. Then he shook the canteen for sixty seconds and set it aside. He handed the thumb-sized bottle to Tony. "Halozone. Tastes better than the iodine tablets."

Both of Tony's canteens were empty, so he accepted what little Tait had left in his two-quart plastic bladder. It was difficult to drink out of the folded top, but the water running down his chin and onto his sweaty jungle fatigues felt good.

Tony dropped two pills through the narrow neck, and started filling his own canteens. "Why didn't you ask to be put into the Construction Battalion? If you were already an engineer and had worked in the field, the CBs could have used you."

"For the same reason you didn't wind up wiring tents and telephone poles back at Duc Pho. I'd have had to sign up for four years to get any kind of a guarantee."

"Even with a college degree?"

Tait smiled whimsically as he shook the canteen again. "It doesn't matter to Uncle Sam what kind of degree you have. If you get drafted, they put you where they want you. Right now they need infantrymen more than they need engineers, so that's where they put me. All in all, I guess it's for the best. I can get my time over with in two years, and go back and pick up where I left off. The government guarantees draftees their old job, including seniority. Otherwise, I'd be thirty years old and starting over again."

They filled the rest of the water bottles and stood around shaking them to hasten the dissolving tablets. Meanwhile, Burns and Wallace, both looking hot and tired, broke into the clearing from one of the paths and looked thirstily at the canteens lined up on the ground.

Wallace picked up one that Tony had just filled. "Gimme a swig o' that."

"I haven't put any tablets in it yet."

Wallace glugged down a quart of water without stopping, and handed the canteen back to Tony. Then he pulled a tiny bottle of pills from his jacket pocket, dumped them into his massive palm, and swallowed two. "I guess they'll do just as good a job in my tummy." He wiped his mouth with the back of his hand. Then he took another canteen and swallowed its contents, this time in two gulps. Like a camel, he was stoking up for the day.

While Tony dipped the bucket into the well for more water, Burns put down his machine gun and took the canteen that Tait offered to him. "I'm so dry I feel like a cotton ball waitin' for Wallace to pluck."

"You don't pluck cotton, you dumb ass. You pick it."

Tait shook his head. "Why do you always wait till you're ready to pass out fore you take a drink?"

" 'Cause that's what it takes to make me drink this dink well water. I keep hoping we'll come across a spring or something, or at least a moving stream."

Wallace said, "I'm gonna make a yellow stream inna minute."

Tait explained patiently, "Well water's cleaner than any creek. The slopes won't shit in them."

"Well, if it ain't Mr. Medic." As Andrews approached, Burns rested one foot on the hardened mortar at the base of the well.

"Have you men been drinking water without taking salt tablets?" He automatically took a small jar out of his medical kit.

"Aw, man, why're you always handin' out pills? I swallowed more pills in the last six months since the day I was born."

He gave each man two salt tablets. "I just don't want anyone to get sick and miss the fun."

"Yeah, well, how about some anti-heat pills."

Andrews took out another bottle and handed him two white tablets. "Take two aspirins and walk slower."

****

Rainbow-hued chickens wandered freely throughout the hamlet of Dong Hoa, clucking wildly as the men from Bravo Company kicked their way through the open spaces between hooches. The dirt was white and hard-packed, trampled by hundreds, perhaps thousands of generations of bare feet. Animal pens with pigs and goats were tacked on to hooches wherever there was room.

"Fuckin' bastards." For five minutes White had been trying to light one of the five cigarettes included in the c-ration sundry pack. He threw the now empty match pad away and reached for another. He read off the back cover, " 'These matches are designed especially for damp climates. But, they will not light when wet, or after long exposure (several weeks) to very damp air.' Now what the fuck's the idea of having waterproof matches that ain't waterproof? They send us out here for a goddamn year, and give us matches that're only good for a week. Don't make no sense."

"Have a piece of tropical chocolate." Tait held out a hand that was a gooey mess. He licked off his fingers more to get rid of the chocolate than to enjoy it.

The main part of the hamlet spread behind them. The hooches were thinning out so that the other platoons could be seen as they walked a jagged parallel line. The sweep had produced no enemy sightings, no contact, and no results. It was another wasted day in the annals of seeking out the enemy and making him mine. Nor had they won the hearts and minds of any people.

The late afternoon sun beat down unmercifully. The company split in half to go around a dense contortion of jungle that invaded the hamlet through neglect. If encroachment was not fought on a daily basis, the jungle crept in and gradually reclaimed what rightfully belonged to it.

Sergeant Miller talked with Yates for a moment, then went back to directing his own squad. In the background, Lieutenant Blake was speaking into the handset of a PRC-10 while the radioman crouched unconcernedly on one knee.

Yates removed his steel pot, wiped sweat. "The lieutenant wants us to check out this patch of jungle. As soon as we're done, we head for home. And they're choppering in hot food for us. So let's not have any grumbling and get it over with. We gotta do it anyway, so let's do it with a smile."

"Why they always gotta pick on us?" Burns complained.

"Yeah, you'd think this is the only platoon that gots to do the hard work," Wallace said.

White humphed. "This is the only platoon Blakey's got, and he got to make a name for hisself before too long, or he'll never make captain."

"Let's knock off the bullshit and get the job done. You keep saying you want to make contact, but you always complain at the chance."

Rodriguiz was quick to respond. "I never said no such thing."

"An' we ain't gonna make no contact in this bamboo patch." Burns swung the machine gun off his shoulder, and cradled it under one arm where it was ready for action. "But we gotta complain, Yates. It's good for morale."

Wallace readjusted the weight of the ammunition belts across his giant frame. "How come the only bush we get to beat is full o' thorns?" He took his bayonet out of its sheath and started slashing the vines that were draped over the snaky branches of a banyan tree.

Slowly, the two squads melted into the jungle, soon to be sweltering in greenhouse heat and swatting swarms of insects. Bayonets slashed back and forth like miniature machetes.

There was a constant battle between swinging at flies, and wielding the blade through the dense foliage and creeping vines.

"They ain't nothin' can even get in here, much less hide here," White said.

Banyan trunks, ten feet in diameter, were surrounded by nearly impregnable stands of bamboo. Knee high, daggerlike grass added to the agony: it wound together like twisted wire and served as a platform for myriads of biting bugs.

"That's what they want you to think." Tait poked his bayonet into the ground near the base of a thicket. The jungle canopy made it unusually dark and foreboding. "There could be spider holes right under your feet and you'd never know it."

Dumbly, White looked down at the tangled vegetation. He bent his ankles outward — the soles of his jungle boots were worn flat, and the leather at the sides was beginning to wear through. "I hope it ain't true, 'cause there ain't no room to run away from 'em in here." His words were punctuated by a sharp cry from ahead that set him back on his heels.

It was Burns. "Hey, I think I found something."

Ammunition belts clattered as Wallace threw off his burden and prepared to reload the machine gun. Yates' voice was muffled by the dense foliage. "Okay, men, spread out and keep in line."

Sergeant Miller was suddenly standing right behind him. "What is it? What've you got?" He shoved through the underbrush toward Burns. "Raymonds, keep close with that Prick-10. Where the hell's the lieutenant?"

The men formed a semicircle behind Burns. Crouched low, they crept forward. The two squads merged, and familiar faces showed the strain of unbroken months in the jungle, months of heat and hard work.

Miller took over tactical control. "All right, Burns. What did you see?"

"There's a spider hole in there. Right in the middle of that bamboo shit."

All the guns, including the platoon's two machine guns, were poised to pour a hail of lethal lead at the prescribed spot, should a head suddenly appear — or a grenade coming flying out. Rodriguiz squatted behind a palm tree, a grenade of his own in his hand and the pin already pulled.

"How do you know?"

"Because, damn it, I saw it. There's a square patch about two feet across cut out."

Miller never took his eyes off the target area. "All right. Cover me."

With catlike steps, the short sergeant slunk through the underbrush, his rifle stuck out in front of him like an erect penis. Drops of sweat collected on his sweatband and trickled down his forehead. His jungle fatigue jacket was soaked and grimy, his boots dusty. But his rifle was sparkling clean, and ready to shoot.

Now there was no talking at all; scarcely a man breathed. Playful bantering gave way to dead seriousness. Every eye was watchful, every trigger finger quivered.

Way in the back, holding his breath, Tony watched the whole scene as if he were not a part of it. He could not understand how, in the face of certain contact, the men overcame their fear and reacted with such — eagerness.

Sergeant Miller dropped from view as he got down on all fours. Tall grass swaying awkwardly was all that gave away his position. He stifled his equipment noise. The natural sounds of birds and insects took back the jungle. Suddenly he stood up and waved his rifle over his head.

"It's all right. Come on in. It's empty."

Tony breathed a sigh of relief — he had been doing a lot of that lately. The joking and bantering started up again as the men closed on the sergeant. He held up a square of carefully woven reeds: the lid that had concealed the abandoned hideout.

"Now tell me there ain't no VC in this goddamn ville."

Burns' voice was drowned out by a scream of pure terror. White leaped forward and hit the ground with a crash: tree limbs snapped under his bulk. The entire platoon went flat. Tony, with fear transmitted to his heart, fell backward and closed his eyes, awaiting the inevitable.

Five seconds passed without a sound; ten seconds. Tony rolled up to a sitting position. His pulse throbbed in his ears. He stood up on shaky legs. Beside him, White lay face down, his strong frame racking uncontrollably. Slowly, the men recovered from the scare.

White gathered himself together. He yanked a piece of vine from around his leg, and thrashed it against a tree. He brought himself under control.

Laughing, Yates stood over him. "What's the matter, get bit by a wild vine?"

"Shit, man. I thought it was a goddamn trip wire."

****

Darkness had almost settled in by the time the men from Bravo Company straggled into camp. Tony unclipped his web harness and let it fall away: he did not have the energy to place it on the ground. If his step had had any spring to it that morning, it had been seared and sweated away during the long, laborious day. His muscles were sore, his throat was dry, his stomach was grumbling. But walking into that sandbagged rice paddy was like coming home.

"White, Giovanni. Set up the claymores."

"Shit, man, we jus' got in. Can't we rest up a bit first?"

Yates was just as tired as anyone else. "Don't give me any fuckin' shit. Just do it."

White backed up a step and stared down his sweaty nose. He held the other's gaze for several seconds, then wordlessly ducked into the bunker and retrieved the squad's two claymores. He handed one to Tony.

"Come on, man. I'll show you how to do this." He unwound the detonation cord and let the coiled loops lie on the ground. At the end of the line he gouged a hole in the sand with the worn heel of his boot, and snugged the antipersonnel mine into it. The claymore squatted just behind a clump of grass, making it invisible from the front. Then he started kicking sand over the cord. Tony mimicked him. "Hey, man, get a load of this."

In his hands he held a gleaming, gold-colored incense burner. "It's solid brass, an' prob'ly a thousand years old."

"Where did you get it?"

White cast a furtive glance over his shoulder. "In that hooch today. Them VC mamasans ain't gonna need it." He stuffed the art object into his fanny pack and pulled the straps down tight. "I collect the stuff, an' send it home every time we come in from patrol. I'm buildin' me a little nest egg outa this war to make up for what Uncle Sam don't pay me."

"What happens if Yates finds out?"

"He knows what's goin' on. But as long as he don' actually see nothin', he lets it go."

"That doesn't make it right."

"It ain't right them mamasans're layin' booby traps, either."

When the detonation cord was buried all the way back to the bunker, White took both ends and tossed them in through the slit opening. He ran the cords out the back door and wedged them between two sandbags while he spliced on the blasting caps. Then he placed the detonators so they could be reached either from the top of the bunker, where the night guards would sit, or from inside.

Tony joined in nightly weapons maintenance. While half the men were designated as guards, the rest fieldstripped their weapons and cleaned out the grime and sand that could cause clogging and misfires. Bullets were removed from their magazines; the shells were wiped and the magazine springs were oiled.

Amid this flurry of activity, Yates ripped open a case of c-rations.

White was the first to complain. "Hey, what about the hot meal you promised us?"

"We got back too late. The chow choppers are all down for the night."

"Shit, man. We're humpin' all day long, an' all we gets is cold C's. What kinda fuckin' war is this, anyhow?"

"Look, I'm just as disappointed as you, but that's the way it is. But we got an extra ration of beer — "

"Big fuckin' deal."

" — and a Red Cross sundry box."

"More razor blades and toothpaste — just what we need."

Yates sighed heavily. "Look, just take what we got and quit complaining."

He dumped the meals so the labels were face down, to prevent the men from picking their favorites and leaving the worst for the others. One at a time they took their chances.

"This ain't the kinda potluck supper I'm usta havin'."

****

Afterwards, Yates allowed the men to go two at a time to the flooded paddy on the north side of camp. With toothbrush and washcloth in hand, Rodriguiz showed Tony the way. At the perimeter, he asked permission to pass through.

Tony munched on a piece of chocolate. "How can you drink that warm beer?"

"Better than none."

"I wouldn't be able stand it, or the soda either. Besides, the way that stuff explodes when you open it doesn't leave much to drink. How often do you get those care packages from the Red Cross?"

"Too often. We got more than we need." Most of the toothpaste, toothbrushes, razors and blades, combs, paperback books, and other items that were equally useless in the field, ended up in the trash dump. Rodriguiz pointed to the slender white slivers that looked like tiny leaves floating near the bottom of the dirty paddy water. "Watch out for the leeches. Not like in *African Queen*, but dirty all the same. They are slow, so not to worry."

Tony looked disdainfully at the brown water, his toothbrush poised. With upturned nose, he bent down and sniffed. "Well, it doesn't seem any worse than that well water we had today from — what's the name of that village? Bung Lao?"

"Dong Hoa. VC village."

Tony slashed his toothbrush through the water where there were the least number of leeches, then squeezed paste onto the bristles. "What makes you say that? We didn't find any Vietcong. And Tait said you'd been through there before and never found anything."

"VC smart. They hide when we come. They hear us a long way off."

"Is that why we didn't see anyone but women and children and old men?"

Rodriguiz nodded slowly as he let water trickle down his face and neck. While he washed, he watched the jungle on the other side of the paddy. His M-16 was leaning against his leg, safety off.

"But that doesn't mean the VC are there."

Rodriguiz shook his head. Just before he stabbed his toothbrush into his mouth, he said, "Rice. Mamasan cook too much rice."

****

Just after dark, a stream of tracers vaulted out of the jungle and spattered into the compound, tossing tufts of dust into the air while the men scrambled frantically for cover.

Within seconds, a thousand rounds of small arms fire plowed into the trees where but twenty had emerged. The men vented their anger not because they had almost been nipped, but because some of their valuable gear had been shot up: a stack of girly magazines was torn to shreds, and once luscious bodies were dismembered.

Captain Collins radioed for an artillery strike. The howitzer crews at Duc Pho were called into action. Five minutes later, high explosive rounds zeroed in on the jungle's edge. Trees were felled, dense underbrush was shredded, and the smell of gunpowder filled the air. Chunks of hot steel flew high into the sky and landed all over camp, thunking into the sand, and sizzling whenever they drowned in puddles of paddy water.

Shaking, and gripped with fear, Tony tried to crawl into his steel pot. The fist-sized shards that were raining all around kept him awake. He crawled under the mosquito mesh fully dressed, lay with his head on his rifle, sweated more from terror than from heat. But when he was tired enough, his mind refused to acknowledge the danger of the falling shrapnel. His eyelids sank lower, and the sound of exploding ordnance faded. Eventually, even the thudding chunks of iron could not keep him awake.

Chapter 91

Tony ate his c-rations quietly in the predawn gloom. A few stars were still visible in the lightening blue; trees in the distance stood like tall sentinels against the eastern sky. To the west, the dense jungle was a solid blur, like a supernatural wall, out of which blurted strident sounds and eerie calls. As the men shoved plastic spoons into the canned breakfast, there was no grumbling, no banter, no camaraderie — only dread anticipation.

The air was still and surprisingly cool. The odor of musk crawled through the camp, the symbol of rotting vegetation only two hundred meters away. The susurration through the upper canopy attested to a gentle breeze at the higher elevation.

Loose equipment rattled during the last minute checkup. Ammunition clips were filled and packed in their canvas pouches. Rifles were locked and loaded, with safeties on. Bayonets were sharpened and sheathed; straps were tested; hand grenades were clipped in place. Each man topped off his canteens, and stored his day's rations in his fanny pack. Included were personal items which, despite the added bulk, found a place: candy bars, ample supplies of cigarettes and matches, letters from home, good luck charms, cameras, even a tape recorder. Weight was not a consideration today.

The sound came first, from the direction of the jungle. It was not a chirp or a howl or a grunt, but the *whup-whup-whup* of helicopter blades. Unlike the chow wagons, these armored knights of the sky bristled with armament: machine guns, miniguns, and rockets.

Dimly the first silhouette appeared, cropping the treetops seemingly with only inches to spare. Behind it flew another, and another, and another. Radio communication sparkled between Captain Collins and the pilots, while platoon leaders got their men in position for the pick-up: one squad per chopper.

The Hueys did not touch down. With their landing skids barely hovering over the dusty terrain, the men charged through the sandstorm that was created by the propwash, leaped aboard, and were in the air within seconds. The Huey kept low and headed out to sea, a Pegasus carrying not one Bellerophon, but eight. Unlike mythology, their Chimaeras were real.

Tony was the last of his squad to clamber aboard the waiting Huey. There was no room inside, so he was forced to sit on the edge with his feet dangling above the runners. The noise of the whirring blades was deafening. He was about to shout that he was not ready when he felt a hand on his shoulder.

"Hold onto this." The door gunner indicated the pedestal base of the M-60. "You'll be okay." Then he said something into his microphone, and the helicopter lifted off the ground with stomach sinking speed.

Tony braced himself as his olive features turned a dull green that matched his jungle fatigues. Yates, sitting behind him, grabbed hold of his belt and secured him in place. He shared his smirk with the rest of the squad.

As soon as the Huey was airborne and moving away, another raced forward to take its place. In less than sixty seconds the entire company was airborne, and two minutes later was winging out high over the South China Sea. They gained altitude until, at five thousand feet, the ocean looked like a blanket of sequins as the now visible sun reflected off the solemn wave tops. White streaks gently brushed the undulating coastline; a few ragged sampans breasted the waves as families of fisherfolk sought an early catch.

The formation of Hueys banked and veered north, keeping well to the east of the white sandy coast. By leaning forward, Tony could see the rest of the hueys, ahead and behind. Abreast, only a few meters away, another man sat on the edge of the adjacent Huey, his feet resting on the skid. He stared down at the blue ocean.

Several minutes later they banked sharply to the left. Tony gasped as the engine whined and the Huey pivoted over on its side. For an instant he was looking straight down at the waves. It seemed that he would fall out any moment, but fear and momentum held him in place.

"Hang on, Giovanni," Yates shouted in his ear as he pulled back on Tony's belt. Tony gulped, and the Huey slid onto an even keel. He put his hand to his mouth.

Maintaining altitude, they flew high over quilted rice paddies for several kilometers. Patches of jungle alternated with the square, cultivated fields, adding green to the white and ocher terrain. As the helicopters started descending, large villages and roads became discernible, then individual buildings, and finally people and carts on the dirt tracts.

The pilots navigated from two thousand feet, the altitude at which small arms fire from the ground became ineffective. Sweeping wide to make sure of their coordinates, the formation zeroed in on one tiny hamlet that was separated from the rest by encircling jungle. From treetop level, the ville was razed with rockets that left fizzling tracks in the air long after the warheads exploded. The Hueys took turns coming in from alternate sides, crisscrossing the hooches with fire. Door gunners had a field day, firing until the barrels of their machine guns glowed cherry red.

Villagers ran in random patterns, like ants when a large boot has disturbed their hill. Farmers in the fields sought cover, while heavy slugs slammed into the water, kicking up spray. Tony did not actually see anyone go down.

The machine gun that was only inches away from his head, deafened him as red tracers zipped through grazing water buffalo. One must have been hit, for it started kicking the air and running in circles to avoid the stinging bees. Nearby, ignoring the bullets, a farmer ran into the field to try to catch the beast's bridle and bring it out of the field of fire.

The Hueys regrouped in the air, selected a dry paddy, and settled down to offload their human cargo. From an airy vantage point, a light colonel watched and directed the assault from the comfort of his private loach, an OH-6 Cayuse light observation helicopter. To him, this was war at its finest.

With engines straining, the Hueys seemed to be putting on brakes as their expert pilots brought them to a dead standstill. Dust kicked up by the madly spinning rotors obscured all sight of the ground. There was nothing below Tony but a beige, swirling cloud. The rat-tat-tat of machine guns unnerved him.

"All right, Giovanni," Yates screamed over the sound of the turbines. "Jump."

Tony leaned out and put one foot on the landing skid. He could still see nothing but a whirlpool of dust. The feeling in the pit of his stomach told him the Huey must still be descending. How high were they?

"Where's the ground?"

The hand that had been holding his belt now became a ramrod. It pushed hard against the small of his back. Caught off guard, he was easily overbalanced. A gasp escaped him as he fell away from the Huey. He braced himself for the long plunge into nothingness.

He fell only half a meter, and hit the ground so unexpectedly that he stumbled and fell forward onto his knees. Almost instantly, Yates leaped out after him and crashed into his back. The rest of the squad was right behind Yates, and Tony was nearly trod underfoot.

The noise of exploding firearms erupted from all around. When Tony stood up, it was only into a low crouch. Yates was yelling, getting the men on line for a frontal assault. Tony looked behind just in time to see the Huey lift off. Then he knew that they were committed.

"Spread out. Keep your interval. Start moving out. Keep in line. Hey, White, not so far in front."

Visibility was reduced to a few meters; Tony could only see one man on each side of him. The sound of Hueys was fading, but the small arms fire continued to hammer from everywhere. None of the men from his squad seemed to be firing — or worrying about it. Tony strained his eyes, looking for targets.

Gradually, the dust settled down and a hedgerow appeared, its leaves dulled to a gray color. There were no villagers anywhere to be seen, but Tony imagined them right on the other side of the thick bush — armed to the teeth.

"Keep in line, I said!"

A grenade exploded to the left, followed by machine gun fire. There was still no sign of the enemy — just the sounds of fighting.

"Rodriguiz! Burns! Spray it!"

A couple of grenades went over the top of the hedgerow at the same time that Burns opened up with the M-60. He let one belt go through the gun, then hollered at Wallace to re-load him.

"That's enough." Yates caught Burns before he went berserk. "Tait. White. Find a way through."

The dust settled now, and all along the line Tony could see other rifle squads beating through the hedgerow. The village was well fortified by the natural barrier. Several minutes passed before the company managed to hack its way inside.

"Rodriguiz. White. Check out that hooch. Tait. Giovanni. Get that one over there."

Burns and Wallace stayed back and provided cover. A few seconds later, four women and half a dozen children came scampering out of a bunker. They chased after the men who were entering the hooches. White shoved them out of the doorway.

"Get these slopes out o' here." He ducked back inside while Yates directed the terrified villagers into a huddle. One of the women was bleeding; she held her arm as she shouted Viet-namese obscenities. The other women joined in the tirade, while the children bawled on the ground.

"Burns, keep an eye on them." Yates swept his M-16 over the heads of the peasants. "If they do anything suspicious, blow them away."

"Okay, granny, stop your babbling an' you won't get hurt. An' you too, mamasan."

There were cries from all over the village as the company infiltrated the hooches and tossed grenades into the reinforced mud bunkers. Hueys flew patterns overhead, and fired inter-mittently along the perimeter to prevent any villagers from escaping. Those who had been caught in the paddies were being herded back by crack Huey pilots toward a dry, open field where an interpreter was challenging them for ID's.

Tony stood guard in the doorway while White rummaged through drawers. Then he pushed past Tony and reported to his squad leader. "No people, no weapons."

"All right. Check out *that* bunker."

Between the two thatched hooches squatted the bunker in which the people had taken refuge. The walls were half a meter thick, and could withstand the force of any artillery round that was not a direct hit. Tony stooped down and started to duck into the low opening. A firm, black hand gripped his shoulder and whipped him back hard.

"That ain't the way to announce yourself." White detached a grenade from his web gear. With his rifle in one hand and the grenade, pin pulled, in the other, he approached the opening from the side. "Lottie! Lottie!"

The corruption of 'lai de' meant 'come here.'

A few seconds later he repeated his command, adding, "Didi! Didi mau!" Run! Run quickly! He opened his hand and let the spring pop out the grenade lever. Tony knew that there was now no way to stop the grenade from detonat-ing. White cooked it off for three seconds, lobbed it inside underhanded, and stepped be-hind the protection of the sidewalls.

"Fire in the hole!"

An explosion rent the air. The doorway belched smoke, dirt, and flying shrapnel. When the dust settled, White lowered his bulky frame and stepped inside with his rifle pointing for-ward. He emerged a moment later and reported directly to Yates.

"Nobody home. But how 'bout givin' the new guy a break an' tellin' him what to do first."

A sneaky smile crawled over Yates' face. "I thought he would learn faster through experi-ence."

"What the fuck you tryin' to do, get him blowed away his third day inna bush?"

"He's got to learn."

"The only thing he got to learn is not to trust you. You been havin' him walk point ever since he landed, so hows about leanin' on somebody else for a change?"

The smirk faded slowly. "Like you, maybe."

"Yeah, like me, maybe. Let 'im learn the ropes before you tie 'im up in knots."

Yates resumed his solemn demeanor. Point-ing his rifle toward another bunker, he said to Tony, "Do that one over there."

"Come on with me." White escorted Tony as they approached the bunker from an angle. "Now, we don't know if Charlie's hidin' in there, or if some mamasans're keepin' their kids outa the way o' the bullets, or if the damn thing is booby trapped. First rule is, don't take no chances."

White unhooked another grenade from the webbing on his chest. "We give 'em the benefit of the doubt by askin' first. If nobody comes out, we toss in some insurance. Then we go in to collect on the policy. An' make sure you look under the boards, 'cause the bastards'll have spider holes under 'em an' Charlie'll plug you in the ass when you're leavin'. Got it?"

Tony found it hard to concentrate with all the shooting, shouting, and explosions ripping through the hamlet. "Got it."

It turned out to be simple — as long as no one was inside.

****

The company was no longer in line; it was a ragged bunch of soldiers performing a hooch-to-hooch search and chasing out women and children and old men. There were no more Hueys flying overhead, and no more small arms fire; just the dull thud of grenades inspecting the bunkers. There was no resistance from the villagers other than the continual crying and pleading.

Most of the children were nearly naked, with their bloated bellies protruding horribly. Young mothers, with pimple-sized breasts, and older mamasans with skin like shriveled leather, herded the tots together to keep them out of the hands of marauding soldiers. It was the elders who spoke out volubly, oblivious of guns waving in their faces. They actually pushed aside the still-warm barrels in order to make their demands known. The old, bearded men, seemingly senile, squatted and clutched their knees and looked around with wide-eyed stares.

Captain Collins divided his attention between HQ on the radio and his interpreter. Lieutenant Thang stood only five-foot-six, but he was as mean looking as a pug-nosed boxer. He wore U.S. issue jungle fatigues, carried an M-16 and web gear, and swung a black, wooden billy club by its leather strap as a way of intimidating his charges.

"They say no VC, no VC."

"I can hear that myself."

Thang stabbed a woman in the rib cage none too gently, and threw a question at her. Collins mumbled something into the radio, then patted the RTO on the back when he replaced the receiver. "Go easy on her, there, lieutenant. Why the hell do they have bomb proof shelters if they aren't VC?"

Lieutenant Blake broke through the throng of soldiers and civilians. He dragged a middle-aged man by his silver-streaked goatee, and hurled him forward so hard and fast that he fell at the captain's feet. The man babbled incessantly, the fall not even slowing down his chatter. The woman who was being poked by the interpreter shouted back at him, completely ignoring the chorused cries of the man at her feet. Her eyes glowed with anger.

"What's she saying? And please, don't hit her so hard."

Lieutenant Blake vied for the CO's attention. "I found this guy in a false partition in that hooch over there. The captain cast a glance in the indicated direction and saw several men setting a roof afire with cigarette lighters. "He was hiding."

"Did he have any papers or weapons on him?"

Thang translated some of the irate woman's words. "She say they peaceful people, raise cow and pig and chicken. Grow rice."

"So why the hell do they have bomb proof shelters?"

"He didn't have any ID, but as soon as he was caught he started waving a chieu hoi pass.

They all carry them, sir. Just in case. I want authority to question him."

"Well, Jesus Christ, question him, dammit." He turned to Thang. "What the hell is she saying now?"

The woman pushed back, holding her arms where the interpreter pounded her with his billy club. He shouted at her, and threatened with his fist.

Blake dragged his prisoner several yards away, and threw him into the fold of two men from Miller's squad. They pinned his arms while another tied a vine around his neck. The peasant began to cry: not real tears, for they were too precious. But his despairing features spoke just as loudly. The lieutenant slapped him across the face while the man ranted in his own tongue.

"She say they want to be left alone. Plant rice, grow pig, raise children."

"Yeah, and ask her where all the young men are." In the other direction: "Lieutenant, bring that man over here and let's hear what he has to say."

The squirming peasant was dragged to where Thang shouted at the woman. She was crying now because of the repeated bludgeoning from his club. He shoved her hard enough so that she stumbled to the ground. Then he feinted his club at her head, scowled when she refused to duck, and turned his back on her.

"She say all gone, all in army."

"She say which one?"

Lieutenant Thang shrugged. Suddenly, the woman jumped to her feet and lunged at the captain, hitting and clawing at him. Instantly, three men including the radiotelephone operator pulled her off, and subdued her with their fists and rifle butts.

"Get that goddamn woman out of here! And go a little easier on the prisoners — I don't want them damaged."

Now the interpreter pulled out his bayonet and held it point-first to the male captive's bewhiskered chin. He released a continuous babble that showed his willingness to cooperate. A dot of red showed where the point of the blade had nicked the skin. The bayonet moved down to his unprotected neck: the interpreter did not like what he was saying.

He pushed the point in until it stretched the skin into a deep dimple. Then he slapped the man across the face. The blow knocked him backward, but the two men held him in place. There was a thickening red line on his neck. He babbled in Vietnamese, reaching out toward the captain with beseeching eyes.

Captain Collins averted his eyes, looked the other way. "All right. Put him over there. He's probably just a goddamn draft dodger."

****

While the rest of the squad cleared out a large hooch, White led Tony to another bunker. He tossed in a grenade, yelled "Lottie" and "Fire in the hole," and counted backwards from five. Tony barely had time to get out of the way before the opening spit dirt and steel splinters. "The idea is to get rid of all your grenades right away so's you don't hafta carry 'em back."

"But you didn't give them time to get out."

"Keeps 'em on their toes." White ducked into the bunker. A moment later he backed out. "Besides, your grenade might have a short fuse."

Rodriguiz showed up a moment later. "White, you are a fucking asshole."

"Oh, well. Not everybody likes me."

In surprisingly short order, the company swept through the hamlet, from one end to the other, and encountered no armed resistance. Most of the villagers marched sheeplike out of their hooches, and gathered in huddled groups as they were directed to do, while the soldiers ransacked their houses, their belongings, their persons. More than one nubile girl was felt up in the process. The people endured the invasion, this one by the Americans.

By ten o'clock the search part of the mission was over. There was no outward sign that this was anything other than a peaceful peasant village. There were no weapons or enemy soldiers, just a lot of suspects.

Then the destroy part of the mission commenced.

The initial rocket assault had burned some of the thatch and wood structures right to the ground. Others had been torched by overzealous soldiers wielding cigarette lighters: the so-called Zippo squad. It was their way of acting out their frustration at not finding signs of the enemy. But that was only a harbinger of what was to come.

Hueys arrived laden with dynamite, fifty pounds to a case. The red sticks were not separated, but carried and detonated by the box. After the explosives were unloaded, the villagers — every man, woman, and child — were put aboard and taken away. They were being permanently removed to a refugee camp, supposedly for their own protection: to save them from the ravages of the Vietcong who came to steal their rice and rape their women.

A team of demolition experts tested some of the dynamite on the A-shaped bunkers. An entire fifty-pound case did little more than shake the roof and drop some dust. Two cases positioned at the opening would collapse the entrance. The bunkers could not be demolished, only damaged.

Then came the backbreaking work of humping the wooden crates throughout the village, while the demolition men plugged in blasting caps that were strung together with primacord.

Tony set down a box and wiped sweat from his forehead, a constant pastime. "I don't understand. Why are we doing this? How do we know these people are VC sympathizers?"

"Because Army Intel says so." Wallace was indifferent as he hefted a box of dynamite inside a bunker entry. He pulled out his canteen, and offered it to Tony first.

Tony took a long, deep drink and passed it back. "I didn't catch the name of this ville. Have you ever been here before?"

Wallace looked around. "No, it don't look familiar. Course, they all begin to look alike after a while — people too." He polished off the canteen and jammed it back in its canvas holder. "Don't know the name of the place, don't know where we are. Don't care, neither. Won't be here tomorrow."

"What happens to the people? How will they live?"

"Won't be helpin' the Cong, that's all I know. We jus' put in our time, do our job, an' get the hell out after our year's up. Jus' do what you're tole an' don't ask no questions."

"An' take what you can while the gettin's good." White walked out of a hooch stuffing coins into his fanny pack. "Here, take a look at these."

He showed them a handful of copper coins that were stamped French Indo-China. A hole had been drilled through each coin so it could be carried on a string and worn around the neck — the Vietnamese rarely used pockets. The coins were dated in the 1930s, during the French occupation.

"They must be worth something to collectors back in the States. An' besides, they ain't gonna need 'em here. They only gonna get blown to smithereens in a coupla hours." He wandered off to pillage another hooch for whatever valuables he could find.

Tait approached Wallace and Tony, shaking his head skeptically. He drawled, "That man's going to come to a bad end."

"I jus' hope he don't take us all with him."

The heavy hauling was accomplished by mid afternoon. The squad regrouped at a stuccoed house that had been erected by the French. Owned by the village chief, it was full of antiques and beautifully wrought furniture. The concrete pad on which it was built must have broken the backs of a large number of peasants, carrying sacks of lime from the nearest trail that passed for a road. It sported a real A-frame roof, and plastered walls and ceiling.

White hefted a load of dynamite onto the hand-carved dining room table. "Man, I sure do wish I could take this stuff with me."

Yates was grim. "White, I can see your pack bulging already, so I know you've been plundering."

"Jus' collectin' a few soovineers."

"I won't stop you this time, but how about helping the rest of the men let the animals loose so they don't burn to death when we set off this ville." White nodded, and grinned. "The man's almost human."

Then Yates had his laugh. "No sense leaving cooked meat for the Cong."

Bravo Company retreated amid a cacophony of pigs and chickens. The explosives team unrolled the last of the primacord, plugged in the last of the blasting caps. The entire hamlet was wired in series. From a safe distance they dropped the plunger.

"I'll huff an' I'll puff an' I'll blow your house down."

The primacord burned at 27,000 feet per second, detonating all the dynamite almost simultaneously. In the blink of an eye, the hamlet erupted with one titanic explosion, lifted into the sky, and settled slowly to the ground. The cloud of dust kept rising.

That was one ville that they would never have to worry about again.

****

"Why us? Why alla time us?" Burns shouted at no one in particular. "Don't the captain got no other platoon? Don't the lieutenant got no other squad?"

Yates sighed as Burns finished his outburst. The machine gunner plumped down heavily in the sand, with legs crossed and the M-60 across his lap. Pouting, he picked up handfuls of dirt and flung them in patterns around his faded jungle boots. He reminded Tony of a kid playing in a sandbox.

"It only seems like us all the time because we're so short-handed, and there's so many details. Didn't First Platoon have to hang back and check out the ville after we blew it? Didn't Fourth Platoon have to stand guard on the river while we crossed it?"

"We shoulda been choppered back," Burns retorted, chorused by Wallace's "Yeah." "They took all those fuckin' gooks back in Hueys, why not us?"

"Yeah."

"Look, maybe Alpha Company needed support and there were no more choppers available. Maybe they needed medevacs for some other company. I don't know." Yates removed his steel pot and ran his fingers through blonde curls that were beginning to grow long. The helmet liner left crosshatch marks where the straps flattened down the hair. His handsome face was covered by a stubble almost invisible as it nearly matched his tanned skin; he always had a clean-shaven look about him. "I don't know what the hell's going on in this war. I only know our little part of it."

Rodriguiz was standing closer than usual. "Nobody knows what the hell's going on in this war."

"Not even the Prez," said White.

"Especially not the Prez," Burns agreed. He was now making circled designs around the toes of his boots. "You think Westmoreland'd tell 'im anything he don't wanna hear?"

"Yeah," Wallace said. "Westy's got his hands tied as it is. The fucker wants ta bomb Hanoi an' cut the dragon's head off, an' Mr. No Guts'll only let 'im clip his toenails."

"Aw, you guys give me a pain." Yates looked out over the bunker in exasperation. "What do *you* think, Tait?"

He pushed his helmet liner back so he could scratch his scalp. "I guess I'll keep my opinions to myself."

"You usually do," Burns said.

"You're no help. I thought you were on my side. Giovanni, what do you think about all this?"

"I'm confused."

"Join the crowd."

"I mean, I haven't figured out who we're fighting yet. All I've seen so far are civilians."

"They're all fuckin' VC as far as I'm concerned." Burns straightened out his legs. "Wait till you been here a while. Then you'll hate 'em as much as I do, every fuckin' slant-eyed one of 'em. Won't stand up an' fight on their own, won't help us do the job. I say let's blow 'em all to kingdom come and get our asses outa the fuck outa here."

Yates said, "You don't make any sense. One minute you want to make contact, the next minute you're griping when we get the chance."

"An all night ambush ain't my idea of makin' contact. You know we ain't gonna see nothin'."

"Yeah."

"That sniper'll know the first second we step on his turf. So he'll stay in his hole an' get a good night's sleep while we make brownie points for the lieutenant."

White said, "The lieutenant's just tryin' to make a name for hisself — an' we're gonna make it for 'im. What's the matter with Miller's squad? He kiss ass better 'an you?"

"Is better we get a good night's sleep." Rodriguiz pushed a cigarette into his mouth. He did not light it, but just sucked on it until it got soggy, tasting the tobacco on his tongue. Then he bit off the wet end, spit it out, and started sucking the dry spot. "Then we be ready for fight instead of half worn out."

White threw his fanny pack, with the day's valuables, into the bunker. "I say let's wait for Sundown Sam to fire his shots an' bomb the shit outa him."

"Did that last night."

"Napalm, then. Air strike. B-52s. Rome plows, and knock the trees down. Send him two tickets to a whore house in Saigon, an' give 'im a week's R 'an R. Pour salt on 'is tail an' — "

"*Shut the fuck up!*" Yates' face turned bright red. "You can argue about it later. For now we got a job to do. And all your complaining isn't going to change it. So let's get on with it before the lieutenant gets on my ass. Okay?"

"You afraid o' him?"

"I'm not afraid of nobody, but this is what we gotta do. You don't have to like it, just do it."

Burns grumbled as he climbed laboriously to his feet. "Don't make sense, feedin' the mosquitoes all night."

At the perimeter, Yates explained his mission to the burly Third Platoon sergeant. "Make sure your men know we're out there. I don't want anybody shooting at us if Sundown Sam starts spitting."

The sergeant scratched the dark stubble on his chin. "Ah hope you boys git 'im. He perturbs me an awful lot." Then, in aside, he added with a wink, " 'Though he does keep my boys on their toes."

Two men on guard watched as C squad streamed past. "Fifty bucks says he don't show tonight."

"Is that greenbacks or MPCs?"

"What difference does it make?"

"Greenbacks are worth double on the black market."

"So what? You ain't never gonna live to spend it."

"Who ain't?"

"You ain't."

"I'll live long enough to eat steak from the cows that graze on your grave."

"You gonna bet or bitch?"

"Shit, I know he ain't gonna show."

"Okay, fifty bucks says he shows."

"Greenbacks or MPCs?"

Once they reached the edge of the jungle, they were forced to hack their way through the dense foliage with machetes — two had been issued for the purpose — and entrenching tools. The lowering sun was just above the trees, but once they entered the jungle canopy, their shadows disappeared. Tall grass and twisting vines grappled at their feet, and sharp, pointed branches snagged their clothing and exposed skin.

Already Tony was being eaten alive by hordes of mosquitoes that were hungry for fresh blood. A copious helping of bug juice kept off as many mosquitoes as a good bout of cursing: sweat kept washing it off.

They broke into a clearing where the sky appeared like a dark blue umbrella. A little searching revealed a narrow swath in the tall grass.

Wallace stared first one way and then the other. "So this is how the little bastard gets out o' here so fast when they start lobbing' shells."

Burns picked up a piece of rusty metal with sharp, nasty edges. "I think he hides in a spider hole when the shrapnel starts fallin'."

Rodriguiz bent and inspected the trail. "This is animal track. It look like tiger."

"Jus' what we need," said White.

"Spoor still fresh."

"All right, get away from that shit and jog up the trail a ways and see where it goes. White, you go with him. Tait, Giovanni, go that way. No more than five minutes, and no noise. Burns, Wallace, set up the machine gun here so it covers the path."

"There's more room over there, an' we got a wider field of view."

"And we'll be shooting right into our own men on the other side of those trees. They'll come back with everything they have."

Wallace started digging a shallow hole and pushing up the dirt. "That's why he's a fire team leader an' you're just a trigger puller."

Burns harrumphed, but dropped the M-60 where he was told, and started clearing the brush from in front of it. "I hate it when he's right."

Tony followed Tait through the tall grass. As soon as they were out of sight of the ambush, Tait held up his hand.

"Why are we stopping here?"

Tait squatted on the dry earth and drew Tony down beside him. Now they were below the brown, waving grass, hidden among the knife-sharp blades. "It don't pay to get too far from help. This is Charlie's country, and he could be lurking right around the corner, waiting for us."

So far Tony took everything for granted. He went along with what the other men did, relying on their experience. He did not always understand what they were doing, he did not always *like* what they were doing. But whatever they were doing, they certainly knew how to do it better than he did. He followed their lead.

Other than that one sniper, there had been no real enemy contact since his arrival with the outfit. He had been lulled into a sense of security by the apparent inaction. He needed to be reminded that this was, indeed, enemy territory. Despite the hardship, this all seemed too much like a family outing or a Boy Scout camping trip. He found it difficult to conceive that there was any real danger.

Tait consulted his watch, reading the luminescent dial in the last glimmering of daylight. Now, while they sat silently, Tony became aware of the nighttime sounds: recurring clicks, chirps, chatters, and screeches. He caught a glimpse of monkeys in the trees, a troop swinging rapidly from limb to limb.

The sun set, and the jungle carried with it a darkness all its own. Tait was a phantom in military garb.

"Who's this Hanes everyone keeps talking about?"

"Shush." Tait clamped a hand over Tony's mouth, and breathed in his direction. "Charlie's sharper than an Indian, and twice as deadly."

For the first time, Tony realized how scared Tait truly was — and how scared he should be himself. It was his ignorance that gave him courage. And he was losing his daring with his innocence.

Tait put his lips close to Tony's ear. "Caught a trip wire tied to a log. A Bouncing Betty blew off one leg and half his groin."

Tony swallowed hard. A Bouncing Betty was an antipersonnel mine which, when triggered, flew up out of the ground and exploded about waist high. It was not intended to kill, but to maim, for by doing so it took more than one man out of action. His buddies had to stop and protect him, medius had to evacuate him, hospitals and doctors and staff had to be maintained to take care of him, therapy clinics had to retrain him. All these were a drain on the intruding country.

"Villagers said they didn't know how it got there."

By now the sky was a deep, pervading purple. A few stars twinkled through lower atmosphere heat inversions, but gave forth precious little light. Tait squeezed Tony's arm, stood up, and led the way back.

"Find anything?"

The disembodied voice from somewhere ahead was crystal clear. Tait stopped in his tracks as if the voice were a brick wall. Tony, walking almost on his heels, slammed into him. The chills that ran up his spine threatened to shake him apart.

A tall figure stepped out of the shadow, as silent as a wraith. The shape of the head looked vaguely familiar. Yates said, "And cover that watch. Gooks'll spot that thing a mile away."

Tait quietly slipped off the band and buttoned the timepiece in his jacket pocket. "Sorry."

Yates handed him a stick of black rouge. "You better take some of that shine off your cheeks, too. And Giovanni, no swatting or throat-clearing from here on out."

Tony nodded, forgetting that Yates could not see him in the dark. He immediately had a strong urge to clear his throat, and suddenly his skin itched from a hundred mosquito bites. He splashed on some more repellent, then covered it with the rouge when Tait finished his make-up job.

Yates unreeled the detonation cord from a secreted claymore. Tony had no idea where the machine gun position was located until he heard a wayward voice.

"Hey, Wallace, smile so I know where you are." There was a sharp thud and a muted "ouch."

"You fuckin' moron. You wanna put a neon sign over your head, too?"

Burns chafed his wound, but did not come back with his usual retort. Two more phantoms appeared out of the gloom. White and Rodriguiz had already applied their own rouge: not an ear lobe or a belt buckle shone.

The men lay flat on the ground, stretched out in a line. Wisps of grass kept touching Tony on the face, making him feel that he was being bitten by insects. Whenever he thought something was crawling over his skin, he slowly pressed the spot with the point of his forefinger. Sometimes he felt the gratifying softness of a crushed mosquito, already fattened with blood; mostly, there was nothing there. The mosquitoes buzzed annoyingly in his ears all night.

Despite the laces that tied his trousers tightly to his boot tops, insects managed to crawl up his legs. He constantly rubbed them together to crush the creeping intruders.

Tropical birds were pretty much settled for the night, but flying insects that grew nearly as large made just as much noise. Leaves and foliage fluttered all the time with the passing of small animals; the trees rattled with the clawing of restless lizards; monkeys stirred in their sleep. Miscellaneous squawks and cries from the nocturnal menagerie emanated from the ground, the air, the upper canopy.

Every now and then, Yates, at the left end of the rank, would dig his elbow lightly into White's side. The signal passed down the line to Tait, at the other end, who would then acknowledge receipt by passing it back. This kindergarten mode of communication was silent and effective.

Tony's muscles began to cramp. Every movement stirred a blade of grass, turned a leaf, cracked a twig. Each tiny noise was an unholy alarm in the stillness. A simple hiccup could result in seven fatalities.

Each man suffered with his thoughts, his delayed aspirations, his remembrances of home and loved ones. Each head was a tiny island of furious dreams. Each gut throbbed for the next meal, each eyelid ached for sleep, each heart prayed for the next beat that would prove that it was still alive.

At first, the sporadic harassment fire from camp — meant to keep sappers on their toes — reminded Tony of the closeness of the company. But he knew that they were too far away to help. This small squad of men was on its own: any trouble that they got into, they had to get themselves out of.

A heavy eyelid closed, a helmeted head fell forward, a loose chin collided with a barely breathing breast, teeth snapped together, and the head pulled up with a jerk. The procedure started over again. The jab in the side became an annoyance that could be passed on perfunctorily without arousing consciousness.

There was nothing to do, nothing to see. The jungle was everlasting. Trees were dark statues seen against a black background. No stars shone through the canopy. No manmade sound broke the breathing of the bush. Anticipation faded, and the earlier fear gave way to monotony, shrouded in lethargy. Nothing happened. Ergo, nothing was going to happen.

Tony's night vision improved. He could make out trunks and weaving vines, the tan grass standing straight in the absence of moving air. For the thousandth time he wiped sweat off his forehead, out of his eyes. Gradually, the shadows melted away and the sky turned from a deep purple to a dark blue.

Then, sounding strange after so many hours of utter silence, Yates spoke in a whisper that was almost sacrilegious. "All right, let's call it a night."

Wearily, Tony rolled over and bunched taut muscles. Canteens were opened and the men drank copiously. The claymores were retrieved. All signs of the ambush site were obliterated: the dirt was replaced, the grass was fluffed up, bushes and branches were scattered over their positions.

Seven haggard men approached the perimeter cautiously until they were recognized. Then they trooped over the mound between the Third Platoon's bunkers.

"Didn't hear no commotion out there."

"Guess you owe me fifty bucks."

"Damn. You want it in cash?"

"Naw, just put it on the tally. I'm still in the hole to you anyway."

"I don't know, this may get you outa the red."

"It's about time."

"Next time *I'm* gonna bet on no show."

"Okay."

The sun rose like a lazy orange eyeball. It winked at Tony.

CHAPTER 92

If there was a landing zone down there in that miasma of rain, fog, and triple canopy jungle, it took better eyes than Tony's to pick it out. From an altitude of five thousand feet, nothing was visible in either direction except for the other Huey and the accompanying loach.

Captain Collins and Lieutenant Colonel Adams, of the Fourth Brigade — Charles Bradey Adams (two Silver Stars, one Medal of Honor, and service in the Korean War) — flew in the light observation helicopter with their pilot. Lieutenant Blake and the men of C squad were crammed together in the huey that had been selected to make the first assault, while Sergeant Miller and A squad flew alongside.

The door gunner relaxed behind his M-60, sucking in the cool air and flinging some of it under his flak jacket, heedless of the rain. Tiny droplets splashed horizontally through the open doors, wetting the men and all their gear. Bronzed, thickly veined hands cupped flash suppressors to keep the barrels from flooding. Their helmets dripped beads of water, like strings of pearls hanging tenaciously to the camouflaged brims. Their skin glistened with moisture; their clothes were soaked, and clung to bodies that shivered in the cramped quarters.

For Tony, it was the first time since his arrival in Vietnam that he had experienced cold.

After fruitless weeks of daily patrols in the low-level country and rice paddy district around Duc Pho, even Tony was looking forward to a change. This long-range operation in the Central Highlands promised different terrain, different strategy, and a welcome break in the routine.

Belonging to another time was the dirt and the dust, the limitless vision of paddies and dikes, the ignorant and lethargic peasants, the dull drudgery and toil of search and destroy missions that found nothing and proved less. Now Command had outlined a tactic geared to find the enemy where he was known to be hiding, preying among the Montagnard tribes.

The whine of the turbine lowered in pitch, the helicopter started descending. The loach sped forward and shot out of sight. Through the mist, the vague greenery that was the top of the jungle came closer, but still there was no sign of a landing zone. The loach came back into view, spiraling down like a Flash Gordon spaceship.

According to intelligence, this patch of unoccupied jungle was supposed to be safe territory. That made it an ideal intrusion point for a company-sized maneuver. Realistically, guerrillas could be anywhere. But the Montagnards were a proud and independent people, hated by the lowlanders and treated as an inferior race. They did not like Vietnamese of any political belief, and so they were extremely cooperative when it came to ousting the NVA from their territory. Many of their tall, muscular men had volunteered for the army in order to protect their autonomy.

Radio waves crackled between the pilots. The loach zoomed up while the Huey veered to the left toward a hill which offered a hole in the treetops. It was barely wide enough to admit the rotating blades. Tony leaned forward and peered down. What he saw was actually an old bomb crater, the result of a B-52 drop that had run short when the primary target could not be found. It was SOP to empty their load before returning to base, since it was not safe for these lumbering freighters to land with full racks. Alternate targets, while not usually precise military goals, at least served to keep the enemy aware of U.S. might — or so the theory went. In any case, the stray bomb had sprayed the tropical boles with ten thousand anti personnel pellets, and converted any man or animal within the half mile kill zone to dead and unrecognizable meat.

"Get ready to jump," Lieutenant Blake called out suddenly, taking his cue over the headphones borrowed from the crew chief. He whipped them off his ears and handed them back.

No one in the Huey moved — no one *could* move. The overloaded gunship sluggishly sought the jungle opening that had been found by the loach pilot. Overhead, the other Huey hovered in readiness. The door gunners merely watched. They had been instructed to return fire only.

The pilot maneuvered the helicopter directly over the blasted out hole, and started dropping straight down. Now the excess weight helped stabilize the craft in this unorthodox approach. Leaves and slender twigs were sheared off with a staccato report that caused the gunship to shudder, and hearts to flutter. There was no flat ground to land on, and the steeply slanted hillside was littered with shattered tree trunks and fallen limbs.

As the Huey neared the ground, Tony saw that because of the angle, the starboard blade was getting perilously close to the ground. If it hit, the Huey would be slammed aside by the powerful torque: a crash would be inevitable.

The pilot expertly settled his craft as close to the ground as he could. The port side, where Tony was looking straight down with great apprehension, was still eight feet from the rocky earth when the next order came.

"First man out!" the lieutenant shouted. He stood up and brought his rifle up to port arms.

Yates leaped out the starboard door while Tait climbed down onto the port skid, hung on for a moment, then jumped. He hit the angled hillside with a roll; his sixty-pound pack levered him onto his back. Tony landed beside him like a cat, grabbed Tait's shoulder, and hefted him out of the way before the giant Wallace landed atop them both. Lieutenant Blake went out the starboard side behind Yates — he merely had to step off the skid onto the ground.

Immediately came a rush of wind as the lightened Huey lifted straight up above the trees, spun around, and screamed for altitude. Scant seconds later, the second Huey slid into the opening and hovered momentarily while Sergeant Miller and the men of A squad disembarked. Then it vaulted into the rain-filled sky. They were last seen winging east with the loach as a sidekick. The *whup-whup-whup* persisted long after the hueys were no longer visible. Then the sound, too, was swallowed up, as if by magic.

Now they were alone.

Lieutenant Blake wasted no time issuing orders. "Miller, Yates, get those men headed for the top of the hill. I want to be there before the colonel reaches base."

"Yes, sir," the two NCOs chorused. They repeated the orders to the men, all of whom were still standing within a thirty-foot radius and had heard the original command. They were already spreading out like seasoned veterans, moving upward.

Within moments both squads were swallowed by the abysmal darkness of the jungle. The tops of the hundred-foot-tall trees were in another world, for Tony could see no higher than the first layer of leaves that sprouted only a few feet overhead. The ground was a contorted mass of thick, rotting vegetation and pulpy ground. Even on a cloudless day no sunlight ever reached this far down: this was a land of perpetual gloom. Water dripped incessantly after following a tortuous path that started at the top of the broad-leafed canopy and wound its way earthward along limbs and vines, each drop like a marble in a vast mechanical mousetrap.

Burns breathed heavily under his load, the machine gun an additional burden. "This ain't exactly what I had in mind for a change of scenery. I was lookin' more for a beach type resort with air-conditioned rooms."

"Cut the chatter," warned Yates, keeping his voice low. "This is supposed to be a combat patrol."

Burns, usually ready with a retort, knew when to keep quiet. He raised the barrel of the M-60 so that it pointed straight ahead, and clicked off the safety. Wallace grinned as he silently shifted the weight of his bandoliers. He gave Burns a wink.

The platoon trudged up the hill through the dense underbrush in a ragged H formation, with one squad on either side and the lieutenant and his radiotelephone operator forming the cross. Monkeys chirped in the treetops as their territory was being invaded. To the experienced jungle fighter this was a welcome sound, for it meant that there were no other intruders in the immediate area.

Or so they hoped.

Lieutenant Blake continued to call to his squad leaders whenever he thought they strayed too far. Tony, only twenty feet away, could barely see his platoon leader. Wallace was a giant in front of him, Rodriguiz a shadow behind. Of the rest of the men he heard only cursing, and tramping through slushy vegetation. The glimpses he had of the lieutenant showed his alertness, his concentration, his seeming obliviousness to the jungle or entangling vines: the personification of performance.

Despite the chilly drizzle, the tough plodding stirred enough of Tony's blood to keep him warm. Plant sap and insect carcasses kept his face and neck sticky. His boots were soaked through, the tread clogged with heavy mud. The weight of the pack bore down on his shoulders like a hod of bricks. He kept readjusting the web gear until every part of his neck and shoulders ached. To make matters worse, the handle of his entrenching tool, protruding below his fanny pack, snagged on every log or vine that he stepped over; there was no opportunity to stop and fix the problem.

White, following too close behind Burns, got smacked in the face by a springing tree limb. He cursed too loudly for conditions, and was soundly chastised by Yates. Burns then turned around and tried to mollify his ego.

"Quit your complainin'," he whispered. "At least nobody ain't shootin' at you."

With that White harrumphed, and a second later a loud retort rang out like a tiny peal of thunder. Instantly, every man hit the loamy, leaf-covered ground; every heart doubled its beat. A grenade automatically appeared in Rodriguez's hand, its pin between clenched teeth.

"Who fired that shot?" Lieutenant Blake shouted, after a couple seconds of silence. From the sound he knew that it was an M-16.

A quaking voice sounded from A squad. "Sorry, sir," PFC Belden answered. "My hand got caught on a vine."

"You fucking idiot," the lieutenant shouted, not bothering to keep his voice down. "Now every gook between here and Cambodia knows where we are."

Tony thought, *None but the deaf could have failed to hear the engines and whirring blades of the Hueys.*

Belden did not repeat his apology.

"Okay, move them out." Lieutenant Blake climbed to his feet and started shoving vines and tree limbs out of his way. Raymonds pushed himself and the radio that he was carrying off the ground, and struggled after him. Slowly, pulse rates dropped, and the men began moving up the hill. "Fucking idiot," he muttered again, so that his two squad leaders could hear him.

Neither deemed to reply.

Tony's skin crawled. They had been told that they were being inserted into uninhabited enemy territory — whatever that was supposed to mean. But all around them grew the unknown: in front, behind, to both sides. To Tony, the unknown was beginning to mean strong apprehension. He shrugged off the complacency that he had come to accept in the paddies. There the enemy had not shown himself. But there must be a reason for their being here — a reason that Command knew, and the rest suspected.

Every safety was in the ready position — no one wanted to chance being a split second too late in firing.

The slope moderated, but the men kept sweating. Insect repellent had long since been washed off, leaving the men naked to the bite of mosquitoes that were thirsting for blood. The jungle thinned as the troops crested the hill. Now they could see where they were going.

"All right," Lieutenant Blake said to his squad leaders. "Let's make a perimeter search. Come on, check it out." Once the orders were given and the men were underway, he helped the radioman out of his harness and placed the waterproof field instrument on the ground. He grabbed the phone from its receiver. "Command Base Zero, this is Firefly. Command Base Zero, this is Firefly. Come in, please."

The radio crackled. The lieutenant repeated his call. "Damn," he cursed, when he still could not get through. After five minutes he picked up part of a message, asked for a repeat, and received nothing but more static. He contained himself while Miller and Yates made their reports — the area was under control.

"All right, set up a perimeter," he said.

"It's already done, sir," Miller replied. He pushed his helmet up over his forehead and wiped off some sweat. "Want us to dig in?"

"Just hang loose till I get through to Command." He keyed in the radio and tried again. Over the course of the next ten minutes he managed to piece together the broken messages that had come through the static. "Damn," he said, for their benefit. "All right, go ahead and tell them to dig in. And tell them why so they stay on their toes."

Back at C Squad, Yates explained to the men as they gathered around, "Okay, here's the story. The weather's gotten bad and the Hueys can't get through. They've cancelled the operation until tomorrow."

'I hope the lieuy told 'em to hurry their ass and get us the fuck outa here," Burns said.

"Never shoulda started out on a day like this no how," Wallace added.

White took a long draft from his canteen now that he did not have to be conservative with it. He passed it to Tony. "Leastways we'll have a hot meal waitin' for us."

"Will you guys wait and let me finish," Yates said, with his usual exasperation. "Didn't you hear me when I said the Hueys couldn't get through? That means they can't get through, either to bring in the engineers or to get us out. So we're digging in for the night — and praying for better weather."

"Are you outa your fuckin' mind?" White said. The rest chimed in with their grievances, far too loud for conditions. Yates let them have their say — he knew that they had to get it out of their systems.

"Look, I don't like it any more than you do. But that's the way it is. We're stuck here and there's nothing we can do about it. Nothing's coming in, nothing's going out. So let's get dug in before Charlie lays his sights on us."

With much grumbling and grunting, the men dug in. The circle they made around the platoon leader was small enough so they could see each other and communicate. The digging was not easy because of the profusion of thick roots that interlaced the compact soil. They had to hack off the roots with an entrenching tool, or slowly cut through them with bayonet blades.

Fields of fire were created with the best advantage. Obscuring brush was cut down, and claymores placed strategically. The rain continued to hammer down and, once the heavy work was done, the men got cold again. Ponchos were staked out over each position not only to help keep them dry, but to catch rain water and funnel it into canteens and open mess kits. They huddled in pairs, prayed for warmth, and wiled away the afternoon as best they could.

Lieutenant Blake was not sitting idle. He and Raymonds dug their own hole in the middle of the perimeter, large enough for both of them, the radio, and a space for one at a time to lie down. Every hour he made a status report, whether or not he thought he was getting through to base. He did not look scared, but by his orders he demonstrated a healthy respect for their perilous position. He actually seemed to be enjoying the responsibility that had been thrust upon him.

Lunchtime arrived. Each man broke out c-rations. Heat tabs were lighted in the bottom of foxholes, and plenty of hot coffee relieved the men of their chills.

"It don't make no sense," White said to Tony, as they crouched in their foxhole. They sat facing each other, their knees interlaced since there was not enough room to spread out. "Why the fuck do they send us out here in bad weather in the first place?"

Tony grunted into his coffee and did not reply for a long time. He tried to control his chattering teeth. "If we had answers to all these questions, we probably wouldn't even be here." He paused, and sipped. The metal canteen cup transmitted the heat of the water and burned his lips, but he sipped anyway.

"What the fuck you talkin' 'bout? I only ast one question."

Humphing, Tony continued, "You only think you did. Actually you asked a whole bunch of questions." He intended to say more, but left it hanging.

A couple minutes later, White said, "You know, sometimes I think you know what you're talkin' 'bout. But you're too smart for your own britches. I hope none of it don't rub off on me. I know too many things already."

After that, they lapsed into silence. They took turns watching the jungle through the mist — and hoping that the vague shapes out there were only phantoms. The afternoon wore on.

The rain slackened and, eventually, stopped, although the sun did not pierce the thick overcast. Even so, the temperature rapidly climbed and it was not long before the troops began to dry out. The mud caked on their clothes, and turned to a fine powder on their skins. But because of the water in the foxholes, their feet stayed wet.

Every time the radio crackled, Tony's ears perked up. Lieutenant Blake received a call from Captain Collins, who told him that the weather at the base was still bad, and that there had been no change in the cancellation of the operation. He was told to hold his position until morning. Under the circumstances, there did not seem to be any other choice.

As night approached, Lieutenant Blake spread the word to maintain a fifty percent alert. Yates climbed out of his hole and made certain that everyone heard the order. "And no smoking after dark."

White packed a little mud under his eyes so his face was not so shiny. "If you think I'm gonna do anythin' to give my position away, you got another think cumin'. An' that goes for my partner, too, don't it?"

"If you think so," Tony agreed with a smile.

"Ah *know* so."

"Good," Yates said, grinning back. "You have enough water?"

Tony pointed. "Full canteens plus most of the mess kit."

Yates eyed the open trays askance. "You'd better drink that stuff before it becomes infested with mosquito larvae."

"We'll just boil it an' mix it with the cocoa," White laughed.

Yates just sneered. "Just make sure Giovanni knows what to do — in case."

"He'll know what to do when the time comes," White assured him.

Yates nodded, then returned to his own foxhole. Tony reached for his pack and pulled out his evening choice of rations: ham and lima beans. He ripped open the carton and started opening the main meal.

"When's he going to start calling me by my first name?" Tony lit another Heatab and poured another cup of water. "Heck, I don't even know *your* first name."

For a moment the expression on White's face faded. "We don't use no first names around here," he said seriously.

Tony looked up with a quizzical expression. "What do you mean?"

"I mean we don't want to get too familiar with each other. Don't do no good to make friends if you're gonna lose 'em." White spat on the ground, pulled a cigarette out of his shirt pocket, and lit up. "The better you know somebody, the worst you feel when he gets his. Me, I'm jus' keepin' to myself, puttin' in my time, an' gettin' the fuck out when my year's up. Ain't nothin' wrong with that."

Tony took some gum out of his c-ration accessory packet. He chewed thoughtfully. Sundown was a long time coming.

****

Just before sunset, when shadows invaded the jungle and disguised their actions, the claymore positions were changed.

That night in the jungle proved to be darker than any night Tony had ever experienced. The dense cloud cover, which blanketed the sky like a shroud, also kept the water in the lower atmosphere trapped close to the ground. The humidity was near a hundred percent. His body was chilled with the lowering temperature, and he longed to sip on a cup of hot coffee.

The silence was unnerving. In comparison, a swish of clothing was a rumble of distant thunder; a cracked twig was a rifle retort; a sneeze was an exploding grenade. But the jungle emitted nothing.

A whisper brought Tony out of deep reverie — or had he fallen asleep at his post?

"How's everything look?" Lieutenant Blake

crouched behind him, at the edge of the foxhole, bright eyes peering into the gloom.

"You scared me," Tony said testily, turning around with a jerk. He hoped he had not kicked White, who was curled up in the bottom of the hole. "Don't sneak up on me like that."

"If you'd been awake you'd have heard me coming," was the lieutenant's quick reply. Tony did not answer the accusation, and Lieutenant Blake did not make an issue of it. "Have you seen or heard anything out there?"

Tony was now fully alert. "I can't see beyond my nose. But I haven't heard a thing. It's quiet."

"Yes, too quiet," the lieutenant added. He removed a flap of tape and consulted the luminescent dial of his watch. "Well, the gooks never start anything till oh-two-hundred. That gives us another ten minutes."

He disappeared into the blackness.

Those ten minutes crept by slowly, with Tony counting each minute as the sweep hand on his watch dial made another circle. He breathed a little easier when two o'clock passed. He took a swig from his canteen, careful to muffle the noise of the pouch snaps, and was just screwing down the cap when he heard a dull *whump* in the distance. A moment later he heard a singsong whistle approaching from somewhere overhead. There was a thud behind him, followed immediately by a tremendous explosion. The flare of light was like a ball of shorted electrical wires on a main buss. Tony was already ducking when typewriter keys tapped against the back of his steel pot.

"What the fuck?" White uncoiled like a jack-in-the-box. The top of his helmet collided with Tony's chin, but neither one noticed. Two more explosions ripped the matted grass from the front of their position and sent a shower of dirt and debris into the air and down onto their heads. White fell back down with Tony on top of him. "Jesus fuckin' Christ."

He tried to push Tony aside, tried to fight off flailing arms and legs. Another explosion took place on the other side of the perimeter, where A squad was dug in. More *whumps* could be heard in the jungle, and by this time the men knew what was soon to follow.

"Mortars," White said under his breath. Silence was hardly necessary. From a squatting position, he reached up and took a handful of poncho and pulled the cover down into the hole. It was too late, for the first blast had riddled it with shrapnel and left it in tatters — else they never would have been rained upon by the rubble from those twin rounds. He stuffed the soggy mess under his feet, careful not to cover the sump hole.

Between *whumps,* he jumped up and took a

quick look around, then ducked just before another mortar landed within the platoon's tiny perimeter. It was obvious that Charlie knew exactly where they were. Cramped as it was, Tony wished that they had made the hole smaller.

"Hey, you all right?" Tony was crouched in the bottom of the hole as limp as a wet dishrag. White shook him violently. "Come out of it, man!"

Tony began to look up when another explosion tore through the nearby jungle. He buried his face in his hands as mud rained down, his ears ringing from the noise. Burns and Wallace cursed out loud as part of their hole caved in, so near did the mortar explode.

White struck a match and held it in front of Tony's face. "Where you hit, man?" he wanted to know. Tony's eyes were glassy, and he was beginning to shake. Blood dripped from his mouth. He had a thundering headache and did not know why. White ran his coal-black hands over Tony's upper body. Then he pulled off his steel pot and felt for head wounds. "I can't find nothin' wrong. Where you hit?".

Lieutenant Blake was screaming, too. "Get me a spare aerial. This one's been blown off."

Tony put his hands over his ears, but could not block out the sounds.

A spring clicked. "Take that, amigo." The explosion was close, as if Rodriguiz had rolled the grenade right in front of him.

The M-60 burped. "They're out there! I see 'em! They're out there!"

"What the fuck you shootin' at. I don't see nothin'."

"Hold your fire, men. Hold your fire."

"I ain't gonna look for the white's o' their eyes, Yates."

Whump. Whump. Whump. Bar-ROOM. *Bar*-ROOM. *Bar*-ROOM.

Lieutenant Blake called base between mortar blasts. "Command Base Zero. Command Base Zero. This is Firefly. Come in."

White struck another match. "Man, I can't find nothin'. What's wrong?" Tony nodded faintly, and muttered something under his breath. White stuck his ear close. "I'm scared."

The match went out. "Shit, man, we all scared," White said through gritted teeth. Then he braced himself as more *whumps* left the jungle, launching their 82-millimeter mortars on their mission of death. This time they landed wide, far on the other side of A squad's position.

Tony crawled to his knees and peeped over the edge of the foxhole. Another, smaller explosion ripped through the bushes in front of Rodriguiz and Tait: a grenade, by the sound of it. A moment later there was a scream. A man from A squad? From the jungle? His ears were

rattled, and it was impossible to tell. As the whine of mortars grew louder, frantic eyes sought movement. He ducked an instant before the explosion shredded the foliage in front of him. Then he was on his feet with his M-16 trained. He emptied a clip into the bushes, while Rodriguiz launched two more grenades, spreading his pattern.

White pulled Tony down into the hole. "Whatchu shootin' at?"

More mortars landed. Roots and tree limbs fell from the sky. "I — I don't know."

Yates yelled. "Goddamn it, hold your fire! You want them to see your muzzle flash?" More grenades sailed out into the trees. During a short lull between mortars, Yates low-crawled from his hole to check on his men. "Hold your fire," he shouted at Rodriguiz, "Until you see something."

"I seen 'em. They're out there waitin' to overrun us. We need artillery or we lost."

"Just make sure you have a target." Yates crawled to the next hole where White was loading the M-203 attached to his rifle. "Hold your fire." He glanced down at Tony at the bottom of the hole. "Hey, is he all right?"

"He's okay, man, just a little shook up cause he took some shrapnel in the back of his helmet."

Yates reached down and placed a warm hand on Tony's shoulder. His fingers contracted in a friendly squeeze. "Take it easy, Giovanni. We'll get out of this all right." He flashed a smile that was barely visible in the dark. Tony saw it and managed a weak grin in return.

A chorus of *whumps* sounded off in the jungle. "Gotta go." Yates jumped up to his knees. If Charlie were close, he would be taking cover from his own mortars. He had half a dozen seconds before they came crashing down. "Hold that machine gun," he shouted over his shoulder. A moment later he smashed into the ground and rolled into the central hole right on top of Lieutenant Blake, who was on top of Sergeant Miller.

The earth shook with the nearness of the explosions, three of which took place within the perimeter. The deafening roar brought with it a cross-weave of dirt, rocks, and jagged steel. The men in the command hole were inundated with debris.

As soon as the barrage ended, Lieutenant Blake was up and shouting into the telephone. "Did you hear that, goddamn it? Now will you believe we're under attack?" The voice crackled back with words that made him apoplectic. "You fucking moron, I need those shells now, or we won't be here when you get the go ahead from your commander. Start lobbing HE at those coordinates and fire for effect. *Now!*"

The *whump* of mortar tubes warned everyone down. Tony listened to the lieutenant pleading. "Goddamn assholes are using the chain of command." Then he added vehemently in true officer style, "Somebody's head's going to roll over this."

Bar-ROOM. *Bar*-ROOM. *Bar*-ROOM.

Tony was coming to his senses, gaining confidence in the protection of the hole. He unclipped a couple of grenades, stood up behind the mound of dirt facing the jungle, and waited next to White.

"Sir, I've got gooks out there on my side," Miller said.

"Mine, too," Yates added.

"Whatever you do, don't blow those claymores till you see the bastards." The lieutenant keyed the microphone again. He propped up the radio and shouted for an artillery barrage. His gentlemanly language was quickly deteriorating.

"Renslow's bleedin' bad. Lieterman's puttin' on compresses as fast as Andrews can get them unwrapped."

"There's no way we're gettin' a dust-off at night."

A rat-tat-tat sounded from the M-60, as Burns poured hot lead into the shrubbery. Yates hit the ground right behind him and jerked him halfway out of the hole.

"You stupid ass," he shouted angrily. "You want to draw Charlie a road map?"

"What the fuck, you don't think he knows where we are?" Burns shrugged out of his squad leader's grip. "I seen gooks not twenty meters away, crawlin' on the ground."

He turned and pulled the trigger, sending a searing blast of tracers through the low grass. Yates rolled aside. If an enemy soldier fired up that red beam, he did not want to be at the end of the bead. He stayed flat, where he was somewhat protected by the hillock of dirt that was piled in front of the hole.

Wallace clipped another belt onto the last cartridge. "They out there, man. And our claymore cord's been shot to hell." For proof he held up a shredded end of wire.

"Then goddamn it, throw grenades."

There was no stopping Burns in a fight. But he was a good man behind a gun. Yates raced back to his own hole before another barrage of mortars screamed out of the overhead darkness.

While Rodriguiz was lining up grenades at the front of his hole, Tait was tensely fixing a bayonet to the barrel of his M-16. There was no telling how this fight was going to go; it paid to be prepared for the worst.

Watching this, Tony began pulling grenades out of his pack. Once he had gotten used to the terrible thundering, and realized that nothing

but a direct hit could hurt them as long as they kept their heads down, he found new strength. Meanwhile, White was firing grenades on a high trajectory that would bring them down a scant fifty meters away. Like Burns with the machine gun, he was laying down a barricade of flying steel all along their squad's tactical area of responsibility.

"Sorry I freaked out on you," Tony said calmly, belying the fear that he was hiding.

"Don't worry 'bout it." White's teeth were a skeletal grin against the black background of his face. He sat back down in the hole, holding his fire until he had something more than shadows to shoot at. "Least you come out o' it."

"What's going to happen now?" Tony wanted to know.

White shrugged. "Don't know how many of 'em are out there, or where they are. The bastards may attack any time, or lay low and try to catch us off guard. But judgin' from the mortars I could hear, I don't think there's more 'an a platoon of 'em. And they can't be sure how many *we* are."

Tony nodded. He peered into the jungle and tried to make out something among the weirdly shaped trees, the hanging vines, the bunched shrubbery. His rifle was cocked at a bush, waiting for it to move.

Then came a whining sound that was ten times as loud as that of the mortars. It came from high in the sky, and seemed as if it were descending right on top of them. "Omigod," White muttered, dragging Tony to the bottom of the hole. The whine became a screech like ten locomotives throwing their massive wheels in reverse and skidding along iron tracks. The screech ended suddenly, engulfed in an explosion so close and so loud that it rivaled Armageddon.

The jungle erupted with a violence of heat and flame that melted Wallace's poncho where it lay on the ground, that blackened the tops of steel pots and singed camouflage covers, that incinerated vegetation, that for a brief moment turned the air to molten fire. Hundreds of pounds of shrapnel sliced through the trees, leaving some leafless, felling others. One fifty-foot trunk crashed right between two foxholes, separating White and Tony from Burns and Wallace, the top sending broken limbs into Lieutenant Blake's hole and tearing his uniform sleeve.

"Right on target, Zero," the lieutenant shouted happily into the mouthpiece. "Now give me another one, one notch to the west."

In the eerie silence that followed, the jungle to the east was smoldering — it was too wet to burn for very long. Tony listened intently for the sound of mortars, knowing that they could resume at any moment. During the lull, Tony saw Raymonds holding a flashlight on a map, saw the lieutenant making calculations on a notepad.

"Then give me everything you got at five zero nine six seven."

The high-pitched whine of shells approached the camp. This time the explosions tore up the jungle a hundred meters in front of A squad's perimeter. A ball of flame boiled up from the ground and chopped the jungle apart with deafening destruction. If there were any soldiers out there, they were either underground — or dead. With two well-placed shots, Lieutenant Blake had called in artillery that straddled his position and cleared the field of the enemy.

Now came another flight of shells that landed on an inclined ridgeline a thousand meters to the east. If that was where the mortar emplacements were located, they were no more. Lieutenant Blake called in for three more volleys, then stopped to listen for activity.

The seconds ticked by like hours, the minutes like days. Renslow, now under Andrews' constant care, was in good condition and joking about his condition.

"I was out taking a leak when I heard the first mortar go off. Startled me for a minute — I didn't know what it was. Then it dawned on me, and I hightailed it back with my peter still hanging out. I was jumping into the hole when it hit. Felt like a hundred pinpricks stabbing me at once. But I was sure glad to find my peter was still where it was supposed to be. I stuffed it in my pants and fainted."

If the troops were relieved during the lull in the fighting, Lieutenant Blake was not. Captain Collins was on the line, receiving the battle report. Tony could hear only one side of the conversation, but it sounded as if contingency plans were being made, should extraction prove to be their only hope of survival.

But back at command center it was still raining, and the cloud cover was as thick as ever. Captain Collins warned his platoon leader that he might have to fend for himself if the Hueys could not fly. Word shot around the tiny outpost like a spark of primacord.

Andrews was worried about Renslow's condition. Even though most of the wounds were superficial, infection could set in so fast in the bush that, without proper medical treatment in a sterile facility, he could end up losing an arm. He filled his patient with penicillin.

White took a long drink from his canteen. "Charlie out there somewhere, gettin' closer. Come dawn, we better not be here."

Chapter 93

The tranquility of the morning was out of proportion to the awful cacophony of only a few hours before. Birds sang in the treetops, and monkeys cavorted through the middle canopy. And, as always, insects buzzed furiously. But as the sky lightened and the mist thinned, the terrible destruction caused by the high explosive shells became evident.

"Christ, you'd think there was a war going on," White commented dryly. He plucked a twig off the tree that had fallen across their perimeter, and chewed on it thoughtfully. In a louder voice, he called out, "Hey, Yates, can I go out there and take a look-see for gooks?"

Yates climbed over the tree and crouched beside him. "Would you keep your fucking voice down?" He glanced toward the lieutenant's hole, but Blake was too engrossed in his maps to make any outburst.

"Shit, man, I jus' wanna take a body count."

"Bullshit. You want souvenirs, and we both know it." A moment later, he added, "If I didn't need your black ass to keep an eye on Giovanni, I'd let you go. But I can't afford to have you blown away."

"Man, there ain't nothin' alive out there, believe me."

"Just sit tight and keep your mouth shut — and your eyes open. You, too, Giovanni. And you keep your eyes on *him*, even though he isn't a pretty sight. What happened to the back of your steel pot?"

With that he left. Tony removed his cover and saw the blackened top and the gouged back. Mortar shrapnel had ripped the canvas camouflage cover and dented the metal.

"Next time somebody says to keep my hat on, I will," he laughed. White joined him, and slapped his shoulders exuberantly. Tony experienced an elation that made the biting insects, the morning cold, the pain, the dirt, and the sleepless throbbing in his eyes a welcome distraction. He was very glad to be alive.

Lieutenant Blake called Yates and Miller to his hole, and gave them a situation report. Tony listened intently. "This is the way it is, and it doesn't look good. Captain Collins says it's blowing like hell and the fog is thick as soup. The Hueys can't even get off the ground. He tried to have some sent in from Pleiku, but a spotter plane sent out to keep an eye on us reported that we're covered in fog below five hundred feet. That means they can't find us anyway."

He paused a moment to let them absorb the information. Both squad leaders were silent. Since last night Tony had gained newfound respect for this gung-ho second lieuy. He had been in country barely a month, but he had already proven himself in battle. Calling in artillery that straddled their own position had called for unbelievable precision in reading co-ordinates, and uncommon courage. Even the tiniest mistake could have resulted in the death of them all.

"So here's what we've got to do." Pointing to the map with a worn pencil stub, he showed them the terrain. "The mortars came from over here, on the other side of this ridge. That means the only way they can get to us is by coming down either side of this cliff and into this draw, then up to the north and around here." Tony wished he could see the map. "We're going to advance to the south, staying clear of yesterday's LZ in case they decide to ambush it, and swing over this other ridge and down this ravine. There's a 'Yard village about fifteen klicks away. If we're lucky we'll get there by nightfall."

Tony wondered what would happen if they did *not* get there, or if they met resistance along the way. What had started out yesterday as a company-sized assault had deteriorated to a half-platoon-sized rout. Now, instead of seeking out the enemy and engaging in hostilities, they were the bait to lead the guerrillas into an ambush.

"The rest of the company will meet us there." Lieutenant Blake folded the map, tucked it into his jacket pocket, and buttoned the flap. "We're moving out now."

"What about breakfast?" Miller wanted to know.

"We'll stop in a couple hours. But we've got to get away from here before Charlie catches us. Let's move it. Quietly."

Minutes later the men were packed and ready to go. They were haggard from lack of sleep, but fully alert to their untenable situation. They were strictly on their own; no one was coming to get them out of this one. With heavy minds and heavier packs, they formed a V with one squad on each leg, and started down the hillside which had been converted to a barren moonscape by 155-millimeter artillery shells.

"Did you guys pick up your claymores?" Yates asked, as the mud-splattered men marched past.

"Didn't find nothing but a piece o' wire," White said, shaking his head. "Even the boulder I propped it up against was gone."

"How many shells were in that salvo?" Tait asked curiously, in his deadpan drawl.

Yates cinched down his web straps. "Enough."

"Is this considered battle damage, or am I going to have to pay for it?" Tony indicated the shrapnel holes and ripped fabric of his pack.

"Next time I'd like my hair cut with scissors instead of shrapnel," was Burns' retort. He showed Yates where the top of his steel pot had been scraped clean by fire and steel.

"At least it wasn't your throat." Wallace stretched to his fullest height. "An' the next time we're diggin' deep enough so's I don't have to put my knees up around my ears."

"At least you — "

"*Knock it off!*" Lieutenant Blake snapped angrily. "Anything I can hear, Charlie can hear."

Burns harrumphed to himself. His arms tensed as he brought the heavy machine gun to a ready position. He could hold it that way for hours on end.

The slope steepened sharply. The men literally had to climb downhill, holding onto brush and vines for support, and leaning against trees to rest. The ground was soft and muddy, the rocks and boulders covered with slippery moss. The thump of falling bodies and the clatter of dropped weapons were punctuated by curses and cries of pain. Renslow had it the worst, for besides being weakened by the loss of blood, the constant twisting and turning rubbed the bandages across wounds that still contained bits of sharp metal.

The jungle was so dense that Tony could not see through the upper canopy to the cloud layer. He knew that dust-off pilots had a reputation for daring, but they could not land where they could not see. And there was something about this lieutenant, as if he wanted to get his men out on his own rather than stoop to asking for help: a matter of pride — or ego.

Soon they reached the bottom of the slope, where a rivulet of dank water coursed over the fern-covered ground. Mosquitoes were thick in the humid air, and flies buzzed in clouds that at times were difficult to see through. More than one man was reduced to coughing spasms when he inhaled a blindly flying insect. Repellent did not seem to be doing much good.

An hour later, Lieutenant Blake called a halt to the ragged patrol. "I want four point coverage and no two men sitting together. You've got ten minutes to chow down. And Andrews," he added, to the medic, "Make sure everyone puts tablets in their water. And no smoking." Then he leaned against a tree and pulled out his map.

Yates and Miller assigned sentries — who were not allowed to eat — and converged on the lieutenant.

"Sir, I think we should radio in our position so command knows where we are," Miller suggested. Several weeks ago his eight-months field experience had been a great boon to this wet-behind-the-ears, recently graduated officer. But in that short time, the training received in officer's candidate school had shown through. The greenhorn lieutenant was already a seasoned veteran, a leader of men. In the exigencies of war, he might make captain before he learned to shave.

"As soon as I get it I'll take care of it, sergeant," he said, somewhat testily. Without looking up, he made calculations in a bent and soggy note pad. The code was in his head, under dark, mottled hair that was plastered down with sweat. Perspiration beaded on his wrinkled brow.

Tony was not appointed for guard duty so, keeping an eye on the lieutenant, he opened a can and spooned out the cold food, not even aware of what he was eating. "Hey, White, what're you doing?"

One boot and sock were already off, and White was kneading his toes with a handful of powder. "Got the rot somethin' awful." His foot was swollen, and open sores spread back from his toes.

"Get that fucking boot back on, you idiot!" Yates hushed through gritted teeth.

"But, it hurts. I gotta — "

"*Now!*"

Reluctantly, White pulled on a dry sock and relaced his jungle boot. "I gotta change the other — "

"Some other time."

"But — "

Yates grabbed a handful of shirt, pulled White close. "You keep those boots on and your eyes open. We're not back in the paddies. This is Charlie's country. And he's out there waiting for us to go slack."

"Aw —"

Yates shoved him back. "Giovanni, stop looking at me and watch that jungle. I want you to see Charlie before he pinches your ass."

Tony swallowed.

When he was done with his work, Lieutenant Blake shoved a candy bar in his mouth as he called for Raymonds to bring the radio. At the same time, he made the squad leaders move away a respectable distance. He called in a report without waiting for acknowledgement of receipt.

At nine and a half minutes, he refilled his own canteen from the trickle of water pouring over the slimy rocks, tossed in two iodine tablets and a packet of Kool-Aid, and shoved the canteen back in the canvas holder. "Let's go." He stood up and marched off.

Although the sky remained cloudy, and the air damp, by mid morning the heat was uncomfortable. The breaks were staggered, but frequent. Many short rests kept the platoon eager and alert, whereas a long one often resulted in loss of momentum, initiative, and energy. Captain Collins reported over the radio that all helicopters were still grounded. Blake reported Renslow's wounds, but said he was holding.

As bayonets swung against the thick greenery, not a word was spoken. Tony watched the tall, vine enshrouded, insect infested trees with vivid imagination. A sniper could be drawing a bead on him this very minute. An ambush could be hidden around the next bend. Guerrillas, or an entire NVA battalion, might be waiting in camouflaged positions, with rifles trained and grenade pins pulled. Or the jungle could be rigged with booby traps.

Crack. The shot that rang out spun Lieterman around like a top and hurled him to the ground. As soon as he hit, he crawled like a spider under the nearest log, rolled onto his left side, and aimed his M-16 toward the spot where the ringing was still echoing in the trees. Everyone else scrambled for cover. Tony found himself lying in a pool of water, with a rock under his belly. But he stayed flat, refusing to move — too scared to move. He held his breath until he was forced to gasp for air. He stared at Lieterman, only a few feet away, squinting with pain.

"Medic," Lieterman called out, his voice trembling with fear. "I'm hit."

There followed an utter silence that lasted an eternity, while anxious eyes scanned the right flank for the sniper. There was no wind; not a leaf fluttered, not a twig cracked. Somewhere out there, one man was in control of the situation; one man held an entire platoon pinned to the ground as effectively as if they had been mired in quicksand. That one man wielded awful power over the lives of others.

Andrews began a slow crawl over rocks and broken tree limbs, slid through the damp, dank undergrowth that concealed his movements as well as other slithering, unknown horrors. As he crawled past, Tony watched him brush aside beetles and centipedes that rivaled mice in size.

No one uttered a word, not even Blake, for to speak was to draw attention — and lead. They could not run, for there might be more waiting, in either direction. This was a game that had to be played with extreme caution.

After an agony of time, Andrews reached his man. "Where are you hit?" he whispered calmly.

"The right side," came the painful groan. "My whole side feels like it's burning."

From behind, Andrews reached around and released Lieterman's web straps. Gently, he pulled the pack off Lieterman's back and pushed it aside, revealing a red stain around the waistline. With his bayonet he cut away the bloody material and inspected the damage. There was a long gash below the rib cage that was disgorging blood like a runaway faucet.

"Ouch!" Lieterman screamed, when Andrews pulled the skin back to see how deep the cut extended.

"It's only a flesh wound," was the medic's opinion. He pulled out some compresses and pressed them firmly over the gouge to stem the flow of blood. "No broken bones and no ruptured organs. It looks like the pack took most of the force, and maybe deflected the bullet." Lieterman continued to groan as Andrews taped the bandages in place.

"Miller. Yates," Lieutenant Blake whispered. He had squirmed to a position from which he was protected on the right by a rounded boulder. "You see where that shot came from?"

"He's too well covered," came Miller's coarse reply. He low-crawled to where the lieutenant was hiding. When his whiskered face was only inches away from Blake's, he added, "Why don't we get fire power on him and hightail it out of here?"

Tony felt stinging sensations on his wrist. He pulled his arms out of the tiny stream and saw several dull gray, sluglike creatures squiggling about: leeches.

Blake readjusted his steel pot. "No, I don't want to make too big a ruckus. Maybe he's the only one who knows where we are, and how many. No, I want to sneak away without giving out any more information. We're going to go up the opposite hill, get away from this damn crick. Make sure the men have their canteens full — there's no telling when we'll get near water again."

Miller crawled away to pass the word. Andrews crept back to the lieutenant, his face streaming with sweat.

Tony pinched the leeches to no avail. They seemed to be glued to his skin. He dragged himself backward in the tall grass, and dumped the contents of his shirt pocket on a bare rock.

"Sir, Lieterman's hit hard, but I think he can make it out on his own steam. But if he loses too much blood we may have to carry him."

"How's Renslow holding out?"

"He's in a lot of pain, but none of his wounds are serious. Of course, he's still full of shrapnel. I cleaned out what I could, but his biggest problem is going to be from infection."

"Okay, stay with them." Looking around, he said, "Where's Raymonds?" When he spotted the radiotelephone operator, he low-crawled to his position. Still lying down, he grabbed the radio on the RTOs back, pointed the antenna into the air, and whispered into the phone.

Tony struck a match, let it flare down, and brought it close to the spots where the ugly leeches were attached. One by one they fell off as he touched them with the flame.

"Yates, I want you to take your men up that hill. Keep low, and out of sight. This may be a lone sniper, or a whole company of NVA. I

don't know. When you get fifty meters out, whistle — and cover for us."

"Yes, sir." Still flat on his belly, he turned and said, "Rodriguiz, you take point. Giovanni, right behind him. Then Burns, Wallace, Tait, and White."

Lieutenant Blake nodded. Rodriguiz moved out immediately, low-crawling up the hill through the dense foliage. He could not possibly see more than a few feet in front of him, and must be relying on other senses to warn him of danger. He stopped after every body length of progress, and listened. Tony stared at the worn soles of his boots. Flies and mosquitoes buzzed incessantly around his face, landing on his skin; a huge wasp, with ponderous abdomen hanging low, whirred around his head then hovered in front of his face. Gnats flew into the glossy white of his eyes. Rodriguiz slid like a snake, with a grenade in his throwing hand and his rifle in his left. He moved with the stealth of an Indian.

Tony was drenched in sweat, and almost frantically beating away the insects that drove him to distraction. He stayed right on Rodriguiz's heels, glancing often to the right and left for signs of the enemy. "Watch out for booby traps," Yates had warned him, and whether or not it was for effect, he was watching out.

The weight of the pack was arching his back painfully. The grenades clipped to the front of his web gear kept catching on vines and tangled brush. The ground was soggy, and slurped at his elbows. His knees sank in as he pushed himself along. Sticks kept poking at his eyes, ants bit his hands and crawled up pants. The constant jungle sounds were a mask that concealed enemy movement.

"Pssst," said Rodriguiz. "I see nothing. Pass it back."

Had they come fifty meters already — or a hundred miles? Like a Boy Scout, he turned and repeated the message. Then he rolled over on his back, humped awkwardly on the pack, and stared upward. Barely visible through the lower canopy, the white shroud that had entrapped them swirled around the treetops. He wished he could see a blue sky and puffy clouds, so he could picture familiar shapes that would remind him . . . remind him of — If only the insects would leave him alone . . .

"Hey," Yates blurted, as he slapped him on the foot. "Quit your daydreaming." Tony stared back silently, then rolled onto his side. "Where's Rodriguiz?"

"Right up ahead, on the other side of that clump."

Yates crawled past. "All right, follow me."

Tony jerked hard on the pack and rolled over, grunting when it pressed down on his back. He waited until Yates was out of sight before crawling after him. He crept slowly through the brush, wishing for the hundredth time that the insects would leave him alone. When he caught up with the squad leader, he was sitting up and looking calmly back at him. The clearing at the top of the hill was about fifty feet across.

A moment later, the rest of the squad crawled out of the underbrush, and Rodriguiz raced to the opposite tree line. He looked around for a moment, then nodded silently to Yates. He clipped the grenade back onto his web strap, but kept his rifle cocked and ready. Yates directed Tony to one side, along with Tait, while he spread the others around until he had a makeshift perimeter. Minutes later, C squad ushered the injured into the ring.

Tony took a good look at Renslow and Lieterman. Renslow's fatigue jacket was stained a dark shade of brown. He winced as his web straps rubbed across his chest. Lieterman stoically refused to groan, knowing that it might give their position away, but the great pain that he was suffering at every movement showed in the strain on his face. He was still losing blood despite Andrews' ministrations.

Lieutenant Blake instructed the rearguard to keep a sharp eye open for the sniper. In the security of the circle he referred to his map. The countryside around them was a convoluted system of hillocks and ravines, thickly overgrown where water flooded through narrow defiles but more open in the high ground.

"Yates, move your men along the crest of this hill until you come to the next ravine, then veer south so we can cross it diagonally. Miller, I want you to bring up the rear. Renslow, Lieterman, keep in the middle with Andrews." Addressing the medic, he added, "Andrews, do what you can to keep these men on their feet. But remember, we can't stop for anything. Charlie's right on our tail."

In expanded V formation, with Rodriguiz walking catlike on point, the foreshortened and beleaguered platoon moved quickly and quietly away from the lone sniper. Beady, Hispanic eyes missed nothing as they swept the ground, the brush, the trees, for signs of the enemy. Tony was glad not to be leading the way. He was overcome with inertia that a single rifle shot could not dispel. He remembered all too well the constant shelling that had kept him awake and on edge all through the night. It had taken only twenty-four short hours to transform the complacency learned in the rice paddies into fearful weariness.

Burns seemed to be happy despite the danger. He had been given a chance to fire his precious machine gun, and eagerly awaited the next opportunity. His sidekick kept close with extra ammunition, prepared at a moment's notice to slap a new belt into the breech. "I wanna kill me some gooks," Wallace had said. His silence was a testimonial to the reversal of roles from hunter to hunted.

An hour later and three hills away, another shot rang out. As a well-trained unit, every man hit the ground in unison.

"Who's hit? Who's hit? I want a report," the lieutenant called out. When no one answered, he feared the worst. "Miller, Yates, check your men. I want a report."

It took only a moment for the squad leaders to ascertain that none of the men had been injured. The shot from behind had gone wild.

"All right, get up and run." Lieutenant Blake jumped to his feet, lifted Raymonds by the radio, and pushed him forward. "Get moving, men. Double time."

It was an odd maneuver, and the men were slow to respond. But when their platoon leader charged ahead in a bold move, they ran to catch up. The lieutenant took point and led his men away from the sniper. This time he was using speed instead of stealth.

Ten minutes later, he called a halt and allowed the men to rest. "Miller, Yates, get point men out on four sides." He pulled the map from his pocket, studied it for five minutes, folded it, tucked it under the flap, and took a drink from his canteen. His blue eyes were bright with excitement, his pulse beat with sheer aliveness. He seemed to be enjoying the situation.

Five minutes later the platoon forged ahead, down a steep hill into a ravine and up the other side. Tony struggled every step of the way — but realized that Renslow and Lieterman must be struggling even more. He had seen Andrews change the dressing at the last rest stop, saw the horrendous gash on Lieterman's side, listened to him groan, and almost felt the torment that he must be enduring. More, he awoke to the fear that the next bullet could have his name on it.

It was mid afternoon when the next shot rang out. Tony heard a peculiar, hollow thud as the air collapsed behind a bullet that was uncomfortably close to his head. It spent itself harmlessly in a tree trunk, ripping off bark in the process. He hit the ground so hard that for a moment he was breathless.

Immediately, Lieutenant Blake unloosed his M-16 into the jungle where the report had originated. "Shoot, men, shoot. I want fire power."

Instantly came a staccato burst from Burns' machine gun, followed closely by the discharge from a dozen rifles, White's grenade launcher, and the other M-60, Kelsey's. In seconds the jungle was ripped apart as the barrage of bullets and exploding shrapnel ate through the foliage like an invisible chain saw. Bushels of shredded leaves and two dead monkeys fluttered to the earth, while a gaggle of wildly plumed birds screeched into the air.

"I think we got 'im," Burns said aloud, when Lieutenant Blake called a halt to the mad minute of fire.

"We ain't got shit," Wallace replied, simply for the sake of argument. Tony pointed with his rifle. "I thought I saw something didiing that way."

"Pickin' up the lingo fast, ain'tchu?" White grinned.

"Want us to check it out?" Miller asked the lieutenant. "He's prob'ly holdin' out in some spider hole."

"We can't take a chance on an ambush." Blake shook his head slowly, scrutinizing the silent jungle. "That may be exactly what they want us to do. Yates, get your men moving. We've got to find a place to dig in while we still have light." He surveyed the gray sky. Night fell fast in the jungle, and the overcast conditions did not help any. "Keep bearing sixty degrees. Move fast, but keep in sight."

Burns was squatting against a tree, his pants down to his knees, groaning. "Burns, get your pants up and get moving," Yates snarled. "You've been shitting all morning."

"I think I got the dys, man. It's that goddamn gook water. I'm hurtin' bad." Burns groaned with the abdominal cramps of dysentery.

"You're gonna hurt worse if you get a slug up your ass. Now move it." The lieutenant helped the wounded men to their feet. "Keep up the good work, men. We'll get out of this yet."

"Any chance for a medevac, sir?" Andrews persisted.

"If there was I'd have called it already," Blake said testily. "Did you give these men any morphine?"

"Of course."

The lieutenant started walking away. "Don't give them any more. We can't afford to be slowed down."

"Yes, sir." Andrews furiously stuffed the medical kit into his pack, and when Blake was out of hearing, Tony overheard the medic grumble, "Goddamn brown bar. Even if he did go to Ranger school, I don't trust him."

Before long they came to a bamboo thicket like none that Tony had ever seen before. These were not the slender poles that were used to stiffen carpet rolls: the stalks were eight inches in diameter and forty feet high, and so dense in some places that one had to squeeze between them as if they were the bars of a cage.

The heat was sweltering. A fine dust that itched like cracker crumbs settled on Tony's skin, and clung to his clothes. Gnats danced in-

terminably in front of his eyes, hypnotized by the bright reflection, and flew into his nose and mouth. He coughed spasmodically when they touched the back of his throat.

Crack! The rifle shot pealed out in the bamboo forest, dropping everyone to his knees. Like a billiard ball, the AK-47 bullet ricocheted off the hard-walled stems.

"Goddamn bastard," White sneered. "Why don't he show himself 'stead o' 'sneakin' aroun' like a goddamn skunk?"

Before anyone could make with a suitable reply, Yates said, "Don't even think of throwing a grenade, Rodriguiz."

Rodriguiz turned, his face a mask. He did not have a grenade in his hand. "Gimme *some* credit, amigo."

In seconds, Burns had his pants down again. "Hey, somebody gimme some TP. I'm all out."

Seconds passed. No other shots were fired, by either side. Lieutenant Blake sidled up to the point man, and asked, "Where did it come from, Rodriguiz?"

Dark, Hispanic eyes stared into the jungle. "Two hundred seventy degrees, ground level."

"Shit," the lieutenant replied. He pulled out his map and studied it for a moment. "All right, take a compass bearing on sixty degrees. I just hope the bastards aren't trying to herd us into an ambush."

Tony handed a packet of toilet paper to Burns. The machine gunner groaned and tooted. "Thanks. What a time to get the shits."

Tony crawled away from the odor. He looked up at the Puerto Rican's swarthy features, and tried to imagine how he would have looked in black pointed shoes and skintight dungarees, holding a switchblade instead of an automatic weapon. Under different circumstances, and in a different place, he would have been terribly afraid of Rodriguiz. But the jungle was no back alley, and Tony viewed Rodriguiz as his protector.

Lieutenant Blake folded his compass. "You want to be relieved?"

Rodriguiz shook his head slowly from side to side.

Tony sighed with relief. He did not want to be picked for point. Rodriguiz was the best man for the position, and the lieutenant undoubtedly knew it. However they would have related to each other back in the States, here in the jungle they shared mutual respect. They both needed each other for survival.

"Okay. But be careful." That was the closest the lieutenant could come to saying thanks.

The game of tag was wearing on everyone's nerves. Near misses were almost as debilitating as a hit.

The platoon moved quickly under Lieutenant

Blake's constant prodding. They rested infrequently. Water had become scarce since they were staying in the higher elevations. Canteens were going dry, throats were becoming parched. There was no time to look for streams. And there was the uncertain knowledge that somewhere out there, Charlie was keeping an eye on them.

Tony had no doubt that the fuzzy-faced lieutenant knew where he was going. He called the shots every time, always predicting where the terrain was going to rise, which way it would slope, even what kind of vegetation would cover the ground. His predictions were uncanny, as if this patch of jungle were the farm on which he had been born, and on which he had played as a kid. It was so late when the lieutenant called a halt, that Tony could hardly see. He struggled out of his pack.

"Have your men dig in right away, and make plenty of noise."

"Sir?" Miller squinted his eyes. He removed his steel pot and wiped sweat off shaggy black hair.

"Charlie already knows where we are. I just want to make sure he knows we're dug in deep."

The top of this hill was fairly clear, and offered a good field of fire. Most of the claymores had been blown up by artillery barrage the night before, but those that had survived were planted as protection while the men dug their foxholes. It was backbreaking work, especially after the strenuous and harrowing day. Muscles close to collapse were forced to continue working; eyes that were bleary from lack of sleep had to be kept open. And there was no chance of rest in sight.

"This is really some shit." With his entrenching tool, White hacked down a bush that was covered with sharp pointed leaves, rubbed his shin where it had been punctured, then got to digging again. "Shouldn't be out here in the first fuckin' place."

Tony pushed some medium-sized bamboo shoots out of the way, breaking them off near the ground. This gave them more clearance in front. "Did you know that bamboo is a grass?"

"Then what we need is a big fuckin' lawn mower to cut this whole damn country down to size. Can't see nothing through this shit."

Tony spaded earth into a pile. "Maybe that's good. Maybe they can't see us, either."

"They can see through anythin', and don' you forget it. This is Charlie's country." White hammered the ground with the point of his entrenching tool, using it like a hole digger. The shaft went up and down like a piston. "Let's not make this abode too big — I only want to spend the night in it, not the rest of the war."

Tony nodded in the semi darkness. He was so tired that he just wanted to be done so he could go to sleep, even if it meant never waking up. Nearby, Burns and Wallace were bantering back and forth as if they were playing croquet instead of wallowing in a war zone. Tait and Rodriguiz worked together quickly and silently, like a well-trained team. Yates puffed on a cigarette, the burning tip hidden from view by the steel pot he held in front of his face. He was not about to make a glowing target of himself.

Lieutenant Blake consulted his map by the quickly fading sunlight. "Raymonds, get command on the radio and give him these coordinates." He shoved over the scrap of paper on which he had scribbled some numbers. While everyone around him was digging, Blake sat back and relaxed for a few moments, sipping precious water from his almost empty canteen. Then he opened his last can of c-rations and watched the work in progress.

Once the digging was done, the men squatted in their holes and scavenged the last of their own rations. Tropical candy bars, the non-melt kind that had been included in the sundry packs, were shared with whomever did not mind licking the sodden mess off the wrappers. Every cracker was consumed, every piece of chewing gum swallowed. The platoon was no longer on short rations — now they were on *no* rations.

Tony chewed thoughtfully on a bamboo shoot that he had split open with his bayonet. It did not taste good at all. "You know, people around here eat this stuff." He spat out a mouthful of pulp. "But I don't know how."

White crouched in the hole with his head below ground level, dragging hard on a cigarette. "They tough people."

Now that they were on fifty percent alert, Tony found himself unable to sleep. The exertion of digging, and the gnawing at the pit of his stomach, kept him unhappily awake. Later, he felt sure, it would all catch up with him. He passed the opportunity to White. After enjoying his smoke, he curled up in the bottom of the hole and went instantly to sleep, as if he had not a care in the world.

Time dragged. Darkness settled in like a pall, shutting out the jungle as completely as if a curtain had been drawn across the front of their position. Because of the thick, overhead canopy there was no silhouette of trees against a deep purple sky — there was just unending blackness all around. The jungle sounds were the only touch with reality besides the persistent biting mosquitoes. Tony felt as if he were in a dream — or a nightmare.

His energy left him as suddenly as if a plug

had been pulled. Now he struggled to keep his eyes open. Ponderous weights dragged down his eyelids. Only his chin banging against his chest kept him from slipping away altogether. That and the fear that Lieutenant Blake would catch him napping and give him hell. That the enemy might be sneaking up on him this very minute, mattered not at all.

Sometime later, rough hands shook him violently. He struggled to open his eyes, saw White's muscular form dimly silhouetted, black on black, above him. He only vaguely remembered waking the Negro, apologizing and telling him that he could stay awake no longer, and dropping into the sanctity of the bottom of the hole. "Wake up, man. We're movin' out."

Tony pushed his fists into his eyes. "Huhn?" He peeled back the black tape, but could not read the dial of his watch because of the matter in his eyes; it did not appear to be morning. He felt as if he had fallen asleep only seconds ago.

"Get your gear on," White was saying. He was crouched over the hole, trying to pull Tony out by the armpits. Before he knew it, he was on his feet and rolling out of the hole onto the damp ground. He lay there for a moment, still groggy. Wet grass pushed against his face, tickled his nose. He had to keep brushing it away. Finally, it was too much effort to move, so he let it tickle. "Come on, Giovanni. We ain't got all night."

With great effort, Tony curled up to a sitting position. Rough hands helped him on with his web gear. "What's happening?"

"The lieutenant thinks we're gonna get 'tacked, like last night only worse."

"So where're we going?"

"Anywhere but here."

In the utter blackness, Tony fumbled with the buckles while the men were forming up around him.

"I want absolute silence," a voice whispered directly into his ear. Lieutenant Blake's tone was low, but commanding.

"Sorry, sir." By that time the platoon leader had disappeared into the shadows. With the pack finally in place, Tony looked around for some direction. In a barely audible whisper, he said, "What's going on?"

It was Corporal Yates who leaned close and said, "We're moving out in single file. Don't get more than arm's reach behind the man in front or you'll lose him. And look over your shoulder once in a while."

Then he was gone, and the column started stretching out like a hesitant caterpillar. Tony humped along like a two-legged segment.

Tree limbs slapped him constantly in the face. Vines and underbrush tangled around his feet with near intelligent intent. The mosqui-

toes became so thick that in desperation he closed his eyes and squirted the last remaining dregs of insect repellent onto his face. He smeared it on his skin with one hand, stuffed the empty plastic container into a pocket.

He first knew that the man in front of him had stopped when he ran into him. He hardly had time to get his breath back before someone crashed into him from behind. The muttered curses were quickly hushed by a curt order from Lieutenant Blake. The men crouched silently while Rodriguiz, on the point, felt for a way through a grove of bamboo.

Soon, Tony found that he had to crawl on hands and knees to get through a tangle of thick stalks that were growing like Pick-Up Sticks across their path. This midnight maneuver seemed like sheer madness — no one could possibly know where he was going, and once lost in this wilderness of jungle there would be no telling one hill from another. Tony knew that the most important thing about map reading was progressive orientation — a constant knowledge of changing locations.

Besides, all he wanted to do was sleep.

Tony bumped into a tree trunk so hard that it knocked off his steel pot. He sat rubbing his head for a moment. Someone said, "Pssst, this way." He recognized White's voice. He turned to the right and felt in the brush for a way through the thicket. His back started to ache from the weight of the pack, and his hands were getting cut from the sharp, bamboo splinters that littered the ground. At least there were no mosquitoes in here.

Lieutenant Blake called a halt in a clearing that was surrounded by the bamboo forest. Tony had no idea where they were, but he was pretty sure that no enemy troops could know either. If that had been the lieutenant's intention, he had succeeded admirably.

"All right, men, go to sleep," Blake said, adding to his squad leaders, "I'll stand guard till midnight, then you two can split the rest of the night." Their nods were invisible in the absolute blackness. Tony needed to hear no more; a moment later he was fast asleep.

Dull explosions seemed to chase him in his dreams. He tried to shake them off, but could not. Finally, he stirred enough to realize that he was not asleep, and that the explosions he heard were real. He sat up, found that the lieutenant was talking on the radio and that the rest of the men were awake, too.

"What's going on now?" he said aloud, his voice almost a shout in the jungle stillness.

"Gooks are mortaring our position," came Tait's unmistakable drawl.

Now it was all becoming clear. He listened intently as Lieutenant Blake alerted command of their situation. The explosions continued for five full minutes, then stopped abruptly. The lieutenant issued an order on the radio. Five minutes passed before incoming rounds could be heard whistling through the nighttime sky. Then the ground shook as salvo after salvo of U.S. artillery shelled their abandoned position — after having allowed enough time for the enemy to make a ground assault.

Muffled cheers ran through the platoon, and much backslapping. If all went according to Blake's calculations, they had just won a great victory over enemy forces — and they had not even been there to do the fighting.

When the noise of the shelling stopped, Lieutenant Blake's voice rang out clearly in the sudden stillness. "Andrews, you can give morphine to the wounded. Raymonds, get on the radio and tell command right on target. As for the rest of you men, you can do what you want, but I'm going to sleep." He knew that no guerrilla, no matter how refined his prowess, was going to find them — or be able to sneak up on them — in this natural bamboo fortress.

Wearily, but with wild elation, Tony curled up on the ground. Using his pack as a pillow, he made himself comfortable and fell into a deep and dreamless sleep.

Chapter 94

The most startling thing about dawn was that it arrived without fear.

Tony rubbed sleep out of his eyes and surveyed the slumbering patrol that was sacked out around him. They looked like the dead, for total exhaustion had sapped their strength and energy. Some lay stretched out, while others lay in curled, fetal positions like so many broken dolls scattered over the earth. Only spasmodic quiverings, or an occasional snore, gave any suspicion that they were in fact alive.

"How do you feel this morning?" Yates leaned against a smooth-barked tree, with his legs crossed in front of him and his rifle lying nonchalantly across his lap. He appeared totally relaxed. His steel pot lay on the ground beside him, but his short, blonde hair was still imprinted with the design of the suspension webbing.

Bleary-eyed, Tony managed a weak smile while blinking away matter that obscured his vision. "I'm sore," he croaked. "Everywhere."

Yates laughed out loud. When Tony's eyes darted around quickly, Yates said, "Don't worry, we're so far into this bamboo thicket that even if Charlie could hear us he'd never find us."

"Does that mean I can go for a walk to take care of some business?"

"By all means." Yates pulled a pack of ciga-rettes from his fatigue jacket, pulled one out and stuck it between his lips, unlit. "And while you're out there, see if you can find some water. There's not a drop left in the whole platoon."

Tony nodded. Leaving the rucksack where it lay, he donned his web gear, with canteens and ammunition pouches, and picked up his rifle by the rear sight. He climbed achingly to his feet; he was sore in more places than he knew he had places. He picked his way over the snoozing bodies to a hole in the thicket. Stooping under angled bamboo shoots, he felt like Alice in Wonderland ducking into the rabbit hole.

He pushed through broad leaves and thorny briars, careful not to get cut in the process. The ground was moist, but the air felt dry. It would not be too difficult to get lost, and it would be impossible to get found.

A minute or two later, the bamboo thinned out and Tony was able to stand up straight. He rolled his shoulders to work out the kinks. He was surprised to find that the claustrophobic bamboo jungle yielded to open forest with large, grassy spaces. Then he noticed something that he had not seen for two days — the sun. The monsoon rains had seceded, and the sky appeared in full, glorious blue. The yellow orb hovered just above the horizon. Sparkling in the airborne dust, beams of light vaulted through the now-thin treetops. The waxy surface of leaves glinted in the sunlight like miniature reflectors.

More important, he noticed that the slanted trunks were those of coconut palms — and that they were bearing fruit. Except for the coconut carved into a hideous caricature, with seashells for ears and eyes, which his parents had brought home from a Florida vacation, he had never seen one before. But he did know something about them: they contained milk, and they were edible. He suddenly forgot about the business he had come to conduct.

Dropping his gear to the ground, he sized up the angle of the tall ribbed trunk. The bark was smooth; when he placed the mud caked soles of his jungle boots against the bole, they slid right off. He was not going to be able to climb the tree native style.

He unstrapped the entrenching tool from the fanny pack, hefted it for a moment. It was thirty feet to the moplike treetop where broad leaves and coconuts sprouted from the otherwise limbless trunk. He hurled the folded tool upward; it fell short and landed with a thud nearby. It took him three more tries before he hit a branch and managed to dislodge one of the coconuts, which then almost domed him. Eagerly, he sliced open the top with his bayonet. It took five minutes of hacking before he had a hole in the thick husk from which he could suck the cool juices. He thought he had never tasted anything so good. In five more minutes he had all he could carry, and rushed back with an armload of much needed provisions.

"Hey, whatchu got there?" White was scooping peanut butter out of a can with his bayonet, and licking it from the blade.

Collapsing to his knees, Tony let his load roll to the ground. He took a quick count and figured that every man could have a half coconut, with one left over so the injured could have a whole one each.

"It's all I could find," he said, apologetically. "There was only one tree and I stripped it bare."

Half the men were awake by this time, and the resulting commotion woke up the rest. Lieutenant Blake, who had been about to report on the radio, dropped the handset and coveted the coconut that Miller handed to him. He wasted no time in hacking a small hole in the husk and sipping the surprisingly cool liquid. Then he let his squad leader finish the rest and slice it in half to get at the white pulp.

Andrews made certain that Renslow and Lieterman got their share, helping the latter because of the difficulty he was having in raising his right arm. Despite another shot of morphine, the wound was causing him great pain.

While the men ate their improvised breakfast, the medic approached Lieutenant Blake. "Sir, Lieterman's in a bad way. That gash needs to be stitched. I'm afraid it's getting infected. Any chance of getting a medevac in here?"

"It's on the way," he said matter-of-factly. "But we've got to find an LZ." Raising his voice, he said, "Giovanni, come here." Tony sidled to the lieutenant's side, and sat down. "What's it look like on the outside of this bamboo fortress? Any place for a chopper to set down?"

"Well, sir, I didn't go too far, but there seem to be clearings all around. It's real open."

"Good. Miller, Yates, get the men on their feet. We're moving out right away." He still would not talk to the men directly.

Within sixty seconds they were underway, packs and web gear hastily donned. The men stuffed their pockets with chunks of coconut meat that was yet in the shell. White was happily spreading peanut butter on his share, and taking big bites as he crawled.

Once the bamboo patch was behind them, the lieutenant ordered a V formation. In the open forest this was easy to maintain, and there were excellent fields of view all the way around. Blake calculated his precise position and radioed it to command. They soon found a suitable LZ, where a large glade afforded plenty of room for whirling helicopter blades, and set up a defense position. They did not have long to wait.

The *whup-whup-whup* of Huey blades cut through the air from the east. Even though the chopper had been sent from Pleiku, to the south, it had circled around so it could appear out of the rising sun. It hugged the treetops to reduce its visibility to ground troops, friendly and enemy alike. At Lieutenant Blake's direction, Miller popped smoke. The pilot reported a sighting of green smoke. After the RTO acknowledged the color, the Huey descended quickly. The door gunners manned their M-60s, ready for action.

"Where the rest of the choppers?" Wallace wanted to know. "We ain't all gonna fit in one."

"This is only a medevac," Yates replied.

Burns shifted his machine gun. "Yeah, well, how long we gotta wait?"

A slow smile broke out on Yates' handsome face. Somehow, he had managed to rub off most of the mud and dirt with a handkerchief, so he looked relatively clean. He had even dry-brushed his teeth. "We're not being flown out of here — we're walking."

"What the fuck you talkin' 'bout, man?" came White's startled comment.

"Where we walkin' to — Cambodia?" Burns practically yelled.

"We ain't got far to go."

Wallace held his rifle menacingly. "Hey, man, I'm flyin' out on that Huey whether you guys come or not."

With the smile still there, Yates explained calmly, "This platoon is going to continue on to its main objective, a Montagnard village about ten klicks from here. A Sidge patrol is on its way out to meet us now."

Further argument was halted by the banshee noise of the Huey's rotor compacting the air. Renslow and Lieterman, without their packs, stood waiting for the skids to touch down in the tall grass. Their buddies carried their gear and, in the seconds before touchdown, were saying their hurried good-byes. Chances were that these men, brought together through combat and hardship, would never see each other again.

The crew chief waved frantically as he kicked several cardboard cartons off the deck; they spilled open when they hit the ground. Renslow and Lieterman, helped by Belden and Norton, climbed aboard. The gear of the injured men was tossed in after them. They shook hands with their companions. Then the men on the ground backed away as the Huey surged forward and swung to the south. It left behind emptiness, and a great silence.

"Glad I didn't know 'em that good," White

said, shrugging.

"I think it stinks," Burns said resentfully. "We should at least — "

"*Do you have a complaint, soldier?*" Lieutenant Blake bellowed. He planted his face several inches in front of the machine gunner's.

"Well, sir, it's just that we've been out for two — "

"We are here to conduct a reconnaissance patrol, with or without the rest of the company. And, by god, we're going to complete the mission as planned. Is that clear?"

Burns knew when he was outdone. "Yes, sir."

"Then let's get on with it." Diverting his attention to his squad leaders, he said, "Miller, Yates, I want that food and ammo distributed immediately. We leave here in five minutes." He returned to the radio and reported the successful medical evacuation.

As the troops gathered around the supply boxes, filling their packs with bullets and c-rations, general discontent was evidenced by the many whispered comments. The men were weary and sore, thirsty and disgruntled. This was no war, but a game of hide and seek. Even now, they would not have minded fighting — if the enemy would show himself, and would stand still and fight. They were tired of fighting phantoms.

"What do we want to go to some goddamn 'Yard ville for?" Burns grumbled. "They're more backward than the paddy people."

For once Wallace disagreed with him. "At least they on our side." From his towering height he scanned the open brush land before them. "What scares me is, what's between us an' them."

"Nothin' scares me," Burns commented dryly. "I just don't see why we gotta walk while the rest of the company's gonna get choppered out."

Walk they did, over gently rolling hills that were for the most part sparsely covered with dead, brown grass and leafless trees. Patches of once-thick jungle reminded Tony of the Poconos in winter: vines were withered and dry, tree limbs were naked, foliage was nonexistent. It was as if the country were suffering an epidemic of plague.

"What's this white powder all over everything?" Tony asked, sniffing a hand that appeared to be covered with flour.

"This area's been prepped," Yates said, walking casually alongside. He wiped sweat off his brow; it was going to be one of those days. "This operation was planned months ago, so they sprayed defoliants wherever they thought Charlie might be hiding. If we have to dig him out, it'll make our job a lot easier."

"Don't mean shit," White said, spitting. "Charlie'll jus' move where they didn't spray. *If* they even sprayed the right place to begin with."

"Why are you always so cynical?"

" 'Cause I ain't gullible like some people."

A few minutes later they entered a denuded forest, and the lieutenant gave the order to set out guards. He promised them thirty minutes for breakfast. The men spread out into defensive positions, staying close to trees and fallen logs. Empty stomachs absorbed the cold meals urgently before an interruption could occur.

"Why the hell didn't they bring us some water 'stead o' ammo?" Burns, the perennial complainer, spoke in a voice that was low enough so the lieutenant could not overhear.

Wallace was quick on the uptake. "That's the army way o' sayin' suck a bullet."

"Yeah, well, I wish Cappy Collins was out here eatin' dry rations 'stead o' loungin' round the base camp waitin' for the weather to break." He looked around at the defoliated, alien landscape. "This place gives me the creeps. I don't think I'm gonna miss Vietnam at all."

"It ain't gonna miss you, either," Wallace quipped. "But one thing is for sure, it ain't gonna never be the same after we leave."

In order to have the last word, Burns added, "We ain't gonna leave no leaves."

Precisely on the minute, Lieutenant Blake rose to his feet and ordered his squad leaders to form up the men. With full bellies but parched throats, they continued on their way.

The sun was a furnace in the blue sky, sending down flames that licked at the ground and burned Tony's heels. Much-needed body moisture poured out as if he were a sponge being squeezed. He became an entity unto himself, lost in his thoughts for water. The rest of the world, the jungle, the war, had no meaning. The only item of importance was assuaging the swollen tongue that filled his mouth like a ball of cotton.

At the point, a fist rose in the air: the signal to halt. Without a word the platoon dropped to a crouch; safeties clicked off. Lieutenant Blake scrambled to where Rodriguiz was staring straight ahead with the intensity of a pointer locating a rabbit.

"What is it? What do you see?"

Rodriguiz waited a moment before answering, "Smoke."

Blake pinched his eyes. "Camp fire?"

After another pause, Rodriguiz said, "It's purple."

Tony saw the thin wisps in the trees, getting closer. Five hundred yards away a man stepped out of cover, waving a smoke flare over his head. With undue certainty he came closer, his rifle held casually to one side. Two more men appeared behind him, then three more.

"It's the Sidge patrol," Lieutenant Blake breathed. Those who were squatting nearest to him heard his assessment, and straightened up. "Get down, you fools," he barked. "Let them come to us."

The six members of the local CIDG — Civilian Irregular Defense Group — approached with great smiles on their faces. Carrying hand-me-down M-1s and faded canvas rucksacks, they were otherwise nearly naked. A loincloth was their only adornment as they walked barefoot across the open plain. All were over six feet tall, with well-defined muscles rippling under dark brown skin. Their eyes were typically epicanthic.

"Goddamn, these 'Yards are big mothers," White said in awe. To him all Vietnamese were puny runts that he could crush between two fingers.

"Bigger than you," Wallace said. "An' blacker, too."

"Knock it off, men," Yates warned. "Remember civilian relations. We don't want them to hear you talking like that."

"They don't speak English, do they?" Burns said.

"I don't think these savages speak at all," Wallace added.

But speak they did, in a strange dialect of Vietnamese that no one could understand. It was not the Oriental singsong language of the paddy peasants, but a more guttural version without specific intonations. When the lead Montagnard reached a point about five meters in front of Lieutenant Blake, who had moved forward to meet them, he gesticulated with large, vein-wrapped hands. His black, shaggy hair billowed in the soft breeze as he ended his short speech with a grin that revealed a mouth almost devoid of dental caries — without teeth one cannot have cavities.

"I think he wants us to follow him," Miller said, as he came up behind the lieutenant.

"I guess you're right, sergeant. But how the hell do I make him understand that I understand?"

"Just nod and smile like crazy." Miller set an example. Several Montagnards returned his gesture with a display of teeth stained brown with betel nut; they crowded forward, overflowing with friendliness. "Works every time."

While the soldiers of two different armies were fraternizing, it did not take long to discover that the Montagnards had something that was desperately needed: water. Out of their packs came leather containers more like carafes than canteens. These were cheerfully passed to their U.S. counterparts. It was not enough to slake everyone's thirst, but it sure took the edge off the desiccated throats.

When the last canteen was emptied, Lieutenant Blake signaled for the tribesmen to lead the way. Taking the point, and jabbering among themselves in their incomprehensible language, they headed back the way they had come. Within an easy hour's marching over rolling but clear ground, the village perimeter came into view.

Blake called a halt while he checked in with Captain Collins over the radio. "All right, men." He faced Miller and Yates but spoke loudly enough so the entire platoon could hear him. "This is where we're spending the night."

An Lap village was a true mountain aerie. It stood broad and proud on the top of a knoll that commanded a scenic view of the rolling hills to the north. It was open and spacious, with all the vegetation cut away so that the huts and animal pens were all visible at a glance. The ground was dry, pummeled to dust by generations of bare feet.

In the center of the village, three elderly, bare-breasted women stood around a mud-walled well. One cranked a thick handle that wound up a manila rope while the other two stooped over wooden tubs in which three naked children splashed water on each other. Chickens clucked and wandered freely, pecking at the ground for scraps of food. The surrounding huts were large and accommodating: they had to be, for several families shared each one. The bamboo walls were covered with woven vine matting to keep out the wind. The roofs were set on rough-hewn A-frames and covered with thatch. All the men had gathered together where they could greet the newcomers with toothy — or toothless — smiles.

Burns let out a wolfish whistle. "Get a load of this set up."

"Topless broads right out in the open," Wallace said.

There was a moment of stunned silence before White could recover from his shock. "You jokers've been out in the woods too long. These mamasans must be a hundred years old — and they're savages to boot."

"But they're *female*," Wallace responded. He and Burns started moving toward them while White stood like a rock, mouth agape. Wallace wrapped his arms around the woman turning the crank, and placed his strong hands over hers, covering them like boxing gloves. He helped her wind up the bucket.

When it reached the top of the well casing, Burns walked around to the other side of the well, pulled out his canteen, and submerged it in the cool water. Laughing uproariously, he poured it over his head, onto his face, into his mouth, gulping as much of it as he could and letting the rest dribble down the front of his shirt. A moment later the rest of the men surged ahead. There followed a wild melee while everyone strove to get his canteen filled.

The three women dragged their children away, smiling all the time at the soldiers' antics as they doused each other playfully. White took his share, but remained sour. "Those jokers outfoxed me."

"All right, men, knock it off." Lieutenant Blake did not make it sound like an order. A sense of camaraderie was needed in the field, but he could not afford to lose his control over his men.

By now they were surrounded by friendly Montagnard tribesmen who were all smiles and rotting teeth. One of them was positively ancient, sporting a great, gray beard that covered dark skin with washboard corrugations. But the eyes twinkled with energy and intelligence. He was the village chief. Lieutenant Blake, using sign language and the few words of Vietnamese that he had picked up during his short time in country, tried to get him to understand that his men needed to establish a defense perimeter. Several hundred meters away there was another hill, connected to the hamlet by a worn path. It had been cleared of trees and would suit his purposes admirably. All he wanted to do was to dig a few holes. . . .

Meanwhile, the other tribesmen mingled with the troops and eyed their clothing and belongings enviously. One of them was smiling and pointing to the chain around Tait's neck. He held up a basket in which he had some fruit, then indicated the chain again.

"Well, I guess Uncle Sam wouldn't mind a little bartering." Tait grinned as he undid the hasp, removed his dog tags, put them in his pocket, and handed over the chain. The tribesman was ecstatic at this connecting bit of metal, and handed the basket to Tait. "Now which piece do I want?" But the Montagnard walked off chattering happily, and left him with the whole basket. "Hell, somehow this doesn't seem quite fair, getting all this fruit for one lousy ten-cent chain."

He picked out a fresh mango, carved into it with his bayonet, and sliced off a chunk. He chewed it longingly, and handed a piece to Tony. The fruit was deliciously cool and sweet, unlike anything he had ever tasted before. He sucked up every bit of juice.

"Hey, let me have one of those bananas." White reached into the basket and plucked out a bent yellow fruit that was firm to the touch. It proved to be impossible to peel, however, so he lopped off the top with his bayonet. A moment later he spat out the white pith. "This thing's not ripe yet. It's sour."

"That's because it's not a banana, you idjit," Wallace laughed. "It's a plantain."

"Looks like a banana to me." White wiped his tongue on his shirtsleeve. "Got a awful aftertaste, too."

By this time the bartering was in full session as the men relieved themselves of any bits of metal they could find. Coins, bracelets, rings, pen knives, even paper clips bought more food than they could carry, ranging from coconuts to fruit to monkey meat to uncooked rice.

Tony rummaged through his pack for trade goods. "My dog tags were stolen out of my footlocker at Fort Dix, and I'm not about to give up *this* chain." He kept a grip on the St. Christopher's medal. "It's silver, and was a gift." The only thing he could find were some French Indo-China coins with holes drilled through them. He had collected them at Dong Hoa before it had been demolished. These were not high on the priority list, but he was able to obtain a fresh coconut that was twice as large as those that he had collected that morning, as well as a split bamboo shoot with the pulp exposed. The Montagnard grinned as he tried to peddle his wares to Rodriguiz, who had stayed apart from the group and watched the proceedings with a disdainful eye.

"You right. This don't seem fair, somehow." Wallace bit into a mango that he had bartered his key chain for. "I feel like a thief."

Burns stuffed fruit into his fanny pack. "What're you worried about, man? Metal's a rare commodity to these savages. An' the fruit don't cost 'em nothin'. They just go out an' pick some more."

Meanwhile, Lieutenant Blake somehow got through the idea that he wanted to encamp on the neighboring hill, and got what he thought was an okay. He ordered Miller and Yates to get the men away from the villagers and get dug in. Grumbling, the two squads sauntered down the shallow depression that separated the two hills. The tribesmen waved as they went, holding aloft more of their wares. But the soldiers had work to do.

Cleared as it was, the hill commanded an excellent field of fire. The jungle came to within two hundred meters of the south side. The jungle veered westward from there, stopping at an open field where the path continued through the foliage. To the east was the village, and to the north the slope ran gently downward to a vast plain that stretched for miles, and was broken only by occasional trees. It was mostly grazing land for the village's water buffalo.

Lieutenant Blake selected the locations for the foxholes. They were widely separated, and made a circle about a hundred yards across.

"Big enough so when the rest of the company gets here we can use it as a base camp."

Yates assigned the men to their positions. "Tait, I want you and Giovanni on this side, overlooking the village. I don't trust any of these other trigger-happy bozos. Burns, set up the machine gun on the far left. Make sure you can cover the trail where it meets the jungle, but be able to sweep the field in front, too. Rodriguiz, White, dig your hole somewhere in the middle where you can reach everywhere with the grenade launcher." He paused for a moment, then added, "And when you're done, you've got the afternoon off."

With that kind of incentive, it did not take long to make defensive positions, erect ponchos for shade, and clear the little bit of brush that might conceal enemy infiltrators. There were no claymores for an outer screen, so Rodriguiz rigged some hand grenades as booby traps, although Yates warned him not to arm them until nightfall. After all, this was a peaceful village, and they did not want any Montagnards to get hurt by accident.

Lying shiftless on the ground, Tait made himself busy by getting a tan in the afternoon sun. He never seemed to sweat, but gladly soaked up the yellow rays from which everyone else was hiding. He was so lean that Tony could easily see his ribs protruding; his skin seemed to hang on him like a salted side of beef. He certainly did not look his age.

"I still don't understand about your wife — er, your ex-wife." Tony sat cross-legged on the ground, playing with tufts of grass as he looked out over the broad valley, where a dozen water buffalo ambled across the grassy plain, oblivious of the clear blue sky and the white, puffy clouds. "Why did she want to get you drafted?"

"Well, it was like this," he explained, in his lazy drawl. "We'd been married for about five years when she ran off with this other guy — then she got it into her head she wanted to move back into our house. I was living there with another gal, and didn't want to move, naturally. I'd done a lot of work on the old place. Fixed it up from little more than a shack, really. Put a couple additions on the place 'cause I was planning on having a family someday." Now he switched time frames without slowing down the story. "But she got a notion into her head that I was moving along too slow. I wasn't advancing fast enough in the firm — she wanted me to move into management where there was more money. But I liked being an engineer."

"Where was this? What state?"

"Oklahoma. In a little town called Wheatland, right outside Oklahoma City." Tait closed his eyes, and conjured up images from the past.

"I can still see that whitewashed house with the stoop in front, and the rickety screen door I never got around to fixing, and the shutters that protected the windows from windstorms and tornadoes. I can even see the improvements that have to be made.

"Well, there was just no way I could please her. She wanted to live in a big house and have maids and have her hair done twice a week and not have to worry about nursing the kids — when they came along. So she went and found somebody else, a guy who was older and used to spread greenbacks around like they were playing cards. Only after she went to live with him she found that he couldn't have kids, and the house he lived in was mostly mortgaged, and the stocks he had were almost worthless. He was living high on the hog, but it was all on borrowed money.

"Now she was sorry she hadn't had any kids by me when we were married. At least she could have taken them with her. And she always did love that house, even though it was small and didn't have room for maids. He had to sell his place to pay off some debts, and she didn't want to live in an apartment, so she went after mine. Claimed that half of it was due her because we'd bought it when we were married."

"Did she work at all?" Gorged on native fruit, Tony twisted tufts of grass into little knots, making a lacework out of them. "I mean, had she done anything to earn any of it?"

"According to the law, a woman don't have to work for anything. If she's married, half of anything her husband makes belongs to her, whether she was a good wife or not. So she hired a lawyer — paid him out of her alimony —"

"You mean, you had to pay alimony even though *she* left *you*?"

"That's what the law says."

"But, she was living with another man."

"Don't matter. She wasn't married to him. And as long as there was nothing legal between 'em, I had to pay."

"But, that doesn't sound fair."

In his soulful, winsome way, Tait said, "I'm not making judgments, and I don't make the law — I only abide by it." He paused to brush a fly off the end of his nose. "Anyhow, the judge ruled that half the place was hers. But you can't cut a house in half, so I either had to come up with the money to buy her out, or sell the place. But she didn't want me to have it — said if she couldn't have it, nobody could. So she went to the draft board in Oklahoma City and told them we were divorced and why wasn't I drafted."

"She went there — personally?" To Tony,

this story was getting weirder and weirder.

"Must have, 'cause when I got my notice to appear, I took my girlfriend with me — I told you this before, didn't I?" Tait said, but kept on with his tale. " — and told them she was my wife. We even had identification to prove it. But they had a copy of the divorce decree, and knew I was lying. A few weeks later I was in the Army."

"But what about your house?" By this time Tony had lost all interest in the lacework of grass.

"I don't know." Tait's eyes twitched, as if he had suffered a twinge of pain. "I left it in the hands of our firm's attorney. He said he would try to block the sale until I could get a loan to buy her out. But being over here, I don't know. There's not much I can do about it from over here."

The sun continued to beat down, endlessly, tirelessly. It was the only thing in this war, in this world, that was unchanging.

****

"Amigo, I t'ink you better move." Rodriguiz spoke calmly as he stuck his spoon into a can of beans and franks, shoved another mouthful into his mouth.

White was asleep. He had piled dirt in front of their foxhole high enough so he could prop himself up against it and stare at the fading sunset. The exertion of the past two days had completely exhausted him, and in the warmth of the rays he had dozed off. His legs stretched out across the beaten path that led to the village, but so far not a single Montagnard had made use of it.

Slightly louder, but without any sense of urgency, Rodriguiz said, "Amigo, you gonna be sorry you don't move soon."

White half-opened his eyes, groaned, and rolled over onto his side. He lay still for perhaps five seconds while his abysmally dark eyes slowly focused on an approaching tank-sized shape. It was not until after he heard the high-pitched wail that he began to move.

A gnomelike, toothless mamasan, who stood barely four feet tall, was chattering away angrily in highland Vietnamese. Except for a loincloth she was completely naked. Her parchmentlike skin was wrinkled like that of an Egyptian mummy. Her tiny breasts hung straight down like two desiccated prunes. In one gnarled hand she held a slender stick which she whipped constantly, and in the other she held a halter fastened to the neck of a fifteen-hundred-pound water buffalo. She beat the beast around the neck and head and dragged it forward against its will.

White was just about to be trampled upon as the old mamasan ignored his presence — and

predicament — on the path. With a sudden yell he contracted his legs and pushed hard as he scrambled to get out of the way. His action took him over the top of the dirt mound, still yelling; he fell headlong into the foxhole.

Burns and Wallace roared with laughter, while Tait merely shook his head. Tony ran forward to see if he could help. Rodriguiz sat placidly, took another bite of food.

With great difficulty, White managed to turn himself around in the narrow hole. He poked his head up in time to see the mamasan punch the water buffalo hard between the eyes, screaming foreign obscenities. They trudged past, toward the village. Behind came three more animals, led by younger and prettier girls who were hardly out of their teens. By contrast their skin was fair and soft, and their hair hung down in tresses to their rounded shoulders. One by one they smiled at the men as they led their beasts of burden along the path. Burns and Wallace were caught between laughing at White's predicament, and leering after the youthful topless females.

The entire scene was brought to a close as Lieutenant Blake, coming along the same path from the village, veered toward the hole where Raymonds had placed the radio set, and directed Yates to alert his men. None of them had seen the incident.

"Looks like we've walked into a rat's nest," Blake said seriously. When no one questioned him, he went on anyway. "Miller was using sign language to talk to the village chief. The old geezer was more than willing to talk about his people, his buffalo, his rice. But the only thing he said that we understood was 'Beaucoup VC. Beaucoup VC.' Seems like the NVA has been pulling operations all around here, and taxing these people in rice and beef to support their army. We may get attacked any time."

The order of the night was fifty percent alert. The Montagnards had been put on a curfew — they were not allowed to leave the village grounds after dark. If any movement was reported, the men were instructed to shoot on sight — no questions asked.

That night, Tony watched the fires burn on the adjacent hill. From his vantage point overlooking the village, he could see people moving by candlelight inside their hooches. He could see what he thought was dancing, and hear the voices of children in song.

These were the happy, innocent people he had come all this way to protect.

Chapter 95

The Hueys landed only a few minutes after dawn. Men, ammunition, and supplies were disembarked onto the huge range where water buffalo had not yet been led out to graze. The grass was flattened and whipped about by a dozen prop washes. What had been bright green a moment before was now olive drab, as troops waded through the field.

Within minutes the helicopters were gone, leaving behind the remnants of Company B and piles of packing cases. Lieutenant Blake ordered his men to stand fast while he and Miller greeted Captain Collins. Since their position was secure, the lieutenant saluted his superior.

Returning the salute smartly, the captain said, "Well done, Lieutenant. You've done a damned fine job and I'm proud of you and your men."

"Thank you, sir." Lieutenant Blake revealed no emotion in his reply. He then briefed the captain on what he had learned so far from the village chief.

Captain Collins told him that the Kit Carson scout, Lieutenant Thang — would conduct an additional interview.

While Blake's platoon stayed in their foxholes and acted as guard, the rest of the company was given the task of carrying the several tons of materiel up the hill: watertight cans of 5.56 mm ammunition for the M-16s, 7.62 mm ammunition and the M-60s; cases of hand grenades, smoke grenades, tear gas grenades, and 40 mm rounds for the M-79 grenade launcher; tripod mounts for the machine guns; scores of c-ration cartons, twelve meals each; and tied bundles of burlap sand bags. A lot of entrenchment was planned.

"What are the gas masks for?" Tony asked Tait, as he watched the antlike procession of supplies being carried past.

"My guess is that Charlie is dug in pretty deep, and we're going to gas him out."

Tony finished brewing a cup of coffee, and placed a can of "ham and eggs chopped" over the Heatab flame. Together they ate a leisurely breakfast while the work went on around them. The command post was designated, and a detail was assigned to dig it and use the dirt to fill the sandbags. Everywhere was a flurry of activity as the platoons were given defensive positions and the men made a perimeter of foxholes.

****

Two Negroes dropped their packs about ten feet away. Tony recognized the men from the chopper ride on his first day in the bush. It seemed like so long ago — or was it only a few weeks? On patrol, there was little fraternization among platoons, each existing almost as a separate unit.

"Hey, dago," Pepper called out. With a toothy grin on his face, he crouched down so he could reach Tony, standing in his foxhole. "Don't remember your name, but it was Eye-

talian, wasn't it?"

Tony held out his hand. "Giovanni."

Pepper shook it vigorously. Tilting his head toward Henderson, he said, "Hey, nigger, come over here."

Henderson put down his entrenching tool and sauntered closer. He nodded down at Tony. "Heard you got into some heavy shit. Two casualties?"

"Renslow and Lieterman, from A squad. Wounded, but not too badly."

Tony pointed with his plastic spoon. "Uh, Tait, this is Pepper, and this is Henderson."

"No, *I'm* Henderson. *He's* Pepper."

"Sorry. Anyway, Renslow took some mortar shrapnel, Lieterman got hit by a sniper."

"What happened to your helmet?" Pepper pointed with his chin. "You using it for a bowling ball?"

Tony grinned, taking pride in the close call. "It was the first night out. The first mortar round landed right behind me. I was a little slow in ducking." He shrugged it off.

"A little slower and you'd a been Swiss cheese," Henderson said. Then, to goad Pepper, he added, "At least it was *enemy* shrapnel."

"Knock it off, nigger," Pepper sneered.

"Who you callin' nigger, nigger?"

"Who the fuck you think I'm callin' nigger, these two white boys?"

"Man, if I didn't think you were gonna save my black ass some day, I'd knock those pearly whites down your goddamn throat."

"Bah," Pepper growled. "You and who's army? Hey, Giovanni, what's the scoop, man? Is this place surrounded by VC like they say it is?"

"I don't know."

"We were hoping *you* could tell us something," Tait said.

Pepper spat on the ground. "They don't tell us grunts nothing. We never know what to 'spect. You'd think it was a big secret that only ocifers are allowed to know."

"We heard the village chief said there were a lot of VC," Tony admitted. "I guess the interpreter will find out the details."

"I don't trust these Vietnamese dudes." Henderson scratched his crotch and pulled his pants away from the skin. "I think half of 'em are on the enemy payroll, collectin' from both sides. Shit, they don't give a shit who wins, as long as they're on the winnin' side."

"You don't trust nobody," Pepper said accusingly.

"And why should I? All these gooks are alike — they just as soon blow you away as look at you."

"Let's cut out this shit, man. We got a hole to dig — before we get both our asses kicked."

"Are you going to dig in over there?" Tony indicated where they had dropped their packs.

"No, our platoon's over on the other side. But we got to dig a hole for your guys, 'cause we're takin' over their hole."

"Those two ball bustin' machine gunners of yours," Henderson added. "They got an act that oughta go on stage."

Even the placid Tait smiled at that. "They do kind of grow on you."

"I wouldn't mind diggin' this hole if Wallace wasn't so damn big." Pepper complained. "We gonna hafta dig half way to China."

"You're almost *in* China," Henderson retorted.

"Then we'll dig our way back home."

For the next hour they swung their entrenching tools furiously, then picked up their gear, waved, and departed. By noontime the whole platoon was back together. Then Lieutenant Blake sent them, a squad at a time, on water detail. Each man went to the village with two five-gallon gerry cans, to be filled from the well. The Montagnards seemed happy to have U.S. troops in their village.

"Ain't these little fellers cute?" White scooped up one naked three-year-old in his great, black palms, and cradled him as if he were his own.

Burns poured water from a bucket into a can. "Hey, White. I never knew you had fatherly instincts."

"Got a couple youngsters of my own back home," White said proudly.

"I didn't even know you were married."

"I ain't. But I love kids — love their mothers, too. Both of 'em. Suppose I'll hafta marry one of 'em when I get home. Don't know which one, though."

The little boy was smiling, and playing with the pocket flaps of White's jungle fatigue jacket. Deftly, he unbuttoned one and brought out a pack of cigarettes. White laughed, and took it away from him. "Try the other one, son." Seeming to understand, the boy did — and to his delight found a candy bar. His eyes lit up like headlamps as he peeled off the wrapper and took a big bite of the tropical chocolate.

Within seconds the men were surrounded by a flock of squawking children, all holding out their hands. White unloaded a lower pocket and, before he could say a word, a dozen tiny hands plucked at the candy he brought out of it.

"Where the hell'd you get all that stuff?" Yates wanted to know.

"Shit, man, they musta brung in ten sundry packs from the Red Cross, an' we ain't never gonna eat it all. Most of it's been melted ten times already an' ain't no good."

White unbuttoned the other pocket with some difficulty because he had to shift the little boy to his other arm. Out came a pile of small toothpaste tubes. One girl, taller than the rest, grabbed his hand, causing him to spill them onto the ground. Then there was pandemonium as the children scrimmaged for the tubes. They soon learned how to unscrew the tops and suck out the mint-flavored paste.

Wallace shook his head. "Never thought I'd see the day you'd be givin' out food."

"You gotta take care o' kids," White said, behind a happy smile. "Nobody else can. That's why I never got no money. I send it home to take care o' the little fellers."

Some of the Montagnard women now crowded around, smiling at the children's excitement. They were either ancient hags, or breastfeeding. All able-bodied women were either working in the fields or tending the livestock.

One young mother approached Tony with a beckoning hand. She was clean and pretty, with skin that was still soft and supple, yet bronzed by the tropical sun. A smile piqued her broad cheeks, framed by long black hair that hung straight down over her shoulders. She wore only a loincloth, and cradled an infant at her breast, immodestly suckling it as if it were the most natural thing in the world. Despite his discomfiture, Tony realized that it *was* the most natural thing in the world.

Tony started fumbling with his jacket pockets, for he suddenly remembered the extra c-ration cans that he had tucked away for later. He found two, and promptly offered them to this smiling, and somehow happy, mother. As she took the cans, mumbling incomprehensively in her native language, Tony's eyes were drawn to the naked baby at her breast.

It was like a wind-up doll, with a little patch of dark hair on its crown. The tiny feet kicked spasmodically, while one hand clutched at the air. It was so small, so defenseless — Tony wished that he had more to give. Then, he turned red in a flush of self-consciousness as he suddenly became aware of where he was staring. He looked up, and the mother did not seem to mind, or even to have noticed. To her it was part of life.

"Hey, how about if y'all get a little closer together." Tait backed away, holding a miniature camera to his eye. "I want to take a picture."

"You got that camera out again?" Burns said loudly. "I haven't seen it for so long I thought you lost it."

Still backing away, panning the camera for composition, Tait said, "Ah haven't seen anything worthwhile taking a picture of." He clicked the shutter once, then backed further away and clicked again. "Now wait a minute," he called out, "let me take one from a different angle."

"How about you get me and mamasan together?" Wallace said, throwing his long arm about an old woman's shoulders and squeezing her tight. She looked up at him — her face was level with his stomach — and smiled.

"Why don't you grab her tit, man?" Burns said, laughing.

"You got a one track mind," was White's perturbed comment. He scowled, then turned to face the camera.

Rodriguiz, for once, became part of the group. His normally frozen features relaxed, his coiled-spring body released its tension. For the moment there was no danger. The closeness of these Montagnard women and children must have reminded him of his life in the tenements of New York City, where he had been crowded into a one-room existence with his mother and two brothers and three sisters. Tony surmised too that the absence of the men folk must have hit on a subconscious level. Rodriguiz was the kind who would not allow himself to feel the abandonment, the loneliness, the inner hatred. That was what gave him such strong self-assurance.

Yates stayed well out of camera range, a scowl on his face. "Let's quit playing around. We've got a job to do. Tait, put that camera away."

There were shouts of "spoilsport," "slave master," and "relax, man," as the men struck appropriate poses.

White gathered the children around him. "Hey, man. These kids have never seen a camera before."

The children did not seem to understand what was. But if it was all right with the adults, it must be acceptable procedure. They, too, smiled at the lens.

Tait snapped several more shots.

"Come on," Yates insisted. "Let's get the water before the lieutenant sends a search party after us."

"Hey, man," Burns said. "You forget, this is the number one squad, and nothing don't happen to us. We go through mortars, artillery, snipers, anything they can throw at us, and we always come through smellin' like a rose."

Before Yates could object, several of the children started chanting, "Numba One GI. Numba One GI."

"You got that right, kid. We're number one. We're gonna go through these hills like Grant took Richmond." The rest of the men cheered him on.

Yates let the mood run its course. After the men had had their fun, they got on with the job of filling the gerry cans. Leading the children like the Pied Piper of Hamelin, the squad debarked up the hill. The mothers showed no anxiety as their youngsters skipped along after them. It was Yates who prevented their further progress by standing in the path and shooing them back to their village. "Screaming little brats. They never want to take orders."

In the matter of a few hours the hilltop had been transformed from a quiet patch of brush to a bustling military outpost. Foxholes now circled the brow of the hill, while in the middle a command post had been dug in the ground and walled in with sandbags. From there Captain Collins was directing construction, studying maps and plotting coordinates, consulting with his platoon leaders, and checking endless details over the radio with Colonel Adams.

When Tony was sent to collect a case of C's for lunch, he hung around long enough to pick up a few details. So far the entire operation had been one big snafu. Captain Collins had advised the colonel to hold back that first day when his Third Platoon had been infiltrated to secure a landing zone. The timing was off, the weather was against them, and intelligence proved faulty. Now the colonel was taking a new tack, placing the companies under his command in different locations where, over the course of the next few weeks, or months, or however long it took, they could seek out the enemy's hiding places and catch him in a pincer movement as the entire brigade closed in from all sides. The colonel wanted this operation to work. It *had* to work, because he was due to rotate soon and he had accomplished nothing of note in ten months of service. If he was going to get a promotion out of this tour, he needed to go out in a blaze of glory. For that he was willing to give it his all, with whatever he had in the way of equipment, ammunition, and personnel. Let it never be said that Lieutenant Colonel Charles Bradey Adams was not willing to sacrifice.

That night, on the hill, in fresh mountain coolness, Tony watched the Montagnards by the light of their fires. The livestock was penned for the night, the tables were laden with fresh fruit, and the men had come home to their families. Children frolicked with their fathers, women with their husbands. It appeared to be such a simplistic life, without mortgage payments, without car insurance, without unemployment.

Andrews tramped along the beaten trail, dragging his medical kit as if it were a ton of bricks. He plopped down next to the foxhole like a deflated blow-up doll. "I'm beat."

Tony held out the canteen cup of coffee. "What were you doing in the village?"

The medic took the cup by the metal handle

and gulped down the brew. "Medical treatments."

"They got wounded down there?" White said.

"No, disease. The people have everything you can imagine: cholera, typhoid, TB, diphtheria. Most of it I can't even recognize. Hell, I'm only a medic, but I know they have typhus 'cause all the dogs have fleas. The men have open wounds, and won't treat it. They believe it comes from a bad wind. I gave every one a tetanus shot. But that goddamned Thang walked out on me. Now I can't even talk to the people. And I don't have the supplies, or the equipment. These people need real help, more than I can give them. I just wish there was more I could do."

Chapter 96

Cambodia, they said, was just around the corner. The company commanders, the platoon leaders, the forward artillery observers, the pilots flying cover: they all had maps and knew coordinates. But the grunt in the field just went where he was pointed and did what he was told. One patch of jungle looked just like any other, was just as hot, had just as many mosquitoes, could be as beautiful or could conceal as many booby traps. The boundaries were political, existing only in the minds of men. Nature did not recognize them.

Central highlands or rice paddy lowlands, the villages looked pretty much the same. As they approached this one in company strength, the people looked up from their work. Soldiers were a common sight to them: their curiosity lasted just long enough to determine which army was invading them now.

Captain Collins gave orders to his platoon leaders to institute a search. While First and Second Platoons looked through the hooches and gathered the inhabitants in a central location, Third Platoon spread out and surrounded the perimeter, beating the bush for escaping VC suspects. It was all pretty much by the book, and no one sweated it out.

Tony was glad that they had left their heavy packs behind. The web gear was heavy enough, especially with the extra ammunition that they had been ordered to carry. With his entrenching tool, he hacked at vines and thickets in his search for enemy signs, mines, or hiding places for men and materiel. As in Dong Hoa, the people here were classified as VC sympathizers.

What that meant in practical terms was that if the people of the village were coerced under threat of death to supply food and shelter for the enemy, they would comply.

Next to an outlying hut stood a storage shed that looked much like an American outhouse, except that the door opened only from about halfway up. It was kept closed by a simple wooden handle that pivoted on a rusty nail.

"Check it out," Yates said to Tony. Yates moved on with the rest of the squad, leaving Tait behind. They were working on the buddy system — no one was allowed to be alone even to perform bodily functions. And if possible, the squads should stay within hearing range of each other.

Tait pointed his M-16 cocked and ready. He nodded for Tony to go ahead. He rotated the latch, swung wide the door, and peered inside. It was filled with rice to within six inches of the sill. Tony remembered the incident in Dong Hoa. He hated to deprive these people of their precious food supply by scattering their rice on the ground.

"It's just rice," he said to Tait.

Tait pursed his lips and nodded. "You heard what the man said. Check it out."

Shrugging, Tony leaned his rifle against the shed. He stuck both hands into the rice and sifted the white grains through his fingers. He tossed it up into the air, inside the bin, taking care that none of it escaped through the open door. The food here would feed the village for many months.

"Hey," he yelped, jerking his hands out quickly. "Something bit me." He looked to Tait for advice.

Tait's eyes narrowed. "Sometimes rats burrow into the rice. Even raise their babies there. Plenty of food."

Tony inspected his finger, saw a tiny scratch. "No, I think this was just a splinter." He reached back into the rice and felt around more carefully. A moment later he brought out a contraption that had bare wires leading out of it. His heart sank as he stared at it, waiting for the device to explode. He was paralyzed.

Tait took it from him, twisting it around to view it from all sides. "Don't know what it is, but we better show it to Yates. Start scooping out the rest of that rice. I'll be right back."

While Tait was looking for Yates, Tony opened his entrenching tool and, with tentative strokes, pushed it into the bin of rice and started making a neat pile on the ground. He had half of the bin empty when Tait returned with Yates in tow.

"Step aside," the squad leader said.

"I haven't found anything else."

Ignoring him, Yates stood in front of the storage shed and with a mighty kick knocked in the bottom boards. Again and again he kicked, until he made a sizeable hole and the rice poured onto the ground. He grabbed Tony's entrenching tool, and, using it as a pick, stabbed into the remaining rice. He pulled the dried grains through the hole until he was scraping the wooden floor.

"Let's knock this thing over. No telling what might be under it."

Tony picked up his rifle and leaned it against a stand of bamboo. All three of them pushed on one side until the shed toppled. It went only partway before the roof crashed into the trunk of a eucalyptus tree. Yates got down on his knees and surveyed the ground under the floor. It appeared to be solid.

A rifle cracked close by, sending a quick chill along Tony's spine. A moment later the village erupted with the sustained roar of machine gun fire, followed by staccato bursts of automatic weapons and the explosion of a grenade.

Yates ran off in a flash, followed by Tait. Tony scrambled to pick up his entrenching tool and his rifle, and chased after them. The machine gun stopped and started again. Tony charged into a wide path that led toward the ruckus, bounded by bamboo shoots and tall shade trees that arched overhead like a covered bridge. He stopped short at a bend in the trail.

He found himself alone, in the open. Before he could even wonder where the other men had gone, he saw a man pop out of a hole in the middle of the worn path. What happened next occurred so fast that it was not until afterward that Tony was able to piece together the proper sequence of events.

A shaggy bush of swept-back hair covered a dirty, slant-eyed face that appeared amazingly calm under the circumstances. The camouflaged jacket was buttoned tightly around a dark-skinned neck. Something round and dull-colored left his hand, came bouncing down the trail like an out-of-bound foul.

Tony dived out of the way. Guns crackled from the brush. Spurts of dust leaped off the soft dirt like raindrops plopping in mud. The body in the spider hole danced in a strange rhythmic pattern that was punctuated by flying lead, seemed to disintegrate as pieces of olive drab material and blood-flecked flesh flew away in a cloud. The eyes closed, the jaw slackened, the head descended into the hole as if on a slow moving elevator. Bamboo smacked against Tony's face, parted, tore at his clothes. Then came a deafening roar, and he was lying on the ground staring up at the sky through reddened eyes, as splinters of metal and wood soared over him.

In the silence that followed, Tony rolled over and found that his worst injury was a bruised forehead and scraped wrists. He was still on his hands and knees when Lieutenant Blake grabbed him by the shoulder and flung him upward.

"Are you okay?"

Tony nodded, and said weakly, "I — I think so."

A voice that was unmistakably Sergeant Miller's, shouted, "Cover me. Cover me." The lieutenant charged into the opening that Tony had made through the thicket, turned and raced along the path. Tony followed him.

By this time Sergeant Miller was already standing over the spider hole, looking down with his rifle only inches away from the shattered lid. Men started crawling out of the bushes. Lieutenant Blake hurried forward, stood opposite Miller, and peered into the dark hole.

"Get him out of there," he ordered.

Both squads surrounded the spider hole. Tony pushed through the tight knot of men to see what was happening. Miller dropped his rifle, got down on both knees, and grabbed the dead guerrilla by the armpits. He pulled him halfway out before Yates got there and lent a hand. Together they yanked the body out, and dropped it on the ground as if it were a sack of flour. There was surprisingly little blood for the amount of holes in the chest and back: it was as if the body had been stung by a hundred maddened wasps, red splotches mute evidence of the painful stings.

Miller jumped into the hole and tossed out the guerrilla's belongings: two Chinese potato masher hand grenades with long stick handles, a worn rucksack, and an entrenching tool. Lieutenant Blake turned the rucksack upside down. It contained precious little: two bananas, a ball of cooked rice, some manioc roots, a green head mask, a hammock, a camouflaged cover under which one could lie in the open and not be seen from the air, and a wallet containing faded black and white pictures of his family. The man had probably not seen his loved ones for months, perhaps years.

"Don't he got no rifle?" White asked, bending low over the hole. Miller climbed out, saying, "Check it out for yourself."

"Not me, man. I ain't no tunnel rat. Tight places scare me."

Burns scowled down at the dead soldier. "What about those tight places you got into back home, where those kids come from?"

"Knock it off," Yates said, scowling.

Burns turned and stepped back, grumbling, "The first gook we see on this op, an' my fuckin' gun jams."

"You said you wanted contact, man," Wallace reminded him.

"Yeah, but I wanna shoot the mother fuckers."

Burns walked straight into Captain Collins. The captain was wearing a face that would melt stone. "Mister, we're out here to win a war, not to kill people for the sake of killing. And you'd better remember that."

Burns wilted slightly, muttering the appropriate "Yes, sir" in a tone that was not at all sincere.

"What have we got here, Lieutenant?"

"Sir, it appears to be a VC guerrilla. It's not in proper uniform and — "

"You mean 'he'." Captain Collins interrupted.

"Sir?"

"*He* appears to be a VC guerrilla."

"Uh, yes, sir. It's not — he's not wearing a proper uniform and, uh, he's not carrying a weapon — just grenades. We got him as he was coming out of the hole throwing — "

"I see." The captain interrupted again, looked around, spotted Raymonds. "Get back to Base Camp and report this. Tell them — " Shouting broke out in another area, followed by gunfire. On the run, he finished, "I'll get back to the colonel later." His voice was fading in the distance as he shouted over his shoulder, "Check him out for ID."

Lieutenant Blake took a step after his commanding officer, and stopped. Slowly, he turned around, his jaw working silently. "Okay, let's get on with it. We got a body count of one, let's see how many more we can add to it. Miller, see if he's got any papers on him."

In a battlefield without front or rear, where the presence of the enemy was the only point of reference, a dead enemy soldier was the only tangible proof that the fight was being won — if not by acquiring land as in conventional warfare, then by attrition.

"For God's sake, spread it out. One grenade would get you all."

Miller checked the dead man's pockets, but found nothing.

"And let's be careful. I don't want nobody hurt."

Before moving out, Tony stared long and hard at the dead man. The face was contorted in pain, and the upper body was so pockmarked with bullet holes that no one person could claim a kill. The sight was an ugly one. Andrews stooped by the lifeless thing — the *he* that was now an *it* — and squeezed the limp wrist, feeling for a pulse. He took the dead man's poncho and covered the face and body. Tony walked away with a sickness in the pit of his stomach. Now he had seen death. And in his mind he could not forget the smiling faces in those pictures that fell from the enemy soldier's knapsack.

The cluster separated and the search went on. They poked and prodded every bush, inspected every bamboo thicket, kicked every piece of ground that had a covering of grass or thatch. Tony, still shaken, was extra cautious; complacency was a thing of the past.

Raymonds reported to the lieutenant. "Sir, I got a call from the captain. He says that shootin' was a case of mistaken identity. First platoon firin' on second platoon. Nobody hurt."

"Don't they know what the hell they're doing?"

"I don't care what the old man says, I wanna kill me some gooks," Burns said, seeking sympathy. "We ain't out here for no Sunday stroll."

"Is that why you joined the Army?" Wallace poked his rifle into a thicket. Despite the calmness of his voice, he moved slowly and deliberately, his finger wrapped around the trigger.

"Wipe your mouth out with soap." Burns let the other men poke the bushes while he kept his machine gun ready to pour support fire where it was needed. "Ain't nobody in his right mind would *ask* for this kinda duty. But as long's I'm here, I'm gonna make sure somebody pays for it."

"Very commendable — an' patriotic," Wallace returned.

"Don't go givin' me no patriotic shit. I don't see you wavin' no flags."

White joined the repartee. "The lieutenant sure ain't got no gripe against killin' the bastards. He wants to beef up his career an' attrite as many gooks as he can."

"Quiet, amigos," came Rodriguiz's sibilant voice. Burns swung the M-60. The short man was poised like a hound dog pointing out a nest of pheasants. The deadly silence lasted for long seconds as every man in the squad stopped in mid stride.

Tait was closest to him. He whispered, "What is it?"

Rodriguiz pointed with his rifle. His flak jacket stirred as he drew in a breath. Slowly, he put one foot forward. His dark eyes scrutinized every blade of grass, every bamboo shoot. If there was a piano wire there, a trip device for a booby trap, he was not going to step on it. But that one patch of ground was suspiciously bare, and unnaturally angled.

Deftly, with one hand, Rodriguiz unclipped a grenade from his harness. He pulled the pin with his teeth, but kept a solid grip on the handle. He took another step forward, brushing limbs aside ever so lightly, ever so quietly. He reached further with his rifle, using it as a pointer. His feet stayed where they were, but his body went into a forward leaning crouch that drew him closer to that patch of bare earth.

The rifle tip touched the ground, drawing a line in the dirt. There was a recognizable bump as it traveled over a hidden groove. Rodriguiz froze for five, ten seconds. Tony could hear his own heart beating like a drum, but Rodriguiz was a picture of serenity and concentration. With maddening slowness he eased the flash suppressor into the groove until it was halted by something hard. The black tip slipped under something solid, he bent the rifle down like a lever, and a crack appeared around an area that measured two feet square.

The trap door flew upward with such abruptness that Tony gasped and fell backward as the Vietcong leaped up screaming, rifle in hand. A shot rang out, then three more. Both Tait and Rodriguiz leaped out of the bush and flattened themselves on the ground, while the rest of the men dropped to their knees and fired. Burns blasted away until a loud explosion knocked him off his feet.

A puff of smoke and a funnel of dirt shot straight up into the air. Shrapnel shredded the overhead leaves like confetti, then rained down harmlessly. Tony heard pieces of hot metal clanging off his steel pot, felt them hit his jacket. He rolled up to a sitting position, his rifle pointed toward the spider hole. There were three other weapons trained there already.

Rodriguiz scrambled to his feet. Another grenade was in his hand, another pin in his mouth. His chest heaved like a bellows, as if he had just run a mile in under five minutes. He looked into the hole for a long time, rifle pointing. Then he pushed the pin back into the grenade and clipped it to his harness.

"You got him right between the eyes," Tait said. The body was huddled at the bottom of the hole like a rag doll that had been torn apart by a wild dog.

"She-ee-t," Wallace breathed, shouldering close for a look.

"How you know it was me, amigo?"

Casually, in his best drawl, Tait said, "Because when I fired I was too busy getting out of the way. My shots must have gone wild." He crouched down next to the hole. He fingered three gouges in the wooden door. "Here's where my rounds hit."

"Man, you got 'im comin' an' goin'," White said, adding a whistle. The grenade had dropped between his legs and gone off underneath him.

"Damn, I missed him completely," Burns said in disgust.

By this time Miller and his squad had run over from one direction, while Lieutenant Blake dashed in from the other. "Goddamn it, will you men get out of here? How many times do I have to tell you not to bunch up? Now move on. Miller, you should know better." He turned to Yates. "All right, get him out of that hole."

Miller bit his lower lip, chafed at being chastised in front of his men, but moved his leering squad elsewhere.

Tait and Rodriguiz each grabbed a limp arm, dragged the body out, and lay it on the ground, face up. A neat, bloodless hole adorned the middle of the forehead, the only damage done to the face. But the body itself was a frothy mess: it had been practically severed around the waist. The hips and legs were twisted around almost backwards, and a snake blob of intestines fell to the ground along with various other organs. Andrews stepped closer for inspection, but did not bother taking this one's pulse. Tony turned away, sickened by the sight and the smell.

"Raymonds, get on the radio and tell the captain we got another one. The bastards are all over the place."

Tony's skin crawled at the thought. He looked around expecting to find Vietcong leering from behind every tree, or popping up out of the ground like rabbits.

"Hey, Giovanni. Check out that thicket over there." Yates pointed with his chin.

Stepping cautiously, Tony rustled through the brambles. Thorns pricked his skin and caught his shirtsleeves, vines grappled for control of his rifle. He looked over the area thoroughly. "I don't see anything suspicious." It did not seem possible that a spider hole could be hidden beneath that tangled mass of vegetation. And even if there were, he was not sure that he wanted to find it.

"It's all right, Giovanni," Yates said, with a smirk across his tanned face. "I already checked it out. I just wanted to be sure."

Tony was quick to respond. "Of what? Me, or the Vietcong?"

Yates laughed. "Don't take it personally."

Gunshots rang out, cutting short Tony's thoughts. Yates wheeled and took off. A moment later Burns and Wallace leaped out of a patch of brush and raced after him. Tony brought up the rear. The firing died out for a few seconds, then started again with renewed vigor: shouts, gunfire, the dull thud of a grenade.

"There he goes. Over there."

Burns leveled his machine gun into a bamboo thicket and let it rip. The thick stalks flew apart like shredded wheat. Rodriguiz fired his M-16 because it was too dangerous to toss a grenade.

"Shoot, goddamn it," Yates yelled as he fired his own weapon. Several seconds passed before Tony realized that Yates was yelling at *him*. Not knowing who or what he was supposed to shoot, he held his rifle to his hip and emptied a magazine into the thicket.

"Hold it, hold it, hold it." Yates advanced toward what was left of the bamboo.

Burns leaned on his trigger a few more seconds before complying. "What is it? What are we shooting at?"

Tait and White appeared from the other side of a banyan tree, gun barrels smoking. Sergeant Miller charged between them, eager for action. Then Lieutenant Blake pushed Tony aside and confronted Yates.

"Did you get him?"

"I didn't even see anything. Rodriguiz, what was it?"

"Don't know. Man with long hair, maybe woman, didiing out of the bush. I tell to her stop, she keep running. I shoot." He shrugged his shoulders.

Wallace climbed into the thicket, looked around, and stepped back out. "No bodies. Whoever it was got away."

"That's great! That's fucking great!" Lieutenant Blake stormed. "Now we've got armed gooks running around behind us." His face was blood red, and he was breathing hard. "All right, I want everyone in the ville. I'm not going to take a chance of getting ambushed out here where we can't get any help. Miller, get your men over here. Yates, post some rear guards while we withdraw. This area's too damn hot."

Punctuating his words came automatic weapons fire from the other side of the village. This time the bull-throated roar of an AK-47 was distinguishable from the M-16s and M-60s.

"Oh, Jesus Christ. Raymonds, get over here with that radio."

Raymonds and Andrews came running together. Miller's squad had them surrounded. Lieutenant Blake called for Captain Collins on the radio.

Static could not hide the urgency of the reply. "Get the hell off the air, Blake, and get over here. We're in trouble."

"All right, men," Lieutenant Blake said, waving his arm over his shoulder. "Follow me."

He took off at a trot, bent low with his rifle tugged tightly against his stomach. One by one the men chased after him. Tony, struggling to get a fresh magazine in his gun, was suddenly all thumbs. When he finally got going he was in the middle of Miller's squad. But at least there was someone friendly at his back.

All hell seemed to have broken loose in the village. As they passed the first hooch, Lieutenant Blake halted his men and spread them out in a defensive line. It seemed as if the shooting was getting closer, as if the enemy was being driven this way.

"Miller, get your men over there. Yates, take cover behind that hooch. Raymonds, goddamn

it, stay close with that radio." Raymonds crouched behind the broad trunk of a banyan tree. The lieutenant joined him, scooped up the handset that Raymonds handed him, but kept peering out. "Hey, I said I wanted a rear guard." He motioned toward Miller. The sergeant scowled, then grabbed Kelsey and Norton and had them set up the machine gun so they could fire down the path.

As Blake was trying to raise the captain on the radio, the men of the second platoon came within shouting distance, although they were still out of sight. Weapons barked almost incessantly. Then something broke cover and squealed in terror, running down the wide path right toward the lieutenant. Before Tony knew it, half a dozen guns barked flame and lead — and a three hundred pound domestic pig rolled through the dust, and died right before Lieutenant Blake's position.

Dead silence followed. A uniformed soldier from the first platoon stepped out of the bush, bullets kicking dust in front of him.

"Don't shoot! Don't shoot! I'm American."

Blake strode across the opening, apoplectic. "Goddamn it, what the hell is going on here? Soldier, you'd better explain yourself."

The hapless grunt stood speechless, mouth open, eyes as large as quarters, staring at the business end of a dozen guns. Then Henderson walked out of a side path, laughing.

"Hey, Pepper, did you get that pig?" His face dropped when he saw the livid lieutenant approaching. His eyes rolled in their sockets as he mumbled, "Uh, oh."

"Soldier, consider yourself on report. Now, where the hell's your platoon leader?"

"I don't fucking believe this," Yates muttered under his breath.

But before anything more could come of the matter, another firefight commenced. Blake rallied his men and charged through the village. Burns was right behind him, undaunted by the weight of the machine gun and the ammunition belts that were slapping against his legs. For a man with a heavy paunch, he could sure move when he wanted to.

They came upon Captain Collins crouched in a clearing bounded by four hooches. He was shouting into the radio. "I need gunships now! The enemy is escaping to the west, through the jungle. I'm trying to flank 'em from the south. Ten to twenty, colonel, but I'm losing contact."

So much fire was pouring out of the jungle opposite the clearing, that Bravo Company could not cross without being shot down.

"Sure, napalm would be better."

"Sir, what can I do to help?" Lieutenant Blake shouted.

The captain turned around, stared blankly for

a moment. "Guard these people." He jerked a thumb at the Kit Carson scout. "Lieutenant Thang will conduct interviews," he said, almost as if the villagers were making job applications.

"Guard the . . . But, sir, we've got them on the run. Why — "

"Yes, that's right, sir. *Lieutenant, do as I say.* Okay, here are the coordinates. . . . " Captain Collins stood, dragged the RTO with him, and marched toward the tree line beyond the row of hooches.

"Ole Blakey ain't gonna get no glory that way."

"An' Collins, he ain't lookin' for glory, jus' doin' his job."

Lieutenant Blake stared blankly at Lieutenant Thang. The Vietnamese scout was expressionless. The platoon leader pointed with his rifle. "Miller, post two men over there. Yates, set up your machine gun along that path. And spread out the men."

Without being retold, Burns and Wallace took a position behind a low mud wall. The hamlet consisted of a few hooches made of bamboo and thatch, but no bunkers as the lowland peasants possessed. Their prisoners consisted of a dozen women, a score of children, and two white haired, long whiskered old men. The adults sat quietly on their haunches, except for one girl who squatted by herself, crying and chanting. The toddlers were herded together in a circle. They stared about with big, dark, questioning eyes that showed pain and horror if not fear.

The rest of the battle died down to sporadic firing a hundred yards away. The advancement halted. Three Air Force A-1 Skyraiders, propeller driven planes, screamed out of the blue in a tight circle around the hamlet.

As he looked around, Tony noticed three bodies lying on the ground in the shade of a stand of palm trees. One was either a young man or a teenager, the other two were middle-aged women. Their clothing was riddled with holes, as if they had been caught in the blast of a grenade, or perhaps in a crossfire. Already, flies were landing on the sagging faces, walking impiously over bloodless lips and unseeing eyes. In death these people had taken on new meaning: they would add to the body count that was now being assembled so the generals in Saigon could show how they were winning the war.

"These people in trouble now," White said to Tony. "Kit Carson there used to have a fambly till the night the NVA tore up his ville. Took all the food they could carry, raped and killed his wife, slaughtered the younguns in their beds, burned down the hooches."

It was the kind of experience that could turn a meek farmer, a loving husband, a doting father, into an enraged killer seeking revenge.

Thang turned toward his charges with a face that was as mean as a Mack truck. He waded into the pool of people and grabbed one old man by his ragged shirtfront and jerked him to his feet. With the back of his hand he slapped the aged peasant across the face. He would have fallen down had the interpreter not held onto his shirt. The material ripped, so he reached for a better hold, this time around the man's throat. Unresisting, the peasant closed his eyes and waited to pass out — or die — from suffocation. It was only when Thang released him, and he took several gasping breaths, that he was addressed with a question.

Tony could not follow the words, but could tell by the yelling and beating that the peasant was not giving the right answers. Thang slapped him first on one side of the face, then on the other. Blood flew out of his cracked lips, and trickled down his chin and neck. Still he denied whatever Thang was asking him.

The planes returned, releasing canisters that tumbled into the jungle. The skyline leaped into flames with the violence of an erupting volcano. Jellied gasoline billowed into the air, a gigantic ball of fire and heat that clung to everything it touched, and burned until nothing was left but blackened cinder. Captain Collins sent his three other platoons into the still-smoking aftermath.

The sounds of shooting were fading, both with distance and in intensity.

If any enemy soldiers had survived the napalm attack, they were doing their best to break contact. This was a guerrilla war, and the only way for a guerrilla army to win was to fight only when he had the advantage, when and where he wanted.

While Lieutenant Blake and the rest of the platoon had their attention riveted on the interrogation, White slipped into one of the hooches. When he emerged, his fanny pack was bulging noticeably. He knelt down and handed out bars of candy. The children took the offerings without enthusiasm; the women stared blankly. Whistling a nontune, he walked to where Tony was standing.

"Man, these people are loaded."

Lieutenant Thang pulled out a forty-five and jammed the barrel hard against the old man's throat. He posed another question in Vietnamese. The peasant did not resist, for resistance was useless. Thang pistol-whipped him. Teeth, brown with betel juice and red with blood, flew out of his mount and onto the ground. The old man whimpered.

"This isn't getting us anywhere." Lieutenant

Blake looked disgusted at the display of brutality. "Kill him and get it over with. The next one will talk."

But Thang refused to kill him. There is no pain in death, only the absence of pain. And he did not want these people to be free of pain. Instead, he lowered his pistol and shot the old man in the foot. He yelped with pain, and fell to the ground when Thang let go of him. And although the man whimpered piteously, there were still no tears.

I think I've seen this before, Tony thought. Only now it seemed to make sense. Before it was in an innocent village, devoid of any sign of enemy infiltration. Here, though, what this man divulged might save an American life — possibly his own. The Vietcong were here, of that he was certain. But then, did these people want them here, or had the enemy moved in by force? How was anyone to know? Was there any one, real truth, or just different facets of the same truth?

Thang continued with his interrogations, beating and bullying. By the time Captain Collins returned at the vanguard of his company, Thang had bloodied every face, brutalized every body, left fear in every heart and hatred in every mind. If these people had not been Vietcong sympathizers before, he had converted them.

"That's enough, Lieutenant." Captain Collins placed a constraining hand on the interpreter's arm in mid swing. He glanced around at the torn clothing, the weeping women, the mangled men. "If you haven't gotten anything out of them by now, you're not going to." Turning to Blake, he said, "Lieutenant, there are choppers on the way to pick up these people. See to it they get aboard safely."

White nudged Tony with his elbow. "Ole stick-his-head-in-a-hole Collins knew what that bastard was gonna do. Just didn't have the guts to stay and watch it."

Tony nodded, thinking: war is an act of cruelty in which the decency of one's actions is judged by a different set of standards.

"And Lieutenant," the captain continued, "Tell your men they did a good job."

****

It was nearly dark by the time Bravo Company trudged back to their bivouac site. The fields below were empty, the nearby jungle whispered with nightlife. Campfires burned brightly in the village of An Loa, but with less activity than usual. And the children did not sing tonight — they wailed.

As the men of C squad dropped their equipment at their foxholes, Yates detoured to the command post to get their c-ration allotment for the evening meal. He returned with news.

"The village chief is dead. His wife, too. Sappers sneaked into his hut last night and cut their throats while they slept. Word has it that it was a reprisal for helping us."

"Poor bastards," Tait said, using a rare swear word. "If they don't get it from one side, they get it from the other."

Chapter 97

The jungle seemed to go on and on: without beginning, without end. Insects buzzed, monkeys howled, vines tripped, sweat clung. For the tenth time that morning Tony reached for a drink; for the third time he discovered that his canteens were empty.

"Tait, do you have any water?"

Before Tait could answer, Yates said, "Hold off on that, Giovanni. We'll be stopping soon."

Tony nodded, and touched his lips with his swollen tongue. A village was supposed to be somewhere nearby. While they were approaching it from the east, Alpha Company was swinging into it from the west. Intelligence confirmed it to be an NVA stronghold, a base from which elements of an enemy artillery battalion were operating. It seemed impossible that wheeled howitzers could be dragged through this kind of terrain, but the NVA were experts at jungle movement.

The next thirty minutes seemed an eternity to Tony. He was weak from dehydration, his arms and legs felt like lead weights. It was an effort to breath. When Lieutenant Blake signaled a rest stop, Tony collapsed in his tracks.

"This'll perk you up." Tait unlimbered the two-quart, clear plastic bladder that he carried in addition to his two canteens.

Tony took it greedily. The bladder did not have a mouth-sized spout, but he did not care about the water that poured over his face and down his chest. It helped to wash away some of the sweat and grime, and the blood trails left by biting mosquitoes.

Tait pulled the bladder away from him. "Slow up, or you'll get sick."

Tony gulped down air, then pulled the container back to his mouth. When it was half empty, he let Tait have it back. Tait took his time, and left some for later. He squeezed the air out of the bladder, folded over the flap, and tucked it into his fanny pack.

"Thanks." Tony checked the tree behind him for ants and, finding none, leaned against it gratefully. He removed his steel pot and rubbed his forearm over his soggy head, ruffling hair that was beginning to sprout. "How do you stand this heat?"

"You get used to it after a while."

"How long's a while?"

"Ten months for me."

Tony dried his eyebrows on the rolled bundles of his sleeves. "Two months to go, huhn?"

"Fifty-seven days."

"You started the final countdown."

Tait simply nodded. He looked up as Andrews plopped down beside them. The medic dumped some pills out of a white plastic bottle onto his palm, and passed them around. "Two salt tablets and one anti-malaria pill."

"I can sure use the salt," Tony breathed. "I'm as weak as a kitten." Andrews poured out another tablet. "Have an extra one. It's on the house."

"Thanks."

Andrews winked, then moved down the line to where Rodriguiz was sitting by himself, staring out into the jungle. Tait pulled out the bladder again; this time they finished the water in swallowing their pills. Before any more perspiration could accumulate, Tony doused himself liberally with insect repellent.

Yates joined them a few minutes later. "The captain says we're on the outskirts of a ville. Alpha Company's already reached the other side. No contact yet."

"I'd just as soon not have any," Tony said. "It's too hot to have a war today."

Yates smiled. "Ain't exactly like Hollywood, is it?"

Tony shook his head. "I'm glad I'm with the good luck squad."

"Let's keep it that way." Yates passed the information on to Andrews and Rodriguiz. On his way back, he said, "Giovanni, you still have that gas mask?"

"Right here." He indicated the pouch that was slung under his arm.

"Okay. Let's get going."

Tony struggled to his feet. The dizziness left him, and his legs were no longer tingling. Under these conditions, water and salt meant as much for survival as food and ammunition.

A few minutes later they reached a tall hedgerow that constituted the outer defense wall of the village. The jungle was thick all around, and seemed to continue on the other side of the thorny barrier. The company fragmented into platoons, and fanned out to penetrate from different paths.

Lieutenant Blake kept tight control over his two squads. With only fifteen men under his command, that was easy to do. The two replacements who had been flown in that morning with the hot, predawn breakfast were having a tough time keeping up with the rest of the men. He pushed them to their fullest.

As the third platoon forged along a narrow path that was almost a tunnel through the thick vegetation, one of the new men was walking point. Tony, three men back, heard a click and

saw something leap up off the ground. A ball of light and a bull fiddle roar sent him instinctively to the ground, flipping the safety switch on before he crashed to his elbows. He saw the new man knocked backward and thrown flat. Norton, who was behind him, dropped to one knee and leveled his rifle over the fallen soldier.

Sergeant Miller jumped past him, took one look at the stricken soldier, and muttered, "Omigod." He gulped, then turned and shouted, "Lieutenant, get up here!"

Blake bounded past while Tony was getting up to his knees. "Jesus Christ," he said, staring down. A moment later, Andrews pushed him aside and knelt by the casualty. It was hard to tell where to start bandaging.

The man's eyes were closed, and his fists were tightly clenched. The moan that issued from his throat was horrible to hear. His chest, abdomen, crotch, and upper thighs were a mass of blood. The fatigues had been completely blown away, along with most of the skin and certain body parts. If he had not been in shock he would have been screaming — if not in pain, then in knowledge of what he had lost.

Andrews started unpacking compresses. His hands were shaking so violently that he could hardly work the buckles of his pack. Tears flooded his eyes, rolled down his cheeks. Over and over he uttered falteringly, "Oh, god. Oh, god. Oh, god."

At last Lieutenant Blake dragged his eyes away from the awful sight. "Miller, guard the front. Raymonds, get on the horn and tell the old man we need a medevac." He looked back at the mangled thing on the ground. "Andrews, is he going to be all right?"

If the medic heard him he made no notice. He was still repeating his "Oh, god" soliloquy and ripping cellophane wrappers apart as fast as his shaking hands would allow.

"Raymonds! We need that medevac on the double," Blake repeated.

The radioman had already given a situation report to the captain's RTO, and was waiting patiently for a reply. He repeated the message for the lieutenant's benefit.

"Yates, get your men up here. Take the lead, and watch out for booby traps."

Tony averted his eyes as he jogged past the wounded man, whose name he had not even learned. For that he was thankful.

Yates stopped abruptly at a place where the hedgerow parted and the path passed through a mass of vegetation. He turned and put his hand on Tony's chest. His blue eyes stabbed deep into Tony's and quivered with — apprehension? Anticipation? Compassion? "Be careful."

He pushed through the opening. Tony followed him slowly, glancing both ways for any sign of movement. They were in a garden that was overgrown with weeds and apparently long abandoned.

Another explosion rent the silence. Tony dropped to one knee and brought his rifle up to bear as the squad bunched behind him. Shouting, but no shots, came from one of the other platoons. Tony tried to see what was going on, but intervening shrubbery prevented him. The village was a warren of passageways through walls of vegetation that were themselves shaded by tall palm trees.

"Another bouncing betty."

White spat. "Like Hanes."

The psychological impact was having its effect on Tony: his palms were slippery with sweat, his legs trembled, his eyes darted. The next explosion was farther away: a friendly grenade.

A moment later Lieutenant Blake scurried to Yates. "This is a hot ville. First Platoon just cornered a gook in a hooch, and two more are on the run. Let's get this platoon into action."

"Yes, sir," Yates said, without moving. He waited until the platoon leader took the point.

The lieutenant charged through the garden to the opposite hedgerow. He made a brief inspection for trip wires, then kept going.

Yates shook his head. "He wants it too bad."

"Wants what?" Tony said.

"Glory. Fame. Death. We're going to stay well behind him." He motioned for the rest to follow. "Keep your interval."

Violent shooting erupted on their flank, punctuated by the explosions of two grenades. Machine gun fire rattled in a long, continuous burst that reverberated loudly in the hot, humid air.

"Somebody's gettin' some action," Burns said.

Lieutenant Blake flattened against a low mud wall; he motioned for silence. He peered through the arched opening into another compound, where a patch of jungle stretched beyond a bamboo hooch. He looked closely for trip wires, ran his hands along the chinks. With a grunt, he tossed a grenade high into the air. It hit with a thud, and exploded a split second later. Jumping up, he ran into the dark cloud of still settling dust.

He charged to the front of the hooch, kicked in the door, and sprayed the interior with an entire magazine from his M-16. No one was inside.

"Secure the area!"

Burns was the first to go after him, running hunched over his machine gun until he reached the lieutenant. Wallace hurried after him, ammunition belts clanging across his broad chest.

"Burns, spread a few rounds in that shrubbery."

The patch of dense jungle was perhaps twenty yards across: large enough to hide an enemy company, or trap doors leading to an underground complex. Reconnaissance by fire was the only safe way to draw the enemy's attention — if they were there.

With short, controlled bursts, Burns sprayed the foliage with lead messengers. He was calmly, almost disinterestedly locking in a new belt that Wallace had handed him when automatic fire was returned from the thick copse. The bullets went wild, soaring into the roof of the hooch, but the reaction was immediate. All three men scrambled to duck behind the tenuous protection of the thatched hut.

With coordinated effort, Yates laid down suppressing fire and rallied the rest of the squad to do the same. White, Tait, and Tony launched short bursts into the shrubbery while return bullets were still whizzing overhead. Rodriguiz hurled two grenades in rapid succession, then started firing his rifle even before the grenades had time to detonate. When they exploded, the compact vegetation absorbed the shrapnel.

By this time Burns had recovered and had his weapon on line. With a little more constraint, he sprayed the shrubbery again, taking over the firepower while the riflemen changed magazines. Rodriguiz tossed in another grenade, then the firing died down to an eerie, clinging silence.

Sergeant Miller arrived with his squad, ready for action. "Where are they?"

"In there." Blake pointed with his chin. "Miller, I want your squad to place cover fire. Yates, split your men up and run down both sides of that thicket."

Yates took White and Rodriguiz with him. Tait led the others along the mud barricade. On hands and knees they advanced, while A squad laid down covering fire. Tony's legs were shaking as he expected at any moment to have a rifle barrel shoved into his face. His heart beat like a drum, painfully thrumming against his rib cage.

"That's enough! That's enough!"

"All right. Let's go." Yates threw himself into the mass of trees, vines, and underbrush. Anyone there was almost assuredly dead, but if he had managed to duck the barrage of lead, they had to find him before he could retaliate. "Be sure of your target before you shoot."

Converging from both sides, the men stayed low and waded into the thicket. Tony advanced in a low crouch. The ground was alive with crawling insects, the air buzzed with flies and mosquitoes. A fine dust filtered through his clenched teeth, clung to the sweat on the back of his neck. The smell of rotting vegetation was nauseating.

Except for thrashing sounds on either side, Tony was alone in this jungle world. He could not see more than a few feet in any direction. He swept aside clinging vines, pushed through thick foliage which snagged his clothes, his rifle, the grenades hanging from his web gear.

He broke into a small clearing where the ground had been swept clean of weeds and roots. Branches and vines covered it like a tent. It was a ten-foot circular retreat, a perfect hide-away. To one side a pajama clad man lay with his rifle pointing directly at Tony.

Tony could not move, could not react. He was frozen in fear, staring at the rifle, waiting for the muzzle flash and the tearing of flesh, expecting death. He hoped mercifully that it would be quick.

The man was dead. It was not just that the eyes were closed; it was the unnatural configuration of the body, the sideways twist in the neck. The rifle had been propped up on one leg, and the man had died in that position.

Tony struggled to find his voice. When he did, his words came out in a crackle. "Here. He's over here. He's dead."

The jungle thrashed, and a massive body engulfed him like a shroud, and bore him to the ground under its weight.

"You fuckin' idjit," Wallace breathed into his ear. "There may be more of 'em."

Tony gulped, but lay still under the giant. He heard the men coming closer. *His* men? A moment later the nearby brush stirred, and Yates stepped out and looked down at them.

"Looks like he's the only one," he said, with a laugh.

"Shit." Burns stooped to examine the body. "M-16 holes."

"Better luck next time." White relieved the body of its weapon. The AK-47, complete with one thirty-round banana clip, was in good condition considering that it had probably been carried by hand all the way from North Vietnam, and had been in field use for years. The automat kalashnikov was the best of Soviet assault rifles and worth a lot of money both to collectors and on the black market. "Too bad I can't keep it."

Rodriguiz and Tait grabbed the body by the shoulders and dragged it through the dense underbrush. Except for Yates, who stayed behind to search the hideout, the rest of the squad followed.

Lieutenant Blake surveyed the body. "Raymonds, get the CO on the horn and tell him what we've got. White, make sure that weapon gets turned in. And get rid of that body. Drop it down the well."

It was a simple way of poisoning the water supply while cleaning up after a firefight. Miller and Yates exchanged frowns. Then, they took it upon themselves to carry out the lieutenant's orders.

"All right, let's keep alert. I don't want any gooks getting away," Lieutenant Blake said. Then, almost as an afterthought, he added, "Oh, and Raymonds, find out what happened to that medevac. I don't like having Andrews back there alone. We might need him."

The sweep continued. There was something claustrophobic about the way this village was constructed. Each area was a separate fortress, surrounded by impenetrable hedgerows or mud walls, and interspersed with patches of thick jungle or compact gardens. Tall palm trees spread their carrotlike tops, offering shade, but adding to the feeling of closeness. The hooches were in disrepair, with doors hanging loose on their hinges and shutters rattling in itinerant breezes.

"Where are all the people?" Tony wanted to know, after a half hour of non-activity. The sporadic shooting was usually reconnaissance by fire but, except for false alarms, only two other people had been found in the otherwise abandoned village. They were white bearded, grubby old men who cowered at the arrival of the soldiers, and who chanted with senile ramblings to the interpreter. Both inhabitants said that they had lived here at one time, before the people had been forced to move away.

"I heard they went through this ville a couple months ago and transported all the gooks to Shantytown," Yates said. "That's the only way you can be sure of clearing out the VC. Take out their suppliers, then kill anybody left behind."

"This is a free fire zone. They oughta kill those two antique papasans. Hey, here's another well." Burns shook his empty canteen. "I can sure use a refill."

"Anybody in this one?" Wallace said.

"Knock it off." Yates unscrewed the cap of his canteen, took a long, last draft.

"I ain't too happy 'bout dumpin' bodies down no wells, even if it do poison their water."

"It was the lieutenant's orders. We do a lot of things in this war I'm not happy about."

"Yeah, like bein' here." Burns set his machine gun down by the circular mud wall. He lowered a wooden bucket on a rotted manila rope while the rest of the men unlimbered canteens and broke out purification tablets. "Man, feel that cold air." A cool draft rose up out of the deep hole.

"Try not to drip your sweat into it," Wallace said.

Burns hauled in the bucket; two frogs leaped out and hopped away. White grabbed one of them, but held it for only a moment before dropping it.

"Goddamn critter peed on my hand."

"I hope they didn't pee in the bucket." Wallace held out his canteen for Burns to fill. He dropped two iodine tablets through the neck, shook the canteen for a few seconds, then downed the entire quart in a single gulp. He grinned as he wiped his bulging lips with the back of his hand. " 'Cause if they did, I jus' drank it."

"Anyone ever tell you, you were a pig, man?" Burns said.

Wallace laughed out loud while the rest of the canteens and plastic bladders were filled. "Not to my face."

"Nobody's tall enough to say it to your face."

Tony caught the frogs and carried them back to the well, holding them by the back, legs jerking. "Frogs are a valuable food source to the Vietnamese. The kids catch them and break their legs so they can't get away." He deposited them into the well. "Frogs also mean that the water is potable."

"What the fuck you doin'?" White said.

Tony was taken aback. "Well, they'll die out of water. Their skins will dry up."

"Don't mean we gotta soak 'em in our drinkin' water. An' where you pick up all that crap 'bout the local yokels?"

Tony shook his canteen, then put it aside to wait the prescribed twenty minutes. "Oh, I read up on the people and the country."

"Man, you are one sick dude."

Burns balanced himself on the edge of the well. "This is fuckin' ridiculous. We're savin' frogs an' killin' people. Shit, I thought we were gonna get lotsa action."

"We got one gook, ain't that enough?" Wallace said.

Tait said, "Fourth platoon got two. I heard it over the radio. And the lieutenant thinks Alpha Company got a bunch."

"Hey, how about somebody taking over for Rodriguiz?" Yates said.

"Giovanni, go stand over there and keep your eyes open."

"You 'spectin' somebody?" Wallace said.

"This is supposed to be a combat patrol," Yates explained patiently, for about the hundredth time. "We already know the bastards are here. And — "

"Somebody's coming," Rodriguiz announced calmly.

A moment later Lieutenant Blake stepped into the glade, with Andrews behind him. No one asked about the new man — Andrews' presence and the fading *whup-whup-whup* of

helicopter blades told them what they wanted to know. Miller and his squad soon crowded around the well.

Kelsey looked exhausted, a combination of the heat, thirst, and carrying around the M-60. He lunged for the bucket that was sitting on the ground, and drank greedily straight from the upturned wooden lip. The lieutenant leaped forward and knocked the bucket out of his mouth, spilling the remaining water.

"Soldier, you put purification tablets in that water first. I'm not losing a man because of dysentery."

Kelsey glared at the lieutenant with reddened eyes. "Goddamn it, I ain't had a drink o' water for two hours."

"I'll see to it that you never drink again unless you take the proper precautions." Blake promptly ignored the machine gunner and turned toward Raymonds. "How close is Alpha Company?"

"Several hundred meters, sir, but still no enemy contact."

The lieutenant pulled out a sheet of paper, unfolded it, and studied the penciled diagram of the village that he had drawn. Shooting erupted nearby. The lieutenant was off and running. The troops straggled after him, weapons clattering and canteens still in their hands. Almost before Tony knew where they were going, Lieutenant Blake held up his hand for them to stop. He crouched behind a hedgerow, parted the tangled branches. Tony did the same. On the other side, the First Platoon was in a hot firefight with an enemy machine gun nest inside a dilapidated hooch. Chance had put the Second Platoon in a perfect, unseen flanking position.

Blake sized up the situation at a glance. "On the count of three I want everyone to throw a grenade over these bushes. Aim for about fifteen meters." The two squads spread out along the hedgerow. The lieutenant took a grenade off his belt, pulled the pin. Tony waited for the order, a strange calm coming over him. "One. Two. *Three.*"

Blindly, Tony estimated the force necessary to throw the one-pound hand grenade a distance of fifty feet. As soon as it left his hand, he planted his face on the ground. A few seconds later, a long, continuous detonation, like a peal of thunder, roared deep-throated from the hooch. Dirt and shrapnel filled the air, steel shards fell like a storm of hail.

"Sands," Blake shouted from his cover, when the noise had died down. "Is that you, Blake?" came the loud reply.

"Yes, sir."

"Good work." The leader of First Platoon stood and walked into the open. Blake found a path through the hedgerow. Tony was right behind him. The bamboo walls of the enemy hooch were splintered with holes, as if from some giant shotgun. The two lieutenants came together. "The bastards had us pinned down behind that wall."

"Looks like we got 'em all." Blake's lips turned into a quirky smile.

The three dead bodies lay strewn in unnatural positions inside the one-room hooch. Lieutenant Sands approached warily, his M-16 trained on the uniformed regulars. They could be faking. He poked one of them in the eye with his gun barrel. The body did not move.

"Want to split the credit?" Lieutenant Sands said, with a smile.

"Always willing to share with a friend. But how are we going to split three of them?"

"Guess we'll have to cut one in half."

The men from the two platoons mingled as the two leaders broke into gales of laughter. It looked as if this was going to be a profitable day for their records.

Without warning, a machine gun rattled so close by that it seemed that it must be one of their own. Before the men realized what was happening, bullets were slamming into the two platoons from the direction of a large grain hut. Some men crouched and opened return fire, some scrambled for protection. Three were knocked down and did not get up. Lieutenant Sands took a direct hit in the temple: he was dead before his body hit the ground.

First platoon took the brunt of the assault as the heavy slugs tore into their flank. Half a dozen wounded men lay crying and bleeding behind the mud wall. Tony found himself on the ground, scrambling for cover. Return fire was sporadic until squad leaders coordinated their efforts. Then two machine guns came on line, one of them Burns'. The deadly crossfire ripped wood chips and bamboo slivers from the hut's facade, but a makeshift bulkhead of thick timbers protected the men inside. Wallace unlimbered the spare belts and added his M-16 to the incredible amount of firepower that was being poured into the stronghold.

"Cover me! Cover me!" someone from First Platoon shouted. An instant later a short black man dashed from the bushes into the open. One of the injured men, lying in the open, moved. Tony, now in control of himself, had to stand in order to shoot over the man's head so as to provide protecting fire superiority. From a crack in the hedgerow, he fired spaced single shots into the grain hut until his magazine was empty.

PFC Pepper flattened himself behind the body of Lieutenant Sands, then crawled to where his partner lay jerking spasmodically. Pepper was in tears as he placed a hand on Henderson's bloodstained face, as if to cover the gaping hole in the jaw. He lifted the heavier man by the shoulders and dragged him straight across the field of battle toward the hedgerow where A squad was sending a blistering hail of fire.

The enemy machine gunner picked dirt his heels, but could fire only a few bursts before he had to duck the combined fusillades from half a company. Pepper crashed through the hedgerow next to Tony. He dropped his rifle and helped pull the wounded man to safety. Andrews appeared out of nowhere.

"Keep shooting, men," Lieutenant Blake shouted, emptying his own magazine. "Keep their heads down."

Rodriguiz pumped grenades toward the grain hut as fast as he could pull the pins, but they bounced off the thatched roof and rolled to the ground before detonating. Now he cooked one off in his hand and released it so that it exploded just as it reached the enemy position. Shrapnel ripped through the thin fabric of bamboo, but without recognizable results. "I got to get closer."

"Outa my way." White slammed a 40 mm grenade into his launcher. "I'll blow the bastards to kingdom come."

Henderson's eyes were open now, bulging in fear and pain. Andrews ripped open a morphine syringe and tried to hold the wounded man's arm steady so he could make the injection. There was little he could do to stop the bleeding. The bullet had entered the left cheek, gone through the mouth, and exited the other side. The tongue was torn but intact, but a sizeable chunk of jawbone had been blown away along with the teeth, gums, and the side of his dirt-smudged face.

"You fuckin' nigger. You fuckin' nigger. I tole you to keep your goddamn mouth shut." Pepper cried while he cradled his friend's head in his lap, rolling back and forth as if he were rocking a baby gently to sleep.

"Where's Raymonds? Where's Raymonds?" Lieutenant Blake screamed. He looked around with the feral eyes of a caged tiger, and sidled along the hedgerow on hands and knees, trying to get closer to the other platoon's position and Sands' RTO.

Tony fastened another magazine to his rifle, and poked the muzzle through the hedgerow. He held his fire because he saw nothing to shoot. Burns clipped away with the machine gun, and was surrounded by a growing pile of brass casings and shreds of the disintegrating belt. There was a frantic moment when a cartridge jammed in the breech. In the brief lull, the enemy machine gun swung around and trimmed the hedges with sustained a burst that was properly elevated. Tony never knew how close he could get to the ground.

Temporarily relieved, those of the First Platoon who had reached the safety of the low wall poured a tremendous amount fire power into the open doorway, silencing the machine gun for the moment, while the rest of the men deployed for better positioning. An uncommon amount of lead streamed out of the grain hut, and now Tony could see that a thin groove had been cut in the bamboo walls to permit a three hundred sixty degree field of fire.

White pulled the trigger of the M-203. A white puff of smoke leaped from the stubby barrel, and a faintly visible streak terminated high in the doorway.

The inch-and-a-half-diameter steel canister cut through the back bamboo wall and exploded harmlessly in the trees fifty yards beyond. "Damn. The range is too short."

"Try ricocheting it inside," Yates suggested. "If it bounces around a little it may be enough to arm it."

Henderson's eyes filmed to an enchanted gaze; he slipped into shock. Andrews slapped a large compress over the ragged opening in the side of Henderson's face, and wrapped tape around the back of his head and across his nose. He tried stuffing another bandage inside the mouth, but the patient started coughing, and what little skin was holding the lips in place started to tear.

"You've got to hold the right side of his head down," Andrews explained to Pepper, through gritted teeth. "Otherwise he'll choke on his own blood."

Lieutenant Blake reached the First Platoon's position, and shouted for the radioman. As ranking senior officer, he was now in charge of both platoons. One of the squad leaders, a dumpy looking, bow-legged sergeant in faded fatigues, slithered on the ground more snake-like than one would figure he could move. He led the lieutenant through a complicated pattern of shrubbery to where the radio had been taken out of the line of fire.

Rodriguiz was flat on his stomach now, directly under Burns' line of fire. He was completely exposed. Only the short, interrupted bursts from the machine gun kept him alive, as if the flying steel was a solid protective wall. He crawled past the two bodies that lay in the open, ignoring their existence, and kept going until he reached the hooch where the three dead NVA soldiers lay in the ruins of their gun position. From there he was only five yards from the doorway of the grain hut.

White plunked another grenade into his launcher, waited for Yates to give him the go-ahead, then stood, aimed, and fired in one smooth motion. The grenade whizzed low across the open ground, past Rodriguiz. It hit the thick wooden door jam with a shower of sparks, ricocheted into the mud barricade that protected the gun crew, and bounced up into the ceiling. It did not have enough power to break through the thatch; nor had it traveled far enough to arm itself. It plunked back down on the floor, harmless.

The enemy machine gun had not fired back for more than a minute, so intense was the return fire. It was just what Rodriguiz needed as he stood for the split second necessary to hurl his death weapon through a slit. The grenade exploded inside. All shooting ceased for a moment as everyone waited to see what effect the sneak attack had. Seconds later, machine gun bullets spit through the bamboo walls as if they were tissue paper, raking both platoons' position blindly, but effectively.

American guns barked back, cutting so many wood chips out of the hut that a cloud of dust covered the entire area. The air reeked with the smell of gunpowder.

By the time Lieutenant Blake got Captain Collins on the radio, the CO had problems of his own. His pincher movement with Alpha Company was closing, and there were straggling Vietcong elements turning tail and trying to squeeze out between them. He could not spare any men at the moment, and told the lieutenant to hold his own.

Raymonds crawled next to Tony. "What the hell is going on?"

"Where've you been?" Tony shouted.

"I stopped to take a shit."

The receiver crackled as Lieutenant Blake called the captain from First Platoon's radio. "Sir, Lieutenant Sands is dead. I'm taking over his command. I'm also engaging an enemy machine gun position."

The message came back clearly. "Lieutenant, Alpha Company is commencing the pincer maneuver. Take tactical control of Lieutenant Sands' platoon and get over here on the double."

"Yes, sir. Out."

Sergeant Miller slapped his hands on Tony's back and flipped him over. Tony had not even heard him approach; he probably would not have heard a tank approach. His awareness had been tunneled by the events of battle.

"Gimme those tear gas grenades." The sergeant yanked them off Tony's harness. He ripped open the pouch hanging by Tony's side, and removed the gas mask. Throwing off his steel pot, Miller donned the mask. "Kelsey. Burns. I want protection."

The machine gunners continued to fire as the ammo bearers clipped on new belts. Yates checked the mask straps for the sergeant. They were cinched down tight. Beads of sweat rolled down from the rubber seals, but the sergeant made no mention of it as he crawled through the hedgerow.

The radio crackled. Yates picked up the handset, and explained the situation to the lieutenant.

"All right, Yates, I'm sending a squad around the other side. Let's get this over with fast."

Tony saw the men sneaking away, on the other side of a hedgerow. The NVA machine gunner followed them around with his barrel spewing lead, and for a moment one side was unprotected. Every man in Second Platoon emptied his clip into the grain bin, to no effect.

"Guy must have armor plating inside that thing."

"*Medic!*"

Andrews climbed over Tony with his medical kit in tow. Norton pointed at his pants leg, stained red with blood.

"Something stung me in the leg. Musta been a wasp or something. It feels numb." Norton sat behind a thick banyan trunk with his injured leg held out stiffly. He attached another belt of cartridges and laid them out so they could feed easily into the breech of Kelsey's machine gun. It was consuming ammunition as if bullets were air.

Tony lay only a few paces from the eight-foot-diameter tree, yet he had not even noticed the machine gun fire. He slapped another magazine into his M-16, poked the flash suppressor through the hedgerow, and fired over Miller's head.

Andrews untied the cuff string from the jungle boot and slowly pushed the material upward. When the entire calf was uncovered, he fingered the two red sting marks, one on each side. Gently he palpated the thick muscle around the bones.

"Ouch!"

Andrews shook his head. "Boy, are you lucky."

"It's not poisonous?"

"No, but I'd say you're good for about two months of R and R." The blood was already clotting around the wounds as Andrews removed two compresses and began taping them over the holes. "A bullet went right through your leg, between the tibia and the fibula. Never touched the bone. Other than a little muscle damage, you're okay."

Norton's jaw dropped. Then, pounding Kelsey on the shoulder, he said cheerfully, "Hey, man, didja hear that? I got me a purple heart an' a vacation outa this hell hole all in one, an' I don't hardly feel a thing."

"Great, man. The million dollar wound."

Norton was still smiling as systemic shock caught up with him and he casually keeled over in a dead faint.

Kelsey shook his head over his companion's unconscious form. "Hey, new guy. Get over here and see these belts don't get tangled up."

Riley was in a daze and hardly able to function. He stared blankly at Kelsey. Yesterday he had been doing close order drill at Pleiku.

Burns' machine gun ran dry. "Yo, Wallace. You gonna play with yourself or gimme some more ammo?"

The First Platoon continued to pour a deadly sheet of lead from three machine guns as Wallace threw another cartridge lei over his head. "I should be slingin' taters 'stead o' bullets."

"It's better to give than to receive."

"Mister, would you get your goddamn platoon leader on the phone?" the radio barked. Tony heard the command just as the lieutenant crawled over his legs. Bullets zinged overhead, cutting sticks out of the hedgerow.

Raymonds held out the instrument. "Sir, the CO wants you."

"I heard him, dammit, but I'm busy."

Despite the racket of bullets and grenades, his voice carried over the transmitter. "*I heard that, goddamn it, and I'm busy, too.*"

The lieutenant scooped up the phone. "Blake here."

"What the hell is going on? I ordered you to get your men here on the double."

"Sir, we're pinned down by a machine gun at the mo — "

"*A machine gun? Two platoons are pinned down by one machine gun?*" The lieutenant held the phone away from his ear. "Lieutenant, I've got most of an NVA company slipping out of my clutches and you're fucking around with one lousy machine gun. If you can't knock it out, leave one squad to keep it engaged — and get the rest the hell out of there. Walk around it if you have to, just *get* here."

Sergeant Miller reached the barricade behind which Rodriguiz was lying. He crawled over a dead soldier as if he were a sandbag, and lay down next to him. The New York Puerto Rican had already expended all his grenades in a futile attempt to destroy the gun position. All he had been able to do was direct machine gun fire toward himself.

The sergeant aimed a hand signal at his own machine gunners. They slacked off for a moment, while all the guns from the First Platoon continued to shred the bamboo facade. Thousands of rounds had already been poured into the grain bin, without any effect other than to chew out gaps in the tubular walls. Miller gave one tear gas grenade to Rodriguiz. They pulled the pins. On the sergeant's nod, they both stood up and tossed the grenades at the grain bin. One went through the slit opening, the other through the doorway.

They ducked just as the machine gun swiveled toward them and ripped chunks of sun-baked mud from the top of the low wall. Quelling fire was returned from both platoons. The canisters detonated with a whoosh, spewing the thick, stinging, eye-watering vapor through the bullet riddled walls. The gun ceased firing.

Lieutenant Blake got off the radio. Now that the two platoons under his command had stopped firing for a moment, awaiting the outcome of the tear gas, Tony could hear the sounds of a firefight that was several hundred meters away.

"Yates, get the men over to the other side of the ville. Meet up with the rest of — " Machine gun fire raked the hedgerow. Bullets thudded into the ground all around them. "What the fuck — "

"Sir, we've got them boxed in now — "

"I said get moving. Those are your orders," the lieutenant screamed. "I'll stay here and take care of this."

"Right, sir." Yates started crawling away, taking the men with him.

The lieutenant's hand clamped down on Tony's shoulder. "You stay here."

Henderson recovered consciousness. He started screaming: a throaty, guttural scream that was the best he could manage with his torn face and blood-clogged throat.

"Leave that man alone and get going."

"But, sir," Pepper cried. "He's ma buddy an' he's hurt bad."

"Goddamn it, soldier. There's a war on. We may all be dead if you don't get your ass in gear. Now get moving."

"I can't leave him, sir. I can't."

Andrews tried to take the wounded man's head into his own lap, but Pepper would not let him. He clung to Henderson like a child hugging his favorite stuffed animal.

Blake slapped Pepper across the face, hard enough to get his attention. "I'm giving you an order, soldier. I'm in charge of this platoon now, and you'll do as I say."

"But he's ma buddy." Tears ran in torrents down Pepper's face. To Blake, "Go fuck yo'-self."

"Soldier, I'm putting you on report. And this time I'll make it stick." The lieutenant turned his attention toward Tony. "All right, get the rest of those gas grenades out to the sergeant."

"*What?*" Tony was distracted by the concurrence of horrible events. "Oh. Yes, sir." He got his knees under him, then ran crouching toward the hole in the hedgerow. He skidded on hun-

dreds of shell casings that littered the ground like roller bearings, and promptly fell down. Any other time it would have been hilarious. Ignoring bruised shins and forearms, he low-crawled with race-winning speed, keeping his buttocks flattened more than he had ever done in basic training.

"*Fire in the hole!*"

Two grenades flew out of the grain bin and rolled across the open ground toward the First Platoon. Tony scuttled to Lieutenant Sands' body and groveled in the armpit just as two thunderous roars rent the air. Shrapnel flew around like flakes in a snowstorm, filling the air with dust and yellow haze, and the smell of cordite. A moment later another explosion rent the inside of the machine gun nest.

Miller shouted through the mask. "What was that? Who threw that grenade?"

Tony raised his head. Sweat poured into his eyes, stinging. A faint wisp of tear gas drifted his way. Rodriguiz started coughing, but the sergeant was still protected.

"Cover me." Sergeant Miller made a mad dash toward the hut and slid to the ground like a ballplayer reaching for home plate.

Rodriguiz fired a few rounds through the door. The flanking squad was in position, but the lieutenant came out from behind the bushes shouting.

"Don't shoot! Don't shoot!"

No one moved. No one fired a weapon. The tear gas was dispersing rapidly through the shot-up bamboo walls. Sergeant Miller eased up his head, then unwound his crouched body so he could peer through the doorway.

The whole side of Lieutenant Sands' head had been blown off. A sticky gray mass of brain matter oozed onto Tony's shirtsleeve. He backed away, vomiting and rubbing dirt on the stain.

"Hey, get up here with that rifle. I'm out of ammo."

Tony wiped his mouth, stumbled toward Sergeant Miller. The tear gas had dissipated. The circular, mud-covered wooden barrier in the center of the hut looked like a well, with the long barrel of a machine gun protruding from it. The barrel still glowed fire engine red from the heat of sustained fire. It pointed uselessly at the roof. Thousands of shell casings built a pile of brass that was inches deep. The gunner lay under the wreckage of the machine gun, practically covered by the littered scrap metal of the disintegrating belt.

Not much was left of him other than a bloody froth. The grenade that he had pulled on himself had emasculated his body, severed both hands and feet, split open his gut, spilled out the intestines, and left his face an unrecognizable pulp.

Rodriguiz said, "How come nobody thought of torching the place?"

Suicide had been better than defeat — or capture.

****

Alpha and Bravo Companies had merged, joined forces, and tried to engage the enemy's rearguard. The firefight that ensued lasted only minutes before Charlie was absorbed into the jungle like water into a sponge. Dead and wounded lay on both sides.

All those mothers, all those wives . . .

Tony was detailed to bring in the dead, their weapons, and papers. It was chance that Tony came across them first.

Two men lay in the knee-deep grass at the jungle's edge. They wore different uniforms, carried different weapons, fought a different war and for different reasons. But they were still men. Each had been a soldier, a son, a husband, a father. Now, they were just chunks of protoplasm, without meaning.

One was whole, but lifeless. The other was torn and bloody, with the clothes ripped away by steel fragments. His leg was bent at an awkward and unnatural angle. The black, curly hair was matted with a thick, red dye that ran over the bridge of a splayed nose and spread over a chocolate brown face. The deep chest struggled under the weight of bandoliers. The Adam's apple bobbed as air rasped through a blood-filled throat.

Tony tried to speak. After several failed attempts, he squeaked, "Dear God." Then, "Medic." In desperation, he screamed, "*Medic! I need a medic.*"

At first he was afraid to touch him, even to feel for a pulse, for fear that he would fall apart like some sawdust-filled doll that was cracked with age. He fumbled with his bayonet, cut away the bandoliers and shirt buttons to take pressure off the heaving rib cage. A sticky fluid seeped from several holes in the hairless chest. Tony poured water onto his hand and pressed it against the dry, quivering lips.

The eyelids fluttered, the creature came to life. Dark, fathomless orbs showed faint recognition. The throat gurgled. "I tole you we'd meet again, bro."

He coughed. Blood foamed from his mouth. Tony did not seem to notice. Black fingers worked up his forearm, grasped him firmly below the elbow with a strength that was the final focusing of energy. All too soon the eyes went blank and rolled up under the lids. A hiss escaped from strained lungs like air from a collapsing balloon. The pressure of the fingers relaxed.

"Bro!" Tony shouted, shaking the retracting arm. It was flaxen, like the plastic appendage of a department store manikin. Tony looked through the eyes, through the familiar skull, into the brain that was the seat of emotion, the soul, the only place of real conflict. "*Bro.*"

There was no answer. Alexander Hays was dead.

Chapter 98

Tony trudged up the hill rubbing his hands over his pockmarked face. His skin was dry and flaky, punctuated by ulcerating sores from insect bites, and a rough stubble that was unfamiliar to him: he had not shaved, or even washed, for days. There had been no time, or energy. The patrols had been long, one after the other. His body was crying for rest.

Again, no insulated containers were waiting for them; another night on c-rations. The coveted Heatabs had run out, and that meant *cold* c-rations. Tony plopped beside his foxhole and swung his legs around so that they dangled over the edge. He took immeasurable pleasure in the simple relief of not being on his feet. As the pain ebbed from his soles, he released the harness straps and let the web gear fall to the ground behind him.

He leaned back on his arms, arched his back, and dreamt of comforts that he used to take for granted: a cool shower and a bar of fresh smelling soap; a drink of iced tea out of a clean, crystal glass; a moment to lounge in the shadow of a dark umbrella without fear of incoming artillery; relief from the constant cloud of annoying mosquitoes.

The days melded together in his mind, as ephemeral as a dream — as ugly as a nightmare. How many dead? How many wounded? How many new faces?

Tait dropped down beside him and held out a meal packet. "I thought I'd spring for dinner tonight."

Tony did not say a word, or look to see what was on the bill of fare. He was too tired to eat. He pulled a dirty, sweat-soaked envelope out of his jacket pocket. He had carried it for two days; there had been no time to read it. Now, as he opened it, he reminded himself that there was another world back home — the real world. Out here, the only reality was the heat, the drudgery, the jungle, the enemy. All else was fantasy.

The letter was from Ben — the first one that Tony had ever received from him. He read the words without enthusiasm. The problems that he wrote about did not seem important any more. Out here, the only personal problem was staying alive.

"Bad news?" Tait unfolded the cardboard box and snatched a meal can. "Might help to talk about it."

Tony licked painful lips. "Everything is so different."

Tait dug into congealed beef slices. "Different how?"

"Nothing's going to be the same when I get home."

"Nothing's ever the same. Things change all the time, you just don't notice because you change along with them. When you're away for a while you're more aware of it, like when you see cousins at a reunion and they're all grown up. You see the change all at once — "

"Hope you boys ain't feelin' sleepy." White approached with his thumbs tucked under his harness like a western marshal. "Cause we is goin' on OP." Clean, white teeth grinned down at them. White seemed to be made of energy; he never tired. Yet, he could fall asleep at a moment's notice.

Tony said, "I thought it was an observation post during the day, and a listening post at night."

"Call it what you want." Yates appeared carrying a fat, tubular object in one hand and a pair of handie-talkies in the other. "But when you've got a starlight scope you'd better take advantage of it."

Tait looked at the instrument appreciatively. "Well, I do declare."

"And take good care of it, or it'll come out of your pay."

White took the expensive scope from Yates, rubbed his hands over it lovingly, and hugged it to his chest. "I'm gonna wear it out in one night, 'cause I'm gonna have my eyeball glued to one end of it. Heared they sneaked into the ville last night an' killed another 'Yard."

Yates nodded grimly. "The gooks are out there, all right." He handed the handie-talkie to Tony. "I'll be taking over your hole for the night, and I'll be on the other end of that. Raymonds, Weston, and Jarvis will be out, too. Make sure you call me every hour, on the hour."

Tony groaned, pushed himself to his feet, dragging his web gear and c-rations with him.

"And don't trip on the claymore wires on your way out."

"Whatta we do if we hafta come in?"

"Pray."

The LP was a shallow depression in the field some fifty meters beyond the company perimeter. It had been dug wide enough so that three men could crouch behind the low dirt barricade that offered protection on three sides. Before them stretched the open range where the village water buffalo were grazed. The amber, knee-high grass waved in an evening zephyr.

White flung down his web gear and fanny pack, and took a seat. "If Charlie gonna 'tack, he gonna come in from the jungle on the other side."

"Makes sense." Tony opened a box of C's and plucked out the cans, lining them up on a dirt shelf. Cold spaghetti did not particularly interest him right now.

The twilight was deepening, and already the brightest stars were visible in the purple sky. The village was in shadow, but scurrying Montagnards were making the most of the feeble light. Their fires were lit, the wood that was gathered during the day was stacked nearby. It was going to be a beautiful, clear night.

"You gonna wear out the ink you keep starin' at it like that."

Tony scowled, folded the letter, tucked it back in the envelope, and slipped it into his pocket. He took a long breath. "A buddy of mine has disappeared."

White wolfed down another can of food. "Whatchu mean, distappeared? He go into hiding?"

Tony stared toward An Lap, watching young mothers gather their children and usher them into the safety of the hooches. "He was an Air Force pilot. They say his plane was shot down, maybe north of the DMZ. They don't know for sure. The official report is that he just never returned from a mission."

"That's tough," White said. "That's really tough."

Silence lingered in the air. The chirping sounds of night insects mingled with the burst of laughter from the direction of the perimeter. Tony slapped angrily at a mosquito on his neck, then perfunctorily took his squeeze bottle of repellent and smeared more of the oily, foul-smelling liquid on his face, neck, and hands.

"I hope you understand why I say this," Tait said softly. "But for his sake, I hope he's dead. I don't like to think of what the Cong do to prisoners."

Tony toyed with his food.

White finished eating and tucked the empty cans in his fanny pack. He picked his teeth with a thick blade of grass. "I think a lot o' that's propaganda, an' I don't say it for your benefit, neither. The gook soldiers hear the same kinda bullshit 'bout us. 'Member that day Sands got his? When that gook run outa ammo, he blew hisself up on his own grenade. Now tell me Ho Chi Minh don't have his men believin' the 'Mericans were gonna torture the shit outa 'em. Damn, that takes balls."

The events of that day were fogged by numerous other incidents, firefights, jungle paths, villages, and patrols. After a while they all ran together — a endless montage of blood, gore, fatigue . . . Tony could no longer picture Sands' face.

"Wasn't that the same day your buddy got wasted?"

Now he remembered. "Yeah." Tony did not want to repeat his name, or even think of it. "We were in Tiger Land together. Might have come to Vietnam together, too, if I hadn't gone AWOL. Most of the guys were assigned to the 25th."

White pulled a shiny metal tube out of his fanny pack and held it out in the fading light. "Not to change the subject, but I got this that day."

"A rifle barrel?"

He pulled the rest of it out: a wooden stock, a trigger mechanism, a banana clip. "It's the AK-47 I took off that dead gook. The lieutenant tole me to turn it in, but I took it apart, field-stripped it right there on the spot, an' hid it in my pack."

"Have you been carrying that thing with you ever since?" Tait asked.

"You think I'm gonna leave it layin' around for someone to steal? This thing's worth some bucks back in the world. I'm gonna ship it home in pieces an' reassemble it when I get back." He carefully stowed the parts. "If I thought — " The handie-talkie clicked, and White picked up the instrument. "What's up, boss?"

Yates' voice came back loud and clear. "You want to light a couple flares so Charlie can *see* you, too? I can hear every word you're saying."

White's jaw dropped. With his hand over the mouthpiece, he whispered, "He's gotta be bull-shittin'." He pressed the voice contact. "Sorry, boss. We'll keep it down from now on."

"I'll be listening. Out."

White grinned, his teeth all that were visible in the descending darkness. "He didn't hear nothin'." But the inflection in his voice hinted at his uncertainty. He threw his arms out in an exaggerated stretch. "Well, I'm gonna get me some shut eye. Wake me in a couple."

"I don't know how he does it." Tait exchanged his food tins for a rifle, and sat up in a comfortable position.

The stars were out in full panoply, as well as the mosquitoes. Some of the repellent had been sweated off, so Tony applied more. He disliked the smelly, oily substance, but it was better than the constant bites. As the tiny blood suckers buzzed around his ears, he opened a can of food and fished out the cold contents with a plastic spoon.

While the sky was bright, the land was shrouded in shadow. The camp was invisible at the top of the rounded knoll. The distant trees across the range were silhouetted like a ragged paper tear against the purple backdrop. In the village, people walked around the yellow glow of campfires.

Tait cocked his M-16 and cradled it across his lap. "I'd like to rest a little myself."

"I don't mind." Tony took a prone position where he could see over the hummock in front, looking downrange, and still keep an eye on the village. "I'm too jittery to sleep. I've got too much on my mind."

"Don't let it get you down. But if that's the way you feel, I'll just relax my eyelids for a bit. They're feeling kind of heavy."

Tony picked up the starlight scope and removed the lens caps. He put the device to his right eye. Light from the stars was funneled into the instrument and intensified so that the field appeared visible as a snowy, crimson fairyland. It was like looking through rose-colored sunglasses that were full of annoying, crosshatched scratches.

Carmen grass waved in the breeze, the distant trees were scarlet sticks on the horizon. The hooches of An Lap were red dominoes standing out faintly against the surrounding, rusting forest. The bonfires were dancing splotches that looked like living Rorschach inkblots tainted with blood. It was the world of Hieronymus Bosch.

He dabbed at sweat that was stinging his sunburned neck, careful not to rub off the repellent. Time trickled by. He rolled over on his back and gazed up at the stars, trying to pick out constellations. Here, only fifteen degrees north of the equator, there were many constellations that were below the horizon from Salisbury. Without the overpowering lights of civilization, stars became visible as soon as they rose above the distant mountains. He looked hard for the Southern Cross that he had read about in his astronomy books, but without success.

Tony called Yates on the handie-talkie. The squad leader answered promptly, his voice clear and alert. He made another report, and another. He was unable to sleep, and saw no reason to wake up anyone else. By two a.m., he was beginning to feel signs of fatigue. And if he were going to be alert on tomorrow's patrol, he would have to get *some* sleep.

White snored peacefully, stretched out. Tait, in a sitting position, rolled fitfully from side to side. Tony kept digging out rocks and clumps of dirt that got under his belly. If he woke them up now, he could probably sleep straight through till dawn.

The fires of An Lap were red embers lying dormant under a pall of ash. With filmy eyes he took one last look through the scope. His vision was beginning to blur, for the trees in the middle distance seemed to waver above the flowing, red grass. He pressed his fists into his sockets, careful not to get any repellent in his eyes, where it stung terribly. It was no use: he could no longer focus properly without seeing phantoms.

"White," he hissed, grabbing hold of his shoulder. The man remained oblivious. Tony shook him harder. "White."

"I'll take over." Tait stretched his arms and legs, and arched his back. His rifle was balanced on his lap. "What time is it?"

"I just made the two o'clock check in."

Tait stifled a yawn. "You should have called me sooner."

Night was the only time he could feel alone. "I needed some air to clean the cobwebs out of my head." He snuggled down and pulled his knees up to his chin. He clutched his rifle with one hand, as if the skin of his palm had grown around the trigger mechanism. As if it were his childhood teddy bear, he wrapped the other arm around it protectively. He and his rifle had become as one: walking together, eating together, sleeping together. It had been a slow, symbiotic progression, until he could no more imagine being without the powerful weapon than he could be without his arm. They took care of each other.

Tait took a look around, swinging the scope casually. Tony felt his body stiffen, then a trembling hand reached down and found his arm. "Giovanni, did you see anything out there?"

"Yeah, but if you squint it'll go away."

"Did you see — people?"

Tony's eyelids flickered. There was alarm in Tait's voice. He became instantly alert. Sure, he had seen phantoms quivering through the imperfect scope, but they had been the imaginings of a drowsy mind.

"Oh, god," Tait said, in a barely audible monotone.

Tony was wide awake now, clutching at the starlight scope. Tait let him have it, then scooped up the handie-talkie. Cupping his hand over his mouth, he pressed the transmitter button twice. Instead of answering vocally Yates returned the code. It came back as two faint clicks.

Tait whispered into the mouthpiece. "We're in deep shit, Yates. We've got slopes all around us, sneaking toward the perimeter. They're crawling through the grass."

The only reply was two more clicks. Tony knew that Yates understood, and even now was passing the alarm. His heart skipped a beat when he realized that some sappers were closer to the camp than the men on listening post. "Can we get back in?"

Tait clamped a hand over White's mouth, and shook him. White woke up swinging. He

bashed a clenched fist against Tait's steel pot, sending him reeling. Tony leaped forward and wrestled the black man down.

"Cut it out," he breathed.

White relaxed his arms, letting Tony hold him down. "What the fuck is goin' on?"

Tait reseated his helmet liner, came close so all their faces were only inches apart. Their breath was strong in Tony's nostrils. "We've got slopes all around us."

White's face showed gradual enlightenment. "Oh, shit."

Two grenades went off: Rodriguiz was already in action. A moment later the M-60 burst into action, spraying lead in such an arc that the three LPs scrambled to the bottom of the depression, and huddled there like three entangled worms.

"Fucking idiot," White cursed, none too loudly. "Don't he know we're out here? If the gooks don't get us, that fuckin' madman with the machine gun will."

Tony whispered in his ear, "It doesn't matter. He's got to shoot."

"Let's get all our grenades out," Tait suggested. "We daren't fire our guns or it'll give our position away."

"You said a mouthful." White pushed out from under his companions and reached for his web gear. "I brought a bunch o' extras with me."

Tony's hands were shaking as he unclipped six grenades from his harness. He was grateful that he had not used any that day. Suddenly, it seemed as if the entire camp was alert to the sneak attack. Automatic weapons fire chattered from all sides. Tony peered over the edge of their hole, ready to toss a grenade at anything that moved — or even if it looked as if it *might* move.

A terrible fusillade poured out of the jungle on the other side of camp, tearing up the positions that were occupied by First and Second Platoons. Tracers flew back and forth like a Fourth of July fireworks display. Enemy mortars *whumped* from the west and landed perilously close to the command center.

"The shit has hit the fan," White said, observing the battle with only his helmet and the rim of one eye above ground level. Lying equally flat, Tony scanned his field of view through the starlight scope. The sappers were keeping their heads low, now that gunfire was being directed down from the top of the hill. "We gonna need planes, artillery, anything we can get our hands on."

"I think they're going to overrun us." Tait's words struck fear into Tony's heart. "Let's heave a couple grenades just to keep ourselves in the clear." He pulled the pin on one, and hurled it a scant fifteen feet down range. It detonated with a roar that sent shrapnel whizzing over their heads.

"There's someone over there," Tony whispered, never taking his eye from the scope. White obliged him by tossing a grenade in the indicated direction. Tony ducked until the dust settled, then sat back up with the scope. "There's no one moving now."

"Yates! Yates! You gotta get us outa here." White hissed into the mouthpiece as loud as he dared. "Yates, goddamn it, answer the fucking phone."

Bullets soared overhead, rifle fire crackled all over the field, and grenades tumbled down the hill toward every shadow suspected of solidity. To raise their heads more than an inch above the surrounding dirt mound was to invite instant death.

"You better keep your asses glued to the ground," came the whispered reply. "Lay low and I'll call back later."

White dropped the instrument and rolled over on his back. "Oh, God, we gonna die," he whimpered. "We gonna die."

Tait punched him hard on the arm. "Shut up, you fool, before you get us all killed."

Tony continued to sweep the field with the scope. He saw no motion, but the noise from the other side of camp attested to the fierceness of the attack that was coming from the jungle. Then came a bright flash of light from where the trees edged the plain. It startled Tony so much that he dropped the scope, but the fireball kept on coming. It passed right overhead and detonated somewhere within the Bravo Company perimeter.

"Rockets," Tait murmured. One after the other they streamed out of the tree line and pounded into camp. "Or recoilless rifles."

"What'll we do?"

"We gonna die. We gonna die."

"Quit it, White." Tait punched him again. "Mount your bayonet in case we have to fight hand-to-hand."

Tony gulped. He had yet to see a living enemy soldier who was close enough to touch. And he knew that he did not want to get that close. Shooting into a hooch or a patch of jungle was one thing. Shoving a steel blade into a human being was another. He fixed his bayonet with palsied hands. White continued to moan, his whole body trembling as if from the cold. Whenever he made a sound, Tait thumped him with his elbow.

Rockets from the north and mortars from the south continued to pummel the camp. Tait said, "They're softening us up for a ground assault."

"Yes, and for now we're safer right where we are."

A moment later, Tony gave a silent cheer as he heard the whining approach of artillery. The first salvo touched down on prearranged coordinates on the opposite side of camp, at the edge of the jungle where most of the fighting was occurring, splattering the no-man's-land with high explosive shells. Then came another salvo, and another.

Keeping a three-point vigil, White, Tait, and Tony lay in their hole and watched the war. Tony kept his eye glued to the starlight scope, saw a 40 mm grenade arc out of the camp into An Lap.

"Hey, they're shooting into the village."

"Damn, I knew I shouldn't have let Rodriguiz have that launcher," White said.

A second grenade landed square in the middle of a thatched hut. It instantly exploded in flames, bright enough so that Tony could see the melee without the aid of the scope. Villagers dashed madly out of the conflagration, only to be shot down from behind.

"There're VC in the village. They're chasing the people out and shooting them."

"The poor bastards are going to get caught in the crossfire," Tait said.

"What about the kids?" White cried. "Fuckin' bastards are killin' the kids."

"Damn it, keep your voice down."

White slammed the ground with his fist. Every day he had gone down to the village after returning from patrol to give leftovers from the sundry packs to the children. In a few weeks, those silent faces had learned to grin whenever they saw their Number One black man approaching. White reached behind him and grabbed for his rifle.

Tait rolled on top of him and pinned his arm. "Are you out of your mind?" White rolled the lighter man off him, but was immediately held back by Tony. "You can't help them. All you'll do is — "

The grass rustled a few meters away. All three froze. Tony stopped breathing, suddenly overcome with an insatiable urge to clear his throat. He kept swallowing, but the urge would not go away. Stars from the sky stabbed down like klieg lights. He wanted to crawl into his steel pot like a turtle into its shell.

The shooting died down for a moment, extending an unearthly silence. An M-60 let loose, lighting up the night with swift, tiny fireflies. More rockets leaped out of the jungle a mile away, skimmed by overhead, and crashed within the perimeter. As if on signal, dark forms stood up in the knee-high grass, and advanced on the fire base, shooting as they went.

Claymores exploded practically in Tony's ear. Tait lobbed a few grenades downhill, to dissuade the Vietcong from walking over their position.

White plucked a grenade from his harness, stared at it for a moment. "We gotta save at least one. We don' wanna be taken prisoner."

Tait lunged on him. "Put that away, you fool."

"I ain't gettin' captured. Not by no gooks. I know what they do to POWs."

"That's just propaganda," Tony hissed. "You said so yourself."

"You call it whatchu want, but they ain't takin' me alive."

Rockets flared past on long, yellow flames, detonated with a roar of dirt and grass and screaming men. Mortars whistled down from the sky. Dark-clad figures hunched over their weapons, ran forward a few meters, hit the ground, rose up again like immortal phantoms. They were close, horribly close.

An airplane droned overhead, navigation lights doused. Half a dozen brilliant, white phosphorus flares burst in the sky with the intensity of a hundred suns. They floated down slowly, casting the distant jungle in glaring contrast against the open field. Scurrying shapes melted into the waving grass.

The Douglas AC-47 swung wide and made another pass. Correcting for trajectory and the forward motion of the twin-engine plane, the craft tilted so that the three multi-barrel miniguns that projected from the port side were directed at the tree line. Each barrel erupted at the rate of 6,000 rounds per minute as the plane executed a pylon turn that kept the guns bearing on target.

The jungle dissolved under a hail of lead. All enemy resistance ceased as the trees were cut down around the fleeing sappers. Tracers streamed toward the ground in such quantity that it looked like the plane was tethered by a continuous bolt of lightning, swinging it around like a balloon on a string.

"Jesus fucking Christ," White muttered, watching the destruction as a kid watches a circus side show.

"Puff the Magic Dragon," said Tait, giving the slang term in a drawl.

Three minutes and fifty thousand rounds later, the plane straightened and flew away in the dark, a quickly moving silhouette masking a succession of stars. The flares hit the ground, burned in the damp grass, and died out. Blackness came, and silence.

A dark figure loomed over the observation post. The swarthy face seemed just as surprised at finding three American soldiers lying on the ground in front of him, as they were when they looked up at the barrel of the AK-47. The frozen tableau lasted for five interminable seconds before Tait raised his rifle and sliced into the stunned sapper on full automatic. Wild bullets shot into the sky as the Vietcong fell backward, clutching the trigger in his death throes.

Tony dropped the starlight scope and picked up his M-16. He sprayed a full clip downhill. White lobbed a grenade in a high arc. It exploded at the same moment that it landed. Someone moaned in the momentary stillness.

White screamed into the handie-talkie. "Yates, get us the fuck outa here. We comin' in." Before Tait could grab him, he scrambled out of the hole and scurried toward the perimeter on hands and knees.

Tony snatched the transmitter and curled it around his face. "Yates. Yates. Don't shoot. White's coming in."

A split second later, Yates called back. "All right, get your asses in here pronto. You're the only OPs still on the air."

Tony released the key. "He said to come in."

Tait needed no further encouragement. He seized the starlight scope and cradled it over his arms, along with his rifle. He flung his elbows forward and started crawling. Tony was right alongside, slithering on the ground like a snake, low enough to pass under a root.

"Halt, who goes there?"

"It's me. White."

"What's the code word?"

"There ain't no fuckin' code word, Yates, now quit fuckin' aroun'."

"All right, come on in."

White dropped head first into Yates' foxhole just as Tait and Tony cleared the tall grass.

"Pssst. Yates. It's me, Tait."

A fireball flew past on a downward trajectory, landed near the command center. The temporary respite over, Tony needed no more incentive. Just as the entire company opened fire again, he and Tait dropped into the hole built for two. The four of them were jammed together like sardines in a can.

White shook violently. "You goddamn motherfucker, asking me for a fuckin' code word."

"How else was I supposed to know who it was? And I'm damn near out of ammo."

A mortar round landed right behind them, spraying deadly steel splinters across the top of the hole. Tony emptied his bandoliers. "Here, I've got plenty. Want me to go get some more?"

The sky descended, and a body the size of a grizzly bear smashed down on top of them. The side of Tony's face went numb as he was punched and crushed into the bottom of the hole.

"What the fuck we got here, a convention?" came Wallace's deep voice. Another mortar landed, closer.

Yates gurgled, "You okay?"

"Yeah, but I felt the breeze of them pellets.

Burns's outa ammo."

"Get your knee out of my stomach," Tony coughed. "I can't breath."

"Sorry 'bout that."

It sounded as if the entire company was shooting on automatic. Flashes of light erupted from the compound as rockets skidded on nearly parallel arcs like caroming billiard balls.

"You got a concussion from my big feet?"

"Yeah, but it doesn't matter, as long as that carcass of yours is safe. You're a hell of a target, you big baboon."

"Time like this I wish I was a baby monkey."

"You're not furry enough."

"What's with the LP's."

"Who the fuck you think you're standin' on?"

"Haven't heard from the others. If they keep their heads low, Charlie might walk right by them and never know it."

"Man, I sure hope they don't try to play hero. Raymonds owes me ten bucks."

"You want to go collect it?"

"Hell, no."

"If I can get him on the ringer I'll tell him you're concerned about his health."

"Listen, man, I'd love to sit and chitchat witchu, but Burns's gonna be pissed if he gets killed before I git back with his ammo. An' I don't want him mad at me when I go to heaven."

"What makes you think you're going there?"

" 'Cause after this war is over, hell's gonna be plumb full."

"Giovanni, go with him and bring us some more grenades — and bullets."

"I can't get up. Somebody's sitting on me."

As the pressure eased, Tony sprang out of the foxhole like a jack-in-the-box. Wallace had a head start, but Tony caught up to him at the sandbag entrance to the command bunker. An 82 millimeter mortar round exploded right outside. Lieutenant Blake dived through the doorway and knocked Tony down like a three hundred pound linebacker mowing down the center after the hike.

"Where's the ammo, man?"

"Sir, we've got smokes comin' up the hill."

"Catlow's got chinks throwing satchel charges right in his face."

Captain Collins wielded his flashlight like Zorro with his sword. The radiotelephone lay on a box of flares in the middle of the bunker, covered with sand that was falling through gouges in the overhead sandbags. "Hold them off with gunfire. Grenades in that corner, bullets over there. Hello, Spenser, we're getting ready for another pass."

"No, I need machine gun belts."

"I can't. They're hiding in the village."

Shrapnel hit the bunker walls with the sound of marbles on a hardwood floor. The shooting intensified on the east side, where the jungle was close and the enemy well protected.

"Goddamn it, where's Charlie Company? They're supposed to be attacking from the rear."

"Hey, grab a couple o' these belts, too."

"Captain Marina said they got separated in the dark. He's tryin' to find the rest of the company."

"Okay. And I'm getting more 40 millimeters for Rodriguiz."

The roof shuddered as a mortar made a direct hit. The triple sandbag layers held, but inside the command bunker, the dust blew thicker than sand in a Sahara windstorm. "I'm afraid the village may be compromised."

"Do what you can, lieutenant."

The radio crackled. "Brimstone here. We're reloaded and ready to go. Got the coordinates?"

"Hey, get your goddamn ammo and get the hell outa here."

"Here, I can take another one under my arm."

"You mind if we wait till the rocket's red glare ain't glarin'?"

"Sir, I'd like to direct some artillery fire over that way."

"I can't do that now, lieutenant. We've got a Spooky in the air."

"But they're breaking through."

"Hold them off with bullets, grenades, spitballs, anything."

During a lull of incoming, Wallace and Tony charged out of the command bunker, burdened down with ammunition. A rocket chased them across the camp, exploded as they dived into a foxhole on top of Burns. Tony dropped one of the ammo cans. The lip snapped open, spilling out its contents. A fragment of hot metal sliced through it and ignited the loose shells like a burning roll of caps. The men kept their heads down while the fireworks detonated inches away.

"Where the fuck you been? Out on a goddamn coffee break?"

Wallace slid out from under eight heavy ammunition belts that crisscrossed his broad chest. "I had to sign for every shell — in triplicate."

Burns ripped a canteen cover from his ammo belt, and used it as a glove. The barrel of the M-60 was glowing like a flaming torch, illuminating the inside of the foxhole. "Thought you were out on LP?"

"It got crowded out there."

Burns extracted the glowing barrel and dropped it hissing and spluttering into the wet mud in the bottom of the hole. "Ain't no picnic in here."

Wallace slammed a magazine into his M-16, and emptied it toward the village of An Lap. "Fuckin' gooks're gonna overrun us, the lieutenant don't get that artillery on its way. Human wave assault. You fire the claymores, yet?"

Tony stuck up his head, started burping off rounds on semiautomatic. Bullets whizzed back so close to his ears that he could hear the popping sounds as they created momentary vacuums and the air clapped together in the wake.

The new barrel was installed. *Rat-tat-tat* went the machine gun. "No, I'm savin' 'em."

"What the fuck for, a rainy day?" Wallace searched for the detonator leads.

"I'm waitin' for 'em to come close."

"What the fuck you wanna do, read their goddamn dog tags for Chrise sake?"

Sappers were popping up everywhere, coming up the hill from the village. Tony burned through another magazine, repacked it from the cardboard boxes. "I've got to get the rest of this ammo distributed."

Wallace twisted the wires onto the blasting cap. "As soon as I blow this mother, you get going." The village was in flames, and enemy soldiers were silhouetted against the flickering crimson glow.

Burns fired a sustained burst. Screws and rivets flew off the breech. "This fuckin' gun is gonna fall apart in my hands pretty soon." Two claymores exploded, sending out thousands of steel pellets. As soon as the backwash subsided, Tony leaped up and dashed to the next hole. He slid into it with enemy bullets on his tail.

"Thought you'd never get here," Yates said.

"Yeah, well, it's rush hour, you know. Where're the rest of the guys?"

"Hiding out in the next hole. White's shakin' so bad he started a landslide."

Tony opened an ammunition can and poured out several boxes of bullets. "Thank God someone had the foresight to order more. How're *their* supplies holding out?"

"They could use a refill."

"As they say in the mental institution, I must be off."

The Spooky dropped more flares, started hammering the jungle in front of First Platoon. Tony felt like a snowman in a coal bin as he raced for the next foxhole.

"You got here just in time. I done shot up all my ammo," White said.

Tait took a great handful of cartridge boxes. "Rodriguiz's over there screaming for grenades."

"Got a whole can full." Invisible rifle fire shot right above his head. The Vietcong were not using tracers. Tony looked for muzzle flashes in the grass, emptied a magazine about

knee high. "Cover me."

Between mortar barrages and rockets, Tony slid into the hole with the Puerto Rican, and handed him a full case. "Did you order a pizza with mustard and extra onions?"

"Man, you been hanging around that vaudeville team too long. Miller's over there crying for ammo."

"Thanks for the tip." Tony slid into the next hole at the same time that Lieutenant Blake got there. He had an ammunition can, too.

The Douglas poured out tons of lead, while tracers from the eastern perimeter arced into the no-man's-land. More rockets cascaded from the western jungle, where the Spooky had already made its pass. The enemy seemed to be unstoppable.

Miller fired obliquely, into the smoking village. "Sir, we gotta do something. The old man don't know how bad it is."

"I tried to tell him, but he wouldn't listen. Where's that radio?" Lieutenant Blake keyed in the mike. "Captain. Blake here. We got smokes breathing down our necks. I'm requesting artillery fire starting from three hundred meters out."

Captain Collins answered immediately. "Lieutenant, are you aware there's a civilian hamlet out there?"

"Sir, the smokes are *in* the hamlet. The only way we can save the village is to blow it up. They're taking cover in the hooches."

"Lieutenant, I can't risk the lives of innocent women and children."

"Their safety is already compromised. And I've got three men out on LP I haven't heard from in an hour. Their lives are more important than a bunch of 'Yards."

"I hate to interrupt this discussion, but I'm hit."

"Lieutenant, get off the air. Brimstone — "

Blake threw down the phone. "The impotent coward. He'll kill us all for a herd of cattle. Hey, leave some ammo and get the hell out of here."

Miller said, "Haven't heard anything from Kelsey. See if he's outa ammo."

The flares from the Spooky continued to throw their stark, white light.

Tony left one can and took the other with him. The air was dense with the odor of gunpowder. Bullets winged by like angry hornets as he hit the ground and rolled into the foxhole. Something squished under his feet. He looked down, gasped, and clambered out of the hole.

He lay flat, next to Kelsey's torso. When he put his hand on the machine gunner's chest, it sank right into the spongy material of his deflated lungs. He jerked back, covered with blood and gore. He stared in shock for only a second, then the last flare died out. Taking advantage of the darkness, Tony jumped up and ran back to the lieutenant's position.

"Sir, they're dead. Both of them. Looks like a mortar fell right into their hole."

Bullets slammed into the dirt around them, and Tony dropped head first between Miller and Blake. The sergeant placed several controlled bursts downrange.

"Damn." Lieutenant Blake picked up the radiotelephone, screamed into it, "Sir, I need those shells now. We may not be able to hold out much longer."

"Lieutenant, you may have tactical control of the artillery. Can you direct it from your position?"

Tony saw teeth in the darkness. "Yes, *sir*." To Tony, "Go warn the men to keep low, 'cause I'm gonna blast everything between here and that ville to kingdom come."

Wordlessly, Tony started crawling along the perimeter. A strange calmness came over him. The utter fear that had gripped him with the first assault, that had engulfed him when they became sealed off from help, that had caused such uncontrollable trembling when he could hear sappers crawling through the grass, had been supplanted by the exigencies of the moment. It was as if a switch had been thrown, casting aside thoughts of danger and replacing them with a dedication for survival.

Fear was useful when it kept one from being overbold. But it became a liability when it served no purpose. This night, Tony passed from the ranks of initiates and entered the ken of soldiers who had reached a peace with their hearts, and from then on could face death squarely in the eyes — and spit on it.

When death did not come as expected, life became all the more exciting. And when the stimulation of the moment died down, the heart yearned for more. Battle now became a self-seeking goal, the only reason for living. Each moment had to be more intense than the last.

With almost orgasmic pleasure, Tony sighted and fired, sighted and fired, feeling a strange sensation in his groin that he had never felt before. He no longer thought about living through the night, he hoped only that he could maintain the feeling of exhilaration. He wanted action. And if it did not come to him, he would have to seek it out.

He plopped into the hole next to Yates. "Hang onto your helmet. Blake's going to drop HE in our laps."

Yates never stopped firing. "You mean Collins?"

"I mean Blake. The captain's afraid of hitting the village, so he's letting Blake take over."

Three mortars whined down from the sky and pummeled the center of the compound. Three more followed. Rockets, leaning forward on long yellow tails, leaped out of the jungle on parallel trajectories. Bullets winged by from somewhere right in front. Tony emptied a magazine, then ducked low to reload another while Yates planted covering fire.

"Captain always was a pussy. Leaves it up to his platoon leaders to do the dirty work."

Tony shot at phantom shapes, never knowing if he hit any, or if they were nothing more than bushes. He just kept firing, firing, firing. His skin tingled, his heart thrilled. He was alive — oh, so alive.

Tracers flew all over the camp, but Tony ignored them as if they were nothing more than annoying insects. The hammering noise of battle had dulled his senses. The odor of cordite and burning flesh was no longer noticeable. It was merely a three dimensional movie, without popcorn.

Incoming artillery shells screamed out of the sky like shooting stars. Tony and Yates ducked into the hole as the first salvo exploded practically in their faces. The concussion hit Tony like a two-by-four across the forehead. The dirt that rained down shortened the depth of the hole by inches. Chunks of hot steel thudded into the ground. The sides of the foxhole caved in around their feet.

The next salvo walked away, toward the still-burning village of An Lap. The no-man's-land was crisscrossed with jagged steel projectiles that must have minced anything that was not underground. Shrubbery was uprooted, grass was burnt, stones were fractured.

Tony stuck up his head, and watched as Burns poured hot lead into the fleeing figures that were dodging among the hooches of An Lap. Whether soldiers or civilians, he could not tell. Tony checked his fire. He wanted to be sure of his target: so many people, running, screaming. Rodriguiz popped grenades from the launcher into the melee.

The high-pitched whine returned. Tons of death and destruction descended upon the once peaceful village. With a gigantic, thundering roar and a flash of heat, the thatched huts were first leveled, then hurled upward in a boiling cauldron of broken, burning bamboo. Scintillating debris showered down, tumbling, blazing, bringing with it the stench of death, and left in its wake complete and utter devastation. It was the grandest, most glorious sight that Tony had ever witnessed.

Afterwards came silence, total and absolute. Vigilance went unrewarded, for after the dried thatch was consumed, nothing moved. For the alert, there was nothing to see. For the wounded, there was pain; and for some, slow death.

For the dead, there was mockery.
****

At the first crack of light, as smoke still hung in the air, three worn men slowly climbed to their feet and waved. A huge grin broke out on Yates' face as the men whom he thought must be dead at their listening post headed wearily for the perimeter, dragging their weapons like lead weights. They were grim-faced and hollow-eyed, and stared vacantly.

"The kids!" White stared at the ruins of An Lap, still smoldering. Not a building was standing, not a soul was moving. He started walking down the hill, along the path, first slowly, then running.

"White!" Tony ran after him, clutched his arm, tried to make him stop. White shrugged him off with powerful muscles that were unweakened by the night's agonies.

"The bastard. He didn't have to bomb 'em."

"He had no choice."

"The fuckin' bastard."

The trees had been blown flat. The water buffalo lay dead in their pens; chickens and pigs were roasted. The well was gone, sheered off level with the ground and covered with debris. The bamboo and thatch were smoking piles of black residue. The stench of charred bodies was pervading, nauseating.

White bent down on' one knee, stared at the blackened remains of a mother, clutching her baby in death as she had nursed it in life. He cried, long and loud. Tony stood by his side, squeezing his shoulder. Tears ran down his own face, making tracks on muddy cheeks.

"Don't look now, but Charlie Company finally showed up," Yates said.

The approaching men seemed clean and fresh, their weapons fully loaded and ready for action. They arrived like Nemesis, but too late to do any good. They tramped through what was left of the village, ponderously, sacrilegiously, to stare goggle-eyed at the men of C Squad.

"Hey, Tony. Tony! It's me. Terry."

A sudden weariness came over Tony. He heard the voice inside his head, dully. It was all he could do to raise his chin. He wavered on his feet, exhausted, slump-shouldered, barely able to keep from dropping his rifle. His eyes focused slowly.

Terry Kurtz stopped in front of him, a smile on his bronzed cheeks. He had not changed much since jungle warfare training, an eternity ago. "Looks like you had a pretty bad night."

Tony did not answer, but stared back fathomlessly.

"We were supposed to reinforce you last night, but we got lost."

Tony's fingered quivered, his arm contract-

ed. The M-16 took on a mind of its own.

"I mean, we got separated. The old man, he had us coming through this fucking jungle in the dark. Some of us lost contact. Man, it was scary."

The rifle barrel rose like an erection, stiffened, thrust forward. The butt was jammed in the crook of Tony's arm.

"I mean scary, man. Couldn't see your hand in front of your face. We had radios, but you couldn't give directions over them. I mean, we couldn't call Triple A for road service. Wandered around all night trying to find the main part of the company. Would have been here sooner but — "

The rifle was aimed at Terry's crotch, his stomach, his chest, his throat. "Hey, it wasn't my fault. We were lost. This goddamn jungle — "

The flash suppressor stopped inches away from Terry's forehead, aimed over the bridge of the nose, right between the eyes. It was rock steady.

A snakelike tongue darted out and licked dry lips. Eyes flickered from Tony to barrel, from barrel to Tony. "I mean, I was *scared*. We were lost — We could hear the rockets, the mortars, but it was thick — The underbrush, the vines — "

After a nighttime of use, of wallowing in the mud, of being pummeled with flying dirt, the trigger squeaked as Tony slowly squeezed it. His eyes were piercing daggers, drilling into Terry's skull.

Tony to barrel, barrel to Tony. "It was *bad*, man. We were lost. It — it wasn't my fault."

Tony's finger kept squeezing with a volition all its own.

"We coulda got here sooner, but — Man, it wasn't my fault."

Tighter.

"It wasn't my fault."

Tony pulled the trigger. The bolt shot home.

Chapter 99

Heat poured off the dry rice paddy in clear, snaky ribbons, making the distant trees seem to sway rhythmically in a hula dance. Tony's feet were being fried on the hot sand while the rest of him baked in the reflection. His fatigues were soaked with sweat. Salty beads dripped off his eyebrows. His puffy tongue licked cracked lips.

Three water buffalo scanned the point squad through jaundiced eyes, warily watching the two-legged creatures that were invading their grazing territory. Longhaired tails swatted continuously at flies; fuzzy ears wiggled annoyingly.

The V formation marched ahead lethargically. Rodriguiz, walking point, kept a vigilant eye on the trees to the left. He ignored the endless stretch of paddy ahead and to the right: no Vietcong would hide in the open. He clutched the handgrip of his M-16, index finger curled around the black trigger.

Thumping hooves sounded from the right. Tony looked around and spotted the charging water buffalo. Long, sharp horns stabbed the air as the beast of burden lumbered toward him on galloping legs. Tony stood his ground, held his rifle out in front of him, and yelled. The animal, momentarily nonplussed, veered away. White, walking behind him, turned screaming as the animal roared past dangerously close. Except for Rodriguiz and Tony, the formation scattered like ten pins as the animal trampled through one leg of the V and out the other.

Tony stood there laughing at the fleeing men. White fell headlong, Burns stepped back and tripped over a low dike. Wallace dropped to one knee, ready to shoot for his life. Tait jumped one way while Yates jumped the other. The big bull grunted loudly as it passed between them. Then it turned, and faced the broken ranks with a direful stare.

Yates retained as much composure as he could, standing tall and erect and aiming his rifle at the beast. But it just stood there; it had made its point.

Burns climbed to his feet, shaking sand out of the machine gun barrel. "That's as much action as we've had in a week."

Wallace eased away from the half-ton animal. "You wanna go back to the highlands?"

"I don't never wanna see another mountain. Had enough action to last me a lifetime. I'll take a flat, quiet rice paddy any day."

The squad regrouped while the rest of the company halted in their tracks and watched their discomfiture. A charging water buffalo was a welcome diversion after endless days and profitless patrols.

Tony laughed. "Hey, Burns, don't take any crap off that buffalo. It's just a lot of bull."

"Son of a bitch knows we ain't gonna shoot it — not with the old man around."

Bravo Company regrouped on the other side of the animals, took a breather in the open by a flooded paddy. Tony cupped his hand in the thin film of scum that floated on the surface, then buried his canteen into the mud so that the spout was underwater. That would keep out most of the unwanted filth. He knew the Vietnamese used human feces for fertilization, but it did not stop him, or anyone else, from taking his fill. Three dull-gray leeches were attached to the olive drab plastic when he pulled out the nearly full canteen; he wiped them off with a stick and plopped two purification tablets

through the neck of the canteen. He waited only ten minutes before gulping down the water. It was hot, but delicious.

Burns leaned against a seven-foot mound of hardened dirt that had only slightly more girth than he had. Half a dozen of these hillocks staggered along the tree line. He leaned the machine gun on his hip and tilted his steel pot back to wipe sweat off his forehead. "Whadda the gooks use these for?"

Tony inspected the spire, picking at it with his bayonet. Several tiny, red ants crawled out of the hole, maddened at the intrusion. "It's an anthill."

Burns jumped as if he had been singed. "Crazy fuckin' country." He wiped crawling bugs off his jacket sleeves. "The gooks live in the ground an' the ants have condos."

"If the VC don't get chu, the wildlife will," Wallace said.

The men drifted away from the insect high-risers and found a safer place to finish their rest period.

Small arms fire crackled from one side of the stretched-out company. Two or three M-16s barked at a grove of trees that stood several hundred meters away. Captain Collins looked up from his map, squinted his eyes in the afternoon sun.

"What's going on, lieutenant?"

Lieutenant Blake was on his feet immediately, even though it was not his platoon that was engaged. His recent field promotion had instilled him with even more incentive to take command of every situation. If he could make first lieutenant by bringing in artillery on an out-of-the-way Montagnard hamlet, he now knew the path to captaincy.

"Three men in white, didiing like crazy."

A sergeant from Lieutenant Catlow's platoon ran back with a report. "Sir, we got some suspicious looking characters out there. Started running away when we fired on 'em."

"Must be VC," Blake said. "Want me to run 'em down?"

"I want your help with these maps. How about detaching a squad to go after them?"

"Yates!" When the squad leader looked over, Lieutenant Blake shouted, "Go check it out."

Tony threw the selector switch and trotted off, rifle ready. He saw the three bobbing, conical hats retreating westward, toward the jungle a mile away. Hand grenades clanged together as his web gear bounced up and down with each step. Squared off sections of rice paddy, some wet and some dry, filled the open area. Peasants worked in the wet paddies, bent over with legs spread and knees straight, ignoring the noise that the Americans were making. A few water buffalo stalked the mud flats, rooting for food. After a minute of hard running, Tony was getting out of breath.

Yates fired from the hip on the fleeing figures, yelling for them to stop. They were far beyond hearing range, and continued to skip over the low dikes. To Tony they did not appear to be armed, or carrying anything.

"Stop them!" Yates brought his rifle up to his shoulder. *Crack! Crack! Crack!* went his M-16. No one else fired a round.

"Hey! Wait a minute! They're unarmed," Tony warned.

Yates kept firing, all his shots going wide. "They're running, and we got to stop them."

Peasants in the line of fire scattered out of the way. Tony raised his rifle, sighted in. At a range of over five hundred meters, he had to elevate the weapon so much that the muzzle prevented him from seeing the three runaways. With expert precision he fired three shots, then lowered his weapon and waited for the bullets to reach their target. He was gratified to see puffs of dust kick up directly in front of the white clad figures. He let loose another three rounds, aiming over their heads.

"After them." Yates swept his arm over his head.

Still, no one else fired. The men fanned out and surged over the dry paddies. Tony ran as fast as his clattering gear and weighted pack would allow. He passed by peasants who were cowering behind the low berms, lying in the water.

Tony continued shooting over the tops of the three conical hats, hoping that the accuracy of his aim would convince them to stop. He could easily have brought them down if they had shown some aggression, or returned his fire. But they just kept running, probably scared.

Way out in front, he raced along a dike between two flooded paddies. He had to pull up the pistol belt, for the swinging grenades threatened to emasculate him. Still half a mile away, the three people blended into the forest. Tony stopped to catch his breath. He was sweating profusely, but the heat hardly bothered him. He had become acclimated — to the weather, if not to the war.

Yates continued to blast away, senselessly. Nearby, a water buffalo was bucking crazily around an old man. Tony thought it must be the noise that was scaring the animal, until he saw puffs of sand kicking up around it.

He started running again. Reaching a perpendicular dike in the maze of squared off paddies, he ran toward the cow and the farmer who was trying to grab her harness. The scrawny Vietnamese was knocked down when the beast thundered past. But he got up and ran after it, ignoring the bullets that were slamming into the ground at his feet. Yates stopped to change magazines.

In the sudden silence, Tony tried to interfere. A group of women lay flat in a dry paddy, crying in their singsong language. Tony raced by as Yates put the rifle up to his shoulder again. A shot cracked the silence, and a puff of dirt kicked up dust only meters beyond the animal. The slug must have passed right under the bulging udder.

"Hold your fire!" Tony yelled.

Another shot rang out. The buffalo danced as if stung by a bee. Now the farmer was trying to get out of her way as she leaped and twisted like a mad Brahman bull at a rodeo.

"Hold your fire!"

The Vietnamese fell down to avoid the high-flying kicks. The beast of burden pirouetted with surprising gainliness for an animal so large and ungainly-looking. The farmer rose, oblivious to the bullets that zinged around him. The water buffalo might have been his sole possession in the world.

"Hold your fire!"

Tony bolted along the dike until he was almost in Yates' line of fire. He held his rifle over his head and waved it back and forth. He was dangerously close to getting shot down by his own squad leader.

Yates paused, and peered over his sights. Tony kept going until he was between Yates and the farmer. The squad leader was forced to throw down his weapon. Tony turned and faced the farmer who was still intent on chasing the wounded animal, which was galloping in fear of the steel jacketed insects that had buzzed past her ears and stung her tough hide.

Tony put his left hand on the old man's bony shoulder. The farmer turned and shouted invectives in his native tongue. Tony did not understand a word of it, but it was obvious that he was not discussing the World Series. Cursing in any language was cursing. The leathery face of the peasant glanced after his water buffalo, and he started to go after her.

Tony grabbed him again. "Mister, you'd better stay put, because that man over there — " He pointed with his M-16. " — would like nothing better than an excuse to shoot you."

The old man jabbered, and pointed toward his galloping water buffalo. "I don't care. You'll have to let it go."

More Vietnamese malediction spouted from the wrinkled corners of the peasant's mouth. He flung his arms around like a signalman.

"I know how you feel, but you have to do what I say. How about showing me some ID. You know, ID. ID. Identification card."

Tony could see that the pajama tops and loose fitting shorts had no pockets. And it was ludicrous to continue the conversation. Neither understood the other, and both were talking as if they did. The old man pointed frantically at his water buffalo, while Tony pointed at his squad leader.

"Mister, he would like nothing better than an excuse to just blow you away." Any dead Vietnamese was automatically Vietcong. "Papasan, unless you want to add to the body count, you'd better be a good boy and come with me."

The farmer jabbered, but refused to follow Tony's motioning hand.

"This is getting us nowhere." Tony lowered his rifle so the barrel pointed at the ground between the peasant's feet. He squeezed the trigger. As the rifle barked, the old man jumped catlike into the air, without flexing a muscle in his scrawny legs. He hit the ground crying, and gesticulating. "Now that I've got your attention, I think you'd better come with me."

Tony pushed the peasant ahead and kept right on his heels. The farmer was sufficiently intimidated, but every few steps he stole a look at the fat cow that, Tony surmised, probably supplied the entire hamlet with milk. The water buffalo lay calmly in the middle of a dry paddy, licking its wounds.

The rest of the squad had gathered around a group of frightened peasants who were slowly rising from behind a dike. Babbling women adjusted their conical hats and retied their chinstraps. One young girl lay on her back while an ancient, gray-bearded papasan knelt by her side, his lower lip quivering silently.

Burns nodded with his chin. "See you scared the shit outa the old man."

"Just like he did to that kid from Charlie Company, 'cept he hadn't run outa ammo," said Wallace.

Yates shoved the crouching papasan away. "Quit the banter and check these people for IDs."

Tony's prisoner gestured toward his water buffalo, talking volubly. He paid no attention to the mud that clung to his naked feet, or the dung that squished between splayed toes. The women continued to wail. Penetrating eyes that had seen too much war, too much innocent bloodshed, stabbed at the soldiers accusingly.

Tony laid his rifle aside and dropped to examine the supine girl. Pearly white shoulders rested on the old farmer's lap, her head cradled in his gnarled hands. She looked up at Tony, spoke in her native tongue in a calm, clear voice. Blood stained the old man's hands.

"What happened to her?"

"Looks like somebody shot her," Yates sneered.

Snapping his head around, Tony snarled, "What do you mean, somebody? You and I were the only ones shooting, and I was aiming over their heads."

Yates was instantly enraged. "What were you doing that for?"

"I was trying to stop them."

"The only way to stop 'em is to drop 'em. When I give orders to fire, I mean shoot to kill."

"At what? Civilians?"

"They were VC."

"What? Were they wearing signs, or something?"

"They were running away, and that proves it."

"It only proves they wanted to stay alive. They've run up against Americans like you before. Look at the way you shot up that water buffalo — and this girl." Tony shook his head slowly. "You just look for an excuse to kill, don't you?"

"That's why we're here, remember?"

"We're supposed to fight the enemy, not civilians. Try acting like a soldier instead of a murderer."

Yates' broad hand reached down, grasped Tony's fatigue jacket, and pulled him to his feet. "Giovanni, that's enough out of you. We're out here to do a job and sometimes the locals get in the way. Sure, some of 'em get killed, but this is their country so they shouldn't mind dying for it. Now let's get the hell out of here while *we're* still alive."

He shoved Tony away. Tony dug his heel into the sandy soil and stared venomously at the squad leader, fists clenched. The hatred that passed between the two was tangible. Tony's teeth ground out the words that he longed to say, his face contorted with the effort. He looked down at the girl, her head rolling back and forth and her jaw working soundlessly. Her eyelids fluttered; she stared up at him with brown, doleful eyes. She was hardly more than a teenager; maybe eighteen at the most.

Almost as old as my wife, Tony thought.

He knelt down by her and the old man. When he saw her tongue lick dry lips, he automatically reached for his canteen, unscrewed the cap, and held the spout to her lips. He tilted it slightly as her mouth closed around the plastic threads. She sucked greedily, her head coming forward to get more of the life-sustaining water.

"Call a medevac," Tony ordered.

"We don't have a radio."

"Then send someone after it."

"I'm not splitting up the squad. This is enemy territory, and if we don't catch up with the rest of the company we may all find ourselves with bullets in our backs."

"So how do we get help?"

"We don't."

Every face in the squad was cast in bronze. "We can't just leave her here."

"Why not? She'll be dead soon anyway."

Tony tasted blood in his mouth. "You'd like that, wouldn't you, you bastard?"

The girl mumbled. Blood trickled through the old man's hands. The girl was wearing faded white shorts, and a pullover that was torn and bloody. Tony took two fistfuls of material and ripped the blouse down the middle. He saw no fear in her eyes, no hope, no longing. Used to living without doctors, without medical facilities, it was commonly accepted that a serious wound resulted in death. She was merely awaiting the inevitable.

Very gently he spread the shirt, revealing two small, delicate breasts with faded pink nipples. Tony swallowed, and flushed: embarrassed that he could not take his eyes off them. The girl did not seem to notice. She uttered something in Vietnamese that was soft and soothing. He slid the right sleeve over her shoulder and carefully pulled her arm out of it. He lifted her slightly, halting when she let out an involuntary moan. With his eyes he said he was sorry, then bent close to the ground to inspect the wound.

The bullet had entered just below the shoulder blade, traveled up through the muscle, and come out her arm. The bones did not appear broken, and the fact that she could not move her left arm might be due to shock, or muscle damage. There was surprisingly little bleeding for a hole made by an M-16 round.

Tony yanked out his first-aid kit, ripped open a package, and slapped a compress over each wound, making the old man hold them in place while he wrapped the material of the shirt around the gauze pads. Then he made a sling around her neck and tied it in front. The wizened old man nodded, parting lips to reveal rotted, blackened teeth.

"Let me take her, now." Tony reached under her back and knees. The old man placed the paralyzed left arm across her naked breast. Tony leaned back to gain a balance point, then stood with the girl in his arms.

She was a fragile bundle of flowers, each pretty petal in danger of being crushed.

"What the hell do you think you're doing?" Yates said gruffly.

"Taking her with us," was the cool reply. There was no defiance in his voice, no incrimination — just a simple statement of fact. "We'll catch up with the company and call for a medevac. It's the least we can do."

Yates' jaw muscles bunched; his face had the pall of a riled tomcat. "What about your weapon?"

The war could be won without guns and bombs and napalm. "Forget it. It's not important."

"It'll come out of your pay."

"I don't need the money."

"You can't leave it here for Charlie."

In all this time, not another man in the squad had uttered a word. Now, Rodriguiz stepped forward. "I take it for you."

Yates glared at him for a moment, fists clenching. After a long silence, he said, "All right, let's get going. And bring these two along. I want them checked out. If they make a false move, waste 'em."

Guns clattered, pointed at the two peasants. They got the idea, and followed the squad leader. From the women left behind there was not a word.

The girl was a feather in Tony's arms. She weighed no more than eighty or ninety pounds. The long tresses of raven, silky hair, now plastered with blood, hung down straight, swinging at every step. Large eyes stared up at him silently. If there was pain behind those eyes, it was well concealed.

The makeshift bandage was soaked through. Tony could feel the sticky fluid where it coagulated on his arm. He paid it no mind, concentrating instead on his footing. He walked along the middle of the dike, while on both sides the squad fanned back in a truncated V. White and Rodriguiz splashed through the water to his left, Burns and Wallace stamped in a dry paddy to his right. Tait stayed behind with the two prisoners.

When they reached the end of the wet paddies, Yates struck out diagonally toward the place where they had left Bravo Company. The girl closed her eyes against the bright sun, notched her face in the crook of Tony's arm. Sweat poured annoyingly down his face, into his eyes, over cracked lips. The salt stung, but he could not wipe off the sweat.

He felt the strain on his arms. He curled his fingers and used them to inch his hands around for a firmer grip. The girl did not seem to notice. The sun beat down relentlessly. Inside his steel pot, Tony's head baked like a potato in an oven. The sweatband gripped his head like a vise. He squinted beads of perspiration out of the corners of his eyes.

The uneven footing became a problem because Tony could not see where his boots were setting down. He constantly misjudged the random corrugations, either catching his toe or stepping into a depression. With the heat, with the weight on his arms, his strength was waning fast. It became an effort to lift his legs, to keep his shoulders straight. The muscles in his back started aching painfully. But he, like the girl, refused to cry out.

The company had moved on. Instead of heading back to the point from which they had separated, Yates led them on an intersecting course. The paddies seemed to go on forever, an endless flatland that was ribbed with dikes and punctuated with stands of trees. Shimmering heat waves danced over the sand like crystal kelp surging in the sea. Tony felt like a crucible holding a delicate chemical over a Bunsen burner. The strain on his arms sent shooting pains all the way down to his fingertips.

They passed peasants working in the field. From bent-over positions they mutely tipped their conical hats to watch the strange parade. Of soldiers they had seen plenty, but never one carrying one of their own.

Tony flexed his muscles and brought the girl closer to his chest. Her dark eyes opened. If she suffered any pain by his movement, she forbore from showing it. Not the slightest complaint escaped her lips. Tony smiled weakly, belying his own agony. Light she might be by human standards, but how far could he carry a sandbag in his arms?

His legs began to falter. With full web gear, gas mask and tear gas grenades, food and ammunition, fanny pack stuffed with poncho and sundries, he was already carrying the normal compliment. He had grown accustomed to that, felt naked without it. He was in the finest physical condition he had ever been — undaunted by heat, lack of sleep, and sheer exertion. But he could not go on forever.

Yates turned around periodically, casting aspersive glances. Tony tried to keep his face a mask, to hide the torment that he felt. He refused to yield, either to his aching muscles or to Yates' insulting jeers.

His foot caught a clump of grass. He stumbled, but caught himself. His arms were painful stumps, no longer part of his body, but mechanical braces that were weakening, bending under the load.

Then he was on the ground, without any idea of how he had gotten there. His knees were jammed into the loam, his arms rested on his thighs. He had kept his fingers curled around the girl's arm and leg; she was still in his grip. He leaned over her body, groaning because his flesh was weaker than his soul. His arms were lead weights tied to the earth.

"I — need — to — rest." He did not want to sound imploring, but was unable to do otherwise.

Yates stopped, no longer in charge of the situation.

A grim satisfaction came over Tony when he realized that the retreat would proceed at *his* pace, at *his* command.

Yates merely nodded.

Tony leaned back and gently pulled his arms out from under the girl's soft body. She stared wide-eyed at him, with warmth and hope — and trust. Even though they spoke different tongues, her face expressed volumes. Tony held his canteen to her lips; he forced her to drink. He finished the rest of the water, then wiped the sweat off his face and forehead with his stained, mud-caked shirttail.

Too soon, Yates uttered, "Let's get going," and, without waiting to see that his orders were carried out, marched off. Tony stood up with his burden. The two Vietnamese men following meekly.

Some of the strength had come back to his arms, but he was in a weakened condition. Only minutes passed before he felt the strain. His back ached, his arms throbbed, he feet dragged along the ground. How much farther did they have to go?

A group of ancient women and goggle-eyed children watched them from a dilapidated hooch that was surrounded by a few sparse trees. In the middle of this vast rice paddy, the oasis of shade was used as a nursery while younger, able-bodied mothers worked in the field.

"Hold up."

Tony sank slowly to his knees, his head spinning. He placed the girl on the ground, careful of her injury, and waited for the kaleidoscopic images to fade. He drew out his arms and flexed his tortured triceps.

One toothless mamasan ushered her charges inside, but the others held their ground. Tony's eyes focused on the makeshift, bamboo door that was tied with thong hinges made of vine. He struggled to his feet and shuffled past the gawking children. He slashed the aged vines, and appropriated the door without asking. He laid it on the ground next to the girl. Carefully, he worked her slender form onto the tubular slats: shoulders first, then hips, then legs and feet.

"You! You! Over here. Like this." Tony indicated how he wanted the two Vietnamese prisoners to carry one end of the door. They were willing to help. Tony stooped at the girl's head, reached behind him, and lifted. The two papasans picked up the other end, and started walking. Yates scowled, motioning the men to follow.

With only half the load to bear, Tony's strength was quickly renewed. But after a few hundred meters this proved to be a false hope. The unnatural position of having his wrists bent backwards against the hacked off, splintered wood was uncomfortable in the extreme. The jagged ends banged into the back of his legs at every step. His lower back ached because of the way he had to hunch over. And still there was the unremitting sun, the waves of heat.

Tony's mouth was dry, his throat parched. His empty canteens hung uselessly at his side. He did not want to give Yates satisfaction by asking for water. He was determined not to give in to purely physical needs. He was resolved not to suffer the ignominy of pleading again for rest. He would continue until he dropped.

"Over this way," Yates said abruptly.

Tony had been walking in a mental fog, staring at the worn leather uppers of his jungle boots. In the middle of this vast field stood a house, made of real boards, and decorated with shutters and doors: probably built by a French landlord when this land was known to English-speaking world as Indo-China. The house was surrounded by a grove of tall shade trees, covering a broad courtyard that thronged with women and children. In the middle was a stone-walled well.

The temperature dropped twenty degrees in the shade, and a cooling breeze rustled leaves on the lower branches. Young mothers kept their youngsters out of the way; children watched the armed squad move in and, without asking, take over the well.

The men were unusually quiet as they raised the bucket from the depths and drank their fill. Even Burns and Wallace made no banter. Tony found a rag on the ground, soaked it with water, and placed it over the wounded girl's forehead. She would drink no water.

One of the household women, of middle age, knelt by her side. They talked sibilantly in Vietnamese. The older woman cast brief glances at Tony. Then Yates grabbed her roughly and pulled her away.

"Get out of here, mamasan. I've got enough trouble without you two passing on intelligence." He stared hard at Tony, then at the rest of the squad. "White, Rodriguiz, you relieve him."

Tony felt no satisfaction over his triumph in the contest of wills. Dominance was not the issue, nor honor, nor dignity, but the propriety of humanity.

The last drink was swallowed, the last of the canteens was filled. Tony took the two rifles from Rodriguiz. Tait stepped forward and took White's. The two prisoners resumed their station at the foot of the door. The children stared curiously after the departing men.

Tony walked alongside the improvised stretcher, keeping between the girl and the blinding sun. He pulled the dampened cloth over her eyes and glanced briefly at her exposed breasts. He could not help but feel the quivering in his groin, the longing in his heart.

The rice paddies stretched unceasingly. Except for the jungle border, two klicks to the east, the flatland continued to the limits of visibility. Only intervening streams, snaking through the fields and made visible by the trees and shrubbery that fed on the precious water that they carried, offered any relief. At incredible distances Tony could see people conducting their daily routine among the waving green stems, content in their work and oblivious to the war that was being waged around them. The peasants' fight was with poverty.

The Americans brought war. The Vietcong brought war. But when they left, the war left with them. The people remained unchanged. Those who survived when the governments and the soldiers got tired of fighting, continued on as they did before: eating, sleeping, having babies, growing rice, eking out a simple existence so their children could do the same. They had no need of guns, or technology, or politics.

Time had no meaning in this country. It was not gauged in hours and minutes and seconds, but in generations and growing seasons.

Later, much later, they came upon the rear guard of Bravo Company. Only when he saw Sergeant Miller did Tony recognize the other half of the platoon. All the rest were new, still-unfamiliar faces, replacements for those who were lost and wounded in that last great assault in the Central Highlands that had decimated their number. Even Andrews, the faithful medic, was gone. For his act of completing the amputation of a leg with a rusty bayonet, he had received the Medal of Honor — posthumously. Only C Squad, the untouchables, had survived unscathed.

Sergeant Miller stepped out of the sea of strange faces, and confronted Yates. "What the hell's going on?"

"I picked up a couple of prisoners — and one wounded."

Miller glanced briefly at the girl. "How'd she get hit?"

Yates shifted his weight, shrugging. "Accident."

"What about those gooks in white?"

"Couldn't catch them. They got to the jungle before we could bring them down."

"Shit. Blake's not gonna like that." Miller looked at the two papasans, shaking his head. "Hey, Fowler, come here."

A tall, thin youth approached. His pale skin and nervous manner gave away his newcomer status. "That's Fulmer, sergeant."

"Whatever. Go find the lieutenant and tell him we've got three prisoners, one wounded. I guess we gonna need a medevac."

"Right, sergeant." Fulmer trotted off, gear clanging.

The makeshift stretcher was set down on the sandy soil. "Thanks for the help," Tony said. White nodded as he backed away. Rodriguiz merely stared. Solemnly he took back his weapon, sweating profusely under the insulating flak jacket. Because of it he was not now on his way home — either in a cast or in a box.

The two Vietnamese prisoners sat on their haunches while Tony knelt by the girl's side. She babbled in a low voice, delirious. With her good arm, she tugged the cloth off her face and stared up at him, speaking softly. One of the papasans indicated the canteen. Tony slid his arm under her head, raised her up to a half reclining position, and held the opening to her lips. She took a few sips, nodding gratefully.

The old man held out gnarled hands, and Tony handed the canteen to him. The two papasans shared the remaining water. Tony spread out the cloth and covered her tiny breasts, more for his sake than for hers.

For the first time, Tony noticed that the girl was more than pretty, she was beautiful. Fathomless, oriental eyes mirrored innocence that could not last in this state of conflict. The shapely features of a model were wasted in a world where there existed no opportunity to become more than a wife, a mother, a tiller of the soil, and old and used before her time. She was embroiled in a struggle in which she had no part, out of which she could derive no benefit. If there was justice in the world, it was not her fate in life to find it.

The *whup-whup-whup* of a helicopter soughed in the air. Whirling blades kicked up a cloud of dust; the red signal smoke was blown away. Two men jumped out of the cargo compartment, pulled a collapsible canvas stretcher after them.

Tenderly, Tony lifted the girl. She squinted stoically against the windblown sand. Her uninjured arm reached out. Dainty fingers that were shriveled from constant submersion, calloused from wielding a hoe, grappled with his shirt. She pulled so hard that the top two buttons popped off. She brought her face close, planted a kiss on his sweaty, exposed chest, then fell back as her energy left her.

The bearers thrust out the stretcher, Tony made his offering. The two papasans were shoved aboard. The engine revved. The Huey lifted, and darted off into the blue sky. Tony stared after it until all sight and sound were gone. He was left with his thoughts for a moment that was all too brief.

A rifle cracked. A grenade exploded. It was time to get back to the business at hand. There was a war going on.

****

There was a reason for killing: food, sport, even for pleasure — if the object were a nagging, malaria-carrying mosquito. But by what reason did one kill people? By what right? By whose authority? Self-defense was a reason. Freedom was a right. A uniform granted authority. But Tony wrestled with the thought that in no way did a license to kill relieve one of moral responsibility.

"What's wrong?" Tait thrust his entrenching tool into the soft soil. He scooped the dirt into the sandbag that White was holding open for him. "You've been in another world ever since we got back."

"Ever since he put that girl on the Huey, you mean. An' it ain't because we gotta dig a new shit pit."

Tony shrugged, tossing a shovel full of sand into the bag. "Well, that's partly it, I guess."

"That's mostly it, I guess. You as happy as I am to get outa them hills. I like the lowlands, land o' inaction. Shit, rifle's gettin' rusty from lack o' use. But you don' see me complainin'."

The brief tragedy of the day had been their only diversion in weeks. But even the drudgery and boredom of search and destroy missions without enemy contact could be exhausting.

"Hey, no shit, Giovanni. You did all right today. You showed Yates up for the bastard he is. I wished I'd a done it long ago."

Tait leaned his entrenching tool against the side of the hole. "If that's what's bothering you, you've got a right to be worried. He isn't likely to forget it. You made him look bad, and he doesn't take to that."

Tony continued to dig. It was almost dark, and he wanted to get some sleep before going on guard duty. "It isn't just that. It's just — I don't know, I can't believe this is really happening. I mean, it seems like yesterday I was going to school, hanging around on street corners, racing cars, going to hamburger stands. And I thought I had problems. Now, all of a sudden, I'm in the middle of a jungle, carrying a gun, shooting at people, and getting shot at. These people here, the Vietnamese, have real problems — not dreamt up American neuroses."

"Welcome to the world." White dropped the sandbag and crouched down low. He said confidentially, "Did you ever see Peter Pan?"

Tony had to rework his thinking processes. "Sure."

"The one with Mary Martin?" Tait said.

"I meant the cartoon, but it don't matter. The point is, this is the part that Peter Pan don't like, the part o' growin' up that makes you wanna be a kid all your life. That's what I like 'bout kids. They're lucky, 'cause they still too little to know what life's got in store for 'em. Sure, they 'fraid o' the boogie man and alligators under the bed, but all that stuff's 'maginary. They close their eyes an' it all goes away. But this. — " He made a sweeping gesture with his hand. "This don' go away. These kids here got a hard world to grow up in. That's why we gotta make it easier for 'em."

"We're not making it any easier by killing off their parents."

"And it doesn't help taking away their homes," Tait added. "None of it makes any sense, when you stop and think about it. Even digging this trash hole doesn't make any sense. They'll only come and dig it up again as soon as we leave, to see what they can find. If we really want to help these people, the best thing we can do is get out of their lives. I learned that a long time ago."

"You sho' said a mouth*ful*, brother. We jus' a thorn in their side. They don' want us here, an' we don' wanna be here. But as long as we is, we gotta make the best o' it. So let's help the people by puttin' a bullet in that mothafucka's helmet — while his head is still in it."

In the last gleaming light of the sun, a long shadow fell across the half-finished trash hole. Yates strode casually, swinging his rifle by the rear sight. "All right, that's enough for tonight. Pack the tools and get back to the bunker."

Tait climbed out and folded his entrenching tool. White tied a knot in the last sandbag, but left it where it lay. Tony picked up his jacket and threw it over his shoulders. As soon as he had it buttoned, he rolled down the sleeves. Then he leaped lightly up to ground level.

Yates put a restraining hand on his shoulder. "Not you." To the others, he said, "Go ahead, we'll be along in a minute."

Tony unscrewed the locking nut, folded the entrenching tool, and retightened. "What's up?"

"What do you think?"

"Look, Yates, I'm not in the mood for any more of your games. If you have something to get off your chest, then say it."

The last rays of the sun refracted through airborne dust, turning the sky into a picture postcard of brilliant red and yellow hues.

"I wouldn't be so smug if I were you. That was quite a stir you caused today."

Pent up anger gushed out like water through a burst dam. Tony jabbed a finger into Yates' broad chest. "You lousy bastard. You didn't get enough blood and guts in the highlands, so you have to go around making your own. If Charlie's not around, you'll shoot water buffalo. When they don't fall like they're supposed to, you go after young girls. What kind of sick mind does it take to do that? Does it make you feel like a man? Are you impotent without a gun? Is that how you get your kicks?"

Yates' voice was surprisingly calm. "I know you think I'm a cold-blooded killer, but I'm not. That girl got hit by accident, and I'm not even sure I did it." Tony started to protest, but Yates went on before he could interrupt. "But that's neither here nor there. Whether one girl lives or dies in this godforsaken country is the least of my worries. There are plenty more where she came from. The important thing to me is whether *I* live or die. You may have some idealistic notion about this war, but I don't. And I'm not going to let anyone jeopardize my chances of getting out of here alive."

"Well, maybe — "

"You shut up and listen. I'm not through yet. You can believe anything you want — about me, about God, about politics, about morality. But when you're in the bush under my command, you damn well better do as I say. And the army will back me up on this. If you want to gripe, take it up with the lieutenant, or the old man, or Colonel Brady, or your congressman. But when I give an order I expect it to be carried out."

"What you're saying is I'm not allowed to make moral judgments about my own actions."

"What I'm saying is you haven't been sent here as a disciple of God. All you're supposed to do is carry out orders — don't make decisions, and don't make judgments. Just do what you're told so we can all live through this and go home."

Debating with Yates was like spitting into the wind. Tony was hot with anger, but knew at the same time that argument was useless. He would serve no purpose by applying reason. "Look, just forget about it, will you?"

"I can't forget about it until you understand that I'm trying to save *your* hide as well as my own. You can hate me as much as you want, but I want your cooperation."

"Yates, I'm not trying to be difficult. I want to live through this as much as you do. But after it's all over, I want to be able to live with myself, too."

"You're taking this war too seriously. Just get it through your head that we're not here to win, we're here to survive. We can't win this war, not the way we're fighting it. We never will. And we're not supposed to. Even the people we're fighting for don't want to win."

"So what are we doing here, then?"

"I don't know the answer to that any more than you do. All I know is that self-preservation is more important to me, right now, than trying to create a philosophy or justification for being here. We're here because we're here. And if we play the game right, we get to go home and protest. So please do me a favor and play along. Okay?"

Tony did not answer — he *could* not answer. Not without getting into another argument. It was easier to let Yates think what he wanted.

Yates let it slide. "Listen, the lieutenant wants to see you. He's at the command bunker."

"What's he want?"

Yates shrugged. "Not to give you a medal, but probably the same thing I want. That's why I got to you first — to sort of warm you up for what's coming. But a word of caution, just so you don't think I'm a total prick — don't talk to him the way you just talked to me. You'll only get yourself into more trouble."

"Thanks for the advice," Tony said, with feigned gratitude. He swung the entrenching tool over his shoulder and sauntered off, rifle in hand.

He met Lieutenant Blake coming out of the sandbagged position. His steel pot was still in his hand, his sandy hair plastered to the top of his head as if it had been slicked down with oil. His steely eyes stabbed at Tony's like twin rapiers en garde.

"Giovanni, I want you to know I heard about your action with that girl today, and I've talked it over with Captain Collins. He hasn't agreed to anything yet, but I think he'll back me up. We can't afford to let a situation like this go unrecognized, so I'm going to put it in my report."

The lieutenant grimaced as he squeezed his head into his helmet liner, his drawn face drew tighter. "I'm recommending you for a general court-martial."

Chapter 100

The broad dike was at least ten feet higher than the surrounding paddies. On one side, rice fields ambled among trees and scattered hooches; on the other, a deep, clear stream flowed past wooden gates that could be lifted to irrigate the paddies during the growing season. Now, the drum-sized tunnels through the dike were dry.

Yates squinted in the bright sun, said in a bored tone, "Check this one out, too."

Tony and White, patrolling opposite sides of the dike, peered at each other through the horizontal shaft. The VC commonly used such places as weapons caches. Any suspicious hole, opening, or recently unearthed ground was investigated: they had been known to bury supplies and ammunition under bodies.

"I hate this," White said. "I don' like crawlin' inna these holes."

"I'll cover you." Tait stood right behind him, holding his rifle casually by the rear sight.

Tony could see him only from the waist down as he crawled into the tunnel from the other side. "Just remember what happened to Alice in Wonderland when she crawled into a hole."

White's reply echoed dully off the earthen walls. "If you see a big rabbit carryin' a watch in there, tell him he's inna wrong fairy tale. *Aaagh!*"

Tony froze, heard movement to one side. An instant later he crawled backward as fast as he could. He popped out the entrance like a cork from a Coke bottle, and rolled sideways. "What was it?"

"There's a goddamn gook in there," White screamed. He scrambled to the top of the dike, stared at Yates with bulging eyes. "I ran right into the mothafucka."

"Giovanni, you clear?"

"Yeah."

"Burns! Throw in a few rounds." Yates slid down the embankment and landed behind Tony. The machine gun roared, and bullets tore out of the hole only inches away from Tony's face. Dust from the blasted walls coughed outward. "Was he armed?"

"Yeah, an' he got a mole on his left cheek. How the fuck should I know? I jus' got the fuck out."

Yates pulled Tony out of the way. "Lai de. Lai de. Didi mau," he shouted into the opening. When there was no answer, and no movement, he shouted, "Burns, keep that hole covered. Giovanni, get your gas mask on. We're taking this guy alive. Tait, go get the lieutenant."

In seconds, Tony tossed off his steel pot, donned the mask, and had a grenade in his hand. "Ready."

Yates backed out of the way. "I'll cover you."

Stooping alongside the entrance, Tony pulled the pin and lobbed the tear gas grenade into the tunnel. He raced back to a tree as the stinging vapor started boiling from the hole.

"Rodriguiz, frag that side of the dike to herd him out this way."

The squad spread out as the Puerto Rican launched his grenade. From the protection of the slender coconut tree, Tony aimed his M-16 and steeled himself for whatever might come out: a grenade, or a desperate guerrilla blasting away with his rifle.

Tony was as surprised, and as relieved, as anyone when he heard an imploring voice calling out in Vietnamese. A moment later, out of the dense cloud of gas, an Oriental appeared with his hands high in the air. Talking constantly, and with his eyes wide open, he did not seem to know that he should be coughing and gagging. He was dressed only in shorts and a loose fitting shirt. He had no weapons, nor any place to conceal one.

Tony ran out from behind the tree. He motioned with his rifle. The man nodded, still talking calmly, and showing no effects from the tear gas.

"Get back here, you fool!" Yates ran to Tony's side, facing the broiling gas cloud. "There might be more in there." A finger of vapor brushed his face, and he coughed uncontrollably, but he stood his ground.

Tony mustered his prisoner up the slope to the top of the dike. Yates, with tears in his eyes, knocked the man down and jumped on his back. Tait and Lieutenant Blake came running, with Sergeant Miller and Captain Collins not far behind.

"Sorry, Yates, I guess I got carried away," Tony said, as he took off the hot mask.

"Don't worry about it. Just remember the next time." He blinked rapidly, tears streaming from his eyes. On the ground, the Vietnamese kept repeating something in his native language, like a broken record. He might never have been gassed.

"Nice going, Yates," Lieutenant Blake kicked the prisoner in the ribs to see how lively he was.

The man grunted once, then maintained his monologue.

"It was Giovanni who did it." Yates wiped his eyes with his shirttail. "He's the gas man."

The lieutenant stared hard at Tony, but said nothing.

By that time Captain Collins had arrived. Sizing up the situation, he turned to Miller and said, "Go get Thang. Tell him we have a prisoner."

"Yes, sir," the sergeant said, as he turned and ran off.

The gas was dissipating. A few thin wisps curled out of both ends of the tunnel. The men stayed in position, keeping a close guard on the openings.

"Corporal, check out that hole for weapons and documents," Captain Collins ordered.

"Yes, sir," Yates said. Without being told, Tony slipped the gas mask back over his head. Yates handed him a flashlight. "We'll throw grenades in from both sides. As soon as the dust settles, you go in."

"Right."

The prisoner was quiet now, awaiting his fate. Captain Collins and Lieutenant Blake watched as the tunnel was prepped. Tony took a deep breath, got down on his hands and knees, and crept in with his rifle held in front, his finger on the trigger.

The weak beam of light barely dispelled the darkness, barely penetrated the still-falling dust. When he reached the middle of the tunnel he saw a hole gouged out on one side. It was little more than an indentation in which a small person could squat so that he could not be seen by a casual glance from either end of the tunnel. The dirt floor concealed no trap doors, the tiny niche held nothing more than a small bag of cooked rice. There were no weapons. The man who had occupied this alcove was nothing more than a peasant hiding from the onslaught of American soldiers.

By the time Tony crawled back out of the hole with his single bag of rice, Lieutenant Thang was already conducting an interview with the prisoner. With a rope tied around the man's neck, he jerked him around and stabbed him with questions. The slipknot strangled the prisoner so he could not answer, could in fact hardly breath. Then Thang loosened the knot, poked the man in the gut with the blunt end of his bayonet, and repeated his question. After the man had sucked in his breath, he gave a curt reply that was not what Thang wanted to hear. The next poke in the ribs was with sharpened steel.

Tony looked away from the brutality. He saw nothing but a simple farmer who had run and hid: an innocent victim of Vietcong intimidation, of American atrocity; a poor peasant who wanted to be left out of the struggle of opposing forces.

"Good work, private — " Captain Collins left the sentence dangling.

"Giovanni, sir," Tony supplied.

The captain stared noncommittally for a moment, then went on, "Yes, I've heard about you." There was no hostility in his voice. "I'd like to have a talk with you. Come around tonight after chow."

"Yes, sir," Tony replied, but the company commander had already turned back to the business at hand. He had a prisoner to interrogate, and intelligence to evaluate. Tony slipped out of the way.

****

"I think it stinks." Burns took a mouthful of turkey loaf, his unfortunate allotment in the c-ration lottery.

"Yeah, you ain't got no right pickin' on Giovanni alla time." Wallace wiped his lips with his shirttail. "You shoulda had the guts to own up to what you did. Instead, you get him in trouble with the old man."

Even normally taciturn Rodriguiz had something to say. "You do that in Harlem, you get your throat cut."

"Knock it off, will you?" Yates said.

"No, you knock it off, man." White leaped up from his seat on the log and jumped in front of the squad leader. "You are a fuckin' rat, man. You didn't hafta go tell the lieutenant nothin'. You kept your mouth shut and Giovanni wouldn't be in no trouble. Man, I taken a lot o' shit off you, but this is too much. If he gets court-martialed, you better take to wearin' a flak jacket with a double layer in back."

"Is that a threat, White?"

"Yeah, man, that's a threat." White shook his fist in front of Yates' face. "You wanna turn me in, too, you fuckin' fink?"

"I'm telling you I had nothing to do with it. I didn't make any recommendations, all I did was tell the story the way it happened. Miller was there, ask *him*."

"Ask your bosom buddy, you mean?" Wallace said. "That fuckin' bastard's worsen you are."

"You gettin' a promotion outa this?" White was still standing in front of Yates, but he had lowered his fist.

"I'm not getting anything. Look, I had to make a report on what happened. That's my job. And whether you believe it or not, those gooks might have been VC guerrillas."

"Bullshit!" Burns yelled. "There ain't a fuckin' VC or NVA within a hundred klicks of this place. We spent months going through these villes an' never found nobody."

"That doesn't mean they're not here now," Yates insisted.

"It doesn't mean you gotta go shootin' little girls." White took a step closer so his black face was right in front of Yates', so his hot breath blew in his face.

"Look, it was an accident."

"Accident, shit. Like shootin' that water buffalo was a accident, huhn?"

There was no holding White back now. His wrath was up and he had plenty to say. "Yates, I been wantin' to tell you this for months, but ain't had the guts till Giovanni paved the way. I think you're a low down, ass kissin', mothafucka who ain't got the guts to own up to what a bastard you are. You lower than whale shit, man, and that's only found at the bottom of the ocean, with the rest of the scum. You — "

Yates came up off the ground like a jack-in-the-box. His fist landed squarely in White's face. The black man saw it coming and was already stepping back when it landed, knocking off his steel pot. He was propelled as much by his own volition as by the concussion. He hit the ground and kept on rolling, and in an instant he was on his feet and charging at the squad leader. White lowered his head and caught Yates full in the chest. The two went down in a heap, jabbing at each other with short, powerful punches.

The rest of the men joined the melee. For a moment it looked like a football pile up: a mass of contorted bodies and flailing arms and legs. Then they started to pull the two scrappers

apart. With Wallace sitting on his chest, Burns across his legs, and Tony holding down one arm, White grunted and struggled. Yates climbed to his feet, but allowed Rodriguiz and Tait to pin his arms.

After he caught his breath, Yates said, "Let him up."

Slowly, White was released. When all the bodies were off him, he stood up. He never took his eyes off Yates. His broad chest heaved like a bellows. "Yates, I hate your fuckin' guts — " he started.

Tony stepped in front of him and placed a restraining hand on his arm. "That's enough, White. Let's go for a walk and cool off."

White went grudgingly. His eyes stayed locked on those of the squad leader as Tony dragged him away by the arm. When they got out of hearing range, White jerked his arm out of Tony's grasp.

"Somebody's gonna shoot that son of a bitch someday."

"Well, let Charlie do it, okay? At least he won't have to go to jail for it."

"He just pisses me off sometimes."

Veering away from the grove of trees, Tony steered White toward an abandoned hooch that was surrounded by a garden. A small group of women worked in a distant rice paddy, while several children played on a nearby dike. Tony was overcome with a haunting feeling of déjà vu.

"Hey, does this place look familiar to you?"

White, still blind from his temper, glanced around. "All these goddamn gook villes look the same." When they got close to a mud bunker and saw that the front was caved in, White whistled. "You're right, man. I recognize it now."

"Isn't this the place where you got the incense burner?"

"Yeah, that's it. Musta been when you first got here. Dong Hoa, it's called. We been through here a bunch o' times. Goddamn."

"And you tripped over a vine and thought it was a trip wire."

"Don' remind me."

"You looked pretty funny — " A gunshot stopped him in mid sentence. After listening for a moment he heard no additional shots. "Do you think we ought to be heading back?"

'I don' wanna tangle with that fuckin' Yates yet. But if there's some action goin' on an' we ain't there, he gonna be really mad. Course, *you* don' hafta worry. They can't court-martial you twice at the same time."

Tony managed a weak grin, then led the way through the village to where they had left the rest of the squad. There were no more shots, however, and before they got there they saw from a distance the interrogation of the peasant whom Tony had captured.

He was bleeding from the nose and mouth. Lieutenant Thang kept a taut grip on the leash around his neck, and jerked it violently whenever he asked a question. Then he fired his pistol close to the man's head.

"Poor bastard."

"Yeah, I'm almost sorry we found him."

They were standing in a garden when a Vietnamese woman approached. She had two children in tow, a girl and a boy, both less than waist high.

"Hey, there, little fella." White reached into his fanny pack for some sundry pack goodies. He brought out a handful of candy bars and two packs of cigarettes. He let the children have the candy, but held onto the smokes. "Don' wanna start 'em off on a bad habit."

While White took care of the youngsters, the mother talked and gesticulated. Tony watched her. He saw that she was pointing toward the prisoner, then at herself and the children. Her voice was calm, almost musical.

"It won't hurt 'em. It's only candy and crackers. Here, I'll even throw in a tube of toothpaste so they won't get no cavities."

"White, I think she's trying to tell us something."

"Beggars are never satisfied."

"No, no. It has something to do with the prisoner." Slowly, following her gestures, comprehension began to dawn on Tony. "Wait a minute. I think I know what she's saying."

"When did you learn to speak gook lingo?"

Paying him no mind, Tony continued. "Look how she's pointing. Don't you see what she means? She's saying that the man is her husband, the father of these children. See, he's not Vietcong after all. He just hid when he saw us coming."

White squinted his eyes, as if they would help him understand any better. "It do kinda make sense."

Tony was overcome with a terrible sense of guilt. Forgetting that he had saved the man's life, he felt nothing but remorse over what he was having to endure at the hands of the sadistic Lieutenant Thang. From here he could see the beatings, hear the thuds of fists on flesh and the screams of pain. Led around on a leash like an animal, the man was suffering for doing nothing more than living in the country of his birth.

"I — I'm sorry," Tony mumbled. From his pockets he took the remainder of his lunch. Suddenly, he was no longer hungry. He handed the olive drab cans to the young woman. She took them with quiet thanks. *Was that an equitable exchange for a human life*, Tony won-

dered? Was that all a man was worth in this country? "Let's get out of here."

"Sho' 'nuf." White seemed as eager as Tony to make believe that this was not really happening.

When Tony last saw her, the mother was standing with the c-ration cans in her hands. The children clutched the material of her skirt, hiding behind the folds, dark eyes peering out of darker faces.

Two rifles cracked, almost simultaneously. One of them burped again. This followed by a mad scramble of men running from a clump of bamboo.

"Fire in the hole!" someone shouted.

Men ducked behind dikes, hid behind trees, or flattened to the ground if they were caught in the open. The explosion threw splinters and shrapnel into the air. Before the dust had settled, a machine gunner propped his gun on its bipod and blasted the thicket with a long, continuous burst. A stealthy silence followed. Leaves fluttered to the ground while men uncovered their faces to see what was happening.

"What the hell was that all about?" White said. He and Tony had hit the ground automatically, even though they were out of range of the grenade.

"I think they've got somebody trapped in a spider hole."

He could see Captain Collins low-crawling out of the line of fire. For a moment it struck Tony funny to see his company commander slithering on his belly. Then he saw Lieutenant Thang and Lieutenant Catlow doing the same. Still roped by the neck, the prisoner was dragged to the safety of a thick stand of areca palms. By now Captain Collins was taking over the situation. He rose from the ground and directed one of the platoon sergeants to spread out his men.

From his half-crouched position, Tony saw members of the First Platoon form a semicircle around the thicket. They kept their distance in case another grenade was tossed out of the hidden hole. The same tactics that had been used so well in the highlands were put to use here. While a blanket of fire was laid down, one man crept close enough to drop a grenade into the hole. They were not taking any prisoners this time.

The dull, earth-dampened thud shot dirt into the air like a blast of steam from Old Faithful. An arm flew up out of the hole — and impossibly, kept rising until it arced at ten feet and fell downs to the ground. After the dust settled, the men dragged out what was left of the body, and dropped it on the ground like a sack of potatoes.

Somebody laughed. "Got more holes in him

than a screen door."

They found no weapons on the body or in the hole.

"Shit, man, that farmer knew right where that gook was hidin'. Sniffed 'em out like a hound dog."

Tony was confused. "But why? He wasn't a soldier, just another farmer."

"Use your head, man. They forced 'em to helpin'. Man with a fambly ain't got much bargainin' power, y'know."

"But why did they kill him?"

"The captain's under pressure to show a body count."

Events proceeded at an ever-quickening pace. Now the peasant was leading the way, pointing with one outstretched arm to another bamboo thicket. He was jerked to the ground while Captain Collins had the First Platoon surround it. The process was repeated. Without much ado, two partially clothed men, bearded and wrinkled with age, were killed with hand grenades and hauled out of the hole.

"Hey, you two. Get over here." It was Yates.

Tony ran up to him with tears in his eyes. "Yates, what're they doing? They're killing innocent civilians."

"Farmers by day, sappers by night."

"But that woman back there — "

"Listen, we haven't got time to argue. We've got to cross the river and cover the other side. According to this gook, there are VC positions all over the place."

"I ain't forgettin' our argument, but we can hash it out later. An' don' think I'm gonna forget about it, neither."

Yates refused to be baited. "All right, just keep your eyes open. There's no telling how many gooks are hiding around here."

"But, Yates, we found out something from a woman in the village." Tony chased the squad leader to where the others were wading in the stream. Burns was halfway across, holding the machine gun over his head even though the water was only knee deep. "That prisoner isn't really a Vietcong. He lives here. That's his wife and children back there."

"Where did you hear that?" Yates halted behind Wallace. Now Tony could see that Rodriguiz and Tait were already on the other side of the narrow band of water, standing guard.

"She told us," Tony said. "His wife. We just ran into her in the village. She — "

The sound of gunfire cut him off. Burns splashed across the stream and flattened himself on the sandy bank before he realized that the shots had not been directed at him. Five guns fired at once only a hundred feet away. Lieutenant Blake and Sergeant Miller charged into a bamboo thicket and let loose with their M-16s, firing down through a concealed trap door. A moment later Miller flipped open the lid, but found it unnecessary to drop his grenade into the hole. The two occupants were already dead, their bodies riddled with bullet wounds. Both of them were women.

"Give us a hand," the lieutenant shouted, waving to the neophytes of Miller's squad. Miller jumped into the hole and started pulling up the bodies to waiting hands. They were dragged out onto the berm that separated the paddy from the stream.

"Jesus Christ, we're really rackin' 'em up today," Wallace said happily.

"Cut the chatter and let's get across the river," Yates called out.

Tony tore his attention away from the action. "Yates, you've got to get them to stop it. These aren't soldiers, these are just — "

A rough hand hit him in the middle of the chest, spun him around. Another shoved him into the stream. "They're fuckin' sympathizers, goddamn it. Now, get moving."

He tripped and went down on one knee. The water was cool as it soaked through his fatigues and filled his jungle boots. Yates picked him up and pushed him onward.

"But you don't know that."

"I know it until they prove otherwise. Hey, fan out along the bank and watch the other side of the river."

The bamboo partially blocked Tony's view of the proceedings. He scrabbled along behind the low dike to where he could see through the brush and watch the other half of the platoon that was working around the spider hole. He lay down on the hot sand, wiped tear-stained cheeks.

"Why don't they chase them out with tear gas? Give them a chance to explain?"

"They're hiding, they're Cong."

Burns clipped another belt onto the tail leading from the machine gun. He swiveled the barrel up and down the riverbank with short, jerky movements.

"Man, we patrolled this place for months and months. Never found nothin'."

" 'Cept for that bouncin' betty got Hanes in the ass," said Wallace.

"I always thought that was a fluke."

"Fluke, hell. It was a goddamn shark an' it up an' bit 'im."

White jammed a cigarette between his lips, but his hands were shaking too badly to light it. Behind them, a couple hundred meters away, peasants ignored the gunfire and continued their work in the field. "Look at those fools, surrounded by killers an' they go 'bout their business as if nothin' was happenin'."

Tony said, "You see. There can't be any VC

around or they'd be running for cover."

"A good point." Tait stripped the wrapping off a candy bar and stuck half of it into his mouth. "They act as if the war's not even happening. They just go on picking their rice like — "

Suddenly, Rodriguiz screamed. "Amigos. On the bank."

Tony flipped over and instinctively wrapped his hand around the trigger. Even before he picked up the rifle, he saw the two, uniformed Vietnamese at the water's edge where none had been before. For a moment he wondered where the ARVN regulars had come from. He noticed the wooden stock rifles that they were carrying just as Burns let loose with the machine gun.

There was pandemonium as his bullets slammed into the opposite bank, just below the men of the Third Platoon. The officers and men hit the ground without ever knowing what was happening. Rodriguiz could not use his precious grenades because of the proximity of his own men. He brought his M-16 to bear and caught the enemy soldiers in a deadly crossfire that drove them into the side of the bank. Another guerrilla was just crawling out of an exit hole at the water's edge when Burns' machine cut him down with a lethal burst.

White bit his cigarette in two, and Tait had chocolate smeared all over his hand and trigger guard. Tony had his gun aimed by now, but the action seemed to be over. Then he saw someone leap out of the spider hole from which the two dead women had just been hauled. He was about to shoot when he recognized Miller.

"This is a goddamn main complex." Miller directed a burst at the opening, then fell backward to the ground beside Lieutenant Blake.

A cold shiver of fear ran along Tony's spine; he had been about to shoot one of his own men. The action telescoped in his mind as events occurred faster than he could comprehend them. Bravo Company was in a flurry of activity as officers shouted orders, men raced back and forth, weapons were fired, grenades exploded, wounded screamed in pain.

"Jesus Christ," he heard Yates mutter, eyes riveted on the melee across the stream. "What the fuck are we into?"

The sounds of shooting were everywhere. Tony saw Captain Collins directing his platoon leaders, saw platoon leaders shouting at their sergeants, saw sergeants trying to make sense out of what was happening. A machine gun fired a long burst that ended only when the belt ran out.

"What's that fuckin' kid doin' out there?" White said. Tony turned and saw where he was looking. A Vietnamese toddler, no older than five or six, walked toward them with his arms folded around his middle as if he were hugging himself. Tears streamed from his eyes, his bawling barely audible above the noise of battle. "I gotta do something." White was up and running at a half crouch, kicking sand with his heels.

"White, get back here," Yates bellowed.

At almost the same time there was a shout from across the stream. "They're poppin' up everywhere." The raucous intermittent sounds of AK-47s blended with the continuous roar of machine guns and M-16s. Uniformed regulars of the North Vietnamese Army evacuated their underground military complex, causing mad confusion. Tony could see Captain Collins shouting on the radio. In the span of a few minutes the situation had gotten completely out of control. Tony found himself shooting, reloading, shooting, the rifle hot in his hands.

"Hey, watch out. They're on the other side of the river."

White reached the child, picked him up and ran with him toward the safety of a grove of trees. Just as the pair reached the grove, there came an ear-shattering blast and a billowing cloud of dust. Tony had a momentary glimpse of White and the boy leaping into the air, impossibly high, then separating into an expanding pattern of limbs, flesh, and blood. Both of them seemed to disintegrate into parts too small to see, and settled with the falling dust.

"*White!*" Tony screamed, rising to his feet.

White had been cheated: instead of getting a million dollar wound, he got one that was worth only ten thousand dollars — to his gray-haired mother in Tallahassee.

Out of the corner of his eye, Tony saw someone running. He would have paid no mind had a gun not fired and kicked up dirt in the paddy in front of him.

"Run for cover," he heard Yates shout.

Oh, how he wanted to take the time to think about what had happened to White; how he wanted to stare paralyzed in shock at the scattered pieces of protoplasm that had once been two human beings; how he wanted to sit down and cry about the cruelty of booby-trapping a baby, how he wanted the whole, bloody mess to go away like a bad dream.

More soldiers suddenly appeared along the banks of the stream. They were climbing out of the soil like the mythical soldiers from the dragon's teeth. Tony spun around in time to see two uniformed Orientals fire in enfilade along the dike, stitching bullets between him and the bamboo thicket that offered the only place of protection. The rest of his platoon was already taking cover.

He leaped to the top of the dike, shooting desperately at two men to his left. He barely got off two rounds when something slammed into his left leg with the force of a battering ram. His feet were torqued out from under him, and in an instant he was lying on the ground. He groaned as he slapped his hand over his thigh, just below the hip. It came away sticky with blood. He looked up at the bamboo and bushes only ten feet away, but when he tried to crawl for cover he found that his wounded leg would not move.

"I'm hit! I'm hit!"

Moaning, Tony glanced around for help, but he was alone on the exposed dike. Fifty feet away, a solitary soldier scuttled along a right-angled dike, crouched over his AK-47. The wooden stock and black banana clip were clearly visible. A pair of dark eyes looked deep into his own.

Twisting in terror, Tony shouted, "Shoot him. Shoot him. He's seen me." Grenades thundered nearby, and the sound of rifle fire was almost continuous. Bravo Company was hotly engaged. Tony's voice was drowned out by the sounds of battle. He was helpless, lying on his rifle.

When he looked again, he saw the enemy soldier sink down to one knee, seat the butt of his rifle against his shoulder, and peer over the metal sights. From such close quarters, Tony noted the professional air of calm, the total lack of expression, the complete discipline that came only with constant drill and years of experience: no guerrilla this, but a highly trained mercenary who had a job to perform.

Tony was looking right into the dark opening of the barrel. He knew that the end was near.

He leaned back to get the rifle out from under him. Resting on one elbow, he swung the rifle around and pointed it the best he could. Time seemed to stop. His finger worked the trigger with the speed of an automatic. He could not aim, he could only try to see where his bullets kicked up dirt, and adjust his fire from that.

He saw nothing, knew that he must be shooting too high. He pushed his arm into the ground, brought the line of bullets lower, saw the Vietcong flinch, caught the flash of light from the muzzle, was slammed into the ground when the high speed bullet drilled through his chest like a pointed icicle, bounced forward like a rag doll so that he lay with his face in the sand, his body hunched over in a twisted, contorted position that would have been uncomfortable had he not been momentarily insensate.

Everything went dark. When the dimness receded, he found himself in a strange position. He could open only one eye; the other was jammed against the rim of his steel pot. His arm was over his head, in the air, jerking — *jerking* — like a puppet on a string, as if some separate entity were in command of his body. Torn muscle fiber and overloaded nerve endings blocked the control paths from his brain.

Was he going to lie there all day while the war went on without him? He had to do something. He had to say something. "Medic." It sounded trite even to him.

The word came out a whisper that he could barely hear. The whole left side of his chest was a mass of pain, the lung deflated. He needed help badly. But Andrews, the faithful medic, had not yet been replaced. And that Vietcong soldier was still out there.

"Help. Help."

Burns' voice trumpeted out of the concealing brush. "Giovanni, lay still and maybe they'll think you're dead."

Part of Tony laughed at the incongruity of the statement. But he could not control that arm. It was still dancing around with a life of its own.

Then Tait was kneeling by his side, rolling him over. Tony groaned with unbelievable pain — his leg, his chest, his shoulder. It hurt just to breath. His eyes stared up at the bright blue sky, infinitely clear.

"Why didn't you shoot him? Why did you leave me out there alone?" Tony muttered in a cracked voice that he hardly recognized.

Guilt washed across Tait's face. "We were pinned down. The gooks are all over the place."

"But he shot me again," Tony said uselessly. Tait was working over him now, ripping off buttons, unclipping gear. Tony screamed in pain. "*Don't move me.*"

"I've got to get your web gear off," Tait said.

"Don't move me."

"I'm not going to move you. When we pick you up the web gear will stay behind." Another face looked down on him. "Take it easy, amigo," Rodriguiz said. "You gonna be all right."

"But it hurts."

"Yeah, but you going home."

The horse blinders left his mind. Tony became aware of the sounds of battle from across the stream: gunfire, explosions, shouting. Someone nearby was crying.

"Yates," came Burns' frantic scream. "Get a fuckin' medevac in here. Wallace got it in the chest."

"Bastard was a good shot," Tait said. All the straps were loose, and he was looking at the tiny puncture where the steel jacketed bullet had entered Tony's rib cage. There was surprisingly little blood. But from an enormous hole in his back, the red fluid was gushing in quantity and soaking into the dry earth.

"Water. I want water," Tony mumbled. "Give me a drink."

Tait cradled Tony's head in his lap, while Rodriguiz held a canteen to his lips. The moisture was pure pleasure on his cracked lips, his swollen tongue, his parched throat. He felt as if he were dying of thirst. He craved more, but Rodriguiz would give him only small amounts.

The air vibrated with the *whup-whup-whup* of Hueys. The sky was full of gunships. So thick were the helicopters that Tony could not see the blue for the cloud of brown that flew overhead like a swarm of locusts. Miniguns roared, rockets flashed, the world was full of noise. Reinforcements were landing.

A Huey settled down in the open paddy, attracted by purple smoke. Stretcher-bearers loomed like leering gargoyles. They set the stick and canvas contraption on the ground next to Tony. One man grabbed him by the legs, the other by the shoulders. Tony screamed as loud as his ruptured lung would allow, as broken bones were squeezed and wrenched out of place. They paid him no mind, but picked up the handles and ran toward the waiting helicopter.

The downdraft washed his face as the men ducked under the whirling blades. They stopped while another team deposited a bawling Wallace onto the metal deck. Tony's head lolled, and he saw another patient waiting to be lifted into the medevac. Lieutenant Blake was hardly recognizable under the bloody froth that covered his face. One leg ended in a stump where the knee should have been. His right arm lay across his stomach, unconnected. It had been severed at the shoulder, along with his career.

Tony closed his eyes to the awful sight. Then he was being loaded onto the deck. A sea of faces looked down at him. His eyes were blurring. He could hear practically nothing over the roar of the whining turbine.

Yates' face swam into view, watching half his squad being taken away. His lips mouthed words. "So long, Tony."

The stretcher was clamped into place. The engine pitch crescendoed. The strain of gravity pressed him flat. As the helicopter banked, Tony had one last look at the battlefield, the rushing figures, the winding stream, the dry paddies.

Blood rushed to his head. Faces dissolved into mist. He passed out.

Tony was on the first leg of his journey home.

EPILOGUE

Tony came home to a country that was both different and indifferent. For him the conflict was over; for many it was just beginning.

Frank Giovanni shaded the bright sun from his eyes. He ignored Elizabeth's rambling questions about the order of military pomp. Patty, silent and stoic, hugged Davey tight to her breast. Teddy watched the oncoming jet in anticipation mixed with anxiety.

The C-141 looked like a silver crossbow, descending through cirrus clouds that dotted the cerulean sky. Heat waves shimmered ghostlike above the runway's hot macadam, causing the aircraft to lose definition so that it waved like a papier-mâché mockup. It was eerily quiet even as it touched the tarmac. Twin puffs of burned rubber pealed off the black landing strip. Only after the jet nosed down, and glided along on tripod pistons, did the faint squeal reach the throng of expectant greeters.

The pilot was praised by applause from the crowd: he had successfully brought home another load of soldiers from the conflict across the sea.

The plane taxied in a wide arc that brought it to a halt on a concrete pad in front of the administration building. Flight officers wearing dress blue — the official welcoming committee — poised in front of a military brass band that played the National Anthem. The ground crew rolled out the stairway and luggage carts. The engines were still whining down when the door opened and the first soldier, a Marine captain, stepped into the heat and noise of the jet's after blast.

Two women broke from the crowd and ran screaming past the small contingent of military police. When the captain stepped off the last rung, his wife and daughter wrapped their arms around him, laughing and crying. They were so weak from the release of pent-up emotion that he had to carry them from the ramp.

Music blared loudly as the four great turbines coughed into silence. Young MPs politely stepped aside and let friends and relatives mingle with the returning marines, soldiers, sailors, and Air Force personnel as they stepped down from the metal stairs. Loved ones anxiously sought out husbands, fathers, and sons.

Frank remained erect, neither moving from his self-allotted place, nor allowing any expression to sweep over his swarthy face.

The plane continued to spew its passengers, all of them bronzed by the tropical sun. Official motion picture cameras rolled, still cameras clicked. Short-sleeved soldiers waved and smiled, some with their arms in slings. Next came the ambulatory patients, wearing hospital pajamas, swathed in gauze or plaster casts, limping or hobbling on wooden crutches. The crowd thinned as stretcher-bearers carried the more seriously wounded. Each man broke into a smile as he emerged from the tubular cocoon.

Frank Giovanni remembered well his brother's return from France, after his travails at Anzio. Harry had been received with full military honors, as well as with a hero's welcome from close friends and relatives. And Frank remembered the pride that he had felt that his very own brother had earned such adulation.

The long line of white stretchers ended. The band stopped playing. The welcoming committee dispersed. The crowd departed. Only the Giovanni's remained; and Teddy, looking resplendent in his dress Marine uniform. Little Davey began to cry.

At the rear of the plane, the ground crew unloaded luggage, leather valises, cardboard boxes, and olive drab duffel bags. Fatigue clad airmen pushed special wheeled dollies, each holding a long aluminum coffin that was draped with the red, white, and blue of the American flag. The long train rattled through the gates where bored sergeants waited with clipboards and triplicate forms in hand.

The movie cameras had stopped rolling; the shutters had ceased clicking.

The pad was empty. The plane was abandoned. A breeze blew loose papers and trash past the mighty flying machine.

Elizabeth dabbed her mascaraed eyes with a tissue, turned and walked slowly after the last of the gruesome parade. Patty whimpered, clutched the baby tighter. Teddy, his face drawn and sallow, wrapped an arm around her shoulders.

Frank continued to watch the plane as the wind tugged at his hair. He would not — could not — look back at the coffins. There had to be more to the homecoming than this. He expected more — he demanded more. He would not be destroyed by someone else's failure. They owed him.

He heard a baby crying at his side — a lonely, lonesome wail. Davey was a gesticulating doll in Patty's perspiring arms.

In a queasy, quivering voice, she whimpered, "Who's gonna take care of me . . . ?"

Gary Gentile wrote a true account of his service in Vietnam, in Book One of his autobiographical history of diving on shipwrecks, *The Lusitania Controversies: Atrocity of War and a Wreck-Diving History*.

The book recounts some of his wartime experiences, including the last firefight in which he was wounded, and his year-long struggle with convalescence.

As a result of wounds received in action in Vietnam, Gary Gentile was given three Purple Hearts (although he declined to accept the third.) He spent thirteen months in military hospitals, recuperating from his wounds.

In 1985, he underwent additional surgery in a VA hospital: another tendon transplant similar to the one that was done in the Army hospital in 1967. Recuperation took six months.

An actual account of his service in Vietnam, his ultimate firefight, subsequent hospitalization and convalescence, and other personal information, was told in Book One of his two-volume history of wreck-diving, *The Lusitania Controversies*.

After his discharge from the Army, Gary worked for ten years as a commercial and industrial electrician. He then embarked on a career as a freelance author and photographer.

Since then, Gary has written 44 books, published more than 3,000 photographs, and led a life of adventure. Many of his most exciting adventures have occurred under water.

Of the thousands of decompression dives that Gary has made, over 180 of them were on the Grand Dame of the Sea: the *Andrea Doria*. He was the first scuba diver to enter the First Class Dining Room, from which he recovered many items of elegant china. He also recovered and restored hundreds of items of jewelry and souvenirs from the Gift Shop, located at a depth of 220 feet. More important, he discovered and recovered a number of ceramic panels that once adorned the walls of the First Class Bar. These colorful panels were the work of famed Italian artist Romano Rui.

In the early 1990's, Gary was instrumental in merging mixed-gas diving technology with wreck-diving. His 1990 dive on the German battleship *Ostfriesland*, at a depth of 380 feet, triggered an unprecedented expansion in the exploration of deep-water shipwrecks, and the advent of helium mixes as a breathing medium. He wrote the first book on technical diving. In 1994, he participated in a mixed-gas diving expedition to the *Lusitania*, which lies at a depth of 300 feet.

Gary has specialized in wreck-diving and shipwreck research, concentrating his efforts on wrecks along the eastern seaboard, from Newfoundland to Key West, and in the Great Lakes. In addition to diving on hundreds of known shipwreck sites, he has made more than forty discovery dives.

He has compiled an extensive library of books, photographs, drawings, plans, and original source materials on ships and shipwrecks. He has conducted surveys on numerous wrecks, some of which have been drawn in the form of large-sized prints that are suitable for framing.

Over the years, he has rescued many thousands of shipwreck artifacts from the ravages of the sea, making him a leading authority in recovery techniques. He has gone to great lengths to preserve and restore these relics from the deep, and to display them to thousands of interested people, divers and nondivers alike. Throughout the years, these artifacts have been displayed at various museums, symposiums, and club-oriented exhibitions.

Gary has written scores of magazine articles, and has published photographs in books, periodicals, newspapers, brochures, advertisements, corporate reports, museum displays, postcards, film, and television. He lectures extensively on underwater topics, and conducts seminars on advanced wreck-diving techniques, high-tech diving equipment, and shipwreck photography.

His 44 books are primarily novels of science fiction and adventure, and nonfiction volumes on wreck-diving and on nautical and shipwreck history. The Popular Dive Guide Series will eventually cover every major shipwreck along the East Coast of the United States.

There is also another side of Gary's life: that of an outdoor adventurer. In this guise he has climbed rock and mountains, backpacked through country high and low, bivouacked in the snow, and paddled his canoe through rapids and down untamed wilderness rivers - often for weeks at a time. His longest trip lasted a month, when he and five companions paddled 380 miles down the George River in Labrador. For three weeks straight they did not encounter another human being, or see signs of civilization. Gary embraces total self-sufficiency in the wilderness.

He has captured on film all of these wonderful outdoor adventures, as well as the splendor of nature's colorful scenery. He has given slide presentations to dive clubs, hiking clubs, canoe clubs, elder hostels, church groups, Cub Scouts, power squadrons, Naval associations, Civil War societies, Masonic lodges, Mensa, corporate functions, scientific organizations, and many, many other groups too numerous to mention.

In 1989, after a five-year battle with the National Oceanic and Atmospheric Administration, Gary won a suit which forced the hostile government agency to issue him a permit to dive on the USS *Monitor*, a protected National Marine Sanctuary. Media attention that was focused on Gary's triumphant victory resulted in nationwide coverage of his 1990 photographic expedition to the Civil War ironclad. Gary continues to fight for the right of access to all shipwreck sites.

The Popular Dive Guide Series

Shipwrecks of Massachusetts: South
Shipwrecks of Rhode Island and Connecticut
Shipwrecks of New York
Shipwrecks of New Jersey (1988)
Shipwrecks of New Jersey: North
Shipwrecks of New Jersey: Central
Shipwrecks of New Jersey: South
Shipwrecks of Delaware and Maryland (1990)
Shipwrecks of Delaware and Maryland (2002)
Shipwrecks of Virginia
Shipwrecks of North Carolina: North
Shipwrecks of North Carolina: South
Shipwrecks of South Carolina and Georgia

Shipwreck and Nautical History

Andrea Doria: Dive to an Era
Deep, Dark, and Dangerous: Adventures and Reflections on the Andrea Doria
The Fuhrer's U-boats in American Waters
Great Lakes Shipwrecks: a Photographic Odyssey
Ironclad Legacy: Battles of the USS Monitor
The Lusitania Controversies (One): Atrocity of War and a Wreck-Diving History
The Lusitania Controversies (Two): Dangerous Descents into Shipwrecks and Law
The Nautical Cyclopedia
USS San Diego: the Last Armored Cruiser
Shadow Divers Exposed
Stolen Heritage: The Grand Theft of the Hamilton and Scourge
Track of the Gray Wolf
Wreck Diving Adventures

Dive Training Manuals

Primary Wreck Diving Guide
Advanced Wreck Diving Guide
Ultimate Wreck Diving Guide
The Technical Diving Handbook

Outdoor Nonfiction

Wilderness Canoeing

Science Fiction

A Different Universe: Tales of Imagination
A Different Dimension: More Tales of Imagination
Entropy
Return to Mars
Silent Autumn
The Time Dragons Trilogy
   A Time for Dragons
   Dragons Past
   No Future for Dragons

Action/Adventure Novels

Memory Lane
Mind Set
The Peking Papers

Supernatural Horror Novel

The Lurking

Vietnam Novel

Lonely Conflict

Videotape (NTSC/VHS)

The Battle for the USS Monitor

Visit the GGP website for availability of titles:

http://www.ggentile.com